'It's all right,' Polly said. She looked down at their hands. Hers, small and slim, was almost lost in his big hand. She saw that, like herself, he wore a plain gold wedding ring. That was unusual, she thought. Not many men did that. She drew in a shaky breath and said, 'I think I'm getting over it a bit now. I mean, so many things have happened and so many people have been killed. You just have to get on with life, don't you?'

'Yes,' he said. 'You do.' There was a moment's silence and then he tucked her hand into the crook of his arm and they walked on. Polly took a deep breath, and then another. Mentioning Johnny always brought an ache to her throat, but she could feel a comfort in the warmth of this big man, with her hand tucked so securely against his body. She had a sudden longing to be held close, to be hugged. No more than that – just to be hugged. To feel the closeness of another human being. To feel the warmth of a living body close to hers.

Oh Johnny, she thought, where are you? What happened to you? And did you think of me, during your last few moments? Did you know how much I loved you – and did it help at all? Or did you forget everything and everyone in those last desperate efforts to stay alive?

The tears came to her eyes and, without knowing it, she tightened her grip on Joe Turner's arm. He glanced down at her but said nothing, and if she had looked up at him then she would have seen that his eyes were wet too.

Lilian Harry grew up close to Portsmouth Harbour, where her earliest memories are of nights spent in an air-raid shelter listening to the drone of enemy aircraft and the thunder of exploding bombs. But her memories are also those of a warm family life shared with two brothers and a sister in a tiny backstreet house where hard work, love and laughter went hand in hand. Lilian Harry now lives on the edge of Dartmoor where she has two ginger cats to love and laugh at. She has a son and daughter and two grandchildren and, as well as gardening, country dancing, amateur dramatics and church bellringing, she loves to walk on the moors and – whenever possible – to go skiing in the mountains of Europe. She has written a number of books under other names, including historical novels and contemporary romances. Visit her website at www.lilianharry.co.uk

By Lilian Harry

Under the Apple Tree

LILIAN HARRY

ORION

An Orion paperback

First published in Great Britain in 2004
by Orion
This paperback edition published in 2004
by Orion Books Ltd,
Orion House, 5 Upper Saint Martin's Lane,
London WC2H 9EA

Third impression 2005

A CIP catalogue record for this book is available
from the British Library.

Printed and bound in Great Britain by
Clays Ltd, St Ives plc

For my dear grandson, Peter

My grateful thanks are due to Rosie Farrant, who suggested the WVS as a subject for this book, and to all members of the WVS (now the WRVS) past and present; to Maurice Flack, who spent his war years watching for aircraft from the rooftop of the Royal Beach Hotel, Southsea (and once got stuck in a lift with one of the staff); to Julie Anderson, who took the time to show us over the hotel, taking Maurice back to the roof for the first time since the war ended; and to all those whose memories, research and chance remarks, have helped me along the way.

Credit is theirs; errors are mine

The words of the song 'Friend O'Mine' were written by Frederick Weatherley, who died in 1929. The song was one which I remember my father singing to my mother at family parties, and never fails to bring tears to my eyes.

Chapter One

The Taylor family already knew what they would find when they crept out of their Anderson air-raid shelter on that bitter morning of 11 January, 1941. Huddling together on the two camp beds that Dick Taylor and his son Terry had set up before Terry had gone away to sea, they had listened in fear to the tumult outside and, when the ground beneath them swelled and shook, when the very air seemed to collapse in the roar of that almost unbelievable explosion, when they knew that their own house must have been hit, they had clutched each other in terror that they were about to be blasted from their hiding-place.

The sheets of corrugated iron that formed a shelter over the hole Dick and Terry had dug, had rattled and shaken about them, and earth had crumbled through the cracks between them. But they had held firm, and when the crash of falling masonry and the smashing of glass had ceased, Dick and Cissie and the others were still alive. Alive – but not yet safe. It was another six hours before the All Clear sounded and they dared to creep out and see, in the cold, grey light, what had been done to their home.

'It's gone,' Cissie whispered, covering her face with both hands. 'Oh Dick, it's all gone. Our home, all our furniture – everything. *Everything.*'

'The bastards,' he said slowly, staring at the huge pile of debris. 'The bloody, bloody *bastards* . . .' He broke into a fit of coughing and bent over, his thin shoulders shaking with the effort, while Cissie steadied him with her arm.

'We might be able to salvage a few things.' Judy took a

step up the garden path. Her fair hair, cut to a short bob, was tousled from the night in the shelter and her eyes were gritty and sore. 'We might be able to get a few bits and pieces out.'

'Bits and pieces!' Cissie shook her head. 'That's all they'll be – bits and pieces. There won't be a thing left whole. It's not even any good searching.'

Judy went forward just the same, with her Aunt Polly close beside her. Polly had been living with the Taylors ever since her husband Johnny had been lost at sea in the early days of the war. At thirty-five she was twelve years younger than Cissie, and the same number of years older than her niece, thus she was more like a sister to twenty-two-year-old Judy and they had long ago dispensed with the title of 'Aunt'. Now, as they crept up the garden path towards the mound of broken beams, shattered glass and tossed bricks, they reached out to each other and touched hands.

'It's awful,' Judy said shakily. 'Everything smashed to bits, just like that. And what for? Why us? The man who dropped that bomb doesn't even know us. Why are they doing it, Poll?'

'It's not just us,' Polly said quietly. 'You know that. Look at what's been happening in London and all those other places. We're all getting it. And I reckon Pompey got it as bad as any last night. Look – you can still see the flames. It looks as if the whole city's on fire. There must be thousands like us, bombed out of their homes. And thousands killed too, I expect. At least we're all alive.' She bit her lip and Judy knew that she must be thinking of Johnny. 'Thank God we were down in the shelter.'

Judy nodded. There had already been over thirty raids on Portsmouth. The people had grown used to the eerie wail of the siren and the frantic dash for shelter. They had heard the thunder of the explosions and felt the earth quake as craters were blasted into roads, and houses demolished. They had emerged into devastated streets, picked their way

2

through the rubble and seen dead and injured lying like broken dolls where they had been flung. They knew what had happened in London and Coventry. Yet they were still not prepared for this terrible Blitz. Perhaps you never can imagine the worst, she thought. Perhaps you always do think it'll never happen to you.

She had almost refused to go down to the shelter the night before. She hated the confinement of the small space half underground, with the corrugated iron curving low over their heads. But the family's insistence had forced her to conquer her fears and now, seeing the ruin of her home, she was thankful. If they'd let me stay indoors, she thought, I'd be dead now, buried in all this rubble.

They paused and lifted their heads. A pall of dust and filth hung about them like a fog, filling their mouths and noses with its grit and stench. The sky was blackened by smoke, shot through with searing flashes of red and orange flame. Judy stared at it and felt her heart gripped by dread.

'And how long are we going to stay alive?' she burst out. 'We were lucky not to get a direct hit on the shelter. They'll come again, Polly, they'll keep on coming till we're all dead.' Tears were pouring down her cheeks. 'Look at that. Our house. Our *home*. Nothing left. All Dad's books and Mum's sewing things, and our Terry's gramophone and all our records, and your Sylvie's dolly that she left to keep you company while she's away, and – and . . .' Sobbing, she ran forward and began to tear at the rubble.

Polly gripped her arm tightly and drew her back.

'Leave it, Judy. Cissie's right – we won't find anything here, and it's dangerous to try. We'd better—' She stopped abruptly and her voice rose with a touch of panic. 'What *do* we do now? What *do* people do when they've got nowhere to go?'

They stared at each other and at the jagged ruins of their entire street, then turned their heads and saw their neighbours, also homeless, coming out of their own shelters,

3

and they heard the wail of fear and grief and anguish that must surely be echoing around the entire city – perhaps in every city in the land.

'It's hopeless,' Judy said, her voice trembling. 'We can't win against this, Polly. They're going to invade. They must be. They might be here already, for all we know. They're going to do the same to us as they've done to all those other countries, and we haven't got a chance.'

Polly stared at her. Her grey eyes, so like Judy's and Cissie's too, hardened, and her mouth drew tight. She shook Judy's arm and her voice was low and fierce.

'Don't say that, Judy! Don't *ever* say that. We're not going to let them win. We're not going to give them the chance. Remember Dunkirk! They didn't beat us then and they won't now. They'll *never* beat us. Never!'

Gradually, the people who had been bombed out of their homes that night began to sort themselves out.

'There was an ARP man round just now with a loud hailer. He says we've all got to go to the church hall,' Mrs Green of number three told Cissie as the Taylors straggled out of the back alley at the end of the street. Everyone was out now, standing and staring in dumb stupefaction at the destruction. Of the houses left standing, none had a single window with glass in it, most had lost their chimneys and several had their fronts torn away, so that the rooms inside were exposed for all to see, like those of a dolls' house. Mrs Green's bedroom wallpaper, that she'd been so proud of when she'd had the room done up just before the war started, was ripped and dirty, and there was a mass of laths and plaster all over the bed. The bath was full of broken slates and the lavatory hung half off the wall, with water pouring out of the cistern above it. The floors had broken away and there were boards, ceiling joists and all manner of rubble piled in the downstairs rooms.

'Look at that,' she said bitterly. 'We put all we had into

4

that house. Our hearts and souls. And look what they done to it. All smashed to bits.' She turned away, her face working. 'We'll never get it back to how it was, never.'

Cissie shook her head. 'How many d'you think have been bombed out like this? What's it like in the rest of Pompey?'

'Gawd knows. That ARP bloke says the whole city's been blasted away. All the big shops out Southsea way have gone – Handley's, Knight & Lee's, all them – and the big Co-op down Fratton has burned to a cinder, *and* the Landport Drapery Bazaar, *and* Woolworth's, *and* C&A.'

'And the Guildhall too,' someone else chimed in. 'He said the Guildhall's still burning. So are the hospitals – the Eye and Ear, and part of the Royal – and the Sailor's Rest, and the Hippodrome and—'

'Blimey, ain't there nothing left?' Dick asked, his chest wheezing.

Judy stepped forward quickly. 'The Guildhall's gone?' She turned to her mother. 'I ought to go there.'

'But we don't know where we'll be. If we've got to go to the church hall . . .' Cissie stared at her, white-faced and frightened. 'What can you do anyway, if it's all burned down? You can't go off now, Judy.' Her voice rose. 'And there's your gran too, all by herself up in April Grove – what about her? Someone ought to go round to see if she's all right.' She shook her head worriedly. 'I just don't know what to do first. I don't know what to do for the best. Oh dear.'

'I'll go to Gran's first, but I really ought to try to get to work. There must be all kinds of stuff to sort out.' Judy gazed back helplessly, and Polly came to her rescue.

'People have got to try to carry on just the same, Cis, you know that. It's the same for me. I ought to go round the salon to make sure things are all right, though I can't think there'll be anyone wanting their hair done today.' Automatically, she put a hand to her own hair, dark like her sister's and still tousled from the night spent in the shelter. It felt

5

gritty from the dust that still hung in the air, and she grimaced. 'Well, maybe there'll be a few. I reckon mine could do with a good wash, for a start . . . But Judy's right, the Guildhall's important, it's where the city's run from. If you can go into Mum's first, Judy, it would set our minds at rest. I'm sure she'll be all right, mind, she's got a good shelter.' She turned back to Cissie and took her arm. 'You and me and Dick'll go to the church hall and see what's what, and Judy can come over once she's found out what's going on. Come on – Dick's getting shrammed with cold, stood out here with all this dust getting down into his lungs and all.'

Cissie stood undecided for a moment, then Dick coughed again and she nodded. 'You're right, it's not doing him no good at all being out in this cold air with all this smoke about.' She glanced up at the blackened sky. 'There's still places on fire, you can see the flames.' A fresh thought struck her and her voice began to rise again. 'And look at us, got nothing but what we're standing up in – my best coat gone, and that nice red frock you made yourself, Poll, and that warm jumper I knitted Dick for Christmas. I don't know what we're going to do, I don't really.'

'Don't worry about that now,' Polly said gently. 'Come on, let's get down the hall into the warm, they'll sort us out. I dare say they've got clothes and other stuff. Come on, Cis.'

Cissie nodded. 'All right. We can't do nothing here, that's for certain.' She took a deep breath and straightened her shoulders. 'Now then, Judy, you make sure you come back the minute you can, and you will look in on your Gran, won't you? She ought to have come up to us like I wanted, not stopped down there by herself where we don't know what's happening to her . . . Dick, are you all right?'

He nodded, though he was holding his chest as if it pained him. 'This blasted dust, it's everywhere. It's plaster dust, you know – it's that fine it gets right down inside.' He coughed again and Cissie clicked her tongue. 'Lot of use I'm going to be,' he said bitterly. 'Useless article.'

'Now you're not to talk like that,' his wife said sharply. 'You did your bit in the last lot, that's why you're like this now. Come on, we're going down the church hall; they'll have somewhere to sit down there and a nice hot cup of tea. That's what we all need.' She started to move away, her hand hooked firmly through her husband's arm, and then turned back to Judy. 'You do whatever you can for your gran, Judy, and come back once you've found out what's happening. If we get sent on anywhere else we'll make sure the people at the hall know the address.'

Judy watched them go, torn with doubt. She wanted to support her mother and help her father and she was racked with fear for her grandmother, all alone in her own small terraced house. But as well as her concern for the family there was her loyalty to her job at the Guildhall offices and her anxiety for the people who spent the nights there – the Lord Mayor himself, who had moved in when the bombing started, and the ARP staff. What had happened to them, if the Guildhall had been destroyed?

She turned and made her way through the streets, passing groups of people scrabbling through the debris in search of possessions or – even worse – for family members or neighbours who had been buried. At every turn, she longed to stop and help, but you couldn't help everyone and her fears for her grandmother grew. Suppose she hadn't gone to the shelter – suppose her house had been bombed before she could get out – suppose the Anderson itself had had a direct hit! Everyone knew they couldn't stand up to that. Suppose her granny was even now lying under a mass of twisted metal and earth and stones, crying for someone to come and rescue her . . .

It was impossible to get through some of the streets, and although she knew the city well, Judy often found herself

7

stopping and gazing helplessly at an unrecognisable landscape. Some streets were blocked off by fire engines and long, snaking hosepipes, with firemen and ARP wardens and police waving at people to get back from craters or suspected unexploded bombs. Time and time again she was turned back and had to find a different way through streets and alleyways she had never seen before, until she began to despair of ever finding a route out of this nightmare.

At last, when she had almost given up hope, she found herself in September Street, at the top of October Street which led down to April Grove, and she broke into a run. There had been some damage here – slates torn off, windows smashed in, and towards the bottom of the street a whole house ripped to pieces, leaving a smoking gap between its neighbours. Her heart in her mouth, Judy came to the little row of houses that ran along the end and then let out a long breath of relief when she saw that the street had been virtually undamaged.

She came to the front door, varnished and polished by her father just before the war had started, and hammered on it, calling at the top of her voice. 'Granny! Gran – it's me, Judy. Are you there? Are you all right?'

'She ain't there, love.' The voice brought her whipping round, to stare in dismay at the wrinkled face of the old woman who lived next door. Then the crumpled lips stretched into a toothless grin. 'She's gorn round the church hall, see if she can 'elp out a bit. Got all the bombed people there, they 'ave, givin' 'em soup and cupsa tea and that. I told her, I could do with a cuppa meself after the night we bin through, but she never bit. Anyway, thass where she's gorn.' She blinked her rheumy eyes at Judy. 'You don't feel like a cuppa tea, I s'pose?'

Judy shook her head. 'I'm on my way to work, Mrs Kinch, but I wanted to make sure Gran was all right first. I'd better go and see if I can find her.'

She ran back up to October Street. The church hall was

about a quarter of a mile away, across the railway line and past the shops. It was crowded with people, all looking bewildered and lost, but she caught sight of the brisk little figure standing behind a long trestle table, wielding a teapot, and pushed her way through the throng.

'Gran! I've been looking for you! Mrs Kinch said you'd be here. We were worried.'

Alice Thomas looked round and gave her granddaughter a quick nod. 'Judy. I was wondering about you, too – thought I'd come up and see once I'd finished here, but the rate we're going it don't look as if we're ever going to finish. Must be thousands bombed out, thousands . . . How d'you get on down home? Any damage round your way? I hear the Guildhall's on fire, and the Landport Drapery Bazaar, where young Jean Foster works, and God knows what else down Commercial Road.'

Judy stared at her miserably. 'Gran, the house was bombed. Everything's gone – everything. Mum and the others have gone to our church hall – we've got nowhere to go. All we've got left is the Anderson!' She began to cry, covering her face with her hands, swept by sudden desolation. 'Oh *Gran*.'

Her grandmother put down her teapot and came quickly round the end of the table. She laid her arm round Judy's shoulders and led her back behind the table, pushing her gently down on a pile of blankets. 'You sit there, love, and I'll get you a cup of tea. I don't suppose you've had a thing to eat yet, have you?'

Judy shook her head. 'There wasn't anything *to* have. And no kettle or anything. Oh Gran, what are we going to do?' She gestured helplessly round the hall. 'All these people – all of us with nowhere to go and nothing left but what we stand up in. What are we going to *do*?'

Alice handed her a thick white cup filled with dark brown tea. 'Drink that, for a start. It's nice and sweet – good for shock. And stop talking about having nowhere to go. Of course you've got somewhere to go! You'll come and stop with me, that's what. Haven't I got a house all to myself? I knew I was right to stay on there instead of giving it up and coming round to you. Fine state we'd have been in if I'd done that! Now, you drink that up and you'll feel better, and then you can give me a hand here.'

Judy shook her head. The tea was hot and warming, and she barely noticed the sweetness. She drew in a long, sobbing breath, then said, 'I can't stop, Gran, I've got to try to get to work. Goodness knows how long it'll take me – it's terrible out there – but I've got to try. And I must find Mum and Dad and Polly first, to tell them you're OK. If we can come to you for a few nights, while we get sorted out . . .'

'Few nights nothing!' Alice said smartly. 'You'll come for the duration. They won't find you nothing better, I can tell you that, not with all these other people needing a place. Now, you're not leaving here without a bit of food inside you. There's some bread and marge at the end of the table, and another cup of tea wouldn't do you any harm.'

'No thanks, Gran, but I'll take the bread to eat on the way.' Judy pulled herself to her feet and bent to give her grandmother a kiss. 'I'll see you later, back in April Grove. Don't overdo it, mind.'

'Cheek!' Alice said, poking out her tongue. 'I could give you youngsters the runaround any day. Mind you tell your mum and dad what I said, now. I'll expect you all for tea at number nine.' She filled her teapot from the steaming urn and turned back to the queue. 'Now then, love, you drink this. It's nice and sweet, good for shock. You'll feel all the better for it . . .'

Judy headed for the exit and set off back to the hall where her mother and father would have gone. After that, she'd get down to Commercial Road and try to find out what was happening at the Guildhall, and where the office staff should be going.

Back outside, it seemed like hours since they had crawled out of the Anderson shelter to find the house blown into oblivion. Yet the sky was still darkened by the pall of stinking smoke, and the streets were still crowded with people, wandering bewildered and stunned by all that had happened during that terrible night. It was as if day had decided not to break, as if the sun had taken one look at what was happening and turned away its face.

The sun would come back though, she thought. It would come back when the sky had cleared, and let light back into their lives. As Polly had said, they weren't going to let the Germans beat them. They wouldn't give them the chance.

Chapter Two

The sight that greeted her as she came down Commercial Road took her breath away.

By then, she'd seen enough damage and heard enough stories to have a fair idea of what was happening. But she still wasn't prepared for the scene of total devastation here – the great shops nothing more than smoking ruins, the road swarming with firemen and police and ARP wardens, the knots of stunned bystanders – and the few shops that hadn't been hit, open and with counter staff valiantly trying to carry on as if nothing had happened.

Worst of all was the Guildhall itself. The great, proud building on the square was still ablaze, its bell tower sending flames high into the sky, shot with flashes of brilliant green fire as the copper of the cupola melted and ran down the tall stone pillars. Judy stopped where she was, on the opposite side of the square, and stared at it. Her eyes filled with tears.

'Terrible, innit,' said a man standing nearby. 'Just terrible. They'll never be able to put it back, you know, not like it was. The whole of Pompey's bin ruined. Never be the same again, never.'

'But what happened to the people inside?' Judy whispered. 'The Lord Mayor was *sleeping* there, so that he could always be on hand if he was needed. And there were staff, and firewatchers on the roof. What happened to them all?'

The man shrugged. 'Don't ask me. Mind, I did hear as they'd all gone out to Southsea, took over a hotel or summat. Fine time to go on their holidays!' He snorted derisively.

Judy stared at him, then turned away. She started to cross the square but was held back by a large policeman. 'Sorry, love, you can't go over there, it's dangerous. We got enough to contend with here, without sightseers getting under our feet. What you doing here anyway? Ain't you got no home to go to?'

'As a matter of fact, I haven't,' Judy said, suddenly angry. 'We were bombed out last night, like a lot of other people.' She ignored his embarrassed flush and went on quickly, 'I work in there – or did till yesterday. I came down to see what I could do. Is it true the Lord Mayor's gone out to Southsea? Is he all right? Are all the staff safe?'

The policeman shook his head. 'I don't know about the staff, love, they ain't told us nothing. The Mayor's all right, I do know that, but what I heard was he'd gone up Cosham.' He lifted his head as someone gave a yell from across the square. 'Look, you can see we're busy, love, just be a good girl and get out of the way, will you? And all you others too,' he added, raising his voice to include the rest of the crowd. 'Go and give a hand to someone what needs it – there's plenty of clearing up to be done.' He turned away and the crowd began to shuffle off, muttering.

Judy stood wondering what to do next. Southsea and Cosham were at opposite ends of the city. Someone must know, she thought. And wherever the Mayor was, he'd need his staff, the secretaries and office workers who knew where everything was kept. Her heart skipped as it suddenly struck her that the offices themselves must have been destroyed, and everything in them. The papers, the files, the type-writers – everything the city depended on to keep it functioning smoothly, would all be gone. How would they ever manage to sort it all out?

'Judy!'

She turned quickly. 'Miss Marsh! Oh, I'm so glad to see you. I couldn't find out what was happening. Someone told me the Mayor was in Southsea, and then the policeman said Cosham and I just didn't know *what* to do.'

The office supervisor came forward quickly and took her arm. 'All right, Judy. Don't worry. We're getting things sorted out gradually.' She rubbed her face wearily. She was carrying a notebook and wearing her office suit and her smart hat with the little veil, and Judy felt suddenly ashamed of her own clothes – the skirt and jumper she'd worn to go to the shelter last night, with her old coat thrown over the top. She began to stammer out an apology, but the supervisor cut her short.

'Don't be silly, child. You've got here, that's the important thing. Was it very difficult, getting through the streets?'

'Well, it was a bit.' Judy thought of the ruined houses, the fires, the devastation on all sides. 'And we were bombed out ourselves.'

'*You* were bombed out? My dear girl!'

'Yes – our house was blown to bits,' Judy told her, nodding miserably. 'There's nothing left at all.' And to her dismay, she began to cry, again the tears pouring down her face as she stood at the edge of the square with the Guildhall and, it seemed, the whole of Portsmouth, in flames around her.

'Judy. Come here, love.' She felt the older woman's arms around her and leaned against the solid body, half amazed at what was happening. Miss Marsh had always been strict and unapproachable, not the sort of person you'd cry on at all – yet here she was, patting Judy's shoulder and murmuring, 'There, there,' just like a mum or an auntie would.

'I'm sorry, Miss Marsh,' Judy said shakily. 'I didn't mean to give way like that – but I was so frightened when I saw the Guildhall, and so worried about the Mayor and everyone, and then when I saw you—'

'It's all right, Judy. You don't have to go on.' Miss Marsh gave her a handkerchief. 'It's not very clean, I'm afraid – there's so much dust in the air. Now, let me get this straight. Your own home was bombed last night, is that right? Was anyone hurt?'

'No.' Judy blew her nose. 'Oh, I'm sorry, I didn't mean to use—'

'Don't be silly. Who else lives in the house? Your mother and father?'

'Yes, and Polly – she's my auntie, my mum's sister – and her little girl Sylvie, only she's evacuated, and my brother, when he's at home, but he's away at sea now. He's in the Navy.'

'So it's just you and your parents and your aunt at home at the moment?' Miss Marsh said, trying to unravel this information. 'And where are they now?'

'They went round to the church hall. They're going to my gran's up at Copnor after, but they had to stay there to register. Someone said there's clothes, and there might even be a bit of money to help get straight again. It's not that we want charity,' Judy said earnestly, 'but we've lost *everything*, and there's the electricity bill to pay, and—'

'Well, all that will be sorted out. And will you be staying with your grandmother in Copnor?'

'Yes. She lives in April Grove, off September Street.'

'I know where you mean. So at least you've got some-where to go tonight?'

'Yes. That's why I thought I ought to come down and see what's happening here.' Judy sniffed and blew her nose again. 'Only it took such a long time getting through the streets, and I know I'm ever so late . . .'

'For heaven's sake, girl, don't apologise for being *late*! I'm amazed you came at all. Now listen, the Lord Mayor's arranging to take over part of the Royal Beach Hotel at Southsea to use as offices – it was closed when the war started and is already being used as a casualty clearing station – so that's where you'll be reporting for work. It's the ARP who have relocated to Cosham. As you've seen, there's been a tremendous amount of damage all over the city, and there's a great deal of work to do. The Lord

Mayor's made arrangements already for people like your-selves who have lost everything – he's managed to find a bank that's open for business and they've released a substantial sum of money for the Air-Raid Distress Fund, so that people can be given some ready cash. The War Emergency Committee will divide it between all their members so that it can be distributed. They'll also be evacuating any homeless women or children who want to leave the city and, as you know, Emergency Centres have been set up in schools and church halls.'

'Yes, that's where Mum and Dad went,' Judy nodded.

'And you remember the Lady Mayoress set up her own Clothing Fund at the beginning of the war, so there will, we hope, be enough clothes to give everyone at least one warm outfit.' Her glance took in Judy's own shabby attire. 'I suppose that's all you have yourself now?'

Judy said glumly, 'I'm afraid it is, Miss Marsh. They're my oldest things, I always change into them, to keep my work clothes nice, and when the siren went—'

'Well, I wouldn't expect you to be dressed in your best for an air raid!' The supervisor's face broke into a rare smile. 'Now, you're not to worry about that. Come to work in whatever you can find. But today, I think you ought to go back and help your family.'

'Oh no! I mean, I ought to be at work – there must be so much to do. And there isn't really anything I can do at home – at Gran's, I mean –' To her horror, she felt the tears gather in her eyes again and blinked them away furiously. 'I'd much rather be doing something useful, Miss Marsh.'

The supervisor looked at her consideringly. 'Very well, then. But you don't have to come all the way out to Southsea, not today. What you can do is stay here and look out for any other Guildhall or Municipal staff like yourself, who come down to find out what's happening. Tell them to report to the Royal Beach.' She sighed. 'We still don't know who is likely to turn up and who isn't. There may be others who've been bombed out, or even hurt in the raids. But those who can, will surely do as you did and come here. Now, do you think you can do that? You know everyone, don't you?' She held out her notebook. 'Write down the names of all the people you see.'

Judy nodded. 'I can do that, Miss Marsh.'

'Good. That enables me to go out to the hotel and get on with the work there. We're having to start completely from scratch. Now, Judy, when you're sure you've seen everyone – everyone who comes here, that is – you're to go back to your grandmother's and be with your family. You've had a dreadful time and you must be exhausted.'

'We didn't get much sleep last night, but I don't really feel tired, Miss Marsh – just sort of light, if you know what I mean.' Judy put her hand to her forehead and swayed slightly. 'I expect I'm just a bit hungry.'

Miss Marsh gave her a sharp glance. 'A cup of tea and something to eat for you, my girl. Come on – there's a stall over there, they'll see to you.' She led Judy over to a makeshift stall where an urn was boiling on a large stove which appeared to have been built out of bricks salvaged from the piles of rubble. A woman in a green uniform was dealing out mugs of tea and sticky buns to the firemen and soldiers who were still desperately trying to put out the fire.

Gratefully, Judy ate a bun, surprised to find just how hungry she was, and swallowed the tea. She smiled a trifle shakily at the supervisor. 'I feel a bit better now. Sorry about that.'

'That's all right. You've got more colour in your cheeks, anyway. Now, I'm off back to Southsea. Don't forget – it's the Royal Beach Hotel – and once you're sure you've seen everyone, you're to go straight home. Don't stay here too long, anyway. If they haven't arrived by mid-afternoon, they won't be coming.' Her face twisted a little and she turned away. 'I'll look for you at the hotel tomorrow morning.'

'Yes, Miss Marsh.' Judy watched her walk briskly away.

She knew well enough what the supervisor had meant. There might be casualties, even deaths, amongst the staff. In the chaos that the raid had caused, nobody knew what might have happened.

How did other places manage when this happened to them? she wondered. Places like London, Bristol, Liverpool, Coventry. They'd been through this as well, yet somehow they still managed to carry on.

Perhaps that was the answer. Perhaps that was all you *could* do. Just carry on.

It was growing dark again as Judy walked wearily down October Street and turned into April Grove. The pall of smoke was still drifting above the rooftops, and with no street-lights and every house blacked out there was no glimmer of cheer in the devastated streets, no hint of warmth in the bitter cold. What will we do if they come again? she wondered. How could we stand another night like last night?

She came to her grandmother's door and knocked. It opened, and her aunt drew back the blackout curtain for Judy to push past. They felt their way down the short, dark passage to the back room, where she found the family sitting round by the glow of a small fire with a kettle resting on the coals, and the light of a single candle. Her mother and grandmother sat in armchairs on each side of the fire, and Dick and Polly were on kitchen chairs in front of it. Dick got up and moved his chair aside, pulling another into the space for Judy.

'That's better,' she said. 'It's horrible outside.' She shrugged off her coat and hung it on the inside of the door to the staircase.

'Oh Judy, thank goodness,' her mother said. 'We were starting to get worried about you.'

'I've been down the Guildhall Square, looking out for the other people at work. They've moved the offices out to Southsea.' Judy sank down on the chair and stretched her hands out to the fire. 'It's awful, Mum. The whole place has gone. The Guildhall's still burning, and they say everything inside's been destroyed. All those lovely pictures, and the wooden panelling, and the carpets – everything. And there's street after street just ruined. You can't get through some of them at all. Someone told me there'd been nearly three thousand fires. Three thousand! How could they hope to put them all out?'

'It's wicked,' Cissie said, her voice trembling. 'Wicked.'

'It's war, Cis,' Dick said. 'There's worse happening than a few pictures and carpets getting burned. People are being killed. Like that young woman just up the road here.'

'What young woman?' Judy looked at him. She'd visited her grandmother often enough to know most of the neighbours in April Grove by sight and from Alice's talk. 'Who's been killed, Dad?'

'I'm not sure if you knew her,' Alice said. She looked down at the black and white cat on her knee, stroking his head. 'She'd only been here a few months – bombed out in the first big raid she was, and came to live in March Street. Kathy Simmons – had two little girls and a baby boy.'

'I remember you talking about her.' Judy stared at her grandmother. 'Wasn't the baby born in the shelter? Don't say she's been killed? Was that her house I saw this morning, bombed flat?'

'That's the one. Olive Chapman as was – you know, she married Derek Harker from the builder's – had just gone over to fetch her to their shelter but Kathy went back indoors to boil some water for her Thermos flask, apparently, just as the bomb fell.' Alice shook her head. Her face creased with sadness. 'They said she couldn't have known anything about it – but still, it's cruel, a young mother like that killed for no reason.'

'Oh, how awful.' Judy put both hands to her face. 'What about the children? Those little girls – and the baby?'

Cissie took out a handkerchief and wiped her eyes. 'Olive

had the girls with her, out in the street. They were blown halfway up the road by the blast, but they weren't hurt, not as such. But the baby – he was with his mummy, poor little scrap.' She stopped, her mouth working. 'Only six months old. It don't bear thinking of.'

Polly put her hand on her sister's arm. 'Don't upset yourself all over again, Cis. It's terrible, I know, but like Mum says, they couldn't have known anything about it.'

'But it's their lives gone, isn't it!' Cissie cried. 'That little baby, with his whole life ahead of him – he never even had the chance to learn to crawl! As for those two girls, they've lost their mother. And they're not the only ones, are they? There's you, Polly, with your Johnny gone, and poor Olive Chapman lost her baby that she was expecting, and others, hundreds and hundreds of others. What was Mrs Shaw along the road telling you about her Gladys, driving that ambulance last night? Went down a cellar she did, and found a whole family dead down there, all except one little girl. How's that poor little soul ever going to get over it? How are *any* of them ever going to get over it? And this is just the beginning!' She pulled her apron up over her face and began to cry. 'I don't think I can stand it any more!' she said in a muffled voice. 'I just don't think I can *stand* it!'

The others gazed at her and then looked at each other miserably in the glow of the fire. There didn't seem to be anything anyone could say, Judy thought. They all felt pretty much the same. But you couldn't give in. You just couldn't.

'Come on, Mum,' she said gently. 'We all depend on you, you know. You're the one that keeps us all going.'

'Well, I'm not much use to you now,' Cissie said bitterly. 'I'm not much use to no one. I've just had enough, that's all. We've been having raids for months, and there's been all those terrible things happening in London and Coventry and the rest, and now it's our turn, and they're just bashing us to pieces, to *pieces* – and what can we do about it, eh? Tell me that. Oh, I know we can bomb them too, but what good's that going to do? It just means a whole lot more people get killed in their own homes, people like us who never wanted a war in the first place. How's it ever going to end?'

'We can't just let them ride roughshod over us,' Judy said. 'You know what they've done in Poland and all those other countries. We can't let that happen here.'

'So it's better to be bombed to bits, is it? It's better to have everything smashed to pieces around us and have little babies killed?' Cissie took the apron from her face and stared at them. 'Oh, I know what they say, I know what they tell us, and I'm just an ordinary person who doesn't know anything about these things – but I just can't see the *sense* of it all.' She took a deep breath. 'I'm sorry, I know we're not supposed to talk like this, but I've just had enough of it all today, that's all.'

'You need a cup of tea.' Judy got up, but her grandmother put out a hand.

'There's no gas, love. The mains got fractured, see, and they turned it off because of the danger. That's why we've got the kettle on the fire.'

Judy sank back. 'No gas and no electricity. It's the same all over the city, I suppose. It's a good thing we've got some coal.' A thought struck her. 'Here, what about *our* coal? From – from home? Hadn't we better get that over here?'

'We've done it, love,' her father said. 'Been going backwards and forwards all day with my old barrow. Had to leave one of us on guard, too. There's people swarming all over the place, looking for anything they can pick up. Not that there was much to find in our place,' he added ruefully.

Judy stared at him. 'You mean they were stealing things?'

'Well, they wasn't offering to pay for them! There's always people out for easy pickings, no matter what's happened.'

She nodded. 'I know. The shops have all got soldiers standing outside them because of looters, but I never

21

thought they'd take stuff from people who'd been bombed out. That's awful.'

'It's all awful,' Polly said, 'but sitting here telling each other about it won't make it any better. Now look, I know we'd all like something hot but we can't, and that's all there is to it – but we can make a few sandwiches. There's plenty of marge and fish paste and some of that blackberry and apple jam Mum made in the autumn, and you'll never guess what else I found in a tin in the cupboard.'

'What?' Judy asked obediently, and her aunt gave a little crow of triumph.

'Christmas cake, that's what! Keeping it for Easter, your Gran was, but I reckon we need it more now. We can all have a really good slice, and thumb our noses at Hitler while we eat it!'

Judy laughed and after a moment or two the others joined in. Their laughter was a little shaky, and sounded dangerously close to crying, but somehow they all felt better for it, and as Dick stoked up the fire and the kettle boiled and Polly began to cut bread, and the Christmas cake was sliced up and handed round, the little gathering began to seem almost like a party.

'I reckon we ought to play a few games,' Judy said. 'Or sing some songs. Cheer ourselves up a bit. Just in case there's any Fifth Columnists listening down the chimney. We don't want them reporting back to Hitler that we're downhearted, do we?'

They ate their sandwiches and cake, then did as she had suggested. But as their voices rose in a wavering rendition of 'Roll Out the Barrel' and 'It's a Long Way to Tipperary', they were each still thinking of the devastation outside, and of the people who were homeless tonight, or who had been killed or injured. They were each thinking of Kathy Simmons and her baby boy, of the two little girls who had lost their mother, and of all those others up and down the country who had had their lives shattered.

Later on, when everyone else had gone to bed – Cissie

22

and Dick upstairs to the front bedroom, Polly to the back room she would share with Judy, and her grandmother Alice to the front room downstairs – Judy sat by the dying fire and tried to write a letter to her fiancé, Sean.

It seemed so long since she had seen him, so long since the night last May when they'd got engaged, only three weeks after they'd met at a dance on South Parade Pier. Dick and Cissie hadn't been at all keen on such a hasty courtship, but Judy was twenty-two, so they couldn't very well say no. And there was no question of a wedding yet, with Sean going back to sea the very next day.

For most of the past eight months, Sean had been in the Northern Atlantic, off Norway and Iceland. During that time, he had sent letters – none for weeks, and then a dozen all arriving at once. Letters that were now buried beneath a heap of rubble in Friday night's blast.

How did you tell your fiancé the sort of things that had happened during the past twenty-four hours? Judy sighed and sucked the end of her grandmother's fountain pen, and started to write.

Dear Sean,
We had a bit of trouble in Pompey last night. There were a lot of aircraft and we got badly bombed. We're all OK but Mum and Dad and Polly and I are staying with Gran up in April Grove. I hope things are OK with you, as they find me here. I'm too tired to write any more now and will close for tonight.
From your loving Judy.

It didn't seem much, but she felt that if she started to tell him what it had really been like, she would still be there come morning.

Chapter Three

Polly got up early next morning and found Judy already downstairs, lighting the fire.

'I know Gran wouldn't usually have a fire in the morning, but there's no other way of making any tea. I wanted to get everyone a hot drink before I go off to work.'

'You're going to work?' Polly looked at her niece in surprise. 'But it's Sunday.'

'Doesn't matter. We've got to get the new offices sorted out. People will be flooding in wanting help, and we can't just tell 'em to go away and come back on Monday. There's all the Emergency Centres to be seen to, and people evacuated or found new homes – any amount of things to be done.' Judy held a sheet of newspaper in front of the fire to make it blaze up. 'It's a good thing you went and got our coal. I don't know how long it'll be before we get the gas and electricity back.'

'It's not just that, either. They were going round telling people to boil water for ten minutes before drinking it in case of typhoid.' Polly put some plates on the table and began to slice the rest of yesterday's loaf. 'Well, at least Jerry gave us a quiet night; we'll all feel better for a few hours' sleep. Me and your mother have got to go round the Emergency Centre again this morning, get new ration books sorted out and see what money they'll give us. They were too busy yesterday, so once we'd registered we just came on here. And there's people we ought to let know – your Auntie May and Uncle Fred, and your mum's friend Mrs Walker. One of us ought to go round and see Jean Foster too, let her know where we are. She's Terry's girlfriend after all, almost one of the family.' She stopped and stared at the loaf in her hand. 'I wish I could go out and see Sylvie.'

'Oh, Polly! She must be wondering if you're all right. They won't know what's been going on, out there in the country.' Judy lowered the newspaper just as it was beginning to scorch in the middle. 'Why don't you go on the train?'

'I don't suppose they're running, do you? Anyway, I don't feel I can leave your mum and dad, not with the way Cis is, and your dad was wheezing all day long yesterday. There's such a lot to see to here. I did send a telegram yesterday, just to say we were all well, but she don't know nothing about the house, of course. There's not much point in telling her, is there – not straight away. She's only seven and I don't want to frighten her.'

'She'll have to know, though, because of addressing her letters.' Judy stood up, irresolute. 'Perhaps I shouldn't go into work, after all . . .'

'No, no, you go, you can't let the office down. We can manage here, and what Sylvie doesn't know won't hurt her. I'll try and go out sometime next week if the trains are running again, and I'll write her a letter. Now, is that fire hot enough for the kettle yet?'

The two of them got together a scrappy breakfast of bread and margarine, just coloured with jam, and by the time the kettle boiled Alice had emerged from the front room where she had slept on the sofa and Cissie had come down from upstairs. 'I told Dick to stay in bed; he's had a terrible night, hacking away. That dust and smoke really got into his chest. How were you on that settee, Mum? I felt proper bad, turning you out of your own bed.'

'Don't be daft, girl, I was snug as a bug in a rug. Stood to reason you two would have to have the double bed. I might be able to get a camp bed or put-u-up for later, but the settee'll do for now.' She bustled through to the lean-to scullery. 'I suppose there's no gas on yet?'

'Nothing's on yet. And we haven't got all that many candles left, neither. I don't know what we're going to do if they don't get things straight soon. There's going to be people desperate.' Polly poured out five cups of tea. 'There, are you going to take Dick's up to him, Cis? There's not much sense in him coming down till the room's warmed up a bit. And look, I'll toast a slice of bread, he needs something hot inside him. Spread some Marmite on it.'

Cissie took her husband's breakfast up the stairs and the others sat round the table, drinking their tea. Polly looked at her mother.

'Cis and me are going down the Centre this morning, see what's what. Are you going to stop here with Dick?'

'I am not!' The old woman looked at her indignantly, her bright eyes snapping. 'Stop here when there's work to be done? No, I'll be helping on the tea-stall, same as yesterday. There'll be plenty glad of a cuppa while they're clearing up.'

'Yes, but I don't want you to overdo it.'

'I'll be the judge of when I've overdone it!' Alice retorted. 'Just because you've moved in here, our Poll, it doesn't mean to say you can start ordering me about. I'd have done as I pleased if you hadn't been here and I'll do as I please now you are, and don't you forget it.'

Judy grinned and Polly shook her head. 'I'm not likely to forget it, you independent old besom! You'll be ordering us all about from your deathbed – that's if you don't outlive us all. All right, you go and pour tea for firemen while me and Cis go and see about our ration books and try to put together a few clothes and things. How about you, Judy, do you want us to try to get you anything?'

Judy shook her head. 'Miss Marsh said there were going to be some things out at the new offices – the Lady Mayoress was going to see to it. After all, if she can't get us a few things from her own Clothing Store, nobody can!' She put down her cup and stood up. 'I'd better be going. Goodness knows how long it'll take me to get all the way out to Southsea. I don't suppose there's any buses running. Better expect me when you see me.' She shrugged into her coat and called up the stairs to her mother. ''Bye, Mum – I'm off now. 'Bye, Dad.'

Polly watched her go. 'I hope she'll be all right. She was tossing and turning all night long. It really upset her, seeing our house bombed to bits and then going down and seeing the Guildhall in flames – not to mention all the other damage. We'll have to keep an eye on her, Mum.'

'She'll be all right. She's made of the right stuff – like you and me. And she knows that the best way to take your mind off things is to get on with your work. No, it's Cis that I worry about, she takes everything so hard. And Dick, too. He was grey when he got round here yesterday, proper grey.'

'Well, with all that smoke and dust about . . .'

'It's not just his chest. It's what it's doing to his mind. It's bringing it all back, you can see that. What he went through before . . . you know what I mean.' The old lady nodded significantly. 'He'll be getting those nightmares again, you see if he don't.'

Polly opened her mouth to reply, then closed it again quickly as they heard the sound of footsteps descending the stairs. By the time Dick appeared at the staircase door in the scullery, Polly was already at the sink, pouring water from the kettle into the enamel bowl. She added a small lump of washing soda and gave him a bright smile.

'Hello, Dick, how're you then? Sleep all right, did you? I must say it was a treat to be allowed to stop in bed all night instead of having to get up and go down the shelter . . . D'you want another cup of tea?'

He shook his head. 'No, thanks. Just going out to the lav.' He opened the back door and a bitter wind scoured into the scullery. 'Strewth, it's like an icebox out here.' The door slammed behind him and he passed the scullery window on his way to the lavatory, tacked on to the back of the lean-to. Polly sighed. It was going to come hard to them all, not having an indoor lavatory any more. And no bathroom either. None of the little two-up, two-down houses in April Grove had a bathroom. They all had a tin bath hanging on a nail outside, which had to be dragged in every Friday or Saturday night and filled with kettles of hot water, or from an Ascot if you were lucky enough to have one. It would be hard on them all, having to go back to that.

'Have you still got that old bath, Mum?' she called. 'Only I was just thinking, you won't be able to come up to us any more of a Friday afternoon for your bath, will you? I wondered if you'd got rid of it.'

'Not got rid of it, as such,' Alice said, coming through and taking a tea-towel from the back door. 'It's still out there – but don't you remember, I got Terry to fill it up with earth and plant potatoes in it. Won't be much cop for bathing in now!'

Polly stared at her and began to laugh. 'Potatoes! Well, we'd better get 'em out. I don't suppose you can buy tin baths for love nor money now.'

'Get 'em out? They're me earlies! I've been looking forward to them for Easter. We'll have to use the small one – stand up and wash ourselves down. You know they're on at us to save water anyway.'

Dick came back indoors, shuddering with cold. 'I could do with that tea now, if there's any left. Did I hear someone talking about a bath?'

'I was just saying, we're going to miss having the lavvy and everything indoors.' Polly dried her hands and poured him a cup of tea. 'There you are, Dick, and don't laugh at it, you'll be old and weak yourself one day . . . Here, guess what, Mum's gone and planted spuds in her old tin bath, and says we'll have to wait till Easter before we can have a good soak. What's it like outside, apart from cold?'

'I never hung about to look. You can still smell the smoke and that. I saw that woman next door, what's her name, the thin scraggy one that hangs round the dockyard gates, but I never said nothing. Wouldn't want her to get the wrong idea.'

Alice laughed. 'Nancy Baxter's all right! She wouldn't bother with you, Dick, she's got her own customers. And you won't get past her old ma without speaking, I can tell you that. Granny Kinch has a word for everyone that goes along the street.'

'I know that, nosy old faggot. What about those nippers? They been evacuated?'

'No such luck,' Alice said. 'Young Micky's as full of mischief as a barrel-load of monkeys; got into trouble with young Gordon Hodges after Christmas last year, but it was only Gordon got sent away though everyone knows it was as much Micky as him. The other one's just a baby – Vera, she's called, and she's as scrawny as her mother.'

Cissie had come downstairs again and was sitting in the back room making more toast over the fire. She called to her husband to come and have some more, and he took his cup of tea through and sat down at the table. They sat in silence, each wrapped in thought.

'It don't seem possible we've lost everything, does it, Dick?' Cissie said at last. 'Our home, and all our furniture and clothes, and the wireless you and Terry built, and all Terry's Meccano and model aeroplanes . . . I can't sort of take it in. I keep remembering things – our photos too, and your Brownie camera . . .' Her voice trembled.

'I know, love. And they'll never be able to give it all back. All we'll get is a few clothes and some cash to tide us over. We'll have to start all over again.'

'But we'll get something from the insurance, won't we? I mean, we've got all the papers – we've got the tin box with everything in, that we always take down the shelter with us. We'll have to look it out, Dick, see what it says, and we'll have to let the collector know where we are too.' She rubbed her face. 'There's so much to *do* – so much to think about. I don't know how we're going to get through it all.'

He was silent for a moment, then he said, 'Nor do I, Cis. It's all too much for me. I keep remembering the last lot – what it was like out in the trenches. Blokes screaming and crying and going off their heads, and then the gas . . .' He coughed, his thin body racked, and gazed at her with red-rimmed eyes. 'I've been dreaming about it all night. I thought I was back there. I don't know how I'm going to face up to it all over again, Cis, I really don't . . .' His voice trailed away to a whisper and he began to shudder.

His wife got up quickly and came round the table to put her arm around his shoulders and draw his head down against her breast. 'Oh Dick,' she said, her voice trembling. 'It's not fair, not when you've been through so much already. But we'll get through it together. We will, really. Look, we're not hurt, any of us, we're all right, and we've got somewhere to live too – we're better off than a lot of people. And our Judy's still home, and we've got Polly too, and Mum as bright as a button still. We've got a lot to be thankful for. We'll face it together, you and me, all of us. And if we've got to start all over again, then that's what we'll do. We're not going to let Hitler get the better of us. We beat the Germans before, didn't we? And we'll beat 'em again!'

Dick stayed still, his head resting heavily against her, for a long time. Then he drew in a deep breath, lifted his head and gave her a shaky grin.

'You're right, love,' he said. 'We didn't give in last time and we won't now. *We'll* give 'em something to remember us by!'

She smiled down at him and he reached for her hand and squeezed it. They looked into each other's eyes with a mixture of pride and defiance. But behind their eyes, each had the same thought.

30

What would happen if they were wrong? What would happen to them all if the Germans really did invade?

Despite his protests that he ought to go to the Centre with them and do his bit, Cissie insisted that Dick should stay at home in the warm. 'I don't want you in bed with your chest again,' she said, winding a long scarf round her neck. 'And you can put the kettle on a bit later so there's a nice cup of cocoa for us when we get back, we'll be shrammed. Tibby'll keep you company.'

Dick looked at the cat, curled up in Alice's chair. 'I'm not sure he doesn't make me cough even more. All right, Cis, I'll stop here, but I'll make meself useful just the same. You can sort out some veg for dinner and I'll set about peeling them. I suppose we can put the saucepans on the fire?'

'It'll make them sooty,' Polly said, 'but we can scrub that off. We've got to have something hot inside us.' She pulled on the woollen mittens Alice had knitted from an old unpicked jumper. 'Come on, Cis. The sooner we get there the sooner we'll be back.'

The two sisters went out into the street. A bitter wind was slicing across the allotments which ran along the back of the houses and came down to the wide part at the end of April Grove. A pleasant-faced woman with beech-brown hair tucked under a dark red hat was pushing a pram up the street, and she nodded and smiled as she came up to them. 'Hello, you're Mrs Thomas's daughters, aren't you? Popped in to see if she's all right, have you?'

Polly shook her head. 'Come to stay, more like. We were bombed out, Friday night. We're going round to the Emergency Centre now to see what they can do for us, but we won't get another house, not when Mum's got this place. It's going to be a bit of a squeeze, though.'

'No! You never were!' The woman looked at them in dismay. 'You poor things. None of you hurt though?'

'No, thank goodness. I hear there was a bit of a tragedy here though. You're Mrs Budd, aren't you?'

The woman nodded. 'That's right, I live in number fourteen. Poor young Kathy Simmons. Such a nice little body, too, and those two little girls. They're in with me now, I've left my Rose looking after them. This little madam's my youngest, Maureen.' They all peered into the pram at the little girl sitting inside, and she beamed back at them. She looked about eighteen months old, Polly thought. Jess Budd went on, 'I'm just going up to my sister's at the end of March Street. Her girl Olive's not very well.' She stopped, folding her lips as if she didn't want to talk about what was wrong with Olive.

'Mum told us,' Polly said gently. 'That's a shame. I know, I've been through it myself – lost two after our Sylvie was born. Well, we'd better not keep you, Mrs Budd. I dare say we'll be seeing you again.'

They walked on up the street, each thinking how lucky they had been to lose no more than their home and possessions. There was no doubt about it, they agreed, you could always find someone worse off than you were yourself. Olive Harker, losing her baby, Kathy Simmons and her baby killed, the two girls left motherless . . . And that was in just one street, with no other damage. What terrible tragedies were happening in all those other streets, where house after house had been destroyed?

'I feel I ought to be doing something to help,' Polly said after a moment or two. 'Ever since Sylvie went off to the country, I've felt I should be doing more than just cutting people's hair. I mean, it's not exactly vital war work, is it?'

'Well, no, but it's good for morale, isn't it? That's what they say. Anyway, what else could you do? You're not thinking of joining one of the women's services, are you?'

'I don't think they'd have me, not at my age. Thirty-five's too old. No, I was thinking of doing something voluntary. I mean, I've got Johnny's pension and if I could work part-time at the salon I'd have enough to live on, and then I could give a bit of time to something else. There must be plenty of things to do. Look at Mum, she's always on the go, doing her bit, and she's getting on for seventy. It makes me feel ashamed.'

Cissie was silent for a minute or two, then she said, 'I suppose I ought to be doing a bit more, too. I mean, there's nothing to stop me.'

'You've got Dick to look after. You know he needs you with him if he gets one of his chests. And there's got to be someone at home to keep the place going, if all the rest of us are out.'

'I suppose so. And I could do knitting and needlework and things.' They were almost at the church hall. 'Look at that, Poll, there's still a crowd of people inside. Looks as if they've been there all night, some of them, poor souls. And those women taking their names, they look worn out, don't they. What a job.'

'Yes,' Polly said, gazing at them. 'What a job.'

Chapter Four

With soldiers, sailors and marines throwing themselves into the work of helping to clear the streets, there were a few buses able to get through and Judy managed to get to Southsea without too much trouble. It took her over an hour all the same, and she thought ruefully of the extra time it would add to her working days while the Council offices were there.

The Royal Beach was a large hotel, directly opposite South Parade Pier. It was eight storeys high and probably one of the grandest hotels in the city, its rooms lavishly decorated and lit with chandeliers. At least, that was what it had been like before the war, Judy thought when she arrived. The chandeliers had all been removed for safety – partly their own and partly because of the danger of flying glass to people if the hotel were bombed – and some of the furniture had been taken away to make room for the makeshift beds and trolleys for the casualties who were brought here after a raid.

Most of these had gone now, for the hotel was being used as a clearing station rather than a hospital, but the big ground-floor lounge, bar and restaurant where they had been brought were littered with blankets and sheets, piled ready for washing, and there was a smell of blood and vomit and disinfectant. First-Aid workers were busy cleaning up and sorting fresh bandages and bedclothes ready for the next raid. They looked exhausted, as if they'd been there ever since the bombs began to fall, and Judy thought they probably had.

'Do you know where the Council offices are going to be?' she asked a woman who was near the door, scrubbing at a patch of what looked like blood on the floor. 'I was told to report here for work.'

The woman, her sleeves rolled up and a scarf wound like a turban round her head, looked up, and to her surprise Judy recognised the face of one of the WVS volunteers who had come to the Guildhall for meetings with the Lady Mayoress. They looked at each other and the woman smiled.

'You didn't expect to see me here, did you! Well, we all have to do our bit. I think the offices are going to be upstairs, though I did hear that the Mayor will have the meeting room on the ground floor as well.' She sat back on her heels and pushed a few straggling hairs out of her eyes. 'I expect you'll get a guided tour, but just in case you don't, the basement's being used as a shelter – the stairs are over there, behind that door – and there's a lookout post on the roof. The Fire Brigade are manning that at the moment, but I did hear they're going to put Observers up there, to see when planes are coming. Anyway, you should find your people on the next floor.'

Judy thanked her and went up the gracious stairs that wound their way from the big foyer all the way to the top of the building. The balustrade was of elegant wrought iron and the well was lit by a single thick flex that hung from the very top, bearing glittering chandeliers at each floor. I suppose it was too difficult to take these away, she thought, looking at the shimmering crystal drops. The touch of luxury sent a little thrill through her body. It was almost like working in a palace.

There wasn't much luxury in the new offices, however. Once comfortable, spacious bedrooms with balconies on which the guests could sit and look out over the sea only yards away, across the road, the rooms were now stark and empty. Beds, dressing-tables and wardrobes had all been removed to make space for utilitarian desks and tables, and plain wooden chairs that looked as if they'd come from the cheapest furniture shop in the city. There were no cabinets, shelves or drawers and people were standing looking a little helplessly about them. Presumably office furniture would be brought in as soon as it could be obtained, but for now they had to make do with what there was.

'How long d'you think we'll be out here?' Judy asked when she found the former bedroom that had been assigned to her department. 'It's taken me ages to get here this morning.'

'It'll be for the duration, I'm afraid,' Miss Marsh said. 'It's the same for us all, Judy.'

'I know.' Judy rubbed her cold hands together. There was no fire in the grate and a bitter wind was scouring in from the sea and finding its way through the windows. 'Well, what is there to do? I suppose none of the office papers were saved?'

'Nothing at all. The Lord Mayor only just managed to get out of the Guildhall before the roof caught fire and fell in, and the ARP were too busy trying to save the building. There were people firewatching up on the roof too, but they got down just in time, thank goodness.' Miss Marsh sat down at a desk that had been brought in from the hotel's reception area, and massaged her forehead with her fingertips. 'We've just got to start from scratch. Organise ourselves as best we can, and try to get things in order again – but it's not going to be easy. Think of all the forms we used to use, all gone; we'll have to get them printed all over again, and I haven't even heard from the printers yet. Most of the phones are out of action, and for all we know they could have been bombed too and all the plates destroyed . . . It's a nightmare, Judy.'

Judy looked at her helplessly. 'But there are people

downstairs already, wanting help – what are we going to tell them?'

'Tell them we'll do our best but it may take time. They can't expect miracles.'

They would though, Judy thought as she went to face the huddle of men and women who were down in the reception area. 'We can't get no information,' one man complained. 'We've had to trek all the way out to Southsea, and you know what the streets is like – and then when we do get here we can't find nothing out. What are we supposed to do? There's no gas, no electricity, not even any water laid on down our way, and nobody seems to know nothing. It's a flipping disaster.'

'Well, so it is,' Judy said. 'You know how much damage there's been. It's bound to take time to sort things out, I'm afraid.'

'And what're we supposed to do in the meantime?' the man demanded again. He had a pugnacious face, with small eyes and a flattened nose, and his ears looked as if they'd been chewed. He glowered at Judy and she took a step back. 'I got a wife an' three nippers to look after. They ain't had a decent meal for two days, only what that WVS stall or whatever it's called has been able to dish out. My missus can't even boil up a kettle to make a cup of tea.'

'I'm really sorry,' Judy said. 'We're doing all we can.'

There was a mutter of discontent from the crowd, and a woman in a brown herringbone coat with a scarf wrapped round her head said, 'Well, what about the Public Assistance, then? Can't they do nothing?'

'They're not here,' Judy said. 'They've been sent somewhere else – I'm not sure where.' She escaped back into the makeshift office. 'They're really upset,' she told Miss Marsh. 'I feel sorry for them but it's not our fault.'

'They won't understand that. They're worried and frightened and a lot of them have lost their homes. Well, you know yourself how they must feel. Look, here are the

37

addresses of the Public Assistance, the Police Headquarters and the Medical Offices. They're spread all over the place, I'm afraid. You'd better put a notice on the wall.'

Judy went back and tacked up the notice, listening to the aggrieved remarks as she did so. She couldn't blame the people for feeling upset – as Miss Marsh had said, they were all under strain – but she did think they ought to make some allowances. After all, nobody had known the Guildhall was going to be destroyed, and all these arrangements had had to be made at a moment's notice. 'I've had to come a long way, too,' she pointed out as one young woman with a baby in her arms started to complain about having to go miles away for Public Assistance. '*And* I was bombed out on Friday night. It's the same for us as for everyone else.'

'Yes, but you're paid to come here,' the woman snapped. 'We've got to find our own shoe-leather.' She hoisted the baby higher on to her hip and glared at Judy before turning to push her way out of the building. Judy looked after her and sighed.

'Never mind, my dear,' said a voice in her ear. 'I don't suppose she means to be nasty. She's just tired and frightened, like the rest of us. Come inside and have a cup of tea. There's something I want to ask you.'

Judy turned and saw to her surprise that it was the Lady Mayoress herself who was speaking to her. She was a familiar figure in the Council offices and had often smiled at Judy as she went by, but had never spoken to her before. Puzzled, Judy followed her back to the office, where the tables were being taken over as desks by various members of staff. The Mayoress walked across to a corner of the room and motioned to Judy to sit down. She gave her a friendly smile. 'I've seen you in the offices quite a lot, haven't I? Your name's Judith Taylor, and you've been working for the Council for some time, haven't you?'

'Yes, madam. Ever since I was sixteen. I worked in a shop when I first left school and did shorthand and typing at night school, and then I saw a job advertised in the Council office and I applied for it.'

'Well done. You're obviously a girl with some initiative.' The Lady Mayoress paused. 'Now, I know just how busy we're all going to be here, and I know how difficult it's going to be for Miss Marsh to get her office organised, but I have a very special request to make. As you probably already know, I'm the local President of the WVS – the Women's Voluntary Service. You may have seen our Head, Lady Reading, when she visited us last July.'

'Yes, madam, I remember her. She came to the Guildhall with another lady.'

'That's right. That was Lady Northampton. Now, the WVS does a lot more work than many people realise – I expect you've seen the stalls giving out tea and buns and soup that have been set up in all the bombed areas. We were there when the men came back from Dunkirk, and we've been helping out at Emergency Centres and First-Aid Posts. But we do a lot of other things, too: we've cooked Christmas dinners for folk who wouldn't otherwise have had anything, we've sorted out coal rations for old people, and we've even enrolled people into the Blood Transfusion Service. In fact, wherever people need help, you're likely to find a WVS volunteer offering it.'

She paused again and Judy gazed at her, wondering where all this was leading. Feeling that she was expected to make some response, she ventured, 'My granny helps on tea-stalls and things, but I don't think she's in the WVS. They have a uniform, don't they?'

'Yes, we wear dark green with a dark red blouse or jumper, and a green beret. But we're not like the women's Services – we don't call people up. We just ask for volunteers. And we pay for our own uniforms,' she added.

Judy began to guess what this was about. 'And you'd like me to be a volunteer? Well, I will, of course, but I can only

39

help out in the evenings. I couldn't do anything in the daytime because of my job.'

The Mayoress shook her head. 'No, my dear, I'm not asking that, although I hope that you will be able to help, in whatever way you can. What I'm asking you to do is work for me – for the WVS – full-time.'

'Full-time?' Judy stared at her. 'I don't understand. I thought it was all volunteers?'

'I'm sorry, I haven't explained properly. Look, my dear, it's obvious that with Portsmouth now under severe attack – we're sure to get more bombing raids like the one on Friday, we're in the front line here – there are going to be a lot of people needing help. Immediate, practical help with things like clothes, rations, food, accommodation – the sort of things the Council would do, certainly *will* do – but the WVS can do so much more quickly, leaving the Local Authority to get on with the job of permanent rehousing, putting the city back to rights and so on. That means we're going to need more volunteers and more office staff to help them. I'd like you, Miss Taylor, to join my staff.'

'Me? But . . .' Judy glanced round the room, looking more like a bustling office now with men and women sitting at tables which were already covered in sheets of paper. Typewriters were being carried in, packets of envelopes being opened. Where had they all come from? she wondered, and felt guilty at not helping. 'But I've already *got* a job, madam, and I ought to be doing it now. I don't want to be rude – I'd really like to be able to help you, and I promise I will, in the evenings and at weekends, but there's going to be so much to do here—'

The Mayoress held up her hand. 'Just wait a minute, Miss Taylor, while I finish explaining. I've already spoken to Miss Marsh and she understands the position. She's agreed to let me have two of her girls to help for as long as I need them. I'm afraid I asked for her best girls,' the Lady Mayoress smiled, 'and she said that in that case one must be

40

you. But of course, this will only be with your agreement –
nobody's going to force you. That's not the WVS way at
all!'

Judy gazed at her, unable to think of anything to say. She
glanced across the room to where Miss Marsh was busy at
her own desk, deep in discussion with two of the senior male
clerks.

'And Miss Marsh doesn't mind?' she asked at last.

'I wouldn't say that – she doesn't want to lose you at all,
and I don't blame her. But she understands the need.' The
Mayoress leaned across the little table. 'You see, the kind of
person I need will be someone who can respond to an
emergency – who can work on her own initiative, and who is
practical and won't mind going out of the office and giving a
hand wherever it's needed. Someone who can organise
anything from the evacuation of small children to collecting
scrap metal. It takes a very special kind of person to do all
that's going to be required in these coming days and
months, Judith – not the sort of girl who just wants to sit at
a desk in a nice warm office all day.'

'And you really think I could do all that?' Judy asked,
with a little twinge of excitement.

The Lady Mayoress gave her a steady look. 'You were
bombed out on Friday night, weren't you? You and your
family lost everything. Yet you still made your way to the
Guildhall – your place of duty – having first made sure that
your family would be cared for at an Emergency Centre.
You even stopped on the way to help others who needed it,
and you then stayed at your post all day, despite the dangers
– there could have been fallen masonry or unexploded
bombs anywhere in the Guildhall Square – to make sure
that everyone from the offices knew the situation here.
Today is Sunday morning, and you're here again, ready to
start work. That's how I know that you're the sort of person
I need.'

41

Judy glanced round the room once more. 'But I'm not the only one, madam. All these others . . .'

The Mayoress smiled again. 'I also like the look of you, Judith. I think we can get along – and that's important too. Now, what do you say? You don't have to agree, and if you do say yes and then find you're not happy with the work – I warn you, it'll be hard, with long hours, and not always as clean and pleasant as you've been accustomed to – then I won't hold you to it. You'll be able to return to normal staff duties. But will you at least give it a try?' She tilted her head a little and lifted her fine eyebrows.

Judy bit her lip, longing to say yes, yet still held back by a sense of loyalty to her workmates. She looked over at Miss Marsh again and the supervisor caught her eye, said something to her companions and came swiftly across the room.

'Well, Judy? Has the Lady Mayoress explained what she wants?'

'Yes, Miss Marsh. I don't know what to say. There's all the work of getting the office together again, and—'

'Say yes,' the older woman advised her. 'It's an opportunity for you, Judy, and I believe you'll be good at it. I can manage with the rest of the girls, and the male clerks, and we may be able to take on extra staff as well. But the Mayoress needs someone with Council experience as well as initiative, and in you she'll have both.'

Judy felt her skin colour. 'Well, if you really think so . . .'

'I do. I'll be sorry to lose you, Judy, but we all have to use our abilities where they're most needed, and the WVS does an excellent job. They'll be needed even more as this war goes on. Now, you'll have to excuse me, I must get back.' She bobbed her head at the Lady Mayoress. 'Let me know if there's anything else you need, madam.'

Left together, the Lady Mayoress and Judy looked at each other. Judy smiled awkwardly and said, 'Well, it looks as if that's settled then, madam. And – and thank you for asking me.'

The Mayoress held out her hand. 'I'm very pleased to have you on my team. Now, I told you that I was stealing two girls from Miss Marsh, but I haven't told you who the other one is. It's Laura Godsall – I think you know her, don't you? She's rather senior to you and will be my secretary, but to all intents and purposes you'll share the work between you. We don't have "hierarchies" in the WVS – we like women to be able to use their own individual skills – so if you have any ideas of your own, or think things could be done differently, you must say so. Now, I've been given the office next door for my own use, so come through and we'll get started.'

'Yes, madam.' Still feeling rather bewildered, Judy followed the Mayoress through to a smaller room where she found another desk and two of the dining tables. Laura Godsall, a tall girl a year or two older than Judy, with long blonde hair rolled up in a thick pleat over her forehead, Betty Grable style, was sitting at one with a pad of notepaper in front of her.

'Here's Miss Taylor come to help us,' the Mayoress said briskly. 'You know each other already, and I'm sure we're all going to get along famously. Now, what's been going on while I've been out of the room, Laura?'

'I'm trying to make lists of all the things we need to do,' Laura said. She had a low, rather musical voice, and Judy remembered that she sang in one of the church choirs in the city. Her father was a vicar. 'If we appeal for more volunteers, we need to be able to give them jobs to do straight away. The tea- and soup-stalls all have a rota, but we need more people for the Emergency Centres, and more Evacuation Helpers. Mrs Daysh was in here just now from the Clothing Fund; she says they're desperate for more clothes—'

'You see why I need help!' the Mayoress said to Judy.

'There's an enormous amount to be done. Now, as Laura says, the first thing we must do is find more volunteers. That means plenty of notices to be put up, and we can't get them printed – the printers have got far too much to cope with – so I think you'd better spend some time making them by hand. Big, bold and simple, there's no time for anything fancy. We'll get them into all the Emergency Centres and First-Aid Posts, and everywhere else we can think of. I've managed to get hold of some large sheets of paper – here, spread them out on the table. Now, I must get down to the Clothing Store. We had a new consignment in last week that I don't think has even been unpacked yet. I'll take Mrs Daysh with me and we can sort them out at once.'

She was gone, leaving the two girls with a pile of paper and a box of crayons between them. They looked at each other and Judy grinned a little ruefully.

'Well, I suppose it's important work.'

'It is,' Laura assured her briskly. 'Even if it does feel a bit like being back at school. Let's see how many we can get done by lunchtime – and what's the betting that by then she'll have thought of something else for us to do!'

As it turned out, by lunchtime the Mayoress had thought of quite a few things for them to do. Most of the women who were already volunteers had gone straight to the Emergency Centres, but some had come to the hotel with its new offices to ask for orders. Laura and Judy, by now inundated with requests for help, were kept busy matching them up, and Judy soon lost any sense of embarrassment at asking a well-dressed woman to take a frail old lady to the lavatory, or sending a young mother with three small children of her own to look after a crowd of bedraggled urchins who didn't seem to have any parents at all.

'They wouldn't volunteer if they didn't mean it,' Laura remarked as she helped an efficient old lady to unload a pile of woollen jumpers that someone had sent in. 'It's like the Mayoress says – if you're in the WVS you've got to be

44

flexible. Ready for anything. I can't see anyone offering if they're not prepared to do whatever they're asked to do.'

'Well, I hope we get lots more offers from these notices,' Judy said, printing WANTED – VOLUNTEERS FOR THE WVS out for the hundredth time. 'It's been busy enough before, it'll be even worse now, especially if we get more raids like Friday's.'

'D'you think we will?' Laura paused in her sorting. 'D'you think they'll bomb us that badly again? I don't know how much more people will be able to stand.'

'We'll stand as much as we've got to,' Judy said grimly. 'We don't have any choice, do we? And the Germans aren't going to stop because they feel sorry for us. They'll hammer and hammer and hammer till they think we'll give in.' She drew a thick black line under the words and looked up. 'We'll get more raids all right, Laura. They haven't finished with Pompey yet – but what they don't know, is that Pompey hasn't finished with *them*.'

Chapter Five

Back at home at last, Judy stretched her toes out to the fire and took a cup of tea from her mother. 'Thanks, Mum. I really need this. It was a horrible journey back. There's any amount of streets still blocked, the bus kept having to go a different way. Some people said they were further away from home when they got off than when they got on!'

'It's a shame you've got to go all the way out to Southsea,' Cissie said, offering her a tin of broken biscuits before settling a saucepan on the coals. 'I hope they manage to get the offices back into town before long.'

Judy shook her head. 'They won't go back now. You haven't seen the damage, Mum. We'll be out at Southsea for the duration, that's what Miss Marsh says.' She nibbled a piece of Rich Tea. 'Anyway, what sort of a day did you have? Did you manage to get the rations sorted out?'

Polly nodded. 'We've got temporary books, and we've registered at the Co-op where Mum gets her rations. They've opened up a grocery store not too far away, being as the big one's been bombed. Had to queue half the day but at least we've got a bit of food in the place now. And we got a bit more coal too, since we couldn't manage to get all ours out, but the woman was a bit funny about that, said it didn't take any more to warm five of us than one. I told her, we've got to have something to cook on while there's no gas, and we've got an invalid in the house too, and she gave way in the end but she didn't like it.'

'She only give us enough for a couple of hours a day

anyway,' Alice observed. 'I could have practically carried it home in my pockets.'

Judy smiled. She was tired and cold after the long journey from Southsea, and it was good to be back with the family again. 'I feel as though I've been working forever,' she said. 'It doesn't seem like Sunday at all today. Did you manage to get to church?'

'Yes, we did, and so did just about everyone else in Pompey,' Polly told her. 'Our church was full and I reckon all the others must have been as well – the ones that are still standing, anyway. The vicar told us there was – how many churches did he say got bombed, Mum?'

'Well, there was the Wesley down Arundel Street, and the one in Elm Grove, and Kent Street and Lane Road – oh yes, and Immanuel too, all Baptist places they were. And the old Unitarian in the High Street, that's nothing but a pile of rubble now, they say.'

'What, old John Pound's church?' Dick said, glancing up from his armchair. He was looking a bit better now, although still with a slight greyish tinge to his face. 'I never heard that. Well, that's a proper shame – bit of history, that church was. It was where old John Pound the cobbler started up his Ragged Schools. Many a time I've looked at the old wall tablet that said about how he used to take kiddies in off the street and teach 'em their letters while he mended shoes. Used his own money to feed 'em too, he did, and put shoes on their feet and clothes on their backs. I call that a real shame.'

'I don't think he actually mended shoes in the church,' Judy began, but was silenced by a glance from her mother. She bit her lip. It hardly mattered anyway. The tragedy was that so many buildings had been bombed, whether they were fine old churches or tiny terraced houses. The city was having its heart torn out.

'Tell you what,' she said. 'I've got a new job!'

The others stared at her. 'A new job? Why? Have you been promoted? You never told us about this, Judy.'

Judy laughed. 'I didn't know, that's why! And it is a kind of promotion, I suppose, in a way. The Lady Mayoress has asked me to work for her, helping with the WVS. You know she's high up in it, and she says they're going to be even busier now, helping in all sorts of ways. She needed some more staff, so she asked Miss Marsh if she could have me and Laura Godsall.'

'But surely they're all volunteers?' Cissie said. 'Does that mean you won't get paid?'

'No, I'll get the same wage as before. She's allowed some paid staff, you see, so that she's always got people who know what's what. And we're stopping out at the Royal Beach because the WVS works with the Local Authority – it's something like the way the Wrens help the Navy and the ATS help the Army, that sort of thing – but we might find ourselves doing all sorts of jobs. I think it sounds interesting,' she said and finished her tea while the others gazed at her.

'Well, fancy the Lady Mayoress herself asking for you, our Judy,' Alice said at last. 'They must think a lot of you.'

Judy shrugged, feeling pleased all the same. 'I don't know about that. I reckon I just came in the door at the right moment.'

Polly's face was bright with excitement. 'So you're going to help with the WVS. Well, what a coincidence. Because I am, too!'

'*You* are?' Judy turned to her. 'How d'you mean, Polly? Are you volunteering?'

'I already have. Put my name down at the Centre this morning.' Polly beamed at her niece. 'I've got to come out to Southsea tomorrow to sign on. I'll come with you on the bus, first thing.'

A huge smile broke out over Judy's face. 'That's smashing! We need lots and lots of volunteers, and it's going to be really interesting work, Poll – you've no idea all the jobs they do. It's not just serving out tea and sorting old clothes. Though those things do have to be done as well, of course,' she added fairly.

'Well, I don't care what I do so long as it's helping the war effort,' Polly declared. 'I've been thinking ever since I let Sylvie go out to the country that I ought to be doing something, but what with having a job and not being able to go in the Services, I didn't really know what to do. But this will suit me – I can put in all the hours I want to and still do a bit of hairdressing as well. I went round to Mrs Mason's this morning to make sure it was all right with her if I just did part-time. We decided afternoons would be best; seems to me it's mornings that volunteers'll be needed most, when there's been a raid overnight.'

'They'll be needed morning, noon and night,' Judy said. 'But whenever you work, you'll be welcome, Polly. You're just the sort they need. I'm really pleased.'

'And I'll still be giving a hand where I can,' Alice chimed in. 'I'm going to go round the Centre regular. Annie Chapman works there – you know, Jess Budd's sister from over the end of March Street, it was her Olive that was with Kathy Simmons – and she says I'll be welcome any time. There's always something to do there. And Peggy Shaw, from down the street, she works in the First-Aid Post and her Gladys drives an ambulance, so we'll all be doing our bit round this way. Well, most of us,' she added as an afterthought. 'I don't suppose that Ethel Glaister will lift a finger to help – wouldn't want to chip her nail varnish – and Nancy Baxter has her own ways of helping, as we all know.'

'Mum!' Cissie protested, amidst laughter from the others. She got up from her chair and bent to lift the lid from the saucepan simmering on the fire. 'I reckon this stew's just about ready now. There's only enough meat in it to cover a half-starved mouse, but plenty of veg, so let's get round the table and tuck in.' She brought the pan to the table and began to spoon stew into the bowls. 'And just in case you think I'm not pulling my weight, I'm going to be doing needlework for the Marine barracks, helping make uniforms, and Dick's going to be making rag rugs for people who are being rehoused and got no furniture.'

'That's right,' Dick said, drawing up a chair. 'It'll be a hive of industry round here. She'll have me knitting next.'

'Well, that wouldn't be anything to be ashamed of,' his mother-in-law told him. 'Plenty of sailors used to do knitting when they were at sea. I don't know where they'd have got new socks from otherwise, when they were away for years at a time.'

They sat round the table, eating their meal. As Cissie had said, there wasn't much meat in it but what there was had given it some flavour, and the vegetables were good. Afterwards they had boiled rice with golden syrup, and while they were eating that Cissie put the kettle on the fire for another cup of tea.

'Wonderful how you can manage when you've got to,' she remarked. 'But I'll be thankful when we've got the gas and power back on. Have you heard anything about that, Judy?'

'I know they're hoping to get the Dockyard generators linked into the city electricity supply,' Judy said, gathering up the dishes. 'If they can do that, everyone will have some power in the next day or two. I don't know about the gas, though.' She hesitated. 'There's going to be a big funeral on Friday – some of the people that were killed. They say there were over a hundred and fifty. They're going to be buried all together at Kingston Cemetery, and the Mayor and all the Corporation are going. I don't know how many of their robes they'll be able to wear; a lot of them were burned in the Guildhall.'

There was a moment of sadness, then Polly said, 'Talking of uniforms, I'll be getting the WVS one. It's quite nice – green with a sort of grey thread running through it. We've got to pay for them ourselves, though.'

'I'm having one too,' Judy told her. 'I don't mind paying for it – I'd have to get some more clothes for work anyway. Did you manage to get much at the Centre, Mum?'

They went on talking as they cleared the table, made tea and put the kettle on the fire yet again for washing up, and then settled down with their knitting. All the women were making something. Judy and Polly had started balaclavas for the Navy, Cissie was unravelling one of Dick's old cardigans to make gloves, and Alice was making squares from scraps of leftover wool, to be sewn together to make blankets. Polly lit an extra candle, to give them more light.

'I'm getting a bit worried about this coal supply,' Cissie said, rolling wool into a ball. 'With all this cooking, and needing water for washing and scrubbing the floors, you've got to keep the fire going but what we've got in the shed's going down really quick, even with those few loads we managed to bring here from home.'

'Well, once the gas is back on we can sit in our coats during the day and just keep the fire for evenings,' Dick said. 'One thing about making rag rugs, they do keep your knees warm while you're working on them!' He glanced at the clock on the mantelpiece. 'Let's put the wireless on – it's nearly time for the nine o'clock news.'

'Good thing I had the accumulator charged last week,' Alice remarked, doing as he asked. 'At least we can still find out what's going on.'

The news, read by Alvar Liddell, was as gloomy and frightening as usual. There had been more Luftwaffe attacks on British warships in the Mediterranean; a destroyer had been damaged, the aircraft-carrier *Illustrious* crippled and another ship, unnamed so far, sunk. In the Netherlands, all Jews had been ordered to register with the authorities. Mr Churchill had insisted to Parliament that assistance to Greece must be given top priority.

'The trouble is, everywhere needs to be top priority,' Dick said, switching it off again. 'We can't be in all those places at once. It's like a disease, breaking out everywhere, and as fast as you try to stop the bleeding in one place it starts somewhere else.'

Cissie shuddered. 'That's horrible, Dick.'

'Well,' he said quietly, 'war *is* horrible.' He looked down at the fire and then pulled his cardigan close around his thin chest. 'I don't know about you, but I'm for bed. I dunno, ever since Friday night I seem to feel so tired I can hardly keep my eyes open. I reckon I'll be a bit warmer there, too. Did you put the bottle in, Cis?'

His wife nodded. 'Half an hour ago. You go up, Dick, and get comfortable. I won't be long.' She waited as he went outside to pay a last visit to the lavatory and then had a quick wash at the scullery sink before climbing slowly upstairs. 'It's the shock,' she said to the others. 'It's knocked him sideways, and I'm not surprised. It's not right, men like him having to go through this all over again.'

'What happened to him in the Great War, Mum?' Judy asked. 'I know he was gassed, but there was more to it than that, wasn't there?'

Cissie looked at her and sighed. 'Well, I suppose it's only right you should know. Not that I know all the ins and outs of it myself, mind – a lot of it, I just had to pick up from what Dick said and what other people have told me. And Dick's never told me the full story, never will. I don't think he can bear to remember it.'

'Bad as it was, I don't think the gas was the worst of it,' Alice said. 'I think it was what else happened to him that upsets him most.'

There was a brief silence, then Cissie said, 'I reckon you might be right, Mum.' She turned back to Judy. 'See – your dad and me were childhood sweethearts – always knew each other, and we always knew we'd get married one day. But there didn't seem to be no hurry till the war broke out, and then when he joined up we thought it'd all be over by Christmas, so we decided to get married then, when he came back. And so we did, only it wasn't all over, and he'd had a taste of the trenches by then and he didn't want to go back.'

'Didn't have no choice, though, did he,' Alice said. 'You either got shot as a deserter or went back and probably got shot by the Germans.'

'That's right. He had an awful time – I only know about it from the nightmares he used to have. Still has, sometimes, specially since this lot started . . . He didn't come home again till the next Christmas – our Terry was three months old then. I tell you, when he walked through that door over there, I didn't even recognise him. He looked like a ghost. No – more like a skeleton, he was so thin and drawn. And he couldn't even talk for three days – just sat and cried in the chair. Wanted me with him all the time, couldn't bear to let the baby out of his sight . . . It was pitiful. Pitiful.'

Judy stared at her, shocked. 'But what was the matter with him?'

'What do you think? He'd had just about all he could take. A lot of them had. They'd been living like rats in holes, being shot at day and night – it wasn't human, what they had to go through. Why, we couldn't even bang a door shut without him jumping out of his skin. Shell-shock, they called it,' Cissie said bitterly. 'Gave him a few weeks' leave to get over it and then dragged him back. He wasn't over it, not by a long way. He isn't over it now – he never will be. It's why he flares up sometimes, all over nothing. Something happens that touches him on the raw and he loses his temper. He never used to be like that. It's all through what happened in the war.'

'And was it after that when he was gassed?' Judy asked quietly.

'That's right. Saved his life, that did.'

'*Saved his life?* But it's left him more or less crippled!'

'And if it hadn't, he'd be dead,' Cissie said bluntly. Judy, accustomed to gentleness from her mother, caught her breath at the harshness of her voice. 'They called it shell-shock when he was home and they wanted him back again, but out there they had a different name for it. Cowardice. And you know what they did to cowards, don't you?' She gave Judy a bitter look. 'They shot them.'

Judy caught her breath. 'You mean they were going to *shoot Dad*?'

'I'm not saying they were going to, but I think that's what he expected. And then they got this gas attack. He only got a whiff, mind – he said there were boys that got a full whack, and they died screaming. It turns your lungs to a sort of mush . . . But your father wasn't too close. It was enough to make him poorly for a bit, mind, and leave his lungs damaged for life, but it got him invalided home and there was no more talk about cowardice. He was all right to work too, for a few years, till it started to get worse, but at least he's still alive. I thank God on my knees every day that he's still alive.'

Judy was silent. She had always known that her father's illness stemmed from the Great War, but had never heard the details before. She glanced at her Aunt Polly.

'I suppose you didn't realise – you were only little then.'

'Nine, when he first came home,' Polly said. 'I was a bridesmaid at the wedding. I was only twelve when the war ended, and Dick went back to his job in the Dockyard – and then our dad died and I don't think I really noticed much. Cis didn't tell me till I was a lot older, when Dick started to get worse.'

'Poor Dad,' Judy said softly. 'Poor, poor Dad.'

'Well, he's got plenty to be thankful for, all the same,' Alice said briskly. 'He's not had such a bad life. The gas didn't kill him, he's got a good wife and two children to be proud of, and there's plenty of others went through the same as he did, and worse. I'm not playing it down, mind, just saying it could have been worse.'

'You're right, Mum,' Cissie said. 'It could have been a lot worse. That's what I thank God for.' She rolled up another ball of crinkly, unravelled wool and got up. 'Well, I'm going up now, too. Don't you be too long, Judy, you look tired. So do you, Poll.'

Fifteen minutes later, Judy and Polly were left alone by the dying fire. Alice had gone into the front room, where a mattress had been put on the floor for her, and a few minutes later they heard her snoring. They looked at each other.

'That's awful, what Mum said about Dad,' Judy said. 'But Gran's right, isn't she? At least he's alive. You must wish you could have your Johnny back, even if he'd been injured.'

'I do,' Polly said quietly. 'But I'm not sure it's what he would have wanted. He was always so proud of being fit and strong – I don't think he could have put up with being an invalid. And I was thinking about you, too. You haven't said anything about Sean, but you must be worried stiff. I saw your face when the newsreader said about the ship that's been sunk in the Med. You were thinking about him then, weren't you?'

Judy bit her lip. 'I don't even know exactly where the *Southampton* is, but she could be out there, Polly. And they wouldn't let me know, would they – not straight away. They'd notify his mum, over in Ireland. I'd have to wait for her to write to me.' She sighed. 'I try not to worry, but sometimes it feels like a great lump of jagged metal inside me. I don't know what I'd do if I lost him, Polly. We knew each other such a short time.'

'I know,' her aunt said softly. 'I know just what it's like. All you can do is wait. That's all any of us can do – wait, and do something useful in the meantime. At least we can do that.'

'Yes,' Judy said. 'At least we can do that.'

Chapter Six

Several of the April Grove residents attended the mass funeral at Kingston cemetery the following Friday. They were there to mourn Kathy Simmons and her baby Thomas. Alice, Cissie and Dick walked down with Freda Vickers, from the end of April Grove. Her husband Tommy was an air-raid warden and had been one of the last men to come down from the roof of the Guildhall when it had caught fire.

It had snowed during the week and the pavements were slippery with ice. They walked carefully, holding on to each other's arms.

'He was named after my hubby, the baby was,' Freda told them sadly. 'Tommy was with her in the air-raid shelter when he was born, see. Took care of Kathy right through, and she was so grateful. Hadn't lived in October Street all that long, but they were a lovely family, and the two little girls are dears.'

'It's terrible,' Cissie said. 'All those people killed, and all the families left behind to grieve. What about her hubby, then – where's he?'

'I told you, Cis,' Alice said. 'He's in the Merchant Navy. On convoys somewhere.'

Judy and Polly were at the funeral too. Judy had gone down from Southsea with Laura and the rest of the Council staff and the Mayor, Mayoress and Corporation, all in ordinary clothes because their grand robes had been lost in the Guildhall fire. The Mayor's regalia, which had been kept in a safe, had been saved, however, and he wore that over his dark suit, while the bishops of both Anglican and

Roman Catholic churches were resplendent in blue and gold, and black, gold and cherry-pink respectively.

The procession was led by the Royal Marine Band, its trombones dazzling, its drums muffled with black crêpe. It was followed by twelve Rolls-Royce and Daimler hearses, each driver wearing a top hat, and the coffins draped in Union Jacks. Beside the hearses, in a slow march, walked the servicemen who were to act as pallbearers, and behind them came a parade of all the Armed Services, including some from the French Navy, as well as members of the ARP and Home Guard. Tommy Vickers was there, his yellow hair glinting in the sunlight when he took off his hat in respect for the dead.

Polly was smart in her new green WVS uniform, standing in line with the other volunteers along the road. The icy pavements were packed with mourners, and a number of people who had just come to watch.

'Sightseers!' Judy said indignantly as they walked back to Southsea afterwards. 'Got nothing better to do. As if watching a lot of coffins being put into a grave was entertainment!'

'Well, I'm sure they were upset about it too,' Polly said. 'And you've got to admit it was a real sight, for all it was so sad. I didn't know Kathy Simmons but I couldn't help shedding a few tears. All those poor souls being put into one grave – and all those people standing there, absolutely quiet, watching. And those words the bishop said, about us being a "proud people" and calling them "Citizens in the City of God". I don't know how they think these things up.'

'Neither do I,' Judy said caustically. 'All that about them being "happy dead" and "winning a victory"! I bet Kathy Simmons isn't happy being dead, and I bet she doesn't think she's won a victory either. It's just *words*, Polly, and they don't mean a thing!' Her cheeks flushed and her eyes brightened with anger. 'Just because he's a bishop, we're meant to believe him and be *proud* that so many people were killed and injured and bombed out of their homes, and I tell you, I'm not! I'm not proud at all!'

Polly looked at her in surprise. Judy had never expressed such feelings before, but when you came to think about it, perhaps she had a point. The bishop's words *had* made her feel proud, but it was true that she hadn't felt like that beforehand. She'd been sad and upset and frightened. She thought for a moment and then said carefully, 'I suppose he's trying to make us all feel better – stronger. Being miserable isn't going to help them, or us. If we can feel better about them dying, perhaps it helps us to carry on.' She sighed. 'Pompey's not the only place hit this week. Plymouth and Bristol have had bad raids too. I suppose this sort of thing's happening there as well. What I wonder is where they get all the coffins from. They surely don't have all that many ready at the undertakers.'

'I reckon they've got places making them specially,' Laura said. She and Judy were also in their new WVS uniforms, with warm greatcoats over their jackets and skirts. 'They won't tell us about them though, because of spreading panic.'

They reached the Royal Beach and went inside. The offices were busy, with half a dozen girls clacking away at a bank of typewriters and clerks sitting at paper-strewn desks and dining tables. All the forms and official documents had to be printed and sent out to homes and businesses all over the city, and on top of that the bombed and damaged premises must be surveyed for repair or rebuilding. There were lists of people who needed rehousing, lists of places where they could be sent, lists of those who had decided to take evacuation, lists of places in the country that could accommodate them. Lists, lists, lists, Judy thought as she pulled off her coat, gloves and hat and hung them on a hook. There's no end to them, but without them we couldn't even begin to get everything done. She sat down at her own desk and gazed at the mound of paper that seemed to have grown during her absence. Each list, each entry, she knew, represented some personal problem or even tragedy – a workman needing new clothes, a family bombed out just as her own had been, two little sisters whose mother had been killed.

'That's Kathy Simmons,' she said, staring at the sheet of paper in her hands. 'She lived just across the road from my gran, where we're staying now. She was killed with her baby boy in her arms, and now the little girls have got no one. Oh, Laura.' Suddenly, she was in tears. The strain of the past week – the horror of seeing her home in ruins, the desperate struggle to get through the streets, the sight of the Guildhall that was the pride of Portsmouth, the funeral of so many people that afternoon – overwhelmed her with a rush of emotion, and she put her elbows on her desk, her face in her hands and shook with sobs.

'Judy!' Laura came and put her arms round Judy's heaving shoulders. 'Oh Judy, don't. I know it's awful.' She held the girl's head against her, stroking the bright hair. 'I've cried, too. I cried all night, thinking of it all. Perhaps it's best to cry. Let it out, Judy, let it out. It'll make you feel better.' She went on murmuring and stroking, and Judy's tears slowly began to subside, until at last she was able to look up and blow her nose and give a small, shaky smile.

'Sorry, I didn't mean to break down like that. It was just seeing their names. It's different when it's someone you know.'

'I know. It makes it so real. Not that we're in any doubt about that,' Laura said with a sigh, glancing round the office. 'I just wish we could wake up and find it was all a dream – a nightmare. But it's not.'

'No. It just seems like one. A nightmare we can't wake up from.' Judy blew her nose again. 'And being sorry for ourselves isn't helping anyone. We've got so much to do – there's so many people needing things.' She drew the sheet of paper towards her again. 'Stella and Muriel Simmons.

They're staying with Mrs Budd, down at the other end of April Grove from Gran, but I suppose they'll have to be evacuated. Poor little scraps. They'd already been bombed out once, you know.'

'Would you like me to see to that?' Laura asked gently, but Judy shook her head.

'No, I'll do it. I can't give up over everything that upsets me, or I'll never get a thing done. It's the same for all of us, after all. We're all going to come across people we know, sometime or other.' She looked at the paper again. 'What do we do, though? Send someone to go and see Mrs Budd, or get their evacuation organised first and then just tell her?'

'Haven't they got any other relatives? A granny or aunties? What about their father?'

'I think he's in the Merchant Navy.' Judy sighed. 'I suppose someone had better go and find out.' She glanced round the room and saw her aunt standing by the window, talking to another WVS volunteer. 'I know – I'll get Polly to do it. We're staying in April Grove after all, and Gran knows Mrs Budd. Polly and Mum grew up there themselves, though I don't think the Budds moved in till after they'd got married and moved out. It's better than sending a stranger though, and we can find out about the girls' family before we do anything else.'

She made a note in the ledger she had been given to keep a record of what action had been taken in each case, and went on to the next, two boys whose mother was in hospital with a broken leg. They ought to have been evacuated too, she thought. She was surprised how many children there still were in the city – children who had been evacuated right at the beginning of the war and then come home when nothing much seemed to be happening, children who had refused to go or whose parents refused to send them, children who were under five and too young to go without their mothers, whose mothers wanted to stay at home with their husbands . . . Surely some of them would go now, she thought. Surely, after this, their parents will see the danger they're in.

But not everyone wanted to be parted from their children. There was Jess Budd, whose boys were at Bridge End. She and her elder daughter Rose, together with the baby Maureen, had all gone out there to begin with, but Jess had come back to look after her husband Frank, who worked in the Dockyard, and naturally the baby had had to come too. And then Rose had wanted to come back with her mother, and after some argument Frank had agreed to her return. He wouldn't hear of the boys coming back though, and they didn't really want to. They were enjoying their stay in the country and, apart from being disgruntled at missing the air raids, they were content to stay there, especially now that there was some snow.

'I thought perhaps Stella and Muriel could go to the vicarage there,' Jess said when Polly went to see her. 'That's where my boys are now, and they're well looked after. The vicar's got a housekeeper who's like a mother to them, and the vicar's like an overgrown boy himself, by all accounts. There's plenty of room there and I'm sure they'd be welcome, and they met Tim and Keith at Christmas.' She took a photograph from the mantelpiece and looked at it fondly. It was a studio portrait and showed the whole family in their best clothes, with baby Maureen seated on Jess's knee and Frank and Rose behind her while the two boys stood straight and proud beside them. 'My Frank had this taken specially, before they went back. He wanted us all together, just in case . . .' She bit her lip, then added brightly, 'You've seen my boys in the street, I expect, before they went away?'

'The whole school went to Bridge End, did they?' Polly asked, trying to get the picture straight in her head.

'That's right. The teachers are there, too – Miss Langrish and the others. They're happy enough there. Well, mostly,' she added, remembering the children like Martin Baker and the little Atkinsons who had not been at all happy. 'They didn't all get good billets, I'm afraid. But the girls would be all right at the vicarage.'

'What about the father? Do they have any other relatives?'

Jess frowned, trying to remember. 'Well, Mr Simmons is in the Merchant Navy, he doesn't get home very often, of course. As for other relatives – well, I got the impression there weren't many. They're not Pompey people anyway. Kathy told me once they both came from Basingstoke. Her parents died when she was a kiddy and she was brought up by her gran, but the old lady's over ninety now. And I think she said her hubby's mother was in a home – doesn't really know what's going on.'

'It doesn't look as if they're going to be much help,' Polly said. She looked down at her notebook. 'They're staying with you at the moment, is that right? But I expect you'd rather they were evacuated.'

'I don't mind having them at all, but I think they ought to be somewhere safe. The poor little mites have been bombed out twice and they're terrified every time we hear a plane go over. We've had to go down the shelter quite a few times already since the big raid, and you can see they're almost out of their minds with fear, especially Muriel, the younger one. And Stella's like a little old woman – you'd think she was carrying the weight of the world on her shoulders. They need to be somewhere they can feel safe and start to be children again.'

Polly nodded. 'We can certainly contact the vicar and see if he'd be willing to take them. What's his name?'

'Mr Beckett. But I think I ought to talk to their father first – he's hoping to be able to get back and see them soon. His ship comes back to Pompey, you see, for supplies. I wouldn't like him to come and find them not here, not when he's lost his wife and baby boy as well.'

'Well, we'll wait a little while,' Polly agreed, 'but we can't leave it too long. As you say, they ought to be somewhere safe.' She put her notebook away and stood up. 'Thanks, Mrs Budd. It's been nice to talk to you.' She glanced around the small room. 'You've got a lovely place here.'

'We do our best to keep it nice,' Jess said modestly. 'Frank does a lot of work on it – woodwork and decorating, and that – at least, he did when you could still get the materials. It's not rented, you see, like most of the houses round here. Frank wanted his own place – likes his independence, and likes to be able to do what he wants with his home. A lot of his mates said he was daft, taking on a mortgage, said it'd be a millstone round his neck, but we've never regretted it. He always says he'd sooner put the money into his own bricks and mortar than pay rent for the rest of his life.' She looked round proudly. 'It's been a real struggle at times, but this house will be ours one day, with no more to pay – well, that's if the Germans let it!'

Polly nodded. Before Johnny was killed, they'd rented two rooms, and even Dick and Cissie's house had been rented. Her mother Alice had been lucky to be able to stay in the house at the other end of the street, where Polly and Cissie had grown up, after her husband had died in the 'flu epidemic after the Great War, but she was still paying rent. Frank and Jess Budd had been sensible, she thought, as well as brave to take on such a commitment.

'Well, let's hope they do,' she said, referring to the Germans. 'It's no picnic, being bombed out, I can tell you.'

Jess's face softened in sympathy. 'Yes, I heard about your trouble. It must have been a terrible shock, coming out of the shelter to find everything gone. Thank goodness you were all down there, though. I've heard of people who just popped indoors to make a cup of cocoa . . . well, look at Kathy, killed in just those few minutes. It doesn't bear thinking of.'

Polly walked back up the icy street towards her mother's house. No it didn't bear thinking of, but you had to think about it when it happened to you. There were a lot of things these days that didn't bear thinking of, but you had to do so all the same. Things like her Johnny, drowning or blown up at sea – she would never know just what had happened to him. And their little daughter Sylvie, out in the country near Romsey, living with strangers. They were kind enough to her, Polly knew that, but it wasn't right, a kiddy of seven living with people she didn't know. And how long was it going to be before she could come home and be with her mummy again? Nobody knew.

'You're Mrs Thomas's girl, Polly!' a cracked voice exclaimed, making her jump. 'I knowed you when you was a little 'un. Come back to stop with your ma then, I hear.'

'Mrs Kinch!' Polly said, stopping. 'Yes, we were bombed out of our house, so me and Cissie and her husband, and their Judy, have all come back to April Grove. It seems funny, being back where I was born,' she added, glancing along the street where she had played so often as a child.

'Ah, I remember you two, skipping and playing two-ball up against the walls.' The old woman looked just the same as always, Polly thought, her thin grey hair wound tightly into metal curlers and covered with a brown net. 'My Nancy often talks about you – she'll be pleased you're back. You can come in and have a cuppa tea with us one of these days, have a bit of a chinwag about old times.' She peered at Polly's green uniform. 'You joined up then, have you? Which Service is that?'

'It's not one of the Armed Services. It's the WVS – the Women's Voluntary Service. Anyone can volunteer,' Polly said proudly. 'We do all sorts of things – help people who've been bombed out, run tea-stalls down by the docks, take children to be evacuated, collect scrap – anything that needs doing. Nancy could join if she wanted to,' she added a little doubtfully.

Granny Kinch cackled. 'My Nancy's already doing her bit towards the war effort,' she said, confirming Alice's remarks about Nancy Baxter. 'But you carry on, young

Polly, there's plenty of other comforts our boys need these days. Anyway, I can't stand here nattering all day, I got our Micky's dinner to get. He does a bit of work down Charlotte Street market; brought home a nice string of pork sausages last night, he did, and he'll expect 'em on the table when he comes in.' She grinned toothlessly at Polly and went indoors.

Polly opened the door of number nine and went inside, smiling. Her brother-in-law was in his armchair, a piece of canvas spread over his knees as he hooked bits of coloured material into it. 'Hello,' he said, 'what's tickled you?'

'Granny Kinch. Just said she couldn't stand nattering at the front door all day. I thought that was all she ever did! You know, she doesn't look a scrap different from how she looked when I was a little girl – I think she must have been born toothless and with curlers in her hair.'

Dick grinned. 'I don't know about the curlers but I expect she was born toothless. Look, what d'you think of my rug? Bit of all right, isn't it? I'm getting proper nifty with this hook.'

'You are,' Polly said, admiring it. 'Some family's going to be pleased with that to put in front of their fire.' She sighed and sat down in the other armchair. 'It's awful, though, Dick, when you think of it. I've just been down to see Mrs Budd about those two little Simmons girls. There must be hundreds of kiddies like them, lost their homes and parents. It's so tragic.'

'You weren't much older when you lost your own dad,' Dick said, 'so you can understand what it's like for them. And it's the same for your Sylvie. D'you reckon you'll be able to get out to see her soon?'

'I hope so. It's just that with everything so upside down all over the city, and now we've got all this snow, there's hardly any trains or buses running and they're needed for getting people evacuated.' She looked into the fire, thinking of her daughter. 'I'm glad I had her home for Christmas. At

65

least we all had a few days together then for Terry's bit of leave, but I'm even more glad I made her go back. I felt awful when she begged me to let her stay, but it was the right thing to do.'

Dick rolled up his work and got up. He went out to the scullery and filled the kettle. The gas was back on now, as well as the electricity, and soon the kettle was whistling and he made the tea and brought in two cups.

'Here. You look a bit done up. It's upset you, talking to Jess Budd.'

'I think it has, a bit.' Polly stirred a saccharin tablet into her tea and sipped it. 'I want to help, Dick, and I'm glad I joined the WVS, but it does bring it home to you what terrible things are happening. Not that we *need* it bringing home to us – I think we've had our share already. But it seems worse, somehow, when it's other people. You can see that some of them just can't cope with it. It's in their eyes – they look sort of lost and bewildered. They're like little children.'

'It's shock,' Dick said. 'I've seen plenty of it, Polly. They'll be all right after a bit – at least, they would be if they had a chance of some peace and quiet. But that's just what we don't get, isn't it?'

She shook her head. 'It's as if the Germans are just banging away at us all the time. They knock us down and then hit us again, just as we're getting up. Nobody gets a chance to recover from one blow before the next one knocks them for six. You just don't know what's going to happen next.' She glanced up at the mantelpiece. 'Is that a letter for our Judy?'

Dick nodded. 'Came by second post. Got an Irish stamp on it. I dare say it's young Sean's mother – she writes now and then, doesn't she?'

'Yes, she does. Perhaps she's got some news from Sean. I know Judy's been a bit worried, not hearing from him just lately.' Polly looked round as the front door opened and closed again. 'I expect that's her now. There's a letter here for you, Judy,' she called.

Judy burst into the room, her face alight. 'A letter? From Sean?' She held out her hand for the envelope Polly was taking down from the mantelpiece, and as she caught sight of the stamp, the colour drained from her face. In the same instant, Polly remembered her remark a few days earlier.

They wouldn't let me know, would they – not straight away. They'd send any telegram to his mum, over in Ireland. I'd have to wait for her to write to me.

'Oh Judy,' she said, getting up quickly. 'Oh, *Judy* . . .'

Chapter Seven

Only Polly could give Judy any comfort during the dark days that followed.

The *Southampton*, a cruiser, had been sunk on 11 January – the day after the Blitz on Portsmouth. Perhaps, Judy thought, Sean had been dying at the very moment she and the family had crawled out of their Anderson and stared in horror at the wreckage of their home. Or, if not then, it must have been at some other moment during that dreadful day – as they walked into the Emergency Centre, perhaps, or while she was struggling to reach the Guildhall, or when she came into the square and saw the great building going up in flames, the copper melting in green streaks of fire down its scorching walls . . . At some time during that day, Sean, the merry Irish sailor she'd met and fallen in love with at a South Parade Pier dance – the laughing young seaman who had swept her off her feet, begged her to marry him and given her the tiny diamond she was wearing on her finger now – had died in the sea he had loved and which had become his killer. Had he been thinking of her as he died? Had he called her name, regretted that he would never see her again? Or had he forgotten everything else in his desperate struggle to stay alive?

'It's no good torturing yourself over it,' Polly told her as they huddled together on the single bed in Alice's back bedroom. 'You've just got to do your grieving and then come to terms with it. It's hard – no one knows that better than me – but you've got to do it.'

'I can't,' Judy sobbed. 'I can't stop thinking about him,

Poll. What was it *like*? If only I knew, if only I could *imagine* it, I could feel I was sharing it with him then. I could feel that perhaps it wasn't so lonely. I know that's stupid, it can't make any difference to him now – it couldn't ever make any difference to him. But it might help me to *understand*.'

'I know. I know just what you mean.' Polly stroked her niece's bright, fair hair. 'I went through it all when I lost Johnny. I felt cheated, somehow. Not just of his life, though that's bad enough, losing the life we were going to have together, but of his death, too.' She looked at Judy, whose sobs had lessened a little. Her face was still buried in her hands but Polly sensed that she was listening. She hesitated, hoping she wouldn't increase the girl's pain, and then went on. 'It's like it says in that old song – you remember, the one your dad used to sing to your mum sometimes, when we were round the piano. My dad used to sing it too. All about sharing the good things in life, and the bad ones too. "Am I not yours for weal or woe? How else can friends prove true? Tell me what breaks and brings you low, And let me stand with you." '

She paused again. Judy lifted her head. Her eyes were red and swollen, her skin puffy, but she looked at Polly and nodded. 'I remember it. The last verse always made me cry.'

'It makes me cry too,' Polly said, her own eyes filling with tears as she thought of the two men who had meant so much to them – both sailors, both lost at sea. I shouldn't go on with this, she thought, it's too heartbreaking – yet that last verse, sad though it was, had expressed so well the loss she had felt, and it had helped her to think that someone else knew and understood that loss. 'Do you remember how it goes?' She sang the words, very softly. ' "So when the night falls tremulous, When the last lamp burns low, And one of us, or both of us, The long, lone road must go . . . Look with your dear old eyes in mine, Give me a handshake true. Whatever fate our souls await, Let me be there – let me be there. There, with you." '

They were both crying now, their tears falling like rain, yet Polly felt that for Judy the tears were healing ones, no less bitter, but the tears of a grief shared and understood. She held her niece's shoulders firmly, feeling the slim body shake against hers, and felt her own grief as fresh and sharp as on the day when she too had received that terrible news. And we're not the only ones, she thought. There are thousands of us, all over the country. All over Europe. And perhaps, before this awful war is finished, all over the world.

Lives torn apart too soon; wives and husbands robbed of a lifetime together. Robbed even of that last goodbye.

Judy felt for a handkerchief. There was scarcely a dry one left in the house, and the one she used now was already sodden. But there was an air of finality as she rubbed her eyes and turned to look at her aunt.

'It'll always make me cry, that song,' she said 'but I'm going to try to stop now. I'm going to do all I can to help people who're worse off than me – and there's plenty of them. I'm going to do it for the war effort, and to beat Hitler, same as before – but I'm going to do it now for Sean as well. So that he won't have died for nothing.'

Polly gave her a shaky smile. 'That's right, Judy. That's what I'm doing. Working for Johnny and my Sylvie – so that he won't have died for nothing, and so that she's got a life to look forward to. A *better* life.'

'There'll never be anyone else for me,' Judy said sadly. 'I don't suppose I'll ever get married and have children now.'

'I thought that, too,' Polly agreed. 'But I don't know, Judy – no one ever knows what life will bring.' She sighed. 'It'll have to bring someone pretty special to take Johnny's place, all the same. And I don't even know that I want it to. Johnny's got his place in my heart – I don't think there's room for anyone else.'

'We'll be old maids together,' Judy said with an attempt at a smile. 'Well, *you* won't be an old maid, because of

Sylvie. But when she's grown up and got her own family, we'll stay together, won't we? You and me?'

Polly hugged her. 'We will. As long as we've got each other, we'll never be really alone, Judy. Never. You will be happy again, Judy – I promise. And we'll always share things. All right?'

'All right,' Judy said, and then her eyes filled again and she cried out in a voice sharp with anguish, 'But I'm going to miss him so much, Polly! I'm going to miss him *so* much . . .'

The end of January 1941 and beginning of February brought several important visitors to Portsmouth.

Winston Churchill was the first. Accompanied by Franklin Roosevelt's Envoy, Mr Harry Hopkins, he went on a tour of the city's bombed areas before arriving at the Royal Beach to meet the City Council members. Judy, lining up with the rest of the staff to greet him, gazed in awe at his stumpy figure and the famous cigar wedged in his mouth. He really does look like a bulldog, she thought – absolutely determined, as if nothing can stop him. If anyone can make us win the war, he can.

He made a speech too, as good as any on the wireless. 'I thought about you a good deal a few weeks ago when we knew how heavily you were being attacked,' he told them, 'and I am very glad to find an afternoon to come to see you here and wish you "Good Luck". Our buildings, our dwellings, may be destroyed, but the spirit of Britain glows warmer and brighter for the tribulations through which we pass. We *shall* come through. We cannot tell when. We cannot tell how. But we *shall come through*.' He paused and seemed to look at every person present, as if calling on each one to live up to his expectations. 'We have – *none of us* – any doubt whatever. And when we have done so, we shall have the right to say,' his voice swelled and deepened, 'that we live in an age that, in all the long history of Britain, was most filled with glorious achievement and most graced by duties done.'

There was a pause as he finished speaking, and then a spontaneous outburst of applause. All the women and many of the men had tears in their eyes. Mr Churchill stood for a moment, smiling broadly, then he nodded his big head and waved his hand, giving them the famous Victory salute, and turned to go out of the room.

'Isn't he wonderful!' Judy said, going back to her desk. 'You can't help but follow a man like that. I mean, even on the wireless he makes you feel you could do anything, but when you see him in person – well, he's like a tidal wave, rushing you along.'

'And the way he puts things,' Laura agreed. 'I used to be good at English at school, but I could never put things the way he does. And it wasn't even a big speech, not to go on the wireless or in Parliament, I mean. It was just to us, here in Pompey.'

'It'll be in the newspapers though,' Judy said. 'The *Evening News* will print it – there was a reporter here taking down every word – and some of the others will too, I expect. Plenty of people will get to know what he said to us.'

They went back to work, heartened by the Prime Minister's words. Judy thought about them, wondering just why they seemed so different from the bishop's during the mass funeral. He, too, had been trying to give them hope, but somehow it hadn't been the same. It was as if he were trying to brush aside and glorify the horrible deaths that so many people had suffered, whereas Mr Churchill seemed to suffer with them. He'd seen deaths like that himself, he knew what they were like and didn't pretend they were glorious or 'happy', but at the same time he seemed to draw strength from them, and hand it on to others. What was it he'd said in that other speech? *'I have nothing to offer you but blood, toil, tears and sweat.'* And, *'We shall fight them in the streets and the hills and on the beaches. We shall never surrender.'* He didn't pretend, but at the same time he gave you hope and some of his own stubborn determination. And he made you feel that, however small a part you played yourself, it was important. It was all a part of the great national effort.

Just at the moment, Judy's part in that effort was trying to set up a system for salvage collections – there had been appeals for binoculars for the Navy, for saucepans and other aluminium goods for making aeroplanes, for clothes, for rags and bones. Nothing, it seemed, was to be thrown away; everything could be put to some use.

'There are going to be special bins for food scraps,' she said. 'They'll be collected for pig swill – pigs will eat anything. There'll be one on the corner of every street to start with.'

'One pig?' Laura was sorting through a pile of temporary ration books to be issued to people who had lost theirs in the bombing.

'One *bin*, twerp!' Judy threw a screwed-up scrap of paper at her and Laura caught it and threw it back.

'I hope you weren't going to waste that – it'll do for one of your collections.' They made faces at each other, grinned and went back to their tasks, feeling more light-hearted.

The next special visitors were the King and Queen themselves. Judy, in a flurry of nerves, made Polly help her drag in the small tin bath the night before, muttering to each other that it would be a good thing when the potatoes could be harvested and the big bath returned to its proper use. They poured in hot water from kettles and added some bath salts Polly had been given for Christmas. Judy got in first, luxuriating in the pleasure of having a bath on a Wednesday instead of the usual Friday or Saturday. Then she got out again and Polly got in, followed by Alice, Cissie and finally Dick. 'We might as well all have a treat,' Alice said. 'No sense wasting the hot water.'

With their hair newly washed and set with Amami lotion,

Judy and Polly joined the rest of the staff and volunteers at the hotel early next morning to receive the Royal visitors. The King, looking serious but ready with a shy, friendly smile, was wearing Naval uniform – he'd actually served during the Great War, Polly whispered to Judy, and been in the Battle of Jutland. The Queen was in a dark costume, with a hat that was swept up away from her face, four rows of pearls around her neck and a fur stole draped over her arms.

All the bigwigs were there too – the Lord Mayor and Lady Mayoress, of course, Admiral Sir William James the Commander-in-Chief of Portsmouth, Brigadier Harter, Major-General Hunton, Colonel Walker and the Town Clerk. The men bowed deeply and the Mayoress dropped a graceful curtsey. As they passed the staff, the latter all bowed or curtseyed as well, most of them terrified that they would fall over or get their hair caught in someone's buttons. As the door of the Mayor's office closed behind the visitors, the staff heaved a general sigh of relief.

'She looks just like a film star!' Judy exclaimed. 'Did you see those pearls? And that fur – it must have been real mink!'

'I can't see why she needs to dress up like that,' remarked Eileen Hall, who didn't really like royalty. 'Especially when she's going to see people who've been bombed out and got nothing. It's just flaunting herself and all her money.'

'No, it's not.' Polly was an avid follower of the Royal Family. 'They can't help being rich, and if they've got nice clothes they might as well wear them. Anyway, she says that if people go to see her they dress up in their best, so why shouldn't she do the same?'

'Oh, know her personally, do you?' Eileen sneered, and Polly flushed angrily.

'No, I read it in the paper, and so could you have done if you didn't have your head buried in penny romances all the time. Anyway, I've got work to do and we'd better not start

74

yelling at each other or they'll hear us in there and a fine impression of Pompey that'll give them!'

They went back to their desks, the excitement of the morning slightly dimmed by the squabble. Polly felt angry with herself for letting Eileen get under her skin. I ought to learn to ignore her, she thought as she tried to sort out lists for the salvage collections, a job she had taken over from Judy who was now busy helping the Mayoress with the Clothing Depot. All the WVS staff and volunteers were extra busy that morning, as they were all going to St Mary's Hospital in the afternoon to meet the Queen again as part of her tour.

'It was lovely,' Judy told her mother that evening as they sat round the supper-table eating bubble and squeak. 'There must have been a couple of hundred of us there, all WVS, and there were some Red Cross nurses too. The Queen's ever so pretty – smaller than you'd think from her pictures, with gorgeous blue eyes – and she was so *interested*. D'you know what I heard her say? "Sunshine will come again," she said. Don't you think that's lovely? She couldn't talk to everyone, of course, but she managed to have a few words with quite a lot. And they did so much during the day. They went and looked at some of the bombed areas down Commercial Road, and the Guildhall, and some of the ordinary streets as well, and she saw our Clothing Depot, and the billeting people, and the welfare offices, and then they went and had lunch on the *Victory*.'

'Oh, that must have been lovely,' Alice broke in. 'And nice for the King, too, him having been in the Navy.'

'Well, I don't think he was ever on a ship like the *Victory*,' Polly said with a grin. 'And after that, he went to see the Gunnery School and she came on to the hospital and some of the First-Aid Posts. They were on the go all day.' She was silent for a moment, then she said, 'I think she's right about dressing up, you know. It wouldn't have been so special if they'd come in old clothes – even if they've got any! And it does make you feel better, knowing someone like that's taken the trouble to look nice for you. It makes you feel as though you matter to them.'

'Yes,' Judy agreed. She was still grieving for Sean, still thought about him all the time, still felt cheated of all they might have known and had together. But Polly was right, she thought. 'It does make you feel better.'

'That bit about sunshine coming again,' Alice said after a moment. She looked at the two faces, showing the same sorrow, and her own face softened in sympathy. 'It's true, you know. You can't go on without letting in a bit of sunshine now and again. You've got to start living again. You've got to.'

Chapter Eight

The raids continued, although all through January and February the concentration was on other cities. Bristol, Plymouth and Swansea all came under heavy attack, and all along the south coast the sirens went night after night, sending people to the shelters to sit listening to the snarl of German bombers overhead, and wonder where they were making for.

The firewatcher's post on the hotel roof had been taken over by the Royal Observers' Corps. Judy had noticed the young men in their RAF uniforms coming in and out several times before she found herself in the lift with one, on her way to the fifth floor with a message. He was tall, with fair hair and blue eyes and a nice smile, and she smiled back and asked, 'What is it you're doing up there? Looking out for enemy aircraft?'

'That's right,' he said. He touched the badge on his arm. It showed a Spitfire in flight. 'The RAF advertised for chaps like me who are keen on spotting aircraft, so I applied and here I am.' He grinned. 'It's like a dream come true, sitting up there in the best place in Southsea, looking for aeroplanes. I used to do it for a pastime and now I'm helping the war effort as well!'

Judy looked at him, so clean and smart in his uniform, obviously enjoying himself on the roof of a nice building, with nothing uncomfortable or difficult to do, and thought of the pilots who risked their lives every day in the air, and the sailors like Sean and Johnny, who died horrible deaths at sea. 'Nice work if you can get it,' she said tartly.

'Well, someone's got to do it!' he said jocularly, and then caught the note in her voice. 'Look, I know it must seem a cushy number – and maybe it is, compared with what some poor blighters have to do – but it's essential work just the same. We're the ones who spot the aircraft first and identify them so that others can shoot them down and stop them bombing Pompey. I know a lot still get through, but that doesn't mean we've just got to sit back and let them all come in. It'd be even worse if we did that.'

'Yes, but why does it have to be people like you? Why not people who can't go on active service? People who've been injured or can't serve for one reason or another?'

'Like poor eyesight?' he asked quizzically. 'Well, don't ask me. I suppose because we're the ones who volunteered. Blokes like me who've always been keen on aeroplane spotting. We're the ones who're good at it. And it does take a bit of skill, you know, to be able to spot an aircraft coming in at twenty thousand feet and be able to recognise what it is. It's not all that safe sometimes either,' he added as if as an afterthought, 'sitting up on top of an eight-storey building right on the beach. We're an easy target.'

'I suppose so,' Judy said a little grudgingly. The lift had arrived at the fifth floor and she got out. The young Observer went on to the top; here he would climb the steel ladder to the roof, originally installed as a fire escape. On her way to one of the offices with her message, Judy passed a room that the Observer Corps was using as a classroom and glanced in through the open door. A row of young men and two or three girls were sitting at desks while an instructor fixed large sheets of paper covered with the silhouettes of aircraft on a board.

I suppose it *is* skilled work, she thought, and I suppose it's a bit dangerous being up there like sitting ducks – but all the same, it doesn't compare with what other people are doing. It doesn't compare in the least with what Sean and Johnny and all those others in action are doing.

Even without the raids, the war news was bad. Malta, its position in the Mediterranean making it a vital possession, was bombarded day and night while the islanders, with only three Spitfires to protect them, dug themselves into caves and catacombs and sat out the raids which all but destroyed their island and capital city.

Meanwhile, the war had spread. Italy had taken over the vital supply ports of Tobruk, Somaliland and Libya, as well as Greece and Albania. Most people in Britain had never even heard of these places and had to search out old school atlases to find where they were, and daily newspapers published large maps of the world which could be pinned on walls. Even then, it was difficult to make sense of what was happening.

'I don't see why it's spread so much,' Cissie said, staring at the coloured pins Dick had put in to mark the progress of the different armies – red for Britain, black for Germany, blue for Italy. 'It was just Poland and Austria, and places like that, to begin with. Why does Africa have to get mixed up in it?'

'It's because of Italy coming in on Hitler's side,' Dick explained. 'They've got all these places in Africa, you see, and so have we, so we've got to defend ours against them.' He paused doubtfully, his chest wheezing a little. It still didn't seem to make much sense. 'Frank Budd was saying the other day that they're getting worried about the Japanese now. They think they might come in.'

'The *Japanese*!' Cissie stared at him. 'Why? Whatever's it got to do with them?'

'Well, nothing, but apparently they don't like America being in the South Pacific. They've got places in Hawaii – naval bases – so they're quite close to Japan really.' He looked at the map again. 'You can see it better on a globe. They look far apart on a map, but if you imagine it sort of bent round the back, then you can see how close they are.'

'But America's not even *in* the war,' Cissie said. 'What's the point of Japan butting in?'

'They think the Americans want their oil. And they'd like to take over China as well, and maybe even go up into Russia, and this would be a good chance, while we're all busy defending everywhere else.' Dick began to cough. His chest was getting worse again and he'd had two mild asthma attacks in the past week or so. 'I don't understand it any more than you do, Cis, but that's what I've heard.'

Cissie shook her head. 'I can't make it out at all. Seems to me they've all gone mad. The whole world's going to be fighting each other at this rate, and what's the good of that? What's going to be left when they finish? What's the point of it all?'

Judy, who had been sitting quietly mending her stockings, looked up and said, 'Freedom, Mum. That's what it's all about. We couldn't let Hitler march all over Europe and take away everyone's freedom like he did to the Jews and all those other poor people. We had to stop him.'

'Yes, but all these others – Africa and Japan and Russia – he wasn't marching into *their* countries. It's like boys fighting in the street. One or two start scrapping and then the rest all pile in just for the sake of it, and in the end no one knows what it was all about. It was the same in the Fourteen-Eighteen War – someone shot that man in Yugoslavia and before we knew where we were, all our men were being marched off to fight. Millions were killed, and thousands like your dad, messed up for the rest of their lives. It's like a disease.' She stopped and stared at them all. 'Like a horrible, mad disease.'

Mike Simmons turned up on Jess Budd's doorstep one day and, after some discussion, agreed that the two little girls should go out to Bridge End and be billeted at the vicarage. 'I wanted them to be evacuated right at the beginning,' he said sadly, 'but Kathy wouldn't hear of them going without her, and she wouldn't go herself because she wanted to stay in Pompey for when I got home. We went over it again and again, but all she would say was that the Queen wouldn't let her girls go to Canada without her, and she wouldn't go because she wanted to be with the King, and it was the same for her. I stopped trying to talk her round in the end. I didn't want to spend all my time arguing.' He shook his head. 'Perhaps I ought to have put my foot down – said she'd *got* to go. But how could I make her, Mrs Budd?' He lifted his head and looked at Jess. 'How could I?'

'Well, it's the same with me,' Jess said a little uncomfortably. 'I feel the same about leaving my Frank, and so of course the baby has to be here, too. And Rose went to start with, but she wanted to come home . . . But I do think your little ones'd be better off out there now, Mr Simmons.'

Polly was given the task of taking Stella and Muriel out to Bridge End on the train. So far, she'd not had any specific job to do in the WVS but had just helped wherever she was needed, but since the Blitz, more and more children who had returned to Portsmouth for Christmas and stayed there – or perhaps not been evacuated at all – were going back, and they all needed escorts. Polly had accompanied several already, and enjoyed the task, though the children varied greatly.

'You should have seen the boys I took last week,' she told Laura when she was in the office collecting the documents that would have to go with the two girls. 'I thought I knew Pompey pretty well, but I've never seen anything like the home they came from. It was no better than a hovel. And their clothes! Well, I've seen better on a scarecrow – toes poking out of their boots, hardly any backside to their trousers – I felt ashamed, I did really, to be taking them to strangers in that state.'

'Weren't there any clothes in the Store they could have had?' Laura asked, shuffling the papers together.

'Yes, there were as it happens, and I got them fitted out

with nice flannel shorts and a jacket and shirt each, and a pair of wellington boots – there weren't any other shoes that would fit them. But that was only one outfit. I just hope they can put something together in the country.' Polly shook her head. 'But it's not just that, Laura. It's the boys themselves. They were sick on the train, all three of them – I don't know why it is that boys are always sick, the girls don't seem to suffer like it – and they'd obviously never seen a hanky before in their lives, their noses never stopped running. And their language! I tell you, I didn't know half the swear words they came out with!'

'How did you know they were swear words then?' Laura asked with a grin and Judy, who was putting some papers away in a filing cabinet in the corner, chuckled.

Polly smiled too, pleased to hear her niece laugh. 'It was the way they said them. And the way they looked at me, too, as if they wanted to see what I'd say – I knew they were swearing all right. I don't suppose they knew what they really meant, though, any more than I did. And I'm not going to repeat them now,' she added firmly as Laura's mouth opened. 'Goodness knows what I might be saying!'

She collected the railway tickets and other papers and went out. She was to deliver the children next day, and went down to Jess Budd's early in the morning to find the two girls waiting for her, neatly dressed in clothes that Jess had found for them amongst her own daughter's old things, with their faces shining and hair brushed.

'Well, you do look smart,' Polly said, gazing at them. 'I should think anyone would be pleased to have two nice little girls like you billeted with them.' The little one, Muriel, was nearly eight, just the same age as her Sylvie, and Stella was ten and old enough to be sensible. They looked back at her and then turned to Mrs Budd.

'Do we have to go, Auntie?' Muriel asked, her bottom lip trembling. 'We like it here with you.'

Jess Budd looked down at them tenderly. 'I like having

you, Muriel, but you'll be safer out in the country. And you'll be with Tim and Keith and the other children.'

'Tim and Keith are *boys*. I'd rather stay here with you and Maureen and Rose. *They're* not going out to the country.'

'I know.' Jess looked helpless. 'But your daddy wants you to go, doesn't he? Don't you remember, he had a talk with you both when he came to see you? He told you then he wanted you to go, so that he wouldn't have to worry about you in the bombing.'

'Well, *I* want to go,' Stella said suddenly. 'I'm fed up with being bombed. And Tim and Keith don't matter, Mu. We don't have to take any notice of them – there'll be plenty of girls to play with.'

Jess and Polly glanced at each other, trying not to smile. Polly picked up one of the little cardboard suitcases. 'Come on, then. We'll catch the train at Hilsea station. Have you been on a train before?'

'I'll come with you,' Jess said, putting Maureen into her pram. 'We'll wave goodbye.' To Polly she said quietly, 'I'll miss the little dears, but it'll be better for them to be away from Pompey. Every time they walk up the street they see the house they lived in – well, the space where it used to be. It's not good for them, being reminded what happened that night.'

Once on the train, the girls perked up and looked out of the window eagerly. Neither had ever seen the countryside before, and they cried out with excitement at seeing cows and sheep in the snowy fields. There were even one or two early lambs skipping about and Muriel turned to Polly, her face alight, and asked if she would be allowed to have one of her own.

'Maureen Budd's got one. The butcher gave it to her.'

'The butcher gave her a *lamb*?' Polly asked in surprise. 'Are you sure?'

'It's not a real one,' Stella said. 'It's the one he used to

83

have standing on his counter. He gave it to her at Christmas.'

'Well, what a lovely present. There can't be many little girls who've got a lamb like that.'

'Yes, but I want a real one,' Muriel persisted. 'Like Bo-Peep.'

'No, that was Mary,' Stella corrected her. 'Bo-Peep *lost* her sheep.'

They started to recite nursery rhymes and then went on to songs. They were on their third rendition of 'Run, Rabbit, Run' when the train arrived at Bridge End station. Polly gathered together their few pieces of luggage and helped them down on to the platform.

'We're supposed to meet Mrs Tupper,' she said, consulting her instructions and glancing around. 'I don't see anyone here, though.' An elderly porter was shovelling snow into piles on the platform and she approached him. 'Do you know if there's been a lady called Mrs Tupper here? She was supposed to meet us.'

He straightened up and pushed back his cap to scratch his forehead. 'Mrs Tupper? Big lady, is she, in charge of the evacuees?'

'I don't know what she looks like,' Polly said, 'but these are evacuees so I expect that's the one. Have we missed her?'

He shook his head. ''Ent coming. Gone down with 'flu, that's what I heard. Message come through on the telephone half an hour ago.' He started to shovel again.

Polly looked at him in exasperation. 'Well, what was the message? Didn't she say what I should do with the girls? I was supposed to hand them over to her.'

He shook his head. 'Wasn't her that telephoned. Told you, she's got the 'flu. Too poorly to come to the telephone, I dare say, so she got someone else to do it for her.'

'Yes, but what did they say? Wasn't there any instruction for me?'

'You?' he repeated blankly.

Polly took a deep breath. I shall laugh about this later, she told herself, but she didn't feel much like laughing now. 'Yes, me. Presumably that's why she – or whoever it was,' she added hastily as his mouth began to open, 'telephoned the station, to let me know that she wouldn't be here. And I expect they left a message to say what I should do. Didn't they?'

'Well, so they might've done,' he muttered resentfully, 'only I don't know who you are, do I? I ent going to give messages to people I don't know. Might be someone else's message, mightn't it? I got a responsible position here,' he told her severely, 'and there's a lot of funny people about. Spies and Fifth Columnists and that. You know what the posters say: *Walls Have Ears*. Well, I ent going to give no messages to nobody, not unless I knows who they are, and that's flat.' He sniffed and made to start shovelling again.

Polly reached out and grasped the handle of his spade. 'All right. Perhaps I should have told you who I was. My name's Mrs Dunn, and I'm escorting these two little girls from Portsmouth to their billet at the vicarage here. We were supposed to be met by Mrs Tupper. Now she's not here and I'd like to know if she left any message for me, or whether I should just take Stella and Muriel straight to the vicarage. And I'd like to know quickly, please, because we've been on the train all morning – goodness knows why it took that long, but it did – and I have to hand them over and then go back. *On the train*,' she added, just to make everything clear, and looked him in the eye.

The porter shrugged and looked away. 'Well, that's all right then, because that's what you're supposed to do. Take 'em to the vicarage. It's straight down the lane, by the church. I dare say they're waiting for them there – Mrs Mudge and the vicar, and those boys they've got there already. Pair of rapscallions,' he added vengefully.

Polly looked at him with a mixture of exasperation and

curiosity. 'What do you mean, rapscallions? And why couldn't you give me the message in the first place?'

'I told you, I wasn't giving out no information till I knowed who you was. And all boys is rapscallions, stands to reason, it's their nature. I was, when I was a boy.' He stared at her, as if defying her to doubt that he'd ever been a boy. 'Anyway, you should see what those two gets up to, leading the vicar astray. Man of his age too. Oughter know better.' He shuffled off down the platform, leaning on his spade rather than shovelling with it, and muttering to himself.

What on earth can he mean? Polly wondered, but it was too cold to stand on the platform any longer. She led the two girls out of the station, each carrying a suitcase and festooned with brown paper bags containing their few possessions.

'It can't be too far to the vicarage,' she said encouragingly. 'You can see the church tower there, look, across the fields. But I'm sure we can get there by the lane,' she added as Muriel stared at the cows over the hedge and began to look alarmed.

'They're ever so big close to, aren't they? They're as big as elephants.'

'Well, not quite.' Polly herself had never been quite so close as this to a cow, and was glad they didn't have to go into the field with them. Sylvie must be quite used to them by now, she thought, and sighed. She'd hoped to get over to Ashwood today to see her. If she could have just handed the little girls over to Mrs Tupper, she could have got straight back on to the train. She sighed again.

A small hand slid into hers. 'Is it a big nuisance having to take us to the vicar's house?' Muriel asked, and Polly looked down at her and felt ashamed.

'No, of course it's not. I'll be pleased to see where you're going, and I can tell Mrs Budd I've seen Tim and Keith as well. I can give them the cake she's sent.'

The church tower, which had been over to their left, had

disappeared behind some trees and then, mysteriously, reappeared on their right. I hope it isn't too far, Polly thought. It's so cold and the girls haven't had anything to eat since breakfast. I hope the housekeeper's got something hot for them.

They began to pass a few cottages. There were one or two on their own, then a small row, then some more in pairs. Some were thatched, some had slate roofs, and with the snow covering them like quilts and their gardens a mysterious jumble of white bumps, they looked like a Christmas card. Polly even spotted a robin sitting on a holly bush and pointed it out to the girls. They nodded glumly, too cold, tired and apprehensive to be excited by Christmas cards.

The lane turned again and the tower appeared directly ahead, at the end of the village street. There were cottages on both sides of the road, which widened to a village green with a small pond in the middle. Beside the pond stood a large snowman, and some boys were sliding on a long strip of ice along the edge of the road.

'Well,' Polly said, 'doesn't this look lovely?'

The two girls regarded the scene without enthusiasm. Poor little scraps, they've had enough, Polly thought. But it did look a happy place, with all these cosy-looking cottages and the snow-covered green and the children playing. They'd be better off here, away from the war and all the terrible things that had happened to them. Polly rather wished she could stay herself.

The vicarage was easy to find – a large house, set back from the road in a big garden with lots of trees, close to the church. Polly opened the iron gates and they went up the path. They climbed a few steps to the front door and Polly lifted the knocker.

'I don't like this place,' Muriel said, putting her thumb in her mouth. 'It's too big.'

Before Polly could reply, the door opened and they saw a

woman standing there. She was as tall as Polly but a good deal rounder, with curly grey hair and very bright eyes. She wore a cherry-red jumper and skirt, covered by a flowery apron, and her sleeves were rolled up as if she'd just been mixing cakes or scrubbing a floor. She beamed at them.

'You're here!' She sounded as though this was the moment she'd been looking forward to all day. 'Come in out of the cold. Come through to the kitchen, it's nice and warm and I've got some good stew simmering ready, and a loaf of bread just out of the oven. Here, let me take your coats. My, what pretty little girls. Mr Beckett's going to be so pleased!'

She swept them along the passage and into the kitchen. It was a big room, almost as big as the rooms at the Royal Beach, and its warmth equalled the warmth of the housekeeper's welcome. Polly, finding herself pressed into a large rocking chair by the stove, felt as if she had been wrapped in a comforting eiderdown. She looked at the girls, who had been ensconced on small stools and were now having their wellington boots removed, and hoped they felt the same.

'The boys are out playing in the snow,' the housekeeper continued, warming Muriel's feet between her hands. 'And the vicar's probably with them if I know anything about it! Nothing more than a boy himself, and that's the truth. My name's Mrs Mudge, by the way. I've looked after the vicar for years – me and my hubby both, before he passed away. Anyway, they'll be in soon clamouring for their dinner. You'll have something before you go back, won't you, Mrs . . . ?'

'Dunn,' Polly said. 'Well, if it's not too much trouble. I don't want to take your rations.'

'Rations!' the housekeeper exclaimed, as if she'd never heard the word before. 'You don't want to worry about rations! My stew's all vegetables from the garden – Mr Beckett and me dug over a big patch as soon as all this started. There's a bit of rabbit in it too, that Mr Knight brought round. There's not a single *ration* been near it!'

'Well, it smells delicious,' Polly said, eyeing the pan simmering on the stove. 'And it will be nice to see the boys – I can go back and tell their mother how they are. They're not being too much trouble, I hope?' she added, remembering her official position.

'Trouble? Tim and Keith?' Mrs Mudge laughed. 'Well, they're boys, aren't they – bound to get into a few scrapes. But no, they're no real trouble, no trouble at all, though young Tim's a bit of a live wire. If there's anyone who's trouble in this house, it's not *them*, I can tell you.' She folded her lips and nodded darkly.

Polly looked at her doubtfully, but before she could ask what the housekeeper meant the back door burst open and they could hear excited voices in the scullery beyond the kitchen. Polly recognised the voices of Tim and Keith Budd, whom she'd often seen playing in April Grove when she'd visited her mother, and decided that the deeper tones must belong to Mr Beckett himself. Aware of a sudden nervous tension in the two little girls, she drew them close and stood up as the vicar entered.

'Why, they're arrived!' he exclaimed, rubbing long thin hands together. He came forward hastily, draping a pair of navy-blue woollen gloves over the rail on the front of the stove before holding one of his hands out to Polly and smiling at the girls. 'I was expecting Mrs Tupper.'

'She couldn't come. She's got 'flu. My name's Polly Dunn, I brought the girls from Portsmouth.'

'How kind of you. How very kind.' The vicar beamed at her, then turned to the girls and dropped to one knee so as to be able to look into their faces. He was like a spider, Polly thought, or one of those stick insects they'd once had in the classroom at school – all long, thin arms and legs that looked as if they ought to have at least two elbows or knees each. But his smile was as wide, as joyous and as unforced as a baby's, as if – like Mrs Mudge – he was really pleased and happy to see them.

'How very good to see you both,' he said, taking one of the girls' hands in each of his. 'How very, *very* good to have you here with us. I hope you'll be very happy here.'

They stared back at him without expression. Then Stella said bluntly, 'Our mummy's dead. She was killed by a bomb. And our baby, too.'

There was a brief, appalled silence. Polly put a hand to her burning face. It was a clear reproach, as if to say *'How do you expect us to be happy, here or anywhere else?'* But Mr Beckett didn't seem at all put out by it. He nodded gravely, his smile put away for the moment, and drew them a little closer.

'I know, my dears, and I'm very, very sorry. You must miss her so much. I lost my own mother when I was just the same age as you.'

They looked at him uncertainly. 'Did you?' Stella asked at last.

'Yes, I did. She was riding a horse and it jumped a fence that was too high. She fell off and her back was broken. She never woke up again.' There was a moment of quiet, then he said, 'I was very unhappy about it for a long time. I'm *still* unhappy about it. But do you know what happened? After a while, I found I could still be happy about *other* things. And that will happen to you too, as time goes on. So I hope you'll be very happy here with us – even though I know you'll never stop being unhappy about your mother, and you'll always miss her.'

There was another moment of quiet. Polly was aware of Tim and Keith standing in the doorway, their eyes fixed on the vicar's thin, stooping back. She was struck by the expression in their eyes. It's the sort of look boys only give to someone they really think a lot of, she thought – an older boy or a teacher, or a father – and a sense of warmth stole across her heart.

Muriel took a deep breath. She nodded matter-of-factly

at the vicar, then let go of his hand and looked up at Mrs Mudge.

'I'm hungry,' she said in her small, clear voice. 'Can we have our dinner now?'

The rabbit stew was, Polly thought, the best meal she had eaten for months. It was followed by a rice pudding and then Mrs Mudge made a large pot of tea and set it on the middle of the table.

'You children can go and play now,' she said. 'Put your wellingtons on, and your coats and scarves. Have both you girls got gloves?'

'Mittens,' Stella said, holding them up. 'Auntie Jess knitted them. She was teaching me,' she added proudly.

'Well, that's good. I'll go on teaching you, then. We can do with some more knitters around here to make things for soldiers and sailors.' Mrs Mudge buttoned Muriel into her coat. 'Tim and Keith will take you out and show you their snowman, won't you, boys? And you can go for a walk round the village. The boys know most of the people here now, so you don't need to worry about anything. You look after them, now, boys.'

Tim, who had been talking about a snowball fight that had been arranged between the evacuees and the village children, looked somewhat disgruntled by this instruction, but the vicar gave him a firm look and he went without argument. In any case, Stella, who had recovered her normal assertiveness, was already taking charge. 'We'll look at the snowman first,' she was saying as they went out through the back door, 'and then you can take us to look at that pond. There were some boys sliding near it . . .'

The door closed behind them and Mr Beckett smiled. 'I foresee a few battles there. Tim won't like being bossed about by a girl, and that's the boys' slide.'

Polly grinned back. 'Not now Stella's here. I haven't known her long, but I can tell you this – anything a boy can do, Stella can do better! I don't think you'll have any problems getting her to settle, Mr Beckett. I'm not so sure about Muriel, though. Stella mothers her a lot, but she's a sensitive little girl and she's been through so much in this past year. She may need some extra care.'

'Well, she's come to the right place for that,' Mr Beckett said, warming his long, thin hands round his cup of tea. 'Mrs Mudge and I have had quite a lot of experience in looking after children now, haven't we, Mrs Mudge? I think both those little girls will settle in very well. They can be safe and happy, and forget about war now. They can be children again, as God intended them to be.'

Polly glanced at the housekeeper and was surprised to catch the expression on her face. She was looking at the vicar in just the same way as Tim and Keith had looked at him when he was talking to the little girls. As if she thought the world of him. And there was an added tenderness in her face that reminded Polly of Jess Budd, when she looked at the photograph of her two sons.

Tenderness, and indulgence for boys and their ways. But Mr Beckett wasn't a boy. He was an elderly man.

Polly finished her tea and thanked them both before gathering together her coat and gloves and getting ready to walk back to the station for the return journey to Portsmouth. As they went outside, she saw the four children careering madly round the big garden, hurling snowballs at each other. One caught Mr Beckett on the shoulder and as Polly gasped in dismay he chuckled and bent to gather up a handful of snow.

'I'll show you!' he yelled, flinging a huge snowball that caught Tim full in the chest. 'I'll show the lot of you!'

Polly and Mrs Mudge looked at each other, and the housekeeper raised her eyes to heaven and spread out her hands.

'Boys!' she said. 'They never grow up . . .'

Chapter Nine

When Polly reached the station the aged porter told her that there wouldn't be a Portsmouth train for another two hours.

'That's if it comes at all,' he added, with some satisfaction. 'Never know where you are with the times these days.'

'Two hours!' Polly looked at the station clock and wondered what to do. She didn't like to go back to the vicarage, even though she was sure Mrs Mudge would be kindness itself, and it was too cold to stand on the icy platform all that time. I suppose I'll just have to go for a walk, she thought. But it'll be getting dark in an hour or so . . .

As she stood there, gazing at the unhelpful face of the porter, she heard the whistle of an approaching train and turned quickly. To her disappointment, it was heading away from Portsmouth, towards Salisbury. A sudden idea struck her.

'Does that train stop at Ashwood? The little halt just before Romsey?'

'It do,' he admitted unwillingly.

'Then I'll get on that and catch the Portsmouth train back from there,' she said. 'I can go and see my daughter.'

'You'll need a ticket.'

'Well, you can sell me one, can't you? A return ticket? Then I can come back here and use my Portsmouth return for the rest of the journey. Hurry *up*,' she urged him as the train drew up at the platform. The guard got out and she waved to him. 'Don't go yet, please! I'm just buying a ticket!' The porter, evidently unable to think of any reason why not, was shuffling reluctantly towards his little office and she ran after him. 'Oh, *please* hurry!'

Begrudgingly, he made out the ticket and Polly handed him the money and ran out on to the platform again. The guard was holding a door open and she leaped aboard and threw herself down into a seat. For once, the train wasn't crowded and there was only one other person in the compartment – a man with wavy, iron-grey hair brushed back from a broad forehead, wearing a shabby greatcoat and khaki woollen gloves. He grinned at her as she flung herself down, and said, 'You only just made it, love.'

Polly looked at him. His voice was deep and warm, with a London accent, and he had a good-natured face, with three corrugated lines on his forehead that somehow added to the twinkle in his dark brown eyes. She smiled back.

'I didn't think the man was going to let me have a ticket. He doesn't seem to like passengers.'

'I 'spect he thinks they make the station look untidy,' the man said. 'You can't see what it's like now, with all the snow and ice, but in spring and summer it's a real picture. He wins prizes for the Best Station Garden – I reckon he thinks trains and passengers are a bit of a nuisance. They get in the way of his garden!'

Polly laughed. 'Well, you'd think he'd have been glad to get rid of me, then. I just think he wanted to be awkward.'

There was a slight pause and then the man said, 'You don't live at Bridge End, then?'

Polly shook her head. 'No, I'm from Portsmouth. I've just been taking two little girls to an evacuation billet.'

He looked concerned. 'But this train ain't going to Portsmouth – it's just come from there. You're going the wrong way, love.'

'No, I'm going on to Ashwood to see my own little girl. There isn't a train back to Portsmouth for two hours, so I thought I'd take the chance. It's only a short journey – I'll just have time to see her before I have to go back. I haven't seen her since Christmas,' she added wistfully, 'and a lot's happened since then.'

'You're telling me.' The corrugated lines on his forehead deepened a little. 'Had a big raid in Pompey last month, didn't you? Were you there through that?'

Polly nodded. 'We were bombed out.' She stopped suddenly, wondering if she had said too much, then decided that even if spies or Fifth Columnists were listening there wasn't much worth reporting back to Hitler about the fact that the Taylors and Polly Dunn had been bombed out, or that little Stella and Muriel Simmons had been sent to Bridge End. All the same, you never knew who you might be talking to and she resolved to watch her words. Portsmouth was an important city and almost any snippet of information might be of use to the enemy.

'Bombed out?' he echoed. 'Here, that's rough. Were you inside the house, or did you manage to get to a shelter?'

'Oh yes, we always went down there. We lost everything, but at least we were all right. We're lucky too, because we could go and stay with my mother. And Sylvie – my little girl – was already out in the country so she wasn't there.'

He shook his head. 'Bloody awful, all the same, if you'll pardon my French.' He glanced at her uniform. 'I see you're in the WVS.'

'Yes, I am,' Polly said, pleased that he had recognised it. 'You know about the WVS, then?'

The man laughed. 'I ought to! My sister works at the Headquarters in London – 41 Tothill Street. She never stops telling me about all the good work they do – if I wasn't a man she'd have recruited me long ago. Mind you, she's right – they do wonderful work. All the things nobody else will do.'

'Well, we're not dogsbodies,' Polly said, 'but I suppose it's true that there just doesn't seem to be anyone else to do a lot of the jobs we take on. But that's because in wartime there are a lot of new jobs to do, like taking children out to the country – it just doesn't happen in peacetime.'

''S right. And we're lucky there are women like you ready to do them.' He grinned at her. 'Tell you what, I reckon this war'll be won by you women. Not by fighting, I don't mean that, but 'cause you're always there on the spot, ready to do whatever's needed to keep the country running. Look at all the young girls who're joining up now, so that the men can go and fight – and all the others like the WVS and that, doing all sorts of work, driving buses and ambulances, farming, you name it – and still managing to keep homes going for their menfolk and kiddies.' He nodded. 'Without them, I reckon the war would've been lost from the very start.'

Polly gazed at him. 'You really mean that?'

'I do. I really do.' Their eyes met and Polly felt a thrill of warmth touch her heart. The man looked out of the window. 'Here, look, we're just coming into Ashwood now. Well, it's been a real pleasure to meet you, love.' He smiled at her again and, as the train slowed down, leaned out to open the door. 'I hope you find your kiddy OK,' he said, 'and good luck. Don't get bombed out again, will you!'

Polly laughed and stepped down on to the platform. 'I'll try not to. Goodbye, and thank you for the things you've said. It's nice to be appreciated.'

'Oh, you are, love,' he said, and his eyes met hers again. 'You don't have to worry about that. You really are.'

The train set off again with a loud snort from the engine, and Polly stood on the platform waving as it steamed off along the track. It rounded a bend and disappeared from sight and she let her arm drop with a sigh. A nice man, she thought. The sort of man you could feel comfortable with. A pity she would never see him again.

All the same, he'd more than made up for the old porter's cantankerousness, and the station clock told her that she had an hour and a half before the Portsmouth train was due.

Sylvie's billet was in a farmhouse only ten minutes' walk away. She would be just coming back from school now, and certain to be there. With a leap of excitement in her heart, Polly turned to walk briskly out of the station, and forgot about the man in the fawn greatcoat, with the warm dark eyes and the corrugated forehead.

'So I had over an hour with her,' Polly told the family later when she finally arrived back at April Grove. 'It was lovely – she was *so* excited to see me. And the people she's billeted with, Mr and Mrs Sutton, they couldn't be nicer. They've got two other evacuees there too, a brother and sister; the boy's Sylvie's age and the girl's a bit older. Jenny and Brian, they're called. They were all playing Ludo when I got there.'

'I didn't know there were other children there,' Cissie said. 'Sylvie's never mentioned them in her letters.'

'Well, you know Sylvie's letters, they're not much more than *Dear Mummy, I hope you're well, I'm well, I hope Granny's well . . .*' Polly said, laughing. 'After all, she can't write all that much. But these two haven't been there long. They were sent out after the Blitz, apparently, like Stella and Muriel.'

'And d'you think they'll settle in all right?' Judy asked. She'd spent most of the day trying to sort out other hasty evacuations. 'We've had complaints from a few people. Some of the parents think their children aren't being looked after properly and some of the country hosts say the children are so badly behaved they can't put up with them. Mostly ones from Rudmore and areas like that,' she added.

'Everyone knows what a slum Rudmore is,' Alice remarked. 'Though they're the salt of the earth just the same. And I dare say there's a few from Old Portsmouth too, with backsides hanging out of their trousers and no shoes. Look at the Hodges family who came here just before the war started. They lived in a pub in Old Portsmouth, so

Tommy Vickers told me, and didn't have a penny to bless themselves with. Mr Hodges works down the Camber dock, steady enough work but you know what the pay's like. And that boy of theirs, the older one – Gordon – you could see from the start he'd be a troublemaker. Got mixed up straight away with Micky Baxter, and now he's in an approved school for pinching stuff from an antique shop. You remember that, don't you? Caused a real rumpus in April Grove.'

'Don't understand why they didn't send Micky away too,' Dick said. 'He was in it just as much as the older one. Wasn't there a younger boy, too?'

Alice nodded. 'Sammy. He's not a bad little chap, helped his mum a lot before she died. Mr Hodges couldn't manage at all after that, left the kiddy on his own for two or three days at a time. If it hadn't been for Freda Vickers giving him his dinners I don't know what would have happened. Anyway, Tommy went down the billeting offices in the end and they took Sammy out to Bridge End, where the other youngsters went.'

'It looks a nice village,' Polly said. 'The vicar's a real gentleman, a bit odd but you expect that of a vicar, don't you, and his housekeeper Mrs Mudge is a proper motherly soul. Stella and Muriel'll be all right there.'

They were just finishing up the tea left in the pot when the familiar wail of the siren rose in the air. It had sounded almost every night since the Blitz, but the raids hadn't been as bad as on that terrible night. All the same, you couldn't take chances and there was a hasty gathering up of coats, blankets and the tin box that contained all the important household papers – insurances, birth certificates and so on – and within five minutes they were all in the Anderson shelter at the bottom of the garden, huddling on the bunks Dick and Terry had fitted there. Dick lit the hurricane lamp and they all looked at each other and shrugged.

'Might as well have a game of cards,' Cissie said, but Polly shook her head.

'I'm going down to the Emergency Centre. I said I would, if there was a raid. What about you, Judy?'

Judy nodded. Like Polly, she was still wearing her WVS uniform. 'You'll be all right here, won't you, Mum? You've got Dad and Gran with you.'

'I'm not worried about us,' Cissie said anxiously. 'It's you, going through the streets in the blackout, in the middle of a raid. Surely they can't expect you to do that?'

'Someone's got to, Mum,' Judy said. 'We were glad enough of the Centre when we got bombed out. Anyway, if we go quickly we'll be there before the planes come – and they might not even be coming here, this time.'

There had been alarms almost every night since the big raid, and a few bombs dropped on the city and its outskirts, but there had never been as much damage again, and nobody had been hurt. More often, the planes went over on their way to London or some other city. You still had to take shelter, just in case, but Portsmouth people were beginning to hope they'd had their share.

'I feel sorry, leaving Cissie like that,' Polly remarked as they groped their way through the pitch-black streets. 'She's always been a bit nervous, but we've got to do our bit.' She grabbed Judy's arm as they heard the first drone of enemy aircraft approaching. 'Oh Lord – here they come!'

They flattened themselves against a wall, staring up at the sky. It was criss-crossed with the long swords of the searchlights, and now and then the dark shape of a plane, high above, was caught in the shining white beam. Immediately, a rattle of ack-ack fire would break out from one or more of the gun emplacements around the city – on Southsea Common, or the slopes of Portsdown Hill – and once the two women saw a burst of orange as a plane was hit, and the streak of flame like a ribbon as it fell to earth.

'Suppose it fell on buildings?' Judy whispered, but she

knew that the gun crews couldn't think of that. It was too important to destroy the plane and its deadly cargo, for if it were allowed to go on its way, many more buildings might be demolished and people killed.

'Come on,' Polly murmured, giving her arm a little tug. 'We're not far away from the Centre now. Let's get there as quickly as we can.'

The Centre was an old church, and its crypt was being used as a shelter. Polly and Judy reached it safely and scrambled down the steps. The basement was already crowded with people, and there were a few hurricane lamps set about, lighting their faces eerily. At the far end someone had set up a long trestle table, and a WVS volunteer was busy with a large steaming urn.

'You can spread this bread with margarine and fish paste,' she directed the two newcomers. 'We're not expecting too much trouble tonight, but you never know. Here, aren't you Alice Thomas's girls? You know me – Mrs Chapman, from the bottom of October Street.'

'Yes, of course.' Polly started to slice the bread. 'The house with the turret. How's your Olive now?'

'Oh, not so bad, considering. She's still cut up about losing the baby, of course, but she's not letting it get her down. Gone back to work at Derek's dad's place, just like before.'

They worked busily, making cocoa and sandwiches. A lot of the people there had no shelters – in some streets, because of the way the water mains and sewers were laid, it was impossible to dig the hole needed for an Anderson, so those who lived there had to go to street shelters or Centres like this. Mostly, they brought their own food and drink with them, but there had to be plenty on tap for anyone who was bombed out, or brought in as casualties. There were First-Aid workers too, and ARP wardens popping in and out to bring news, glad of a hot drink and a 'wad', so one way and another they were kept busy enough even if there were no bombs.

Peggy Shaw, who lived next door to Jess Budd, joined them and began talking about her daughter Gladys, who drove an ambulance. 'Well, a bread-van, to be honest, converted. She's on standby all the time in air raids. And it's not just driving, neither. She got a kiddy out of a ruined cellar in the Blitz, saved her life, she did. Dug some poor boy out of a pile of rubble, took I don't know how many to hospital, and then came home for a wash, changed her clothes and went straight off to work.'

Peggy shook her head. 'I had to hand it to her, I did really.'

'But you must have been worried to death,' Annie said 'knowing she was out in all that bombing.'

Peggy laughed. 'Worried? I was out there with her! And I can tell you this, there was no time for worrying – no more than you had when you were sorting out all the people who got bombed out.' She picked up a fresh loaf and held it against her chest as she sliced it. 'Anyway, there's no use worrying, is there? If a bomb's got your name on it, it'll find you, wherever you are. That's what I think. Doesn't matter whether you're down the air-raid shelter or standing on top of the Guildhall like Tommy Vickers was that night. If it's got your name on it, it'll find you.'

Polly glanced up as a plane snarled overhead. There had been several explosions already, and the roar of aircraft had been increasing. The rattle of ack-ack fire came from Portsdown Hill. 'I don't know about you,' she said, 'but it seems to me it's getting worse.'

They all lifted their heads and listened for a moment. There were obviously a lot of planes overhead, their nasal snarl unmistakable as German craft. At that moment, a tremendous explosion rocked the hall, and Judy put out a hand involuntarily to Polly's arm. They looked at each other.

'You're right,' Annie Chapman said grimly. 'This is going to be a bad one. It'll be more than cocoa and hot soup we'll be needing before it's over. Here come the first ones now, look.'

People had begun to straggle into the hall. There were already plenty who had come in for shelter when the siren had first sounded, but these were men and women, and children too, who looked frightened and bewildered. Some were covered with dust and others were injured, limping or holding their arms, or with blood running down their faces and staining their clothes. Polly, who had just finished a First-Aid course, went over at once to take charge.

'She's as good as my Gladys,' Peggy said, watching her. 'Hey-up, what's happening now?'

The door burst open and one of the Rover Scouts, the older members of the Boy Scouts who ran messages between the Centres, came panting in.

'They want someone to go and open an Incident Centre in Portsea,' he told them. 'It's bad down there – any amount of places bombed. People all over the place, don't know what to do. A copper sent me on my bike to fetch someone to take charge.' He looked from Annie to Judy. 'Come *on*!'

'All right, young man, no need to get so aeriated,' Annie said severely. She started to take off her apron. 'I'd better go.'

'No, I will. I can run faster.' Judy was pulling on her coat and hat as she spoke. She looked at the boy. 'Or I'll ride your bike, and you can do the running.'

'But it's got a crossbar!'

'So what? Think I can't manage it? I've been riding my brother's bike since I was ten years old.' She hustled him out of the church and grabbed the handlebars of his bike, hoisting up her skirt to cock her leg over the bar. 'Which way?'

Portsea was, as the Scout had said, badly bombed. The streets presented the now familiar sight of ruined houses, rubble-blocked roads, fire engines and ambulances – and pathetic knots of people huddled together in shocked bewilderment, or wandering in a daze, calling out for family members or friends.

'Joanie! Where's our Joanie?'

'My Fred – has anyone seen my Fred?'

Others were scrabbling desperately at piles of rubble. 'Our Brenda's down there somewhere; she was under the stairs and it's all fell in on top of her. Oh my *God*, my *God*, she'll be killed. We've got to get her out! *Help* me, for God's sake, *help* me. Our Brenda's in there, our *Brenda*!'

The Scout pushed Judy past them and through a doorway. The building had been a small church with a meeting-room at the back. The windows had been shattered but the glass had been safely caught by the criss-crossing of brown paper and the thick blackout curtains, and it was otherwise intact. Judy cast a nervous glance at the remaining walls, wondering what damage had been done to them unseen, and if another blast was all that was needed to bring them tumbling down. But there was nowhere else fit to use, and already a short, chubby man in an overcoat and dog-collar was setting up trestle tables and brushing dust off them with his sleeve.

'I'm WVS,' Judy said, joining him. 'Judy Taylor. I've come to set up an Incident Enquiry Centre.'

'Oh, bless you, it's so good to see you.' He grasped her hand briefly in his. 'Look, we've started to take information – the wardens are bringing in news all the time. They tell us which Emergency Centre people have gone to, or which hospital. Then, as people come in to enquire about their family and friends, we know where to direct them.' He shook his head. 'All too often, it's the mortuary, I'm afraid. Let's see if we can get an urn of tea on the go; there's nothing like a cup of hot sweet tea for shock. Where have you come from, my dear?'

'Copnor.' Judy felt a pang of anxiety, wondering how her

parents and grandmother were faring amongst all the bombing. The noise now was almost unbearable, each explosion sending shock waves through the ground and up through your whole body. Even bombs falling a mile or more away could be felt – and Portsmouth was a small area, the island of Portsea on which it was situated only five miles long and half as wide. Every now and then there was a duller thud which meant a bomb had landed in one of the two harbours, sending mud and sea water flying into the air. Portsdown Hill, to the north, was alight with incendiary bombs.

However, there was no time for thinking about the family, or bombs, or anything but the people who were straggling into the meeting-room, their faces lost and confused. Another woman had arrived, who seemed to know the clergyman and to be familiar with the battered tea urn, so Judy left her to it and sat down at one of the tables, drawing a sheet of paper towards her.

'You'll need to go to the Emergency Centre – there's one about half a mile away. If you're not hurt, you'd best get into a shelter until the raid's over, and then go. Give me your name first, in case anyone comes looking for you . . . There's a First-Aid Post at the infants' school round the corner – take him there and they'll bandage him up and see if he needs to go to hospital. Give me your name and address first.'

An air-raid warden pushed past the queue and bent to speak in her ear. He gave her a scrap of paper, covered with dirty fingerprints, and Judy read it quickly. She looked at him in consternation.

'You think his parents will come in here?'

'More'n likely, ducks. They'll be looking for him, see? Stands to reason, dunnit. You'll have to tell 'em.'

Judy bit her lip and looked down again at the scrap of paper. It bore the details of a child found dead in the street – a boy of no more than three years old, horribly injured, who must have run from a bombed house and then been caught by a second explosion. There was a brief description – chubby, with fair, curly hair, wearing blue pyjamas and still clutching a teddy-bear. The body had been taken to the local morgue.

Tears came to Judy's eyes but the warden had already gone, called by a shout from the doorway. The next minute, someone was standing before her holding out a length of thick string. The other end was attached to a wire-haired terrier of some indeterminate breed, leaping and barking hysterically.

'Found 'im wandering about outside, miss. The ARP man said to bring 'im in 'ere.'

Judy glanced helplessly at the clergyman, who nodded briskly. 'Put him in the church, my dear. We've already got quite a menagerie in there.' He turned away to attend to someone else and Judy took the makeshift lead and dragged the frantic dog through the door leading into the main church where, as the minister had said, there were already several animals including two black cats who leaped up on to the altar and began spit and hiss furiously.

'I hope to goodness you don't all get free and start fighting,' Judy muttered, tying the dog to the leg of a pew. The church was very plain, with little ornamentation, and she hadn't even known it was here until this evening. She found two large cardboard boxes and having – with some difficulty – caught the two terrified cats, she crammed them in and then hurried back to the meeting-room where a queue of people was building up, some wanting to know where they should go, some desperate to find family or friends they had lost.

Judy recorded all the new arrivals and checked her list to see if the missing had already been sent on.

'Yes, he had a head injury, they took him to the Royal. No, it didn't look too bad, really . . . A black cat? Yes, we've had two brought in. They're in boxes in the church through that door, but please be careful not to let any of the other animals out ... The whole family were sent to the Emergency Centre – yes, they're all quite safe, not hurt at all ... A little boy?' She looked up, her heart sinking, and saw the fear in the face of the woman standing before her.

'He's called Bobbie,' the woman said. Her voice was rough, her eyes huge and dark, her cheeks drawn with fear. 'We were in the shelter – next door was hit. I looked out to see what was going on, and he just slipped past me. He hated being in the shelter. I couldn't find him nowhere, and then another bomb . . .' She stopped, the tears running down her face, and stared at Judy piteously. 'Has he been brought in here, miss? Have you seen him?'

Judy swallowed, not knowing how to find the words to tell her. 'Was – was he wearing blue pyjamas?' she asked, praying that the woman would say no. But she nodded her head and with a sick sense of doom, Judy went on. 'And – and did – does he have fair, curly hair? And – and a teddy-bear?'

'Yes! Yes, he never goes anywhere without it, screams the place down if we take it away! Oh, where is he, where's my Bobbie?' the woman cried eagerly, and then her voice faded to a whisper and she stared at Judy with terror in her eyes. *'Where is he?'*

'I'm dreadfully sorry,' Judy said wretchedly. 'It might not be your little boy – I didn't see him myself – but the warden told me there was a little boy like that found a few streets away . . .'

'Where is he? Tell me!' The woman leaned forward. 'For God's sake! *Tell me where my Bobbie is*!'

'It might not be him,' Judy repeated. 'But the – the little boy the warden told me about – they had to take him to the – the mortuary.' She bit her lips, angry with herself for breaking the news so badly, for not being able to find the right words. 'I – I'm so sorry. He couldn't have known anything about it.'

'The *mortuary*? You mean he's *dead*?'

Judy nodded miserably, tears filling her eyes. The woman stared at her. Then she banged her fist on the table. 'My Bobbie? *Dead*?' She stared wildly at Judy. 'But he was only *three*. It was his birthday last week – I made him a cake. He *can't* be dead. He can't, he can't, he *can't*. I won't let him be dead!' Her voice rose to a shriek and she turned and began to scream at the queue. 'I won't *let* him be dead! I won't, I *won't*!'

'I'm very sorry,' Judy said, crying almost as much as the woman herself. 'It's terrible. I'm very, very sorry.'

The clergyman came round the table and laid a hand gently on the woman's shoulder. 'Come along, my dear. Come and sit over here for a few minutes. I'll bring you a cup of tea. Then I'll go with you to see if it is your little boy. Come along . . .'

She stared at him, and for a moment Judy was afraid she was going to hit him. Then her face crumpled, and she covered it with her hands and began to weep. She allowed him to lead her into a corner, where she sank on to a chair, sobbing as if her heart were broken. Which, Judy thought, it probably was.

She watched them ruefully. Well, a fine job I made of *that*, I don't think! she told herself. She groped for a hanky and rubbed her face fiercely, then looked up to see who was next in the queue.

The raid became known as Portsmouth's Second Blitz. Thousands of incendiaries and nearly three hundred high-explosive bombs were dropped on the city. Fourteen hundred people were made homeless, just under a hundred killed and over two hundred injured. Had it not been for the shelters, there would have been many, many more.

Polly and Judy met as they both made their way wearily along September Street. They stopped for a moment, tears of thankfulness filling their eyes as they hugged. 'I've been so worried,' Polly said, and Judy gave a shaky laugh. 'I was just going to say the same thing!' Their eyes met, and each knew what the other was thinking. What had been happening in April Grove?

Stumbling with fatigue, they continued along the street. The shops were already beginning to open. Mrs Marsh was polishing the dairy windows, and Alice Brunner was opening the door of the newsagent's to take in a pile of newspapers. She looked tired and unhappy, and Judy remembered that her husband Heinrich had been interned as an alien. They said good morning to her and she nodded, a wavery smile briefly lighting her pale face.

'It doesn't look as if there's been any damage round here,' Polly said as they turned down October Street. Near the bottom, the ruin of Kathy Simmons's house made an ugly gap between the houses, but apart from a few slates in the road and a broken window or two, there seemed to be nothing worse. With a sigh of relief, they turned the corner at the bottom and saw that number nine was still intact.

'Oh, thank goodness,' Judy said, and nearly ran the last few steps, eager to be indoors with her family again. With Polly close behind her, she unlocked the door and went inside.

Cissie was hurrying along the passage to meet them, her face drawn.

'Don't look like that, Mum,' Judy said. 'We're back safe and sound.'

'It's not that,' Cissie said, her voice shaking. 'It's your dad. He's having an asthma attack – a bad one. I think he needs to go to the hospital.'

Chapter Ten

Polly took one look at Dick, who was sitting hunched over the dining table, gasping desperately for breath, then turned round and went straight down to Peggy Shaw's house, where she and Gladys were just crawling into bed. Gladys put on her clothes and came out again, dashing off through the streets to fetch the converted baker's van. Alice had been out in the scullery making tea, and they all had a quick cup while they waited. By the time Gladys came back, Judy and her mother were bending over Dick, trying to get him to breathe out by pressing on the sides of his chest.

'Can't – breathe,' he wheezed, his eyes filled with panic. 'Got to – get me – *breath*. Ahh – ahh – ahh . . .'

'You've got to breathe *out*, lovey,' Cissie urged him, pressing harder as he tried ineffectually to shake her off. 'You know that's what the doctor said. You can't get any more breath in, you've got to let it out first. Now calm down, Dick, and try – please, just for me.'

'Can't – *breathe*,' he wheezed again. '*Cis*.' He stared at her with pleading, terrified eyes and beat feebly on the table with his hands. 'Cis!'

'It's all right, Dick.' She spoke calmly, trying to still her own panic. Dick had had enough attacks over the years for the family to become accustomed to them, but they were always frightening. You could see that Dick was afraid he was never going to be able to breathe again, and when he was as bad as this Cissie feared that he might be right. She pressed his chest again, signalling to Judy to do the same and suddenly Dick began to cough, his thin body torn with the violence of his retching. A gobbet of dark yellow phlegm spat out of his mouth and landed on the tablecloth, and they stared at it in horror. It was tinged with black dust, like soot, and there were streaks of blood in it as well.

'Dad!' Judy gasped, and looked wildly round for Polly. 'Is Gladys coming? He's got to go to hospital!'

'She's here.' Polly came in swiftly, followed by Gladys Shaw. 'Come on, Dick – let's get you out to the ambulance.' She helped Judy and Cissie lift him to his feet.

Dick, still wrenched with coughing, was trying frantically to breathe. He leaned on the table, his face almost blue.

'Hot,' he gasped. 'Too hot.' He tried to throw off the blankets, but Cissie firmly wrapped them round him again.

'You've got a temperature,' she said anxiously. 'If you take all those off you'll catch a chill. Come on, now, let's get you outside.'

'Keep him wrapped up,' Polly said, 'it's bitter out here.' They half carried him along the passage to the front door and lifted him into the van. 'That's it, Dick. You'll be all right now. Shall I come with you, Cis?'

'No, you stop here, you need your rest.' But it was clear that Cissie needed company. Polly and Judy glanced at each other, and Judy said quickly, 'I'll go, you've been up all night and you were travelling all day yesterday. Look, I'll get to work as soon as I can, but you can explain if I'm late. I can't leave Mum by herself.'

'No, she's got to have one of us.' Polly chewed her lips. Gladys had started the engine and was in the driver's seat now, impatient to be off, and Polly leaned in through the window. 'I just hope to God they'll take him in at the hospital. They must be crowded out with casualties as it is. Knock on the door when you get back, Gladys, would you? And thanks for turning out again.'

Gladys nodded and Judy jumped up beside her. Cissie was already in the back, kneeling beside the makeshift bed.

The van jolted off down the road and Polly and her mother went back indoors.

'I dunno,' Alice said, sitting down and picking up the cup of tea she'd poured before Gladys had arrived. 'It's just one thing after another. I've never seen Dick as bad as that, never. This tea's gone cold.'

'I'll make you some more,' Polly said. 'It's all these nights down the shelter. It's so cold and damp, it's bound to set him off. And then the worry of it all. He's never got over what happened to him in the Great War, you know. It brings it all back, hearing the planes go over and bombs falling. It was a bad raid tonight, too – as bad as that big one in January, I wouldn't wonder.'

Alice nodded. 'Don't trouble about the tea, Poll. I can't be bothered. I just want to go to bed, though whether I'll be able to sleep is another matter.'

She went into the front room. They'd got a bed-settee in there now, bought with the money Cissie and Dick had been given for being bombed out. It was more comfortable than the old sofa and could be folded away during the day. Polly heard it creak a bit as Alice got into it, and then silence.

She sat gazing at the ashes in the grate, her coat pulled round her shoulders for warmth, thinking over the long day. It seemed a lifetime since she'd collected young Stella and Muriel from Jess Budd and taken them on the train. Then there'd been the surly porter and the walk to the vicarage through the snowy lanes, and the warm welcome given them by Mrs Mudge and the vicar. That rabbit stew had been the best Polly had tasted for a long time – and not a 'ration' in it, she thought, smiling. And then there'd been the sudden decision to go on to Romsey to see Sylvie, the pleasant man on the train, and the joy of seeing her daughter again, even though it meant the pain of parting only an hour later.

'I wish you could come out and stay here too,' Sylvie had whispered, burying her face against Polly's coat. 'I miss you ever so much.'

'I miss you too,' Polly had said, brushing away the tears before they fell on to Sylvie's blonde curls. 'But I've got work to do in Portsmouth, and it's safer for you to be out here. And you're having a nice time, aren't you? Mr and Mrs Sutton are looking after you well, and you've got Jenny and Brian to play with.'

'They're all right,' Sylvie said dismissively, for all the world as if she hadn't been engrossed in a game of Ludo with them when Polly had arrived. 'But I'd rather be home with you.'

'Well, I expect all the children feel like that. And let's hope it won't be long before you can come back.' Gently, Polly unwound the child's fingers from her coat. 'Now, give me a big kiss and say you'll be a good girl for Mummy, and I'll come back and see you as soon as I possibly can. And tell Mrs Sutton I'll write again soon.'

Sylvie nodded and sniffed hard. A large tear rolled out of her eye and down her cheek. Polly bit her lips fiercely, hugged her and then turned away. She closed the kitchen door behind her and walked swiftly down the garden path.

It must be the hardest thing anyone has to do in this war, she thought, feeling the ache of tears in her throat again as she stared at the cold ashes. Saying goodbye to your children. It must be just as bad when they're grown up too, and going off to fight like Terry, serving on one of Britain's biggest battle cruisers, and Annie Chapman's boy Colin. Just as bad as saying goodbye to your husband, not knowing whether you'll ever see him again. And knowing, when that telegram comes, that you've said goodbye for the last time ever.

The sorrow of it all – of leaving her little girl with strangers, however kind, of losing her husband at sea, of knowing that this anguish was multiplied a thousand times up and down the country, and now, on top of it all, the worry over Dick – surged over her like a tidal wave and, worn out by her day and by a hopeless, overwhelming misery, Polly put down her head and wept.

'It's pneumonia,' Cissie said later to Freda Vickers, who had called to ask how Dick was. 'Well, what can you expect, with his lungs being so bad anyway. They were ever so kind – stretchers and injured people everywhere, but they still took him in straight away and put him in an oxygen tent. Wouldn't let me and Judy stop, of course. Said I could go in and see him at visiting time – that's three this afternoon.' She blinked away tears. 'I don't know as they can do much for him, though. I mean, there's not much you *can* do for pneumonia, is there? Only keep him warm and look after him till the crisis happens, and even then it can go either way.'

'I think they can drain the fluid off from his lungs, can't they?' Freda said doubtfully. 'Stop it building up, like. And if he's on oxygen, that'll help the breathing. Anyway, he's in the best place, Cis. At least he won't have to spend any more nights in a hole in the ground for a while.'

Cissie sighed. 'That's true, but I shall worry all the time, not knowing what's happening to him. I hope we don't get any raids while he's in there.' She turned as they heard the tapping of high heels coming along the pavement behind them, and nodded at the woman in a powder-blue suit and feathery hat. 'Morning, Mrs Glaister.'

Ethel Glaister gave them both a cool look. 'Good morning,' she said in her rather sharp voice. 'I'm surprised you've got time to stand gossiping after a night like last night. I'm going up to the butcher's shop – he had some fresh stewing steak brought in yesterday, I've heard, and I mean to get some.'

'Mum's gone up there already,' Cissie said. 'And Mrs Vickers just called to enquire after my hubby. He was taken into hospital with pneumonia this morning.'

'Oh.' Ethel Glaister looked slightly taken aback. 'Well, I

hope he'll soon be better. Of course, he doesn't work, does he?' She stepped past them, leaving the two women open-mouthed.

'Well!' Cissie said at last. 'And just what do you suppose she meant by that? That he's some sort of parasite? No loss if he doesn't get better? I've a good mind to go after her and give her a piece of my mind!'

'She's not worth it,' Freda said, although she looked equally indignant. 'And I don't suppose she meant anything by it, not really. She's just got to say something and she can't help saying it in a nasty way. That's Ethel Glaister all over.'

'Well, you won't catch me giving her the time of day again,' Cissie said, turning away. 'Anyway, I'm going in now – I thought I might have a bit of a lay-down. If I'm going to see Dick this afternoon I want to look a bit brighter for him. I caught sight of myself in the mirror just now and I look like death warmed up.'

She went indoors and stood for a moment looking around the room where she had grown up. It still felt funny to be back, with so many of the neighbours she had known as a child. Ethel Glaister, who had always thought herself a cut above the rest of April Grove – Granny Kinch and her daughter Nancy, who most people thought were a cut below – and good, friendly people like Freda and her husband Tommy, and Peggy Shaw and her daughters, and Jess and Frank Budd. It was a good place to be, she thought. And there were so many streets like this in Pompey – streets of small terraced houses, where families lived all their lives and got to know each other, always ready to help out, with just the odd one or two like the Glaisters and the Kinches and Baxters, who didn't quite fit in with the rest yet were still part of the pattern. So many streets like this, in every city in the land.

We may not have much, Cissie thought, going upstairs to lie down on the bed she and Dick shared, but we've got a lot more than some. We've got ourselves – family, friends and neighbours. That's what you need most in times like these.

Judy had gone to work straight from the hospital. There was so much to do that she felt that even if she did go to bed she wouldn't rest. Getting there through the newly bombed streets was the usual problem and she wondered if Polly would like the idea of looking for a couple of second-hand bikes so that they could cycle to Southsea. It would be better than having to rely on the uncertain bus service.

As usual after a raid, the casualty station on the ground floor was frantically busy and there was plenty to be done for those who had come looking for help, grumbling as always about having to trek all the way out to Southsea where the nobs were living in luxury in one of the best hotels. The staff were used to these complaints by now and tried to ignore them and get on with the business as cheerfully as possible, understanding that most of the grumblers were shocked and bewildered by what had happened to them.

As she came through the front door, Judy had encountered the young Observer she had met in the lift a few weeks earlier. The staff were accustomed to seeing the RAF uniforms about the building now, and knew most of them by sight, if not by name. Judy had discovered that most of them – the night staff in particular – were volunteers, with other jobs during the day, and her antagonism had faded. She looked at the tired young face with sympathy.

'Have you been up there all night?' she asked, looking up at the roof of the big building. 'It must have been pretty scary.'

He nodded. His eyes were bloodshot with fatigue and rimmed with red. 'I suppose it is. You don't think about it at the time, though. You just have to get on with the job. I hope we managed to get a few of the blighters.'

'It was a bad raid. I've been at an Incident Enquiry

Centre. There was this little boy . . .' She swayed and put out a hand to steady herself against the wall. 'I don't know how they can do it – bomb people like this. I just don't know how they can *do* it.'

'It's the same for us,' he said quietly. 'We're doing the same to them.' He ran his fingers through his fair hair. It was straight and thick, and looked as if it could do with cutting. If he'd been in the Army, Judy thought irrelevantly, he'd have been marched off to the barber's, but the RAF didn't seem to bother so much about that sort of thing, and what did it matter anyway?

'You look all in,' she said, and he gave her a wry grin.

'So do you. Pity really, or I'd have asked you for a date.'

'A *date*?'

'Yes – you know, when a bloke takes a girl out. To the pictures or for a drink, that sort of thing.' He grinned again, and the grin reached his eyes. They were nice eyes, she thought, very blue and a bit shy despite the cheekiness of his grin. 'I've been thinking about it for a while now but I never seem to catch you. And now I have, we're both too whacked even to think about it.'

'I can't think about it anyway,' Judy said, her tone more brusque than she had intended. She turned quickly away. 'I've got to go now. Sorry.' She went through to the office and shut the door behind her. Laura glanced up in surprise.

'Hullo, what's been eating you? Didn't I see you talking to Chris Barrett in the corridor? He surely hasn't upset you, has he?'

'Is that his name?' Judy said off-handedly. 'I've never bothered to ask. I don't like him much.'

'Don't like him?' Laura asked in astonishment. 'Why, half the girls in the building are head over heels about him. He's gorgeous!'

Judy shrugged. 'He's all right, I suppose. Thinks a bit too much of himself, that's all. Anyway, I've got more important things to think about. My dad was taken into hospital this morning – he's had a really bad asthma attack. I've got to find Polly and tell her what's happened, and then I've got a load of work to do.'

Laura looked concerned. 'Oh Judy, that's awful. I am sorry. Look, Polly's in the small office – you go and see her first. And don't take any notice of Chris, it's just his way. He's a nice chap, and if he asked you for a date he meant it. He wouldn't fool about. I tell you what, he wouldn't have to ask me twice!'

Judy shrugged again. She found Polly and gave her a brief account of what had happened at the hospital, then went to her desk and started to deal with the pile of papers that seemed to have appeared overnight. The Lady Mayoress was there this morning, interviewing some new recruits and Judy was in charge of sending them in. After a time, Polly came over and asked if she could have a few minutes, too.

'Why, you're not thinking of resigning, are you?' Judy looked at her aunt in alarm. She knew that seeing Sylvie yesterday had upset her and she wondered if Polly was thinking of going out to the country to be with her daughter. 'I suppose you could get a transfer,' she added doubtfully. 'The WVS does a lot of work in country places as well.'

Polly shook her head. 'I'm not thinking of that. But there's a notice up about a driving course and I thought I'd go in for it. It was seeing Gladys Shaw with that ambulance last night – I'd like to do something like that, something really active. I mean, I know helping at the Centres and taking kiddies out to the country is valuable work too, and I expect I could still do that as well. But I'd like to do something *more*.'

She went in to see the Mayoress and asked if there was any chance of her becoming a driver. 'I don't really mind what I do, madam. I'll do anything to help. But I did do a bit of driving before the war – my hubby was a mechanic and he used to get a car and take me out in the country sometimes of a Sunday and give me a lesson round the lanes – and I think I'd pick it up quite quick. And when I saw the notice . . .'

'Yes.' The Lady Mayoress regarded her thoughtfully. 'Yes, I think you could do well as a driver. You'd have to learn to drive in the blackout as well, you know.'

'Yes, I understand that. Not that it's very dark when the raids are on,' Polly added, thinking of the red glow that had lit Portsmouth during the night of the Blitz. But the Mayoress shook her head.

'Not just during raids. At other times too. You see, we have a car pool and we get called upon to use it for all kinds of things, at any time of the day or night. Last week, for instance, one of our volunteers had to meet a visiting Minister at the railway station and bring him here for a meeting. Before the meeting was over she was asked to take a bundle of clothes to the Clothing Depot at the warehouse then on the way back she was flagged down by a man whose wife was in labour and had to be taken urgently to St Mary's Hospital to have her baby. She still managed to get back in time to return the Minister to the station – where she found herself collecting a load of sandbags to go to the canteen in Commercial Road! All that was during the day, of course,' she added, 'but she could equally well have been asked to do similar journeys during the night, without lights to guide her.'

'I think I could do that,' Polly said. 'I know Portsmouth like the back of my hand.' She looked at the Mayoress. 'I want to do something that – that sort of asks a lot of me,' she said quietly. 'You see, I lost my hubby over a year ago – his ship was one of the first to go down – and I feel I want to make it up to him, somehow. I can't explain it any better than that, but I want something more *difficult* to do.'

The Mayoress looked at her steadily, then nodded her head. 'Yes, I understand completely, my dear. I'll put you down for the driving course, and I'm sure you'll be a credit to us. And to your husband,' she added. 'I know that wherever he is now, he's proud of you.'

Polly went out of the room and stood for a moment taking deep breaths and blinking away her tears. She was still there when Judy emerged from the main office and looked at her enquiringly.

'Well? Did she say yes?'

Polly grinned a little shakily at first, then her smile broadened. 'Yes! She did. She's putting me in straight away. I'm going to learn to drive, Judy! I'm going to learn to drive a car!'

Polly's lessons began almost at once. Determined to learn quickly, she begged to go out as often as possible and soon passed the test and gained her licence. But before she was allowed to join the WVS pool or drive an ambulance, she had to master the art of driving in pitch darkness with only two narrow slits of light to guide her.

'Honestly, it's like driving with a blindfold on!' she reported, coming home after her first lesson. 'You don't know what you're going to bump into! I was frightened to go more than five miles an hour – the instructor said it would be faster on a push-bike! It's not so bad when there's something light-coloured to pick out, but some streets are so black you could be out in the middle of the countryside for all you know.'

'Is that why all the trees along Copnor Road have got white bands painted round their trunks?' Cissie asked, and Polly nodded.

'People were forever driving into them before they did that. Still, I'll get used to it – and, as I said to Mrs Parker, there's plenty of light to see by during the raids, what with searchlights and fires and everything!'

Alice went out to the scullery and returned with a steaming casserole. She'd managed to get some oxtail from the butcher yesterday and it had been simmering all day with vegetables from the garden. She'd skimmed off most of the fat and put it aside for dripping, and it was a rich, gleaming brown.

'My, that looks good,' Polly said, drawing up her chair. 'I've been looking forward to this all day.'

Alice nodded. 'It's so tasty, oxtail – makes a lovely gravy. I just wish Dick could have some, it would build him up. Say what you like, hospital food doesn't have the nourishment you get at home.'

'How is he today?' Polly asked her sister. 'You said he was a bit better yesterday afternoon.'

Cissie lifted her shoulders a little. 'Well, they had him out of the oxygen tent then for a while, but he's back in it again today. He's still poorly. They think the crisis will come any time now.' She laid down her fork and stared at the tablecloth. 'I wish they'd let me stop with him. I can't bear to think of him so ill, and me not there. And – and when the crisis comes – he could *die*. He could die, and me not there . . .'

Polly and Judy gave each other a swift glance, remembering their own shared grief, and the words of the song Dick used to sing to Cissie. 'Let me be there with you . . .' Simultaneously, they reached across the table and laid their hands on Cissie's. Alice too laid a hand on her daughter's arm.

'Dad's not going to die, Mum,' Judy said in a shaking voice. 'He's *not*. By the time you go back tomorrow, he'll have passed the worst and be on the mend. I know he will. I can *feel* it.'

'I can too,' Polly said. 'We'll have him back here before you know it. All the same, it's a shame you can't stop with him. He must want you there.'

'Well, that's the way hospitals are,' Cissie said, wiping her eyes. 'They have their visiting hours and you've got to stick to them. But I'll be there on the dot tomorrow, you see if I'm not.'

'And I'll go with you,' Judy said. 'I know they probably won't let me in to see him but you need someone with you, Mum. Just—' She bit her lip and stopped, but they all knew she'd been going to add, '*Just in case.*' They knew that however strongly they hoped for Dick to get better, however strongly they believed that he would, he really was dangerously ill.

'We'll say our prayers for him tonight,' Polly said soberly. 'We all will.'

Once Polly had satisfied her instructor that she was competent to drive at night as well as by day, she was assigned a number of duties. Mostly she undertook these in an old van that had been converted to act as an ambulance, but could also transport various bulky items or people, but sometimes she found herself driving one of the cars that had been donated to the pool 'for the duration' as the expression was. On these occasions she usually had a passenger of some importance – the Lord Mayor himself, going to meet some visiting dignitary at the railway station, or a high-ranking official arriving from London. Once, she found herself holding a baby while its mother, the wife of a Naval Captain, struggled to get twin toddlers off the train. 'It may be the last chance for them to see their daddy for a long time,' she explained to Polly, lifting them down to the platform. 'There you are, darlings, now just stand still while this nice lady helps us with all our bags. It's just not possible to travel light with three little ones,' she said, brushing her ash-blonde hair back from her forehead while she tried to count the pieces of luggage strewn around them. 'I don't know how I'd have managed if all these kind people hadn't been so helpful.' She indicated the two blushing sailors and a middle-aged man who had formed a chain to get the suitcases and naval holdalls off the train and were now apparently awaiting further orders. 'But people always are, don't you find?'

Polly smiled and nodded, but she wondered privately if the Captain's wife would have been offered so much help if she'd been elderly and rather less glamorous. Her pearl-grey suit was probably at least three years old, yet the quality of its cut and fabric ensured that it still looked smart, and the stole draped carelessly round her shoulders looked like ocelot. Her hair was styled with the latest rolled-up pleat at the front, and her fingers glittered with diamonds. But her face was friendly and the smile she bestowed upon her helpers so dazzling that they almost reeled.

'You've got a *car*?' she said to Polly, as if she'd expected to be guided to a truck. 'Oh, how kind. If you wouldn't mind carrying Benjamin for a little bit longer . . . He's been most dreadfully spoilt on the train,' she continued, wafting down the platform in a cloud of scent. '*Everyone* wanted to hold him. And the twins have been treated like princesses. We couldn't have had a nicer journey. Oh, just *look* at that!' She stopped at the entrance to the station and gazed rapturously across the harbour.

Polly followed her gaze. I suppose it does look quite interesting, she thought, although having lived all her life with this view on her doorstep she had never taken much notice of it. Now she looked more attentively at the wide expanse of shimmering water, its green, broken surface speckled with white foam, and at the craft tossing about on its waves. Tugs, Isle of Wight paddle-steamers, Gosport ferry-boats, naval pinnaces and, towering over them all, the ships of the Royal Navy, sleek and grey, anchored in the middle of the harbour or tied to the dockyard jetties with the Semaphore Tower and the masts of HMS *Victory* behind them.

'It's splendid,' the Captain's wife said. 'Quite splendid. You're so lucky to live here. We've always been based at Chatham, so we've made our home there, but I should just *love* to live in Portsmouth. The harbour is *so* much a part of the town, don't you agree?'

By the time Polly dropped her at the hotel where she was to spend a few days with her husband, she felt that she was seeing her home town with new eyes. The Captain's wife, who seemed no older than Polly herself, was so interested, so enthusiastic and so sympathetic over the raids they had suffered that Polly felt as if they'd been friends for years. She helped her into the hotel, and said goodbye with regret.

'Now, you must come to see us,' the Captain's wife said, pressing her hand. 'Milly and Mandy have obviously taken you to their hearts and I don't think Benjamin would mind at all if you took him home with you! I know your name, and I know where you work, so I'll be in touch. Thank you *so* much, Mrs Dunn.'

'It's quite all right. It's been a pleasure.' Polly looked at her and hesitated. She didn't really believe that the other woman would contact her again. It was just the way people like her talked. But she really did seem very nice. 'I hope everything goes well with you and your husband,' she said with a rush. 'I hope it isn't too long before – well, you know, before he comes home again.'

The dazzling smile faltered a little and Polly caught a glimpse of the fear that lay behind it. She's as scared as the rest of us, she thought. She knows he could die at sea, just like my Johnny, just like Judy's Sean, but she's doing her best to hide it; she's doing her best to make things nice for other people, even if all she can do is smile at them. I bet everyone who's met her today feels better for it.

'It won't be any time at all,' the Captain's wife said firmly. 'And meanwhile, we can find plenty to do to keep ourselves busy, can't we?' She cast a humorous glance at her little brood, the twin girls standing on either side of her, clutching her pearl-grey skirt, and the baby cradled in her arms. 'Even if it's only wiping noses and changing nappies.

Speaking of which . . .' She wrinkled her nose and laughed, and Polly smiled back, then turned and hurried out.

It was time to go back to the Royal Beach and take on her next assignment. Within half an hour the Captain's wife would be almost forgotten. But her smile, and the warmth with which she bestowed it on all who came within her orbit, would not be forgotten. They would remain in every heart.

We can all do that, Polly thought. We can all do our bit, just by putting a smile on our faces and helping each other. That's what Mr Churchill means when he says we'll come through. That's what he means by the spirit of Britain.

Chapter Eleven

Dick had, at last, passed the crisis of his illness. Cissie and Judy had gone to the Royal Hospital, dreading what they might find, and had been overwhelmed with relief to see him out of his tent and sleeping more peacefully than he had done since the night of the asthma attack. Cissie, looking at his white face, had broken down in tears and the nurse had come to lead her to a chair and even brought them both a cup of tea.

'It's been a hard time,' she said sympathetically. 'He was seriously ill – Doctor was worried about him – but he's turned the corner now. He'll still need a lot of nursing before he's back to strength again, mind.'

'So long as he's on the mend,' Cissie said through her tears. 'Oh, I'm so thankful. We've got used to the asthma attacks over the years, but this one was so bad, and then when we found he'd got pneumonia as well . . .'

'Well, his chest condition makes him very vulnerable,' the nurse said. 'And I dare say he's been spending nights in an Anderson, too; the damp and cold are bound to have an effect. And then there's all the worry of the raids.'

'We were bombed out in January,' Cissie said. 'And he was gassed in 1917 – and shell-shocked too. He's not been a well man since.'

'You'll have him home again soon,' the nurse told her cheerfully. 'And let's hope we don't have any more raids like that one. That was terrible.'

Judy stayed with her mother until she was sure Cissie was fit to go home alone, then she made her way out to the Royal

Beach. She had sent a message via Polly to say she would be late, knowing that the Mayoress would understand, but she was anxious not to waste a minute. She arrived to find the place in uproar.

'We've lost an important document,' Laura explained breathlessly as Judy came into the main office. 'It was supposed to go to the top office and nobody can find it. You don't happen to know where it is, do you?'

'Which one was it?' Judy asked, and turned pale as Laura told her. 'Oh my goodness! I had it yesterday – I slipped it into my drawer for safety. It must still be there.' She ran to her desk and pulled open the drawer. 'Is – is this it?'

'Yes!' Laura snatched it away from her and raced over to the Lady Mayoress, who was sitting at her desk searching through a huge box file. 'Here it is, madam. Judy had it all the time.'

'*Judy* did?' The Lady Mayoress stared at her. 'But what on earth? Why? No, don't bother to explain. Just take it up to Mr Williams at once – you know where he is, don't you – on the eighth floor. And then come straight to me when you get back.' She shook her head as if in despair and Judy, scarlet-faced, took the file back from Laura and scurried out of the room.

She was almost in tears as she stepped into the lift. It was the first serious mistake she had made, and she had never seen the Mayoress look so annoyed. I didn't know it was so important, she thought as she waited for the door to close, and I didn't know I was going to be late this morning. Oh, please don't let her be really angry with me. Please don't let her say I'm no use to her and I've got to go back to my old job. What if Miss Marsh doesn't want me any more? What if she says I'm no use either? Oh, *why* won't this wretched door *close*?

Judy hated the lift. It was small and creaky and you could see the walls through the cage-like structure. When you were inside it, moving slowly up or down, it was like being in a long vertical tube with no windows. She always felt as if the sides were closing in on her and, if she could, used the stairs. But now, with a document to be delivered urgently to the eighth floor, she had no choice.

She wrenched at the iron door but nothing happened; she was just about to step out and face the long climb up eight flights of stairs when a cheery voice said, 'Hey, don't take it out on the door! What harm did it ever do you?' and she looked up and saw Chris Barrett, the fair-haired Observer, grinning at her from the corridor.

'It won't shut, that's what harm it's doing!' she retorted savagely. 'I've got to get an important file up to Mr Williams and I'm going to have to climb up all those stairs, and – and if you want to know the truth, I've just about had enough!' Then, to her fury, she burst into tears.

'Hey.' He came a little closer. 'Hey, come on. Don't cry. It can't be that bad. Let me have a go.' He stepped into the lift beside her, pressed the button and the door slid across immediately. 'There you are! Chocks away and ready for take-off. You just need to press the button, that's all, it won't know otherwise. Where d'you want to go? Floor eight?'

'Yes.' Judy scowled at the buttons. 'I did press it. It took no notice.'

'Well, it is a bit temperamental. It's refused to start a couple of times lately. I think they're sending out a maintenance crew from somewhere, but what with everything else . . .' He smiled down at her. 'Your name's Judy, isn't it? Judy Taylor?'

Judy admitted that it was. 'And you're Chris Barrett. Someone in the office told me. I didn't *ask* her,' she added quickly, just in case he might think she was interested in him. 'She just saw us talking and told me.'

The lift creaked slowly upwards. It might have been quicker to walk anyway, Judy thought, and then she wouldn't have had to stand in this tiny space with this cheeky airman. She stood gazing fixedly at the floor, determined not to glance up and catch Chris Barrett's eye. She was sure he was staring at her. There was a silence.

'So how are you getting on, up there on the roof?' she asked eventually, unable to stand it any longer. 'I suppose you've been pretty busy lately.'

'Pretty well,' he agreed. 'There are planes about all the time, even when there's no raid. We have to spot our own as well as theirs, you see. And we have to be able to recognise them straight away. It's not much good to HQ if you can't tell a Spit from a Messerschmitt.'

Judy nodded. They were passing the fourth floor now. She could see the corridor through the iron gates, its carpet taken up to leave bare boards, the doors that had once led to luxurious bedrooms open to show glimpses of the offices within. She wondered what sort of people used to come and stay here. Entertainers who were appearing in the theatre at the end of the long pier over the road, probably. People like Joe Loss, Ambrose, Max Miller. It was funny to think that she might be standing in a lift that had once carried a famous comedian or band leader . . . She tried to imagine he was here now, instead of this tall, fair-haired young Observer and, just as she was drifting off into a dream of being recognised by a famous band leader and becoming a singer like Anne Shelton or Vera Lynn, the lift gave a loud creak and shuddered to a halt. They were between floors and all they could see through the gates was the wall of the lift-shaft.

Judy and the Observer stared at each other. A worm of panic stirred deep in her stomach.

'It's stopped.' She put out her hand and pressed the button hard. 'What's happened? Why's it stopped?' The worm twisted a little. She began to shake the gates.

'Don't do that. It might be dangerous.' He gripped her wrist and pulled back her arm sharply. 'I'm not surprised. This thing's been on its last legs for years.'

'But what shall we do?' Her voice was rising. 'I've got an important document to deliver. I was late in this morning anyway. The Mayoress will be furious!'

'No, she won't. It's not your fault the lift's broken down. Don't get in a flap, Judy.' He laid his hand on her arm again, more gently this time. 'Look, there's nothing we can do. Someone will notice pretty soon and they'll send for that maintenance crew I was talking about. They'll get us out.'

'And what are we supposed to do in the meantime?' Judy demanded, her voice shaking. 'Tell each other stories? Sing songs?'

'Well, we could do worse.' He grinned. 'Come on, Judy, it's not the end of the world. A lot worse things than this have happened.'

Judy flung him a look of fear. 'I know. It's just that I – I hate being shut in tiny spaces. I've never liked using this lift – I always use the stairs if I can. And – and so many awful things have happened, and this is the last straw. I know it's a small thing really, but that's what straws are, aren't they?' She covered her face with her hands. 'I was late in this morning because I went to the Royal Hospital to see my dad. He's had pneumonia. He's getting better now but we – we thought he was going to die.' Her voice shook and she began to cry.

There was a moment's pause and then Chris put his arm across her shoulder. 'Hey, hey, come on. He's getting *better*. That's what you've got to think of. He's *not* going to die. And you're not going to have to spend the rest of your life stuck in this lift with me.' He peered upwards through the gates, trying to see to the next floor. 'At least, I hope not!'

Judy looked around. The walls of the shaft could be seen on each side. They were roughly built, not finished with plaster, and were dingy and draped with cobwebs. She shuddered.

'It's horrible. Nobody ever cleans these walls. I feel as if I'm shut in a zoo, or going down a mine.'

'It's just the lift-shaft,' he said soothingly. 'I expect they used to clean it when it was a hotel but we don't have time for those things now. Tell you what, soon as we get out of here I'll fetch a bucket and mop and clean the whole thing myself, from top to bottom. How's that?' He grinned at her.

Judy looked at his open, friendly face, his twinkling eyes and smiling mouth, and drew in a deep breath. I'm being an idiot, she thought. Letting it all get on top of me. He's right – it's just a lift-shaft and soon someone will come and get us out. There's nothing to be frightened of. She repeated the words firmly in her mind. *There's nothing to be frightened of.* And the thought of Chris with a bucket and mop, cleaning the entire eight floors of it, brought an unexpected bubble of laughter to her lips.

'Sorry, it just sort of came over me for a minute.' She managed a smile and felt a little better. 'Well, you wanted a date. Looks like you've got your way!'

'So it does.' He grinned. 'Though I had thought of taking you somewhere a bit more glamorous than this – a British Restaurant, perhaps!'

'Or a WVS Emergency Centre,' Judy said, and he laughed. He had a nice laugh, she thought, his blue eyes crinkling at the corners and his smile widening to show very white teeth. Polly's right, she thought, he *is* good-looking. It was easy to imagine other girls finding him attractive.

'We might as well sit down, I suppose,' he said, indicating the dusty floor. 'Sorry I can't offer you anything more comfortable. But if we're going to be here a while . . .'

'Why, how long d'you think it could be?' She glanced upwards, her anxiety returning. 'I don't think anyone's even noticed yet!'

A yell sounded from above and they heard the distant rattle of gates. Chris grinned at her. 'I think they have now! But they'll just think some twerp's left the gates open on another floor. It'll be a while before they realise it's stuck.'

He moved closer to the gate and shouted up the shaft. 'Hey! We're stuck – the lift's stuck! Get some help, will you?'

There was a brief silence. The yells from above sounded again, together with an even more impatient rattling. Chris renewed his own shouting and eventually a voice sounded from somewhere closer. 'Where are you?'

'Where d'you think we are?' Chris bellowed. 'We're stuck in the flipping lift!'

'Yes, but what floor? We can't tell.'

'I don't know.' He glanced at Judy.

'I know we went past the fourth floor,' she said doubtfully. 'I'm not sure about the fifth.'

'Well, we're pretty high anyway. It's no use rattling the gates like that,' he shouted. 'Get the maintenance crew, they'll know what to do.'

There was some muted conversation from above, as if several more people had joined the first. Then a new voice shouted, echoing hollowly in the shaft.

'We're sending for the maintenance people. Soon have you out.'

'What a good idea,' Chris said sardonically, and Judy giggled. 'I'd never have thought of that.'

'Who's in there?' the new voice called.

'Chris Barrett, ROC, and Judy Taylor, WVS. You'd better let our people know.'

'We'll let your people know,' the voice shouted, overriding Chris's last words. He rolled his eyes and Judy giggled again. Her panic seemed to have vanished and the humour of their situation was beginning to strike her. She followed his advice and sat down in a corner, wrapping her arms about her knees. Chris looked down at her, then sat down in another corner.

'I think we're going to be here quite a while. I don't know where the maintenance chaps are coming from, but I don't think they're on permanent duty here. Hope you're not hungry.' He gave her a wry look.

'Not really.' It was some time since her breakfast of Shredded Wheat and toast, and thank goodness she had been to the lavatory when she'd arrived at the hotel. Judy pushed her fingers through her hair and sighed. 'Oh, this *would* happen. Just when we're so busy. And Mr Williams wanted this file urgently.' She touched the brown folder.

'Well, he'll have to manage without it a bit longer. I don't suppose it was that important, anyway. People make a lot of fuss about things like that, and then it turns out they don't matter at all.' He cocked his head to one side. 'Cheer up, Judy. The worst that can happen is that you've got to spend a couple of hours alone with me. And even that's not too bad. I'm quite a gentleman really, you know. I won't take advantage of you.' He grinned wickedly. 'Not unless you want me to!'

Judy gave him a cold look. 'Well, I *don't* want you to.' Then she relented and smiled reluctantly. 'All right, I won't keep moaning. We're here and we might as well make the best of it. Tell me some more about what you do up there on the roof. It sounds quite interesting.'

'It is.' His face lit up with enthusiasm. 'We're all mad keen about spotting aircraft, you see. That's why we answered the adverts.'

'I'd have thought you'd have been called up anyway,' she said, with a touch of tartness in her voice as she thought again of Sean and Johnny. 'Why aren't you in one of the Services? Active, I mean.'

'Because most of us are in reserved occupations. I'm in the Dockyard. I filled in my papers,' he said, looking at her earnestly. 'I took them in and everything, but the foreman told me I could forget it – none of us Yardies'll be called up. And he was right, I haven't heard a thing, so when this came up – well, I wanted to do my bit so I slapped in my application straight away.'

Judy looked at him and felt ashamed. She said, 'What sort of qualifications did you have to have, then?'

'Just good sight and being able to recognise aircraft. That's all that's needed. You've got to be able to think pretty quickly too,' he added. 'But really, they just wanted blokes who already knew their stuff.'

'But there's a classroom – I've seen it. They're training people now.'

'Yes, we still have to train. We're training all the time. We've got to keep the skills up, and we've got to be able to recognise new aircraft. We have competitions too,' he added. 'Master tests, they're called. We do them once a quarter and we compete with spotters from all over the country.'

'Competitions? How do they run them? I mean, you can't actually use aircraft, can you?'

'No, they use a flashtrainer – a screen and epidiascope. You sit in a room looking at a screen, and then the bloke says, "Blink" and you blink, and they flash a silhouette up on the screen. It's only there for a hundredth of a second, and you have to be able to identify the plane in that time. If you get ninety per cent right, you get this Spitfire badge, and if you do that three times in a row you get a red badge, and then you're a Master Spotter.' He paused and then added modestly, 'I've done it twice so far.'

'A hundredth of a second?' Judy stared at him. 'I didn't think they could measure time as small as that. I can't even imagine what it is.'

'It's just a flash,' he said. 'You can barely see it. But if you're good, you can recognise a shape in that time.'

'But aeroplanes – they're not that different, surely? I mean, they've all got two wings and a tail – how can you possibly tell what they are in that time?'

'Oh, there are lots of differences. Tails, rudders, wing shapes – they're all a little bit different. That's why we've got to be able to recognise them instantly, you see. If we see a plane coming in over the coast we've got to know what it is straight away so that we can phone through to the Ops room at Winchester. We've got to know what direction it's coming from, where it's heading, and we've got to plot its position. Then they can match that up with reports from other observation posts and see what's happening in the sky. There might be just one, you see, or there might be hundreds. That's how they know where to send our own aircraft to intercept them, and whether to sound the air-raid sirens or not.'

Judy gazed at him, fascinated. She had almost forgotten that they were stuck in a lift and that Mr Williams was waiting for his important document. 'How many of you are there doing this? At one time, I mean.'

'Two. One to look at the sky and one to write the log. We write down what's happening every minute, and then our logbook can be compared with all the others so that Ops know that all aircraft in the vicinity are being observed.' He glanced at his watch. 'They'll be getting in a flap over me pretty soon, but I dare say they'll pull someone out of the classroom to stand in for me.'

There were sounds from above. Someone was rattling the lift gates. A voice yelled down, 'You OK in there?'

'Oh, we're fine,' Chris called back. 'Having a wonderful time. Always wanted to be stuck in a lift with a pretty girl!'

'You behave yourself,' the voice commanded. 'If he gives you any trouble, miss, you just scream. Anyway, you'd better make up your minds for a bit of a wait. We've got to get someone out from naval barracks to see to the mechanism. Nobody here seems to know how the bl— blooming thing works.'

'Well, don't hurry on my account,' Chris returned, winking at Judy. He settled himself more comfortably in his corner and said, 'What about you? What d'you do?' He glanced at her green uniform. 'I know you're WVS but I'm not sure what that is.'

'Women's Voluntary Service,' Judy said. 'It's run by the Lady Mayoress here in Portsmouth, but there are branches everywhere. It started in 1938 to help women get involved in air-raid precautions and then it just expanded. Now, we do whatever we're asked to do. We never say no,' she finished proudly, and then caught the glint in his eye and wished she hadn't.

'I won't take you up on that!' he said with a grin. 'But I wouldn't go around saying that to some of the other oiks we've got – they're not all as gentlemanly as me. So what sort of things have you done so far?'

Judy shrugged. 'Anything and everything. We set up Enquiry Centres when a raid starts, for people to come to if they're worried about members of their family, and we open Emergency Centres for people who've been bombed out. We take hot drinks and sandwiches round to the air-raid shelters. We go into bombed areas and do whatever we can – we build fireplaces with bricks from the rubble and brew up tea, or we take warm clothes out to people who've been bombed out in their nightclothes. All sorts of things. And we have a car pool, to drive people wherever they need to go. My auntie's learned to drive 'specially – she's driven all sorts of important people – and she drives an ambulance in the raids too.'

'That's pretty good,' he said admiringly. 'And all this without getting paid?'

'Yes, everyone's a volunteer. Well, *I* get paid,' she added honestly, 'because I'm "borrowed" from the Council. But I do a lot of voluntary work as well. I don't just work office hours.'

'Well, I think that's smashing,' Chris said. He hesitated and then said, 'I think you're pretty smashing, too, Judy.'

There was an awkward pause. Judy looked down at the ring on her finger, wondering if Chris had noticed it. For the first time since Sean had died, she wished that she had not been wearing it, and guilt immediately washed over her at the thought. She could feel Chris's eyes on her and she wanted to say something about Sean, to tell him what had happened, but before she could speak they heard another rattling from above. A voice shouted down, a voice they hadn't heard before. This one was firm and positive, as if it belonged to someone who knew what he was doing.

'The cavalry's arrived,' Chris said ironically.

'You OK?' the voice shouted. Judy imagined a naval mechanic, big and brawny, with a 'full set' of beard and moustache. 'Hold on, we'll have you out soon. Have to go up on the roof to sort out the motor. Don't worry if the whole caboodle shakes about a bit. We won't let you drop.'

'You'd better not, mate,' Chris called back. 'We're just getting to know each other in here.' He winked at Judy and settled back. 'Won't be long now.' There was a short pause, then he asked, 'Whereabouts do you live?'

The moment for telling him about Sean had passed. 'I used to live in Portchester Road but we were bombed out. We're with my gran now, in April Grove.'

'April Grove? Is that up Copnor Road?'

Judy nodded. 'That's right, just off September Street. Well, at the end of March Street and October Street, really. It runs along the bottom, by the allotments.' She was gabbling, she knew, thankful to be relieved of the necessity of talking about Sean. 'They're just two-up, two-down houses so it's a bit of a squash, but we were lucky to have somewhere to go. And since Sylvie's out in the country—'

'Sylvie?'

'My niece. Her mum's my Aunt Polly, but I never call her that because she's only twelve years older than me. She – she lost her husband early in the war. At sea.' I could tell him now, she thought, but the words were hard to find and she added instead, 'So there's just the five of us – me and Polly, Mum and Dad, and Gran. It's all right.'

Chris nodded. 'Like you say, we're lucky to have somewhere to live these days. There's a hell of a lot of people been bombed out. Far more than anyone expected.'

'The Council's had a lot of complaints about that,' Judy

136

said. 'People criticising because we weren't properly prepared. But you don't know what's going to happen in a war, do you? They thought there'd be thousands killed, and instead of that they've been made homeless. It must mean that the shelters are working, yet people don't think how lucky they are to survive, they just moan because they've got nowhere to live. Well, it *is* awful, I know,' she added. 'It's horrible, not having a home. But we're doing our best — people *are* being rehoused, somehow or other. And they are still alive. That's the main thing.'

The lift shook and rattled, and Judy put her hand on the floor to steady herself. It trembled beneath her and she felt suddenly scared. Suppose something went wrong. Suppose the lift suddenly plunged to the bottom of the shaft — somewhere down in the basement. That was at least five floors . . . She looked at Chris in alarm.

'It's all right,' he said, moving a little closer. 'They're just working on the motor.'

'But if it gives way . . .' She could hear the shake in her voice. 'It'll be like being dropped off the roof in a box. We wouldn't have a chance.'

'It won't give way. Here, let me put my arm round you.' He slid his arm round her shoulders and held her firmly. Judy pressed her face against his shoulder. He smelt of blue serge and coal-tar soap and sweat. She breathed in the scent of him, feeling a sudden quickening of her pulse. Sean had smelt a little like this, but there was a difference . . . the lift shook again and she gasped and pressed closer.

'It's all right.' Chris's voice was soft and soothing. His fingers gripped her shoulder and he put his other arm around her and stroked her back. 'It's all right, Judy. You're safe. We're not going to fall. It's all right.'

They sat very still, pressed close together. Judy could feel her heart beating. Her cheek was against his neck and she could feel his pulse beneath the warm skin. His fair hair tickled her face. She gripped his shoulders tightly.

I *will* tell him about Sean, she decided. After we've got out of here, when everything's all right again, I'll tell him about Sean. It won't make any difference. I don't want another sweetheart, not yet, not for a long time, maybe not ever. But I would like to be friends, and I want him to know about Sean. I want him to know the important things . . .

The lift gave a huge shudder. For a moment, it hung trembling, as if undecided as to what to do next. Judy held her breath and pressed her face hard against Chris's shoulder. She felt his arms tighten about her. The cables creaked, the lift groaned and there was a shiver of movement. Then, slowly and complainingly, it began to rise.

'It's all right,' Chris whispered. 'Judy, it's all right.'

She lifted her head to look at him. 'We're going up! Oh, *Chris*.'

'Thank God for that,' he said, and grinned a little shakily. 'I don't mind admitting, even I was a bit worried there for a minute!'

They laughed with relief. Their eyes met and as she saw his pupils darken Judy felt a quick surge of excitement. She lifted her face towards him and, when he bent closer and his lips met hers, she closed her eyes and relaxed against his body. For a brief, whirling moment, she forgot where they were, forgot the creaking lift, forgot Mr Williams's important document and the fact that there was likely to be a reception committee awaiting them when they arrived. It was only the sound of ironic cheering that brought her out of her daze and then she blinked, stared through the gates at the little cluster of people waiting at the foot of the steel stairway, and jerked herself out of his arms.

'For goodness sake!' Scarlet with embarrassment, she brushed back her hair, grabbed the brown folder and scrambled to her feet. Mr Williams was there himself, his hand held out, a frown of disapproval on his face. So was

Laura, her lips twitching with amusement. So were half a dozen other Observers, all applauding – all except one.

The one not applauding was a girl of Judy's own age. Tall and slim, with the sort of auburn hair Judy would have given her eye teeth for, and eyes as green as a cat's, she was dressed in the Air Force blue uniform and sported a Spitfire badge like the one Chris wore on his sleeve. She was leaning against the wall, her arms folded, her lips tight, and as she glanced from Judy to Chris her eyes flashed with temper.

Why, she's his girlfriend, Judy thought indignantly. And there he was kissing me, for all to see! The *rotter*!

She turned away angrily and found herself confronting the two sailors who had rescued them. They were packing away their tools into canvas bags and straightened up to grin at her. One was tall and thin, the other shorter than Judy herself, with a bald head and button nose.

'Well, that wasn't too bad, was it, love?' he said, and she recognised the voice that had shouted down to them, the one that she had envisaged as belonging to a big, brawny matelot with beard and moustache. 'You seem to have passed the time all right, anyway!'

Judy stared at him. Then, still scarlet, she turned her back and without even thanking him set off down the stairs, back to the ground floor.

It'll be a long time before I trust that lift again, she reflected grimly. And even longer before I trust one of those beastly Observers!

For the next few days, Judy did her best to avoid Chris Barrett.

It wasn't easy. She couldn't find out when his shifts were without attracting comment; the story of their incarceration in the lift, and the attitude in which they'd been caught when it arrived, had gone all round the building and Judy found herself the butt of a good deal of teasing. She did her best to take it in good part and it soon died down, but she knew that even to mention his name would be enough to start it all over again. To be seen talking to him would be even worse, so whenever she caught sight of him she darted through the nearest doorway, making some excuse if she found herself in an office she didn't normally visit. Once she had to wait for several minutes in a cluttered broom cupboard, as a series of footsteps went by, before emerging in the hope that the corridor was empty.

To make matters worse, Chris didn't seem to have the same inhibitions. Time and time again he tried to speak to her, until at last Judy was forced to face him on the hotel steps, where she'd met him as she hurried out. He stood just below her, the sun on his hair as he looked up, and his blue eyes laughing.

'Judy! I was beginning to think you were trying to avoid me.'

'Well, you were right,' she retorted waspishly. 'Look, I'm sorry, I'm in a hurry—'

'Don't rush off,' he begged. 'There's something I want to say to you.'

'I've got a bus to catch.'

'No, you haven't. You come by bike, I've seen you. Look, this won't take a minute.' He reached out and touched her arm and Judy jumped away as if she'd been stung.

'Don't do that! Haven't you caused enough trouble?' Pink with anger, she tried to push past him, but his hand tightened on her sleeve and she glared at him. 'Let me go!'

'Not until you listen to what I want to say. Judy, about the lift—'

'I don't want to talk about it,' she broke in, thrusting him away and walking across the road with tight, quick steps. He followed her and she turned at the top of the beach and began to stride along the promenade, too angry to notice the glint of sunshine on the rippling waves or the green rolling hills of the Isle of Wight. 'It's taken days to live it down, and if people see us here like this it'll start all over again. D'you realise how embarrassing it was for me? All those people watching – I thought I'd die, I did really.'

'I just want to say I'm sorry. I never meant to upset you.'

'Well, you shouldn't have done it, then. You should have behaved like a gentleman.'

'Oh, come on,' he said, beginning to sound angry in his turn. 'It was only a kiss, for Pete's sake. I wasn't asking you to marry me!'

Judy looked down at his hand. She plucked it away from her sleeve, then she met his eyes coldly.

'That's just as well,' she said in a tight, icy tone, 'because I wouldn't marry you if you were the last man on this earth. And I don't want to be stuck in a lift with you again, either. I don't even want to *talk* to you.'

'But why not?' he asked in bewilderment. 'Look, I thought we were getting on really well when we were in that lift together. And when I kissed you – well, you kissed me as well. At least, that's what it felt like. And it wasn't the end of the world when everyone saw us, was it? We weren't doing anything wrong. So why was it so terrible?'

Judy looked at him. 'And what did your girlfriend think about it? Didn't *she* think it was terrible – seeing you kissing another girl?'

'My girlfriend?' He stared at her. 'What on earth are you talking about now? I haven't got a girlfriend.' He glinted a wink at her. 'I was hoping when we were in the lift that that was about to change!'

Judy gave him a chilly look. 'So who was that redhead if she's not your girlfriend? The one who was looking so furious when we got out of the lift? If looks could kill, you'd have dropped dead on the spot.'

'You mean Joyce? Oh Judy,' his face broke into laughter, 'Joyce isn't my girlfriend! She's engaged to a bloke at HQ in Winchester. She wouldn't give me the time of day, let alone go out with me. And if you want to know why she was furious, it was because she couldn't go off duty until I was there – and she was waiting to go off on a forty-eight-hour pass for a dirty weekend! It was bad enough that I kept her waiting, but the thought that I might have *enjoyed* being stuck – well, that took the biscuit. I tell you, the way she laid into me you'd think I'd done it deliberately!'

'Oh,' Judy said blankly. 'Oh.' She stared at him for a moment, then turned away and looked out over the sea. There was a light breeze, just enough to blow the tops off the waves into a spray of glittering foam. 'Oh – well, I'm sorry. I thought . . .'

'I know what you thought,' he said, grinning. 'So now will you think again? Give me a smile now and then? Say hello – that sort of thing?'

She laughed. 'Of course I will! I'm sorry, Chris. It was just that—'

'Just that we seemed to be getting on so well together,' he said quietly. He took her left hand and raised it, looking at the ring. 'I did notice it, in case you were wondering. That's why I didn't ask to see you again – though I wanted to, right from the start. To tell you the truth, I couldn't believe my luck when that lift got stuck – and before you ask, no, I didn't arrange it!' His eyes laughed at her again. 'But then, when we kissed – well, I felt that there could be something more between us.' He looked at the ring again. 'This chap you're engaged to – is it really that serious?'

Judy bit her lip and looked down. She could walk away from Chris now. She could let him think she was still engaged, that she wasn't interested in any other man. She knew that he wouldn't pester her. He would accept it, and it really would be just a matter of a casual 'hello' now and then, a smile as they passed in the corridor.

But Sean was dead. He was never going to come back, and was she to spend the rest of her life alone? The next sixty years, perhaps, recalling a young sailor she had known and loved for just a few weeks?

Chris might not ever be more than a friend. They might fall in love for a little while and then part. But as she looked down at the ring with its tiny diamond, she remembered her grandmother's words. *'You've got to start living again some-time, Judy. You've got to.'*

Perhaps she could start with Chris.

She made up her mind and lifted her face to look him in the eye. He was watching her with a tinge of anxiety.

'I want to tell you about it,' she said, 'but not now – not here. Perhaps we could meet one evening, after your duty – go for a walk or something.'

'All right,' he said. 'What about Saturday – oh blast, I can't – we've got my uncle and aunt coming down from London and Mum'll throw a fit if I'm not there. How about Sunday? I'm on duty in the afternoon but I'm off at six – we could go and have some tea and then maybe see a film. That's if you'd like to do that,' he added with that touch of anxiety again.

Judy nodded and smiled. 'That'll be fine,' she said. 'I'll write down my address. Come and call for me at six.'

I've made a date, she thought with amazement as she cycled home. I've made a date! It might not lead to anything – I'm not sure I even want it to – but it's a date and I don't feel guilty about Sean, I don't feel guilty at all. He wouldn't have wanted me to live my life as if half of it was over. He'd have wanted me to start living again.

She glanced down at her left hand and saw his ring, winking up at her. On a sudden impulse, she stopped and took it off her finger and put it on her right hand instead. There, she thought. I'll still wear it for you, in remem-brance. But I know now that it can never be more than that. It's not a promise any more.

With a heart lighter than it had been for many months, she pushed down the pedal and cycled the rest of the way home.

*

On 27 April, the Sunday when Judy had been due to meet Chris, the Luftwaffe came again.

The raid began early in the evening, just when the people of Portsmouth had finished their Sunday tea and were looking forward to an evening spent playing cards or listening to the wireless. The sirens wailed, cutting into their comfortable plans, and once more they ran down their gardens to huddle in their shelters, or went out to fight the fires that tore through their homes and workplaces. Once more, ambulances and fire engines raced through streets blocked with rubble; once more, the Emergency Centres were filled with homeless people while First-Aid Posts tended the injured.

It was going to be another bad night. They knew it from the incessant snarl of German aircraft overhead, from the open roar of Allied planes, from the silvery net of searchlights lighting up the sky, from the staccato rattle of ack-ack. And, most of all, from the thunderous explosions that shook the ground, rattling doors and windows, making the very walls tremble. By dawn, there would be more hundreds made homeless, more families bereaved, more patients crowding in the city's hospitals – and if the hospitals themselves were hit, as each one had been in previous raids, more desperation as to where they could be taken.

Gladys Shaw was out with her ambulance, racing through streets that were lit by incendiaries and fire. Peggy was at her First-Aid Post. Annie Chapman and Judy were at the Emergency Centre, making an endless supply of hot soup, cocoa and tea for the people who straggled in, lost and bewildered, often bleeding, their homes damaged or destroyed, their lives shattered.

As usual, Judy was ready to help in any capacity – manning a canteen somewhere amidst all the bombs, rushing off to set up an Enquiry Centre somewhere for people to report to, or to start the hunt for missing relatives, helping with First Aid for those who stumbled in, hurt, but not seriously enough to be sent to hospital.

She was bandaging a cut head for an old woman who had been sheltering under her stairs when she heard her name spoken and glanced up. 'Polly!'

'Judy.' Polly was looking anxious. 'I came in to see if there was anyone who could come on the van with me. The Red Cross nurse never turned up. But it looks as if you're pretty busy here.'

'I don't know – there are a few more volunteers here now.' Judy glanced around and called to one that she knew: 'Susan, could you take over here? My aunt needs someone on her ambulance – I'll go with her.' She followed Polly into the fire-raddled, bomb-torn night and they scurried out to the old van that had been converted to an ambulance. Polly had been out at night quite a lot by now, learning to see in what little glow was allowed from the narrow slits of light from her headlamps. It was almost a luxury, she thought, having all this light from the fires and the incendiaries, but not a luxury she welcomed. Every raddled glow meant someone's home or property on fire, every gleam of light a broken heart.

There was no other light to be had. With the first stick of bombs, the city's electricity system had failed and the city was plunged into darkness. Only those places, such as hospitals, which possessed their own emergency generators, still had light. For the rest, out came the hurricane lanterns, the candles, the torches with their precious, dwindling batteries. None of these things would last for ever, and nobody knew where the next candle, battery or half-pint of paraffin would come from. If you could manage without light, you did.

They were accustomed to the sirens going almost every night, accustomed to nights when just a few bombs fell, accustomed to nights when there was no bombing at all and you just listened to planes going over on their way to raid some other unfortunate city, and waited for the All Clear to sound. But tonight had a worse feeling about it. It was frighteningly similar to those other two nights when the bombing had been so severe it had been called a 'Blitz'. The aircraft filled the night sky with their roar, as if there were a huge cloud of them up there, blacking out the stars and the moon – the 'Bomber's Moon' – each one loaded with bombs and letting them fall over Portsmouth. It was as if it didn't matter any more whether they fell on the Dockyard, on the ships in the harbour, on the Naval establishments and military barracks, or on simple two-up, two-down terraced homes like those in April Grove. It was as if so long as people were injured and killed, so long as buildings were damaged and destroyed, the pilots could go home satisfied at having done their job.

Gladys Shaw was out in her ambulance as well. Polly and Judy had seen it as they set off – a battered old van in even worse condition than theirs – and Gladys had given them a murderous look as she swung the crank-handle. 'I'm fed up with this!' she'd yelled. 'Bloody *fed up*! I was going out with Graham tonight, and, now flaming Hitler's messed it all up again. I'm sick of him – bloody *sick* of him!'

She'd swung the van out into the road and Polly and Judy gave each other a grimace. 'We're all fed up,' Polly said, starting her own van. 'We've had nearly enough of this, Judy. But we've got to carry on, all the same.'

'She doesn't mean she's giving in,' Judy said, scrambling into the seat beside her. 'She just means she'd like to wring his neck.' So would I, she thought, thinking regretfully of her own date with Chris and wondering if he had been the first to spot and identify the new wave of attacking aircraft. 'Who's Graham, anyway?'

Polly put her foot cautiously on the accelerator. The van was liable to pretend it wasn't going to move, then suddenly leap forward, to the danger of anyone who happened to be standing near. 'I think it's Graham Philpotts, that young matelot Betty Chapman knocked about with for a while. His family used to live round here when I was still at home, before they moved over to Gosport. Where are we supposed to be going, Judy?'

'Maddens. It's on fire.' Maddens was a big hotel on the corner of the Guildhall Square. If that had been hit, there were bound to be casualties, unless they'd all got into the shelter before the bombing started. Whether the ambulance would ever get there or not was another question: they were sure to pass other emergencies on their way to the city centre, and you couldn't just drive past people desperate to get some injured friend to a First-Aid Post or hospital. There was the added problem of finding your way through streets that had been bombed already and were blocked with fallen masonry, or full of other ambulances as well as fire engines with hoses tangled like snakes all over the road – and all this in pitch darkness lit only by jagged flames or roaring infernos that warned you to reverse swiftly out of their heat. It took hours to get anywhere, and more than once Polly stopped while Judy tried to find out exactly where they were. 'I thought I knew this place,' she said despairingly, 'but we could be in the middle of Liverpool for all I can recognise now.'

At last they reached their destination, only to find that the casualties had already been removed. A fireman, his reddened eyes staring out of a face streaked with soot, yelled at them to get out of the way, Polly slammed the van into reverse once more to get out of range of the flames, then jerked to a stop and leaped out as a man jumped out in front of the van, waving his arms. 'What is it? Someone hurt?'

'It's me mum,' he shouted. His voice was drowned by the roar of the planes and the thunder of the bombs, but she could read the message in his lips and see the terror in his eyes. 'She's got caught under something – oh my God, it's awful. Come and help, miss, please, you gotta help!' He had hold of Polly's arm, dragging her across the road. Judy snatched up the First-Aid haversack and scurried after them, her heart thumping. They ran down a narrow alley and found themselves in a huddle of old houses, hidden behind the Theatre Royal and the small shops and offices that occupied the buildings along the main road. *I never even knew all this existed,* Judy thought, her old fear of confined spaces returning as she stared up at the high walls that surrounded them, but there was no time for panic. The man was tugging her towards a tall building, one of several around a tiny, dank courtyard that probably never saw the light of day. The building was half-collapsed, its front wall sagging dangerously over the paving stones, and the lower floor was in ruins.

'She's in *there*?' Polly asked, stopping, and Judy, close behind her, stared in dismay at the wreckage. 'Your mother's in *there*?'

He jerked her arm impatiently. 'That's what I said, innit? She's got a coupla rooms there – there's no shelter or nothing, and she wouldn't go down the public, says there's rats. For Gawd's sake, can't you do nothing? She's trapped, there's summat over her leg, I can't get her out and she's crying and moaning something awful.' He stared at the two women, his face working with fear. 'I arst a fireman but they're all too busy with Maddens and all round there. The station's bin hit, and the Post Office and McIlroy's – it's bloody chaos – and the ARP ain't no good, too bloody busy going round telling people to put lights out. *Lights!*' He cast a bitter glance at the raddled glow of the sky. 'There ain't no bloody lights to *put* out, they done in the electric again, and my poor old mum . . .' Once again, he jerked Polly's arm. 'Can't you do nothing?'

Polly shook herself and hurried forward. The wall of the house sloped out perilously above her; she gave it one glance and decided not to look again. The man urged her through the doorway of the building and she crouched to scramble under the leaning architrave. The door was stuck half-open

148

and she had to wriggle past it, praying all the time that the building was not about to collapse on top of her. Behind her, she could feel Judy following, and a moment later the room was lit by the thin beam of the torch.

'Oh, my God,' Polly breathed, and heard Judy draw in her breath.

The room was small and you could see that even before the bomb had fallen it had been no more than a slum. The walls had old cracks as well as new – cracks that were thick with black dirt and mould. The one wall that was left undamaged was encrusted with a huge patch of damp, riddled with fungus. Half the ceiling had come down in a muddle of laths and plaster. The fireplace was filled with soot and rubble from the chimney, and didn't look as if there had been a fire in it for months, despite the bitter weather. The only furniture was an old table, now smothered with dust and rubble, a broken armchair and a chamber pot.

In one corner was a heap of what looked like old blankets and possibly a mattress, and on this lay an old woman. She was crumpled like a broken toy, her face creased with fear and pain, and across the lower part of her body lay a large beam of wood which had fallen in from the wall. There was more rubble all around her, and it was a miracle that her upper body had not been crushed as well.

Polly and Judy scrambled across the room and knelt beside her. Polly touched the withered cheek.

'My name's Polly Dunn. I've come to help you. Tell me where it hurts.'

'Every bleedin' where,' the woman muttered. Her voice sounded like a creaking gate and every word came with difficulty. 'Bleedin' Jerries.'

Polly cast a swift glance over the woman's chest and shoulders. There was no blood and she ran gentle fingers over her. Apart from a few swear words, the woman made no response. There didn't appear to be anything broken there, and Polly heaved a sigh of relief.

The pelvis and legs were a different matter. From the waist down, the old woman was pinned beneath the beam and a mound of bricks and mortar. There were probably dreadful injuries there, and even moving the weight from her body could cause more harm. Polly stared at the sight, biting her lips and wondering what to do. She glanced uncertainly at Judy and as she did so the woman groaned and began to vomit.

'She's bleeding, look,' Judy whispered, pointing at the rubble, and Polly saw a stream of blood trickling between the bricks and soaking the dust and plaster. 'If we don't manage to stop it—'

Polly nodded sharply. The woman would bleed to death. 'We've got to get the stuff off her. But carefully. Where's the son?'

'I'm here.' The man came forward, staring fearfully at the mess. 'Is she going to be all right? Ma?'

'I don't know. We'll do our best, but it's dangerous – we don't know what the injuries are. We've got to stop the bleeding, so the first thing to do is get some of this rubble off her. It's heavy, but we've got to be very careful not to hurt her any more, or even take things off too suddenly. You stay beside her, make sure all that sick's wiped away out of her mouth.'

Polly began to lift bricks away, passing them to Judy to toss into the corner of the room. Together they worked while the man cradled his mother's head in his hands, imploring her not to go, not to leave him, not to die, for *Gawd's* sake, not to die . . .

The blood continued to seep from under the rubble, soaking their clothes. How much has she got in her, Judy wondered, and how much can she afford to lose? She tried to remember what she'd been taught in the First-Aid classes all the WVS staff and volunteers had done. Was it eight pints? A gallon? But this woman looked so tiny and withered, she surely couldn't have that much blood in her body. And how much had she lost already? She's going to die, she thought suddenly, and her heart seemed to drop. She's going to die.

The old woman was rambling now, swearing at the Germans, at the Government, at the bombers, at the ARP. She called out for people she must have known during her life – Johnny, our Moll, Fred and Rags, presumably the family dog. She went further back and cried for her father and mother, who must have been dead for years. Her son pleaded with her to come back to the present, to know that he was with her: 'It's your Jack, Mum, don't you know me, your Jack what's looked after you all these years. Don't say you don't know me, Ma, I can't bear it . . . It's your Jack, your *Jack* . . .'

Their voices went on and on, calling and shouting against each other, and the anguish of it tore at Polly's heart. It might be a slum, but this was a mother and son who'd stuck together through who knew what bad times, and now they'd come to this terrible end. Like Judy, she was sure the old woman was going to die. Too much blood was being lost, too much injury suffered. And yet she could not give up. As long as the old heart could still beat, as long as the tattered lungs could still draw breath to scream, there must be hope. While there was life, there must still be hope . . .

At last there was nothing left on the crumpled body but the beam itself. It lay across the woman's abdomen, crushing her body and one leg which was curled beneath her. Polly stared at it. She saw the mess of torn flesh and broken bone, the twisted internal organs that should never be revealed, and wondered sickly how the old woman had survived this long.

'Oh Polly,' Judy whispered in her ear. 'Whatever are we going to do?'

*

Chris had been the first to spot the approaching wave of bombers.

He had been working overtime in the Dockyard until noon, then gone home for his Sunday dinner. He'd had a wash at the sink, grabbed his tin helmet, fastened his brassard to his arm and then cycled out to the hotel, looking forward to his date with Judy later on. She was a real smasher, he thought, his heart quickening a little, but it was a shame she was engaged. Still, she'd agreed to go for a walk with him so maybe it wasn't really that serious. If it was, Chris wouldn't push things, but he couldn't help hoping . . .

He arrived at the hotel and went straight up in the lift, thinking of the hour or so he and Judy had spent trapped inside. Good old lift, he thought affectionately, watching the walls as it creaked its way up. At least *you* were on my side. The lift shuddered to a stop and he got out and climbed the fire-escape ladder to the roof.

The roof was a large, flat area with a variety of small, square buildings planted apparently at random over it. Some were water tanks, one was the Fire Brigade lookout and one was the ROC Observation Post – little more than a shack, with a table inside on which lay a map with the pivoting plotting instrument mounted on top. The Observers also had a small wooden 'caboose' where they had a chair or two, a stove and a kettle. Spud Murphy, Chris's fellow Observer, was already inside, brewing up.

Chris took a quick look around. The view from up here must be the best in Pompey, he thought. To the north, you could see the green bulk of Portsdown Hill, pocked with chalk pits, with the whole city spread between. You could see all the bomb damage – streets of demolished houses, huge piles of rubble, the ruins of churches, shops and, worst of all, the Guildhall, a gutted shell amidst the desolation. His heart grew cold as he gazed at it.

Turning west, he could see the broad, glittering harbour, always crowded with naval ships, and the Camber, driving into the heart of Old Portsmouth, where the fishermen and small commercial ships came. The square, white tower of the cathedral looked deceptively strong and tranquil in the late afternoon light and he wondered how long it would be before that too was blasted to smithereens.

The Royal Beach faced south, over the Solent towards the Isle of Wight. On an April Sunday afternoon in peacetime this would have been thronged with yachts and sailing dinghies and the beach crowded with families bathing and having picnics on the shingle beach. Today there were just a few, probably people who lived close by. Most of the others who might have come out would be staying at home, wanting to be within reach of shelter in case of a raid, and South Parade Pier itself was almost deserted. Chris had been to a good few dances there; like most young men and women he was keen on the big bands and had never failed to be there when Joe Loss, Ambrose or Sid Phillips were performing. He wondered if Judy had been there on those nights too – maybe with that fiancé of hers – and thought wistfully of taking her himself. He hoped that nothing would happen to spoil their date tonight.

Spud poked his head out of the caboose. 'Tea up, mate. Anything in sight?'

Chris shook his head, turning to gaze eastwards across the sweep of Langstone Harbour, smaller and shallower than the main harbour and used mostly by fishermen and leisure sailors. It was from that direction, over Hayling Island, that enemy attackers usually came, or sometimes from the Isle of Wight. The two Observers who had been on duty came out of the shack. There was nothing to report, they said, and clattered off down the steel ladder, leaving Chris and Spud in charge.

The ROC had been formed in the 1920s, almost entirely of volunteers like Chris. Until only a fortnight ago, it had been simply the 'Observer Corps', the title 'Royal' having been conferred upon it in recognition of its services during the Battle of Britain, last September. There was talk of their being allowed to wear RAF uniform as well and Chris hoped this would happen. He still felt disappointed at not being able to join up, and to wear His Majesty's uniform and be seen to be a part of it all would go a long way to make up for that.

Carrying their mugs of tea, Chris and Spud went into the lookout post. As well as the table with the map and plotting instrument, there was a telephone and a large pair of binoculars. It was one Observer's job to scan the skies, keeping a constant watch for aircraft, while the other plotted their position and course. The details were then telephoned through to the Winchester Observation Centre, where the plotters worked at their large central table, using long poles to move the counters that represented the aircraft into their positions. With information coming through headphones from three posts at once, each observing the same aircraft, it was possible for the controllers on the dais overlooking the table to see exactly what was happening in the sky many miles away, and to take appropriate action.

Chris picked up his binoculars and immediately spotted a plane, heading for the Fleet Air Arm airfield at Lee-on-the-Solent. 'Friendly Fleet Air Arm,' he reported, and Spud quickly plotted its position and wrote it in the log book. *Friendly civil. Friendly coastal.* Each one was plotted and reported to Winchester. The overall picture was important, even when there were no raiders.

The afternoon wore on, the few people who were still on the beach went home and the sun began to dip towards the horizon. It looked as though his date with Judy would be safe. Spud took his turn with the binoculars and Chris made another mug of tea and began to relax.

His four-hour duty was almost over when he picked up the glasses for the last time and caught sight of the dark spots far away over Hayling Island.

'Raiders,' he said sharply, and Spud, who was writing up

the log book, snapped to attention. 'Blimey, there's bloody hundreds of them . . . Get their positions plotted, quick!'

Spud bent over the map which covered the table. It was marked with Ordnance Survey grid references and, with the pivoting mapping instrument mounted in the centre, he could estimate the attackers' present position as well as their direction. At the same time, reports began to come in from the post further along the coast, giving details of the invaders as they passed, and Spud began to set the Micklethwait in position. 'Altitude?'

'Around 10,000 feet. Junker Ju88As . . . Dornier Do17s . . . Heinkels . . . They're sending the bloody lot over – this is going to be a big one . . . Coming in fast now – get on to HQ . . .'

Spud grabbed the phone and spoke urgently. '3M.3 calling, numerous planes seen 7592, flying north, height 10,000 feet.' By the time he had finished, Chris was spitting out more information. Continuing to operate the Micklethwait, Spud relayed the details, knowing that in Winchester everyone would be agog, watching the development of what must be a big raid. But a big raid over which city? 'It's going to be Pompey,' he said, taking a quick look through the window. 'Bugger it, Chris, it's going to be us!'

Almost before he had finished speaking, the sirens began to wail. The steel ladder rattled and the Chief Observer thrust his way into the tiny shelter. 'What's going on?'

'Large formation over Hayling, sir.' Chris handed him the spare set of binoculars. 'Looks like a hell of a raid.'

'You've been on to Winchester?'

The question was unnecessary. Spud was still on the phone, reporting the progress of the invaders. 'Looks like they're coming here, sir.' He thought regretfully of his date with Judy. 'Blimey, they're like a flock of bloody starlings coming home to roost!' The sky was darkening with the mass of aircraft. In a few moments, the drone of their engines would be audible; a few moments after that and the bombs would begin to fall. 'Hey, look, ours are up now!' A flock of wings had risen into the air down the coast, somewhere near Chichester. 'That'll see them off! Atta boy!'

The three men watched tensely. Chris had forgotten about going off duty. The chances were that his relief wouldn't get here now. Like most of the Observers, the next two on duty were Portsmouth boys and able to live at home. If the raid were bad, they might well get caught or be unable to make it through the streets. Observers had been known to be stuck in their posts for hours, sometimes days, especially during the snowstorms of January, and you never left your post until relief arrived – not if you wanted to remain an Observer.

Chris continued to watch the planes, still rapping out estimates of position and altitude to Spud who swiftly checked them on the map and relayed them to the plotting rooms at Winchester. There was no time for anyone to think about being off duty. No time to think of anything else but the raiders, and the urgent need to prevent their deadly progress.

'One's down!' Chris could see the balloon of black smoke and the spurt of flame as a Dornier spiralled into the sea. 'Oh, bloody well done!' But one was not enough. Ten would not be enough, nor twenty, out of the mass of aircraft still steadily approaching. 'There's bloody hundreds of them,' he said again. 'Bloody *hundreds.*'

The siren had wailed into silence. The hotel was almost certainly deserted now, with everyone in it sheltering in the basements, just as all those in Portsmouth would now be crouching in their Andersons or pushing into the street shelters. Those who could not would be huddled under the stairs, while some who refused to shelter at all would be sitting defiantly in their own back rooms, convinced that if a bomb had their name on it, it would find them wherever they were. And some, ignoring the danger, would be preparing to go out into the streets, ready to put out incendiaries, fight fires, rescue the trapped from bombed buildings or give First Aid to the injured.

Judy would be doing that, Chris thought. Judy would be out there now, setting up an Incident Enquiry Centre or out on an ambulance somewhere. Oh God, he prayed, keep her safe. Don't let her be hurt.

The planes were almost overhead. The men jammed their tin helmets on their heads and watched tautly as one streaked low, heading straight for South Parade Pier. The roar of its engine shook the wooden turret, shook the hotel itself. Frozen, Chris stared as a stick of bombs fell away from its belly – four of them in a line, each falling into the sea and sending up a huge spray of foam and shingle. Then he saw that the plane was coming over the pier and straight for the hotel. There'll be another bomb, he thought, it'll be a direct hit. Someone grabbed his arm and he turned to see the Chief yelling at him, the words inaudible but the meaning clear. *'Get downstairs, you fool!'* He found himself pushed unceremoniously towards the steel ladder and tumbled down it, ducking into the rest-room at the bottom just as the explosion shook the building.

'Hell's teeth!' Spud muttered in his ear as the noise died slowly away. 'That was flaming close.'

Cautiously, they got to their feet. There were only the three of them there; everyone else had gone down to the base- ment, leaving mugs of tea and half-eaten buns on the tables. Two mugs had fallen to the floor, spreading their contents on the linoleum, while one had stayed miraculously upright, its surface barely rippled. The windows had shattered and when Chris removed his tin helmet a mass of broken glass showered to the floor. He found shards embedded in his jumper, and wondered briefly what would have happened if he had been in shirtsleeves.

'Right, let's get back up to the post,' the Chief said

tersely. 'Winchester will be wondering what the hell's going on.'

They scrambled up the ladder. The wooden shack was still standing. But there was a gaping hole in its roof now, and as they crowded through the doorway they realised at once what a narrow escape they had had.

The fifth bomb of the stick had landed behind the hotel. Apart from the shattered windows there was little damage. But it had dug a crater in the street below, and a paving slab had been blown high into the air and had landed on the table where, a few seconds earlier, Chris had been staring through binoculars and Spud had been plotting the positions of the enemy aircraft.

Cissie and Alice huddled in the Anderson, clutching each other's hands in the darkness. Both were worried about Polly and Judy, somewhere out there amongst all the bombs, and both were anxious about Dick, still in the Royal Hospital. It had been damaged once already in the first Blitz and patched up again, but who was to say it wouldn't be hit again? 'They don't bomb the same place twice,' Alice said, trying to be a comfort to her daughter, but Cissie shook her head and a hot tear fell on to the back of her hand.

'I can't believe that, Mum. All these thousands of bombs –' they both ducked lower at the roar and vibration of a bomb falling not far away '– they've got to land somewhere. I don't see how they can miss a big place like the Royal.'

'But aren't they more likely to aim for the Dockyard? I mean, the ships are more vital to them, aren't they, and the repair shops. I reckon anywhere else just gets hit by accident.'

'Mum, they don't care where they hit now. All that stuff about only aiming for military targets – that's all gone by the board. They just want to destroy and kill wherever they can. And if they can't kill us, they'll frighten us to death. It's what they call terror bombing.' Cissie clutched her hand even more tightly as another explosion rocked the earth and the corrugated iron roof of the Anderson shifted and screeched. 'Oh my God, my God! Oh, Dick – where are you? I want him back, Mum, I want him home!'

Alice was in tears. 'He's better off where he is, Cis. He's being looked after, he's safe.'

'He's not! He's not! The Royal's already been bombed once. He could be being bombed now, this very minute.' Cissie had lost all control. 'At least if he was home I'd know what was happening, I could look after him myself. I'm going to get him, Mum.' She half rose to her feet, crouching in the low space, and Alice groped for her and grasped her coat.

'You can't! Don't be daft, our Cis! Sit down at once and pull yourself together!' Her voice sharpened, became a reminder of the days when Cissie had been a child and her mother a strict disciplinarian. *'Sit down this minute!'*

Shaken out of her hysteria, Cissie sank back on to the narrow bunk, trembling with sobs. Alice put her arm around her and drew her close, and Cissie leaned her head on her mother's shoulder, feeling the comfort of her mother's embrace just as a moment ago she had felt her authority.

'Oh, Mum,' she said brokenly. 'Oh Mum, I don't know that I can stand any more of this.'

'I know, love,' Alice murmured, stroking her hair. 'I know. This is the worst we've ever known, and we've been through enough in our time, heaven knows. One world war already, the 'flu epidemic that took your dad, the hard times we went through in the thirties – and now this. But we've got to bear up, Cis. It's no use giving way to it all. We've got to keep going somehow, and keep a smile on our lips while we do. It don't do none of us no good to let it get on top of us.'

'A *smile*!' Cissie said, with an attempt at a laugh. 'I don't reckon anyone feels like smiling tonight.' The noise was still going on outside – the drone of planes, the rattle of anti-aircraft fire, the sudden shattering roar of exploding bombs. 'I don't see how anyone *can* feel like smiling.'

'Doesn't matter what we feel like,' Alice said with a return to her sharpness. 'It's putting a smile on our faces that counts, not what we feel like inside. It makes you *feel* better, smiling does, and it makes other people feel better to see you do it. So you try it now, Cis. Come on.'

'Oh Mum!' This time, the laugh was unforced. 'Who's going to see me? It's pitch dark in here. Who's going to know if I'm smiling or not?'

'*You'll* know,' Alice said firmly. 'And so will I. We'll keep each other cheerful, Cis, same as we've done all those other times. Now come on, put a smile on your face and let's play a game of something to pass the time.'

'A game?' Cissie repeated, but Alice heard the wobbly grin in her voice. 'And just what game d'you think we ought to play, Mum – *I Spy With My Little Eye?*'

'What are we going to do?' Judy repeated. She stared around at the dimly lit room, the shadowy corners heaped with rubbish, at the torn, broken walls, at the heavy beam that still lay across the crushed body. The darkness and the squalor of it pressed in on her and she felt the familiar worm of panic.

'I don't know,' Polly whispered back. 'I don't know what to do. I don't know what anyone can do.' She turned and saw the woman's son staring too. 'We need help. We need men – a doctor.'

'She's 'ad it,' he said tonelessly. 'She's 'ad it, ain't she? Nobody can't get her out of this.'

'We'll fetch help,' Polly said again, and turned to Judy. 'Go and see if you can find someone. Bring them here. Say they must come. We need at least two men, strong men, and a doctor. We've *got* to have help.'

Judy stared at her. 'But I can't leave you.'

'Go!' Polly shouted, and her voice was edged with fear. 'Go on, go! Get some help! We can't do it by ourselves. *Please*, Judy!'

Judy's face crumpled but she turned and scurried out of the building. Outside, the sky was crimson with flames and even the beams of the searchlights were dimmed. She could still hear planes overhead, and the sudden reverberation of exploding bombs. No one will come, she thought despairingly. Not for one old woman.

She ran out of the alley and looked both ways. Several shops and offices were ablaze now, surrounded by firemen. Over the road, she could see a huddle of people round something on the pavement. She ran over and caught at an arm. 'What's happening? Is there a doctor anywhere here?'

'Kiddy hurt,' a man said briefly. 'Doctor's looking after her now.'

'Oh.' Judy gazed helplessly at the scene. The child was stretched on the pavement, clearly unconscious, and a woman was kneeling beside her. She must be the doctor – Judy had heard of the young woman doctor who had been so brave in the bombing, coming out to help whatever the danger. She wanted to go to her, beg her to come and help the old woman who was dying in the slum room nearby, but she knew she could not. This was a child, in equal or perhaps worse danger. The doctor wouldn't leave her, and Judy couldn't ask it.

A van screeched to a halt and Judy looked round and saw Gladys Shaw scrambling down from the driver's seat. Her mother Peggy came round from the passenger's side. 'What's the trouble? Does anyone need taking to the hospital?' She looked down at the child on the pavement and the young woman doctor beside her, then pulled open the back doors of the van and dragged out a stretcher. 'Get her into the ambulance. I'll take her straight away.' Carefully, the doctor and two or three helpers began to lift the small body on to it.

'I'll go with her,' someone volunteered. 'I'm her auntie, I'll look after her.' There was a hasty consultation with the doctor, and then she pulled herself up into the van with the little girl. The crowd sighed thankfully and began to hurry away to find shelter.

The doctor stood up and pushed back her hair. Judy grabbed her arm. 'Don't go! Please – there's an old woman in a building over there. She's trapped by a wooden beam and she's bleeding terribly. My aunt's in there and we've been lifting stuff off her, but we can't manage any more. We need help.' She called out to some of the departing crowd: 'Can some of you come – *please*? She'll die if we can't get her out.'

A couple of men turned and came back. 'Who is it? Where is she?'

'Over there.' Judy pointed. 'Her son's in there with her, and my auntie. We're both WVS, she drives an ambulance, too – it's that van over there. The ceiling's all fallen in and the old lady's in a terrible way, crying and screaming and being sick.' They were all hurrying across the road now, leaping across the snaking hoses of the firemen, dodging past vehicles and fallen masonry. Judy ducked down the dark little alleyway and led them into the courtyard. 'She's in there.'

There was a brief pause. The two men, the doctor and Judy all stood for a moment, staring at the building, at the wall that still leaned outwards, looking as if it might topple at any moment. Then the doctor turned to Judy and began to speak.

Judy never knew what she had been going to say. At that moment, there was a tremendous explosion as a bomb fell only a few streets away. What glass there was left in the surrounding windows blew outwards, spattering them with lethal shards. One of the men screamed and clapped both hands over his eyes, and the other jerked him and Judy to the ground. The doctor dropped beside her and then cried out and dragged them all to their feet again, pointing wildly at the building above them.

The wall that had been leaning so precariously outwards seemed to shiver and bend in the flickering light of the flames that burned the sky. It buckled slowly and began to fall into the courtyard. There was a shattering roar, and Judy and the others scuttled back into the alleyway just in time.

The narrow passage was filled with dust; thick, fine, choking dust. Judy retched and struggled for breath. She could see nothing in the sudden swirling darkness; she could feel only the urgent hands of the young doctor, thrusting her towards the entrance to the alleyway, towards what fresh air there was. Her mind was filled with the compelling need to breathe, to stay alive. I've got to get out of here, she thought, I've got to get out. And then, following swiftly, another thought: *But Polly's still inside . . .*

'Polly!' She turned and tried to run back into the alley. 'Polly – my aunt – she was in there! *She was in that building!* We've got to go back in and get her out!'

Chapter Twelve

By daybreak, the city once again lay devastated. The mine that had destroyed Maddens Hotel had also damaged the town railway station and the main Post Office. Kingston Prison had been hit, and the railway line behind it blocked. There were massive fires in the Dockyard and many homes and businesses were hit. Over a hundred people had been killed and hundreds more injured. Once again, the Emergency Centres were busy finding homes for those who had been bombed out.

Cissie and her mother crept out of their Anderson soon after dawn. April Grove had escaped damage, and people all along the row of long, narrow gardens leading to the allotments were making their way up their paths, hoping the gas was on so that they could make tea. Cissie went straight through the house to the front, hoping to see Polly and Judy coming home. Alice followed her.

There were quite a few people out there already. Frank Budd, who had spent the night firewatching, was already setting off to go to work in the Dockyard and Tommy Vickers was coming down the street, stumbling a little with weariness. The two men paused for a moment and Alice and Cissie joined them.

'Bad night,' Frank said, shaking his head. 'There'll be all sorts of damage done. You could read a newspaper by the light of the flames. I suppose it was the city centre and the Yard got it worst again.'

Tommy looked at him. Usually a bright, cheery man with a quip for every occasion, he looked, as Frank put it later, 'proper done in'. His eyes were red-rimmed with smoke and fatigue, his face drawn and grey. He rubbed a hand across his face.

'I just come from Powerscourt Road. There've been more bombs there.' He shook his head slowly. 'Kids – boys – in the cellar of one of those houses that were bombed last year. Where young Kathy Simmons lived before she come to October Street.' His voice was trembling a little. 'Reckon they had some sort o' den there – you know what boys are. Collecting stuff – shrapnel, that sort of thing.' He took a deep breath while Frank stared at him. 'Seems like they had a bomb in there with them – unexploded. They must have found it and took it there.' He stopped.

'A bomb?' Frank said. 'Why, the silly young fools. Didn't they realise it could go off at any time?' He stopped and looked more closely at Tommy. 'What is it, Tom? What happened?'

'The place was hit again,' Tommy said wearily, 'and the bomb went off as well. They'd got out of the cellar, they were out in the garden when it went, but . . . ' He looked at Frank and the women as if begging them to say it wasn't true. 'They were youngsters from round here, that's the worst of it. That Micky Baxter. And young Jimmy Cross. And that little Nash boy – Cyril, is it? – the one that always looks as if butter wouldn't melt in his mouth. Not that we found much of him,' he added bitterly. 'Blown to bits, poor little tyke. And Jimmy Cross – well, he's lost a leg, blown clean off, and they reckon he'll be lucky if that's all the damage.'

Cissie stared at him. 'But youngsters like that ought to have been down in their shelters. What on earth were they doing out there? What were their mums and dads *thinking* of?'

'I don't suppose Nancy Baxter even knew Micky was out,' Alice said. 'She's not home herself at night all that much. But the other two – well, I'd have thought they'd be better looked after.'

'It'll have been that Micky Baxter who was the ring-leader,' Frank said grimly. 'There's always trouble where that boy is. What about him, Tom? Was he hurt?'

'I dunno. I don't think he was, much, just knocked out by the blast.' Tommy rubbed his face again. 'But those other two – I tell you, I don't never want to see nothing like that again. That little Cyril Nash – he used to come round here with his guy, Firework Night, asking for pennies. My Freda always used to give him something, she said he had such a sweet face. I dunno how she's going to take this.'

'And Jimmy Cross too,' Alice said sadly. 'I used to live in the same street as his grandpa when I was little – played together, we did. They were a nice family, the Crosses. What a terrible thing.'

Tommy went indoors and Frank continued on his way. Alice and Cissie looked at each other.

'I'm worried sick about our Polly and Judy,' Cissie said, her voice shaking. 'Something's happened to them, Mum, I'm sure of it. Something awful's happened to them.'

'I just don't know what we ought to do,' Alice said. She'd managed to persuade Cissie to come back indoors and boil up a kettle for some tea; just for once, the gas supply seemed to have survived the raid. That didn't mean it wouldn't be cut off later, of course, if there was danger from an unexploded bomb or some fracture further along the mains. But for now, you could at least make a hot drink. Alice put a couple of slices of bread under the grill too, but when she spread margarine and Marmite on the toast Cissie shook her head.

'I couldn't eat a thing, Mum, not till I know what's happened to them. And there's Dick as well, he's supposed to be coming out of hospital in the next day or two. What

166

am I going to tell him when I go in at visiting time if our Judy still isn't home?'

'She'll be back by then.' Alice spoke with more conviction than she felt. 'Bound to be. But I don't know what we can do about it anyway, Cis. I suppose we could go down the Emergency Centre. They'll know what's what.'

Cissie began to get to her feet. 'I'll go now.'

'You'll eat your breakfast first.' Once again, Alice's voice was stern, reminding Cissie of her childhood. 'You don't take a step out of this house without something inside you. Eat up your toast now, there's a good girl. You don't want me to waste it, do you?'

If she'd really been the child her mother seemed to think she was, Cissie would have retorted that she hadn't wanted her to make it. But she was a grown woman, for all her nervousness, and knew that you couldn't afford to waste good food these days. Alice was right – she did need something to eat before she went out. So she picked up the toast and nibbled it, then realised that she really was hungry and ate it without further argument. She drank the tea and then got up again.

'I'll go down the Centre now, Mum. You're right, they'll know what's happened. They might even be there, our Judy and Polly, having a rest before they come home. They must have been so busy last night . . .' Her voice wavered again and then strengthened as Alice too began to make ready for going out. 'No, you stop here. You need a rest too and I'd rather there was someone here in case they come while I'm gone.'

She shrugged on her jacket and let herself out into the street again. April Grove was busy now, with women at their doors washing their steps and delivery vans already beginning to arrive with bread, milk and vegetables. It was a marvel how people just got on with their lives even after a night like they'd just been through, Cissie reflected. Mind you, the baker's van didn't seem to have many loaves to hand out, and old Mr Briggs who drove it seemed to be operating his own rationing system ('No, Mrs Kinch, you 'ad one yesterday, you can't 'ave got through that already'), while his horse seemed nervous, as if it had been frightened all night, which it probably had. But the milkman was whistling cheerfully and the burly man from the greengrocer's was weighing out potatoes as if he didn't have a care in the world. So perhaps the raid hadn't been so bad after all, she thought hopefully as she hurried along.

It was a different matter when she came out into the main road. There were no buses running, and she could see a pall of smoke further south, over Portsea. A woman walked past crying, with a handkerchief held up to her face, and there was a group of workmen standing on a corner looking stunned. Cissie began to feel anxious again, a heavy sense of dread settling over her like a cloud. She thought again of the little boy who had been killed and the one who would be 'lucky if he only lost a leg'. How many others were there like that?

Her chest and throat tight with anxiety, Cissie almost ran along the pavement. I ought to go to the hospital too, she thought, and let Dick know we're all right. Even if they don't let me in, I ought to go. But I don't *know* that we're all right, she reminded herself. Until I know where Polly and my Judy are, I don't know that at all.

Dick would be all right, anyway, tucked up in bed and well looked after. He was over the worst now, and yesterday they'd told her he'd be home in a few days. He'd be worrying about them, she was sure, and the minute she knew about Polly and Judy she'd go straight to the Royal and get a message to him, but just for now her sister and daughter came first.

She arrived at the Centre at last. It was thronged with people and as Cissie came round the corner and saw the queue her heart leaped with relief. Not for all those poor souls who'd been bombed out, of course, but just because she knew that if there were so many people needing help it was no wonder Polly and Judy hadn't been able to get home. They'd been there all night, handing out cocoa and sandwiches, and probably that's where they were still. Some of the daytime volunteers might have been bombed as well, or just couldn't get through the streets to take over. That was all it was. She'd see them the minute she went through the door, looking tired but cheerful, glad as always to be able to lend a hand.

Getting through the door wasn't so easy, however. The people waiting were reluctant to let her through. 'Oy, no queue-jumping if you don't mind! Go to the back. It's first come, first served.'

'I need to see my daughter.'

'You've got a wait, then,' said a woman with pinched lips and a deep vertical line between her eyebrows. 'Gawd knows what they're doing in there, but whatever it is they're handing out there's not going to be much left for us poor buggers. We bin here since five, and hardly moved.'

'No, she's a volunteer – a helper. She's been out all night. I just want to make sure she's all right. And my sister too, she drives an ambulance. Please let me through,' Cissie begged. 'I've got my hubby in hospital, too, in the Royal, he's had pneumonia. I've got to go and let him know we're all right.'

'In the Royal?' A man standing just in front of them turned. 'Well, you'd better go and see if *he's* all right too. Didn't you know it got hit last night?'

'The Royal?' Cissie stared at him, her heart suddenly cold. 'The Royal Hospital got hit?'

''S right. Mine fell on it. Hundreds killed, so I heard. There was ambulances backwards and forwards all night, and what I heard was, the Casualty Ward got the worst of it. Maybe that's where your girl's gone, if your sis was one of the drivers.'

Cissie felt sick. She put out one hand and leaned against

the door jamb, swept by a wave of dizziness. The woman who had been reluctant to let her through steadied her with one arm.

'Here, hold on, ducks. I dare say your girl's all right, and your sister too. They're probably in here now, dishing out tea and filling up forms. And if it was just the Casualty that got hit, your hubby'll be all right. Don't you worry. Now look, you go on in and make sure they're here and then pop off to the Royal. Let her through,' she said, raising her voice to those in front. 'Let this lady through, she's got a girl and a sister in the volunteers, and her hubby's down the Royal. Come on, move yourselves!'

The queue shifted, some of those at the front grumbling a little but, as the details were passed along the line, changing dramatically as they went, Cissie was allowed to pass. By the time she reached the head of the queue the whispers had arrived before her, and she was receiving sympathetic glances. 'Lost her hubby and daughter and sister in the raid,' someone murmured as she passed, and Cissie swayed again. Suppose it were true! Oh, let it not be true, she begged.

To her relief, the woman pouring tea was Annie Chapman. 'Cis! Whatever are you doing here? I thought you'd be at the hospital.'

Cissie stared at her. 'At the hospital? You mean the Royal?'

'Well, no. They were taking people to Queen Alexandra or St James's. The Royal was hit, you know.' Annie's hand flew to her mouth in consternation. 'Oh, my goodness. Your hubby's in there, isn't he? How is he? Have you been to see?'

'No – I didn't even know about it till a few minutes ago.' Cissie put her hand to her head. 'I was looking for Polly and Judy – they never came home. I thought I'd find them here, but . . .' Annie's words sank in and she caught her breath.

'D'you mean to say *they've* been taken to hospital, too? They've been hurt?'

Annie looked dismayed. 'Cis, I'm ever so sorry to break it to you like this. That's what I heard, anyway. They were in some building when it collapsed. They can't have been killed,' she added swiftly. 'They can't, can they, or they wouldn't have been taken to hospital. But that's all I've heard. I'm sorry.'

Cissie felt as if all her surroundings – the hall full of people, the noise, the clatter of kettles and teacups – had fallen away from her, leaving her swinging giddily over a yawning abyss. For a moment she was aware of nothing but a deadly fear, a horror of the roaring darkness that rushed in upon her. Then hands gripped her and she felt herself guided to a chair and her head pressed gently between her knees. Someone put a cup to her lips and she tasted cold water. She spluttered and swallowed, and gradually the sickness receded and she was aware once more of the clatter in the hall, the hubbub of voices. Slowly, she lifted her head. Annie was crouching beside her.

'I'm ever so sorry, Cis,' she said again. 'All we heard was that they'd gone to hospital – we don't know which one it was ourselves. They'll let us know later, but it was such a bad night, everything's just an awful muddle.'

Cissie nodded. 'What am I going to do?' she asked bleakly. 'I don't know where to go first. Someone said there was hundreds killed in the Royal. I've got to find out what's happened to Dick. But if Judy's been hurt – and our Poll – and they might be in QA or St James's . . .' A fresh thought struck her. 'St *James's*! That's the mental hospital! Does that mean—?'

'It just means they were taking casualties there,' Annie said firmly. 'It doesn't mean anything else at all. Cis, I don't know what to tell you. We can't even ring up – the telephones are mostly out of action again, and what lines there are they need for the emergency services. It's like a madhouse out there.' She bit her lip, obviously regretting that choice of phrase, and turned as someone called her. 'Look, I'm sorry, Cis, I'll have to go. You can see how we're placed here. Tell you what I think, you might as well go to the Royal first, since it's nearest, and then when you've made sure your Dick's all right, you could go on up to St James's or QA. But why not pop in home first, because they might be back by then. A lot of people who aren't hurt bad are being sent home, and I dare say that's what's happened to your two.'

Cissie nodded and stood up. She handed the cup back to one of the other volunteers and made her way out of the hall, not hearing the anxious enquiries from those who had let her through. They looked at her stricken face and shook their heads sadly. 'Shame, poor soul,' the whisper ran, but Cissie heard nothing. She ran blindly through the streets, seeing nothing of the damage, anxiety beating at her mind like a bird with broken wings. Dick – Polly – Judy – what had happened to them all? And she was gripped by a dark certainty that they were all dead.

The Royal Hospital had been hit by a mine. It had blown the Casualty Ward apart, and the entrance where patients were being brought by ambulance. Everyone in the reception area was killed. There'd been several ambulances arriving at the time but most of the drivers had been outside and blown clear. Those who had been hurt had been taken to St James's.

'But what about my hubby?' Cissie asked desperately. She didn't know where to go. The hospital forecourt was a mass of rubble and splintered wood and glass, and there were soldiers, sailors and ARP men pulling at it, trying both to clear the forecourt and to find anyone who might have been buried. Their faces were set and Cissie saw to her horror that there was already a row of objects lying on the ground nearby, humped under torn and bloody blankets. Bodies, she thought, and panic edged her voice.

One of the ARP men looked up. His face was grimed with dust and his eyes were red and sore-looking. He rubbed the back of his hand across his face and said, 'What's up, love? Who're you looking for?'

'My husband. He's in hospital here.' She glanced fearfully at the row of bodies. 'How can I find out if he's all right?'

'Brought in last night, was he?'

She shook her head. 'No, he's been here for weeks now. He had pneumonia. I don't know where to go.'

'He'll have been took down the basements,' the man said. 'He wouldn't have been up here. You'll have to go and ask.' He turned away. 'Sorry, love, but we're busy here, you can see.' Someone called out and he went across to help a small knot of men who were carefully lifting a beam away from a heap of smashed bricks. Cissie made to follow him, then stopped abruptly as she caught sight of red, bloodstained flesh, the jagged end of a bone and a fragment of the blue serge worn by sailors.

Sickened, she turned away. Picking her way through the rubble, avoiding the bodies, she eventually reached a door where a crowd of people were gathering, all seeking information about friends and relatives who were patients. Three or four nurses were sitting at makeshift desks with lists in front of them, looking harassed. Cissie joined the queue, listening anxiously.

'No, nobody in that ward was hurt. All the patients from that part of the hospital who could walk went down to the basements. There were several people in the reception area when the mine hit, and they were all killed – a doctor, some nurses, some new patients coming in and a sailor who was helping on one of the ambulances. Yes, there were some women ambulance drivers as well, they were taken to St James's.' The nurse looked up as Cissie reached the head of the queue. 'Men's Medical? If he was able to walk he'd have gone to the basement. They took quite a lot of bed patients there too, before the hospital was struck. Oh, a *chest* patient . . .' She consulted her list, then turned to the nurse sitting beside her. 'Where did chest patients go, Morrison? Weren't they going through the hallway on their way to the shelter?'

The other nurse nodded. 'They'd just gone through. Nobody was hurt,' she added quickly, seeing Cissie's face, 'but some were affected by the dust. The worst patients it could happen to,' she murmured to the first nurse, and then looked up at Cissie again. 'Go down that corridor and through the double doors at the end. Someone there will help you.'

Cissie thanked them both and set off, walking as quickly as she could and wishing she dared break into a run. Affected by dust – the worst patients it could happen to . . . Oh Dick, she thought, please don't get pneumonia all over again. Please don't suffer any more.

Through the double doors, things were quieter. The hubbub of the crowd's anxious questions and the noise of people working outside was shut out, and Cissie's footsteps sounded suddenly loud. A Sister put her head out of a door and looked at her, frowning. Cissie stopped.

'I've come to find out about my husband. He's been in with pneumonia. I was worried after the raid.'

'Name?' the Sister asked briskly.

'Dick Taylor. *Richard* Taylor. He was a chest patient.'

The woman gave her a look as if to say she knew that a man with pneumonia was likely to be a chest patient, and Cissie felt herself blush. But when the Sister spoke again her voice was kind. 'He'll be in there. It was unfortunate that they were rather close to the area affected by the bomb, but nobody was hurt. You can slip in and see him, but please don't stay long. It isn't visiting time, you know.'

'I know. But I just had to find out if he was all right.'

Cissie's voice wobbled. 'I've got to try to find my sister too, she was driving an ambulance last night – and my daughter. She didn't come home either.' A sob caught in her throat and she turned away hastily. 'I won't stay long, just to see he's all right.'

The Sister touched her shoulder. 'Don't worry too much. It was such a bad raid, they're probably still helping somewhere. There must be hundreds of people who haven't managed to get home yet.' She gave Cissie a brief smile and then turned away as a man pushing a trolley thrust his way through the doors and hastened towards them. There was a small girl on the trolley, her face covered in blood and her legs bent at an unnatural angle.

Cissie pushed through the ward door, tears running down her cheeks. So many people hurt and killed, so many almost out of their minds with worry. Just inside the ward, she stood for a moment looking this way and that, trying to make sense of the turmoil of beds hastily squashed in together, the hurrying nurses and the paraphernalia of drips, bedpans and trolleys.

A nurse came up to her, obviously about to order her out, but Cissie forestalled her. 'I've come to see my husband. The Sister outside said I could, just for a few minutes, just to make sure he's all right.'

The nurse looked as if this was highly irregular but for once Cissie stood her ground. She hadn't come this far to be balked now. The woman obviously read this in her face, for she shrugged and said, 'Well, just for a minute or two, then. What's his name?'

'Taylor. Richard Taylor.'

'Oh yes, he's over there.' She pointed to a corner. 'He's rather poorly, I'm afraid. Only a minute, mind,' she added as Cissie started forwards. 'We're very busy.'

Rather poorly! Cissie barely heard the nurse's last words. She almost ran across to the bed in the corner and stared down at her husband. 'Dick! Dick, whatever's happened to you?'

The figure in the bed stared up at her. 'Cis? Is that you?' His voice was as rough as sandpaper.

'Yes, of course it is.' She fell on her knees, gripping his thin hands. 'What's wrong? What's the matter with you? They said no one was hurt.'

'I wasn't.' He could manage only a few words at a time. 'Got a faceful of dust and muck. Breathed it in. Felt like sandpaper, it did. Been coughing all night.' He coughed again, painfully, as if to demonstrate. 'Reckon I've still got some in me lungs. It could turn to pneumonia again, Cis.' He clung to her hand. 'I was coming home tomorrow. Coming *home*.'

'I know.' She gazed at him in distress. 'Oh *Dick*.'

'Want to come home,' he wheezed. 'Take me home, Cis. I don't want to be here any more.'

'Dick, I can't. If you discharge yourself, they won't take you back again. And if you do get pneumonia . . .'

He fixed his eyes on her pleadingly and she stared back in despair. The ward was full of noise. It smelt of urine and faeces and blood, of disinfectant and medicines – the 'hospital' smell that all the wards seemed to share. Nurses were hurrying to and fro, their shoes clattering on the linoleum floor. Voices called out, some demanding, some filled with pain, some in obvious delirium. I wouldn't want to be here either, Cissie thought.

'I'll take you home the first minute I can,' she promised. 'But you'll have to wait for the doctor to say so. I'm sorry, love.'

He looked at her and then turned his head away and stared at the wall. Cissie stroked his hand desperately. 'Dick. Dick, don't look like that. I *can't* take you home now. You might be ill again – you could *die*.' Her voice rose in anguish. 'Dick, I'd take you this minute if I could, but—'

'I'm afraid you'll have to go.' An authoritative voice broke in and she turned quickly to find a tall, weary-looking man standing beside her. Hastily, Cissie let go of Dick's hand and scrambled to her feet. The man looked at her severely. 'I don't know who let you in now, but you'll have to come back at visiting time. That's three o'clock this afternoon.'

'I know, thank you. I've been coming in for the past three weeks.' Cissie looked back towards the bed. 'My husband – is he . . .'

'I haven't examined him yet,' the doctor stated. 'Sister will give you any information this afternoon. Now, if you'd please go.'

'Yes,' Cissie muttered, defeated. She turned back to Dick and felt for his hand once more. 'Bye now, love. I'll be back this afternoon. You'll be all right – I'm sure you'll be all right.' She caught the doctor's eye again, dropped his hand and moved away, walking uncertainly out of the ward. At the door she stopped again. The doctor was bent over Dick, his stethoscope placed on the thin chest. Blinded by tears, Cissie turned away.

Three o'clock this afternoon. *I'll be back*, she promised Dick silently.

But before then, she had to find out what had happened to Judy and Polly.

Chapter Thirteen

The noise as the front of the building fell into the courtyard had been the worst explosion Judy had ever heard. It had reverberated around the tall, narrow space between the other buildings, blasting her eardrums and filling her head with a roar that she thought would never stop. A great cloud of thick, choking dust rose into the air and she buried her face in her sleeve, trying not to breathe in too deeply, the foul, gritty powder coating her tongue and teeth and making her gag and retch to get rid of it. I can't stand this, she thought, I can't stand it any more. Make it go away. *Make it go away*.

Someone pulled her sleeve and she lifted her face away cautiously and saw the young doctor mouthing something at her. Panic gripped her as she realised that she could hear nothing. She tried to yell back, but even inside her head her words sounded distorted and meaningless. She shook her head, terrified, but there was nothing but a strange, roaring silence.

She looked around. Dust was swirling around the narrow space and even the crimson light of the flames outside could only just penetrate the darkness. With another leap of fear, she wondered if the buildings here had caught fire, but could see no fresh flames. It could surely be no more than a matter of time, though. All this wood and plaster needed only a spark to set it off, and even as the thought entered her head she saw a gobbet of flame drift past high above. We've got to get out of here, she thought, and turned to see if the entrance had been blocked.

Polly! For a few seconds, she had forgotten her aunt and the old woman and her son, still trapped in the collapsed building. She whirled back, to find her arm grasped again by the doctor.

Judy shook her off angrily, and tried to shout again, but her voice seemed to have no power. I can't even hear myself, she thought in despair, but there was no time to think about that now. She jabbed her finger urgently at the fallen masonry and made her mouth shape the words, 'My aunt – my aunt –' Whether the other woman understood, she didn't know, but she evidently remembered that they had come here to help someone who was trapped, and nodded quickly before turning herself to follow Judy's pointing finger.

The two men were getting to their feet as well, shaking their heads and rubbing their ears. We've all gone deaf, she thought, and grabbed their arms to drag them in the direction of the fallen house. Even now there were still bricks and slates and slabs of mortar tumbling down from the splintered edges of the roof that was still left, hanging drunkenly from the adjoining buildings. It only wants one of them falling on your head to kill you, Judy thought, but she couldn't give up now. Polly was in there somewhere, and if she left her she would never forgive herself.

Together, the four of them went cautiously forwards, each keeping an eye on the wreckage above. To her amazement, Judy saw that even though almost the entire front of the building had fallen, the doorway itself was still standing. The architrave must have been especially strong – perhaps old oak from an ancient sailing ship, strengthened from years of immersion in salt water. Tentatively, she pushed at the splintered door and it swung open a foot or so, then stopped, blocked by rubble. Judy began to wriggle through the narrow space.

A touch on her arm made her turn. The doctor was shaking her head, obviously warning her of the danger, but

Judy shook her own head in reply. *I'm going in there, whatever happens.* She eased herself very carefully round the edge of the door and picked her way over a pile of bricks.

It hadn't been far to the room where the old woman had lain, but it was now almost pitch dark in there, with only the faintest red glow from the flame-lit sky. Judy tried to remember which way she had gone, and moved very slowly, feeling her way. If only she had a torch . . .

As if in answer to a prayer, a thin beam of light flickered in one corner and her heart jumped. Polly had had a torch! Was she still there, still miraculously alive, perhaps calling out unheard by her deafened rescuers, shining the torch to show them the way? Judy tried again to shout, without any idea as to whether her voice could be heard. Behind her, she was aware of someone following, one of the men or perhaps the doctor. The light had disappeared, but she pointed and felt, rather than saw, the nod of the head, then groped for her companion's arm. The warmth and solidity reassured her, and they went on side by side, taking slow, careful steps and scrabbling with their hands at the mounds of bricks and plaster.

Something soft met Judy's questing fingers. She froze, half afraid of what it might be, then moved her hands cautiously, feeling the softness of fabric coated with gritty dust. It was a garment of some kind, but was it something that had been taken off and flung down, or was it still wrapped around a body? A *body*, she thought in panic, and almost tore her hands away. At the same moment, the fabric shifted under her hands and the light shone again.

'*Polly!*' The name was a thought rather than a cry, but Judy hardly cared now whether she was deaf or not, for there at her feet, half-buried in rubble, lay her aunt, her small torch gripped in one hand and shining towards her grime-coated face. There was blood on her forehead and in her hair, but her eyes were open, and as Judy bent towards her a faint smile curved her lips.

Judy almost fell on her, half laughing, half crying. Beside her, the doctor bent swiftly to press her fingers against Polly's neck and then looked up at Judy and indicated the rubble. Her mouth moved and Judy read the silent message: '*She's alive! We've got to get this off her.*'

Judy began to pull away bricks and slivers of wood. To her immense relief they were all small, or at least within her ability to lift, but she was so thankful to find Polly alive that she felt she could have moved a mountain to get her out. By now, the two men were also in the small space, and together they worked feverishly to free the trapped woman. Oh, let her be all right, Judy prayed. Let her not be hurt too badly. It was uncanny, working in the silence, uncannier still to know that the air must be filled with sound, with the cacophony of aircraft overhead, the roar of exploding bombs, the rattle of ack-ack guns. The raid was still going on – at any moment they might all be blasted to oblivion or burned to death in a firestorm – yet the most important thing in the world now was to get Polly out of her prison, to bring her out alive.

They had shifted all the small stuff now and by the flickering light of Polly's torch, Judy saw with dismay that there was a large beam of wood across her body. Oh God, if she's been crushed . . . she thought in horror, but almost before the thought had formed in her mind she saw that it was balanced on two other lumps of broken masonry, and didn't touch Polly at all. In fact, it had probably saved her life, making a cage around her over which the rubble had fallen, while inside she was barely scratched.

As soon as she was able, Polly began to struggle out from underneath the beam. She was filthy and bedraggled, one leg was dragging and there was still blood trickling down her face, but her eyes were bright and she hugged Judy fervently. Her mouth moved in some question, but Judy shook her head and pointed to her ears. '*I can't hear,*' she mouthed. And then, hoping that Polly could hear her, *'What about the others? The man and his mother?'*

Either Polly heard her or read her lips, for she glanced round the devastated room and shook her head slightly, the movement obviously paining her. The others had already begun to try to dig through the rubble and the two women joined them, but it was clear that there was little chance of finding any other survivors. Eventually, one of the men straightened up and wiped his forehead. *'We can't move any more. We'll have to get help. It's all big stuff, too heavy . . . I don't reckon there's anyone alive in here now anyway.'*

Reluctantly, they turned and battled their way out through the cluttered courtyard. Outside, the raid was still going on, although it seemed to have lessened. We must have shot down some of their planes, surely, Judy thought, and rubbed her ears, suddenly afraid that she was never going to be able to hear again. I'm deaf, she thought in panic.

The young doctor saw the gesture and looked at her in concern. *'Are you still deafened?'* she mouthed, and Judy nodded. The doctor glanced at Polly, parted her hair gently with her fingers to look at the wound in her head, and bent to give her dragging leg a swift examination. Then she straightened up and looked around.

The street was still full of people trying to fight the fires that had broken out. Soldiers, sailors and civilians alike were rushing to and fro with stirrup pumps, buckets, anything that could hold a few drops of water. At least the mains didn't seem to have been fractured this time. Judy moved to go and help, but the doctor gripped her arm.

'Hospital,' she mouthed. *'You both need to go to hospital. We need an ambulance.'* She glanced around again and then pointed to a vehicle which had apparently been abandoned at the side of the road, and a sob of hysteria rose in Judy's throat as she recognised their own old van.

One of the men who had helped her came forwards and

spoke in the doctor's ear. She nodded briskly. *'This man will take you.'* She helped Polly, who was beginning to sway, into the back of the van. Judy, more anxious for her aunt than for herself, followed, and they crouched together on the makeshift bunk fitted inside.

The journey seemed to take hours. Swaying, jerking and bumping through the bombed streets, they had no idea where they were going. Polly was looking dazed and sick, and Judy was unable to communicate with the driver. Exhaustion overtook her, her ears hurt almost unbearably, and she sagged against the cold metal walls of the van. She was unaware of their arrival at the Royal Hospital and the devastation that caused them to be turned away and sent to St James's, and when they finally stumbled out of the van she had no idea where they were.

Once in the foyer, she and Polly stood leaning against one another, almost too bewildered and exhausted to care what happened to them now. The place was in chaos, crowded with nurses, doctors and injured people. Stretchers and trolleys cluttered every space. Judy and Polly found themselves being hustled into a corner where a harassed young nurse began to question them.

'I can't hear.' Judy pointed to her ears and then held her hands over them to show that they were painful. The nurse turned at once to Polly and evidently asked about her injuries. Polly pointed to her head and then her leg, and the nurse pushed her gently on to a bed and began to examine her.

Judy watched anxiously. The head wound seemed to have stopped bleeding and was soon washed and bandaged. The leg seemed to be no worse than a superficial cut on the skin, but it was unpleasantly jagged and might have got germs in it. Having attended to these, the nurse turned her attention to Judy, but all Judy could do was mouth at her, *'I'm not hurt. It's just my ears – the blast – I've gone deaf.'* Tears came to her eyes and she shook her head angrily, furious with herself, but once started they could not be stopped and she crumpled, her hands to her face, her shoulders shaking. *I've gone deaf. I've gone deaf. I'm never going to be able to hear anything again . . .*

'Thank God I've found you.' Cissie collapsed on to a wooden chair beside Polly's bed and stared at her sister. 'Oh, thank God. I thought you and our Judy were both . . .' She couldn't say the word. Tears brimmed out of her eyes and she wiped them away and sniffed, her mouth both smiling and trembling.

'I don't know why they're keeping me in here,' Polly said grumpily. She was sitting up in bed, swathed in a huge white gown. 'I'm all right, it's just a bit of a cut on my leg and a graze on the head. But they want to keep an eye on me in case of concussion, the doctor said. I'm coming out tomorrow though, thank goodness.' She glanced around the overcrowded ward. 'They're doing their best, I know, but it's horrible in here.' She looked at her sister. 'Have you seen Judy yet?'

Cissie nodded. 'She's in a poor way. Oh, not hurt as such, but it's her ears; she can't hear a thing and she thinks she's gone deaf permanent. She's really cut up about it. I had a word with the Sister and she says they'll keep her in for a day or two to make sure there's no other damage, but she thinks the hearing'll come back pretty soon. She says it's a common effect of the blast. They get any amount of people in here just the same way, she said.'

'Oh, I hope she'll be all right. It'd be awful if she was permanently deaf, a young girl like that.' Polly lay back on her pillows. She was white and exhausted still and her voice trembled as she went on, 'She saved my life, you know, Cis. I wouldn't be here now if Judy hadn't come in and dug me out, and got those men and that young doctor to help. I'd have died in there, in all that filth and dust and –' Her voice broke and she began to cry helplessly. 'Oh Cis.'

'Polly. Polly.' Cis slipped her arms about her sister's body and held her like a baby. She always was my baby too, she thought tenderly, remembering her delight when Alice had told her she had a new sister. At twelve years old, Cissie had been of an age to be of real help, cuddling Polly and helping to wash and dress her – although she'd drawn the line at changing nappies, she remembered with a smile. She remembered too her pride as she'd pushed the pram up the street, attracting envious attention from all her friends, and her pleasure in watching the baby grow to a toddler and then a little girl, always looking up to her sister, always ready to be a companion.

Later, when Cissie had married, Polly was her bridesmaid, and when Cissie's own children had been born Polly was more like a big sister than an aunt to them. She and Judy had always been special friends, and had formed an additional link between Polly and Cissie herself. The thought that Judy had saved her aunt's life brought a lump to Cissie's throat.

'I'm sorry, Cis,' Polly wept. 'I can't seem to stop crying. I'm so ashamed – but the doctor says it's natural, it's shock. But whenever I think of being buried like that – oh, I can't tell you what it was like, it was so horrible.'

'There, there,' Cissie said soothingly. 'It's all right, Polly. You're all right now. You have a good cry. The doctor's right, it's a natural reaction. Anyone would cry after a thing like that – anyone. You just let it all out and you'll feel better.' She rocked her sister's body in her arms and went on murmuring to her, though her heart was heavy. Polly, her bright, laughing sister, reduced to this sobbing wreck. Her daughter Judy, frantic with the terror of being deaf. Her husband Dick, only just over pneumonia, choking with the dust of yet another bombing and reliving the nightmare of his experiences in the First World War. What are we coming to, she wondered, and what's going to become of us all before this is over?

'I'll have to go soon,' she whispered as Polly's sobs eased. 'I want to pop in on Judy again, and I must be back at the Royal in time to see Dick, and Mum doesn't even know where I am. By the way, you know you've got company in here from April Grove, don't you? I saw Peggy Shaw and Gladys up the other end of the ward. They were at the Royal when it got bombed last night. Peggy was thrown into some rose bushes, and Gladys has got a broken arm.' She hesitated, then decided not to tell her sister that young Graham Philpotts, the sailor who used to go out with Betty Chapman and had been calling round for Gladys just lately, had been killed. He'd been helping with the ambulance, so Peggy had told her quietly when she stopped to have a word with them, and Gladys was blaming herself. But Polly didn't need to know that – not just yet.

This awful war, she thought, making her way slowly out of the ward, sadly aware of the people around her – injured, bereaved, homeless and bewildered. This *awful* war.

Chapter Fourteen

By the beginning of May, Dick, Judy and Polly were all home again, each still somewhat shaken by their experiences. To Cissie's relief, Dick's chest hadn't been as badly affected by the dust as they had feared, but his nerves were a different matter. The violence of the raid and the close proximity of the mine that had hit the hospital had brought back all the old terrors, and his nights, and therefore Cissie's too, were broken by nightmares. In fact, she told Alice privately, that was one of the reasons they'd sent him home from the hospital – his cries and screams were keeping other patients awake. He was nervous and on edge during the day, too, likely to flare up over the least little thing, and although Cissie did her best to remember that this was all part of his illness, she couldn't help getting upset sometimes.

'Where's my glasses gone?' he demanded. 'You've been tidying up again, Cis – I can't find nothing. You've hid them deliberately.'

'Dick, of course I haven't! I wouldn't do a thing like that. I expect you've put them down somewhere and forgotten them.'

'Oh yes, it's bound to be *my* fault, isn't it! Everything that happens in this house has got to be *my* fault. Neither use nor ornament, that's me. I dare say you got on a lot better when I was in that hospital. Better send me back.' He sat down, staring angrily into space. Cissie took a deep breath and put her arms around his shoulders.

'Dick. Please don't talk like that. You know it's not true. All I want is to have you at home and feeling well again.' He had covered his face with his hands and she tried to prise them away. 'Dick, look at me. Please. Let me give you a kiss. Come on, now,' she coaxed him, talking softly, stroking his thin cheek with her fingers. 'Come on. You know you don't mean those things. And look,' she laughed suddenly, 'there are your glasses – on top of your head! They've been there all the time!'

For a moment, he looked even angrier and she was afraid that she'd upset him even more by laughing at him. Then the sense of humour that had always saved them came to the rescue again and his lips pulled into a grin. He pulled her close.

'Sorry, Cis. I'm a twerp. I dunno how you put up with me.'

'Nor do I,' she said, hugging him in relief. 'But just you thank your lucky stars I do, because I don't think you'll find another woman at your age!'

'Don't you be too sure,' he warned her, his temper over as quickly as it had arisen. 'That Ethel Glaister's been giving me some funny looks just lately!' And they both dissolved into laughter.

Polly too was plagued by nightmares. Half a dozen times a night she woke, convinced she was buried under a pile of bricks and rubble, and threw off her blankets, coughing and choking in distress. As soon as she was awake, she realised that it had been a dream, but it took several minutes to regain control of her breathing, and she lay staring into the darkness, almost afraid to go to sleep again.

Judy, who shared the small back bedroom, couldn't help her for she had still not regained her hearing. The few sounds she could hear seemed to come to her through a thick fog of distorted mush, and it was almost worse than not being able to hear at all. The normal family chatter with the wireless on in the background almost drove her demented, and she couldn't understand what anyone said unless they spoke very slowly and exaggerated their lip movements so that she could try to read them.

Even that wasn't very successful.

'Time for tea,' Cissie mouthed, and Judy stared at her blankly.

'By the sea? What's by the sea?'

Sometimes she could see the funny side of it, and laughed, but too often she became upset and angry. 'I'm fed up with this!' she cried, beating her fists together. 'I'm never going to be able to hear again, never – you don't know how awful it is! I'm going to be like this for the rest of my life, and it's like being in prison. I'm caged in all the time – it's *horrible*!'

The doorbell rang and Polly went to answer it. She came back and said to Judy, 'It's someone for you. Chris Barrett, from the Observers.' Judy stared at her uncomprehendingly, and she wrote it down on the little blackboard they'd found in Sylvie's toybox.

'I don't want to see him.'

'But he's come all this way specially.'

'Then he can go back,' Judy said abruptly. 'I don't want to see him – I don't want to see *anyone*, not while I'm like this. What d'you think he's going to say when he realises what I'm like – deaf, half out of my mind? He'll never come again anyway, so there's no point. Tell him to go away.' Her lips trembled and Polly gazed at her anxiously. Judy turned her face aside, but not before the others had seen the tears on her cheeks. 'Tell him to just go away!'

'Perhaps she'll feel a bit more up to it in a week or two,' Polly said gently to the disappointed young man. 'She's had a terrible shock, and she's really not feeling well.'

Chris shrugged. 'All right, Mrs Dunn. Shall I come back, then?'

Polly hesitated. She had no idea what the situation was between him and her niece. 'Better leave it perhaps,' she said, hoping she was doing the right thing. 'I see you out at the Beach, anyway. I can always let you know when she's feeling better.'

Shame, she thought, watching him walk off up the street. He was a nice young man and it would have done Judy good. But Judy didn't seem interested in him. Her deafness seemed to be taking over her life. Time and again she dissolved into tears of frustration and despair, and Cissie began to be seriously worried about her.

'I think she's going to have a nervous breakdown if something can't be done soon,' she told Polly as they ate a hasty breakfast of cornflakes. 'She says it makes her feel so useless. She can't go to work because she can't hear what anyone says to her or use the phone or anything, and when people talk to each other they leave her out, and that's hurtful. She feels as if she's being treated as if she's stupid.'

'I know. And she seems to be shutting herself away from everything. I mean, take that Chris Barrett – nice young feller, he is, and he's obviously a bit struck with our Judy. I was hoping they'd get together, but no. He's asked after her a few times, wanted to come round again and see her but she won't have it. Says nobody'd be interested in a deaf girl. Says it's no use him coming, she won't even go to the door to say hello. And it's not just the deafness, you know,' Polly went on. 'It's Sean as well. She's never grieved properly over him, just pushed it away. You can't do that. I should know. I tried it myself when Johnny died, but you can't put it off for ever.'

'I don't know what we ought to do about her,' Cissie said. 'She needs to get away from all this bombing. Well, we all do. Raids night after night – you know last Tuesday's was the fiftieth, don't you? It was in the *Evening News*. I mean, how are we supposed to stand it?'

'We're not,' Polly said wryly. 'But you're right, Judy needs some peace and quiet. I wonder if the people Sylvie's staying with could put her up for a few days?'

Cissie stared at her in surprise. 'Surely not! They've got those other two kiddies there too, haven't they? I don't suppose they've got room.'

'Well, she could sleep in with Sylvie. Or maybe that nice vicar where I took the Simmons girls could take her, there seemed to be plenty of rooms there. Honestly, Cis, it would do her so much good to be out in the country for a few days, and it'd be lovely there now it's May. Look, I'll talk to the Mayoress. She's really kind and helpful, and she might know of somewhere.' Polly glanced at the clock on the mantelpiece. 'Talking of the Mayoress, I'd better get a move on or I shall be late. I'm going into the main Clothing Store today, we're moving some of the stock to a church hall near Elm Grove. Apparently the Queen wrote to the Mayoress after they came here that time and said we ought to have a few more stores in case the main one got bombed. The Mayoress was already seeing to it, of course, but it just shows the Queen really thinks about these things, doesn't it?'

She gathered up her jacket, bag and gas mask, and hurried out, still limping a little. As soon as she had gone, Judy came down the stairs and Cissie heard her take the lid off the teapot to see if there was any tea left. She put her head round the scullery door.

'Has Polly gone to work?' She had accepted the fact that her voice could be heard by others, although she didn't seem able to get the level right and either whispered or shouted. It was one of the reasons why others found her so hard to talk to, Cissie thought, and felt a fresh wave of sympathy.

'Yes, she's going to the Clothing Store.' She bit her lip, aware that she'd spoken too quickly and without turning her face to Judy's. She tried again, mouthing the words with some exaggeration. '*Clothing – Store.*'

Judy flushed and Cissie knew that the exaggeration itself had upset her. She left the room quickly and then returned with a cup of tea. She put it on the table, sat down, stared at it for a few moments, then leaned her head on her hands and burst into tears.

Cissie moved swiftly round the table and took her in her arms. 'Oh you poor, poor love.' She patted her daughter's shoulders helplessly, brushed her fair hair out of her eyes, wiped her face with her hanky. 'Oh, I know you can't hear me. If only I could help you. Oh my poor, poor love – what are we going to do? What are we going to do?'

'Sorry,' Judy choked. 'Sorry, Mum. Didn't mean to start again.' She dragged in a long, sobbing breath, and leaned her head wearily on one hand while she felt for her own hanky with the other. 'I'm so *useless*. No good to anyone. I wanted to do so much.'

'Don't talk rubbish!' Cissie twisted her round so that she could see her face. Even though her daughter couldn't hear her words, she went on, knowing that she could read the expression on her face. 'That's silly and you know it! You're not useless!' She exaggerated the words. '*Not – useless*. You saved Polly's life, and you're alive too. That's what matters. And your hearing *will* come back. You're not going to be deaf for ever. The doctor said so.' She held Judy by the shoulders, looking intently into her grey eyes. Judy stared back, almost frozen, and Cissie went on more quietly, 'It's not just that, though, is it? It's not just your ears. It's Sean, isn't it?'

'Sean,' Judy whispered, showing that she had understood, and the wide grey eyes flooded with fresh tears. 'Sean – oh, *Sean*.' Once again, she bent her head and began to sob. 'Oh Mum, he's dead! Sean's dead. He's never coming back. We're never going to be married, or have babies, or *anything*. We never had any time together.' She looked down at the ring, now back on her left hand, its tiny diamond winking in the morning light, and twisted it round so that the diamond was hidden and it looked like a wedding band. 'Oh, Mum.'

'I know.' Cissie cradled her head again. Her own eyes

were wet. She and Dick hadn't been keen on the hasty engagement, so soon after the young couple had met, but it was obvious they were head over heels in love, and it was wartime. And now it was over, so swiftly it was easy to forget it had ever happened. But Judy had not forgotten.

'You'll get over it,' she whispered. 'You'll get over it, in time.'

But she knew that Judy could not hear her, and wouldn't believe her if she could.

The Lady Mayoress agreed that Judy must have some time off to recover from the shock of the raid and give her hearing a chance to return. 'She needs some peace and quiet away from these incessant raids.' She gave a small, wry smile and echoed Cissie's words: 'We all do, don't we! But Judy's had a sad time lately. You say her fiancé was lost at sea?'

'Yes. They hadn't known each other long. They wanted to get married before he went away, but there just wasn't time and my sister and her husband weren't keen. Not that they could have stopped her, of course, because she's over twenty-one, but Judy wouldn't have wanted to go against their wishes. Now she blames herself because she didn't just go ahead. She says she feels she let Sean down, and what difference would it have made, as things turned out?'

'Poor girl,' the Mayoress said. 'She must certainly have a few days off, and I agree that it would be ideal for her to get away from Portsmouth for a while. You say you think your own little girl's foster parents might take her in?'

'Yes, they might. And it would be nice for Sylvie to have her there. I'll write and ask them.' Polly went back to sorting clothes, feeling more optimistic. A week or two in the country – it sounded like bliss and would surely be just what Judy needed to set her back on her feet. She's been through too much too quickly, Polly thought. And just because the rest of us have suffered, too, doesn't mean she shouldn't be given the chance to get over it.

The main Clothing Store had been split into several different sections, each situated in a different part of the city so that even if there were another major raid, at least some of them should survive. Polly was working this morning in the Children's Swap Store, where mothers could come with the clothes their own children had grown out of and exchange them for larger sizes.

'My Johnny's right out of these flannel shorts and he can hardly get into this jacket. He's growing so fast these days.'

'Have you got a pretty party frock for my Joan? It's her twelfth birthday next week and I want to give her a nice party, with jelly and everything.'

'Look, I got this skirt and jumper here last week for my Dottie and it's all holes already. I'd have thought you'd have better quality than this, what with it being the Lady Mayoress's pigeon and all.'

Polly was constantly amazed by the requests, and even more so by the quality of some of the clothes brought for 'swapping'. 'This pullover looks as if it's been in a cupboard for years,' she said indignantly to one woman who had tipped a pillowcase full of clothes on to the long trestle table. 'And a damp cupboard, at that. Look, that's green mould, that is.'

'So what?' the woman demanded belligerently. She was a big woman, with a bosom like a shelf and a dark, mannish face. 'It's clothes, innit? You got a notice outside saying you'll swap clothes, aincher? Well, I brought some clothes to swap.'

'Yes, but,' Polly hesitated. 'They're supposed to be swapped for children. I mean,' she corrected herself, aware of a tittering amongst the queue, 'for children's clothes. This is a man's pullover. You can't just come with old clothes that nobody's used for years and take away better ones. How old are your children?'

The woman looked at her and Polly knew at once that she had no children but had simply cleared out a cupboard. Probably she would sell the clothes and then boast about having 'done the Council'. A little worm of anger stirred in Polly's stomach.

'I got six,' the woman declared. 'Six, from a six-month-old baby up to a boy of twelve, and they all needs clothes.' She waved a muscular arm to indicate the festering heap of rags on the table. 'You can see what they've had to put up with ever since this bloody war started. Running about in rags, they are, running about in rags.'

'I'm surprised they're still in Portsmouth,' Polly said boldly, determined to call the woman's bluff. 'Haven't they been evacuated?'

The woman hesitated. 'No. Yes. Well, they *was* – but they come back, see, when there wasn't no raids. Anyway, the baby couldn't go without me, now could she, and what with my hubby being away at sea since the war broke out I got lonely on me own, and—'

'Didn't stay lonely for long then, did you?' someone in the queue butted in. 'Not if the baby's only six months old! Come on, Madge Perkins, you know you never got no kids, so why don't you take your rubbish and get out? Runs a rag-and-bone shop down Rudmore, she does,' the speaker continued indignantly, as the woman turned with a fearsome expression on her face and bunched a massive fist. 'And her hubby died years ago – it was the only way he could get away from her. And you needn't wave your fists at me, neither,' she added, squaring up as the queue joined in with resentful muttering. 'I can fight me corner as well as anyone.'

'Not in here though, please,' Polly intervened hastily. She scooped the rags back into the pillowcase and thrust it at Madge Perkins. 'Take this with you and go, please. If you have clothes to donate – decent clothes, in reasonable condition – one of the other Clothing Stores will be pleased to receive them.'

'And give me nothing for 'em!' The big woman snatched up the bag and glared at her. 'I can't afford to go giving stuff away. I'm not rolling in money. Call this a charity? You Council people, you're all the same, take it all off us in rates and then wants the clothes off our backs as well. I tell you, I'm doing good work with my trade, work for the war effort. And as for you, Jean Barstow,' she turned on the woman who had challenged her, 'I'll have something to say to your Billy next time he comes round wanting to sell me rags and bones. I give him too much for the last lot, out of the goodness of me heart, and look how you repays me!'

She stalked out furiously and the queue made way for her, glowering and muttering. Mrs Barstow poked her tongue out at her departing back and then turned to Polly.

'You don't want to take no notice of Madge Perkins, missus. She'd try it on with anyone. She'll be round all the stores with that lot, trying to get something for it, and it's all stuff that other people have chucked out. Trying to get summat better and then sell it on, that's what she was doing. Talk about working for the war effort!'

'That's right,' someone else chimed in. 'Trying to make money out of the war. Unpatriotic, I call it.'

The queue murmured in agreement and Polly inspected the clothes that Mrs Barstow had brought in. There were two pairs of boys' flannel shorts, a jacket and a girl's skirt and cardigan, both home made. They had all seen better days and she wasn't at all sure that she'd be able to pass them on to anyone else, but she was grateful to the woman for sending Mrs Perkins packing and wanted to help her.

'How many children d'you have?'

'Boy and girl, both ten. They're twins,' she added unnecessarily. 'They're not identical though, see, 'cause they're a boy and girl.'

'Well, I can let you have one pair of shorts and a jacket

for the boy, and there are some skirts over there that might suit your little girl, and some jumpers and cardigans. I'm afraid you can only have one of each garment,' she added apologetically. 'Not everything we get brought in is suitable to be passed on.'

'Not as bad as Madge's stuff, though,' Mrs Barstow said cheerfully. 'OK, missus, I'll have a look through and pick summat out. The boy's things'll be easy enough, but my Susie's getting a bit fussy about what she wears now. I tell her there's a war on and she'll have to be grateful for what she can get, but you know what kiddies are, they don't really understand, do they?' She moved along the table, turning over the neatly folded garments while Polly turned her attention to the next customer.

As soon as she had finished, she went home to write to Mrs Sutton to ask if she could put Judy up for a few days. *I know it's asking a lot,* she wrote, *but my niece really does need some peace and quiet, and I don't know where else to try. We'd pay for her keep of course, and I know she'd give a hand wherever she could.* She chewed the end of her pen, wondering how to end the letter. Whatever else she thought of sounded as if she were trying to make it difficult for Mrs Sutton to refuse, and she didn't want to do that. In the end, she just wrote, *Yours sincerely, P.M. Dunn* and left it at that.

The reply came two days later. It was waiting for Polly when she came home from the hairdresser's, where she was now working for just two or three hours each day after her stint at the Clothing Store. Worn out with standing all day, she dropped into a chair and opened the letter while Cissie brought her a cup of tea.

'Well, isn't that lovely!' She raised a smiling face as Cissie came in from the scullery. 'Mrs Sutton says Judy will be welcome to go and stay with them, so long as she doesn't mind sleeping in the same room as the two girls. She won't mind that, will she?'

'I'm sure she won't,' Cissie was beginning, when Judy herself interrupted them. Her face was flushed and angry.

'You're talking about me – I know you are! What are you saying? What's that letter about?' She jumped up from her chair, trembling. 'You're sending me away. You think I'm mental as well as deaf, and you're sending me away! Aren't you? *Aren't* you?'

'Judy, *no*!' Polly and Cissie spoke together, gazing at her in distress. 'It's not that at all,' Cissie went on, speaking far too quickly for Judy to follow, but Polly brushed her aside and held out the letter. 'Here, read it for yourself. It's from Mrs Sutton,' she said, speaking slowly and clearly so that Judy could read her lips. 'Mrs Sutton. Where Sylvie is. Read it, Judy.'

Judy took the letter, still gazing at her face, a slight, puzzled frown creasing her forehead. She looked down at the sheet of paper and then sat down slowly. Polly heaved a sigh of relief and sank back into her own chair, taking the cup of tea Cissie was still holding out.

'Mrs Sutton,' Judy said in her odd, painful voice. 'Mrs Sutton – she says I can go and stay there?' She looked at Polly. 'You wrote to her.'

'Yes, I wrote the day before yesterday and she's answered straight away.' Polly forgot to speak slowly. 'Isn't that kind of her? You'll like her, Judy, and Sylvie will be so pleased to have her auntie there. And it'll be lovely there now, all the spring flowers will be out and there'll be lambs and—'

'You wrote to her,' Judy said, ignoring her. 'You wrote and told her about me.'

'Well – yes.' Polly began to feel uncomfortable. Judy didn't seem pleased at all. 'I was worried about you, Judy. We all are. We think you need a few days away, out in the country where you can—' She recalled that Judy could barely follow one word in three of this. 'We want you to have a holiday,' she enunciated. 'Some peace and quiet. To help you get better.'

She stopped uncertainly. Judy seemed to understand, but she didn't look any more pleased. She stared from Polly to her mother, then back at the letter in her hand. 'Why didn't you ask me?' she said. 'Why didn't you tell me you were writing?'

Polly glanced helplessly at her sister and Cissie said, 'We only wanted to do what was best for you, love.'

'But why didn't you *ask* me? I've been here all the time. I've still got a brain, you know – I can still decide what I want to do! What if I don't want to go? What if I'd rather stay here?' Her voice trembled. 'I want to go back to work. I want to be *useful*. I don't want to be sent away to the country like a – like a little child. And don't you understand? Don't *any* of you understand what it'll be like for me? Not being able to hear what people say? Being with strangers, and not being able to hear what they say?'

Cissie and Polly looked at each other. Polly put her teacup back on the table and spoke again, very slowly, looking directly into Judy's eyes.

'Judy. Nobody is treating you like a child. We want to help you get better. You need to be away from Portsmouth – away from the bombs. Away from noise. Please go. Just for a few days. That's all we want you to do. *Please*. And the Suttons will understand – I know they will. They're kind people, Judy.'

There was a long silence. Judy looked down at the letter again. Her face was pale. Then she said, 'Just for a few days?'

'Yes. That's all, really. Just to see if it helps.'

'And I'd see Sylvie. It seems so long since I saw Sylvie.'

'She'd love to see you,' Polly said quietly, thinking how long it was since she herself had seen her daughter. Not since that brief hour when she'd taken Stella and Muriel to Bridge End. When the children had first been evacuated, all the parents had expected to be able to visit them regularly – you could even get the fare paid for two or three visits – but once the raids had started there just hadn't been the chance. Railways stations were full of posters – *Is Your Journey Really Necessary?* – and there was so much to do at home. 'I'd feel happier about her if I knew you'd had a chance to spend a few days there,' she said to Judy.

Judy seemed to understand the gist of what she was saying. She nodded and her mouth twisted into a wry smile. 'Well, I suppose I'd better go, then. But only for a few days,' she added warningly. 'I'm not being sent away for ever.'

'Of course not!' Cissie threw her arms around her and kissed her. 'Oh Judy, I'm so glad! It'll do you good, I know it will. And they have much better food out in the country too – lots of milk, and butter and proper eggs. You need a bit of building up. You've been looking so peaky and washed-out lately. Now, we'd better sort out what you're going to take with you. There's that blue skirt you got from the Clothing Store after we were bombed, and you can take my best blouse, and—'

'Wait a minute!' Judy cried, only half understanding what her mother was saying. 'Can't you wait to get rid of me? I didn't say I'd go this minute.'

'No, but there's no point in waiting, is there? Mrs Sutton says she's expecting you any day. And we're just having a spell of nice weather too, so you may as well make the most of it.' Cissie was not to be deflected. She ran upstairs and began pulling open cupboards and drawers. Judy glanced at Polly and smiled ruefully.

'You're determined to make me go, aren't you? But what about Dad? He's the one who's been ill – he could do with a few days in the country. Where is he, anyway?'

'He's gone for a walk,' Polly said. 'You might not have noticed it, but he's really improving with this nice sunny spell. He's gone over to Langstone Harbour – said he just wants to rest his eyes on some water. It's months since he was on the shore.' She saw Judy's face and repeated the main words more slowly, until Judy understood. Then she said, 'You won't feel too awkward, will you, Judy, when you're at the Suttons'? They know about what's happened. And your hearing is getting better, isn't it? You can hear some things now.'

Judy shrugged. 'No, not really. I'm just getting a bit better at lip-reading.'

'Well, I still think this is what you need.' Polly looked into her cup and then stood up. 'This tea's gone cold. I'll make some more, and then help Cissie with supper.' She bent and gave Judy an awkward kiss. 'I'm glad you're going. It'll do you so much good.'

Judy shrugged. 'Perhaps. But it's not going to bring Sean back, is it?' She looked at her aunt. 'I may get my hearing back, but I'll never have my sweetheart again.'

Chapter Fifteen

The whole family walked down to the tiny station next morning to wave Judy off. With a small suitcase from the store, her gas mask in its cardboard box, and two brown paper carrier bags, she looked like a waif as she climbed aboard the train, and there were tears in all the women's eyes. Even Dick cleared his throat rather often, and hugged his daughter tightly before letting her go.

'It's only for a week or so,' she said, leaning out of the window. 'You don't have to look as if you're never going to see me again.'

'Don't talk like that,' Cissie begged her, but what with her deafness and the noise the engine was making, there was no chance of Judy's hearing her. However, she had learned to lip-read surprisingly well and grinned impudently at her mother.

'I might not want to come back. I might decide to stay.'

'Don't you dare! Not but what it wouldn't be good to know you were safe.' The whistle of the engine drowned her words and the train began to pull away. Suddenly crying in earnest, Cissie waved frantically and turned to her husband to bury her face against his shoulder. 'Oh Dick, she's gone! Oh, I hope she'll be all right, going all by herself. I hope we've done the right thing.'

'Of course we've done the right thing – and she's only going to Ashwood. It's not the other end of the world. You're going on as if she was off to the Front.'

'I know.' She sniffed and laughed a little. 'I'm being silly. It's just that so much has happened, and you never know what's going to happen next, and just saying goodbye, even for only a week, makes you think about all the people who go away and never come back, or perhaps there's no home to come back *to*. Oh, I know I'm being silly, I'm talking a lot of nonsense.'

'It's all right, love,' Dick said quietly. 'You're not talking nonsense. We've been through some terrible times, you're bound to worry. And I know you worry about our Terry too, same as I do. We don't know where he is half the time, and all we can do is hope we don't hear it's his ship that's got sunk. It's worry we never thought we'd have, and more than anyone should have to put up with. And I'm not a lot of help to you,' he added ruefully.

'You mustn't say that.' They had begun to walk away from the station. 'You don't know how empty the house seemed while you were in hospital. I feel like I'm just half a person when you're not there.' Cissie stopped and looked into his eyes. 'You're only ill because of what happened to you in the Great War. That was cruel, and you've been suffering ever since. It's not your fault.' She took hold of both his hands. 'Shall I tell you what I think? You're *still* serving your country. Every time you wheeze or cough, you're serving your country, because you wouldn't be like it if you hadn't gone to serve it then. And I thank God on my knees every day – *every day* – that you came home. So don't ever say you're no use. *Ever.*'

'And so say all of us,' Alice said fervently, and Polly agreed.

'We'll go home and have a cup of tea,' she said, 'and then I'll be off down to the Centre.' She lifted her face to the May sunshine. 'Do you realise, we've had five nights now without a raid? Five nights of peace in our own beds. I can't believe it.'

'Nor can I,' Dick said, 'but it won't last. Mark my words, the Germans haven't finished with us yet.' He, too, looked at the blue, innocent sky with its drifting fleet of silver barrage balloons. 'They'll be back. Sure as God made little chickens, they'll be back.'

Judy sat on the train, feeling a little sick. She had refused both her mother's and her aunt's offers to come with her, insisting that she could manage – 'I've only got to get off the train and walk down the lane to the farm' – but inside she felt apprehensive. Suppose the train broke down, or went the wrong way, or she didn't recognise the station when they arrived there? All the signs had been taken down, and she had only Polly's description to go by, and the stations all looked more or less the same. Because she wouldn't be able to hear any announcements, they'd taken the precaution of asking the guard to make sure she got off there, but suppose he forgot? And suppose someone got into the compartment and tried to talk to her? Suppose she got lost and had to ask for directions? Tears came into her eyes as she reflected that even a simple thing like a train journey seemed almost impossible when you were deaf.

Angrily, she brushed the tears away. She had seen enough injuries, and enough death too, during the air raids and in hospital, to know that she had escaped quite lightly in comparison with others. Awake night after night, she'd told herself over and over again that losing her hearing was nothing – *nothing* – and if it really did get better, as the doctors thought it would, then she had no reason to complain. No reason at all to be sorry for herself. No reason for this incessant weeping that kept overtaking her. No reason to get so angry with her mother and aunt just because they tried to help. No reason to feel so *useless*.

Yet everything seemed to be so difficult. The simplest tasks – going shopping, answering the door – seemed suddenly to be almost impossible. Making herself understood was easier, although she suspected her voice was coming out oddly, either too quiet or too loud, but trying to make out what others were saying drove her into a frenzy of frustration. I'll have to learn sign language, she thought, but that was only any use if everyone else learned it too. And she felt left out of conversations. You couldn't expect people to say everything slowly; you just had to sit by, knowing they were talking and laughing but with no idea what the subject or the joke was. It was even worse when they listened to the wireless and you could see them looking dismayed by the news or laughing at *ITMA* or Arthur Askey. It was like living in a glass cage.

There I go again, she thought impatiently, feeling sorry for myself. I've just got to grow up and get on with it. There are worse things than being deaf. Being blind, for instance. Not being able to see this lovely countryside, the cows and sheep and the lambs, skipping about in the grass. The trees all coming into fresh green leaf. The blossom on the wild cherries and the apple trees that had grown beside the track, from cores people had thrown out years ago.

But other people were different when you were blind. They were helpful, considerate. They still treated you as a human being, they took your arm and guided you along, they *talked* to you.

If you were deaf, they treated you as though you were stupid. They talked to you for a few minutes, making big shapes with their mouths, and then they left you out. After a while, it was as if you weren't there at all. As if you were invisible.

The train trundled through the countryside, stopping at every small station and halt and sometimes in between for unexplained rests. The actual distance to the village where Sylvie lived wasn't very great, but the journey took almost two hours and at every stop someone got on or off. There were servicemen and women, Land Girls, civilians in shabby coats or smart suits, workmen carrying bags of tools, and a vicar. He was a tall, spindly man with long arms and legs, and he smiled kindly at Judy as he sat in the corner opposite her. As she had dreaded someone would, he began to make conversation.

'I'm sorry,' she said, pointing at her ears. 'I can't hear.'

His mouth made an 'oh dear' shape, and he looked concerned. *'Since birth?'* he mouthed. *'Or an accident?'*

'Bomb blast,' Judy said briefly. 'In Portsmouth.'

'Portsmouth?' He said something she couldn't catch, then mouthed again. *'I have evacuees from Portsmouth.'*

Judy nodded. She didn't really want the struggle of conversation with a stranger but the vicar was clearly trying hard not to let her feel ignored. The other passengers had stopped their own conversation and were watching and listening. Feeling self-conscious, she said, 'There are some children in our street evacuated out this way somewhere. A village called Bridge End.'

'Bridge End? But that's where I live!' He leaned forwards and repeated his words more slowly. 'Perhaps you know them. Tim and Keith Budd.'

The names were easy to read. Judy forgot her self-consciousness and nodded eagerly. 'I know them! They live in April Grove. My granny lives there too, and we went to stay with her when we were bombed out.' She remembered her aunt's visit here. 'You've got Stella and Muriel Simmons too.'

'That's right.' He looked enormously pleased to have found this point of contact. 'Such sweet girls, and such a sad story. But they're settling in very well.'

'It was my auntie who brought them to you,' Judy said, not really understanding all his words but able to pick up a few. 'Polly Dunn. Do you remember her?'

'Mrs Dunn! Of course I remember! Such a nice woman. So you're her niece.' He sat back and smiled broadly. 'Well, how very pleasant. Are you coming to Bridge End on a visit?'

Once again, she was able to recognise the important words. Perhaps it was because he was a vicar, and used to talking clearly in church. 'No, I'm going on to Ashwood. My niece Sylvie – Polly's little girl – is evacuated there. I'm going to stay with her foster family for a while. The doctors think it might help me get my hearing back.' She had forgotten her shyness, delighted to find someone so easy to talk to, someone who had met Polly and knew people she knew. 'It's shock, you see, and blast, not actual damage.'

'Then I'm sure a stay at Ashwood will do you the world of good. And why don't you try to bring Sylvie over to Bridge End to see us one day? I'm sure Stella and Muriel would like to see an old friend.'

'I don't think they'd know her,' Judy said, having disentangled this invitation. 'But she'd like to come, I'm sure. I'll see if we can manage it.'

The train arrived at yet another small station and the vicar glanced out of the window and jumped to his feet, knocking his head on the luggage rack as he did so. He rubbed his head ruefully and smiled at Judy. 'I'm always doing that. I can never remember how tall I am. Now, don't forget, bring Sylvie over to see us the first chance you get. I'm very easy to find. The vicarage is right beside the church, and my name's Mr Beckett. Everyone knows me.' The train had stopped and he opened the door, tumbling out on to the platform in a tangle of arms and legs. Judy smiled and waved at him, and the other occupants of the compartment laughed.

'I just bet everyone knows him!' said a woman who happened to be looking Judy's way as she spoke. 'A real character, he is.' The rest of the conversation was lost as she turned away and the other passengers joined in, but for once Judy didn't feel left out. She sat back in her corner and smiled to herself, still feeling the warmth of the vicar's conversation and the attention he'd paid to her. Some people understood, then, she thought. Some people understood what it was to be deaf.

*

Ashwood station was only a few miles further down the line and the guard remembered to walk along the platform and open the compartment door for her. Judy smiled her thanks and scrambled down, lugging her suitcase and carrier bags. She stood for a moment on the platform, gathering her thoughts, and then turned quickly as she felt someone tap her arm.

'Sylvie!' With a cry of delight, she scooped the little girl into her arms. 'Oh Sylvie, how lovely! How did you know I'd be on this train?'

Sylvie hugged her aunt and beamed up at her, her lips moving quickly as she chattered. Judy felt a swift lurch of dismay; she'd known she wouldn't be able to hear Sylvie's voice, of course she'd known, but somehow the realisation seemed to hit her more bitterly than since she'd first found she was deaf. 'I'm sorry, Sylvie,' she said regretfully. 'I don't know what you're saying. You have to speak very slowly, and make sure I can see your mouth move. Like this.' She mouthed a few words and to her surprise Sylvie burst into giggles.

'Auntie Judy! You are funny!'

'Funny?' For a moment, Judy felt indignant. Nobody had dared suggest she was funny – indeed, she was sure nobody had even thought so. But suddenly, looking down at the child's bright face, innocent of either embarrassment or the wish to hurt, she laughed. Maybe she *was* funny! Maybe that was the best way to treat this affliction – laugh at it. She bent again and hugged her niece, lifting her in her arms to whirl her round in the air.

'Whee!' The child's scream of pleasure vibrated against her body and Judy set her down again, trembling a little. It was almost like hearing. Perhaps it would come back after all, she thought with a lift of hope.

Sylvie was urging her to come with her now, picking up one of the carrier bags in one hand and dragging Judy by the other. Together, they hurried out of the station and along the lane. Judy looked around her and felt her heart move.

Born and brought up in Portsmouth, she had never been far into the countryside. Before the war started, the family had gone up on Portsdown Hill sometimes for picnics, or caught a bus out to Denmead or Catisfield. Once or twice they'd gone to Petersfield and wandered by the lake, and they'd found bluebell woods and come home with arms full of scented flowers. But for the past eighteen months such jaunts had been impossible, and it was a long time since they'd had a family picnic. Now, the feeling of space and the sense of peace was like a balm to the soreness of her mind.

The lane leading from the station was wide enough for a horse and cart and roughly metalled. It ran between hedges laced with fresh new green, and mossy banks clothed like a king's robes with the gold and purple of primroses and violets. The hedges were alive with birds, darting in and out of the branches, their beaks stuffed with worms and insects. They must all have nests in there, Judy thought in wonder. And I expect they're singing too. It's lovely!

The sky was a soft blue and the sun warm. Sylvie skipped beside her, one hand still clasped in Judy's. Every now and then she peeped up at her aunt and laughed, and Judy laughed back. Mum and Polly were right, she thought. This is what I need. But then, it's probably what *everyone* needs.

In ten minutes, they were at the farmyard gate. Sylvie stopped to unfasten it, putting down the bag to do so, and Judy went through, looking about her with interest. She had never been in a farmyard before, and her knowledge came mostly from picture-books she had had as a child, showing chickens and ducks scratching about the yard, cows in the fields and maybe a horse looking over a stable door.

To her astonishment, that was exactly what it did look like. There was even a big, swaggering rooster, its head crowned with a scarlet cockscomb, its tail spraying out like an iridescent rainbow behind it. It stared at Judy, tilting its head, and she stopped for a moment, feeling as if she had actually strayed into her own childhood picture-book, and gave a laugh of pure pleasure.

I'm laughing! she thought in amazement. I'm actually *laughing*!

The farmhouse itself was a long, low building with a thatched roof and a row of small windows like eyes set beneath curved arches in the thatch. A wide doorway gave it the appearance of a smiling face, and there were flowers growing along its walls. On the far side of the yard there was a well, with a little roof over it, and a woman who was winding up the handle turned at the click of the latch and her face broke into a smile. Hastily, she brought the bucket up to the top, unhooked it and set it on the ground before hurrying over, wiping wet hands on her flowery pinafore.

'Miss Taylor! So you're here! Sylvie's been down to the station all morning, hoping you'd come soon. It's a pleasure to see you, it really is.' She remembered Judy's deafness and repeated her words more slowly, smiling all the time. Her face was round and rosy, her silver-grey hair scraped back into a bun, her figure as comfortable as a cushion. She took both Judy's hands in hers and clasped them warmly.

'Thank you,' Judy said, liking Mrs Sutton at once. No wonder Polly felt happy about her daughter being here. 'It's so kind of you to let me come and stay. And please, call me Judy. Everyone does.'

'Judy. That's a nice name. Now, come in and I'll make some tea.' Mrs Sutton was still speaking slowly, but when she turned away her words were lost. Judy followed her in, ducking her head to go through the low doorway, and standing for a moment to let her eyes get accustomed to the darkness. Sylvie, beside her, squeezed her hand.

It's like a house in a fairytale, she thought, looking about her. The room was not very big – perhaps a couple of feet all round larger than the rooms in April Grove – but it was different from any room she had ever been in. The walls were almost three feet thick and built of huge, uneven blocks of stone. The fireplace was like a small room in itself, sunk deep into the wall and with two stone shelves like seats at the sides. Above one was a small iron door with a handle, and Judy stared at it, wondering what it could be.

Over the fireplace was a lintel that could have made a respectable tombstone, with another great slab down one side. There was no fire burning, but a pile of logs on a mound of ash indicated that cold nights would be cosy in here. A couple of shabby armchairs, placed in the alcoves on either side and covered with chintz in a faded flower pattern, seemed to throw out an invitation to sink into them and rest.

There were other chairs too, and a couple of stools as well as a squashed and battered pouffe that looked as if it had been used by generations of children. In one corner stood a small grandfather clock, its swinging brass pendulum shining like a beacon, and a shelf ran round the room about a foot below the ceiling, with jugs of all colours and sizes ranged upon it. The floor was of stone flags, warmed by colourful rag rugs; the walls were washed a rich cream, broken by wooden beams, and the ceiling was supported by similar beams.

Mrs Sutton had bustled through another door to a room at the back of the house. Sylvie gave Judy a gentle push and she went obediently after her hostess and found her in a large kitchen, with a kitchen range at one end. Judy sat down at the big kitchen table and looked at the dresser with its rows of blue and white striped crockery, thinking how cheerful it all looked.

Sylvie placed herself in front of Judy and spoke slowly and importantly. 'This is the kitchen. We have our dinner here. This is Bossy.' She lifted a large tabby cat from one of the chairs and held him up for inspection. He hung like a rag doll in her arms, sleepy eyes barely open, and Judy stroked his big striped head. Sylvie dumped him down on the chair again like a pile of washing. 'We've got a dog too.'

She was still remembering to speak slowly and clearly. 'He's called Flash. He's out with Uncle Bob. He collects sheep.'

Judy had a vision of the dog with his collection of sheep, poring over them as her brother Terry used to do with his stamp collection. She laughed and Mrs Sutton, standing at the range and pouring water from a kettle into a big brown teapot, looked round and smiled. She said something Judy couldn't hear, but she looked pleased and Judy thought she could guess what the remark had been. Polly had told her that she was low in her spirits, and the farmer's wife was glad to hear her laugh.

All the same, it was no easier to take part in conversations here than it had been at home. The country accent was difficult for Judy to read, and when Mr Sutton came in for dinner with the collie dog Flash at his heels she found that he talked almost without opening his mouth, so that it was almost impossible to read his words. He was welcoming enough and shook her hand warmly, but he seemed shy and wouldn't look her full in the face, which made it even harder to understand him. When he was followed in by Jenny and Brian, the other two evacuees, the chatter became impossible to follow and Judy's initial optimism faded a little. She sat looking at the table, scarred with many years of use, while the conversation flowed about her unheard.

Dinner was toad-in-the-hole with cabbage and potatoes, followed by rice pudding. Afterwards, she helped wash up and then Sylvie took her upstairs to show her where she was to sleep.

The room was the same size as the one downstairs, its uneven walls distempered in a sunny yellow and with yellow gingham curtains at the low window. There was a cupboard in one corner and a chest of drawers. Against one wall were two bunks, both neatly made with patchwork quilts spread over them.

'This is where me and Jenny sleep. My bed's the bottom one. But you're going to sleep in it now, and I'm going to be on the floor.' A mattress had been laid under the window. It looked comfortable enough, and Sylvie knelt on it to lean on the wide windowsill and gaze down into the garden. She turned after a moment and looked enquiringly at her aunt, and Judy realised she must have said something.

She pointed at her ears. 'I didn't hear you. Say it again.' But Sylvie shrugged and shook her head, as if what she had said wasn't worth repeating.

Judy felt a familiar flash of irritation. This happened time and time again. People made casual remarks but when they were unheard, couldn't be bothered to repeat them. It made her feel even more cut off – as if she had no choice in what she was allowed to hear, as if she didn't matter. It made no difference that on the occasions when someone did repeat their casual remarks she thought herself that they weren't worth repeating – she just wanted to *hear*. She wanted to hear *everything* – like other people. Like she had before. She wanted to be able to make up her own mind about what was worth hearing.

The irritation quickly faded, however. It wasn't Sylvie's fault, and she'd been very good about talking directly to Judy. She was pointing down into the garden now, saying something about an apple tree. Judy knelt beside her and found that she was gazing out into an orchard at the back of the house. She gave a little gasp of delight.

The orchard contained a dozen or so trees, every one smothered in blossom. A foam of pale pink and white seemed to wash like waves on the seashore right up to the walls of the house, reaching just below the window. Their scent drifted in through the open window, filling the room with delicate fragrance. Below them, revealed only in glimpses, the grass was sprinkled with late daffodils and Judy saw the cat, Bossy, who had been ejected from his chair at dinnertime, slumbering in a corner, warmed by sunlight.

Judy felt a warmth steal over her body and into her heart.

I'm going to be happy here, she thought. It was the right thing to do. If I can get better anywhere, it will be here.

She gave her cousin a hug. 'Show me the rest of the farm,' she said. 'Show me *everything*.'

Chapter Sixteen

It was not until she experienced the peace of the countryside that Judy realised just how much she had been affected by the terror of the raids on Portsmouth.

For a few days, she just roamed about in a dream. The weather stayed fine and after she had helped Mrs Sutton to tidy the bedrooms and wash some of the everlasting supply of dirty clothes from the children and Mr Sutton, she was free to go outside and lift her face to the sunshine. Often, she took a bowl of vegetables out into the garden and sat on an old chair, preparing them, but more than that Mrs Sutton refused to allow her to do. 'You're here to get built up, not do housework,' she said, making her meaning plain. 'You go for a nice walk. There might be a few bluebells starting to come out.'

The children were at school in the mornings, and Judy wandered alone down the lanes, drinking in the scent of the flowers that bordered the way, and wishing she could hear the song of the birds. She came to the village and stood for a moment gazing at the green with its pond, alive with tadpoles, but turned away quickly when she saw an old man hobbling her way. She wasn't ready to meet strangers, who wouldn't understand her deafness. On her own, with no need to strain to hear, she felt herself again.

Arriving at a crossroads, she took a different way and found herself close to some woods. As Mrs Sutton had suggested, they were filled with early bluebells just beginning to come out – a sea of misty colour rippling in the green dappled light that filtered down through the leaves above. Judy gave a little gasp of pleasure and dropped down amongst them, stretching herself out and breathing in their fragrance. She turned over and gazed up through the leaves at the sky. I could be happy in a place like this, she thought. I could be happy here for ever.

Back in Portsmouth, on the night after Judy left, there was a raid which was concentrated on the Hilsea area, with several high-explosive bombs being dropped close to the gasworks and on the main railway line. A lot of houses were hit too, and three people killed, one of them a friend of Polly's.

'I knew her at school. We used to sit next to each other when we were in Miss Jenkins's class. She went to work at Lipton's, and then she got married to a chap from Tipnor way – dockyardman, he was till he went in the Army.' Polly wiped her eyes. 'They had two boys, must be about my Sylvie's age. I suppose they were evacuated, poor little souls.'

'It's awful for kiddies, losing their mums and dads,' Cissie said. 'Like those two little Simmons girls. Our Judy's going to try to get across to see them, you know. It's not far.'

'She'll see Jess Budd's boys too, then,' Dick observed. 'Not bad nippers, though the older one's a bit of a scamp. He used to knock about with Micky Baxter, you know, when his mother wasn't looking. I should think she's glad to have him out of the way. That boy's a bad influence.'

'Oh, he's not so bad,' Alice said. 'I saw him down Charlotte Street the other day, working on one of the stalls. He told me he's been given a delivery bike, got a little round of his own. Said he wants to join the Army soon as he's old enough – wants to be a hero.'

'Hero!' Dick snorted. 'Dunno what sort of a hero that boy'd be! Look at the trouble he got those other poor little tykes into – Jimmy Cross with one leg blown off, and that Nash boy killed outright. I'd be glad to have *my* youngster out of his way, I can tell you.'

Now that the weather was better, Dick's health had improved and he was able to get out into the back garden and do some digging. The patch where Alice had grown lupins, sweet williams and bunny-rabbits was now entirely given over to vegetables and a couple of currant bushes. Frank Budd, from number fourteen, had given Dick some cabbage seedlings from his allotment, and he had already harvested several pounds of new potatoes and baby carrots. He had also managed to get some sticks for a row of peas and runner beans.

'Dig for Victory,' he said, going out to the shed to fetch his gardening tools. 'Well, at least I can be a bit of use around the place.'

Polly was working almost full-time now as a WVS volunteer. She still did some hairdressing, but it was mostly during the evenings or on Saturday afternoons. For the rest of the time she found herself carrying out a huge variety of tasks – from organising salvage drives to collecting saucepans, jelly moulds and kettles for their aluminium, to sweeping up nuts and bolts from factory floors for re-use. Every time the air-raid warning went, she hurried off to present herself at the Emergency Centre, where she collected her old ambulance van and prepared to dash off to the site of the nearest bomb damage.

Often, the raid came to very little, with the planes droning overhead on their way to London, Bristol or some other city. But you never knew when the siren went whether this would be such a night, or whether it was the beginning of another ferocious attack. And you never knew if they might jettison some leftover bombs on the way back. You could never feel safe. Not until the 'Raiders Passed' – or, as most people now called it, the 'All Clear' – sounded its comforting wail.

Cissie and Alice too were doing their bit for the war effort. Alice went to the Centre on the days after a raid and spent her time making tea and sandwiches. On other days she and Cissie presented themselves at one of the two communal feeding centres, where meals were provided for all those who couldn't cook their own, or were unable to get groceries from the shops. There wasn't much variety – just soup at a penny a cup or a plate of minced beef and potatoes at three or fourpence a time – but customers arrived in droves, and when the tables and chairs were all occupied they sat on the floor, the stairs and even outside in the street to eat. The Centres were invariably sold out by one o'clock.

It did seem, however, as if the raids were easing off. After the one on the night following Judy's departure to Ashwood, there was a lull. People began to look and feel better. It was almost summer, they were getting more sleep and some of the bomb damage was being patched up. You could almost think about smiling again.

Not that there was much else to smile about. The war was looking bad in Europe. Yugoslavia and Greece had both been overrun, with Allied forces having to be evacuated from Greece and Crete – 'just like Dunkirk all over again,' Dick said bitterly – and at home there had been devastating raids on Plymouth, Liverpool, Newcastle and Bristol. At this rate, there wouldn't be a city left in the whole country. It wouldn't be worth invading.

Yet the fear of invasion was still very strong. All around the coasts barbed wire was being put up along the beaches, so you couldn't even go for a swim any more, and the Home Guard was on permanent alert. The signal for an invasion was the ringing of the church bells, so they were silenced on every other occasion and Sunday mornings were quiet. You didn't know how much you'd enjoyed hearing the bells till they weren't there any more, Cissie remarked.

At Ashwood, Judy would have welcomed hearing anything at all. She went for walks every day, wishing she could hear the birds singing or the rustling of leaves and the whisper of grass. She avoided meeting the village people or even the other evacuees, knowing they would be embarrassed by her deafness or even think there was something 'strange' about her. They probably think that anyway, she thought sadly, noticing a small group of children cross to the other side of the lane as she approached. They'll be saying I'm mental, or a witch or something. She wondered how many people in the past had become objects of fear or derision simply because they were deaf, or frail in some other way. Lonely old women, stuck in tumbledown cottages because people were afraid to help them. Grumpy old men, surly because they were hurt by their neighbours' treatment of them.

Is this going to happen to me? she wondered. Suppose I never get my hearing back? Am I going to spend the rest of my life like this, avoiding people just because I'm afraid they'll treat me like a leper?

The thought of Sean haunted her still. She grieved for him, yet she had an uneasy feeling that her grief should have been deeper. I *loved* him, she thought, twisting the little ring on her finger. I ought to be even unhappier . . . yet to her dismay she could barely remember what he looked like. She hadn't even a photograph to remember him by. The only person in the family to own a camera was Dick, who had had a box Brownie, lost in the bombing, and with film so hard to come by he had never taken a picture of Sean. Judy tried to capture Sean's face in her mind but it was elusive, fading away every time she thought she had conjured it up. Perhaps it was because they had known each other such a short time; there were so few memories.

She stopped and leaned on a field gate. Another memory came into her mind – a brief glimpse of a tall, fair-haired young man in RAF uniform with a Spitfire badge on his arm. Chris Barrett. She thought of his ready grin, the flash of white teeth and the crinkling of blue eyes. She thought of the hour or so they had spent together trapped in the lift, the easy conversation, the feeling of comfort he had given her.

She thought of his kiss.

With an angry shrug, she pushed the memory away and stared into the field where lambs were playing tag around their mothers' stolid bodies. One jumped up on top of its mother's back, and stood there for all the world as if it were laughing at its playmates. Half a dozen raced off to a grassy knoll and began to skip up to the top and then down again. Another little gang began running races from one side of the field to the other, and soon all had joined in, breaking off after a few minutes to rush back to their mothers for a drink.

Judy watched them and laughed suddenly. I can't hear them but I can still see them, she thought. There's still plenty of joy to be had, and it doesn't help Sean or anyone else to pretend it isn't there. And, with sudden energy, I *don't* have to be sorry for myself – I can still do things to help. I'm fit and strong, and I shouldn't be drifting about as if I'm on holiday. The WVS works even out here in the country, and I ought to be doing something too. I'll find out who's in charge.

She waved goodbye to the lambs and began to walk rapidly down the lane back to the village. Mrs Sutton would know, she thought, and went back to the farmhouse. The farmer's wife was busy making bread, and looked up with a smile.

'Had a nice walk?' She had learned quickly to shape the words so that Judy could read them, and Judy nodded and sat down at the table, watching her hostess's hands knead the floury dough.

'I want to do something to help.'

Mrs Sutton shook her head. 'No, love, you go out and enjoy the sunshine. You've done all the jobs that need doing here. You go and get some roses in your cheeks.'

'No, I mean I want to do something more. In Portsmouth, I was in the WVS. I helped in the raids. I want to do something like that here.'

'But we don't have the raids here, love. Only the odd bomb dropped by mistake, and that usually goes into a field. Old Walter Hart had a couple of cows killed a while back, but that's all.'

'But there must be something,' Judy persisted. 'I thought of offering to help on the farm, but I really ought to see the local WVS organiser. Do you know who she is?'

The floury hands paused. 'Well now, who would that be? It was a Mrs Tupper who brought the evacuee children out at the beginning of the war. She was WVS, or I suppose she was, so she'd know. But I don't know where she lives, so that's not much use to you.' She gazed at Judy, her forehead creased, and then her expression cleared. 'I know who could help you! The vicar – he'd be bound to know. Come to think of it, I do believe Mrs Hazelwood herself's in the WVS. There now!' She beamed. 'That's the answer. She's bound to be high up. Why didn't I think of it before? I'll just set this bread to rise and we'll go round to the vicarage straight away.' She repeated her last words slowly and then began to pound the dough again with vigour.

'No, I'll go by myself.' Judy stood up. 'I've got to start being more independent – I won't be any use if I can't do things for myself. And you're busy, anyway.' She touched Mrs Sutton's arm. 'Thank you. I'll be back at dinnertime.'

The vicarage was a large Victorian house close to the church. Its garden had been given over entirely to the cultivation of vegetables, of which there were neat rows already beginning to flourish. A large man, dressed in rough working clothes, was working with a hoe, and as Judy approached he straightened up and turned round. He was well over six feet tall with a large, black, bushy beard and moustache and to her surprise, she saw that he was wearing a dog-collar.

Judy looked at him and her heart sank. I can't even *see* his lips, she thought, let alone read them. But his eyes looked kind and she plunged into her explanation.

'I'm sorry to bother you. I'm Judy Taylor, I'm staying at the Suttons' farm for a while. I'm in the WVS and wondered if there's anything I can do to help while I'm here. Mrs Sutton says your wife is the local organiser.' Belatedly, she added, 'I'm afraid I can't hear what you say – I'm deaf. Bomb blast.'

The beard moved and she guessed he was speaking. 'I can't read your lips either,' she added apologetically, and was surprised to see that he was laughing. He reached out a big hand and ushered her inside the house. Judy, slightly disconcerted, found herself in a wide hallway, its floor patterned with black and white tiles. An old coat-stand stood near the door and there was a long settle that looked suspiciously like a church pew against the wall. The vicar led her through the door to her right, and she found herself in a big room with a bay window overlooking the garden, shabbily but comfortably furnished with a battered three-piece suite, a large cluttered desk and sundry other mismatched chairs and small tables. The walls were lined with bookshelves.

Mr Hazelwood spoke again and then pushed her gently into a chair. He pulled a sheet of paper across the desk and began to write on it.

You do the talking. I'll do the writing!

Judy laughed and nodded, feeling suddenly at ease with this big man who looked more like a farmhand than a vicar. She said, 'Well, it's just as I said. I work for the WVS in Portsmouth, helping the Lady Mayoress. I was out on an ambulance during the raid a fortnight ago, and we got caught in the bombs. We were all deafened, but the others got their hearing back. The doctor thought I needed a rest. He says it should come back, but no one knows for certain. Anyway, I just thought I ought to be doing something while

I'm here, and Mrs Sutton said that your wife runs the WVS in this area.'

She does, he wrote, *but is that quite what the doctor meant by 'having a rest'?*

'But I'm perfectly well,' Judy protested. 'I feel as if I'm shirking. There must be something I could do.'

I'm sure there is. He paused and looked at her thoughtfully, then seemed to make up his mind. *She's out at the moment, but she'll be back soon. Why don't you go and sit in the garden until she comes back? I'll make you a cup of coffee.*

Judy didn't much like the liquid Camp coffee mixture that most people used. 'Water would be fine,' she said, and he nodded and led her through to a big kitchen where he poured her a cup of water. Carrying this, he opened the back door and she found herself in a tiny garden that had not been taken over for vegetables. There was a patch of lawn with a pond filled with squiggling tadpoles which were being attentively watched by a large black cat with huge yellow eyes. The garden was bounded by a warm brick wall with a flower border that seemed to sweep up to it like a tide of colour, and in the middle was an gnarled apple tree covered with deep pink blossom. It was a tiny patch of tranquillity; a haven from the world outside.

The vicar indicated an old wooden seat under the tree and Judy sat down and accepted the water. He smiled at her and vanished round the corner of the house, and she leaned back her head, closed her eyes and felt the warmth of the sun on her face. After a moment or two, a furry paw touched her knee and the cat jumped on to her lap. She laid her hand on its sun-warmed back and smiled.

When she opened her eyes, a young man was sitting on the grass watching her. Judy started and spilled some water over the cat, which leaped off her lap and sat down a few yards away, shaking its head indignantly.

The man spoke. He looked about the same age as Judy, with dark hair brushed back from his forehead and very blue eyes under heavy black brows. He was frowning slightly and Judy realised that he must have been speaking for some moments.

'I'm sorry,' she said. 'I can't hear you. I'm deaf.'

'Oh,' he said, and looked nonplussed. Judy held out the sheet of paper the vicar had given her, and he looked at it and smiled. He took the pencil and wrote, *I'm Ben Hazelwood. You must be waiting for my mother.*

Judy nodded. 'My name's Judy Taylor. I'm from Portsmouth.'

He held out his hand and she shook it. His grasp was firm and cool. They looked at each other for a moment, neither quite knowing what to do next. His smile was rather wicked and very attractive, Judy thought. It seemed to light up his rather dark face, which she suspected might be forbidding when he frowned and lowered those heavy brows over the bright blue eyes. But his mouth was wide and curled up at the corners, so that he looked as if he were about to break into a chuckle.

'Are you in the Services?' she asked and he twisted his mouth wryly and shook his head.

I'm not old enough. I'm thinking about lying about my age and volunteering!

'Not old enough?' Judy said in surprise, reading this. 'I thought . . .' She stopped and blushed, and he grinned and held up both hands, fingers stretched, then one hand and only two fingers of the other. 'Seventeen? You look older.'

Eighteen in September. But I want to go before then. I want to fly.

'Fly?' She glanced up at the cloudless sky, remembering the dogfights of last summer and the Battle of Britain that had raged across the South of England. Pilots, many of them barely more than boys, had been dying every day, yet there seemed to be a never-ending supply of young men willing to take their place. She looked at the youthful face, noting now the signs of immaturity – the softness of his cheeks and lips, the eager innocence of his eyes – and thought of him fighting in the skies, perhaps being hit, his plane in flames, spiralling out of control . . .

The sudden vision shook her and she closed her eyes, trying to push it away. When she opened them he was watching her with some concern. She spoke quickly, at random, 'What do your parents think about it?'

He grimaced. *Haven't told them yet. Know I want to join the RAF – don't know I'm thinking of volunteering.* He looked suddenly anxious and started scribbling again. *You won't tell them, will you?*

Judy smiled and shook her head. 'No. I won't tell them.'

Ben looked up suddenly as if he had heard something, and quickly screwed up the piece of paper and stuffed it into his pocket. A moment or two later a tall, rather thin woman came round the corner of the house. She was evidently expecting to see Judy there and smiled and held out her hand, saying something. Ben spoke to her and she nodded.

'Miss Taylor. I'm very pleased to meet you, my dear.' She spoke carefully and Judy guessed that she would have a clear, rather pleasant voice. 'I see you've met my son.'

Judy nodded. Mrs Hazelwood sat down beside her and Ben went into the house, returning a few moments later with a fresh sheet of paper. He smiled at Judy and went away again.

Ben's home from school at the moment, Mrs Hazelwood wrote. *He has a week for Whitsun. Tell me what I can do for you.*

Judy nodded. One of the things you missed when you were deaf, she thought, was the more casual part of conversation – the little asides that didn't really matter, the humorous comments and quips, the remarks that made chatting a pleasurable experience. When you were deaf, it was so difficult for people to get across to you the information they wanted you to have – either by slowly mouthing the words or by writing them down – that they kept it to the bare minimum. It was like receiving a series of telegrams.

'I'm in the WVS in Portsmouth,' she said. 'I work for the Lady Mayoress. I thought perhaps there was something I could do while I'm at Ashwood.'

Mrs Hazelwood's eyes rested on her for a moment. They were a cool grey, set wide apart in a face that was made to look more narrow by pulling back the silver hair into a French pleat. She had a wide mouth too, rather like her son's, with a humorous curve to the lips, and her expression was compassionate.

'Are you here for a rest?' she said carefully.

'Well – yes,' Judy said. 'But there's nothing wrong with me. Apart from my ears, I mean. I'm not ill or anything. Just tired and – and things have been a bit difficult lately.' She felt her eyes fill with tears. 'I'm sorry.'

'There's no need to apologise.' The curved lips were easy to read. 'I know just how difficult things have been in Portsmouth. Was your home bombed?'

Judy nodded and bit her lip, trying to hold back the tears. 'In the first Blitz,' she whispered. 'We were in the shelter – Mum and Dad and Polly – she's my aunt, she's lived with us since her husband was killed. We went to live with my grandmother, and then Sean – *Sean* . . .' To her horror, the tears spilled over and a huge sob forced its way up from her throat. She put her head into her hands, appalled but unable to control the weeping any more, and the sobs tore themselves from her body; hard, painful sobs that wrenched at her chest and shoulders and made her throat feel raw and scraped.

'I'm sorry,' she choked.

She felt Mrs Hazelwood's hand laid gently on her shoulders. It was firm and soothing, and a strength seemed to flow from it into Judy's body. She found a large handkerchief pressed into her hand and after a while the sobs eased and she was able to blow her nose and sit up. She gave her hostess a faint, wobbly smile.

'I'm sorry. I didn't mean to do that.'

'I've told you, there's no need to apologise. You're not the first person to have wept in this garden.' The vicar's wife glanced around the tranquil little haven. 'It's meant for peace, but there are some griefs that have to be expressed in order to find peace. Was Sean your sweetheart?'

Judy nodded, understanding only the last part of this little speech. 'We only knew each other for a short while. We wanted to get married, but there wasn't time.' She looked down at the ring he had given her, with its tiny scrap of diamond. 'I can't seem to believe he's gone. I keep thinking about it, trying to imagine . . .' Her voice shook again. 'He was at sea, like Polly's husband. It must have been so awful.'

'Yes, it must.' Mrs Hazelwood's hand gave her shoulder a final squeeze, then dropped gently away. 'It must be so awful for so many people. For you as well.'

Judy shook her head at once. 'No – *I've* hardly suffered at all. I wasn't hurt in the bombing, I've got somewhere to live and my family are still there. I've been helping, until this happened.' She touched one of her ears. 'I want to help again. I need to *do* something – I can't just spend my time going for country walks and being looked after by other people. It feels wrong. It feels wrong *not* to have suffered.'

Mrs Hazelwood looked at her thoughtfully. 'But perhaps you need to be looked after for a while. There are more kinds of illness than the physical ones, you know.' This was a difficult sentence to read, and she wrote it down. Judy flushed and she shook her head vehemently.

'I'm not mad! Just because I can't hear—'

'No, no, my dear, I didn't mean that at all.' She wrote again. *You've had terrible shocks. You need rest to get over them. You mustn't feel guilty about that.*

'I don't know if I feel guilty or not,' Judy said, 'but I do know I want to do something to help. Please, isn't there anything? I don't mind what it is.'

Mrs Hazelwood looked at her steadily, and then smiled. It was a warm, friendly smile and Judy felt comforted by it. In fact, she thought, she felt comforted simply by being here, in this small, peaceful garden with its flowers and its sheltering walls. 'I hope the vicar never grows vegetables in here,' she said.

'I won't let him. It's a healing place, and that's just as important as cabbages. Food for the soul,' the vicar's wife said, and smiled again. 'Now, let's think what you could do. Have you ever made scrim?' She laughed at Judy's blank expression and wrote it down.

'Scrim?' The word still meant nothing. Judy shook her head. 'I've never heard of it.'

'I don't suppose you have! Nor had we until the war started. Come with me – I'll show you.'

Judy got up and followed her. Scrim! she thought. Whatever can it be? But it didn't really matter. Whatever it was, she was going to be doing something to help the war effort. She was going to be able to feel useful again.

Chapter Seventeen

'Scrim' turned out to be strips of dull green, khaki and grey fabric which had to be woven into huge nets to make camouflage material for the Army. The work was being carried out in a large barn, where a number of women were standing at wide wooden frames on which the net was stretched. The fabric was laid out on the earthen floor and they were painstakingly threading the strips through the netting. They looked up and smiled as the two newcomers arrived, and spoke to the vicar's wife, but in the dim shadows of the barn it was impossible for Judy to read what they were saying.

'It's not quite as easy as it looks,' Mrs Hazelwood said. 'You see, it has to look as real as possible so you have to fade out the edges and make the corners turn so that there are no sudden sharp lines. It's called "breaking shadow". Think of the dappled light of sun falling through trees, and you'll understand. It's rather dirty, tedious work, I'm afraid,' she added apologetically, 'but we all take a turn at it. There are other jobs to do as well, in between.'

Judy found that while she didn't catch all of Mrs Hazelwood's words, she could read enough to understand the gist. She stood beside an elderly woman wearing a pinafore, with a strip of the fabric wound round her head in a turban, watching to see how the work was done.

Mrs Hazelwood spoke to the other women and then smiled at Judy and left the barn. She had evidently explained Judy's problem and they didn't attempt to talk to her, but gave her friendly looks and showed her what to do.

One of them wound some fabric round her fair hair to keep it clean, and in a little while she felt confident enough to join in on her own section of netting.

As Mrs Hazelwood had said, it was dirty work. The air was full of dust and fluff from the fabric, so that she found herself sneezing every few minutes and soon understood why they all wore turbans. It was also hard on the fingers, which were soon sore from twisting the fabric through the stiff, oily netting. Yet even so, the work itself was strangely soothing. And you could take pride in weaving in the subdued colours, making dappled patterns and shadows here, a pool of light there. It's almost like painting, she thought. We're making a picture. And we might be saving soldiers' lives as well.

The other women were mostly elderly, one or two of them sitting on chairs as they worked. There was one enormously plump woman with swollen legs who could have done few other tasks, and another who could only work with one arm. It's a job for the weak and feeble – like me, Judy thought, and she smiled. Anyone and everyone could help the war effort in some way.

It was also a very sociable job. There was no machinery to make a noise and she could see that the other women were enjoying a good gossip and plenty of laughter. She sighed, wishing she could join in, but she was beginning to get accustomed to this sense of isolation now. Accustomed to being deaf, she thought in dismay. And I'm only twenty-two. Am I going to be like this for the rest of my life?

For a moment, she was swept with the sense of desolation that had also become painfully familiar – and then she took a grip on herself. I am *not* going to give way to self-pity, she told herself firmly. I'm fit and well and I'm working again. Plenty of people are far worse off than me.

She picked up another strip of fabric and wove it into the netting. This is a wood, she thought. It's a wood somewhere in Europe, and there are British soldiers creeping through the undergrowth. They're making dugouts to sleep in and they need this camouflage netting to hide them and keep them safe. Or they want to cover a tank or a lorry with it, so that the enemy doesn't know they're advancing. They're depending on me to make a really good camouflage. Someone out in Germany or France is depending on me – Judy Taylor. They're depending on me to keep them alive – and it doesn't matter a scrap to them whether I'm deaf or not.

By the time Mrs Hazelwood returned she had completed a whole frame. Pleased with her work, she stood back to admire it, just as an artist might stand back to assess a painting, and Mrs Hazelwood smiled her approval.

'You've done well, my dear. Now it's time for a break. I dare say Mrs Sutton will be expecting you back for dinner.'

'Goodness, is it that time already?' They came out into the sunlight and Judy glanced up at the church clock. 'I'll come back this afternoon and do some more.'

Mrs Hazelwood shook her head. 'No, I've got something else for you to do, outside in the sunshine. Most people only pop in for an hour or so, or even less, in between their other jobs. Come back at two o'clock and you can help collect sphagnum moss.'

Judy looked at her in bewilderment, totally unable to make out the last two words, Mrs Hazelwood just smiled and said, 'I'll explain when you come back,' so she smiled back a little uncertainly and went off down the lane in the direction of the farm.

'So you've been making scrim?' Mrs Sutton said, serving her a helping of cottage pie. 'I've done a bit of that too. Filthy work, but it's got to be done. And are you going back this afternoon?'

'Not to make scrim,' Judy said, watching her face carefully to read the words. 'I don't know what I'll be doing. I couldn't understand.'

The three children were back from morning school and

sitting up at the table, watching the big dish of cottage pie eagerly and squabbling about who would have the crispy bits round the edges. Sylvie nudged Judy and said, 'Perhaps you'll be digging up acorns. They did that last year, for pigs.'

'Acorns?' Judy said in surprise. 'Why? Can't the pigs dig up their own acorns?'

Mr Sutton, who was washing at the sink, laughed and said, 'That's what the women said, but they were just told to get on with it,' and Brian said scornfully, 'You don't collect acorns in May, silly. Anyway, they got them all last year. There won't be any more till after the summer. I expect it's rosehips for making juice for babies.'

'Well, that just shows who's silly, then!' Sylvie retorted. 'There aren't any rosehips either, so yah boo!'

'That's quite enough of that,' Mrs Sutton said severely. 'We'll have none of that kind of language at the table, Sylvie, if you don't mind.' To Judy, who had missed most of this exchange, she said, 'Perhaps you're going to be collecting moss. I've heard they use it for injuries. Put it on cuts and bruises,' she added, demonstrating.

This time, Judy understood. 'It might have been moss that Mrs Hazelwood said,' she said doubtfully, 'but they don't really put it on people, do they? What good would that do?'

'Don't ask me. It's a wonder what they can do, these days. Why, the vicar himself told me they use spiders' webs in telescopes and submarine periscopes and such, to give them sightings. Spiders' webs! I wouldn't have believed it if anyone else had told me. But he'd know, because he was in the Army. Chaplain, he was.'

Judy gave up on all these complicated words, and fastened instead on the mention of the vicar. 'I met their son in the garden. Ben.'

'Oh, Ben!' Mrs Sutton face broke into a smile. 'Their youngest, he is. Late baby – the others are all quite a few years older. In the Services, all of them – Ian in the Army, chaplain like his father, Alexandra gone for a nurse, Peter in the Navy. It must be a worry for the vicar and his poor wife, but at least they know Ben's safe at school.'

Judy followed this carefully and decided to say nothing about Ben's intentions. Brian, who had been concentrating on his cottage pie, looked up and said, 'Is it true they use spiders' webs for telescopes? Do they pay people to collect them? I could get lots.'

'Yeugh!' Sylvie said. 'Don't you bring them indoors. I hate spiders.'

'That's because you're a girl,' he said dismissively. 'All girls are scared of spiders.' He grinned evilly and made a spidery shape with his fingers, and Sylvie gave a little scream and cowered away.

'That's enough, now,' Mrs Sutton said, and held out the cottage pie dish. 'Does anyone want more of this? It's macaroni pudding for afters.'

'Bags the skin!' the three children shouted in unison, and she handed the dish to Mr Sutton, who scraped his fork round the edges and cleaned out every last scrap.

Judy walked back to the vicarage feeling well-fed and warmed by the cheerful company. The children were certainly better off in the country, she thought. Milk straight from the cow, home-made butter, home-baked bread and fresh eggs such as were rarely seen in the shops in Portsmouth. And peace. Freedom from the raids. Freedom from the wail of the siren, the roar of aircraft, the thunder of exploding bombs. Freedom from fear.

She took a deep breath of clean, country air, and wondered if she really was going to spend the afternoon collecting moss to put on soldiers' wounds.

It turned out to be true. With half a dozen other women, some of them the same age as herself, Judy was directed to a wood a mile or so from the village. The little group strolled along the lane, laughing and joking, and although Judy couldn't hear them she felt less left out than usual. They smiled at her and one, a lanky, red-haired girl with freckles and a ready grin, linked arms with her as they swung along. She smiled back, feeling a little as if she were a foreigner who didn't understand the language, but aware that they were friendly.

After a while they left the lane and crossed two or three fields. In the distance, Judy could see a church tower which she thought must be at Bridge End. She wondered how Stella and Muriel were getting along. She would have liked to go and see them, but her deafness made it too difficult. She still shrank from new situations and encounters.

The wood lay in a hollow, and in the centre of it was a swampy area, with tussocks of tough grass and reeds growing in shallow water. Judy could see the moss growing in thick, soft cushions of bright green everywhere. She looked at it with interest, wondering just why it was so valuable.

'The moss has healing properties,' Mrs Hazelwood had told them as they set off. 'It stops wounds from going septic. We send it out to the troops.'

Everyone was wearing Wellington boots and they set down their baskets on tussocks and began to work. It was quite pleasant, Judy discovered, once you'd got used to plunging your hands into the cool, damp cushions and pulling them up to pack into your basket. It didn't take long to fill them, and within an hour or so they were on their way back, each swinging two tightly packed baskets. As they crossed the fields, they paused to gather wool left on the fences by sheep and crammed it in with the moss. Mrs Hazelwood received them with approval.

'That's excellent. We'll have another moss-gathering party tomorrow.' Most of the women had meals to prepare for menfolk and children, the evacuees as well as their own, so could only spare an hour or two each day. But it was surprising how much could be achieved in a short time, Mrs Hazelwood told Judy, inviting her in for a cup of tea before returning to the farm. An hour or so making scrim in the mornings, another hour spent gathering moss or wool in the afternoon, and it all added up to a substantial contribution towards the war effort.

She took Judy into the garden again. The sun was warm and they took their tea to the seat under the apple tree. Mrs Hazelwood talked carefully, facing Judy so that she could read her words. She talked about her children – Ian, who had taken Orders and followed his father into the Army as a chaplain, Peter who was a Lieutenant in the Navy, and Alexandra who had volunteered as a VAD nurse and was at present working at Haslar Naval Hospital in Gosport.

'It's good to have her so close. She comes home when she can manage it, for her day off. But they've been so busy during the last few months, with all the bombing . . .' She fell silent and sat gazing at the black cat, who was stretched out on his back in the sun, soaking up the warmth. 'I'm glad to know they're all being useful, though,' she said at last.

Judy sipped her tea and thought how difficult it must be for mothers like Mrs Hazelwood, knowing that their children were in danger and unable to do anything to keep them safe. She thought about Ben, who was as safe as anyone could be at his school in Winchester, yet wanted to leave that safety and take to one of the most dangerous of occupations as an RAF pilot. How would the Hazelwoods feel when he took that step, without even consulting them? They'll be upset about it, she thought, but they'll be proud too. And we all have to put our worries away in this war, because it's got to be fought, to save the whole of Europe, maybe the whole world, from tyranny, and none of us is really safe.

A shadow fell across the lawn and Ben himself appeared, tall and loose-limbed in grey flannel trousers and white, open-necked shirt. He grinned at his mother, winked at

Judy, and flung himself down on the grass beside the cat. There were some extra cups on the tray and he poured himself some tea.

Mrs Hazelwood stood up. 'I'll leave you to finish your tea,' she said to Judy. 'And please come back tomorrow if you'd like to do some more – but don't feel you have to. You're here for a rest, remember.'

She walked away across the lawn, her skirt swaying around her lean figure, and Judy watched her, thinking how kind she was, how kind everyone was in this village. She glanced at Ben uncertainly and he reached out a hand and pulled her to her feet.

'Come for a walk. Or are you worn out from all your moss-gathering?'

Judy shook her head. 'I feel I ought to be doing more.'

'Well, we'll take some baskets,' he declared, 'in case we find something useful.' He led her across the garden to the shed where the baskets were kept and handed her one, taking another for himself. Side by side, they strolled off between the green hedges.

A little way along the lane, Ben turned off to the left down a track Judy hadn't noticed before. It was roughly metalled and ran between hawthorn hedges frothed with white blossom. The grassy banks beneath them were misted with bluebells and here and there were patches of starry white wild garlic flowers. Now and then the lane was shaded by a spreading oak, ginger with new leaves just about to burst, or a stand of tall elms crowded with rooks. There were a couple of farm cottages, with small children playing in the dust, and then the lane wound down a hill and forded a river before climbing up out of the valley through woods on the other side.

There was a narrow wooden bridge over the river, and Ben crossed halfway and then sat down, swinging his legs over the side. Judy joined him and they sat quietly for a while, watching the brown water ripple beneath them.

'I suppose there are birds singing,' she said thoughtfully after a moment or two. 'Wish I could hear them.'

'You will,' he said, and she could tell by his expression that his voice was firm, as if he knew that what he said was true. Judy shrugged.

'I hope so. But nobody knows for sure. I might be deaf always.'

He shook his head. 'You won't. You'll hear again. I know you will.' He smiled, full of confidence. 'You've just got to want it badly enough – you've got to believe it.'

Startled, she stared at him, and then, suddenly angry, began to get to her feet. 'Don't say that. Don't you realise, I *do* want to hear again – I want it more than anything in the world! But it's my *ears* – there's something wrong with them, something damaged. Just *believing* isn't going to make any difference.' She scrambled up, but Ben caught her hand and drew her back down beside him.

'I'm sorry. Please don't go, Judy. I didn't mean to upset you.' She looked into his face, reading only some of the words but understanding his expression, and suddenly he looked so young, so pleading, that she burst out laughing.

'All right. But please don't talk like that. It's silly.' She sat down and looked at him again. 'You *don't* know, Ben. You can't. Even the doctors don't know for sure. I could be deaf for the rest of my life. And even if I am,' she paused, 'it can't possibly matter to you.'

Ben opened his mouth and then shut it again. He looked away from her, down into the brown, rippling water, and she saw his mouth move, but he didn't look back at her to repeat his words. She felt a sudden sense of frustration, wanting to be able to talk to him, freely and naturally. I *do* want to be able to hear him, she thought with despair. I want to be able to hear everyone. But wanting isn't enough.

Ben suddenly gripped her hand more tightly, indicating something with his head. Judy followed his gaze and stifled a little cry of delight. A bird was sitting on a branch a few yards further up the river – a bird with brilliant, electric-blue wings and a flame-red breast. As Judy watched, it dived into the water and reappeared a moment later with a small fish struggling in its beak. It flew back to its branch, gave a few quick glances around, and then disappeared into a hole in the bank.

'A kingfisher!' Judy exclaimed. 'I've never seen one before. It was beautiful. But why did it go into that hole? Is it hiding?'

Ben shook his head. 'That's its nest. It must have young in there.' He smiled his wicked, curving smile at her. 'Now are you glad we came?'

Judy nodded, and felt the easy rapport between them return. The moment of uncertainty had disappeared in their shared pleasure. 'Yes, I'm glad. It's a lovely spot. Thank you for bringing me. But I ought to be going back to the farm now. I promised to help Mrs Sutton with the supper.'

He nodded and got to his feet, helping Judy up. They stood facing each other on the narrow bridge for a moment, then Judy turned away and walked back to the bank. Ben caught her up as she bent to pick up the baskets they had left on the grass. He laid his hand on her shoulder. 'You're not cross with me, are you, Judy?'

'No. I'm not cross.' Their eyes met again and she relaxed and smiled. 'I'm not cross at all,' she said softly, and began to walk back up the track.

Ben fell into step beside her. They did not speak again until he left her at the gate to the Suttons' farm.

Chapter Eighteen

It really did seem as if the raids over Portsmouth were easing. There were only four during May, spaced several days or even a week or two apart, and they were light in comparison to the savagery of the three Blitzes. Some houses at Tipnor were damaged and the main railway line put out of action, but many of the bombs fell into the sea and there were only three people killed and just a handful injured.

The Luftwaffe had not given up, however. Liverpool had been cut off by seven nights of continuous bombing, with fires raging uncontrollably throughout, the worst of all being at the Bryant & May match factory. The city centre had been reduced to rubble, and a ship loaded with bombs and ammunition had been set on fire by a barrage balloon which fell blazing from the sky; the explosion sank six other ships and destroyed the dock area. A hospital had received a direct hit, killing sixty staff and patients, and a hundred and sixty children had died when their school shelter was bombed. By the end of the week, almost fifteen hundred people had been killed and seventy thousand were without homes.

London was attacked again. Under a cruelly bright 'Bomber's Moon', the heaviest raid yet left the House of Commons, Westminster Abbey, the Tower of London and the Royal Mint in flames. Every main railway terminus was out of action, over three thousand people were killed or injured and a hundred and fifty thousand homes had no gas, water or electricity.

'They're having a terrible time coping with the homeless,'

the Mayoress told Polly as they walked out of the Royal Beach into the sunshine a few days after the raid. She had been asked to go to London for a meeting at WVS Head Office in Tothill Street. The main railway line had been put out of action and, since the trains weren't running, she had decided to use the official car and asked Polly to drive it.

Polly was rather excited at the prospect. Driving a nice car in daylight would make a welcome change from dashing through blacked-out streets in a converted van. She was looking forward to seeing London, too – she'd only been there three or four times, long before the war had begun, when Alice had taken her and Cissie to visit a cousin. Johnny had talked about taking her to see the sights, but somehow, what with Sylvie's birth and the miscarriages later, it had never happened. Now some of those sights were gone for ever, she thought, and others might not last much longer.

The Lady Mayoress was still talking about the problem of the homeless in London. 'They don't seem to have foreseen such a situation, you see. They expected far more people to be killed – over six hundred thousand were estimated, I believe – and in the event there have been only twenty thousand in London and forty thousand in the entire country. Well,' she caught herself up and gave Polly a wry look, 'one can hardly say *only*, but still it's nothing like as many as were expected. Whereas they did nothing to plan for the homeless, and they already number over two million. It's a terrible problem.'

'And not all of them as lucky as us, with relatives to go to,' Polly said. 'Whatever will happen to them all?' She opened the passenger door of the car and the Mayoress got in. Polly cranked the engine and as it hiccuped and then purred into life she slid into the driver's seat.

The Mayoress sighed. 'I really don't know where they'll all go. That's partly what this meeting is about. It seems a strange time to go to London, with all the devastation there, but it's at this time they need us most. Now, do we have enough petrol? I've got some vouchers so that we can get more if we need it, but of course I'd rather not use them.'

'I think there's enough.' Polly put the car into gear and nosed it carefully out on to the road. South Parade Pier shone as if it had been iced, and the sun was glinting on the sea, turning the waves to white-flecked blue. The fenced-off common was crowded with servicemen and girls, walking arm-in-arm or sitting on the grass. Because it was May, the sailors were all wearing their white cap-covers – one of the first signs of spring, Polly had always thought it. The sight reminded her of Johnny and brought an ache to her heart.

She had looked up the route to London and laid a set of directions on the seat beside her. It was the first time she had driven so far; she had never been further than the Queen Alexandra Hospital before, and driving over Portsdown Hill was like entering new territory. She knew the road to Petersfield from having been on charabanc outings out that way before the war, but from there it became a real adventure.

'You drive very well, Polly,' the Mayoress commented, and Polly blushed and thanked her.

'I like it. My husband could drive and he let me go very slowly in bottom gear in a field once or twice – but I never thought we'd have a car of our own. And even if we had, I don't suppose I'd have driven it. Women don't, do they? Or didn't, before the war,' she added.

'No, and I dare say they'll go back to being passengers once the war's over,' the Lady Mayoress said thoughtfully. 'The men will want their own places back then. And they'll need help to find them, I think. It will be very strange for them to come home to wives who've learned to manage without them. Women will have to take a back seat, even if they don't want to, just to help their men feel at home again.'

'I suppose so. I know I'd be so glad to have my Johnny

back that I wouldn't care if I never touched a car again. I'd just want to look after him, like a wife should.' Polly stopped, aware that if she continued to think and talk about Johnny the tears would come, and she couldn't drive with tears in her eyes. 'It's a lovely morning, madam.'

'It is.' The Mayoress gazed out of the window and sighed. 'You know, on a day like this, driving through the countryside with the sun shining and the birds singing, it's hard to believe we're at war. And then you remember the raids and all those poor souls without a home – well, *you* must feel for them especially, Polly, having been in just the same position. You've dealt with it all so well, I'm afraid I tend to forget.'

'Not all that well, madam,' Polly said, thinking of the nightmares and the tears that soaked her pillow. 'But you can't let it get you down, can you? You just have to carry on.'

'And how's Judy? Is the countryside helping her?'

'I think it is. We had a letter this morning – she still can't hear much, but she seems to be more settled in herself. She's found the local WVS organiser and she's doing some work – says she's making scrim!'

'Scrim? Whatever's that?'

'It's camouflage netting, madam,' Polly grinned. 'Apparently the nets are stretched over big frames and you have to weave in strips of fabric. She says it's the filthiest job she's ever done, but she quite likes it because she's making pictures to send to the troops! I'm not sure what she means by that, to tell you the truth. And she's been out collecting some kind of moss; she says they use it like a sort of bandage.'

'Oh yes, I've heard of that. Sphagnum moss, I think it's called. Well, that's excellent news, but I hope she won't overdo it. She's supposed to be having a rest.'

'Oh, Judy's like our Gran,' Polly said. 'She doesn't agree

with resting. What I'm afraid of is that she'll get to like being out there and not want to come home!'

'It's more likely that they won't want to lose her,' the Lady Mayoress said. 'Judy's an excellent worker, and no WVS organiser is going to let someone like that slip through their fingers. I wonder now if I was wise to let her go!'

Polly laughed. 'Well, so long as she's helping the war effort one way or another, it doesn't really matter, does it? It's like our Gran says, cream always rises to the top.'

They drove on. Polly's confidence was increasing and she found herself enjoying the drive along country roads and through small towns and villages. After a while, she said, 'It looks as if the weather's changing, madam. There's a big black cloud ahead, see?'

The Mayoress stared at it. 'I don't think it's an ordinary cloud, Polly,' she said quietly. 'It's smoke. We've seen just the same over Portsmouth after a raid. There must be fires still burning. You'll have to go carefully – we may not be able to get all the way in by car.'

Sobered, they drove on. There was damage in the outskirts of London and, as they approached the city itself, they began to see the devastation of the raids beneath the pall of smoke and dust that darkened the sky.

Buildings on all sides were destroyed or damaged, their roofs splintered and caving in, their walls torn down like a child's sandcastle. Some were smouldering, some still in flames, and although there were firemen and engines everywhere it was clear that it was impossible to deal with them all. Some houses had been just left to burn, with their occupants watching in despair. In one street, Polly saw a housewife in pinny and curlers, hurling buckets of water at the walls of her house. Others seemed to be reasoning with her, trying to get her to leave it, but her face was twisted with anguish and it was as if she barely knew they were there. She shook them off and ran back to the standpipe for more water, crying and screaming in her blind distress. The sight caught at Polly's heart and she remembered her own pain as she and the rest of the family had crept out of their shelter to find their own house in ruins. It isn't fair, she thought helplessly. What had we done to deserve that? What did this poor soul do to deserve it? What in the world is it all for?

'It's dreadful,' the Mayoress said as, having been diverted down street after street, they drove at last through Westminster. 'Worse even than Portsmouth. Row after row of houses, completely demolished. These poor people!'

Polly was almost in tears. 'It gets worse the further in you get,' she said. 'Isn't there anywhere left standing? Oh look – isn't that Westminster Abbey, with its tower all smashed down? And Parliament too! I never realised how bad it was.'

'The House of Commons, yes,' the Mayoress said as they drove slowly past, negotiating the fire engines and hoses. 'They're still burning. Dreadful. Polly, *look*! Surely that's Mr Churchill himself!'

Polly, who had been keeping her eyes on the cluttered road, risked a glance and saw the stumpy figure making his way through the firemen towards the devastated building. He was unmistakable, from the many times she had seen him in newspaper pictures or on film newsreels, and of course from the time he had visited the Royal Beach. He looked just the same, dressed in an overcoat and trilby and with the inevitable cigar gripped between his teeth, and somehow just the sight of his determined, pugnacious figure seemed to instil a little of the defiant hope that his words so often brought to the country. What did he feel like inside? she wondered. Surely even he, at a moment like this, must feel some despair. 'He must be so upset. What will they do now? They'll have to find somewhere else to have Parliament.' A thought struck her. 'They're homeless – same as the rest of us.'

'So they are.' The Mayoress looked out of the window. 'Turn left here, Polly. Tothill Street is the next on the right

– that's it. And there's number forty-one. Thank goodness that seems to have escaped the bombing.' She smiled at Polly. 'Well done. Now, I'm sure if you come in there'll be a cup of coffee for you, and then if you like you can walk through to St James's Park. It used to be very pleasant there – the lake was always full of ducks. I expect they're still there.'

Polly drew the car to a halt beside the kerb. There were a few other cars there, mostly official ones like her own; with petrol so severely rationed, most people who had their own cars had put them on blocks in garages 'for the duration'. She supposed that the other cars had brought people like the Mayoress for the meeting, and there might be some other drivers like herself who would be at a loose end for a few hours. At any other time, the prospect of some free time in London would have been an exciting one. Now, looking at the devastation around her, it was heart-breaking.

Number forty-one Tothill Street was a large house, turned into offices and meeting rooms. They were welcomed into a hall that had probably once seen debutantes setting off to be presented to the King, and top-hatted men and women in evening dress departing for the opera. A graceful stairway rose on one side, and there were tall, heavy doors leading into what had no doubt once been drawing rooms.

The hallway and drawing rooms were now full of bustling women in WVS uniform, or smart tweed or city suits. Polly glimpsed an office very like the one at the Royal Beach, with filing cabinets and girls seated at desks, typing or going through papers. Before she could see more, she was led through to the back regions and found herself in a dining room with a long table and about a dozen chairs, some of them occupied by women drinking coffee and eating toast; and beyond that a large kitchen where someone was busy preparing food and someone else was washing up.

'I might as well help,' Polly said, but the Mayoress shook her head.

'You're to have a cup of coffee and some fresh air. You've had quite a difficult drive. I'll just see how long my meeting's likely to take.' She strode briskly from the room and Polly found herself seated at the table, a cup of steaming coffee in front of her and a plate of toast pushed under her nose.

'It's all right,' said a woman of about her own age with a grin. 'Breakfast goes on until lunchtime here. We're coming and going all the time, you see, and after a bad night people just dash in whenever they've got the chance. My name's Daphne, by the way – Daphne Mallow. Have you driven up from somewhere?'

'Portsmouth.' Polly took a slice of toast and spread it with margarine and marmalade. 'I'm Polly Dunn. I'm with the Lady Mayoress. I'm a driver mostly, but of course I help out wherever I can.'

The other woman nodded. 'That's what's so good about the WVS. We'll turn our hands to anything, we never say no, and we're not bogged down by silly rules and red tape. I hope I'll be able to stay in it for the duration, not get called up into one of the Forces.'

'Why, d'you think we're likely to, at our age? They'll only take the younger ones, surely, in their twenties?'

Daphne shrugged. 'Who knows? The longer it goes on, the more help they'll need. Of course, if it came to it I'd go – that goes without saying – but I'd much rather do my bit with the WVS. All that marching and drilling – seems a waste of time to me.'

Polly nodded. She'd never thought about it before, but it now seemed to her that Daphne might be right. After all, if you were spending your time learning to march in step, you weren't spending it in helping people, and surely that was what doing your bit for the war effort was really all about. 'It's because of discipline, though, isn't it?' she said, trying to remember what Johnny had told her about being in the Navy. 'If you get used to obeying orders without question – even if it's just orders about marching – you'll do it when you're in an emergency and it's really important. I mean, my hubby was at sea, and he told me that if an officer shouted an order it wouldn't be any good if half the men started to argue about it. It could mean the ship being sunk.'

'Well, of course everyone must be sensible about it,' Daphne said. 'But then women are, on the whole. We don't need to have it drilled into us like that. And in the WVS we can think for ourselves. You're not always allowed to do that in the Services.' She glanced at the clock on the wall and jumped up. 'I must go! I've got to deliver a message to an office in Whitehall. See you later, perhaps.' She grinned again at Polly, crammed her green beret on her head, and was gone.

Polly finished her toast and coffee thoughtfully and took the empty plate and cup through to the kitchen. There was a plump woman of around fifty washing up and Polly offered her help. The woman smiled her thanks and Polly collected the rest of the crockery and picked up a tea-towel.

'So you're from Portsmouth?' the woman, who had introduced herself as Mrs Cousins, observed after they had chatted for a few moments. 'I've got an auntie near there. Gosport, she lives in – I dare say you know it.' She had a pleasant face, with warm brown eyes and greying hair.

Polly nodded. 'It's across the harbour. You can get there by ferry – I've been a couple of times, but there's not much there. It's not like Pompey. We've got all the best shops.' She paused, then added, 'At least, we *did* have, before the Germans decided to change things.'

Mrs Cousins gave her a wry look. 'I know, you've had some terrible raids. But it's the same story everywhere – raids and Blitzes, people killed or made homeless. And there don't seem to be no end in sight, neither.' She scrubbed at a large pan that seemed to have been used for making porridge. 'What it is, we've never had this kind of thing in Britain. We've always sent our armies off to fight in other countries, and then gone on much the same as usual at home. But now, with all these air raids, we're all mixed up in it together, and it's children and old people as much as soldiers and sailors.' She regarded the pan and then turned it upside down on the draining board. 'That's what sticks in my craw – seeing little nippers hurt and killed and frightened. Not that there ought to be any here by now,' she added grimly. 'Ought to be out in the country, where they'd be safe.'

Polly began to wipe the pan with her teacloth. 'I know. I don't understand why their parents keep them in towns. My little girl went straight away, right at the beginning. I know a lot of people brought their kiddies back when nothing much seemed to be happening, but surely with the way things are . . .'

'Oh, there are still people who think they know best. And there are plenty who don't really care all that much, to tell you the truth.' Mrs Cousins swished water round in the enamel washbasin and then tipped it down the sink. 'Some of the slums up the East End are a real eye-opener – youngsters in rags who don't see soap and water from one week's end to another, scavenging for food while their parents are in the pub drowning their sorrows in gin or beer and don't know where they are half the time. Mind you, I don't say they're all like that,' she added fairly. 'There are some who try to keep decent no matter how poor they are, but there are plenty who just have no idea. No idea at all. We do our best to help them, of course, but it's an uphill struggle.' She ran water over a dishcloth, squeezed it out and began to wipe down the scrubbed wooden draining boards. 'Well, that's breakfast done and dusted, time to start the dinner things.' She opened the door of a larder and began to heave out a bag of potatoes.

'I'll help you,' Polly offered, but Mrs Cousins shook her head.

'No, I heard the Mayoress tell you to go out and get some fresh air. That meeting's going on till about three – you can either come back and have a bite here, or have something while you're out. There's a Lyons' Corner House not far away – try that. You can always get a decent meal there at a reasonable price, and it's the sort of place a woman can go on her own and not feel conspicuous.'

Polly nodded and found her beret and shoulder bag. At the last minute, she remembered her gas-mask in its cardboard box, and slipped that over her shoulder too. She had still never really got used to taking it with her everywhere she went and often forgot, but here in London with the evidence of the Blitz wherever you looked, it seemed unlucky to go without it. The Germans hadn't used gas so far, but that didn't mean they wouldn't – and she knew from Dick's experiences in the 1914–1918 war just how terrible it could be. He'd had only a whiff and was still suffering; those who had been badly gassed had died in agony.

She walked out of the front door and stood for a moment looking about her. The sun was shining and she had a sudden, unexpected feeling of holiday. For a few hours, she had nothing to do and no one to please save herself. She was in London – a bombstruck, half-ruined London, it was true, but London nevertheless – and there were still sights to see. She decided to do as the Mayoress had suggested and go first to St James's Park.

Really, she thought a few minutes later, having crossed Birdcage Walk and gone through the park gates, you'd hardly know there was a war on. Well, provided you ignored the gun emplacements and trenches, and didn't look up at the fleet of drifting barrage balloons that had been supposed to prevent the enemy aircraft from getting through . . . But apart from those things, the grass was green, the cherry trees a foam of pink blossom, and the ducks on the lake were quacking about their business apparently without a care in the world. I wonder what they make of the bombing, she thought, leaning over the bridge and wishing she'd brought some stale bread. I wonder if it frightens them or if they just accept it as part of everyday life. I wonder how many have been killed . . .

'Hello.' The voice made her jump. 'Aren't you the young lady I met on the train for Ashwood? Whatever are you doing here?'

Polly turned, startled. Beside her, leaning on the railing of the bridge, stood a man – a long-legged man with wavy, iron-grey hair brushed back from a broad forehead, wearing a tweed jacket and grey flannel trousers. His voice was deep and warm, and she remembered it at once and smiled up at him.

'I've come up to WVS Headquarters with my boss – she's at a meeting. I drove her up and now I've been sent out to get some fresh air and exercise.' She laughed self-consciously. 'I feel a bit like a little girl who's been sent out to play!'

He raised his eyebrows, so that his forehead creased into the three crinkly lines that she remembered. Not frown lines, she thought, but humour lines. And there were other little ones too, splayed out from the corners of his dark brown eyes. It was a cheerful, crumpled face, a face that looked as if it had been lived in, and had found something to enjoy in much of what it had seen.

'What a bit of luck,' he said. 'Is this your first time in the Smoke?'

'Mum brought me and my sister a few times when we were children. She had a cousin in St John's Wood.' Polly laughed. 'I was so disappointed the first time I came – I was expecting a real wood! But she showed us St Paul's and the Tower, things like that. It's a long time ago now.' She sighed a little. 'I was going to come with my hubby, but we never got round to it.'

He looked at her for a moment, then said, 'Well, why don't you let me show you a few of the sights now – those that the Germans have left us, anyway. Buckingham Palace ain't far. And then we could walk up Piccadilly and back down Regent Street. What time d'you have to be back?'

'I think they expect the meeting to end at three. But I really ought to go and help. There's a lady there cooking dinner all by herself.'

'She won't be for long,' he said, grinning so that his face crinkled into a million tiny lines. 'My sister will make sure that everyone who walks through the door will lend a hand! I told you she works there, didn't I? She's in charge of the kitchen. In fact, it was probably her you saw – Edna Cousins, her name is.'

'That's right! She told me her name was Mrs Cousins.' Polly gazed at him. 'I can see the likeness now, too.' She put out her hand. 'My name's Polly Dunn.'

'And I'm Joe Turner.' His hand was big and warm, with stubby fingers. 'Pleased to meet you, Polly Dunn.'

They shook hands and then stood looking a little uncertainly at each other. After a minute or two, he said, 'Well, how about it? Going to let me show you the sights?'

'Well, if you think it will be all right,' Polly said, a little doubtfully. 'I still feel a bit guilty, as if I'm taking time off when I ought to be working.'

'You've driven up from Portsmouth,' he said. 'You're going to drive back. You've had some bad raids recently and I'll bet my bottom dollar you've been out night and day, helping and probably risking your life. If your boss has told you to get some fresh air, I think that's what you ought to do!' His face crinkled.

Polly laughed. 'Well, if you put it like that! And I *would* like to see Buckingham Palace – that's if you've got time. You've got other things to do, surely?'

'Not for an hour or two,' he said. 'I'm like you – snatching a bit of time to try to forget the war. We've all got to do that sometimes,' he added, looking down at her as they began to walk slowly through the park, alongside the lake with its crowds of colourful ducks. 'Keeps us from going round the bend.'

They strolled along quietly for a while. Polly wondered what he did. Despite his greying hair and crinkly face, he didn't seem too old to be in the Forces; in fact, when she had met him before, she had put him down as a soldier – a Sergeant, perhaps. Now she noticed that he walked with a stick, favouring his right leg, and wondered if he'd been injured and was on recuperation leave.

'Sorry to be a bit slow,' he said, as if reading her mind, 'but I've got a bit of a gammy leg. Copped it on the beach at Dunkirk. I've applied to go back to my regiment but they seem to think I'd be a liability.' He looked at Polly. 'You've got a kiddy, haven't you, a little girl? You were going to see her at Ashwood. I bet she was tickled pink to see you, wasn't she? Is she OK where she is?'

'Yes, she's with some really nice people. We're lucky, not all the evacuees are in such good billets. Actually, my niece is out there at the moment, too. We thought she needed a break, like you were saying just now.'

'Your niece? Wasn't she evacuated at the same time as your kiddy, then?'

Polly shook her head. 'No, Judy's in her twenties now.'

'Go on! You're not old enough to have a niece in her twenties!'

'I am,' Polly said with dignity, and then grinned. 'I'm quite a bit younger than my sister, Judy's mum, Cissie. There's the same difference between me and Judy as there is between me and Cissie.'

'Don't tell me any more,' he said, 'or I'll start working out your age, and that ain't the way to behave with a lady. And what about your hubby – serving, is he?'

'No. He's dead,' Polly said quietly. 'He was in the Navy, and his ship was sunk right at the beginning of the war.'

'Oh, blimey!' Joe stopped again and took her hand. 'That's me all over – open me big mouth and put me blooming foot straight in it. Sorry, love. Just tell me to shut up.'

'It's all right,' Polly said. She looked down at their hands. Hers, small and slim, was almost lost in his big hand. She saw that, like herself, he wore a plain gold wedding ring. That was unusual, she thought. Not many men did that. She drew in a shaky breath and said, 'I think I'm getting over it a bit now. I mean, so many things have happened and so many people have been killed. You just have to get on with life, don't you?'

'Yes,' he said. 'You do.' There was a moment's silence and then he tucked her hand into the crook of his arm and they walked on. Polly took a deep breath, and then another. Mentioning Johnny always brought an ache to her throat, but she could feel a comfort in the warmth of this big man, with her hand tucked so securely against his body. She had a sudden longing to be held close, to be hugged. No more than that – just to be hugged. To feel the closeness of another human being. To feel the warmth of a living body close to hers.

Oh Johnny, she thought, where are you? What happened to you? And did you think of me, during your last few moments? Did you know how much I loved you – and did it help at all? Or did you forget everything and everyone in those last desperate efforts to stay alive?

The tears came to her eyes and, without knowing it, she tightened her grip on Joe Turner's arm. He glanced down at her but said nothing, and if she had looked up at him then she would have seen that his eyes were wet too.

Chapter Nineteen

Polly and Joe walked right through St James's Park to Buckingham Palace. They stood by the Queen Victoria Memorial, gazing at the iron railings and the rows of windows. The sentries were not dressed in red jackets and tall busbies, as Polly recalled having seen them years ago, but in tin hats and combat uniform. They looked grimly prepared to fight to protect their King and Queen.

'They were bombed too, weren't they?' she said, looking at the big courtyard, and Joe Turner nodded.

'Copped it two or three times, back in March. There was craters there you could've dropped a house into, and there was some damage round the back of the building, too. You gotta hand it to Their Majesties, they didn't let it scare 'em off. Been out round the bombed areas every day, they have, talking to people and shaking their hands. Not just London, neither – Liverpool, Plymouth, anywhere that's been hit.'

'They came to Portsmouth,' Polly said. 'We saw them in our offices and then all the WVS workers went out to one of the hospitals and met the Queen there. She's lovely. She told us that sunshine would come again.'

'Well, she was right. It's come today, for a start,' Joe Turner said, looking at her, and Polly felt her cheeks blush slightly. 'Let's cut across Green Park now and go down Pall Mall.'

'You seem to know London very well,' Polly said as they crossed the park and made their way through a maze of streets. 'Is it where you grew up?'

''S right. Whitechapel, that's my old stamping ground.'

'Does that make you a Cockney? I don't know much about London,' Polly confessed.

'Well, not far off. I reckon you can hear Bow Bells on a good day, with the wind in the right direction. I don't live there now, though.' He closed his mouth, as if he didn't want to say any more, and Polly fell silent. After a few minutes they came to Pall Mall. 'This is where all the posh people hang out. Or used to – most of 'em have gone now, got places out in the country.' He fished an old chain watch from his pocket. 'Tell you what, I'm getting a bit peckish – how about a bite to eat at the Corner House? They do a decent dinner there.'

Polly nodded. 'Mrs Cousins told me that. She said it was the sort of place a woman could go to on her own.'

'Well, so it is, but I hope you ain't going to do that.' He kept her hand pressed firmly between his arm and his body. 'It ain't every day I gets a nice young woman to step out with. And I'll get you back to Tothill Street afterwards in good time to pick up your boss.' They continued along the wide road and then through to Trafalgar Square and Charing Cross. Joe Turner was walking more slowly now, and Polly wondered if his leg pained him. Perhaps we shouldn't have come so far, she thought, but didn't like to say so. She knew from Dick that men could be very funny about admitting to a weakness.

Charing Cross railway station was closed as, it seemed, was every other big station in London, and all the way around Polly could see signs of the massive Blitz. Fires were still smouldering, buildings destroyed, rubble blocking the roads, cars crushed beneath a weight of fallen masonry, and yet amongst it all life was struggling to continue as normal. People were coming out of offices and shops, dressed in their working clothes, as if it were any other lunchtime. And many of them were heading for the imposing white building of the Lyons Corner House.

'It's enormous!' she said, staring up at it. 'Is it all one restaurant?'

''S right. You've heard of Corner Houses, haven't you? And the Nippies – the waitresses there? They're famous, they are.' They joined the queue and moved slowly towards the big doors. 'I'm surprised your mum never brought you here when you come up to see the sights.'

'We couldn't afford restaurants. We always took a few sandwiches.' They were at the doors now, and as they passed through they were met by a smiling young girl who showed them to a table. Polly sat down, feeling rather awed. She had seldom been to a restaurant and thought that Mrs Cousins was wrong. She would never have had the nerve to come in here on her own.

'Mind, they used to be really grand before the war started,' Joe Turner told her. 'Big glass chandeliers, they had, and a gipsy band playing – almost as good as the Café de Paris, they were. And they always had a decent menu, see, not too pricey. So that ordinary people like you and me could come in.' He gazed around for a moment. 'Had to take all that away, of course, in case of bomb damage. You couldn't have glass flying all over the place, getting in the soup.'

Polly stared at him, then caught the twinkle in his eye and laughed. 'I never know whether you're being serious or not,' she said, picking up the menu.

'Oh, you'll know when I am.' He glanced at her for a moment. 'But it ain't very often, so don't look so worried. Now, what're you going to have? You're only allowed one protein per meal, if I remember rightly.'

They both chose shepherd's pie and peas. The peas might even be fresh instead of tinned, he said without much hope, but in any case it would be good. They might not be able to get all the best ingredients now, like they used to, but whatever it was it would be well cooked and the Nippy who served it would have a smile on her face and wouldn't keep them hanging about.

'That's why they're called Nippies,' Joe said. 'But I dunno how much longer they'll last. A lot of them are going into the Wrens and ATS and that now. If the war goes on much longer, we'll all have to queue up and help ourselves, like in a blooming canteen!'

Polly laughed. 'Oh, I'm sure there'll still be plenty of women who'll want waitressing jobs. It won't seem like going out if you have to carry your own tray.' Their own Nippy arrived at that moment and set their plates down before them. As Joe had expected, the peas were tinned but the mashed potato was good and the gravy rich and tasty. Joe had asked for a glass of beer as well, while Polly stuck to water, and they settled hungrily to their food.

This is the first time I've been out with a man since Johnny died, Polly thought – the first time I've been out with *anyone* except Johnny. Yet somehow there seemed to be nothing awkward about it, nothing to make her feel uncomfortable. Of course, it hadn't been arranged, it wasn't a proper date or anything like that, and she didn't suppose she'd ever see him again. To her surprise, the thought of never seeing him again seemed disappointing. He's a nice man, she thought, the sort of man I could be friends with. But of course, she couldn't be – he was a married man. And she still felt herself to be a married woman.

'D'you reckon you'll be coming up to London again with your boss?' he asked, once again seeming to read her thoughts. 'I mean, if she's going to come to meetings regular, she might want you to drive her, same as today. Only, I was thinking, if you could let me know, we might do this again. Have a bit of a walk together, and a bite to eat. If you felt like it, I mean,' he added quickly.

'Well . . .' Polly felt flustered. 'I don't know. I mean, I don't know if the Mayoress – she's never said anything about it before, she usually comes on the train. And anyway, won't you be back with your regiment?'

He shook his head. 'No chance of that.' He glanced down at his leg, stuck awkwardly out from the table. 'Told you I'd got a gammy leg, didn't I? Well, to tell you the truth, it ain't my leg at all. Well, it *is* mine – they give it me, see? At the hospital.' He caught her glance and nodded. 'Wooden one. The other one got shot off just below the knee. They won't want me back on service, that's the truth of it. Pensioning me off.'

'Oh,' Polly said blankly. 'Oh Mr Turner, I'm so sorry. That's awful.'

'Well, it weren't much fun,' he admitted. 'And the name's Joe. I'd take it kindly if you'd call me that.' He looked at her and his face crinkled. 'And I'd like to call you Polly, if you wouldn't mind.'

'No,' she said, 'I wouldn't mind at all.' He reached his hand across the table and she took it. They shook hands formally, as if they'd only just met, and then both laughed a little. 'But what will happen now? I mean, what will you do?'

'Oh, they'll find me things to do,' he said. 'Polish up the knocker on the big front door, that sorta thing. Just for the minute I'm still with my old boss, doing for him, but when he goes overseas again he'll get a new batman. I'm training up a new young chap now. Can't let the Colonel go back with no one to shine his buttons up for him.'

'I'm really sorry,' Polly said inadequately. 'You must be very disappointed. Were you in the Army before the war started?'

He nodded. 'Enlisted as a boy, went through the ranks, finished up as Sergeant. I was in the regimental band – trumpeter. Give you a tune one day, if you like.' He winked. 'Thought I might get a place in a dance band, bit of the old Glenn Miller stuff – "Moonlight Serenade", that sorta thing.'

'Oh, I love Glenn Miller,' Polly exclaimed. 'I like Ambrose, Joe Loss – all those sort of bands. We have the wireless on at home whenever they're on. I live with my sister and her husband,' she added, 'and my niece, Judy. And when we were bombed out we went to live with Mum. It's a bit of a squash but it's better to be all together.'

'Yes,' he said, 'it must be.'

There was an odd note in his voice and Polly gave him a curious glance. For once, he didn't meet her eyes but stared down at his empty plate, scraped almost clean of gravy and potato. Before either of them could speak again, the Nippy was at their side, swiftly removing the plates and asking if they'd like pudding. 'There's tapioca or plums and custard.'

'I'll have the plums,' Polly said, and Joe nodded in agreement. He looked up at last and grinned at her.

'We seem to have the same tastes. Music, food . . .'

'Same tastes as a lot of other people, then,' Polly said, a flicker of panic making her voice come out a little sharply. 'I dare say nearly everyone in the country likes Glenn Miller – and Lyons wouldn't put shepherd's pie and plums on the menu if they didn't think a lot of people would like them.'

'Ouch,' he said. 'Sorry – talking out of turn.'

'No, *I'm* sorry,' Polly told him, feeling ashamed of her sharpness. She gave him a smile. 'You're right, it is nice to meet someone who seems to like the same sort of things as you do. But . . .' she hesitated.

'But don't expect anything to come of it,' he said quietly.

'No, I don't. I don't think we can expect anything at all these days. You've only got to look around you and see all the bomb damage to know that. Here today, gone tomorrow, that's what they say, ain't it – and they never said a truer word. Never.' Once again there was that strained note in his voice. He looked at her, his face suddenly grave, the crinkles no longer of laughter, and said, 'Look, Polly, there's summat I want to tell you. I know I might be talking out of turn again, and I want you to know I wouldn't do this in the ordinary way – let out all my business to someone I've only just met. But somehow – well, it's as if we've known each other a long time. That day we met on the train – I felt it then, a bit. I was sorry you got off so soon. And then, bumping into you again today – well, it seemed to me as if it was meant. I don't feel as if I want to let this chance go by me.'

He stopped as the Nippy appeared again and set two bowls of plums and custard in front of them. Polly stared at him. Her heart was beating fast and she cast a panic-stricken glance around the restaurant. 'Mr Turner—' she began. 'Joe . . .' But he raised one hand to stop her.

'Let me have me say out, Polly. If you don't like it, you can get up and walk out, and I swear I'll never bother you again – but just let me say it. Please.'

His dark brown eyes were fixed on her face, like those of a big, anxious dog. Polly couldn't help smiling at him, and he grinned back, but the grin faded quickly and his eyes were serious again. When he spoke, his voice was husky.

'Maybe I oughter told you before, only it ain't summat I talks about a lot.'

'We've only really known each other a couple of hours,' Polly pointed out, thinking how strange that seemed. 'You've hardly had time.'

'Well, I know, but you told me about your old man, didn't you? I could've told you then.' He paused. 'It's the same for me, see. I lost my missus. Early on in the war – November thirty-nine. So – so I know what it's like.'

Polly gazed at him. The crinkles were all of pain now, a pain she understood all too well. She put out her hand and covered his. 'Joe, I'm so sorry,' she said softly. 'I'm ever so sorry. What happened?'

'It was in the blackout,' he said heavily. 'When it first started. There wasn't no lights allowed at all. Cars and buses were going about in the pitch dark, and you know what London's like for fogs – it was a real pea-souper. Couldn't see your hand in front of your face. Anyway, my Rosie, she had to go out one night, round to her mum's; the old girl'd been poorly for a week or two and took a turn for the worse. Rosie told the woman next door she was worried about her and made up her mind to go round and see if she was all right, settle her down for the night. Only she never got there. Knocked down by a car, she was, two streets away. Banged her head, never knew nothing about it – that was the only comfort.' He stared at their hands, still clasped together on the table. 'Never knew nothing about it.'

'Oh Joe,' Polly whispered. There was a long pause. Then she said, 'Where were you when it happened? Were you away?'

He nodded. 'In France. Couldn't come back, neither, not straight off. They got me back first chance they could, but it was all over by then. Her sister had done everything, the funeral and that, and the nippers were out in the country.'

'*Nippers*? You mean you've got children, too?'

'Two boys,' he said. 'That's where I was going the day we met on that train. They're down in Devon, smashing place, right on the edge of Dartmoor, think they're on a flipping holiday. Well, it hit 'em hard, losing their ma like that, I won't say it didn't, but you know what kids are, they get over it better than we do. Nine and seven, they are,' he said with a touch of pride in his voice. 'Billy and George. Couple of scallywags, too.'

'And what about your wife's mother?' Polly asked, trying to take all this in. 'What happened to her? Did she get better?'

He shook his head. 'Rosie was right. She was poorly. She'd had a bit of a stroke a day or two before, only they didn't realise it, see, and she wouldn't hear of getting the doctor. But when she heard what had happened to Rosie, she had another one and they had to take her into hospital. She died a couple of days later. So that was *two* funerals poor Annie had to sort out. She had 'em both buried in the same plot,' he added. 'It was all over by the time I come home.'

'It must have been dreadful,' Polly said, shaking her head. 'Dreadful.'

'Well, it wasn't a bundle of laughs,' he said. 'But I had the boys home for Christmas – that was when I got leave – and Annie and her hubby had us round there for the day, and it wasn't too bad. They didn't really want to go back to Devon after that – a lot of nippers didn't go back, there was nothing much happening over here then – but Annie couldn't have them and I wanted them out of the way if London did get bombed. And I had to give up me quarters, too. So they went back to Meavy, down in Devon, and I went back to France, and the next time I come home to Blighty it was on a stretcher with half me leg blown away.'

The Nippy appeared beside them again and looked down at their pudding bowls. 'Is there something the matter with the plums?'

Polly jumped and looked guilty. 'I'm sorry, I'd forgotten all about them.' She picked up her spoon, not feeling in the least like eating but guiltily aware that good food mustn't be wasted. The Nippy looked anxious.

'Only there's a lot of people waiting for tables.'

'We'll be finished in a minute or two.' They spooned plums rapidly into their mouths, scarcely tasting their sharpness, and it was not until they were out in the street again that they resumed their conversation. By now, Polly had regained some of her composure. She turned to her companion and tucked her hand into his arm again.

'It's a terribly sad story, Joe. I'm really sorry. But I'm glad you told me, all the same.'

'I just wanted you to know.' He looked down at her and seemed about to add more, then changed his mind. 'I'd like us to be pals, Polly, and pals ought to know the big things about each other.'

'Yes.' They walked in silence for a moment or two. They

were going down Whitehall now, past the great offices of the Government. Soon they would be back in Tothill Street; it was nearly time for the meeting to end. They would have to say goodbye.

'I dunno about you,' he said, 'but I ain't got so many pals I can pass up the chance of another one. So what d'you say? Keep in touch, shall we? Meet up now and then? Write to each other?' His fingers were big and warm about hers and she found herself wondering again what it would be like to be hugged by him. 'Will you say yes to that, Poll?'

Poll. It was as if she had always known him, as if he had always called her that. She nodded, smiling, and his face broke into a big, crinkly grin, his eyes almost disappearing amongst the wrinkles. He flung his arms around her and hugged her tightly.

It was just as she had known it would be. Warm and comforting. Strong. It was all that she had been missing, ever since Johnny went away.

But he was not Johnny. He never would be. And she would never be Rose.

Polly and Joe walked in silence for the rest of the way, past Downing Street where Mr Churchill lived and worked, past the Cenotaph with its list of men killed during the Great War of 1914–1918, and back to Parliament Square where the tower of Big Ben still rose proudly over the bombed House of Commons. They were sobered by both the devastation they could see on every side, and by the story Joe had told, which seemed to bring that wider devastation down to ordinary human terms – the anguish that had been suffered by so many people since this war had begun. It didn't matter whether you were killed by a bomb or by simply walking down the street in the blackout, Polly thought, it was the war that had done it. And her heart went out to the big man beside her, with his crinkly, humorous

263

face and his stoical acceptance of the tragedies he had suffered.

Yet she knew that however stalwart he seemed, deep down he was lonely and bewildered. Her hand was still tucked through his arm, as if he were the stronger, but she could sense that deep need for comfort. I understand it because I feel it too, she thought. We're two lonely people who have met and think we could be friends – and so we could be. But neither of us is ready for any more than that. Perhaps we never will be.

They came to the WVS Headquarters and rang the doorbell. It was Edna Cousins herself who came to answer it, and she stared at them in surprise, her eyebrows lifted.

'Well, you don't need to look so flummoxed, our Edna,' her brother admonished her. 'Me and Mrs Dunn are old acquaintances. Bumped into each other in the park, we did, and been up to the Lyons' Corner House for a bite of dinner, and me being a gentleman I've walked her back here.'

'Where you were coming anyway,' Mrs Cousins told him, unimpressed by his claim. 'Well, trust you to find yourself some nice company. Don't you take no notice of him, love,' she said to Polly. 'He's full of blarney, that one. Our mum had an uncle who came from Ireland, that's where we reckon he got it from.'

'Don't be daft, Uncle Pat wasn't no relation to us, he was only our uncle by marriage to Auntie Margie and she had no more Irish blood in her than this door. Speaking of which, are you going to let us in or ain't you? This foot of mine's had enough, if you want to know the truth.'

'Come on, then.' They walked into the hallway and Polly glanced about a little anxiously, afraid that she might have kept the Mayoress waiting. But the door to the meeting room was still closed and she could hear the murmur of voices within. Joe disappeared into the cloakroom and she followed Mrs Cousins through to the kitchen, where she had evidently just finished washing up after the midday meal. Polly felt a pang of guilt.

'Look at that mountain of crocks! I ought to have stayed and helped you.'

'I told you, you've done your job and you've still got to drive back to Portsmouth. Now, how d'you fancy a cup of tea? I've got the kettle on for them in there and I dare say you're ready for one after your walk. Specially if you've had to put up with *him* nattering on,' she added, with a humorous glance.

Polly hesitated, then said quietly, 'He told me about his wife. It must have been dreadful.'

'He never did! Well!' The cook sat down suddenly, looking upset. 'He don't talk about it much,' she said. 'I wish he would, sometimes, it'd do him good to let it out, but he was always one for keeping cheerful – well, we were brought up that way, all of us. I'm surprised he'd tell someone he's only just met.' A small frown creased her brow and she looked very like her brother. 'But didn't he say you already knew each other?'

'Well, not really. We met on a train a few months ago.' Quickly, Polly recounted the story of their meeting. 'I wouldn't say we *knew* each other.'

Edna Cousins's eyes rested on her thoughtfully. 'Well, there must be something, to make him come out with it like that.' The kettle started to whistle and she got up and began to make the tea. 'You don't want to take no notice of what I says about him,' she said over her shoulder. 'That's just the way we go on. If you've got any brothers, you'll know what I mean.'

'I haven't,' Polly said. 'But I've got a sister, and she's got a son and daughter, so I know what you mean. And I know how he feels too,' she added in a rush. 'I lost my hubby, early in the war. It knocks you sideways, but you've got to carry on. You've got to do your best for the war, for their sake.'

'That's right,' Edna said. 'The hard thing for our Joe is that there don't seem to be nothing he can do, not with his foot. He says he's no use to the Army any more. It's daft – a man who can walk the distance he's walked today could do any amount of jobs – but he's a soldier, see; he wants to go and fight – that's what a soldier *does*, he says – and that's what they won't let him do.'

'But other jobs are as important,' Polly said. 'There must be hundreds of things he can do.'

'Try telling him that,' the cook said, and began to pour milk into a row of cups already set on a big tray.

They heard Joe's footsteps coming along the hall then and the conversation ceased. Polly took the tray into the meeting room and found the Mayoress at the head of a long table with a dozen other women around it. They thanked her for the tea and the Mayoress told her that the meeting would be over soon and she would be ready to go back to Portsmouth. Polly went back to the kitchen, where she found Joe and his sister drinking tea and talking about his boys in Devon.

'Bit different to Blighty, where they are,' he said. 'Little village, it is, proper picture postcard place – church, pub, village green with a big old oak tree, and a lot of little cottages all round. You go up the lane a bit and you're out on Dartmoor.' He pulled a face. 'Don't fancy it meself, big wide open spaces like that with hardly so much as a tree in sight, and all them rocks, but the nippers think they're in paradise. Do what they like, see – roam about making dens and playing cowboys and indians, and nobody to tell 'em to bu— shove off and play somewhere else. Don't reckon as they'll ever want to come home, once it's all over.'

'Don't be silly, Joe,' Edna said. 'You know they wanted to stay with you after Christmas.'

'Yeah, but they went back and had all that snow, didn't they, and since then there's been all the lambs getting born, and I don't know what else, and I reckon they've got their feet well under the table with that woman what's looking after them. She's a widow,' he explained to Polly. 'Never had no nippers, so she treats 'em like they're her own. Stands to reason they'd rather stop with someone like that than come back to their dad with his foot blowed off and no proper job to do, nor even a decent home for them.'

Polly looked at him in dismay. It was the nearest he had come to appearing sorry for himself. Before she could speak, however, his sister said sharply, 'Now you know it's no use talking like that, Joe. It doesn't matter how good Mrs Ellacombe is, she isn't their mum, nor ever will be. Blood's thicker than water and they'll want to come back to their dad once it's safe. It's like you always say – this evacuation's like holiday for them, and nobody wants to be on holiday for ever.'

There was a small silence. Polly glanced at Joe and wondered if the widow Ellacombe had ideas of becoming the boys' stepmother. No doubt she knew of the tragedy of their mother's death, and if she found Joe a congenial companion when he went to visit them she might well have allowed the thought to cross her mind.

The kitchen door opened and the Mayoress appeared. She smiled round at the little gathering and said to Polly, 'We've finished the meeting and I'll be ready to leave in about ten minutes. I just want a word in the office first.' She disappeared and they heard her go into the room where all the typewriters were still clattering away. Polly got up and pushed her chair under the table.

'I'll get my coat. Thanks for the tea, Mrs Cousins.' She hesitated, not knowing quite how to say goodbye to Joe. He stood up too and held out his hand.

'Good luck, Polly. And mind you remember what we said, eh? Keep in touch.' He fished in his pocket and drew out an envelope. 'Look, here's my address. Or you could send a letter here, care of Edna. And tell me your address – I'll write it down.' He tore the back off the envelope and found a stub of pencil.

'It's number nine, April Grove,' Polly said, feeling a little embarrassed under Edna Cousins's gaze. 'Portsmouth, Hants. And – and if you're ever down that way, mind you call in. There's usually someone in.'

They nodded at each other, smiling a little uncertainly, and then shook hands. Polly thought wistfully of the hug they had shared so spontaneously out in the street, for all the world to see, but in here it seemed different. She saw the same thought in his eyes, and then they heard the Mayoress's footsteps approaching again and the moment passed.

He came out of the front door with them, helped both women into the car and then stood on the steps to wave farewell. His sturdy figure, looking suddenly lonely as he leaned on his stick, was the last thing Polly saw as she turned the corner.

'He seems a very nice man,' the Mayoress remarked as they drove slowly through the streets, still blocked with rubble and smoky from the fires that still burned. 'Have you known him long?'

'No,' Polly said. 'Not very long.' But, somehow, she felt that she had.

Chapter Twenty

It was nearly a fortnight before the next raid on Portsmouth, and then it was almost laughable compared with what had gone before, with just a few bombs being dropped into the sea at Spithead, injuring no one and causing no damage except, perhaps, to the fish. 'Bombing sprats and herrings now!' Tommy Vickers said scornfully when Cissie met him in the street. 'I reckon we've seen 'em off, don't you?'

'I don't know, Tommy.' Cissie shivered, despite the warmth of the sunshine. 'I wouldn't put anything past that Hitler. They say he's developing a secret weapon – something worse than anything he's used before.'

'The only secret weapon Hitler's got is fear,' Tommy told her. 'And it hasn't done much for him so far. All right, we're frightened – every time the air-raid warning goes, my backbone turns to ice – but we don't let it stop us doing what we got to do. And I reckon we're doing the same for the Germans anyway; our lads are bombing them to bits every night, same as he's been doing to us.'

Cissie nodded. She couldn't feel glad about that, though. They were ordinary people, she thought, people with homes and families just like in England. Kiddies in their prams, old folk like her mother, men like Dick who were still suffering from the First War. They didn't deserve to be 'bombed to bits' any more than the people at home.

Jess Budd felt the same. She had invited Cissie down to number fourteen to tea once or twice, and when Cissie went into the cosy little back room, crowded with Jess's piano against one wall, two armchairs beside the fire and a square dining table in the middle, she found several other neighbours there too – Jess's sister Annie Chapman, from the end of March Street, Tommy's wife Freda and, since it was early closing day, white-haired old Mrs Seddon who kept the little shop on the corner of October Street. The women all had some knitting to do – nobody sat down these days without a piece of work in their hands. Maureen Budd, who was nearly two years old, was playing on the rug in front of the fireplace with some coloured bricks that had belonged to her brothers.

'Your boys getting on all right out at Bridge End?' Freda asked, and Jess nodded.

'Seem to be. I didn't think they'd take to it, mind, living with a vicar – our Tim's never been one for church, couldn't ever keep still long enough – but Mr Beckett seems to have a way with boys. Girls too,' she added. 'Stella and Muriel have settled down well, in spite of everything.'

'Didn't your Polly take them out there?' Annie asked Cissie, passing her a plate of broken biscuits that Mrs Seddon had brought over.

'Yes. She liked the old man, and his housekeeper – she's the one that looks after them really. Treats the vicar like another boy, so Polly said.'

Jess smiled. 'That's what he is, I reckon. I knew him a bit when I was there, right at the beginning. Always riding round on that old bike of his, dressed up in his cassock like a great big bat. And sometimes, when he took the early service, you could see he was still in his pyjamas underneath! But he's a really kind man, and sort of *wise* too, if you know what I mean. I always felt he understood a lot more than he let on. And you could tell him anything – he'd never be shocked or think you weren't worth helping. He's a real Christian, I suppose.' She sounded half embarrassed. Most of those present went to church, if not every week, but none of them would have felt easy in discussing their beliefs. It was almost as bad as talking about sex, or cancer.

'And how about your Judy?' Mrs Seddon asked. 'I always remember her popping into the shop as a little girl, when you came round to see your mum. Such a dear, polite little soul, holding out her ha'penny and asking for a cone of lemon drops. Not like some of the children these days,' she added, and they all knew who she was thinking about. Micky Baxter, who lived almost opposite the shop, hardly knew the words 'please' and 'thank you'.

'Well, you know she's out at Ashwood, with little Sylvie, at the moment,' Cissie said. 'We're hoping the change will do her good, and some fresh air and country cooking. They say you can even get butter out there! But of course, that can't help her hearing. I don't know if anything can.'

'It's a crying shame.' Annie Chapman, who had an opinion on everything, spoke forcefully. 'Terrible thing to happen to a young girl. And not long after her young man had died too. I don't know what the world's coming to.'

'Nor do I,' Jess Budd said. She looked down at Maureen, who had built a rather lopsided castle with the bricks. 'Little children being bombed – and it's not just here, it's over there too. I mean, they may be German, but they're still kiddies. It doesn't seem right to me, and even Mr Churchill himself can't tell me it is.'

'It's war,' Annie said a little sharply. She was worrying about her daughter Betty, who was a Land Girl out near Bishop's Waltham, and getting more friendly with a young man than Annie and her husband Ted liked. The young man was called Dennis and there was something funny about him; neither of them could understand why he was working on a farm, when most young men of his age were in the Forces. Ted had wondered once or twice if he was a conscientious objector and told Annie in no uncertain terms that young Betty needn't think she could bring him home if that was the case, because he wouldn't have him in the house. Annie couldn't argue with him, partly because Ted was going through a bad patch at present himself, and partly

271

because she agreed with him. Instead, she lay awake at night, going over it all in her mind and not even telling Jess about her suspicions.

There was a ring on the doorbell and Peggy Shaw's voice called out. A moment later she was in the room, looking flushed and excited. 'You'll never guess what's happened!' She looked round at them all. 'Our Gladys is getting a medal! The British Empire Medal! It's for what she did the night of the big raid, when the Royal Hospital got blown up. Can you credit it – our Gladys with a medal, presented by the King himself!'

The others stared at her. 'Well, that's a turn-up for the book, and no mistake,' Annie said at last. 'Someone in April Grove getting a medal! You must be ever so pleased, Peggy.'

'I am.' Peggy sat down on one of the dining chairs and took the cup of tea Jess had poured out. 'Thanks, Jess. Yes, I am pleased, and proud as Punch. So's Bert. But our Gladys doesn't seem too thrilled about it.'

'Why ever not?' The other women stared at her.

'Well, you know she got a bit knocked about – broken arm and that – and I suppose she's still a bit shocked. But she says she doesn't deserve it. Says there were plenty of others did things just as brave – your Polly for one, and Judy,' she said to Cissie. 'And she says it's Graham Philpotts that ought to be given it, because he didn't even need to be there, he was just helping her, and he got killed. She's really upset about that.'

'Well, *I* think she deserves it,' Annie said staunchly, 'and so do our Olive and Betty. They were talking about Gladys yesterday, when Betty came down from Bishop's Waltham for her day off. And look at it this way – they can't give *everyone* medals, so those that do get them are getting them on behalf of all those others that deserve them. It's Graham's and Polly's and Judy's medal, just as much as it's Gladys's, but she happens to be the one that's been picked out. That's all it is.'

Peggy nodded. The flush had faded a little and now she looked worried. 'The other thing is, she's made up her mind to volunteer. Wants to go into the Wrens. She says it'll make up a bit for getting Graham killed. My Bert's none too pleased, but what can you do? They've all had to sign on anyway but they don't actually have to go into the Services till they're called up. But Gladys wants to go now. And on top of that, young Diane's gone and got herself a job at Airspeed – says she wants to learn to fly, of all things!'

'Fly?' Jess echoed. 'I shouldn't think she's got much hope of that – why, she's barely sixteen, surely. They're not going to take young girls as pilots.'

'I dunno,' Peggy said with a sigh. 'I dunno what they'll do. Everything seems turned upside down now.' She looked down at the toddler on the rug. 'Sometimes I wish mine were all this age again. At least you could have a bit of a say in what happens to them and what they do. What with Gladys and Diane, and our Bob away in the Army, I just wonder what it's all about. It's not the life we wanted for them, Jess. It's not at all.'

'I wonder if anyone ever does have the life their parents want for them,' Jess commented sadly. 'Look at us. We had to go through the First War and now, just when we're getting on our feet, along comes this one to mess it all up again. And there's not a thing we can do about it. It's out of our hands.'

Mrs Seddon looked at the little group of women with their sad faces. She too had been through the Great War, and could remember even further back, to the Boer War and other conflicts of the nineteenth and twentieth centuries. 'What we have to realise,' she said in her soft voice, 'is that this *is* life. All these things that go wrong – little things at home and great things overseas, squabbles in the family and quarrels between nations – they're *part* of life, they happen over and over again. They always have and they always will. The important thing, I think, is not what happens to us, but

273

what we do about it.' She paused and the women gazed at her. 'The young people are rising to the occasion, just as we'd want them to,' she said. 'It might not be what we wanted for them – but they're acting in just the ways we would have hoped. I think you can *all* feel proud – of your children and yourselves.' A little pink in the cheeks, she held out her cup. 'Is there any more tea in that pot, Mrs Budd?'

The little tea-party broke up soon after that. The women rolled up their knitting and left to start preparing tea for their husbands. Mrs Seddon, who was a widow, went off saying that she was going to change the window display – not that there was much to display these days, but a new jar of sherbet lemons had come in this morning and she wanted to give it pride of place. She crossed the road to her door, and Cissie, Freda and Annie Chapman walked up the street together.

'That was nice, what Mrs Seddon said, wasn't it?' Cissie said. 'She's a lovely old lady. All the kiddies love her, you know.'

'Well, she's part of April Grove, isn't she,' Annie said. 'I can't remember a time when she wasn't there in that little shop, weighing out biscuits and sweets and dried fruit. I wonder sometimes how she manages to make a living, now that everything's on ration. But I reckon she's right, you know, about all this being a part of life. Wars always have happened and I don't suppose they'll ever stop happening. Look at what they said about the last one – the "war to end all wars", they called it. And here we are again, barely twenty years later, worse than ever. Not that the youngsters seem to mind all that much. Our Betty's having the time of her life out in the country, even though the work's hard. Her dad and me wonder sometimes what she gets up to out there.'

'I think a lot of the young women are getting the sort of freedom they'd never have had otherwise,' Freda agreed.

'Our Eunice is the same, proper let off the leash she is, in the ATS. If it hadn't been for the war they'd have all stopped at home, under their parents' eyes, till they got married. Now you don't know what they're doing.'

'And some of them aren't getting the lives they thought they'd have,' Cissie said quietly. 'Look at our Polly, a widow at thirty-five. And Judy, deaf at twenty-two.' She looked at Annie Chapman. 'And what about your Olive? It must have been ever so hard for her to say goodbye to her husband only a day or two after their wedding.'

The others nodded soberly. There was no making sense of it all, they agreed. They came to Alice Thomas's front door and said goodbye. Cissie went indoors and found Dick sitting in his usual chair, his latest rag rug spread over his knees.

'I dunno as I'll be able to go on with this much more in the hot weather,' he said, looking up. 'It's like having a blanket over me. Have a good natter?'

Cissie nodded and went through to the scullery to start getting tea ready. 'Gladys Shaw's getting a medal,' she called. 'The British Empire Medal, it is, for what she did in the raids. She says she doesn't deserve it, that there's plenty of others did just as much, but she'll have to go and be presented with it all the same. And Peggy says she's going in the Wrens now.'

'Peggy Shaw? She's too old, surely!'

'Not Peggy, Gladys. And Diane, their youngest, she's got a job at Airspeed, wants to learn to fly.'

'They'll never let her. What is she, sixteen? Mind you, she's always been the *flighty* one!' Dick laughed at his joke and rolled up the rug. 'I've had enough of this, Cis, it's making my eyes go funny. What's for tea?'

'I thought we'd have sardines on toast. I got a tin yesterday.' Cissie came in and looked at him a little anxiously. 'You feeling all right, Dick?'

'More or less. I'm just a bit hot. And it's all these

different colours, dazzling me. I dunno who's going to get this one, but they'd better like bright colours.' He grinned again and Cissie laughed too but put her hand on his forehead. 'It's all right, Cis, I haven't got a temperature.'

'No, but all the same . . . It's not long since that pneumonia, Dick. You've got to be careful.'

'Careful!' he said. 'I don't know how I could be any more careful than I am now. All I do is sit in this chair all day making blinking rugs and listening to the wireless.'

'You go for a walk every day.'

'Yes, up to the end of the street and back. Well, I tell a lie, this morning I walked all the way up to the newsagent's shop. That Alice Brunner, she's looking a bit better these days. Gave me a nice smile, she did. I reckon that girl of hers told her to pull herself together.'

'Joy's a big help to her mum,' Cissie said, 'and Alice has had a lot of worry, with Heinrich being taken away like that. I ask you!' she went on indignantly, coming through the door and waving a bread-knife. 'Interning a man like Heinrich Brunner who's been in England and running his own business all those years! As if he was a spy. It's criminal. And then sending him off on that ship and getting him torpedoed. It's no wonder poor Alice nearly had a nervous breakdown.'

'Well, you needn't stab me to death because of it,' Dick said, pretending to cower in his chair. 'But you're right, Cis, it was a bad do. There must have been hundreds like Heinrich Brunner, been living here for years not doing no harm to nobody, and all put in prison like common criminals. It was like a sort of panic.'

'They've let a lot of them out now,' Cissie said, going back to the scullery. 'But that doesn't help men like poor Mr Brunner, who got killed on that ship.'

She went on getting the tea ready. Presently, Alice came in from her own afternoon spent helping at the local Clothing Store, and then Polly arrived. She had been working at the salon, cutting and setting hair. With no raids for a fortnight, and then just a few bombs dropped in the sea, it seemed almost as if normal life was beginning to return.

'There's another letter for you, Poll,' Dick said, nodding at the mantelpiece. It had come by second post, not long after Polly had left for the salon, and Cissie and he had indulged in some conjecture about it before placing it behind the photo of Terry in his naval uniform. Letters weren't all that common unless they were from Sylvie out at Ashwood or Terry, somewhere at sea, and this wasn't from either of them. It bore a London postmark, and it wasn't the first to have arrived in the last couple of weeks.

Polly took it and blushed. 'I'll just slip upstairs and change out of this skirt and blouse,' she said, trying to sound casual, and Dick winked at Cissie who had come through from the scullery.

'Reckon she's found herself a fancy man?' he asked in a whisper.

'Well, I don't know. That's the third, isn't it? But I never thought she'd be interested again, not this soon after losing Johnny.'

'It's eighteen months or more,' Dick pointed out. 'And she's not old, Cis.'

Cissie pursed her lips. 'Well, I wouldn't object myself, but you know what Mum is like about second marriages. She wouldn't like it if Polly got serious about another man.'

'Yes, but that's just being old-fashioned. People aren't so strict these days, and with so many men getting killed—'

'Ssh.' Cissie put her finger to her lips. Alice was coming in from the outside lavatory, already beginning to tell them about a woman she'd had in the Clothing Store that afternoon, trying to exchange a tattered old jacket for a good three-piece suit. Cissie gave Dick a warning glance and went back to the scullery where she was spreading margarine on bread and getting out a new pot of jam from the store Alice had made last summer.

When Polly came down in her old skirt and blouse, they all sat down round the table. Cissie set the plates of sardines on toast in front of them and looked at her sister, hoping for some remark about the letter. But Polly didn't mention it. Instead, she said, 'I had that Ethel Glaister from number fifteen in for a perm this afternoon. What a cat she is! Doesn't have a good word to say for a soul. Seems to think she's too good for April Grove or anyone in it.'

'Dunno why she goes on living here then,' Dick remarked. 'If she's so posh, why doesn't she move up to Hilsea or somewhere?'

'Oh, she says they were just going to when the war started, and then of course everything stopped. Her hubby was in the Territorials and he went straight off into the regular Army. Honestly, you'd think he did it just to spite her.' Polly giggled. 'I dare say he was glad of the excuse to get away! It must have seemed like a dream come true to him when war broke out.'

'Polly! That's a terrible thing to say,' Cissie reproved her, but the others were laughing and she had to smile. 'Well, I can't say I'd like to live with Ethel Glaister for long. How did you do her hair, Poll?'

'Oh, the latest fashion of course – Marcel waves. And I'll tell you something else.' Polly leaned over the table and glanced from side to side as if there might be a spy lurking behind a chair. 'That hair of hers isn't really yellow at all! It's practically grey! We have to touch up the roots every six weeks to stop it showing through.'

'*Dyed*! Well, I always suspected it,' Alice said disapprovingly. 'You know, I sometimes wonder about Ethel Glaister and where she goes off to every afternoon in her smart suit and high heels. Now I wonder even more. If you ask me, she's no better than Nancy Baxter.'

'Well, you'd better not say so,' Polly advised her. 'You

could get into trouble. And don't any of you dare tell anyone about her hair. I'd get the sack if Mrs Carson knew I'd let out something like that about one of the ladies.'

'Why?' Dick asked. 'It's not that bad, surely. Plenty of women dye their hair.'

'Not decent women,' Alice retorted, but Polly shook her head.

'It's because they don't want people to know they're going grey. Women like Ethel Glaister who think they're smart and glamorous,' the family hooted with laughter, 'they like people to think it's natural, see? So that everyone thinks they're younger than they really are.'

'As if it mattered,' Alice said in disgust. 'We've all got to get older. It's nothing to be ashamed of. If you ask me, people like Ethel Glaister haven't got enough to do. Ought to come down the Clothing Store of an afternoon with me and do a hand's turn to help. That'd take her mind off being *glamorous*.'

The evening passed quietly with a game of whist, and at nine o'clock they switched on the wireless to hear the news. No matter how quiet it might have been in Portsmouth, there was always news of some terrible event somewhere else. A bombing raid on another city, a battle in Africa or the Mediterranean, a ship sunk by a U-boat in the Atlantic.

'*What was that?*' Cissie gasped, her hand at her throat.

They stared at her, then at each other. Polly opened her mouth but Dick gestured to her to be silent. In horror, they listened again to the newsreader's words, and then the bulletin ended and Dick reached out a slow, trembling hand and turned the knob.

'I can't believe it,' Alice whispered, her face as white as paper. 'HMS *Hood*, blown up and sunk in just four minutes. There can't be anyone left alive, there *can't* be.'

'Our Terry,' Cis whimpered, covering her face with her hands. 'He said it was the best ship in the whole of the Fleet. Dick,' blindly, she reached a hand out to her husband, 'Dick, our Terry's been killed. Our *Terry's* been killed.'

'We don't know that, love.' But his voice was shaking and tears were trickling down his cheeks. 'We don't know it for sure. They haven't said everyone was killed. There might've been survivors.'

'When it was blown up and sunk in *four minutes?*' She shook her head. 'How could anyone have lived through that? Oh Dick.' She began to cry, while the others wept as well. Despite Dick's words, they all knew that Terry's chances were very low. Even if he had survived the explosion, how could he have lived more than a few minutes in the icy waters off Greenland where the battle had taken place? People said you froze to death almost at once. And none of the family had any faith in the Germans having picked up men in the water. That's what they were supposed to do, but would they have done it?

There was little sleep that night in number nine. Cissie could not stop crying. Every time her sobs eased a little, she thought of the news announcement, or some little reminder of her son, and started all over again. She took his photo down from the mantelpiece and wept afresh, stroking his laughing face with her fingertips. 'It's the only one we've got,' she sobbed. 'All those pictures of him at school and that lovely one that photographer took of him out at Southsea, with that parrot on his arm, we lost all those in the Blitz. And all his toys and things, his Meccano and his comics that he wanted saved – they've all gone. We've got nothing left. It's as if he never existed.'

'Of course it's not, Cis.' Polly, her own eyes red and swollen, tried to comfort her sister. 'It'll never be as if he never existed, never. We'll all remember him all our lives, and so will lots of other people. All the neighbours who knew him, and Dick's brother and his family, and Jean Foster.'

'Jean!' Cissie lifted her face and stared at her. 'She'll have heard the news too. Oh, poor Jean – he was talking about asking her to get engaged, last time he was home. I'll have to go round and see her.'

'Tomorrow.' Alice, looking grey and weary, came in with a cup of cocoa for them all. 'Drink this, Cis. It'll make you feel better and help you to sleep. Come on, now, it's no use making yourself ill. And like Dick said, we don't *know* he's dead. Miracles do happen.' She sighed and Polly, glancing at her, knew that in spite of her words, she too had almost given up hope. 'Drink it up and let's go to bed,' she said gently.

Still sobbing, Cissie managed to drink her cocoa and the family gathered up the cards that had been lying forgotten on the table and prepared for bed. One by one, they went outside to the lavatory, washed at the sink, cleaned their teeth, each going through the motions like an automaton. Then Cissie and Dick went slowly up the stairs and Polly and her mother were left alone.

'She's taking this very hard,' Alice said, shaking her head. 'Not that you can blame her. That's three good men we've lost at sea in this family. Three good men! Where's it going to end, Poll?'

Polly shook her head. 'I don't know, Mum. But I tell you what – I think we'd better get our Judy back home, don't you? It's the only thing that'll help Cis through this, having her back. It's a shame, because I think it's doing her good to be out in the country, but I reckon it's the best thing to do.'

'You're right,' Alice said. 'And I wouldn't be surprised if she turns up tomorrow without even being sent for. I bet she's packing her bags at this very minute.'

Chapter Twenty-One

It was not Judy who arrived next day, however. It was somebody else who turned up, quite unexpectedly, on the doorstep of number nine.

After all her crying, Cissie had fallen into a deep sleep and woke late, heavy-eyed and feeling as if she'd been crying even in her dreams. Dick had slept badly, tossing and turning as his mind filled again with the horrific memories of his own war experiences. He was pale and shaky when he stumbled downstairs to find Polly making tea and Alice sitting at the table, looking shrunken and grey in an old dressing-gown.

'Dick, you look like death warmed up,' Polly said, and then closed her eyes. 'Oh, I'm sorry – I could bite my tongue off sometimes. Have a cup of tea, and take one up for Cis. Is she awake yet?'

'Just stirring.' He rested against the door to the staircase. 'Tell you the truth, Poll, I don't feel too good at all. Don't tell Cis, though. She's got enough to upset her.'

'Don't feel too good?' Polly stopped with the teapot raised and looked at him closely. 'What is it? One of your attacks?'

'No, it's not like that. Just sort of tingly, and I've got a sort of ache—' He stopped as they heard movements from above, and opened the staircase door to call up: 'You stop in bed a bit longer, Cis. I'm just bringing you a cuppa.' To Polly, he said, 'I don't suppose it's anything much. Shock, probably, and I didn't sleep too well.'

'I don't suppose any of us did.' Polly handed him a cup

and went through to her mother. 'Here you are, Mum. Drink that down. It's hot, if nothing else. We're nearly out of tea again. I'll go up the street in a minute, see if there's anything in the papers.'

She looked through the cupboards to see what they could have for breakfast. There was half a packet of cornflakes, the end of a loaf that was going stale, some dried egg and some margarine and the pot of jam they'd started yesterday. Normally they wouldn't dream of having jam for breakfast, but this was her mother's own blackberry and apple, made last autumn with blackberries from Hilsea Lines, and Cissie was especially fond of it. It wasn't that a slice of bread and jam would make up for losing Terry, Polly thought, that would be daft, but a little treat at a time like this couldn't do any harm. She lit the grill to make toast and put some cornflakes in a bowl. Cissie could have breakfast in bed.

Dick came treading down the stairs again. He looked as grey as Alice, and was breathing heavily. Polly glanced at him and wondered if he could after all be heading for an asthma attack. It wasn't all that long since his pneumonia, and shock could bring it on. It looks as if I'm going to have to look after the lot of them, she thought, glancing from Dick's ashen face to her mother's. While I'm up the street getting the papers, I'd better ring up and let the office know I won't be able to go in today.

She went to the telephone box first, searching for pennies for the call, and then walked along to the newsagent's. Alice Brunner's daughter Joy was there, sorting the papers. Polly looked at the headlines: SINK THE BISMARCK.

She read the report beneath. It was the *Bismarck* which had presented such a serious threat to Allied shipping that a flotilla of ships had set off from Scapa Flow in pursuit – HMS *Hood*, *Prince of Wales*, *King George V*, *Victorious* and a number of others. It was the *Bismarck* which, with just one shell, had sunk the *Hood*, penetrating the weak armour of its sides and striking the store of ammunition within to cause the huge and devastating explosion that had destroyed the ship and killed almost fifteen hundred men. Few, if any, could have been saved.

Now the hunt was on in earnest for the killer ship. The order had gone out – she was to be sunk at all costs. And that meant more men killed, Polly thought, trudging back down October Street with an armful of newspapers and a heavy heart. More young men like Terry and Johnny and Sean. And it wouldn't bring even one of them back. Not one.

Nobody had been able to eat much breakfast. Cissie had come downstairs, saying she couldn't stop in bed, and after they'd washed up, feeling as if nothing was really worthwhile doing but not knowing what else to do, she and Dick set off to see Jean Foster, who had been Terry's sweetheart since they'd been at school. Jean had worked in the Landport Drapery Bazaar, in Guildhall Square, but since the bombing the shop had re-opened in several different places in town, and now she was in Lake Road. Since they would pass it on the way to her home, they called in there first to see if she had come to work.

Jean was serving a customer. She looked a little plumper than when they had last seen her, during Terry's Christmas leave, but her clear skin was glowing, her brown hair springing with natural curls and her pretty face smiling as she talked to the customer. Cissie and Dick looked at each other in dismay.

'She doesn't know,' Cissie mouthed. 'Oh Dick, we've got to tell her ourselves.' Her lips trembled. 'I don't think I can.'

'I dunno what else we can do, love.' Dick half turned awkwardly, as if to slip out again, but at that moment Jean glanced up and saw them. She hesitated, looking embarrassed, and then finished giving the customer her change and came over.

'Mrs Taylor! Mr Taylor – I didn't expect to see you

here.' She looked flushed and embarrassed and they gazed at her silently, taken aback by her manner. 'I don't know who's told you,' she went on quickly, 'but I haven't done anything wrong. We'd been going steady for a long time, and what with Christmas and Terry going away, and us never knowing when we'd see each other again, well . . .' she tilted her chin a little defiantly '. . . it just happened, that's all, and there's nothing anyone can do about it now, I've written to tell Terry and—'

Dick interrupted her. 'We don't know what you're talking about, Jean. We just came to see if you'd heard the news. It was on last night. Haven't you heard?'

The girl stared at them. She seemed to notice their swollen eyes for the first time and her colour faded. Nervously, she said, 'News? What news? I haven't heard no news.'

'The *Hood*,' Cissie said in a dry, aching voice. 'She's been sunk. D'you mean to say you hadn't heard? It's all over the papers.'

Jean turned white. 'The *Hood*? Sunk? But – oh, *no*.' She reached out a hand and laid it against the wall, swaying a little. 'But – Terry – isn't he all right? Wasn't he saved?'

'We don't know,' Dick said quietly. 'We don't think he could have been. The ship went down in four minutes.'

'Four minutes?' The ashen white turned to a sickly green and Dick stepped forwards quickly to catch the girl as she crumpled. He staggered beneath her weight and the shop supervisor noticed what was happening and came quickly across to help. Between them, they got Jean on to the chair put beside the counter for customers. Cissie pressed her head down to her knees while Dick steadied her and the supervisor hurried off for a cup of water.

'Drink this.' She held the cup beneath Jean's lips. 'Just a sip or two. It'll make you feel better.' They all watched anxiously as Jean sipped and took a couple of shuddering breaths. The supervisor looked at Dick and Cissie. 'Has she had bad news?'

Cissie nodded. 'We all have.' Her eyes filled with tears again. 'The *Hood*,' she said, chokingly. 'On the news last night.'

The woman nodded. 'I heard it. It's in the papers this morning. Terrible.' Her eyes sharpened. 'You mean, someone was on it? Someone Jean knew – was fond of?'

'Our son was one of the crew,' Dick said hoarsely. 'And Jean and him – well, they've been going steady ever since they left school. He was hoping they'd get engaged, the next time he got leave.' He looked down at the girl's bent head. 'We'd have been pleased. We're fond of Jean – we'd have been proud to have her as a daughter-in-law.'

The supervisor's eyes softened. 'Oh, I'm so sorry. That's dreadful. But Jean never said. She's been just the same as usual this morning, a bit quiet, but then she has been just lately. Missing her sweetheart, naturally. I'd no idea.'

'I don't think she knew,' Cissie said. 'That's why it was such a shock to her when we told her just now.'

'The poor girl. And you as well.' The woman hesitated, then glanced down at the bent head. 'Jean,' she said kindly, 'when you feel well enough, I think you'd better go home for the rest of the day. We can manage without you. Take the rest of the week off and come back on Monday, when you've had time to get over the shock. I know just how you must be feeling.' She said quietly, 'I lost my brother a few months ago, so I do understand.'

Jean looked up at last. Her face was like parchment, her eyes like bruises against the yellowish-green tinge of her normally rosy cheeks. She looked at them all with a dull, hopeless stare and said in a flat voice that seemed to have been drained of all feeling, 'You *don't* understand, Miss Browning. Nobody does.' Her eyes went to Dick's face and then to Cissie's. 'It's not just Terry, you see. I'm in trouble anyway. Bad trouble.' She took a deep breath, as if gathering courage, and then said in a rush, 'I'm expecting. I'm in the family way. And now Terry's never coming back, I don't know what to do.' Her voice wavered and cracked, and she broke into a storm of crying. 'I just don't know what I'm going to do!'

Locked behind her wall of silence, Judy had no idea what had happened.

She had gone to bed early the night before, just as the family was sitting down to listen to the nine o'clock news. It was one of the most frustrating times for her, watching their faces and wondering what was going on in the world. They would tell her, of course, Mrs Sutton either mouthing the words carefully or writing them down on a scrap of paper – but she was sure they didn't tell her everything they heard. It was too laborious, too much trouble. She had formed the habit of going outside to sit under the apple tree, watching the sky deepen from soft blue to deep purple, streaked and patterned with glowing crimson as the sun dipped below the wooded hill. Tomorrow, she would read the newspaper to find out what had happened; tonight she would sleep in peace.

On this night, however, it was dull and there was a drizzle in the air. Judy had been making scrim almost all day and had come home tired and dirty. While the family were listening to the wireless, she shut herself in the scullery for a good wash, and then went straight up to bed, calling her goodnight through the half-open door. She tiptoed into the room she shared with Sylvie, checked that her niece was asleep and properly covered, and then slipped into bed.

She had been here for a fortnight now, and it seemed like home. Although she missed her family, the Suttons had been so kind that she felt almost as if she had found a second family, and the cottage and the countryside around were like a balm to her unhappy soul. It was a balm she had needed desperately. The loss of first her brother-in-law and then her fiancé had struck at her heart, the bombing of her home had left her feeling lost and disoriented, and her deafness had been a final cruel blow. Over and over again she told herself how lucky she was – she still had her parents, her sister, her little niece and her grandmother, her brother Terry was serving on one of Britain's greatest ships, she had been able to come to this peaceful village and stay with these kind people – yet she could not rid herself of the deep, searing loneliness of her silent world. If only I could hear again, she thought. If *only* . . .

It was strange that the one person with whom she felt completely at ease was Ben Hazelwood, the boy who seemed so much older than seventeen, who had taken her down to the river and shown her a kingfisher and told her she would hear again. She had seen him again several times over the next few days. He had come to the farm and sat with her under the apple tree in the orchard, looking intently into her eyes as he talked. With him, she had felt her pain begin to ease and the scars in her mind begin to heal.

He had gone back to school in Winchester now, but he had written to her and she had written back. It was strange to strike up so close a friendship with a boy still at school, yet he didn't seem so young, and in any case there were boys not much older serving at this moment in the Armed Forces. If Ben got his way – and she felt sure he would – he would soon be one of them.

Her mind drifted to another young man whose eyes had looked into hers as he talked, who had held her for a while with his magnetism. Chris Barrett, the Observer who spent his time on the roof of the Royal Beach searching for enemy aircraft, and who had sat with her on the floor of the lift, his arms around her in comfort; who had kissed her to the sound of cheers as the lift arrived at the eighth floor. She thought of the way she had treated him after that – hiding in a cupboard when she saw him coming, pushing past him in the corridors, snapping his head off when she'd met him on

288

the steps. I wasn't very nice to him, she thought. And I really think all he wanted to do was say sorry. Polly said in her letter that he's asked after me two or three times and wanted her to send his good wishes to me. I really ought to send mine back, just to show no hard feelings. It wasn't his fault the lift arrived when it did. He was a nice chap. And it was a lovely kiss . . .

She lay in bed, thinking of Chris and thinking of Ben until, smiling a little, she fell asleep.

There was no time to read a newspaper next morning. It was always busy then, because of the milking, but today one of the cows was having difficulty calving and Judy was sent down to a neighbouring farm to get help. She came back to find that Sylvie had been sick and was back in bed, looking pale and miserable, so she ate a hasty breakfast and went up to look after her. The newspaper, brought from the station by a neighbouring farmer, was tossed into a corner where Mrs Sutton dropped a bundle of washing on top of it, and if the wireless was on at all Judy didn't hear it. She didn't even wonder what the news might have been. It was always the same anyway, she thought, sponging Sylvie's face gently. Bombing, and more bombing. Deaths, and more deaths.

There were believed to have been just three survivors from the *Hood*.

'Three mothers will be happy, at least,' Alice said as Polly switched off the wireless after listening to the one o'clock news. 'But I don't think our Cis'll be one of them. I mean, I know one of those boys *could* have been our Terry – but you know what they say. Things go in threes. First your Johnny, then Sean and now Terry. It seems like fate, somehow.'

Polly nodded. She didn't really believe in superstition and refused to throw spilled salt over her shoulder, or avoid the cracks in pavements, but now she had the same feeling as her mother, that it wasn't likely that Terry was one of the three who had survived that terrible blast. For one thing, he worked in the engine rooms so he would almost certainly have been below decks when it happened. Terry wouldn't have had a chance.

'At least it must have been quick,' she said, trying to find a crumb of comfort. 'He wouldn't have known anything about it. He wouldn't have been floating about in the sea for hours.' Like Johnny, she thought. Like Johnny and, probably, Sean.

Alice nodded, but the comfort wasn't enough to stop her face crumpling again and the tears welling up in her eyes. 'Our Terry,' she said, choking on his name. 'It don't seem possible, Poll. He was always so full of life, so bright and breezy all the time. I can't believe all that's gone. I can't believe we'll never see him again.'

'Oh Mum.' Polly moved to put her arm round her mother's shoulders. She was as thin as a bird, she thought, feeling the tiny bones beneath her hands. She's getting smaller, I'm sure. 'There's still a chance,' she murmured. 'He could have been one of those saved.'

'No,' Alice wept, shaking her head so that the grey hair, not yet properly brushed and pinned up that morning, straggled across her brow. 'No, he's not. We'd have heard, you know that. If they know there's three saved, they must know their names and they'd have sent someone round. He's gone, Polly, and we've got to face up to it. But it's so hard.' She broke down in a storm of sobs. 'Oh Poll, it's so *hard*, losing all our men like this. It's so *cruel*.'

Polly could not speak. The tears were pouring down her cheeks and she was holding her mother now as much to gain comfort as to give it. For some time they clung to each other, weeping as if their hearts were broken, and then at last Alice gave a sniff and felt for a hanky. She blew her nose hard, drew a deep, shuddering breath and looked at her daughter with wet but determined eyes.

'Well, we can't sit here piping our eyes all day, Poll. We've still got to do our jobs, same as usual. Cis and Dick'll be home any minute for their dinner, and we haven't even done the potatoes.' She glanced at the clock. 'Look at the time! Wherever can they be?'

'They were going to see Jean.' Polly frowned anxiously. 'I hope Dick hasn't had an attack. He hasn't been looking at all well lately, and what with the shock and upset and everything . . .'

'That would just about put the tin lid on things.' Alice wiped her eyes again and then looked up in relief as the doorbell shrilled. 'Oh, that'll be them now. Go and let them in, Poll.'

'But they'd have a key.' Her heart thumping with anxiety, Polly hurried to the front door. Something had happened, she was sure of it. Then a new thought occurred to her. Judy – it must be Judy, rushing home as soon as she had heard the news. She opened the door, a smile of welcome battling with the grief still pulling at her face.

For a moment, she did not recognise the man who stood there. She stared at him as if at a stranger, half-recognised, dimly remembered. It seemed a lifetime since he had played any part in her thoughts. Blankly, she shook her head.

'Well, Poll,' Joe Turner said, his crinkly face spread all over with delight, 'don't you know me no more?'

Chapter Twenty-Two

Joe's first reaction, on hearing the news, was to leave immediately. Polly had asked him in, embarrassed because the house was in a 'state' – nothing yet done, breakfast things still piled by the sink, Alice's bed in the front room not yet made – and he'd realised at once there was something wrong. It had needed only a few words to tell him what it was.

'Blimey, that's a facer and no mistake,' he said, staring from one to the other. 'No wonder you looked at me as if I'd just fell down from the moon. Here,' he turned towards the door. 'You won't want me around. I'll get out of your way.'

'No!' Polly reached out a hand involuntarily. 'No, don't rush off, not after you've taken the trouble to come all this way. Stop and have a cup of tea at least.'

'Well . . .' He hesitated. 'Maybe I could do something to help. Not that there's much anyone can do at a time like this, but – you know, I could take a message somewhere, do a bit of shopping, whatever you like. Go and get you some fish and chips for your dinner. Anything. Just say the word.'

Polly looked at him. 'Well, there is something you can do. It's Cis and Dick. They went to see Terry's girlfriend, Jean – she works at the Landport.' She realised that this meant nothing to him. 'In a shop. Only they've been gone hours and we're getting, worried. Dick's a bit of an invalid, you see; he gets asthma and he's only just got over pneumonia and we're afraid he might have had an attack. I was thinking of going to look for him, but I don't like leaving Mum.' She gestured at the old woman, who seemed to have lost all her sprightliness and sunk into a small, crumpled heap of misery. 'She's taking it very hard,' Polly whispered.

'I'll go,' he offered. 'Just tell me where. Only, I don't know Portsmouth at all, see, never been here in me life. Where do I start looking?' Then he grimaced. 'Come to that, who do I look for?'

'Oh dear, you don't even know what they look like, do you? So that's no good.' Polly went out to the scullery and filled the kettle. 'You'd better have a cup of tea anyway – we all will. And I was just going to start doing some potatoes for dinner. You'd better stop and have a bite with us.' He had followed her and stood leaning against the door-jamb. She looked at him regretfully. 'I'm sorry you had to find us all at sixes and sevens like this. It's just been such a shock, you see, and now with Cis and Dick not coming home I hardly know what I'm doing.'

'That's all right,' he said quietly. His crinkly face was soft with compassion. He hesitated for a moment, then stepped forwards and held out his arms. Polly stared at him. Her mouth drew itself down at the corners, her lips trembled and her eyes filled once again with hot, stinging tears. Without being aware that she had moved, she found herself leaning against his chest, her face against his shoulder, weeping as he held her close, weeping as she had not wept since Johnny had died. 'Oh Joe,' she sobbed, holding him tightly.

'There,' he murmured, stroking her back with a big, warm hand. 'There, there. You have a good cry, Poll, you just have a good cry. Let it all out – that's right. It'll do you good. And now you sit yourself down by your mum and I'll make that tea. I'll peel the spuds as well, and get you a bit of dinner, and then if your sis hasn't come back we'll think what to do next. You need someone to look after you. You all do.'

He led her back into the other room and pushed her gently into Dick's armchair. Polly sniffed, and blew her nose and wiped her eyes, and looked at him gratefully as he placed a cup of tea beside her. 'You don't have to do all that, Joe.'

'Don't see why not,' he said. 'I come all this way to see you, I ain't going to turn round and go without making meself a bit useful. Unless you wants me to, of course,' he added quickly. 'You've only got to say the word, if that's what you'd rather.'

'No. No, I don't want you to go.' She gave him a watery smile and he grinned at her and went back to the scullery.

Polly looked at her mother. Alice had recovered a little and was sipping her tea. She gave her daughter a quizzical look, almost like her old self.

'I must say, he seems a nice feller, Poll – but who is he? You never mentioned no Joe Turner before.'

Polly blushed, aware that Joe could hear everything they said. 'I met him that day I went to London with the Mayoress, Mum. His sister's the cook at WVS Headquarters. I said if he ever came down to Pompey he ought to come and see us, and I suppose that's what he's done.'

'Hm. Come down special, just for a cup of tea?' Alice gave her a sideways glance. 'And I dare say that's where those letters have been coming from too, is it? The ones you don't say nothing about?' Then she seemed to remember the trouble they were in and her face crumpled again. 'Not that it seems to matter much now,' she said despondently. 'Nothing seems to matter now.'

'Oh Mum . . .' But whatever Polly had been about to say was lost in the sound of the front door being opened, and voices as Cissie and Dick came into the passage. The two women looked at each other with relief, and Polly jumped to her feet.

'Cissie! Dick!' she cried as they came through to the back room. 'Wherever have you been? We've been so worried.' She caught the expression on their faces and stopped.

'What's happened now? What's the matter? Is it Jean? Is she ill?'

Cissie sat down on the nearest chair, as if her legs refused to hold her up any longer. She leaned her elbow on the table and supported her head in her palm. She heaved a huge sigh and Dick stood beside her, resting his hand on her shoulder, although he too looked grey and shocked. Polly stared at them in alarm. 'What's happened? Tell me what's happened!'

'Not ill, as such,' Cissie said, shaking her head. 'We had to take her home from the shop – she fainted when we told her the news. But it wasn't just that that made her faint,' she added bitterly, as Polly gave a little exclamation of pity. 'And I don't reckon it was the first time she done it, neither.' She raised her eyes and looked at her sister. 'The silly girl – the silly, *silly* girl – she's gone and got herself into trouble. She's *expecting*, Poll. She's expecting our Terry's baby – and what's she going to do now, I ask you! What in heaven's *name* does she think she's going to do now?'

In the first few moments after Cissie's announcement, Polly forgot all about Joe, still out in the scullery. It was only when a sound of swishing water made them all look round that she remembered he was there, presumably peeling potatoes. Her hand to her mouth, she went swiftly out and brought him through.

'This is Joe Turner,' she announced to her bewildered sister and brother-in-law. 'He – he popped down to see me. From London.' She could feel her face flooding with scarlet. 'We ran into each other when I went up with the Mayoress that time.'

'Popped in?' Dick echoed, his glance taking in Joe's rolled-up sleeves and the potato peeler in his hand. 'From *London*? But what the flipping heck is he doing in our scullery?'

'I was just helping with the dinner,' Joe explained. 'Poll

told me about your lad – I thought I'd give a bit of a hand. But you don't want me now, I can see that. Right, I'll be off.' He looked at Polly. 'Some other time, eh?'

She stared at him, distressed, and then turned to Cissie. 'I asked him to stop for a bite to eat, him having come all that way. But now . . .'

'It don't matter,' Joe said, shrugging into the jacket he'd slipped off when he began work. 'I can see you're in trouble. I just wanted to help, but if there's nothing else I can do . . .'

'No,' Dick said, his eyes hard and suspicious. 'There isn't.'

The women looked at him in surprise. Polly flushed again, and began, 'There's no need—' but Cissie interrupted her.

'Wait a mo.' She looked at Joe. 'It's a lot to ask, but if you really wouldn't mind . . . It's our Judy – my daughter. She's out in the country, and we don't know if she's heard about the ship. You see, she's deaf.'

He nodded. 'I know. Polly told me.'

'Well, we ought to let her know. I meant to send a telegram while we were out, but we went to see Jean first and then when she told us about her trouble –' Cissie coloured, embarrassed first by the trouble itself and then by the realisation that Joe must have heard her blurt it out, 'well, it went right out of my mind. But if you wouldn't mind doing that for us, I'd be really grateful. I'll give you the money,' she added, reaching for her purse.

'Don't you worry about that,' Joe said. 'And I tell you what, I won't send a telegram – I'll go out there meself, on the train. I dare say she'll want to come home, and she'll need someone with her, 'specially with her being deaf and all.' He looked at Polly. 'Ashwood, isn't it? Give me her address and I'll go straight away.'

'Oh, but you can't,' Polly began, glancing from him to Dick, who was still looking unfriendly.

'Don't see why not. You write out a note for her, so she knows I'm kosher. Look, I got nothing else to do. And don't worry about the fare, we'll sort all that out after. The main thing is to let her know what's happened and see what she wants to do.' He buttoned his jacket and found the cap he'd been wearing, while Polly scribbled a hasty note. She handed it to him and he held her hand for a brief second, his eyes meeting hers. 'Don't you worry, Poll,' he said quietly. 'She'll be all right with me.'

The door closed behind him and they all stared at each other. Dick sat down heavily beside his wife and Polly sank back into the armchair.

'Well!' he said. 'And who was that, might I ask? Coming in here, taking over, saying what's to be done and all. Well, Polly?'

'You needn't look at me as if I'd done something wrong, Dick Taylor,' she said with asperity. 'Joe's a decent man. His sister's Cook at the WVS Headquarters in London—'

'I don't care if his sister's the Queen of England,' Dick broke in. 'What I want to know is, who is he, and what's he doing here in my house?'

'My *mother's* house,' Polly reminded him sharply, getting to her feet. 'Just because you're Cissie's husband . . .'

'Look, I may not be much cop as far as you're concerned, but I'm the man around here and I'm head of the family!' Dick's voice rose. 'And I don't much like coming home and finding some other bloke what I've never seen before nor heard of, making free with my kitchen – all right, your *mother's* kitchen. I don't say there's anything wrong with the bloke, I don't say that, I just don't like it, that's all. 'Specially when we got our own private family business to talk about. You don't know what he might have heard before we knew he was out there. And now he's gone off to fetch our Judy from the country, for all the world as if he's one of the family himself. It's all too quick, that's what it is, and *I don't like it*.'

'Dick,' Cissie begged, 'don't upset yourself.' She cast an anxious glance towards Polly. 'You know what he's like when he gets upset.'

Polly bit her lip and sat down again. She knew very well what happened when Dick got upset. He didn't lose his temper often, but he could blow up quite unpredictably, and then he would be quite unreasonable, keeping a row going for hours and only ending it with an asthma attack. Over the years, they had all grown accustomed to fending off any situation which might cause an outbreak, but the present troubles were too great to be ignored.

'Let's forget about Joe,' she said quietly. 'He's a decent man and he just wants to help. I'll tell you about him later, but we've got other things to worry about now. Tell me about Jean. Is it true what you said? Is she really expecting?'

Cissie nodded miserably. 'She said it happened the last night he was on leave at Christmas. You know he stopped over at their house because they were out late. She said they just couldn't help it. He was going away, and they didn't know when they might see each other again, and they wanted to get engaged – they wanted to get married but there wasn't time. And they were there in her mum's front room, saying goodnight, and everyone else had gone to bed and – and . . .' She started to cry and Dick's hand moved on her shoulder. 'Oh Polly, it was just the once, she swears it was just the once.'

'But once is enough,' Dick said grimly. 'And you can guess who did the leading on.'

'Dick, we don't know that.'

'Don't we? Look, our Terry was a decent boy. We always brought him up to know right from wrong same as we did our Judy, and when he went off to join the Army I had a talk with him. Keep yourself decent, I told him, and you'll never have no trouble. I know what it's like when these young chaps get off in a gang in foreign parts. There's a lot of temptation and—'

'But Terry wasn't in foreign parts,' Polly said. 'He was home with Jean.'

Dick glared at her and she remembered suddenly that he was fifteen years older than she, and had known her as a little girl. Perhaps he still thought of her that way. 'There's no need to get clever, Polly,' he said heavily. 'The facts speak for themselves. Our Terry's dead, and young Jean Foster's carrying his baby, and it don't matter which way round you look at it, they been daft and done wrong, both of them. But I know what it's like to be a young bloke going off to war, and I know it don't take much to—' He closed his mouth abruptly. 'Well, never you mind. I just know it wasn't all our Terry's fault, that's all.'

'I don't see as it matters whose fault it was,' Alice said suddenly, speaking for the first time. 'What we've got to think about now is what we're going to do about it.'

There was a short silence. They looked at her, and then at each other. Cissie was the first to find her voice.

'Do about it, Mum? Why, what can we do about it? It's for Jean to make up her mind about that. It's her baby. Not but what we won't do what we can to help, of course,' she added. 'I mean, we'll make it a few clothes and that sort of thing, we can't let it go naked. But I dare say she'll get it adopted, won't she? There's not much else she can do.'

'Get it adopted?' Alice stared at them. 'Your grandchild? My great-grandchild? The first I'll have – maybe the only one I'll ever have? Get it *adopted*?'

They were silent again, astonished by her outburst. Then Polly said in a reasonable tone, 'But what else can she do, Mum? I mean, she can't keep it, can she, not without a man to stand by her. How could she afford to? And what would everyone say? You know what it's like for a girl in her position.'

'I know what people would say,' the old lady said grimly. 'I know it wouldn't be easy for her. But she's not the first one to have a baby born the wrong side of the blanket and she won't be the last, neither. And I reckon there'll be a lot more kiddies like this before this lot's over. Children who won't ever know their daddies, but still need their mothers – *and* their grandparents and great-grandparents too,' she added forcefully. 'Why should they have to go to strangers when they've got a family already? Why shouldn't they be with their own family, with the people who'll love them just because they're their own flesh and blood? Don't they have no say in the matter – don't they have no rights? And don't the rest of the family have no rights neither? This is *our Terry's* baby,' she said, fixing them all with a brilliant stare. 'Our Terry's. It might look like him. It might be him all over again. We've found out about it only a few hours after we've heard about Terry. Doesn't it seem to you as if it's meant? How can you talk about giving it away?'

The silence this time was longer. They glanced at each other uneasily. Dick was staring at the table, his lips tight, his jaw clenched. Cissie was crying again, silently, the tears running down her face. Polly felt a huge lump in her throat, a lump that wouldn't go away.

'But Mum,' she said, trying to talk past it, 'it's going to be so hard for Jean. You know what people are like. They won't talk to her. They won't have anything to do with her. How's she going to manage?' She glanced at Cissie. 'What do her own mum and dad think about it? What do they say?'

'People forget,' Alice said before Cissie could answer. 'They might cross the street when they see her coming at first, but they'll get used to it. And babies bring their love with them. Once it's born and she's pushing a pram, people will want to stop and look at it. They might be funny at first, but they'll come round.'

'Not all of them,' Cissie said. 'Some people will stay funny all their lives.'

'Well,' Alice said, 'they're not worth bothering about then. They'll only be people like Ethel Glaister down the road and who takes any notice of her?'

They had to smile at this. Nobody liked Ethel Glaister, who had a sharp word to say about everything and made no bones about letting folk see that she thought herself better than they. But Cissie's smile faded quickly and she frowned.

'I still don't see what we can do about it, Mum. It's for Jean and her mum and dad to work out. It's not really our business, is it?'

Alice thumped her wrinkled hand on the arm of her chair and spoke forcefully. 'Of *course* it's our business! Isn't that just what I've been trying to say? It's *our* baby too – *our* flesh and blood. We can't just stand by and let it be given away to strangers. It's our Terry's little boy or girl. *Think* about it!'

They stared at her. Polly thought about the baby, still a tiny being curled up in its mother's womb. She thought of how it would look after it was born – streaked with blood and mucus, screaming its way into life and, later, bathed and wrapped in soft white clothes, sleeping peacefully in its mother's arms. She thought of it as a toddler, running about with its fingers into everything. Looking like Terry had looked. Laughing like Terry had laughed, crying as he had cried.

'Mum's right,' she said, feeling the ache of loss in her breast even though just an hour ago she hadn't even known of the baby's existence. 'If it's Terry's baby, it's ours too.' She hesitated. 'What I don't understand is why nobody knew. I mean – it was Christmas, wasn't it? And now it's May. That's five months. Isn't she showing?'

'Well, she's just started to,' Cissie admitted. 'But you know Jean, she's a plump little thing and if you don't have any reason to suspect anything, you'd just think she was putting on a bit more weight. Her mum was beginning to wonder, I think, but it would've been another couple of weeks before she could be sure.'

'And how did she take it?' Alice asked. 'Her dad wasn't there, I suppose, so they'll need to talk it over when he comes home from work, but how did her mum seem?'

'Well, what d'you think? She was proper upset. I thought she was going to hit Jean for a minute. Then she started to cry, and Jean started again, and –'

'And you joined in,' Dick said. 'I had to go and make them all a cup of tea,' he told Alice. 'Me! In someone else's kitchen and all. Couldn't get no sense out of any of 'em, so I said to Cis we ought to come away and leave 'em to it. Say what you will, Ma, it's their business more than it's ours. It's Jean who's in the family way, and it's them who'll have to decide what to do about it.' He set his jaw grimly.

Alice took no notice. 'We can still put our point of view. We'd better go round there one evening and talk it over. And we'd better make it soon, in case they turn her out.'

'They wouldn't do that,' Cissie said. 'Not Mrs Foster.'

'Mr Foster might,' Alice said with a glance at Dick. 'Men are harder about these things. And Mrs Foster always struck me as one who'd set a lot of store on what the neighbours say. They might not turn her out as such, but they might send her to one of them homes for unmarried mothers, where they can stop until the baby's born. And you know what happens then. They give the babies up and never see them again.' She drew in a ragged breath and her eyes filled with tears. 'I don't want that to happen, Cis, I really don't. It's as if it's *meant* – finding out about it the very day we lose our Terry. I can't bear to think of losing his baby without even setting eyes on its dear little face.'

Cissie and Polly began to cry again in sympathy. They moved to sit together, their arms about each other as they wept for Terry and for the baby he had left behind, the baby he had not even known existed.

Dick stared at them. There was a lump in his throat too, and an uncomfortable feeling that he was the outsider, the one who didn't fit in, the one who had let himself down in some way. I've only said what any other bloke with a sense of decency would say, he told himself rebelliously. The girl probably *did* lead Terry on. It was in her house it happened.

And it *is* for her and her mum and dad to sort out. They probably won't thank us for interfering if we do go round there.

And yet, he couldn't ignore the pictures conjured up by Alice's words. Like Polly, he had seen the baby in its cot, the laughing toddler staggering about the room. He had also seen the boy that Terry had been, that his baby might become. The schoolboy, his socks down round his ankles, kicking a ball along the street, the twelve-year-old riding an old bike, the sixteen-year-old out at work, on a Dockyard apprenticeship perhaps, turning into a young man . . .

'Blimey,' he said in disgust, surveying the women. 'It'll be like a blooming swimming pool in here in a minute. I suppose I'd better go and make another cup of tea.'

Judy was out in the orchard with Sylvie when Joe Turner arrived. The little girl was feeling better and had managed to eat a piece of dry toast for her dinner, and was now lying on an old blanket in the shade of the apple tree. Its new leaves whispered above her, and she had fallen asleep while Judy sat beside her on a cushion, darning socks.

She looked up at the click of the gate, wondering who the stranger was who was standing there with Mrs Sutton. He was stocky, with a face that looked as if someone had screwed it up in a ball and then tried to iron out the creases. But she could see that it was a friendly, good-humoured face, even though just at present it looked grave. The farmer's wife too was looking upset, and Judy felt a sudden pang of dread.

'What is it?' she asked, and started to scramble to her feet. 'What's happened?'

'This is Mr Turner,' Mrs Sutton said. 'He's come to see you, Judy.'

'To see me? But why?' Judy stared from one to the other. Joe Turner produced a letter and she looked at it uneasily. 'What is it? What's happened? Have they had another raid in Portsmouth?' She felt herself shrink away from the note as if by not reading it she could push away whatever dreadful news he had brought. 'Has Grandma's house been bombed? Has – has anyone been hurt?'

'No!' She could see just how forceful the word was, and felt her body sag with relief. But his face was still solemn. 'Not anyone at home, anyway.' He nodded at the letter. 'You'd better read it. I'm sorry.'

'That's right, love,' Mrs Sutton said. 'Read the letter.'

Slowly, Judy reached out to take it. It was addressed in her aunt's writing and began by introducing Joe Turner as a friend. You can trust him, Polly had said. And then, as if she found the words difficult to write, came the news that had brought Joe to Ashwood. The news of HMS *Hood*.

Judy stared at the words. They blurred and danced in front of her eyes, and the orchard and the grass and the sunshine seemed to fall away into darkness. She shook her head, feeling sick and frightened, and found a cup of water pressed to her lips. Mrs Sutton must have brought it with her, knowing she would need it. She sank down again on the cushion and reached a hand out to Sylvie, who was still fast asleep. Her tears beginning to fall, she whispered, 'Let's go somewhere else. I don't want Sylvie to see. She'll be frightened.'

The others nodded and Joe Turner helped Judy to her feet. She found her legs shaking, and leaned upon him as they went softly from the orchard. Sylvie would probably sleep for an hour or two yet, and would not be alarmed to find herself alone when she woke. They went into the cool, dim kitchen and Mrs Sutton shifted the kettle on to the hot plate.

'I can't believe it,' Judy said in bewilderment, staring at the letter. 'Our Terry. It's awful.' She shook her head and looked at Mrs Sutton. 'I went to bed early last night, before the news. Did you hear it? Did you know the *Hood* had been sunk?'

'Well, yes, I did,' the farmer's wife confessed. 'We both heard it. But we didn't know your brother was on board. All we knew was that he was in the Navy.' She spoke slowly and clearly, so that Judy could follow her, and wrote it down to make sure. 'I'm so sorry,' she added in shaky handwriting, and tears fell on to the paper.

'Our Terry,' Judy said. 'Oh, I don't think I can bear it!' She bent her head and burst into tears, sobbing wildly. 'It's not fair! First Johnny, and then Sean – and now Terry! It's just not *fair*!'

'Judy, Judy.' She felt Mrs Sutton's arms around her and her head was drawn down on to the warm cushion of her bosom. A comforting hand stroked her hair and another, harder and hornier but just as comforting, patted her hand. She could feel the vibrations in the woman's body that meant she was speaking, and although she couldn't hear the words, she knew what they must be. 'Poor love. You poor, poor love. There, there. Cry it out, now, cry it out. Poor, poor love.'

At length, with no more tears in her for the time being, Judy hiccuped into silence. She screwed up the third of the hankies Mrs Sutton had pressed into her hand, and gazed at it through swollen eyes. Then she looked up at the two who watched her so sympathetically.

'I'll have to go home. They'll want me there.'

Mrs Sutton nodded. 'I thought you'd say that. Mr Turner here says he'll take you back as soon as you like.' She glanced at the clock. 'There's a train in an hour – you can pack your things while I get some tea ready for you. And you can take some fresh eggs and butter back for your family. I dare say they'll be glad of them. I'll put in a few slices of bacon as well.'

Judy barely followed this, but understood that she was to go and pack and that Joe Turner would take her back to Portsmouth. She looked at him doubtfully and he gave her his crinkly grin. 'Go on, love. I'll wait for you here.' He seemed to realise why she was doubtful and added, 'I'm a friend of your Aunt Polly's. Met her in London when she come up to WVS Headquarters a couple of weeks back. My sister's the cook there.' He followed Mrs Sutton's example and wrote the words down and Judy read them, nodding.

'Are you sure you want to bother? I could manage on my own.'

He laughed. 'Well, I can't stop out here, can I! I've got to go back to Pompey, so I might as well see you safe back home. Anyway, I don't reckon me and Polly would be friends any more if I didn't.' He saw that she hadn't followed this and said gently and more slowly, 'You go and get yourself ready, love. We'll go back to Portsmouth together.'

Judy gave in and went upstairs. She stood at the door of the room she had shared with Sylvie, the room that had become so familiar and so dear. The walls were distempered a sunny yellow, there were yellow curtains flowered with blue at the window and yellow cushions on the low, deep windowsill. It was a room that seemed filled with sunshine on even the dullest of days, and here, as she had sat on that windowsill gazing down into the orchard, she had found comfort and healing. Now she was to leave it and go back to the grey, ruined streets of Portsmouth, and she felt torn between a desire to see her family again and a longing to stay here for ever.

She crossed the room and looked down into the orchard. Sylvie was still asleep on her blanket under the apple tree. How many times have I sat under that tree in the past two weeks? Judy thought. By myself, with Sylvie – and with Ben. She thought of the tall, dark-haired boy with his bright blue eyes beneath the heavy brows. They had shared an easy understanding, a ready friendship, and she had found it difficult to believe that he was only seventeen. He seemed so much older, so much more mature. He felt it himself too, with his restless desire to leave school and join the RAF. He was ready for manhood.

She turned her mind away from that disturbing thought and lifted her suitcase down from the top of the wardrobe. Then she took her few clothes from the cupboard and drawers and began to fold them on the bed.

Chapter Twenty-Three

During their light meal of sliced ham, early lettuce and beetroot, Judy noticed that Joe Turner seemed uneasy, as if there were something else on his mind. He said nothing, however, until Judy had made her tearful farewells and Sylvie, who had come in yawning and hungry after her sleep, had accompanied them to the station where they could catch the train back to Portsmouth. The little girl clung to her aunt, begging to be allowed to go back to Portsmouth with her, and Judy had been in tears yet again as she gently unwound the small arms from around her neck.

'You're better off here. We're still getting raids – it's not safe. And you know you're happy here with the Suttons and the other children.'

'I'd rather be home with you and Mummy,' Sylvie said mutinously.

'You will be,' Judy promised, hoping it was true. 'Once all this bombing's over you'll come back straight away, I promise.' Her words were lost as the train arrived, huffing to a stop beside the platform. 'I'll have to go now, Sylvie. Be good for me, won't you? And look after Cavalier.' Cavalier was the farmyard rooster, so named for his spectacular feathers. She gave Sylvie a final hug and then turned away quickly, dashing the tears from her eyes. I don't know where they all come from, she thought, but I wish I could smile as much as I cry.

Joe opened the carriage door and helped her up into an empty compartment, following with her case. He pulled down the window so that she could lean out and wave goodbye to Sylvie, then the train gathered speed and surged out of the station. In another moment the platform was out of sight and Judy sat down and heaved a trembling sigh.

Joe Turner looked at her. 'You all right, love?'

Judy nodded. He had such an expressive face, she found him easy to understand. 'I suppose so. It's just a bit much to take in. A couple of hours ago I was sitting under the apple tree darning socks without a care in the world – well, not too many anyway,' she amended, thinking ruefully of Sean and her deafness. 'I suppose I was used to the ones I had! And now, here I am on my way back home, and – and I've lost my brother.' Her voice trembled. 'Oh dear, I'm going to start crying again. I'm sorry.'

'It's all right, love.' He handed her a large khaki handkerchief. 'You cry all you want. You've been through a lot.'

'So have other people,' Judy wept. 'It's no worse for me than it is for Mum and Dad – or Polly, or Grandma. We've all been through the same.'

'And you've all had a good cry,' he said. 'It's natural.'

Judy gathered control of herself, glad that there was no one else in the compartment. She gazed out of the window at the fields and woods, thinking how strange it was that war was being waged less than a hundred miles away – not much further than it was from Portsmouth to London – yet here it seemed so peaceful, and so lovely. 'Why do people have to hate each other?' she asked. 'Why do they have to fight? Why can't people just live peacefully together, like we used to?'

Joe shrugged. 'Not for us to ask that, love,' he said. 'It's up to them that lead us.' He hesitated and then said carefully, 'You'll need to prepare yourself for another bit of news when you get home.'

Judy stared at him. 'Another bit of news? Why, what else

has happened?' Her eyes sharpened. 'You said everyone was all right.'

'They are, love. They're all fine – well, as fine as can be expected, in the circs. But there's summat else – look, it ain't for me to tell you. I just thought you ought to be prepared, that's all.'

'I can't follow all this,' Judy said despairingly. 'You'll have to write it down. Oh, I *hate* being deaf!'

He looked at her sympathetically and felt in his pockets for paper and a pencil. But all he had was the train tickets, and neither of them had anything to write with. They gave up and sat helplessly gazing at each other. Something else? Judy thought. What can it be? Oh, I wish he hadn't said it! And yet, she knew that it was better for her to be prepared. It would make it easier for the family to tell her.

The train rumbled on through Botley and Fareham, and then along the top of the harbour. Judy stared out at the expanse of water stretching away to the south, and thought of Terry's last leave. She had seen the great ship he was on, and stood on the Sallyport to watch it sail away through the narrow neck of the harbour. Now it was at the bottom of the sea, somewhere off Greenland, and only three of its great crew of almost fifteen hundred men would ever return.

Judy stared at her mother in disbelief. 'Jean Foster's having a *baby*?'

Now, more than ever, she hated her deafness. To have to stare at people's mouths as they spoke, unable to understand any but the most obvious words, or wait while they wrote things down, pausing as they wondered how to spell the words – all that was bad enough. But now, with everyone talking at once about these new events, so important to them all, turning to each other and speaking too quickly for her to follow, was nothing short of agonising. I wish I'd never gone back to that building, she thought bitterly. It didn't do any good, and we nearly lost Polly as well.

'What are you saying?' she asked loudly, so that they all stopped talking and turned to her. 'What's the use of me coming back if you won't even tell me what's going on?' Her shock and distress over Terry, the hurried return home and now the news of the baby had left her shaken and on edge, ready either to burst into tears all over again or to lose her temper completely. 'Don't I matter any more?' she went on, aware that she was shouting. 'Can't anyone even be bothered to *look* at me when they're talking? I feel as if I'm in a glass jar – I can see your mouths moving, but all I can hear is a sort of *woolly* sound. I can't make out any words, and I feel so left out, and it's awful. *Awful*!' Temper and tears came together then, and she buried her face in her hands, sobbing wildly. 'You don't know what it's like! None of you knows what it's like!'

'Oh, Judy!' Arms came around her and hands patted her back. Over her head, Cissie and Polly looked at each other. 'She's right,' Polly said in a low voice, although there was no danger of Judy's overhearing her. 'We do leave her out, and it's not fair. Terry was her brother and she's just as upset about it all as we are. We've got to do our best to help her.'

'It's not that I don't want to,' Cissie said in distress. 'I'd do anything I can to help her. But I can't help just saying what comes into my head, and I forget to look at her all the time.' She tightened her arms around Judy's bent shoulders. 'To be honest, I wonder if it was a bit selfish to ask her to come home. I want her here, I really do, but maybe it was better for her to be out in the country. She seemed to be settling down so well out there.'

'I think she'd have come whatever we said,' Polly said. 'Joe told me it was the first thing she said, that she'd come home. She said we'd need her.'

She sighed. Joe had refused even to stop for a cup of tea after delivering Judy at the door. 'You've got your own troubles,' he'd told her on the doorstep of number nine.

'You don't want strangers around. I'll be in touch.' And then he'd gone, limping away up the street and turning at the corner to wave a cheery hand, and she realised that she didn't even know what he was going to do next. Would he get a train back to London, or was he staying somewhere in Portsmouth? She had followed Judy indoors feeling frustrated.

'And so we do need her,' Cissie said. 'I need her, and so does Dick. We all need her.' She put her hand under Judy's chin and lifted the wet, swollen face, speaking slowly and clearly. 'Judy, we're all glad you've come home. We need you here. Do you understand that? We *need* you.'

Judy drew in a ragged breath and nodded, trying to smile. 'OK, Mum. Sorry. It's just – well, it's all been such a shock.' She twisted her lips ruefully. 'It must have been an awful shock for you too, hearing that from Jean. What's she going to do?'

'We don't know yet. We only found out this morning.' Cissie shook her head wonderingly. It seemed as if an age had passed since they had spoken to Jean in the shop. 'Your grandma thinks we ought to help her to keep the baby.'

'Keep it?' It was a moment or two before Judy fully understood what she was saying. 'But how could she, all on her own? What about her parents?'

Alice had been writing on an old envelope, and passed it to Judy. She read the words aloud. '*It's Terry's baby, and there'll never be another one. It's my great-grandchild. I don't want it to go to strangers.* Oh Gran,' she said. 'Oh Gran, of course you don't.'

Dick spoke up from his corner. He had been silent during the halting conversation, retreating there after first greeting Judy with a brief kiss. 'That's all very well. But it's not easy for a young woman on her own with a little 'un.'

'You don't have to tell *me* that!' Alice's voice was sharp. She had not yet forgiven him for his assumption that, in *her*

312

house and *her* kitchen, he was the master. 'I brought up two on my own after my hubby died. Of course it's not easy!'

'Yes, but they were the right side of the blanket,' Dick retorted. 'Not by-blows, like Jean's is going to be!'

For a moment, it looked as if the quarrel would break out again. Alice and Dick glared at each other, while Judy stared at them in uncomprehending astonishment. Then Cissie put both hands on their shoulders and spoke with unusual firmness.

'Now, you needn't start that all over again! We had all that out before our Judy got here and she didn't come all this way to watch you two squabbling. Just you calm down, Dick, you'll make yourself ill getting your rag out like that, and we've got enough on our plates without having you back in hospital. And while I'm thinking about it, you might say sorry to Polly for the way you behaved to Mr Turner. I'm sure he never wanted to intrude on family problems, and he's been a real help, going out to fetch our Judy and all, but from the way you acted, anyone would have thought he'd come to pinch all the family silver. Supposing we'd got any to pinch,' she added, and Dick, who had been staring at her in astonishment, suddenly laughed. 'There,' she said, smiling, 'that's better.'

'Well, I suppose you're right, Cis,' he said, and looked over at Polly. 'Sorry, Poll, but I didn't know what to think when I found him here, and what with the shock over Terry and then Jean, I was knocked all of a heap . . . And I'm sorry to you too, Ma,' he went on, turning to Alice. 'You're right, we ought to give the girl a hand. It's not the time to start argufying over things that can't be altered.' He glanced at Judy, who was once again watching them in bewilderment. 'And here we are, leaving our Judy out again. Don't worry, gal, we haven't forgot you. We're glad to have you home again.'

'I've been thinking,' Polly said. 'Judy and Jean are pretty good friends. Why don't we ask her to go round and have a talk? Tell her what we've been thinking, see if we can do anything.'

'That's a good idea,' Alice said at once, and when they conveyed this idea to Judy she nodded.

'I will, if she wants to see me. She might feel awkward, though.'

'Not with you. You've known each other all your lives. You were in the same class at school.'

'I mean, because of me not being able to hear,' Judy said, but they shook their heads and Polly said she would let Judy use the writing-pad she'd been saving for writing to Sylvie.

'All right, I'll go round tomorrow. It's too late now.'

'You're right,' Alice said, looking at the clock. 'It's almost nine o'clock. Time for the news.'

They looked at each other. It was on last night's news that they'd heard of the sinking of HMS *Hood*. Only twenty-four hours ago!

'It seems like a lifetime,' Polly said soberly, and the others nodded. This time last night, they'd been more or less happy, thinking that Terry was still alive. Now, knowing not only that he must be dead but that he'd left his sweetheart pregnant, everything had changed.

Nobody had the heart to switch the wireless on for tonight's news. They'd had enough of news for a while, Polly thought as she went out to the scullery to make cocoa. Enough for a long time. In fact, if she had her way she'd never listen to the news again.

You couldn't just ignore it, though. You had to know what was going on. You had to care about other people as well as yourself, or why should they care about you? And even if you'd never wanted the war in the first place, even though nobody had asked your opinion nor listened if you gave it, you were still a part of it all. You had to stand by what was right.

And that went for what was happening in the family too. You had to stand by what was right – and Gran was right about this. Jean Foster's baby – Terry's baby – was a part of their family, a part that would be all they had left of Terry himself. What was done was done, and they would all do their best by the girl Terry had loved, and the baby she bore.

What's done is done, Polly repeated to herself. Who knows? Maybe in the end we'll be glad of it.

Judy went round to see Jean Foster the next evening, thinking that she would probably have gone to work as usual in the morning. She found her friend looking wan and red-eyed, picking listlessly at a plate of boiled fish and mashed potatoes.

'Perhaps you can talk some sense into her,' Mrs Foster said, leading Judy past a door leading to a front room that looked like a furniture shop showroom, with a three-piece suite daintily attired in lace antimacassars and a small occasional table with china figurines arranged upon it. She took her into an almost equally tidy back room. 'Done nothing but cry her eyes out, she has, ever since she heard, but I've told her, it's no use letting it all get on top of you. You've made your bed, my girl, and now you've got to lay in it,' she said to her daughter in a sharp, exasperated voice. 'And it's no good piping your eye all day over what can't be mended.'

Judy heard none of this but could tell from Mrs Foster's expression and gestures what sort of thing she was saying. She gave Jean a sympathetic smile and touched her ears. 'I've brought some paper for you to write on. It makes things easier. Could we go up to your bedroom or somewhere, so we don't disturb everyone else?'

'Oh, don't mind me,' Mrs Foster cried. 'Jean doesn't tell *me* what she's doing. Nor her dad, neither. Well, go on then,' she snapped, seeing that Judy had not understood. '*I* don't mind doing the washing-up, I'm sure, seeing as you've got company.'

Judy followed the other girl up the stairs. Mr Foster was a foreman in the Dockyard on a good wage and the Fosters' house was larger than Alice's, with three bedrooms and an indoor lavatory (which Mrs Foster called the WC) and bathroom. It had nice front rooms too, with rounded bay windows, and a little patch of front garden. Jean's room was at the back, overlooking a larger garden with a patch of lawn, and a small, neat vegetable plot, together with the inevitable Anderson shelter. I bet they've got proper chairs and a table down there, Judy thought, with a fresh white tablecloth every Sunday!

The girls sat down on Jean's bed, rumpling the bright green satin bedspread, and Jean drew in a deep breath and burst into tears. Judy put her arm around her shoulders, but her own grief overtook her and they wept together for several minutes, mourning the brother and the sweetheart who had been taken from them. I seem to have been here before, Judy thought, remembering the pain of losing Sean, and she held Jean tightly against her, scarcely knowing whether she did so to give comfort or to receive it.

'I *did* love him,' Jean sobbed. 'I really did. I still do! It wasn't just being wicked, like Mum says. We couldn't help it – we *loved* each other. He was going away, and we just couldn't bear it. We had to do what we did.'

'Jean, I'm sorry, I can't hear you,' Judy said gently. She rummaged in her bag for the writing-pad. 'Write it down. It doesn't matter what it is – just write it down. I get so fed up with people only putting down *bits* of what they're saying,' she added with feeling.

Jean wrote down what she had said, and then added, *It was only once. But I wish now it had been lots of times – so there!* and looked at Judy with an expression that was half-apologetic, half-defiant.

Judy grinned despite her unhappiness. 'I'll tell you something, Jean – I wish me and Sean had done it, too! He wanted to, I know, though he wouldn't ask me. We'd only known each other a little while, and Mum and Dad nearly hit the roof about our getting engaged. But now – well, I wish we had. Just so that he could have had that to remember.' And me, too, she thought. I'd like to have it to remember as well.

'You wouldn't,' Jean said tonelessly. 'Not if you'd found yourself in the mess I'm in now.' She scribbled the words quickly and handed the pad to Judy again.

'No, maybe not. But that's why I've come to see you. Mum and Dad and Gran – and me and Polly too, come to that – we've been wondering what you're going to do. Have you thought about it yet?' She made a face. 'That's a daft thing to say – you can't have been thinking about anything else since you realised.' Involuntarily, her glance drifted to Jean's stomach, beginning to show a swelling beneath her loose dress.

'I haven't, actually,' Jean confessed, and wrote down her next words. *I tried to push it out of my mind. I suppose I hoped it would go away! Stupid, but that's how it was.*

'But now your parents know, what do they think you should do?'

Mum was all for turning me out straight away! Dad wouldn't let her, though. He said if I went, he'd go too. Jean looked apprehensive, as though she thought it might really come to that, and Judy remembered that Jean Foster had always been the apple of her father's eye. *So Mum stopped saying it, but she's hardly spoken to me since. I don't know what I'm going to do.*

'That's why I've come round. We want you to know that you can always live with us, if it comes to it. I don't know where we'd put you, mind,' she added with a grin. 'You might have to sleep in the Anderson! But Gran said we'll do whatever we can, for Terry's sake, and because the baby's her great-grandchild and she doesn't want it going to strangers.'

Once again, Jean dissolved into tears. 'Oh Judy, I don't

317

know what to say. I didn't think anyone would want anything to do with me. I thought I'd be sent away, and have to give my baby up.' Unconsciously, her hand moved protectively to her stomach. 'I mean, I knew if Terry could come home it would be all right because he'd stand by me, but I didn't know how long he'd be away. This horrible war's going on and on and it doesn't look as if it's *ever* going to end, and I was so scared. I thought, What'll happen to me if he doesn't come home? And then yesterday, when I found out he *wasn't* going to – well, I just didn't know what I was going to do. And Mum's been so awful – we had such a terrible row last night over it – and I've been missing Terry so much, and now I'm never going to see him again, and – and . . .' The storm of weeping overtook her again and she sobbed uncontrollably.

Judy held her tightly, not needing to hear the words, her tears once more mingling with the frightened girl's. As the weeping eased again, she said, 'Look, Jean, you don't have to worry any more. We'll stand by you, since Terry can't. We're your family now too. It's your baby, and you've got to decide what you want to do, but whatever you decide, we'll help you.' She hesitated. 'If you want to give it up for adoption, we won't stand in your way, but we don't want you to do that. It's our Terry's baby as well as yours, and we want it to be part of our family.'

Jean wiped her face and blew her nose. She looked at Judy gratefully and attempted a smile. 'Thanks, Judy. It's really helped, having you come round. And I don't want to give my baby away either. It's just that, I don't really know how I'll manage. How am I going to be able to keep it? How can I *afford* to? There's so much a baby needs – a pram and a cot, and lots of clothes and nappies – and how could I go to work with a baby to look after? How can I earn a living for us both?' The tears were falling again as she picked up the pencil. *How am I going to manage, Judy?*

'We'll work it out,' Judy promised, managing to follow

the gist of Jean's tearful questions. 'We'll all put our heads together, and we'll work it out. I'm sure Mum and Gran will help, and I expect your mum'll come round, once she gets used to the idea. Anyway, just remember this, Jean – you're not on your own. We're all going to help you.' She wondered if she ought to say it, then added quietly, 'I almost wish it *had* happened to me, in some ways. I'd like to have something of Sean to remember him by – his baby, a part of him. As it is, all I've got is a ring and a few memories, and even those are starting to fade.'

It's better to have loved and lost than never to have loved at all, Jean wrote with shaking fingers. *I just wish it didn't hurt so much, Judy – having loved and lost. I wish everything didn't seem so hopeless.*

'It's not,' Judy said, wondering if she believed it. 'There's always hope, Jean. That's what Gran says. While there's life, there's hope.' She touched her friend's stomach wonderingly. 'That's where our hope is – in there. Your baby. Terry's baby. *Our* baby.'

'Hope,' Jean said, also touching her stomach. 'That's what I'll call it – if it's a girl. Hope.'

Judy looked at the name, written on a single sheet in the writing-pad. *Hope*. It was an unusual name but a good one. Perhaps this baby would be a turning point for them all. A new life, to make up for the one that had been lost.

'I'll tell them at home,' she said. 'They'll like that. It's what we all need, Jean. Hope.'

Chapter Twenty-Four

'I might have known you'd come home with some fancy ideas,' Dick said disgustedly as they sat round the supper-table that evening. 'Hope! Trouble, more like. It isn't going to be as easy as you all seem to think, not for young Jean anyway. A baby costs money, and it goes *on* costing money. How's a girl like Jean, working in a shop for – what? Fifteen bob a week? – how's she going to be able to afford to bring up a nipper? I mean, if they'd been married she'd have had a pension, but as it is she can't expect nothing from the Army, nothing at all. And we haven't got the means to help her out.'

The women looked at each other. They knew Dick was right: his own income was a war pension, and Cissie had had to take in dressmaking for years to make ends meet. It was easier once Terry and Judy were old enough to leave school and go out to work, and Terry had been sending money home regularly since he joined the Army, but now that would stop. Alice too had only her small pension. There wasn't anything left over for a baby.

'Well, we're going to have to do something,' Polly said with determination. 'Like Gran says, the baby is part of our family, and if Jean wants to keep it, we've got to help her. I don't mind chipping in a bit. There's always something I can go without.'

'Well, I dunno what it is, then,' Dick said. 'We're going without just about everything already.' He sighed. 'If you're all so set on it there's nothing more I can say, is there? I never had much chance with three women lined up against me, anyway. You'd better tell young Jean to come round here for tea on Sundays.' A thought struck him. 'I bet her mum doesn't go much on all this, does she? I remember her as a girl at the dances down the Oddfellows – stuck-up piece, she was. What did she have to say about all this?'

He looked interrogatively at Judy and she stared back blankly. Polly mouthed at her, 'Mrs Foster. What did she say?'

'Oh, Jean's mum,' Judy said, and made a face. 'Jean says she's been awful. They've had a really bad row over it, and Jean thought she was going to turn her out, but her dad wouldn't let her. I don't know what she'll say about Jean keeping the baby, though. I can't see her letting them stay there.'

'No, nor can I,' Cissie said. 'And she won't have the same feeling about it that we have. After all, Jean could have other children, in wedlock. But if she does keep the baby, it might spoil her chances of getting married at all.'

Polly sighed. 'What a problem. I don't know what to suggest. We really haven't got room for her here, we're like sardines as it is.' She stood up and started to gather the plates together. 'Let's clear this away and listen to the news. Perhaps they'll have caught the *Bismarck* by now. That might cheer us up a bit.'

The pursuit of the German ship was the topic on everyone's lips. It had become an ogre in everyone's minds, a symbol of the terror that stalked the world. It was as if nothing more could be achieved until it had been hunted down and destroyed. To the family in number nine, as to so many other families in the country, it seemed a personal retribution – a just reprisal for the terrible loss they had suffered – yet the need was almost as great to those who had not known any of the crew. The *Hood* represented something vital to the national sense of strength, and its loss must be balanced by an equal loss to the Germans.

'An eye for an eye, a tooth for a tooth,' Dick said grimly. 'That's what it is. And a ship for a ship.'

'And a thousand mothers' sons for a thousand mothers' sons,' Cissie said sadly. 'I don't know, it seems wrong to me, looking at it that way. The whole thing about war – leaders like Hitler sending ordinary young men to do his dirty work for him and the rest of us having to join in and send ours to stop them – well, it doesn't seem Christian to me.'

'But there've always been wars,' Polly said. 'The Bible's full of them. It's full of talk about God smiting people down.'

'Well, I can't understand it,' Cissie said. 'But there, I suppose it's not for folk like us to understand, we haven't got the education. We just have to do as we're told. And send our lads to be killed,' she added bitterly.

The wireless began its burbling warm-up and a moment or two later the announcer's voice came through. 'This is the nine o'clock news, and this is Alvar Liddell reading it. The hunt for the German battleship *Bismarck* goes on as she evades the British Force sent to engage her. There has been more heavy fighting on the island of Crete which was invaded three days ago by almost five hundred Junker transport planes bringing thousands of paratroopers. Lord Louis Mountbatten's ship HMS *Kelly* has been reported sunk, together with her sister ship HMS *Kashmir*. Many of the survivors, including Lord Mountbatten, were rescued by HMS *Kipling*, after being machine-gunned in the water. More fighter aircraft have been delivered to the besieged island of Malta, which has been under heavy attack from the Luftwaffe. HMS *Ark Royal* and HMS *Furious* between them brought a total forty-eight Hurricanes. German High Command is believed to be building up a massive attack force on the Russian Front. There were no reports of air raids over Britain over the past twenty-four hours . . .'

'That's one bit of good news anyway,' Alice said as they switched off the wireless and stared at each other. 'I shouldn't think they had enough planes to raid us anyway. They seem to be everywhere!'

'It's terrible,' Cissie said, 'Lord Mountbatten being machine-gunned in the water! And all those poor souls on Malta. I heard yesterday that they're just living in holes in the ground, frightened to come out. And Crete – they can't leave our boys there, surely? They'll have to go and get them out.'

'It's another Dunkirk,' Dick said. He shook his head. 'I can't see how we can beat them this time. They've been getting ready for it for years, while we've been shutting our eyes to what's been going on.'

'Well, I believe in Mr Churchill,' Alice said staunchly, 'and if *he* says we'll win, I reckon we will.'

Dick looked at her gravely. 'I'm not sure that's what he has said, Ma,' he said in a quiet voice. 'He's said we'll fight them. He's said we'll fight them on the beaches and in the streets and in the hills. He's said we'll never surrender. But I don't think he's ever said we're going to *win*.'

The *Bismarck* was sunk two days later, after a desperate chase across the Atlantic, pursued by over a hundred ships. She was finally caught a few hundred miles off the coast of Brittany and hit, first by torpedoes from the *Ark Royal*, which destroyed her steering gear, and then by shells fired from the numerous ships which were closing in upon her. In the end, defiant to the last, the German Commander ordered that she be scuttled, and the great ship turned over and sank, with the loss of over two thousand men.

Britain breathed a sigh of relief. The seas were a little less dangerous now, even though there were still plenty of enemy ships patrolling them, but it was mainly a sense of justice that caused them to celebrate. An eye for an eye. A tooth for a tooth. A ship for a ship . . .

'It's just like children squabbling in a playground,' Cissie said privately to Polly, but they didn't repeat these sentiments to others. April Grove was full of people stopping to congratulate each other on the victory, and you didn't want to be thought either a 'conchie' or a Fifth Columnist. It only needed some busybody like Ethel Glaister to hear you saying something like that, and you could find yourself in prison!

All the same, Cissie couldn't help feeling glad that the men who had killed her Terry were now themselves dead, even though she knew that in Germany there were a lot of mothers suffering the same grief as herself. It doesn't make sense, she thought. How can I be glad and sorry both at the same time? But then, nothing about war really made sense.

Jean Foster came round to see them the day after the *Bismarck* had been sunk. She was pale, red-eyed and nervous, obviously both grieving for Terry and in a panic over her own situation. She looked a different girl from the pleasant, smiling shop assistant Dick and Cissie had seen the day before. She also looked plumper, as if her figure were blossoming by the day, and she told them she was sure some of the neighbours were beginning to look at her a bit funny.

'Mum says I've got to go away before they notice,' she said, 'but where can I go? And what shall I do for money? I don't know what I'm going to do, I don't really.' She sat on one of the dining chairs and stared at them all fearfully. 'I'm ever so sorry, Mrs Taylor, for bringing all this trouble on you. I never meant – me and Terry, we just – well, we never thought that just *once* . . .'

'It only takes once,' Dick said grimly. 'And we brought our Terry up to know right from wrong.'

'Well, *I* know right from wrong too, Mr Taylor.' Jean's cheeks flushed. 'We both did. But he was going away the next day, and we loved each other so much. We just couldn't help ourselves.' She began to cry again. 'I know what you think of me – I know what everyone'll say, that I'm a hussy and a trollop and all the rest of it – but we couldn't help it, we *couldn't*, and I tell you what, I'm glad we did it. I never meant it to be like this and nor did Terry, but I'm glad all the same. At least he was happy when he went away, and *I made him happy*.' She lifted her chin and gave Dick a challenging stare. 'He said so. And I'm *glad*.'

There was a short silence. Dick flushed too but he let his eyes drop. He glanced down sideways into the empty fireplace and his jaw clenched. Cissie watched him, biting her lip, afraid that he was going to give way to a burst of temper, and Alice seemed to square her shoulders as if she too were ready to join in the fray. Judy, unable to follow their words, glanced anxiously at Polly, who gave her a small smile, as if to say that she thought Jean had got the better of the angry man.

Dick took a breath. He turned his eyes back to Jean's defiant face.

'All right, young lady,' he said stonily. 'So you're glad. You're going to look after yourself then, are you? You won't come looking for help from no one else?'

Jean's defiance faded a little. 'I'm not saying that, Mr Taylor,' she said. 'I'd do that if I could. And maybe I will, if I can find a way. Maybe I can get a job somewhere, where I can have my baby with me. I thought it was only right to come and see you, but I'm not asking for help from anyone who doesn't want to give it,' she added with a flash of spirit. 'If you don't want me round here, just say so and I'll go. It was only that Judy said you and her mum would like to see me.' She began to get up. 'If you don't, I'll be off.'

'No! No, don't go.' Cissie looked at her husband. 'Dick'll be the one to go if he doesn't want you here, won't you, Dick? You can take yourself out for a walk if you don't want anything to do with young Jean, but just remember what Mum said – this is our Terry's baby, come what may, and our grandchild, and there's never going to be another, not from Terry. All right, they did wrong, but it's Jean who's got to carry the can, and with our Terry not here to stand by her – and he *would* have done, you know he would – then we've got to do it in his place. So you'd better make up your mind: are you going to stop here and give the girl some support with the rest of us, or are you going to make yourself scarce?'

Their eyes met. The others watched them, knowing that Cissie rarely opposed Dick like this. Partly because she held to the view that a wife must love, honour and *obey*, just as it said in the marriage service, and partly because she had always been extra careful with Dick owing to his illness, she always tried to steer clear of arguments. But this time she was standing firm, and they could all see that there would be no moving her.

Dick saw it too. A look of wary admiration came into his eyes and he seemed to settle back in his chair. He wasn't giving in too readily, though.

'All right,' he said with a shrug. 'Have it your own way. You always do, anyway. Bloke doesn't have a chance in a house full of women.' It was an old war cry, spoken usually in jest, and they looked at each other a little uncertainly and then decided to ignore the touch of bitterness in his tone and take it as one now. They smiled and Cissie leaned across and patted his knee.

'That's better,' she said, and gave him her loving smile. 'Now we can start to think what to do next.' She turned to Jean and asked tentatively, 'How about your mum, Jean? How's she taking it now?'

Jean lifted her shoulders hopelessly. 'She's either going on and on at me or she's not speaking to me at all, and I don't know which is worse. All the usual things: always brought me up to be decent, what will the neighbours say, never be able to hold up her head again in public . . . And then she starts to cry, and she won't let me say anything, or even touch her, and after that she goes out to the kitchen and won't speak to me. She won't even let me help get dinner ready. It's as if she's pretending I'm not there – don't even exist.'

There was a note of real pain in her last words and Polly experienced a moment of insight into the girl's frightened mind. Poor little mite, she thought compassionately. She's lost the man she loves – and Judy and me both know what *that* feels like – and on top of that she's in the worst trouble a girl can be in, without any chance of her chap standing by her, and her own mother's trying to make out she doesn't exist. She doesn't know where to turn.

She went swiftly across to Jean and put her arms around her. 'Well, you exist here,' she said firmly, 'and we'll help you all we can. Now, what we've got to do first is think what you want to do, and then see how you can do it. That's the best way, isn't it?'

'Trust you, Polly,' her mother said admiringly. 'You could always see right to the nub of things.'

'Well, being in the WVS helps,' Polly admitted. 'You get used to solving problems. Now, what do you want most, Jean – apart from what we all know you can't have,' she added hastily as Jean's eyes filled with tears. 'We've all got to face up to not having our Terry back again.'

'I want to keep my baby,' the girl whispered. 'Terry and me were going to get married the next time he came home. It would have been all right then, and we'd have been a family.' She raised anguished eyes to Polly's face. 'I can't lose our baby as well as Terry. I *can't*.'

'No, you can't,' Polly said. She looked around at the others. 'You can all see that, can't you? She can't give the baby away. And we don't want her to. It's Terry's.'

Nobody spoke for a moment, and then Judy said a little plaintively, 'I wish somebody'd tell me what you're all saying.'

As if it were a relief, they all began to talk at once, and Judy shook her head helplessly. 'It's no use! You *know* I can't hear you. Write it down, someone – please. Oh,' she clapped her hands over her ears, 'it's awful not being able to

327

hear. You just get left out of *everything*, and I'm *fed up* with it!'

'Judy, I'm sorry,' Polly said, and found some paper. Hastily, she wrote a brief account of what was happening, finishing with the words, *and we're going to help Jean all we can*. Judy read them and nodded.

'That's all right, then. So what are we going to do?'

'That's what we've got to decide,' Polly said, remembering to look at her and speak clearly. Judy could still not lip-read a great deal, but could usually manage to pick up the gist, as much from the speaker's expression as from the carefully articulated words. Polly looked at Jean, who was controlling her sobs and wiping her eyes on an already sodden handkerchief. 'Now then, Jean. You want to keep your baby. What we've got to do is work out how you can do that.'

Jean nodded. 'But I don't see how,' she whispered. 'If Mum says I've got to go, and you can't have me here, what am I going to do? There's nowhere else I can think of.'

'Are you sure your mum won't come round? It's early days yet, and it must have been a shock for her.' Cissie spoke kindly, but with some feeling for the other mother. It had been a shock for her, to know that Terry had gone against his upbringing, and it was all the worse when it was a daughter, who would carry the evidence of her wrong-doing. 'What about your dad?'

'Oh, Dad's all right. He's upset, I know he is, but,' she glanced at them apologetically, 'he's more angry with Terry than he is with me. He hasn't said too much about that because of Terry being killed, but I know he is. I've told him it was just as much me as him,' she added.

Dick cleared his throat. 'Well, I can understand that. I know how I'd feel if some bloke had taken advantage of one of my girls and then left her in the lurch.' There was an immediate outcry from all except Judy and he raised one hand. 'All right, all right, I'm not saying that's what our

Terry did, but I can understand Mr Foster thinking that way. Any father would.'

'So you agree we've got to do what Terry would do if he was here?' Cissie challenged him. 'You're ready to stand by and help Jean?'

Dick glowered for a moment, then said, 'I've already said so, haven't I? Course I will!' He glanced at the girl. 'I won't say I'm pleased about what you've done,' he said heavily, 'and if our Terry was here I'd give him the rough edge of my tongue. But there's no doubt he'd have stood by you and married you if he was here, and since he isn't nor ever will be,' a flicker of pain twisted his lips but he went on with determination, 'then we'll look after you and the baby as best we can. Only it's like Polly says, we've got to work out how to do it. I don't see how we can have you here, not without someone having to sleep out in the shed!'

The little flash of humour made them all smile and eased the tension. Cissie went out to the scullery to make some tea, and Polly said, 'How are you feeling in yourself, Jean? Have you been to a doctor yet?'

Jean shook her head. 'I've felt really well. To tell you the truth, I never even realised what had happened till I'd,' she glanced at Dick and blushed, 'till I'd missed twice. Then I started to wonder, but I still didn't think it could be true. I was never sick, or anything like that. I did feel a bit tired for a while, but that passed off and I felt better than ever. And then when I missed again – well, I felt too scared to go to a doctor. I suppose I didn't want to know it was true.' She looked round at their faces. 'It is true, though. I know it is, and soon everyone else will know as well.'

'Well, there's nothing we can do about that.' Polly spoke briskly. If there was one thing she'd learned during her service with the WVS it was that problems were best solved by looking at them straight in the face, without emotion. 'If you're going to keep this baby, everyone's going to know anyway, and the sooner the better if you ask me. They won't have so much time to wonder and gossip, and they can start getting used to the idea. I tell you what, Jean, you're not the first girl to be caught like this and you won't be the last. I reckon there'll be plenty more in the position you're in, with a baby whose father's never coming home. As for those folk who look down their noses and cross the street when they see you coming, well, all I can say is, good luck to 'em and it makes more room on the pavements for the rest of us!'

Everyone else laughed. Judy looked at them and opened her mouth in exasperation, but Polly cut in swiftly. 'I'm sorry, Judy, I can't write it all down. We're just saying we'll do all we can to help Jeanie, that's all.'

'But you *laughed*,' Judy said. 'You all did. You made a joke and everyone else laughed, and I don't know what it was. It's the worst thing of all,' she added, 'not knowing what jokes are. I never get anything to laugh at now.'

There was a brief silence. Then Polly wrote down some words quickly and Judy read them and flushed with anger. She bit her lip, and then sighed and nodded.

'Sorry, Poll. You're right, I'm getting sorry for myself. And it's Jean we've got to be thinking about.' She turned to Jean. 'Look, I was wondering – if you want to go away, maybe we could ask Mrs Sutton to have you for a while. She's our Sylvie's foster-mother, out at Ashwood. I've just come back from there and she's ever so nice.' She looked at Polly. 'What d'you think?'

'Well, it's an idea,' Polly said. Cissie came in with the tea and passed cups round. 'Judy just suggested Jean might go out to the Suttons'.'

'I know, I heard her.' Cissie sat down again. 'But would Mrs Sutton want her? Not that she'd be nasty at all,' she added quickly. 'I mean, I haven't met her myself but Judy and Polly both say what a nice woman she is. But she's already taken our Judy in, and I don't know that we could ask her to take Jean. She's not running a convalescent home, after all. And she couldn't do it for nothing. Where would the money come from to pay her?'

'And Jean would have to sleep in with Sylvie,' Polly added dubiously. 'She hasn't got another spare room.'

Jean sipped her tea. She was looking better now, the colour back in her cheeks, although her eyes were still swollen. It would be a day or two before that went down, Polly thought, even if she didn't cry any more, and she probably would. 'What about your job?' she asked suddenly. 'Do they know why you haven't gone in to work today?'

Jean nodded. 'Well, they know about Terry, of course, because that's where I was when Mr and Mrs Taylor came to tell me. And I think Miss Anstruther must have realised, when I fainted. She's passed one or two remarks lately about my figure. I needed a new black frock for working in the shop, and I had to have a bigger size. She's been putting two and two together for a week or two now, I think.'

'What will she do? Will she let you go on working there?'

'I don't know,' Jean said miserably. 'She might if I was in the office or the stores, but I don't know about serving the public. It gives the shop a bad name, see.'

'Perhaps she'll let you change over to something else.'

'But I couldn't work in the stores because of lifting things,' Jean pointed out. 'And I don't know anything about office work. I can't type, and I don't understand invoices – and they're not going to teach me, are they, not when they know I'll have to leave soon anyway.'

'But you're going to need a job afterwards,' Polly said. 'Will she take you back then?'

'I don't know,' Jean said again. 'And anyway, I'll have the baby then, won't I? I don't know what I'll be able to do.'

They gazed at her, beginning to realise the difficulties of her situation. Then Judy was struck by an idea.

'But you'll be eligible for evacuation! If you've got a baby, you can go out to the country. You can go to Ashwood, if there's anyone who can take you in, and Mrs Sutton will help look after you, and you can see Sylvie too. I know you've still got to pay the billeting money,' she added doubtfully, 'but can't you get National Assistance or something?' She looked at Polly. 'They'll know at the office, won't they?'

'Of course they will. And even if there isn't anything official, the WVS will help. It's what we're for. One of the things we're for, anyway. Look, I'm going in tomorrow, I'll find out whatever I can and come straight round to your house to tell you, Jean. That's if it'll be all right to do that,' she added, remembering Mrs Foster's attitude.

'It'll be all right,' Jean said. 'I still live there, after all. At least, I suppose I do.' Her mouth creased. 'I don't think Dad will let Mum turn me out that easy.'

'Poor Jean,' Cissie said after she had gone. 'It's only when you start to think about it that you realise what a terrible position she's in. In a lot of ways, it'd be easier for her to give the baby away and start afresh.'

'And could you have done that?' Polly demanded. 'Given Judy or Terry away, just because it wasn't convenient to have them? I know I wouldn't ever have parted with my Sylvie, no matter what it cost to keep her. And now I've had to part with her anyway,' she added sadly, thinking of the months it had been since Sylvie had lived at home and wondering how many more months, perhaps even years, it would be before she could return. 'But at least she's still mine.'

Cissie glanced at Judy and her eyes filled with tears. 'You're right, Polly. I know it would have torn me to bits to let my babies go. But this is different, isn't it? We didn't have the problems Jeanie's got.'

'It'd still hurt her just as much,' Polly said. 'Maybe even more.'

They were silent for a while. Cissie gathered up the cups and took them out to the scullery. Judy joined her there and said, 'I'll do these, Mum, and then get the supper ready.

You go in with the others. You've got a lot to talk about and I'm not much use at that, the way I am.'

'Judy, don't talk like that! Of course you're useful. Why, it was you who suggested Jean could be evacuated.' But Cissie knew that Judy was right. It was too difficult to include her in discussions between several people, and you couldn't write down everything. She laid her hand on her daughter's arm. 'I know how hard this is for you, love,' she said, speaking slowly. 'It's horrible for you. I just wish there was something we could do about it.'

Judy gave her a wry smile. 'Well, the doctor said it might come back all of a sudden, so perhaps it will. She said a sudden loud noise might do it – or a shock – or just nothing at all. I might wake up one morning and be able to hear all the rude things you're saying about me!'

Cissie laughed, even though she felt more like crying – a sensation that was becoming all too familiar these days – and went back to the others. Polly and Alice were discussing the possibility of Jean's being evacuated, while Dick listened. He was looking grey again, Cissie noticed, and breathing as if it hurt.

'Are you all right?' she asked, and he nodded impatiently. She folded her lips and made up her mind to keep an eye on him. The last thing they wanted now was for Dick to be ill again. They had quite enough on their plates, without that.

'Well then,' she said, sitting on one of the straight-backed dining chairs and looking around the room. 'Let's start making plans. We're going to have a new baby in the family, and I for one want to make sure we're ready to welcome the poor little mite as we should!'

Chapter Twenty-Five

When Polly arrived at the Royal Beach next morning, she went straight to the Lady Mayoress's office and asked to speak to her. The Mayoress was busy with a list of all the personnel of HMS *Hood*, trying to arrange visits to all the families who lived in Portsmouth, but she stopped what she was doing to listen to Polly's story.

'Jean knows they did wrong,' Polly finished. 'But I think it's understandable, madam, and I don't suppose they're the only ones, not by a long chalk. It was just Jean's bad luck to get caught.'

The Mayoress nodded. 'Poor child. She must be in a terrible state, hardly able to grieve properly over losing her sweetheart because of the trouble she's in. Well, it won't help anyone to be judgemental over it, Polly. What we have to do now is think how best to help her. You say she's determined to keep the baby?'

'Yes, madam, and we want to help her. It's our Terry's baby, you see – none of us wants it to go to strangers.'

'You realise that the baby itself will face difficulties as it grows up? There's a terrible stigma to being illegitimate.'

'I know, madam.' Polly flushed at the use of the word they had all avoided. 'But there's going to be such a lot of kiddies without fathers, we thought perhaps after a while nobody will think too much of it. I mean, they'll just think he was lost in the war. As he *was*. And Jeanie could call herself Mrs, couldn't she? It's not against the law, is it?'

'No, although she couldn't use it on legal documents. Well, those are problems for the future. So long as you're all aware of them.' The Mayoress tapped her teeth thoughtfully with her pencil. 'Now, you've suggested the idea of evacuation. I think that would be a good idea, if only for the girl's own safety and that of her child. And she'll certainly be eligible.'

'It's money that's the problem,' Polly ventured. 'She doesn't think she'll be able to keep her job at the Landport, you see, and we haven't got much to spare. I don't know about her own family, but if Mrs Foster isn't willing to help . . .'

'I expect she'll come round,' the Mayoress said. 'Mothers usually do, especially once the baby's born. It's fathers who are usually the problem. But I think we can find some help for her in one of our funds, and I'm sure she'll be entitled to National Assistance. The people to ask about that are the Citizens' Advice Bureau. The Misses Kelly will know, although I believe they're snowed under with requests for help.' She sighed. 'One Bureau in a city that needs at least five! If only we could have a little respite – just time to get ourselves properly organised. We seem to lurch from one crisis to another.'

Polly had heard a great many complaints about this. The townspeople of Portsmouth were forever grumbling about the Council offices being 'all the way out at Southsea' and the Citizens' Advice Bureau practically unfindable. They seemed to have no idea how difficult it was to run a city in wartime, especially one that had been bombed as heavily as Portsmouth. You never knew what was going to happen next, what new situation would face you, what needs there would be. She thought of the plans the authorities had made to treat the injured and bury the dead – hundreds of thousands of them – when what they should have been planning was how to help the homeless. But how could they have known that? There had never been a war like this in the entire history of the world. No country had been

335

subjected to these massive and sustained air raids. Nobody had known what the effects would be.

'Nobody knew there was going to be a war,' she said, trying to comfort the other woman. 'Nobody knew we were going to have to do all this.'

'But we *should* have done! We were warned enough. Mr Churchill himself tried to warn us, and what happened? He was laughed at. Treated with scorn. Now he's leading us, and we all realise at last what a great leader he is – but we could have lost him, you know, Polly. We could have thrown away the only man who seems able to reach the people, to touch our hearts and to give us strength to carry on.'

She sighed again, her face creased with worry, and then seemed to pull herself physically together. With a brisk lift of her head, she looked up at Polly and said, 'Well, we must get on. We'll do whatever we can to help your brother's fiancée. And we have a lot of other tasks this morning too, but before you go, tell me about Judy. How is she now?'

'I'm not sure really,' Polly said, pausing in the doorway. 'She came home as soon as we told her about Terry, of course. I think it did her good, being in the country – she looks a lot better – but she still can't hear anything much, and it's making her so miserable. She feels left out of everything. She's been working out there though, making camouflage, and collecting moss for soldiers. It heals their wounds, apparently. I'm not sure *I'd* want a lump of dirty moss slapped on a cut, mind you, but they say it really helps to heal them.'

'Well, I'm sure it will be good for her, working out in the fresh air. When is she going back?'

'Oh, she's not. She wants to stay at home now. She says she'd like to come back to work if you'll have her.'

'Have her? I'll be delighted. Tell her to come in as soon as she feels ready and we'll find work for her to do. And now,' the Mayoress drew a pile of papers towards her 'I really must attend to these. Thank you for coming in, Polly.'

'Thank *you*, madam.' Polly withdrew. Evidently there was going to be no driving for her to do that day, so she began to collect tasks from the other women in the office and then went to her desk.

Judy was planning to fetch Jean and bring her out to Southsea that afternoon. Before beginning on any of her tasks, Polly started to investigate the help that Jean could ask for, and the possibilities of evacuation.

If she could go out to Ashwood, or Bridge End, where there were already people they knew, Polly was sure she would find kindness and warmth. Country people, in her experience, were more likely to accept you for what you were and not what they might think you ought to be. There, with people like the Suttons, she would be able to grieve properly for Terry and look forward to the birth of her baby – the baby called Hope.

Crete had fallen and, as Dick had predicted, there was an evacuation not very different from that of Dunkirk. Fighting on the island had been bitter, but the German invaders had been too powerful and the Royal Navy had been sent in to bring out as many men as possible. This time, many of the Allied soldiers who were killed or rescued were from New Zealand and Australia. Once again, there were stories of heroism and suffering and, once again, there was grieving over men who had been lost.

'I can't bear to think about it,' Cissie said. 'Mothers in Australia and New Zealand feeling just as bad as me and all the rest of us who've lost their boys. Wives like you, Polly, and girls like our Judy. Kiddies like Sylvie.'

'Don't,' Polly begged. 'It's no good going on like that, Cis. It just makes you feel worse. You've got to try and think about other things.'

'Other things?' Cissie was pale and drawn. Her eyes were

dull and her hair lank and straggly, with signs of grey. 'How can I think of other things? I've lost my boy. The boy I carried for nine months inside me, and fed with my own milk, and loved and looked after – he's *gone*, Polly. I'm never going to see him again. He's never going to come through that door again and say, "Hello, Mum," and sit down at that table and eat the food I've cooked for him. He's never going to ask to scrape out the bowl when I've made a cake, or take the last roast potato, or bring in the coal or—'

'*Cissie*! You've got to stop this or you'll make yourself ill.' Polly cut in across the rising voice and put her hands on her sister's shoulders. 'Look, I *know* what you're going through – I've already lost my man, remember? And I've had to send my little girl away to strangers, not knowing when I'll be able to have her with me again. I'm upset about Terry too – we all are. But we've got to carry on. Going over it all, over and over again, won't do any of us any good. It won't bring him back. What we've got to think about now is the living. The rest of us here – the things we can do to help. And Jean and her baby,' she added in a low voice.

Cissie stared at her and then seemed to sag. She turned away and sank into a chair.

'I know, Poll. I know all that, but it just comes over me. I've *got* to cry for him. I've got a *right* to cry for him – he was my boy. I never expected him to die before me. I thought he'd still be alive when I went myself. I thought he'd always be here – a part of my life, a part of me. It's not what you have children for,' she said, looking up at her sister. 'Seeing them go off to war, knowing they've died, hundreds of miles away, not even able to be with them at the end. It's not what you ever think of. Not when they never meant it themselves. It's different if they went into the Forces beforehand, but when they've been conscripted . . .'

'I know,' Polly said. 'I know you've got to grieve for him, Cis. You always will – that's never going to stop. It's the worst thing in the world, losing a child, but you can't let it get on top of you.'

'But I feel I want to. Just for a little while, Poll. I feel I want to let go and let it all wash over me.' Cissie put her head into her hands and rocked to and fro. 'I just want to cry and cry and cry, and there doesn't seem to be *time*. There's always so much to do, so much to worry about, and I can't even have time to grieve properly over my own boy. It doesn't seem fair.'

'Well, I think we've got to stop thinking about what's fair,' Polly said ruefully. 'Nothing's fair, these days. In fact, I wonder whether it ever was. There's always been unfair things happening, Cis.'

On the last day of May, there was another raid on Portsmouth. Two houses in Tipnor were completely destroyed and a number of others badly damaged. Once again the fire engines were out and the bomb disposal squad called in, but the residents had reached safety in their shelters and nobody was hurt. Instead, the WVS found themselves back at their old task of handing out food and hot drinks to people who were homeless, giving them clothes from the Lady Mayoress's Clothing Store, and searching for places for them to live.

The newspapers were full of the scandal of the Jewish internees who had fled from Hitler's regime and been taken to Australia almost a year earlier. Polly read it and thought of her words to Cissie, that nothing seemed to be fair. But it doesn't have to be this unfair, she thought angrily. People don't have to be this cruel to each other.

'Those poor souls!' she said indignantly. 'Kept down below decks like slaves in a slave ship, and when they got to Australia all their luggage was taken away from them and they were treated like criminals. And these are the people we're supposed to be fighting for! I don't understand it, I really don't.'

'What it boils down to,' Dick said, 'is that there's good

and bad in most countries. And I don't know what it is, but nobody seems to like refugees. It doesn't matter how bad they've been treated in their own countries, nor how much we say they ought to be helped, nobody seems to want them. It's not even as if Australia was crowded with people, like we are here – there's space enough for all.'

'I don't think it was the Australians that did this, though. It's the British soldiers who were in charge of them who've been court-martialled.' Polly sighed and folded the newspaper. 'I've had enough of reading this. It's all misery, wherever you look. Who wants to go to the pictures?'

The cinema was only partially an escape, though, for between the two films – the 'big' picture that everyone went to see and the 'little' picture that you saw whether you wanted to or not – they sandwiched the *Pathé Pictorial News*. This showed a résumé of the week's events with, inevitably, most of it about the war. The news you had heard on the wireless over the past few days came dramatically to life as you watched shots of soldiers marching in the desert, ships at sea and bomb damage. Sometimes you saw the bombs actually falling and exploding, and people clambering over the wreckage afterwards as they searched for their family, friends and belongings. The scenes were all too familiar to Portsmouth folk.

All the same, it was good to go and be entertained for a few hours and the whole family went to see George Formby when he came to the Odeon to put on a fund-raising show for air-raid victims one afternoon. He sprang on to the stage with his ukelele, singing his cheeky songs 'When I'm Cleaning Windows' and 'Sitting in the Maginot Line', and had them all laughing within seconds. They were still laughing as they came out into the sunlight after the show had ended, and returned home feeling better than they had since before Terry's death. Even Judy had enjoyed it.

Polly had received another letter from Joe Turner. He was still working in the offices at Whitehall, although he was vague about what he was actually doing. She thought of his rueful words – 'polishing up the knocker on the big front door' – and wondered what a man with only one foot could do, apart from such menial tasks. He had been down to Devon again to see his boys and said they were well and happy, spending all their spare time either helping around the farm or out on the moors playing cowboys and Indians. *They'll forget they were ever Cockneys*, he wrote wryly.

Polly thought about Joe as she went about her tasks. She could hardly believe that another man could be important to her after Johnny's death, and she reminded herself that he had offered her nothing but friendship – a shoulder to cry on, a helping hand when she'd needed it. Yet how many friends, especially ones so newly made, would have done all that Joe Turner had done? He'd come all the way from London to see her, and he'd been a real help in their time of trouble, making cups of tea, doing the veg and going out to fetch Judy home. And when he'd held out his arms to her and hugged her against him, she'd felt a deep, warm closeness between them that she hadn't known since Johnny had gone away. For a moment, it had been like coming home.

But since then, he seemed to have cooled off. His letter was no more than a letter that any casual friend or acquaintance might have written – pleasant, friendly, chatty. No more than that. No mention of another visit.

Perhaps seeing me at home made some sort of difference, she thought. Perhaps I was different from what he'd thought. Perhaps since he's been down to Devon again and seen that Mrs Ellacombe who's looking after his boys, he's got more interested in her.

It didn't matter. He was a man she'd met briefly a couple of times, had a pleasant day with and who'd been helpful to her family when they were in trouble. That was all there was to it. Probably he wouldn't bother to write again. She decided to put him out of her mind.

Judy had had a letter too. Hers was from Ben, still at school in Winchester. He wrote of school activities – lessons, exams, sports – with impatience. *Only a few more weeks to go*, he wrote, *and I can leave for ever.* He had already applied to join the RAF and expected to be called up almost as soon as the school holidays began. Judy wondered what the Hazelwoods would say about that. She was sure that Ben hadn't mentioned his plans to his parents.

It was strange, she thought, that a boy of eighteen could go to fight in a war without asking his parents' permission, whereas he couldn't get married, vote or even stay out late without it until he was twenty-one.

Chapter Twenty-Six

Life was still a lonely, silent affair for Judy. She spent her days working in the Clothing Store, keeping a check on what garments they had. It was even more important now, for on the first day of June, clothing rationing was announced and people weren't so ready to give away unwanted items. Instead, they would have to take old winter coats to bits to make new ones for children, cut down frocks that had got too tight round the bodice to make skirts, and unpick jumpers that had gone at the elbows to make pullovers or gloves. There were complaints, of course – Ethel Glaister was especially bitter about the new rules against pleats and frills – but it was just one more thing to put up with. In fact, Alice remarked, it probably didn't hit the people of April Grove as hard as the smarter ones who lived in better streets and had bigger houses. They weren't used to make do and mend, while for April Grove folk it had always been a way of life.

However, apart from the clothes rationing and a series of raids, including one night when it was announced that there had been more alarms than on any other since the beginning of the war, June did bring a few items of good news. The first was when the news ran round the Clothing Store that the Lord Mayor had been knighted in the King's Birthday Honours list.

'You mean he'll be a Sir?' Judy asked when this had been explained to her by Laura, who was also working in the store. 'Instead of Lord Mayor?'

'No, he'll still be Lord Mayor, but he'll be "Sir" as well.

And the Lady Mayoress will be "Lady", even after she stops being Lady Mayoress. Isn't it smashing!' Laura finished sorting a pile of children's jumpers and set them aside. 'It just shows that the King thinks a lot of him. It's for services to Civil Defence.'

'I've never known a knight before.' Judy's ideas of knights of the realm were mostly gained from a hotchpotch of children's stories, and legends from St George to King Arthur. She tried to imagine the Lord Mayor in armour and failed. 'Will he have to wear special clothes and go to Buckingham Palace and all that?'

'Well, to be knighted, I suppose he will.' Laura didn't know much about it herself. 'I don't suppose he'll be all that different the rest of the time.'

The *Evening News* was full of the new appointment and recounted messages of congratulation from all over England as well as running an article on all the many things the Mayor and his wife had done to help the city and its people during the hardships of the past two years. But even this news couldn't compete for long with the war itself, and it seemed almost like a deliberate insult when the Luftwaffe came again that very night and dropped high explosive and oil bombs on several of the city's military establishments, including the RAOC camp in Copnor Road where a number of soldiers were killed. The families in April Grove huddled in their shelters, hearing the bombs explode frighteningly close, and dreading the thought of being made homeless again. I couldn't bear it, Cissie thought, not a second time, and reached for her husband's hand. Alice, too, looked fearful by the flickering light of the hurricane lamp, and all three were thinking of Polly and Judy, out together in the ambulance. I don't know how our Judy stands it, Cissie thought, nor our Polly, not after what's already happened to them. They're brave as lions, the pair of them. They ought to be knighted too, only they don't knight women, but they ought to get medals at least. All those girls and women ought to get medals.

However, despite the damage and the tragedy of the RAOC camp, there was not much more damage in the area and April Grove lived – as Granny Kinch put it, standing at her door as usual in her steel hair curlers – to fight another day.

'We're bound to get some good news soon,' she said staunchly. 'Bound to. Old Hitler can't have things all his own way.'

And her words were proved true only two days later, when Jess Budd came down the street in a state of high excitement, almost dragging little Maureen along by one hand, and reported that Heinrich Brunner had come home.

'I saw him out in the street first,' she told Cissie, who was scrubbing the front doorstep. 'I never even recognised him! He's gone ever so thin, and his hair's grey and he's got these shaggy whiskers, and he looks as if he's been sleeping rough. I did think he looked a bit familiar but then I thought he was some old tramp that I might have seen before. And then he came into the shop. Alice and Joy were both there, marking up the papers, the trains were late and half the paper boys hadn't turned up and Alice was saying how they'd all be late and people would be complaining – and they looked at him for a minute as if they didn't recognise him either! And he looked as if he hardly knew where he was. And then he said, "Alice, don't you know me?" and we all realised who he was. Well, you should have seen Alice Brunner's face! She looked as if the sun had come out just behind her eyes. And then he sort of swayed a bit and she came round the counter like a flash of lightning and caught him, and he said, "It's me, Alice, it's Heinrich, I've come home," and they all started crying . . .' Jess wiped her own eyes and her voice broke a little '. . . and I came away. I don't think people will be getting their papers till teatime today, if they get them at all!'

'Well, isn't that wonderful.' Cissie stood up with her scrubbing brush in her hand, gazing at Jess. 'That's really good news. It was never right, putting people like Heinrich Brunner in prison. I mean, what harm would he do? He'd been in England for years. And poor Alice has had a hard time running that shop by herself.'

'I know. Mind, I'm not sure as he's going to be much help to her, not to start with anyway. He looks as if he's going to need a bit of looking after himself. But I don't suppose she'll mind that. Just having him back is going to make all the difference.' She pulled Maureen away from Cissie's bucket of water. 'Leave that alone, Maureen. We're going to see Auntie Annie now and tell her. D'you know, Cissie, it's really done me good, seeing something nice happen for a change!'

It's done me good, too, Cissie thought, picking up her bucket and going back indoors. I just wish it could have been my Terry. It was three weeks now since the *Hood* had been sunk, and her secret hope that he might have been one of the three men saved had been dashed. Yet she still couldn't rid herself of the feeling that he might yet come back. A mistake might have been made. There could have been four survivors. One might have been taken prisoner by one of the German ships. Or he might somehow have managed to reach Greenland or Iceland and been saved by Eskimos who were even now taking care of him in some isolated igloo . . . During the daytime, she knew that none of these miracles had happened, but as she lay awake at night or sat in the Anderson listening to the drone of aircraft or the '*crump*' of an exploding bomb, anything seemed possible. Miracles *did* happen. Look at Heinrich Brunner. Everyone had thought him lost in the torpedoing of the ship that had been transporting him and other internees to Canada. Now here he was, returned from the dead. If it could happen to him, couldn't it happen to Terry?

'Heinrich Brunner's come back,' she said to her mother

346

and Dick as she went into the back room. 'He came down September Street looking like a tramp, Jess Budd said, and nobody knew him at first. Alice Brunner's over the moon, she's shut the shop for the day and left the papers in a pile outside for people to collect for themselves, and Jess Budd says she's sent up a tin of salmon she's had put by, for their tea.'

'I don't suppose poor Mr Brunner's seen tinned salmon for months and months,' Alice said, beaming. 'Well, what lovely news. It's like an answer to all our prayers. He never ought to have been taken away in the first place. I thought he was gone for good.'

'So did Mrs Brunner. She's been looking terrible just lately, letting herself go and leaving the shop to young Joy to manage. She'll buck up now.'

'Well, I don't know as it's something to get all that fussed about,' Dick said from his corner. He had started on a new rag rug but the canvas had slipped off his knees and was lying on the floor. 'Whether he was a spy or not, they had to intern all the aliens just in case, it stands to reason. You can't trust foreigners, not at a time like this.'

'But Mr Brunner wasn't a foreigner! He's been in England for twenty years.'

'He's a foreigner,' Dick stated. 'He's a German. He's got a German name and he speaks with a German accent. You can't get round that.'

Cissie opened her mouth to argue, then glanced at her mother and folded her lips. When Dick was in this mood, there was no reasoning with him. He knew Heinrich Brunner as well as they did, he'd been in and out of the newsagent's shop ever since he'd first come to April Grove to court Cissie, he'd laughed and joked with the man and watched young Joy grow up from a baby. She knew that deep down he agreed with them, but his mood lately had been growing more and more morose. It was as if no matter what you said, he had to take the opposite view.

It's all been too much for him, she thought, going out to the scullery to empty her bucket and start on the next chore. It's getting him down, all of it, the air raids, the shortages, and then his illness. He couldn't even get any rest from the bombing in hospital. It was enough to send anybody crackers.

Not that Dick was crackers! He was just miserable. Depressed and miserable – and who could blame him?

Jean was six months pregnant now and beginning to show. Nobody could be in any doubt about her condition and the supervisor at the shop had told her that she'd have to leave.

'It's not decent, not with mothers bringing their children in, and you getting more and more obvious, without even a ring on your finger. You'd better take a week's wages and go now.'

Jean had stared at her, shocked and hurt. 'You mean straight away? Without even time to say goodbye?'

'I don't suppose anyone wants to say goodbye to you anyway,' the supervisor said brusquely. 'You're an embarrassment, the way you are. A lot of people would have given you your cards before this.'

Jean turned and ran out of the shop. She saw some of the other assistants staring as she hurried past, and one girl put out her hand to stop her. But Jean shook her head and pushed past, the tears streaming down her face. I'll never go there again, she thought, never. I'll never buy anything in that horrible place again, not as long as I live.

On the pavement, well away from the door, she stopped, wondering what to do next. The thought of going home and admitting she'd been sacked was unbearable. She'd have to do it eventually, of course, but not now, at only half past nine in the morning. Her mother would have enough to say as it was, when she found out, and Jean didn't want to spend the entire day listening to her recriminations.

She wandered through the streets, wiping away her tears,

and after a while found herself outside the church hall that was being used for one of the Lady Mayoress's Clothing Stores. Glancing through the open door, she caught sight of Judy sorting a pile of clothes, and as she hesitated Judy looked up and saw her.

'Jean! Whatever are you doing here?' She hurried out into the sunshine, gazing at her friend in concern. 'What's the matter? You look awful. Come in and sit down – I'll get you a glass of water.' She guided Jean to a chair and pushed her into it, then disappeared for a moment, returning with a cup which she held to Jean's lips. 'Here. Sip this. It's – it's not the baby, is it?'

Jean shook her head. 'No, she's all right.' She was quite certain it would be a girl. 'Kicking me to death as usual!' She laid her hand on her stomach. 'Judy, I've been given the sack.'

'What?' Judy stared at her and Jean bit her lip. For a few minutes she had forgotten that Judy couldn't hear. She repeated her words more carefully and saw by Judy's face that she understood. 'The *sack*? But why? Because of the baby?'

Jean nodded. 'I'm too embarrassing to have in the shop any more. I knew it would happen, of course, but I didn't think it would be like this.' Her voice shook and tears brimmed over again. 'She was so horrible to me, Judy. Said I wasn't decent and that nobody would want to talk to me. She wouldn't even let me say goodbye to the others. And now they'll all know, and nobody *will* want to speak to me and – and I don't know how I'm going to tell Mum, she'll start going on at me all over again, and Dad will be upset, and – and I just don't think I can bear it, Judy. I don't know what I'm going to do.' She put down her cup and leaned forwards, sinking her face into her hands.

Judy didn't need to hear to know what Jean was saying and feeling. She knelt beside the distraught girl, putting her arms around the shaking shoulders and drawing her close.

'It's all right, Jean. It's all right. Everything's going to be all right. We'll stand by you – all of us. We'll look after you. Don't worry. Don't be frightened. You've still got us. We're your family now, too, and we won't let you down.'

'Oh, Judy.' The weeping girl turned and buried her face against Judy's shoulder. 'It's so awful. I never thought it would be like this. I never thought it would lead to all this trouble, and people hating me and not wanting to know me. And Terry would never have wanted me to do it if he'd known. We just didn't think, we wanted to love each other so much, it seemed so right and natural at the time – and now he's gone and he's never coming back.' Her words were lost in a series of hiccuping sobs.

'Sssh, sssh, it'll be all right.' Judy held her close, murmuring comforting words. One of the other volunteers came over and looked questioningly at her, and she shook her head. 'It's all right, thanks. I can manage. I know her. It's all right, Jean, we'll look after you. Don't worry, it's going to be all right, I promise.'

Gradually, the sobs eased. Judy found a hanky and pressed it into Jean's hand. Jean wiped her face and blew her nose, then drew in a shaky breath. She looked at Judy.

'I'm sorry. I shouldn't have come here, making a scene.'

'Don't be silly.' Once again, Judy could guess at what she was saying. 'Look, you just sit here and rest for a bit. I've got to finish this job and then I'll take you home. *My* home,' she added firmly as Jean began to protest. 'You know Mum and Gran and Polly are all on your side as well as me. Dad too,' she added with slightly less conviction. Dick seemed to veer from one point of view to another these days, for no apparent reason. 'And you know we've written to Mrs Sutton to see if there's anywhere in the village you can stay. Why, there might be a letter there now, for all we know. Anyway, you've got to stop worrying. Everything's going to be all right.'

She went back to her work, hoping that what she had said

was true. However much the family rallied round to help, Jean's path was not going to be an easy one to tread. Being an unmarried mother, even in wartime when quite a few young women were finding themselves in the same position, was no picnic. There were plenty of people all too ready to criticise, plenty who would turn the other way or cross the street to avoid speaking to the girl whose sin was so obvious. And having to manage on your own, with no breadwinner to support the family, was so difficult that not many girls even tried. They gave their babies up for adoption, hoping that the new family would be able to give the child all that they couldn't provide, and then got on with their lives and tried to forget.

I don't know how you could forget though, Judy thought as she went back to sorting children's clothes. I don't know how you could *ever* forget having a baby.

When Polly came home from the Royal Beach that day she found the whole family waiting for her, with Jean ensconced in Dick's armchair, looking pale and red-eyed. She stopped in the doorway.

'What's up? What's happened?'

'It's all right, Poll,' Alice said quickly. 'Nothing's wrong. Well,' she glanced at Jean, 'nothing too serious, anyway. Jean's been put out of her job, that's what it is. It's not as if it wasn't expected.'

'Put out? Oh Jean!' Polly crossed the room quickly and took the girl's hands. 'Didn't they even give you proper notice?'

Jean shook her head. 'Miss Browning told me I was getting embarrassing and I'd better go. She said she'd give me a week's wages, but I was so upset, I just rushed out. I suppose I'll have to go back for my cards.'

'One of us will do that,' Polly said firmly. 'You don't have to go anywhere near the place again. Spiteful old cat!'

'I don't know why she was so nasty,' Jean said woefully.

'She seemed to understand at first, when we first heard about Terry. She was so nice. But since she found out about the baby . . .'

The others glanced at each other. 'Well, you're going to have to put up with a lot of that,' Alice said reasonably. 'You've got to get used to it. It's the baby I'm sorry for.' She stopped and bit her lip, and Jean looked up at her in dismay.

'You mean people will be nasty to her as well? My baby? But it's not her fault.'

'Some people will be,' Polly said. 'There's always some people who take every chance of being spiteful. But you don't have to worry about them. Remember what we used to say as kiddies? "Sticks and stones may break my bones, but names will never hurt me!" That's what you've got to remember. And I think there's going to be more than one girl in your position before this war's over, so we're all going to have to be a bit more understanding. Anyway, that doesn't matter now. What we've got to do now is decide what's going to happen next.'

'We've been talking about that,' Cissie said. 'We think she ought to go out to Ashdown straight away. You said she could be evacuated, didn't you, Polly? And there's a letter for you here, look, with an Ashdown postmark. Maybe it's from Mrs Sutton herself with some news.'

'You mean you've been sitting here all day and never opened it?' Polly snatched the envelope. 'Honestly, I wouldn't have minded.' She tore it open and scanned the sheet of paper inside. 'Yes, it is! She says she's been talking to the vicar's wife – Mrs Hazelwood – about Jean, and Mrs Hazelwood says she can go there.' She lifted her head and looked at them with sparkling eyes. 'To the vicarage itself. Isn't that kind of them!'

'The vicarage?' Jean repeated doubtfully. 'Oh, I don't think – I mean, I hardly ever go to church. Do they know

352

about me?' She touched her stomach. 'Do they know about the baby?'

'Of course they know about you. That's why she's offered to have you.' Polly glanced round and caught sight of Judy, sitting in the corner trying to follow the excited chatter. She passed the letter across. 'Read this, Judy. Isn't it lovely?'

'Yes,' Judy said, but there was a tinge of uncertainty in her voice. 'Yes, it is. But – I don't understand. They've already got a houseful, with Mr Hazelwood's old parents and two Army officers billeted there. The only other room is Ben's. What's he going to do when he comes home from school?'

Jean stared at her. 'You mean they haven't got room? I can't stay there?'

'Of course you can,' Polly said. 'Mrs Hazelwood says so, doesn't she?' She looked at Judy. 'Didn't you say he wanted to go into the RAF?'

'Yes, but he hadn't even discussed it with his parents. And he's not old enough. I don't understand.' She looked at the letter again. 'Mrs Hazelwood says Jean can go out as soon as she likes.'

'Then that's all right,' Polly said, and turned back to Jean. 'Is that what you want to do? Go out to Ashwood straight away?'

Jean nodded. 'Yes, but it would help if someone could go with me. I mean, I don't know anyone there and—'

'I'll go with you,' Judy said, before anyone else could speak. They weren't even sure whether she had understood Jean's plea, or whether she was still speaking her own thoughts. She looked at the letter in her hand and then at Jean. 'I'll go with you. I can introduce you to everyone. I'm not much use here, after all.' And as they all looked at her, opening their mouths to deny it, she added, 'It'll be nice to see them all again anyway.'

Then, to herself she added, *And I can find out what's happening to Ben.*

Chapter Twenty-Seven

Jean and Judy travelled out to Ashwood the next day. The Fosters had been taken aback and not very pleased to find that the whole thing had been discussed and decided without their presence, but as Jean had said, they'd made it clear that they didn't approve anyway, so what was the point? 'You'd rather I gave my baby away,' she said, wrapping her arms across her stomach. 'You'd rather I went away and had it and then came back and pretended it had never happened. Well, I *am* going away and you can pretend that if you want to, but I won't be coming back. Not until I can bring my baby with me.'

Mrs Foster had looked angry and told Jean that she wasn't going to be told what to do in her own house, and if that was the way she felt she'd better pack her things and go. And when Mr Foster tried to reason with her she had turned on him asking how Jean could possibly keep the baby, what would they live on and what, oh *what* would the neighbours say when they saw her walking down the street pushing a pram?

'That was what finished it for me,' Jean said, her face white. 'My own mother putting more store on what spiteful cats like Mrs Barrow next door and Mrs Parry over the road think than on what happens to her own daughter.' She looked at Cissie. 'You're my mum now, Mrs Taylor. You're my family.'

Cissie looked as if she might begin to cry, and Dick cleared his throat and said gruffly, 'You didn't ought to talk like that, Jean. They're your mum and dad and nothing can change that. But we'll do what we can for you, all the same. And I reckon it'll be better for you when you get out to Ashwood. There's no need for folk there to know what's happened. No need to know you're not married, I mean,' he added, glancing away from Jean's plump figure.

'No, there's not,' Alice said. 'And if you've got a ring on your finger, they won't even wonder. Here.' She pulled the gold ring from her own finger and held it out. 'Wear that. That'll put paid to any gossip. You can just tell them the truth about what happened to Terry, and nobody will ask any more questions.'

'*Mum!*' Cissie exclaimed, and Alice looked at her defiantly.

'All right, our Cis, you needn't look like that. It's not your dad's ring. It's your gran's – my mum's. I've had it on me finger since the day she died, but now I reckon it'll do more good passed down the family to Jean. I was going to offer it to Terry anyway, so she'd have had it if he'd lived.'

Jean took the ring and stared at it. It was thin, its edges soft with many years of wear, but it was still bright. Her eyes filled with tears. 'I can't take this, Mrs Thomas.'

'I've told you, I'd have given it to Terry anyway.' Nobody knew if this were really true, but Alice's look dared them to question it. 'Now, put it on – never mind if it feels like a lie. You and Terry were married in the sight of God, that's how I look at it, and you're one of the family now. And no more calling me Mrs Thomas, neither. I'm Gran to young Judy here and I'll be Gran to you as well, all right?'

'Yes, Mrs – Gran,' Jean said, and her voice broke. 'Thank you. Thank you very much.'

Jean spent the night in Judy's bed, while Judy slept on cushions on the floor, and next morning they all walked down to the little halt, carrying the two suitcases that held all Jean's belongings, with a few clothes pushed in for Judy. She was going to stay a few days, just to see Jean settled in, she said, but after the train had pulled away Polly remarked to Cissie that she wouldn't be surprised if the girl didn't stay on. 'She's never properly settled back home, you know. She seems to feel left out of things so much. It was different out in the country, where there's not so many people anyway. I reckon she felt easier there, somehow.'

'I thought she might have got her hearing back by now,' Cissie said. 'The last doctor she saw said there was nothing really wrong with her ears. It was to do with the blast – a sort of shock.'

'I can tell you what it is,' Dick said. 'It's nerves. It's like she doesn't *want* to hear any more.'

'Dick!' Cissie said. 'How can you say that? Of *course* she wants to hear! It's awful for her, being deaf. Anyone can see that.'

'I don't mean it's deliberate. She can't help it. But it's like we had in the First War – shell-shock. That night it happened,' he looked at Polly, 'there was a lot of noise, wasn't there? Explosions and ack-ack and planes going over, all that sort of thing.'

'Of course there was. And buildings crashing down, and flames crackling and roaring – no end of din. But—'

'And then you were buried and she thought you were dead. Well, I think she *was* deafened to begin with, same as a lot of people are when bombs drop, but it didn't wear off like it usually does because she found out that if she was deaf she didn't have to hear all those things that reminded her of when she thought you'd been killed.' He stopped. 'You don't have to stare at me like that. I just think that's what it is, that's all. I've thought so all along, to tell you the truth. And you know what she's always been like about being shut in small spaces. Well, I reckon that was what it felt like to her then. Shut in, and all that din going on round her.'

'Dick!' Cissie said again. 'Wherever did you get all them ideas?'

'I heard a talk about it on the wireless. This what d'you

call 'em, psychologist, he was talking about nerves and what we used to call shell-shock, and the way he explained it, I thought, That's what's happened to our Judy. Only it was just after that I got pneumonia so I never got a chance to say nothing, and I didn't think you'd believe me anyway. But I think that's what it is, all the same.'

'I suppose it might be,' Polly said thoughtfully. 'But if it is, will she ever get better? I mean, if there's nothing actually wrong, and she doesn't know she's doing it, how can she ever stop? I can't see her believing it, Dick. She'd be ever so upset if you told her she could hear if she wanted to. She'd think you were saying she was putting it on.'

'That's why I've never said nothing,' he said. 'And I don't know what would make her better. Maybe another shock, but I don't know what sort. Bombs'd only make it worse.'

'Rest and peace and quiet, that's what'll help her,' Alice said firmly. 'I don't know if Dick's right or not, but I do know they're what our Judy needs most. I hope she does decide to stay out in the country. It's the best thing for her, whichever way you look at it.'

Judy thought so too, as the train chuffed to a halt at Ashdown station. She stood up and got Jean's suitcases down from the rack, then helped her drag them out on to the platform. They stood for a moment breathing in the fresh, warm air, and Jean smiled.

'It's lovely,' she said, turning to face Judy so that her lips could be read. 'I can hear birds singing – oh, Judy, I'm sorry!' She put her hand to her mouth. 'I never meant—'

'It's all right.' Judy wasn't sure what she'd said anyway, only that it was clearly something to do with hearing. She picked up the cases. 'Come on. It's not far to walk.'

'Well, you can let me carry one of the cases then.' Jean took the lighter one and they strolled along between the leafy hedges. There had been primroses and violets here a

357

few weeks ago, Judy reflected, and bright, sunshiny celandines. Now the grass had grown and a froth of wild parsley on both banks almost met across the narrow way, so that it was almost like walking through a shower of foam. Small birds were dustbathing in shallow potholes, and a rabbit scuttled into a hole as the two girls rounded a corner. Above them, the sky was a deeper blue than it had been in the spring, and the sun hotter. You don't notice the seasons half as much in a town, Judy thought, yet here everything seems to have changed in just a few weeks.

The vicarage garden had changed too. The big vegetable patch was flourishing, with rows of lettuces already big enough to pick, and runner beans climbing vigorously up a row of tall poles. A shorter row was bushing out with peas and there were several furrows of potatoes which had already been dug over, and a line of feathery carrots. Judy looked at them enviously. Some of the men in April Grove had allotments and grew vegetables like these but Dick had never been strong enough to do heavy gardening, and in any case until they'd moved to Alice's house they'd lived too far away. Except for a few things Alice and Cissie had planted in the small garden at the back of the house, the Taylors were dependent upon vegetables from Atkinson's, the greengrocer's in September Street.

'You're going to eat well here,' she said to Jean. 'It'll be good for you and good for the baby.'

She opened the small wicket gate into the patch of garden that the Hazelwoods had kept for relaxation. Here too the flowers had grown and the apple trees had lost their blossom and now bore small green fruits. Beneath the one where she had been sitting on the day that she had first met Ben, there was a deckchair and at the sight of it, Judy stopped short. '*Ben!*'

The lanky figure stretched in the chair stirred. A pair of dark, rather heavy brows lifted enquiringly and bright blue

358

eyes met hers. The wide mouth spread into a curling grin and Ben unfolded himself and came to his feet.

'Judy! I thought you were never coming.' He pulled her into his long arms and hugged her tightly.

Judy, laughing, expostulated, 'Ben, don't be silly. What are you doing here? Shouldn't you be at school? Oh, it *is* good to see you.'

He let her go, making a rueful face. 'Well, that puts me in my place. *Shouldn't you be at school*, indeed! Just when I was hoping to impress this lovely lady you've brought with you.'

'I don't know what you're saying but I'm sure it's ridiculous,' Judy said firmly. 'Ben, this is Jean Foster. She's come to stay here for a while. But we thought – well, *I* thought you'd be away at school. I thought she'd be having your bedroom.' She stopped, feeling her face turn pink, and Ben laughed.

'Well, so she can.' He spoke clearly so that she could understand. 'I'm leaving today – that's why I was hoping you'd arrive this afternoon. I didn't want to miss you.'

'Leaving?' Judy stared at him. 'Going back to school, you mean?'

He sighed. 'There you go again. No, I've left school. I've joined the RAF.' Excitement broke out over his face. 'I'm going to train to be a pilot, Judy! A *pilot*!' He spread his arms and tilted from side to side, like a small boy playing Spitfires, then flung his hands skywards. 'I'm going to be up there, flying my own aeroplane and doing my bit for the war at last!'

Judy stared at him. Even when the words escaped her, it was easy to understand what Ben was saying, and how pleased he was to be saying it. But Judy couldn't feel pleased for him. A cold fear settled round her heart. Not another one going off to be killed, she thought. Not another boy like Sean and Terry and Johnny, setting off full of hope and courage, to die in some horrible way without ever having really had his chance at life . . .

Ben had turned to Jean and was shaking her hand, obviously welcoming her to the vicarage and Jean, who had been standing shyly by, was flushed and smiling as she responded. Judy wondered how much he knew about her condition. Had his mother and father discussed it in front of him? Did he know enough to notice that she was pregnant? She watched them a little sadly, the boy who was about to risk his life and the girl who had lost her sweetheart. It all seemed so peaceful and innocent, standing in the sunshine in this tranquil garden, yet the shadow of death was reaching out to them both.

'What am I doing, keeping you standing out here?' Ben exclaimed, picking up both suitcases. 'Come in and we'll find Mother. She'll want to make you a cup of tea or a glass of lemonade or something. It won't be real lemonade, of course,' he went on, striding off towards the French windows. 'We can't get lemons now, although I did hear a consignment of oranges has arrived in Southampton. But the stuff we make with those crystals isn't too bad.' He went on talking as he led them through the cool house, but for once Judy didn't feel left out. She looked about her, glad to be back here, glad to be at Ashdown, glad to be with Ben.

I've missed them all while I've been back in Portsmouth, she thought with some surprise. I've missed the peace and quiet. And then she caught herself up in surprise.

How could a deaf person say that she missed the peace and quiet?

Back at the Royal Beach, Polly was kept busy with a variety of jobs. Sometimes she found herself driving round the city all day, delivering messages or packages, at others she was in one of the Clothing Stores, or on another day she might be driving the Lady Mayoress or some important visitor. There were no more trips to London, however, and Joe Turner didn't seem to be likely to visit Portsmouth again.

Polly had tried to put him out of her mind, but without

success. There was nothing special about him, she told herself – he was no oil painting, he was several years older than she, and he was a widower with two sons to bring up. Yet his face was friendly, his eyes warm and his presence comforting. She could not forget how he had taken her into his arms to comfort her, and how she had felt as if she had come home. Oh Johnny, she thought, would you mind very much? Would you be very hurt if I found someone else to love? It wouldn't make any difference to you and me – I could never forget how we loved each other. But there are so many years ahead, so many years to spend alone, and if I could just have the sort of comfort Joe Turner gave me, it would make the years so much easier to bear.

And then she shook herself. Joe Turner had never given her any reason to suppose that he wanted or would offer anything more than friendship. And look at the last time he came here – flung headlong into a family crisis, sent off into the countryside to fetch home an unknown girl, and one who couldn't even hear him when he talked to her? He wasn't likely to risk that again!

Deep in thought, she mounted the steps to the Royal Beach and jumped, startled, as someone touched her on the arm. She looked up and recognised the young Observer who had been stuck in the lift with Judy.

'Hello, you're Chris Barrett, aren't you?'

'That's right,' he said, 'and you're Mrs Dunn – Judy Taylor's aunt.'

'Polly,' she said, smiling at him. 'I feel we're almost family after what happened to you and Judy.'

He looked rueful. 'I'm never going to hear the last of that. It would start at just that moment! I never meant to embarrass her, you know, Mrs Dunn. I didn't even mean to make a pass – it just happened. We were talking, and then—'

'It's *Polly*. Please.' She hesitated. 'I think you should forget about that. It wasn't really that important, after all.'

'I know.' He lifted his shoulders. 'I suppose I ought to put Judy out of my mind – I know she's engaged – but somehow, I can't. How is she, Mrs Dunn? Is she all right? Will she get better?'

Polly stared at him. 'Better? You mean her ears? Well, we hope so, but nobody really knows. But – what was that you said about her being engaged?'

'Well, she is, isn't she? She was wearing a ring anyway, that day in the lift.' He stared at her, a small frown creasing his brows. 'She said she was going to tell me about it – we were going to go out together, but it was the Sunday of the big raid and I had to stay on duty. And after that – well, she wouldn't see me again. And I've been away for a while, on a training course. When I came back, I didn't know what to do next.'

Polly remembered Judy coming home a few days before the raid, different somehow, her eyes brighter and her face more alive than it had looked for weeks. Was that because she had made a date with Chris Barrett? Was it then that she had moved Sean's ring over to her right hand? Had she been going to tell Chris about the young Irish sailor?

But if so, they had never had their date and she had never told him. Polly remembered the young man's attempts to come and see Judy in April Grove, and her refusal even to go to the door. Perhaps she had regretted agreeing to see him. Or perhaps she really did believe he would no longer be interested in her. And then she'd moved the ring back again.

'Judy was engaged,' she said, making up her mind. 'But her fiancé died – he was lost at sea around the time of the first Blitz. I expect that was what she was going to tell you.'

He gazed at her. 'So we could have gone out together. She wasn't being disloyal or anything. But why won't she see me again? What happened to make her decide not to have anything more to do with me?'

'It's not just you,' Polly said gently. 'She's had a bad

time. That's why we got her to go out to the country – for some peace and rest. You see, she's not as strong as she likes to think. She has this terrible fear of being shut in.'

'I know,' he said. 'She was scared stiff in the lift, but she tried hard not to show it. I thought she was really brave.'

'She is, but in the Blitz that night we were trapped in a building with high walls all around. It was terrible – there was a woman dying, we were trying to get her out and then the building was bombed again – we thought we weren't going to get out at all. Judy was a heroine, she saved me. I wouldn't be here now if it weren't for her, but afterwards she seemed to go right down. The doctors say there's nothing wrong with her ears, nothing physical. And my brother-in-law thinks it's like shell-shock. It's as if she doesn't want to hear, as if she's shut everything out – the noise and the fear, everything.'

'But that's terrible,' he said. 'She's shut herself into a worse space than ever.'

'I know,' Polly said. 'That's why we're so worried about her. But out in the country – well, she seems more able to manage. She seems stronger.'

Chris nodded. Then he said, 'D'you think she'd see me if I went out there? D'you think she'd send me away?'

Polly looked at him. His fair, open face was troubled. She said carefully, 'I think you ought to leave her for a while, Chris. She needs time to get over Sean. She needs the peace and quiet of the countryside, with no more complications. Perhaps in a few weeks, if you still feel the same . . .'

'I'll still feel the same,' he said. He met her eyes candidly. 'I think a lot of Judy, Mrs Dunn – Polly. The first time I saw her, I thought, That's the girl for me. That's the girl I want to marry.' He paused. 'I don't know if she could ever come to feel anything for me, but when we were in the lift it was as if there was something between us, something special. So, I'd like to try again. I'd like to see if there is a chance. And I'm ready to wait.'

'And suppose she's deaf for the rest of her life?' Polly asked. 'It isn't easy, you know, for anybody.'

'She'll still be Judy,' he said simply. 'She'll still be the girl for me.'

Chapter Twenty-Eight

Jean settled into the vicarage more quickly than anyone had thought possible. The arrangement was that she would have her board and lodging in return for whatever household duties she could manage, and Mrs Hazelwood found herself continually remonstrating with her for doing too much. 'You're not supposed to slave from morning till night, my dear. You're expecting a baby – you ought to be putting your feet up.'

'I did.' Jean was cleaning the French windows with a screwed-up newspaper. 'I was out there in the deckchair for nearly an hour. Then I noticed the glass was all smeary where the cat was trying to get out to chase the birds, and once I'd started—'

'Once you'd started you decided to clean every window in the house.' Mrs Hazelwood took away the newspaper and spoke firmly. 'Jean, I do not expect you to work all day long. If you'll just help out a bit in the mornings with some cleaning – *light* cleaning – and doing the vegetables for lunch, that will be quite enough. I mean it.'

'But it's not enough! I know it isn't. A great big house like this,' Jean waved her hand at the sprawling Victorian house, built in an age when vicars were expected to have large families. 'It needs a lot of looking after. And I'm supposed to be working for my keep. Just doing a bit of sweeping and peeling a few potatoes isn't enough for that.'

'Well,' Mrs Hazelwood hesitated. 'If you really want to do more, you could take over the ironing. The vicar needs a clean shirt every day, and there's his dog-collars and his surplices – there always seems to be a mountain of ironing waiting to be done. But I don't want you to stand for long periods. You can sit on a high stool to do it, and you must promise me that you'll stop at once if you feel tired or your back starts to ache.'

'I'll do that,' Jean promised. 'I quite like ironing anyway. And I thought I might look after the ornaments in the morning room as well. All those lovely pieces of china – I'd really enjoy dusting them. That's if you'll trust me not to drop them,' she added hastily.

Mrs Hazelwood smiled. 'Of course I trust you, my dear. And I'd just like to say how much the vicar and I enjoy having you with us. You seem to have fitted in so well – it's hard to believe you've only been here a week. And with Ben gone, the house would seem so empty.'

Ben had written already from his RAF training camp, and seemed to be enjoying it very much. He had written to Judy as well, telling her rather more than he told his parents, and she read his letter two or three times and then put it in a drawer beside her bed. He seemed so young, she thought, so young to be a pilot and risk his life. She thought of her brother Terry, only a few years older and dead already. Ben was a bit like a younger brother; she hoped he would survive. Surely some of them must. Or would the war just go on and on until there was nobody left to fight?

There had been more raids on Portsmouth and Polly wrote to tell her that a huge bomb had fallen in Torrington Road, not far from September Street, and buried itself beneath a house. The bomb disposal squad had come to defuse it and announced that, although it was now safe, it couldn't be moved. There just wasn't time, when there were so many other bombs all over the city. It wasn't a danger to anyone so could be left where it was for the time being.

I wouldn't like it, though, Polly had written. *Imagine knowing there was a bomb under your floor! I mean, how do they know for certain it's safe?*

Towards the end of the month Hitler invaded Russia. He sent in three million troops – three *million*! Judy thought in astonishment – and kept only six hundred thousand to cover Europe and North Africa. Even that sounded a lot. Mr Churchill immediately proposed an alliance with Russia and Stalin accepted. It seemed very strange, when you remembered that Russia had once been on Germany's side, but this war seemed to grow stranger and stranger as time went on. Friends one day, enemies the next, and then the whole lot ganging up on someone else. Like children in a playground, Judy thought, only these games were much more dangerous.

Now that she was out in the country, she felt her anxiety begin to diminish again. The peace she had known when she was here before stole over her heart again, and the panic that never seemed far away when she was in Portsmouth receded. She felt ashamed, thinking of all those she had left behind to face the bombing and the dangers, and threw herself even more whole-heartedly into her voluntary work.

'You could help with the pie scheme,' Mrs Hazelwood suggested when Judy went to ask what she could do. 'We always seem to need volunteers for that.'

'The pie scheme?'

'Yes. It's called the Hampshire County Pie Scheme and it's approved by the Ministry of Food. A baker in Romsey makes the pies and we pay him threepence-ha'penny each. The public pays fourpence, so we make a ha'penny profit, which we pay into our bank account and then send on to Winchester. We're allowed to deduct our expenses – postage, telephone calls and so on. We can order up to three hundred pies a week, but if we need more we have to apply for the baker to be permitted extra fat and meat.'

'But what happens to the pies?' Judy asked when she had digested this information, conveyed by a mixture of clear speaking and written notes. 'Who has them all?'

'Oh, all sorts of people. Land Girls, farmers, villagers, old people who can't manage to cook a meal any more. The pies are very much appreciated, I can tell you. We collect them in the mornings when they're baked and take them all around the village and quite a long way into the outlying countryside. It helps the rations along and saves people cooking at lunchtime.'

'Lunchtime' to Judy had always been 'dinnertime', when she was used to having the main meal of the day. She could see that it would be helpful to farmers' wives not to have to cook a large midday meal for all the farmworkers, and would save their having to return to the house from distant fields. 'So would you want me to take pies round?' she asked a little doubtfully. 'I mean, I don't really know the area that well. I might get lost and wouldn't be able to find my way back, what with all the signposts being taken down and not being able to ask the way. And I'm not sure how many pies I could carry on my bike.'

'No, we wouldn't expect you to do that. We use one of the vans in the car pool. But if you could just take over the paperwork?'

A few hours later, Judy found herself poring over a large box filled with forms and letters. 'I can see why you always need volunteers for this,' she said ruefully, and Mrs Hazelwood looked a little apologetic.

'I know. It's dreadful, isn't it, all that paperwork just for a few pies. But the Ministry insists, and I suppose they know best.' She glanced at the heap of letters. 'You wouldn't think there was a paper shortage, would you!'

'I should think this is the reason *why* there's a paper shortage,' Judy said grimly, beginning to sort through. 'It's worse than Portsmouth Corporation!'

The pie scheme was meticulously recorded. First, there was a letter telling Mrs Hazelwood that approval had been given for Ashwood to be a part of it, and explaining the prices. Enclosed with this had been the forms for making out monthly returns which must be sent in together with the bakers' receipts and paying-in slips (in duplicate). Then there was a paying-in book (in triplicate) which must be used every time money was paid into the bank. There was a licence for the baker to make meat pies, listing the ingredients he was permitted to use and a large number (including such items as syrup, table jellies and crystallised fruits) which could not by any stretch of the imagination be found in meat pies. Some of them Judy had not seen since before the war; some, like soya flour, she had never even heard of.

Well, it was probably meant to cover all contingencies, not just meat pies. She turned to the next letter, which appeared to be a stern reproof to someone for not enclosing the baker's receipt with the previous return. This was followed by an equally severe reminder that *on no account* must the baker be asked for pies beyond the number for which he was licensed, and then a request that another form be completed to show the number of pies distributed each week during the eight weeks of April and May. The weeks were numbered one to eight (that's clever! Judy thought sarcastically) and the pies should be entered in the column headed *subs. meals* (what did that mean when it was at home?) and no other entry was required, other than a signature. Judy tried hard but could not think of any other entry that the unfortunate filler-in might be tempted to make. On the other hand, she thought, maybe I can.

The correspondence went on. Someone had noticed that some months had five weeks and there was a letter about this. A form had been sent out to ask for an overdue return – there must have been quite a few, Judy thought, for them to make a special form about them – and a somewhat plaintive note that not so many pies had been distributed during the previous month. Were the people who received them less keen on the pies? Was there something wrong with the pies? Perhaps it would be better to have pies only twice a week instead of three times, or even just on Fridays. Returns would, of course, still have to be made and the money paid in as usual. Oh, and a shilling too much had been paid in last week and could the sender please deduct this amount next time. By the time Mrs Hazelwood came in again with a cup of coffee Judy's head was spinning and she felt that she never wanted to see a meat pie again in the whole of her life.

'Listen to this!' she said, barely acknowledging the coffee and biscuit that had been placed beside her. 'Just listen! *You have entered 1/- as Petty Cash and instead of deducting it from the ha'penny levy of £1.5.6d you have added it on and paid in £1.6.6d, which of course is 2/- too much, and there is also the 1/- paid in excess last month, so that altogether you appear to have paid in 3/- too much. Perhaps you will be good enough to adjust this when you next pay money in to the Pie Account.* Someone,' she said, looking indignantly at Mrs Hazelwood, 'has spent time – precious, valuable *time* – working out what's been paid in and what hasn't and where it should have been instead. It must cost more to do that than they ever get back in profit. Why do they bother? And look – just *look* at this return. It's worse than an exam. It'll take half the afternoon just to fill it in, let alone add this and deduct that, and get it all right! And it doesn't matter how often they write,' she went on, scrabbling amongst the papers, 'or what the letter's about, it always ends up with *I enclose a few monthly returns.* What do they think we do with them all, *eat* them? Or maybe they think we put them into the pies. Honestly, I can see why nobody sticks this job for long.'

Mrs Hazelwood was almost helpless with laughter. She sank into a chair and wiped her streaming eyes while Judy continued to stare at her indignantly. Then Judy's lips began to twitch and she began to giggle. She turned the box upside down and tipped the papers out on to the floor.

'There! That's what I think of that! Still, I suppose it'll have to be done, or the poor people who buy these pies will have to go without. But honestly, Mrs Hazelwood, is it really doing any good?'

'Well, it isn't as successful as it was expected to be,' the vicar's wife admitted. 'But even if only one person who needs pies gets them it will be worthwhile. And who knows what the poor woman who writes these letters feels about it all? If she believes she's doing useful work towards the war effort, then it's good for her, isn't it?'

Judy managed to get the gist of this and bent to scoop up the papers. 'I suppose so. But if they make all this fuss and write all these letters about a few pies, how on earth do they manage to run a war? Anyway, I'm sure we don't need all these letters now, Mrs Hazelwood. Is it all right if I throw the old ones away?'

'I should think so. But don't just put them in the bin, will you? They are official correspondence and we ought to dispose of them carefully. You'd better put the important ones into a box and store it in a cupboard somewhere, and then take the rest down to the end of the garden. Mr Honey's having a bonfire.'

Judy drank her coffee and sorted through the papers again, setting aside those she considered worth keeping (including the monthly returns) and piling the others on her desk. Then she set off to the end of the garden, where the ancient man who came in three days a week to tend the vegetables was stoking up a bonfire of prunings and spring clippings.

'Ah,' he said when Judy approached. 'Come to have a bit of a warm, have 'ee?' He laughed uproariously while Judy smiled politely, having no idea what he had said. He saw the papers in her arms. 'Want to put them papers on the fire?'

'Yes, please. Shall I throw them on now?'

He shook his head decisively. 'No, that'll do no good, they'll just scorch round the edges if you puts 'em on in a pile, see, and then drift about all over the village in the wind.' He tapped the side of his nose. 'Secret papers, be they?'

'Not really; no,' Judy said, catching on to the last phrase.

'But they've got to be disposed of.' She made to throw them on but the old man caught her arm.

'I told 'ee, not all in a heap. Put 'em on one be one, look, like this here.' He took a letter and crumpled it in his fist, throwing it into the heart of the fire where it caught and quickly burned away. 'See? That's the way you wants to do it.'

'All right.' Judy began to follow his example, screwing up each letter separately and throwing them into the flames. Well, that should keep the country's secrets safe, she thought, dusting her hands off and watching the last paper shrivel to nothing. I wonder what vital task I'll be asked to do next.

She stood for a moment watching the fire revert to its normal fare of twigs and dried grass clippings. To her surprise, she was feeling better than she had for some time. It's being out in the country again, she thought. The war's still on and we're all still as anxious about it, but it isn't the only thing there is. In the towns and cities, where you live in fear of bombing all the time, where you can't put your head out of doors without seeing the damage, it seems to be the only thing that matters. But out here, where you can see trees coming into leaf and vegetables growing and where an old man can spend his afternoon with a bonfire – out here, you remember what life is all about. And it isn't about war at all, not really. It's about peace.

Mr Honey was leaning on a gnarled stick, watching the flames. He feels it too, she thought. He's seen war himself – he must have been through the Great War – and he knows that it's peace which is important. He knows the truth.

He turned suddenly and looked into her eyes. For a moment, as their eyes met, they were in perfect accord. Then Judy smiled at him and turned, going back to the house to see what she might do next to help, in however small a way, so that England might once again be at peace.

Chapter Twenty-Nine

As the summer continued, Jean and Judy became closer than ever. Always friends, they were now more like sisters. And so we would have been, Judy thought, if Terry had lived.

She was now working on several different tasks for the local WVS. As well as the pie scheme, which seemed to have settled down since she had sorted out the paperwork, she had gone back to making scrim and going out on the sphagnum moss parties. Jean came too, although her figure was now making it difficult for her to bend easily, and they took bottles of lemonade and a few sandwiches and made a picnic of it.

'I never thought I'd like it in the country,' Jean said, sitting on a fallen tree and unwrapping the sandwiches. 'I always thought it was just trees and fields, with nothing to do.' She lowered her voice and glanced around to make sure that nobody was listening. 'And I thought country people were all a bit stupid. But they're not. They're nice.'

Judy's lip-reading skills had increased, particularly with people she knew well, and she understood most of what Jean was saying. 'They're just different,' she agreed. 'They've got more time, that's why they seem slow. But they're not stupid. They just know different things.'

Jean nodded. 'The children like it here, too – most of them. They've settled in really well.'

There were a number of evacuees in Ashdown. Judy's cousin Sylvie and many of her schoolmates were scattered around the village and attended classes in the local school, sharing it turn and turn about with the local children. There had been some difficulties with this arrangement to begin with – the local children resented the newcomers coming into their classrooms and using their desks – but when they realised that the new timetables meant they only had to attend for half the day, they soon saw the advantages. Over the months, the two factions had become warily friendly, although the evacuees still tended to band together. It was only natural, Mrs Sutton observed, for kiddies to stick with their own.

The children from the April Grove area, being from a different school, were at Bridge End. Judy went over to see Stella and Muriel Simmons so that she could report back to Polly and Mrs Budd. Tim and Keith Budd were there as well, and the four children were busy picking strawberries in the vicarage garden when Judy arrived. They looked happy and occupied, and Judy was able to write a cheerful report to her aunt. She saw some of the other children from the April Grove area too – Brian Collins, living on a farm, Sammy Hodges who was staying with a young widow, and a cluster of others. They were wary of Judy at first, finding her deafness difficult to cope with, but once Tim had told them she had been in a bombing raid they looked at her with more respect.

'Wish I could've been in Pompey in the raids,' one boy said enviously. ''S not fair, being sent out here where there's nothing happening. I could help, I could. I could watch out for Jerries and put out incendiaries.'

Judy also went to visit some refugee families who were staying in the village. The invasion of the Low Countries a year before had brought thousands over to England, and they too had to be billeted. There were a number in a large country house nearby, and Judy spent one or two afternoons a week there, helping in the kitchens. It was just another job she could do without having to talk to people.

I wonder if I'll ever be able to hear again, she thought wistfully. Here in the country, people seemed to have more time to listen to her and try to communicate their own thoughts. Yet she was still miserably aware of how isolated she was, especially in a crowd. Apart from her work, she spent almost all her time alone, or with Jean or Sylvie.

Much of this time, she spent thinking of Sean. He seemed very far away now, as if he were slowly receding into the distance. She tried to recapture the sound of his voice or the look of his face, but her memory was patchy and the harder she concentrated the more difficult it became to picture him. We didn't know each other long enough, she thought sadly. There aren't enough memories. Oh Sean . . .

Another face came more readily to her mind – a fair, open face with glinting blue eyes and a laughing mouth. Irritated, she tried to push it away, but the memory of the two hours she had spent in the lift with Chris Barrett were sharper than any of those she had tried to recapture of Sean. She could recall every word of their conversation, hear every laugh as he tried to cheer her up and feel again the comfort he had given her as he slipped his arm around her to drive away her fears. And she could remember the kiss. The only kiss they had ever shared. The only kiss, she thought sadly, they ever would share, for she had refused to see him when he came to the door after that terrible raid, and by now he would have forgotten all about her.

By now, he would be kissing some other girl.

As it happened, Judy was wrong about Chris. He was not kissing some other girl. As he stood in his wooden turret on top of the Royal Beach peering incessantly over the Solent through his binoculars to watch for enemy aircraft, his thoughts were not of other girls, but of Judy herself, and he was growing more and more impatient.

'How long's it going to be before she gets better?' he demanded. 'I saw her aunt again this morning and asked her, and she says there's been no change. It doesn't seem

375

right, a lovely girl like that deaf for the rest of her life. Can't they do anything for her?'

Spud Murphy shrugged. 'No good asking me, mate. I dunno nothing about it.'

'Well, I'm getting fed up with it,' Chris said. He stared moodily out across the glittering sea towards the Island. 'We were going to go out together. I reckon there was a good chance for us – we got on all right when we were stuck in that lift.'

'So we all noticed!' Spud said with a grin.

'I thought there was something really special about her,' Chris went on, ignoring him. He had come in for so much ribbing over that episode that he barely noticed it now. 'You know how you do, sometimes? I thought she was a real smasher.'

'Yeah, but that's months ago now. If she'd wanted to see you she'd have let you know. If you ask me,' Spud advised from a store of experience which comprised a different girlfriend every week, 'you oughter forget her and find yourself some other little popsie. There's plenty around. Come to the dance over on the Pier on Saturday, why don't you? I'll fix you up with someone.'

'No thanks. I don't want to be fixed up with someone. I want to see Judy again.'

Spud eyed him. 'Well, if it's that bad, why don't you do that? Go out and see her. Talk to her. Tell her how you feel. And if she can't hear you, tell her some other way.' He winked. 'I'm sure you can think of something!'

Chris put down the binoculars and stared at him. Then he took Spud's pencil to take his turn at writing the log and said, 'You're right, Spud! It's not very often you're right, but you're right this time. That's what I'll do. I'll go out to wherever it is she's staying, in the country, and this time I won't take no for an answer. I'll *make* her see me. If she's not interested after that, I'll leave her alone – but at least I'll have tried.'

376

'Atta boy!' Spud said, grinning. He picked up the binoculars and trained them on the view. 'Hey, look! What's that coming in over the Island? Is it a Dornier or a Heinkel?'

Chris grabbed the glasses back. He stared for a minute, then punched his friend on the arm.

'You twerp! It's a bloody *seagull*!'

The summer was hot and long, as if to make up for the bitter winter. In July, it was declared that London had just had the sunniest day of the century – almost sixteen hours of it. If there hadn't been a war on, it would have meant long, lazy afternoons on the beach at Southsea or walks on Portsdown Hill. The harbour would have been filled with sailing dinghies and yachts, and the Solent would have been a mass of white sails, especially during Cowes Week when the big yacht races were held and you felt you could almost walk across to Cowes on their decks, without getting your feet wet. But all that was just a memory. The last time the Solent had been filled with little boats was during the Dunkirk evacuation, and it was now grey warships that forged their way through the Channel.

But the war was still very much on. The air-raid sirens were still sounding, although the raids weren't as heavy as before. The end of June and beginning of July saw thousands of incendiaries showered on the city and on Portsdown Hill, starting a blaze of gorse fires, and a number of high-explosive bombs were dropped into the sea off Stamshaw. In August it was announced that tunnels had been driven deep into Portsdown Hill, beneath the chalk pits, and three thousand people would be given tickets. Mothers with children, and people without their own bunked shelters would get first choice. Jess Budd, who had her baby Maureen at home, was entitled to go, and so was Nancy Baxter, who had Micky and Vera, but Jess said she was happy with the Anderson, and Nancy had her own reasons for not wanting to be stuck in a tunnel all night.

Everyone was wondering if America would come into the war. Already their aircraft were patrolling the North Atlantic, searching for U-boats, and their forces had joined British and Canadian troops in Iceland to help its defence. All young American men of twenty-one and over were compelled to register for the 'draft' and it seemed as if they might be preparing to join the Allies. Yet still they held off. The Japanese threat was one they didn't want to confront, and it was feared that if they declared war on Germany it would open the way for fighting in the Far East.

'It's all so complicated,' Cissie complained. 'The Japanese are attacking China now. I mean, what do *they* have to do with it all? Why make it all worse?'

'That's just what they want to do, isn't it?' Dick said, blowing his nose. The summer weather helped his chest but now he had hay fever and hardly dared venture outdoors to enjoy the sunshine. 'They reckon if they go into China now, while we're all busy in Europe and Africa, nobody will be able to stop them. And they don't like the Yanks having all those bases in the South Pacific, either. It's a bit too close to home for them.'

Cissie was reading the local paper. 'The *Evening News* says we've got to register for new ration books, by the end of this week, or we won't get them. What would someone do who didn't know, or forgot? Would they just starve to death?'

'Nobody'll be able to forget, with notices up everywhere and the paper putting in these big adverts,' Polly said. 'And the WVS and Citizens' Advice Bureau are helping people who can't manage on their own.' She lay back in her chair and closed her eyes. It had been an exhausting day, filled with irritating tasks that never seemed to get done properly. She had been sent on several errands, delivering messages to people who weren't there, meeting others who didn't arrive, searching for documents that had mysteriously disappeared and answering innumerable questions from Portsmouth residents who had trekked complainingly out to the Royal Beach only to find that the Council office they needed was in a different building, as often as not one that they'd passed on their way. Polly could understand their frustration but wished they could in turn understand the difficulties the Corporation had faced in finding and setting up new premises after the bombing of the Guildhall. We had to start from scratch, she thought, and we still haven't got it all organised, but they just won't accept that.

'There's a letter here for you,' Cissie said, handing her an envelope. 'Looks like it's from your friend Mr Turner.'

Polly took it and turned it over. Joe had written a few times and she'd written back, but their letters had been no more than the letters of friends – brief descriptions of their lives, mention of more important events, a joke or two. They were pleasant to receive, but didn't seem to be going anywhere and once or twice lately Polly had wondered if they were worth going on with. Yet she knew that she would miss having him in her life, however tenuously. So long as he was there, she had a small hope that one day things might change.

She opened the letter and gave an exclamation. Cissie and Dick both looked at her, and Alice popped her head round the scullery door. 'What's going on? What's our Poll squeaking about?'

'It's that Joe Turner,' Dick said. He still harboured a strange disapproval of the man his sister-in-law had met, and there was a grumbling note in his voice whenever he mentioned him. 'Been writing to her again.'

'Oh.' Alice came right into the room, wiping her hands on her pinny, and they all gazed expectantly at Polly. She looked up and met their eyes.

'Well, I don't know what you lot think you're staring at! I've had letters from Joe before.'

'Yes, but you haven't looked like that before,' Alice said shrewdly. 'Come on, what's he say?'

'Like what? I don't know what you mean,' Polly said, blushing.

'Like a young girl who's just come in from her first date,' Cissie laughed. 'Come on, Polly, out with it!'

She gave them a look of exasperation. 'There's no privacy in this family, none at all. Everyone wants to know everyone else's business. Well, if you must know, he's coming down to Pompey again and wants to take me out to tea, and *that's all*. Nothing out of the ordinary in that, is there? Nothing to make a song and dance about?'

'Well, I wouldn't have said so,' Alice said, 'but it's not me who's looking ten years younger all of a sudden. More's the pity,' she added, touching her grey hair.

Polly laughed and shook her head. 'You're awful, all of you. Look, Joe and me, we're just friends, that's all. I can be pleased a friend's coming to see me, can't I, without you turning it into something more than what it is?'

'Well, maybe we are and maybe we're not,' Cissie said. 'Time will tell. So when's he coming, Poll?'

'Next Tuesday,' she said, looking at the letter again. 'He's coming down on the afternoon train and staying overnight.'

'Where?' Dick broke in. 'I hope he's not expecting us to put him up here. I hope you've told him we haven't got room, Poll.'

'Of course he's not expecting to stay here. He's been here, hasn't he? He knows what the house is like. I don't know where he's staying, he doesn't say. He just says he'd like to take me out to tea and maybe to the pictures or for a walk or something.' She raised her eyes again. 'There's no harm in that, is there? You don't think you ought to come too, Dick, just to make sure he doesn't take advantage of me?'

'There's no need to talk like that,' he began, his colour rising, and Cissie intervened hastily.

'Now, don't you two start getting all aeriated. Dick's just concerned about you, Polly, you know that. He doesn't mean anything by it.'

'Well, he doesn't have to be concerned,' Polly said resentfully. 'I'm not a young girl and he's not my father. I've been a married woman—'

'And now you're a widow,' Dick said. 'And I've got a responsibility towards you, Polly. You're living in my house –' he caught Alice's sharp movement and amended his words hastily '– all right, it's not my house now, but you were living in my house till we got bombed out, and that gives me a responsibility. I took it on when Johnny died and I'm not taking it lightly.'

There was a silence. Then Polly said in a tight voice, 'You don't have to remind me I'm a widow, Dick. I remember it every day of my life. And you don't have to take responsibility for me, either. I'm not a child, I'm thirty-six years old, I'm doing responsible work and I can take responsibility for myself, thank you very much. And if you don't like it,' she rose to her feet and looked down at him with a glint of challenge in her eye, 'maybe it's time for me to find somewhere else to live!'

She marched out of the room and they heard her feet going up the stairs. For a moment or two there was complete silence and then Cissie turned on Dick, her eyes filled with angry tears.

'There!' she said furiously. '*Now* see what you've done! And you needn't start coughing and sneezing neither, because you've brought it on yourself and just for once I'm not sorry for you. Not a *bit* sorry!'

Judy was walking home from the big house where the refugee families were living, having spent the afternoon preparing vegetables and making pastry for their evening meal of meat and vegetable pie (more vegetable than meat), when she paused on the hill above the railway cutting, and sat down in the shade of an oak tree.

The sky was cloudless and the air stirred by only the faintest of breezes. Below, deep in the cutting, the railway lines shimmered in the heat. The grass had grown long and in the fields the corn was a deep gold, almost ready to harvest. Bees hovered over the mauve and cream globes of clover, and Judy watched them wistfully, knowing that the air must be filled with their humming. I *wish* I could hear them, she thought. I wish so much that I could hear them . . .

A movement caught her eye and she saw a train pull in at the station. The ancient station master came out of his office and someone in the guard's van threw a few parcels on to the platform. Two or three passengers alighted: a man in a suit, a woman with several shopping bags, and a tall young man in RAF uniform.

Judy watched. She saw the woman drop one of the parcels and the young airman stoop to pick it up. He handed it back to her, then took two of the bags to carry. They walked out of the station and along the lane, talking animatedly.

I wonder who he is, Judy thought. For a moment, as he had first alighted, he had reminded her sharply of Chris Barrett, and her heart had skipped a beat. Surely not . . . But as she saw him walking along with the woman, carrying her bags, she dismissed the thought. It must be someone from the village, come home on leave. Her heart sank a little and she shrugged away the brief disappointment. I don't want it to be him anyway, she told herself sharply. I don't want it to be anyone I know.

The two had disappeared between the hedges that bordered the lane. Now they appeared again, directly below her, and she could see their faces clearly. The woman was a spinster who lived at the other end of the village with her elderly mother. And the young man –

'Chris!' she breathed, and her whole body turned cold and then flushed with warmth. 'Chris . . .'

'I didn't know if you'd want to see me,' he said. He'd looked up and seen Judy at the same moment, almost thrusting the bags back at the spinster in his haste to come racing up the hill. He saw the incomprehension in her face and repeated slowly, enunciating his words. 'I – didn't – know – if – you'd – want – to see – me.'

'So why did you come?' He'd caught her hands, his whole face glowing with delight, and she withdrew them quickly. She felt a turmoil of strange emotions – pleasure at seeing him, wonder that he should have bothered to come, dismay and embarrassment at her own condition. I didn't want him to see me like this, she thought, and then came anger that he had caught her unawares and she hadn't had time to hide. 'Why didn't you let me know?'

'And what would you have done?' he asked simply, and then said more slowly. 'You would not have seen me. You would have hidden away. Like you did before. Wouldn't you?' He looked at her accusingly.

Judy understood. She met his eyes and said, 'Yes.'

'But why?' His frustration showed in the crease of his brows, the brightness of his eyes. 'Why don't you want to see me, Judy? What have I done?'

'It's not you. It's me. I'm *deaf*, Chris. I can't hear you. I can't hear anyone – or anything.' She waved her hand at the trees, the hedges, the railway. 'There could be all sorts of sounds – trains coming, birds singing, cows and sheep, people in the lane – but I can't hear a thing. It's just a sort of mushy sound all the time. It's horrible.' She paused and stared at him. 'It's horrible for everyone else too. Having to speak slowly, having to make sure I can see them. Even then, most of the time I can't understand them. Some people don't open their lips much, they don't make any shape at all with their words – I shall *never* understand people like that. And they have to write it down for me, and then I can't read their writing or they can't spell the words and then they're even more embarrassed. You don't know what it's like, Chris. *Nobody* knows what it's like.'

'Isn't there a sort of sign language?' he asked doubtfully. 'I'm sure I've heard of something.' Once again, forgetting already, he had spoken too quickly and Judy looked at him in exasperation.

'You see? You see how difficult it is?'

Chris bit his lip and repeated his words, determined to be understood, and Judy shrugged.

'Yes, I think so. But I don't see what use it is. It's no use just me learning it, is it? Everyone else would have to know it too.'

'I'd learn it,' he said quickly, and Judy shook her head.

'It's no use, Chris. I don't know why you bothered to come. You'd better go back.'

'No!' He was angry now. 'I came because I wanted to see you. We had a date, remember? We were going to go out together – have a walk, talk to each other, get to know each other.' Once again, he saw her look of incomprehension, and was forced to speak more slowly. 'We had a *date*, Judy. I've come for my *date*.'

Judy's eyes met his and the penny dropped. 'You said more than that,' she said dully. 'This is another thing that happens. People can't be bothered to talk properly to me. They just talk in a sort of shorthand. It's not like proper talking at all.'

Chris stared at her. Then he caught both her hands in his again and shook them. 'Judy! You've got to stop feeling sorry for yourself!' Her eyes flicked up at him again, shocked by the fierceness of his grip and the anger in his face. '*Stop feeling sorry for yourself*,' he enunciated, watching her eyes to make sure that she understood. 'Deafness isn't the end of the world. You're young – you're pretty – *I* think you're beautiful – and there's nothing else wrong with you. Being deaf isn't the worst thing that can happen to you.' He waved at the countryside about them, then put his hands to his eyes. 'Suppose you were blind. Suppose you couldn't see

384

all this? Suppose you couldn't walk anywhere without someone to guide you?'

Judy understood his meaning. She looked down at their hands, then around at the banks. They were thick with ragged robin and campions, guelder roses and a froth of wild parsley. Queen Anne's Lace, Mrs Sutton called it. She looked at the ash trees just breaking into leaf, later than all the other trees, and caught a glimpse of a thrush sitting on a branch, its beak open and its throat swelling as it sang the song she knew she would never hear again.

'It would be awful,' she agreed quietly, 'but it's *not* as awful as being deaf. People take trouble with a blind person. They look after them and talk to them, and they tell them things they can't see. When you're deaf, people only care for a while, and after that you're left alone. You can't take part in any conversations. You can't listen to the wireless and laugh when they laugh. You can't be part of the family any more, not in the same way. You're just a nuisance.'

There was a long silence. Chris looked at her as if he didn't know what to do next. After a while, he said in a low voice, 'I care, Judy. I care a lot. I'd like to look after you, and I wouldn't leave you out of things.'

'You wouldn't be able to help it,' she said. 'Look at the Suttons – they're really kind, but they can't help leaving me out. They've got things to talk about – the farm, the war, village things – they can't just look at *me* all the time they're talking. It's the same with everyone. I don't mean they don't care,' she added, frowning as she tried to explain. 'I don't mean they're deliberately unkind. But they just can't do it. Nobody can. It's just too difficult.'

Again, they were silent. Then Chris said, 'But won't you let me try, Judy? Won't you at least let me try? May I come and see you sometimes – take you out? We could learn the sign language – we could talk then.'

Judy hesitated. She looked at the fair, open face, the anxious blue eyes, the mouth that could curl so easily into a

385

grin, the lips that had kissed hers. For a moment, she longed to say yes, to see the face light up with joy, the eyes dance, the mouth break into a laugh. She yearned to be in his arms and to be kissed again as he had kissed her in the lift.

She took a deep breath and then shook her head.

'No. Please, Chris, don't ask me. I can't see *anyone*, not in that way. It's too hard. All the repeating and the writing down and the misunderstandings and the worry of it all. I can't do it. I just can't.' She pulled away and began to walk quickly along the lane. 'I'm sorry, Chris. I'm sorry we ever met. I'm sorry we agreed to have a date. I'm sorry you've come all this way. Please – just go away now. Forget me. There are plenty of other girls – girls who can *hear* what you say. Go and ask one of them out.' She was aware that he was close behind her and turned swiftly to face him. 'Go *away*, Chris,' she said, and pointed down the embankment towards the railway line. 'Look. There's a train coming – you can catch it now and go back to Portsmouth and forget you ever saw me. Go on. Go *away*.'

He stood his ground. 'Tell me that's what you *want* me to do,' he said and then shouted at her in his frustration. '*Tell me!* Tell me you *want* me to go away!'

Judy's eyes filled with tears. She looked into his face and said, 'There, you see? That's what it's like. That's what it *would* be like.' And then she turned and walked away from him.

This time, Chris did not follow her. He knew there was nothing more he could say. Burning with shame, his head bowed, he walked back to the station where the train was just pulling in. The station master stared at him.

'Quick visit,' he said. 'Didn't she want you, then?'

Chris gave him a furious glare and climbed aboard the train without answering. He dropped into the seat and gazed morosely out of the window. As the train pulled out of the station, he could just see the lane and there, between the froth of Queen Anne's Lace, the figure of a young woman walking slowly and doggedly up the sloping lane in the opposite direction.

Chris stared at her, willing her to turn. If she does, he thought, I'll get off the train at the next station and come straight back. And this time I won't take no for an answer.

But Judy did not turn. Not until the train was almost out of sight and Chris had given up and slumped back into the seat. At just that moment, as she came to the crest of the slope, she paused and looked back and, as the train disappeared round a bend and into a wood, she lifted her hand and waved, even though her eyes were too full of tears to see.

Chapter Thirty

Joe came straight out to the Royal Beach to meet Polly from work. She walked down the steps to see him standing on the other side of the road, near the entrance to South Parade Pier, and she paused for a moment, her heart skipping a little. He was leaning on the railing, staring out to sea, and she had a moment or two to observe him. She came slowly down to the pavement.

There was nothing special about him, she thought, nothing at all. He was just an ordinary man, a friend, come to see her and take her for a cup of tea. Nothing more than that. He was certainly not in the least like Johnny, the laughing young sailor who had swept her off her feet and married her and promised to spend the rest of his life with her. He wasn't tall or handsome, he probably wasn't all that clever – but then, neither was she. I don't know what I'd do with a man who was clever, she thought.

And yet – there was something about him that quickened her heart. Something that reached out to her, something to which she responded. And when he turned and saw her standing there, the way his face lit up told her that he felt it too. And that what they shared – or could share – was not at all ordinary.

'Polly!' He crossed the road swiftly, limping a little, and she ran towards him. They met in the middle and hesitated, neither knowing quite which way to go next. A trolley-bus coming towards them sounded its horn and Joe gripped her arm and hurried her back to the pavement on the pier side, and then they stood looking into each other's eyes and laughing.

'Blimey, I thought he was going to run us down!' Joe said. 'I bet he felt like it, an' all! How are you, Polly? It's good to see you again, by golly it is.'

'It's good to see you too, Joe.' She smiled at him, and saw the warmth in his dark brown eyes. This is what's special about him, she thought. He's so warm, so good-hearted. You can see it in his face. It wraps itself around you, like a lovely blanket. Impulsively, she put both hands on his shoulders, stood on tiptoe and kissed him.

Joe looked startled and she saw his skin colour. 'Blimey, Poll, I didn't expect that. That's a real welcome, that is. Thanks.' He tucked her hand into his arm and turned to walk her along the promenade. 'Where's a good place for tea?'

'There's a café a bit further on.' They strolled along the top of the beach, arm in arm, lifting their faces to the sunshine. Once again, Polly had that sensation of being at home. 'How long are you down here for, Joe?'

'Just a day or two.' He hesitated. 'I've got summat to tell you, Poll. That's why I came. I wanted to see you – to tell you face to face, like. Then I'm going on down to Devon to see my boys.'

'What?' She stopped and looked at him, pierced by sudden anxiety. 'What is it? What's happened?'

'Don't look like that, love. It's nothing bad – at least, I don't think it is.' He grinned at her. 'But there's summat I want to ask you as well. I meant to leave it till later on, but now I've started I might as well come out with the lot.' They stopped and she felt him take a deep breath. 'D'you reckon you could get a day or two off, Poll? I mean, right now? Day after tomorrow, perhaps?'

'A day or two off?' she repeated in bewilderment. 'I might be able to. Now that all the new ration books have been issued we're not quite so pushed, though there's always a lot of work to do. But why? What do you want me to do? You're not asking me to go to Devon with you, are you?'

'That's right,' he said. 'I want you to meet my nippers. I want them to meet you.' He sighed and rubbed a hand over his face. 'I'm doing this all the wrong way round. Look, what I want to tell you is, I'm being moved. My bloke, the one I've been batman to, is going overseas with the regiment. I can't go – I've asked enough, I've told him a tin foot's as good as any other for polishing up his kit, and better if it comes to being shot again – but it's not on. So I'm coming down to Pompey – well, Gosport really – to St George's Barracks. Looks like I'll be there permanent. And that means we'll be able to see a bit of each other. If that's what you want,' he added anxiously.

'You're coming down to Gosport? You'll be just across the harbour!' A flicker of excitement ran through her. 'Joe, that's lovely! Of course we'll be able to see each other. But—'

'It's more than that,' he interrupted, taking her hands and gripping them tightly. 'See, it's like this. I've never been what they call a ladies' man. Even when I was a youngster, I was never one for clicking with the girls. I met my Rosie and that was it, we both knew straight off we were right for each other, and I never bothered with no one else.' He looked down into her eyes. 'I felt the same when I first saw you, Polly. That first time on the train, I felt it then. I didn't think it would ever come to anything, of course, 'cause I didn't think I'd ever see you again. But I just knew that you were someone I could get along with. I knew you could be special.'

Polly stared at him. Her heart was beating fast. She whispered, 'I think I felt it too, Joe. But I couldn't – it was too soon after Johnny.'

'I know. And I hadn't long lost my Rosie neither. It just seemed too soon, like you say. But when we met again, well,

390

I reckoned maybe there was summat in it. Summat meant. And then, when I come down and you were in all that trouble, I thought, Better back off a bit, Joe Turner, she don't want you muddling things up. So that's what I did. I just wrote to you like a pal, just to try to keep the door open. But now, seeing you again, I don't reckon I want to back off any more. And if I'm going to be down here permanent, I want to know if you feel the same. If there's any hope. 'Cause I don't think I could manage to see you regular just as a friend. I know I'd want more than that, and if it's never going to be, well, we'd be better not to start. Sorry,' he finished, 'I haven't put any of that the way I wanted to, and if you want to tell me to go to hell you'd better say so. I know I'm not the bloke your hubby was, nor ever will be.'

'No, you won't,' Polly said quietly, looking down at his hands. 'But you don't have to be, Joe. You're *you* – and that's all that matters now.' She lifted her eyes. 'I can't say for sure what's going to happen to us, but I'm willing to give it a try. Can you take it like that, Joe? No promises – just hope?'

'Hope,' he said, smiling at her. 'I like that, Polly. Hope. And will you come down with me to see the boys? It's important, see. They're mine, and if I'm going to be seeing someone regular . . .'

'You might be putting someone else into their mother's place,' Polly nodded. 'It's a test, isn't it? If they don't like me, or I don't like them . . .'

'I didn't think of it like that,' he said. 'I just wanted you to see them, and I wanted them to see you. It's not a test.'

'But you'll feel better about it if we all like each other,' Polly said. She thought for a moment, and then nodded. 'All right. I'll ask the Mayoress tomorrow if I can have time off. I'm sure it will be all right. And now,' she looked at him with a teasing smile, 'what about that cup of tea you promised me?'

'Tea?' he exclaimed, and she saw with a little leap of

delight that his face had suddenly lost its creases, the lines of worry had gone from his brow and he looked almost like a boy again, the boy he had been when he first met his Rosie, and as laughing and merry as Johnny had been when she first knew him. 'Tea? It's not tea we oughter be having now – it's bloody champagne! Pardon my French,' he added with a guilty look, and Polly laughed and took his arm again, leading him across the road.

'Tea will do for now, Joe. And the way I'm feeling, I think it will taste like champagne anyway. Oh Joe,' she drew him to a stop, right in the middle of the road, 'I *am* glad we met that day on the train!'

A honking noise made them both jump and they looked round to see a trolley-bus approaching, its driver glaring down at them. Joe pulled her quickly out of its way and they scurried across to the pavement, almost convulsed with giggles.

'It was the same flipping driver!' he panted as they reached the kerb. 'Blimey, he must think we're a couple of lunatics!'

'I feel like one,' Polly said, laughing up at him. 'I don't know what it is about you, Joe, but when I'm with you, that's exactly how I feel!'

Jean was growing bigger and heavier by the day. She still did as much as possible in the house, but Mrs Hazelwood insisted that she rest. 'Are you sure this baby's not due until September?' she asked worriedly, looking at Jean's bulging stomach. 'You couldn't have got your dates wrong?'

Jean shook her head. 'It can't be. It was just after Christmas we –' she blushed '– well, it was only the once anyway. I've never – it was the first time I ever . . .'

'All right, Jean, I understand. But I think it would be a good idea to get the midwife in to have a look at you, just the same. She'd be coming in a week or two anyway.'

The midwife was a middle-aged woman, thin as a strand

of wire, with iron-grey hair and a beaky nose. She gave Jean a quick examination, felt her stomach all over and gave a sharp nod. 'Nothing wrong there. Going to be a big lad, though. Might be a week or two early.'

'It's not a lad,' Jean said. 'It's a girl.'

'Oh, and how d'you know that? Done the wedding-ring test, have you?' Her glance strayed to Jean's left hand and Jean felt thankful for the wedding ring Alice Thomas had given her.

'The wedding-ring test?'

'That's right. You tie the ring to a bit of cotton and someone holds it over your belly to see which way it swings. If it goes backwards and forwards it's a boy, if it goes round in a circle, it's a girl. Do it now, if you like.' She took Jean's hand and made to pull off the ring.

Jean snatched her hand away. 'No! I don't want to. I don't want to take my ring off – and anyway, it's a girl.' She stared defiantly at the midwife. 'I don't need to do any tests at all. I *know* it's a girl.'

The midwife shrugged. 'Hoity-toity!' she sniffed. 'Well, have it your own way. But if it's a girl, it's a mighty big one. You'd better get yourself decent again. I'll come back in a fortnight, see how you are.'

Jean watched her go, half-annoyed, half-frightened. Later, telling Judy about it, she said, 'I didn't like her much. I don't really want her there when the baby's born.'

'You'll have to have her though, won't you?' Judy asked. 'I mean, suppose something goes wrong? And if the baby really is going to be big . . .'

'Oh, I know I'll have to have her. And I expect she's all right really. Mrs Hazelwood says she's delivered any amount of babies round the village. I just didn't like her much.'

'Well, never mind,' Judy said comfortably. 'It's weeks away yet, anyway.'

They were sitting on a blanket and some cushions in the

garden, beneath the apple tree where Judy had first met Ben. The small green apples which had followed the blossom were growing fast and some were beginning to redden. By the time Jean's baby was born they would be ready to pick and eat, and Mrs Hazelwood said they were good keepers. A heavy crop would see them right through the winter.

Ben had almost completed his training as a pilot. He wrote to Judy once or twice, his letters enthusiastic, his desire to get into the air throbbing through every line. She read the letters a little sadly, wondering how long he would survive once he did. So many young men were being killed in the air, some of them on their first mission. She prayed that wouldn't happen to Ben. He was so young, so ardent, so full of life. And he had told her once that she would hear again.

I wish I could, she thought. I wish I could, just for him. Just to hear his voice. I've never heard his voice.

There were so many voices she had never heard. And even those she knew well were beginning to fade. Maybe even if I did get my hearing back, she thought, I wouldn't know them. They could come up behind me and speak – Jean, or Mum and Dad, Gran, Polly, Chris – and I wouldn't know who they were. I'd have to learn them all over again.

The thought of Chris brought back the memory of that last meeting, when he had told her not to be sorry for herself. Judy had walked away from the train that day feeling hurt and angry. Why shouldn't I be sorry for myself? she had wondered. I'm entitled to be . . . But slowly she had begun to see the sense of his words. She began to realise that she had changed during the past few months. Locked in her own, silent world, she had forgotten that other people had feelings too, forgotten that they had problems as great as hers. The old man who lived in a tumbledown cottage down the lane and crept about, too crippled with arthritis to be able to draw a bucket of water from the well, his hands too gnarled and stiff to cut a slice of bread. The woman in the broken-down hovel who had four children under seven and whose husband had been killed at Dunkirk. The Hazelwoods, afraid of losing their youngest son. Polly, widowed at thirty-five. Her own parents, losing Terry . . . But I lost him too, she argued, and then reminded herself sharply that this was exactly what she was doing wrong. Always looking for her own griefs and sorrows, dismissing those of other people.

I'm sorry, Chris, she thought sadly. You were right, and I was wrong. And she regretted, bitterly, that she had sent him away. He won't come back now, she thought. Even if I wrote and begged him – he wouldn't come back now.

·'Judy!'

Jean grabbed her arm and Judy turned quickly. At the look on her friend's face, she gasped. 'What is it? What's wrong?'

'I don't know. I got this sudden pain.' Jean's face twisted again and she bent and pressed both hands to her back.

'Is it the baby? It can't be, surely.' Judy was on her feet, glancing wildly towards the house. 'It's much too soon.'

'She said it might come early.' The pain seemed to have faded and Jean was breathing quickly. 'But it was in my back, not my stomach. It's gone off a bit now anyway.' She lay back on the cushions. 'I suppose it was just a twinge.'

'It looked as if it was more than a twinge.' Judy sat down again, looking at her doubtfully. 'Do you think I ought to fetch someone?'

'Not yet. It takes hours and hours for a baby to be born. There's no one to fetch, anyway. The vicar's gone to Bridge End and Mrs Hazelwood's at the WI meeting. And everyone else is out in the fields, haymaking.'

Jean understood only the shaking head and the words 'WI' and 'haymaking' but they were enough. Anyway, Jean looked better now. Perhaps it had been no more than a twinge. She'd had a number of aches and pains by now –

her back hurt if she walked too far or tried to do too much work, she had heartburn after meals, and she'd had a fierce stabbing pain down one leg that Mrs Sutton said was sciatica. It was caused by the baby lying on a nerve, apparently. There must be other nerves the baby could lie against, especially now that it was getting so big.

'*Ouch*!' Jean exclaimed, her face contorting again. 'Oh no, no, *no*.'

'What is it?' Judy was on her feet again, thoroughly alarmed. Jean was half sitting, half lying, leaning one elbow on the cushions, the other arm held tightly over her stomach as she rocked with pain. 'Oh Jeanie, what's happening? I'd better get someone.'

'No!' Jean reached out a hand to stop her. 'Don't go away! Don't leave me!' She pulled at her skirt and stared down in horror at the blanket. 'Look!'

Appalled and frightened, Judy looked down and saw a dark stain spreading over the rug. 'What is it? Whatever is it?'

'It's my waters,' Jean said, forgetting to look Judy in the face as she spoke. She remembered and raised her head. 'My *waters*. They've *broken*.'

Judy gazed at her helplessly. 'I don't understand.'

'It means the baby's coming.' The pain seemed to have receded, and Jean lay back again, breathing heavily.

'I'll have to fetch someone.'

'No! Don't go! It's coming now – I can feel it. Oh!' Jean's voice rose to a scream and she fell back and flailed wildly with her arms. 'Oh Judy, Judy, Judy – it hurts so much! Aaaah! *Aaaaaaah*!'

Judy knelt beside her, terrified. She had never seen a baby being born, had no idea what happened. She had been only ten years old when Sylvie was born and had not even known that Polly was expecting a baby until the day it happened. What she knew about 'the facts of life' had been gleaned gradually over the years from other girls, equally ignorant, much of the knowledge distorted, and although she now understood about sex she still had very little idea how the baby that had been conceived would actually be born. Jean herself didn't know very much more.

'What shall we do?' Judy asked when the pain faded again. 'How quickly will it come?'

'I don't know.' Jean's face was white and beaded with sweat. 'Oh Judy, it hurts so much. People say it can go on for hours – even days. I don't think I'll be able to stand it.' Tears came into her eyes. 'I'll die. I'm going to die.'

'No!' Judy's terror pierced her voice. 'No, you're not going to die, Jean, you can't. I'll *have* to get someone—'

'It's starting again!' Jean clutched her arm, digging her fingers in like talons. Her nails bit into Judy's bare flesh. 'Oh God – here it comes – ah – aaah – *aaaaaah*! I can't do it!' she yelled, twisting frantically on the blanket. *'I can't bloody do it! Aaaaaaaah! Aaaaaah! Aaaaaaah!'*

Judy put her hands on the writhing body and tried to hold her still. One of Jean's hands was still gripping her arm, the other flailing in the air, beating on the ground, pulling at her own hair. Judy reached across and grabbed it, holding it tightly, trying to calm the desperate girl. She could hear none of Jean's cries but knew from her face that she was making a lot of noise. Perhaps someone will hear, she thought. Perhaps she's shouting loudly enough for someone to hear and come.

'What shall we do?' she asked when the pain subsided. 'What do we have to do?'

'Better get my knickers off. It's got to be able to come out, and they're soaking wet anyway.'

'Out here?' Judy was scandalised. She looked around the garden. It was in full sight of the vicarage, and anyone passing by could look over the wall. She forgot for a moment that she had been praying for someone to do just that.

Jean threw her a scornful glance. 'I don't care if we're in

the Lord Mayor's parlour! I'm having a baby. Judy – quick, it's starting again. Get them off. Oh . . .' The two girls scrabbled frantically and dragged off the sodden garment, tossing it out of the way. They were just in time. The pain came again, a fresh wave even stronger than before, and Jean lay back, crying out again, reaching for Judy's hands. As Judy caught them in hers, she realised that something else was happening. Jean was using all her strength to tense her body, arching her back so that the swollen stomach rose like a whale, her screams now as much groans of effort as cries of pain.

Dimly, Judy remembered hearing the phrase 'bear down'. You had to 'bear down' when you were having a baby. She had had no idea what it meant, but now she thought she understood. 'Bearing down' was pushing, pushing the baby out, and you did it when the pain gripped you, when it was at its fiercest. She knelt beside the twisting, screaming girl and spoke in her ear.

'That's it, Jean. That's it. Bear down. Push. That's right. Keep going, keep trying.' She risked a quick glance beneath the rucked-up skirt and caught a glimpse of a mass of fair pubic hair and something else – something swollen, like a massive growth, protruding from Jean's body. For a moment she stared, horrified, and then Jean relaxed as the pain faded, and the growth drew back inside. In that second, she realised what it was.

'It's the baby! I can see its head! Oh Jean, Jean, I can see the baby's head!' Beside herself with terror and excitement, she gripped Jean's hands. 'Jean, the baby's almost born! *I can see its head*!'

'I don't want it!' Jean yelled. 'I don't want it any more! It hurts too much! It bloody well *hurts*! Take it away! Take it *away*! I don't *want* it! Oh – oh – *ohhhh*!'

'You *do* want it. You *do*. Oh, *please* let someone come, let someone come soon.' Judy was crying now, gripping Jean's hands as the wave of pain rose once more. 'Oh Jean, keep trying, just keep trying. It'll be over soon. It's coming soon, I know it is, and it'll all be over and you'll have a lovely little baby girl – or maybe a boy, you wouldn't really mind if it was a boy, would you – and – and – oh Jean, Jean, that's right, bear down, push hard – it's coming now, I can see it.' She wrenched her hands from Jean's grasp and caught at her thighs, parting them so that the baby's head could push its way out. It was clear now, a round, hard little ball, wet and dark and slimy, and as Jean screamed she saw it surge suddenly forward, thrusting itself out into the world – head, shoulders, body and legs – and Judy reached out and caught it in her hands, a thrill juddering through her whole body as she felt the warm, slippery, squirming flesh. A baby, she thought wonderingly, a *baby*, and I'm the first one ever in the whole world to hold it. But there was no time for wonder. With the baby came a rush of water and blood, and she lifted it clear and saw to her horror that there was something else – a thick, twisted rope that was attached to the baby's stomach and seemed to disappear back into Jean's body. At that moment the baby began to cry, its mouth opening to a square in its tiny red face, and Judy stared at it in wonder.

'Is it all right?' Jean was leaning up on one elbow, panting. She stared down at Judy and reached out one hand. 'My baby? Is it all right? Is it a girl?'

'Yes.' Judy gave a quick look to make sure. 'Yes, it is. Oh, Jean, you've got a little girl. But there's this thing, this sort of rope . . .'

'It's the cord. Let me hold her.' Jean reached out her arms and Judy, a little doubtful as to whether the cord would reach, laid the baby on her mother's breast. She dragged the cushions from where they had been flung and heaped them behind Jean's back, and Jean rested against them, smiling. For a moment they stayed there, recovering their breath, gazing in wonder at the baby, so small and so new, already turning its face into its mother's breast, seeking the nipple.

'She's beautiful,' Jean whispered. 'Oh Judy, she's so beautiful.'

Judy, looking at the crumpled red face, peaceful now, at the hair plastered wetly against the little skull, at the naked body that was grey with slime and flecked with blood, thought that beautiful was perhaps an odd word to use. And yet it was the right word. It was exactly the right word. And then she caught her breath as she realised what else had happened.

'Jean,' she whispered disbelievingly.

Jean turned her head and met her eyes enquiringly. Judy went on, in a voice that trembled, 'Jean, I can *hear*. I heard the baby cry. I can hear what you're saying to me. I can hear birds singing – and the leaves rustling – and people calling to each other in the hayfield. Jean – *I can hear again.*'

Chapter Thirty-One

It was only a few moments after that when help began to arrive. Someone had heard Jean's final scream and was hurrying down the lane. Mrs Hazelwood had come back from the Women's Institute meeting. In seconds it seemed that Jean was surrounded by people, people who knew what to do. The midwife was called. There was a flurry of activity as the afterbirth was expelled, and then the midwife arrived, clucking as she saw what had happened, and the cord was cut and tied. Jean was lifted and carried into the house, where she and the baby were both bathed, and by the time Judy saw her again an hour or two later she was in bed, the baby dressed in a fresh white nightgown and cradled in the crook of one arm.

'Thanks, Judy,' she said, smiling sleepily. 'I don't know what I'd have done without you.'

'I didn't do much. I didn't know what to do.' The miracle of her hearing seemed almost as great to Judy as the miracle of new life before her. 'Oh Jean, I'm glad I was there. I'm so glad. It was awful – but it was wonderful too. She's a lovely baby.' She smiled. 'You were right. It *is* a girl.'

'And I'm calling her Hope, just like I said.' Jean was quiet for a moment, gazing at her baby and stroking her head gently. 'You'll let everyone know, won't you? Mum and Dad, and your family. They'll be surprised she's so early.'

'But she's all right, isn't she? It doesn't matter about her coming so soon?'

'Well, she's very small. I'll have to take a lot of care of her. But the midwife says she'll be all right. And Mrs

Hazelwood is going to get the doctor to come and make sure.' Jean looked at her. 'And you really can hear, Judy?'

Judy nodded. 'I can hear just as well as I ever could. I think Dad was right, you know – it was a shock that stopped me hearing, and it's a shock that's brought it back again. A nice one, though.' She smiled and touched the baby gently with one finger. 'And I wanted to hear again so much – just to hear her cry.'

Jean was almost asleep and Judy tiptoed out of the room. She went into the garden and sat down on the old bench, and began to think of all the people she must telegraph about the new arrival.

The warm late-summer sky was deepening into evening. The sun was going down beyond the wall and the woods, casting an apricot glow on the old stones and lighting the first few golden tints of autumn in the trees. A blackbird was singing at the top of the tree, and Judy tilted her head, listening to it. Next to the baby's cry that had been her first realisation that she could hear again, and she thought it must be the most beautiful sound in the world.

I'll have to go back to the farm soon, she thought. And I'll have to decide what to do next. Everything's different now – the baby's here and Jean's so happy with her, and I can hear again, I can do all the things I did before. But – will there still be a place for me, back in Portsmouth? I've been happy here in the country, as happy as I could be while I was locked away in that silent world. Will I be able to go back?

She listened again to the blackbird's song and decided to put away all her worries until tomorrow. Just for now, she would be content to sit here, watching the sun set and listening to the sounds she had thought never to hear again. Just for now, there was no better place to be than here – under the apple tree, where Hope had been born.

For a few days, all was quiet at Ashdown. Judy had sent off telegrams to both families and her mother had written back at once to both her and Jean. Cissie had never been much of a letter-writer and these must have been awkward letters for her to write, Judy thought, reading the rather stilted congratulations to Jean. However pleased she must be to have a grandchild, you couldn't get around the fact that Hope was illegitimate and that life was never going to be easy for her or her mother. And nobody could forget that Terry, the baby's father, Cissie's only son, was dead, had died even before he knew she was on the way. I expect they hoped the baby would be a boy, she thought, a boy who'd be like Terry, and they haven't even got that.

Polly wrote too, rather more warmly. She had set aside her own feelings about the rights and wrongs of it all, and poured out all her sympathy to Jean, the sympathy that came from having lost her own husband and knowing what it was like to be a woman alone with a child to bring up. *But you have a family who will help you through this*, she wrote, *and we'll always stand by you and your baby*. She added that she would be coming out to see them all as soon as possible – she and Joe.

Joe was at St George's Barracks by now, and he and Polly had been down to Devon to see the boys. They were living in a small cottage with the widow who 'looked after them as if they were her own'. Polly was secretly relieved to find that she was a comfortable woman in her fifties who was friendly with a local farmer – he was there when she and Joe arrived – and that she clearly took the view that the boys had been loaned to her for an indefinite period but would one day be going back to their father. She had set a tea such as Polly had not seen for years – salad with thick slices of real ham, hard-boiled eggs, a mound of potatoes, a loaf of bread fresh from the oven and stewed plums with rich, yellow clotted cream.

It seems awful to think of all those poor people in Leningrad, starving to death, Polly wrote to Judy, *when we had all that put in front of us. But it doesn't do them any good for us not to*

*eat it, does it? And there are people in our own cities who aren't
a lot better off – not starving, but not well-fed either. I feel a bit
guilty about them too.*

Mrs Ellacombe had given her some eggs and a jam jar full
of clotted cream to take back to the family, but it wasn't the
food that interested Polly most about the visit. She'd been
nervous about meeting Joe's sons, she didn't mind admitting
it to Judy, but thank goodness there hadn't been any
problem at all. They'd been out playing on the moor when
she arrived and came in muddy and dirty, carrying baskets
of blackberries, their shirts hanging out of their shorts and
their socks down round their ankles just like any other little
boys, and had flung themselves at their father, obviously
thrilled to bits to see him again.

They'd been a bit shy with Polly at first, but once they'd
found out she drove an ambulance during the raids and had
seen lots of bombs falling, they had pelted her with
questions and obviously thought her a fitting friend for their
father. *I don't suppose they think any further than that*, she
wrote, *and there's no need to for a long time yet. Me and Joe
want to take things slowly. We're not in any hurry.* But it was
clear to Judy that they both knew perfectly well where they
wanted their relationship to go, and she folded her letter
wistfully, thinking sadly of the young Observer she had sent
away and wondering what would have happened, had she let
him stay.

There was a strange feeling of expectation in the air.
Everyone was waiting for America to decide to come into
the war. Japan seemed to be making preparations, and
American patrol ships were being attacked off Iceland.
Britain was bombing major cities such as Hamburg while
German troops were invading Russia. There was a shared
belief that, however bad it was now and however much was
happening, there was worse to come.

Yet nothing could take away the joy that Hope had
brought with her. She was well-named, Mrs Hazelwood said

as she wheeled out the old pram and set it under the apple tree. You could swear she was smiling, even at two weeks old – surely such a lovely, happy expression couldn't be just wind! – and she hardly ever cried. When Jean was allowed out of bed to come and sit with her in the garden, it was like the beginning of the world itself – a woman who had given birth, at peace with her child.

Judy was with her one afternoon at the beginning of September, the month when Hope should have been born. She had been making scrim all morning. She'd scrubbed her hands and face but there were still traces of dark green and brown dye on them and even though she'd been wearing a turban there was still dust in her hair.

'I sometimes think I'll never be clean again,' she said ruefully. 'I'd much rather collect sphagnum moss, or even acorns – it'll be time for them again soon.'

'I ought to be doing something too,' Jean said, stirring restlessly. 'I'm sick of being treated like an invalid. Honestly, I feel better than I ever have in all my life – just getting rid of that huge bump and not getting backache or heartburn any more is wonderful, but the midwife says I mustn't do too much. And of course Hope needs a lot of attention. She's so tiny.' She touched the blanket that had been spread over the baby to keep her warm, even though there wasn't a chill in the air. For the first few days of her life, Hope's smallness and premature birth had caused a little anxiety, but she had made up her birthweight again and was obviously thriving. 'But I don't know what I *should* be doing. I can't put upon the Hazelwoods for ever. And I'm not doing any real war work.'

'You could always make scrim!' Judy joked. The charm of weaving camouflage had quickly worn off and she now loathed the job as much as the other women did. 'But you'll be helping Mrs Hazelwood again, like you did before, won't you? Didn't they say you could stay on after the baby was born?'

'Yes, but it's not fair to expect them to keep me *and* Hope.' Jean sighed. 'I don't know where else I could go, though. Not back to Pompey, that's for sure!'

'You still haven't heard from your mum or dad, then?'

Jean shook her head. 'Nor likely to, I reckon. They've washed their hands of me, just like Mum said they would.' She paused, then said, 'Judy, there's something I want to ask you.'

She sounded a little diffident and Judy looked at her in surprise.

'What is it?' she asked.

'I'd like you to be Hope's godmother. Mr Hazelwood says she ought to be christened in a few weeks. I want it done here at Ashwood and I'd like you and Polly to be godmothers. You can't be related to her in any other way,' she went on sadly, 'and you'd have been her aunts if Terry and me had been married. So – will you?'

'Oh Jean, I'd love to.' Judy's eyes filled with tears. 'But we still *are* her aunts, Jean.' She grinned suddenly. 'And Polly's her great-aunt! I wonder if she's thought of that? It sounds so old, doesn't it! Who will you ask to be godfather?'

'I thought I'd ask Ben.' Jean blushed a little. 'You know he came home last weekend and he seemed to just fall in love with her. And we got on well too,' the blush deepened, 'and as the Hazelwoods have been so kind to me – well, it seemed a good idea . . .' She floundered to a stop and Judy laughed.

'It *is* a good idea! And Ben'll be a good friend to you both.' She eyed Jean, wondering about that blush, but before she could say any more she heard voices and they both looked up to see Mrs Hazelwood coming through the French doors and into the garden. There were two other people with her, and at the sight of them Judy gasped and Jean turned pale; but before either of them could say anything, one of the newcomers came forward, speaking in a quick, high voice as if she were embarrassed and upset and happy all at once.

'Jean!'

'*Mum!*' Jean sprang to her feet. 'Mum, I didn't think you'd come. You didn't write –'

'I didn't know what to say.' Mrs Foster stopped a foot or two away and the two gazed at each other, neither knowing quite what to do next. 'I did try. I tried a few times, but the words just wouldn't come out right. And then your dad said why not just come here and see you, so we got on the train – and here we are.' She moved towards the pram and looked down at the sleeping baby.

'She's called Hope,' Jean said, putting her hand on the baby's blanket.

'I know. Judy told us in the telegram. Oh Jeanie.' Mrs Foster bent closer. She touched the blanket, drawing it away from the baby's face, and stared down at her. Tears began to slip down her cheeks and she whispered in a breaking voice, 'Jeanie, she's so lovely.'

She turned suddenly and caught her daughter in her arms. Jean, who had been standing a little stiffly, crumpled against her and the two held each other close, sobbing. Mr Foster cleared his throat and came forward to look down into the pram, and Judy saw that his eyes too were bright and wet with tears.

'She's been breaking her heart over this,' he murmured. 'Thought we'd lost our Jeanie for good and it was all her fault. I said to her, "You're the girl's mother, she'll want to make it up" – but she was that upset, she made up her mind that Jeanie wouldn't want to know. It took a lot for her to come out here.' He reached out a hand and touched the baby's face with the tip of one finger. 'Hope,' he murmured. 'Our Jean's baby. Our granddaughter. Well, what a little peach you are. What a little beauty.' He turned to his daughter. 'Come here, girl, and give your dad a kiss.'

Judy caught Mrs Hazelwood's eye. The vicar's wife nodded to her and they both tiptoed back into the house. 'They'll need to be alone,' Mrs Hazelwood said. 'I'll take out some tea in a little while. I think things will be all right now.'

'Yes,' Judy said, and glanced out through the French windows at the little group under the apple tree. 'I think they will.'

Once the Fosters had been to see their daughter and new granddaughter, Judy felt more at a loose end than ever. There was plenty to do, for they were making desert scrim now, the colour of sand, and instead of black and green their hands were stained with pink and brown. The sphagnum collecting was still going on and there were blackberries and mushrooms coming along. Nothing could be wasted; even though in the country fresh food was more plentiful than in town, anything that couldn't be produced locally or had to be imported was just as strictly rationed. And even some of the local foods were under threat. The Suttons were desperately anxious about their cows, many of whom would have to be slaughtered when winter came because no grain was being imported and there would be no feed for them.

'That means a shortage of milk and butter and no cream at all,' Mrs Sutton said. 'And the hens'll have to go too, though they can live on scraps – if there are any.' She sighed. 'I don't know what we're all going do, I'm sure. I don't know what the world's coming to.'

Judy went out into the orchard and looked up at the apple trees. The fruit was swelling and ripening now, little globes of gold and scarlet amongst the leaves. She thought back to the first time she had stood under these trees, when they had been smothered in pink and white blossom, its scent strong enough to waft through her open window at night. So short a time ago, and yet so much had happened. The bombing – that terrible raid in which Polly had been trapped in that collapsed building – her deafness – Terry's death – Jean's pregnancy and now the birth of Hope. All in a few months.

And the war was not yet over. It was clear now that it

would go on for months, maybe years. If America came in, and Japan attacked, what would happen then? Like Mrs Sutton, she didn't know what the world was coming to.

Other things had happened too, she thought. Sean had died, and she'd met Chris Barrett. Chris, who had come out here to Ashdown to find her. Whom she'd sent away because she was deaf and couldn't hear his voice.

What a stupid reason, she thought, suddenly and savagely. What a stupid, *stupid* reason!

A sound made her turn. Mrs Hazelwood was coming into the orchard. She smiled at Judy and came over to her.

'Mrs Sutton told me you were here.' She was carrying a folder and some papers. 'There's something I want to ask you, Judy. Can we sit down for a moment?'

Judy led her to the old seat that stood against the wall where it could catch the last of the evening sun. Mr Sutton, who seldom rested, occasionally sat here with a glass of cider after the day's work was over. 'What is it? What's happened? Is Jean all right – and the baby?'

'Yes, yes, they're both well. And Jean's starting to work again in the house and helping with some of the local war work as well. I've told her she can stay as long as she likes – we're glad to have her – and I think that's what she's going to do,' Mrs Hazelwood said. 'No, the reason I came was to ask what you were going to do now, Judy. I've thought just lately that you seemed a little uncertain – as if you felt that now you had your hearing back, you ought to be doing more.'

'Well, I do.' Judy met her eyes. 'And I should, shouldn't I? I'm fit and healthy – there's nothing wrong with me now. I ought to be doing my bit, same as everyone else my age. I mean, I don't mind making scrim – not more than anyone else does, anyway – but I ought to be doing something more than that.'

'And have you thought what that might be?' the vicar's wife asked quietly. She tapped the folder on her lap. 'I have a few suggestions to make, if you haven't made up your mind. The women's Services – you may well be called up soon anyway, and it's better to volunteer so that you have a choice. But the WVS can always find a place for young women like you, energetic and capable, and if you feel you'd like to stay here with us, I can certainly offer you plenty of work. Perhaps you'd like to think about it.'

Judy gazed at her. She looked around the orchard and up into the rippling leaves of the tree, lit by its gleaming fruits. She thought of the devastation of Portsmouth, the nights of fear and destruction, the terror of thinking Polly dead and the nightmare of her deafness. She thought of Sean and Terry and Johnny, all dead, and then of Chris, who was still alive.

'No,' she said slowly, and then again as certainty grew in her mind, 'no, Mrs Hazelwood. Thank you, but I can't stay in the country. I love it here – I hope I'll come back to see you all, lots of times, when peace comes. But for now, I've got to go back. I've got a job in Portsmouth, with the Lady Mayoress. There's work for me to do there. And – and there's someone I have to see as well.'

There was a small silence. Then, with the thought of Chris filling her mind and warming her heart, she added quietly, 'That's where my life is – in Portsmouth. That's where I belong.'

Chapter One

'No! Don't!' You mustn't!'

The man just about to lower a sack into the choppy waters of Portsmouth Harbour turned in surprise as a girl rushed towards him, her dark curls flying out from under the scarf she wore around her head. With half a dozen others, she had been walking through the Naval Armament Depot of Priddy's Hard, on her way to the shifting room, when through the dim morning mist she had seen Sam Reece stride past, carrying the sack. From the size and shape of it, and the way something inside wriggled, she knew just what he was about to do.

'He's drowning the kittens!' Forgetting all about work, she pushed past the other girls and rushed across to the Camber. Sam was almost at the quayside now, a shadowy figure bending to find a space between the barges where he could drop his burden into the waves that slapped against the wall. Kate screamed at the top of her voice, and several men, at work loading the lighters to take munitions across the harbour, straightened up and stared at her. Sam Reece himself jumped like a naughty boy caught in the act of mischief, and then flushed a dark, angry red. He was a squat, swarthy man with small, permanently bloodshot eyes and a surly scowl, and he'd never approved of bringing women in to work at Priddy's Hard.

'You yelling at me, girl?'

'Yes, I am!' Kate was beside him now, breathless, her

1

eyes spitting blue fire. She snatched at the bag and tried to pull it away from him. 'You're going to drop them in, aren't you? Our Tibby's kittens – you're going to drop them in the water.'

'Yeah. What of it?' He dragged the sack back and a chorus of faint mewing sounds rose from inside. Kate's eyes filled with tears. 'You know we can't keep all the bloody kittens that are born here. Leave go, and get over to the shifting room, or you'll be late clocking on.'

'I don't care if I am!' It would mean a dock in her pay but Kate ignored that. 'You're not drowning these kittens.'

'For cripes' sake—' Sam was beginning, when another voice broke in and they both turned to see the office manager bearing down upon them. Thank goodness, Kate thought, seeing the tall, broad figure. It's Mr Milner – he'll understand. She let go of the sack and stepped towards him.

'What's going on here?' Arthur Milner stopped and stared at them both. 'I could hear the shouting back in the office. Why aren't you getting ready for work, young lady, and what's in that bag?'

'It's the kittens, Mr Milner,' Kate began, but Sam's voice overrode hers, taking on an indignant whine. 'I'm just trying to carry out orders, sir. It's nothing to do with this young woman. She just flew at me, started on about how I mustn't do this, can't do that – if you ask me, it's a pity they ever brought women into the yard. Nothing but trouble, they bin, ever since they first walked in the gates!'

'Well, that's a matter of opinion,' Mr Milner said, cutting in on the flow. 'We'd be in a poor way without them. Anyway, you haven't answered my question. What's in the bag and what were you going to do with it?'

'It's the *kittens*,' Kate began again, but the manager lifted his hand to silence her and looked at Sam.

'Well?'

The workman thrust out his lower lip. 'All right, so it's kittens. I was going to drop 'em over the side – it's what we

2

always do when there's too many. Blooming cats bin popping off all over the place the past few weeks; we can't let 'em all live, now can we?' He appealed to Mr Milner, as man to man. 'I mean, I likes animals as much as the next bloke – got a cat of me own at home, Ginger he's called and soft as butter 'cept when another tom comes sniffing round – but anyone with any sense'd see that we can't just let 'em breed willy-nilly. Wouldn't be able to move for the little perishers, now would we? So when we gets a new litter, we just puts 'em in an old sack with a couple of stones and drops 'em over the side, nice and tidy. It's the best way. They don't know nothing about it.'

'Of course they know about it!' Kate burst out. 'They're *drowning*! It must be horrible for them. It's *cruel*.'

Arthur Milner looked uncomfortable. 'Yes, but Reece has got a point,' he said. 'We'd be overrun with cats if we let them all live. We need a few to keep down rats, and if anyone wants to give a kitten a home they're welcome to take them, but apart from that they've got to be put down. And they don't suffer much, not if it's done almost as soon as they're born.'

Kate stared at him. 'You mean you're going to let him *do* it?' She snatched the bag and Sam, taken unawares, released his grip. Kate untied the bit of string that was knotted around its neck and peered inside. 'I knew it! *These* haven't just been born – they're nearly six weeks old! They're Tibby's kittens, from our hut. We've been helping her look after them.' She cradled the bag against her and looked fiercely at the two men. 'You're not drowning Tibby's kittens.'

There was a moment's silence. Kate was suddenly aware of the clatter going on around her – the noise of the munitions factory at work, the clanging and shouting as the lighters were loaded with crates of shells, the sounds of the great harbour that lay beyond the jetties of the little dock. In a few moments she should be clocking on, and even

3

one minute late would mean the loss of half a day's pay. She stood her ground, meeting the manager's eye, and he sighed.

'These kittens ought to have been dealt with before,' he told Reece. 'Five weeks is too late – they're almost ready to leave their mother. Why wasn't this done sooner?'

'It's them bleeding girls,' the man grumbled. 'You heard what she said. Bin looking after them, they have. Hiding them in a locker, I dare say, bringing in food for 'em, giving the mother milk. You knows what girls are.'

Mr Milner glanced at Kate and she felt her face colour. 'We were going to find homes for them all,' she said defensively. 'And they're so pretty. One of them's a tortoiseshell – look – and one's black with a white bib and paws, just as if he was going to a posh party. And this one's pure white. Look, see how fluffy—'

'Yes, yes, all right,' Mr Milner said hastily as she drew out the tiny creatures, one after another, to display their charms. 'They're pretty little mites, but they still ought to have been dealt with sooner.' He sighed. 'You say you've found homes for them all?'

'Well, I'm having the tortoisehell,' Kate said eagerly, seeing victory within her grasp. 'Maxine Fowler wants the white one, Elsie Philpotts says she'll have the fluffy ginger one, and I'm sure someone will have the black and white one.' She looked up at him, opening her dark blue eyes very wide. '*You* wouldn't like him, would you, Mr Milner? He's got ever such a sweet face. And they're almost ready to go – we were going to take them home on Friday.' She put her head on one side. 'Don't let him drown them, Mr Milner. Please don't let him drown them.'

The office manager hesitated. Sam Reece heaved a loud, heavy sigh. Kate cuddled the tortoiseshell kitten against her breast and kissed the top of its head, then looked up at Mr Milner from under her lashes. He pursued his lips in resignation.

'All right. You can take them back. So long as they're not

in a dangerous place – dangerous to the job and the workers, I mean. They've got to be out on Friday, mind – and if the mother cat gives birth again you must let your supervisor know at once, and leave them to be disposed of. Understood?'

For a moment, Kate struggled with her feelings. Then she nodded. 'Yes, sir.'

Mr Milner glanced at Sam Reece. 'Right. You'd better both get back to work. The whistle will be going at any minute and we've got a big job on. Nobody's going to have time to worry about kittens for the next few weeks, I can tell you that.'

He turned and strode away. Kate and the workman looked at each other.

'Bleedin' kittens!' he said disgustedly. 'Bleedin' *girls*!'

The other girls looked at Kate as she strode towards the shifting room, triumphantly holding up the sack of wriggling, mewing kittens. 'You did it! You stopped him! What did Mr Milner say?'

'He said they were too old to drown. But next time Tibby has kittens, we've got to let someone know, so they can be "disposed of".' She snorted. 'Disposed of! He means drowned, just like these would've been. It's cruel.'

'My dad always drowns our Micky's kittens,' one of the girls said sadly. 'He says they don't feel it when they're so young. He leaves her one though, otherwise she's got nothing to take the milk, see.'

'Well, I don't believe it. Of course they feel it.' Kate carried the sack over to the corner just outside the long shed, where the mother cat had a nest made of old rags in a disused wooden bomb crate. Tibby wasn't there – she'd probably gone hunting – and wouldn't even know that her babies had been missing. Kate opeend the sack and tipped the kittens gently into the crate, watching them as they scrambled about in a heap of fur.

'Come on, Kate.' Maxine Fowler, Kate's best friend, was at her elbow. 'The whistle will be going any minute and you're nowhere near ready. They'll be all right now.'

Kate nodded and opened her locker. Each girl had one, a green-painted metal cupboard where she could put her outdoor clothes and valuables while she was at work. Not that anyone had anything of real value, except for wedding or engagement rings, but even these must be put into the locker. Anything made of metal could cause a spark and blow the entire site sky-high. It had happened years ago – her grandfather, who had also worked here, still talked about the men who had been killed then – and again, in 1921, when her father had been here. Four men had been killed then, all Gosport chaps, and it had brought home to everyone on the site the dangers of the materials they worked with.

The shriek of the whistle broke into her thoughts. She closed the locker door and followed the others into the shifting room. They had five minutes now, to take off their jumpers and skirts and hang them up, then step across the painted red line in their underclothes into the 'clean' area and put on their magazine clothing – loose brown overalls and a cloth cap. Some of the caps bore a red spot, denoting that its wearer worked with gunpowder, while those who worked with more modern explosives were marked by a black spot.

'I feel like Blind Pugh,' Kate observed when she was first given her cap, and when the others looked blank she explained, 'You know. The old pirate in *Treasure Island*.' They nodded then. The story had been read to most of them at school and they remembered the sinister tap-tap-tap of the blind man's stick, and the horror of having the 'black spot' laid on you. It had haunted Kate for a week, and she'd been unable to sleep at nights, certain that every little tapping sound was Blind Pugh coming for her. Her brother Ian had discovered this and stood outside her bedroom door

6

when she was in bed, tapping on the stairs and driving her into nightmares from which she woke screaming, but she'd never told her mother what was frightening her so much. She didn't want her complaining to the teacher who read the story to them, in case he stopped.

From the shifting room, the girls trooped through to the laboratory and took their places at the benches where they would spend the next twelve hours inspecting and putting together ammunition. As soon as the chargehand's back was turned, Kate ducked down and lifted a section of floorboard to reveal her tea can. She pushed in the paper bag of sandwiches she had brought with her, replaced the board swiftly and stood up, winking at Maxine. 'That's for tea-break. We'll make a cuppa from the outlet pipe when old Fred goes up to the office.'

'You'll get caught one of these days,' Maxine said, but Kate shrugged.

'Everyone does it – reckon they know, anyway. They never search us for food. A couple of Marmite sandwiches won't set the cordite off – and I haven't noticed you turning your nose up when I offer you one!'

Maxine grinned. 'Matter of fact, I've got a bit of cake this morning. Mum found a packet of sultanas at the back of the cupboard and made one at the weekend.' She didn't add that she'd deliberately refused a piece when it was offered her at Sunday tea-time, just to upset her mother, Clarrie, and only grudgingly accepted it for her lunch-box.

'*Fruit* cake!' Kate rolled her eyes. 'You'll share it around, naturally.'

'Only with my best friend,' Maxine said, and then turned hastily to her work as the chargehand bore down upon them.

They worked steadily through the morning, stopping only for the illicit tea-break when the supervisor was out of the way, and then for their official lunchtime at twelve. By then, Kate's legs were aching from having stood for nearly

7

six hours, and she was glad to push her way out with the rest of the girls and get a bit of fresh air.

Set on a peninsula of land on the western shores of Portsmouth Harbour, the armament depot covered a large area of what had once been waste ground, a 'hard' area of solid mud, its channels washed twice a day by the tide, and covered with tough grass and furze bushes which burst into golden flowers every spring. Until it had been taken over by the government nearly two hundred years ago, the area had been more or less wild, with the grassy ramparts of Gosport Lines – the earthern fortifications once constructed to ward off possible invasion by the French – forming a long low hill across its neck.

Before then, Naval munitions had been made and loaded at the Gunwharf, on the Portsmouth side of the harbour, but that had been considered too dangerous for the fleet of ships coming through the narrow entrance and mooring at the jetties, so the work had been transferred to Gosport. By 1777, the huge Magazine had been built and munitions were being shipped across the harbour by barge, or lighter, just as they were now.

The ramparts were still there, making a good buffer against possible explosions, and other hillocks had been pushed up between the sheds so that each was protected from the others. What with these and the old moats that ran between the Lines, with blackberry bushes growing along their banks, and the groves of walnut trees that had been planted to provide wood for rifle butts and pistol grips, it was almost like being out in the country.

'They say you can't see Piddy's from the air at all, with all the roofs being painted green to match the grass,' Maxine observed. 'That's why we don't get bombed. Makes you wonder why they don't paint everyone's roofs green, doesn't it.' She looked up at the sky and unbuttoned her brown herringbone tweed coat. 'Look – sunshine!'

'Don't blink, it'll be gone in a minute,' Kate advised. 'It's only the first of March, you know, not Midsummer Day.' She grinned as a chilly wind sprang up and Maxine hurriedly pulled her coat around her again. 'Not a bad day really, though: in like a lion, out like a lamb, they say, don't they? Don't really know what today is like, it's just sort of grey and draughty. Like a seagull, perhaps,' she added as half a dozen birds flew over, cackling.

'It'd be quite nice if you pushed away the clouds and switched off the wind,' Hazel Jackman remarked. 'At least it's not raining.' She gazed across the harbour at the warships that lay at the jetties, awaiting their load of ammunition. 'Did you hear Mr Churchill was in Pompey last Monday? My Uncle Joe came round last night for a game of cards, and he said heaps of people saw him walking round looking at the bomb damage. He was smoking a cigar and he gave them the V-sign and everything.'

'Well, *I'm* more interested in all those Canadians who arrived at the weekend,' Maxine declared with a wink. 'Reckon it'll be worth taking a trip over the water on Saturday? I bet there'll be quite a few on the lookout for a nice girl to show them the sights, and they'll have plenty of money to spend as well.'

'Maxine! You're awful.' Kate poked her friend in the ribs. 'You'll get into trouble one of these days, the way you go on.'

'Not me! I may not always be good, but I'm *always* careful.' Maxine tossed her blonde curls and giggled. 'Why don't you come too? It's only a bit of fun – they're decent blokes, most of them.'

'Sad to say,' another girl put in, and they all laughed. 'Let's all go. Safety in numbers and all that. What about it?'

Maxine nodded vigorously. 'I'm on! Hazel? Janice? Val? Kate, you'll come, won't you?'

'I don't know,' Kate said, and the others stared at her in surprise. 'I'll be taking Topsy home on Friday. She'll be lonely – I can't really leave her to Mum.'

9

'For goodness' sake, you can't stay in all weekend for a *kitten*! She'll be all right – probably sleep most of the time anyway. Look, you'll have all Saturday afternoon to play nursemaid, and you can come out with us in the evening – what about that? We'll go over to South Parade Pier, there's bound to be a dance on and they always have a good band. You don't even need to *talk* to a boy if you don't want to.'

'Well, that sounds like a really good night out,' Kate said. 'I can sit on a chair being a wallflower and not open my mouth all evening, while the rest of you get off with rich Canadians. Thanks a lot!'

Maxine laughed. 'I can't really see you doing that! You talk more than all the rest of us put together. Anyway, I thought maybe we could get some of them to take us to the pictures on Sunday. That new Bob Hope and Bing Crosby film's on at the Gaiety – *Road to Zanzibar*. They say it's ever so good. It's got Dorothy Lamour in it as well, she's really glamorous. But if you're not interested . . .'

Kate clutched her arm. 'I didn't mean it! I was only joking. I'll come. Only – I don't want to come home on my own, all right? No malarkey – you'll have to promise to catch the last boat with me.'

'Well, what else d'you think we're going to do? Of course we'll catch the last boat, dope!' The irrepressible blue eyes gleamed. 'There's plenty of time for a bit of malarkey before then.' Maxine grinned. 'Don't worry, Kate, *we'll* be good. Won't we, girls? The question is – will *you*?'

The others giggled and nudged each other. Val said, 'We might find ourselves a nice rich husband, what about that? I wouldn't mind going to live in Canada.'

'Gosh, yes! That'd be nearly as good as America – better, because they're still British. Part of the Empire, anyway.' Maxine stretched her arms above her head. 'Just think of it, no food rationing, plenty of nylons, plenty of *everything*.'

'That's just greed,' Kate protested. 'You wouldn't marry someone just for nylons. You'd have to love him.'

'Well, I would love him,' Maxine said. 'I'd love anyone who could give me a new pair of nylons every day!'

They screamed with laughter, and Kate gave them a reproving look. 'Well, *I'm* not going to look for a rich Canadian to marry. I'm not looking for a steady boy at all. Not till the war's over, and maybe not even then.'

'We'll all be old by the time the war's over,' Hazel told her. 'Nobody will look at us. You've got to take your chances when they come, Kate. There's a Mr Right for all of us. You never know when you might meet him. Anyway, I'm just looking for a bit of fun – a good dance, and a nice kiss and cuddle at the end of it.'

'And that's all?' Janice asked slyly, and they laughed again.

Kate shrugged but joined in their laughter, while privately making up her mind that although she was happy to dance with boys, British *or* Canadian, and even go to the pictures with them, any goodnight kisses would be just that – a kiss and no more. And there would be no question of finding 'Mr Right'.

I wish I *could* be like the others, she thought, eating her sandwiches and gazing out across the grey, choppy waters. I wish I *could* believe that there's a boy out there who's meant for me. But I just can't. I can't forget what happened before, and I can't believe it won't happen again.

It would take one very special man to make her believe in love again. Perhaps there really was one somewhere, and one day she would meet him.

Perhaps.

All Orion/Phoenix titles are available at your local bookshop or from the following address:

Mail Order Department
Littlehampton Book Services
FREEPOST BR535
Worthing, West Sussex, BN13 3BR
telephone 01903 828503, *facsimile* 01903 828802
e-mail MailOrders@lbsltd.co.uk
(Please ensure that you include full postal address details)

Payment can be made either by credit/debit card (Visa, Mastercard, Access and Switch accepted) or by sending a £ Sterling cheque or postal order made payable to *Littlehampton Book Services*.
DO NOT SEND CASH OR CURRENCY

Please add the following to cover postage and packing

UK and BFPO:
£1.50 for the first book, and 50p for each additional book to a maximum of £3.50

Overseas and Eire:
£2.50 for the first book plus £1.00 for the second book and 50p for each additional book ordered

---

BLOCK CAPITALS PLEASE

name of cardholder .... *delivery address*
.... *(if different from cardholder)*
address of cardholder ....
....
....
....
postcode .... *postcode* ....

☐ I enclose my remittance for £ ....

☐ please debit my Mastercard/Visa/Access/Switch (delete as appropriate)

card number ⬚⬚⬚⬚⬚⬚⬚⬚⬚⬚⬚⬚⬚⬚⬚⬚

expiry date ⬚⬚⬚⬚ Switch issue no. ⬚⬚

signature ....

prices and availability are subject to change without notice

Dennis Lehane was born and raise   chester, Massachusetts. He is the award-winn   of seven novels: *A Drink Before the War*; *Do   My Hand*; *Sacred*; *Gone, Baby, Gone*; *Prayers for   River*; *Shutter Island* and a short-story collectio   . Before becoming a full-time writer, Lehane   a counsellor with mentally handicapped and   dren, waited tables, parked cars, drove limos,   bookstores and loaded tractor-trailers. He lives in   area.

The GIVEN DAY

Dennis Lehane

BLACK SWAN

TRANSWORLD PUBLISHERS
61–63 Uxbridge Road, London W5 5SA
A Random House Group Company
www.rbooks.co.uk

THE GIVEN DAY
A BLACK SWAN BOOK: 9780552775571

First published in Great Britain
in 2008 by Doubleday
an imprint of Transworld Publishers
Black Swan edition published 2009

A CIP catalogue record for this book
is available from the British Library.

Addresses for Random House Group Ltd companies outside the UK
can be found at: www.randomhouse.co.uk
The Random House Group Ltd Reg. No. 954009

The Random House Group Limited supports The Forest Stewardship
Council (FSC), the leading international forest certification organisation.
All our titles that are printed on Greenpeace approved FSC certified paper
carry the FSC logo. Our paper procurement policy can be found at
www.rbooks.co.uk/environment

Typeset in 10/12.5pt Giovanni Book by
Falcon Oast Graphic Art Ltd.
Printed in the UK by CPI Cox & Wyman, Reading, RG1 8EX.

2 4 6 8 10 9 7 5 3 1

for Angie,
my home

When Jesus comes a calling, she said,
He's coming 'round the mountain on a train.

—JOSH RITTER, "Wings"

CAST OF CHARACTERS

Luther Laurence—houseman, athlete
Lila Waters Laurence—Luther's wife

Aiden "Danny" Coughlin—Boston police officer
Captain Thomas Coughlin—Danny's father
Connor Coughlin—Danny's brother, assistant district
  attorney, Suffolk County
Joe Coughlin—Danny's youngest brother
Ellen Coughlin—Danny's mother
Lieutenant Eddie McKenna—Danny's godfather
Nora O'Shea—domestic help for the Coughlin household
Avery Wallace—domestic help for the Coughlin household

Babe Ruth—baseball player, Boston Red Sox
Stuffy McInnis—Ruth's teammate
Johnny Igoe—Ruth's agent
Harry Frazee—owner, Boston Red Sox
Steve Coyle—Danny Coughlin's patrol partner
Claude Mesplede—alderman of the Sixth Ward
Patrick Donnegan—boss of the Sixth Ward

Isaiah and Yvette Giddreaux—heads of Boston chapter of the
  NAACP
"Old" Byron Jackson—head of the bellmen's union, Hotel
  Tulsa

Deacon Skinner Broscious—gangster, Tulsa

Dandy and Smoke—enforcers for Deacon Broscious

Clarence Jessup "Jessie" Tell—numbers runner, Luther's friend, Tulsa

Clayton Tomes—houseman, friend of Luther's, Boston

Mrs. DiMassi—Danny Coughlin's landlady

Frederico and Tessa Abruzze—Danny's neighbors

Louis Fraina—head of the Lettish Workingman's Society

Mark Denton—Boston Police Department patrolman, union organizer

Rayme Finch—agent, Bureau of Investigation

John Hoover—lawyer, Department of Justice

Samuel Gompers—president of the American Federation of Labor

Andrew J. Peters—mayor of Boston

Calvin Coolidge—governor of Massachusetts

Stephen O'Meara—Boston police commissioner until December 1918

Edwin Upton Curtis—O'Meara's successor as Boston police commissioner

Mitchell Palmer—attorney general of the United States

James Jackson Storrow—Boston power broker, former president of General Motors

The

GIVEN DAY

BABE RUTH *in* OHIO

PROLOGUE

Due to travel restrictions placed on major league baseball by the War Department, the World Series of 1918 was played in September and split into two home stands. The Chicago Cubs hosted the first three games, with the final four to be held in Boston. On September 7, after the Cubs dropped game three, the two teams boarded a Michigan Central train together to embark on the twenty-seven-hour trip, and Babe Ruth got drunk and started stealing hats.

They'd had to pour him onto the train in the first place. After the game, he'd gone to a house a few blocks east of Wabash where a man could find a game of cards, a steady supply of liquor, and a woman or two, and if Stuffy McInnis hadn't known where to look for him, he would have missed the trip home.

As it was, he puked off the rear of the caboose as the train chugged out of Central Station at a little after eight in the evening and wound its way past the stockyards. The air was woolen with smoke and the stench of butchered cattle, and Ruth was damned if he could find a star in the black sky. He took a pull from his flask and rinsed the vomit from his mouth with a gargle of rye and spit it over the iron rail and watched the spangle of Chicago's skyline rise before him as he slid away from it. As he often did when he left a place and his body was leaden with booze, he felt fat and orphaned.

He drank some more rye. At twenty-three, he was finally

becoming one of the more feared hitters in the league. In a
year when home runs in the American League had totaled
ninety-six, Ruth had accounted for eleven. Damn near 12 percent. Even if someone took into account the three-week
slump he'd suffered in June, pitchers had started to treat him
with respect. Opposing hitters, too, because Ruth had pitched
the Sox to thirteen wins that season. He'd also started fifty-nine
games in left and thirteen at first.

Couldn't hit lefties, though. That was the knock on him.
Even when every roster had been stripped to its shells by the
players who'd enlisted in the war, Ruth had a weakness that
opposing managers had begun to exploit.

Fuck 'em.

He said it to the wind and took another hit from his flask,
a gift from Harry Frazee, the team owner. Ruth had left the
team in July. Went to play for the Chester Shipyards team in
Pennsylvania because Coach Barrow valued Ruth's pitching
arm far more than his bat, and Ruth was tired of pitching. You
threw a strikeout, you got applause. You hit a home run,
you got mass eruption. Problem was, the Chester Shipyards
preferred his pitching, too. When Frazee threatened them
with a lawsuit, Chester Shipyards shipped Ruth back.

Frazee had met the train and escorted Ruth to the backseat
of his Rauch & Lang Electric Opera Coupe. It was maroon
with black trim and Ruth was always amazed by how you
could see your reflection in the steel no matter the weather or
time of day. He asked Frazee what it cost, a buggy like this,
and Frazee idly fondled the gray upholstery as his driver
pulled onto Atlantic Avenue. "More than you, Mr. Ruth," he
said and handed Ruth the flask.

The inscription etched into the pewter read:

RUTH, G. H.
CHESTER, Penna.
7/1/18–7/7/18

He fingered it now and took another swig, and the greasy odor of cows' blood mixed with the metallic smell of factory towns and warm train tracks. *I am Babe Ruth*, he wanted to shout off the train. And when I'm not drunk and alone at the back of a caboose, I am someone to be reckoned with. A cog in the wheel, yes, and you bet I know it, but a diamond-crusted cog. The cog of cogs. Someday . . .

Ruth raised his flask and toasted Harry Frazee and all the Harry Frazees of the world with a string of lewd epithets and a bright smile. Then he took a swig and it went to his eyelids and tugged them downward.

"I'm going to sleep, you old whore," Ruth whispered to the night, to the skyline, to the smell of butchered meat. To the dark midwestern fields that lay ahead. To every ashen mill town between here and Governor's Square. To the smoky starless sky.

He stumbled into the stateroom he shared with Jones, Scott, and McInnis, and when he woke at six in the morning, still fully clothed, he was in Ohio. He ate breakfast in the dining car and drank two pots of coffee and watched the smoke pour from the stacks in the foundries and steel mills that squatted in the black hills. His head ached and he added a couple of drops from his flask to his coffee cup and his head didn't ache anymore. He played canasta for a while with Everett Scott, and then the train made a long stop in Summerford, another mill town, and they stretched their legs in a field just beyond the station, and that's when he first heard of a strike.

It was Harry Hooper, the Sox team captain and right fielder, and second baseman Dave Shean talking to the Cubs' left fielder Leslie Mann and catcher Bill Killefer. McInnis said the four of them had been thick as thieves the whole trip.

" 'Bout what?" Ruth said, not really sure he cared.

"Don't know," Stuffy said. "Muffing flies for a price, you think? Tanking?"

Hooper crossed the field to them.

"We're going to strike, boys."

Stuffy McInnis said, "You're drunk."

Hooper shook his head. "They're fucking us, boys."

"Who?"

"The Commission. Who do you think? Heydler, Hermann, Johnson. Them."

Stuffy McInnis sprinkled tobacco into a slip of rolling paper and gave the paper a delicate lick as he twisted the ends. "How so?"

Stuffy lit his cigarette and Ruth took a sip from his flask and looked across the field at a small fringe of trees under the blue sky.

"They changed the gate distribution of the Series. The percentage of receipts. They did it last winter, but they didn't tell us till now."

"Wait," McInnis said. "We get sixty percent of the first four gates."

Harry Hooper shook his head and Ruth could feel his attention begin to wander. He noticed telegraph lines stretched at the edge of the field and he wondered if you could hear them hum if you got close enough. Gate receipts, distribution. Ruth wanted another plate of eggs, some more bacon.

Harry said, "We *used to* get sixty percent. Now we get fifty-five. Attendance is down. The war, you know. And it's our patriotic duty to take five percent less."

McInnis shrugged. "Then it's our—"

"Then we forfeit forty percent of that to Cleveland, Washington, and Chicago."

"For what?" Stuffy said. "Kicking their asses to second, third, and fourth?"

"Then, then another ten percent to war charities. You seeing this now?"

Stuffy scowled. He looked ready to kick someone, someone small he could really get his leg into.

Babe threw his hat in the air and caught it behind his back.

He picked up a rock and threw it at the sky. He threw his hat again.

"It'll all work out," he said.

Hooper looked at him. "What?"

"Whatever it is," Babe said. "We'll make it back."

Stuffy said, "How, Gidge? You tell me that? How?"

"Somehow." Babe's head was beginning to hurt again. Talk of money made his head hurt. The world made his head hurt—Bolsheviks overthrowing the Czar, the Kaiser running roughshod over Europe, anarchists tossing bombs in the streets of this very country, blowing up parades and mailboxes. People were angry, people were shouting, people were dying in trenches and marching outside factories. And it all had something to do with money. The Babe understood that much. But he hated thinking about it. He liked money, he liked it just fine, and he knew he was making plenty and he stood to make plenty more. He liked his new motor scooter, and he liked buying good cigars and staying in swell hotel rooms with heavy curtains and buying rounds for the bar. But he hated thinking about money or talking about money. He just wanted to get to Boston. He wanted to hit a ball, paint the town. Governor's Square teemed with brothels and good saloons. Winter was coming; he wanted to enjoy it while he could, before the snow came, the cold. Before he was stuck back in Sudbury with Helen and the smell of horses.

He clapped Harry on the shoulder and repeated his estimation: "Somehow it'll all be fine. You'll see."

Harry Hooper looked at his shoulder. He looked off into the field. He looked back at Ruth. Ruth smiled.

"Go be a good Babe," Harry Hooper said, "and leave the talk to the men."

Harry Hooper turned his back on him. He wore a straw boater, tilted back slightly from his forehead. Ruth hated boaters; his face was too round for them, too fleshy. They made him look like a child playing dress-up. He imagined

19

taking Harry's boater off his head and flinging it onto the roof of the train.

Harry walked off into the field, leading Stuffy McInnis by the elbow, his chin tilted down.

Babe picked up a rock and eyed the back of Harry Hooper's seersucker jacket, imagined a catcher's mitt there, imagined the sound of it, a sharp rock against a sharp spine. He heard another sharp sound replace the one in his head, though, a distant crack similar to the crack of a log snapping in the fire-place. He looked east to where the field ended at a small stand of trees. He could hear the train hissing softly behind him and stray voices from the players and the rustle of the field. Two engineers walked behind him, talking about a busted flange, how it was going to take two hours, maybe three, to fix, and Ruth thought, Two hours in this shithole? and then he heard it again—a dry distant crack, and he knew that on the other side of those trees someone was playing baseball.

He crossed the field alone and unnoticed and he heard the sounds of the ball game grow closer—the singsong catcalls, the rough scuff of feet chasing down a ball in the grass, the wet-slap thump of a ball sent to its death in an outfielder's glove. He went through the trees and removed his coat in the heat, and when he stepped out of the grove they were chang-ing sides, men running in toward a patch of dirt along the first base line while another group ran out from a patch by third.

Colored men.

He stood where he was and nodded at the center fielder trotting out to take his spot a few yards from him, and the center fielder gave him a curt nod back and then appeared to scan the trees to see if they planned on giving birth to any more white men today. Then he turned his back to Babe and bent at the waist and placed his hand and glove on his knees. He was a big buck, as broad-shouldered as the Babe, though not as heavy in the middle, or (Babe had to admit) in the ass.

20

The pitcher didn't waste any time. He barely had a windup, just long goddamn arms, and he swung the right one like he was unleashing a rock from a slingshot meant to travel an ocean, and Babe could tell even from here that the ball crossed the plate on fire. The batter took a nice clean cut and still missed it by half a foot.

Hit the next one, though, hit it solid, with a crack so loud it could have only come from a busted bat, and the ball soared straight at him and then went lazy in the blue sky, like a duck deciding to swim the backstroke, and the center fielder shifted one foot and opened his glove and the ball fell, as if relieved, right into the heart of the leather.

Ruth's vision had never been tested. He wouldn't allow it. Ever since he was a boy, he could read street signs, even those painted on the corners of buildings, from distances far greater than anyone else. He could see the texture of the feathers on a hawk a hundred yards above him, in hunt, streaking like a bullet. Balls looked fat to him and moved slow. When he pitched, the catcher's mitt looked like a hotel pillow.

So he could tell even from this distance that the batter who came up next had a fucked-up face. A small guy, rail thin, but definitely something on his face, red welts or scar tissue against toffee brown skin. He was all energy in the box, bouncing on his feet and his haunches, a whippet standing over the plate, trying to keep from busting out of his skin. And when he connected with the ball after two strikes, Ruth knew this nigra was going to fly, but even he wasn't prepared for how fast.

The ball hadn't finished arcing toward the right fielder's feet (Ruth knew he'd miss it before he did) and the whippet was already rounding first. When the ball hit the grass, the right fielder bare-handed it and didn't so much as stutter-step before he planted and let her loose, that ball leaving his hand like he'd caught it sleeping with his daughter, and no time to blink before it hit the second baseman's glove. But the whippet, he was already standing on second. Standing tall.

21

Never slid, never dove. Waltzed on in there like he was picking up the morning paper, stood looking back out to center field until Ruth realized he was looking at him. So Ruth tipped his hat, and the boy flashed him a grim, cocky smile.

Ruth decided to keep his eyes on this boy, knowing whatever he was going to do next, it would have the feel of something special.

The man on second had played for the Wrightville Mudhawks. His name was Luther Laurence, and he'd been cut loose from the Mudhawks in June, after he got into a fight with Jefferson Reese, the team manager and first baseman, big-toothed, smiley Tom who acted like a perfumed poodle around white folks and badmouthed his own people in the house where he worked just outside Columbus. Luther heard the specifics one night from this girl he ran around with, some fine young woman named Lila, who worked in that same house with Jefferson Reese. Lila told him Reese was pouring soup from the tureen in the dining room one night, the white folks going on and on about uppity niggers in Chicago, the way they walked the streets so bold, didn't even drop their eyes when a white woman passed. Old Reese, he piped in with, "Lawse, it's a terrible shame. Yes, suh, the Chicago colored ain't no more'n a chimpanzee swinging from the vine. No time for churching. Want to drink hisself outta Friday, poker hisself out of Saturday, and love some other man's woman straight through Sunday."

"He said that?" Luther asked Lila in the bathtub of the Dixon Hotel, Coloreds Only. He got some froth going in the water, swept the suds up over Lila's small hard breasts, loving the look of them bubbles on her flesh, flesh the color of unpolished gold.

"Said a lot worse," Lila told him. "Don't you go 'fronting that man now, though, baby. He a cruel one."

When Luther confronted him anyway in the dugout at Inkwell Field, Reese stopped smiling right quick and got this

22

look in his eyes—a hard, ancient look that spoke of not being far enough removed from sun-torture in the fields—that made Luther think, *Uh oh*, but by then, Reese was on him, his fists like the butt end of a bat on Luther's face. Luther tried to give as good as he got, but Jefferson Reese, more than twice his age and ten years a house nigger, had some fury in him gone so deep that when it finally let go it came out all the hotter and harder for having been kept down in the darkness for so long. He beat Luther into the ground, beat him fast and mean, beat him till the blood, mixed with the dirt and chalk and dust of the field, came off him in strings.

His friend Aeneus James said to Luther while he was in the charity ward of St. John's, "Shit, boy, fast as you are, whyn't you just run when you see that crazy old man get that look in his eye?"

Luther'd had a long summer to consider that question, and he still didn't have an answer. Fast as he was, and he'd never met a man faster, he wondered if he was just heartsick of running.

But now, watching the fat man who reminded him of Babe Ruth watching him from the trees, Luther found himself thinking, *You think you seen some running, white man? You ain't. 'Bout to see some now, though. Tell your grandkids.*

And he took off from second just as Sticky Joe Beam came out of that octopus throwing motion of his, had a hair of a moment to see the white man's eyes bulge out big as his belly, and Luther's feet moved so fast the ground ran under him more than he ran over it. He could actually feel it moving like a river in early spring, and he pictured Tyrell Hawke standing at third, twitching because he'd laid out all night drinking, and Luther was counting on that because he wasn't just settling for third today, no sir, thinking *that's right, you best believe baseball is a game of speed and I'm the speediest son of a bitch any ya'll ever see*, and when he raised his head, the first thing he saw was Tyrell's glove right beside his ear. The next thing he saw, just to his left, was the ball, a shooting star gone sideways and pouring smoke. Luther shouted "Boo!" and it came out sharp and high and, yep, Tyrell's glove jerked up three inches. Luther ducked, and that ball sizzled under Tyrell's glove and kissed the hairs on the back of Luther's neck, hot as the razor in Moby's Barbershop on Meridian Avenue, and he hit the third base bag with the tiptoes of his right foot and came barreling up the line, the ground shooting so fast under his feet he felt like he might just run out of it, go off the edge of a cliff, right off the edge of the world maybe. He could hear the catcher, Ransom Boynton, shouting for the ball, shouting, "Hea' now! Hea' now!" He looked up, saw Ransom a few yards ahead, saw that ball coming in his eyes, in the tightening of his kneecaps, and Luther took a gulp of air the size of an ice block and turned his calves into springs and his feet into pistol hammers. He hit Ransom so hard he barely felt him, just went right over him and saw the ball slap into the wooden fence behind home at the exact moment his foot hit the plate, the two sounds—one hard and clean, the other scuffed and dusty—wrapping around each other. And he thought: Faster than any of y'all even *dream* of being.

He came to a stop against the chests of his teammates. In their pawing and hooting, he turned around to see the look on the fat white man's face, but he wasn't at the tree line anymore. No, he was almost at second base, running across the field *toward* Luther, little baby's face all jiggly and smiling and his eyes spinning in their sockets like he'd just turned five and someone had told him he was getting a pony and he couldn't do nothing to control his body, had to just shake and jump and run for the happiness of it.

And Luther got a real look at that face and thought: No.

But then Ransom Boynton stepped up beside him and said it out loud:

"Ya'll ain't gonna believe this, but that there is Babe Ruth running toward us like a fat fucking freight train."

*   *   *

24

C an I play?"
    No one could believe he'd said it. This was after he'd
run up to Luther and lifted him off the ground, held him over
his face, and said, "Boy, I seen some running in my day, but I
ain't never—and I mean ever—seen anyone run like you."
And then he was hugging Luther and clapping him on the
back and saying, "Me oh my, what a sight!"

And it was after they'd confirmed that he was, really, Babe
Ruth. He was surprised so many of them had even heard of
him. But Sticky Joe had seen him once in Chicago, and
Ransom had caught him in Cleveland twice, seen him pitch
and play left. The rest of them had read about him in the
sports pages and *Baseball Magazine*, and Ruth's eyebrows went
up at that, like he couldn't quite believe there were darkies on
the planet who knew how to read.

Ruth said, "So you'll be wanting some autographs?"

No one appeared too interested in that, and Ruth grew long
in the mouth as everyone found reasons to look at their
shoes, study the sky.

Luther thought about telling Ruth that standing here before
him were some pretty great players themselves. Some bona
fide legends. That man with the octopus arm? He went 32–2
last year for the Millersport King Horns of the Ohio Mill
Workers League—32–2 with a 1.78 ERA. Touch that. And
Andy Hughes, playing shortstop for the opposing team of the
hour, this being a scratch game, man was hitting .390 for the
Downtown Sugar Shacks of Grandview Heights. And, besides,
only white folks liked autographs. What the hell was an auto-
graph anyway, but some man's chicken scrawl on a scrap of
paper?

Luther opened his mouth to explain this, but got one good
look at Ruth's face and saw it wouldn't make no difference:
man was a child. A hippo size, jiggling child with thighs so
big you'd expect them to sprout branches, but a child all the
same. He had the widest eyes Luther'd ever seen. Luther
would remember that for years after, as he saw them change

over time in the papers, saw those eyes grow smaller and darker every time he saw a new picture. But then, in the fields of Ohio, Ruth had the eyes of a little fat boy in the school yard, full of hope and fear and desperation.

"Can I play?" He held out his St. Bernard paws. "With you-all?"

That just about busted everyone up, men bending over from the snickering, but Luther kept his face still. "Well . . ." He looked around at the rest of the men, then back at Ruth, taking his time. "Depends," he said. "You know much about the game, suh?"

That put Reggie Polk on the *ground*. Bunch of other players cackled, swiped arms. Ruth, though, he surprised Luther. Those wide eyes went small and clear as the sky, and Luther got it right away: With a bat in his hand, he was as old as any of them.

Ruth popped an unlit cigar in his mouth and loosened his tie. "Picked up a thing or two in my travels, Mr. . . . ?"

"Laurence, suh. Luther Laurence." Luther still giving him that stone face.

Ruth put an arm around him. Arm the size of Luther's bed. "What position you play, Luther?"

"Center field, suh."

"Well, boy, you don't have to worry about nothing then but tilting your head."

"Tilting my head, suh?"

"And watching my ball fly right over it."

Luther couldn't help himself; the grin blew across his face.

"And stop calling me 'suh,' would you, Luther? We're baseball players here."

Oh, it was something the first time Sticky Joe whiffed him! Three strikes, all right down the pipe like thread following the needle, the fat man never once touching cowhide.

He laughed after the last one, pointed his bat at Sticky Joe

26

and gave him a big nod. "But I'm learning you, boy. Learning you like I'm awake in school."

No one wanted to let him pitch, so he subbed for a player each inning in the rest of the field. Nobody minded sitting for an inning. Babe Ruth—Lord's sake. Might not want no sad little signature, but the stories would buy some drinks for a long time.

One inning he played left and Luther was over in center and Reggie Polk, who was pitching for their side, was taking his sweet time between pitches like he was apt to do, and Ruth said, "So what do you do, Luther, when you're not playing ball?"

Luther told him a bit about his job in a munitions factory outside of Columbus, how war was a terrible thing but it sure could help a man's pocket, and Ruth said, "That's the truth," though it sounded to Luther like he said it just to say it, not because he really understood, and then he asked Luther what had happened to his face.

"Cactus, Mr. Ruth."

They heard the crack of the bat and Ruth chased down a soft-fade fly ball, moving like a ballerina on his stumpy little tiptoes and throwing the ball back into second.

"Lotta cactus in Ohio? Hadn't heard that."

Luther smiled. "Actually, Mr. Ruth sir, they be called 'cacti' when you talking 'bout more'n one. And, sho', there's great fields of them all over the state. Bushels and bushels of cacti."

"And you, what, fell into one of these fields?"

"Yes, suh. Fell hard, too."

"Looks like you fell from an airplane."

Luther shook his head real slow. "Zeppelin, Mr. Ruth."

They both had a long soft laugh over that, Luther still chuckling when he raised his glove and stole Rube Gray's shot right out of the sky.

The next inning, some white men straggled out of the trees, and they recognized a few of them right off—Stuffy McInnis, no lie; Everett Scott, Lord; and then a couple of Cubs, dear

Jesus—Flack, Mann, a third guy no one knew by face, could have played for either team. They worked their way along right field, and pretty soon they were standing behind the rickety old bench along the first base line, wearing suits and ties and hats in the heat, smoking cigars, occasionally shouting to someone named "Gidge," confusing the hell out of Luther until he realized that's what they called Ruth. Next time Luther looked, he saw they'd been joined by three more—Whiteman of the Sox and Hollocher, the Cubs shortstop, and some skinny boy with a red face and a chin that stuck out like an extra flap of skin who no one recognized, and Luther didn't like that number—eight of them plus Ruth comprising a full team.

For an inning or so everything was fine and the white men kept mostly to themselves, couple of them making ape sounds and a few more calling out, "Don't miss that ball, tar baby. Coming in *hot*," or "Should've got under it more, jigaboo," but shit, Luther'd heard worse, a lot worse. He just didn't like how every time he looked over, the eight of them seemed to have moved an inch or two closer to the first base line, and pretty soon it was hard to run that way, beat out a throw with white men so close on your right you could smell their cologne.

And then between innings, one of them said it: "Why don't you let one of us have a try?"

Luther noticed Ruth looking like he was trying to find a hole to climb into.

"Whadaya say, Gidge? Think your new friends would mind if one of us played a few? Keep hearing how good these nigras are supposed to be. Run faster'n butter on the porch in July is the rumor."

The man held out his hands to Babe. He was one of the few no one recognized, must have been a bench warmer. Big hands, though, a flattened nose and axe-head shoulders, the man all hard boxy angles. Had eyes Luther'd seen before in the white poor—spent his whole life eating rage in place of

28

food. Developed a taste for it he wouldn't lose no matter how regular he ate for the rest of his life.

He smiled at Luther like he knew what he was thinking. "What you say, boy? Maybe let one of us fellas take a cut or two?"

Rube Gray volunteered to sit a spell and the white men elected Stuffy McInnis as their latest trade to the Southern Ohio Nigra League, haw-hawing in that donkey laugh big white men seemed to share, but Luther had to admit it was fine with him: Stuffy McInnis could *play*, boy. Luther'd been reading up on him since he'd broken in back in '09 with Philadelphia.

After the inning's final out, though, Luther came jogging in from center to find the other white men all lined up by home plate, the lead guy, Chicago's Flack, resting a bat on his shoulder.

Babe tried, at least for a moment, Luther'd give him that. He said, "Come on now, fellas, we were having us a game."

Flack gave him a big, bright smile. "Gonna have us a better game now, Ruth. See how these boys do against the best in the American and National Leagues."

"Oh, you mean, the white leagues?" Sticky Joe Beam said. "That what ya'll talking about?"

They all looked over at him.

"What'd you say, boy?"

Sticky Joe Beam was forty-two years old and looked like a slice of burnt bacon. He pursed his lips, looked down at the dirt, and then up at the line of white men in such a way that Luther figured there'd be a fight coming.

"Said let's see what you got." He stared at them. "Uh, suhs."

Luther looked over at Ruth, met his eyes, and the big baby-faced fat boy gave him a shaky smile. Luther remembered a line from the Bible his grandmother used to repeat a lot when he was growing up, about how the heart be willing but the flesh be weak.

That you, Babe? he wanted to ask. That you?

* * *

29

Babe started drinking as soon as the black guys picked their nine. He didn't know what was wrong—it was just a ball game—but he still felt sad and filled with shame. It didn't make no sense. It was just a game. Some summer fun to wait out the train repair. Nothing more. And yet, the sadness and the shame wouldn't leave, so he unscrewed his flask cap and took a healthy swig.

He begged off pitching, said his elbow was still sore from game one. Said he had a World Series record to think about, the scoreless-innings-pitched record, and he wasn't risking that for some bush league pickup game in the sticks.

So Ebby Wilson pitched. Ebby was a mean, flap-jawed boy from the Ozarks, who'd been playing for Boston since July. He smiled when they put the ball in his hands. "That's right, boys. Be done with these niggers 'fore you know it. 'Fore they know it, too." And he laughed even though no one laughed with him.

Ebby started it off throwing high heat and burned right through the top of their order in no time. Then Sticky Joe came to the mound, and that nigra had no other gear but full on, and when he uncorked that loping, tentacle-swing delivery, god knew what was coming at you. He threw fastballs that went invisible; screwballs that had eyes—soon as they saw a bat, they ducked, winking at you; curveballs that could circle a tire; breaking balls that exploded four inches before the plate. He whiffed Mann. He whiffed Scott. And he got McInnis out to end the inning on a pop-up to second.

It was a pitchers' duel there for a few innings, not much hit past the mound, and Ruth starting to yawn out in left, taking longer sips from the flask. Still, the coloreds scored a run in the second and another in the third, Luther Laurence turning a run from first to second into a run from first to home, tear-assing so fast across the infield it took Hollocher by surprise and he muffed the relay from center and by the time he stopped bobbling the ball, Luther Laurence was crossing the plate.

What had started as a joke game went from surprised respect ("Ain't ever seen *anyone* put mustard on the ball like that ol' nigra. Even you, Gidge. Hell, even Walter Johnson. Man's a marvel") to nervous joking ("Think we'll score a run before we got to get back to, you know, the World Fucking Series?") to anger ("Niggers own this field. That's what it is. Like to see them play Wrigley. Like to see them play Fenway. Shit").

The coloreds could bunt—good Lord could they bunt; ball would land six inches from the plate and stop moving like it'd been shot. And they could run. They could steal bases like it was as simple as deciding you liked standing on second more than first. And they could hit singles. By the bottom of the fifth, it looked like they could hit singles all day long, just step up and poke another one out of the infield, but then Whiteman came over to the mound from first and had a chat with Ebby Wilson, and from that point Ebby stopped trying to play cute or clever, just unloaded heat like he didn't care if it put his arm in the sling through winter.

Top of the sixth, the coloreds ahead 6–3, Stuffy McInnis took a first-pitch fastball from Sticky Joe Beam and hit it so far over the trees that Luther Laurence didn't even bother looking for it. They got another ball from the canvas bag beside the bench, and Whiteman took that one long, got into second standing up, and then Flack took two strikes and fought off six more for fouls, and then pooched a single to shallow left and it was 6–4, men on first and third, no one out.

Babe could feel it as he wiped his bat down with a rag. He could feel all their bloodstreams as he stepped to the plate and horse-pawed the dirt with his shoe. This moment, this sun, this sky, this wood and leather and limbs and fingers and agony of waiting to see what would *happen* was beautiful. More beautiful than women or words or even laughter.

Sticky Joe brushed him back. Threw a hard curve that came in high and inside and would have taken Babe's teeth on a journey through Southern Ohio if he hadn't snapped his head back from it. He leveled the bat at Sticky Joe, looked down it like he was looking down a rifle. He saw the glee in the old man's dark eyes, and he smiled and the old man smiled back, and they both nodded and Ruth wanted to kiss the old man's bumpy forehead.

"You all agree that's a ball?" Babe shouted, and he could see even Luther laughing, way out in center field.

God, it felt good. But, oh, hey, here it comes, a shotgun blast of a breaking ball and Ruth caught the seam with his eye, saw that red line dive and started swinging low, way lower than where it was, but knowing where it was going to be, and sumbitch, if he didn't connect with it, tore that fucking ball out of space, out of time, saw that ball climb the sky like it had hands and knees. Ruth started running down the line and saw Flack take off from first, and that was when he felt certain that he hadn't gotten all of it. It wasn't pure. He yelled, "Hold!" but Flack was running. Whiteman was a few steps off third, but staying in place, arms out in either direction as Luther drifted back toward the tree line, and Ruth saw the ball appear from the same sky into which it had vanished and drop straight down past the trees into Luther's glove.

Flack had already started back from second, and he was fast, and the moment Luther fired that ball toward first, Whiteman tagged up from third. And Flack, yes, Flack was very fast, but Luther had some sort of cannon in that skinny body of his and that ball shrieked over the green field and Flack trampled the ground like a stagecoach and then went airborne as the ball slapped into Aeneus James's glove, and Aeneus, the big guy Ruth had first encountered playing center field when he'd come out of the trees, swept his long arm down as Flack slid on his chest toward first and the tag hit him high on the shoulder and then his hand touched the bag.

Aeneus lowered his free hand to Flack, but Flack ignored it and stood up.

Aeneus tossed the ball back to Sticky Joe.

Flack dusted off his pants and stood on the first base bag. He placed his hands on his knees and planted his right foot toward second.

Sticky Joe stared over at him from the mound.

Aeneus James said, "What you doing, suh?"

Flack said, "What's that?" his voice a little too bright.

Aeneus James said, "Just wondering why you still here, suh."

Flack said, "It's where a man stands when he's on first, boy."

Aeneus James looked exhausted suddenly, as if he'd just come home from a fourteen-hour workday to discover somebody'd stolen his couch.

Ruth thought: Oh, Jesus, no.

"You was out, suh."

"Talking about, boy? I was safe."

"Man was safe, nigger." This from Ebby Wilson, standing beside Ruth all of a sudden. "Could see it from a mile off."

Now some colored guys came over, asking what the holdup was.

Aeneus said, "Man says he was safe."

"*What?*" Cameron Morgan ambled over from second. "You've got to be funning."

"Watch your tone, boy."

"I watch whatever I want."

"That so?"

"I do believe."

"Man was safe. With change."

"That man was out," Sticky Joe said softly. "No disrespect to you, Mr. Flack, but you were out, sir."

Flack placed his hands behind his back and approached Sticky Joe. He cocked his head at the smaller man. He took a sniff of the air for some reason.

"You think I'm standing on first because I got confused? Huh?"

33

"No, sir, I don't."

"What do you think, then, boy?"

"Think you was out, sir."

Everybody was at first base now—the nine guys from each team and the nine coloreds who'd taken seats after the new game had been drawn up.

Ruth heard "out." He heard "safe." Over and over. He heard "boy" and "nigger" and "nigra" and "field hand." And then he heard someone call his name.

He looked over, saw Stuffy McInnis looking at him and pointing at the bag. "Gidge, you were closest. Flack says he's safe. Ebby had a good eye on it, and *he* says he's safe. You tell us, Babe. Safe or out?"

Babe had never seen so many angry colored faces this close. Eighteen of them. Big flat noses, lead-pipe muscles in their arms and legs, teardrops of sweat in their tight hair. He'd liked everything he'd seen in these ones, but he still didn't like how they looked at you like they knew something about you that they weren't going to tell. How those eyes sized you up fast and then went all droopy and faraway.

Six years back, major league baseball had had its first strike. The Detroit Tigers refused to play until Ban Johnson lifted a suspension on Ty Cobb for beating a fan in the stands. The fan was a cripple, had stumps for arms, no hands to defend himself, but Cobb had beaten him long after he was on the ground, applying his cleats to the poor bastard's face and ribs. Still, Cobb's teammates took his side and went on strike in support of a guy none of them even liked. Hell, everyone hated Cobb, but that wasn't the point. The point was that the fan had called Cobb a "half-nigger," and there wasn't much worse you could call a white man except maybe "nigger lover" or just plain "nigger."

Ruth had still been in reform school when he heard about it, but he understood the position of the other Tigers, no problem. You could jaw with a colored, even laugh and joke with one, maybe tip the ones you laughed with most a little

34

something extra around Christmas. But this was still a white man's society, a place built on concepts of family and an honest day's work. (And what *were* these coloreds doing out in some field in the middle of a workday, playing a game when their loved ones were probably home going hungry?) When all was said and done, it was always best to stick with your own kind, the people you had to live with and eat with and work with for the rest of your life.

Ruth kept his gaze on the bag. He didn't want to know where Luther was, risk looking up into that crowd of black faces and accidentally catching his eye.

"He was safe," Ruth said.

The coloreds went nuts. They shouted and pointed at the bag and screamed, "Bull*shit*!" and that went on for some time, and then, as if they'd all heard a dog whistle none of the white men could hear, they stopped. Their bodies slackened, their shoulders lowered, they stared right through Ruth, as if they could see out the back of his head and Sticky Joe Beam said, "Awright, awright. That's how we're playing, then that's how we're playing."

"That's how we're playing," McInnis said.

"Yes, suh," Sticky Joe said. "That's clear now."

And they all walked back and took their positions.

Babe sat on the bench and drank and felt soiled and found himself wanting to twist Ebby Wilson's head off his neck, throw it on a stack with Flack's beside it. Didn't make no sense—he'd done the right thing by his team—but he felt it all the same.

The more he drank, the worse he felt, and by the eighth inning, he considered what would happen if he used his next at bat to tank. He'd switched places with Whiteman by this point, was playing first. Luther Laurence waited on deck as Tyrell Hawke stood in the box, and Luther looked across at him like he was just another white man now, giving him those nothing-eyes you saw in porters and shine boys and bell boys, and Babe felt a shriveling inside of himself.

35

Even with two more disputed tags (and a child could guess who won the disputes) and a long foul ball the major leaguers deemed a home run, they were still down to the coloreds by a score of 9–6 in the bottom of the ninth when the pride of the National and American Leagues started playing like the pride of the National and American Leagues.

Hollocher ripped one down the first base line. Then Scott punched one over the third baseman's head. Flack went down swinging. But McInnis tore one into shallow right, and the bases were loaded, one out, George Whiteman coming to the plate, Ruth on deck. The infield was playing double-play depth, and Sticky Joe Beam wasn't throwing nothing George could go long on, and Babe found himself praying for one thing he'd never prayed for in his life: a double-play so he wouldn't have to bat.

Whiteman feasted on a sinker that hung too long, and the ball roared off into space and then hooked a right turn somewhere just past the infield, hooked hard and fast and foul. Obviously foul. Then Sticky Joe Beam struck him out on two of the most vicious fastballs Ruth had seen yet.

Babe stepped up to the plate. He added up how many of their six runs had come from clean baseball and he came up with three. Three. These coloreds who nobody knew, out in some raggedy field in Shitheel, Ohio, had held some of the best players in the known world to three measly runs. Hell, Ruth himself was hitting one-for-three. And he'd been trying. And it wasn't just Beam's pitching. No. The expression was: Hit 'em where they ain't. But these colored boys were everywhere. You thought there was a gap, the gap vanished. You hit something no mortal man could chase down, and one of these boys had it in his glove and wasn't even winded.

If they hadn't cheated, this would be one of the great moments of Ruth's life—facing off against some of the best players he'd ever come across with the game in his hands, bottom of the ninth, two out, three on. One swing, and he could win it all.

And he *could* win it all. He'd been studying Sticky Joe for a while now, and the man was tired, and Ruth had seen all his pitches. If they hadn't cheated, the air Ruth sucked through his nostrils right now would be pure cocaine.

Sticky Joe's first pitch came in too loose and too fat and Ruth had to time his swing just right to miss it. He missed it big, trying to sell it, and even Sticky Joe looked surprised. The next one was tighter, had some corkscrew in it, and Ruth fouled it back. The one after that was in the dirt, and the one that followed was up by his chin.

Sticky Joe took the ball back and stepped off the mound for a moment and Ruth could feel all the eyes on him. He could see the trees behind Luther Laurence and he could see Hollocher and Scott and McInnis on their bases, and he thought how pretty it would have been if it had been clean, if the next pitch was one he could, in good conscience, send toward God in heaven. And maybe . . .

He held up a hand and stepped out of the box.

It was just a game, wasn't it? That's what he'd told himself when he decided to tank. Just a game. Who cared if he lost one silly ball game?

But the reverse was true as well. Who cared if he won? Would it matter tomorrow? Of course not. It wouldn't affect anyone's *life*. Now, *right* now, it was a case of two down, three on, bottom of the ninth.

If he serves me a meatball, Ruth decided as he stepped back to the box, I'm going to eat. How can I resist? Those men on their bases, this bat in my hand, the smell of dirt and grass and sun.

It's a ball. It's a bat. It's nine men. It's a moment. Not forever. Just a moment.

And here was that ball, coming in slower than it should have, and Ruth could see it in the old Negro's face. He knew it as soon as it left his hand: it was fat.

Babe thought about whiffing, sliding over it, doing the fair thing.

The train whistle blew then, blew loud and shrill and up through the sky, and Ruth thought, That's a sign, and he planted his foot and swung his bat and heard the catcher say, "Shit," and then—that *sound*, that gorgeous sound of wood against cowhide and that ball disappeared into the sky.

Ruth trotted a few yards down the line and stopped because he knew he'd gotten under it.

He looked out and saw Luther Laurence looking at him, just for a split second, and he felt what Luther knew: that he'd tried to hit a home run, a grand slam. That he'd tried to take this game, unfairly played, away from those who'd played it clean.

Luther's eyes left Ruth's face, slid off it in such a way that Ruth knew he'd never feel them again. And Luther looked up as he faded into position under the ball. He set his feet. He raised his glove over his head. And that was it, that was the ball game, because Luther was right under it.

But Luther walked away.

Luther lowered his glove and started walking toward the infield and so did the right fielder and so did the left fielder and that ball plopped to the grass behind them all and they didn't even turn to look at it, just kept walking, and Hollocher crossed home, but there was no catcher there waiting. The catcher was walking toward the bench along third base and so was the third baseman.

Scott reached home, but McInnis stopped running at third, just stood there, looking at the coloreds ambling toward their bench like it was the bottom of the second instead of the bottom of the ninth. They congregated there and stuffed their bats and gloves into two separate canvas bags, acting like the white men weren't even there. Ruth wanted to cross the field to Luther, to say something, but Luther never turned around. Then they were all walking toward the dirt road behind the field, and he lost Luther in the sea of coloreds, couldn't tell if he was the guy up front or on the left and Luther never looked back.

The whistle blew again, and none of the white men had so much as moved, and even though the coloreds had seemed to walk slow, they were almost all off the field.

Except Sticky Joe Beam. He came over and picked up the bat Babe had used. He rested it on his shoulder and looked into Babe's face.

Babe held out his hand. "Great game, Mr. Beam."

Sticky Joe Beam gave no indication he saw Babe's hand.

He said, "Believe that's your train, suh," and walked off the field.

B abe went back onto the train. He had a drink at the bar. The train left Ohio and hurtled through Pennsylvania. Ruth sat by himself and drank and looked out at Pennsylvania in all its scrabbled hills and dust. He thought of his father who'd died two weeks ago in Baltimore during a fight with his second wife's brother, Benjie Sipes. Babe's father got in two punches and Sipes only got in one, but it was that one that counted because his father's head hit the curb and he died at University Hospital a few hours later.

The papers made a big deal of it for a couple of days. They asked for his opinion, for his feelings. Babe said he was sorry the man was dead. It was a sad thing.

His father had dumped him in reform school when he was eight. Said he needed to learn some manners. Said he was tired of trying to teach him how to mind his mother and him. Said some time at Saint Mary's would do him good. Said he had a saloon to run. He'd be back to pick him up when he learned to mind.

His mother died while he was in there.

It was a sad thing, he'd told the papers. A sad thing.

He kept waiting to feel something. He'd been waiting for two weeks.

In general, the only time he felt anything, outside of the self-pity he felt when very drunk, was when he hit a ball. Not when he pitched it. Not when he caught it. Only when he hit

39

it. When the wood connected with the cowhide and he swiveled his hips and pivoted his shoulders and the muscles in his thighs and calves tightened and he felt the surge of his body as it finished the swing of the black bat and the white ball soared faster and higher than anything on the planet. That's why he'd changed his mind and taken the swing this afternoon, because he'd *had to*. It was too fat, too pure, just sitting there. That's why he'd done it. That's all there was to that story. That's all there was.

He got in a poker game with McInnis and Jones and Mann and Hollocher, but everyone kept talking about the strike and the war (no one mentioned the game; it was as if they'd all agreed it never happened), so he took a long, long nap and when he got up, they were almost through New York and he had a few more drinks to cut the sludge in his brain, and he took Harry Hooper's hat off his head while he was sleeping and put his fist through the top of it and then placed it back on Harry Hooper's head and someone laughed and someone else said, "Gidge, don't you respect nothing?" So he took another hat, this one off Stu Springer, head of the Cubs' sales department, and he punched a hole in that one and soon half the car was flinging hats at him and egging him on and he climbed up on top of the seats and crawled from one to the next making "hoo hoo hoo" sounds like an ape and feeling a sudden, unexplainable pride that welled up through his legs and arms like stalks of wheat gone mad with the growing, and he shouted, "I am the ape man! I am Babe Fucking Ruth. I will eat you!"

Some people tried to pull him down, some people tried to calm him, but he jumped off the seat backs and did a jig in the aisle and he grabbed some more hats and he flung some and punched holes in a few more and people were clapping, people were cheering and whistling. He slapped his hands together like a wop's monkey and he scratched his ass and went "hoo hoo hoo," and they loved it, they loved it.

Then he ran out of hats. He looked back down the aisle.

They covered the floor. They hung from the luggage racks. Pieces of straw stuck to a few windows. Ruth could feel the litter of them in his spine, right at the base of his brain. He felt addled and elated and ready to take on the ties. The suits. The luggage.

Ebby Wilson put his hand on his chest. Ruth wasn't even sure where he'd come from. He saw Stuffy standing up in his seat, raising a glass of something to him, shouting and smiling, and Ruth waved.

Ebby Wilson said, "Make me a new one."

Ruth looked down at him. "What?"

Ebby spread his hands, reasonable. "Make me a new hat. You broke 'em up, now make me another one."

Someone whistled.

Ruth smoothed the shoulders of Wilson's suit jacket. "I'll buy you a drink."

"Don't want a drink. I want my hat."

Ruth was about to say "Fuck your hat," when Ebby Wilson pushed him. It wasn't much of a push, but the train went into a turn at the same time, and Ruth felt it buckle, and he smiled at Wilson, and then decided to punch him instead of insult him. He threw the punch, saw it coming in Ebby Wilson's eyes, Wilson not so smug anymore, not so concerned with his hat, but the train buckled again, and the train shimmied and Ruth felt the punch go wide, felt his whole body lurch to the right, felt a voice in his heart say, "This is not you, Gidge. This is not you."

His fist hit the window instead. He felt it in his elbow, felt it in his shoulder and the side of his neck and the hollow just below his ear. He felt the sway of his belly as a public spectacle and he felt fat and orphaned again. He dropped into the empty seat and sucked air through his teeth and cradled his hand.

Luther Laurence and Sticky Joe and Aeneus James were probably sitting on a porch somewhere now, feeling the night heat, passing a jar. Maybe they were talking about him, about

41

the look on his face when he saw Luther walking away from that ball as it fell through the air. Maybe they were laughing, replaying a hit, a pitch, a run.

And he was out here, in the world.

I slept through New York, Babe thought as they brought a bucket of ice and placed his hand in it. And then he remembered this train didn't run past Manhattan, only Albany, but he still felt a loss. He'd seen it a hundred times, but he loved to look at it, the lights, the dark rivers that circled it like carpet, the limestone spires so white against the night.

He pulled his hand from the ice and looked at it. His pitching hand. It was red and swelling up and he couldn't make a fist.

"Gidge," someone called from the back of the car, "what you got against hats?"

Babe didn't answer. He looked out the window, at the flat scrub of Springfield, Massachusetts. He placed his forehead against the window to cool it and saw his reflection and the reflection of the land, the two of them intertwined.

He raised his swollen hand to the glass and the land moved through it, too, and he imagined it healing the aching knuckles and he hoped he hadn't broken it. Over something as silly as hats.

He imagined finding Luther on some dusty street in some dusty town and buying him a drink and apologizing and Luther would say, Don't you worry about it none, Mr. Ruth, suh, and tell him another tale about Ohio cacti.

But then Ruth pictured those eyes of Luther's, giving nothing away but a sense that he could see inside you and he didn't approve of what was there, and Ruth thought, Fuck you, boy, and your approval. I don't need it. Hear me?

I don't need it.

He was just getting started. He was ready to bust wide open. He could feel it. Big things. Big things were coming. From him. From everywhere. That was the feeling he got lately, as if the whole world had been held in a stable, him included.

But soon, soon it was going to bust out all over the place.

He kept his head against the window and closed his eyes, and he felt the countryside moving through his face even as he began to snore.

The MILK RUN

CHAPTER *one*

On a wet summer night, Danny Coughlin, a Boston police officer, fought a four-round bout against another cop, Johnny Green, at Mechanics Hall just outside Copley Square. Coughlin–Green was the final fight on a fifteen-bout, all-police card that included flyweights, welterweights, cruiserweights, and heavyweights. Danny Coughlin, at six two, 220, was a heavyweight. A suspect left hook and foot speed that was a few steps shy of blazing kept him from fighting professionally, but his butcher-knife left jab combined with the airmail-your-jaw-to-Georgia explosion of his right cross dwarfed the abilities of just about any other semi-pro on the East Coast.

The all-day pugilism display was titled Boxing & Badges: Haymakers for Hope. Proceeds were split fifty-fifty between the St. Thomas Asylum for Crippled Orphans and the policemen's own fraternal organization, the Boston Social Club, which used the donations to bolster a health fund for injured coppers and to defray costs for uniforms and equipment, costs the department refused to pay. While flyers advertising the event were pasted to poles and hung from storefronts in good neighborhoods and thereby elicited donations from people who never intended to actually attend the event, the flyers also saturated the worst of the Boston slums, where one was most likely to find the core of the criminal element—the plug-uglies, the bullyboys, the knuckle-dusters, and, of course, the Gusties, the city's most powerful and fuck-out-of-their-minds street gang, who headquartered in South Boston but spread their tentacles throughout the city at large.

The logic was simple:

The only thing criminals loved almost as much as beating the shit out of coppers was watching coppers beat the shit out of each other.

Coppers beat the shit out of each other at Mechanics Hall during Boxing & Badges: Haymakers for Hope.

Ergo: criminals would gather at Mechanics Hall to watch them do so.

Danny Coughlin's godfather, Lieutenant Eddie McKenna, had decided to exploit this theory to the fullest for benefit of the BPD in general and the Special Squads Division he lorded over in particular. The men in Eddie McKenna's squad had spent the day mingling with the crowd, closing outstanding warrant after outstanding warrant with a surprisingly bloodless efficiency. They waited for a target to leave the main hall, usually to relieve himself, before they hit him over the head with a pocket billy and hauled him off to one of the paddy wagons that waited in the alley. By the time Danny stepped into the ring, most of the mugs with outstanding warrants had been scooped up or had slipped out the back, but a few—hopeless and dumb to the last—still milled about in the smoke-laden room on a floor sticky with spilt beer.

Danny's corner man was Steve Coyle. Steve was also his patrol partner at the Oh-One Station House in the North End. They walked a beat from one end of Hanover Street to the other, from Constitution Wharf to the Crawford House Hotel, and as long as they'd been doing it, Danny had boxed and Steve had been his corner and his cut man.

Danny, a survivor of the 1916 bombing of the Salutation Street Station House, had been held in high regard since his rookie year on the job. He was broad-shouldered, dark-haired and dark-eyed; more than once, women had been noted openly regarding him, and not just immigrant women or those who smoked in public. Steve, on the other hand, was squat and rotund like a church bell, with a great pink bulb of a face and a bow to his walk. Early in the year he'd joined a barbershop quartet in order to attract the fancy of the fairer sex, a decision that had served him in good stead this past spring, though prospects appeared to be dwindling as autumn neared.

Steve, it was said, talked so much he gave aspirin powder a headache. He'd lost his parents at a young age and joined the department without any connections or juice. After nine years on the job, he was still a flatfoot. Danny, on the other hand, was BPD royalty, the son of Captain Thomas Coughlin of Precinct 12 in South Boston and the godson of Special Squads Lieutenant Eddie McKenna. Danny had been on the job less than five years, but every cop in the city knew he wasn't long for uniform.

"Fuckin' taking this guy so long?" Steve scanned the back of the hall, hard to ignore in his attire of choice. He claimed he'd read somewhere that Scots were the most feared of all corner men in the fight game. And so, on fight nights, Steve came to the ring in a kilt. An authentic, red tartan kilt, red and black argyle socks, charcoal tweed jacket and matching five-button waistcoat, silver wedding tie, authentic gillie brogues on his feet, and a loose-crowned Balmoral on his head. The real surprise wasn't how at home he looked in the getup, it was that he wasn't even Scottish.

The audience, red-faced and drunk, had grown increasingly agitated the last hour or so, more and more actual fights breaking out between the scheduled ones. Danny leaned against the ropes and yawned. Mechanics Hall stank of sweat and booze. Smoke, thick and wet, curled around his arms. By all rights he should have been back in his dressing room, but he didn't really have a dressing room, just a bench in the maintenance hallway, where they'd sent Woods from the Oh-Nine looking for him five minutes ago, told him it was time to head to the ring.

So he stood there in an empty ring waiting for Johnny Green, the buzz of the crowd growing louder, buzzier. Eight rows back, one guy hit another guy with a folding chair. The hitter was so drunk he fell on top of his victim. A cop waded in, clearing a path with his domed helmet in one hand and his pocket billy in the other.

"Why don't you see what's taking Green?" Danny asked Steve.

"Why don't you climb under my kilt and pucker up?" Steve chin-gestured at the crowd. "Them's some restless sots. Like as not to tear my kilt or scuff my brogues."

"Heavens," Danny said. "And you without your shine box." He bounced his back off the ropes a few times. Stretched his neck, swiveled his hands on the wrists. "Here comes the fruit."

Steve said, "What?" and then stepped back when a brown head of lettuce arced over the ropes and splattered in the center of the ring.

"My mistake," Danny said. "Vegetable."

"No matter." Steve pointed. "The pretender appears. Just in time."

Danny looked down the center aisle and saw Johnny Green framed by a slanted white rectangle of doorway. The crowd sensed him and turned. He came down the aisle with his trainer, a guy Danny recognized as a desk sergeant at the One-Five, but whose name escaped him. About fifteen rows back, one of Eddie McKenna's Special Squads guys, a goon named Hamilton, grabbed a guy off his feet by his nostrils and dragged him up the aisle, the Special Squads cowboys apparently figuring all pretense could be chucked now that the final fight was about to begin.

Carl Mills, the BPD press spokesman, was calling to Steve from the other side of the ropes. Steve went to one knee to talk to him. Danny watched Johnny Green come, not liking something that floated in the guy's eyes, something unhooked. Johnny Green saw the crowd, he saw the ring, he

50

saw Danny—but he didn't. Instead, he looked at everything and looked *past* everything at the same time. It was a look Danny had seen before, mostly on the faces of three-bottles-to-the-wind drunks or rape victims.

Steve came up behind him and put a hand on his elbow. "Mills just told me this is his third fight in twenty-four hours."

"What? Whose?"

"Whose? Fucking Green's. He had one last night over at the Crown in Somerville, fought another this morning down at the rail yards in Brighton, and now here he is."

"How many rounds?"

"Mills heard he went thirteen last night for sure. And lost by KO."

"Then what's he doing here?"

"Rent," Steve said. "Two kids, a pregger wife."

"Fucking *rent*?"

The crowd was on its feet—the walls shuddering, the rafters shimmying. If the roof suddenly shot straight up into the sky, Danny doubted he'd feel surprise. Johnny Green entered the ring without a robe. He stood in his corner and banged his gloves together, his eyes staring up at something in his skull.

"He doesn't even know where he is," Danny said.

"Yeah, he does," Steve said, "and he's coming to the center."

"Steve, for Christ's sake."

"Don't 'Christ's sake' me. Get in there."

In the center of the ring, the referee, Detective Bilky Neal, a former boxer himself, placed a hand on each of their shoulders. "I want a clean fight. Barring that, I want it to look clean. Any questions?"

Danny said, "This guy can't see."

Green's eyes were on his shoes. "See enough to knock your head off."

"I take my gloves off, could you count my fingers?"

Green raised his head and spit on Danny's chest.

Danny stepped back. "What the fuck?" He wiped the

spittle off on his glove, wiped his glove on his shorts.

Shouts from the crowd. Beer bottles shattered against the base of the ring.

Green met his eyes, Green's sliding like something on a ship. "You want to quit, you quit. In public, though, so I still get the purse. Just grab the megaphone and quit."

"I'm not quitting."

"Then fight."

Bilky Neal gave them a smile that was nervous and furious at the same time. "They's getting restless out there, gents."

Danny pointed with a glove. "Look at him, Neal. Look at him."

"He looks fine to me."

"This is bullshit. I—"

Green's jab caught Danny's chin. Bilky Neal backed up, top speed, and waved his arm. The bell rang. The crowd roared. Green shot another jab into Danny's throat.

The crowd went crazy.

Danny stepped into the next punch and wrapped Green up. As Johnny delivered half a dozen rabbit punches into Danny's neck, Danny said, "Give it up. Okay?"

"Fuck you. I need . . . I . . ."

Danny felt warm liquid run down his back. He broke the clinch.

Johnny cocked his head as pink foam spilled over his lower lip and dribbled down his chin. He'd stood like that for five seconds, an eternity in the ring, arms down by his side. Danny noticed how childlike his expression had become, as if he'd just been hatched.

Then his eyes narrowed. His shoulders clenched. His hands rose. The doctor would later tell Danny (when he'd been stupid enough to ask) that a body under extreme duress often acts out of reflex. Had Danny known that at the time, maybe it would have made a difference, though he was hard-pressed to see how. A hand rising in a boxing ring rarely meant anything but what one naturally assumed. Green's left fist entered the space between their bodies, Danny's shoulder twitched, and his right cross blew up into the side of Johnny Green's head.

Instinct. Purely that.

There wasn't much left of Johnny to count out. He lay on the canvas kicking his heels, spitting white foam, and then gouts of pink. His head swayed left to right, left to right. His mouth kissed the air the way fish kissed the air.

Three fights in the same day? Danny thought. You fucking kidding?

Johnny lived. Johnny was fine. Never to fight again, of course, but after a month he could speak clearly. After two, he'd lost the limp and the left side of his mouth had thawed from its stricture.

Danny was another issue. It wasn't that he felt responsible—yes, sometimes he did, but most times he understood the stroke had already found Johnny Green before Danny threw his counterpunch. No the issue was one of balance—Danny, in two short years, had gone from the Salutation Street bombing to losing the only woman he'd ever loved, Nora O'Shea, an Irishwoman who worked for his parents as a domestic. Their affair had felt doomed from the start, and it had been Danny who had ended it, but since she'd left his life, he couldn't think of one good reason to live it. Now he'd almost killed Johnny Green in the ring at Mechanics Hall. All of this in twenty-one months. Twenty-one months that would have led anyone to question whether God held a grudge.

H is woman took off," Steve told Danny two months later. It was early September, and Danny and Steve walked the beat in the North End of Boston. The North End was predominantly Italian and poor, a place where rats grew to the size of butchers' forearms and infants often died before their first steps. English was rarely spoken; automobile sightings unlikely. Danny and Steve, however, were so fond of the neighborhood that they lived in the heart of it, on different floors of a Salem Street rooming house just blocks from the Oh-One Station House on Hanover.

"Whose woman?"

"Now don't blame yourself," Steve said. "Johnny Green's."

"Why'd she leave him?"

"Fall's coming. They got evicted."

"But he's back on the job," Danny said. "A desk, yeah, but back on the job."

Steve nodded. "Don't make up for the two months he was out, though."

Danny stopped, looked at his partner. "They didn't *pay* him? He was fighting in a department-sponsored smoker."

"You really want to know?"

"Yeah."

"Because the last couple months? A man brings up Johnny Green's name around you and you shut him down surer than a chastity belt."

"I want to know," Danny said.

Steve shrugged. "It was a Boston Social Club-sponsored smoker. So technically, he got hurt off the job. Thus . . ." He shrugged again. "No sick pay."

Danny said nothing. He tried to find solace in his surroundings. The North End had been his home until he was seven years old, before the Irish who'd laid its streets and the Jews who'd come after them had been displaced by Italians who populated it so densely that if a picture were taken of Napoli and another of Hanover Street, most would be hard-pressed to identify which had been taken in the United States. Danny had moved back when he was twenty, and planned never to leave.

Danny and Steve walked their beat in sharp air that smelled of chimney smoke and cooked lard. Old women waddled into the streets. Carts and horses made their way along the cobblestone. Coughs rattled from open windows. Babies squawked at so high a pitch Danny could imagine the red of

54

their faces. In most tenements, hens roamed the hallways, goats shit in the stairwells, and sows nestled in torn newspaper and a dull rage of flies. Add an entrenched distrust of all things non-Italian, including the English language, and you had a society no Americano was ever going to comprehend.

So it wasn't terribly surprising that the North End was the prime recruiting area for every major anarchist, Bolshevik, radical, and subversive organization on the Eastern Seaboard. Which made Danny love it all the more for some perverse reason. Say what you would about the people down here—and most did, loudly and profanely—but you sure couldn't question their passion. In accordance with the Espionage Act of 1917, most of them could be arrested and deported for speaking out against the government. In many cities they would have been, but arresting someone in the North End for advocating the overthrow of the United States was like arresting people for letting their horses shit on the street—they wouldn't be hard to find, but you'd better have an awfully large truck.

Danny and Steve entered a café on Richmond Street. The walls were covered with black wool crosses, three dozen of them at least, most the size of a man's head. The owner's wife had been knitting them since America had entered the war. Danny and Steve ordered espressos. The owner placed their cups on the glass countertop with a bowl of brown sugar lumps and left them alone. His wife came in and out from the back room with trays of bread and placed them in the shelves below the counter until the glass steamed up below their elbows.

The woman said to Danny, "War end soon, eh?"

"It sounds like it."

"Is good," she said. "I sew one more cross. Maybe help." She gave him a hesitant smile and a bow and returned to the back.

They drank their espressos and when they walked back out of the café, the sun was brighter and caught Danny in the

55

eyes. Soot from the smokestacks along the wharf seesawed through the air and dusted the cobblestone. The neighborhood was quiet except for the occasional roll-up of a shop grate and the clop-and-squeak of a horse-drawn wagon delivering wood. Danny wished it could stay like this, but soon the streets would fill with vendors and livestock and truant kids and soapbox Bolsheviks and soapbox anarchists. Then some of the men would hit the saloons for a late breakfast and some of the musicians would hit the corners not occupied by the soapboxes and someone would hit a wife or a husband or a Bolshevik.

Once the wife beaters and husband beaters and Bolshevik beaters were dealt with, there would be pickpockets, penny-to-nickel extortions, dice games on blankets, card games in the back rooms of cafés and barbershops, and members of the Black Hand selling insurance against everything from fire to plague but mostly from the Black Hand.

"Got another meeting tonight," Steve said. "Big doings."

"BSC meeting?" Danny shook his head. " 'Big doings.' You're serious?"

Steve twirled his pocket billy on its leather strap. "You ever think if you showed up to union meetings, maybe you'd be bumped to Detective Division by now, we'd all have our raise, and Johnny Green'd still have his wife and kids?"

Danny peered up at a sky with glare but no visible sun. "It's a social club."

"It's a union," Steve said.

"Then why's it called the Boston Social Club?" Danny yawned up at the white leather sky.

"A fine point. The point of the matter, in fact. We're trying to change that."

"Change it all you want and it's still just a union in name. We're cops, Steve—we've got no rights. The BSC? Just a boys' club, a fucking tree house."

"We're setting up a meeting with Gompers, Dan. The AF of L."

Danny stopped. If he told his father or Eddie McKenna

about this, he'd get a gold shield and be bumped up out of patrol the day after tomorrow.

"The AF of L is a national union. You crazy? They'll never let cops join."

"Who? The mayor? The governor? O'Meara?"

"O'Meara," Danny said. "He's the only one that matters."

Police Commissioner Stephen O'Meara's bedrock belief was that a policeman's post was the highest of all civic posts and therefore demanded both the outward and inward reflection of honor. When he'd taken over the BPD, each precinct had been a fiefdom, the private reserve of whichever ward boss or city councilman got his snout into the trough faster and deeper than his competition. The men looked like shit, dressed like shit, and didn't give shit.

O'Meara purged a lot of that. Not all of it, Lord knows, but he'd fired some deadwood and worked to indict the most egregious of the ward bosses and councilmen. He'd set the rotted system back on its heels and then pushed, in hopes it would fall over. Didn't happen, but it teetered on occasion. Enough so he could send a good number of the police back out into their communities to get to know the people they served. And that's what you did in O'Meara's BPD if you were a smart patrolman (with limited contacts)—you served the people. Not the ward bosses or the midget czars with the gold bars. You looked like a cop and you carried yourself like a cop and you stepped aside for no man and you never bent the basic principle: you were the law.

But even O'Meara, apparently, couldn't bend City Hall to his will in the latest fight for a raise. They hadn't had one in six years, and that raise, pushed through by O'Meara himself, had come after eight years of stalemate. So Danny and all the other men on the force were paid the fair wage of 1905. And in his last meeting with the BSC, the mayor had said that was the best they could look forward to for a while.

Twenty-nine cents an hour for a seventy-three-hour week. No overtime. And that was for day patrolmen like Danny and

Steve Coyle, the plum assignment. The poor night guys were paid a flat two bits an hour and worked eighty-three hours a week. Danny would have thought it outrageous if it hadn't been steeped in a truth he'd accepted since he could first walk: the system fucked the workingman. The only realistic decision a man had to make was if he was going to buck the system and starve, or play it with so much pluck and guts that none of its inequities applied to him.

"O'Meara," Steve said, "sure. I love the old man, too, I do. Love him, Dan. But he's not giving us what we were promised."

Danny said, "Maybe they really *don't* have the money."

"That's what they said last year. Said wait till the war's over and we'll reward your loyalty." Steve held his hands out. "I'm looking, and I don't see no reward."

"The war isn't over."

Steve Coyle made a face. "For all intents and purposes."

"So, fune, reopen negotiations."

"We *did*. And they turned us down again last week. And cost of living has been climbing since June. We're fucking starving, Dan. You'd know it if you had kids."

"You don't have kids."

"My brother's widow, God rest him, she's got two. I might as well be married. Wench thinks I'm Gilchrist's on store-credit day."

Danny knew Steve had been putting it to the Widow Coyle since a month or two after his brother's body had entered the grave. Rory Coyle's femoral artery had been sliced by a cattle shear at the Brighton stockyards, and he'd bled out on the floor amid some stunned workers and oblivious cows. When the stockyard refused to pay even a minimal death benefit to his family, the workers had used Rory Coyle's death as a rallying cry to unionize, but their strike had only lasted three days before the Brighton PD, the Pinkertons, and some out-of-town bat swingers had pushed back and turned Rory Joseph Coyle right quick into Rory Fucking Who.

Across the street, a man with an anarchist's requisite watch cap and handlebar mustache set up his wood crate under a street pole and consulted the notebook under his arm. He climbed up on the crate. For a moment Danny felt an odd sympathy for the man. He wondered if he had children, a wife.

"The AF of L is national," he said again. "The department will never—fucking *ever*—allow it."

Steve placed a hand on his arm, his eyes losing their usual blithe light. "Come to a meeting, Dan. Fay Hall. Tuesdays and Thursdays."

"What's the point?" Danny said as the guy across the street started shouting in Italian.

"Just come," Steve said.

After their shift, Danny had dinner alone and then a few too many drinks in Costello's, a waterfront saloon favored by police. With every drink, Johnny Green grew smaller, Johnny Green and his three fights in one day, his foaming mouth, his desk job and eviction notice. When Danny left, he took his flask and walked through the North End. Tomorrow would be his first day off in twenty, and as usually happened for some perverse reason, his exhaustion left him wide awake and antsy. The streets were quiet again, the night deepening around them. At the corner of Hanover and Salutation streets, he leaned against a streetlamp pole and looked at the shuttered station house. The lowest windows, those that touched the sidewalk, bore scorch marks, but otherwise you'd be hard-pressed to guess anything violent had ever happened inside.

The Harbor Police had decided to move to another building a few blocks over on Atlantic. They'd told the papers the move had been planned for over a year, but nobody swallowed it. Salutation Street had ceased being a building where anyone felt safe. And illusions of safety were the least a populace demanded of a police station.

One week before Christmas 1916 Steve had been felled by a case of strep. Danny, working solo, had arrested a thief coming off a ship moored amid the ice chunks and gray sea chop of Battery Wharf. This made it a Harbor Police problem and Harbor Police paperwork; all Danny had to do was the drop-off.

It had been an easy pinch. As the thief strolled down the gangplank with a burlap sack over his shoulder, the sack clanked. Danny, yawning into the end of his shift, noticed that this guy had neither the hands, the shoes, nor the walk of a stevedore or a teamster. He told him to halt. The thief shrugged and lowered the sack. The ship he'd robbed was set to depart with food and medical supplies for starving children in Belgium. When some passersby saw the cans of food spill onto the dock, they spread the word, and just as Danny put the cuffs on, the beginnings of a mob congregated at the end of the wharf. Starving Belgian children were the rage that month, the papers filled with accounts of German atrocities against the innocent, God-fearing Flemish. Danny had to draw his pocket billy and hold it above his shoulder in order to pull the thief through the crowd and head up Hanover toward Salutation Street.

Off the wharves, the Sunday streets were cold and quiet, dusted from snow that had been falling all morning, the flakes tiny and dry as ash. The thief was standing beside Danny at the Salutation Street admitting desk, showing him his chapped hands, saying a few nights in the slammer might be just the thing to get the blood circulating again in all this cold, when seventeen sticks of dynamite detonated in the basement.

The exact character of the explosion was something neighborhood people would debate for weeks. Whether the blast was preceded by two muffled thuds or three. Whether the building shook before the doors flew off their hinges or afterward. Every window on the other side of the street blew out, from ground floor to fifth story, one end of the block to

60

the other, and that made its own racket, impossible to distinguish from the original explosion. But to those inside the station house, the seventeen sticks of dynamite made a very distinctive sound, quite different from all those that would follow when the walls split and the floors collapsed.

What Danny heard was thunder. Not the loudest thunder he'd ever heard necessarily, but the deepest. Like a great dark yawn from a great wide god. He would have never questioned it as anything *but* thunder if he hadn't recognized immediately that it came from below him. It loosed a baritone yowl that moved the walls and shimmied the floors. All in less than a second. Enough time for the thief to look at Danny and Danny to look at the duty sergeant and the duty sergeant to look at the two patrolmen who'd been arguing over the Belgian war in the corner. Then the rumble and the building-shudder deepened. The wall behind the duty sergeant drizzled plaster. It looked like powdered milk or soap flakes. Danny wanted to point so the sergeant could get a look at it, but the sergeant disappeared, just dropped past the desk like a condemned man through a scaffold. The windows blew out. Danny looked through them and saw a gray film of sky. Then the floor beneath him collapsed.

From thunder to collapse, maybe ten seconds. Danny opened his eyes a minute or two later to the peal of fire alarms. Another sound ringing in his left ear as well, a bit higher-pitched, though not as loud. A kettle's constant hiss. The duty sergeant lay across from him on his back, a slab of desk over his knees, his eyes closed, nose broken, some teeth, too. Danny had something sharp digging into his back. He had scratches all over his hands and arms. Blood flowed from a hole in his neck, and he dug his handkerchief out of his pocket and placed it to the wound. His greatcoat and uniform were shredded in places. His domed helmet was gone. Men in their underwear, men who'd been sleeping in bunks between shifts, lay in the rubble. One had his eyes open and looked at Danny as if Danny could explain why he'd woken up to this.

Outside, sirens. The heavy slap of fire engine tires. Whistles.

The guy in his underwear had blood on his face. He lifted a chalky hand and wiped some of it off.

"Fucking anarchists," he said.

That had been Danny's first thought, too. Wilson had just been reelected on a promise that he'd keep them out of all Belgian affairs, all French and German affairs. But a change of heart had apparently taken place somewhere in the corridors of power. Suddenly it was deemed necessary for the United States to join the war effort. Rockefeller said so. J. P. Morgan said so. Lately the press had said so. Belgian children were being treated poorly. Starving. The Huns had a reputed fondness for atrocity—bombing French hospitals, starving more Belgian children. Always the children, Danny had noticed. A lot of the country smelled a rat, but it was the radicals who started making a ruckus. Two weeks back there'd been a demonstration a few blocks away, anarchists and socialists and the IWW. The police—both city and harbor—had broken it up, made some arrests, cracked some heads. The anarchists mailed threats to the newspapers, promised reprisals.

"Fucking anarchists," the cop in his underwear repeated. "Fucking terrorist Eye-talians."

Danny tested his left leg, then his right. When he was pretty sure they'd hold him, he stood. He looked up at the holes in the ceiling. Holes the size of beer casks. From here, all the way down in the basement, he could see the sky.

Someone moaned to his left, and he saw the top of the thief's red hair sticking out from beneath mortar and wood and a piece of door from one of the cells down the hall. He pulled a blackened plank off the guy's back, removed a brick from his neck. He knelt by the thief as the guy gave him a tight smile of thanks.

"What's your name?" Danny asked, because it suddenly seemed important. But the life slid off the thief's pupils as if falling from a ledge. Danny would have expected it to rise. To flee upward. But instead it sank into itself, an animal retreating into its hole until there was nothing left of it. Just a not-quite-guy where the guy had lain, a distant, cooling thing. He pressed the handkerchief harder against his neck, closed the thief's eyelids with his thumb, and felt an inexplicable agitation over not knowing the man's name.

At Mass General, a doctor used tweezers to pull whiskers of metal from Danny's neck. The metal had come from the piece of bed frame that hit Danny on its way to imbedding itself in a wall. The doctor told Danny the chunk of metal had come so close to his carotid artery that it should have sheared it in half. He studied the trail of it for another minute or so and told Danny that it had, in fact, missed the artery by roughly one–one thousandth of a millimeter. He informed Danny that this was a statistical aberration on a par with getting hit in the head by a flying cow. He then cautioned him against spending any future time in the kinds of buildings that anarchists were fond of bombing.

A few months after he left the hospital, Danny began his dire love affair with Nora O'Shea. On one of the days of their secret courtship, she kissed the scar on his neck and told him he was blessed.

"If I'm blessed," he said to her, "what was the thief?"

"Not you."

This was in a room at the Tidewater Hotel that overlooked the boardwalk of Nantasket Beach in Hull. They'd taken the steamboat from downtown and spent the day at Paragon Park, riding the carousel and the teacups. They ate saltwater taffy and fried clams so hot they had to be waved through the sea breeze before they could be swallowed.

Nora bested him in the shooting gallery. One lucky shot, true, but a bull's-eye and so it was Danny who was handed the stuffed bear by the smirking park vendor. It was a raggedy thing, its split seams already disgorging pale brown stuffing and sawdust. Later, in their room, she used it to defend herself during a pillow fight, and that was the end of the bear. They swept up the sawdust and the stuffing with their hands.

Danny, on his knees, found one of the late bear's button eyes under the brass bed and placed it in his pocket. He hadn't intended to keep it beyond that day, but now, over a year later, he rarely left his rooming house without it.

Danny and Nora's affair had begun in April of 1917, the month the United States entered the war against Germany. It was an unseasonably warm month. Flowers bloomed earlier than predicted; near the end of the month their perfume reached windows high above the streets. Lying together in the smell of flowers and the constant threat of a rain that never fell, as the ships left for Europe, as the patriots rallied in the streets, as a new world seemed to sprout beneath them even quicker than the blooming flowers, Danny knew the relationship was doomed. This was even before he'd learned her bleaker secrets, back when the relationship was in the first pink blush of itself. He felt a helplessness that had refused to leave him since he'd woken on the basement floor of Salutation Street. It wasn't just Salutation (though that would play a large role in his thoughts for the rest of his life), it was the world. The way it gathered speed with every passing day. The way the faster it went, the less it seemed to be steered by any rudder or guided by any constellation. The way it just continued to sail on, regardless of him.

D anny left the boardedup ruin of Salutation and crossed the city with his flask. Just before dawn, he made his way up onto the Dover Street Bridge and stood looking out at the skyline, at the city caught between dusk and day under a scud of low clouds. It was limestone and brick and glass, its lights darkened for the war effort, a collection of banks and taverns, restaurants and bookstores, jewelers and warehouses and department stores and rooming houses, but he could feel it huddled in the gap between last night and tomorrow morning, as if it had failed to seduce either. At dawn, a city had no finery, no makeup or perfume. It was sawdust on the floors, the overturned tumbler, the lone shoe with a broken strap.

"I'm drunk," he said to the water, and his foggy face stared back at him from a cup of light in the gray water, the reflection of the sole lamp lit under the bridge. "So drunk." He spit down at his reflection, but he missed it.

Voices came from his right and he turned and saw them—the first gaggle of the morning migration heading out of South Boston and up onto the bridge: women and children going into the city proper for work.

He walked off the bridge and found a doorway in a failed fruit wholesalers building. He watched them come, first in clumps and then in streams. Always the women and children first, their shifts an hour or two before the men's so they could return home in time to get dinner ready. Some chatted loudly and gaily, others were quiet or soggy with sleep. The older women moved with palms to their backs or hips or other aches. Many were dressed in the coarse clothing of mill and factory laborers, while others wore the heavily starched, black-and-white uniforms of domestics and hotel cleaners.

He sipped from his flask in the dark doorway, hoping she'd be among them and hoping she wouldn't.

Some children were herded up Dover by two older women who scolded them for crying, for scuffling their feet, for holding up the crowd, and Danny wondered if they were the eldest of their families, sent out at the earliest age to continue the family tradition, or if they were the youngest, and money for school had already been spent.

He saw Nora then. Her hair was covered by a handkerchief tied off behind her head but he knew it was curly and impossible to tame, so she kept it short. He knew by the thickness of her lower eyelids she hadn't slept well. He knew she had a blemish at the base of her spine and the blemish was scarlet red against pale white skin and shaped like a dinner bell. He knew she was self conscious about her Donegal brogue and had been trying to lose it ever since his father had carried her into the Coughlin household five years ago on Christmas Eve after finding her half-starved and frostbitten along the Northern Avenue docks.

She and another girl stepped off the sidewalk to move around the slower children and Danny smiled when the other girl passed a furtive cigarette to Nora and she cupped it in her hand and took a quick puff.

He thought of stepping out of the doorway and calling to her. He pictured himself reflected in her eyes, his eyes swimming with booze and uncertainty. Where others saw bravery, she would see cowardice.

And she'd be right.

Where others saw a tall, strong man, she'd see a weak child.

And she'd be right.

So he stayed in the doorway. He stayed there and fingered the bear's-eye button in his pants pocket until she was lost in the crowd heading up Dover Street. And he hated himself and hated her, too, for the ruin they'd made of each other.

CHAPTER *two*

Luther lost his job at the munitions factory in September. Came in to do a day's work, found a yellow slip of paper taped to his workbench. It was a Wednesday, and as had become his habit during the week, he'd left his tool bag underneath the bench the night before, each tool tightly wrapped in oilcloth and placed one beside the other. They were his own tools, not the company's, given to him by his Uncle Cornelius, the old man gone blind before his time. When Luther was a boy, Cornelius would sit on the porch and take a small bottle of oil from the overalls he wore whether it was a hundred in the shade or there was frost on the woodpile, and he'd wipe down his tool set, knowing each one by touch and explaining to Luther how that wasn't no crescent wrench, boy, was a monkey wrench, get it straight, and how any man didn't know the difference by touch alone ought just use the monkey wrench, 'cause a monkey what he be. He took to teaching Luther his tools the way he knew them himself. He'd blindfold the boy, Luther giggling on the hot porch, and then he'd hand him a bolt, make him match it to the box points of a socket, make him do it over and over until the blindfold wasn't fun no more, was stinging Luther's eyes with his own sweat. But over time, Luther's hands began to see and smell and taste things to the point where he sometimes suspected his fingers saw colors before his eyes did. Probably why he'd never bobbled a baseball in his life.

Never cut himself on the job neither. Never mashed no thumb working the drill press, never sliced his flesh on a propeller blade by gripping the wrong edge when he went to lift it. And all the while, his eyes remained somewhere else, looking at the tin walls, smelling the world on the other side, knowing someday he'd be out in it, way out in it, and it would be wide.

The yellow slip of paper said "See Bill," and that was all, but Luther felt something in those words that made him reach below his bench and pick up the beat-on leather tool bag and carry it with him as he crossed the work floor toward the shift supervisor's office. He was holding it in his hand when he stood before Bill Hackman's desk, and Bill, sad-eyed and sighing all the time, and not so bad for white folk, said, "Luther, we got to let you go."

Luther felt himself vanish, go so damn small inside of himself that he could feel himself as a needlepoint with no rest of the needle behind it, a dot of almost-air that hung far back in his skull, and him watching his own body stand in front of Bill's desk, and he waited for that needlepoint to tell it to move again.

It's what you had to do with white folk when they talked to you directly, with their eyes on yours. Because they never did that unless they were pretending to ask you for something they planned to just take anyway or, like now, when they were delivering bad news.

"All right," Luther said.

"Wasn't my decision," Bill explained. "All these boys are going to be coming back from the war soon, and they'll need jobs."

"War's still going on," Luther said.

Bill gave him a sad smile, the kind you'd give a dog you were fond of but couldn't teach to sit or roll over. "War's as good as over. Trust me, we know."

By "we," Luther knew he meant the company, and Luther figured if anyone knew, it was the company, because they'd been giving Luther a steady paycheck for helping them make weapons since '15, long before America was supposed to have anything to do with this war.

"All right," Luther said.

"And, yeah, you did fine work here, and we sure tried to find you a place, a way you could stay on, but them boys'll be coming back in buckets, and they fought hard over there, and Uncle Sam, he'll want to say thanks."

"All right."

"Look," Bill said, sounding a bit frustrated, as if Luther were pitching a fight, "you understand, don't you? You wouldn't want us to put those boys, those patriots, out on the street. I mean, how would that look, Luther? Wouldn't look right, I'll tell you right now. Why you yourself would be unable to hold your head high if you walked the street and saw one of them boys pass you by looking for work while you got a fat paycheck in your pocket."

Luther didn't say anything. Didn't mention that a lot of those patriotic boys who risked their lives for their country were colored boys, but he'd sure bet that wasn't who was taking his job. Hell, he'd bet if he came back to the factory a year from now, the only colored faces he'd see would belong to the men working the cleanup shift, emptying the office wastebaskets and sweeping the metal shavings off the work floors. And he didn't wonder aloud how many of those white boys who'd replace all these here coloreds had actually served overseas or got their ribbons for typing or some such in posts down in Georgia or around Kansas way.

Luther didn't open his mouth, just kept it as closed as the rest of him until Bill got tired of arguing with himself and told Luther where he'd need to go to collect his pay.

So there was Luther, his ear to the ground, hearing there might, just might maybe be some work in Youngstown, and someone else had heard tell of hirings in a mine outside of Ravenswood, just over the other side of the river in West

69

Virginia. Economy was getting tight again, though, they all said. White-tight.

And then Lila start talking about an aunt she had in Greenwood.

Luther said, "Never heard of that place."

"Ain't in Ohio, baby. Ain't in West Virginia or Kentucky neither."

"Then where's it at?"

"Tulsa."

"Oklahoma?"

"Uh-huh," she said, her voice soft, like she'd been planning it for a while and wanted to be subtle about letting him think he made up his own mind.

"Shit, woman." Luther rubbed the outsides of her arms. "I ain't going to no Oklahoma."

"Where you going to go then? Next door?"

"What's next door?" He looked over there.

"Ain't no jobs. That's all I know about next door."

Luther gave that some thought, feeling her circling him, like she was more than a few steps ahead.

"Baby," she said, "Ohio ain't done nothing for us but keep us poor."

"Didn't make us poor."

"Ain't going to make us rich."

They were sitting on the swing he'd built on what remained of the porch where Cornelius had taught him what amounted to his trade. Twothirds of the porch had washed away in the floods of '13, and Luther kept meaning to rebuild it, but there'd been so much baseball and so much work the last few years, he hadn't found the time. And it occurred to him—he was flush. It wouldn't last forever, Lord knows, but he did have some money put away for the first time in his life. Enough to make a move in any case.

God, he liked Lila. Not so's he was ready to see the preacher and sell all of his youth quite yet; hell, he was only twenty-three. But he sure liked smelling her and talking to her and he

70

sure liked the way she fit into his bones as she curled alongside of him in the porch swing.

"What's in this Greenwood 'sides your aunt?"

"Jobs. They got jobs all over the place. A big, hopping town with nothing but coloreds in it, and they all doing right well, baby. Got themselves doctors and lawyers, and the men own their own fine automobiles and the girls dress real nice on Sundays and everyone owns their own home."

He kissed the top of her head because he didn't believe her but he loved that she wanted to think something *should be* so bad that half the time she convinced herself it *could* be.

"Yeah, uh?" He chuckled. "They got themselves some white folk that work the land for them, too?"

She reached back and slapped his forehead and then bit his wrist.

"Damn, woman, that's my throwing hand. Watch that shit."

She lifted his wrist and kissed it and then she laid it between her breasts and said, "Feel my tummy, baby."

"I can't reach."

She slid up his body a bit, and then his hand was on her stomach and he tried to go lower but she gripped his wrist.

"Feel it."

"I'm feeling it."

"That's what else is going to be waiting in Greenwood."

"Your stomach?"

She kissed his chin.

"No, fool. Your child."

They took the train from Columbus on the first of October, crossed eight hundred miles of country where the summer fields had traded their gold for furrows of night frost that melted in the morning and dripped over the dirt like cake icing. The sky was the blue of metal that'd just come off the press. Blocks of hay sat in dun-colored fields, and Luther saw a pack of horses in Missouri run for a full mile, their bodies as gray as their breath. And the train streamed through it all, shaking the ground, screaming at the sky, and Luther huffed his breath into the glass and doodled with his finger, drew baseballs, drew bats, drew a child with a head too big for its body.

Lila looked at it and laughed. "That's what our boy gonna look like? Big old head like his daddy? Long skinny body?"

"Nah," Luther said, "gonna look like you."

And he gave the child breasts the size of circus balloons and Lila giggled and swatted his hand and rubbed the child off the window.

The trip took two days and Luther lost some money in a card game with some porters the first night, and Lila stayed mad about that well into the next morning, but otherwise Luther was hard-pressed coming up with a time he'd cherished more in his life. There'd been a few plays here and there on the diamond, and he'd once gone to Memphis when he was seventeen with his cousin, Sweet George, and they'd had themselves a time on Beale Street that he'd never forget, but riding in that train car with Lila, knowing his child lived in her body—her body no longer a singular life, but more like a life-and-a-half—and that they were, as he'd so often dreamed, out in the world, drunk on the speed of their crossing, he felt a lessening of the anxious throb that had lived in his chest since he was a boy. He'd never known where that throb came from, only that it had always been there and he'd tried to work it away and play it away and drink it away and fuck it away and sleep it away his whole life. But now, sitting on a seat with his feet on a floor that was bolted to a steel underbelly that was strapped to wheels that locked onto rails and hurtled through time and distance as if time and distance weren't nothing at all, he loved his life and he loved Lila and he loved their child and he knew, as he always had, that he loved speed, because things that possessed it could not be tethered, and so, they couldn't be sold.

* * *

72

They arrived in Tulsa at the Santa Fe rail yard at nine in the morning and were met by Lila's Aunt Marta and her husband, James. James was as big as Marta was small, both of them dark as dark got, with skin stretched so tight across the bone Luther wondered how they breathed. Big as James was, and he was the height some men only reached on horseback, Marta was, no doubt, the dog who ate first.

Four, maybe five, seconds into the introductions, Marta said, "James, honey, git them bags, would you? Let the poor girl stand there and faint from the weight?"

Lila said, "It's all right, Auntie, I—"

"James?" Aunt Marta snapped her fingers at James's hip and the man hopped to. Then she smiled, all pretty and small, and said, "Girl, you as beautiful as you ever was, praise the Lord."

Lila surrendered her bags to Uncle James and said, "Auntie, this is Luther Laurence, the young man I been writing you about."

Though he probably should have figured as much, it took Luther by surprise to realize his name had been placed to paper and sent across four state lines to land in Aunt Marta's hand, the letters touched, however incidentally, by her tiny thumb.

Aunt Marta gave him a smile that had a lot less warmth in it than the one she gave her niece. She took his hand in both of hers. She looked up into his eyes.

"A pleasure to meet you, Luther Laurence. We're church-goers here in Greenwood. You a churchgoer?"

"Yes, ma'am. Surely."

"Well, then," she said and gave his hand a moist press and a slow shake, "we're to get along fine, I 'spect."

"Yes, ma'am."

Luther was prepared for a long walk out of the train station and up through town to Marta and James's house, but James led them to an Olds Reo as red and shiny as an apple just pulled from a water bucket. Had wood spoke wheels and a black top that James rolled down and latched in the back. They piled the suitcases in the backseat with Marta and Lila, the two of them already talking a mile a minute, and Luther climbed up front with James and they pulled out of the lot, Luther thinking how a colored man driving a car like this in Columbus was just asking to get shot for a thief, but at the Tulsa train station, not even the white folk seemed to notice them.

James explained the Olds had a flathead V8 engine in it, sixty horsepower, and he worked the shift up into third gear and smiled big.

"What you do for work?" Luther asked.

"Own two garages," James said. "Got four men working under me. Would love to put you to work there, son, but I got all the help I can handle right now. But don't you worry—one thing Tulsa's got on either side of the tracks is jobs, plenty of jobs. You in oil country, son. Whole place just sprung up overnight 'cause of the black crude. Shoot. None of this was even here twenty-five years ago. Wasn't nothing but a trading post back then. Believe that?"

Luther looked out the window at downtown, saw buildings bigger than any he'd seen in Memphis, big as ones he'd seen only in pictures of Chicago and New York, and cars filling the streets, and people, too, and he thought how you would have figured a place like this would take a century to build, but this country just didn't have time to wait no more, no interest in patience and no reason for it either.

He looked forward as they drove into Greenwood, and James waved to some men building a house and they waved back and he tooted his horn and Marta explained how coming up here was the section of Greenwood Avenue known as the Black Wall Street, lookie here . . .

And Luther saw a black bank and an ice cream parlor filled with black teenagers and a barbershop and a billiard parlor and a big old grocery store and a bigger department store and a law office and a doctor's office and a newspaper, and all of it occupied by colored folk. And then they rolled past the movie theater, big bulbs surrounding a huge white marquee, and Luther looked above that marquee to see the name of the place—The Dreamland—and he thought, That's where we've come. Because all this had to be just that indeed.

By the time they drove up Detroit Avenue, where James and Marta Hollaway owned their own home, Luther's stomach was starting to slide. The homes along Detroit Avenue were red brick or creamy chocolate stone and they were as big as the homes of white folk. And not white folk who were just getting by, but white folk who lived good. The lawns were trimmed to bright green stubble and several of the homes had wraparound porches and bright awnings.

They pulled into the driveway of a dark brown Tudor and James stopped the car, which was good, because Luther was so dizzy he worried he might get sick.

Lila said, "Oh, Luther, couldn't you just die?"

Yeah, Luther thought, that there is one possibility.

The next morning Luther found himself getting married before he'd had breakfast. In the years that followed, when someone would ask how it was he came to be a married man, Luther always answered:

"Hell if I know."

He woke that morning in the cellar. Marta had made it plenty clear the evening before that a man and a woman who were not husband and wife didn't sleep on the same floor in her house, never mind the same room. So Lila got herself a nice pretty bed in a nice pretty room on the second floor and Luther got a sheet thrown over a broke-down couch in the cellar. The couch smelled of dog (they'd had one once; long since dead) and cigars. Uncle James was the culprit on that score. He took his after dinner stogie in the basement every night because Aunt Marta wouldn't allow it in her house.

Lot of things Aunt Marta wouldn't allow in her house— cussing, liquor, taking the Lord's name in vain, card playing, people of low character, cats—and Luther had a feeling he'd just scratched the surface of the list.

So he went to sleep in the cellar and woke up with a crick in his neck and the smells of long-dead dog and too-recent cigar in his nostrils. Right off, he heard raised voices coming from upstairs. Feminine voices. Luther'd grown up with his mother and one older sister, both of whom had passed on from the fever in '14, and when he allowed himself to think of them it hurt enough to stop his breath because they'd been proud, strong women of loud laughter who'd loved him fiercely.

But those two women had fought just as fierce. Nothing in the whole world, in Luther's estimation, was worth entering a room where two women had their claws out.

He crept up the stairs, though, so he could hear the words better and what he heard made him want to trade places with the Hollaway dog.

"I'm just feeling under the weather, Auntie."

"Don't you lie to me, girl. Don't you *lie*! I know morning sickness when I see it. How long?"

"I'm not pregnant."

"Lila, you my baby sister's child, yes. My goddaughter, yes. But, girl, I will strap the black straight offa your body from head to toe if you lie to me again. You hear?"

Luther heard Lila break out in a fresh run of sobbing, and it shamed him to picture her.

Marta shrieked, "James!" and Luther heard the large man's footfalls coming toward the kitchen, and he wondered if the man had grabbed his shotgun for the occasion.

"Git that boy up here."

Luther opened the door before James could and Marta's eyes were flashing all over him before he crossed the threshold.

"Well, lookit himself. Mr. Big Man. I done told you we are churchgoers here, did I not, Mr. Big Man?"

Luther thought it best not to say a word.

76

"Christians is what we are. And we don't abide no sinning under this here roof. Ain't that right, James?"

"Amen," James said, and Luther noticed the Bible in his hand and it scared him a lot more than the shotgun he'd pictured.

"You get this poor, innocent girl impregnated and then you expect to what? I'm talking to you, boy? What?"

Luther tilted a cautious eye down at the little woman, saw a fury in her looked about to take a bite out of him.

"Well, we hadn't really—"

"You 'hadn't really,' my left foot." And Marta stomped that left foot of hers into the kitchen floor. "You think for one pretty second that any respectable people are going to rent you a house in Greenwood, you are mistaken. And you won't be staying under my roof one second longer. No, sir. You think you can get my only niece in the family way and then go off galavanting as you please? I am here to tell you that *that* will not be happening here today."

He caught Lila looking at him through a stream of tears.

She said, "What're we going to do, Luther?"

And James, who in addition to being a businessman and a mechanic, was, it turned out, an ordained minister and justice of the peace, held up his Bible and said, "I believe we have a solution to your dilemma."

CHAPTER *three*

The day the Red Sox played their first World Series home game against the Cubs, First Precinct Duty Sergeant George Strivakis called Danny and Steve into his office and asked them if they had their sea legs.

"Sergeant?"

"Your sea legs. Can you join a couple of Harbor coppers and visit a ship for us?"

Danny and Steve looked at each other and shrugged.

"I'll be honest," Strivakis said, "some soldiers are sick out there. Captain Meadows is under orders from the deputy chief who's under orders from O'Meara himself to deal with the situation as quietly as possible."

"How sick?" Steve asked.

Strivakis shrugged.

Steve snorted. "*How* sick, Sarge?"

Another shrug, that shrug making Danny more nervous than anything else, old George Strivakis not wanting to commit to the slightest evidence of knowledge aforethought.

Danny said, "Why us?"

"Because ten men already turned it down. You're eleven and twelve."

"Oh," Steve said.

Strivakis hunched forward. "What we would like is two bright officers to proudly represent the police department of the great city of Boston. You are to go out to this boat, assess

78

the situation, and make a decision in the best interest of your fellow man. Should you successfully complete your mission, you will be rewarded with one half-day off and the everlasting thanks of your beloved department."

"We'd like a little more than that," Danny said. He looked over the desk at his duty sergeant. "With all due respect to our beloved department, of course."

In the end, they struck a deal—paid sick days if they contracted whatever the soldiers had, the next two Saturdays off, and the department had to foot the next three cleaning bills for their uniforms.

Strivakis said, "Mercenaries, the both of you," and then shook their hands to seal the contract.

The USS *McKinley* had just arrived from France. It carried soldiers returning from battle in places with names like Saint-Mihiel and Pont-à-Mousson and Verdun. Somewhere between Marseilles and Boston, several of the soldiers had grown ill. The conditions of three of them were now deemed so dire that ship doctors had contacted Camp Devens to tell the colonel in charge that unless these men were evacuated to a military hospital they would die before sundown. And so on a fine September afternoon, when they could have been working a soft detail at the World Series, Danny and Steve joined two officers of the Harbor Police on Commercial Wharf as gulls chased the fog out to sea and the dark waterfront brick steamed.

One of the Harbor cops, an Englishman named Ethan Gray, handed Danny and Steve their surgical masks and white cotton gloves.

"They say it helps." He smiled into the sharp sun.

"Who's they?" Danny pulled the surgical mask over his head and down his face until it hung around his neck.

Ethan Gray shrugged. "The all-seeing they."

"Oh, them," Steve said. "Never liked them."

Danny placed the gloves in his back pocket, watched Steve do the same.

The other Harbor cop hadn't said a word since they'd met on the wharf. He was a small guy, thin and pale, his damp bangs falling over a pimply forehead. Burn scars crept out from the edges of his sleeves. Upon a closer look, Danny noticed he was missing the bottom half of his left ear.

So, then, Salutation Street.

A survivor of the white flash and the yellow flame, the collapsing floors and plaster rain. Danny didn't remember seeing him during the explosion, but then Danny didn't remember much after the bomb went off.

The guy sat against a black steel stanchion, long legs stretched out in front of him, and studiously avoided eye contact with Danny. That was one of the traits shared by survivors of Salutation Street—they were embarrassed to acknowledge one another.

The launch approached the dock. Ethan Gray offered Danny a cigarette. He took it with a nod of thanks. Gray pointed the pack at Steve but Steve shook his head.

"And what instructions did your duty sergeant give you, Officers?"

"Pretty simple ones." Danny leaned in as Gray lit his cigarette. "Make sure every soldier stays on that ship unless we say otherwise."

Gray nodded as he exhaled a plume of smoke. "Identical to our orders as well."

"We were also told if they try to override us using some federal-government-at-time-of-war bullshit, we're to make it very clear that it may be their country but it's your harbor and our city."

Gray lifted a tobacco kernel off his tongue and gave it to the sea breeze. "You're Captain Tommy Coughlin's son, aren't you?"

Danny nodded. "What gave it away?"

"Well, for one, I've rarely met a patrolman of your age who

had so much confidence." Gray pointed at Danny's chest. "And the name tag helped."

Danny tapped some ash from his cigarette as the launch cut its engine. It rotated until the stern replaced the bow and the starboard gunwale bounced off the dock wall. A corporal appeared and tossed a line to Gray's partner. He tied it off as Danny and Gray finished their cigarettes and then approached the corporal.

"You need to put on a mask," Steve Coyle said.

The corporal nodded several times and produced a surgical mask from his back pocket. He also saluted twice. Ethan Gray, Steve Coyle, and Danny returned the first one.

"How many aboard?" Gray asked.

The corporal half-saluted, then dropped his hand. "Just me, a doc, and the pilot."

Danny pulled his mask up from his throat and covered his mouth. He wished he hadn't just smoked that cigarette. The smell of it bounced off the mask and filled his nostrils, permeated his lips and chin.

They met up with the doctor in the main cabin as the launch pulled away from the dock. The doctor was an old man, gone bald halfway up his scalp with a thick bush of white that stood up like a hedge. He didn't wear a mask and he waved at theirs.

"You can take them off. None of us have it."

"How do you know?" Danny said.

The old man shrugged. "Faith?"

It seemed silly to be standing there in their uniforms and masks while still trying to find their sea legs as the launch bounced through the chop. Ridiculous, really. Danny and Steve removed their masks. Gray followed suit. Gray's partner, though, kept his on, looking at the other three cops like they were insane.

"Peter," Gray said, "really."

Peter shook his head at the floor and kept that mask on.

Danny, Steve, and Gray sat across from the doctor at a small table.

"What are your orders?" the doctor said.

Danny told him.

The doctor pinched his nose where his glasses had indented. "So I assumed. Would your superiors object to us moving the sick by way of army ground transport?"

"Move them where?" Danny said.

"Camp Devens."

Danny looked over at Gray.

Gray smiled. "Once they leave the harbor, they are no longer under my purview."

Steve Coyle said to the doctor, "Our superiors would like to know what we're dealing with here."

"We're not exactly sure. Could be similar to an influenza strain we saw in Europe. Could be something else."

"If it is the grippe," Danny said, "how bad was it in Europe?"

"Bad," the doctor said quietly, his eyes clear. "We believe that strain may have been related to one that first appeared at Fort Riley, Kansas, about eight months ago."

"And if I may ask," Gray said, "how serious was that strain, Doctor?"

"Within two weeks it killed eighty percent of the soldiers who'd contracted it."

Steve whistled. "Fairly serious, then."

"And after?" Danny asked.

"I'm not sure I understand."

"It killed the soldiers. Then what did it do?"

The doctor gave them a wry smile and a soft snap of his fingers. "It disappeared."

"Came back, though," Steve Coyle said.

"Possibly," the doctor said. He pinched his nose again. "Men are getting sick on that ship. Packed together like they are? It's the worst possible environment for preventing transmission. Five will die tonight if we can't move them."

"Five?" Ethan Gray said. "We'd been told three."

The doctor shook his head and held up five fingers.

On the *McKinley*, they met a group of doctors and majors at the fantail. It had grown overcast. The clouds looked muscular and stone gray, like sculptures of limbs, as they moved slowly over the water and back toward the city and its red brick and glass.

A Major Gideon said, "Why would they send patrolmen?" He pointed at Danny and Steve. "You have no authority to make public health decisions."

Danny and Steve said nothing.

Gideon repeated himself. "Why send patrolmen?"

"No captains volunteered for the job," Danny said.

"You find amusement in this?" Gideon said. "My men are sick. They fought a war you couldn't be bothered to fight, and now they're dying."

"I wasn't making a joke." Danny gestured at Steve Coyle, at Ethan Gray, at the burn-scarred Peter. "This was a volunteer assignment, Major. *No one* wanted to come here except us. And we do, by the way, have the authority. We have been given clear orders as to what is acceptable and unacceptable action in this situation."

"And what is acceptable?" one of the doctors asked.

"As to the harbor," Ethan Gray said, "you are allowed to transport your men by launch and launch only to Commonwealth Pier. After that, it's BPD jurisdiction."

They looked at Danny and Steve.

Danny said, "It's in the best interest of the governor, the mayor, and every police department in the state that we not have a general panic. So, under cover of night, you are to have military transport trucks meet you at Commonwealth Pier. You can unload the sick there and take them directly to Devens. You can't stop along that journey. A police car will escort you with its sirens off." Danny met Major Gideon's glare. "Fair?"

Gideon eventually nodded.

"The State Guard's been notified," Steve Coyle said. "They'll set up an outpost at Camp Devens and work with your MPs to keep anyone from leaving base until this is contained. That's by order of the governor."

Ethan Gray directed a question to the doctors. "How long will it take to contain?"

One of them, a tall, flaxen-haired man, said, "We have no idea. It kills who it kills and then it snuffs itself out. Could be over in a week, could take nine months."

Danny said, "As long as it's kept from spreading to the civilian population, our bosses can live with the arrangement."

The flaxen-haired man chuckled. "The war is winding down. Men have been rotating back in large numbers for the last several weeks. This is a contagion, gentlemen, and a resilient one. Have you considered the possibility that a carrier has already reached your city?" He stared at them. "That it's too late, gentlemen? Far, far too late?"

Danny watched those muscular clouds slough their way inland. The rest of the sky had cleared. The sun had returned, high and sharp. A beautiful day, the kind you dreamed about during a long winter.

The five gravely ill soldiers rode back on the launch with them even though dusk was still a long way off. Danny, Steve, Ethan Gray, Peter, and two doctors stayed in the main cabin while the sick soldiers lay on the port deck with two other doctors attending. Danny had seen the men get lowered to the launch by line and pulley. With their pinched skulls and caved-in cheeks, their sweat-drenched hair and vomit-encrusted lips, they'd looked dead already. Three of the five bore a blue tint to their flesh, mouths peeled back, eyes wide and glaring. Their breaths came in huffs.

The four police officers stayed down in the cabin. Their jobs had taught them that many dangers could be explained away—if you didn't want to got shot or stabbed, don't befriend people who played with guns and knives; you didn't want to get mugged, don't leave saloons drunk beyond seeing; didn't want to lose, don't gamble.

But this was something else entirely. Could happen to any of them. Could happen to all of them.

Back at the station house, Danny and Steve gave their report to Sergeant Strivakis and separated. Steve went to find his brother's widow and Danny went to find a drink. A year from now, Steve might still be finding his way to the Widow Coyle, but Danny could have a much harder time finding a drink. While the East Coast and West Coast had been concerned with recession and war, telephones and baseball, anarchists and their bombs, the Progressives and their ole-time-religion allies had risen out of the South and the Midwest. Danny didn't know a soul who had taken the Prohibition bills seriously, even when they'd made it to the floor of the House. It seemed impossible, with all the other shifts going on in the country's fabric, that these prim, self-righteous "don't dos" had a chance. But one morning the whole country woke up to realize that not only did the idiots have a chance, they had a foothold. Gained while everyone else paid attention to what had seemed more important. Now the right of every adult to imbibe hung in the balance of one state: Nebraska. Whichever way it voted on the Volstead ratification in two months would decide whether an entire booze-loving country climbed on the wagon.

Nebraska. When Danny heard the name, about all that came to mind was corn and grain silos, dusk blue skies. Wheat, too, sheaves of it. Did they drink there? Did they have saloons? Or just silos?

They had churches, he was fairly certain. Preachers who struck the air with their fists and railed against the godless Northeast, awash, as it was, in white suds, brown immigrants, and pagan fornication.

Nebraska. Oh, boy.

Danny ordered two shots of Irish and a mug of cold beer. He removed the shirt he wore, unbuttoned, over his undershirt. He leaned into the bar as the bartender brought his drinks. The bartender's name was Alfonse and he was rumored to run with the hoolies and bullyboys on the city's east side, though Danny had yet to meet a copper who could pin anything specific on him. Of course, when the suspect in question was a bartender known to have a generous hand, who'd try hard?

"True you stopped the boxing?"

"Not sure," Danny said.

"Your last fight, I lose money. You both supposed to last to the third."

Danny held up his palms. "Guy had a fucking stroke."

"Your fault? I see him lift his arm, too."

"Yeah?" Danny drained one of his whiskies. "Well, then it's all fine."

"You miss it?"

"Not yet."

"Bad sign." Alfonse swept Danny's empty glass off the bar. "A man don't miss what a man forgot how to love."

"Jeesh," Danny said, "what's your wisdom fee?"

Alfonse spit in a highball glass and walked it back down the bar. It was possible there was something to his theory. Right now, Danny didn't love hitting things. He loved quiet and the smell of the harbor. He loved drink. Give him a few more and he'd love other things— working girls and the pigs' feet Alfonse kept down the other end of the bar. The late summer wind, of course, and the mournful music the Italians made in the alleys every evening, a block-by-block journey as flute gave way to violin giving way to clarinet or mandolin. Once Danny got drunk enough, he'd love it all, the whole world.

A meaty hand slapped his back. He turned his head to find Steve looking down at him, eyebrow cocked.

"Still receiving company, I hope."

"Still."

"Still buying the first round?"

"The first." Danny caught Alfonse's dark eyes and pointed at the bar top. "Where's the Widow Coyle?"

Steve shrugged off his coat and took a seat. "Praying. Lighting candles."

"Why?"

"No reason. Love, maybe?"

"You told her," Danny said.

"I told her."

Alfonse brought Steve a shot of rye and a bucket of suds. Once he'd walked away, Danny said, "You told her what exactly? About the grippe on the boat?"

"A little bit."

"A little bit." Danny threw back his second shot. "We've been sworn to silence by state, federal, and maritime authorities. And you tell the widow?"

"It wasn't like that."

"What was it like?"

"All right, it was like that." Steve downed his own shot. "She grabbed the kids, though, and run right off to church. Only word she'll say is to Christ Himself."

"And the pastor. And the two priests. And a few nuns. And her kids."

Steve said, "It can't stay hidden long, in either case."

Danny raised his mug. "Well, you weren't trying to make detective anyway."

"Cheers." Steve met the mug with his bucket and they both drank as Alfonse replenished their shots and left them alone again.

Danny looked at his hands. The doctor on the launch had said the grippe sometimes showed there, even when there were no other signs in the throat or head. It yellowed the flesh along the knuckles, the doctor told them, thickened the fingertips, made the joints throb.

Steve said, "How's the throat?"

Danny removed his hands from the bar. "Fine. Yours?"

"Tip-top. How long you want to keep doing this?"

"What?" Danny said. "Drinking?"

"Laying our lives on the line for less than a streetcar operator makes."

"Streetcar operators are important." Danny raised a glass. "Vital to municipal interests."

"Stevedores?"

"Them, too."

"Coughlin," Steve said. He said it pleasantly, but Danny knew the only time Steve called him by his last name was when he was irate. "Coughlin, we need you. Your voice. Hell, your glamour."

"My glamour?"

"Fuck off, ya. You know what I mean. False modesty won't help us a duck's fart right now and that's God's truth."

"Help who?"

Steve sighed. "It's us against them. They'll kill us if they can."

"Forget the singing." Danny rolled his eyes. "You need to find an acting troupe."

"They sent us out to that boat with nothing, Dan."

Danny scowled. "We get the next two Saturdays off. We get—"

"It fucking *kills*. And we went out there for what?"

"Duty?"

"Duty." Steve turned his head away.

Danny chuckled. Anything to lighten the mood, which had grown sober so quickly. "Who would risk us? Steve. On the Blessed Mother? Who? With your arrest record? With my father? My uncle? Who would risk us?"

"They would."

"Why?"

"Because it'd never occur to them that they couldn't."

Danny gave that another dry chuckle, although he felt lost

suddenly, a man trying to scoop up coins in a fast current.

Steve said, "Have you ever noticed that when they need us, they talk about duty, but when we need them, they talk about budgets?" He clinked his glass quietly off Danny's. "If we die from what we did today, Dan, any family we leave behind? They don't get a fucking dime."

Danny loosed a weary chuckle on the empty bar. "What are we supposed to do about it?"

"Fight," Steve said.

Danny shook his head. "Whole world's fighting right now. France, fucking Belgium, how many dead? No one even has a *number*. You see progress there?"

Steve shook his head.

"So?" Danny felt like breaking something. Something big, something that would shatter. "The way of the world, Steve. The way of the goddamn world."

Steve Coyle shook his head. "The way of *a* world."

"Hell with it." Danny tried to shake off the feeling he'd had lately that he was part of some larger canvas, some larger crime. "Let me buy you another."

"Their world," Steve said.

CHAPTER *four*

On a Sunday afternoon, Danny went to his father's house in South Boston for a meeting with the Old Men. A Sunday dinner at the Coughlin home was a political affair, and by inviting him to join them in the hour after dinner was served, the Old Men were anointing him in some fashion. Danny held out hope that a detective's shield—hinted at by both his father and his Uncle Eddie over the past few months—was part of the sacrament. At twenty-seven, he'd be the youngest detective in BPD history.

His father had called him the night before. "Word has it old Georgie Strivakis is losing his faculties."

"Not that I've noticed," Danny said.

"He sent you out on a detail," his father said. "Did he not?"

"He offered me the detail and I accepted."

"To a boat filled with plagueridden soldiers."

"I wouldn't call it the plague."

"What would you call it, boy?"

"Bad cases of pneumonia, maybe. 'Plague' just seems a bit dramatic, sir."

His father sighed. "I don't know what gets into your head."

"Steve should have done it alone?"

"If need be."

"His life's worth less than mine then."

"He's a Coyle, not a Coughlin. I don't make excuses for protecting my own."

90

"Somebody had to do it, Dad."

"Not a Coughlin," his father said. "Not you. You weren't raised to volunteer for suicide missions."

" 'To protect and serve,' " Danny said.

A soft, barely audible breath. "Supper tomorrow. Four o'clock sharp. Or is that too healthy for you?"

Danny smiled. "I can manage," he said, but his father had already hung up.

So the next afternoon found him walking up K Street as the sun softened against the brown and red brick and the open windows loosed the smell of boiled cabbage, boiled potatoes, and boiled ham on the bone. His brother Joe, playing in the street with some other kids, saw him and his face lit up and he came running up the sidewalk.

Joe was dressed in his Sunday best—a chocolate brown knickerbocker suit with button-bottom pants cinched at the knees, white shirt and blue tie, a golf cap set askew on his head that matched the suit. Danny had been there when his mother had bought it, Joe fidgeting the whole time, and his mother and Nora telling him how manly he looked in it, how handsome, a suit like this, of genuine Oregon cassimere, how his father would have dreamed of owning such a suit at his age, and all the while Joe looking at Danny as if he could somehow help him escape.

Danny caught Joe as he leapt off the ground and hugged him, pressing his smooth cheek to Danny's, his arms digging into his neck, and it surprised Danny that he often forgot how much his baby brother loved him.

Joe was eleven and small for his age, though Danny knew he made up for it by being one of the toughest little kids in a neighborhood of tough little kids. He hooked his legs around Danny's hips, leaned back, and smiled. "Heard you stopped boxing."

"That's the rumor."

91

Joe reached out and touched the collar of his uniform. "How come?"

"Thought I'd train you," Danny said. "First trick is to teach you how to dance."

"Nobody dances."

"Sure they do. All the great boxers took dance lessons."

He took a few steps down the sidewalk with his brother and then whirled, and Joe slapped his shoulders and said, "Stop, stop."

Danny spun again. "Am I embarrassing you?"

"Stop." He laughed and slapped his shoulders again.

"In front of all your friends?"

Joe grabbed his ears and tugged. "Cut it out."

The kids in the street were looking at Danny as if they couldn't decide whether they should be afraid, and Danny said, "Anyone else want in?"

He lifted Joe off his body, tickling him the whole way down to the pavement, and then Nora opened the door at the top of the stoop and he wanted to run.

"Joey," she said, "your ma wants you in now. Says you need to clean up."

"I'm clean."

Nora arched an eyebrow. "I wasn't asking, child."

Joe gave a beleaguered good-bye wave to his friends and trudged up the steps. Nora mussed his hair as he passed and he slapped at her hands and kept going and Nora leaned into the jamb and considered Danny. She and Avery Wallace, an old colored man, were the Coughlins' domestic help, though Nora's actual position was a lot more nebulous than Avery's. She'd come to them by accident or providence five years ago on Christmas Eve, a clacking, shivering gray-fleshed escapee from the northern coast of Ireland. What she'd been escaping from had been anyone's guess, but ever since Danny's father had carried her into the home wrapped in his greatcoat, frostbitten and covered in grime, she'd become part of the essential fabric of the Coughlin home. Not quite family, not ever *quite* that, at least not for Danny, but ingrained and ingratiated nonetheless.

"What brings you by?" she asked.

"The Old Men," he said.

"A planning and a plotting, are they, Aiden? And, sure, where do you fit in the plan?"

He leaned in a bit. "Only my mother calls me 'Aiden' anymore."

She leaned back. "You're calling me your mother now, are you?"

"Not at all, though you would make a fine one."

"Butter wouldn't melt in your mouth."

"You would."

Her eyes pulsed at that, just for a moment. Pale eyes the color of basil. "You'll need to go to confession for that one, sure."

"I don't need to confess anything to anyone. You go."

"And why would *I* go?"

He shrugged.

She leaned into the door, took a sniff of the afternoon breeze, her eyes as pained and unreadable as always. He wanted to squeeze her body until his hands fell off.

"What'd you say to Joe?"

She came off the door, folded her arms. "About what?"

"About my boxing."

She gave him a small sad smile. "I said you'd never box again. Simple as that."

"Simple, uh?"

"I can see it in your face, Danny. You've no love for it anymore."

He stopped himself from nodding because she was right and he couldn't stand that she could see through him so easily. She always had. Always would, he was pretty sure. And what a terrible thing that was. He sometimes considered the pieces of himself he'd left scattered throughout his life, the other Dannys—the child Danny and the Danny who'd once thought of becoming president and the Danny who'd wanted to go to college and the Danny who'd discovered far too late that he was in love with Nora. Crucial pieces of himself, strewn all over, and yet she held the core piece and held it absently, as if it lay at the bottom of her purse with the white specks of talc and the loose change.

"You're coming in then," she said.

"Yeah."

She stepped back from the door. "Well, you best get started."

The Old Men came out of the study for dinner—florid men, prone to winking, men who treated his mother and Nora with an Old World courtliness that Danny secretly found grating.

Taking their seats first were Claude Mesplede and Patrick Donnegan, alderman and boss of the Sixth Ward, as paired up and cagey as an old married couple playing bridge.

Sitting across from them was Silas Pendergast, district attorney of Suffolk County and the boss of Danny's brother Connor. Silas had a gift for looking respectable and morally forthright but was, in fact, a lifelong toady to the ward machines that had paid his way through law school and kept him docile and slightly drunk every day since.

Down the end by his father was Bill Madigan, deputy chief of police and, some said, the man closest to Commissioner O'Meara.

Sitting beside Madigan—a man Danny had never met before named Charles Steedman, tall and quiet and the only man to sport a three-dollar haircut in a room full of fifty-centers. Steedman wore a white suit and white tie and two-toned spats. He told Danny's mother, when she asked, that he was, among other things, vice president of the New England Association of Hotels and Restaurants and president of the Suffolk County Fiduciary Security Union.

Danny could tell by his mother's wide eyes and hesitant

smile that she had no idea what the hell Steedman had just said but she nodded anyway.

"Is that a union like the IWW?" Danny asked.

"The IWW are criminals," his father said. "Subversives."

Charles Steedman held up a hand and smiled at Danny, his eyes as clear as glass. "A tad different than the IWW, Danny. I'm a banker."

"Oh, a *banker*!" Danny's mother said. "How wonderful."

The last man to sit at the table, taking a place between Danny's brothers, Connor and Joe, was Uncle Eddie McKenna, not an uncle by blood, but family all the same, his father's best friend since they were teenage boys running the streets of their newfound country. He and Danny's father certainly made a formidable pair within the BPD. Where Thomas Coughlin was the picture of trim—trim hair, trim body, trim speech—Eddie McKenna was large of appetite and flesh and fondness for tall tales. He oversaw Special Squads, a unit that managed all parades, visits from dignitaries, labor strikes, riots, and civil unrest of any kind. Under Eddie's stewardship the unit had grown both more nebulous and more powerful, a shadow department within the department that kept crime low, it was said, "by going to the source before the source got going." Eddie's ever-revolving unit of cowboy-cops— the kind of cops Commissioner O'Meara had sworn to purge from the force—hit street crews *on their way* to heists, rousted ex-cons five steps out of the Charlestown Penitentiary, and had a network of stoolies, grifters, and street spies so immense that it would have been a boon to every cop in the city if McKenna hadn't kept all names and all history of interactions with said names solely in his head.

He looked across the table at Danny and pointed his fork at his chest. "Hear what happened yesterday while you were out in the harbor doing the Lord's work?"

Danny shook his head carefully. He'd spent the morning sleeping off the drunk he'd earned elbow to elbow with Steve Coyle the night before. Nora brought out the last of the dishes, green beans with garlic that steamed as she placed it on the table.

"They struck," Eddie McKenna said.

Danny was confused. "Who?"

"The Sox and the Cubs," Connor said. "We were there, me and Joe."

"Send them all to fight the Kaiser, I say," Eddie McKenna said. "A bunch of slackers and Bolsheviks."

Connor chuckled. "You believe it, Dan? People went bughouse."

Danny smiled, trying to picture it. "You're not having me on?"

"Oh, it happened," Joe said, all excited now. "They were mad at the owners and they wouldn't come out to play and people started throwing stuff and screaming."

"So then," Connor said, "they had to send Honey Fitz out there to calm the crowd. Now the mayor's at the game, okay? The governor, too."

"Calvin Coolidge." His father shook his head, as he did every time the governor's name came up. "A Republican from Vermont running the Democratic Commonwealth of Massachusetts." He sighed. "Lord save us."

"So, they're at the game," Connor said, "but Peters, he might be mayor, but no one cares. They've got Curley in the stands and Honey Fitz, two ex-mayors who are a hell of a lot more popular, so they send Honey out with a megaphone and he stops the riot before it can really get going. Still, people throwing things, tearing up the bleachers, you name it. Then the players come out to play, but, boy, no one was cheering."

Eddie McKenna patted his large belly and breathed through his nose. "Well, now, I hope these Bolshies will be stripped of their Series medals. Just the fact that they give them 'medals' for playing a game is enough to turn the stomach. And I say, Fine. Baseball's dead anyway. Bunch of slackers without the guts to fight for their country. And Ruth the worst of them. You hear he wants to hit now, Dan? Read it in this morning's paper—doesn't want to pitch anymore, says he's going to sit out if they don't pay him more *and* keep him off the mound at the same time. You believe that?"

"Ah, this world." His father took a sip of Bordeaux.

"Well," Danny said, looking around the table, "what was their beef?"

"Hmm?"

"Their complaint? They didn't strike for nothing."

Joe said, "They said the owners changed the agreement?" Danny watched him cock his eyes back into his head, trying to remember the specifics. Joe was a fanatic for the sport and the most trustworthy source at the table on all matters baseball. "And they cut them out of money they'd promised and every other team had gotten in other Series. So they struck." He shrugged, as if to say it all made perfect sense to him, and then he cut into his turkey.

"I agree with Eddie," his father said. "Baseball's dead. It'll never come back."

"Yes, it will," Joe said desperately. "Yes, it will."

"This country," his father said, with one of the many smiles in his collection, this time the wry one. "Everyone thinks it's okay to hire on for work but then sit down when that work turns out to be hard."

He and Connor took their coffee and cigarettes out on the back porch and Joe followed them. He climbed the tree in the backyard because he knew he wasn't supposed to and knew his brothers wouldn't call this to his attention.

Connor and Danny looked so little alike people thought they were kidding when they said they were brothers. Where Danny was tall and dark-haired and broad-shouldered, Connor was fair-haired and trim and compact, like their father. Danny had gotten the old man's blue eyes, though, and his sly sense of humor, where Connor's brown eyes and disposition—a coiled affability that disguised an obstinate heart—came entirely from their mother.

"Dad said you went out on a warship yesterday?"

Danny nodded. "That I did."

"Sick soldiers, I heard."

Danny sighed. "This house leaks like Hudson tires."

"Well, I do work for the DA."

Danny chuckled. "Juiced-in, eh, Con'?"

Connor frowned. "How bad were they? The soldiers."

Danny looked down at his cigarette and rolled it between his thumb and forefinger. "Pretty bad."

"What is it?"

"Honestly? Don't know. Could be influenza, pneumonia, or something no one's ever heard of." Danny shrugged. "Hopefully, it sticks to soldiers."

Connor leaned against the railing. "They say it'll be over soon."

"The war?" Danny nodded. "Yeah."

For a moment, Connor looked uncomfortable. A rising star in the DA's office, he'd also been a vocal advocate of American entrance into the war. Yet somehow he managed to miss the draft, and both brothers knew who was usually responsible for "somehows" in their family.

Joe said, "Hey down there," and they looked up to see that he'd managed to reach the second-highest branch.

"You crack your head," Connor said, "Ma will shoot you."

"Not going to crack my head," Joe said, "and Ma doesn't have a gun."

"She'll use Dad's."

Joe stayed where he was, as if giving it some thought.

"How's Nora?" Danny asked, trying to keep his voice loose.

Connor waved his cigarette at the night. "Ask her yourself. She's a strange bird. She acts all proper around Ma and Dad, you know? But she ever go Bolsheviki on you?"

"Bolsheviki?" Danny smiled. "Ah, no."

"You should hear her, Dan, talking about the rights of the workers and women's suffrage and the poor immigrant children in the factories and blah, blah, blah. The old man'd keel over if he heard her sometimes. I'll tell you that's going to change, though."

"Yeah?" Danny chuckled at the idea of Nora changing, Nora so stubborn she'd die of thirst if you ordered her to drink. "How's that going to happen?"

Connor turned his head, the smile in his eyes. "You didn't hear?"

"I work eighty hours a week. Apparently I missed some gossip."

"I'm going to marry her."

Danny's mouth went dry. He cleared his throat. "You asked her?"

"Not yet. I've talked to Dad about it, though."

"Talked to Dad, but not to her."

Connor shrugged and gave him another wide grin. "What's the shock, brother? She's beautiful, we go to shows and the flickers together, she learned to cook from Ma. We have a great time. She'll make a great wife."

"Con'—" Danny started, but his younger brother held up a hand.

"Dan, Dan, I know something . . . *happened* between you two. I'm not blind. The whole family knows."

This was news to Danny. Above him, Joe scrambled around the tree like a squirrel. The air had cooled, and dusk settled softly against the neighboring row houses.

"Hey, Dan? That's why I'm telling you this. I want to know if you're comfortable with it."

Danny leaned against the rail. "What do you think 'happened' between me and Nora?"

"Well, I don't know."

Danny nodded, thinking: She'll never marry him.

"What if she says no?"

"Why would she say that?" Connor tossed his hands up at the absurdity of it.

"You never know with these Bolshies."

Connor laughed. "Like I said, that'll change quick. Why

99

wouldn't she say yes? We spend all our free time together. We—"

"The flickers, like you said. Someone to watch a show with. It's not the same."

"Same as what?"

"Love."

Connor narrowed his eyes. "That *is* love." He shook his head at Danny. "Why do you always complicate things, Dan? A man meets a woman, they share common understandings, common heritage. They marry, raise a family, instill those understandings in them. That's civilization. That's love."

Danny shrugged. Connor's anger was building with his confusion, always a dangerous combination, particularly if Connor was in a bar. Danny might have been the son who'd boxed, but Connor was the true brawler in the family.

Connor was ten months younger than Danny. This made them "Irish twins," but beyond the bloodline, they'd never had much in common. They'd graduated from high school the same day, Danny by the skin of his teeth, Connor a year early and with honors. Danny had joined the police straightaway, while Connor had accepted a full scholarship to Boston Catholic College in the South End. After two years doubling up on his classes there, he'd graduated summa cum laude and entered Suffolk Law School. There'd never been any question where he'd work once he passed the bar. He'd had a slot waiting for him in the DA's office since he'd worked there as an office boy in his late teens. Now, with four years on the job, he was starting to get bigger cases, larger prosecutions.

"How's work?" Danny said.

Connor lit a fresh cigarette. "There's some very bad people out there."

"Tell me about it."

"I'm not talking about Gusties and garden-variety plug-uglies, brother. I'm talking about radicals, bombers."

Danny cocked his head and pointed at the shrapnel scar on his own neck.

100

Connor chuckled. "Right, right. Look who I'm talking to. I guess I just never knew how . . . how . . . fucking evil these people are. We've got a guy now, we'll be deporting him when we win, and he actually threatened to blow up the Senate."

"Just talk?" Danny asked.

Connor gave that an irritated head shake. "No such thing. I went to a hanging a week ago?"

Danny said, "You went to a . . . ?"

Connor nodded. "Part of the job sometimes. Silas wants the people of the Commonwealth to know we represent them all the way to the end."

"Doesn't seem to go with your nice suit. What's that color—yellow?"

Connor swiped at his head. "They call it cream."

"Oh. Cream."

"It wasn't fun, actually." Connor looked out into the yard. "The hanging." He gave Danny a thin smile. "Around the office, though, they say you get used to it."

They said nothing for a bit. Danny could feel the pall of the world out there, with its hangings and diseases, its bombs and its poverty, descend on their little world in here.

"So, you're gonna marry Nora," he said eventually.

"That's the plan." Connor raised his eyebrows up and down.

He put his hand on his brother's shoulder. "Best of luck then, Con'."

"Thanks." Connor smiled. "Heard you just moved into a new place, by the way."

"No new place," Danny said, "just a new floor. Better view."

"Recently?"

"About a month ago," Danny said. "Apparently some news travels slow."

"It does when you don't visit your mother."

Danny placed a hand to his heart, adopted a thick brogue. "Ah, 'tis a fierce-terrible son, sure, who doesn't visit his dear old mudder every day of the week."

101

Connor chuckled. "You stayed in the North End, though?"

"It's home."

"It's a shit hole."

"You grew up there," Joe said, suddenly dangling from the lowest branch.

"That's right," Connor said, "and Dad moved us out as soon as he was able."

"Traded one slum for another," Danny said.

"An Irish slum, though," Connor said. "I'll take it over a wop slum anytime."

Joe dropped to the ground. "This isn't a slum."

Danny said, "It ain't up here on K Street, no."

"Neither's the rest of it." Joe walked up on the porch. "I know slums," he said with complete assurance and opened the door and went inside.

In his father's study, they lit cigars and asked Danny if he wanted one. He declined but rolled a cigarette and sat by the desk beside Deputy Chief Madigan. Mesplede and Donnegan were over by the decanters, pouring themselves healthy portions of his father's liquor, and Charles Steedman stood by the tall window behind his father's desk, lighting his cigar. His father and Eddie McKenna stood talking with Silas Pendergast in the corner, back by the doors. The DA nodded a lot and said very little as Captain Thomas Coughlin and Lieutenant Eddie McKenna spoke to him with their hands on their chins, their foreheads tilted low. Silas Pendergast nodded a final time, picked his hat off the hook, and bade good-bye to everyone.

"He's a fine man," his father said, coming around the desk. "He understands the common good." His father took a cigar from the humidor, snipped the end, and smiled with raised eyebrows at the rest of them. They all smiled back because his father's humor was infectious that way, even if you didn't understand the cause of it.

"Thomas," the deputy chief said, speaking in a tone of

deference to a man several ranks his inferior, "I assume you explained the chain of command to him."

Danny's father lit his cigar, clenching it in his back teeth as he got it going. "I told him that the man in the back of the cart need never see the horse's face. I trust he understood my meaning."

Claude Mesplede came around behind Danny's chair and patted him on the shoulder. "Still the great communicator, your father."

His father's eyes flicked over at Claude as Charles Steedman sat in the window seat behind him and Eddie McKenna took a seat to Danny's left. Two politicians, one banker, three cops. Interesting.

His father said, "You know why they'll have so many problems in Chicago? Why their crime rate will go through the roof after Volstead?"

The men waited and his father drew on his cigar and considered the brandy snifter on the desk by his elbow but didn't lift it.

"Because Chicago is a new city, gentlemen. The fire wiped it clean of history, of values. And New York is too dense, too sprawling, too crowded with the nonnatives. They can't maintain order, not with what's coming. But Boston"—he lifted his brandy and took a sip as the light caught the glass—"Boston is small and untainted by the new ways. Boston understands the common good, the way of things." He raised his glass. "To our fair city, gentlemen. Ah, she's a grand old broad."

They met their glasses in toast and Danny caught his father smiling at him, in the eyes if not the mouth. Thomas Coughlin alternated between a variety of demeanors and all coming and going with the speed of a spooked horse that it was easy to forget that they were all aspects of a man who was certain he was doing good. Thomas Coughlin was its servant. The good. Its salesman, its parade marshal, catcher of the dogs who nipped its ankles, pallbearer for its fallen friends, cajoler of its wavering allies.

The question remained, as it had throughout Danny's life, as to what exactly the good was. It had something to do with loyalty and something to do with the primacy of a man's honor. It was tied up in duty, and it assumed a tacit understanding of all the things about it that need never be spoken aloud. It was, purely of necessity, conciliatory to the Brahmins on the outside while remaining firmly anti-Protestant on the inside. It was anticolored, for it was taken as a given that the Irish, for all their struggles and all those still to come, were Northern European and undeniably white, white as last night's moon, and the idea had never been to seat every race at the table, just to make sure that the last chair would be saved for a Hibernian before the doors to the room were pulled shut. It was above all, as far as Danny understood it, committed to the idea that those who exemplified the good in public were allowed certain exemptions as to how they behaved in private.

His father said, "Heard of the Roxbury Lettish Workingman's Society?"

"The Letts?" Danny was suddenly aware of Charles Steedman watching him from the window. "Socialist workers group, made up mostly of Russian and Latvian émigrés."

"How about the People's Workers Party?" Eddie McKenna asked.

Danny nodded. "They're over in Mattapan. Communists."

"Union of Social Justice?"

Danny said, "What's this, a test?"

None of the men answered, just stared back at him, grave and intent.

He sighed. "Union of Social Justice is, I believe, mostly Eastern European café intellectuals. Very antiwar."

"Anti-everything," Eddie McKenna said. "Anti-American most of all. These are all Bolshevik fronts—all of them— funded by Lenin himself to stir unrest in our city."

"We don't like unrest," Danny's father said.

"How about Galleanists?" Deputy Chief Madigan said. "Heard of them?"

Again, Danny felt the rest of the room watching him.

"Galleanists," he said, trying to keep the irritation out of his voice, "are followers of Luigi Galleani. They're anarchists devoted to dismantling all government, all property, all ownership of any kind."

"How do you feel about them?" Claude Mesplede said.

"Active Galleanists? Bomb throwers?" Danny said. "They're terrorists."

"Not just Galleanists," Eddie McKenna said. "All radicals."

Danny shrugged. "The Reds don't bother me much. They seem mostly harmless. They print their propaganda rags and drink too much at night, end up disturbing their neighbors when they start singing too loud about Trotsky and Mother Russia."

"Things may have changed lately," Eddie said. "We're hearing rumors."

"Of?"

"An insurrectionary act of violence on a major scale."

"When? What kind?"

His father shook his head. "That information carries with it a need-to-know designation, and you don't need to know yet."

"In due time, Dan." Eddie McKenna gave him a big smile. "In due time."

" 'The purpose of terrorism,' " his father said, " 'is to inspire terror.' Know who said that?"

Danny nodded. "Lenin."

"He reads the papers," his father said with a soft wink.

McKenna leaned in toward Danny. "We're planning an operation to counter the radicals' plans, Dan. And we need to know exactly where your sympathies lie."

"Uhhuh," Danny said, not quite seeing the play yet.

Thomas Coughlin had leaned back from the light, his cigar gone dead between his fingers. "We'll need you to tell us what's transpiring with the social club."

"What social club?"

Thomas Coughlin frowned.

"The Boston Social Club?" Danny looked at Eddie McKenna. "*Our union?*"

"It's not a union," Eddie McKenna said. "It just wants to be."

"And we can't have that," his father said. "We're policemen, Aiden, not common laborers. There's a principle to be upheld."

"Which principle is that?" Danny said. "Fuck the working-man?" Danny took another look around the room, at the men gathered here on an innocent Sunday afternoon. His eyes fell on Steedman. "What's your stake in this?"

Steedman gave him a soft smile. "Stake?"

Danny nodded. "I'm trying to figure out just what it is you're doing here."

Steedman reddened at that and looked at his cigar, his jaw moving tightly.

Thomas Coughlin said, "Aiden, you don't speak to your elders in that tone. You don't—"

"I'm here," Steedman said, looking up from his cigar, "because workers in this country have forgotten their place. They have forgotten, young Mr. Coughlin, that they serve at the discretion of those who pay their wages and feed their families. Do you know what a ten-day strike can do? Just ten days."

Danny shrugged.

"It can cause a medium-size business to default on its loans. When loans are in default, stock plummets. Investors lose money. A lot of money. And they have to cut back *their* business. Then the bank has to step in. Sometimes, this means the only solution is foreclosure. The bank loses money, the investors lose money, *their* companies lose money, the original business goes under, and the workers lose their jobs anyway. So while the idea of unions is, on the surface, rather heart-warming, it is also quite unconscionable for reasonable men to so much as discuss it in polite company." He took a sip of his brandy. "Does that answer your question, son?"

"I'm not exactly sure how your logic applies to the public sector."

"In triplicate," Steedman said.

Danny gave him a tight smile and turned to McKenna. "Is Special Squads going after unions, Eddie?"

"We're going after subversives. Threats to this nation." He gave Danny a roll of his big shoulders. "I need you to hone your skills somewhere. Might as well start local."

"In *our* union."

"That's what you call it."

"What could this possibly have to do with an act of 'insurrectionary violence'?"

"It's a milk run," McKenna said. "You help us figure out who really runs things in there, who the members of the brain trust are, et cetera, we'll have more confidence to send you after bigger fish."

Danny nodded. "What's my end?"

His father cocked his head at that, his eyes diminishing to slits.

Deputy Chief Madigan said, "Well, I don't know if it's that—"

"Your end?" his father said. "If you succeed with the BSC and *then* succeed with the Bolsheviks?"

"Yes."

"A gold shield." His father smiled. "That's what you wanted us to say, yes? Counting on it, were you?"

Danny felt an urge to grind his teeth. "It's either on the table or it isn't."

"*If* you tell us what we need to know about the infra-structure of that alleged policeman's union? And *if* you then infiltrate a radical group of our choosing and then come back with the information necessary to stop any act of concerted violence?" Thomas Coughlin looked over at

107

Deputy Chief Madigan and then back at Danny. "We'll put you first in line."

"I don't want first in line. I want the gold shield. You've dangled it long enough."

The men traded glances, as if they hadn't counted on his reaction from the outset.

After a time, his father said, "Ah, the boy knows his mind, doesn't he?"

"He does," Claude Mesplede said.

"That's plain as the day, 'tis," Patrick Donnegan said.

Out beyond the doors, Danny heard his mother's voice in the kitchen, the words indecipherable, but whatever she said caused Nora to laugh and the sound of it made him picture Nora's throat, the flesh over her windpipe.

His father lit his cigar. "A gold shield for the man who brings down some radicals and lets us know what's on the mind of the Boston Social Club to boot."

Danny held his father's eyes. He removed a cigarette from his pack of Murads and tapped it off the edge of his brogan before lighting it. "In writing."

Eddie McKenna chuckled. Claude Mesplede, Patrick Donnegan, and Deputy Chief Madigan looked at their shoes, the rug. Charles Steedman yawned.

Danny's father raised an eyebrow. It was a slow gesture, meant to suggest he admired Danny. But Danny knew that while Thomas Coughlin had a dizzying array of character traits, admiration wasn't one of them.

"Is this the test by which you'd choose to define your life?" His father eventually leaned forward, and his face was lit with what many people could mistake for pleasure. "Or would you prefer to save that for another day?"

Danny said nothing.

His father looked around the room again. Eventually he shrugged and met his son's eyes.

"Deal."

*

By the time Danny left the study, his mother and Joe had gone to bed and the house was dark. He went out on the front landing because he could feel the house digging into his shoulders and scratching at his head, and he sat on the stoop and tried to decide what to do next. Along K Street, the windows were dark and the neighborhood was so quiet he could hear the hushed lapping of the bay a few blocks away.

"And what dirty job did they ask of you this time?" Nora stood with her back to the door.

He turned to look at her. It hurt, but he kept doing it. "Wasn't too dirty."

"Ah, wasn't too clean, either."

"What's your point?"

"My point?" She sighed. "You've not looked happy in a donkey's age."

"What's happy?" he said.

She hugged herself against the cooling night. "The opposite of you."

It had been more than five years since that Christmas Eve when Danny's father had brought Nora O'Shea through the front door, carrying her in his arms like firewood. Though his face was pink from the cold, her flesh was gray, her chattering teeth loose from malnutrition. Thomas Coughlin told the family he'd found her on the Northern Avenue docks, beset by ruffians she was when he and Uncle Eddie waded in with their nightsticks as if they were still first-year patrol men. Sure now, just look at the poor, starving waif with nary an ounce of meat on her bones! And when Uncle Eddie had reminded him that it was Christmas Eve and the poor girl managed to croak out a feeble "Thank ye, sir. Thank ye," her voice the spitting image of his own, dear departed Ma, God rest her, well wasn't it a sign from Christ Himself on the eve of His own birthday?

Even Joe, only six at the time and still in thrall to his father's grandiloquent charms, didn't buy the story, but it put the family in an extravagantly Christian mood, and Connor went to fill the tub while Danny's mother gave the gray girl with the wide, sunken eyes a cup of tea. She watched the Coughlins from behind the cup with her bare, dirty shoulders peeking out from under the greatcoat like damp stones.

Then her eyes found Danny's, and before they passed from his face, a small light appeared in them that seemed uncomfortably familiar. In that moment, one he would turn over in his head dozens of times in the ensuing years, he was sure he'd seen his own cloaked heart looking back at him through a starving girl's eyes.

Bullshit, he told himself. Bullshit.

He would learn very quickly how fast those eyes could change—how that light that had seemed a mirror of his own thoughts could go dull and alien or falsely gay in an instant. But still, knowing the light was there, waiting to appear again, he became addicted to the highly unlikely possibility of unlocking it at will.

Now she stared at him carefully on the porch and said nothing.

"Where's Connor?" he said.

"Off to the bar," she said. "Said he'd be at Henry's if you were to come looking."

Her hair was the color of sand and strung in curls that hugged her scalp and ended just below her ears. She wasn't tall, wasn't short, and something seemed to move beneath her flesh at all times, as if she were missing a layer and if you looked close enough you'd see her bloodstream.

"You two are courting, I hear."

"Stop."

"That's what I hear."

"Connor's a boy."

"He's twenty-six. Older'n you."

She shrugged. "Still a boy."

"Are you courting?" Danny flicked his cigarette into the street and looked at her.

"I don't know what we're doing, Danny." She sounded

weary. Not so much of the day, but of him. It made him feel like a child, petulant and easily bruised. "Would you like me to say that I don't feel some allegiance to this family, some weight for what I could never repay your father? That I know for sure I won't marry your brother?"

"Yes," Danny said, "that's what I'd like to hear."

"Well, I can't say that."

"You'd marry out of gratitude?"

She sighed and closed her eyes. "I don't know what I'd do."

Danny's throat felt tight, like it might collapse in on itself. "And when Connor finds out you left a husband behind in—"

"He's dead," she hissed.

"To you. Not the same as dead, though, is it?"

Her eyes were fire now. "What's your point, boy?"

"How do you think he's going to take that news?"

"All I can hope," she said, her voice weary again, "is that he takes it a fair sight better than you did."

Danny said nothing for a bit and they both stared over the short distance between them, his eyes, he hoped, as merciless as hers.

"He won't," he said and walked down the stairs into the quiet and the dark.

CHAPTER *five*

A week after Luther became a husband, he and Lila found a house off Archer Street, on Elwood, little one-bedroom with indoor plumbing, and Luther talked to some boys at the Gold Goose Billiard Parlor on Greenwood Avenue who told him the place to go for a job was the Hotel Tulsa, across the Santa Fe tracks in white Tulsa. Money be falling off trees over there, Country. Luther didn't mind them calling him Country for the time being, long as they didn't get too used to it, and he went over to the hotel and talked to the man they'd told him to see, fella by the name of Old Byron Jackon. Old Byron (everyone called him "Old Byron," even his elders) was the head of the bellmen's union. He said he'd start Luther as an elevator operator and see where things went from there.

So Luther started in the elevators, and even that was a gold mine, people giving him two bits practically every time he turned the crank or opened the cage. Oh, Tulsa was swimming in oil money! People drove the biggest motorcars and wore the biggest hats and the finest clothes and the men smoked cigars thick as pool cues and the women smelled of perfume and powder. People walked fast in Tulsa. They ate fast from large plates and drank fast from tall glasses. The men clapped one another on the back a lot and leaned in and whispered in each other's ears and then roared with laughter.

And after work the bellmen and the elevator operators and

the doormen all crossed back into Greenwood with plenty of adrenaline still ripping through their veins and they hit the pool halls and the saloons down near First and Admiral and there was some drinking and some dancing and some fighting. Some got themselves drunk on Choctaw and rye; others got higher than kites on opium or, more and more lately, heroin.

Luther was only hanging with them boys two weeks when someone asked if he'd like to make a little something extra on the side, man as fast as he was. And no sooner was the question asked than he was running numbers for the Deacon Skinner Broscious, the man so called because he was known to carefully watch over his flock and call down the wrath of the Almighty if one of them strayed. The Deacon Broscious had once been a Louisiana gambler, the story went, won himself a big pot on the same night he killed a man, the two incidents not necessarily unrelated, and he'd come to Greenwood with a fat pocket and a few girls he'd immediately put up for rent. When those original girls got themselves in a partnership frame of mind he cut them in for a slice each and then sent them out for a whole new string of younger, fresher girls with no partnership frame of mind whatsoever and then the Deacon Broscious branched out into the saloon business and the numbers business and the Choctaw and heroin and opium business and any man who fucked, fixed, boozed, or bet in Greenwood got right familiar with either the Deacon or someone who worked for him.

The Deacon Broscious weighed north of four hundred pounds. With plenty change. More often than not, if he took the night air down around Admiral and First, he did so in a big old wooden rocker that somebody'd strapped wheels to. The Deacon had him two high-boned, high-yellow, knob-jointed, thin-as-death sons of bitches working for him, name of Dandy and Smoke, and they pushed him around town at all hours of the night in that chair, and plenty nights he'd take to singing. He had a beautiful voice, high and sweet and strong, and he'd sing spirituals and chain gang songs and even did a version of "I'm a Twelve O'Clock Fella in a Nine O'Clock Town" that was a hell of a lot better than the white version you heard Byron Harlan singing on the disc record. So there he'd be, rolling up and down First Street, singing with a voice so beautiful some said God had kept it from his favorite angels so as not to encourage covetousness in their ranks entire, and Deacon Broscious would clap his hands, and his face would bead with sweat and his smile would become the size and shine of a trout, and folks would forget for a moment who he was, until one of them remembered because he owed the Deacon something, and that one, he'd get to see behind the sweat and smile and the singing and what he saw there left an imprint on children he hadn't even sired yet.

Jessie Tell told Luther that the last time a man had seriously fucked with the Deacon Broscious—"I mean lack-of-*all*-respect type of fucking?" Jessie said—Deacon up and sat on the son of a bitch. Squirmed in place until he couldn't hear the screams no more, looked down and saw that the dumb nigger'd given up the ghost, just lay in the dirt looking at nothing, mouth wide open, one arm stretched and reaching.

"Mighta told me this before I took a job from the man," Luther said.

"You running numbers, Country. You think you do that sort of thing for a *nice* man?"

Luther said, "Told you not to call me Country no more."

They were in the Gold Goose, getting loose after a long day smiling for white folk across the tracks, and Luther could feel the liquor reaching that level in his blood where everything slowed down right nice and his eyesight sharpened and he felt nothing was impossible.

Luther would soon have ample time to consider how he'd fallen into running numbers for the Deacon, and it would take him a while to realize that it had nothing to do with money—hell, with the tips he made at the Hotel Tulsa he was making nearly twice what he'd made at the munitions factory. And it wasn't like he hoped to have any future in the rackets. He'd seen enough men back in Columbus who'd thought they could climb that ladder; usually when they fell from it, they fell screaming. So why? It was that house on Elwood, he guessed, the way it crowded him until he felt the eaves dig into his shoulders. And it was Lila, much as he loved her—and he was surprised to realize how much he did sometimes, how much the sight of her blinking awake with one side of her face pressed to the pillow could fire a bolt through his heart. But before he could even get his head around that love, maybe enjoy it a little bit, here she was carrying a child, she only twenty and Luther just twenty-three. A child. A rest-of-your-life responsibility. A thing that grew up while you grew old. Didn't care if you were tired, didn't care if you were trying to concentrate on something else, didn't care if you wanted to make love. A child just *was*, thrust right into the center of your life and screaming its head off. And Luther, who'd never really known his father, was damn sure certain he'd live up to his responsibility, like it or not, but until then he wanted to live this here life at full tilt, with a little danger thrown in to spice it up, something to remember when he sat on his rocker and played with his grandkids. They'd be looking at an old man smiling like a fool, while he'd be remembering the young buck who'd run through the Tulsa night with Jessie and danced just enough on the other side of the law to say it didn't own him.

Jessie was the first and best friend Luther had made in Greenwood, and this would soon become the problem. His given name was Clarence, but his middle name was Jessup, so everyone called him Jessie when they weren't calling him Jessie Tell, and he had a way about him that drew men to him as much as women. He was a bellhop and fill-in elevator operator at the Hotel Tulsa, and he had a gift for keeping everyone's spirits up on his own high level and that could sure make a day fly. Much as Jessie'd been given a couple nicknames himself, it was only fair, since he'd done the same to everyone he met (it was Jessie who, at the Gold Goose, had first called Luther "Country"), and those names left his tongue with so much speed and certainty that usually a man started going by Jessie's nickname no matter how long he'd been called by any other on this earth. Jessie would move through the lobby of the Hotel Tulsa pushing a brass cart or lugging some bags and calling out, "Happening, Slim?" and "You *know* it's the truth, Typhoon," and following that with a soft "heh heh right," and before suppertime people were calling Bobby Slim and Gerald Typhoon and most felt better for the trade-off.

Luther and Jessie Tell had them some elevator races when times were slow and they bet on bag totals every day they worked the bell stand, hustled like mad with smile and shine for the white folk who called 'em both George even though they wore brass name tags clear as day, and after they'd crossed back over the Frisco tracks into Greenwood and retired to the saloons or the galleries down around Admiral, they kept their raps up, because they were both fast in the mouth and fast on their feet and Luther felt that between the two of them lay the kinship he'd been missing, the one he'd left behind in Columbus with Sticky Joe Beam and Aeneus James and some of the other men he'd played ball with and drank with and, in pre-Lila days, chased women with. Life—*life*—was lived here, in the Greenwood that sprung up at night with its snap of pool balls and its three-string guitars and saxophones and liquor and men unwinding after so many hours of being called George, called son, called boy, called whatever white folk felt a mind to call them. And a man could not only be forgiven, he could be *expected* to unwind with other men after days like they had, saying their "Yes, suhs" and their "How dos" and their "Sho 'nuffs."

Fast as Jessie Tell was—and he and Luther both ran the

same numbers territory and ran it fast—he was big too. Not near as big as Deacon Broscious but a man of girth, nonetheless, and he loved him his heroin. Loved him his chicken and his rye and his fat-bottomed women and his talk and his Choctaw and his song, but, man, his heroin he loved above all else.

"Shit," he said, "nigger like me got to have something slow him down, else whitey'd shoot him 'fore he could take over the world. Say I'm right, Country. Say it. 'Cause it's so and y'know it."

Problem was, a habit like Jessie had—and his habit was like the rest of him, large—got expensive, and even though he cleared more tips than any man at the Hotel Tulsa, it didn't mean much because tips were pooled and then dealt out evenly to each man at the end of a shift. And even though he was running numbers for the Deacon and that was most definitely a paying proposition, the runners getting two cents on every dollar the customers lost and Greenwood customers lost about as much as they played and they played at a fearsome rate, Jessie still couldn't keep up by playing straight.

So he skimmed.

The way running numbers worked in Deacon Broscious's town was straight simple: ain't no such thing as credit. You wanted to put a dime on the number, you paid the runner eleven cents before he left your house, the extra penny to cover the vig. You played for four bits, you paid fifty-five. And so on.

Deacon Broscious didn't believe in chasing down country niggers for their money *after* they'd lost, just couldn't see the sense in that. He had real collectors for real debt, he couldn't bother fucking up niggers' limbs for pennies. Those pennies, though, you added it up and you could fill some mail bags with it, boy, could fill a barn come those special days when folks thought luck was in the air.

Since the runners carried that cash around with them, it stood to reason that Deacon Broscious had to pick boys he

117

trusted, but the Deacon didn't get to be the Deacon by trusting anybody, so Luther had always assumed he was being watched. Not every run, mind you, just every third or so. He'd never actually seen someone doing the watching, but it sure couldn't hurt matters none to work from that assumption.

Jessie said, "You give Deacon too much credit, boy. Man can't have eyes everywhere. 'Sides, even if he did, those eyes are human, too. They can't tell if you went into the house and just Daddy played or if Mama and Grandpa and Uncle Jim all played, too. And you sure don't pocket all four of them dollars. But if you pocket one? Who's the wiser? God? Maybe if He's looking. But the Deacon ain't God."

He surely wasn't that. He was some other thing.

Jessie took a shot at the six ball and missed it clean. He gave Luther a lazy shrug. His buttery eyes told Luther he'd been hitting the spike again, probably in the alley while Luther'd used the bathroom a while back.

Luther sank the twelve.

Jessie gripped his stick to keep him up, then felt behind him for his chair. When he was sure he'd found it and centered it under his ass, he lowered himself into it and smacked his lips, tried to get some wet into that big tongue of his.

Luther couldn't help himself. "Shit going to kill you, boy."

Jessie smiled and wagged a finger at him. "Ain't going to do nothing right now but make me feel right, so shush your mouth and shoot your pool."

That was the problem with Jessie—much as the boy could talk at you, weren't no one could talk to him. There was some part of him—the core, most likely—that got plumb irritated by reason. Common sense *insulted* Jessie.

"Just 'cause folks be doing a thing," he said to Luther once, "don't make that thing a good fucking idea all to itself, do it?"

"Don't make it bad."

Jessie smiled that smile of his got him women and a free drink more often than not. "Sure it do, Country. Sure it do."

Oh, the women loved him. Dogs rolled over at the sight of him and peed all over their bellies, and children followed him when he walked Greenwood Avenue, as if gold-plated jumping jacks would spring from his trouser cuffs.

Because there was something unbroken in the man. And people followed him, maybe, just to see it break.

Luther sank the six and then the five, and when he looked up again, Jessie had gone into a nod, a bit of drool hanging from the corner of his mouth, his arms and legs wrapped around that pool stick like he'd decided it would make him a right fine wife.

They'd look after him here. Maybe set him up in the back room if the place got busy. Else, just leave him where he sat. So Luther put his stick back in the rack and took his hat from the wall and walked out into the Greenwood dusk. He thought of finding himself a game, just sit in for a few hands. There was one going on right now upstairs in the back room of Po's Gas Station, and just picturing it put an itch in his head. But he'd played in a few too many games already during his short time in Greenwood and it was all he could do hustling for tips at the hotel and running for the Deacon to keep Lila from getting any idea how much he'd lost.

Lila. He'd promised her he'd come home tonight before sunset and it was well past that now, the sky a deep dark blue and the Arkansas River gone silver and black, and while it was just about the last thing he wanted to do, what with the night filling up around him with music and loud, happy catcalls and such, Luther took a deep breath and headed home to be a husband.

Lila didn't care much for Jessie, no surprise, and she didn't care much for any of Luther's friends or his nights on the town or his moonlighting for Deacon Broscious, so the small house on Elwood Avenue had been getting smaller every day since.

A week ago when Luther had said, "Where the money

119

going to come from then?" Lila said she'd get a job, too. Luther laughed, knowing that no white folk was going to want a pregnant colored scrubbing their pots and cleaning their floors because white women wouldn't want their husbands thinking about how that baby got in there and white men wouldn't like thinking about it either. Might have to explain to the children how come they'd never seen a black stork.

After supper tonight, she said, "You a man now, Luther. A husband. You got responsibilities."

"And I'm keeping 'em up, ain't I?" Luther said. "Ain't I?"

"Well, you are, I'll grant you."

"Okay, then."

"But still, baby, you can spend some nights at home. You can get to fixing those things you said."

"What things?"

She cleared the table and Luther stood, went to the coat he'd placed on the hook when he'd come in, fished for his cigarettes.

"Things," Lila said. "You said you'd build a crib for the baby and fix the sag in the steps and—"

"And, and, and," Luther said. "Shit, woman, I work hard all day."

"I know."

"Do you?" It came out a lot harder than he'd intended.

Lila said, "Why you so cross all the time?"

Luther hated these conversations. Seemed like it was the only kind they had anymore. He lit a cigarette. "I ain't cross," he said, even though he was.

"You cross all the time." She rubbed her belly where it had already begun to show.

"Well why the fuck not?" Luther said. He hadn't meant to cuss in front of her, but he could feel the liquor in him, liquor he barely noticed drinking when he was around Jessie because Jessie and his heroin made a little whiskey seem as dangerous as lemonade. "Two months ago, I wasn't a father-to-be."

"And?"

"And what?"

"And what's that supposed to mean?" Lila placed the dishes in the sink and came back into the small living room.

"Shit mean what I said," Luther said. "A month ago—"

"What?" She stared at him, waiting.

"A month ago I wasn't in Tulsa and I wasn't shotgun-wed and I wasn't living in some shit little house on some shit little avenue in some shit little town, *Lila*. Now was I?"

"This ain't no shit town." Lila's voice went up with her back. "And you weren't shotgun-wed."

"May as well."

She got up into him, staring with stoked-coal eyes and curled fists. "You don't want me? You don't want your child?"

"I wanted a fucking choice," Luther said.

"You have your choice and you take it every night out on the streets. You ain't ever come home like a man should, and when you do, you drunk or high or both."

"Got to be," Luther said.

Her lips were trembling when she said, "And why's that?"

" 'Cause it's the only way I can put up with—" He stopped himself, but it was too late.

"With what, Luther? With me?"

"I'm going out."

She grabbed his arm. "With me, Luther? That it?"

"Go on over to your auntie's now," Luther said. "Ya'll can talk about what an un-Christian man I am. Tell yourselves how you gonna God me up."

"With me?" she said a third time, and her voice was small and soul sick.

Luther left before he could get the mind to bust something.

They spent Sundays at Aunt Marta and Uncle James's grand house on Detroit Avenue in what Luther'd come to think of as the Second Greenwood.

No one else wanted to think of it that way, but Luther knew

121

there were two Greenwoods, just like there were two Tulsas. Which one you found yourself in depended on whether you were north or south of the Frisco depot. He was sure white Tulsa was several different Tulsas when you got under the surface, but he wasn't privy to any of that, since his interactions with it never got much past "Which floor, ma'am?"

But in Greenwood, the division had become a whole lot clearer. You had "bad" Greenwood, which was the alleys off Greenwood Avenue, well north of the intersection with Archer, and you had the several blocks down around First and Admiral, where guns were fired on Friday nights and passersby could still catch a whiff of opium smoke in the Sunday-morning streets.

But "good" Greenwood, folks liked to believe, made up the other 99 percent of the community. It was Standpipe Hill and Detroit Avenue and the central business district of Greenwood Avenue. It was the First Baptist Church and the Bell & Little Restaurant and the Dreamland Theater where the Little Tramp or America's Sweetheart ambled across the screen for a fifteen-cent ticket. It was the *Tulsa Star* and a black deputy sheriff walking the streets with a polished badge. It was Dr. Lewis T. Weldon and Lionel A. Garrity, Esquire, and John and Loula Williams who owned the Williams Confectionery and the Williams One-Stop Garage and the Dreamland itself. It was O. W. Gurley, who owned the grocery store, the mercantile store, and the Gurley Hotel to boot. It was Sunday-morning services and these Sunday-afternoon dinners with the fine china and the whitest linen and something classical and delicate tinkling from the Victrola, like the sounds from a past none of them could point to.

That's where the other Greenwood got to Luther most—in that music. You only had to hear but a few bars to know it was white. Chopin, Beethoven, Brahms. Luther could just picture them sitting at their pianos, tapping away in some big room with polished floors and high windows while the servants tiptoed around outside. This was music by and for men who whipped their stable boys and fucked their maids and went on weekend hunts to kill small animals they'd never eat. Men who loved the sound of baying hounds and sudden fiight. They'd come back home, weary from lack of work, and compose or listen to music just like this, stare up at paintings of ancestors as hopeless and empty as they were, and preach to their children about right and wrong.

Uncle Cornelius had spent his life working for men like those before he'd gone blind, and Luther had met more than a few himself in his day, and he was content to step out of their path and leave them to themselves. But he couldn't stand the idea that here, in James and Marta Hollaway's dining room on Detroit Avenue, the dark faces assembled seemed determined to drink, eat, and money themselves white.

He'd much rather be down around First and Admiral right now with the bell boys and the liverymen and the men who toted shine boxes and toolboxes. Men who worked and played with equal effort. Men who wanted nothing more, as the saying went, than a little whiskey, a little dice, a little pussy to make things nice.

Not that they'd know a saying like that up here on Detroit Avenue. Hell no. Their sayings fell more along the lines of "The Lord hates a . . ." and "The Lord don't . . ." and "The Lord won't . . ." and "The Lord shall not abide a . . ." Making God sound like one irritable master, quick with the whip.

He and Lila sat at the large table and Luther listened to them talk about the white man as if he and his would soon be sitting here on Sundays alongside them.

"Mr. Paul Stewart himself," James was saying, "come into my garage the other day with his Daimler, says, 'James, sir, I don't trust no one on the other side of them tracks the way I trust you with this here car.' "

Lionel Garrity, Esquire, piped up a little later with, "It's all just a matter of time 'fore folks understand what our boys did in the war and say, It's time. Time to put all this silliness behind us. We all people. Bleed the same, think the same."

And Luther watched Lila smile and nod at that and he wanted to rip that disc record off the Victrola and break it over his knee.

Because what Luther hated most was that behind all this—all this finery, all this newfound nobility, all the wing collars and preaching and handsome furniture and new-mown lawns and fancy cars—lay fear. Terror.

If I play ball, they asked, will you let me be?

Luther thought of Babe Ruth and those boys from Boston and Chicago this summer and he wanted to say, No. They won't let you be. Comes the time they want something, they will take whatever they fucking please just to teach you.

And he imagined Marta and James and Dr. Weldon and Lionel A. Garrity, Esquire, looking back at him, gape jawed and hands out in pleading:

Teach us what?

Your place.

CHAPTER *six*

D anny met Tessa Abruzze the same week people started to get sick. At first the newspapers said it was confined to soldiers at Camp Devens, but then two civilians dropped dead on the same day in the streets of Quincy, and across the city people began to stay inside.

Danny arrived on his floor with an armful of parcels he'd carried up the tight stairwell. They contained his clothes, freshly laundered, wrapped in brown paper, and tied off with a ribbon by a laundress from Prince Street, a widow who did a dozen loads a day in the tub in her kitchen. He tried maneuvering the key into the door with the parcels still in his arms, but after a couple of failed attempts, he stepped back and placed them on the floor, and a young woman came out of her room at the other end of the hall and let out a yelp.

She said, "*Signore, signore,*" and it came out tentatively, as if she weren't sure she was worth the trouble. She leaned one hand against the wall and pink water ran down her legs and dripped off her ankles.

Danny wondered why he'd never seen her before. Then he wondered if she had the grippe. Then he noticed she was pregnant. His lock disengaged and the door popped open, and he kicked his parcels inside because nothing left behind in a hallway in the North End would stay there long. He shut the door and came down the hall toward the woman and saw that the lower part of her dress was soaked through.

125

She kept her hand on the wall and lowered her head and her dark hair fell over her mouth and her teeth were clenched into a grimace tighter than Danny had seen on some dead people. She said, "*Dio aiutami. Dio aiutami.*"

Danny said, "Where's your husband? Where's the midwife?"

He took her free hand in his and she squeezed so tight a bolt of pain ran up to his elbow. Her eyes rolled up at him and she babbled something in Italian so fast he didn't catch any of it, and he realized she didn't speak a word of English.

"Mrs. DiMassi." Danny's holler echoed down the stairwell. "Mrs. DiMassi!"

The woman squeezed his hand even harder and screamed through her teeth.

"*Dove e il vostro marito?*" Danny said.

The woman shook her head several times, though Danny had no idea if that meant she had no husband or if he just wasn't here.

"The . . . *la* . . ." Danny searched for the word for "midwife." He caressed the back of her hand and said, "Ssssh. It's okay." He looked into her wide, wild eyes. "Look . . . look, you . . . the . . . *la ostetrica!*" Danny was so excited that he'd finally remembered the word he immediately reverted to English. "Yes? Where is . . . ? *Dove e? Dove e la ostetrica?*"

The woman pounded her fist against the wall. She dug her fingers into Danny's palm and screamed so loudly that he yelled, "Mrs. *DiMassi!*" feeling a kind of panic he hadn't felt since his first day as a policeman, when it had sunk in that he was all the answer the world saw fit to give to someone else's problems.

The woman shoved her face into his and said, "*Faccia qualcosa, uomo insensato! Mi aiuti!*" and Danny didn't get all of it, but he picked up "foolish man" and "help" so he pulled her toward the stairs.

Her hand remained in his, her arm wrapped around his abdomen, the rest of her clenched against his back as they made their way down the staircase to the street. Mass General was too far to make on foot and he couldn't see any taxis or even any trucks in the streets, just people, filling it on market day, Danny thinking if it was market day there should be some fucking trucks, shouldn't there, but no, just throngs of people and fruit and vegetables and restless pigs snuffling in their straw along the cobblestone.

"Haymarket Relief Station," he said. "It's closest. You understand?"

She nodded quickly and he knew it was his tone she was responding to and they pushed their way through the crowds and people began to make way. Danny tried a few times, calling out, *"Cerco un' ostetrica! Un' ostetrica! Cè qualcuno che conosce un' ostetrica?"* but all he got were sympathetic shakes of the head.

When they broke out on the other side of the mob, the woman arched her back and her moan was small and sharp and Danny thought she was going to drop the child onto the street, two blocks from Haymarket Relief, but she fell back into him instead. He scooped her up in his arms and started walking and staggering, walking and staggering, the woman not terribly heavy, but squirming and clawing the air and slapping his chest.

They walked several blocks, time enough for Danny to find her beautiful in her agony. In spite of or because of, he wasn't sure, but beautiful nevertheless. The final block, she wrapped her arms around his neck, her wrists pressing against the muscle there, and whispered, *"Dio, aiutami. Dio, aiutami,"* over and over in his ear.

At the relief station, Danny pushed them through the first door he saw and they ended up in a brown hallway of dark oak floors and dim yellow lights and a single bench. A doctor sat on the bench, his legs crossed, smoking a cigarette. He looked at them as they came up the corridor. "What are you doing here?"

Danny, still holding the woman in his arms, said, "You serious?"

"You came in the wrong door." The doctor stubbed out his cigarette in the ashtray and stood. He got a good look at the woman. "How long's she been in labor?"

"Her water broke about ten minutes ago. That's all I know."

The doctor placed one hand under the woman's belly and another to her head. He gave Danny a look, calm and unreachable. "This woman's going into labor."

"I know."

"In your arms," the doctor said, and Danny almost dropped her.

"Wait here," the doctor said and went through some double doors halfway up the corridor. Something banged around back there and then the doctor came back through the doors with an iron gurney, one of its wheels rusted and squeaking.

Danny placed the woman on the gurney. Her eyes were closed now, her breath still puffing out through her lips in short bursts, and Danny looked down at the wetness he'd been feeling on his arms and waist, a wetness he'd thought was mostly water but now saw was blood, and he showed his arms to the doctor.

The doctor nodded and said, "What's her name?"

Danny said, "I don't know."

The doctor frowned at that and then he pushed the gurney past Danny and back through the double doors and Danny heard him calling for a nurse.

Danny found a bathroom at the end of the hall. He washed his hands and arms with brown soap and watched the blood swirl pink in the basin. The woman's face hung in his mind. Her nose was slightly crooked with a bump halfway down the bridge, and her upper lip was thicker than her lower, and she had a small mole on the underside of her jaw, barely noticeable because her skin was so dark, almost as dark as her hair. He could hear her voice in his chest and feel her thighs and lower back in his palms, see the arch of her neck as she'd ground her head into the gurney mattress.

He found the waiting area at the far end of the hall. He entered from behind the admitting desk and came around to sit among the bandaged and the sniffling. One guy removed a black bowler from his head and vomited into it. He wiped his mouth with a handkerchief. He peered into the bowler, and then he looked at the other people in the waiting room; he seemed embarrassed. He carefully placed the bowler under the wooden bench and wiped his mouth again with the handkerchief and sat back and closed his eyes. A few people had surgical masks over their faces, and when they coughed the coughs were wet. The admitting nurse wore a mask as well. No one spoke English except for a teamster whose foot had been run over by a horse drawn cart. He told Danny the accident had happened right out front, else he'd have walked to a real hospital, the kind fit for Americans. Several times he glanced at the dried blood covering Danny's belt and groin, but he didn't ask how it had gotten there.

A woman came in with her teenage daughter. The woman was thick-waisted and dark but her daughter was thin and almost yellow and she coughed without stopping, the sound of it like metal gears grinding under water. The teamster was the first of them to ask the nurse for a surgical mask, but by the time Mrs. DiMassi found Danny in the waiting area, he wore one, too, feeling sheepish and ashamed, but they could still hear the girl, down another corridor and behind another set of double doors, those gears grinding.

"Why you wear that, Officer Danny?" Mrs. DiMassi sat beside him.

Danny took it off. "A very sick woman was here."

She said, "Lot of people sick today. I say fresh air. I say go up on the roofs. Everyone say I crazy. They stay inside."

"You heard about . . ."

"Tessa, yes."

"Tessa?"

Mrs. DiMassi nodded. "Tessa Abruzze. You carry her here?"

Danny nodded.

Mrs. DiMassi chuckled. "Whole neighborhood talking. Say you not as strong as you look."

Danny smiled. "That so?"

She said, "Yes. So. They say your knees buckle and Tessa not heavy woman."

"You notify her husband?"

"Bah." Mrs. DiMassi swatted the air. "She have no husband. Only father. Father a good man. Daughter?" She swatted the air again.

"So you don't hold her in high regard," Danny said.

"I would spit," she said, "but this clean floor."

"Then why are you here?"

"She my tenant," she said simply.

Danny placed a hand to the little old woman's back and she rocked in place, her feet swinging above the floor.

By the time the doctor entered the waiting room, Danny had put his mask back on and Mrs. DiMassi wore one as well. It had been a man this time, midtwenties, a freight yard worker by the looks of his clothes. He'd dropped to a knee in front of the admitting desk. He held up a hand as if to say he was fine, he was fine. He didn't cough, but his lips and the flesh under his jaw were purple. He remained in that position, his breath rattling, until the nurse came around to get him. She helped the man to his feet. He reeled in her grip. His eyes were red and wet and saw nothing of the world in front of him.

So Danny put his mask back on and went behind the admitting desk and got one for Mrs. DiMassi and a few others in the waiting room. He handed them out and sat back down, feeling each breath he exhaled press back against his lips and nose.

Mrs. DiMassi said, "Paper say only soldiers get it."

Danny said, "Soldiers breathe the same air."

"You?"

Danny patted her hand. "Not so far."

He started to remove his hand, but she closed hers over it. "Nothing get you, I think."

"Okay."

"So I stay close." Mrs. DiMassi moved in against him until their legs touched.

The doctor came out into the waiting room and, though he wore one himself, seemed surprised by all the masks.

"It's a boy," he said and squatted in front of them. "Healthy."

"How is Tessa?" Mrs. DiMassi said.

"That's her name?"

Mrs. DiMassi nodded.

"She had a complication," the doctor said. "There's some bleeding I'm concerned about. Are you her mother?"

Mrs. DiMassi shook her head.

"Landlady," Danny said.

"Ah," the doctor said. "She have family?"

"A father," Danny said. "He's still being located."

"I can't let anyone but immediate family in to see her. I hope you understand."

Danny kept his voice light. "Serious, Doctor?"

The doctor's eyes remained weary. "We're trying, Officer."

Danny nodded.

"If you hadn't carried her here, though?" the doctor said. "The world would, without question, be a hundred ten pounds lighter. Choose to look at it that way."

"Sure."

The doctor gave Mrs. DiMassi a courtly nod and rose from his haunches.

"Dr. . . ." Danny said.

"Rosen," the doctor said.

"Dr. Rosen," Danny said, "how long are we going to be wearing masks, you think?"

Dr. Rosen took a long look around the waiting room. "Until it stops."

"And it isn't stopping?"

"It's barely started," the doctor said and left them there.

Tessa's father, Federico Abruzze, found Danny that night on the roof of their building. After the hospital, Mrs. DiMassi had berated and harangued all her tenants into moving their mattresses up onto the roof not long after the sun went down. And so they assembled four stories above the North End under the stars and the thick smoke from the Portland Meat Factory and the sticky wafts from the USIA molasses tank.

Mrs. DiMassi brought her best friend, Denise Ruddy-Cugini, from Prince Street. She also brought her niece, Arabella and Arabella's husband, Adam, a bricklayer recently arrived from Palermo sans passport. They were joined by Claudio and Sophia Mosca and their three children, the oldest only five and Sophia already showing with the fourth. Shortly after their arrival, Lou and Patricia Imbriano dragged their mattresses up the fire escape and were followed by the newly-weds, Joseph and Concetta Limone, and finally, Steve Coyle.

Danny, Claudio, Adam, and Steve Coyle played craps on the black tar, their backs against the parapet, and Claudio's homemade wine went down easier with every roll. Danny could hear coughing and fever-shouts from the streets and buildings, but he could also hear mothers calling their children home and the squeak of laundry being drawn across the lines between the tenements and a man's sharp, sudden laughter and an organ grinder in one of the alleys, his instrument slightly out of tune in the warm night air.

No one on the roof was sick yet. No one coughed or felt flushed or nauseated. No one suffered from what were rumored to be the telltale early signs of infection—headache or pains in the legs—even though most of the men were exhausted from twelve-hour workdays and weren't sure their bodies would notice the difference. Joe Limone, a baker's assistant, worked fifteen-hour days and scoffed at the lazy twelve-hour men, and Concetta Limone, in an apparent effort to keep up with her husband, reported for work at Patriot Wool at five in the morning and left at six-thirty in the evening. Their first night on the rooftop was like the nights during the Feasts of the Saints, when Hanover Street was laureled in lights and flowers and the priests led parades up the street and the air smelled of incense and red sauce. Claudio had made a kite for his son, Bernardo Thomas, and the boy stood with the other children in the center of the roof and the yellow kite looked like a fin against the dark blue sky.

Danny recognized Federico as soon as he stepped out on the roof. He'd passed him on the stairs once when his arms were filled with boxes—a courtly old man dressed in tan linen. His hair and thin mustache were white and clipped tight to his skin and he carried a walking stick the way landed gentry did, not as an aid, but as a totem. He removed his fedora as he spoke to Mrs. DiMassi and then looked over at Danny sitting against the parapet with the other men. Danny rose as Federico Abruzze crossed to him.

"Mr. Coughlin?" he said with a small bow and perfect English.

"Mr. Abruzze," Danny said and stuck out his hand. "How's your daughter?"

Federico shook the hand with both of his and gave Danny a curt nod. "She is fine. Thank you very much for asking."

"And your grandson?"

"He is strong," Federico said. "May I speak with you?"

Danny stepped over the dice and loose change and he and Federico walked to the eastern edge of the roof. Federico removed a white handkerchief from his pocket and placed it on the parapet. He said, "Please, sit."

Danny took a seat on the handkerchief, feeling the waterfront at his back and the wine in his blood.

"A pretty night," Federico said. "Even with so much coughing."

"Yes."

133

"So many stars."

Danny looked up at the bright splay of them. He looked back at Federico Abruzze, getting the impression of tribal leader from the man. A small-town country mayor, perhaps, a dispenser of wisdom in the town piazza on summer nights.

Federico said, "You are well known around the neighborhood."

Danny said, "Really?"

He nodded. "They say you are an Irish policeman who holds no prejudice against the Italians. They say you grew up here and even after a bomb exploded in your station house, even after you've worked these streets and seen the worst of our people, you treat everyone as a brother. And now you have saved my daughter's life and the life of my grandson. I thank you, sir."

Danny said, "You're welcome."

Federico placed a cigarette to his lips and snapped a match off his thumbnail to light it, staring at Danny through the flame. In the flare of light, he looked younger suddenly, his face smooth, and Danny guessed him to be in his late fifties, ten years younger than he looked from a distance.

He waved his cigarette at the night. "I never leave a debt unpaid."

"You don't owe a debt to me," Danny said.

"But I do, sir," he said. "I do." His voice was softly musical. "But the cost of immigrating to this country has left me of modest means. Would you, at the very least, sir, allow my daughter and I to cook for you some night?" He placed a hand to Danny's shoulder. "Once she is well enough, of course."

Danny looked into the man's smile and wondered about Tessa's missing husband. Was he dead? Had there ever been one? From what Danny understood of Italian customs, he couldn't imagine a man of Federico's stature and upbringing allowing an unwed, pregnant daughter to remain in his sight, let alone his home. And now it seemed the man was trying to engineer a courtship between Danny and Tessa.

How strange.

"I'd be honored, sir."

"Then it's done." Federico leaned back. "And the honor is all mine. I will leave word once Tessa is well."

"I look forward to it."

Federico and Danny walked back across the roof toward the fire escape.

"This sickness." Federico's arm spanned the roofs around them. "It will pass?"

"I hope so."

"I do as well. So much hope in this country, so much possibility. It would be a tragedy to learn to suffer as Europe has." He turned at the fire escape and took Danny's shoulders in his hands. "I thank you again, sir. Good night."

"Good night," Danny said.

Federico descended through the black iron, the walking stick tucked under one arm, his movements fluid and assured, as if he'd grown up with mountains nearby, rocky hills to climb. Once he was gone, Danny found himself still staring down, trying to give a name to the odd sense he had that something else had transpired between them, something that got lost in the wine in his blood. Maybe it was the way he'd said *debt*, or *suffer*, as if the words had different meanings in Italian. Danny tried to snatch at the threads, but the wine was too strong; the thought slipped off into the breeze and he gave up trying to catch it and returned to his craps game.

A little later in the night, they launched the kite again at Bernardo Thomas's insistence, but the twine slipped from the boy's fingers. Before he could cry, Claudio let out a whoop of triumph, as if the point of any kite were to eventually set it free. The boy wasn't immediately convinced and stared after it with a tremble in his chin, so the other adults joined in at the edge of the roof. They raised their fists and shouted. Bernardo Thomas began to laugh and clap, and the other children joined in, and soon they all stood in celebration and urged the yellow kite onward into the deep, dark sky.

By the end of the week, the undertakers had hired men to guard the coffins. The men varied in appearance—some had come from private security companies and knew how to bathe and shave, others had the look of washed-up footballers or boxers, a few in the North End were low-rung members of the Black Hand—but all carried shotguns or rifles. Among the afflicted were carpenters, and even if they'd been healthy, it was doubtful they could have kept up with the demand. At Camp Devens, the grippe killed sixty-three soldiers in one day. It rooted its way into tenements in the North End and South Boston and the rooming houses of Scollay Square and tore through the shipyards of Quincy and Weymouth. Then it caught the train lines, and the papers reported outbreaks in Hartford and New York City.

It reached Philadelphia on the weekend during fine weather. People filled the streets for parades that supported the troops and the buying of Liberty Bonds, the Waking Up of America, and the strengthening of moral purity and fortitude best exemplified by the Boy Scouts. By the following week, death carts roamed the streets for bodies placed on porches the night before and morgue tents sprang up all over eastern Pennsylvania and western New Jersey. In Chicago it took hold first on the South Side, then on the East, and the rails carried it out across the Plains.

There were rumors. Of an imminent vaccine. Of a German submarine that had been sighted three miles out in Boston Harbor in August; some claimed to have seen it rise out of the sea and exhale a plume of orange smoke that had drifted toward shore. Preachers cited passages in Revelations and Ezekiel that prophesied an airborne poison as punishment for a new century's promiscuity and immigrant mores. The Last Times, they said, had arrived.

Word spread through the underclass that the only cure was

garlic. Or turpentine on sugar cubes. Or kerosene on sugar cubes if turpentine wasn't available. So the tenements reeked. They reeked of sweat and bodily discharges and the dead and the dying and garlic and turpentine. Danny's throat clogged with it and his nostrils burned, and some days, woozy from kerosene vapors and stuffed up from the garlic, his tonsils scraped raw, he'd think he'd finally come down with it. But he hadn't. He'd seen it fell doctors and nurses and coroners and ambulance drivers and two cops from the First Precinct and six more from other precincts. And even as it blasted a hole through the neighborhood he'd come to love with a passion he couldn't even explain to himself, he knew it wouldn't stick to him.

Death had missed him at Salutation Street, and now it circled him and winked at him but then settled on someone else. So he went into the tenements where several cops refused to go, and he went into the boardinghouses and rooming houses and gave what comfort he could to those gone yellow and gray with it, those whose sweat darkened the mattresses.

Days off vanished in the precinct. Lungs rattled like tin walls in high wind and vomit was dark green, and in the North End slums, they took to painting Xs on the doors of the contagious, and more and more people slept on the roofs. Some mornings, Danny and the other cops of the Oh-One stacked the bodies on the sidewalk like shipyard piping and waited into the afternoon sun for the meat wagons to arrive. He continued to wear a mask but only because it was illegal not to. Masks were bullshit. Plenty of people who never took them off got the grippe all the same and died with their heads on fire.

He and Steve Coyle and another half-dozen cops responded to a suspicion-of-murder call off Portland Street. As Steve knocked on the door, Danny could see the adrenaline flare in the eyes of the other men in the hallway. The guy who eventually opened the door wore a mask, but his eyes were red with it and his breaths were liquid. Steve and Danny looked at the knife haft sticking out of the center of his chest for twenty seconds before they realized what they were seeing.

The guy said, "Fuck you fellas bothering me for?"

Steve had his hand on his revolver but it remained holstered. He held out his palm to get the guy to take a step back. "Who stabbed you, sir?"

The other cops in the hall moved on that, spreading out behind Danny and Steve.

"I did," the guy said.

"You stabbed yourself?"

The guy nodded, and Danny noticed a woman sitting on the couch behind the guy. She wore a mask, too, and her skin was the blue of the infected and her throat was cut.

The guy leaned against the door, and the movement brought a fresh darkening to his shirt.

"Let me see your hands," Steve said.

The guy raised his hands and his lungs rattled with the effort. "Could one of you fellas pull this out of my chest?"

Steve said, "Sir, step away from the door."

He stepped out of their way and fell on his ass and sat looking at his thighs. They entered the room. No one wanted to touch the guy, so Steve trained his revolver on him.

The guy placed both hands on the haft and tugged, but it didn't budge, and Steve said, "Put your hands down, sir."

The guy gave Steve a loose smile. He lowered his hands and sighed.

Danny looked at the dead woman. "You kill your wife, sir?"

A slight shake of his head. "Cured her. Nothing else I could do, fellas. This thing?"

Leo West called from the back of the apartment. "We got kids in here."

"Alive?" Steve called.

The guy on the floor shook his head again. "Cured them, too."

"Three of 'em," Leo West called. "Jesus." He stepped back out of the room. His face was pale and he'd unbuttoned his collar. "Jesus," he said again. "Shit."

Danny said, "We need to get an ambulance down here."

Rusty Aborn gave that a bitter chuckle. "Sure, Dan. What's it taking them these days—five, six hours?"

Steve cleared his throat. "This guy just left Ambulance Country." He put his foot on the guy's shoulder and gently tipped the corpse to the floor.

Two days later, Danny carried Tessa's infant out of her apartment in a towel. Federico was nowhere to be found, and Mrs. DiMassi sat by Tessa as she lay in bed with a wet towel on her forehead and stared at the ceiling. Her skin had yellowed with it, but she was conscious. Danny held the infant as she glanced first at him and then at the bundle in his arms, the child's skin the color and texture of stone, and then she turned her eyes to the ceiling again and Danny carried the child down the stairs and outside, just as he and Steve Coyle had carried Claudio's body out the day before.

Danny made sure to call his parents most every night and managed to make one trip home during the pandemic. He sat with his family and Nora in the parlor on K Street and they drank tea, slipping the cups under the masks Ellen Coughlin demanded the family wear everywhere but in the privacy of their own bedrooms. Nora served the tea. Normally Avery Wallace would have performed that duty, but Avery hadn't shown up for work in three days. Had it bad, he'd told Danny's father over the phone, had it deep. Danny had known Avery since he and Connor were boys, and it only now occurred to him that he'd never visited the man's home or met his family. Because he was colored?

There it was.

Because he was colored.

He looked up from his teacup at the rest of the family and the sight of them all—uncommonly silent and stiff in their gestures as they lifted their masks to sip their tea—struck him and Connor as absurd at the same time. It was as if they were still altar boys serving mass at Gate of Heaven and one look from either brother could cause the other to laugh at the least appropriate moment. No matter how many whacks on the ass they took from the old man, they just couldn't help it. It got so bad the decision was made to separate them, and after sixth grade, they never served mass together again.

The same feeling gripped them now and the laugh burst through Danny's lips first and Connor was a half step behind. Then they were both possessed by it, placing their teacups on the floor and giving in.

"What?" their father said. "What's so funny?"

"Nothing," Connor managed, and it came out muffled through the mask, which only made Danny laugh harder.

Their mother, sounding cross and confused, said, "What? What?"

"Jeeze, Dan," Connor said, "get a load of himself."

Danny knew he was talking about Joe. He tried not to look, he did, but then he looked over and saw the little kid sitting in a chair so big his shoes barely reached the edge of the cushion. Joe, sitting there with his big wide eyes and the ridiculous mask and the teacup resting on the lap of his plaid knickerbockers, looking at his brothers like they'd provide an answer to him. But there wasn't any answer. It was all so silly and ridiculous and Danny noticed his little brother's argyle socks and his eyes watered as his laughter boomed even harder.

Joe decided to join in and Nora followed, both of them uncertain at first but gathering in strength because Danny's laughter had always been so infectious and neither could remember the last time they'd seen Connor laugh so freely or helplessly and then Connor sneezed and everyone stopped laughing.

A fine spray of red dots peppered the inside of his mask and bled through to the outside.

Their mother said, "Holy Mary Mother of Jesus," and blessed herself.

"What?" Connor said. "It was a sneeze."

"Connor," Nora said. "Oh God, dear Connor."

"What?"

"Con'," Danny said and came out of his chair, "take off your mask."

"Oh no oh no oh no," their mother whispered.

Connor took off the mask, and when he got a good look at it, he gave it a small nod and took a breath.

Danny said, "Let's me and you have a look in the bathroom."

No one else moved at first, and Danny got Connor into the bathroom and locked the door as they heard the whole family find their legs and assemble out in the hall.

"Tilt your head," Danny said.

Connor tilted his head. "Dan."

"Shut up. Let me look."

Someone turned the knob from the outside and his father said, "Open up."

"Give us a second, will ya?"

"Dan," Connor said, and his voice was still tremulous with laughter.

"Will you keep your head back? It's not funny."

"Well, you're looking up my nose."

"I know I am. Shut up."

"You see any boogers?"

"A few." Danny felt a smile trying to push through the muscles in his face. Leave it to Connor—serious as the grave on a normal day and now, possibly facing that grave, he couldn't keep serious.

Someone rattled the door again and knocked.

"I picked it," Connor said.

"What?"

"Just before Ma brought out the tea. I was in here. Had half my hand up there, Dan. Had one of those sharp rocks in there, you know the ones?"

Danny stopped looking in his brother's nose. "You what?"

"Picked it," Connor said. "I guess I need to cut my nails."

Danny stared at him and Connor laughed. Danny slapped

141

the side of his head and Connor rabbit-punched him. By the time they opened the door to the rest of the family, standing pale and angry in the hall, they were laughing again like bad altar boys.

"He's fine."

"I'm fine. Just a nosebleed. Look, Ma, it stopped."

"Get a fresh mask from the kitchen," their father said and walked back into the parlor with a wave of disgust.

Danny caught Joe looking at them with something akin to wonder.

"A nosebleed," he said to Joe, drawing the word out.

"It's not funny," their mother said, and her voice was brittle.

"I know, Ma," Connor said, "I know."

"I do, too," Danny said, catching a look from Nora now that nearly matched their mother's, and then remembering her calling his brother "dear" Connor.

When did that start?

"No, you don't," their mother said. "You don't at all. The two of you never did." And she went into her bedroom and closed the door.

By the time Danny heard, Steve Coyle had been sick for five hours. He'd woken that morning, thighs turned to plaster, ankles swollen, calves twitching, head throbbing. He didn't waste time pretending it was something else. He slipped out of the bedroom he'd shared last night with the Widow Coyle and grabbed his clothes and went out the door. Never paused, not even with his legs the way they were, dragging under the rest of him like they might just decide to stay put even if his torso kept going. After a few blocks, he told Danny, fucking legs screamed so much it was like they belonged to someone else. Fucking wailed, every step. He'd tried walking to the streetcar stop then realized he could infect the whole car. Then he remembered the streetcars had stopped running anyway. So a walk, then. Eleven blocks from the Widow

142

Coyle's cold-water flat at the top of Mission Hill all the way down to the Peter Bent Brigham Hospital. Damn near crawling by the time he reached it, folded over like a broken match, cramps ballooning up through his stomach, his chest, his throat for Christ's sake. And his head, Jesus. By the time he reached the admitting desk, it was like someone hammered pipe through his eyes.

He told all this to Danny from behind a pair of muslin curtains in the infectious disease ward of the intensive care unit at the Peter Bent. There was no one else in the ward the afternoon Danny came to see him, just the lumpen shape of a body beneath a sheet across the aisle. The rest of the beds were empty, the curtains pulled back. Somehow that was worse.

They'd given Danny a mask and gloves; the gloves were in his coat pocket; the mask hung at his throat. And yet he kept the muslin between him and Steve. Catching it didn't scare him. These past few weeks? If you hadn't made peace with your maker, then you didn't believe you'd been made. But watching it drain Steve to the ground powder of himself—that would be something else. Something Danny would pass the cup on if Steve allowed him. Not the dying, just the witnessing.

Steve spoke like he was trying to gargle at the same time. The words pushed up through phlegm and the ends of sentences often drowned. "No Widow. Believe that?"

Danny said nothing. He'd only met the Widow Coyle once, and his sole impression was one of fussiness and anxious self-regard.

"Can't see you." Steve cleared his throat.

Danny said, "I can see you, pal."

"Pull it back, would ya?"

Danny didn't move right away.

"You scared? I don't blame ya. Forget it."

Danny leaned forward a few times. He hitched his pants at the knees. He leaned forward again. He pulled back the curtain.

143

His friend sat upright, the pillow dark from his head. His face was swollen and skeletal at the same time, like dozens of the infected, living and dead, that he and Danny had run across this month. His eyes bulged from their sockets, as if trying to escape, and ran with a milky film that pooled in the corners. But he wasn't purple. Or black. He wasn't hacking his lungs up through his mouth or defecating where he lay. So, all in all, not as sick as one feared. Not yet anyway.

He gave Danny an arched eyebrow, an exhausted grin.

"Remember those girls I courted this summer?"

Danny nodded. "Did more than court some of them."

He coughed. A small one, into his fist. "I wrote a song. In my head. 'Summer Girls.' "

Danny could suddenly feel the heat coming off him. If he leaned within a foot of him, the waves found his face.

" 'Summer Girls,' eh?"

" 'Summer Girls.' " Steve's eyes closed. "Sing it for you someday."

Danny found a bucket of water on the bedside table. He reached in and pulled out a cloth and squeezed it. He placed the cloth on Steve's forehead. Steve's eyes snapped up to him, wild and grateful. Danny moved down his forehead and wiped his cheeks. He dropped the hot cloth back into the cooler water and squeezed again. He wiped his partner's ears, the sides of his neck, his throat and chin.

"Dan."

"Yeah?"

Steve grimaced. "Like a horse is sitting on my chest."

Danny kept his eyes clear. He didn't remove them from Steve's face when he dropped the cloth back in the bucket. "Sharp?"

"Yeah. Sharp."

"Can you breathe?"

"Not too good."

"Probably I should get a doctor, then."

Steve flicked his eyes at the suggestion.

Danny patted his hand and called for the doctor.

"Stay here," Steve said. His lips were white.

Danny smiled and nodded. He swiveled on the small stool they'd wheeled over to the bed when he arrived. Called for a doctor again.

Avery Wallace, seventeen years the houseman for the Coughlin family, succumbed to the grippe and was buried at Cedar Grove Cemetery in a plot Thomas Coughlin had bought for him a decade ago. Only Thomas, Danny, and Nora attended the short funeral. No one else.

Thomas said, "His wife died twenty years ago. Children scattered, most to Chicago, one to Canada. They never wrote. He lost track. He was a good man. Hard to know, but a good man, nonetheless."

Danny was surprised to hear a soft, subdued grief in his father's voice.

His father picked up a handful of dirt as Avery Wallace's coffin was lowered into the grave. He tossed the dirt on the wood. "Lord have mercy on your soul."

Nora kept her head down, but the tears fell from her chin. Danny was stunned. How was it that he'd known this man most of his life and yet somehow had never really seen him?

He tossed his own handful of dirt on the coffin.

Because he was colored. That's why.

Steve walked out of the Peter Bent Brigham Hospital ten days after he'd walked in. Like thousands of others infected in the city, he'd survived, even as the grippe made its steady way across the rest of the country, crossing into California and New Mexico the same weekend he walked with Danny to a taxi.

He walked with a cane. Always would, the doctors promised. The influenza had weakened his heart, damaged his brain. The headaches would never leave him. Simple speech would sometimes be a problem, strenuous activity of any kind would probably kill him. A week ago he'd joked about that, but today he was quiet.

It was a short walk to the taxi stand but it took a long time.

"Not even a desk job," he said as they reached the front taxicab in the line.

"I know," Danny said. "I'm sorry."

" 'Too strenuous,' they said."

Steve worked his way into the cab and Danny handed him his cane. He came around the other side and got in.

"Where to?" the cabdriver asked.

Steve looked at Danny. Danny looked back, waiting.

"You guys deaf? Where to?"

"Keep your knickers cinched." Steve gave him the address of the rooming house on Salem Street. As the driver pulled off the curb, Steve looked over at Danny. "You help me pack up my room?"

"You don't have to leave."

"I can't afford it. No job."

"The Widow Coyle?" Danny said.

Steve shrugged. "Ain't seen her since I got it."

"Where you going to go?"

Another shrug. "Got to be somebody looking to hire a heartsick cripple."

Danny didn't say anything for a minute. They bumped along Huntington.

"There's got to be some way to—"

Steve put a hand on his arm. "Coughlin, I love ya, but there's not always 'some way.' Most people fall? No net. None. We just go off."

"Where?"

Steve was quiet for a bit. He looked out the window. He pursed his lips. "Where the people with no nets end up. That place."

146

CHAPTER *seven*

Luther was shooting pool alone in the Gold Goose when Jessie came around to tell him the Deacon wanted to see them. It was empty in the Goose because it was empty all over Greenwood, all over Tulsa, the flu having come in like a dust storm until at least one member of most families had gotten it and half of those had died. It was against the law right now to go outside without a mask, and most businesses in the sinners' end of Greenwood had closed up shop, though old Calvin, who ran the Goose, said he'd stay open no matter what, said if the Lord wanted his tired old ass, He could just come get it for all the good it would do Him. So Luther came by and practiced his pool, loving how crisp the balls snapped in all that quiet.

The Hotel Tulsa was closed until people stopped turning blue, and nobody was betting numbers, so there wasn't no money to be made right now. Luther forbade Lila to go out, said they couldn't risk it for her or the baby, but this had meant he'd been expected to stay home with her. He had, and it was mostly better than he would have imagined. They fixed up the place a bit and gave every room a fresh coat of paint and hung the curtains Aunt Marta had given them as a wedding present. They found time to make love most every afternoon, slower than ever before, gentler, soft smiles and chuckles replacing the hungry grunts and groans of summer. He remembered in those weeks how deeply he loved this

147

woman and that loving her and having her love him back made him a worthy man. They built dreams of their future and their baby's future, and Luther, for the first time, could picture a life in Greenwood, had formed a loose ten-year plan in which he'd work as hard as a man could and keep socking away the money until he could start his own business, maybe as a carpenter, maybe as the owner/operator of a repair shop for all the different gadgets that seemed to sprout out from the heart of this country damn near every day. Luther knew if you built something mechanical, sooner or later it broke, and when it did most wouldn't know how to fix it, but a man with Luther's gifts could have it back in your house and good as new by nightfall.

Yeah, for a couple weeks there, he *could* see it, but then the house started closing in on him again and those dreams went dark when he pictured growing old in some house on Detroit Avenue, surrounded by people like Aunt Marta and her ilk, going to church, laying off the liquor and the billiards and the fun until one day he woke up and his hair was speckled white and his speed was gone and he'd never done nothing with his life but chase someone else's version of it.

So he went down to the Goose to keep the itching in his head from coming out through his eyes and when Jessie came in, that itch spread into a warm smile in his head because, boy, he'd missed their days together—just two weeks ago, but it felt like a couple years—when they'd all poured over the tracks from White Town and had them some play, had them some *times*.

"I went by your house," Jessie said, pulling off his mask.

"Fuck you taking that thing off for?" Luther said.

Jessie looked over at Calvin, then at Luther. "You both wearing yours, so what's *I* got to worry about?"

Luther just stared at him because for once Jessie made a bit of sense and it annoyed him that he hadn't thought of it first.

Jessie said, "Lila told me you might be here. I 'spect that woman don't like me, Country."

"You keep your mask on?"

"What?"

"With my wife? You keep your mask on when you talked to her?"

"Hell, yeah. 'Course, boy."

"All right then."

Jessie took a sip from his hip flask. "Deacon needs to see us."

"Us?"

Jessie nodded.

"What for?"

Jessie shrugged.

"When?"

" 'Bout half an hour ago."

"Shit," Luther said. "Whyn't you get here sooner?"

" 'Cause I went to your house first."

Luther placed his cue in the rack. "We in trouble?"

"Nah, nah. Ain't like that. He just want to see us."

"What for?"

"I told you," Jessie said, "I don't know."

"Then how you know it ain't bad?" Luther said as they walked out of the place.

Jessie looked back at him as he tied the mask off behind his head. "Tighten your corset, woman. Show some grit."

"Put some grit up your ass."

"Talking it ain't walking it, Negro," Jessie said and shook his big ass at him as they ran up the empty street.

Ya'll take a seat over here by me now," the Deacon Broscious said when they entered the Club Almighty. "Right over here now, boys. Come on."

He wore a broad smile and a white suit over a white shirt and a red tie the same color as his velvet hat. He sat at a round table at the back of the club near the stage and he waved them over through the dim light as Smoke snapped the lock on the door behind them. Luther felt that snap vibrate in his Adam's

149

apple. He'd never been in the club when it wasn't open for business, and its tan leather booths and red walls and cherry-wood banquettes felt less sinful but more threatening at noon.

The Deacon kept waving his arm until Luther took the chair on the left and Jessie the one on the right, and the Deacon poured them each a tall glass of bonded, prewar Canadian whiskey and slid the glasses across the table and said, "My boys. Yes, indeed. How ya'll doing now?"

Jessie said, "Right fine, sir."

Luther managed, "Very good, sir, thanks for asking."

The Deacon wasn't wearing his mask, though Smoke and Dandy were, and his smile was big and white. "Aw, that's music to my ears, I do swear." He reached across the table and managed to clap both of them on a shoulder. "Ya'll making the money, right? Heh heh heh. Yeah. You liking that, right? Making them greenbacks?"

Jessie said, "We trying, sir."

"Trying, hell. *Doing* is what I see. Ya'll the best runners I got."

"Thank you, sir. Things been a little tight of late because a that flu. So many people sick, sir, they ain't got no heart for the numbers right now."

The Deacon waved that away. "People get sick. What you gone do? Am I right? They sick and their loved ones be dying? Bless us, Heavenly Father, it tries the heart to see so much suffering. Everyone walking the streets with masks on and the undertakers running out of coffins? Lord. Times like these, you puts the bidness aside. You just puts it up on a shelf and pray for the misery to end. And when it do? When it do, then you go right back to bidness. Damn sure you do. But not"— he pointed his finger at them—"*until* then. Can I get an 'amen' on that, my brothers?"

"Amen," Jessie said, then lifted his mask and ducked his glass under there and slammed back his whiskey.

"Amen," Luther said and took a small drink from his glass.

"Shit, child," the Deacon said. "You supposed to drink that not romance it."

Jessie laughed and crossed his legs, getting comfy.

Luther said, "Yes, sir," and threw the whole thing back and the Deacon refilled their glasses and Luther realized that Dandy and Smoke now stood behind them, no more than a step away, though Luther couldn't have said when it was they'd arrived in that spot.

The Deacon took a long slow drink from his own glass and said, "Ahhh," and licked his lips. He folded his hands and leaned into the table. "Jessie."

"Yes, sir?"

"Clarence *Jessup* Tell," Deacon Broscious said, turning those words into song.

"In the flesh, sir."

The Deacon's smile returned, brighter than ever. "Jessie, let me ask you something. What's the most memorable moment of your life?"

"Sir?"

The Deacon raised his eyebrows. "You ain't got one?"

"I'm not sure I understand, sir."

"The most memorable moment of your life," the Deacon repeated.

Luther felt sweat bathe his thighs.

"Everyone's got one," the Deacon said. "Could be a happy experience, could be sad. Could be a night with a girl. Am I right? Am I right?" He laughed, his face folding all over his nose with the effort. "Could be a night with a boy. You like boys, Jessie? In my profession, we don't cast aspersions on what I like to call specified taste."

"No, sir."

"No sir what?"

"No, sir, I don't like boys," Jessie said. "No, sir."

The Deacon showed them his palms in apology. "A girl, then, yeah? Young, though, am I right? You never forget 'em when you were young and they were, too. Nice piece of

151

chocolate with a ass you could pound all night and it still don't lose its shape?"

"No, sir."

"No sir you don't like a fine young woman's ass?"

"No, sir, that's not my memorable moment." Jessie coughed and took another slug of whiskey.

"Then what *is*, boy? Shit."

Jessie looked away from the table, and Luther could feel him composing himself. "My most memorable moment, sir?"

The Deacon clapped the table. "*Most* memorable," he thundered and then winked at Luther, as if, whatever this con was, Luther was somehow in on it with him.

Jessie lifted his mask and took another swig. "Night my pops died, sir."

The Deacon's face strained with the weight of compassion. He dabbed his face with a napkin. He sucked air through pursed lips and his eyes grew large. "I am so sorry, Jessie. How did the good man pass?"

Jessie looked at the table, then back into the Deacon's face. "Some white boys in Missouri, sir, where I was reared?"

"Yes, son."

"They come and said he'd snuck onto their farm and killed their mule. Said he'd meant to cut it up for food but they'd caught him at it and run him off. These boys, sir? They showed up at our house next day and dragged my pops out the house and beat him something fierce, all in front of my mama and me and my two sisters." Jessie drained the rest of his glass and then sucked back a great wet hunk of air. "Aw, shit."

"They lynch your pops?"

"No, sir. They done left him there and he died in the house two days later from a busted-up skull. I was ten year old."

Jessie lowered his head.

The Deacon Broscious reached across the table and patted his hand. "Sweet Jesus," the Deacon whispered. "Sweet sweet sweet sweet Jesus." He took the bottle and refilled Jessie's glass and gave Luther a sad smile.

"In my experience," the Deacon Broscious said, "the most memorable thing in a man's life is rarely pleasant. Pleasure doesn't teach us anything but that pleasure is pleasurable. And what sort of lesson is that? Monkey jacking his own penis know that. Nah, nah," he said. "The nature of learning, my brothers? Is pain. Ya'll think on this—we hardly ever know how happy we are as children, for example, until our childhood is taken from us. We usually can't recognize true love until it's passed us by. And then, then we say, My *that* was the thing. That was the truth, ya'll. But in the moment?" He shrugged his enormous shoulders and patted his forehead with his handkerchief. "What molds us," he said, "is what maims us. A high price, I agree. But"—he spread his arms and gave them his most glorious smile—"what we *learn* from that is priceless."

Luther never saw Dandy and Smoke move, but when he turned at the sound of Jessie's grunt, they'd already clamped his wrists to the table and Smoke had Jessie's head held fast in his hands.

Luther said, "Hey, ya'll wait a—"

The Deacon's slap connected with Luther's cheekbone and busted up through his teeth and his nose and eyes like shards of broken pipe. The Deacon's hand didn't leave his head, either. He clenched Luther's hair and held his head in place as Dandy produced a knife and sliced it along Jessie's jawbone from his chin up to the base of his ear.

Jessie screamed long after the knife had left his flesh. The blood climbed out of the wound like it had been waiting its whole life to do so, and Jessie howled through his mask and Dandy and Smoke held his head in place as the blood poured onto the table and Deacon Broscious yanked on Luther's hair and said, "You close your eyes, Country, I'll take them home with me."

Luther blinked from the sweat, but he didn't shut his eyes, and he saw the blood flow over the lip of the wound and off Jessie's flesh and spill all over the table, and he could tell by a fleeting glimpse of Jessie's eyes that his friend had exited the place where he was worried about the wound to his jaw and had realized these could be the first moments of a long, last day on earth.

"Give that pussy a towel," the Deacon said and pushed Luther's head away.

Dandy dropped a towel on the table in front of Jessie, and then he and Smoke stepped back. Jessie grabbed the towel and pressed it to his chin and sucked through his teeth and wept softly and rocked in his chair, his mask gone red up the left side, and that went on for some time, no one saying anything and the Deacon looking bored, and when the towel was redder than the Deacon's hat, Smoke handed Jessie another one to replace it and tossed the bloody one behind him to the floor.

"Your thieving old man getting killed?" the Deacon said. "Nigger, that's now the second most memorable moment of your life."

Jessie clenched his eyes shut and pressed the towel so hard against his jaw Luther could see his fingers turn white.

"Can I get an 'amen' on that, brother?"

Jessie opened his eyes and stared.

The Deacon repeated his question.

"Amen," Jessie whispered.

"Amen," the Deacon said and clapped his hands. "Way I figure it, you been skimming ten dollars a week from me for two years now. What that add up to, Smoke?"

"One thousand forty dollar, Deacon, sir."

"A thousand forty." The Deacon turned his gaze on Luther. "And you, Country, you either in on it or known about it and didn't tell me, which make it your debt, too."

Luther didn't know what else to do so he nodded.

"You don't need to nod like you *confirming* something. You ain't confirming shit to me. I say something is, and it very much is." He took a sip of whiskey. "Now, Jessie Tell, can you pay me my money or it all done got shot up your arm?"

Jessie hissed, "I can get it, sir, I can get it."

154

"Get what?"

"Your thousand forty dollars, sir."

The Deacon widened his eyes at Smoke and Dandy and all three of them chuckled at the same time and stopped chuckling just as fast.

"You don't understand, dope ho', do you? The only reason you alive is because, in my beneficence, I kindly decided to call what you took a loan. I loaned you the thousand forty. You didn't steal it. If I was to have decided you stole it, that knife be in your throat right now and your dick be in your mouth. So say it."

"Say what, sir?"

"Say it was a loan."

"It was a loan, sir."

"Indeed," the Deacon said. "So, as to the terms of that loan, let me enlighten you. Smoke, what we charge a week for vig?"

Luther felt his head spin and he swallowed hard to keep his vomit down.

"Five percent," Smoke said.

"Five percent," the Deacon told Jessie. "Compounded weekly."

Jessie's eyes, which had gone hooded with the pain, snapped open.

"What's the weekly vig on a thousand forty?" the Deacon said.

Smoke said, "I believe it work out to fifty-two dollars, Deacon, sir."

"Fifty-two dollars," the Deacon said slowly. "Don't sound like much."

"No, Deacon, sir, it don't."

The Deacon stroked his chin. "But shit, wait, what's that per month?"

"Two hundred eight, sir," Dandy chimed in.

The Deacon showed his real smile, a tiny one, having himself a time now. "Per year?"

"Two thousand four hundred ninety-six," Smoke said.

"And doubled?"

"Ah," Dandy said, sounding desperate to win the game, "that be, um, that be—"

"Four thousand nine hundred ninety-two," Luther said, not even sure he was speaking or why until the words left his mouth.

Dandy slapped the back of his head. "I *had* it, nigger."

The Deacon turned his full gaze on Luther and Luther saw his grave in there, could hear the shovels in the dirt.

"You ain't dumb at all, Country. I knew that first time I saw you. Knew the only way you'd get dumb is hanging around fools like this one bleeding all over my table. It was my mistake to allow your fraternization with said Negro, and that's to my everlasting regret." He sighed and stretched his great bulk in his chair. "But it's all spilt milk now. So that four thousand nine hundred ninety-two added to the original loan come out to . . . ?" He held up a hand to stop anyone else from answering and pointed at Luther.

"Six thousand thirty-two."

The Deacon slapped the table. "It *do*. Dang. And before ya'll think I'm a merciless man, ya'll need to understand that even in this, I was more than kind because ya'll need to consider what you'd owe if, like Dandy and Smoke suggested, I'd added the vig *into* the principal every week as I did my computations. You see?"

No one said anything.

"I said," the Deacon said, "do you see?"

"Yes, sir," Luther said.

"Yes, sir," Jessie said.

The Deacon nodded. "Now how you gone pay back six thousand thirty-two dollars of my money?"

Jessie said, "Somehow we'll—"

"You'll what?" The Deacon laughed. "You stick up a bank?"

Jessie said nothing.

"You go over to White Town maybe, rob every third man you see all day and all night?"

Jessie said nothing. Luther said nothing.

"You can't," the Deacon said softly, his hands spread out on the table. "You just can't. Dream all you want, but some things ain't in the realm of possibility. No, boys, there's no way you can come up with my—oh, shit, it's a new week, I almost forgot—my six thousand *eighty-four* dollars."

Jessie's eyes slid to the side and then forced their way back to the center. "Sir, I need a doctor, I think."

"Need you a fucking mortician if'n we don't figure your way out this mess, so shut the fuck up."

Luther said, "Sir, just tell us what you want us to do and we'll sure do it."

It was Smoke who slapped him in the back of the head this time, but the Deacon held up a hand.

"All right, Country. All right. You cut to the chase, boy, and I respect that. So I will respect you in kind."

He straightened the lapels of his white jacket and leaned into the table. "I got a few folks owe me large change. Some of them in the country, some of them right here downtown. Smoke, give me the list."

Smoke came around the table and handed the Deacon a sheet of paper and the Deacon looked at it and then placed it on the table so Luther and Jessie could see it.

"There's five names on that list. Each one is into me for at least five hundred a week. You boys gone go get it today. And I know what you're thinking in your whiny-assed head-voices. You thinking, 'But, Deacon, sir, we ain't *muscle*. Smoke and Dandy supposed to handle the hard cases.' You thinking that, Country?"

Luther nodded.

"Well, normally Smoke and Dandy or some other hard-headed, can't-fucking-scare-'em sons a bitches *would* be handling this. But this ain't normal times. Every name on that list has someone in their house with the grippe. And I ain't losing no important niggers like Smoke or Dandy here to that plague."

Luther said, "But two unimportant niggers like us . . ."

Deacon reared his head back. "This boy is finding his *voice*. I was right about you, Country—you got talent." He chuckled and drank some more whiskey. "So, yeah, that's the size of it. You gone go out and collect from these five. You don't collect it all, you better be able to make up the difference. You bring it on back to me and keep going out and bringing it on back until this flu is over, I'll wipe your debt back to the principal. Now," he said, with that big broad smile of his, "what you think of that?"

"Sir," Jessie said, "that grippe be killing people in one *day*."

"That's true," the Deacon said. "So, if you catch it, you surely could be dead this time tomorrow. But if you don't get my money? Nigger, you surely will be dead tonight."

The Deacon gave them the name of a doctor to see in the back room of a shooting gallery off Second and they went there after they got sick in the alley behind the Deacon's club. The doctor, a drunken old high-yellow with his hair dyed rust-colored, stitched Jessie's jaw as Jessie sucked air and the tears ran quietly down his face.

In the street, Jessie said, "I need something for the pain."

Luther said, "You even think about the spike, I'll kill you myself."

"Fine," Jessie said. "But I can't think with this pain, so what you suggest?"

They went up into the back of a drugstore on Second, and Luther got them a bag of cocaine. He cut two lines for himself to keep his nerve up and four for Jessie. Jessie snorted his lines one after the other and took a shot of whiskey.

Luther said, "We going to need some guns."

"I got guns," Jessie said. "Shit."

They went back to his apartment and he handed the long-barreled .38 to Luther and slid the .45 Colt behind his back and said, "You know how to use that?"

Luther shook his head. "I know if some nigger try to beat me out his house I'll point this in his face."

"What if that ain't enough to stop him?"

"I ain't dying today," Luther said.

"Then let me hear it."

"Hear what?"

"If it ain't enough to stop him, you going to do what?"

Luther put the .38 in his coat pocket. "I'm going to shoot the son of a bitch." "Then shit, Negro," Jessie said, still talking through gritted teeth, although now it was probably more from the cocaine than the pain, "let's get working."

They were a scary sight. Luther would admit that much as he caught their reflection in the window of Arthur Smalley's living room as they walked up the steps to his house—two wound-up colored men with masks that covered their noses and mouths, one of them with a row of black stitches sticking out of his jaw like a spiked fence. Time was, the look of them would have been enough to terror the money out of any God-fearing Greenwood man, but these days it didn't mean much; most folks were scary sights. The high windows of the small house had white Xs painted on them, but Luther and Jessie had no choice but to walk right up on the old porch and ring the bell.

By the looks of the place, Arthur Smalley had at one time tried to have a go at farming. Off to his left, Luther could see a barn in need of painting and a field with a skinny horse and a pair of knobby-looking cows wandering in it. But nothing had been tilled or reaped out there in some time and the weeds stood tall in midautumn.

Jessie went to ring the bell again and the door opened and they looked through the screen at a man about Luther's size but near twice his age. He wore suspenders over an undershirt yellowed by old sweat, the mask over his face yellowed with it, too, and his eyes were red from exhaustion or grief or the flu.

"Who you-all?" he said, and the words came out airless, as if whatever they answered wouldn't make no difference to him.

"You Arthur Smalley, sir?" Luther said.

The man slid his thumbs under his suspenders. "What you think?"

"I had to guess?" Luther said. "I'd say yeah."

"Then you'd guess right, boy." He leaned into the screen. "What ya'll want?"

"The Deacon sent us," Jessie said.

"Did he now?"

In the house behind him someone moaned, and Luther got a whiff of the other side of that door. Sharp and sour at the same time, as if someone had left the eggs, the milk, and the meat out of the icebox since July.

Arthur Smalley saw that smell hit Luther in the eyes and he opened the screen door wide. "Ya'll want to come in? Maybe set a spell?"

"Nah, sir," Jessie said. "What say you just bring us the Deacon's money?"

"The money, uh?" He patted his pockets. "Yeah, I got some, drew it fresh this morning from the money well. It's still a little damp, but—"

"We ain't joking here, sir," Jessie said and adjusted his hat back off his forehead.

Arthur Smalley leaned over the threshold and they both leaned back. "I look like I been working of late?"

"No, you don't."

"No, I don't," Arthur Smalley said. "Know what I been doing?"

He whispered the words and Luther took another half-step back from the whisper because something about the sound of it was obscene.

"I buried my youngest in the yard night before last," Arthur Smalley whispered, his neck extended. "Under an elm tree. She liked that tree, so . . ." He shrugged. "She was thirteen. My other daughter, she in bed with it. And my wife? She ain't been awake in two days. Her head as hot as a kettle just come to boil. She gone die," he said and nodded. "Tonight most likely. Else tomorrow. You sure you don't want to come in?"

Luther and Jessie shook their heads.

"I got sheets covered in sweat and shit need washing. Sure could use a hand."

"The money, Mr. Smalley." Luther wanted off this porch and away from this sickness and he hated Arthur Smalley for not washing that undershirt.

"I don't—"

"The money," Jessie said, and the .45 was in his hand, dangling beside his leg. "No more bullshit, old-timer. Get the fucking money."

Another moan from inside, this one low and long and huffing, and Arthur Smalley stared at them so long Luther started to think he'd fallen into some sort of trance.

"Ya'll got no decency at all?" he said and looked first at Jessie and then at Luther.

And Luther told the truth. "None."

Arthur Smalley's eyes widened. "My wife and child are—"

"The Deacon don't care about your domestic responsibilities," Jessie said.

"But you-all? What you care about?"

Luther didn't look at Jessie and he knew Jessie wasn't looking at him. Luther pulled the .38 from his belt and pointed it at Arthur Smalley's forehead.

"Care about the money," he said.

Arthur Smalley looked into that barrel and then he looked in Luther's eyes. "Boy, how does your mama walk the street knowing she birthed such a creature?"

"The *money*," Jessie said.

"Or what?" Arthur said, which is exactly what Luther had been afraid he'd say. "You gone shoot me? Shit, I'm *fine* with that. You want to shoot my family? Do me the favor. Please. You ain't gone do—"

"I'll make you dig her up," Jessie said.

"You what?"

"You heard me."

Arthur Smalley sagged into the doorjamb. "You didn't just say that."

"I damn well did, old man," Jessie said. "I will make you dig your daughter out her grave. Else I'll tie your ass up, make you watch me do it. Then I'll fill it back in, while she lying beside it, so you'll have to bury her twice."

We're going to hell, Luther thought. Head of the line.

"What you think about that, old man?" Jessie put his .45 behind his back again.

Arthur Smalley's eyes filled with tears and Luther prayed they wouldn't fall. Please don't fall. Please.

Arthur said, "I ain't got no money," and Luther knew the fight was gone from him. "What you got then?" Jessie said.

Jessie followed in his Model T as Luther drove Arthur Smalley's Hudson out from behind the barn and crossed in front of the house as the man stood on his porch and watched. Luther shifted into second gear and put some juice into it as he passed the small fence at the edge of the dirt yard, and he told himself he didn't see the freshly turned dirt under the elm. He didn't see the shovel that stuck upright from the dark brown mound. Or the cross made from thin planks of pine and painted a pale white.

By the time they'd finished with the men on the list, they had several pieces of jewelry, fourteen hundred dollars in cash, and a mahogany hope chest strapped to the back of what had once been Arthur Smalley's car.

They'd seen a child gone blue as twilight and a woman no older than Lila who lay on a cot on a front porch with her bones and her teeth and her eyes lunging toward heaven. Saw a dead man sitting against a barn, blacker than black could ever get, as if he'd been struck by lightning through his skull, his flesh all bumpy with welts.

Judgment Day, Luther knew. It was coming for all of them. And he and Jessie were going to go up and stand before the

Lord and have to account for what they'd done this day. And there was no possible accounting for that. Not in ten lives.

"Let's give it back," he said after the third house.

"What?"

"Give it back and run."

"And spend the rest of our short fucking lives looking over our shoulders for Dandy or Smoke or some other broke-down nigger with a gun and nothing left to lose? Where you think we'd hide, Country? Two colored bucks on the run?"

Luther knew he was right, but he also knew it was eating Jessie up as awful as it was eating him.

"We worry about that later. We—"

Jessie laughed, and it was the ugliest laugh Luther'd ever heard from him. "We do this or we dead, Country." He gave him an open-armed, wide-shouldered shrug. "And you know that. Less you want to kill that whale, sign you and your wife's death warrant in the process."

Luther got in the car.

The last one, Owen Tice, paid them in cash, said he wouldn't be around to spend it no way anyhow. Soon as his Bess passed, he was going to get his shotgun and ride that river with her. He'd had him a raw throat since noon and it was starting to burn and without Bess there wasn't no fucking point to it anyway. He wished them well. He said, sure he understood. He did. Man had to make a living. Wasn't no shame in that.

Said, My whole fucking family, you believe that shit? A week ago we all in the pink, eating dinner 'round the table— my son and daughter-in-law, my daughter and son-in-law, three grandchildren, and Bess. Just sitting and eating and jawing. And then, then, it was like God Hisself reached through the roof and into their house and closed his hand 'round the whole family and squeezed.

Like we was flies on the table, he said. Like that.

* * *

They drove up an empty Greenwood Avenue at midnight and Luther counted twenty-four windows marked by Xs and they parked the cars in the alley behind the Club Almighty. There was no light coming from any of the buildings along the alley and the fire escapes hung above them and Luther wondered if there was anything left of the world or if it had all gone black and blue and seized up with the grippe.

Jessie put his foot on the running board of his Model T and lit a cigarette and blew the smoke in a stream toward the back door of the Club Almighty, nodding his head every now and then, as if he heard music Luther couldn't and then he looked over at Luther and said, "I walk."

"You walk?"

"I do," Jessie said. "I walk and the road is long and the Lord ain't with me. Ain't with you neither, Luther."

In the time they'd known each other, Jessie had never, not once, called Luther by his Christian name.

"Let's unload this shit," Luther said. "Yeah, Jessie?" He reached for the straps that held Tug and Ervina Irvine's hope chest to the back of Arthur Smalley's car. "Come on now. Let's get this shit done."

"Ain't with me," Jessie said. "Ain't with you. Ain't in this alley. I think He done left this world. Found Hisself another one to be more concerned with." He chuckled and took a long drag on his cigarette. "How old you think that blue child was?"

"Two," Luther said.

" 'Bout what I guessed, too," Jessie said. "Took his mama's jewelry, though, didn't we? Got her wedding ring right here in my pocket." He patted his chest and smiled and said, "Heh heh yeah."

"Why don't we just—"

"I tell you what," Jessie said and tugged his jacket, then shot his cuffs. "Tell you what," he said and pointed at the back door of the club, "if that door be unlocked, you can forget what I said. That door open, though? God be in this alley. Yes indeed."

And he walked to it and turned the knob and the door opened.

Luther said, "Don't mean shit, Jessie. Don't mean nothing but someone forgot to lock the door."

"You say," Jessie said. "You say. Let me ask you— You think I'd a forced that man to dig up his girl's grave?"

Luther said, " 'Course not. We were hot. That's all. Hot and scared. Got crazy."

Jessie said, "Let go of them straps, brother. We ain't lifting nothing right now."

Luther stepped away from the car. He said, "Jessie."

Jessie reached out so fast his hand could have slapped Luther's head off his neck but instead it landed soft on Luther's ear, barely touching. "You good kin, Country."

And Jessie went into the Club Almighty and Luther followed and they walked through a foul back hallway that stank of piss and came out near the stage through a black velvet curtain. The Deacon Broscious sat just where they'd left him at the table at the base of the stage. He sipped milky white tea from a clear glass, and he gave them the kind of smile told Luther there was more than milk in the tea.

"Stroke of twelve," the Deacon said and waved at the darkness all around him. "Ya'll done come at the stroke of twelve itself. Should I put my mask on?"

"Nah, sir," Jessie said. "Ya'll don't need to worry."

The Deacon reached beside himself, as if he was looking for his mask anyway. His movements were thick and jumbled and then he waved his hands at the whole idea and beamed at them with the sweat beading on his face thick as hail.

"Haw," he said. "You niggers look *tired*."

"Feel tired," Jessie said.

"Well, come on over here and sit, then. Tell the Deacon about your travails."

Dandy came out of the shadows on the Deacon's left, carrying a teapot on a tray and his mask flapping from the

165

overhead fan, and he took one look at them and said, "What ya'll doing coming through the back door?"

Jessie said, "Just where our feets took us, Mr. Dandy," and cleared the .45 from his belt and shot Dandy in his mask and Dandy's face disappeared in a puff of red.

Luther crouched and said, "Wait!" and the Deacon held up his hands and said, "Now—" but Jessie fired and the fingers of the Deacon's left hand came free and hit the wall behind him and the Deacon shouted something Luther couldn't understand and then the Deacon said, "Hold it, okay?" Jessie fired again and the Deacon didn't seem to have any reaction for a moment and Luther figured the shot had hit the wall until he noticed the Deacon's red tie widening. The blood bloomed across his white shirt and the Deacon got a look at it for himself and a single wet breath popped out of his mouth.

Jessie turned to Luther and gave him that big Jessie-smile of his and said, "Shit. Kinda fun, ain't it?"

Luther saw something he barely knew he saw, something move from the stage, and he started to say "Jessie," but the word never left his mouth before Smoke stepped out between the drums and the base stand with his arm extended. Jessie was only half turned toward him when the air popped white and the air popped yellow-and-red and Smoke fired two bullets into Jessie's head and one into his throat and Jessie went all bouncy.

He toppled into Luther's shoulder, and Luther reached for him and got his gun instead and Smoke kept shooting, and Luther raised an arm across his face, as if it could stop the bullets, and he fired Jessie's .45 and felt the gun jumping in his hand and saw all the dead and blackened and blue from today and heard his own voice yelling, "No please no please," and pictured a bullet hitting each of his eyes and then he heard a scream—high-pitched and shocked—and he stopped firing and lowered his arm from his face.

He squinted and saw Smoke curled on the stage. His arms

were wrapped around his stomach and his mouth was open wide. He gurgled. His left foot twitched.

Luther stood in the middle of the four bodies and checked himself for wounds. He had blood all over his shoulder, but once he unbuttoned his shirt and felt around in there, he knew that the blood was Jessie's. He had a cut under his eye, but it was shallow and he figured that whatever had ricocheted off his cheek hadn't been a bullet. His body, though, did not feel like his own. It felt borrowed, as if he shouldn't be in it, and whoever it might belong to sure shouldn't have walked it into the back of the Club Almighty.

He looked down at Jessie and felt a part of him that just wanted to cry but another part that felt nothing at all, not even relief at being alive. The back of Jessie's head looked as if an animal had taken bites from it, and the hole in his throat still pumped blood. Luther knelt on a spot of floor the blood hadn't reached yet and cocked his head to look into his friend's eyes. They looked a little surprised, as if Old Byron had just told him the night's tip pool had turned out bigger than expected.

Luther whispered, "Oh, Jessie," and used his thumb to close his eyes, and then he placed his hand to Jessie's cheek. The flesh had begun to cool, and Luther asked the Lord to please forgive his friend for his actions earlier today because he'd been desperate, he'd been compromised, but he was, Lord, a good man at heart who'd never before caused anyone but himself any pain.

"You can . . . make this . . . right."

Luther turned at the sound of the voice.

"Sm-smart boy like . . like you." The Deacon sucked at the air. "Smart boy . . ."

He rose from Jessie's body with the gun in his hand and walked over to the table, coming around to stand on the Deacon's right so the fat fool had to roll that big head of his in order to see him.

"You go get that doctor you . . . you . . . saw this afternoon."

167

The Deacon took another breath and his chest whistled. "Go get him."

"And you'll just forgive and forget, uh?" Luther said.

"As . . . as God is my witness."

Luther removed his mask and coughed in the Deacon's face three times. "How about I fucking cough on you till we see if I got me the plague today?"

The Deacon used his good hand to reach for Luther's arm, but Luther pulled it away.

"Don't you *touch* me, demon."

"Please . . ."

"Please what?"

The Deacon wheezed and his chest whistled again and he licked his lips.

"Please," he said again.

"Please *what*?"

"Make . . . this right."

"Okay," Luther said and put the gun into the folds under the Deacon's chin and pulled the trigger with the man looking in his eyes.

"That fucking do?" Luther shouted and watched the man tip to his left and slide down the back of the booth. "Kill my *friend*?" Luther said and shot him again, though he knew he was dead.

"Fuck!" Luther screamed at the ceiling, and he grabbed his own head with the gun clutched against it and screamed it again. Then he noticed Smoke trying to pull himself across the stage in his own blood and Luther kicked a chair out of his way and crossed to the stage with his arm extended and Smoke turned his head and lay there, looking up at Luther with no more life in his eyes than Jessie's.

For what felt like an hour—and Luther would never know how long he stood there exactly—they stared at each other.

Then Luther felt a new version of himself he wasn't even sure he liked say, "If you live, you'll have to come kill me, sure as sin."

Smoke blinked his eyelids once, real slow, in the affirmative.

Luther stared down the gun at him. He saw all those bullets he'd scored in Columbus, saw his Uncle Cornelius's black satchel, saw the rain that had fallen, warm and soft as sleep, the afternoon he'd sat on his porch, willing his father to come home when his father was already four years five hundred miles away and not coming back. He lowered the gun.

He watched the surprise flash across Smoke's pupils. Smoke's eyes rolled and he burped a thimbleful of blood down his chin and onto his shirt. He fell back to the stage and the blood flowed from his stomach.

Luther raised the gun again. It should have been easier, the man's eyes no longer on him, the man probably slipping across the river right at this moment, climbing the dark shore into another world. All it would take was one more pull of the trigger to be sure. He'd had no hesitation with the Deacon. So why now?

The gun shook in his hand and he lowered it again.

Wouldn't take the people the Deacon associated with long to put all this together, to put him in this room. Whether Smoke lived or died, Luther and Lila's time in Tulsa was done.

Still . . .

He raised the gun again, gripped his forearm to stop the shakes and stared down the barrel at Smoke. He stood there a good minute before he finally faced the fact that he could stand there for an hour and he'd still never pull that trigger.

"Ain't you," he said.

Luther looked at the blood still leaking out of the man. He took one last look behind him at Jessie. He sighed. He stepped over Dandy's corpse.

"You simple sons of bitches," Luther said as he headed for the door. "You brought this on yourselves."

CHAPTER *eight*

After the flu had passed on, Danny returned to walking the beat by day and studying to impersonate a radical at night. In terms of the latter duty, Eddie McKenna left packages at his door at least once a week. He'd unwrap them to find stacks of the latest socialist and Communist propaganda rags, as well as copies of *Das Kapital* and *The Communist Manifesto*, speeches given by Jack Reed, Emma Goldman, Big Bill Haywood, Jim Larkin, Joe Hill, and Pancho Villa. He read thickets of propaganda so dense with rhetoric it may as well have been a structural engineering manual for all it spoke to any common man Danny could imagine. He came across certain words so often—*tyranny, imperialism, capitalist oppression, brotherhood, insurrection*—that he suspected a knee-jerk vocabulary had become necessary to ensure a dependable shorthand among the workers of the world. But as the words lost individuality, so they lost their power and gradually their meaning. Once the meaning was gone, Danny wondered, how would these noodle heads—and among the Bolshie and anarchist literature, he had yet to find someone who wasn't a noodle head—as one unified body, successfully cross a street, never mind overthrow a country?

When he wasn't reading speeches, he read missives from what was commonly referred to as the "front line of the workers' revolution." He read about striking coal miners burned in their homes alongside their families, IWW workers tarred and feathered, labor organizers assassinated on the dark streets of small towns, unions broken, unions outlawed, workingmen jailed, beaten, and deported. And always it was they who were painted as the enemies of the great American Way.

To his surprise, Danny felt occasional stirrings of empathy. Not for everyone, of course—he'd always thought anarchists were morons, offering the world nothing but steel-eyed bloodlust, and little in his reading changed his opinion. Communists, too, struck him as hopelessly naïve, pursuing a utopia that failed to take into consideration the most elemental characteristic of the human animal: covetousness. The Bolshies believed it could be cured like an illness, but Danny knew that greed was an organ, like the heart, and to remove it would kill the host. The socialists were the smartest—they acknowledged greed—but their message was constantly entwined with the Communists' and it was impossible, at least in this country, for it to be heard above the red din.

But for the life of him Danny couldn't understand why most of the outlawed or targeted unions deserved their fate. Time and again what was renounced as treasonous rhetoric was merely a man standing before a crowd and demanding he be treated as a man.

He mentioned this to McKenna over coffee in the South End one night and McKenna wagged a finger at him. "It's not those men you need to concern yourself with, young protégé. Ask yourself instead, 'Who's funding those men? And to what end?'"

Danny yawned, tired all the time now, unable to remember the last time he'd had a true night's sleep. "Let me guess—Bolsheviks."

"You're goddamned right. From Mother Russia herself." He widened his eyes at Danny. "You think this is mildly amusing, yeah? Lenin himself said that the people of Russia will not

171

rest until all the peoples of the world join their revolution. That's not idle talk, boyo. That's a clear fucking threat against these shores." He thumped his index finger off the table. "My shores."

Danny suppressed another yawn with his fist. "How's my cover coming?"

"Almost there," McKenna said. "You join that thing they call a policemen's union yet?"

"Going to a meeting Tuesday."

"What took so long?"

"If Danny Coughlin, son of Captain Coughlin and no stranger himself to the selfish, politically motivated act, were to suddenly ask to join the Boston Social Club, people might be a bit suspicious."

"You've a point. Fair enough."

"My old partner, Steve Coyle?"

"The one who caught the grippe, yeah. A shame."

"He was a vocal supporter of the union. I'm letting some time pass so it'll seem I passed a few long dark nights of the soul over him getting sick. Finally my conscience caught up, so I had to check out a meeting. Let them think I have a soft heart."

McKenna lit the blackened stub of a cigar. "You've always had a soft heart, son. You just hide it better than most."

Danny shrugged. "Starting to hide it from myself, then, I guess."

"Always the danger, that." McKenna nodded, as if he were intimate with the dilemma. "Then one day, sure, you can't remember where you left all those pieces you tried so hard to hold on to. Or why you worked so hard at the holding."

Danny joined Tessa and her father for dinner on a night when the cool air smelled of burning leaves. Their apartment was larger than his. His came with a hot plate atop an icebox, but the Abruzzes' had a small kitchen with a Raven stove. Tessa cooked, her long dark hair tied back, limp and shiny from the heat. Federico uncorked the wine Danny had brought and set it on a windowsill to breathe while he and Danny sat at the small dining table in the parlor and sipped anisette.

Federico said, "I have not seen you around the building lately."

Danny said, "I work a lot."

"Even now that the grippe has passed on?"

Danny nodded. It was just one more of the beefs cops had with the department. The Boston police officer got one day off for every twenty. And on that day off, he wasn't allowed to leave city limits in case an emergency arose. So most of the single guys lived near their stations in rooming houses because what was the point in getting settled when you had to be at work in a few hours anyway? In addition, three nights a week, you were required to sleep at the station house, in the fetid beds on the top floor, which were lice- or bug-ridden and had just been slept in by the poor slob who would take your place on the next patrol.

"You work too much, I think."

"Tell my boss, would you?"

Federico smiled, and it was a hell of a smile, the kind that could warm a winter room. It occurred to Danny that one of the reasons it was so impressive was that you could feel so much heartbreak behind it. Maybe that's what he'd been trying to put his finger on that night on the roof—the way Federico's smile didn't mask the great pain that lay undoubtedly in his past; it embraced it. And in that embracing, triumphed. A soft version of the smile remained in place as he leaned in and thanked Danny in a low whisper for "that unfortunate business," of removing Tessa's dead newborn from the apartment. He assured Danny that were it not for his own work, they would have had him to dinner as soon as Tessa had recovered from the grippe.

Danny looked over at Tessa, caught her looking at him. She lowered her head, and a strand of hair fell from behind her ear and hung over her eye. She was not an American girl, he reminded himself, one for whom sex with a virtual stranger could be tricky but not out of the question. She was Italian. Old World. Mind your manners.

He looked back at her father. "What is it that you do, sir?"

"Federico," the old man said and patted his hand. "We drink anisette, we break bread, it must be Federico."

Danny acknowledged that with a tip of his glass. "Federico, what is it you do?"

"I give the breath of angels to mere men." The old man swept his hand behind him like an impresario. Back against the wall between two windows sat a phonograph cabinet. It had seemed out of place to Danny as soon as he'd entered. It was made of fine grain mahogany, designed with ornate carvings that made Danny think of European royalty. The open top exposed a turntable perched on purple velvet inlay, and below, a two-door cabinet looked to be hand carved and had nine shelves, enough to hold several dozen disc records.

The metal hand crank was gold plated, and while the disc record played, you could barely hear the motor. It produced a richness of sound unlike anything Danny had ever heard in his life. They were listening to the intermezzo from Mascagni's *Cavalleria Rusticana*, and Danny knew if he'd entered the apartment blind he would have assumed the soprano stood in the parlor with them. He took another look at the cabinet and felt pretty sure it cost three or four times what the stove had.

"The Silvertone B-Twelve," Federico said, his voice, always melodious, suddenly more so. "I sell them. I sell the B-Eleven as well, but I prefer the look of the Twelve. Louis the Sixteenth is far superior in design to Louis the Fifteenth. You agree?"

"Of course," Danny said, though if he'd been told it was Louis the Third or Ivan the Eighth, he'd have had to take it on faith.

"No other phonograph on the market can equal it," Federico said with the gleaming eyes of the evangelical. "No

174

other phonograph can play every type of disc record—Edison, Pathé, Victor, Columbia, *and* Silvertone? No, my friend, this is the only one so capable. You pay your eight dollars for the table model because it is less expensive"—he crinkled his nose downward—"and *light*—bah!—*convenient*—bah!—*space saving*. But will it sound like this? Will you hear angels? Hardly. And then your cheap needle will wear out and the discs will skip and soon you will hear crackles and whispers. And where will you be then, except eight dollars the poorer?" He spread his arm toward the phonograph cabinet again, as proud as a first-time father. "Sometimes quality costs. It is only reasonable."

Danny suppressed a chuckle at the little old man and his fervent capitalism.

"Papa," Tessa said from the stove, "do not get yourself so . . ." She waved her hands, searching for the word. ". . . *eccitato*."

"Excited," Danny said.

She frowned at him. "Eggs-y-sigh . . . ?"

"Ex," he said. "Ex-ci-ted."

"Eck-cited."

"Close enough."

She raised her wooden spoon. "English!" she barked at the ceiling.

Danny thought of what her neck, so honey-brown, would taste like. Women—his weakness since he'd been old enough to notice them and see that they, in turn, noticed him. Looking at Tessa's neck, her throat, he felt beset by it. The awful, delicious need to possess. To own—for a night—another's eyes, sweat, heartbeat. And here, right in front of her father. Jesus!

He turned back to the old man, whose eyes were half closed to the music. Oblivious. Sweet and oblivious to the New World ways.

"I love music," Federico said and opened his eyes. "When I was a boy, minstrels and troubadours would visit our village

175

from the spring through the summer. I would sit until my mother shooed me from the square—sometimes with a switch, yes?—and watch them play. The sounds. Ah, the sounds! Language is such a poor substitute. You see?"

Danny shook his head. "I'm not sure."

Federico pulled his chair closer to the table and leaned in. "Men's tongues fork at birth. It has always been so. The bird cannot lie. The lion is a hunter, to be feared, yes, but he is true to his nature. The tree and rock are true—they are a tree and rock. Nothing more, but nothing less. But man, the only creature who can make words—uses this great gift to betray truth, to betray himself, to betray nature and God. He will point to a tree and tell you it is not a tree, stand over your dead body and say he did not kill you. Words, you see, speak for the brain, and the brain is a machine. Music"—he smiled his glorious smile and raised his index finger—"music speaks for the soul because words are too small."

"Never thought of it that way."

Federico pointed at his prized possession. "That is made of wood. It is a tree, but it is not a tree. And the wood is wood, yes, but what it does to the music that comes from it? What is that? Do we have a word for that kind of wood? That kind of tree?"

Danny gave him a small shrug, figuring the old man was getting a bit tipsy.

Federico closed his eyes again and his hands floated up by his ears, as if he were conducting the music himself, willing it forth into the room.

Danny caught Tessa looking at him again and this time she did not drop his gaze. He gave her his best smile, the slightly confused, slightly embarrassed one, the small boy's smile. A flush spread under her chin, and still she didn't look away.

He turned back to her father. His eyes remained closed, his hands conducting, even though the disc record had ended and the needle popped back and forth over its innermost grooves.

* * *

176

Steve Coyle smiled broadly when he saw Danny enter Fay Hall, the meeting place of the Boston Social Club. He worked his way down a row of folding chairs, one leg dragging noticeably after the other. He shook Danny's hand. "Thanks for coming."

Danny hadn't counted on this. It made him feel twice as guilty, infiltrating the BSC under false pretenses while his old partner, sick and unemployed, showed up to support a fight he wasn't even part of anymore.

Danny managed a smile. "Didn't expect to see you here."

Steve looked back over his shoulder at the men setting up the stage. "They let me help out. I'm a living example of what happens when you don't have a union with negotiating power, you know?" He clapped Danny's shoulder. "How are you?"

"Fine," Danny said. For five years he'd known every detail of his partner's life, often on a minute-to-minute basis. It was suddenly odd to realize he hadn't checked in on Steve in two weeks. Odd and shameful. "How you feeling?"

Steve shrugged. "I'd complain, but who'd listen?" He laughed loud and clapped Danny's shoulder again. His beard stubble was white. He looked lost inside his newly damaged body. As if he'd been turned upside down and shaken.

"You look good," Danny said.

"Liar." Again the awkward laugh followed by an awkward solemnity, a look of dewy earnestness. "I'm really glad you're here."

Danny said, "Don't mention it."

"Turn you into a union man yet," Steve said.

"Don't bet on it."

Steve clapped him on the back a third time and introduced him around. Danny knew about half of the men on a surface level, their paths having crossed on various calls over the years. They all seemed nervous around Steve, as if they hoped he'd take whatever afflicted him to another policemen's union in another city. As if bad fortune were as contagious as the grippe. Danny could see it in their faces when they shook Steve's hand—they'd have preferred him dead. Death allowed for the illusion of heroism. The maimed turned that illusion into an uncomfortable odor.

The head of the BSC, a patrolman named Mark Denton, strode toward the stage. He was a tall man, almost as tall as Danny, and rail thin. He had pale skin, as hard and shiny as piano keys, and his black hair was slicked back tight against his skull.

Danny and the other men took their chairs as Mark Denton crossed the stage and placed his hands on the edges of the dais. He gave the room a tired smile.

"Mayor Peters canceled the meeting we had scheduled at the end of the week."

Groans broke out in the room, a few catcalls.

Denton held up a hand to quiet them. "There're rumors of a streetcar workers strike, and the mayor believes that's of more pressing importance right now. We have to go to the back of the line."

"Maybe we should strike," someone said.

Denton's dark eyes flashed. "We don't talk of strike, men. That's just what they want. You know how that would play in the papers? Do you really want to give them that kind of ammunition, Timmy?"

"No, I don't, *Mark*, but what are our options? We're fucking starving out here."

Denton acknowledged that with a firm nod. "I know we are. But even whispering the word *strike* is heresy, men. You know it and I know it. Our best chance right now is to *appear* patient and open up talks with Samuel Gompers and the AFL."

"That really happening?" someone behind Danny asked.

Denton nodded. "In fact, I was planning to put a motion to the floor. Later tonight, I'll grant you, but why wait?" He shrugged. "All those in favor of the BSC opening up charter talks with the American Federation of Labor, say aye."

178

Danny felt it then, an almost tactile stirring of the blood throughout the room, a sense of collective purpose. He couldn't deny his blood jumped along with everyone else's. A charter in the most powerful union in the country. Jesus.

"Aye," the crowd shouted.

"All against?"

No one spoke.

"Motion accepted," Denton said.

Was it actually possible? No police department in the nation had ever pulled this off. Few had dared try. And yet, they could be the first. They could—quite literally—change history.

Danny reminded himself he wasn't part of this.

Because *this* was a joke. This was a pack of naïve, overly dramatic men who thought with enough talk they could bend the world to their needs. It didn't work that way, Danny could have told them. It worked the other way.

After Denton, the cops felled by the flu paraded onstage. They talked of themselves as the lucky ones; unlike nine other officers from the city's eighteen station houses, they'd survived. Of twenty onstage, twelve had returned to duty. Eight never would. Danny lowered his eyes when Steve took the dais. Steve, just two months ago singing in the barbershop quartet, had trouble keeping his words straight. He kept stuttering. He asked them not to forget him, not to forget the flu. He asked that they remember their brotherhood and fellowship to all who'd sworn to protect and to serve.

He and the other nineteen survivors left the stage to loud applause.

The men mingled by the coffee urns or stood in circles and passed around flasks. Danny quickly got a feel for the basic personality breakdown of the membership. You had the Talkers—loud men, like Roper from the Oh-Seven, who rattled off statistics, then got into high-pitched disagreements over semantics and minutiae. Then there were the Bolshies and the Socies, like Coogan from the One-Three and Shaw who worked Warrants out of headquarters, no different from all the radicals and alleged radicals Danny had been reading up on lately, always quick to spout the most fashionable rhetoric, to reach for the toothless slogan. There were also the Emotionals—men like Hannity from the One-One, who had never been able to hold his liquor in the first place and whose eyes welled up too quickly with mention of "fellowship" or "justice." So, for the most part, what Danny's old high school English teacher, Father Twohy, used to call men of "prattle, not practice."

But there were also men like Don Slatterly, a Robbery detective, Kevin McRae, a flatfoot at the Oh-Six, and Emmett Strack, a twenty-five-year warhorse from the Oh-Three, who said very little but who watched—and saw—everything. They moved through the crowd and dispensed words of caution or restraint here, slivers of hope there, but mostly they just listened and assessed. The men watched their wake the way dogs watched the space their masters had just vacated. It would be these men and a few others like them, Danny decided, who the police brass should worry about if they wanted to avert a strike.

At the coffee urns, Mark Denton suddenly stood beside him and held out his hand.

"Tommy Coughlin's son, right?"

"Danny." He shook Denton's hand.

"You were at Salutation when it was bombed, right?"

Danny nodded.

"But that's Harbor Division." Denton stirred sugar into his coffee.

"The accident of my life," Danny said. "I'd pinched a thief on the docks and was dropping him off at Salutation when, you know . . ."

"I'm not going to lie to you, Coughlin—you're pretty well known in this department. They say the only thing Captain Tommy can't control is his own son. That makes you pretty popular, I'd say. We could use guys like you."

"Thanks. I'll think about it."

Denton's eyes swept the room. He leaned in closer. "Think quickly, would you?"

Tessa liked to take to the stoop on mild nights when her father was on the road selling his Silvertone B-XIIs. She smoked small black cigarettes that smelled as harsh as they looked, and some nights Danny sat with her. Something in Tessa made him nervous. His limbs felt cumbersome around her, as if there were no casual way to rest them. They spoke of the weather and they spoke of food and they spoke of tobacco, but they never spoke of the flu or her child or the day Danny had carried her to Haymarket Relief.

Soon they left the stoop for the roof. No one came up on the roof.

He learned that Tessa was twenty. That she'd grown up in the Sicilian village of Altofonte. When she was sixteen, a powerful man named Primo Alieveri had seen her bicycling past the café where he sat with his associates. He'd made inquiries and then arranged to meet with her father. Federico was a music teacher in their village, famous for speaking three languages but also rumored to be going *pazzo*, having married so late in life. Tessa's mother had passed on when she was ten, and her father raised her alone, with no brothers or money to protect her. And so a deal was struck.

Tessa and her father made the trip to Collesano at the base of the Madonie Mountains on the Tyrrhenian coast, arriving the day after Tessa's seventeenth birthday. Federico had hired guards to protect Tessa's dowry, mostly jewels and coins passed down from her mother's side of the family, and their first night in the guesthouse of Primo Alieveri's estate, the throats of the guards were cut as they slept in the barn and the dowry was taken. Primo Alieveri was mortified. He scoured the village for the bandits. At nightfall, over a fine dinner in the main hall, he assured his guests he and his men were closing in on the suspects. The dowry would be returned and the wedding would take place, as planned, that weekend.

When Federico passed out at the table, a dreamy smile plastered to his face, Primo's men helped him out to the guesthouse, and Primo raped Tessa on the table and then again on the stone floor by the hearth. He sent her back to the guesthouse where she tried to rouse Federico, but he continued to sleep the sleep of the dead. She lay on the floor beside the bed with the blood sticky between her thighs and eventually fell asleep.

In the morning, they were awakened by a racket in the courtyard and the sound of Primo calling their names. They came out of the guesthouse where Primo stood with two of his men, their shotguns slung behind their backs. Tessa's and Federico's horses and their wagon were gathered on the court-yard stones. Primo glared at them.

"A great friend from your village has written to inform me that your daughter is no virgin. She is a *puttana* and no suitable bride for a man of my stature. Be gone from my sight, little man."

In that moment and several that followed, Federico was still wiping the sleep from his eyes. He seemed bewildered.

Then he saw the blood that had soaked his daughter's fine white dress while they slept. Tessa never saw how he got to the whip, if it came from his own horse or from a hook in the courtyard, but when he snapped it, he caught one of Primo Alieveri's men in the eyes and spooked the horses. As the second man bent to his comrade, Tessa's horse, a tired, orange mare, broke from her grasp and kicked the man in the chest. The horse's reins raced through her fingers and the beast ran out of the courtyard. Tessa would have given chase, but she was too entranced by her father, her sweet, gentle, slightly *pazzo* father as he whipped Primo Alieveri to the ground, whipped him until strips of his flesh lay in the courtyard. With one of the guards (and his shotgun), Federico got her dowry back. The chest sat in plain view in the master bedroom, and from there, he and Tessa tracked down her mare and left the village before dusk.

Two days later, after using half the dowry for bribes, they boarded a ship in Cefalu and came to America.

Danny heard this story in halting English, not because Tessa could not grasp the language yet, but because she tried to be precise.

Danny chuckled. "So that day I carried you? That day I was losing my mind trying to speak my broken Italian, you could understand me?"

Tessa gave him arched eyebrows and a faint smile. "I could not understand anything that day except pain. You would expect me to remember English? This . . . crazy language of yours. Four words you use when one would do. Every time you do this. Remember English that day?" She waved a hand at him. "Stupid boy."

Danny said, "Boy? I got a few years on you, sweetheart."

"Yes, yes." She lit another of her harsh cigarettes. "But you a boy. You a country of boys. And girls. None of you grow up yet. You have too much fun, I think."

"Fun with what?"

"This." She waved her hand at the sky. "This silly big country. You Americans—there is no history. There is only now. Now, now, now. I want this *now*. I want that *now*."

Danny felt a sudden rise of irritation. "And yet everyone seems in a hell of a hurry to leave their country to get here."

"Ah, yes. Streets paved with gold. The great America where every man can make his fortune. But what of those who don't? What of the workers, Officer Danny? Yes? They work and work and work and if they get sick from the work, the company says, 'Bah. Go home and no come back.' And if they hurt themselves on the work? Same thing. You Americans talk of your freedom, but I see slaves who think they are free. I see companies that use children and families like hogs and—"

Danny waved it away. "And yet *you're here*."

She considered him with her large, dark eyes. It was a careful look he'd grown used to. Tessa never did anything

183

carelessly. She approached each day as if it required study before she'd form an opinion of it.

"You are right." She tapped her ash against the parapet. "You are a much more . . . *abbondante* country than Italia. You have these big—whoosh—cities. You have more automobiles in one block than all of Palermo. But you are a very young country, Officer Danny. You are like the child who believes he is smarter than his father or his uncles who came before."

Danny shrugged. He caught Tessa looking at him, as calm and cautious as always. He bounced his knee off hers and looked out at the night.

One night in Fay Hall, he sat in back before the start of another union meeting and realized he had all the information his father, Eddie McKenna, and the Old Men could possibly expect from him. He knew that Mark Denton, as leader of the BSC, was just what they feared—smart, calm, fearless, and prudent. He knew that the most trusted men under him—Emmett Strack, Kevin McRae, Don Slatterly, and Stephen Kearns—were cut from the same cloth. And he knew who the deadwood and the empty shirts were as well, those who would be most easily compromised, easily swayed, easily bribed.

At that moment, as Mark Denton once again strode across the stage to the dais to start the meeting, Danny realized that he'd known all he needed to know since the first meeting he'd attended. That was seven meetings ago.

All he had left to do was to sit down with McKenna or his father and give them his impressions, the few notes he'd taken, and a concise list of the leadership of the Boston Social Club. After that, he'd be halfway to his gold shield. Hell, maybe more than halfway. A fingertip's reach away.

So why was he still here?

That was the question of the month.

Mark Denton said, "Gents," and his voice was softer than normal, almost hushed. "Gents, if I could have your attention."

There was something to the hush of his voice that reached every man in the room. The room grew quiet in blocks of four or five rows until the silence reached the back. Mark Denton nodded his thanks. He gave them a weak smile and blinked several times.

"As many of you know," Denton said, "I was schooled on this job by John Temple of the Oh-Nine Station House. He used to say if he could make a copper out of me there'd be no reason left not to hire dames."

Chuckles rippled through the room as Denton lowered his head for a moment.

"Officer John Temple passed this afternoon from complications connected to the grippe. He was fifty-one years old."

Anyone wearing a hat removed it. A thousand men lowered their heads in the smoky hall. Denton spoke again: "If we could also give the same respect to Officer Marvin Tarleton of the One-Five, who died last night of the same cause."

"Marvin's dead?" someone called. "He was getting better."

Denton shook his head. "His heart quit last night at eleven o'clock." He leaned into the dais. "The preliminary ruling from the department is that the families of neither man receive death benefits because the city has already ruled on similar claims—"

Boos and jeers and overturned chairs temporarily drowned him out.

"—because," he shouted, "because, *because*—"

Several men were pulled back down into their seats. Others closed their mouths.

"—because," Mark Denton said, "the city says the men did not die in the line."

"How'd they get the fucking flu, then?" Bob Reming shouted. "Their dogs?"

Denton said, "The city would say yes. Their dogs. They're dogs. The city believes they could have contracted the grippe on any number of occasions unrelated to the job. Thus? They

185

did not die in the line. That's all we need to know. That's what we have to accept."

He stepped back from the dais as a chair went airborne. Within seconds, the first fistfight broke out. Then the second. A third started in front of Danny and he stood back from it as shouts filled the hall, as the building shook from anger and despair.

"Are you angry?" Mark Denton shouted.

Danny watched Kevin McRae wade into the mob and break up one of the fights by pulling both men off their feet by their hair.

"Are you angry?" Denton shouted again. "Go ahead—fucking hit *one another*."

The room began to quiet. Half the men turned back toward the stage.

"That's what they want you to do," Denton called. "Beat yourselves to a pulp. Go ahead. The mayor? The governor? The city council? They *laugh* at you."

The last of the men stopped fighting. They sat.

"Are you angry enough to *do* something?" Mark Denton asked.

No one spoke.

"Are you?" Denton shouted.

"Yes!" a thousand men shouted back.

"We're a union, men. That means we come together as one body with one purpose and we take it to them where *they* live. And we demand our rights as men. Any of you want to sit this out? Then fucking sit. The rest of you—show me what we are."

They rose as one—a thousand men, some with blood on their faces, some with tears of rage bubbling in their eyes. And Danny rose, too, a Judas no longer.

He met his father as his father was leaving the Oh-Six in South Boston.

"I'm out."

His father paused on the station house steps. "You're out of what?"

"The union-rat job, the radicals, the whole thing."

His father came down the stairs and stepped in close. "Those radicals could make you a captain by forty, son."

"Don't care."

"You don't care?" His father gave him a withered smile. "You turn this chance down, you'll not get another shot at that gold shield for five years. If ever."

Fear at that prospect filled Danny's chest, but he jammed his hands deeper in his pockets and shook his head. "I won't rat on my own men."

"They're subversives, Aiden. Subversives within our own department."

"They're cops, Dad. And by the way, what kind of father are you to send me into that kinda job? You couldn't find some-one else?"

His father's face grew gray. "It's the price of the ticket."

"What ticket?"

"For the train that never runs out of track." He rubbed his forehead with the heel of his hand. "Your grandchildren would have ridden it."

Danny waved it off. "I'm going home, Dad."

"Your home's here, Aiden."

Danny looked up at the white limestone building with its Grecian columns. He shook his head. "Your home is."

That night he went to Tessa's door. He knocked softly, looking up and down the hall, but she didn't answer. So he turned and walked toward his room, feeling like a kid carrying stolen food under his coat. Just as he reached his door, he heard hers unlatch.

He turned in the corridor and she was coming down the hallway toward him with a coat thrown over her shift, barefoot, her expression one of alarm and curiosity.

When she reached him, he tried to think of something to say.

"I still felt like talking," he said.

She looked back at him, her eyes large and dark. "More stories of the Old Country?"

He thought of her on the floor of Primo Alieveri's great hall, the way her flesh would have looked against the marble as the light of the fire played on her dark hair. A shameful image, really, in which to find lust.

"No," he said. "Not those stories."

"New ones, then?"

Danny opened his door. It was a reflexive gesture, but then he looked in Tessa's eyes and saw that the effect had been anything but casual.

"You want to come in and talk?" he said.

She stood there in her coat and the threadbare white shift underneath, looking at him for a long time. He could see her body underneath the shift. A light sheen of perspiration dotted the brown flesh below the hollow of her throat.

"I want to come in," she said.

CHAPTER *nine*

The first time Lila ever laid eyes on Luther was at a picnic on the outskirts of Minerva Park in a green field along the banks of the Big Walnut River. It was supposed to be a gathering of just the folks who worked for the Buchanan family at the mansion in Columbus, while the Buchanans themselves were on vacation in Saginaw Bay. But someone had mentioned it to someone and that someone mentioned it to someone else and by the time Lila arrived in the late morning of that hot August day there were at least sixty people going full-out for high times down along the water. It was a month after the massacre of coloreds in East St. Louis, and that month had passed slow and winter-bleak among the workers at the Buchanan house, pieces of gossip trickling in here and there that contradicted the newspaper accounts and, of course, the conversation among the white folk around the Buchanan dinner table. To hear the stories—of white women stabbing colored women with kitchen knives while white men burned the neighborhood down and strung their ropes and shot the colored men—was plenty reason to have a dark cloud drift down into the heads of everyone Lila knew, but four weeks later, it seemed folks had decided to retire that cloud for a day, to have fun while there was fun to be had.

Some men had cut an oil drum in half and covered the halves in cattle wire and started barbecuing and folks had brought tables and chairs and the tables were covered with plates of fried catfish and creamy potato salad and deep brown drumsticks and fat purple grapes and heaps and heaps of greens. Children ran and folks danced and some men played baseball in the wilting grass. Two men had brought their guitars and were cutting heads against each other like they were standing on a street corner in Helena, and the sounds of those guitars was as sharp as the sky.

Lila sat with her girlfriends, housemaids all—'Ginia and CC and Darla Blue—and they drank sweet tea and watched the men and the children play and it wasn't no trick at all to figure out which men were single because they acted more childish than the children, prancing and bowing up and getting loud. They reminded Lila of ponies before a race, pawing the dirt, rearing their heads.

Darla Blue, who had all the sense of a barn door, said, "I like that one there."

They all looked. They all shrieked.

"The snaggle-toothed one with the big ol' bush for a head?"

"He cute."

"For a dog."

"No, he—"

"Look at that big spilly belly on him," 'Ginia said. "Go all the way to his knees. And that butt look like a hundred pounds of warm taffy."

"I like a little roundness in a man."

"Well, that be your true love, then, 'cause he all round all the time. Round as a harvest moon. Ain't nothing hard in that man. Ain't nothing going to *get* hard neither."

They shrieked some more and clapped their thighs and CC said, "What about you, Miss Lila Waters? You see your Mr. Right?"

Lila shook her head, but the girls were having none of it.

Yet no matter how much shrieking and jawing they did to get it out of her, she kept her lips sealed and her eyes from wandering because she'd seen him, she'd seen him just fine, could see him now out of the corner of her eye as he moved across the grass like the breeze itself and snatched a ball from the air with a flick of his glove so effortless it was almost cruel. A slim man. Looked like he had cat in his blood the way he moved, as if where other men had joints, he had springs. And they were oiled to a shine. Even when he threw the ball, you didn't notice his arm, the piece of him that had done it, so much as you saw every square inch of him moving as a whole.

Music, Lila decided. The man's body was nothing less than music.

She'd heard the other men call his name—Luther. When he came running in to take his turn at bat, a small boy ran along-side him in the grass and tripped as they reached the dirt. The child landed on his chin and opened his mouth to wail, but Luther scooped him up without breaking stride and said, "Hear now, boy, ain't no crying on *Saturday.*"

The child's mouth hung open and Luther smiled wide at him. The child let loose a yelp and then laughed like he might never stop.

Luther swung the boy in the air and then looked straight at Lila, taking her breath on a ride down to her knees with how fast his eyes locked on hers. "Yours, ma'am?"

Lila tuned her eyes in to his and didn't blink. "I don't have no children."

"Yet," CC said and laughed loud.

That stopped whatever was about to come out of his mouth. He placed the child's feet on the ground. He dropped his eyes from hers and gave a smile to the air, his jaw slanted to the right. Then he turned back and looked right at her again, cool as you please.

"Well, that's some pretty news," he said. "Yes, sir. That's pretty as this here day itself, ma'am."

And he tipped his hat to her and walked over to pick up the bat.

By the end of the day, she was praying. Lying against

Luther's chest under an oak tree a hundred yards upriver from the party with the Big Walnut dark and sparkling in front of them, she told the Lord that she feared she could love this man too much one day. Even if she were struck blind in her sleep, she would know him in a crowd by his voice, by his smell, by the way air parted around him. She knew his heart was wild and thumping, but his soul was gentle. As he ran his thumb along the inside of her arm, she asked the Lord to forgive her for all she was about to do. Because for this wild, gentle man, she was fit to do whatever would keep him burning inside of her.

So the Lord, in His provenance, forgave her or condemned her, she could never be sure, because He gave her Luther Laurence. He gave him to her, in the first year of their knowing each other, about twice a month. And the rest of the time, she worked at the Buchanan house and Luther worked at the munitions factory and ran through life as if he were being clocked at it.

Oh, he was wild. Yet, unlike so many men, wildness wasn't a choice for Luther, and he meant no harm by it. He'd have corrected it if you could have explained to him what it was. But that was like explaining stone to water, sand to air. Luther worked at the factory and when he wasn't working he was playing ball and when he wasn't playing ball he was fixing something and when he wasn't fixing something he was running with his boys through the Columbus night and when he wasn't doing that he was with Lila, and she had the full force of his attention because whatever Luther focused on, he focused on it to the exclusion of all else, so that when it was Lila he was charming, he was making laugh, he was pouring his full self at, she felt that nothing, not even the warmth of the Lord, projected such light.

Then Jefferson Reese gave him the beating that put him in the hospital for a week and took something from him. You couldn't right say exactly what that something was, but you noticed the lack of it. Lila hated to picture what her man must have looked like curled in the dirt trying to protect himself while Reese pounded him and kicked him and unloosed all his long-bottled savagery. She'd tried to warn Luther off Reese, but Luther hadn't listened because some part of him needed to buck against things. What he'd found out, lying in the dirt while those fists and feet rained down on him, was that if you bucked certain things—the mean things—they didn't just buck back. No, no, that wasn't enough. They crushed you and kept crushing and the only way you escaped alive was through pure luck, nothing else. The mean things of this world had only one lesson—we are meaner than you'd ever imagine.

She loved Luther because that kind of mean was not in him. She loved Luther because what made him wild was the same thing that made him kind—he loved the world. Loved it the way you loved an apple so sweet you had to keep taking bites from it. Loved it whether it loved him back or not.

But in Greenwood, that love and that light of Luther's had started to dim. She couldn't understand it at first. Yes, there were better ways to get married than the way they did, and the house on Archer was small, and then the plague had come to town, and all of this in a short eight weeks—but still, still they were in paradise. They were in one of the few places in the whole world where a black man and a black woman walked tall. The whites not only left them alone, they respected them, and Lila agreed with Brother Garrity when he declared that Greenwood would be a model for the rest of the country and that ten to twenty years from now there'd be Greenwoods in Mobile and Columbus and Chicago and New Orleans and Detroit. Because the blacks and whites had figured out how to leave one another be in Tulsa, and the peace and prosperity that came with that was too good for the rest of the country not to sit up and take notice.

Luther saw something else, though. Something that ate away at his gentleness and his light, and Lila had begun to fear that their child would not reach the world in time to save its father. For on her more optimistic days, she knew that's all it would take—for Luther to hold his child so he'd realize once and for all that it was time to be a man.

She ran a hand over her belly and told the child to grow faster, grow faster, and she heard a car door slam and knew by the sound of it that it was that fool Jessie Tell's car and that Luther must have brung that sorry man home with him, the two of them probably high as balloons that had lost their strings, and she got up from her chair and put her mask on and tied it behind her head as Luther came through the door.

It wasn't the blood she noticed first, even though it covered his shirt and was splashed up along his neck. What she noticed first was that his face was all wrong. He didn't live behind it no more, not the Luther she'd first seen on the ball field, not the Luther who smiled down into her face and brushed back her hair as he moved in and out of her on a cold Ohio night, not the Luther who'd tickle her until she screamed herself hoarse, not the Luther who drew pictures of his child in the window of a speeding train. That man did not live in this body anymore.

Then she noticed the blood and came toward him, saying, "Luther, baby, you need a doctor. What happened? What happened?"

Luther held her back. He gripped her shoulders as if she were a chair he needed to find a place for and he looked around the room and said, "You need to pack."

"What?"

"Blood ain't mine. I ain't hurt. You need to pack."

"Luther, Luther, look at me, Luther."

He looked at her.

"What happened?"

"Jessie's dead," he said. "Jessie's dead and Dandy, too."

"Who's Dandy?"

"Worked for the Deacon. Deacon's dead. Deacon's brains all over a wall."

She stepped back from him. She touched her hands to her

throat because she didn't know where else to put them. She said, "What have you done?"

Luther said, "You got to pack, Lila. We got to run."

"I ain't running," she said.

"What?" He cocked his head at her, only a few inches away, but she felt as if he was a thousand miles on the other side of the world.

"I ain't leaving here," she said.

"Yes you are, woman."

"No, I'm not."

"Lila, I'm serious. Pack a fucking bag."

She shook her head.

Luther clenched his fists and his eyes were hooded. He crossed the room and put his fist through the clock hanging above the couch. "We are *leaving*."

She watched the glass fall to the top of the couch, saw that the second hand still ticked. So she'd repair it. She could do that.

"Jessie's dead," she said. "That's what you come home to tell me? Man got himself killed, near got you killed, and you expect me to say you my man and I'm'a pack a bag right quick and leave my home because I love you?"

"Yes," he said and took her shoulders in his hands again. "Yes."

"Well, I ain't," she said. "You a fool. I told you what running with that boy and running with the Deacon would get you and now you come in here covered in the wages of your sin, covered in other men's blood, and you want *what*?"

"Want you to leave with me."

"You kill tonight, Luther?"

His eyes were lost and his voice a whisper. "I killed the Deacon. I shot him straight up through his head."

"Why?" she said, her voice a whisper now, too.

"Because he the reason Jessie dead."

"And who'd Jessie kill?"

195

"Jessie killed Dandy. Smoke killed Jessie and I shot Smoke. He probably die, too."

She could feel the anger building in her, washing over the fear and the pity and the love. "So Jessie Tell kill a man and then a man shoot him and then you shoot that man and then kill the Deacon? Is that what you're telling me?"

"Yes. Now—"

"Is that what you're telling me?" she yelled and beat his shoulders and his chest with her fists and then slapped him hard across the side of the head and would have kept on going if he didn't grab her wrists in his.

"Lila, listen—"

"Get out of my house. Get out of my house! You've taken life. You are foul in the eyes of the Lord, Luther. And He *will* punish you."

Luther stepped back from her.

She stayed where she was and felt their child kick inside her womb. It wasn't much of a kick. It was soft, hesitant.

"I have to change these clothes and pack some things."

"Then pack," she said and turned her back on him.

As he tied his belongings to the back of Jessie's car, she stayed inside, listening to him out there, and thinking how a love like theirs couldn't possibly end no other way because it had always burned too bright. And she apologized to the Lord for what she now saw so clearly was their greatest sin: They had searched for heaven in this world. A search of that kind was steeped in pride, the worst of the seven deadly sins. Worse than greed, worse than wrath.

When Luther came back, she remained sitting on her side of the room.

"This is it?" he said softly.

"I guess it is."

"This is how we end?"

"I believe so."

"I . . ." He held out his hand.

"What?"

"I love you, woman."

She nodded.

"I said I love you."

She nodded again. "I know that. But you love other things more."

He shook his head, his hand still hanging in the air, waiting for her to take it.

"Oh, yes, you do. You're a child, Luther. And now all your playing brought this bloodshed home to roost. That was you, Luther. It wasn't Jessie and it wasn't the Deacon. It was you. All you. You. You, with your child in my womb."

He lowered his hand. He stood in the doorway a long time. Several times he opened his mouth, as if to say something, but the words wouldn't come.

"I love you," he said again, and his voice was hoarse.

"I love you, too," she said, though she did not feel it in her heart at that moment. "But you need to go before someone comes here looking for you."

He walked out the door so fast she'd never be able to say she'd seen him move. One moment he was there, the next his shoes were hard against the wooden planks and then she heard the engine turn over and the car idled for a short time.

When he depressed the clutch and shifted into first the car made a loud clanking and she stood but didn't move toward the door.

When she finally stepped out on the porch, he was gone. She looked up the road for his taillights, and she could just make them out, far off down the road in the dust the tires raised in the night.

Luther left Arthur Smalley's car keys on his front porch on top of a note that said "Club Almighty alley." He left another note saying the same thing to let the Irvines know where to find their hope chest, and he deposited jewelry and cash and most everything else they'd taken on the porches of the sick. When he got to Owen Tice's house, he could see the man through his screen door, sitting dead at the table. After he'd pulled the trigger, the shotgun had bounced back in his hands. It stood straight up between his thighs, his hands still gripping it.

Luther drove back through the graying night and let himself into the house on Elwood. He stood in the living room and watched his wife sleep in the chair where he'd left her. He went into the bedroom and lifted the mattress. He placed most of Owen Tice's money under there and then he went back out into the parlor and stood and looked at his wife some more. She snored softly and groaned once and pulled her knees closer to her belly.

She'd been right in everything she'd said.

But, oh, she'd been cold. She'd seen to breaking his heart as much as he, he now realized, had broken hers these last months. This house he'd feared and bristled at was something he now wished he could wrap his arms around and carry out to Jessie's car and take with him wherever he was going.

"I do so love you, Lila Waters Laurence," he said and kissed the tip of his index finger and touched it to her forehead.

She didn't stir, so Luther leaned over and kissed her belly and then he left his home and went back to Jessie's car and drove north with the dawn rising over Tulsa and the birds waking from their sleep.

CHAPTER *ten*

For two weeks, if her father wasn't home, Tessa came to Danny's door. They rarely slept, but Danny wouldn't call what they did making love. A bit too raw for that. On several occasions, she gave the orders—slower, faster, harder, put it there, no there, roll over, stand up, lie down. It seemed hopeless to Danny, the way they clawed and chewed and squeezed each other's bones. And yet he kept returning for more. Sometimes, walking the beat, he'd find himself wishing the uniform weren't so coarse; it rubbed parts of him that had already been scratched to the last layer of flesh. His bedroom on those nights gave off the feel of a lair. They entered and tore at each other. And while the sounds of the neighborhood did reach them—an occasional car horn, the shouts of children kicking a ball in the alleys, the neighs and huffs from the stables behind their building, even the clank of footsteps on the fire escape of some other tenants who'd discovered the attraction of the roof he and Tessa had abandoned—they seemed the sounds of an alien life.

For all her abandon in the bedroom, Tessa withheld herself when the sex was finished. She would sneak back to her room without a word and never once fell asleep in his bed. He didn't mind. In fact, he preferred it this way—heated yet cold. He wondered if his part in all of this unleashing of unnameable fury was tied into his feelings for Nora, his urge to punish her for loving him and leaving him and continuing to live.

There was no danger he would fall in love with Tessa. Or she with him. In all their snakelike commingling he sensed contempt above all, not just she for him, or he for her, but both of them for their barren addiction to this act. Once, when she was on top, her hands clenched against his chest, she whispered, "So young," like a condemnation.

When Federico was in town, he invited Danny over for some anisette and they sat listening to opera on the Silvertone while Tessa sat on the davenport, working on her English in primers that Federico brought back from his trips across New England and the Tri-States. At first Danny worried that Federico would sense the intimacy between his drinking companion and his daughter, but Tessa sat on the davenport, a stranger, her legs tucked under her petticoat, her crepe blouse cinched at the throat, and whenever her eyes found Danny's they were blank of anything but linguistic curiosity.

"Dee-fine *avar-iss*," she said once.

Those nights, Danny would return to his rooms feeling both the betrayer and the betrayed, and he'd sit by his window and read from the stacks provided by Eddie McKenna until late into the evening.

He went to another BSC meeting and still another, and little about the men's situation or prospects had changed. The mayor still refused to meet with them, while Samuel Gompers and the American Federation of Labor seemed to be having second thoughts about granting a charter.

"Keep the faith," he heard Mark Denton say to a flatfoot one night. "Rome wasn't built in a day."

"But it *was* built," the guy said.

Then one night, when he returned after two solid days of duty, he found Mrs. DiMassi dragging Tessa and Federico's rug down the stairs. Danny tried to help her, but the old woman shrugged him off and dropped the rug into the foyer and let loose a loud sigh before looking at him.

"She's gone," the old woman said, and Danny saw that she knew what he and Tessa had been up to and it colored how she would look at him as long as he lived here. "They go without a word. Owe me rent, too. You look for her, you will not find her, I think. Women of her village are known for their black hearts. Yes? Witches, some think. Tessa have black heart. Baby die, make it blacker. You," she said as she pushed past him to her own apartment, "you probably make it blacker still."

She opened her door and looked back at him. "They waiting for you."

"Who?"

"The men in your room," she said and entered her apartment.

He unsnapped the leather guard on his holster as he walked up the stairs, half of him still thinking of Tessa, of how it might not be too late to find her if the trail wasn't too cold. He thought she owed him an explanation. He was convinced there was one.

At the top of the stairs, he heard his father's voice coming from his apartment and snapped the guard back on his holster. Instead of going toward the voice, though, he went to Tessa and Federico's apartment. He found the door ajar. He pushed it open. The rug was gone, but otherwise the parlor looked the same. Yet as he walked around it, he saw that all the photographs had been removed. In the bedroom, the closets were empty and the bed was stripped. The top of the dresser where Tessa had kept her powders and perfumes was bare. The hat tree in the corner sprouted empty pegs. He walked back into the parlor and felt a cold drop of sweat roll behind his ear and then down the back of his neck: they'd left behind the Silvertone.

The top was open and he went to it, smelling it suddenly. Someone had poured acid onto the turntable, and the velvet inlay had been eaten down to nothing. He opened the cabinet to find all of Federico's beloved record discs smashed into shards. His first instinct was that they must have been murdered; the old man would have never left this behind or allowed anyone to vandalize it so obscenely.

Then he noticed the note. It was glued to the right cabinet door. The handwriting was Federico's, identical to that on the note he'd left inviting Danny to dinner that first night; Danny suddenly felt nauseated.

> Policeman,
> Is this wood still a tree?
> Federico

"Aiden," his father said from the doorway. "Good to see you, boy."

Danny looked over at him. "What the hell?"

His father stepped into the apartment. "The other tenants say he seemed like such a sweet old man. Your opinion of him as well, I assume?"

Danny shrugged. He felt numb.

"Well, he isn't sweet and he isn't old. What's the note he left you all about?"

"Private joke," Danny said.

His father frowned. "Nothing about this is private, boy."

"Why don't you tell me what's going on?"

His father smiled. "Elucidation awaits in your room."

Danny followed him down the hall to find two men waiting in his apartment. They wore bow ties and heavy rust-colored suits with dark pinstripes. Their hair was plastered to their skulls by petroleum jelly and parted down the middle. Their shoes were a flat brown and polished. Justice Department. They couldn't have been more obvious if they'd worn their badges pinned to their foreheads.

The taller of the two looked over at him. The shorter one sat on the edge of Danny's coffee table.

"Officer Coughlin?" the tall man said.

"Who're you?"

"I asked first," the tall man said.

"I don't care," Danny said. "I live here."

202

Danny's father folded his arms and leaned against the window, content to watch the show.

The tall man looked over his shoulder at the other man and then back at Danny. "My name's Finch. Rayme Finch. Rayme. No 'ond.' Just Rayme. You can call me Agent Finch." He had the look of an athlete, loose-limbed and strong of bone.

Danny lit a cigarette and leaned against the doorjamb. "You got a badge?"

"I already showed it to your father."

Danny shrugged. "Didn't show it to me."

As Finch reached into his back pocket, Danny caught the little man on the coffee table watching him with the kind of delicate contempt he'd normally associate with bishops or showgirls. He was a few years younger than Danny, maybe twenty-three at the most, and a good ten years younger than Agent Finch, but the pockets beneath his bulging eyes were pendulous and darkly pooled like those of a man twice his age. He crossed his legs and picked at something on his knee.

Finch produced his badge and a federal ID card stamped with the seal of the United States government: Bureau of Investigation.

Danny took a quick glance at it. "You're BI?"

"Try saying it without a smirk."

Danny jerked his thumb at the other guy. "And who's this exactly?"

Finch opened his mouth but the other man wiped his hand with a handkerchief before extending the hand to Danny. "John Hoover, Mr. Coughlin," the man said, and Danny's hand came away with sweat from the handshake. "I work with the antiradical department at Justice. You don't cotton to radicals, do you, Mr. Coughlin?"

"There're no Germans in the building. Isn't that what Justice handles?" He looked back at Finch. "And the BI is all about bankruptcy fraud. Yeah?"

The doughy lump on the coffee table looked at Danny like he wanted to bite the tip of his nose. "Our purview has expanded a bit since the war started, Officer Coughlin."

Danny nodded. "Well, good luck." He stepped over the threshold. "Mind getting the fuck out of my apartment?"

"We also deal with draft dodgers," Agent Finch said, "agitators, seditionists, people who would make war on the United States."

"It's a living, I'd guess."

"A good one. Anarchists in particular," Finch said. "Those bastards are tops on our lists. You know—bomb throwers, Officer Coughlin. Like the one you were fucking."

Danny squared his shoulders to Finch's. "I'm fucking who?"

Agent Finch took a turn leaning against the doorjamb. "You *were* fucking Tessa Abruzze. At least that's how she called herself. Am I correct?"

"I know Miss Abruzze. What of it?"

Finch gave him a thin smile. "You don't know shit."

"Her father's a phonograph salesman," Danny said. "They had some trouble back in Italy but—"

"Her *father*," Finch said, "is her husband." He raised his eyebrows. "You heard me right. And he couldn't give a damn about phonographs. Federico Abruzze is not even his real name. He's an anarchist, and more particularly he's a Galleanist. You know what that term means or should I provide help?"

Danny said, "I know."

"His real name is Federico Ficara and while you've been fucking his wife? He's been making bombs."

"Where?" Danny said.

"Right here." Rayme Finch jerked his thumb back down the hall.

John Hoover crossed one hand over the other and rested them on his belt buckle. "I ask you again, Officer, are you the kind of man who cottons to radicals?"

"I think my son answered the question," Thomas Coughlin said.

204

John Hoover shook his head. "Not that I heard, sir."

Danny looked down at him. His skin had the look of bread pulled too early from the oven and his pupils were so tiny and dark they seemed meant for the head of another animal entirely.

"The reason I ask is because we are closing the barn door. After the horses have left it, I'll grant you, but before the barn has burned to the ground. What the war showed us? Is that the enemy is not just in Germany. The enemy came over on ships and availed himself of our wanton immigration policies and he set up shop. He lectures to mine workers and factory workers and disguises himself as the friend of the worker and the downtrodden. But what he really is? What he really is is a prevaricator, an inveigler, a foreign disease, a man bent on the destruction of our democracy. He must be ground into dust." Hoover wiped the back of his neck with his handkerchief; the top of his collar had darkened with sweat. "So I'm going to ask you a third time—are you a coddler of the radical element? Are you in effect, sir, an enemy of my Uncle Samuel?"

Danny said, "Is he serious?"

Finch said, "Oh yes."

Danny said, "John, right?"

The round man gave him a small nod.

"You fight in the war?"

Hoover shook his large head. "I did not have the honor."

"The honor," Danny said. "Well, I didn't have the *honor* either, but that's because I was deemed essential personnel on the home front. What's your excuse?"

Hoover's face reddened and he pocketed his handkerchief. "There are many ways to serve your country, Mr. Coughlin."

"Yes, there are," Danny said. "I've got a hole in my neck from serving mine. So if you question my patriotism again, John? I'll have my father duck and throw you out that fucking window."

Danny's father fluttered a hand over his heart and stepped away from the window.

Hoover, though, stared back at Danny with the coal-blue clarity of the unexamined conscience. The moral fortitude of a knee-high boy who played at battle with sticks. Who grew older, but not up.

Finch cleared his throat. "The business at hand, gents, is bombs. Could we return to that?"

"How would you have known about my association with Tessa?" Danny said. "Were you tailing me?"

Finch shook his head. "Her. Her and her husband, Federico, were last seen ten months ago in Oregon. Beat the holy shit out of a railroad porter who tried to inspect Tessa's bag. Had to jump off the train while it was going a good head of steam. Thing was, they had to leave the bag behind. Portland PD met the train, found blasting caps, dynamite, a couple of pistols. A real anarchist's toolbox. The porter, poor suspicious bastard, died from his injuries."

"Still haven't answered my question," Danny said.

"We tracked them here about a month ago. This is Galleani's home base, after all. We'd heard rumors she was pregnant. The flu was running the show then, though, so that slowed us up. Last night a guy, let's say, we count on in the anarchist underground coughed up Tessa's address. She must have got word, though, because she got into the wind before we could get here. You? You were easy. We asked all the tenants in the building if Tessa had been acting suspicious lately. To a man or woman they all said, 'Outside of fucking the cop on the fifth floor? Why no.'"

"Tessa a bomber?" Danny shook his head. "I don't buy it."

"No?" Finch said. "Back in her room an hour ago, John found metal shavings in the floor cracks and burn marks that could have only come from acid. You want a look? They're making bombs, Officer Coughlin. No, correct that—they've made bombs. Probably used the manual Galleani wrote himself."

Danny went to the window and opened it. He sucked in the cold air and looked out at the harbor lights. Luigi

Galleani was the father of anarchism in America, publicly devoted to the overthrow of the federal government. Name a major terrorist act in the last five years and he'd been fingered as the architect.

"As for your girlfriend," Finch said, "her real name *is* Tessa, but that's probably the only true thing you know about her." Finch came over to the window beside Danny and his father. He produced a folded handkerchief and opened it. "See this?"

Danny looked into the handkerchief and saw white powder.

"That's fulminate of mercury. Looks just like table salt, doesn't it? Put it on a rock and hit the rock with a hammer, though, and both the rock and the hammer will explode. Probably your arm, too. Your girlfriend was born Tessa Valparo in Naples. She grew up in a slum, lost her parents to cholera, and started working in a bordello at twelve. She killed a client when she was thirteen. With a razor and an impressive imagination. Fell in with Federico shortly after that and they came here."

"Where," Hoover said, "they quickly made the acquaintance of Luigi Galleani just north of here in Lynn. They helped him plan attacks in New York and Chicago and play sob sister to all those poor helpless workers from Cape Cod to Seattle. They worked on that disgraceful propaganda rag *Cronaca Sovversiva* as well. You're familiar with it?"

Danny said, "You can't work in the North End and not see it. People wrap their fish in it, for Christ's sake."

"And yet it's illegal," Hoover said.

"Well, it's illegal to distribute through the mail," Rayme Finch said. "I'm the reason it's so actually. I raided their offices. I've arrested Galleani twice. I guarantee you, I'll deport him before the year's out."

"Why haven't you deported him already?"

"The law thus far favors subversives," Hoover said. "Thus far."

Danny chuckled. "Eugene Debs is in jail for giving a fucking *speech*."

"One that advocated violence," Hoover said, and his voice was loud and strained, "against this country."

Danny rolled his eyes at the chunky little peacock. "My point is, if you can jail a former presidential candidate for giving a speech, why can't you deport the most dangerous anarchist in the country?"

Finch sighed. "American kids and an American wife. That's what got him his sympathy votes last time. He's going, though. Trust me. He's fucking going next time."

"They're all going," Hoover said. "Every last unwashed one of them."

Danny turned to his father. "Say something."

"Say what?" his father said mildly.

"Say what you're doing here."

"I told you," his father said, "these gentlemen informed me that my own son was shacking up with a subversive. A bomb maker, Aiden."

"Danny."

His father pulled a pack of Black Jack from his pocket and offered it to the room. John Hoover took a piece, but Danny and Finch declined. His father and Hoover unwrapped their sticks of gum and popped them in their mouths.

His father sighed. "If it hit the papers, *Danny*, that my son was taking the favors, shall we say, of a violent radical while her husband built bombs right under his nose—what would that say about my beloved department?"

Danny turned to Finch. "So find 'em and deport 'em. That's your plan, right?"

"Bet your ass. But until I find them and until they go," Finch said, "they're planning on making some noise. Now we know they've got some things planned for May. I understand your father already briefed you on that. We don't know where or who they're going to hit. We have some ideas, but still, radicals aren't predictable. They'll go after the usual list of judges and politicians, but it's the industrial targets we have trouble protecting. Which industry will they choose? Coal, iron, lead, sugar, steel, rubber, textiles? Will they hit a factory? Or a distillery? Or an oil derrick? We don't know. But what we do know is that they're going to hit something big right here in your town."

"When?"

"Could be tomorrow. Could be three months from now." Finch shrugged. "Or they might wait until May. Can't tell."

"But we assure you," Hoover said, "their insurrectionary act will be loud."

Finch reached into his jacket, unfolded a piece of paper, and handed it to Danny. "We found this in her closet. I think it's a first draft."

Danny unfolded the page. The note was composed of letters cut from the newspaper and glued to the page:

> *Go-Head!*
> *Deport us! We will dynamite you.*

Danny handed the note back.

"It's a press release," Finch said. "I'd bank on it. They just haven't sent it out yet. But when it does hit the streets, you can be sure a boom is going to follow."

Danny said, "And you're telling me all this, why?"

"To see if you have an interest in stopping them."

"My son is a proud man," Thomas Coughlin said. "He wouldn't stand for word to get out on something like this and sully his reputation."

Danny ignored him. "Anyone in their right mind would want to stop them."

"But you're not just anyone," Hoover said. "Galleani tried to blow you up once."

Danny said, "What?"

"Who do you think ordered the bombing of Salutation Street?" Finch said. "You think that was random? It was revenge for the arrest of three of theirs in an antiwar protest the month before. Who do you think was behind those ten cops got blown up in Chicago last year? Galleani, that's who. And his minions. They've tried to kill Rockefeller. They've tried to kill judges. They've blown up parades. Hell, they exploded a bomb in St. Patrick's Cathedral. Galleani and his Galleanists. At the turn of the century people of this exact same philosophy killed President McKinley, the president of France, the prime minister of Spain, the empress of Austria, and the king of Italy. All in a six-year span. They may blow themselves up occasionally, but they're not comical. They're murderers. And they were making bombs right here under your nose while you were fucking one of them. Oh, no, let me amend that—while she was fucking you. So how personal does it have to get, Officer Coughlin, before you wake up?"

Danny thought of Tessa in his bed, of the guttural sounds they'd made, of her eyes widening as he'd pushed into her, of her nails tearing his skin, her mouth spreading into a smile, and outside, the clank of the fire escape as people moved up and down it.

"You've seen them up close," Finch said. "If you saw them again, you'd have a second or two's advantage over anyone who was going off a faded photograph."

"I can't find them here," Danny said. "Not here. I'm an American."

"This is America," Hoover said.

Danny pointed at the floorboards and shook his head. "This is Italy."

"But what if we can get you close?"

"How?"

Finch handed Danny a photograph. The quality was poor, as if it had been reproduced several times. The man in it looked to be about thirty with a thin, patrician nose and eyes narrowed to slits. He was clean-shaven. His hair was fair, and his skin appeared pale, though that was more of a guess on Danny's part.

"Doesn't look like a card-carrying Bolshie."

"And yet he is," Finch said.

Danny handed the photograph back. "Who is he?"

"Name's Nathan Bishop. He's a real beaut'. A British doctor and radical. These terrorists accidentally blow off a hand or slip away from a riot with wounds? They can't just stroll into an emergency room. They go to see our friend here. Nathan Bishop's the company quack for the Massachusetts radical movement. Radicals don't tend to fraternize outside their individual cells, but Nathan's the connective tissue. He knows all the players."

"And he drinks," Hoover said. "Quite copiously."

"So get one of your own men to cozy up to him."

Finch shook his head. "Won't work."

"Why?"

"Honestly? We don't have the budget." Finch looked embarrassed. "So we came to your father, and he told us you've already begun the prep work to go after a radical cell. We want you to circle the entire movement. Get us license plate numbers, membership counts. All the while, you keep your eyes peeled for Bishop. Your paths will cross sooner or later. You get close to him, you get close to the rest of these sons-a-bitches. You heard of the Roxbury Lettish Workingman's Society?"

Danny nodded. " 'Round here they're just called the Letts."

Finch cocked his head, as if this were news to him. "For whatever bullshit sentimental reason, they seem to be Bishop's favorite group. He's friends with the guy who runs it, a Hebe name of Louis Fraina with documented ties to Mother Russia. We're hearing rumors Fraina might be the lead plotter in all this."

"All what?" Danny said. "I was kept in the dark on a need-to-know basis."

Finch looked over at Thomas Coughlin. Danny's father raised his hands, palms up, and shrugged.

"They may be planning something big in the spring."

"What exactly?"

"A national May Day revolt."

Danny laughed. No one else did.

"You're serious."

His father nodded. "A bomb campaign followed by armed revolt, coordinated among all the radical cells in all the major cities across the country."

"To what end? It's not like they can storm Washington."

"That's what Nicholas said about St. Petersburg," Finch said.

Danny removed his greatcoat and the blue coat underneath, stood there in his T-shirt as he unbuckled his gun belt and hung it on the closet door. He poured himself a glass of rye and didn't offer anyone else the bottle. "So this Bishop fella, he's connected to the Letts?"

A nod from Finch. "Sometimes. The Letts have no ostensible connection to the Galleanists, but they're all radicals, so Bishop has connections to both of them."

"Bolsheviks on one hand," Danny said, "anarchists on the other."

"And Nathan Bishop linking them together."

"So I infiltrate the Letts and see if they're making bombs for May Day or—what—if they're connected to Galleani in some way?"

"If not him, then his followers," Hoover said.

"And if they're not?" Danny said.

"Get their mailing list," Finch said.

Danny poured himself another drink. "What?"

"Their mailing list. It's the key to breaking any group of subversives. When I raided the offices of *Cronaca* last year? They'd just finished printing their latest issue. I got the names of every single person they were sending it to. Based on that list, the Justice Department managed to deport sixty of them."

"Uh-huh. I heard Justice once deported a guy for calling Wilson a cocksucker."

"We tried," Hoover said. "Unfortunately the judge decided jail was more fitting."

212

Even Danny's father was incredulous. "For calling a man a cocksucker?"

"For calling the president of the United States a cocksucker," Finch said.

"And if I see Tessa or Federico?" Danny caught a whiff of her scent suddenly.

"Shoot 'em in the face," Finch said. "Then say, 'Halt.' "

"I'm missing a link here," Danny said.

His father said, "No, you're fine."

"The Bolsheviks are talkers. The Galleanists are terrorists. One doesn't necessarily equal the other."

"Nor do they necessarily cancel one another out," Hoover said.

"Be that as it may, they—"

"*Hey.*" Finch's tone was sharp, his eyes too clear. "You say 'Bolsheviks' or 'Communists' like there are nuances here the rest of us are too thick to grasp. They're not *different*—they're fucking terrorists. Every last one. This country's heading for one hell of a showdown, Officer. We think that showdown will happen on May Day. That you won't be able to swing a cat without hitting some revolutionary with a bomb or a rifle. And if that occurs, this country will tear itself apart. Picture it—the bodies of innocent Americans strewn all over our streets. Thousands of kids, mothers, workingmen. And for what? Because these cocksuckers hate the life we have. Because it's better than theirs. Because *we're* better than *them*. We're richer, we're freer, we've got a lot of the best real estate in a world that's mostly desert or undrinkable ocean. But we don't hoard that, we share. Do they thank us for sharing? For welcoming them to our shores? No. They try to kill us. They try to tear down our government like we're the fucking Romanovs. Well, we're not the fucking Romanovs. We're the only successful democracy in the world. And we're done apologizing for it."

Danny waited a moment and then clapped.

Hoover looked ready to bite him again, but Finch took a bow.

213

Danny saw Salutation Street again, the wall transformed into a white drizzle, the floor vanishing underfoot. He'd never talked about it to anyone, not even Nora. How did you put words to helplessness? You didn't. You couldn't. Falling from the first floor straight through to the basement, he'd felt seized with the utter certainty that he'd never eat again, walk a street again, feel a pillow against his cheek.

You own me, he'd thought. To God. To chance. To his own helplessness.

"I'll do it," Danny said.

"Patriotism or pride?" Finch arched one eyebrow.

"One of the two," Danny said.

After Finch and Hoover left, Danny and his father sat at the small table and took turns with the bottle of rye.

"Since when did you let federal cops shoehorn in on BPD business?"

"Since the war changed this country." His father gave him a distant smile and took a sip from the bottle. "If we'd come out on the losing side, maybe we'd still be the same, but we didn't. Volstead"—he held up the bottle and sighed—"will change it further. Shrink it, I think. The future is federal, not local."

"Your future?"

"Mine?" His father chuckled. "I'm an old man from an even older time. No, not my future."

"Con's?"

His father nodded. "And yours. If you can keep your penis at home where it belongs." He corked the bottle and slid it across to Danny. "How long will it take you to grow a beard fit for a Red?"

Danny pointed at the thick stubble already sprouting from his cheeks. "Guess."

His father rose from the table. "Give your uniform a good brushing before putting it away. You won't be needing it for a while."

"You saying I'm a detective?"

"What do you think?"

"Say it, Dad."

His father stared across the room at him, his face blank. Eventually, he nodded. "You do this, you'll have your gold shield."

"All right."

"I hear you showed up at a BSC meeting the other night. *After* you told me you wouldn't rat on your own."

Danny nodded.

"So you're a union man now?"

Danny shook his head. "Just like their coffee."

His father gave him another long look, his hand on the doorknob. "You might want to strip that bed of yours, give those sheets a good washing." He gave Danny a firm nod and left.

Danny stood by the table and uncorked the rye. He took a sip as his father's footsteps faded in the stairwell. He looked at his unmade bed and took another drink.

CHAPTER *eleven*

Jessie's car only got Luther as far as central Missouri before one of the tires blew out just past Waynesville. He'd been sticking to back roads, driving at night as much as possible, but the tire blew out close to dawn. Jessie, of course, hadn't packed a spare, so Luther had no choice but to drive on it. He crawled along the side of the road in first gear, never getting above the speed an ox pulled a plow, and just as the sun entered the valley, he found a filling station and pulled in.

Two white men came out of the mechanic's shed, one of them wiping his hands on a rag, the other pulling from a bottle of sassafras. It was that one who said it sure was a nice car and asked Luther how he'd come by it.

Luther watched them spread out on either side of the hood, and the one with the rag wiped his brow with it and spit some chaw into the dirt.

"I saved up," Luther said.

"Saved up?" the one with the bottle said. He was lean and lanky and wore a sheepskin coat against the cold. He had a thick head of red hair but up top he had a bald spot the size of a fist. "What kind of work you do?" He had a pleasant voice.

"Work in a munitions factory for the war effort," Luther said.

"Uh-huh." The man walked around the car, taking a good

216

look, squatting from time to time to check the body lines for dents that might have been hammered out and painted over. "You were in a war once, weren't you, Bernard?"

Bernard spit again and wiped his mouth and ran his stubby fingers along the edge of the hood looking for the latch.

"I was," Bernard said. "Haiti." He looked at Luther for the first time. "They dropped us off in this one town, said kill any natives give you a funny look."

"You get a lot of funny looks?" the redheaded man asked.

Bernard popped the hood. "Not once we started shooting."

"What's your name?" the other man asked Luther.

"I'm just looking to fix this here flat."

"That's a long name," the man said. "Wouldn't you say, Bernard?"

Bernard stuck his head out from behind the hood. "It's a mouthful."

"My name's Cully," the man said, and reached out his hand.

Luther shook the hand. "Jessie."

"Pleased to meet you, Jessie." Cully walked around the back of the car and hitched his pants to squat by the tire. "Oh, sure, there it is, Jessie. You want to look?"

Luther walked down the car and followed Cully's finger, saw a jagged tear the width of a nickel in the tire right by the rim.

"Probably just a sharp stone," Cully said.

"Can you fix it?"

"Yeah, we can fix it. How far'd you drive on it?"

"Couple miles," Luther said. "But real slow."

Cully took a close look at the wheel and nodded. "Don't seem to be any damage to the rim. How far you come, Jessie?"

The whole time he'd been driving, Luther kept telling himself he needed to come up with a story, but as soon as he'd start trying, his thoughts would drift to Jessie lying on the floor in his own blood or the Deacon trying to reach for his arm or Arthur Smalley inviting them into his home or Lila

217

looking at him in the living room with her heart closed to him.

He said, "Columbus, Ohio," because he couldn't say Tulsa.

"But you came from the east," Cully said.

Luther could feel the cold wind biting the edges of his ears and he reached in and took his coat from the front seat. "I went to visit a friend in Waynesville," Luther said. "Now I'm heading back."

"Took a drive through the cold from Columbus to Waynesville," Cully said as Bernard closed the hood with a hard clank.

"That'll happen," Bernard said, coming down the side of the car. "Nice coat."

Luther looked at it. It had been Jessie's, a fine wool cheviot carovette overcoat with a convertible collar. For a man who loved to dress, he'd been prouder of this coat than anything he owned.

"Thank you," Luther said.

"Might roomy," Bernard said.

"What's that?"

"A bit big for you is all," Cully said with a helpful smile as he straightened to his full height. "What you think, Bern'? Can we fix this man's tire?"

"Don't see why not."

"How's that engine looking?"

Bernard said, "Man takes care of his car. Everything under that hood is cherry. Yes, sir."

Cully nodded. "Well, Jessie, we're happy to oblige you then. We'll get you up and running in no time." He took a stroll around the car again. "But we got some funny laws in this county. One says I can't work on a colored man's car until I check his license against the registration. You got a license?"

The man smiled all pleasant and logical.

"I misplaced it."

Cully looked over at Bernard, then out at the empty road, then back at Luther. "That's unfortunate."

"It's just a flat."

"Oh, I know, Jessie, I do. Hell, it was up to me we'd have you fixed up and on the road five minutes from last Tuesday. We surely would. If it was up to me, I'll tell you true, there'd be a whole lot less laws in this county. But they got their ways of doing things and it's not my place to tell them different. I tell you what—it's a slow day. Why don't we let Bernard get to working on the car and I'll drive you down to the county courthouse and you can just fill out an application and see if Ethel will make you up a new license on the spot?"

Bernard ran his rag down along the hood. "This car ever been in an accident?"

"No, suh," Luther said.

"First time he said 'suh,'" Bernard said. "You notice that?"

Cully said, "It did catch my attention." He spread his hands to Luther. "It's okay, Jessie. We're just used to our Missouri coloreds showing a bit more deference. Again, makes no difference to me, you see. Just the way of things."

"Yes, suh."

"Twice!" Bernard said.

"Whyn't you grab your things," Cully said, "and we'll take that ride?"

Luther took his suitcase from the backseat and a minute later he was in Cully's pickup truck and they were driving west.

After about ten minutes of silence, Cully said, "You know I fought in the war. You?"

Luther shook his head.

"Damnedest thing, Jessie, but I couldn't tell you now what it was exactly we were fighting about. Seems like back in 'fourteen, that Serbian fella shot that Austrian fella? And next thing you know, in 'bout a *minute*, Germany was threatening Belgium and France was saying, well, you can't threaten Belgium and then Russia—'member when they were in it?—they're saying you can't threaten France and before you know it, everyone's shooting. Now you, you say

219

you worked in a munitions factory, so I'm wondering—did *they* tell you what it was about?"

Luther said, "No. To them I think it was just about munitions."

"Hell," Cully said with a hearty laugh, "maybe that's what it was about for all of us. Maybe that's all indeed. Wouldn't that be something?" He laughed again and nudged Luther's thigh with his fist and Luther smiled in agreement because if the whole world were that stupid then it truly was something indeed.

"Yes, suh," he said.

"I read a bunch," Cully said. "I hear at Versailles that they're going to make Germany surrender something like fifteen percent of her coal production and near fifty percent of her steel. *Fifty* percent. Now how's that dumb country supposed to ever get back on its feet? You wonder that, Jessie?"

"I'm wondering it now," he said, and Cully chuckled.

"They supposed to give up, like, another fifteen percent of their territory. And all this for backing the play of a friend. All that. And the thing is, who amongst us picks our friends?"

Luther thought of Jessie and wondered who Cully was thinking of as he stared at the window, his eyes gone wistful or rueful, Luther couldn't tell.

"No one," Luther said.

"Exactly. You don't *pick* friends. You *find* each other. And any man don't back a friend gives up the right to call himself a man in my opinion. And I understand, you gots to pay if you back a bad play by your friend, but do you have to be ground into the dirt? I don't think so. World apparently thinks different, though."

He settled back in his seat, his arm loose against the wheel, and Luther wondered if he was expected to say something.

"When I was in the war," Cully said, "a plane flies over this field one day, starts dropping grenades? Whew. That's a sight I try to forget. Grenades start hitting the trenches and everyone's jumping out and the Germans start firing from their trenches and I'll tell you, Jessie, wasn't no way to tell hell from hell that day. What would you do?"

"Suh?"

Cully's fingers rested lightly on the wheel. He looked over. "Stay in the trench with grenades falling on you or jump out into a field where boys were shooting at you?"

"I can't imagine, suh."

"I suspect you can't. Hideous really, the cries boys make when they're dying. Just hideous." Cully shuddered and yawned at the same time. "Yes, sir. Sometimes life don't give you a choice but between the hard thing and the harder thing. Times like that, man can't afford to lose much time thinking. Just got to get doing."

Cully yawned again and went silent and they drove that way for another ten miles, the plains spread out around them, frozen stiff under a hard white sky. The cold gave everything the look of metal that had been rubbed with steel wool. Gray wisps of frost swirled along the edges of the road and kicked up in front of the grille. They reached a railroad crossing and Cully stopped the truck in the middle of the tracks, the engine giving off a low chug as he turned in his seat and looked over at Luther. He smelled of tobacco, though Luther had yet to see him smoke, and small pink veins sprouted from the corners of his eyes.

"They string coloreds up here, Jessie, for doing a lot less than stealing a car."

"I didn't steal it," Luther said and immediately thought about the gun in his suitcase.

"They string 'em up just for driving cars. You in Missouri, son." His voice was soft and kind. He shifted and placed an arm up on the seat back. "Now it's like a lot of things have to do with the law, Jessie. I might not like it. Then again maybe I do. But even if I don't, it ain't for me to say. I just go along to get along. You understand?"

Luther said nothing.

"You see that tower?"

221

Luther followed the jut of Cully's chin, saw a water tower about two hundred yards down the track.

"Yeah."

"Dropping the 'suh' again," Cully said with a small lift of his eyebrows. "I like that. Well, boy, in about three minutes, a freight train is going to come down these tracks. It'll stop and take on water for a couple minutes and then head toward St. Louis. I recommend you get on it."

Luther felt the same coldness he'd felt when he'd pressed the gun under Deacon Broscious's chin. He felt ready to die in Cully's truck if he could take the man with him.

"That's my car," Luther said. "I own it."

Cully chuckled. "Not in Missouri you don't. Maybe in Columbus or wherever bullshit place you claim to come from. But not in Missouri, boy. You know what Bernard started doing soon as I pulled out of my station?"

Luther had the suitcase on his lap and his thumbs found the latches.

"He got on the horn, started calling around, telling folks about this here colored fella we met. Man driving a car he can't afford. Man wearing a nice coat too big for him. Ol' Bernard, he killed him some darkies in his time and he'd like to kill more, and right about now, he's organizing a party. Not a party you'd cotton to much, Jessie. Now I ain't Bernard. I got no fight with you and lynching a man ain't something I've ever seen and not something I ever want to see. Stains the heart, I suspect."

"It's my car," Luther said. "Mine."

Cully went on like Luther hadn't spoken. "So you can avail yourself of my kindness or you can get plumb stupid and stick around. But what you—"

"I own—"

"—can't do, Jessie," Cully said, his voice suddenly loud in the truck. "What you can't do is stay in my truck one more second."

Luther met his eyes. They were bland and unblinking.

222

"So get out, boy."

Luther smiled. "You just a good man who steals cars, that it, Mr. Cully, suh?"

Cully smiled, too. "Ain't going to be a second train today, Jessie. You try the third box car from the back. Hear?"

He reached across Luther and opened the door.

"You got a family?" Luther asked. "Kids?"

Cully leaned his head back and chuckled. "Oh ho. Don't push it, boy." He waved his hand. "Just get out my truck."

Luther sat there for a bit and Cully turned his head and stared out the windshield and a crow cawed from somewhere above them. Luther reached for the door handle.

He climbed out and stepped onto the gravel and his eyes fell on a stand of dark trees on the other side of the tracks, thinned by winter, the pale morning light passing between the trunks. Cully reached across and pulled the door shut and Luther looked back at him as he spun the truck around, crunching the gravel. He waved out the window and drove back the way he'd come.

The train went beyond St. Louis, crossing over the Mississippi and into Illinois. It turned out to be the first stroke of good luck Luther'd had in some time—he'd been heading for East St. Louis in the first place. It was where his father's brother, Hollis, lived, and Luther had hoped to sell the car here and maybe lie low for a while.

Luther's father, a man he couldn't remember knowing in the flesh, had left the family for East St. Louis when Luther was two. He'd run off with a woman named Velma Standish, and they'd settled here and Timon Laurence had eventually set up a shop that sold and repaired watches. There had been three Laurence brothers—Cornelius, the eldest, and then Hollis, and lastly, Timon. Uncle Cornelius had often told Luther he wasn't missing out on much growing up without Tim around, said his youngest brother had been a man born feckless and weak for women and liquor since about the time

223

he learned what the two were. Threw away a fine woman like Luther's mother for nothing more than junk pussy. (Uncle Cornelius had pined throughout Luther's life for Luther's mother with a love so chaste and patient it couldn't help but be taken for granted and grow, through the years, entirely unremarkable. It was his lot in life, he'd told Luther not long after he'd gone fully blind, to have a heart no one wanted except in pieces and never as a whole, while his youngest brother, a man of no definable principles, culled love to him as easily as if it fell through the rain.)

Luther grew up with a single tin-plated photograph of his father. He'd touched it so many times with his thumbs that his father's features had softened and blurred. By the time Luther grew to manhood there was no way to tell if his own features bore a resemblance. Luther had never told anyone, not his mother or his sister or even Lila, how deep it cut to grow up knowing his father never gave him a thought. That the man had glanced at this life he'd brought into the world and said to himself: I'm happier without it. Luther had long imagined he'd meet him one day and stand before him a proud young man of great promise and watch regret fill his father's face. But it hadn't worked out that way.

His father had died sixteen months ago, along with near a hundred other colored folk while East St. Louis burned around them. Luther got the word from Hollis, the man's block letters looking pained and cramped on a sheet of yellow paper:

Yor Daddy shot ded by white men. Sorry to tell you.

Luther walked out of the freight yard and into downtown as the sky was beginning to darken. He had the envelope Uncle Hollis had sent his letter in with his address scrawled on the back, and he pulled it from his coat and held it in his hand as he walked. The deeper he traveled into the colored section the less he could believe what he saw. The streets were

224

empty, and much of the reason, Luther knew, had to do with the flu, but it was also because there wouldn't seem to be much point to walk streets where all the buildings were either blackened or crumbled or lost forever beneath rubble and ash. It reminded Luther of an old man's mouth, where most of the teeth were missing, a couple broken in half, and the few that remained leaning to the side and useless. Whole blocks were nothing but ash, great piles of it that the early-evening breeze blew from one side of the street to the other, just trading it back and forth. So much ash that not even a tornado could have erased it all. Over a year since the neighborhood had burned, and those piles stood tall. On those blown-out streets, Luther felt as if he were surely the last man alive, and he figured that if the Kaiser had managed to send his army across the ocean, with all their planes and bombs and rifles, they couldn't have done more damage.

It had been over jobs, Luther knew, the white working-class folks getting more and more convinced that the reason they were poor was because the colored working-class folks were stealing their jobs and the food off their tables. So they'd come down here, white men and white women and white children, too, and they'd started with the colored men, shooting them and lynching them and setting them afire and even driving several into the Cahokia River and then stoning them to death when they tried to swim back, a job they'd left mostly to the children. The white women pulled colored women off the streetcars and stoned them and stabbed them with kitchen knives, and when the National Guard came, they just stood around and watched it go on.

July 2, 1917.

"Your daddy," Uncle Hollis said, after Luther showed up at the door of his juke joint and Uncle Hollis took him into the back office and poured him a drink, "was trying to protect that little shop of his never made him a dime. They lit it on fire and called for him to come out and once all four walls were burning down around him, he and Velma came out.

Someone shot him in the knee and he lay there on the street for a while. They handed Velma over to some women, and they beat her with rolling pins. Just beat her about the head and face and hips and she die after crawling into an alley, like a dog gone under a porch. Someone come up to your father, and the way I was told, he try to get to his knees, but he can't even do that and he keep tipping over and pleading and finally a couple white men just stand there and shoot him until they run out of bullets."

"Where's he buried?" Luther said.

Uncle Hollis shook his head. "Wasn't nothing to bury, son. They got done shooting him, they picked him up, one on each end, and they tossed him back into his own store."

Luther got up from the table and went over to a small sink and got sick. It went on for some time, and he felt as if he were puking up soot and yellow fire and ash. His head eddied with flashes of white women swinging rolling pins onto black heads and white faces shrieking with joy and fury and then the Deacon singing in his wheelchair-rocker and his father trying to kneel in the street and Aunt Marta and the Honorable Lionel A. Garrity, Esquire, clapping their hands and beaming big smiles and someone chanting, "Praise Jesus! Praise Jesus!" and the whole world burning with fire as far as the eye could see until the blue skies were painted half black and the white sun vanished behind the smoke.

When he finished, he rinsed his mouth and Hollis gave him a small towel and he dried his lips on it and wiped the sweat from his brow.

"You hot, boy."

"No, I'm okay now."

Uncle Hollis gave him another slow shake of the head and poured him another drink. "No, I said you are *hot*. There's people looking for you, sending word up and down and across this here Midwest. You kill a bunch of coloreds in a Tulsa joint? You kill Deacon Broscious? You fucking out your mind?"

"How'd you hear?"

"Shit. It's burning up the wires, boy."

"Police?"

Uncle Hollis shook his head. "Police think some other fool did it. Clarence Somebody."

"Tell," Luther said. "Clarence Tell."

"That's the name." Uncle Hollis stared across the table at him, breathing heavy through his flat nose. " 'Parently you left one of them alive. One they call Smoke?"

Luther nodded.

"He in a hospital. Ain't nobody sure if he gone get well or not, but he told people. He fingered you. Gunners from here to New York looking for your head."

"What's the price on it?"

"This Smoke say he pay five hundred dollars for a photograph of your corpse."

"What if Smoke dies?"

Uncle Hollis shrugged. "Whoever take over the Deacon's business, he going to have to make sure you dead."

Luther said, "I ain't got no place to go."

"You got to go east, boy. 'Cause you can't stay here. And stay the fuck out of Harlem, that's for sure. Look, I know a boy up in Boston can take you in."

"Boston?"

Luther gave that some thought and quickly realized that thinking about it was a waste of time because there wasn't any choice in the matter. If Boston was all that was left of "safe" in this country, then Boston it would have to be.

"What about you?" he asked. "You staying here?"

"Me?" Uncle Hollis said. "I didn't shoot nobody."

"Yeah, but what's here anymore? Place been burned to nothing. I hear all the coloreds are leaving or trying to."

"To go where? Problem with our people, Luther, is they bite into hope and keep their teeth clenched to it the rest of their lives. You think any place is going to be better than here? Just different cages, boy. Some prettier than others but cages

227

just the same." He sighed. "Fuck it. I'm too old to move and this right here, this right here is as much home as I know."

They sat in silence and finished their drinks.

Uncle Hollis pushed back his chair and stretched his arms above his head. "Well, I got a room upstairs. We'll get you situated for a night while I make some calls. In the morning . . " He shrugged.

"Boston," Luther said.

Uncle Hollis nodded. "Boston. Best I can do."

In the boxcar, with Jessie's fine coat covered in hay to ward off the cold, Luther promised the Lord he would atone. No more card games. No more whiskey or cocaine. No more associating with gamblers or gangsters or anyone who even *thought* of doing heroin. No more giving himself over to the thrill of the night. He would keep his head down and call no attention to himself and wait this out. And if word ever came that he could return to Tulsa, then he would return a changed man. A humble penitent.

Luther had never considered himself a religious man, but that had less to do with his feelings about God than it did with his feelings about religion. His grandmother and his mother had both tried to drum the Baptist faith into him, and he had done what he could to please them, to make them believe he believed, but it had taken no more hold of him than any of the other homework he claimed to be doing. In Tulsa he'd grown even less inclined toward Jesus, if only because Aunt Marta and Uncle James and all their friends spent so much time praising Him that Luther figured if Jesus was, in fact, hearing all those voices He'd just as soon prefer silence every now and then, maybe catch Himself up on some sleep.

And Luther had passed many a white church in his day, heard them singing their hymns and chanting their "Amens" and seen them gather on a porch or two afterward with their lemonade and piety, but he knew if he ever showed up on their steps, starving or injured, the only response he'd get to a plea for human kindness would be the amen of a shotgun pointed in his face.

So Luther's arrangement with the Lord had long stood along the lines of You go Your way and I'll go mine. But in the boxcar, something took hold of him, a need to make sense of his own life, to give it a meaning lest he pass from the face of the earth having left behind no heavier footprint than that of a dung beetle.

He rode the rails across the Midwest and back through Ohio and then on into the Northeast. Although the companions he met in the boxcars weren't as hostile or dangerous as he'd often heard and the railway bulls never rousted or hassled them, he couldn't help but be reminded of the train ride he'd taken to Tulsa with Lila and he grew sad to the point where he felt swollen with it, as if there were no space for anything else in his body. He kept to himself in the corners of the boxcars, and he rarely trusted himself to speak unless one of the other men fairly demanded it of him.

He wasn't the only man on the train running from something. They ran from court dates and policemen and debts and wives. Some ran toward the same things. Some just needed a change. They all needed a job. But the papers, of late, had been promising a new recession. The boom times, they said, were over. War industries were shutting down and seven million men were about to hit the streets. Four million more were returning from overseas. Eleven million men about to enter a job market that was tapped out.

One of those eleven million, a huge white guy named BB, with a left hand mashed by a drill press into a pancake-flap of useless flesh, woke Luther his final morning on the train by throwing open the door so that the wind blew into Luther's face. Luther opened his eyes and saw BB standing by the open door as the countryside raced past him. It was dawn, and the moon still hung in the sky like a ghost of itself.

"Now that's a sweet picture, isn't it?" BB said, his large head tilting up toward the moon.

Luther nodded and caught his yawn in his fist. He shook the sleep from his legs and joined BB in the doorway. The sky was clear and blue and hard. The air was cold but smelled so clean Luther wished he could put it on a plate and eat it. The fields they passed were frozen and the trees were mostly bare, and it felt as if he and BB had caught the world at sleep, as if no one else, anywhere, bore witness to this dawn. Against that hard blue sky, as blue as anything Luther had ever seen, it all looked so beautiful that Luther wished he could show it to Lila. Wrap his arms around her belly and tuck his chin into her shoulder and ask her if she'd ever seen anything so blue. In your life, Lila? Have you ever?

He stepped back from the doorway.

I let it all go, he thought. I let it all go.

He found the fading moon in the sky and he kept his eyes on it. He kept his eyes on it until it had faded altogether and the wind had bitten clear through his coat.

BABE RUTH *and the* WORKERS' REVOLUTION

CHAPTER *twelve*

The Babe spent his morning giving out candy and baseballs at the Industrial School for Crippled and Deformed Children in the South End. One kid, covered ankles-to-neck in plaster, asked him to sign the cast, so Babe signed both arms and both legs and then took a loud breath and scrawled his name across the torso from the kid's right hip to his left shoulder as the other kids laughed and so did the nurses and even some of the Sisters of Charity. The kid in the cast told Ruth his name was Wilbur Connelly. He'd been working at the Shefferton Wool Mill in Dedham when some chemicals got spilled on the work floor and the vapors met the sparks from a shearing machine and set him on fire. The Babe assured Wilbur he'd be fine. Grow up someday and hit a home run in the World Series. And wouldn't his old bosses at Shefferton go purple with jealousy that day? Wilbur Connelly, getting sleepy, barely managed a smile but the other kids laughed and brought more things for Babe to sign—a picture torn from the sports pages of *The Standard*, a small pair of crutches, a yellowed nightshirt.

When he left with his agent, Johnny Igoe, Johnny suggested they pop over to the St. Vincent Orphan Asylum just a few blocks away. Couldn't hurt, Johnny said, add to the positive press and maybe give Babe an edge in his latest round of bargaining with Harry Frazee. Babe felt weary, though—weary of bargaining, weary of cameras snapping in his face, weary of orphans. He loved kids and orphans in particular, but boy oh boy those kiddos this morning, all hobbled and broken and burned, really took something out of him. The ones with the missing fingers wouldn't grow them back and the ones with sores on their faces wouldn't look in a mirror someday and find the scars vanished and the ones in wheelchairs wouldn't wake up one morning and walk. And yet, at some point, they'd be sent out into the world to make their way, and it had overwhelmed Babe this morning, just sucked the juice out of him.

So he ditched Johnny by telling him he needed to go buy a gift for Helen because the little woman was angry with him again. This was partly true—Helen *was* in a snit, but he wasn't shopping for a gift, not in any store leastways. He walked toward the Castle Square Hotel instead. The raw November breeze spit drops of sharp, random rain, but he was warm in his long ermine coat, and he kept his head tilted down to keep the drops from his eyes and enjoyed the quiet and anonymity that greeted him on deserted streets. At the hotel, he passed through the lobby and found the bar almost as empty as the streets, and he took the first seat inside the door and shrugged off his coat and laid it over the stool beside him. The bartender stood down at the far end of the bar, talking to the other two men in the place, so Ruth lit a cigar and looked around at the dark walnut beams and inhaled the smell of leather and wondered how in the hell this country was going to get along with any dignity now that Prohibition looked a dead certainty. The No-Funs and the Shouldn't-Dos were winning the war, and even if they called themselves Progressives, Ruth couldn't see much progress in denying a man a drink or shuttering a place of warm wood and leather. Hell, you worked an eighty-hour week for shit pay it seemed the least to ask that the world give you a mug of suds and a shot of rye. Not that Ruth had worked an eighty-hour week in his life, but the principle still applied.

The bartender, a wide man with a thick mustache curled up

so violently at the edges you could hang hats on it, came walking down the bar. "What can I get you?"

Still feeling a glow of kinship with the workingman, Ruth ordered two beers and a shot, make it a double, and the bartender placed the drafts before him and then poured a healthy glass of whiskey.

Ruth drank some beer. "I'm looking for a man named Dominick."

"That'd be me, sir."

Ruth said, "I understand you own a strong truck, do some hauling."

"That I do."

Down the other end, one of the men rapped the edge of a coin off the bar top.

"Just a second," the bartender said. "Them's some thirsty gents, sir."

He walked back down the bar and listened to the two men for a moment, nodding his large head, and then he went to the taps and after that to the bottles, and Ruth felt the two men watching him, so he watched them back.

The one on the left was strapping tall, dark-haired and dark-eyed, and so glamorous (it was the first word that popped into Babe's head) that Babe wondered if he'd seen him in the flickers or in the pages of the papers devoted to returning war heroes. Even from down the other end of a long bar, his simplest gestures—raising a glass to his lips, tapping an unlit cigarette on the wood—achieved a grace that Ruth associated with men of epic deeds.

The man beside him was much smaller and less distinct. He was milky and dour and the bangs of his mousy brown hair kept falling over his forehead; he brushed them back with an impatience Ruth judged feminine. He had small eyes and small hands and an air of perpetual grievance.

The glamorous one raised his glass. "A great fan of your athleticism, Mr. Ruth."

Ruth raised his glass and nodded his thanks. The mousy one didn't join in.

The strapping man clapped his friend on the back and said, "Drink up, Gene, drink up," and his voice was the baritone of a great stage actor hitting the back row.

Dominick placed fresh drinks in front of them and they returned to their conversation, and Dominick came back to Ruth and topped off his whiskey, then leaned back against the cash register. "So you need something hauled, do you, sir?"

Babe sipped his whiskey. "I do."

"And what would that be, Mr. Ruth?"

Babe took another sip. "A piano."

Dominick crossed his arms. "A piano. Well, that's not too—"

"From the bottom of a lake."

Dominick didn't say anything for a minute. He pursed his lips. He stared past Ruth and seemed to listen for the echo of an unfamiliar sound.

"You've got a piano in a lake," he said.

Ruth nodded. "Actually it's more like a pond."

"A pond."

"Yeah."

"Well, which is it, Mr. Ruth?"

"It's a pond," Babe said eventually.

Dominick nodded in a way that suggested past experience with such a problem and Babe felt a thump of hope in his chest. "How does a piano manage to get itself submerged in a pond?"

Ruth fingered his whiskey. "You see, there was this party. For kids. Orphans. My wife and I held it last winter. You see, we were having work done on our house, so we'd rented a cottage on a lake not too far away."

"On a pond you mean, sir."

"On a pond, yeah."

Dominick poured himself a small drink and threw it back.

"So, anyway," Babe said, "everyone was having a fine old

time, and we'd bought all the little tykes skates and they were stumbling around the pond—it was frozen."

"I gathered, sir, yes."

"And um, I, well, I sure do like playing that piano. And Helen sure does as well."

"Helen's your wife, sir?"

"She is."

"Noted," Dominick said. "Proceed, sir."

"So myself and some of the fellows decided to take the piano from the front room and push it down the slope onto the ice."

"A fine idea at the time, I'm sure, sir."

"And that's what we did."

Babe leaned back in his chair and relit his cigar. He puffed until he got it going and took a sip of his whiskey. Dominick placed another beer in front of him and Babe nodded his thanks. Neither of them said anything for a minute and they could hear the two men at the other end talking about alienated labor and capitalist oligarchies and it could have been in Egyptian for all that Babe understood it.

"Now here's the part I don't understand," Dominick said.

Babe resisted the urge to cringe on his barstool. "Go ahead."

"You've got it out on the ice. And does it crack through the ice, taking all those tads on skates with it?"

"No."

"No," Dominick said softly. "I believe I would have read about that. So, my question then, sir— How did it manage to go through the ice?"

"The ice melted," Ruth said quickly.

"When?"

Babe took a breath. "It was March, I believe."

"But the party . . . ?"

"Was in January."

"So the piano sat on the ice for two months before it sank."

"I kept meaning to get to it," Babe said.

237

"I'm sure you did, sir." Dominick smoothed his mustache. "The owner—"

"Oh, he was mad," the Babe said. "Hopping. I paid for it, though."

Dominick drummed his thick fingers on the bar. "So if it's paid for, sir . . ."

Babe wanted to bolt the bar. This was the part he hadn't quite worked out in his head yet. He'd installed a new piano in both the rental cottage and the restored house on Dutton Road, but every time Helen looked at that new piano she'd look at Ruth in a way that made him feel as attractive as a hog in its own filth. Since that new piano had taken residence in the house, neither of them had played it once.

"I thought," Ruth said, "if I could pull that piano from the lake, I—"

"The pond, sir."

"The pond. If I could pull that piano back up and, you know, restore it, it would make a swell anniversary gift for my wife."

Dominick nodded. "And what anniversary would that be?"

"Our fifth."

"Isn't wood usually the appropriate gift?"

Babe said nothing for a moment, thinking that one through.

"Well, it's made of wood."

"Point taken, sir."

Babe said, "And we've got some time. It's not for six months, my anniversary."

Dominick poured them each another drink and raised his in toast. "To your unbridled optimism, Mr. Ruth. It's what makes this country all that it is today."

They drank.

"Have you ever seen what water does to wood? To ivory keys and wire and all those little delicate parts in a piano?"

Babe nodded. "I know it won't be easy."

"Easy, sir? I'm not sure it'll be possible." He leaned into the bar. "I have a cousin. He does some dredging. He's worked the seas most of his life. What if we were to at least establish the location of the piano, how deep it actually is in the lake?"

"The pond."

"The pond, sir. If we knew that, well, then we'd be somewhere, Mr. Ruth."

Ruth thought about it and nodded. "How much will this cost me?"

"Couldn't say without talking to my cousin, but it could be a bit more than a new piano. Could be less." He shrugged and showed Ruth his palms. "Although, I make no guarantees as to the final fee."

"Of course."

Dominick took a piece of paper and wrote down a telephone number and handed it to Ruth. "That's the number of the bar. I work seven days from noon to ten. Call me Thursday, sir, and I'll have some details for you."

"Thanks." Ruth pocketed the number as Dominick went back down the bar.

He drank some more and smoked his cigar as a few more men came in and joined the two down at the other end of the bar and more rounds were purchased and toasts given to the tall, glamorous one, who was apparently giving some kind of speech soon at the Tremont Temple Baptist Church. Seemed like the tall man was big noise of a sort but Ruth still couldn't place him. Didn't matter—he felt warm here, cocooned. He loved a bar when the lights were dim and the wood was dark and the seats were covered in soft leather. The kids from this morning receded until they felt several weeks in his past, and if it was cold outside, you could only imagine it because you sure couldn't feel it.

Midautumn through winter was hard on him. He never knew what to do, couldn't gauge what was expected of him when there were no balls to hit, no fellow players to jaw with. Every morning he was confronted with decisions—how to please Helen, what to eat, where to go, how to fill his time, what to wear. Come spring, he'd have a suitcase packed with his traveling clothes and most times he'd just have to step in front of his locker to know what he was going to wear; his uniform would be hanging there, fresh from the team laundry. His day would be mapped out for him—either a game or a practice or Bumpy Jordan, the Sox travel secretary, would point him to the line of cabs that would take him to the train that would carry him to whichever city they were going next. He wouldn't have to think about meals because they'd all been arranged. Where he was going to sleep never crossed his mind—his name was already written in a hotel ledger, a bellman standing by to transport his bags. And at night, the boys were waiting in the bar and the spring leaked without complaint into summer and the summer unfurled in bright yellows and etched greens and the air smelled so good it could make you cry.

Ruth didn't know how it was with other men and their happiness, but he knew where his lay—in having the days mapped out for him, just as Brother Matthias used to do for him and all the other boys at St. Mary's. Otherwise, facing the humdrum unknown of a normal domestic life, Ruth felt jumpy and mildly afraid.

Not here, though, he thought, as the men in the bar began to spread out around him and a pair of large hands clapped his shoulders. He turned his head to see the big fellow who'd been down the end of the bar smiling at him.

"Buy you a drink, Mr. Ruth?"

The man came around to his side and Ruth again caught a whiff of the heroic from him, a sense of scale that couldn't be contained by anything as small as a room.

"Sure," Ruth said. "You're a Red Sox fan, then?"

The man shook his head as he held up three fingers to Dominick, and his smaller friend joined him at the bar, pulling out a stool and dropping into it with the heaviness of a man twice his size.

"Not particularly. I like sport but I'm not beholden to the idea of team allegiance."

Ruth said, "Then who do you root for when you're at a game?"

"Root?" the man said as their drinks arrived.

"Cheer for?" Ruth said.

The man flashed a brilliant smile. "Why, individual achievement, Mr. Ruth. The purity of a single play, a single display of adroit athleticism and coordination. The team is wonderful as a concept, I grant you. It suggests the brotherhood of man and unionism of a single goal. But if you look behind the veil, you see how it's been stolen by corporate interests to sell an ideal that is the antithesis of everything this country claims to represent."

Ruth had lost him halfway through his spiel, but he raised his whiskey and gave what he hoped passed for a knowing nod and then he took a drink.

The mousy guy leaned into the bar and looked past his friend at Ruth and mimicked Ruth's nod. He tipped back his own drink. "He doesn't have a fucking clue what you're on about, Jack."

Jack placed his drink on the bar. "I apologize for Gene, Mr. Ruth. He lost his manners in the Village."

"What village?" Ruth said.

Gene snickered.

Jack gave Ruth a gentle smile. "Greenwich Village, Mr. Ruth."

"It's in New York," Gene said.

"I know where it is, bub," Ruth said, and he knew that as big as Jack was, he'd be no match for Babe's strength if he decided to push him aside and tear that mousy hair off his friend's head.

"Oh," Gene said, "the Emperor Jones is angry."

"What'd you say?"

"Gentlemen," Jack said. "Let's remember we're all brothers. Our struggle is a shared one. Mr. Ruth, Babe," Jack said, "I'm something of a traveler. You name the countries of this world, there's probably a sticker on my suitcase for every one."

"You some kind of salesman?" Babe took a pickled egg from the jar and popped it in his mouth.

Jack's eyes brightened. "You could say that."

Gene said, "You honestly have no idea who you're talking to, do you?"

"Sure I do, Pops." Babe wiped his hands off each other. "He's Jack. You're Jill."

"Gene," the mousy one said. "Gene O'Neill, in point of fact. And this is Jack *Reed* you're talking to."

Babe kept his eyes on the mouse. "I'm sticking with 'Jill.' "

Jack laughed and clapped them both on their backs. "As I was saying, Babe, I've been all over. I've seen athletic contests in Greece, in Finland, in Italy and France. I once saw a polo match in Russia where no small number of the participants were trampled by their own horses. There's nothing purer or more inspirational, truly, than to see men involved in contest. But like most things that are pure, it gets sullied by big money and big business and put to the service of more nefarious purpose."

Babe smiled. He liked the way Reed talked, even if he couldn't understand what he meant.

Another man, a thin man with a profile that was hungry and sharp, joined them and said, "This is the slugger?"

"Indeed," Jack said. "Babe Ruth himself."

"Jim Larkin," the man said, shaking Babe's hand. "I apologize, but I don't follow your game."

"No apologies necessary, Jim." Babe gave him a firm shake.

"What my compatriot here is saying," Jim said, "is that the future opiate of the masses is not religion, Mr. Ruth, it's entertainment."

"That so?" Ruth wondered if Stuffy McInnis was home right now, if he'd answer the phone, maybe meet Babe in the city somewhere so they could get a steak and talk baseball and women.

"Do you know why baseball leagues are sprouting up all

over the country? At every mill and every shipyard? Why just about every company has a workers' team?"

Ruth said, "Sure. It's fun."

"Well, it is," Jack said. "I'll grant you. But to put a finer point on it, companies like fielding baseball teams because it promotes company unity."

"Nothing wrong with that," Babe said, and Gene snorted again.

Larkin leaned in close again and Babe wanted to lean back from his gin-breath. "And it promotes 'Americanization,' for lack of a better word, among the immigrant workers."

"But most of all," Jack said, "if you're working seventy-five hours a week and playing baseball another fifteen or twenty, guess what you're probably too tired to do?"

Babe shrugged.

"Strike, Mr. Ruth," Larkin said. "You're too tired to strike or even think about your rights as a worker."

Babe rubbed his chin so they'd believe he was thinking about the idea. Truth was, though, he was just hoping they'd go away.

"To the worker!" Jack shouted, raising his glass.

The other men—and Ruth noticed there were nine or ten of them now—raised their glasses and shouted back, "To the worker!"

Everyone took a strong slug of liquor, including Ruth.

"To the revolution!" Larkin shouted.

Dominick said, "Now now, gents," but he was lost in the clamor as the men rose on their seats.

"Revolution!"

"To the new proletariat!"

More shouts and cheers and Dominick gave up trying to impose order and started rushing around to refill drinks.

Boisterous toasts were made to comrades in Russia and Germany and Greece, to Debs, Haywood, Joe Hill, to the people, the great united working peoples of the world!

As they whipped themselves into a preening frenzy, Babe

243

reached for his coat, but Larkin blocked the chair as he hoisted his drink and shouted another toast. Ruth looked at their faces, sheened with sweat and purpose and maybe something beyond purpose, something he couldn't quite name. Larkin turned his hip to the right and Babe saw an opening, could see the edges of his coat and he started reaching for it again as Jack shouted, "Down with capitalism! Down with the oligarchies!" and Babe got his hand into the fur, but Larkin inadvertently bumped his arm and Babe sighed and started to try again.

Then the six guys walked in off the street. They were dressed in suits, and maybe on any other given day, they'd have seemed respectable types. But today, they reeked of alcohol and anger. Babe knew with one look at their eyes that the shit was going to hit the fan so fast the only hope would be to duck.

Connor Coughlin was in no fucking mood for subversives today. In truth he was in no fucking mood in general, but particularly not for subversives. They'd just had their heads handed to them in court. A nine-month investigation, over two hundred depositions, a six-week trial, all so they could deport an avowed Galleanist named Vittorio Scalone, who'd spoken to anyone within earshot of blowing up the State House during a meeting of the Senate.

The judge, however, didn't think that was enough to deport a man. He'd stared down from his bench at District Attorney Silas Pendergast, Assistant District Attorney Connor Coughlin, Assistant District Attorney Peter Wald, and the six ADAs and four police detectives in the rows behind them and said, "While the issue of whether the state has the right to pursue deportation measures at a county level is, in some minds, debatable, that is not the issue before this court." He'd removed his glasses and stared coldly at Connor's boss. "As much as District Attorney Pendergast may have tried to make it so. No, the issue is whether the defendant committed any treasonous act whatsoever. And I see no evidence that he did any more than make idle threats while under the influence of alcohol." He'd turned and faced Scalone. "Which, under the Espionage Act, is still a serious crime, young man. For which I sentence you to two years at the Charlestown Penitentiary, six months time served."

A year and a half. For treason. On the courthouse steps, Silas Pendergast had given all his young ADAs a look of such withering disappointment that Connor knew they'd all be sent back to petty crimes and would not see the likes of this type of case for eons. They'd wandered the city, deflated, popping into bar after bar until they'd stumbled into the Castle Square Hotel and walked in on this. This . . . *shit*.

All the talking stopped when they were noticed. They were met with nervous, patronizing smiles, and Connor and Pete Wald went up to the bar and ordered a bottle and five glasses. The bartender spread the bottle and the glasses on the bar, and still no one spoke. Connor loved it—the fat silence that ballooned in the air before a fight. It was a unique silence, a silence with a ticking heartbeat. Their brother ADAs joined them at the bar rail and filled their glasses. A chair scraped. Pete raised his glass and looked around at the faces in the bar and said, "To the Attorney General of these United States."

"Hear! Hear!" Connor shouted, and they threw back their drinks and refilled them.

"To deportation of undesirables!" Connor said, and the other men joined in chorus.

"To the death of Vlad Lenin!" Harry Block shouted.

They joined him as the other crowd of men started booing and hooting.

A tall guy with dark hair and picture-show looks was suddenly standing beside Connor.

"Hi," he said.

"Fuck off," Connor said and threw back his drink as the other ADAs laughed.

"Let's all be reasonable here," the man said. "Let's talk this out. Hey? You might be surprised how many times our views intersect."

Connor kept his eyes on the bar top. "Uh-huh."

"We all want the same thing," the pretty boy said, and patted Connor's shoulder.

Connor waited for the man to remove his hand.

He poured himself another drink and turned to face the man. He thought of the judge. Of the treasonous Vittorio Scalone walking out of court with a smirk in his eyes. He thought of trying to explain his frustration and feelings of injustice to Nora, and how that could go either way. She might be sympathetic. She might be distant, indistinct. You could never predict. She seemed to love him sometimes, but other times she looked at him as if he were Joe, worthy only of a pat on the head and a dry kiss good night on the cheek. He could see her eyes now—unreadable. Unreachable. Never quite true. Never quite seeing him, really seeing him. Or anyone for that matter. Something always held in reserve. Except, of course, for when she turned those eyes on . . .

Danny.

The realization came suddenly, but at the same time it had lived in him for so long, he couldn't believe he'd just faced it. His stomach shriveled and the backs of his eyeballs felt as if a razor scraped across them.

He turned with a smile to face the tall pretty boy and emptied his shot glass into his fine black hair and then butted him in the face.

As soon as the mick with the pale hair and matching freckles poured his drink over Jack's head and drove his forehead into his face, Babe tried grabbing his coat off the chair and making a run for it. He knew as well as anyone, though, that the first rule of a bar fight was to hit the biggest guy first, and that happened to be him. So it wasn't any surprise when a stool hit the back of his head and two large arms wrapped over his shoulders and two legs folded over his

246

hips. Babe dropped his coat and spun with the guy on his back and took another stool to his midsection from a guy who looked at him funny and said, "Shit. You look like Babe Ruth."

That caused the guy on his back to loosen his grip, and Ruth surged for the bar and then pulled up short just before he hit it and the guy flew off his back and over the bar and hit the bottles behind the cash register with a great crash.

Babe punched the guy nearest him, realizing only too late but with complete satisfaction that it was the mousy prick, Gene, and Gene went spinning backward on his heels, flailing his hands as he fell over a chair and dropped to his ass on the floor. There might have been ten Bolsheviks in the room, and several of them were of good size, but the other guys had a rage on their side the Bolshies couldn't touch. Babe saw the freckled one drop Larkin with a single punch to the center of his face and then step right over him and catch another with a jab to the neck. He suddenly remembered the only piece of advice his father had ever given him: Never go toe to toe with a mick in a bar fight.

Another Bolshie took a running leap at Babe from the top of the bar, and Babe ducked him the way he'd duck a tag, and the Bolshie landed on a tabletop that quivered for just a second before collapsing under the weight.

"You are!" someone called, and he turned to see the jake who'd hit him with the stool, a smear of blood on the guy's mouth. "You're Babe Fucking Ruth."

"I get that all the time," Babe said. He punched the guy in the head, grabbed his coat off the floor, and ran out of the bar.

WORKING CLASS

CHAPTER *thirteen*

In the late autumn of 1918, Danny Coughlin stopped walking a beat, grew a thick beard, and was reborn as Daniel Sante, a veteran of the 1916 Thomson Lead Miners Strike in western Pennsylvania. The real Daniel Sante had been close to Danny's height and had the same dark hair. He'd also left behind no family members when he'd been conscripted to fight in the Great War. Shortly after his arrival in Belgium, however, he'd come down with the grippe and died in a field hospital without ever firing a shot.

Of the miners in that '16 strike, five had been jailed for life when they'd been tied, however circumstantially, to a bomb that had exploded in the home of Thomson Iron & Lead's president, E. James McLeish. McLeish had been taking his morning bath when his houseman carried in the mail. The houseman tripped crossing the threshold and juggled a cardboard package wrapped in plain brown paper. His left arm was later discovered in the dining room; the rest of him remained in the foyer. An additional fifty strikers were jailed on shorter sentences or beaten so badly by police and Pinkertons that they wouldn't be traveling anywhere for several years, and the rest had met the fate of the average striker in the Steel Belt—they lost their jobs and drifted over the border into Ohio in hopes of hiring on for companies that hadn't seen the blackball list of Thomson Iron & Lead.

It was a good story to establish Danny's credentials in the

workers-of-the-world revolution because no well-known labor organizations—not even the fastmoving Wobblies—had been involved. It had been organized by the miners themselves with such speed it probably surprised them. By the time the Wobblies did arrive, the bomb had already exploded and the beatings had commenced. Nothing left to do but visit the men in the hospital while the company hired fresh recruits from the morning cattle calls.

So Danny's cover as Daniel Sante was expected to hold up fine under the scrutiny of the various radical movements he encountered. And it did. Not a single person, as far as he could tell, had questioned it. The problem was that even if they believed it, his story still didn't make him stand out.

He went to meetings and wasn't noticed. He went to the bars afterward and was left alone. When he tried to strike up a conversation, he was met with polite agreement of anything he said and just as politely turned away from. He'd rented rooms in a building in Roxbury, and there, during the day, he brushed up on his radical periodicals—*The Revolutionary Age, Cronaca Sovversiva, Proletariat,* and *The Worker.* He reread Marx & Engels, Reed & Larkin, and speeches by Big Bill Haywood, Emma Goldman, Trotsky, Lenin, and Galleani himself until he could recite most of it verbatim. Mondays and Wednesdays brought another meeting of the Roxbury Letts followed by a boozy gathering at the Sowbelly Saloon. He spent his nights with them and his mornings with a curl-up-and-cry-for-your-momma hangover, nothing about the Letts being frivolous, including their drinking. Bunch of Sergeis and Borises and Josefs, with the occasional Peter or Pyotr thrown in, the Letts raged through the night with vodka and slogans and wooden buckets of warm beer. Slamming the steins on scarred tables and quoting Marx, quoting Engels, quoting Lenin and Emma Goldman and screeching about the rights of the workingman, all the while treating the barmaid like shit.

They brayed about Debs, whinnied about Big Bill Haywood, thumped their shot glasses to the tables and pledged retribution for the tarred-and-feathered Wobblies in Tulsa, even though the tarring and feathering had taken place two years ago and it wasn't like any of them were going to go wipe it off. They tugged their watch caps and huffed their cigarettes and railed against Wilson, Palmer, Rockefeller, Morgan, and Oliver Wendell Holmes. They crowed about Jack Reed and Jim Larkin and the fall of the house of Nicholas II.

Talk, talk, talk, talk, talk, talk, talk, talk.

Danny wondered if his hangovers came from the booze or the bullshit. Christ, the Bolshies blabbed until your eyes crossed. Until you dreamed in the harsh chop of Russian consonants and the nasal drag of Latvian vowels. Two nights a week with them and he'd only seen Louis Fraina once, when the man gave a speech and then vanished under heavy security.

He'd crisscrossed the state, looking for Nathan Bishop. At job fairs, in seditionist bars, at Marxist fund-raisers. He'd gone to union meetings, radical gatherings, and get-togethers of utopists so pie-eyed their ideas were an insult to adulthood. He noted the names of the speakers and faded into the background but always introduced himself as "Daniel Sante," so that the person whose hand he shook would respond in kind—"Andy Thurston" as opposed to just "Andy," "Comrade Gahn" as opposed to "Phil." When the opportunity presented itself, he stole a page or two of the sign-in sheets. If cars were parked outside the meeting sites, he copied down the license numbers.

City meetings were held in bowling alleys, pool halls, afternoon boxing clubs, saloons, and cafés. On the South Shore, the groups met in tents, dance halls, or fairgrounds abandoned until summer. On the North Shore and in the Merrimack Valley, the preference was for rail yards and tanneries, down by water that boiled with runoff and left a copper froth clinging to the shoreline. In the Berkshires, orchards.

If you went to one meeting, you heard about others. The fishermen in Gloucester spoke of solidarity for their brothers in New Bedford, the Communists in Roxbury for their comrades in Lynn. He never heard anyone discuss bombs or specific plans to overthrow the government. They spoke in vague generalizations. Loud, boastful, as ineffectual as a willful child's. The same held for talk of corporate sabotage. They *spoke of* May Day, but only in terms of other cities and other cells. The comrades in New York would shake the city to its foundation. The comrades in Pittsburgh would light the first match to ignite the revolution.

Anarchists' meetings were usually held on the North Shore and were sparsely attended. Those who used the megaphone spoke dryly, often reading aloud in broken English from the latest tract by Galleani or Tommasino DiPeppe or the jailed Leone Scribano, whose musings were smuggled out of a prison south of Milan. No one shouted or spoke with much emotion or zeal, which made them unsettling. Danny quickly got the sense that they knew he was not of them—too tall, too well fed, too many teeth.

After one meeting in the rear of a cemetery in Gloucester, three men broke away from the crowd to follow him. They walked slow enough not to close the distance and fast enough to not let it widen. They didn't seem to care that he noticed. At one point, one of them called out in Italian. He wanted to know if Danny had been circumcised.

Danny skirted the edge of the cemetery and crossed a stretch of bone white dunes at the back of a limestone mill. The men, about thirty yards back now, began to whistle sharply through their teeth. "Aww, honey," it sounded like one of them was calling. "Aww, honey."

The limestone dunes recalled dreams Danny'd had, ones he'd forgotten about until this moment. Dreams in which he hopelessly crossed vast moonlit deserts with no idea how he'd gotten there, no idea how he'd ever find his way home. And weighing down on him all the heavier with every step was the growing fear that home no longer existed. That his family and everyone he knew was long dead. And only he survived to wander forsaken lands. He climbed the shortest of the dunes, scrabbling and clawing up it in a winter quiet.

"Aww, honey."

He reached the top of the dune. On the other side was an ink sky. Below it, a few fences with open gates.

He reached a street of disgorged cobblestone where he came upon a pest house. The sign above the door identified it as the Cape Ann Sanatorium, and he opened the door and walked in. He hurried past a nurse at the admitting desk who called after him. She called after him a second time.

He reached a stairwell and looked back down the hall and saw the three men frozen outside, one of them pointing up at the sign. No doubt they'd lost family members to something that waited on the upper floors—TB, smallpox, polio, cholera. In their awkward gesticulating Danny saw that none would dare enter. He found a rear door and let himself out.

The night was moonless, the air so raw it found his gums. He ran full-out back across the white gravel dunes and the cemetery. He found his car where he'd left it by the seawall. He sat in it and fingered the button in his pocket. His thumb ran over the smooth surface and he flashed on Nora swinging the bear at him in the oceanfront room, the pillows scattered all over the floor, her eyes lit with a pale fire. He closed his eyes and he could smell her. He drove back to the city with a windshield grimed by salt and his own fear drying into his scalp.

One morning, he waited for Eddie McKenna and drank cups of bitter black coffee in a café off Harrison Avenue with a checkered tile floor and a dusty ceiling fan that clicked with each revolution. A knife sharpener bumped his cart along the cobblestones outside the window, and his display blades swung from their strings and caught the sun. Darts of light slashed Danny's pupils and the walls of the café. He turned in his booth and flicked open his watch and got it to stop jumping in his hand long enough to realize McKenna was late, though that wasn't surprising, and then he took another glance around the café to see if any faces were paying too much or too little attention to him. When he was satisfied it was just the normal collection of small businessmen and colored porters and Statler Building secretaries, he went back to his coffee, near certain that even with a hangover, he could spot a tail.

McKenna filled the doorway with his oversize body and obstinate optimism, that almost beatific sense of purpose that Danny had seen in him all his life, since Eddie'd been a hundred pounds lighter and would drop by to see his father when the Coughlins lived in the North End, always with sticks of licorice for Danny and Connor. Even then, when he'd been just a flatfoot working the Charlestown waterfront with saloons that were judged the city's bloodiest and a rat population so prodigious the typhus and polio rates were triple those of any other district, the glow around the man had been just as prominent. Part of department lore was that Eddie McKenna had been told early in his career that he'd never work undercover because of his sheer presence. The chief at the time had told him, "You're the only guy I know who enters a room five minutes before he gets there."

He hung his coat and slid into the booth across from Danny. He caught the waitress's eye and mouthed "coffee" to her.

"Holy Mary, Mother of God," he said to Danny. "You smell like the Armenian who ate the drunken goat."

Danny shrugged and drank some more coffee.

"And then puked it back up on yourself," McKenna said.

"Praise from Caesar, sir."

McKenna lit the stub of a cigar, and the reek of it went straight to Danny's stomach. The waitress brought a cup of coffee to the table and refilled Danny's. McKenna watched her ass as she walked away.

He produced a flask and handed it to Danny. "Help yourself."

Danny poured a few drops into his coffee and handed it back.

McKenna tossed a notepad on the table and placed a fat

256

pencil as stubby as his cigar beside the notepad. "I just came from meeting a few of the other boys. Tell me you're making better progress than they are."

The "other boys" on the squad had been picked, to some degree, for their intelligence, but mostly for their ability to pass as ethnics. There were no Jews or Italians in the BPD, but Harold Christian and Larry Benzie were swarthy enough to be taken for Greeks or Italians. Paul Wascon, small and dark-eyed, had grown up on New York's Lower East Side. He spoke passable Yiddish and had infiltrated a cell of Jack Reed's and Jim Larkin's Socialist Left Wing that worked out of a basement in the West End.

None of them had wanted the detail. It meant long hours for no extra pay, no overtime, and no reward, because the official department policy was that terrorist cells were a New York problem, a Chicago problem, a San Francisco problem. So even if the squad had success, they'd never get credit, and they sure wouldn't get overtime.

But McKenna had pulled them out of their units with his usual combination of bribery, threat, and extortion. Danny had come in through the back door because of Tessa; God knows what Christian and Benzie had been promised, and Wascon's hand had been caught in the cookie jar back in August, so McKenna owned him for life.

Danny handed McKenna his notes. "License plate numbers from the Fishermen's Brotherhood meeting in Woods Hole. Sign-in sheet from the West Roxbury Roofers Union, another from the North Shore Socialist Club. Minutes of all the meetings I attended this week, including two of the Roxbury Letts."

McKenna took the notes and placed them in his satchel. "Good, good. What else?"

"Nothing."

"What do you mean?"

"I mean I got nothing," Danny said.

McKenna dropped his pencil and sighed. "Jesus' sakes."

"What?" Danny said, feeling a hair better with the whiskey

in his coffee. "Foreign radicals—surprise—mistrust Americans. And they're paranoid enough to at least *consider* that I could be a plant, no matter how solid the Sante cover is. And even if they are sold on the cover? Danny Sante ain't looked on as management material yet. Least not by the Letts. They're still feeling me out."

"You seen Louis Fraina?"

Danny nodded. "Seen him give a speech. But I haven't met him. He stays away from the rank and file, surrounds himself with higher-ups and goons."

"You seen your old girlfriend?"

Danny grimaced. "If I'd seen her, she'd be in jail now."

McKenna took a sip from his flask. "You been looking?"

"I've been all over this damn state. I even crossed into Connecticut a few times."

"Locally?"

"The Justice guys are crawling all over the North End looking for Tessa and Federico. So the whole neighborhood is tense. Closed up. No one is going to talk to me. No one's going to talk to any Americano."

McKenna sighed and rubbed his face with the heels of his hands. "Well, I knew it wasn't going to be easy."

"Nope."

"Just keep plugging."

Jesus, Danny thought. This—*this*—was detective work? Fishing without a net?

"I'll get you something."

"Besides a hangover?"

Danny gave him a weak smile.

McKenna rubbed his face again and yawned. "Fucking terrorists, I swear to Christ." He yawned again. "Oh, you never came across Nathan Bishop, did you? The doctor."

"No."

McKenna winked. "That's 'cause he just did thirty days in the Chelsea drunk tank. They kicked him loose two days ago. I asked one of the bulls there if he's known to them and they

258

said he likes the Capitol Tavern. Apparently, they send his mail there."

"The Capitol Tavern," Danny said. "That cellar-dive in the West End?"

"The same." McKenna nodded. "Maybe you can earn a hangover there, serve your country at the same time."

Danny spent three nights at the Capitol Tavern before Nathan Bishop spoke to him. He'd seen Bishop right off, as he came through the door the very first night and took a seat at the bar. Bishop sat alone at a table lit only by a small candle in the wall above it. He read a small book the first night and from a stack of newspapers the next two. He drank whiskey, the bottle on the table beside the glass, but he nursed his drinks the first two nights, never putting a real dent in the bottle, and walking out as steadily as he'd walked in. Danny began to wonder if Finch and Hoover's profile had been correct.

The third night, though, he pushed his newspapers aside early and took longer pulls from the glass and chain-smoked. At first he stared at nothing but his own cigarette smoke, and his eyes seemed loose and faraway. Gradually his eyes found the rest of the bar and a smile grew on his face, as if someone had pasted it there too hastily.

When Danny first heard him sing, he couldn't connect the voice to the man. Bishop was small, wispy, a delicate man with delicate features and delicate bones. His voice, however, was a booming, barreling, train-roar of a thing.

"Here he goes." The bartender sighed yet didn't seem dissatisfied.

It was a Joe Hill song, "The Preacher and the Slave," that Nathan Bishop chose for his first rendition of the night, his deep baritone giving the protest song a distinctly Celtic flavor that went with the tall hearth and dim lighting in the Capitol Tavern, the low baying of the tugboat horns in the harbor.

"Long-haired preachers come out every night," he sang.

"Try to tell you what's wrong and what's right. But when asked how 'bout something to eat, they will answer in voices so sweet: 'You will eat, bye and bye, in that glorious land above the sky way up high. Work and pray, live on hay, you'll get pie in the sky when you die.' That's a lie, that's a lie . . ."

He smiled sweetly, eyes at half-mast, as the few patrons in the bar clapped lightly. It was Danny who kept it going. He stood from his stool and raised his glass and sang out, "Holy Rollers and Jumpers come out, and they holler, they jump and they shout. 'Give your money to Jesus,' they say. 'He will cure all diseases today.' "

Danny put his arm around the guy beside him, a chimney sweep with a bad hip, and the chimney sweep raised his own glass. Nathan Bishop worked his way out from behind his table, making sure to scoop up both his whiskey bottle and his whiskey glass, and joined them at the bar as two merchant marines jumped in, loud as hell and way off key, but who cared as they all swung their elbows and their drinks from side to side:

> "If you fight hard for children and wife
> Try to get something good in this life,
> You're a sinner and bad man, they tell,
> When you die you will sure go to hell."

The last line came out in shouts and torn laughs, and then the bartender rang the bell behind the bar and promised a free round.

"We're singing for our supper, boys!" one of the merchant marines cried out.

"You're getting the free drink to stop singing!" the bartender shouted over the laughter. "Them's the terms and none other."

They were all drunk enough to cheer to that and then they bellied up for their free drinks and shook hands all around— Daniel Sante meet Abe Rowley, Abe Rowley meet Terrance

Bonn and Gus Sweet, Terrance Bonn and Gus Sweet meet Nathan Bishop, Nathan Bishop meet Daniel Sante.

"Hell of a voice there, Nathan."

"Thank you. Good on yours as well, Daniel."

"Habit of yours, is it, to just start singing out in a bar?"

"Across the pond, where I'm from, it's quite common. It was getting fairly gloomy in here until I took up the cause, wouldn't you say?"

"I wouldn't argue."

"Well, then, cheers."

"Cheers."

They met their glasses, then threw back their shots.

Seven drinks and four songs later they ate the stew that the bartender kept cooking in the fireplace all day. It was horrid; the meat was brown and unidentifiable and the potatoes were gray and chewy. If Danny had to guess, he'd bet the grit it left on his teeth came from sawdust. But it filled them. After, they sat and drank and Danny told his Daniel Sante lies about western Pennsylvania and Thomson Lead.

"That's just it, isn't it?" Nathan said, rolling his cigarette from a pouch on his lap. "You ask for anything in this world and the answer is always 'No.' Then you're forced to take from those who themselves took before you—and in much bigger slices, I might add—and they dare call you a thief. It's fairly absurd." He offered Danny the cigarette he'd just rolled.

Danny held up a hand. "Thanks, no. I buy 'em in the packs." He pulled his Murads from his shirt pocket and placed them on the table.

Nathan lit his. "How'd you get that scar?"

"This?" Danny pointed to his neck. "Methane explosion."

"In the mines?"

Danny nodded.

"My father was a miner," Nathan said. "Not here."

"Across the pond?"

"Just so." He smiled. "Just outside of Manchester in the North. It's where I grew up."

"Tough country I've always heard."

"Yes, it is. Sinfully dreary, as well. A palette of grays and the occasional brown. My father died there. In a mine. Can you imagine?"

"Dying in a mine?" Danny said. "Yes."

"He was strong, my father. That's the most unfortunate aspect of the whole sordid mess. You see?"

Danny shook his head.

"Well, take me for instance. I'm no physical specimen. Uncoordinated, terrible at sports, nearsighted, bowlegged, and asthmatic."

Danny laughed. "You leave anything out?"

Nathan laughed and held up a hand. "Several things. But that's it, you see? I'm physically weak. If a tunnel collapsed and I had several hundred pounds of dirt on me, maybe a half-ton wood beam in the mix, a terribly limited supply of oxygen, well, I'd just succumb. I'd die like a good Englishman, quietly and without complaint."

"Your father, though," Danny said.

"Crawled," Nathan said. "They found his shoes where the walls had collapsed on him. It was three hundred feet from where they found his corpse. He crawled. With a broken back, through hundreds, if not thousands, of pounds of dirt and rock while the mining company waited two days to begin excavation. They were worried that rescue attempts could put the walls of the main tunnel at risk. Had my father known that, I wonder if it would have stopped his crawling sooner or pushed him on another fifty feet."

They sat in silence for a time, the fire spitting and hissing its way along some logs that still held a bit of dampness. Nathan Bishop poured himself another drink and then tilted the bottle over Danny's glass, poured just as generously.

"It's wrong," he said.

"What's that?"

"What men of means demand of men without them. And then they expect the poor to be grateful for the scraps. They have

262

the cheek to act offended—morally offended—if the poor don't play along. They should all be burned at the stake."

Danny could feel the liquor in him turning sludgy. "Who?"

"The rich." He gave Danny a lazy smile. "Burn them all."

Danny found himself at Fay Hall again for another meeting of the BSC. On tonight's agenda, the department's continued refusal to treat influenza-related sickness among the men as work related. Steve Coyle, a little drunker than one would have hoped, spoke of his ongoing fight to get some kind of disability payments from the department he'd served twelve years.

After the flu discussion was exhausted, they moved on to a preliminary proposal for the department to assume part of the expense of replacing damaged or severely worn uniforms.

"It's the most innocuous salvo we can fire," Mark Denton said. "If they reject it, then we can point to it later to show their refusal to grant us any concessions at all."

"Point for who?" Adrian Melkins asked.

"The press," Mark Denton said. "Sooner or later, this fight will be fought in the papers. I want them on our side."

After the meeting, as the men milled by the coffee urns or passed their flasks, Danny found himself thinking of his father and then of Nathan Bishop's.

"Nice beard," Mark Denton said. "You grow cats in that thing?"

"Undercover work," Danny said. He pictured Bishop's father crawling through a collapsed mine. Pictured his son still trying to drink it away. "What do you need?"

"Huh?"

"From me," Danny said.

Mark took a step back, appraised him. "I've been trying to figure out since the first time you showed up here whether you're a plant or not."

"Who'd plant me?"

Denton laughed. "That's rich. Eddie McKenna's godson,

263

Tommy Coughlin's son. Who'd plant you? Hilarious."

"If I was a plant, why'd you ask for my help?"

"To see how fast you jumped at the offer. I'll admit, you not jumping right away gave me pause. Now here you are, though, asking *me* how you can help out."

"That's right."

"I guess it's my turn to say I'll think about it," Denton said.

Eddie McKenna sometimes conducted business meetings on his roof. He lived in a Queen Anne atop Telegraph Hill in South Boston. His view—of Thomas Park, Dorchester Heights, the downtown skyline, the Fort Point Channel, and Boston Harbor—was, much like his persona, expansive. The roof was tarred and flat as sheet metal; Eddie kept a small table and two chairs out there, along with a metal shed where he stored his tools and those his wife, Mary Pat, used in the tiny garden behind their house. He was fond of saying that he had the view and he had the roof and he had the love of a good woman so he couldn't begrudge the good Lord for forsaking him a yard.

It was, like most of the things Eddie McKenna said, as full of the truth as it was full of shit. Yes, Thomas Coughlin had once told Danny, Eddie's cellar was barely able to hold its fill of coal, and yes, his yard could support a tomato plant, a basil plant, and possibly a small rosebush but certainly none of the tools needed to tend them. This was of little import, however, because tools weren't all Eddie McKenna kept in the shed.

"What else?" Danny had asked.

Thomas wagged a finger. "I'm not that drunk, boy."

Tonight, he stood with his godfather by the shed with a glass of Irish and one of the fine cigars Eddie received monthly from a friend on the Tampa PD. The air smelled damp and smoky the way it did in heavy fog, but the skies were clear. Danny had given Eddie his report on meeting Nathan Bishop, on Bishop's comment about what should be done to the rich, and Eddie had barely acknowledged he'd heard.

But when Danny handed over yet another list—this one half names/half license plates of a meeting of the Coalition of the Friends of the Southern Italian Peoples, Eddie perked right up. He took the list from Danny and scanned it quickly. He opened the door to his garden shed and removed the cracked leather satchel he carried everywhere and added the piece of paper to it. He put the satchel back in the shed and closed the door.

"No padlock?" Danny said.

Eddie cocked his head. "For tools now?"

"And satchels."

Eddie smiled. "Who in their right mind would ever so much as approach this abode with less than honest intentions?"

Danny gave that a smile, but a perfunctory one. He smoked his cigar and looked out at the city and breathed in the smell of the harbor. "What are we doing here, Eddie?"

"It's a nice night."

"No. I mean with this investigation."

"We're hunting radicals. We're protecting and serving this great land."

"By compiling lists?"

"You seem a bit off your feed, Dan."

"What's that mean?"

"Not yourself. Have you been getting enough sleep?"

"No one's talking about May Day. Not how you expected them to anyway."

"Well, it's not like they're going to go a galavanting about, shouting their nefarious aims from the rooftops, are they? You've barely been on them a month."

"They're talkers, the lot of them. But that's all they are."

"The anarchists?"

"No," Danny said. "*They're* fucking terrorists. But the rest? You've got me checking out plumbers unions, carpenters, every toothless socialist knitting group you can find. For what? Names? I don't understand."

"Are we to wait until they *do* blow us up before we decide to take them seriously?"

"Who? The plumbers?"

"Be serious."

"The Bolshies?" Danny said. "The socialists? I'm not sure they have the capacity to blow up anything outside of their own chests."

"They're terrorists."

"They're dissidents."

"Maybe you need some time off."

"Maybe I just need a clearer sense of exactly what the hell we're doing here."

Eddie put an arm around his shoulder and led him to the roof edge. They looked out at the city—its parks and gray streets, brick buildings, black rooftops, the lights of downtown reflecting off the dark waters that coursed through it.

"We're protecting this, Dan. This right here. That's what we're doing." He took a pull of his cigar. "Home and hearth. And nothing less than that indeed."

With Nathan Bishop, another night at the Capitol Tavern, Nathan taciturn until the third drink kicked in and then:

"Has anyone ever hit you?"

"What?"

He held up his fists. "You know."

"Sure. I used to box," he said. Then: "In Pennsylvania."

"But have you ever been physically pushed aside?"

"Pushed aside?" Danny shook his head. "Not that I can remember. Why?"

"I wonder if you know how exceptional that is. To walk through this world without fear of other men."

Danny had never thought of it like that before. It suddenly embarrassed him that he'd moved through his entire life expecting it to work for him. And it usually had.

"It must be nice," Nathan said. "That's all."

"What do you do?" Danny asked.

"What do you do?"

"I'm looking for work. But you? Your hands aren't those of a laborer. Your clothes, either."

Nathan touched the lapel of his coat. "These aren't expensive clothes."

"They're not rags either. They match your shoes."

Nathan Bishop gave that a crooked smile. "Interesting observation. You a cop?"

"Yes," Danny said and lit a cigarette.

"I'm a doctor."

"A copper and a doctor. You can fix whoever I shoot."

"I'm serious."

"So am I."

"No really."

"Okay, I'm not a copper. You a doctor, though?"

"I was." Bishop stubbed his cigarette out. He took a slow pull of his drink.

"Can you quit being a doctor?"

"You can quit anything." Bishop took another drink and let out a long sigh. "I was a surgeon once. Most of the people I saved didn't deserve to be saved."

"They were rich?"

Danny saw an exasperation cross Bishop's face that he was becoming familiar with. It meant Bishop was heading for the place where his anger would dominate him, where he couldn't be calmed down until he'd exhausted himself.

"They were oblivious," he said, his tongue lathering the word with contempt. "If you said to them, 'People die every day. In the North End, in the West End, in South Boston, in Chelsea. And the thing that's killing them is *one thing*. Poverty. That's all. Simple as that.' " He rolled another cigarette and leaned over the table as he did, slurped his drink from the glass with his hands still in his lap. "You know what people say when you tell them that? They say, 'What can *I* do?' As if

267

that's an answer. What can you do? You can very well fucking help. *That's* what you can do, you bourgeois piece of shit. What can you *do*? What *can't* you do? Roll up your fucking sleeves, get off your fat fucking arse, and move your wife's fatter fucking arse off the same cushion, and go down to where your mates—your brother and sister fellow fucking human beings—are quite authentically starving to death. And *do* whatever you need to do to help them. *That's* what the bloody fuck you can bloody well fucking do."

Nathan Bishop slammed back the rest of his drink. He dropped the glass to the scarred wood table and looked around the bar, his eyes red and sharp.

In the heavy air that often followed one of Nathan's tirades, Danny said nothing. He could feel the men at the nearest table shift in awkwardness. One of them suddenly began talking about Ruth, about the newest trade rumors. Nathan breathed heavily through his nostrils while he reached for the bottle and placed his cigarette between his lips. He got a shaky hand on the bottle. He poured himself another drink. He leaned back in his chair and flicked his thumbnail over a match and lit his cigarette.

"That's what you can do," he whispered.

In the Sowbelly Saloon, Danny tried to see through the crowd of Roxbury Letts to the back table where Louis Fraina sat tonight in a dark brown suit and a slim black tie sipping from a small glass of amber liquor. It was only the blaze of his eyes behind a pair of small round spectacles that gave him away as something other than a college professor who'd entered the wrong bar. That, and the deference the others showed him, placing his drink carefully on the table in front of him, asking him questions with the jutting chins of anxious children, checking to see whether he was watching when they expounded on a point. It was said that Fraina, Italian by birth, spoke Russian as close to fluently as could be asked of one not raised in the Motherland, an assessment rumored to have been first delivered by Trotsky himself. Fraina kept a black moleskin notebook open on the table in front of him, and he'd occasionally jot notes in it with a pencil or flip through the pages. He rarely looked up, and when he did, it was only to acknowledge a speaker's point with a soft flick of his eyelids. Not once had he and Danny exchanged so much as a glance.

The other Letts, though, had finally stopped treating Danny with the amused politeness one reserved for children and the feeble-minded. He wouldn't say they trusted him yet, but they were getting used to having him around.

Even so, they spoke in accents so thick they'd soon tire of conversation with him and jump ship as soon as another Lett interrupted in the mother tongue. That night, they had a full docket of problems and solutions that had carried over from the meeting into the bar.

Problem: The United States had launched a covert war against the provisional Bolshevik government of the new Russia. Wilson had authorized the detachment of the 339th, who'd joined up with British forces and seized the Russian port of Archangel on the White Sea. Hoping to cut the supplies of Lenin and Trotsky and starve them out during a long winter, the American and British forces were instead facing an early winter freeze and were rumored to be at the mercy of their White Russian allies, a corrupt group of warlords and tribal gangsters. This embarrassing quagmire was just one more instance of Western Capitalism attempting to crush the will of the great people's movement.

Solution: Workers everywhere should unite and engage in civil unrest until the Americans and the British withdrew their troops.

Problem: The oppressed firemen and policemen of Montreal were being violently devalued by the state and stripped of their rights.

Solution: Until the Canadian government capitulated to the police and firemen and paid them a fair wage, workers everywhere should unite in civil unrest.

Problem: Revolution was in the air in Hungary and Bavaria and Greece and even France. In Germany, the Spartacists were moving on Berlin. In New York, the Harbor Workers Union had refused to report for duty, and across the country unions were warning of "No Beer, No Work" sit-downs if Prohibition became the law of the land.

Solution: In support of all these comrades, the workers of the world should unite in civil unrest.

Should.

Could.

Might.

No actual plans for revolution that Danny could hear. No specific plotting of the insurrectionary deed.

Just more drinking. More talk that turned into drunken shouts and shattered stools. And it wasn't just the men shattering stools and shouting that night but the women as well, although it was often hard to tell them apart. The workers revolution had no place for the sexist caste system of the United Capitalist States of America—but most women in the bar were hard-faced and industrial-gray, as sexless in their coarse clothes and coarse accents as the men they called comrades. They were without humor (a common affliction among the Letts) and, worse, politically opposed to it—humor was seen as a sentimental disease, a by-product of romanticism, and romantic notions were just one more opiate the ruling class used to keep its masses from seeing the truth.

"Laugh all you want," Hetta Losivich said that night. "Laugh so that you look like fools, like hyenas. And the industrialists will laugh at you because they have you exactly where they want you. Impotent. Laughing, but impotent."

A brawny Estonian named Pyotr Glaviach slapped Danny on the shoulder. "Pampoolats, yes? Tomorrow, yes?"

Danny looked up at him. "I don't know what the hell you're talking about."

Glaviach had a beard so unruly it looked as if he'd been interrupted swallowing a raccoon. It shook now as he tilted his head back and roared with laughter. He was one of those rare Letts who laughed, as if to make up for the paucity in the rest of the ranks. It wasn't a laughter Danny particularly trusted, however, since he'd heard that Pyotr Glaviach had been a charter member of the original Letts, men who'd banded together in 1912 to pitch the first guerrilla skirmishes against Nicholas II. These inaugural Letts had waged a campaign of hit-and-hide against czarist soldiers who'd outnumbered them eighty to one. They lived outdoors during the Russian winter on a diet of half-frozen potatoes and massacred whole villages if they suspected a single Romanov sympathizer lived there.

Pyotr Glaviach said, "We go out tomorrow and we hand out pampoolat. For the workers, yes? You see?"

Danny didn't see. He shook his head. "Pampoo-what?"

Pyotr Glaviach slapped his hands together impatiently. "Pampoolat, you donkey man. Pampoolat."

"I don't—"

"Flyers," a man behind Danny said. "I think he means flyers."

Danny turned in his booth. Nathan Bishop stood there, one elbow resting on the top of Danny's seat back.

"Yes, yes," Pyotr Glaviach said. "We hand out flyers. We spread the news."

"Tell him 'okay,' " Nathan Bishop says. "He loves that word."

"Okay," Danny said to Glaviach and gave him a thumbs-up.

"Ho-kay! Ho-kay, meester! You meet me here," Glaviach said. He gave him a big thumbs-up back. "Eight o'clock."

Danny sighed. "I'll be here."

"We have fun," Glaviach said and slapped Danny on the back. "Maybe meet pretty women." He roared again and then stumbled away.

Bishop slid into the booth and handed him a mug of beer. "The only way you'll meet pretty women in this movement is to kidnap the daughters of our enemies."

Danny said, "What are you doing here?"

"What do you mean?"

"You're a Lett?"

"Are you?"

"Hoping to be."

Nathan shrugged. "I wouldn't say I belong to any one organization. I help out. I've known Lou for a long time."

"Lou?"

"Comrade Fraina," Nathan said and gestured with his chin. "Would you like to meet him some day?"

"Are you kidding? I'd be honored."

Bishop gave that a small, private smile. "You have any worthwhile talents?"

"I write."

"Well?"

"I hope so."

"Give me some samples, I'll see what I can do." He looked around the bar. "God, that's a depressing thought."

"What? Me meeting Comrade Fraina?"

"Huh? No. Glaviach got me thinking. There really isn't a good-looking woman in any of the movements. Not a . . . Well, there's one."

"There's one?"

He nodded. "How could I have forgotten? There is one." He whistled. "Bloody gorgeous, she is."

"She here?"

He laughed. "If she were here, you'd know it."

"What's her name?"

Bishop's head moved so swiftly Danny feared he'd blown his cover. Bishop looked him in the eyes and seemed to be studying his face.

Danny took a sip of his beer.

Bishop looked back out at the crowd. "She has lots of them."

CHAPTER *fourteen*

Luther got off the freight in Boston, where Uncle Hollis's chicken-scratch map directed him and found Dover Street easily enough. He followed it to Columbus Avenue and followed Columbus through the heart of the South End. When he found St. Botolph Street, he walked down a row of redbrick town houses along a sidewalk carpeted in damp leaves until he found number 121 and he went up the stairs and rang the bell.

The man who lived at 121 was Isaiah Giddreaux, the father of Uncle Hollis's second wife, Brenda. Hollis had married four times. The first and third had left him, Brenda had died of typhus, and about five years back Hollis and the fourth had kind of mutually misplaced each other. Hollis had told Luther that as much as he missed Brenda, and he missed her something terrible on many a day, he sometimes missed her father just as much. Isaiah Giddreaux had moved east back in '05 to join up with Dr. Du Bois's Niagara Movement, but he and Hollis had remained in touch.

The door was opened by a small slim man wearing a dark wool three-piece suit and a navy-blue tie speckled with white dots. His hair was speckled with white, too, and cropped close to his skull, and he wore round spectacles that revealed calm, clear eyes behind their panes.

He extended his hand. "You must be Luther Laurence."

Luther shook the hand. "Isaiah?"

Isaiah said, "Mr. Giddreaux if you please, son."

"Mr. Giddreaux, yes, sir."

For a small man Isaiah seemed tall. He stood as straight as any man Luther had ever seen, his hands folded in front of his belt buckle, his eyes so clear it was impossible to read them. They could have been the eyes of a lamb lying down in the last spot of sun on a summer evening. Or those of a lion, waiting for the lamb to get sleepy.

"Your Uncle Hollis is well, I trust?" He led Luther down the front hall.

"He is, sir."

"How's that rheumatism of his?"

"His knees ache awful in the afternoons but otherwise he feels in top form."

Isaiah looked over his shoulder as he led him up a wide staircase. "He's done marrying I hope."

"I believe so, sir."

Luther hadn't been in a brownstone before. The breadth of it surprised him. He'd have never been able to tell from the street how deep the rooms went or how high the ceilings got. It was as nicely appointed as any of the homes on Detroit Avenue, with heavy chandeliers and dark gumwood beams and French sofas and settees. The Giddreauxs had the master bedroom on the top floor, and there were three more bedrooms on the second, one of which Isaiah led Luther to and opened the door long enough for him to drop his bag on the floor. He got a glimpse of a nice brass bed and walnut dresser with a porcelain wash pot on top before Isaiah ushered him back out again. Isaiah and his wife, Yvette, owned the whole place, three floors and a widow's walk on top that looked out over the entire neighborhood. The South End, Luther discerned from Isaiah's description, was a budding Greenwood unto itself, the place where Negroes had carved out a little something for themselves with restaurants served their kind of food and clubs played their kind of music. Isaiah told Luther the neighborhood had been born out of a need for servant housing, the servants being those who attended to the needs of the rich old-money folk on Beacon Hill and in Back Bay, and the reason the buildings were so nice—all red brick town houses and chocolate bowfront brownstones—was that the servants had taken pains to live in the style of their employers.

They took the stairs back down to the parlor, where a pot of tea waited for them.

"Your uncle speaks highly of you, Mr. Laurence."

"He does?"

Isaiah nodded. "He says you have some jackrabbit in your blood but sincerely hopes that one day you'll slow down and find enough peace to be an upstanding man."

Luther couldn't think of a reply to that.

Isaiah reached for the pot and poured them each a cup, then handed Luther's to him. Isaiah poured a single drop of milk into his cup and stirred it slowly. "Did your uncle tell you much about me?"

"Only that you were his wife's father and you were at Niagara with Du Bois."

"*Doctor* Du Bois. I was."

"You know him?" Luther asked. "Dr. Du Bois?"

Isaiah nodded. "I know him well. When the NAACP decided to open an office here in Boston he asked me to run it."

"That's quite an honor, sir."

Isaiah gave that a tiny nod. He dropped a cube of sugar into his cup and stirred. "Tell me about Tulsa."

Luther poured some milk into his tea and took a small sip. "Sir?"

"You committed a crime. Yes?" He lifted his cup to his lips. "Hollis deigned not to be specific what that crime was."

"Then with all due respect, Mr. Giddreaux, I . . . deign the same."

Isaiah shifted and tugged his pant leg down until it covered the top of his sock. "I've heard folks speak of a shooting in a

275

disreputable nightclub in Greenwood. You wouldn't know anything about that, would you?"

Luther met the man's gaze. He said nothing.

Isaiah took another sip of tea. "Did you feel you had a choice?"

Luther looked at the rug.

"Shall I repeat myself?"

Luther kept his eyes on the rug. It was blue and red and yellow and all the colors swirled together. He supposed it was expensive. The swirls.

"Did you feel you had a choice?" Isaiah's voice was as calm as his teacup.

Luther raised his eyes to him and still said nothing.

"And yet you killed your own kind."

"Evil got a way of not caring about kinds, sir." Luther's hand shook as he lowered his cup to the coffee table. "Evil just muck things around till things go all sideways."

"That's how you define evil?"

Luther looked around this room, as fine as any in the fine houses on Detroit Avenue. "You know it when you see it."

Isaiah sipped his tea. "Some would say a murderer is evil. Would you agree?"

"I'd agree some would say it."

"You committed murder."

Luther said nothing.

"Ergo . . ." Isaiah held out his hand.

"All due respect? I never said I committed anything, sir."

They sat silent for a bit, a clock ticking behind Luther. A car horn beeped faintly from a few blocks away. Isaiah finished his tea and placed the cup back on the tray.

"You'll meet my wife later. Yvette. We've just purchased a building to use as the NAACP office here. You'll volunteer there."

"I'll what?"

"You'll volunteer there. Hollis tells me you're good with your hands, and we have repairs that need seeing to in the building before we can open for business. You'll pull your weight here, Luther."

Pull my weight. Shit. When's the last time this old man pulled any weight outside of lifting a teacup? Seemed the same shit Luther had left behind in Tulsa—moneyed colored folk acting like their money gave them the right to order you around. And this old fool acting like he could see inside Luther, talking about evil like he'd know it if it sat down beside him and bought him a drink. Man was probably a step or two away from whipping out a Bible. But he reminded himself of the pledge he'd made in the train car to create the New Luther, the better Luther, and promised he would give it time before he made up his mind about Isaiah Giddreaux. This man worked with W.E.B. Du Bois, and Du Bois was one of only two men in this country that Luther felt worthy of his admiration. The other, of course, was Jack Johnson. Jack didn't take shit from no one, black or white.

"I know of a white family that needs a houseman. Could you handle that work?"

"Can't see why not."

"They are good people as far as whites can be." He spread his hands. "There is one caveat—the household in question is headed by a police captain. If you were to attempt an alias, I suspect he would ferret it out."

"No need," Luther said. "Trick is to never mention Tulsa. I'm just Luther Laurence, late of Columbus." Luther wished he could feel something beyond his own weariness. Spots had started popping in the air between him and Isaiah. "Thank you, sir."

Isaiah nodded. "Let's get you upstairs. We'll wake you for dinner."

Luther dreamed of playing baseball in floodwaters. Of outfielders washed away in the tide. Of trying to hit above the waterline and men laughing every time his bat head slapped off the muddy water that rose above his waist, up over his ribs, while Babe Ruth and Cully flew past in a crop duster, dropping grenades that failed to explode.

He woke to an older woman pouring hot water into the wash pot on his dresser. She looked back over her shoulder at him, and for a moment he thought she was his mother. They were the same height and had the same light skin speckled with dark freckles over the cheekbones. But this woman's hair was gray and she was thinner than his mother. Same warmth, though, same kindliness living in the body, like the soul was too good to be kept covered.

"You must be Luther."

Luther sat up. "I am, ma'am."

"That's good. Be a frightful thing if some other man stole up here and took your place." She lay a straight razor, tub of shaving cream, brush and bowl by the pot. "Mr. Giddreaux expects a man to come to the dinner table clean-shaven, and dinner's almost served. We'll work on cleaning up the rest of you afterward. Sound right?"

Luther swung his legs off the bed and suppressed a yawn. "Yes, ma'am."

She held out a delicate hand, so small it could have been a doll's. "I'm Yvette Giddreaux, Luther. Welcome to my home."

While they waited for Isaiah to hear back from the police captain, Luther accompanied Yvette Giddreaux to the proposed NAACP offices on Shawmut Avenue. The building was Second Empire style, a baroque monster of chocolate stone skin with a mansard roof. First time Luther'd seen the style outside of a book. He stepped in close and looked up as he walked along the sidewalk. The lines of the building were straight, no bowing, no humps, either. The structure had shifted with the weight of itself, but no more so than would be expected from a building Luther guessed dated back to the 1830s or so. He took a good look at the tilt of the corners and decided the foundation hadn't racked, so the shell was in good shape. He stepped off the sidewalk and walked along the edge of the street, looking up at the roof.

"Mrs. Giddreaux?"

"Yes, Luther."

"Seem to be a piece of this roof missing."

He looked over at her. She held her purse tight in front of her and gave him a look of such innocence it could only be a front.

She said, "I believe I heard something to that effect, yes."

Luther continued moving his gaze from the point on the ridgeline where he'd spotted the gap, and he found a dip exactly where he was hoping he wouldn't—in the center of the spine. Mrs. Giddreaux was still giving him that wide-eyed innocence, and he placed his hand softly under her elbow as he led her inside.

Most of the first-floor ceiling was gone. What remained leaked. The staircase just to his right was black. The walls were missing their plaster in half a dozen places, the lathes and studs exposed, and scorched black in half a dozen more. The floor was so eaten away by fire and water that even the sub-flooring was damaged. All the windows were boarded.

Luther whistled. "You buy this place at auction?"

"About so," she said. "What do you think?"

"Any way you can get your money back?"

She slapped his elbow. The first time, but he was sure it wouldn't be the last. He resisted the urge to hug her to him, the way he'd done with his mother and sister, loving that they'd always fought him, that it had always cost him a shot to the ribs or the hip.

"Let me guess," Luther said, "George Washington never slept here, but his footman did?"

She bared her teeth at him, little fists placed to little hips. "Can you fix it?"

Luther laughed and heard the echo bounce through the dripping building. "No."

She looked up at him. Her face was stony. Her eyes were gay. "But of what usefulness does that speak, Luther?"

"Can't nobody *fix* this. I'm just amazed the city didn't condemn it."

"They tried."

Luther looked at her and let out a long sigh. "You know how much money it'll take to make this livable?"

"Don't you worry about money. Can you fix it?"

"I honestly don't know." He whistled again, taking it all in, the months, if not years, of work. "Don't suppose I'll be getting much in the way of help?"

"We'll round up some volunteers every now and then, and when you need something, you just make a list. I can't promise we'll get you everything you need or that any of it will arrive in the time you need it, but we'll try."

Luther nodded and looked down into her kind face. "You understand, ma'am, that the effort this will take will be *biblical*?"

Another slap on the elbow. "You best set to it then."

Luther sighed. "Yes, ma'am."

Captain Thomas Coughlin opened the door to his study and gave Luther a wide, warm smile. "You must be Mr. Laurence."

"Yes, sir, Captain Coughlin."

"Nora, that'll be all for now."

"Yes, sir," the Irish girl Luther'd just met said. "Nice to meet you, Mr. Laurence."

"You, too, Miss O'Shea."

She bowed and took her leave.

"Come in, come in." Captain Coughlin swung the door wide, and Luther entered a study that smelled of good tobacco, a recent fire in the hearth, and the dying autumn. Captain Coughlin led him to a leather chair and went around the other side of a large mahogany desk and took his seat by the window.

"Isaiah Giddreaux said you're from Ohio."

"Yes, suh."

280

"I heard you say 'sir.' "

"Suh?"

"Just a moment ago. When we met." His light blue eyes glittered. "You said 'sir,' not 'suh.' Which will it be, son?"

"Which do you prefer, Captain?"

Captain Coughlin waved an unlit cigar at the question. "Whichever makes you comfortable, Mr. Laurence."

"Yes, sir."

Another smile, this one not so much warm as self-satisfied. "Columbus, correct?"

"Yes, sir."

"And what did you do there?"

"I worked for the Anderson Armaments Corporation, sir."

"And before that?"

"I did carpentry, sir, some masonry work, piping, you name it."

Captain Coughlin leaned back in his chair and propped his feet on the desk. He lit his cigar and stared through the flame and the smoke at Luther until the tip was fat with red. "You've never worked in a household, however."

"No, sir, I have not."

Captain Coughlin leaned his head back and blew smoke rings at the ceiling.

Luther said, "But I'm a fast learner, sir. And there's nothing I can't fix. And I look right smart, too, in tails and white gloves."

Captain Coughlin chuckled. "A sense of wit. Bully for you, son. Indeed." He ran a hand over the back of his head. "It's not a full-time position that's being offered. Nor do I offer any lodging."

"I understand, sir."

"You would work roughly forty hours a week, and most of it would be driving Mrs. Coughlin to mass, cleaning, maintenance, and the serving of meals. Do you cook?"

"I can, sir."

"Not a bother. Nora will do most of that." Captain

Coughlin gave another wave of his cigar. "She's the lass you just met. She lives with us. She does chores as well, but she's gone most of the day, working at a factory. You'll meet Mrs. Coughlin soon," he said, and his eyes glittered again. "I may be the head of the household, but God was remiss in telling her. You follow my meaning? Anything she asks, you hop to."

"Yes, sir."

"Stay on the east side of the neighborhood."

"Sir?"

Captain Coughlin brought his feet off the desk. "The east side, Mr. Laurence. The west side is fairly infamous for its intolerance of coloreds."

"Yes, sir."

"Word will get out, of course, that you work for me and that's fair warning, sure, to most ruffians, even west-siders, but you can never be too careful."

"Thank you for the advice, sir."

The captain's eyes fell on him through the smoke again. This time they were part of the smoke, swirling in it, swimming around Luther, looking into his eyes, his heart, his soul. Luther had seen hints of this ability in cops before—they didn't call them copper's eyes for nothing—but Captain Coughlin's gaze achieved a level of invasion Luther had never come across in a man before. Hoped to never come across twice.

"Who taught you to read, Luther?" The captain's voice was soft.

"A Mrs. Murtrey, sir. Hamilton School, just outside of Columbus."

"What else she teach you?"

"Sir?"

"What else, Luther?" Captain Coughlin took another slow drag from his cigar.

"I don't understand the question, sir."

"What else?" the captain said for a third time.

"Sir, I'm not following you."

"Grew up poor, I imagine?" The captain leaned forward ever so slightly, and Luther resisted the urge to push his chair back.

Luther nodded. "Yes, sir."

"Sharecropping?"

"Not me so much, sir. My mother and father, though, yeah."

Captain Coughlin nodded, his lips pursed and pained. "Was born into nothing myself. A two-room thatched hut we shared with flies and field rats, it was. No place to be a child. Certainly no place to be an intelligent child. You know what an intelligent child learns in those circumstances, Mr. Laurence?"

"No, sir."

"Yes, you do, son." Captain Coughlin smiled a third time since Luther had met him, and this smile snaked into the air like the captain's gaze and circled. "Don't muck about with me, son."

"I'm just not sure what kind of ground I'm standing on, sir."

Captain Coughlin gave that a cock of his head and then a nod. "An intelligent child born to less than advantageous surroundings, Luther, learns to charm." He reached across the desk; his fingers twirled through the smoke. "He learns to hide behind that charm so that no one ever sees what he's really thinking. Or feeling."

He went to a decanter behind his desk and poured two helpings of amber liquid into crystal scotch glasses. He brought the drinks around the desk and handed one to Luther, the first time Luther'd ever been handed a glass by a white man.

"I'm going to hire you, Luther, because you intrigue me." The captain sat on the edge of the desk and clinked his glass off Luther's. He reached behind him and came back with an envelope. He handed it to Luther. "Avery Wallace left that for whoever replaced him. You'll note its seal has not been tampered with."

Luther saw a maroon wax seal on the back of the envelope. He turned it back over, saw that it was addressed to: MY REPLACEMENT. FROM AVERY WALLACE.

Luther took a drink of scotch. As good as any he'd ever tasted. "Thank you, sir."

Captain Coughlin nodded. "I respected Avery's privacy. I'll respect yours. But don't ever think I don't know you, son. I know you like I know the mirror."

"Yes, sir."

" 'Yes, sir,' what?"

"Yes, sir, you know me."

"And what do I know?"

"That I'm smarter than I let on."

The captain said, "And what else?"

Luther met his eyes. "I'm not as smart as you."

A fourth smile. Cocked up the right side and certain. Another clink of the glasses.

"Welcome to my home, Luther Laurence."

Luther read the note from Avery Wallace on the streetcar back to the Giddreauxs.

To my replacement,

If you are reading this, I am dead. If you are reading this, you are also Negro, as was I, because the white folk on K, L, and M Streets only hire Negro housemen. The Coughlin family is not so bad for white folk. The Captain is never to be trifled with but he will treat you fair if you don't cross him. His sons are mostly good. Mister Connor will snap at you every now and again. Joe is just a boy and will talk your ear off if you let him. Danny is a strange. He definitely does his own thinking. He is like the Captain, though, he will treat you fair and like a man. Nora is a funny thinker herself but there is not any wool over her eyes. You can trust her. Be careful with Mrs. Coughlin. Do what she asks and never question her. Stay well clear of the Captain's friend, Lieutenant McKenna. He is something the Lord should have dropped. Good luck.

Sincerely,
Avery Wallace

Luther looked up from the letter as the streetcar crossed the Broadway Bridge while the Fort Point Channel ran silver and sluggish below.

So this was his new life. So this was his new city.

Every morning, at six-fifty sharp, Mrs. Ellen Coughlin left the residence at 221 K Street and ventured down the stairs, where Luther waited by the family car, a six-cylinder Auburn. Mrs. Coughlin would acknowledge him with a nod as she accepted his hand and climbed into the passenger seat. Once she was settled, Luther would close the door as softly as Captain Coughlin had instructed and drive Mrs. Coughlin a few short blocks to the seven o'clock mass at Gate of Heaven Church. He would remain outside the car for the duration of the mass and often chat with another houseman, Clayton Tomes, who worked for Mrs. Amy Wagenfeld, a widow who lived on M Street, South Boston's most prestigious address, in a town house overlooking Independence Square Park.

Mrs. Ellen Coughlin and Mrs. Amy Wagenfeld were not friends—as far as Luther and Clayton could tell, old white women didn't have friends—but their valets eventually formed a bond. Both were from the Midwest—Clayton grew up in Indiana not far from French Lick—and both were valets for employers who would have had little use for them had they placed just one foot in the twentieth century. Luther's first job after returning Mrs. Coughlin to her household every morning was to cut wood for the stove, while Clayton's was to haul coal to the basement.

"This day and age?" Clayton said. "Whole country—'least

what can afford it—is going electrical, but Mrs. Wagenfeld, she want no part of it."

"Mrs. Coughlin neither," Luther said. "Enough kerosene in that house to burn down the block, spend half my day cleaning gas soot off the walls, but the captain say she won't even discuss the subject. Said it took him five years to convince her to get indoor plumbing and stop using a backyard privy."

"White women," Clayton would say, then repeat it with a sigh. "White women."

When Luther took Mrs. Coughlin back to K Street and opened the front door for her, she would give him a soft, "Thank you, Luther," and after he'd served her breakfast, he'd rarely see her for the rest of the day. In a month, their interactions consisted solely of her "thank you" and his "my pleasure, ma'am." She never asked where he lived, if he had family, or where he hailed from, and Luther had gleaned enough about the employer–valet relationship to know it was not his place to initiate conversation with her.

"She's hard to know," Nora said to him one day when they went to Haymarket Square to purchase the weekly groceries. "I've been in that house five years, I have, and I'm not sure I could tell you much more about her than I could the night I arrived."

"Long as she ain't finding fault with my work, she can stay silent as a stone."

Nora placed a dozen potatoes in the sack she carried to market. "Are you getting on well with everyone else?"

Luther nodded. "They seem a nice family."

She nodded, though Luther couldn't tell if it was a nod of agreement or if she'd just decided something about the apple she was considering. "Young Joe's certainly grown a fondness for you."

"Boy loves his baseball."

She smiled. " 'Love' may not be a strong enough word."

Once Joe had discovered Luther had played some baseball in his time, the after-school hours became games of catch and pitching and fielding instruction in the Coughlins' small backyard. Dusk coincided with the end of Luther's shift, so the final three hours of his workday were spent mostly at play, a situation Captain Coughlin had immediately approved. "If it keeps the boy out of his mother's hair, I'd let you field a team should you ask, Mr. Laurence."

Joe wasn't a natural athlete, but he had heart and he listened well for a child his age. Luther showed him how to drop his knee when he fielded grounders and how to follow through on both his throws and the swings of his bat. He taught him to spread and then plant his feet beneath a pop-up and to never catch it below his head. He tried to teach him how to pitch, but the boy didn't have the arm for it, nor the patience. He just wanted to hit and hit big. So Luther found one more thing to blame Babe Ruth for—turning the game into a smash-ball affair, a circus spectacle, making every white kid in Boston think it was about ooohs and aaahs and the cheap soaring of an ill-timed dinger.

Except for the morning hour with Mrs. Coughlin and the late day hours with Joe, Luther spent most of his workday with Nora O'Shea.

"And how do you like it so far?"

"Doesn't seem much for me to do."

"Would you like some of my work, then?"

"Truth? Yeah. I drive her to and from church. I bring her breakfast. I wax the car. I shine the captain's and Mr. Connor's shoes and brush their suits. Sometimes I polish the captain's medals for dress occasions. Sundays, I serve the captain and his friends drinks in the study. Rest of the time, I dust what don't need to be dusted, tidy what's already tidy, and sweep a bunch of clean floors. Cut some wood, shovel some coal, stoke a small furnace. I mean, what's that all take? Two hours? Rest of the day I spend trying to look busy till either you or Mr. Joe get home. I don't even know why they hired me."

She put a hand lightly on his arm. "All the best families have one."

"A colored?"

Nora nodded, her eyes bright. "In this part of the neighborhood. If the Coughlins didn't hire you, they'd have to explain why."

"Why what? Why they haven't updated to electric?"

"Why they can't keep up appearances." They climbed East Broadway toward City Point. "The Irish up here remind me of the English back home, they do. Lace curtains on the windows and trousers tucked into their boots, sure, as if they know from work."

"Up here maybe," Luther said. "Rest of this neighborhood . . ."

"What?"

He shrugged.

"No, what?" She tugged his arm.

He looked down at her hand. "That thing you doing now? You don't ever do that in the rest of this neighborhood. Please."

"Ah."

"Like to get us both killed. Ain't any lace curtains part of that, I'll tell you what."

Every night he wrote to Lila, and every few days the letters came back unopened.

It was near to breaking him—her silence, being in a strange city, his self as unsettled and nameless as it had ever been—when Yvette brought the mail to the table one morning and placed two more returned letters softly by his elbow.

"Your wife?" She took a seat.

Luther nodded.

"You must have done something fierce to her."

He said, "I did, ma'am. I did."

"Wasn't another woman, was it?"

"No."

"Then I forgive you." She patted his hand, and Luther felt the warmth of it find his blood.

288

"Thank you," he said.

"Don't worry. She still cares for you."

He shook his head, the loss of her draining him to his root. "She doesn't, ma'am."

Yvette shook her head slowly at him, a smile spread thin across her lips. "Men are fine for many things, Luther, but none of you know the first thing about a woman's heart."

"That's just it," Luther said, "she don't want me to know her heart anymore."

"Doesn't."

"Huh?"

"She *doesn't* want you to know her heart."

"Right." Luther wanted a cloak to hide in, duck in. Cover me, cover me.

"I beg to differ with you, son." Mrs. Giddreaux held up one of his letters so he could see the back of the envelope. "What's that along the sides of the flap?"

Luther looked; he couldn't see anything.

Mrs. Giddreaux traced her finger down the flap. "See that cloud there along the edges? The way the paper is softer underneath it?"

Luther noticed it now. "Yes."

"That's from steam, son. Steam."

Luther reached for the envelope and stared at it.

"She's opening your letters, Luther, and then sending them back like she hasn't. I don't know if I'd call that love," she squeezed his arm, "but I wouldn't call it indifference."

CHAPTER *fifteen*

Autumn yielded to winter in a series of wet gales that carved their way across the eastern seaboard, and Danny's list of names grew larger. What the list told him, or anyone for that matter, about the likelihood of a May Day uprising was a mystery. Mostly he just had the names of ass-fucked workingmen looking to unionize and deluded romantics who actually thought the world welcomed change.

Danny began to suspect, though, that between the Roxbury Letts and the BSC, he'd become addicted to the strangest of things—meetings. The Letts and their talk and their drinking led to nothing he could see but more talk and more drinking. And yet, on the nights there were no meetings, no saloon afterward, he felt at loose ends. He'd sit in the dark of his cover apartment, drinking and rubbing the button between his thumb and index finger with such agitation, it seemed a miracle in retrospect that it never cracked. So he'd find himself at another meeting of the Boston Social Club at Fay Hall in Roxbury. And another after that.

It wasn't much different from a meeting of the Letts. Rhetoric, rage, helplessness. Danny couldn't help marvel at the irony—these men who'd served as strikebreakers finding themselves backed into the same corners as the men they'd manhandled or beaten outside factories and mills.

Into another bar one night, and more talk about workers' rights, but this time with the BSC—brother policemen, patrolmen, foot stampers and beat walkers and nightstick maestros filled with the stunted rage of the perpetually pushed-aside. Still no negotiations, still no decent talk of decent hours and a decent wage, still no raise. And word was that across the border in Montreal, just 350 miles north, the city had broken off negotiations with police and firemen and a strike was unavoidable.

And why not? the men in the bar said. Fucking starving, they said. Ass-fucked and broke-down and handcuffed to a job that gives us no way to feed our families and no way to see them properly either.

"My youngest," Francie Deegan said, "my youngest, boys, is wearing clothes he got from his brothers and I'm shocked to discover the older ones ain't wearing 'em still because I'm working so much I think they're in second grade, but they're in fifth. I think they're at my hip, but they're at me fuckin' nipple, boys."

And when he sat back down amid the hear-hears, Sean Gale piped up with:

"Fucking dockworkers, boys, are making three times as much as us coppers who bust them on drunk-and-disorderlies on Friday nights. So somebody better start thinking of how to pay us what's right."

More shouts of "Hear! Hear!" Someone nudged someone and that someone nudged someone else and they all looked over to see Boston police commissioner Stephen O'Meara standing at the bar, waiting for his pint. Once the pint had been drawn and the quiet had fallen over the bar, the great man waited for the tender to shave off the foam with a straight razor. He paid for the pint and waited for his change, his back to the room. The bartender rang up the sale and handed the coins back to Stephen O'Meara. O'Meara left one of those coins on the bar, pocketed the rest, and turned to the room.

Deegan and Gale lowered their heads, awaiting execution.

O'Meara made his way carefully through the men, holding

his pint aloft to keep it from spilling, and took a seat by the hearth between Marty Leary and Denny Toole. He looked at the assembled men with a soft sweep of his kind eyes before he sipped at his beer, and the foam crept into his mustache like a silkworm.

"Cold out there." He took another sip of his beer and the logs crackled behind him. "A fine fire in here, though." He nodded just once but seemed to encompass each of them with the gesture. "I've no answer for you, men. You aren't getting right-paid and that's a fact."

No one dared speak. The men, who just moments before had been the loudest, the most profane, the angriest and most publicly injured, averted their eyes.

O'Meara gave them all a grim smile and even nudged Denny Toole's knee with his own. "It's a fine spot, isn't it?" His eyes swept them again, searching for something or someone. "Young Coughlin, is that you under that beard?"

Danny found those kind eyes meeting his and his chest tightened. "Yes, sir."

"I'll take it you're working undercover."

"Yes, sir."

"As a bear?"

The room broke out in laughter.

"Not quite, sir. Close."

O'Meara's gaze softened and was so stripped of pride Danny felt as if they were the only two men in the room. "I've known your father a long time, son. How's your mother?"

"She's fine, sir." Danny could feel the eyes of the other men now.

"As gracious a woman as any who ever lived. Tell her I said hello, would you?"

"I will, sir."

"If I may inquire—what is your position on this economic stalemate?"

The men turned in his direction while O'Meara took another sip of his beer, his eyes never leaving Danny's.

292

"I understand," Danny began, and then his throat went dry. He wished the room would go dark, pitch-black, so that he could stop feeling their eyes. Christ.

He took a sip from his own pint and tried again. "I understand, sir, that cost of living is affecting the city and funds are tight. I do."

O'Meara nodded.

"And I understand, sir, that we are not private citizens but public servants, sworn to do our duty. And that there is no higher calling than that of the public servant."

"None," O'Meara agreed.

Danny nodded.

O'Meara watched him. The men watched him.

"But . . ." Danny kept his voice level. "There was a promise made, sir. A promise that our wages would freeze for the duration of the war, but that we would be rewarded for our patience with a two-hundred-a-year increase as soon as the war ended." Danny dared look around the room now, at all the eyes fixed upon him. He hoped they couldn't see the tremors that rippled down the backs of his legs.

"I sympathize," O'Meara said. "I do, Officer Coughlin. But that cost-of-living increase is a very real thing. And the city is strapped. It's not simple. I wish it were."

Danny nodded and went to sit back down and then found he couldn't. His legs wouldn't let him. He looked back at O'Meara and could feel the decency that lived in the man like a vital organ. He caught Mark Denton's eye, and Denton nodded.

"Sir," Danny said, "we have no doubt that you sympathize. None whatsoever. And we know the city is strapped. Yes. Yes." Danny took a breath. "But a promise, sir, is a promise. Maybe that's what all this is about in the end. And you said it wasn't simple, but it is, sir. I would respectfully submit that it is. Not easy. Quite hard. But simple. A lot of fine, brave men can't make ends meet. And a promise is a promise."

No one spoke. No one moved. It was as if a grenade had

been lobbed into the center of the room and had failed to go off.

O'Meara stood. The men hastily cleared a path as he crossed in front of the hearth until he'd reached Danny. He held out his hand. Danny had to place his beer on the mantel above the hearth and then he placed his own shaky hand in the older man's grip.

The old man held it fast, not moving his arm up or down.

"A promise is a promise," O'Meara said.

"Yes, sir," Danny managed.

O'Meara nodded and let go of his hand and turned to the room. Danny felt the moment freeze in time, as if woven by gods into the mural of history—Danny Coughlin and the Great Man standing side by side with the fire crackling behind them.

O'Meara raised his pint. "You are the pride of this great city, men. And I am proud to call myself one of you. And a promise *is* a promise."

Danny felt the fire at his back. Felt O'Meara's hand against his spine.

"Do you trust me?" O'Meara shouted. "Do I have your faith?"

A chorus rose up: "Yes, sir!"

"I will not let you down. I will not."

Danny saw it rise in their faces: love. Simply that.

"A little more patience, men, that's all I ask. I know that's a tall order, sure. I do. But will you indulge an old man just a little longer?"

"Yes, sir!"

O'Meara took a great breath through his nose and raised his glass higher. "To the men of the Boston Police Department—you have no peers in this nation."

O'Meara drained his pint in one long swallow. The men erupted and followed suit. Marty Leary called for another round, and Danny noticed that they had somehow become children again, boys, unconditional in their brotherhood.

O'Meara leaned in. "You're not your father, son."

Danny stared back at him, unsure.

"Your heart is purer than his."

Danny couldn't speak.

O'Meara squeezed his arm just above the elbow. "Don't sell that, son. You can't ever buy it back in the same condition."

"Yes, sir."

O'Meara held him with his gaze for one more long moment and then Mark Denton handed them each a pint and O'Meara's hand dropped from Danny's arm.

After he'd finished his second pint, O'Meara bade the men good-bye and Danny and Mark Denton walked him out into a thick rain that fell from the black sky.

His driver, Sergeant Reid Harper, exited the car and covered his boss with an umbrella. He acknowledged Danny and Denton with a nod as he opened the rear door for O'Meara. The commissioner rested an arm on the door and turned to them.

"I'll speak to Mayor Peters first thing in the morning. I'll convey to him my sense of urgency and arrange a meeting at City Hall for negotiations with the Boston Social Club. Do either of you have any objections to representing the men at that meeting?"

Danny looked over at Denton, wondering if O'Meara could hear the thumps of their hearts.

"No, sir."

"No, sir."

"Well, then." O'Meara held out his hand. "Allow me to thank you both. Sincerely."

They each shook the hand. "You're the future of the Boston policemen's union, gentlemen." He gave them a gentle smile. "I hope you're up to the task. Now get out of the rain."

He climbed in the car. "To home, Reid, else the missus will think I've turned tomcat."

Reid Harper pulled away from the curb as O'Meara gave them a small wave through the window.

295

The rain soaked their hair and fell down the backs of their necks.

"Jesus Christ," Mark Denton said. "Jesus Christ, Coughlin."

"I know."

"You know? Do you understand what you just did in there? You saved us."

"I didn't—"

Denton wrapped him in a bear hug and lifted him off the sidewalk. "You fucking saved us!"

He spun Danny over the sidewalk and hooted at the street and Danny struggled to break free but he was laughing now, too, the both of them laughing like lunatics on the street as the rain fell into Danny's eyes, and he wondered if he'd ever, in his life, felt this good.

He met Eddie McKenna one night in Governor's Square, at the bar of the Hotel Buckminster.

"What have you got?"

"I'm getting closer to Bishop. But he's cagey."

McKenna spread his arms in the booth. "They suspect you of being a plant, you think?"

"Like I said before, it's definitely crossed their minds."

"Any ideas?"

Danny nodded. "One. It's risky."

"How risky?"

He produced a moleskin notebook, identical to the one he'd seen Fraina use. He'd been to four stationers before he'd found it. He handed it to McKenna.

"I've been working on that for two weeks."

McKenna leafed through it, his eyebrows going up a few times.

"I stained a few pages with coffee, even put a cigarette hole in one."

McKenna whistled softly. "I noticed."

"It's the political musings of Daniel Sante. What do you think?"

McKenna thumbed through it. "You covered Montreal and the Spartacists. Nice. Oooh—Seattle and Ole Hanson. Good, good. You got Archangel in here?"

"Of course."

"The Versailles Conference?"

"You mean as a world-domination conspiracy?" Danny rolled his eyes. "You think I'd miss that one?"

"Careful," Eddie said without looking up. "Cocky gets undercover men hurt."

"I've gotten nowhere in weeks, Eddie. How could I possibly be cocky? I got the notebook and Bishop said he'll show it to Fraina, no promises. That's it."

Eddie handed it back. "That's good stuff. You'd almost think you believed it."

Danny let the comment pass and put the notebook back in his coat pocket.

Eddie flicked open his watch. "Stay away from union meetings for a while."

"I can't."

Eddie closed his watch and returned it to his vest. "Oh, that's right. You *are* the BSC these days."

"Bullshit."

"After the meeting you had with O'Meara the other night, that is the rumor, trust me." He smiled softly. "Almost thirty years on this force and I'll bet our dear commissioner doesn't even know my name."

Danny said, "Right place at the right time, I guess."

"Wrong place." He frowned. "You better watch yourself, boy. Because others have started watching *you*. Take some advice from Uncle Eddie—step back. There are storms imminent everywhere. Everywhere. On the streets, in the factory yards, and now in our own department. Power? That's ephemeral, Dan. More so now than ever before. You keep your head down."

"It's already up."

Eddie slapped the table.

Danny leaned back. He'd never seen Eddie McKenna lose his slippery calm.

"If you get your face in the paper meeting with the commissioner? The mayor? Have you thought of what that means to *my* investigation? I can't use you if Daniel Sante, apprentice-Bolshevik, becomes Aiden Coughlin, face of the BSC. I need Fraina's *mailing list*."

Danny stared across at this man he'd known his whole life. Seeing a new side to him, a side he'd suspected was there all along but had never actually witnessed.

"Why the mailing lists, Eddie? I thought we were looking for evidence of May Day uprising plans."

"We're looking for both," Eddie said. "But if they're as tight-lipped as you say, Dan, and if your detecting capabilities are a little less substantial than I'd hoped, then you just get me that mailing list before your face is all over the front page. Could you do that for your uncle, pal?" He stepped out of the booth and shrugged into his coat, tossed some coins on the table. "That should do it."

"We just got here," Danny said.

Eddie worked his face back into the mask it had always been around Danny—impish and benign. "City never sleeps, boy. I've got business in Brighton."

"Brighton?"

Eddie nodded. "Stockyards. Hate that place."

Danny followed Eddie toward the door. "Bracing cows now, Eddie?"

"Better." Eddie pushed open the door into the cold. "Coloreds. Crazy dinges are meeting right now, after hours, to discuss their rights. You believe that? Where does it end? Next thing, the chinks'll be holding our laundry hostage."

Eddie's driver pulled to the curb in his black Hudson. Eddie said, "Give you a lift?"

"I'll walk."

"Walk off that booze. Good idea," he said. "Know anyone by the name of Finn by the bye?" Eddie's face was blithe, open.

Danny kept his the same way. "In Brighton?"

Eddie frowned. "I said I was going to Brighton on a coon hunt. 'Finn' sound like a colored name to you?"

"Sounds Irish."

" 'Tis indeed. Know any?"

"Nope. Why?"

"Just wondering," Eddie said. "You're sure?"

"Just what I said, Eddie." Danny turned up his collar against the wind. "Nope."

Eddie nodded and reached for the car door.

"What he do?" Danny said.

"Huh?"

"This Finn you're looking for," Danny said. "What'd he do?"

Eddie stared into his face for a long time. "Good night, Dan."

" 'Night, Eddie."

Eddie's car drove up Beacon Street and Danny thought of going back in and calling Nora from the phone booth in the hotel lobby. Let her know that McKenna could be sniffing around her life. But then he pictured her with Connor—holding his hand, kissing him, maybe sitting on his lap when no one else was in the house to see—and he decided there were a lot of Finns in the world. And half of them were either in Ireland or Boston. McKenna could have been talking about any one of them. Any at all.

CHAPTER *sixteen*

The first thing Luther had to do at the building on Shawmut Avenue was make it weather-tight. That meant starting with the roof. A slate beauty, she was, fallen on ill fortune and neglect. He worked his way across her spine one fine cold morning when the air smelled of mill smoke and the sky was clean and blade-blue. He collected shards of slate the firemen's axes had sent to the gutters and added them to those he'd retrieved from the floor below. He ripped sodden or scorched wood from their lathes and hammered fresh planks of oak in their places and covered it all with the slate he'd salvaged. When he ran out of that he used the slate Mrs. Giddreaux had somehow managed to procure from a company in Cleveland. He started on a Saturday at first light and finished up late of that Sunday afternoon. Sitting on the ridgeline of the roof, slick with sweat in the cold, he wiped his brow and gazed up at the clean sky. He turned his head and looked at the city spread out around him. He smelled the coming dusk in the air, though his eyes could see no evidence of it yet. As smells went, though, few were finer.

Luther's weekday schedule was such that by the time the Coughlins sat for dinner, Luther, who'd set the table and helped Nora prepare the food, had already left. But on Sundays, dinners were all-day affairs, ones that occasionally reminded Luther of the ones at Aunt Marta and Uncle James's on Standpipe Hill. Something about recent church attendance and Sunday finery brought out an inclination for pronouncements, he noticed, in white folk as well as black.

Serving drinks in the captain's study, he sometimes got the feeling they were pronouncing *for* him. He'd catch sidelong glances from one of the captain's associates as he pontificated about eugenics or proven intellectual disparities in the races or some similar bullshit only the truly indolent had time to discuss.

The one who spoke the least but had the most fire in his eyes was the one Avery Wallace had warned him about, the captain's right-hand man, Lieutenant Eddie McKenna. A fat man, given to breathing heavily through nostrils clogged with hair, he had a smile as bright as the full moon on a river, and one of those loud, jolly natures Luther believed could never be trusted. Men like that always hid the part of themselves that wasn't smiling and hid it so deep it got all the hungrier, like a bear just come out of hibernation, lumbering out of that cave with a scent in its nose so focused it couldn't ever be reasoned with.

Of all the men who joined the captain in the study on those Sundays—and the roster changed from week to week— it was McKenna who paid Luther the most attention. At first glance, it seemed welcome enough. He always thanked Luther when Luther brought him either a drink or a refill, whereas most of the men simply acted as if his servitude was their due and rarely acknowledged him at all. Upon entering the study, McKenna usually asked after Luther's health, his week, how he was adapting to the cold weather. "You ever need an extra coat, son, you let us know. We usually have a few spares down at the station house. Can't promise they'll smell too fine, though." He clapped Luther on the back.

He seemed to assume Luther was from the South and Luther saw no reason to dissuade him from the impression until it came up one late afternoon at Sunday dinner.

301

"Kentucky?" McKenna said.

At first Luther didn't realize he was being addressed. He stood by the sideboard, filling a small bowl with sugar cubes.

"Louisville, I'm guessing. Am I right?" McKenna gazed openly at him as he placed a slice of pork in his mouth.

"Where I hail from, sir?"

McKenna's eyes glimmered. "That's the question, son."

The captain took a sip of wine. "The lieutenant prides himself on his grasp of accents, he does."

Danny said, "Can't lose his own, though, uh?"

Connor and Joe laughed. McKenna wagged his fork at Danny. "A wiseacre since diapers, this one." He turned his head. "So which is it, Luther?"

Before Luther could answer, Captain Coughlin raised a hand to him. "Make him guess, Mr. Laurence."

"I did guess, Tom."

"You guessed wrong."

"Ah." Eddie McKenna dabbed his lips with his napkin. "So, not Louisville?"

Luther shook his head. "No, sir."

"Lexington?"

Luther shook his head again, felt the whole family looking at him.

McKenna leaned back, one hand caressing his belly. "Well, let's see. You don't have a deep enough drawl for Mis'sipi, tha's fo' sho'. And Gawgia is right out. Too deep for Virginia, though, and too fast, I think, for Alabama."

"I'm guessing Bermuda," Danny said.

Luther caught his eye and smiled. Of all the Coughlins, he had the least experience with Danny, but Avery had been right—you felt no lying in the man.

"Cuba," Luther said to Danny.

"Too far south," Danny said.

They both chuckled.

The gamesmanship left McKenna's eyes. His flesh pinkened. "Ah, a bit a sport the lads are having now." He smiled at Ellen Coughlin down the other end of the table. "A bit of sport," he repeated and cut into his roast pork.

"So what's the guess, Eddie?" Captain Coughlin speared a potato slice.

Eddie McKenna looked up. "I'll have to give Mr. Laurence a bit more thought before I hazard any more idle conjecture on that point."

Luther turned back to the coffee tray, but not before he caught another look from Danny. Not an entirely pleasant look, one bearing a hint of pity.

Luther shrugged into his topcoat as he came out onto the stoop and saw Danny leaning against the hood of a nut-brown Oakland 49. Danny raised a bottle of something in Luther's direction, and when Luther reached the street he saw that it was whiskey, the good stuff, prewar.

"A drink, Mr. Laurence?"

Luther took the bottle from Danny and raised it to his lips. He paused, looking at him, making sure sharing a bottle with a colored was what the man wanted. Danny gave him a quizzical arch of his eyebrow, and Luther tilted the bottle to his lips and drank.

When Luther handed it back, the big cop didn't wipe the bottle with his sleeve, just tilted it to his own lips and took himself a healthy snort. "Good stuff, uh?"

Luther remembered how Avery Wallace had said this Coughlin was a strange who did his own thinking. He nodded.

"Nice night."

"Yeah." Crisp but windless, the air a bit chalky with the dust of dead leaves.

"Another?" Danny handed the bottle back.

Luther took a drink, eyeing the big white man and his open, handsome face. A lady-killer, Luther bet, but not the kind to make it his life's work. Something going on behind those eyes that told Luther this man heard music others didn't, took direction from who knew where.

"You like working here?"

Luther nodded. "I do. You've a nice family, suh."

Danny rolled his eyes and took another swig. "Think you could drop the 'suh' shit with me, Mr. Laurence? Think that's possible?"

Luther took a step back. "What do you want me to call you then?"

"Out here? Danny'll do. In there?" He gestured with his chin at the house. "I guess Mr. Coughlin."

"What's your complaint against 'suh'?"

Danny shrugged. "It sounds like bullshit."

"Fair enough. You call me Luther, then."

Danny nodded. "Drink to it."

Luther chuckled as he lifted the bottle. "Avery warned me you were different."

"Avery came back from the grave to tell you I was different?"

Luther shook his head. "He wrote a note to his 'replacement.'"

"Ah." Danny took the bottle back. "Whatta you think about my Uncle Eddie?"

"Seems nice enough."

"No, he doesn't." Danny's voice was soft.

Luther leaned against the car beside Danny. "No, he doesn't."

"You feel him circling you in there?"

"I felt it."

"You got a nice clean past, Luther?"

"Clean as most, I guess."

"That ain't too clean."

Luther smiled. "Fair point."

Danny handed the bottle over again. "My Uncle Eddie? He reads people better than any man alive. Stares right through their heads and sees whatever it is they don't want the world to find out. They got a suspect in one of the station houses nobody can break? They call in my uncle. He gets a confession every time. Uses whatever it takes to get one, too."

Luther rolled the bottle between his palms. "Why you telling me this?"

"He smells something he doesn't like about you—I can see it in his eyes—and we took that joke in there too far for his comfort. He started thinking we were laughing *at* him and that's not good."

"I appreciate the liquor." Luther stepped away from the car. "Never shared a bottle with a white man before." He shrugged. "But I best be getting home."

"I'm not working you."

"You ain't, uh?" Luther looked at him. "How do I know that?"

Danny held out his hands. "Only two types of men in this world worth talking about—a man who is as he appears and the other kind. Which do you think I am?"

Luther felt the whiskey swimming beneath his flesh. "You about the strangest kind I've come across in this city."

Danny took a drink, looked up at the stars. "Eddie might circle you for a year, even two. He'll take all the time in the world, believe me. But when he finally *does* come for you? He'll have left you no way out." He met Luther's eyes. "I've made my peace with whatever Eddie and my father do to achieve their ends with plug-uglies and grifters and gunsels, but I don't like it when they go after civilians. You understand?"

Luther placed his hands in his pockets as the crisp air grew darker, colder. "So you're saying you can call off this dog?"

Danny shrugged. "Maybe. Won't know until the time comes."

Luther nodded. "And what's your end?"

Danny smiled. "My end?"

Luther found himself smiling in return, feeling both of *them* circling now, but having fun with it. "Ain't nothing free in this world but bad luck."

"Nora," Danny said.

Luther stepped back to the car and took the bottle from Danny. "What about her?"

"I'd like to know how things progress with her and my brother."

Luther drank, eyeing Danny, then let loose a laugh.

"What?"

"Man's in love with his brother's girl and he says 'what' to me." Luther laughed some more.

Danny joined him. "Let's say Nora and I have a history."

"That ain't news," Luther said. "I only been in the same room with you both this one time but my blind, dead uncle could have seen it."

"That obvious, uh?"

"To most. Can't figure out why Mr. Connor can't see it. He can't see a lot when it comes to her."

"No, he can't."

"Why don't you just ask the woman for her hand? She'll jump at it."

"No, she won't. Believe me."

"She will. That rope? Shit. That's love."

Danny shook his head. "You ever known a woman acted logically when it came to love?"

"No."

"Well, then." Danny looked up at the house. "I don't know the first thing about them. Can't tell you what they're thinking from minute to minute."

Luther smiled and shook his head. "I 'spect you get along just fine all the same."

Danny held up the bottle. "We got about two fingers left. Last swig?"

"Don't mind if I do." Luther took a snort and handed the bottle back, watched Danny drain it. "I'll keep my eyes and ears open. How's that?"

"Fair. Eddie makes a run at you, you keep me informed."

Luther held out his hand. "Deal."

Danny shook his hand. "Glad we could get to know each other, Luther."

"The same, Danny."

Back at the building on Shawmut Avenue, Luther checked and re-checked for leaks, but nothing came down through the ceilings, and he found no moisture in the walls. He ripped all the plaster out, first thing, and saw that plenty of the wood behind it could be salvaged, some with little more than hope and tenderness, but hope and tenderness would have to do. Same with the flooring and the staircase. Normally a place that had been this fucked-up by neglect and then fire and water damage, the first thing you'd do would be to gut it to its skin. But given their limited finances and beg-borrow-steal approach, the only solution in this case was to salvage what could be salvaged, right down to the nails themselves. He and Clayton Tomes, the Wagenfelds' houseman, worked similar hours in their South Boston-households and even had the same day off. After one dinner with Yvette Giddreaux, Clayton had been enlisted into the project before he knew what hit him, and that weekend, Luther finally had some help. They spent the day carrying the salvageable wood and metal and brass fixtures up to the third floor so they could get to work on installing the plumbing and electrical next week.

It was hard work. Dusty and sweaty and chalky. The pull of pry bars and the tear of wood and the wrench of the hammer's claw. Kind of work made your shoulders tighten hard against your neck, the cartilage under your kneecaps feel like rock salt, dug hot stones into the small of your back and bit the edges of your spine. Kind of work made a man sit down in the middle of a dusty floor and lower his head to his knees and whisper, "Whew," and keep his head down and his eyes closed a bit longer.

After weeks in the Coughlin house doing almost nothing, though, Luther wouldn't have traded it for anything. This was work of the hand and of the mind and of muscle. Work that left some hint of itself and yourself behind after you were gone.

Craftsmanship, his Uncle Cornelius had once told him, was just a fancy word for what happened when labor met love.

"Shit." Clayton, lying on his back in the entrance hallway, stared up at the ceiling two stories above. "You realize that if she's committed to indoor plumbing—"

"She is."

"—then the waste pipe, Luther—the waste pipe *alone*—that going to have to climb up from the basement to a roof vent? That's four stories, boy."

"Five-inch pipe, too." Luther chuckled. "Cast iron."

"And we got to run *more* pipes off *that* pipe on every floor? Two maybe off the bathrooms?" Clayton's eyes widened to saucers. "Luther, this shit's *crazy.*"

"Yeah."

"Then why you smiling?"

"Why you?" Luther said.

What about Danny?" Luther asked Nora as they walked through Haymarket.

"What about him?"

"He doesn't seem to fit that family somehow."

"I'm not sure Aiden fits anything."

"How come sometimes you-all call him Danny and other times Aiden?"

She shrugged. "It just happened. You don't call him *Mister* Danny, I've noticed."

"So?"

"You call Connor 'Mister.' You even do it with Joe."

"Danny told me not to call him 'Mister,' 'less we were in company."

"Fast friends you are, yeah?"

Shit. Luther hoped he hadn't tipped his hand. "Don't know I'd call us friends."

308

"But you like him. It's clear on your face."

"He's different. Not sure I ever met a white man quite like him. Never met a white woman quite like you, though."

"I'm not white, Luther. I'm Irish."

"Yeah? What color they?"

She smiled. "Potato-gray."

Luther laughed and pointed at himself. "Sandpaper-brown. Pleased to meet you."

Nora gave him a quick curtsy. "A pleasure, sir."

After one of the Sunday dinners, McKenna insisted on driving Luther home, and Luther, shrugging into his coat in the hall, couldn't think of a reply quick enough.

" 'Tis awful cold," McKenna said, "and I promised Mary Pat I'd be home before the cows." He stood from the table and kissed Mrs. Coughlin on the cheek. "Would you pull my coat from the hook, Luther? There's a fine lad."

Danny wasn't at this dinner and Luther looked around the room, saw that no one else was paying much attention.

"Ah, we'll see you soon, folks."

" 'Night, Eddie," Thomas Coughlin said. " 'Night, Luther."

" 'Night, sir," Luther said.

Eddie drove down East Broadway and turned right on West Broadway where, even on a cold Sunday night, the atmosphere was as raucous and unpredictable as anything in Greenwood had been on a Friday night. Dice games being played out in the open, whores leaning out of windowsills, loud music from every saloon, and there were so many saloons you couldn't count them all. Progress, even in a big, heavy car, was slow.

"Ohio?" McKenna said.

Luther smiled. "Yes, sir. You were close with Kentucky. I figured you'd get it that night, but . . ."

"Ah, I knew it." McKenna snapped his fingers. "Just the wrong side of the river. Which town?"

Outside, the noise of West Broadway dunned the car and

the lights of it melted across the windshield like ice cream. "Just outside Columbus, sir."

"Ever been in a police car before?"

"Never, suh."

McKenna chuckled loud, as if he were spitting rocks. "Ah, Luther, you may find this hard to believe but before Tom Coughlin and I became brothers of the badge, we spent a fair amount of time on the wrong side of the law. Saw us some paddy wagons we did and, sure, no small amount of Friday-night drunk tanks." He waved his hand. "It's the way of things for the immigrant class, this oat sowing, this figuring out of the mores. I just assumed you'd taken part in the same rituals."

"I'm not an immigrant, suh."

McKenna looked over at him. "What's that?"

"I was born here, suh."

"What's that supposed to mean?"

"It doesn't mean anything. It's just . . . you said it was the way of things for immigrants, and that may be so, but I was saying that I'm not—"

"What may be so?"

"Sir?"

"What may be so?" McKenna smiled at him as they rolled under a streetlight.

"Suh, I don't know what you—"

"You *said*."

"Suh?"

"You *said*. You said jail may be the way of things for immigrants."

"No, suh, I didn't."

McKenna tugged on his earlobe. "Me head must be filled with the wax then."

Luther said nothing, just stared out the windshield as they stopped at a light at the corner of D and West Broadway.

"Do you have something against immigrants?" Eddie McKenna said.

"No, suh. No."

"Think we haven't earned our seat at the table yet?"

"No."

"Supposed to wait for our children's children to achieve that honor on our behalf, are we?"

"Suh, I never meant to—"

McKenna wagged a finger at Luther and laughed loudly. "I got you there, Luther. I pulled your leg there, I did." He slapped Luther's knee and let loose another hearty laugh as the light turned green. He continued up Broadway.

"Good one, suh. You sure had me."

"I sho' did!" McKenna said and slapped the dashboard. They drove over the Broadway Bridge. "Do you like working for the Coughlins?"

"I do, suh, yes."

"And the Giddreauxs?"

"Suh?"

"The Giddreauxs, son. You don't think I know of them? Isaiah's quite the high-toned-Negroid-celebrity up in these parts. Has the ear of Du Bois, they say. Has a vision of colored equality, of all things, in our fair city. Won't that be something?"

"Yes, suh."

"Sure, that'd be grand stuff indeed." He smiled the warmest of smiles. "Of course, you'd find some folk who would argue the Giddreauxs are not friends to your people. That they are, in fact, enemies. That they will push this dream of equality to a dire conclusion, and the blood of your race will flood these streets. That's what some would say." He placed a hand to his own chest. "Some. Not all, not all. 'Tis a shame there has to be so much discord in this world. Don't you think?"

"Yes, suh."

"A tragic shame." McKenna shook his head and tsk-tsked as he turned onto St. Botolph Street. "Your family?"

"Suh?"

McKenna peered at the doors of the homes as he rolled

slowly up the street. "Did you leave family behind in Canton?"

"Columbus, suh."

"Columbus, right."

"No, suh. Just me."

"What brought you all the way to Boston, then?"

"That's the one."

"Huh?"

"The Giddreauxs' house, suh, you just passed it."

McKenna applied the brakes. "Well, then," he said. "Another time."

"I look forward to it, suh."

"Stay warm, Luther! Bundle up!"

"I will. Thank you, suh." Luther climbed out of the car. He walked around behind it and reached the sidewalk, hearing McKenna's window roll down as he did.

"You read about it," McKenna said.

Luther turned. "Which, suh?"

"Boston!" McKenna's eyebrows were raised happily.

"Not really, sir."

McKenna nodded, as if it all made perfect sense to him. "Eight hundred miles."

"Suh?"

"The distance," McKenna said, "between Boston and Columbus." He patted his car door. "Good night to you, Luther."

"Good night, suh."

Luther stood on the sidewalk and watched McKenna drive off. He raised his arms and got a look at his hands—shaking, but not too bad. Not too bad at all. Considering.

CHAPTER *seventeen*

Danny met Steve Coyle for a drink at the Warren Tavern in the middle of a Sunday afternoon, the day more winter than autumn. Steve made several jokes about Danny's beard and asked him about his case, even though Danny had to repeat, with apologies, that he couldn't discuss an open investigation with a civilian.

"But it's me," Steve said, then held up a hand. "Just kidding, just kidding. I understand." He gave Danny a smile that was huge and weak at the same time. "I do."

So they talked about old cases, old days, old times. Danny had one drink for every three Steve had. Steve lived in the West End these days in a windowless room of a rooming-house basement that had been partitioned into six sections, all of which smelled thickly of coal.

"No indoor plumbing still," Steve said. "Believe that? Out to the shed in the backyard like it was 1910. Like we're in western Mass., or jigaboos." He shook his head. "And if you're not in the house by eleven? The old geezer locks you out for the night. Some way to live." He gave Danny his big weak smile again and drank some more. "Soon as I get my cart, though? Things'll change, I'll tell you that."

Steve's latest employment plan involved setting up a fruit cart outside Faneuil Hall Marketplace. The fact that there were already a dozen such carts owned by some very violent, if not outright vicious, men didn't seem to dissuade him. The fact

313

that the fruit wholesalers were so leery toward new operators they charged "inaugural" rates for the first six months, which made it impossible to break even, was something Steve dismissed as "hearsay." The fact that City Hall had stopped giving out merchant medallions for that area two years ago didn't trouble him either. "All the people I know at the Hall?" he'd said to Danny. "Hell, they'll pay *me* to set up shop."

Danny didn't point out that two weeks earlier Steve had told Danny he was the only person from the old days who answered his calls. He just nodded and smiled his encouragement. What else could you do?

"Another?" Steve said.

Danny looked at his watch. He was meeting Nathan Bishop for dinner at seven. He shook his head. "Can't do it."

Steve, who'd already signaled the bartender, covered the dejection that flashed across his eyes with his too-big smile and a laugh-bark. "All set, Kevin."

The bartender scowled and removed his hand from the tap. "You owe me a dollar twenty, Coyle. And you best have it this time, rummy."

Steve patted his pockets but Danny said, "I got it."

"You sure?"

"Sure." Danny slid out of the booth and approached the bar. "Hey, Kevin. Got a sec'?"

The bartender came over like he was doing a favor. "What?"

Danny placed the dollar and four nickels on the bar. "For you."

"Must be my birthday."

When he reached for the money, Danny caught his wrist and pulled it toward him.

"Smile or I break it."

"What?"

"Smile like we're chatting about the Sox or I'll break your fucking wrist."

Kevin smiled, his jaw clenched, eyes starting to bulge.

"I ever hear you call my friend 'rummy' again, you fucking

bartender, I'll knock out all your teeth and feed them back to you through your ass."

"I—"

Danny twisted the flesh in his hand. "Don't you do a fucking thing but nod."

Kevin bit his lower lip and nodded four times.

"And his next round's on the house," Danny said and let go of his wrist.

They walked up Hanover in the fading of the day's light. Danny planned to slip into his rooming house and grab a few pieces of warmer clothing to bring back to his cover apartment. Steve said he just wanted to wander through his old neighborhood. They'd reached Prince Street when crowds ran past them toward Salem Street. When they reached the corner where Danny's building stood, they saw a sea of people surrounding a black Hudson Super Six, a few men and several boys jumping on and off the running boards and the hood.

"What the hell?" Steve said.

"Officer Danny! Officer Danny!" Mrs. DiMassi waved frantically at him from the stoop. Danny lowered his head for a moment—weeks of undercover work possibly blown because an old woman recognized him, beard and all, from twenty yards away. Through the throng, Danny saw that the driver of the car had a straw hat, as did the passenger.

"They try and take my niece," Mrs. DiMassi said when he and Steve reached her. "They try and take Arabella."

Danny, with a fresh angle on the car, could see Rayme Finch behind the wheel, tooting the horn as he tried to move the car forward.

The crowd wasn't having it. They weren't throwing anything yet, but they were yelling and clenching their fists and shouting curses in Italian. Danny saw two members of the Black Hand moving along the edges of the mob.

"She's in the car?" Danny said.

"In back," Mrs. DiMassi cried. "They take her."

Danny gave her hand a tug of encouragement and began pushing his way through the crowd. Finch's eyes met his and narrowed. After about ten seconds, recognition found Finch's face. It was quickly replaced, though. Not with fear of the crowd, just stubborn determination as he kept the car in gear and tried to inch forward.

Someone pushed Danny, and he almost lost his balance but was buffeted by a pair of middle-aged women with beefy arms. A kid climbed a streetlamp pole with an orange in his hand. If the kid had a decent throwing arm this would get scary fast.

Danny reached the car, and Finch cracked the window. Arabella was curled up on the backseat, her eyes wide, her fingers grasping her crucifix, her lips moving in prayer.

"Get her out," Danny said.

"Move the crowd."

"You want a riot?" Danny said.

"You want some dead Italians in the street?" Finch banged on the horn with his fist. "Get them the fuck out of the way, Coughlin."

"This girl knows nothing about anarchists," Danny said.

"She was *seen* with Federico Ficara."

Danny looked in at Arabella. She looked back at him with eyes that comprehended nothing except the growing fury of the mob. An elbow pushed off Danny's lower back and he was pressed hard against the car.

"Steve!" he called. "You back there?"

"About ten feet."

"Can you get me some room?"

"Have to use my cane."

"Fine with me." Danny turned back, pressed his face into the crack of window Rayme Finch had afforded him, and said, "You saw her with Federico?"

"Yes."

"When?"

"About half an hour ago. Down by the bread factory."

"You personally?"

"No. Another agent. Federico ducked him, but we got a positive ID on this girl."

The top of someone's head drove itself into Danny's back. He swatted at it, tagged a chin.

He pressed his lips to the window crack. "If you leave with her, and then return her to the neighborhood, Finch? She will be assassinated. You hear me? You're killing her. Let her out. Let me handle it." Another body jostled his back and a man climbed up on the hood. "I can barely breathe out here."

Finch said, "We can't back down now."

A second guy climbed on the hood and the car began to rock.

"Finch! You've already fucked her by putting her in the car. Some people are going to think she *is* an informant, no matter what. But we can save this situation if you let her out now. Otherwise . . ." Another body slammed into Danny's. "Jesus, Finch! Unlock the fucking door."

"You and me are going to have a talk."

"Fine. We'll talk. Open the door."

Finch gave him one last long look to let him know this wasn't over, not by a damn sight, and then he reached back and unlocked the rear door and Danny got his hand on the handle and turned to the crowd. "There's been a mistake. *Ci è stato un errore.* Back up. *Sostegno! Sostegno!* She's coming out. *Sta uscendo.* Back up. *Sostegno!*"

To his surprise, the crowd took a few steps back and Danny opened the door and pulled the shaking girl across the seat. Several people let out whoops and claps, and Danny hugged Arabella to his body and headed for the sidewalk. She clutched her hands to her chest and Danny could feel something hard and square under her arms. He looked in her eyes, but all he saw there was fear.

Danny held tight to Arabella and nodded his thanks to the people he passed. He gave Finch one last look and gestured up the street with his head. Another smattering of cheers broke out and the crowd began to thin around the car. Finch nudged the car forward a few feet and the mob backed up farther and the tires rolled. Then the first orange hit. The fruit was cold and sounded more like a rock. That was followed by an apple, then a potato, and then the car was pelted with fruit and vegetables. But it made steady progress up Salem Street. Some urchins ran alongside, shouting at it, but there were smiles on their faces and the jeers from the crowd had a festive air to them.

Danny reached the sidewalk and Mrs. DiMassi took her niece from him and led her toward the stairs. Danny watched the taillights of Finch's Hudson reach the corner. Steve Coyle stood beside him, wiping his head with a handkerchief and looking out at the street littered with half-frozen fruit.

"Calls for a drink, uh?" He handed Danny his flask.

Danny took a drink but said nothing. He looked at Arabella Mosca huddled in her aunt's arms. He wondered whose side he was on anymore.

"I'm going to need to talk to her, Mrs. DiMassi."

Mrs. DiMassi looked up into his face.

"Now," he said.

Arabella Mosca was a small woman with wide almond eyes and short blue-black hair. She didn't speak a word of English outside of *hello*, *good-bye*, and *thank you*. She sat on the couch in her aunt's sitting room, her hands still clenched within Mrs. DiMassi's, and she had yet to remove her coat.

Danny said to Mrs. DiMassi, "Could you ask her what she's hiding beneath her coat?"

Mrs. DiMassi glanced at her niece's coat and frowned. She pointed and asked her to open her coat.

Arabella tilted her chin down toward her chest and shook her head vehemently.

"Please," Danny said.

Mrs. DiMassi wasn't the type to say "please" to a younger

relative. Instead, she slapped her. Arabella barely reacted. She lowered her head farther and shook it again. Mrs. DiMassi reared back on the couch and cocked her arm.

Danny stuck his upper body between them. "Arabella," he said in halting Italian, "they will deport your husband."

Her chin came off her chest.

He nodded. "The men in straw hats. They will."

A torrent of Italian flew from Arabella's mouth and Mrs. DiMassi held up a hand, Arabella talking so fast even she seemed to be having trouble following. She turned to Danny.

"She said they can't do this. He has job."

"He's an illegal," Danny said.

"Bah," she said. "Half this neighborhood illegal. They deport everyone?"

Danny shook his head. "Just the ones who annoy them. Tell her."

Mrs. DiMassi held her hand out below Arabella's chin. *"Dammi quel che tieni sotto il cappotto, o tuo marito passera'il prossimo Natale a Palermo."*

Arabella said, "No, no, no."

Mrs. DiMassi cocked her arm again and spoke as fast as Arabella. *"Questi Americani ci trattano come cani. Non ti permettero'di umiliarmi dinanzi ad uno di loro. Apri il cappotto, o te lo strappo di dosso!"*

Whatever she said—Danny caught "American dogs" and "don't disgrace me"—it worked. Arabella opened her coat and removed a white paper bag. She handed it to Mrs. DiMassi who handed it to Danny.

Danny looked inside and saw a stack of paper. He pulled out the top sheet:

While you rest and kneel, we worked. We executed.
This is the beginning, not the end. Never the end.
Your childish god and childish blood run to the sea.
Your childish world is next.

319

Danny showed the note to Steve and said to Mrs. DiMassi, "When was she supposed to distribute these?"

Mrs. DiMassi spoke to her niece. Arabella started to shake her head, then stopped. She whispered a word to Mrs. DiMassi who turned back to Danny. "Sundown."

He turned back to Steve. "How many churches have a late mass?"

"In the North End? Two, maybe three. Why?"

Danny pointed at the note. " 'While you rest and kneel.' Yeah?"

Steve shook his head. "No."

"You rest on the Sabbath," Danny said. "You kneel in church. And at the end—your blood runs to the sea. Gotta be a church near the waterfront."

Steve went to Mrs. DiMassi's phone. "I'm calling it in. What's your guess?"

"There's only two churches that fit. Saint Teresa's and Saint Thomas's."

"Saint Thomas doesn't have an evening mass."

Danny headed for the door. "You'll catch up?"

Steve smiled, phone to his ear. "Me and my cane, sure." He waved Danny off. "Go, go. And, Dan?"

Danny paused at the door. "Yeah?"

"Shoot first," he said. "And shoot often."

St. Teresa's stood at the corner of Fleet and Atlantic across from Lewis Wharf. One of the oldest churches in the North End, it was small and starting to crumble. Danny bent to catch his breath, his shirt drenched in sweat from his run. He pulled his watch from his pocket: five-forty-eight. Mass would end soon. If, like Salutation, the bomb was in the basement, about the only thing to do would be to rush into the church and order everyone out. Steve had made the call, so the bomb squad couldn't be far off. But if the bomb was in the basement, why hadn't it detonated? Parishioners had been in there for over forty-five minutes. Ample time to blow out the floor beneath them. . . .

Danny heard it then, off in the distance, the first siren, the first patrol car leaving the Oh-One, surely followed by others.

The intersection was quiet, empty—a few jalopies parked in front of the church, none of them more than a step removed from a horse-drawn cart, though a couple had been maintained with pride. He scanned the rooftops across the street, thinking: Why a church? Even for anarchists, it seemed political suicide, especially in the North End. Then he remembered that the only reason any churches in the neighborhood offered early-evening mass had been to cater to workers deemed so "essential" during the war they couldn't be afforded a day off on the Sabbath. "Essential" meant some connection, however broad, to the military—men and women who worked with arms, steel, rubber, or industrial alcohol. So this church wasn't just a church, it was a military target.

Inside the church, dozens of voices rose in hymn. He had no choice—get the people out. Why the bomb hadn't gone off yet, he couldn't say. Maybe he was a week early. Maybe the bomber was having trouble with the detonation—anarchists often did. There were dozens of plausible reasons for the lack of an explosion, but none of them would mean shit if he let the worshippers die. Get them to safety, *then* worry about questions or possible egg on his face. For now, just get them the fuck out.

He started across the street and noticed that one of the jalopies was double-parked.

There was no need for it. There were plenty of spaces on both sides of the street. The only stretch of curb that wasn't free was directly in front of the church. And that's where the car was double-parked. It was an old Rambler 63 coupe, probably 1911 or '12. Danny paused in the middle of the street, just froze as the skin along his throat and under his arms grew clammy. He expelled a breath and moved again, quicker now. As he drew closer to the car, he could see the driver slouched low behind the wheel, a dark hat pulled down his forehead. The sound of the siren grew sharper and was joined by several more. The driver sat up. His left hand was on the wheel. Danny couldn't see his right.

Inside the church, the hymn ended.

The driver cocked his head and turned his face toward the street.

Federico. No gray in his hair anymore, and he'd shaved his mustache, his features somehow leaner because of the changes, hungrier.

He saw Danny but his eyes didn't display recognition, just a vague curiosity at this large Bolshevik with the beastly beard crossing a street in the North End.

The doors to the church opened.

The lead siren sounded like it was a block away. A boy came out of a shop four doors down, a tweed scally cap on his head, something under his arm.

Danny reached into his coat. Federico's eyes locked on Danny's.

Danny pulled his gun from his coat as Federico reached for something on the car seat.

The first parishioners reached the church steps.

Danny waved his gun. He shouted, "Get back inside!"

No one seemed to realize he was talking to them. Danny stepped to his left, swung his arm, and fired a round into Federico's windshield.

On the church steps, several people screamed.

Danny fired a second time and the windshield shattered.

"Back inside!"

Something hot hissed just beneath his earlobe. He saw a white muzzle flash off to his left—the boy, firing a pistol at him. Federico's door popped open; he held up a stick of dynamite, the wick sparking. Danny cupped his elbow in his hand and shot Federico in the left kneecap. Federico yelped and fell against the car. The stick of dynamite dropped onto the front seat.

Danny was close enough now to see the other sticks piled in the backseat, two or three bundles of them.

A chunk of cobblestone spit off the street. He ducked and fired back at the boy. The boy hit the ground and his cap fell off and long caramel hair cascaded out from under it as the boy rolled under a car. No boy. Tessa. Out of the corner of his eye, he saw movement from the Rambler and he fired again. The bullet hit the running board, an embarrassing shot, and then his revolver clicked on empty. He found bullets in his pocket and emptied his shells onto the street. He ran in a crouch over to a streetlamp pole and placed his shoulder to it and tried to reload his revolver with shaking hands as bullets thunked off the cars nearest to him and hit the lamp pole.

In a plaintive, despairing voice, Tessa called Federico's name and then shouted, "*Scappa, scappa, amore mio! Mettiti in salvo! Scappa!*"

Federico twisted his way off the front seat, his good knee hitting the street, and Danny stepped from behind the lamp pole and fired. The first shot hit the door, but the second caught Federico in the ass. Again, the strange yelp as the blood sprouted and darkened the back of his pants. He flopped against the seat and crawled back inside. Danny got a sudden flash of the two of them in Federico's apartment, Federico smiling that warm and glorious smile of his. He pushed the image away as Tessa screamed, a guttural wail of broken hope. She had both hands on the pistol when she fired. Danny dove to his left and rolled on the street. The rounds ripped up the cobblestone, and he kept rolling until he reached a car on the other side of the street and heard Tessa's revolver dry-fire. Federico lunged out of the Rambler. He arched his back and turned. He pushed off the car door, and Danny shot him in the stomach. Federico fell back into the Rambler. The door closed against his legs.

Danny fired where he'd last seen Tessa, but she wasn't there anymore. She'd run several doors down from the church, and she pressed a hand to her hip and the hand was red. Tears poured down her face, and her mouth was open in a noise-less howl. As the first prowl car came around the corner, Danny gave her one last look and ran toward the cruiser with his hands raised, trying to wave it off before it got too close.

The blast bubbled outward as if it came from under water. The first wave knocked Danny's legs out from under him and he landed in the gutter and watched the Rambler jump four feet in the air. It came back to earth almost exactly where it had left it. The windows blew out, and the wheels collapsed, and a portion of the roof peeled back like a can. The front steps of the church splintered and disgorged limestone. The heavy wooden doors fell off their hinges. The stained glass windows collapsed. Debris and white dust floated in the air. Flames poured out of the car. Flames and oily black smoke. Danny stood. He could feel blood dripping out of his ears.

A face loomed in front of his. The face was familiar. The face mouthed his name. Danny held up his hands, one of them still holding his revolver. The cop—Danny remembered his name now, Officer Glen Something, Glen Patchett—shook his head: No, you keep your gun.

Danny lowered the gun and placed it in his coat. The heat of the flames found his face. He could see Federico in there, blackened and afire, leaning against the passenger door, as if sleeping, a guy along for a drive. With his eyes closed, he reminded Danny of that first night they'd broken bread together, when Federico, seemingly enraptured by music, had closed his eyes and mock-conducted the music spilling from his phonograph. People began to exit the church, coming around from the sides, and Danny could hear them suddenly, as if from the bottom of a hole a mile deep.

He turned to Glen, "If you can hear me, nod."

Patchett gave him a curious look but nodded.

"Put out an APB on a Tessa Ficara. Twenty years old. Italian. Five five, long brown hair. She's bleeding from the right hip. Glen? She's dressed as a boy. Tweed knickers,

324

plaid shirt, suspenders, brown work shoes. You got that?"

Patchett scribbled in his notebook. He nodded.

"Armed and dangerous," Danny said.

More scribbling.

His left ear canal opened with a pop, and more blood sluiced down his neck, but now he could hear and the sounds were sudden and painful. He placed a hand to the ear. "Fuck!"

"You hear me now?"

"Yeah, Glen. Yeah."

"Who's the crisper in the car?"

"Federico Ficara. He's got federal warrants out on him. You probably heard about him at roll call about a month ago. Bomber."

"Dead bomber. You shoot him?"

"Three times," Danny said.

Glen looked at all the white dust and debris as it fell into their hair, onto their faces. "Hell of a way to fuck up a Sunday."

Eddie McKenna arrived on-scene about ten minutes after the explosion. Danny sat amid the rubble on what remained of the church steps and listened as his godfather talked to Fenton, the Bomb Squad sergeant.

"Best we can figure, Eddie? The plan was to detonate the dynamite in the car once all the people were out front, you know, milling about for ten minutes afterward, the way these people do. But when the wops start coming out of the church, Coughlin's kid over there yells at them to go back inside. Makes his point by discharging his weapon. So the people run back inside and Coughlin starts firing at the asshole in the Rambler. Someone else comes into play around then— I'm hearing from Tactical that it's a woman, believe that?—and he's drawing her fire, too, but hell if he's letting that asshole out of the car. Makes him blow up with his own bombs."

"A delicious irony, that," McKenna said. "Special Squads will take over from here, Sergeant."

"Tell that to Tactical."

"Oh, I will. Rest assured." He placed a hand on Fenton's shoulder before he could walk off. "In your professional opinion, Sergeant, what would have happened if that bomb had gone off while the parishioners congregated on the street?"

"Twenty dead minimum. Maybe thirty. The rest wounded, maimed, what have you."

"What have you, indeed," McKenna said. He walked over to Danny, shaking his head with a smile. "You have so much as a scratch?"

"Doesn't appear so," Danny said. "Fucking ears hurt like hell, though."

"First Salutation, then working the flu like you did, and now this?" McKenna sat on the church steps and hitched his pant legs at the knee. "How many near misses can one man have, boy?"

"Apparently, I'm putting the question to the test."

"Rumor is you winged her. This Tessa cunt."

Danny nodded. "Caught her in the right hip. Mighta been my bullet, mighta been ricochet."

"You got dinner in an hour, don't you?" McKenna said.

Danny cocked his head. "You don't honestly expect me to go, do you?"

"Why not?"

"The guy I'm supposed to meet for dinner is probably sewing Tessa up as we speak."

McKenna shook his head. "She's a soldier, she is. She shan't panic and cross the city before full dark while she's bleeding. She's holed up somewhere right now." His eyes scanned the buildings around them. "Probably still in this neighborhood. I'll put a major presence on the street tonight; it should pin her in. At least it'll keep her from traveling far. Also, your friend Nathan is hardly the only dirty doctor in the game. So

I think the dinner should go ahead as planned. Sure now, it's a calculated risk, but one worth taking."

Danny searched his face for the joke.

"You're *this* close," McKenna said. "Bishop asked for your writing. You gave it to him. Now he's asked you to dinner. Fraina, I bet you all the gold in Ireland, will be there."

"We don't know that for—"

"We do," McKenna said. "We can infer it. And if all the stars align and Fraina takes you up to the offices of *Revolutionary Age*?"

"What? You want me to just say, 'Hey, while we're all chummy, mind giving me the mailing list of your entire organization?' Something like that?"

"Steal it," McKenna said.

"What?"

"If you get inside the offices, fucking steal it, lad."

Danny stood, his balance still a little off, one of his ears still plugged up. "What is so all-important about these lists?"

"They're a way to keep tabs."

"Tabs."

McKenna nodded.

"You're so full of shit you could fill a barn." Danny walked down the steps. "And I'm not going to be anywhere near the offices. We're meeting in a restaurant."

McKenna smiled. "All right, all right. Special Squads will give you some insurance, make sure these Bolshies don't even think of looking at you funny for a couple of days. Will that make you happy?"

"What kind of insurance?"

"You know Hamilton from my squad, yes?"

Danny nodded. Jerry Hamilton. Jersey Jerry. A goon; all that separated him from a prison cell was a badge.

"I know Hamilton."

"Good. Keep your eyes peeled tonight and be on the ready."

"For what?"

"You'll know it when it happens, believe you me." McKenna stood and slapped at the white dust on his pants. It had been falling steadily since the explosion. "Now go and clean yourself up. You've got tracks of blood running down your neck. You've got this dust all over you, you do. Covering your hair, your face. Look like one of them Bushmen I've seen in the picture books."

CHAPTER *eighteen*

When Danny arrived at the restaurant, he found the door locked and the windows shuttered.

It's closed on Sundays." Nathan Bishop stepped out of a darkened doorway into the weak yellow light cast by the nearest street-lamp. "My mistake."

Danny looked up and down the empty street. "Where's Comrade Fraina?"

"At the other place."

"What other place?"

Nathan frowned. "The other place we're going."

"Oh."

"Because this place was closed."

"Right."

"Have you always suffered Mongoloidism, or did you just come down with it?"

"Always."

Nathan held out his hand. "Car's across the street."

Danny saw it now—an Olds Model M, Pyotr Glaviach behind the wheel looking straight ahead. He turned the key, and the rumble of the heavy engine echoed up the street.

Nathan, walking toward the car, looked back over his shoulder. "You coming?"

Danny hoped McKenna's men were somewhere he couldn't see, watching, not boozing it up in a bar around the corner until they decided to stroll on over to the restaurant and make whatever move they had planned. He could picture it—Jersey Jerry and some other thug with a tin shield, both of them standing outside the darkened restaurant, one of them looking at the address he'd written on his own hand, then shaking his head with a five-year-old's befuddlement.

Danny stepped off the curb and walked toward the car.

They drove a few blocks and then turned onto Harrison as a light rain fell. Pyotr Glaviach turned on his wipers. Like the rest of the car, they were heavy things, and the back-and-forth slap of them found Danny's chest.

"Quiet tonight," Nathan said.

Danny looked out at Harrison Avenue, its empty sidewalks. "Yeah. Well, it's Sunday."

"I was talking about you."

The restaurant was called Oktober, the name appearing solely on the door in red lettering so small that Danny had passed it several times over the last couple of months without ever knowing it was there. Three tables inside, and only one of them was set. Nathan led Danny to it.

Pyotr threw the lock on the front door and then took a seat by it, his large hands lying in his lap like sleeping dogs.

Louis Fraina stood at the tiny bar, speaking rapidly on the phone in Russian. He nodded a lot and scribbled furiously in a notepad as the barmaid, a heavyset woman in her sixties, brought Nathan and Danny a bottle of vodka and a basket of brown bread. Nathan poured them each a drink and then raised his in toast. Danny did the same.

"Cheers," Nathan said.

"What? No Russian?"

"Good Lord, no. You know what Russians call Westerners who can speak Russian?"

Danny shook his head.

"Spies." Nathan poured them a refill and seemed to read Danny's thoughts. "You know why Louis is an exception?"

"Why?"

"Because he's Louis. Try the bread. It's good."

From the bar, an explosion of Russian, followed by a surprisingly hearty laugh, and then Louis Fraina hung up the phone. He came to the table and poured himself a drink.

"Good evening, gentlemen. Glad you could make it."

"Evening, Comrade," Danny said.

"The writer." Louis Fraina held out his hand.

Danny shook it. Fraina's grip was firm but not to the point of trying to prove anything. "Pleased to meet you, Comrade."

Fraina sat and poured himself another vodka. "Let's dispense with the 'Comrade' for now. I've read your work, so I don't doubt your ideological commitment."

"Okay."

Fraina smiled. This close, he gave off a warmth that wasn't even hinted at in his speeches or the few times Danny had seen him holding court at the back of the Sowbelly. "Western Pennsylvania, yes?"

"Yes," Danny said.

"What brought you all the way to Boston?" He tore a piece of dark bread from the loaf and popped it in his mouth.

"I had an uncle who lived here. By the time I arrived, he was long gone. I'm not sure where."

"Was he a revolutionary?"

Danny shook his head. "He was a cobbler."

"So he could run from the fight in good shoes."

Danny tipped his head to that and smiled.

Fraina leaned back in his chair and waved at the barmaid. She nodded and disappeared into the back. "Let's eat," Fraina said. "We'll talk revolution after dessert."

They ate a salad in vinegar and oil that Fraina called *svejie ovoshy*. That was followed by *draniki*, a potato dish, and *zharkoye*, a meal of beef and still more potatoes. Danny'd had no idea what to expect, but it was quite good, far better than the gruel served nightly in the Sowbelly would have led him to believe. Still, throughout dinner, he had trouble concentrating. Some of it was due to the ringing in his ears. He only heard half of what was said and dealt with the other half by smiling or shaking his head where it seemed appropriate. But it wasn't the hearing loss, ultimately, that pulled his interest away from the table. It was the feeling, all too familiar lately, that his job was the wrong fit for his heart.

He had woken up this morning, and because of that, a man was now dead. Whether the man deserved to die or not—and he did, he did—wasn't what concerned Danny at the moment. It was that *he'd* killed him. Two hours ago. He'd stood in the street and shot him like an animal. He could hear those high-pitched yelps. Could see each of the bullets enter Federico Ficara—the first through the knee, the second through the ass, the third into the stomach. All painful, the first and the third, however, exceptionally so.

Two hours ago, and now he was back on the job and the job was sitting with two men who seemed, at best, over-impassioned but hardly criminal.

When he'd shot Federico in the ass (and that was the one that bothered him the most, the indignity of it, Federico trying to scramble out of that car like forest prey) he'd wondered what created a situation like this—three people shooting it out on a city street near a car laden with dynamite. No god had ever designed such a scenario, even for the lowest of his animals. What created a Federico? A Tessa? Not god. Man.

I killed you, Danny thought. But I didn't kill *it*.

He realized Fraina was speaking to him.

"I'm sorry?"

"I said for a writer of such impassioned polemic, you're quite taciturn in person."

Danny smiled. "I like to leave it all on the page."

Fraina nodded and glanced his glass off Danny's. "Fair enough." He leaned back in his chair and lit a cigarette. He blew out the match as a child would blow out a candle, with pursed lips and an air of purpose. "Why the Lettish Workingman's Society?"

"I'm not sure I understand your question."

"You're an American," Fraina said. "You need only to walk half a mile across the city to find Comrade Reed's American Communist Party. And yet you chose to be among Eastern Europe ans. Are you uncomfortable with your own kind?"

"No."

Fraina tilted one palm in Danny's direction. "Then?"

"I want to write," Danny said. "Comrade Reed and Comrade Larkin are not known for letting newcomers break in on their paper."

"But I am?"

"That's the rumor," Danny said.

"Candor," Fraina said. "I like it. Some of them are quite good, by the way. Your musings."

"Thank you."

"Some are, well, a bit overwrought. Turgid, one could say."

Danny shrugged. "I speak from the heart, Comrade Fraina."

"The revolution needs people who speak from the head. Intelligence, precision—these are what are most valued in the party."

Danny nodded.

"So you would like to help out with the newspaper. Yes?"

"Very much so."

"It is not glamorous work. You'd write occasionally, yes, but you'd be expected to work the press and to stuff envelopes and type names and addresses onto those envelopes. This is something you can do?"

"Certainly," Danny said.

Fraina pulled a piece of tobacco off his tongue and dropped it in the ashtray. "Come by the offices next Friday. We'll see how you take to it."

Just like that, Danny thought. Just like that.

Leaving the Oktober, he found himself behind Louis Fraina

and Pyotr Glaviach as Nathan Bishop trotted across the sidewalk to open the back of the Olds Model M. Fraina stumbled and a gunshot report echoed in the empty street. Pyotr Glaviach knocked Fraina to the ground and covered his body. The smaller man's glasses fell off the curb and into the gutter. The gunman stepped out of the building next door, one arm extended, and Danny took the lid off a trash can and knocked the pistol out of his hand and the gun went off again and Danny hit him in the forehead. Sirens rang out. They were drawing closer. Danny hit the gunman another time with the metal lid and the man fell on his ass.

He turned back as Glaviach shoved Fraina into the backseat of the Model M and stood on the running board. Nathan Bishop hopped up front. Bishop waved his arm frantically at Danny. "Come on!"

The shooter grabbed Danny by his ankles and pulled his legs out from under him. Danny hit the sidewalk so hard he bounced.

A police cruiser turned onto Columbus.

"Go!" Danny called.

The Model M squealed as it pulled away from the curb.

"Find out if he a White!" Glaviach shouted from the running board as the cruiser drove over the curb in front of the restaurant and the Model M took a sharp left out of sight.

The first two coppers on the scene ran into the restaurant. They pushed back the barmaid and two men who'd ventured out. They shut the door behind them. The next cruiser arrived on their heels and banged to a stop halfway up the curb. McKenna climbed out, already chuckling at the absurdity of it all, as Jersey Jerry Hamilton let go of Danny's ankles. They got to their feet. The two patrolmen with McKenna came over and manhandled them over to the cruiser.

"Realistic enough, you think?" McKenna said.

Hamilton rubbed his forehead several times and then he punched Danny's arm. "I'm bleeding, you fuck."

Danny said, "I kept away from the face."

334

"Kept away from the . . . ?" Hamilton spit blood onto the street. "I should ram your—"

Danny stepped in close. "I could hospitalize you right fucking here, right now. You want that, mug?"

"Hey, why's he think he can talk to me like this?"

"Because he can." McKenna clapped their shoulders. "Assume the positions, gents."

"No, I'm serious," Danny said. "You want to two-step with me?"

Hamilton looked away. "I was just saying."

"You were just saying," Danny said.

"Gents," McKenna said.

Danny and Jersey Jerry placed their palms on the hood of the cruiser and McKenna made a show of frisking them.

"This is bullshit," Danny whispered. "They'll see through it."

"Nonsense," McKenna said. "Ye of little faith."

McKenna placed loose cuffs on their hands and pushed them into the back of the cruiser. He got behind the wheel and drove them all back down Harrison.

In the car, Hamilton said, "You know? If I ever see you off the job—"

"You'll what?" Danny said. "Cry yourself stupider?"

McKenna drove Danny back to his cover apartment in Roxbury and pulled to the curb a half block up from the building.

"How you feeling?"

Truth was, Danny felt like weeping. Not for any particular reason, just a general and all-consuming exhaustion. He rubbed his hands over his face.

"I'm okay."

"You shot the bejesus out of an Eye-tie terrorist under extraordinary duress just four hours ago, then went right into an undercover meeting with another possible terrorist and—"

335

"Fucking Eddie, they're not—"

"What'd you say?"

"—fucking terrorists. They're Communists. And they'd love to see us fail, yes, see this whole government collapse and cascade into the ocean. I grant you that. But they're not bomb throwers."

"You're naïve, lad."

"So be it." Danny reached for the door handle.

"Dan." McKenna put a hand on his shoulder.

Danny waited.

"Too much has been asked of you this last couple of months. I agree, as God is my judge. But it won't be much longer 'til you'll have your gold shield. And all, all will be perfectly brilliant then."

Danny nodded so Eddie would let go of his shoulder. Eddie dropped his hand.

"No, it won't," Danny said and got out of the car.

The next afternoon, in the confessional of a church he'd never entered before, Danny knelt and blessed himself.

The priest said, "You smell like liquor."

"That's because I've been drinking, Father. I'd share, but I left the bottle back at my apartment."

"Have you come to confess, son?"

"I don't know."

"How can you not know? You either sinned or you didn't."

"I shot a man to death yesterday. Outside a church. I figure you've heard about it by now."

"I have, yes. The man was an anarchist. You . . . ?"

"Yes. I shot him three times. *Tried* five times," Danny said, "but I missed twice. Thing is, Father? You'll tell me I did right. Yeah?"

"That's for God to—"

"He was going to blow up a church. One of yours."

"Correct. You did right."

"But he's dead. I removed him from this earth. And I can't shake the feeling . . ."

A long silence followed, made all the longer by the fact that it was church silence; it smelled of incense and oil soap and was hemmed in by thick velvet and dark wood.

"What feeling?"

"The feeling that we—me and the guy I shot?—we're just living in the same barrel? See?"

"No. You're being obtuse."

"Forgive me," Danny said. "There's this big barrel of shit. See? And it's—"

"Watch your language."

"—where the ruling class and all the Haves *don't* live, right? It's where they fucking throw every consequence they don't want to think about. And the idea—"

"You are in a house of God."

"—the idea is, Father? The idea is that we're supposed to play nice and go away when they're done with us. Accept what they give us and drink it and eat it and clap for it and say, 'Mmmm, more, please. *Thanks.'* And, Father, I gotta tell you, I've about had my fucking fill."

"Leave this church at once."

"Sure. You coming?"

"I think you need to sober up."

"And I think you need to leave this mausoleum you're hiding in and see how your parishioners really live. Done that lately, Father?"

"I—"

"Ever?"

"Please," Louis Fraina said, "take a seat."

It was just past midnight. Three days since the manufactured assassination attempt. At around eleven, Pyotr Glaviach had called Danny and given him the address of a bakery in Mattapan. When Danny arrived, Pyotr Glaviach stepped from the Olds Model M and waved Danny into an alley that ran between the bakery and a tailor. Danny followed him around to the back and into the storeroom. Louis Fraina waited in a hard-backed wooden chair with its twin directly across from him.

Danny took that seat, close enough to the small, dark-eyed man to reach out and stroke the whiskers of his neatly trimmed beard. Fraina's eyes never left Danny's face. They were not the blazing eyes of a fanatic. They were the eyes of an animal so used to being hunted that some boredom had settled in. He crossed his legs at the ankles and leaned back in his chair. "Tell me what happened after we left."

Danny jerked a thumb behind him. "I've told Nathan and Comrade Glaviach."

Fraina nodded. "Tell me."

"Where is Nathan, by the way?"

Fraina said, "Tell me what happened. Who was this man who tried to kill me?"

"I never got his name. Never even spoke with him."

"Yes, he seems quite the ghost."

Danny said, "I tried to. The police attacked immediately. They hit me, they hit him, they hit me some more. Then they threw us both in the back of the car and drove us to the station house."

"Which one?"

"Roxbury Crossing."

"And you exchanged no pleasantries with my assailant on the ride there?"

"I tried. He didn't respond. Then the copper told me to shut my hole."

"He said that? Shut your *hole*?"

Danny nodded. "Threatened to run his nightstick through it."

Fraina's eyes sparkled. "Vivid."

The floor was caked with old flour. The room smelled of yeast and sweat and sugar and mold. Large brown tins, some the height of a man, stood against the walls, and bags of flour

338

and grain were stacked between them. A bare lightbulb dangled from a chain in the center of the room and left pools of shadow where rodents squeaked. The ovens had probably been shut off since noon, but the room was thick with heat.

Fraina said, "A matter of feet, wouldn't you say?"

Danny put a hand in his pocket and found the button among some coins. He pressed it to his palm and leaned forward. "Comrade?"

"The would-be assassin." He waved at the air around him. "This man no one can find a record of. This man who went unseen, even by a comrade I know who was in the holding cell at Roxbury Crossing that night. A veteran of the first czarist revolution, this man, a true Lett like our comrade, Pyotr."

The big Estonian leaned against the large cooler door, his arms crossed, and gave no indication he'd heard his name.

"He didn't see you there, either," Fraina said.

"They never put me in the holding pen," Danny said. "They had their fun and shipped me in a paddy wagon to Charlestown. I told Comrade Bishop as much."

Fraina smiled. "Well, it's settled, then. Everything is fine." He clapped his hands. "Eh, Pyotr? What did I tell you?"

Glaviach kept his eyes on the shelving behind Danny's head. "Everything fine."

"Everything is fine," Fraina said.

Danny sat there, the heat of the place finding his feet, the underside of his scalp.

Fraina leaned forward, elbows on his knees. "Except, well, this man was only seven or eight feet away when he fired. How do you miss at that range?"

Danny said, "Nerves?"

Fraina stroked his beard and nodded. "That's what I thought at first. But then I began to wonder. There were three of us clustered together. Four, if we count you bringing up the rear. And beyond us? A big, heavy touring car. So, I put it to you, Comrade Sante, where did the bullets go?"

"The sidewalk, I'd guess."

Fraina clucked his tongue and shook his head. "Unfortunately, no. We checked there. We checked everywhere within a two-block radius. This was easy to do, because the police never checked. They never looked. A gun fired within city limits. Two shots discharged? And the police treated it as if it were no more than a hurled insult."

"Hmm," Danny said. "That is—"

"Are you federal?"

"Comrade?"

Fraina removed his glasses and wiped them with a handkerchief. "Justice Department? Immigration? Bureau of Investigation?"

"I don't—"

He stood and placed his glasses back on. He looked down at Danny. "Or local, perhaps? Part of this undercover dragnet we hear is sweeping the city? I understand the anarchists in Revere have a new member who claims to be from the north of Italy but speaks with the accent and cadence of one from the south." He strolled around to the back of Danny's chair. "And you, Daniel? Which are you?"

"I'm Daniel Sante, a machinist from Harlansburg, Pennsylvania. I'm no bull, Comrade. I'm no government slug. I am exactly who I say I am."

Fraina crouched behind him. He leaned in and whispered in Danny's ear, "What other response would you give?"

"None." Danny tilted his head until he could see Fraina's lean profile. "Because it's the truth."

Fraina placed his hands on the back of the chair. "A man tries to assassinate me and just happens to be a terrible shot. You come to my rescue because you just happen to be exiting at the same time as I. The police just happen to arrive within seconds of the gunshot. Everyone in the restaurant is detained and yet none are questioned. The assassin vanishes from police custody. You are released without charge and, in the height of providence, just happen to be a writer of some talent." He strolled around to the front of the chair again and tapped his temple. "You see how fortunate all these events are?"

"Then they're fortunate."

"I don't believe in luck, Comrade. I believe in logic. And this story of yours has none." He crouched in front of Danny. "Go now. Tell your bourgeois bosses that the Lettish Workingman's Society is above reproach and violates no law. Tell them not to send a second rube to prove otherwise."

Danny heard footsteps enter the storeroom behind him. More than a pair. Maybe three pair, all told.

"I am exactly who I say," Danny said. "I am dedicated to the cause and to the revolution. I'm not leaving. I refuse to deny who I am for any man."

Fraina raised himself from his haunches. "Go."

"No, Comrade."

Pyotr Glaviach used one elbow to push himself away from the cooler door. His other arm was behind his back.

"One last time," Fraina said. "Go."

"I can't, Comrade. I—"

Four pistols cocked their hammers. Three came from behind him, the fourth from Pyotr Glaviach.

"Stand!" Glaviach shouted, the echo pinging off the tight stone walls.

Danny stood.

Pyotr Glaviach stepped up behind him. His shadow spilled onto the floor in front of Danny, and that shadow extended one arm.

Fraina gave Danny a mournful smile. "This is the only option left for you and it could expire at a moment's notice." He swept his arm toward the door.

"You're wrong."

"No," Fraina said. "I am not. Good night."

Danny didn't reply. He walked past him. The four men in the rear of the room cast their shadows on the wall in front of him. He opened the door with a fiery itch at the base of his skull and exited the bakery into the night.

* * *

The last thing Danny did in the Daniel Sante rooming house was shave off his beard in the second floor bathroom. He used shears to cut away the majority of it, placing the thick tufts in a paper bag, and then soaked it with hot water and applied the shaving cream in a thick lather. With each stroke of the straight razor, he felt leaner, lighter. When he wiped off the last stray spot of cream and the final errant hair, he smiled.

Danny and Mark Denton met with Commissioner O'Meara and Mayor Andrew Peters in the mayor's office on a Saturday afternoon.

The mayor struck Danny as a misplaced man, as if he didn't fit in his office, his big desk, his stiff, high-collared shirt and tweed suit. He played with the phone on his desk a lot and aligned and realigned his desk blotter.

He smiled at them once they'd taken their seats. "The BPD's finest, I suspect, eh, gents?"

Danny smiled back.

Stephen O'Meara stood behind the desk. Before he'd said a word, he commanded the room. "Mayor Peters and I have looked into the budget for this coming year and we see places we could move a dollar here, a dollar there. It won't, I assure you, be enough. But it's a start, gentlemen, and it's a little more than that—it's a public acknowledgment that we take your grievances seriously. Isn't that right, Mr. Mayor?"

Peters looked up from his pencil holder. "Oh, absolutely, yes."

"We've consulted with city sanitation crews about launching an investigation into the health conditions of each and every station house. They've agreed to commence within the first month of the new year." O'Meara met Danny's eyes. "Is that a satisfactory start?"

Danny looked over at Mark and then back at the commissioner. "Absolutely, sir."

Mayor Peters said, "We're still paying back loans on the Commonwealth Avenue sewer project, gentlemen, not to mention the streetcar route expansions, the home fuel crisis during the war, and a substantial operating deficit for the public schools in the white districts. Our bond rating is low and sinking further. And now cost of living has exploded at an unprecedented rate. So we do—we very much do—appreciate your concerns. We do. But we need time."

"And faith," O'Meara said. "Just a bit more of that. Would you gentlemen be willing to poll your fellow officers? Get a list of their grievances and personal accounts of their day-to-day experiences on the job? Personal testimonials as to how this fiscal imbalance is affecting their home lives? Would you be willing to fully document the sanitation conditions at the station houses and list what you believe are repeated abuses of power at the upper chains of command?"

"Without fear of reprisal?" Danny said.

"Without *a one*," O'Meara said. "I assure you."

"Then certainly," Mark Denton said.

O'Meara nodded. "Let's meet back here in one month. In that time, let's refrain from voicing complaints in the press or stirring up the bees' nest in any way. Is that acceptable?"

Danny and Mark nodded.

Mayor Peters stood and shook their hands. "I may be new to the post, gentlemen, but I hope to reward your confidence."

O'Meara came from around the desk and pointed at the office doors. "When we open those doors, the press will be there. Camera flashes, shouted questions, the like. Are any of you undercover at the moment?"

Danny couldn't believe how quick the smile broke across his face or how inexplicably proud he felt to say, "Not anymore, sir."

In a rear booth at the Warren Tavern, Danny handed Eddie McKenna a box that contained his Daniel Sante clothes and rooming-house key, various notes he'd taken that hadn't been included in his reports, and all the literature he'd studied to inform his cover.

Eddie pointed at Danny's clean-shaven face. "So, you're done."

"I am done."

McKenna picked through the box, then pushed it aside. "There's no chance he could change his mind? Wake up after a good night's sleep and—?"

Danny gave him a look that cut him off.

"Think they would have killed you?"

"No. Logically? No. But when you hear four hammers cock at your back?"

McKenna nodded. "Sure that'd make Christ Himself revisit the wisdom of His convictions."

They sat in silence for a while, each to his own drink and his own thoughts.

"I could build you a new cover, move you to a new cell. There's one in—"

"Stop. Please. I'm done. I don't even know what the fuck we were doing. I don't know why—"

"Ours is not to reason why."

"*Mine* is not to reason why. This is your baby."

McKenna shrugged.

"What did I do here?" Danny's gaze fell on his open palms. "What was accomplished? Outside of making lists of union guys and harmless Bolsheviki—"

"There are no harmless Reds."

"—what the fuck was the point?"

Eddie McKenna drank from his brown bucket of beer and then relit his cigar, one eye squinting through the smoke. "We've lost you."

"What?" Danny said.

"We have, we have," Eddie said softly.

"I don't know what you're on about. It's me. Danny."

McKenna looked up at the ceiling tiles. "When I was a boy,

I stayed with an uncle for a time. Can't remember if he was on me mother's side or me da's, but he was gray Irish trash just the same. No music to him a'tall, no love, no light. But he had a dog, yeah? Mangy mutt, he was, and dumb as peat, but *he* had love, he had light. Sure he'd dance in place when he saw me coming up the hill, his tail awagging, dance for the sheer joy of knowing I'd pet him, I'd run with him, I'd rub his patchy belly." Eddie drew on his cigar and exhaled slowly. "Became sick, he did. Worms. Started sneezing blood. Time comes, me uncle tells me to take him to the ocean. Cuffs me when I refuse. Cuffs me worse when I cry. So I carry the cur to the ocean. I carry him out to a point just above me chin and I let him go. I'm supposed to hold him down for a count of sixty, but there's little point. He's weak and feeble and sad and he sinks without a noise. I walk back into shore, and me uncle cuffs me again. 'For what?' I shout. He points. And there he is, that feeble brick-headed mutt, swimming back in. Swimming toward me. Eventually, he makes it to shore. He's shivering, he's heaving, he's sopping wet. A marvel, this dog, a romantic, a hero. And he looks at me just in time for me uncle to bring the axe down on his spine and cut him in half."

He sat back. He lifted his cigar from the ashtray. A barmaid removed half a dozen mugs from the next table over. She walked back to the bar, and the room was quiet.

"Fuck you tell a story like that for?" Danny said. "Fuck's wrong with you?"

"It's what's wrong with you, boy. You've got 'fair' in your head now. Don't deny it. You think it's attainable. You do. I can see it."

Danny leaned in, his beer sloshing down the side of his bucket as he lowered it from his mouth. "I'm supposed to fucking learn something from the dog story? What—that life is hard? That the game is rigged? You think this is news? You think I believe the unions or the Bolshies or the BSC stand a spit of a chance of getting their due?"

"Then why are you doing it? Your father, your brother,

me—we're worried, Dan. Worried sick. You blew your cover with Fraina because some part of you wanted to blow it."

"No."

"And yet you sit there and tell me you know that no reasonable or sensible government—local, state, or federal—will ever allow the Sovietizing of this country. Not *ever*. But you continue to get deeper and deeper into the BSC muck and further and further from those who hold you dear. Why? You're me godson, Dan? Why?"

"Change hurts."

"That's your answer?"

Danny stood. "Change hurts, Eddie, but believe me, it's coming."

"It isn't."

"It's got to."

Eddie shook his head. "There are fights, m' boy, and there is folly. And I fear you'll soon learn the difference."

CHAPTER *nineteen*

In the kitchen with Nora late of a Tuesday afternoon, Nora just back from her job at the shoe factory, Luther chopping vegetables for the soup, Nora peeling potatoes, when Nora said, "You've a girl?"

"Hmm?"

She gave him those pale eyes of hers, the sparkle of them like a flickering match. "You heard what I said. Have you a girl somewhere?"

Luther shook his head. "No, ma'am."

She laughed.

"What?"

"Sure, you're lying."

"Uh? What makes you say that?"

"I can hear it in your voice, I can."

"Hear what?" She gave him a throaty laugh. "Love."

"Just 'cause I love someone don't mean she's mine."

"Now that's the truest thing you've said all week. Just because you love someone doesn't mean . . ." She trailed off and went back to humming softly as she peeled the potatoes, the humming a habit of hers Luther was fairly certain she was unaware of.

Luther used the flat of the knife to push the chopped celery off the cutting board and into the pot. He sidestepped Nora to pull some carrots from the colander in the sink and took them back down the counter with him, chopped off their tops before lining them up and slicing them four at a time.

"She pretty?" Nora asked.

"She's pretty," Luther said.

"Tall? Short?"

"She kinda small," Luther said. "Like you."

"I'm small, am I?" She gave Luther a look over her shoulder, one hand holding the peeler, and Luther, as he had before, got the sense of the volcanic from her in the most innocent of moments. He didn't know too many other white women and no Irishwomen, but he'd long had the feeling that Nora was a woman worth treading very carefully around.

"You ain't big," he said.

She looked over at him for a long time. "We've been acquainted for months, Mr. Laurence, and it occurred to me at the factory today that I know next to nothing, I do, about you."

Luther chuckled. "Pot calling the kettle black if ever I did hear it."

"You've some meaning you're keeping to yourself over there?"

"Me?" Luther shook his head. "I know you're from Ireland but not where exactly."

"Do you know Ireland?"

"Not a whit."

"Then what difference would it make?"

"I know you came here five years ago. I know you are courting Mr. Connor but don't seem to think about it much. I—"

"Excuse me, boy?"

Luther had discovered that when the Irish said "boy" to a colored man it didn't mean what it meant when a white American said it. He chuckled again. "Hit a nerve there, I did, lass?"

Nora laughed. She held the back of her wet hand to her lips, the peeler sticking out. "Do that again."

"What?"

"The brogue, the brogue."

"Ah, sure, I don't know what you're on about."

She leaned against the side of the sink and stared at him. "That is Eddie McKenna's voice, right down to the timbre itself, it 'tis."

Luther shrugged. "Not bad, uh?"

Nora's face sobered. "Don't ever let him hear you do that."

"You think I'm out my mind?"

She placed the peeler on the counter. "You miss her. I can see it in your eyes."

"I miss her."

"What's her name?"

Luther shook his head. "I'd just as soon hold on to that for the moment, Miss O'Shea."

Nora wiped her hands on her apron. "What're you running from, Luther?"

"What're you?"

She smiled and her eyes sparkled again but this time from the wet in them. "Danny."

He nodded. "I seen that. Something else, though, too. Something further back."

She turned back to the sink, lifted out the pot filled with water and potatoes. She carried it to the sink. "Ah, we're an interesting pair, Mr. Laurence. Are we not? All our intuition used for others, never ourselves."

"Lotta good it does us, then," Luther said.

S he said that?" Danny said from the phone in his rooming house. "She was running from me?"

"She did." Luther sat at the phone table in the Giddreauxs' foyer.

"She say it like she was tired of running?"

"No," Luther said. "She said it like she was right used to it."

"Oh."

"Sorry."

"No. Thanks, really. Eddie come at you yet?"

"He let me know he's on his way. Not how or what yet, though."

"Okay. Well, when he doe . . ."

"I'll let you know."

"What do you think of her?"

"Nora?"

"Yeah."

"I think she's too much woman for you."

Danny's laugh was a booming thing. Could make you feel like a bomb went off at your feet. "You do, uh?"

"Just an opinion."

" 'Night, Luther."

" 'Night, Danny."

One of Nora's secrets was that she smoked. Luther had caught her at it early in his time at the Coughlin house, and it had since become their habit to sneak out for one together while Mrs. Ellen Coughlin prepared herself for dinner in the bathroom but long before Mr. Connor or Captain Coughlin had returned from work.

One of those times, on a high-sun-deep-chill afternoon, Luther asked her about Danny again.

"What of him?"

"You said you were running from him."

"I did?"

"Yeah."

"I was sober?"

"In the kitchen that time."

"Ah." She shrugged and exhaled at the same time, her cigarette held up in front of her face. "Well, maybe he ran from me."

"Oh?"

Her eyes flashed, that danger you sensed in her getting closer to the surface. "You want to know something about your friend Aiden? Something you'd never guess?"

Luther knew it was one of those times silence was your best friend.

Nora blew out another stream of smoke, this one coming

350

out fast and bitter. "He seems very much the rebel, yeah? Very independent and free-thinking, he does, yeah?" She shook her head, took another hard drag off her cigarette. "He's not. In the end, he's not a'tall." She looked at Luther, a smile forcing its way onto her face. "In the end, he couldn't live with my past, that past you're so curious about. He wanted to be, I believe the word was, 'respectable.' And I, sure, I couldn't give him that."

"But Mr. Connor, he don't strike me as the type who—"

She shook her head repeatedly. "Mr. Connor knows nothing of my past. Only Danny. And look how the knowledge tossed us in the fire." She gave him another tight smile and stubbed out her cigarette with her toe. She lifted the dead butt off the frozen porch and placed it in the pocket of her apron. "Are we done with the questions for the day, Mr. Laurence?"

He nodded.

"What's her name?" she said.

He met her gaze. "Lila."

"Lila," she said, her voice softening. "A fine name, that."

Luther and Clayton Tomes were doing structural demolition in the Shawmut Avenue building on a Saturday so cold they could see their breath. Even so, the demo was such hard work—crowbar and sledgehammer work—that within the first hour they'd stripped down to their undershirts.

Close to noon, they took a break and ate the sandwiches Mrs. Giddreaux had prepared for them and drank a couple beers.

"After this," Clayton said, "we—what?—patch up that subflooring?"

Luther nodded and lit a cigarette, blew out the smoke in a long, weary exhale. "Next week, week after, we can run the electrical up back of them walls, maybe get around to some of them pipes you so excited about."

"Shit." Clayton shook his head and let out a loud yawn.

"All this work for nothing but a higher ideal? Place for us in Nigger Heaven, sure."

Luther gave him a soft smile but didn't say anything. He'd lost comfort with saying "nigger," even though the only time he'd ever used it was around other colored men. But both Jessie and the Deacon Broscious had used it constantly, and some part of Luther felt he'd entombed it with them back at the Club Almighty. He couldn't explain it any better than that, just that it didn't feel right coming off his tongue any longer. Like most things, he assumed, the feeling would pass, but for now . . .

"Well, I guess we might as well—"

He stopped talking when he saw McKenna stroll through the front door like he owned the damn building. He stood in the foyer, looking up at the dilapidated staircase.

"Damn," Clayton whispered. "Police."

"I know it. He's a friend of my boss. And he act all friendly, but he ain't. Ain't no friend of ours, nohow."

Clayton nodded because they'd both met plenty of white men that fit that description in their lives. McKenna entered the room where they'd been working, a big room, nearest to the kitchen, probably had been a dining room fifty years ago.

The first words out of McKenna's mouth: "Canton?"

"Columbus," Luther said.

"Ah, right enough." McKenna smiled at Luther, then turned to Clayton. "I don't believe we've met." He held out a meaty hand. "Lieutenant McKenna, BPD."

"Clayton Tomes." Clayton shook the hand.

McKenna gripped his hand, kept shaking it, his smile frozen to his face, his eyes searching Clayton's and then Luther's, seeming to look right into his heart.

"You work for the widow on M Street. Mrs. Wagenfeld. Correct?"

Clayton nodded. "Uh, yes, suh."

"Just so." McKenna dropped Clayton's hand. "She's

rumored to keep a small fortune in Spanish doubloons beneath her coal bin. Any truth to this, Clayton?"

"I wouldn't know anything about that, sir."

"Wouldn't tell anyone anyway if you did!" McKenna laughed and slapped Clayton on the back so hard Clayton stumbled forward a couple of steps.

McKenna stepped close to Luther. "What brought you here?"

"Suh?" Luther said. "You know I live with the Giddreauxs. This is going to be the headquarters."

McKenna shot his eyebrows at Clayton. "The headquarters? Of what?"

"The NAACP," Luther said.

"Ah, grand stuff," McKenna said. "I remodeled me own house once. A constant headache, that." He moved a crowbar to the side with his foot. "You're in the demolition phase, I see."

"Yes, suh."

"Coming along?"

"Yes, suh."

"Almost there, I'd say. 'Least on this floor. My original question, Luther, however, did not pertain to your working in this building. No. When I asked what brought you here, the 'here' I referred to was Boston herself. For instance, Clayton Tomes, where do you hail from, son?"

"The West End, sir. Born and raised."

"Exactly," McKenna said. "Our coloreds tend to be home-grown, Luther. Few come here without a good reason when they could find much more of their kind in New York or, Lord knows, Chicago or Detroit. So what brought you here?"

"A job," Luther said.

McKenna nodded. "To come eight hundred miles just to drive Ellen Coughlin to church? Seems funny."

Luther shrugged. "Well, then, I guess it's funny, suh."

" 'Tis, 'tis," McKenna said. "A girl?"

"Suh?"

"You got yourself a girl up these parts?"

"No."

McKenna rubbed the stubble along his jaw, looked over at Clayton again, as if they played this game together. "See, I'd believe you came eight hundred miles for cunny. Now that's a valid story. But, as it is?"

He stared at Luther for a long time with that blithe, open face of his.

Once the silence had gone on into its second minute, Clayton said, "We best get back at it, Luther."

McKenna's head turned, as if on a slow swivel, and he gave the open gaze to Clayton Tomes who quickly looked away.

McKenna turned back to Luther. "Don't let me hold you up, Luther. I'd best be getting back to work myself. Thank you for the reminder, Clayton."

Clayton shook his head at his own stupidity.

"Back out to the world," McKenna said with a weary sigh. "These days? People who make a good wage think it's okay to bite the hand that feeds them. Do you know what the bedrock of capitalism is, gents?"

"No, suh."

"Sure don't, sir."

"The bedrock of capitalism, gentlemen, is the manufacture or mining of goods for the purpose of sale. That's it. That's what this country is built on. And so the heroes of this country are not soldiers or athletes or even presidents. The heroes are the men who built our railroads and our automobiles and our cotton mills and factories. They keep this country running. The men who work for them, therefore, should be grateful to be a part of the process that forms the freest society in the known world." He reached out and clapped Luther on both shoulders. "But lately they're not. Can you believe that?"

"There isn't much of a subversive movement among us colored, Lieutenant, suh."

McKenna's eyes widened. "Where have *you* lived, Luther?

354

There's quite the lefty movement going on in Harlem right now. Your high-toned colored got himself some education and started reading his Marx and his Booker T. and his Frederick Douglass and now you got men like Du Bois and Garvey and some would argue they're just as dangerous as Goldman and Reed and the atheistic Wobblies." He held up a finger. "*Some* would argue. Some would even claim that the NAACP is just a front, Luther, for subversive and seditionist ideas." He patted Luther's cheek softly with a gloved hand. "Some."

He turned and looked up at the scorched ceiling.

"Well, you've your work cut out for you, lads. I'll leave you to it."

He placed his hands behind his back and strolled across the floor, and neither Luther nor Clayton took a breath until he'd exited the foyer and descended the front steps.

"Oh, Luther," Clayton said.

"I know it."

"Whatever you did to that man, you got to undo it."

"I didn't do nothing. He just that way."

"What way? White?"

Luther nodded.

"And mean," Luther said. "Kinda mean just keeps eating till the day it dies."

CHAPTER *twenty*

After leaving Special Squads, Danny returned to foot patrol in his old precinct, the Oh-One on Hanover Street. He was assigned to walk his beat with Ned Wilson, who at two months shy of his twenty, had stopped giving a shit five years ago. Ned spent most of their shift drinking or playing craps at Costello's. Most days, he and Danny saw each other for about twenty minutes after they punched in and five minutes before they punched out. The rest of the time Danny was free to do as he chose. If he made a hard bust, he called Costello's from a call box and Ned met up with him in time to march the perp up the stairs of the station house. Otherwise, Danny roamed. He walked the entire city, dropping in on as many station houses as he could reach in a day—the Oh-Two in Court Square, down to the Oh-Four on LaGrange, across to the Oh-Five in the South End and as far up the line as he could go on foot in the eighteen station houses of the BPD. The three in West Roxbury, Hyde Park, and Jamaica Plain were left for Emmett Strack; the Oh-Seven in Eastie, for Kevin McRae; Mark Denton covered Dorchester, Southie, and the One-Four in Brighton. Danny worked the rest—downtown, the North and South Ends, and Roxbury.

The job was recruitment and testimony. Danny glad-handed, cajoled, harangued, and persuaded a solid one-third of all the cops he approached into writing down an accurate account of his workweek, his debts versus his income, and the conditions of the station house in which he worked. In his first three weeks back on the beat, he roped in sixty-eight men to meetings of the Boston Social Club at Fay Hall.

Whereas his time in Special Squads had been marked by a self-loathing so acute he now wondered how he'd managed to do any of it, his time doing BSC work in hopes of forming a union with true bargaining power made him feel a sense of purpose that bordered on the evangelical.

This, he decided one afternoon as he returned to the station house with three more testimonials from patrolmen in the One-Oh, was what he'd been looking for since Salutation Street: a reason why he'd been spared.

In his box, he found a message from his father asking him to come by the house that night after his shift. Danny knew few good things had ever come from one of his father's summonses, but he caught the streetcar out to South Boston just the same and rode across the city through a soft snow.

Nora answered the door, and Danny could tell she hadn't expected him to be on the other side of it. She pulled her house sweater tight across her body and took a sudden step back.

"Danny."

"Evening."

He'd barely seen her since the flu, barely seen anyone in the family except for the Sunday dinner several weeks back when he'd met Luther Laurence.

"Come in, come in."

He stepped over the threshold and removed his scarf. "Where's Ma and Joe?"

"Gone to bed," she said. "Turn around."

He did and she brushed the snow off the shoulders and back of his coat.

"Here. Give it to me now."

He removed the coat and caught a faint whiff of the

perfume she wore ever so sparingly. It smelled of roses and a hint of orange.

"How are you?" Danny looked in her pale eyes, thinking: I could die.

"Just fine. Yourself?"

"Good, good."

She hung his coat on the tree in the hallway and carefully smoothed his scarf with her hand. It was a curious gesture, and Danny stopped breathing for a moment as he watched her. She placed the scarf on a separate hook and turned back to him and just as quickly dropped her eyes, as if she'd been caught at something, which, in a way, she had.

I would do anything, Danny wanted to say. Anything. I've been a fool. First with you, then after you, and now as I stand here before you. A fool.

He said, "I—"

"Hmm?"

"You look great," he said.

Her eyes met his again and they were clear and almost warm. "Don't."

"Don't?"

"You know what I mean." She looked at the floor, hugging her elbows.

"I'm . . ."

"What?"

"Sorry."

"I know." She nodded. "You've apologized enough. More than enough. You wanted to be"—she looked up at him—"respectable. Yes?"

Christ—not that word again, thrown back in his face. If he could remove one word from his vocabulary, erase it so that it had never taken hold and thus he never could have used it, it would be that one. He'd been drunk when he said it. Drunk and taken aback by her sudden and sordid revelations about Ireland. About Quentin Finn.

Respectable. Shit.

He held out his hands, at a loss for words.

"Now it's my turn," she said. "I'll be the respectable one."

He shook his head. "No."

And he could tell by the fury that sprang into her face that she'd misinterpreted his meaning yet again. He had meant to imply that respectability was a goal unworthy of her. But she took it to mean it was something she could never attain.

Before he could explain, she said, "Your brother's asked me to marry him."

His heart stopped. His lungs. His brain. The circumnavigation of his blood.

"And?" The word came out as if strangled by vines.

"I told him I'm thinking about it," she said.

"Nora." He reached for her arm but she stepped away.

"Your father's in the study."

She walked away down the hall, and Danny knew, yet again, that he'd failed her. He was supposed to have responded differently. Faster? Slower? Less predictably? What? If he'd dropped to his knees and made his own proposal, would she have done anything but run? Yet he felt he was supposed to have made some kind of grand gesture, if only so she *could* have turned it down. And that would have somehow balanced the scales.

The door to his father's study opened as he stood there. "Aiden."

"Danny," he corrected him through gritted teeth.

In his father's study, the snow falling through the black beyond the windows, Danny sat in one of the leather armchairs that faced the desk. His father had a fire going and it reflected off the hearth and gave the room a glow the color of whiskey.

Thomas Coughlin still wore his uniform, the tunic open at the neck, his captain's bars sitting atop the blue shoulders while Danny wore street clothes and felt those bars smirking at him. His father handed him a scotch and sat on the corner of the desk.

His blue eyes cut through his glass as he drained it. He poured a refill from the decanter. He rolled the glass back and forth between his palms and considered his son.

"Eddie tells me you went native."

Danny caught himself rolling his own glass between his palms and dropped his left hand to his thigh. "Eddie over-dramatizes."

"Really? Because I've been given cause to wonder lately, Aiden, if these Bolshies didn't rub off on you." His father gave the room a soft smile and sipped his drink. "Mark Denton is a Bolshevik, you know. Half the BSC members are."

"Gosh, Dad, they just seem like cops to me."

"They're Bolsheviks. Talking of a strike, Aiden? A *strike*?"

"No one's said that word in my presence, sir."

"There's a principle to be honored here, boy. Can you appreciate that?"

"And which one is that, sir?"

"Public safety above all other ideals for men who hold the badge."

"Putting food on the table, sir, that's another ideal."

His father waved at the sentence like it was smoke. "Did you see the paper today? They're rioting in Montreal, trying to burn the city wholesale right to the ground. And there's no police to protect the property or the people and there's no firemen to put out the fires because they're all out on strike. It might as well be St. Petersburg."

"Maybe it's just Montreal," Danny said. "Maybe it's just Boston."

"We're not *employees*, Aiden. We're civil servants. We protect and we serve."

Danny allowed himself a smile. It was rare he could watch the old man get worked up needlessly and be the one holding the key to his release. He stubbed out his cigarette and a chuckle escaped his lips.

"You laugh?"

He held up a hand. "Dad, Dad. It's not going to be Montreal. Really."

His father's eyes narrowed and he shifted on the edge of the desk. "How so?"

"You heard what, exactly?"

His father reached into his humidor and removed a cigar. "You confronted Stephen O'Meara. My son. A Coughlin. Speaking out of turn. Now you're going from station house to station house, collecting affidavits regarding substandard working conditions? You're recruiting for your purported 'union' on city time?"

"He thanked me."

His father paused, the cigar cutter wrapped around the base of the cigar. "Who?"

"Commissioner O'Meara. He thanked me, Dad, and he asked Mark Denton and me to *get* those affidavits. He seems to think we'll resolve the situation very soon."

"O'Meara?"

Danny nodded. His father's strong face drained of color. He'd never seen this coming. In a million years, he couldn't have guessed it. Danny chewed on the inside of his mouth to keep a smile from breaking wide across his face.

Got you, he wanted to say. Twenty-seven years on this planet and I finally got you.

His father surprised him even further when he came off the desk and held out his hand. Danny stood and took it and his father's grip was strong and he pulled Danny to him and clapped him once on the back.

"God, you made us proud, then, son. Damn proud." He let go of his hand and clapped his shoulders and then sat back on the desk. "Damn proud," his father repeated with a sigh. "I'm just relieved it's all over, this whole mess."

Danny sat down. "Me, too, sir."

His father fingered the blotter on his desktop and Danny watched the strength and guile return to his face like a second

361

layer of skin. A new order of business in the offing. His father already beginning to circle.

"How do you feel about Nora and Connor's impending nuptials?"

Danny held his father's gaze and kept his voice steady. "Fine, sir. Just fine. They're a handsome couple."

"They are, they are," his father said. "I can't tell you what a trial it's been for your mother and me to keep him from sneaking up to her room at night. Like children, they are." He walked around to the back of the desk and looked out at the snow. Danny could see both their faces reflected in the window. His father noticed it, too, and smiled.

"You're the spitting image of my Uncle Paudric. Have I ever told you that?"

Danny shook his head.

"Biggest man in Clonakilty," his father said. "Oh, he could drink something fierce and he'd get a sight unreasonable when he did. A publican once refused him service? Why, Paudric tore out the bar between them. Heavy oak, Aiden, this bar. And he just tore a piece of it out and went and poured himself another pint. A legendary man, really. Oh, and the ladies loved him. Much like you in that regard. Everyone loved Paudric when he was sober. And you? Everyone loves you, don't they, son? Women, children, mangy Italians and mangy dogs. Nora."

Danny put his drink on the desk. "What did you say?"

His father turned from the window. "I'm not blind, boy. You two may have told yourselves one thing, and she may very well love Con' in a different way. And maybe it's the better way." His father shrugged. "But you—"

"You're on thin fucking ice, sir."

His father looked at him, his mouth half open.

"Just so you know," Danny said and could hear the tightness in his own voice.

Eventually his father nodded. It was the sage nod, that one that let you know he was acknowledging one aspect of your

362

character while pondering flaws in another. He took Danny's glass. He carried it to the decanter with his own and refilled them.

He handed Danny his glass. "Do you know why I allowed you to box?"

Danny said, "Because you couldn't have stopped me."

His father clinked his glass with his own. "Exactly. I've known since you were a boy that you could occasionally be prodded or smoothed, but you could never be molded. It's anathema to you. Has been since you could walk. Do you know I love you, boy?"

Danny met his father's eyes and nodded. He did. He always had. Strip away all the many faces and many hearts his father showed the world when it suited him, and that face and that heart were always evident.

"I love Con', of course," his father said. "I love all my children. But I love you differently because I love you in defeat."

"Defeat?"

His father nodded. "I can't rely on you, Aiden. I can't shape you. This thing with O'Meara is a perfect example. *This* time it worked out. But it was imprudent. It could have cost you your career. And it's a move I never would have made or allowed you to make. And that's the difference with you, of all my children—I can't predict your fate."

"But Con's?"

His father said, "Con' will be district attorney someday. Without a doubt. Mayor, definitely. Governor, possibly. I'd hoped you'd be chief of police, but it's not in you."

"No," Danny agreed.

"And the thought of you as mayor is one of the more comical ideas I've ever imagined."

Danny smiled.

"So," Thomas Coughlin said, "your future is something you're hell-bent on writing with your own pen. Fine. I accept defeat." He smiled to let Danny know he was only half serious. "But your brother's future is something I tend to like a garden." He hoisted himself up on the desk. His eyes were bright and liquid, a sure sign that doom was on the way. "Did Nora ever talk much about Ireland, about what led her here?"

"To me?"

"To you, yes."

He knows something.

"No, sir."

"Never mentioned anything about her past life?"

Maybe all of it.

Danny shook his head. "Not to me."

"Funny," his father said.

"Funny?"

His father shrugged. "Apparently you two had a less intimate relationship than I'd imagined."

"Thin ice, sir. Very thin."

His father gave that an airy smile. "Normally people talk about their pasts. Particularly with close . . . friends. And yet Nora never does. Have you noticed?"

Danny tried to formulate a reply but the phone in the hall rang. Shrill and loud. His father looked at the clock on the mantel. Almost ten o'clock.

"Calling *this* home after nine o'clock?" his father said. "Who just signed his own death warrant? Sweet Jesus."

"Dad?" Danny heard Nora pick up the phone in the hall. "Why do you—?"

Nora knocked softly on the door and Thomas Coughlin said, "It's open."

Nora pushed open the doors. "It's Eddie McKenna, sir. He says it's urgent."

Thomas scowled and pushed himself off the desk and walked out into the hall.

Danny, his back to Nora, said, "Wait."

He came out of the chair and met her in the doorway as they heard his father pick up the phone in the alcove off the kitchen at the other end of the hall and say, "Eddie?"

"What?" Nora said. "Jesus, Danny, I'm tired."

"He knows," Danny said.

"What? Who?"

"My father. He knows."

"What? What does he know? Danny?"

"About you and Quentin Finn, I think. Maybe not all of it, but something. Eddie asked me last month if I knew any Finns. I just chalked it up to coincidence. It's a common enough name. But the old man, he just—"

He never saw the slap coming. He was in too close and when it connected with his jaw, he actually felt his feet move beneath him. All five foot five of her, and she nearly knocked him to the floor.

"You told him." She practically spit the words into his face.

She started to turn and he grabbed her wrist. "Are you fucking crazy?" It came out a harsh whisper. "Do you think I would ever—*ever*, Nora—sell you down the river? Ever? Don't look away. *Look at me*. Ever?"

She stared back into his eyes and hers were those of a hunted animal, darting around the room, searching for safety. One more night alive.

"Danny," she whispered. "Danny."

"I can't have you believe that," he said, and his voice cracked. "Nora, I can't."

"I don't," she said. She pressed her face to his chest for a moment. "I don't, I don't." She pulled back and looked up at him. "What do I do, Danny? What?"

"I don't know." He heard his father replace the receiver in the cradle.

"He knows?"

"He knows *something*," Danny said.

His father's footfalls came down the hall toward them and Nora broke away from him. She gave him one last wild, lost look and then turned into the hall.

"Sir."

"Nora," her father said.

"Will you need anything, sir? Tea?"

"No, dear." His father's voice sounded shaky as he turned into the room. His face was ashen and his lips trembled. "Good night, dear."

"Good night, sir."

Thomas Coughlin closed the pocket doors behind him. He walked to the desk in three long strides and drained his drink and immediately poured himself another. He mumbled something to himself.

"What?" Danny said.

His father turned, as if surprised to find him there. "Cerebral hemorrhage. Went off in his head like a bomb."

"Sir?"

He held out his glass, his eyes wide. "Struck him to the floor of his parlor and he was off to see the angels before his wife could even get to the phone. Jesus H."

"Sir, you're not making sense. Who are you—?"

"He's dead. Commissioner Stephen O'Meara is dead, Aiden."

Danny put his hand on the back of a chair.

His father stared out at the walls of his study as if they held answers. "God help this department now."

CHAPTER *twenty-one*

Stephen O'Meara was laid to rest at Holyhood Cemetery in Brookline on a white, windless morning. When Danny searched the sky he found neither birds nor sun. Frozen snow covered the ground and the treetops in a marble white cast that matched the sky and the breath of the mourners gathered around the grave. In the sharp air, the echo of Honor Guard's twenty-one-gun salute sounded less like an echo and more like a second volley of gunfire from another, lesser burial on the other side of the frozen trees.

O'Meara's widow, Isabella, sat with her three daughters and Mayor Peters. The daughters were all in their thirties and their husbands sat to their left followed by O'Meara's grandchildren, who shivered and fidgeted. At the end of that long line sat the new commissioner, Edwin Upton Curtis. He was a short man with a face the color and texture of a long-discarded orange peel and eyes as dull as his brown shirt. Back when Danny was just out of diapers, Curtis had been mayor, the youngest in the history of the city. He was neither now—young nor mayor—but in 1896 he'd been a fair-haired Republican naïf who'd been fed to the rabid Democratic ward bosses while the Brahmins searched for a longer-term solution of more substantial timber. He'd left the highest office in City Hall one year after he entered it and the appointments that followed for him had so diminished in stature that two decades later, he'd been working as a customs clerk when outgoing Governor McCall appointed him to replace O'Meara.

"I can't believe he had the guff to show up," Steve Coyle said later at Fay Hall. "Man hates the Irish. Hates police. Hates Catholics. How're we going to get a fair shake from him?"

Steve still called himself "police." He still attended meetings. He had nowhere else to go. Still, his was *the* question at Fay Hall that morning. A megaphone had been placed on a stand in front of the stage for the men to give testimonials to their late commissioner, while the rest of the rank and file milled among the coffee urns and beer kegs. The captains and lieutenants and inspectors were holding their own memorial across town with fine china and French cuisine at Locke-Ober, but the foot soldiers were here in Roxbury, trying to voice their sense of loss for a man they'd barely known. So the testimonials had begun to fade as each man told a story about a chance meeting with the Great Man, a leader who was "tough but fair." Milty McElone was up there now, recounting O'Meara's obsession with uniforms, his ability to spot a tarnished button from ten yards out in a crowded squad room.

On the floor, the men sought out Danny and Mark Denton. The price of coal had jumped another penny in the last month. Men returned from work to icy bedrooms puffed with vapor clouds from their children's mouths. Christmas was just around the corner. Their wives were sick of darning, sick of serving thinner and thinner soup, angry that they couldn't shop the Christmas sales at Raymond's, at Gilchrist's, at Houghton & Dutton. Other wives could—the wives of trolley drivers, of teamsters, of stevedores and dockworkers—but not the wives of policemen?

"I'm fed up being put out of my own bed," one patrolman said. "I only sleep there twice a week as it is."

"They're our wives," someone else said, "and they're only poor because they married us."

The men who took the megaphone began to express

similar sentiments. The testimonials to O'Meara faded away. They could hear the wind pick up outside, see the frost on the windows.

Dom Furst was up at the megaphone now, rolling up the sleeve of his dress blues so they could all see his arm. "These are the bug bites I got at the station just last night, boys. They jump to our beds when they're tired of riding the backs of the rats. And *they* answer our gripes with *Curtis*? He's one of them!" He pointed off in the general direction of Beacon Hill, his bare arm peppered with red bites. "There's a lot of men they could have picked to replace Stephen O'Meara and send the message 'We don't care.' But picking Edwin Up-Your-Arse Curtis? That's saying, 'Fuck *you*!'"

Some men banged chairs off the walls. Some threw their coffee cups at the windows.

"We better do something here," Danny said to Mark Denton.

"Be my guest," Denton said.

"Fuck you?" Furst shouted. "I say, 'Fuck *them*.' You hear me? Fuck them!"

Danny was still working his way through the crowd toward the megaphone when the whole room picked up the chant:

Fuck them! Fuck them! Fuck them! Fuck them!

He gave Dom a smile and a nod and stepped behind him to the megaphone.

"Gentlemen," Danny tried but was drowned out by the continuous chant.

"Gentlemen!" he tried again. He saw Mark Denton in the crowd giving him a cocked eyebrow and a cocked smile.

One more time. "Gentlemen!"

A few looked his way. The rest chanted and slashed their fists through the air and spilled beer and coffee on one another.

"*Shut. The fuck. Up!*" Danny screamed it into the megaphone. Danny took a breath and looked out at the room. "We

369

are your union reps. Yes? Me, Mark Denton, Kevin McRae, Doolie Ford. Let us *negotiate* with Curtis before you go off half-crazed."

"When?" someone shouted from the crowd.

Danny looked out at Mark Denton.

"Christmas Day," Denton said. "We've a meeting at the mayor's office."

Danny said, "He can't be taking us lightly, he wants to meet on Christmas morn, can he, boys?"

"Could be he's half-kike," someone shouted, and the men broke up laughing.

"Could be," Danny said. "But it's a solid step in the right direction, boys. An act of good faith. Let's give the man the benefit of the doubt until then, yeah?"

Danny looked out at the several hundred faces; they were only half-sold on the idea. A few shouted "Fuck them!" again from the back of the hall and Danny pointed at the photograph of O'Meara that hung on the wall to his left. As dozens of eyes followed his fingers, he realized something terrifying and exhilarating at the same time:

They *wanted* him to lead them.

Somewhere. Anywhere.

"That man!" he shouted. "That great man was laid to rest today!"

The room quieted, no more shouts. They all looked to Danny, wondering where he was going with this, where he was taking them. He wondered himself.

He lowered his voice. "He died with a dream still unfulfilled."

Several men lowered their heads.

Jesus, where was he coming up with this stuff?

"That dream was our dream." Danny craned his head, looked out at the crowd. "Where's Sean Moore? Sean, I saw you earlier. Raise a hand."

Sean Moore raised one sheepish hand in the air.

Danny locked eyes with him. "You were there that night,

Sean. In the bar, the night before he died. You were with me. You met the man. And what did he say?"

Sean looked at the men around him and shifted on his feet. He gave Danny a weak smile and shook his head.

"He said . . ." Danny's eyes swept the room. "He said, 'A promise is a promise.' "

Half the room clapped. A few whistled.

"A promise is a promise," Danny repeated.

More clapping, a few shouts.

"He asked whether we had faith in him. Do we? Because it was his dream as much as it was ours."

Bullshit, Danny knew, but it was working. Chins lifted all over the room. Pride replaced anger.

"He raised his glass—" And here Danny raised his own glass. He could feel his father working through him: the blarney, the appeal to sentiment, the sense of the dramatic. "And he said, 'To the *men* of the Boston Police Department, you have no peers in this nation.' Will you drink to that, boys?"

They drank. They cheered.

Danny dropped his voice several octaves. "If Stephen O'Meara knew we were without peer, Edwin Upton Curtis will know it soon enough."

They started chanting again, and it took Danny several moments to recognize the word they chanted because they'd broken it into two syllables so it sounded like two words, and he felt blood rush up his face so quickly it felt cold and newly born:

"Cough-lin! Cough-lin! Cough-lin!"

He found Mark Denton's face in the crowd and saw a grim smile there, a confirmation of something, of previously held suspicions maybe, of fate.

"Cough-lin! Cough-lin! Cough-lin!"

"To Stephen O'Meara!" Danny shouted, raising his glass again to a ghost, to an idea. "And to his dream!"

When he stepped away from the megaphone, the men

besieged him. Several even tried to lift him above the fray. It took him ten minutes to reach Mark Denton, who placed a fresh beer in his hand and leaned in to shout into his ear above the crowd noise. "You set a hell of a table."

"Thanks," Danny shouted back.

"You're welcome." Mark's smile was taut. He leaned in again. "What happens if we don't deliver, Dan? You thought of that? What happens?"

Danny looked out at the men, their faces sheened with sweat, several reaching past Mark to slap at Danny's shoulder, to raise their glasses to him. Exhilarating? Hell, it made him feel like kings must feel. Kings and generals and lions.

"We'll deliver," he shouted back at Mark.

"I sure as hell hope so."

Danny had a drink with Eddie McKenna at the Parker House a few days later, the two of them lucky to find chairs by the hearth on a bitter evening of black gusts and shuddering window frames. "Any news on the new commissioner?"

McKenna fingered his coaster. "Ah, he's a lackey for the fucking Brahmins, through and through. A purple-veined whore wearing virgin's clothes, he is. You know he went after Cardinal O'Connell himself last year?"

"What?"

McKenna nodded. "Sponsored a bill at the last Republican Convention to pull all public funding from parochial schools." He raised his eyebrows. "They can't take our heritage, they go after our religion. Nothing's sacred to these Haves. Nothing."

"So the likelihood of a raise . . ."

"The raise is not something I'd concern myself with for a bit."

Danny thought of all the men in Fay Hall the other morning chanting his name and he resisted the urge to punch something. They'd been so close. So close.

Danny said, "I got a meeting with Curtis and the mayor in three days."

McKenna shook his head. "There's only one thing to do during regime change—keep your head down."

"What if I can't?"

"Ready it for a new hole."

Danny and Mark Denton met to discuss strategy for their morning meeting with Mayor Peters and Commissioner Curtis. They sat at one of the tables in the back of the Blackstone Saloon on Congress Street. It was a dive, a well-known cops' bar where the other men, sensing that Mark and Danny held keys to their fate, left them alone.

"A raise of two hundred a year is no longer enough," Mark said.

"I know," Danny said. Cost of living had risen so dramatically in the last six months that all that prewar figure would do was restore the men to the poverty level. "What if we come in asking for three hundred?"

Mark rubbed his forehead. "It's tricky. They could get to the press before us and say we're greedy. And Montreal definitely hasn't helped our bargaining position."

Danny reached through the stack of papers Denton had fanned across the table. "But the numbers bear us out." He lifted the article he'd clipped from last week's *Traveler* on the leaps in the prices of coal, oil, milk, and public transportation.

"But if we ask for three hundred when they're still digging in their heels on two?"

Danny sighed and rubbed his own forehead. "Let's just throw it on the table. When they balk, we can come down to two-fifty for veterans, two-ten for new recruits, start building a scale."

Mark took a sip of his beer, the worst in the city, but also the cheapest. He rubbed the foam off his upper lip with the back of his hand and glanced at the *Traveler* clipping again.

"Might work, might work. What if they flat out rebuff us? They say there's no money, none, zip?"

"Then we have to come at them on the company-store issue. Ask if they think it's right that policemen have to pay for their own uniforms and greatcoats and guns and bullets. Ask them how they expect a first-year patrolman working for the 1905 wage and paying for his own equipment to feed his children."

"I like the children." Mark gave him a wry smile. "Be ready to play that up if we meet any reporters on the way out and it hasn't gone our way."

Danny nodded. "Another thing? We've got to bring the average workweek down by ten hours and get time-and-a-half for all special details. The president's coming back through here in a month, right? Getting off the boat from France and parading right through these streets. You *know* they're going to put every cop on that regardless of what he's already worked that week. Let's demand time-and-a-half starting there."

"We're going to put their backs up with that."

"Exactly. And once their backs are up, we say we'll forgo *all* these demands if they just give us the raise they promised plus the cost-of-living increase."

Mark stewed on that, sipping his beer, looking out at the snow falling past the graying windows of late afternoon. "We've got to hit them with the health code violations, too," he said. "I saw rats at the Oh-Nine the other night looked like bullets wouldn't *stun* them. We hit them with that, the company-store thing, and the special details?" He sat back. "Yeah, I think you're right." He clinked his glass off Danny's. "Now remember something—they *will not* say yes tomorrow. They'll hem and haw. When we meet the press afterward, we act conciliatory. We say some progress has been made. But we also call attention to the issues. We mention that Peters and Curtis are fine men who are honestly trying to help us with the company-store problem. To which the reporters will say . . . ?'"

"What company-store problem?" Danny smiled, seeing it now.

"Precisely. Same thing on the cost of living. 'Well, we know Mayor Peters surely hopes to address the disparity between what the men earn and the high price of coal.'"

"Coal's good," Danny said, "but it's still a bit abstract. The children are our aces."

Mark chuckled. "You're getting a real feel for this."

"Lest we forget"—Danny raised his glass—"I am my father's son."

In the morning he dressed in his only suit, one Nora had picked out during their secret days of courting in '17. It was dark blue, a French-back, double-breasted pinstripe and, given the weight he'd lost trying to look like a hungry Bolshevik, too big for him. Still, once he added his hat and ran his fingers along the welt-edge brim to get the curl the way he wanted it, he looked smart, dapper even. As he fiddled with his high collar and made the knot in his tie a little wider to compensate for the gap between the collar and his throat, he practiced somber looks in the mirror, serious looks. He worried he looked *too* dapper, too much the young rake. Would Curtis and Peters take him seriously? He removed the hat and furrowed his brow. He opened and closed his suit jacket several times. He decided it looked best closed. He practiced the brow-furrow again. He added more Macassar oil to his hair and put the hat back on.

He walked to headquarters at Pemberton Square. It was a beautiful morning, cold but windless, the sky a bright band of steel and the air smelling of chimney smoke, melting snow, hot brick, and roast fowl.

He ran into Mark Denton coming along School Street. They smiled. They nodded. They walked up onto Beacon Hill together.

"Nervous?" Danny asked.

"A bit," Mark said. "I left Emma and the kids home alone

375

on Christmas morning, so it better be for something. How about you?"

"I choose not to think about it."

"Wise."

The front of headquarters was empty, no reporters on the steps. No one at all. They would have expected to see the mayor's driver, at least, or Curtis's.

"Around back," Mark Denton said with an emphatic nod. "Everyone's around back, probably already nipping from Christmas flasks."

"That's it," Danny said.

They went through the front door and removed their hats and topcoats. They found a small man in a dark suit and red bow tie waiting for them, a slim valise on his lap. His eyes were too big for his small face and gave him a demeanor of perpetual surprise. He was no older than Danny, but his hairline had receded halfway up his head, and the exposed skin was still a bit pink, as if the balding had all occurred last night.

"Stuart Nichols, personal secretary to Commissioner Curtis. If you'll follow me."

He didn't offer his hand or meet their eyes. He rose from the bench and climbed the wide marble stairs and they fell into place behind him.

"Merry Christmas," Mark Denton said to his back.

Stuart Nichols looked quickly over his shoulder, then straight ahead.

Mark looked over at Danny. Danny shrugged.

"Merry Christmas to you, too," Danny said.

"Why, thank you, Officer." Denton barely suppressed a smile, reminding Danny of his and Connor's days as altar boys. "And a Happy New Year to you, sir."

Stuart Nichols was either oblivious or didn't care. At the top of the stairs he led them down a corridor and then stopped outside a frosted glass door with the words BPD COMMISSIONER stenciled in gold leaf. He opened the door and led them into a small anteroom and went behind the desk and lifted the phone.

"They're here, Commissioner. Yes, sir."

He hung up the phone. "Take a seat, gentlemen."

Mark and Danny sat on the leather couch across from the desk and Danny tried to ignore the feeling that something was askew. They sat there for five minutes as Nichols opened his valise, removed a leather-bound notebook, and jotted in it with a silver fountain pen, the nib scratching across the page.

"Is the mayor here yet?" Mark asked, but the phone rang.

Nichols picked it up, listened, and replaced it in the cradle. "He'll see you now."

He went back to his notebook and Danny and Mark stood facing the oak door that led into the office. Mark reached for the brass knob and turned it and Danny followed him over the threshold into Curtis's office.

Curtis sat behind his desk. His ears seemed half as big as his head, the lobes hanging down like flaps. His flesh was florid and splotchy and breath exited his nose with an audible rasp. He flicked his eyes at them. He said, "Captain Coughlin's son, yes?"

"Yes, sir."

"The one who killed the bomber last month." He nodded, as if the killing were something he'd planned himself. He looked at some papers spread across his desk. "It's Daniel, is that right?"

"Aiden, sir. But people call me Danny."

Curtis gave that a small grimace.

"Take a seat, gentlemen." Behind him an oval window took up most of the wall. The city lay beyond, sharp and still on Christmas morning, white fields and red brick and cobblestone, the harbor stretching off the end of the landmass like a pale blue pan as fingers of chimney smoke climbed and quivered through the sky.

"Patrolman Denton," Curtis said. "You're with the Ninth Precinct. Correct?"

377

"Yes, sir."

Curtis scribbled something on a notepad and kept his eyes there as Danny took his seat beside Mark. "And Patrolman Coughlin—the First Precinct?"

"Yes, sir."

Another scratch of the pen.

"Is the mayor on his way, sir?" Denton draped his coat across his knee and the right arm of the chair.

"The mayor is in Maine." Curtis consulted a piece of paper before writing again in his notepad. "It's Christmas. He's with his family."

"Then, sir . . ." Mark looked over at Danny. He looked back at Curtis. "Sir, we had a meeting scheduled for ten o'clock with yourself and Mayor Peters."

"It's Christmas," Curtis repeated and opened a drawer. He rummaged for a bit and came out with another piece of paper which he placed to his left. "A Christian holiday. Mayor Peters deserves a day off, I would think, on our Lord's birthday."

"But the meeting was scheduled for—"

"Patrolman Denton, it's come to my attention that you've missed several roll calls on the night shift at the Ninth Precinct."

"Sir?"

Curtis lifted the piece of paper to his left. "This is your watch commander's duty report. You've missed or been tardy for nine roll calls in as many weeks."

He met their eyes for the first time.

Mark shifted in his chair. "Sir, I'm not here as a patrolman. I'm here as the chief officer of the Boston Social Club. And in that capacity, I respectfully submit that—"

"This is a clear dereliction of duty." Curtis waved the paper in the air. "It's in black and white, Patrolman. The Commonwealth expects its peace officers to earn their pay. And yet you haven't. Where have you been that you couldn't attend nine roll calls?"

"Sir, I don't think this is the issue at hand. We're going down a—"

"It very much is the issue at hand, Patrolman. You signed a contract. You swore to protect and serve the people of this great Commonwealth. You swore, Patrolman, to abide by and fulfill the duties assigned to you by the Boston Police Department. One of those duties, expressly stated in Article Seven of that contract, is attendance at roll call. And yet I have sworn affidavits from both the watch commander and the duty sergeant at the Ninth Precinct that you have elected not to perform this essential duty."

"Sir, I respectfully submit that there were a few occasions when I was unable to attend roll call due to my duties with the BSC but that—"

"You don't have *duties* with the BSC. You *elect* to perform labor on its behalf."

"—but that . . . In all cases, sir, I was given clearance by both the watch commander and the duty sergeant."

Curtis nodded. "May I finish?" he said.

Mark looked at him, the muscles in his cheek and jaw gone taut.

"May I finish?" Curtis repeated. "May I speak without fear of interruption? Because I find it rude, Patrolman. Do you find it rude to be interrupted?"

"I do, sir. That's why I—"

Curtis held up a hand. "Let me dispel the notion that you hold some moral high ground, Patrolman, because you most certainly do not. Your watch commander and your duty sergeant both admitted that they overlooked your tardiness or outright absence from roll call because they themselves are both members of this social club. However, they did not possess the right to make such a decision." He spread his hands. "It's not within their purview. Only a rank of captain or higher can make such allowances."

"Sir, I—"

"So, Patrolman Denton—"

379

"Sir, if I—"

"I am not finished, sir. Would you please allow me to *finish*?" Curtis propped his elbow on the desk and pointed at Mark. His splotchy face shook. "Did you or did you not show gross indifference to your duties as a patrol officer?"

"Sir, I was under the impress—"

"Answer the question."

"Sir, I believe—"

"Yes or no, Patrolman. Do you think the people of this city want excuses? I've talked to them, sir, and they do not. Did you, or did you not, fail to appear at roll call?"

He hunched his shoulder forward, the finger still pointed. Danny would have thought it comical if it had come from any other source, on any other day, in any other country. But Curtis had come to the table with something they'd never expected, something they would have thought outmoded and out-lived in the modern age: a kind of fundamental right-eousness that only the fundamental possessed. Unfettered by doubt, it achieved the appearance of moral intelligence and a resolute conscience. The terrible thing was how small it made you feel, how weaponless. How could you fight righteous rage if the only arms you bore were logic and sanity?

Denton opened up his attaché case and pulled out the pages he'd been working on for weeks. "Sir, if I could turn your attention to the raise we were promised in—"

"We?" Curtis said.

"Yes, the Boston Police Department, sir."

"You dare claim to represent these fine men?" Curtis scowled. "I've spoken to many a man since taking office, and I can tell you that *they* do not elect to call you 'Leader,' Patrolman Denton. They are tired of you putting words in their mouths and painting them as malcontents. Why, I spoke to a flatfoot at the Twelfth just yesterday and you know what he said to me? He said, 'Commissioner Curtis, we police at the One-Two are proud to serve our city in a time of need, sir.

You tell the folks out there in the neighborhoods that we won't go Bolsheviki. We're police officers.' "

Mark removed his own pen and notebook. "If I could have his name, sir, I'd be happy to speak with him regarding any grievances he may have with me."

Curtis waved it away. "I have talked to several dozen men, Patrolman Denton, from all over the city. Several dozen. And none of them, I promise you, is Bolsheviki."

"Nor am I, sir."

"Patrolman Coughlin." Curtis turned over another sheet of paper. "You were on special duty of late, as I understand it. Investigating terrorist cells in the city?"

Danny nodded.

"And how did that progress?"

"Fine, sir."

"Fine?" Curtis tugged at the flesh over his wing collar. "I've read Lieutenant McKenna's duty reports. They're padded with ambiguous projections with no basis in any reality. That led me to study the files of his previous Special Squads and once again I'm at a loss to discern any return on the public's trust. Now this, Officer Coughlin, is exactly the kind of busywork that I find detracts from a police officer's sworn duties. Could you describe for me specifically what kind of progress you feel you made with these—what are their names?—Lettish Workers before your cover was blown?"

"Lettish Workingman's Society, sir," Danny said. "And the progress is a bit difficult to ascertain. I was undercover, attempting to get closer to Louis Fraina, the leader of the group, a known subversive, and the editor of *Revolutionary Age*."

"To what end?"

"We have reason to believe they're planning an attack in this city."

"When?"

"May Day seems a likely target date, but there have been whispers that—"

"Whispers," Curtis said. "I question whether we have a terrorist problem at all."

"Sir, with all due respect, I—"

Curtis nodded half a dozen times. "Yes, you shot one. I am quite aware of it, as I'm sure your great-great-grandchildren will be. But he was one man. The only one, in my opinion, operating in this city. Are you trying to scare businesses away from this city? Do you think if it becomes common knowledge that we're engaged in some far-flung operation designated to expose *dozens* of terrorist sects within our city limits that any reasonable-minded company would set up shop here. Why, they'll run to New York, men! To Philadelphia! Providence!"

"Lieutenant McKenna and several members of the Justice Department," Danny said, "believe that May Day is a target date for national revolt."

Curtis's gaze remained on his desktop and in the silence that followed Danny wondered if he'd heard anything he'd said.

"You had a pair of anarchists making bombs right under your nose. Yes?"

Mark looked over at him. Danny nodded.

"And so you took this assignment to atone and managed to kill one of them."

Danny said, "Something like that, sir."

"Do you have a blood thirst for subversives, Officer?"

Danny said, "I don't like the violent ones, sir, but I wouldn't call it a blood thirst."

Curtis nodded. "And what of subversives right now within our own department, men who are spreading discontent among the ranks, men who would Russianize this honorable protectorate of the public interest? Men who gather and talk of striking, of putting their petty interests before the common good?"

Mark stood. "Let's go, Dan."

Curtis narrowed his eyes and they were dark marbles of

wasted promise. "If you do not sit, I will suspend you—right here and right now—and you can fight your battle for re-instatement through a judge."

Mark sat. "You are making a grave mistake, sir. When the press hear about—"

"They stayed home today," Curtis said.

"What?"

"Once they were informed late last night that Mayor Peters would not be in attendance and that the main order of business would have very little to do with this 'union' you call a social club, they decided to spend time with their families. Do you know any well enough to possess their home telephone numbers, Patrolman Denton?"

Danny felt numb and sickly warm as Curtis turned his attention back to him.

"Patrolman Coughlin, I feel you are wasted in street patrol. I would like you to join Detective Sergeant Steven Harris in Internal Affairs."

Danny felt the numbness leave him. He shook his head. "No, sir."

"You're refusing a request from your commissioner? You, who slept with a bomb thrower? A bomb thrower who, as far as we know, is still lurking in our streets?"

"I am, sir, but respectfully."

"There is no respect in the denial of a superior's request."

"I'm sorry you see it that way, sir."

Curtis leaned back in his chair. "So you're a friend of the workingman, of the Bolsheviki, of the subversive who mas-querades as the 'common man.' "

"I believe the Boston Social Club represents the men of the BPD, sir."

"I do not," Curtis said. He drummed his hand on the desktop.

"That's clear, sir." This time Danny stood up.

Curtis allowed himself a pinched smile as Mark stood as well. Danny and Mark donned their topcoats and Curtis leaned back in his chair.

"The days of this department being run, sub rosa, by men like Edward McKenna and your father are over. The days the department capitulates to the demands of Bolsheviki are long gone as well. Patrolman Denton, stand at attention if you please, sir."

Mark turned his shoulders and placed his hands behind his back.

"You are reassigned to Precinct Fifteen in Charlestown. You are to report there immediately. That means this afternoon, Patrolman, and begin your duties on the split shift from noon to midnight."

Mark knew exactly what that meant: There'd be no way to hold meetings at Fay Hall if he was locked down in Charlestown from twelve to twelve.

"Officer Coughlin, at attention. You are reassigned as well."

"To, sir?"

"A special detail. You're familiar with those as a matter of record."

"Yes, sir."

The commissioner leaned back in his chair and ran his hand over his belly. "You're on strike detail until further notice. Anytime the workingman walks out on the good men who deem to pay him, you will be there to ensure that no violence takes place. You'll be loaned out on an as-needed basis to police departments across the state. Until further notice, Officer Coughlin, you're a strike breaker."

Curtis placed his elbows on the desk and peered at Danny, waiting for a reaction.

"As you say, sir," Danny said.

"Welcome to the new Boston Police Department," Curtis said. "You're dismissed, gentlemen."

Walking out of the office, Danny was in such a state of shock that he assumed nothing else could add to it, but then he saw the men waiting their turn in the anteroom:

Trescott, recording secretary for the BSC.

McRae, treasurer.

Slatterly, vice president.

Fenton, press secretary.

It was McRae who stood and said, "What the hell's going on? I got a call half an hour ago telling me to report to Pemberton immediately. Dan? Mark?"

Mark looked shell-shocked. He placed a hand on McRae's arm. "It's a bloodbath," he whispered.

Outside, on the stairs, they lit cigarettes and tried to regain their composure.

"They can't do this," Mark said.

"They just did."

"Temporary," Mark said. "Temporary. I'll call our lawyer, Clarence Rowley. He'll scream bloody murder. He'll get an injunction."

"What injunction?" Danny said. "He didn't suspend us, Mark. He just reassigned us. It's within his power. There's nothing to sue over."

"When the press hears, they'll . . ." His voice drifted off and he took a drag off his cigarette.

"Maybe," Danny said. "If it's a slow news day."

"Jesus," Mark said softly. "Jesus."

Danny stared out at the empty streets and then up at the empty sky. Such a beautiful day, crisp and windless and clear.

CHAPTER *twenty-two*

Danny, his father, and Eddie McKenna met in the study before Christmas dinner. Eddie wouldn't be staying; he had his own family to join at home on Telegraph Hill a few blocks away. He took a long gulp from his brandy snifter. "Tom, the man's on a crusade. And he thinks we're the infidels. He sent an order to my office last night that I'm to *retrain* all my men on crowd control and riot procedure. He wants them requalified for mounted duty as well. And now he's going after the social club?"

Thomas Coughlin came to him with the brandy decanter and refilled his glass. "We'll ride it out, Eddie. We've ridden out worse."

Eddie nodded, bolstered by the pat of Thomas Coughlin's hand on his back.

Thomas said to Danny, "Your man, Denton, he's contacting the BSC lawyer?"

Danny said, "Rowley, yeah."

Thomas sat back against the desk and rubbed his palm over the back of his head and frowned, a sign he was thinking furiously. "He played it smart. If he'd suspended you, that's one thing, but reassignment—while it may *look* bad—is a card he can play very well if you buck back against him. And lest we forget—he's got you on that terrorist you shacked up with."

Danny refilled his own drink, noticing the last one had

gone down rather quickly. "And how's he know about that? I thought it was suppressed."

His father's eyes widened. "It didn't come from me, if that's what you're implying. You, Eddie?"

Eddie said, "You had some kind of dustup, I heard, with some Justice agents a few weeks back. On Salem Street? Pulled some girl out of a car?"

Danny nodded. "It's how I found Federico Ficara."

McKenna shrugged. "Justice leaks like a freshly failed virgin, Dan. Always has."

"Fuck." Danny slapped the side of a leather chair.

"As far as *Commissioner* Curtis sees it right now," Thomas said, "it's vendetta hour. Payback, gentlemen. For every time he took it up the behind from Lomasney and the ward bosses when he was mayor. For every lowly position he was farmed out to across the Commonwealth since 1897. For all the dinners he wasn't invited to, all the parties he found out about after the fact. For every time his missus looked embarrassed to be seen with him. He is a Brahmin, gents, through and through. And until a week ago, he was a Brahmin in disgrace." His father swirled the brandy in his glass and reached into the ashtray for his cigar. "That would give any man an unfortunate sense of the epic when it came to settling his accounts."

"So what do we do, Thomas?"

"You bide your time. Keep your head down."

"Same advice I gave the boy just last week." Eddie smiled at Danny.

"I'm serious. You, Eddie, you will have to swallow a lot of pride in the coming months. I'm a captain—he can call me on the carpet for a few things but my ship is tight and my precinct has seen a six percent drop in violent crime since I took over. That's here," he said and pointed at the floor, "at the Twelfth, historically the most crime-ridden nonwop district in the city. He can't do much to me unless I give him ammunition, and I will be resolute in my refusal to do so. But you're a lieutenant and you don't keep open books. He's going to put the screws to you, boy, something hard. Twist them tight, he will."

"So . . . ?"

"So, if he wants you warming up the horses and keeping your men standing at parade rest until the return of the Christ, you hop to. And you," he said to Danny, "you steer clear of the BSC."

"No." Danny drained his drink and stood to refill it.

"Did you just hear what I—"

"I'll do his strikebreaking for him and I won't complain. I'll polish my buttons and shine my shoes, but I'm not turning tail on the BSC."

"He'll crucify you then."

There was a soft knock on the door. "Thomas?"

"Yes, dear."

"Dinner in five minutes."

"Thank you, love."

Ellen Coughlin's footfalls receded as Eddie took his coat from the stand. "Looks to be a hell of a New Year, gents."

"Buck up, Eddie," Thomas said. "We are the wards and the wards control this city. Don't forget it."

"I won't, Tom, thanks. Merry Christmas."

"Merry Christmas."

"To you as well, Dan."

"Merry Christmas, Eddie. Our best to Mary Pat."

"Sure, she'll be glad to hear that, she will."

He let himself out of the office and Danny found his father's gaze on him again as he took another pull from his drink.

"Curtis really took the wind out of you, didn't he, boy?"

"I'll get it back."

Neither said anything for a moment. They could hear the scrape of chairs and the bump of heavy bowls and plates on the dining room table.

"Von Clausewitz said that war is politics by other means."

Thomas smiled softly and took a drink. "I've always felt he got it backward."

Connor had returned from work less than an hour ago. He'd been detached to a suspected arson and still smelled of soot and smoke. A four-alarm fire, he said, passing the potatoes to Joe, two dead. And obviously for the insurance which added up to a few hundred more than the owners could have gotten in a legitimate sale. The Polish, he said with a roll of his eyes.

"You have to be more careful," his mother said. "You're not just living for yourself anymore."

Danny saw Nora blush at that, saw Connor throw her a wink and a smile.

"I know, Ma. I know. I will. I promise."

Danny looked at his father, sitting to his right at the head of the table. His father met his eyes and his were flat.

"Did I miss an announcement?" Danny said.

"Oh, sh—" Connor looked at their mother. "Shoot," he said and looked at Nora, then back at Danny. "She said yes, Dan. Nora. She said yes."

Nora lifted her head and her eyes met Danny's. They were charged with a pride and vanity that he found repulsive.

It was her smile that was weak.

Danny took a sip of the drink he'd carried with him out of his father's office. He cut into his slice of ham. He felt the eyes of the whole table on him. He was expected to say something. Connor watched him, waiting with an open mouth. His mother looked at him curiously. Joe's fork froze above his plate.

Danny put down his fork and knife. He plastered a smile on his face that felt big and bright. Hell, it felt huge. He saw Joe relax and his mother's eyes lose their confusion. He willed the smile into his eyes, felt them widen in their sockets. He raised his glass.

"That's just great!" He raised his glass higher.

"Congratulations to the both of you. I'm so happy for you."

Connor laughed and raised his own glass.

"To Connor and Nora!" Danny boomed.

"To Connor and Nora!" The rest of the family raised their glasses and met them in the center of the table.

It was between dinner and dessert that Nora found him as he was coming back out of his father's study with another refill of scotch.

"I tried to tell you," she said. "I called the rooming house three times yesterday."

"I didn't get home till after six."

"Oh."

He clapped one hand on her shoulder. "No, it's great. It's terrific. I couldn't be more pleased."

She rubbed her shoulder. "I'm glad."

"When's the date?"

"We thought March seventeenth."

"Saint Patrick's Day. Perfect. This time next year? Heck, you might have a child for Christmas."

"I might."

"Hey—twins!" he said. "Wouldn't that be something?"

He drained his glass. She stared up into his face as if searching. Searching for what, he had no idea. What was left to search for? Decisions, clearly, had been made.

"Do you—"

"What?"

"Want to, I don't know what to say . . ."

"So, don't."

"Ask anything? Know anything?"

"Nope," he said. "I'm going to get another drink. You?"

He walked into the study and found the decanter and noticed how much less was in it than when he'd arrived earlier in the afternoon.

"Danny."

"Don't." He turned to her with a smile.

"Don't what?"

"Say my name."

"Why can't I—?"

"Like it means anything," he said. "Change the tone. All right? Just do that. When you say it."

She twisted her wrist in one hand and then dropped both hands to her sides. "I . . ."

"What?" He took a strong pull from his glass.

"I can't abide a man feels sorry for himself."

He shrugged. "Heavens. How Irish of you."

"You're drunk."

"Just getting started."

"I'm sorry."

He laughed.

"I am."

"Let me ask you something—you know the old man is looking into things back in the Old Sod. I told you that."

She nodded, her eyes on the carpet.

"Is that why you're rushing the wedding?"

She raised her head, met his eyes, said nothing.

"You really think it'll save you if the family finds out you're already married?"

"I think . . ." Her voice was so soft he could barely hear it. "I think if I'm wed to Connor, your father will never disown me. He'll do what he does best—whatever is necessary."

"You're that afraid of being disowned."

"I'm that afraid of being alone," she said. "Of going hungry again. Of being . . ." She shook her head.

"What?"

Her eyes found the rug again. "Helpless."

"My, my, Nora, quite the survivor, eh?" He chuckled. "You make me want to puke."

She said, "I what?"

"All over the carpet," he said.

Her petticoat swished as she crossed the study and poured herself an Irish whiskey. She threw back half of it and turned to him. "Who the fuck are you, then, boy?"

"Pretty mouth," he said. "Gorgeous."

"I make you want to vomit, Danny?"

"At the moment."

"And why's that, then?"

He crossed to her. He thought of lifting her up by her smooth white throat. He thought of eating her heart so it could never look back through her eyes at him.

"You don't love him," he said.

"I do."

"Not the way you loved me."

"Who says I did?"

"You did."

"You say."

"*You* say." He took her shoulders in his hands.

"Off me now."

"*You* say."

"Off me now. Unhand me."

He dropped his forehead to the flesh just below her throat. He felt more alone than when the bomb landed on the floor of Salutation Street Precinct, more alone and more sick of his very self than he'd ever expected to feel.

"I love you."

She pushed his head back. "You love yourself, boy. You—"

"No—"

She gripped his ears, stared into him. "Yes. You love yourself. The grand music of it. I'm tone-deaf, Danny. I couldn't keep up."

He straightened and sucked air in through his nostrils, cleared his eyes. "Do you love him? Do you?"

"I'll learn," she said and drained the rest of her glass.

"You didn't have to learn with me."

"And look where that got us," she said and walked out of his father's study.

They had just sat down again for dessert when the doorbell rang.

Danny could feel the booze darkening his blood, growing thick in his limbs, perched dire and vengeful in his brain.

Joe answered the bell. After the front door had been open long enough for the night air to have reached the dining room, Thomas called, "Joe, who is it? Shut the door."

They heard the door shut, heard a soft muffled exchange between Joe and a voice Danny didn't recognize. It was low and thick, the words unintelligible from where he sat.

"Dad?" Joe stood in the doorway.

A man came through the doorway behind him. He was tall but stoop-shouldered, with a long, hungry face covered in a dark, matted beard shot through with tangles of gray over the chin. His eyes were dark and small but somehow managed to protrude from their sockets. The hair on the top of his head was shaven to a white stubble. His clothes were cheap and tattered; Danny could smell them from the other side of the room.

He gave them all a smile, his few remaining teeth the yellow of a damp cigarette left drying in the sun.

"How are you God-fearing folk tonight? Well, I trust?"

Thomas Coughlin stood. "What's this?"

The man's eyes found Nora.

"And how are you, then, luv?"

Nora seemed struck dead where she sat, with one hand on her teacup, her eyes blank and unmoving.

The man held up a hand. "Sorry to disturb you folks, I am. You must be Captain Coughlin, sir."

Joe moved carefully away from the man, sliding along the wall until he reached the far end of the table near his mother and Connor.

"I'm Thomas Coughlin," he said. "And you're in my home on Christmas, man, so you best get to telling me your business."

The man held up two soiled palms. "My name's Quentin Finn. I believe that's my wife sitting at your table there, sir."

393

Connor's chair hit the floor when he stood. "Who the—?"

"Connor," their father said. "Hold your temper, boy."

"Aye," Quentin Finn said, "that's her sure as it's Christmas, it is. Miss me, luv?"

Nora opened her mouth but no words left it. Danny watched parts of her grow small and covered up and hopeless. She kept moving her mouth, and still no words would come. The lie she'd given birth to when she'd arrived in this city, the lie she'd first told when she'd been sitting naked and gray with her teeth clacking from the cold in their kitchen five years before, the lie she'd built every day of her life on since, spilled. Spilled all over the room until the mess of it was reconstituted and reborn as its opposite: truth.

A hideous truth, Danny noted. At least twice her age. She'd kissed that mouth? Slid her tongue through those teeth?

"I said—you miss me, luv?"

Thomas Coughlin held up a hand. "You'll need to be clearer, Mr. Finn."

Quentin Finn narrowed his eyes at him. "Clearer about what, sir? I married this woman. Gave her me name. Shared title to me land in Donegal. She's my wife, sir. And I've come to take her home."

Nora had gone too long without speaking. Danny could see that clearly—in his mother's eyes, in Connor's. If she'd ever held hope of denial, the moment had passed.

Connor said, "Nora."

Nora closed her eyes. She said, "Ssshh," and held up her hand.

" 'Ssshh'?" Connor repeated.

"Is this true?" Danny's mother said. "Nora? Look at me. Is this true?"

But Nora wouldn't look. She wouldn't open her eyes. She kept waving her hand back and forth, as if it could ward off time.

Danny couldn't help but be perversely fascinated by the man in the doorway. *This*, he wanted to say? You fucked *this*?

He could feel the liquor sledding through his blood and he knew some better part of himself waited behind it, but now the only part he could reach was the one who'd placed his head to her chest and told her he loved her.

To which she'd replied: You love yourself.

His father said, "Mr. Finn, take a seat, sir."

"I'll stand, sure, Captain, if it's all the same to ya."

"What do you expect is going to happen here tonight?" Thomas said.

"I expect to walk back out that door with my wife in tow, I do." He nodded.

Thomas looked at Nora. "Raise your head, girl."

Nora opened her eyes, looked at him.

"Is it true. Is this man your husband?"

Nora's eyes found Danny's. What had she said in the study? *I can't abide a man feels sorry for himself.* Who's feeling sorry now?

Danny dropped his eyes.

"Nora," his father said. "Answer the question, please. Is he your husband?"

She reached for her teacup but it tottered in her grip and she let it go.

"He was."

Danny's mother blessed herself.

"Jesus *Christ!*" Connor kicked the baseboard.

"Joe," their father said quietly, "go to your room. And don't dare argue, son."

Joe opened his mouth, thought better of it, and left the dining room.

Danny realized he was shaking his head and stopped himself. *This?* He wanted to shout the word. You married this grim, grisly joke? And you dared talk down to me?

He took another drink as Quentin Finn took two sideways steps into the room.

"Nora," Thomas Coughlin said, "you said *was* your husband. So I can assume there was an annulment, yes?"

Nora looked at Danny again. Her eyes had a shine that could have been mistaken, under different circumstances, for happiness.

Danny looked over at Quentin again, the man scratching at his beard.

"Nora," Thomas said, "did you get an annulment? Answer me, girl."

Nora shook her head.

Danny rattled the ice cubes in his glass. "Quentin."

Quentin Finn looked over at him. He raised his eyebrows. "Yes, young sir?"

"How'd you find us?"

"A man has ways," Quentin Finn said. "I've been searching for this lass for some time now."

Danny nodded. "You're a man of means then."

"Aiden."

Danny lolled his head to look at his father, then lolled it back to Quentin. "To track a woman across an ocean, Mr. Finn, that's quite a feat. Quite a costly feat."

Quentin smiled at Danny's father. "I see the boy's been in his cups, yah?"

Danny lit a cigarette with the candle. "Call me 'boy' again, Paddy, and I'll—"

"Aiden!" his father said. "Enough." He turned back to Nora. "Have you any defense, girl? Is he telling a lie?"

Nora said, "He is not my husband."

"He says he is."

"Any*more*."

Thomas leaned into the table. "They don't grant divorces in Catholic Ireland."

"I didn't say I got me a divorce, sir. I just said he was my husband no longer."

Quentin Finn laughed at that, a loud *haw* that tore the air in the room.

"Jesus," Connor whispered over and over again. "Jesus."

"Pack your things now, luv."

396

Nora looked at him. There was hate in her eyes. And fear. Disgust. Disgrace.

"He bought me," she said, "when I was thirteen. Man's my cousin. Yeah?" She looked at each of the Coughlins. "Thirteen. The way you buy a cow."

Thomas extended his hands across the table toward her. "A tragic state," he said softly. "But he is your husband, Nora."

"Fookin' right on that, Cap'n."

Ellen Coughlin blessed herself and placed a hand to her chest.

Thomas kept his eyes on Nora. "Mr. Finn, if you use profanity in my home again? In front of my wife, sir?" He turned his head, gave Quentin Finn a smile. "Your path home will, I promise, become far less predictable."

Quentin Finn scratched his beard some more.

Thomas tugged Nora's hands gently until he covered them, and then he looked over at Connor. Connor had the heels of his hands pressed to his lower eyelids. Thomas turned next to his wife, who shook her head. Thomas nodded. He looked at Danny.

Danny looked back into his father's eyes, so clear and blue. The eyes of a child with irreproachable intelligence and irreproachable intent.

Nora whispered, "Please don't make me leave with him."

Connor made a noise that could have been a laugh.

"Please, sir."

Thomas ran his palms over the backs of her hands. "But you will have to leave."

She nodded and one tear fell from her cheekbone. "Just not now? Not with him?"

Thomas said, "All right, dear." He turned his head. "Mr. Finn."

"Yes, Cap'n."

"Your rights as a husband have been noted. And respected, sir."

"Thank ye."

"You'll leave now and meet me tomorrow morning at the Twelfth Precinct on East Fourth Street. We'll properly adjudicate the issue then."

Quentin Finn was shaking his head before Thomas had half finished. "I didn't cross the bloody ocean to be put off, man. No. I'll be taking me wife now, thank ye."

"Aiden."

Danny pushed back his chair and stood.

Quentin said, "I have rights as a husband, Cap'n. I do."

"And those will be respected. But for tonight, I—"

"And what of her child, sir? What's he to think of—"

"She has a kid?" Connor raised his head from his hands.

Ellen Coughlin blessed herself again. "Holy Mary Mother of Jesus."

Thomas let go of Nora's hands.

"Aye, she has a little nipper back at home, she does," Quentin Finn said.

"You abandoned your own child?" Thomas said.

Danny watched her eyes dart, her shoulders hunch. She pulled her arms in tight against her body—prey, always prey, searching, plotting, tensing for the mad dash.

A child? She'd never said a word.

"He's not mine," she said. "He's *his*."

"You left a child behind?" Danny's mother said. "A child?"

"Not mine," Nora said and reached for her but Ellen Coughlin pulled her arms back into her lap. "Not mine, not mine, not mine."

Quentin allowed himself a smile. "The lad's lost, he is, without his mother. Lost."

"He's not mine," she said to Danny. Then to Connor: "He's not."

"Don't," Connor said.

Danny's father stood and ran his hand through his hair, scratched the back of his head, and let out a heavy sigh. "We trusted you," he said. "With our son. With Joe. How could you have put us in that position? How could you have misled us? Our *child*, Nora. We trusted you with our child."

"And I did well by him," Nora said, finding something in herself that Danny had seen in fighters, usually the smaller ones, in the late rounds of a bout, something that went far deeper than size and physical strength. "I did well by him and well by you, sir, and well by your family."

Thomas looked at her, then at Quentin Finn, then back at her, and finally at Connor. "You were going to marry my son. You would have embarrassed us. Besmirched my name? *This* name of *this* house that gave you shelter, gave you food, treated you like family? How dare you, woman? How dare you?"

Nora looked right back at him, the tears finally coming now. "How dare I? This home is a coffin to that boy." She pointed back in the direction of Joe's room. "He feels it every day. I took care of him because he doesn't even know his own mother. She—"

Ellen Coughlin stood from the table but moved no farther. She placed her hand on the back of her chair.

"Close your mouth," Thomas Coughlin said. "Close it, you banshee."

"You whore," Connor said. "You filthy whore."

"Oh, dear Lord," Ellen Coughlin said. "Stop. Stop!"

Joe walked into the dining room. He looked up at them all. "What?" he said. "What?"

Thomas said to Nora, "Leave this house at once."

Quentin Finn smiled.

Danny said, "Dad."

But his father had reached a place most sensed in him but few ever saw. He pointed at Danny without looking at him. "You're drunk. Go home."

"What?" Joe said, his voice thick. "Why's everyone yelling?"

"Go to bed," Connor said.

Ellen Coughlin held out a hand for Joe, but he ignored it. He looked to Nora. "Why's everyone yelling?"

"Come now, woman," Quentin Finn said.

Nora said to Thomas, "Don't do this."

"I said close that mouth."

"Dad," Joe said, "why's everyone *yelling*?"

Danny said, "Look—"

Quentin Finn crossed to Nora's chair and pulled her out of it by her hair.

Joe let out a wail and Ellen Coughlin screamed and Thomas said, "Everyone just calm down."

"She's my *wife*." Quentin dragged her along the floor.

Joe took a run at him, but Connor scooped him up in his arms and Joe batted his fists against Connor's chest and shoulders. Danny's mother fell back into her chair and wept loudly and prayed to the Holy Mother.

Quentin pulled Nora tight to him so that her cheek was pressed against his and said, "If someone would gather her effects, yah?"

Danny's father held out his hand and shouted, "No!" because Danny's arm was already cocked as he came around the table and smashed his scotch glass into the back of Quentin Finn's head.

Someone else screamed, "Danny!"—maybe his mother, maybe Nora, could have even been Joe—but by that point he'd hooked his fingers into the socket-bones above Quentin Finn's eyes and used them to ram the back of his head into the dining room doorway. A hand grabbed at his back but fell away as he spun Quentin Finn into the hallway and ran him down the length of it. Joe must have left the front door unlatched because Quentin's head popped the door wide as he went through it and out into the night. When his chest hit the stairs, it pushed through a fresh inch of snow and he landed on the sidewalk where the flakes fell fast and fat. He bounced on the cement and Danny was surprised to see him stumble to his feet for a few steps, his arms pinwheeling, before he slipped in the snow and fell with his left leg folded under him against the curb.

Danny came down the steps gingerly because the stoop was built of iron and the snow was soft and slick. The sidewalk had some slush in the places Quentin had slid through and Danny caught his eye as Quentin made it to his feet.

"Make it fun," Danny said. "Run."

His father grabbed him by the shoulder, spinning him halfway around, and Danny saw something in his father's eyes he'd never seen before—uncertainty, maybe even fear.

"Leave him be," his father said.

His mother reached the doorway just as Danny lifted his father by his shirt lapels and carried him back to a tree.

"Jesus, Danny!" This from Connor, on top of the stoop now as Danny heard Quentin Finn's shoes slap through the slush in the middle of K Street.

Danny looked into his father's face, pressed his back gently against the tree. "You let her pack," he said.

"Aiden, you need to calm yourself."

"Let her take whatever she needs. This is not a negotiation, sir. We firm on that?"

His father stared back into his eyes for a long time and then eventually gave him a flick of his eyelids that Danny took for assent.

He placed his father back on the ground. Nora appeared in the doorway, her temple scraped from Quentin Finn's nails. She met his eyes and he turned away.

He let out a laugh that surprised even him and took off running up K Street. Quentin had a two-block head start, but Danny cut off through the backyards of K Street and then I Street and then J, vaulting fences like he was still altar-boy age, knowing that Quentin's only possible destination was the streetcar stop. He came barreling out of an alley between J and H and hit Quentin Finn up at the shoulders and brought him sliding down into the snow in the middle of East Fifth Street.

Christmas lights had been strung up in garlands above the street, and candles lit the windows of half the homes along the block as Quentin tried to box with Danny before Danny ended a series of light jabs to both sides of his face with a torrent of body blows that finished with the one-two snap of a right and left rib. Quentin tried to run again, but Danny caught him by his coat and swung him around in the snow a few times before releasing him into a streetlamp pole. Then he climbed on top of him and broke bones in his face and broke his nose and snapped a few more ribs.

Quentin wept. Quentin begged. Quentin said, "No more, no more." With each syllable he spat another fine spray of blood up into the air and back down onto his face.

When Danny felt the ache bite into his hands, he stopped. He sat back on Quentin's midsection and then wiped his knuckles off on the man's coat. He rubbed snow into the man's face until his eyes snapped open.

Danny took a few gulps of air. "I haven't lost my temper since I was eighteen years old. You believe that? True. Eight years. Almost nine . . ." He sighed and looked out at the street, the snow, the lights.

"I won't . . . be a . . . bother to ya," Quentin said.

Danny laughed. "You don't say?"

"I . . . just want . . . me . . . w-wife."

Danny took Quentin's ears in his hands and softly banged his head off the cobblestone for a bit.

"As soon as you're released from the charity ward, you get on a boat and leave my country," Danny said. "Or you stay and I call this assault on a police officer. See all these windows? Half of them belong to cops. You want to pick a fight with the Boston Police Department, Quentin? Spend ten years in an American prison?"

Quentin's eyes rolled to the left.

"Look at me."

Quentin's eyes fixed in place and then he vomited on the collar of his coat.

Danny waved at the fumes. "Yes or no? Do you want the assault charge?"

Quentin said, "No."

"Are you going home as soon as you get out of a hospital?"

"Yah, yah."

"Good lad." Danny stood. "Because if you don't, God is my witness, Quentin?" He looked down at him. "I'll send you back to the Old Sod a fucking cripple."

Thomas was out on the stoop when Danny returned. The taillights of his father's car glowed red as his driver, Marty Kenneally, braked at an intersection two blocks up.

"So Marty's driving her someplace?"

His father nodded. "I told him I don't want to know where."

Danny looked at the windows of their home. "What's it like in there?"

His father appraised the blood on Danny's shirt, his torn knuckles. "You leave anything for the ambulance driver?"

Danny rested his hip against the black iron railing. "Plenty. I already called it in from the call box on J."

"Put the fear of God into him, I'm sure."

"Worse than God." He fished in his pockets and found his Murads and shook one out of the pack. He offered one to his father and his father took it and Danny lit both with his lighter and leaned back against the railing.

"Haven't seen you get like that, boy, since I had you locked up in your teens."

Danny blew a stream of smoke into the cold air, feeling the sweat beginning to dry on his upper chest and neck. "Yeah, it's been a while."

"Would you have honestly hit me?" his father said. "When you had me against the tree?"

Danny shrugged. "Might have. We'll never know."

"Your own father."

Danny chuckled. "You had no problem hitting me when I was a kid."

"That was discipline."

"So was this." Danny looked over at his father.

Thomas shook his head softly and exhaled a blue stream of smoke into the night.

"I didn't know she left a child behind back there, Dad. Had no idea."

His father nodded.

"But you did," Danny said.

His father looked over, the smoke sliding out of the corner of his mouth.

"You brought Quentin here. Left a trail of bread crumbs and he found our door."

Thomas Coughlin said, "You give me too much credit."

Danny rolled his dice and told the lie. "He told me you did, Dad."

His father sucked the night air through his nostrils and looked up at the sky. "You'd have never stopped loving her. Connor either."

"What about Joe? What about what he just saw in there?"

"Everyone has to grow up sometime." His father shrugged. "It's not Joe's maturing I worry about, you infant. It's yours."

Danny nodded and flicked his cigarette into the street.

"You can stop worrying," he said.

CHAPTER *twenty-three*

Late Christmas afternoon, before the Coughlins had sat for dinner, Luther took the streetcar back to the South End. The day had started with a bright sky and clear air, but by the time Luther boarded the streetcar, the air had turned indistinct and the sky had folded back and fallen into the ground. Somehow the streets, so gray and quiet, were pretty, a sense that the city had gone privately festive. Soon the snow began to fall, the flakes small and listing like kites at first, riding the sudden wind, but then as the streetcar bucked its way over the hump of the Broadway Bridge, the flakes grew thick as flower heads and shot past the windows in the black wind. Luther, the only person sitting in the colored section, accidentally caught the eye of a white man sitting with his girlfriend two rows up. The man looked weary in a satisfied way, and his cheap wool flat cap was tilted down just so over his right eye, giving a little bit of nothing a little bit of style. He nodded, as if he and Luther shared the same thought, his girlfriend curled against his chest with her eyes closed.

"Looks like Christmas should, don't it?" The man slid his chin over his girl's head and his nostrils widened as he smelled her hair.

"Sure does," Luther said, surprised it didn't come out "Sure do" in an all-white car.

"Heading home?"

"Yeah."

"To family?" The white guy lowered his cigarette to his girl's lips and she opened her mouth to take a drag.

"Wife and child," Luther said.

The man closed his eyes for a second and nodded. "That's good."

"Yes, sir, it is." Luther swallowed against the wave of solitude that tried to rise in him.

"Merry Christmas," the man said and took his cigarette from his girl's lips and put it between his own.

"Same to you, sir."

In the Giddreauxs' foyer, he removed his coat and scarf and hung them, wet and steaming, on the radiator. He could hear voices coming from the dining room and he smoothed the snow into his hair with his palms and then wiped his palms on his coat.

When he opened the door into the main house, he heard the overlapping laughter and overlapping chatter of several conversations. Silverware and glasses clinked and he smelled roast turkey and maybe a deep-fried one as well and some kind of cinnamon scent that might have come from hot cider. Four children came running down the stairs toward him, three colored, one white, and they laughed maniacally in his face when they reached the first floor and then ran full-out down the hall toward the kitchen.

He opened the pocket doors to the dining room and the guests turned to look at him, women mostly, a few older men and two about Luther's age whom he took to be the sons of Mrs. Grouse, the Giddreauxs' housekeeper. Just over a dozen people, all told, and half of them white, and Luther recognized the females who helped out at the NAACP and assumed the males were their husbands.

"Franklin Grouse," a younger colored man said and shook Luther's hand. He extended a glass of eggnog. "You must be Luther. My mother told me about you."

"Nice to meet you, Franklin. Merry Christmas." Luther raised his glass of eggnog and took a drink.

It was a wonderful dinner. Isaiah had returned from Washington the night before and promised he wouldn't talk politics until after dessert, so they ate and drank and chided the children when they got a little too boisterous and the talk jumped from the latest picture shows to popular books and songs and then to the rumor that war radios would become a consumer item that would broadcast news and voices and plays and songs from all over the world, and Luther tried to picture how a play could be performed through a box, but Isaiah said it was to be expected. Between phone lines and telegraphs and Sopwith Camels, the future of the world was air. Air travel, air communication, air ideas. Soil was played out, ocean, too; but air was like a train track that never met the sea. Soon we'd be speaking Spanish and they'd be speaking English.

"That a good thing, Mr. Giddreaux?" Franklin Grouse said.

Isaiah tilted his hand from left-to-right, left-to-right. "It's what man makes of it."

"White man or black man?" Luther asked, and the table broke out laughing.

The happier and more comfortable he became, the sadder he felt. This could be his life—should be his life—with Lila, right now, not as a guest at the table but as the head of it and maybe some of those children would have been his, too. He caught Mrs. Giddreaux smiling at him, and when he met her smile with his own, she gave him a wink, and he could see her soul again, the supple grace of it, and it was lit with blue light.

At the end of the evening, after most of the guests had left and Isaiah and Yvette were taking their brandy with the Parthans, two old friends since his days at Morehouse and hers at Atlanta Baptist, Luther excused himself and went up to the roof with his own glass of brandy and let himself out onto the widow's walk. The snow had stopped falling, but all the roofs were thick with it. Horns bayed from the harbor and the lights of the city spread a yellow band across the lowest reaches of the sky. He closed his eyes and sucked in the smell of the night and the snow and cold, the smoke and soot and brick dust. He felt as if he were snorting the sky right off the outermost curve of the earth. He kept his eyes shut tight and blocked out the death of Jessie and the stone-ache in his heart that had only one name: Lila. He asked only for this moment, this air that he held in his lungs, that filled his body and swelled in his head.

But it didn't work—Jessie came crashing through, turning to Luther to say, "Kinda fun, huh?" and less than a second later pieces of his head went popping off and he fell to the floor. The Deacon, too, the Deacon of all people, surfaced in the wave that followed Jessie, and Luther saw him clutching at him, heard him saying, "Make this right," and his eyes bulged with the universal plea not to be extinguished, not today, as Luther shoved the gun under his chin, and those bulging eyes said *I'm not ready to go. Wait.*

But Luther hadn't waited. And now the Deacon was somewhere with Jessie and Luther was up here, aboveground. It took only a second for another to arrive on the same path as yours and change your life to a point it couldn't change back. One second.

"Why won't you write me, woman?" Luther whispered it to the starless sky. "You carrying my child, and I don't want him growing up without me. Don't want him knowing that feeling. No, no, girl," he whispered, "there's only you. Only you."

He lifted his brandy off the brick ledge and took a drink that singed his throat and warmed his chest and widened his eyes.

"Lila," he whispered and took another drink.

"Lila." He said it to the yellow slice of moon, to the black sky, to the smell of the night and the roofs covered in snow.

"Lila." He put it on the wind, like a fly he didn't have the heart to kill, and willed it to carry itself to Tulsa.

"Luther Laurence, meet Helen Grady."

Luther shook the older woman's hand. Helen Grady had a grip as firm as Captain Coughlin's and a similar trim build, gunmetal hair, and a fearless gaze.

"She'll be working with you from here on out," the captain said.

Luther nodded, noticing she wiped her hand on her pristine apron as soon as she took it back from his grip.

"Captain, sir, where's—?"

"Nora has left our employ, Luther. I noted a fondness between the two of you, and so I inform you of her dismissal with a measure of empathy for the bond you shared, but she is never to be spoken of in this home again." The captain placed a firm hand on Luther's shoulder and gave him a smile just as firm. "Clear?"

"Clear," Luther said.

Luther found Danny as Danny was returning to his rooming house one night. He stepped out from the building and said, "Fuck did you do?"

Danny's right hand drifted toward his coat, and then he recognized Luther. He dropped his hand.

"No 'Hi'?" Danny said. " 'Happy New Year'? Anything like that?"

Luther said nothing.

"Okay." Danny shrugged. "First, this ain't the best neighborhood to be a colored in, or haven't you noticed?"

"I've been out here an hour. I noticed."

"Second," Danny said, "are you fucking crazy talking to a white man like that? A cop?"

Luther took a step back. "She was right."

"What? Who?"

"Nora. She said you were an act. You play the rebel. Play the man who says he don't believe in being called 'suh,' but now you tell me where it's okay for a nigger like me to go in this city, tell me how I's supposed to talk to your whiteness in public. Where's Nora?"

Danny held out his arms. "How do I know? Why don't you go see her at the shoe factory? You know where it is, don't you?"

"'Cause our hours *conflict*." Luther stepped to Danny, realizing people were starting to notice them. It would hardly be unreasonable for someone to whack him in the back of the head with a stick or just flat out shoot him for stepping up to a white man like this in an Italian neighborhood. In any neighborhood.

"Why do you think I had anything to do with Nora leaving the house?"

"Because she loved you and you couldn't live with it."

"Luther, step back."

"You step back."

"Luther."

Luther cocked his head.

"I'm serious."

"You're serious? Anyone in the world looked close at that girl, they saw a whole country of pain had already paid its respects to her. And you, you—what?—you added to it? You and your whole family?"

"My family?"

"That's right."

"You don't like my family, Luther, take it up with my father."

"Can't."

"Why not?"

"'Cause I need the fucking job."

"Then I guess you should go home now. Hope you still have it in the morning."

Luther took another couple of steps back. "How's your union going?"

"What?"

"Your dream of a workers brotherhood? How's that?"

410

Danny's face flattened, as if it had been run over. "Go home, Luther."

Luther nodded. He gulped some air. He turned and started walking.

"Hey!" Danny called.

Luther looked back at him standing by his building in the early evening cold.

"Why'd you come all the way out here? To dress down a white man in public?"

Luther shook his head. He turned to start walking again.

"Hey! I asked you a question."

"Because she's better than your whole fucking family!" Luther took a bow in the middle of the sidewalk. "Got that, white boy? Go grab your noose, string me up, whatever the fuck you Yankees do up here. And you do? I'll know I died speaking truth to your fucking lie. She is better than your whole family." He pointed at Danny. "Better than you, especially."

Danny's lips moved.

Luther took a step toward him. "What? What's that?"

Danny put a hand on his doorknob. "I said you're probably right."

He turned the knob and entered his building and Luther stood alone on the steadily darkening street, raggedy Italians stabbing him with their almond eyes as they passed.

He chuckled. "Shit," he said. "I got him and his horseshit where it *lived*." He smiled at an angry old lady trying to slide past him. "Don't that beat all, ma'am?"

Yvette called to him soon as he entered the house. He came into the parlor with his coat still on because her voice sounded fearful. But as he entered, he saw that she was smiling, as if she'd been touched by a divine joy.

"Luther!"

"Ma'am?" Luther used one hand to unbutton his topcoat.

She stood there, beaming. Isaiah came through the dining

room and entered the parlor behind her. He said, "Evening, Luther."

"Evening, Mr. Giddreaux, sir."

Isaiah wore a small private smile as he took a seat in the armchair by his teacup.

"What?" Luther said. "What?"

"Did you have a good 1918?" Isaiah said.

Luther looked away from Yvette's bursting smile and met Isaiah's tiny one. "Uh, sir, in point of fact, no, I did not have a good 1918. Bit troublesome if you need to know the truth, sir."

Isaiah nodded. "Well, it's over." He glanced at the clock on the mantelpiece: ten-forty-three. "Almost twenty-four-hours over." He looked over at his wife. "Oh, stop your teasing, Yvette. It's starting to torture *me*." He gave Luther a look— *women*—and then he said, "Come on now. Give it to the boy."

Yvette crossed the floor to him and for the first time Luther noticed that she'd kept her hands behind her back since he'd entered the room. Her body was rippling, and her smile kept sliding, topsy-turvy, all over her face.

"This is for you." She leaned in and kissed him on the cheek and placed an envelope in his hand. She stepped back.

Luther looked down at the envelope—simple, cream-colored, standard in every way. He saw his name in the center. Saw the Giddreauxs' address below it. He recognized the lettering—the way it managed to be tight and looping at the same time. He recognized the postmark over the stamp: Tulsa, Okla. His hands shook.

He looked in Yvette's eyes.

"What if it's good-bye?" He felt his lips tighten hard against his teeth.

"No, no," she said. "She already *said* good-bye, son. You said she'd closed her heart. Closed hearts don't write letters to men who love them, Luther. They just don't."

Luther nodded, his head as shaky as the rest of him. He thought of Christmas night, of putting her name on the breeze.

412

"I—"

They watched him.

"I'm going to read it upstairs," he said.

Yvette patted his hand. "Just promise me you won't jump."

Luther laughed, the sound coming out high, like something that had been popped. "I . . . I won't, ma'am."

As he climbed the stairs, terror struck him. Terror that Yvette was wrong, that plenty of women wrote to say goodbye. He thought of folding the letter and putting it into his pocket and not reading it for a while. Until he was stronger, say. But even as the thought occurred to him he knew he had a better chance of waking up white tomorrow than waking up with that envelope still sealed.

He stepped out onto the roof and stood with his head down for a moment. He didn't pray, but he didn't quite not-pray either. He kept his head lowered and closed his eyes and let his fear wash over him, his horror at being without her for life.

Please don't hurt me, he thought, and opened the envelope carefully and just as carefully pulled out her letter. Please don't. He held it between the thumb and index finger of each hand, letting the night breeze dry his eyes, and then he unfolded it:

Dear Luther,

It is cold here. I now wash laundry for folks that send it down from Detroit Avenue in big gray bags. It is a kindness I can thank Aunt Marta for since I know folks can get there laundry cleaned any old way. Aunt Marta and Uncle James have been my salvation and I know the Lord works through them. They said to tell you they wish you well—

Luther smiled, doubting all hell out of that.

—and hope you are all right. My belly is big. It is a boy Aunt Marta says for my belly points to the right. I feel this to. His

413

feet are big and kicking. He will look like you he will need
you to be his daddy. You have to find your way home.

Lila. Your wife.

Luther read it six more times before he could say for sure
that he took a breath. No matter how many times he closed
his eyes and opened them in hopes she had signed it *"Love,"*
that word did not appear on the page.

And yet . . . *You have to find your way home* and *he will need*
you to be his daddy and *Dear Luther* and most important . . .
Your wife.

Your wife.

He looked back at the letter. He unfolded it again. Held it
taut between his fingers.

You have to find your way home.

Yes, ma'am.

Dear Luther.

Dear Lila.

Your wife.

Your husband.

414

BABE RUTH *and the* WHITE BALL

CHAPTER *twenty-four*

At noon on the fifteenth of January, 1919, the United States Industrial Alcohol company's molasses tank exploded in the North End. A vagrant child, standing beneath the tank, was vaporized, and the molasses flooded into the heart of the slum in waves three stories high. Buildings were heaved to the side as if by a callous hand. The railway trestle that ran along Commercial was hit with a scrap of metal the size of a truck. The center of the trestle collapsed. A firehouse was hurled across a city square and turned on its end. One fireman perished, a dozen were injured. The cause of the explosion was not immediately clear, but Mayor Andrew Peters, the first politician to arrive on the scene, stated that there was little doubt terrorists were to blame.

Babe Ruth read every newspaper account he could lay his mitts on. He skipped any long stretches where words like *municipal* and *infrastructure* were commonly used, but otherwise it tickled him to his core. Astounded him. Molasses! Two million gallons! Fifty-foot waves! The streets of the North End, closed off to automobiles, carts, and horses, stole the shoes of those who tried to walk them. Flies battled for pavement in swarms as dark and thick as candied apples. In the plaza behind the city stables, dozens of horses had been maimed by rivets that had flown like bullets from the exploding tank. They'd been found mired in the muck, neighing hideously, unable to rise from the sticky mess. In the middle of that afternoon, forty-five police gunshots punctuated their execution like the last blasts of a fireworks show. The dead horses were lifted by cranes and placed on the flatbeds of trucks and transported to a glue factory in Somerville. By the fourth day, the molasses had turned to black marble and residents walked with their hands pressed to walls and street-lamp poles.

Seventeen confirmed dead now and hundreds injured. Good God—the looks that must have been on their faces when they turned and saw those black waves curl up by the sun. Babe sat at the soda counter in Igoe's Drugstore and Creamery in Codman Square waiting for his agent, Johnny Igoe. Johnny was in the back, primping for their meeting with A. L. Ulmerton, probably going too heavy on the petroleum jelly, the cologne, the toilet water. A. L. Ulmerton was the big cheese of Old Gold cigarettes ("Not a cough in a carload!") and he wanted to talk to Babe about possible endorsements. And now Johnny was going to make them late with his show-girl fussing in back.

Babe didn't really mind, though, because it gave him time to leaf through more stories on the flood and the immediate response to it: the crackdown on all radicals or subversives who might have been involved. Agents of the Bureau of Investigation and officers of the Boston Police Department had kicked down doors at the headquarters of the Lettish Workingman's Society, the Boston chapter of the IWW, and Reed and Larkin's Left Wing of the Socialist Party. They filled holding pens across the city and sent the overflow to the Charles Street Jail.

At Suffolk County Superior Court, sixty-five suspected sub-versives were brought before Judge Wendell Trout. Trout ordered the police to release all who had not been formally charged with a crime, but signed eighteen deportation orders for those who could prove no U.S. citizenship. Dozens more were held pending Justice Department review of their immigration status and criminal history, actions Babe found perfectly reasonable, though some others did not. When the labor lawyer James Vahey, twice a Democratic candidate for governor of the Commonwealth, argued before the federal magistrate that internment of men who had not been charged with a crime was an affront to the Constitution, he was upbraided for his harsh tone and the cases were continued until February.

In this morning's *Traveler*, they'd compiled a photo essay that took up pages four through seven. Even though authorities weren't confirming yet whether their wide net had caught the terrorists responsible, and that made Babe mad, the anger flared only for the briefest moment before it was tamped out by a delicious, itchy trill that thumped the top of his spine as he marveled at the sheer wreckage of it: a whole neighborhood smashed and tossed and smothered in the black-iron slathering of that liquid mass. Pictures of the crumpled fire house were followed by one of bodies stacked along Commercial like loaves of brown bread and another of two Red Cross workers leaning against an ambulance, one of them with a hand over his face and a cigarette between his lips. There was a shot of the firemen forming a relay line to remove the rubble and get to their men. A dead pig in the middle of a piazza. An old man sitting on a stoop, resting the side of his head on a dripping-brown hand. A dead end street with the brown current up to the door knockers, stones and wood and glass floating on the surface. And the people— the cops and firemen and Red Cross and doctors and immigrants in their shawls and bowlers, everyone with the same look on their faces: how the fuck did *this* happen?

Babe saw that look on people's faces a lot lately. Not for any particular reason, either. Just in general. It was like they were all walking through this crazy world, trying to keep pace but knowing they couldn't, they just couldn't. So part of them waited for that world to come back up behind them on a second try and just roll right over them, send them—finally— on into the next one.

419

A week later, another round of negotiations with Harry Frazee. Frazee's office smelled like whorehouse perfume and old money.

The perfume came from Kat Lawson, an actress starring in one of the half dozen shows Frazee had running in Boston right now. This one was called *Laddy, Be Happy* and was, like all Harry Frazee productions, a light romantic farce that played to SRO crowds night after night. Ruth had actually seen this one, allowing Helen to drag him to it shortly after the new year began, even though Frazee, true to the rumors of his Jew heritage, had failed to comp the tickets. Ruth had to endure the disconcerting experience of holding his wife's hand in the fifth row while he watched another woman he'd slept with (three times actually) prance back and forth across the stage in the role of an innocent cleaning woman who dreamed of making it as a chorus girl. The obstacle to those dreams was her no-good Irish blatherskite of a husband, Seamus, the "laddy" of the title. At the end of the play, the cleaning woman contents herself by becoming a chorus girl on the New England stage and her "laddy" makes his peace with her pipe dreams, as long as they remain on a local level, and even lands a job of his own. Helen stood and applauded after the final number, a full-cast reprise of "Shine My Star, I'll Shine Your Floors," and Ruth applauded, too, though he was pretty sure Kat Lawson had given him the crabs last year. It seemed wrong that a woman as pure as Helen should be cheering one as corrupt as Kat, and truth be told, he was still plenty sore about not getting the tickets comped.

Kat Lawson sat on a leather couch under a big painting of hunting dogs. She had a magazine on her lap and her compact out as she reapplied her lipstick. Harry Frazee thought he was putting one over on his wife, thought Kat was a possession to be envied by Ruth and the other Sox (most of whom had slept with her at least once). Harry Frazee was an idiot, and Ruth didn't need any more confirmation than the man leaving his mistress in the room during a contract negotiation.

Ruth and Johnny Igoe sat before Frazee's desk and waited for him to shoo Kat from the room, but Frazee made it clear she was here to stay when he said, "Can I get you anything, dear, before these gentlemen and I discuss business?"

"Nope." Kat smacked her lips together and snapped the compact closed.

Frazee nodded and sat behind his desk. He looked across at Ruth and Johnny Igoe and shot his cuffs, ready to get down to business. "So, I understand—"

"Oh, hon'?" Kat said. "Could you get me a lemonade? Thanks, you're a pip."

A lemonade. It was early February and the coldest day of the coldest week of the winter thus far. So cold Ruth had heard that kids were skating on frozen molasses in the North End. And she wanted lemonade.

Harry Frazee kept his face stone-still as he pushed the intercom button and said, "Doris, send Chappy out for a lemonade, would you?"

Kat waited until he'd released the intercom button and sat back.

"Oh, and an egg-and-onion."

Harry Frazee leaned forward again. "Doris? Tell Chappy to pick up an egg-and-onion sandwich, too, please." He looked over at Kat, but she'd gone back to her magazine. He waited another few seconds. He released the intercom button.

"So," he said.

"So," Johnny Igoe said.

Frazee spread his hands, waiting, one eyebrow arched into a question mark.

"Have you given any more thought to our offer?" Johnny said.

Frazee lifted Ruth's contract off his desk and held it up. "This is something you're both familiar with, I take it. Mr. Ruth, you are signed for seven thousand dollars this season.

That's it. A bond was forged. I expect you to hold up your end."

Johnny Igoe said, "Given Gidge's previous season, his pitching in the Series, and, may I mention, the explosion in cost of living since the war ended, we think it only fair to reconsider this arrangement. In other words, seven thousand's a bit light."

Frazee sighed and lay the contract back down. "I gave you a bonus at the end of the season, Mr. Ruth. I did not have to do that and yet I did. And it's still not enough?"

Johnny Igoe began ticking points off on his fingers. "You sold Lewis and Shore to the Yanks. You unloaded Dutch Leonard on Cleveland. You let Whiteman go."

Babe sat up straight. "Whiteman's gone?"

Johnny nodded. "You're flush, Mr. Frazee. Your shows are all hits, you—"

"And because of that, I'm to renegotiate a signed contract made in good faith by *men*? What kind of principle is that? What kind of ethic is that, Mr. Igoe? In case you haven't been following the news, I am locked in a battle with Commissioner Johnson. I am fighting to have our World Series medals rightfully given to us. Those medals are being withheld because your boy there had to strike before game five."

"I had nothing to do with that," Babe said. "I didn't even know what was going on."

Johnny quieted him with a hand to his knee.

Kat piped up from the couch. "Honey, could you ask Chappy to also get me a—"

"Hush," Frazee said to her. "We're talking business, bubble-head." He turned back to Ruth as Kat lit a cigarette and blew the smoke hard through her thick lips. "You've got a contract for seven thousand. That makes you one of the highest-paid players in the game. And you want what now?" Frazee held his exasperated hands up to the window, the city beyond it, the bustle of Tremont Street and the Theater District.

"What I'm worth," Babe said, refusing to back down to this slave driver, this supposed Big Noise, this theater man. Last Thursday in Seattle, thirty-five thousand ship workers had walked out on strike. Just as the city was trying to get its noggin around *that*, another twenty-five thousand workers walked off the job in a sympathy strike. Seattle stopped dead—no streetcars, no icemen or milkmen, no one to come pick up the garbage, no one cleaning the office buildings or running the elevators.

Babe suspected this was just for starters. This morning the papers had reported that the judge conducting the inquest into the collapse of the USIA molasses tank concluded that the cause of the explosion was not anarchists but company negligence and the poor inspection protocols set up by the city. USIA, in a rush to convert its molasses distillation from industrial purposes to commercial ones, had overfilled the poorly constructed tank, never guessing unseasonably high temperatures in the middle of January would cause the molasses to swell. USIA officials, of course, angrily denounced the preliminary report, charging that the terrorists responsible were still at large and thus the cleanup costs were the responsibility of the city and its taxpayers. Ooooh, it made Babe hot under the collar. These bosses, these slave drivers. Maybe those guys in the bar fight a few months back at the Castle Square Hotel had been right—the workers of the world were tired of saying "yes, sir" and "no, sir." As Ruth stared across the desk at Harry Frazee, he felt swept up in a rich wave of brotherhood for his fellow workers everywhere, his fellow citizen-victims. It was time for Big Money to be held accountable.

"I want you to pay me what I'm worth," he repeated.

"And what's that, exactly?"

It was Babe's turn to put a hand on Johnny's leg. "Fifteen for one or thirty for three."

Frazee laughed. "You want fifteen thousand dollars for *one* year?"

"Or thirty for three years." Babe nodded.

"How about I trade you instead?"

That shook something in Babe. A trade? Jesus Christ. Everyone knew how chummy Frazee had become with Colonel Ruppert and Colonel Huston, the owners of the Yankees, but the Yankees were cellar dwellers, a team that had never been near contention in the Series era. And if not the Yanks, then who? Cleveland? Baltimore again? Philadelphia? Babe didn't want to move. He'd just rented an apartment in Governor's Square. He had a good thing going—Helen in Sudbury, him downtown. He owned this burg; when he walked its streets, people called his name, children gave chase, women batted their eyes. New York on the other hand—he'd vanish in that sea. But when he thought of his brother workers again, of Seattle, of the poor dead floating in the molasses, he knew the issue was larger than his own fear.

"Then trade me," he said.

The words surprised him. They definitely surprised Johnny Igoe and Harry Frazee. Babe stared back into Frazee's face, let him see a resolve that appeared (Babe hoped) twice as strong because of the effort it took to contain the fear that lay behind it.

"Or, you know what?" Babe said. "Maybe I'll just retire."

"And do what?" Frazee shook his head and rolled his eyes.

"Johnny," Babe said.

Johnny Igoe cleared his throat again. "Gidge has been approached by various parties who believe he has a big future on the stage or in the flickers."

"An *actor*," Frazee said.

"Or a boxer," Johnny Igoe said. "We're fielding a lot of offers from them quarters as well, Mr. Frazee."

Frazee laughed. Actually laughed. It was a short, donkey-bray of a sound. He rolled his eyes. "If I had a nickel for every time an actor tried to hold me up with stories of other offers during the middle of a show's run, why, I'd own my own country by now." His dark eyes glittered. "You'll honor your contract." He took a cigar from the humidor on his desk, snipped the end, and pointed the cigar at Ruth. "You work for me."

"Not for coon wages, I don't." Babe stood and took his beaver-fur coat from the hook on the wall by Kat Lawson. He took Johnny's, too, and tossed it across the room to him. Frazee lit his cigar and watched him. Babe put his coat on. He buttoned it up. Then he bent over Kat Lawson and gave her a loud smooch on the kisser.

"Always good to see you, doll."

Kat looked shocked, like he'd run his hand over her Hoover or something.

"Let's go, Johnny."

Johnny walked toward the door, looking as shocked as Kat.

"You walk out that door," Frazee said, "and I'll see you in court, Gidge."

"Then you'll see me in court." Babe shrugged. "Where you won't see me, *Harry*? Is in a fucking Red Sox uniform."

In Manhattan, on February 22, officers of the NYPD Bomb Squad and agents of the Secret Service raided an apartment on Lexington Avenue where they arrested fourteen Spanish radicals of Grupo Pro Prensa and charged them with plotting the assassination of the president of the United States. The assassination had been planned for the following day in Boston, where President Wilson would arrive from Paris.

Mayor Peters had called for a city holiday to celebrate the president's arrival and taken the necessary steps to hold a parade, even though the president's route from Commonwealth Pier to the Copley Plaza Hotel was classified by the Secret Service. After the arrests in New York, every window in the city was ordered closed and federal agents armed with rifles lined the rooftops along Summer Street, Beacon, Charles, Arlington, Commonwealth Avenue, and Dartmouth Street.

Various reports had placed the location of Peters's "secret" parade at City Hall, Pemberton Square, Sudbury Square, and Washington Street, but Ruth strolled up to the State House because that's where everyone else seemed to be going. It wasn't every day you got a chance to see a president, but he hoped if anyone ever tried to kill *him* someday, the powers that be would do a better job keeping his movements private. Wilson's motorcade rolled up Park Street at the stroke of twelve and turned left onto Beacon at the State House. Across the street on the lawn of the Common, a bunch of bughouse suffragette dames burned their girdles and their corsets and even a few bras and shouted, "No vote, no citizenship! No vote, no citizenship!" as the smoke rose from the pyre and Wilson kept his eyes straight ahead. He was smaller than Ruth would have expected, thinner, too, as he rode in the back of an open-air sedan and waved stiffly to the crowd—one flick of the wrist to the left side of the street, one to the right, back to the left again, his eyes never making contact with anything but high windows and treetops. Which was probably good for him, because Ruth saw a dense mob of rough-looking, grimy men being held back by police along the Joy Street entrance to the Common. Had to be thousands of these guys. They held up banners that identified them as the Lawrence Strike Parade and shouted obscenities at the president and the police as the coppers tried to push them back. Ruth chuckled as the suffragettes rushed behind the motorcade, still screaming about the vote, their legs bare and raw in the cold because they'd torched their bloomers, too. He crossed the street and passed their burning pile of clothing as the motorcade rode down Beacon. Halfway across the Common, he heard fearful shouts from the crowd and turned to see the Lawrence strikers going at it with the cops, lots of stumbling and awkward punches and voices pitched high with outrage.

I'll be damned, Ruth thought. The whole world's on strike.

The motorcade appeared in front of him, rolling slowly down Charles Street. He kept a leisurely pace as he followed it through the throngs while it snaked around the Public

Garden and then along Commonwealth. He signed a few autographs as he went, shook a few hands, but it was nice how his celebrity diminished in light of much larger star power. Folks were less clamorous and clingy with him that afternoon, as if, in the bright sun cast by Wilson's fame, Babe was just one of the common folk. He might be famous, but he wasn't the reason rifles were pointing down at their heads. That was a mean kind of famous. His was a friendly kind of famous, a regular famous.

By the time Wilson climbed a podium in Copley Square, Babe had grown bored, though. The president might have been powerful and book-smart and all, but he sure didn't know much about public speaking. You had to give them a show, a little razzle here and some dazzle there, tell a few jokes, make them think you took as much pleasure in their company as they did in yours. But Wilson looked tired up there, old, his voice a thin, reedy thing as he droned on about League-of-Nations this and new-world-order that and the great responsibilities that come with great might and great freedom. For all the big words and big ideas, he smelled of defeat, of something stale and weary and broken beyond fixing. Ruth worked his way out of the crowd and signed two more autographs on the fringe of it and then walked up Tremont and went looking for a steak.

He came home to his apartment a few hours later and found Harry Frazee waiting for him in the lobby. The doorman went back outside and Ruth pushed the button and stood by the brass doors of the elevator.

"I saw you at the president's speech," Frazee said. "I couldn't reach you through the crowd."

"Sure was thick," Ruth said.

"If only our dear president knew how to play the press like you do, Mr. Ruth."

Babe swallowed the smile that threatened to creep up his face. He had to hand it to Johnny Igoe on that one—Johnny had sent Babe out to orphanages and hospitals and old-lady homes, and the papers ate it up. Men had flown in from Los Angeles to give Babe screen tests, and Johnny talked up the offers he'd told Babe were coming in from the flickers business. Actually, just about the only thing that could have pushed Babe off the front pages this week was Wilson. Even the shooting of the Bavarian prime minister went under the fold when Babe's deal to star in a short flicker called *The Dough Kiss* was announced. When reporters asked if he'd be going to spring training or not, Ruth kept saying the same thing, "If Mr. Frazee thinks I'm worthy of a fair wage, I'll be there."

Spring training was three weeks off.

Frazee cleared his throat. "I'll meet your price."

Babe turned and met Frazee's eyes. Frazee gave him a curt nod.

"The papers have been drawn up. You can sign them at my office tomorrow morning." Frazee gave him a thin smile. "You won this round, Mr. Ruth. Enjoy it."

"Okay, Harry."

Frazee stepped in close. He smelled good in a way that Ruth associated with the very rich, the ones who knew things he'd never know in a way that went beyond secret handshakes. They ran the world, men like Frazee, because they understood something that would always escape Babe and men like him: money. They planned its movements. They could predict its moment of passage from one hand to another. They also knew other things Babe didn't, about books and art and the history of the earth. But money most importantly—they had that down cold.

Every now and then, though, you got the better of them.

"Have fun at spring training," Harry Frazee said to Babe as the elevator doors opened. "Enjoy Tampa."

"I will now," Babe said, picturing it. The waves of heat, the languid women.

The elevator man waited.

Harry Frazee produced a money roll held fast by a gold

clip. He peeled off several twenties as the doorman opened the door and a woman who lived on six, a pretty dame with no shortage of suitors, came down the marble floor, her heels clicking.

"I understand you need money."

"Mr. Frazee," Babe said, "I can wait until the new contract's signed."

"Wouldn't hear of it, son. If one of my men is in arrears, I aim to help him out."

Babe held up a hand. "I've got plenty of cash right now, Mr. Frazee."

Babe tried to step back, but he was too slow. Harry Frazee stuffed the money into the inside pocket of Babe's coat as the elevator man watched and the doorman and the pretty woman on six saw it, too.

"You're worth every penny," Harry Frazee said, "and I'd hate to see you miss a meal."

Babe's face burned and he reached into his coat to give the money back.

Frazee walked away. The doorman trotted to catch up. He held the door for him, and Frazee tipped his hat and walked out into the night.

Ruth caught the woman's eye. She lowered her head and got in the elevator.

"A joke," Ruth said as he joined her and the elevator man shut the cage door and worked the crank. "Just a joke."

She smiled and nodded, but he could see she pitied him.

When he got up to his apartment, Ruth put in a call to Kat Lawson. He convinced her to meet him for a drink at the Hotel Buckminster, and after they'd had their fourth round he took her to a room upstairs and fucked her silly. Half an hour later, he fucked her again, doggie-style, and whispered the foulest language he could imagine into her ear. After, she lay on her stomach, asleep, her lips speaking softly to someone in her dreams. He got up and dressed. Out the window lay the Charles River and the lights of Cambridge beyond, winking and watching. Kat snored softly as he put on his coat. He reached into it and placed Harry Frazee's money down on the dresser and left the room.

West Camden Street. Baltimore.
Ruth stood on the sidewalk outside what had been his father's saloon. Closed now, distressed, a tin Pabst sign hanging askew behind a dusty window. Above the saloon was the apartment he'd shared with his parents and his sister Mamie, who'd been barely toddling when Ruth was shipped off to Saint Mary's.

Home, you could say.

Babe's memories of it as such, however, were dim. He remembered the exterior wall as the place he'd learned to throw dice. He recalled how the smell of beer never left the saloon or the apartment above it; it rose through the toilet and the bathtub drain, lived in the floor cracks and in the wall.

Home, in truth, was St. Mary's. West Camden Street was an idea. An on-deck circle.

I came here, Babe thought, to tell you I've made it. I'm Big Noise. I'll earn ten thousand dollars this year, and Johnny says he can get me another ten in endorsements. My face will be on the kind of tin plate you'd have hung in the window. But you wouldn't have hung it, would you? You would have been too proud. Too proud to admit you had a son who makes more money in a year than you could make in ten. The son you sent away and tried to forget. George Junior. Remember him?

No, I don't. I'm dead. So's your mother. Leave us alone.

Babe nodded.

I'm going to Tampa, George Senior. Spring training. Just thought I'd stop by and let you see I'd made something of myself.

Made something of yourself? You can barely read. You fuck whores. You get paid whore's wages to play a whore's game. A game. Not man's work. Play.

430

I'm Babe Ruth.

You're George Herman Ruth Junior, and I still wouldn't trust you to work behind the bar. You'd drink the profits, forget to lock up. No one wants to hear your bragging here, boy, your stories. Go play your games. This is not your home anymore.

When was it?

Babe looked up at the building. He thought of spitting on the sidewalk, the same sidewalk where his father had died from a busted melon. But he didn't. He rolled it all up—his father, his mother, his sister Mamie, who he hadn't talked to in six months, his dead brothers, his life here—rolled it all up like a carpet and tossed it over his shoulder.

Good-bye.

Don't let the door hit your fat ass on the way out.

I'm going.

So go then.

I am.

Start walking.

He did. He put his hands in his pocket and walked up the street toward the taxi he'd left idling at the corner. He felt as if he wasn't just leaving West Camden Street or even Baltimore. He was steaming away from a whole country, the motherland that had given him his name and his nature, now wholly unfamiliar, now foreign ash.

Plant Field in Tampa was surrounded by a racetrack that had been out of use for years but still smelled of horseshit when the Giants came to town to play an exhibition game against the Red Sox and the white-ball rule went into effect for the first time.

The implementation of the white-ball rule was a big surprise. Even Coach Barrow hadn't known it was coming this early. Rumors floating through the leagues had held that the new rule wouldn't be employed until opening day, but the home plate umpire, Xavier Long, came into the dugout just before the game to tell them today was the day.

431

"By order of Mr. Ban Johnson, no less. Even provided the first bag, he did."

When the umps emptied that bag in the on-deck circle, half the boys, Babe included, came out of the dugout to marvel at the creamy brightness of the leather, the sharp red stitching. Christ's sake, it was like looking at a pile of new eyes. They were so alive, so clean, so white.

Major league baseball had previously dictated that the home team provide the balls for every game, but it was never stated what condition those balls had to be in. As long as they possessed no divots of marked depth, those balls could, and were, played until they passed over a wall or someone tore the cover off.

White balls, then, were something Ruth had seen on opening day in the first few innings, but by the end of the first game, that ball was usually brown. By the end of a three-game series, that ball could disappear in the fur of a squirrel.

But those gray balls had almost killed two guys last year. Honus Sukalowski had taken one to the temple and never talked right again. Bobby Kestler had also taken one to the bean and hadn't swung a bat since. Whit Owens, the pitcher who'd hit Sukalowski, had left the game altogether out of guilt. That was three guys gone in one year, and during the war year to boot.

Standing in left, Ruth watched the third out of the game arc toward him like a Roman candle, a victim of its own brilliance. He was whistling when he caught it. As he jogged back in toward the dugout, God's fingertips found his chest.

It's a new game.

You can say that twice.

It's your game now, Babe. All yours.

I know. Did you see how white it is? It's so . . . *white*.

A blind man could hit it, Babe.

I *know*. A blind kid. A blind girl kid.

432

It's not Cobb's game anymore, Babe. It's a slugger's game.

Slugger. That's a swell word, boss. Always been fond of it, myself.

Change the game, Babe. Change the game and free yourself.

From what?

You know.

Babe didn't, but he kind of did, so he said, "Okay."

"Who you talking to?" Stuffy McInnis asked as he reached the dugout.

"God."

Stuffy spit some tobacco into the dirt. "Tell Him I want Mary Pickford at the Belleview Hotel."

Babe picked up his bat. "See what I can do."

"Tuesday night."

Babe wiped down his bat. "Well, it is an off day."

Stuffy nodded. "Say around six."

Babe walked toward the batter's box.

"Gidge."

Babe looked back at him. "Call me 'Babe,' okay?"

"Sure, sure. Tell God to tell Mary to bring a friend."

Babe walked into the batter's box.

"And beer!" Stuffy called.

Columbia George Smith was on the mound for the Giants, and his first pitch was low and inside and Babe suppressed a giggle as it passed over the toe of his left foot. Jesus, you could count the stitches! Lew McCarty threw the ball back to his pitcher and Columbia George threw a curveball next that hissed past Babe's thighs for a strike. Babe had been watching for that pitch because it meant Columbia George was stair climbing. The next pitch would be belt high and a hair inside, and Babe would have to swing but miss if he wanted Columbia George to throw the high heat. So he swung, and even trying to miss, he foul-tipped the ball over McCarty's head. Babe stepped out of the box for a moment, and Xavier Long took the ball from McCarty and examined it. He wiped at it with his hand and then his sleeve and he found something there he didn't like because he placed it in the pouch over his groin and came back out with a brand-spanking new ball. He handed it to McCarty, and McCarty rifled it back to Columbia George.

What a country!

Babe stepped back into the box. He tried to keep the glee from his eyes. Columbia George went into his windup, and, yup, his face corked into that telltale grimace it got whenever he brought the fire, and Babe gave it all a sleepy smile.

It was not cheers he heard when he scorched that fresh white ball toward the Tampa sun. Not cheers or oohs or aahs.

Silence. Silence so total that the only sound that could fill it was the echo of his bat against cowhide. Every head in Plant Field turned to watch that miraculous ball soar so fast and so far that it never had time to cast its shadow.

When it landed on the other side of the right field wall, five hundred feet from home plate, it bounced high off the race-track and continued to roll.

After the game, one of the sports scribes would tell Babe and Coach Barrow that they'd taken measurements, and the final tally was 579 feet before it came to a full stop in the grass. Five hundred and seventy-nine. Damn near two football fields.

But in that moment, as it soared without shadow into a blue sky and a white sun and he dropped his bat and trotted slowly down the first base line, tracking it, willing it to go farther and faster than anything ever could or ever had or maybe ever would in so short a time, Babe saw the damnedest thing he'd ever seen in his life—his father sitting atop the ball. Riding it really, hands clenched to the seams, knees pressed to the leather, his father tumbling over and over in space with that ball. He howled, his father did. He clenched his face from the fear.

Tears fell from his eyes, fat ones, and hot, Babe assumed. Until, like the ball, he disappeared from view.

Five hundred and seventy-nine feet, they told Ruth.

Ruth smiled, picturing his father, not the ball. All gone now. Buried in the saw grass. Buried in Plant Field, Tampa.

Never coming back.

CHAPTER *twenty-five*

I f Danny could say nothing else positive about the new commissioner, he could at least say the man was true to his word. When the molasses flood tore through the heart of his neighborhood, Danny was spending the week keeping the peace forty miles away at a box factory strike in Haverhill. Once the workers there were brought to heel, he moved on to ten days at a fishery strike in Charlestown. That whimpered to an end when the AFL refused to grant a charter because they didn't deem the workers skilled labor. Danny was loaned out next to the Lawrence PD for a textile workers' strike that had been going on for three months and could already claim two dead, including a labor organizer who'd been shot through the mouth as he left a barbershop.

Through these strikes and those that followed throughout the late winter and into early spring—at a clock factory in Waltham, among machinists in Roslindale, a mill in Framingham—Danny was spat at, screamed at, called a goon and a whore and a lackey and pus. He was scratched, punched, hit with eggs, hit with sticks, and once, in Framingham, caught a hurled brick with his shoulder. In Roslindale, the machinists got their raise but not their health benefits. In Everett, the shoe workers got half their raise, but no pension. The Framingham strike was crushed by the arrival of truckloads of new workers and the onslaught of police. After they'd made the final push and the scabs had gone through the gates, Danny looked around at the men they'd left in their wake, some still curled on the ground, others sitting up, a few raising ineffectual fists and pointless shouts. They faced a sudden new day with far less than they'd asked for and much less than they'd had. Time to go home to their families and figure out what to do next.

He came upon a Framingham cop he'd never met before kicking a striker who offered no resistance. The cop wasn't putting much into the kicks anymore, and the striker probably wasn't even conscious. Danny put his hand on the guy's shoulder and the guy raised his nightstick before he recognized the uniform.

"What?"

"You've made your point," Danny said. "Enough."

"Ain't no *enough*," the cop said and walked away.

Danny rode back to Boston in a bus with the other city cops. The sky hung low and gray. Scraps of frozen snow gripped the scalp of the earth like crabs.

"Meeting tonight, Dan?" Kenny Trescott asked him.

Danny had almost forgotten. Now that Mark Denton was rarely available to attend a BSC meeting, Danny had become the de facto head of the union. But it wasn't really a union anymore. It was, true to its original roots and its given name, a social club.

"Sure," Danny said, knowing it would be a waste of time. They were powerless again and they knew it, but some child's hope kept them coming back, kept them talking, kept them acting as if they had a voice that mattered.

Either that, or there was no place else to go. He looked in Trescott's eyes and patted his arm. "Sure," he said again.

One afternoon on K Street, Captain Coughlin returned home early with a cold and sent Luther home.

"I have it from here," he said. "Go enjoy what's left of the day."

It was one of those sneaky days in late winter where spring

came along to get a lay of the land. The gutters gurgled with a stream of melted snow; sun prisms and small rainbows formed in windows and on slick black tar. But Luther didn't give himself over to the idle stroll. He walked straightaway into the South End and made it to Nora's shoe factory just as her shift ended. She walked out sharing a cigarette with another girl, and Luther was immediately shocked at how gray she looked. Gray and bony.

"Well, look at himself," she said with a broad smile. "Molly, this is Luther, the one I used to work with."

Molly gave Luther a small wave and took a drag off her cigarette.

"How are you?" Nora asked.

"I'm fine, girl." Luther felt desperate to apologize. "I couldn't get here before now. I really couldn't. The shifts, you know? They didn't—"

"Luther."

"And I didn't know where you lived. And I—"

"Luther." This time her hand found his arm. "Sure, it's fine. I understand, I do." She took the cigarette from Molly's hand, a practiced gesture between friends, and took a quick drag before handing it back. "Would you walk me home, Mr. Laurence?"

Luther gave her a small bow. "Be my pleasure, Miss O'Shea."

She didn't live on the worst street in the city, but it was close. Her rooming house was on Green Street in the West End, just off Scollay Square, in a block of buildings that catered primarily to sailors, where rooms could often be rented by the half hour.

When they reached her building, she said, "Go 'round back. It's a green door in the alley. I'll meet you there."

She went inside and Luther cut down the alley, all his wits about him, all senses turned up as high and awake as they got. Only four in the afternoon, but already Scollay Square

438

was banging and bouncing, shouts echoing along the rooflines, a bottle breaking, a sudden burst of cackling followed by off-key piano playing. Luther reached the green door and she was waiting for him. He stepped in quickly, and she shut it behind him and he followed her back down the hallway to her room.

It must have been a closet once. Literally. The only thing that fit in it was a child's bed and a table fit for holding a single potted plant. In place of a plant, she had an old kerosene lamp and she lit it before closing the door. She sat up at the head of the bed, and Luther took a seat at the foot. Her clothes were neatly folded and placed on the floor across from his feet and he had to be careful not to step on them.

"Ah now," she said, raising her hands to the room as if to a mansion, "we're in the lap of luxury, we are, Luther."

Luther tried to smile, but he couldn't. He'd grown up poor, but this? This was fucking grim. "I heard the factories never pay the women enough to support themselves."

"No," she said. "And they'll be cutting our hours, we hear."

"When?"

"Soon." She shrugged.

"What'll you do?"

She chewed a thumbnail and gave him another shrug, her eyes strangely gay, as if this was some lark she was trying out. "Don't know."

Luther looked around for a hot plate. "Where do you cook?"

She shook her head. "We gather at our landlady's table every night—promptly, mind you—at five sharp. Usually it's beets. Sometimes potatoes. Last Tuesday, we even had meat. I don't know what kind of meat it 'twas exactly, but I assure you it was meat."

Outside, someone screamed. Impossible to tell if it was from pain or enjoyment.

"I won't allow this here," Luther said.

"What?"

He said it again. "I won't allow this. You and Clayton the only friends I made in this town. I won't abide this." He shook his head. "No, sir."

"Luther, you can't—"

"Know I killed a man?"

She stopped chewing her thumb and looked at him with big eyes.

"That's what brought me here, missy-thing. Shot a man straight up through his head. Had to leave behind my wife and she's pregnant with my child. So I've *been doing* some hard things, some hard *time* since I got here. And damned if anyone—you included—is gonna tell me what I can and can't do. I can damn well get you some food. Put some meat back on you. That I can do."

She stared at him. Outside, catcalls, the honking of horns.

She said, " 'Missy-thing'?" and the tears came with her laughter, and Luther hugged the first white woman he'd ever hugged in his life. She smelled white, he thought, starchy. He could feel her bones as she wept into his shirt, and he hated the Coughlins. Hated them outright. Hated them wholesale.

In early spring, Danny followed Nora home from work. He kept a city block behind her the whole way, and she never once looked back. He watched her enter a rooming house off Scollay Square, maybe the worst section of the city in which a woman could live. Also the cheapest.

He walked back toward the North End. It wasn't his fault. If she ended up destitute and a ghost of herself, well, she shouldn't have lied, should she?

Luther received a letter from Lila in March. It came in an eight-by-eleven envelope and there was another envelope, a small white one, that had already been opened, in there alongside a newspaper clipping.

Dear Luther,

Aunt Marta says babys in the belly turn a womans head upside down and make her see things and feel things that dont make a lick of sense. Still I have seen a man lately to many times to count. He has Satans smile and he drives a black Oakland 8. I have seen him outside the house and in town and twice outside the post office. That is why I will not write for a while for the last time I caught him trying to look at the letters in my hand. He has never said a word to me except hello and good morning but I think we know who he is Luther. I think it was him who left this newspaper article in the envelope at the door one day. The other article I clipped myself. You will know why. If you need to contact me please send mail to Aunt Martas house. My belly is huge and my feet ache all the time and climbing stairs is a chore but I am happy. Please be careful and safe.

Love,
Lila

Even as he felt dread at the rest of the letter and fear of the newspaper clippings, still folded, that he held in his hand, Luther stared at one word above all others—*love.*

He closed his eyes. Thank you, Lila. Thank you, Lord.

He unfolded the first clipping. A small article from the *Tulsa Star*:

DA DROPS CHARGES AGAINST NEGRO

Richard Poulson, a Negro bartender at the Club Almighty in Greenwood, was released from state custody when District Attorney Honus Stroudt refused to press charges in return for the Negro Poulson's pleading guilty to illegal use of a firearm. The Negro Poulson was the sole survivor of Clarence Tell's shooting rampage in the Club Almighty on the night of November 17 of last year. Slain in the shooting were Jackson Broscious and Munroe Dandiford, both

Greenwood Negroes and reputed purveyors of narcotics and prostitution. Clarence Tell, also a Negro, was killed by the Negro Poulson after he received the Negro Tell's fire. DA Stroudt said, "It is clear that the Negro Poulson fired in self-defense for fear of his life and nearly succumbed to wounds inflicted by the Negro Tell. The people are satisfied." The Negro Poulson will serve three years' probation for the weapons charge.

So Smoke was a free man. And a reasonably healthy one. Luther played it back in his head for the umpteenth time—Smoke lying in a growing pool of blood on the stage. His arm outstretched, the back of his head to Luther. Even now, knowing what he knew would come of it, he still doubted he could have pulled that trigger. Deacon Broscious was a different thing, a different circumstance—looking Luther in the eye, talking his bullshit talk. But could Luther have shot what he'd believed was a dying man in the back of the head? No. And yet he knew he probably should have. He turned over the envelope and saw his name and nothing else written across it in a male's blocky handwriting. He opened the envelope and looked at the second clipping and decided to remove "probably" from his thoughts. *Should* have. Without question or regret.

A photo clipping reprinted in the January 22 issue of the *Tulsa Sun* described the great molasses flood under the headline "Boston Slum Disaster."

There was nothing special about the article—just one more on the North End disaster that the rest of the country seemed humored by. The only thing that made this clipping special was that every time the word *Boston* was used—a total of nine times—it had been circled in red.

Rayme Finch was carrying a box to his car when he found Thomas Coughlin waiting for him. The car was government issue and was, as befit a government department that was underfunded and undervalued, a heap of shit. He'd left the engine idling, not only because the ignition often refused to engage but also because he secretly hoped someone would steal it. If that wish were granted this morning, however, he'd regret it—the car, shit heap or no, was his only transport back to Washington.

No one would be stealing it for the moment, though, not with a police captain leaning against the hood. Finch acknowledged Captain Coughlin with a flick of his head as he placed the box of office supplies in the trunk.

"Shoving off, are we?"

Finch closed the trunk. " 'Fraid so."

"A shame," Thomas Coughlin said.

Finch shrugged. "Boston radicals turned out to be a bit more docile than we'd heard."

"Except for the one my son killed."

"Federico, yes. He was a believer. And you?"

"Sorry?"

"How's your investigation going? We never did hear much from the BPD."

"There wasn't much to tell. They're hard nuts to crack, these groups."

Finch nodded. "You told me a few months ago they'd be easy."

"History's ledger will judge me overconfident on that entry, I admit."

"Not one of your men has gathered any evidence?"

"None substantial."

"Hard to believe."

"I can't see why. It's no secret we're a police department caught in a regime change. Had O'Meara, God rest him, not perished, why, you and I, Rayme? We'd be having this lovely conversation while watching a ship depart for Italy with Galleani himself shackled in her bowels."

Finch smiled in spite of himself. "I'd heard you were the slipperiest sheriff in this slippery one-horse town. Seems my sources weren't embellishing."

443

Thomas Coughlin cocked his head, his face narrowed in confusion. "I think you have been misinformed, Agent Finch. Sure, we've more than one horse in this town. Dozens actually." He tipped his hat. "Safe travels."

Finch stood by the car and watched the captain walk back up the street. He decided he was one of those men whose greatest gift lay in the inability of others ever to guess what he was truly thinking. That made him a dangerous man, to be sure, but valuable, too, pricelessly so.

We'll meet again, Captain. Finch entered the building and climbed the stairs toward his last box in an otherwise empty office. No doubt in my mind, we will definitely meet again.

D anny, Mark Denton, and Kevin McRae were called into the police commissioner's office in the middle of April. They were led into the office, which was empty, by Stuart Nichols, the commissioner's secretary, who promptly left them alone.

They sat in stiff chairs in front of Commissioner Curtis's vast desk and waited. It was nine o'clock at night. A raw night of occasional hail.

After ten minutes, they left their chairs. McRae walked over to a window. Mark stretched with a soft yawn. Danny paced from one end of the office to the other.

By nine-twenty, Danny and Mark stood at the window while Kevin paced. Every now and then the three of them exchanged a look of suppressed exasperation, but no one said anything.

At nine twenty-five, they took their seats again. As they did, the door to their left opened and Edwin Upton Curtis entered, followed by Herbert Parker, his chief counsel. As the commissioner took up a post behind his desk, Herbert Parker briskly passed in front of the three officers and placed a sheet of paper on each of their laps.

Danny looked down at it.

"Sign it," Curtis said.

"What is it?" Kevin McRae said.

"That should be evident," Herbert Parker said and came around the desk behind Curtis and folded his arms across his chest.

"It's your raise," Curtis said and took his seat. "As you wished."

Danny scanned the page. "Two hundred a year?"

Curtis nodded. "As to your other wishes, we'll take them into consideration, but I wouldn't hold out hope. Most were for luxuries, not necessities."

Mark Denton seemed stricken of the power of speech for a moment. He raised the paper up by his ear, then slowly lowered it back to his knee. "It's not enough anymore."

"Excuse me, Patrolman?"

"It's not enough," Mark said. "You know that. Two hundred a year was a 1913 figure."

"It's what you asked for," Parker said.

Danny shook his head. "It's what the BSC coppers in the 1916 negotiations asked for. Cost of living has gone up—"

"Oh cost of living, my eye!" Curtis said.

"—seventy-three percent," Danny said. "In seven months, sir. So two hundred a year? Without health benefits? Without sanitary conditions changing at the station houses?"

"As you well know, I've created committees to look into those issues. Now—"

"Those committees," Danny said, "are made up of precinct captains, sir."

"So?"

"So they have a vested interest in not finding anything wrong with the station houses they command."

"Are you questioning the honor of your superiors?"

"No."

"Are you questioning the honor of this department's chain of command?"

Mark Denton spoke before Danny could. "This offer is not going to do, sir."

"It very well *will* do," Curtis said.

445

"No," Mark Denton said. "I think we need to look into—"

"Tonight," Herbert Parker said, "is the only night this offer will be on the table. If you don't take it, you'll be back out in the cold where you'll find the doors locked and the knobs removed."

"We can't agree to this." Danny flapped the page in the air. "It's far too little and far too late."

Curtis shook his head. "I say it's not. Mr. Parker says it's not. So it's not."

"Because you *say*?" Kevin McRae said.

"Precisely," Herbert Parker said.

Curtis ran his palms over his desktop. "We'll kill you in the press."

Parker nodded. "We gave you what you asked for and you turned it down."

"That's not how it is," Danny said.

"But that's how it'll play, son."

Now it was Danny, Kevin, and Mark's turn to trade glances. Eventually, Mark turned back to Commissioner Curtis. "No fucking deal."

Curtis leaned back in his chair. "Good evening, gentlemen."

Luther came down the Coughlins' steps on his way to the streetcar when he noticed Eddie McKenna about ten yards up the sidewalk, leaning against the hood of his Hudson.

"And how's that fine building restoration going? Coming along, she is?" McKenna came off the car and walked toward him.

Luther forced a smile. "Coming along right well, Lieutenant, sir. Right well."

That was, in fact, the truth. He and Clayton had been on a tear lately. Aided on several occasions by men in NAACP chapters all over New England, men Mrs. Giddreaux found a way to get up or down to Boston on weekends and occasional weeknights, they finished the demo weeks ago, ran the electrical through the open walls and throughout the house, and were working on the water pipes that branched off the kitchen and the bathrooms to the main water pipe, a clay beauty they'd run from the basement to the roof a month back.

"When do you suppose she'll open?"

Luther'd been wondering that himself lately. He still had plenty of pipe to run and was waiting on a shipment of horse-hair plaster before he could start sealing the walls. "Hard to say, sir."

"Not 'suh'? Usually you get a bit more southern for my benefit, Luther, something I noticed back in the early days of winter."

"I guess it's 'sir,' tonight," Luther said, feeling a different edge in the man than he'd felt before.

McKenna shrugged. "So how long you think?"

"Till I'm done? A few months. Depends on a lot of things, sir."

"I'm sure. But the Giddreauxs must be planning a ribbon cutting, that sort of thing, a gathering of their ilk."

"Again, sir, I'm hoping to be done summer's end, some-where thereabouts."

McKenna placed his arm on the wrought-iron railing that curved out from the Coughlin stoop. "I need you to dig a hole."

"A hole?"

McKenna nodded, his trench coat flapping around his legs in the warm spring breeze. "A vault, really. I'll want you to be sure to make it weather-tight. I'd recommend poured con-crete, if I could be so bold."

Luther said, "And where do you want me to build this vault? Your house, sir?"

McKenna leaned back from the suggestion, an odd smile on his face. "I'd never let your kind in my home, Luther. Good Lord." He exhaled a small whoop at the entire idea, and Luther could see the weight of carrying a fake self for Luther's benefit leave him, the man finally ready to show Luther his depths. With pride. "An ebon on Telegraph Hill? Ha. So, no, Luther, the vault is not for my home. It's for these 'head-quarters' you're so nobly aspiring to build."

"You want me to put a vault in the NAACP?"

"Yes. Under the floor. I believe last time I was over there, you'd yet to lay in the floor of the rear room in the east corner. Used to be a kitchen, I believe?"

Last time he was over there?

"What of it?" Luther said.

"Dig the hole there. The size of a man, we'll say. Weatherproof it, then cover it with the flooring of your choice, but make sure that flooring is easy to lift. I don't pre-sume to tell you how to do your job, but you may consider hinges in that regard, an inconspicuous handle of some sort."

Luther, standing on the sidewalk by now, waited for the punch line. "I don't understand, Lieutenant, sir."

"You know who's proven my most irreplaceable intelligence source these last couple of years? Do you?"

"No," Luther said.

"Edison. They're grand ones for tracking the movements of a person." McKenna lit a half-smoked cigar and waved at the air between them once he got it going. "You, for example, terminated your electric service in Columbus in September. Took my Edison friends some time to discover where you started it up again, but eventually we got it. In Tulsa, Oklahoma, in October. It's still being supplied to your Tulsa address, so I can only assume you left a woman there. Maybe a family? You're on the run, Luther. Knew it the moment I laid eyes on you, but it was nice to have it confirmed. When I asked the Tulsa PD if they had any unsolved crimes of note, they mentioned a nightclub in niggertown that someone shot the hell out of, left three dead. A full day's labor someone did."

Luther said, "Don't know what you're talking about, sir."

"Of course, of course." McKenna nodded. "Tulsa PD said folks there don't get too riled up when their niggers start

448

shooting each other, 'specially when they can put the blame on one of the dead niggers. Far as they're concerned, it's a closed case with three coons in the grave no one'll miss. So on that score, you are in the clear." McKenna raised his index finger. "Unless I were to call Tulsa PD back and ask them, as a professional courtesy, to question the sole survivor of said bloodbath and in the course of questioning mention that a certain Luther Laurence, late of Tulsa, was living up here in Boston." His eyes glittered. "Then I'd have to wonder how many places you've got left to hide."

Luther felt all the fight in him just roll up and die. Just lie down. Just wither away. "What do you want?"

"I want a vault." McKenna's eyes sparkled. "Oh, I want the *Crisis* mailing list."

"What?"

"The *Crisis*. The newsletter of the National Association for the Advancement of Chimpanzees."

"I know what it is. Where would I get the mailing list?"

"Well, Isaiah Giddreaux must have access to it. There must be a copy of it somewhere in that nigger-bourgeoisie palace you call home. Find it."

"And if I build your vault and find your mailing list?"

"Don't adopt the tone of someone who has options, Luther."

"Fine. What do you want me to put in this vault?" Luther asked.

"You keep asking questions?" McKenna draped his arm over Luther's shoulders. "Maybe it'll be you."

Leaving another ineffectual BSC meeting, Danny was exhausted as he headed for the el stop at Roxbury Crossing, and Steve Coyle fell in beside him as Danny knew he would. Steve was still coming to meetings, still making people wish he'd go away, still talking about grander and grander fool-ambitions. Danny had to report for duty in four hours and wished only to lay his head to his pillow and sleep for a day or so.

"She's still here," Steve said as they walked up the stairs to the el.

"Who?"

"Tessa Ficara," Steve said. "Don't pretend you've forgotten her."

"I'm not pretending anything," Danny said, and it came out too sharp.

"I've been talking to people," Steve said quickly. "People who owe me from when I worked the streets."

Danny wondered just who these people could be. Cops were always under the misguided impression that people felt gratitude or indebtedness toward them when nothing could be further from the truth. Unless you were saving their lives or their wallets, people resented cops. They did not want you around.

"Talking to people is a bit dangerous," he said. "In the North End particularly."

"I told you," Steve said, "my sources owe me. They trust me. Anyway, she's not in the North End. She's over here in Roxbury."

The train entered the station with screaming brakes, and they boarded it and took seats on the empty car. "Roxbury, uh?"

"Yeah. Somewhere between Columbus and Warren, and she's working with Galleani himself on something big."

"Something bigger than the landmass between Columbus and Warren?"

"Look," Steve said as they burst from a tunnel and the lights of the city suddenly dipped below them as the track rose, "this one guy told me he'll get me an exact address for fifty bucks."

"Fifty bucks?"

"Why do you keep repeating what I say?"

Danny held up a hand. "I'm tired. Sorry. Steve, I don't have fifty bucks."

"I know, I know."

"That's over two weeks' pay."

"I said I know. Jesus."

"I could lay my hands on three. Maybe four?"

"Yeah, sure. I mean, whatever you can do. I mean, we want to get this bitch, right?"

Truth was, ever since he'd shot Federico, Danny hadn't given Tessa a sole thought. He couldn't explain why that was, just that it was.

"If we don't get her," he said, "someone else will, Steve. She's a federal problem. You understand."

"I'll be careful. Don't you worry."

That wasn't the point, but Danny'd grown used to Steve missing the point lately. He closed his eyes, head back against the window, as the el car bumped and rattled along.

"You think you can get me the four bucks soon?" Steve asked.

Danny kept his eyes closed because he feared Steve would see the contempt in them if he opened them. He kept them closed and nodded once.

At Batterymarch station, he declined Steve's offer of a drink, and they went their separate ways. By the time Danny reached Salem Street, he was starting to see spots. He could picture his bed, the white sheets, the cool pillow . . .

"And how've you been keeping then, Danny?"

Nora crossed the street toward him, stepping between a horse-drawn wagon and a sputtering tin lizzy that chucked great bursts of ink-colored smoke from its tailpipe. When she reached the curb, he stopped and turned fully toward her. Her eyes were false and bright and she wore a pale gray blouse he'd always liked and a blue skirt that left her ankles exposed. Her coat looked thin, even for the warming air, and her cheekbones were too pronounced. Her eyes sat back in her head.

"Nora."

She held out a hand to him in a manner he found

451

comically formal and he shook it as if it were a man's.

"So?" she said, still working the brightness into her eyes.

"So?" Danny said.

"How've you been keeping?" she said a second time.

"I've been fair," he said. "You?"

"Tip-top," she said.

"Swell news."

"Aye."

Even at eight in the evening, the North End sidewalks were thick with people. Danny, tired of being jostled, took Nora by the elbow and led her to a café that was nearly empty. They took a seat by the small window that overlooked the street.

She removed her coat as the proprietor came out of the back, tying his apron on, and caught Danny's eye.

"*Due caffè, per favore.*"

"*Sì, signore. Venire a destra in su.*"

"*Grazie.*"

Nora gave him a hesitant smile. "I forgot how much pleasure that gave me."

"What's that?"

"Your Italian. The sound of it, yeah?" She looked around the café and then out at the street. "You seem at home here, Danny."

"It is home." Danny suppressed a yawn. "Always has been."

"And now how about that molasses flood?" She removed her hat and placed it on a chair. She smoothed her hair. "They're saying it was definitely the company's fault?"

Danny nodded. "Looks to be the case."

"The stench is awful still."

It was. Every brick and gutter and cobblestone crack in the North End held some residual evidence of the flood. The warmer it got, the worse it smelled. Insects and rodents had tripled in number, and the disease rate among children erupted.

The proprietor returned from the back and placed their coffees in front of them. "*Qui andate, signore, signora.*"

"Grazie così tanto, signore."

"Siete benvenuti. Siete per avere così bello fortunato una moglie, signore." The man clapped his hands and gave them a broad smile and went back behind the counter.

"What did he say?" Nora said.

"He said it was a nice night out." Danny stirred a lump of sugar into his coffee. "What brings you here?"

"I was out for a walk."

"Long walk," he said.

She reached for the cup of sugar between them. "How would you know how long a walk it is? That would mean you know where I live."

He placed his pack of Murads on the table. Christ, he was fucking exhausted. "Let's not."

"What?"

"Do this back-and-forth."

She added two lumps to her own coffee and followed it with cream. "How's Joe?"

"He's fine," Danny said, wondering if he was. It had been so long since he'd been by the house. Work kept him away mostly, meetings at the social club, but something more, too, something he didn't want to put his finger on.

She sipped her coffee and stared across the table with her too-happy face and her sunken eyes. "I half thought you'd have paid me a visit by now."

"Really?"

She nodded, her face beginning to soften from its cast of false gaiety.

"Why would I do that, Nora?"

Her face grew gay again, constricted. "Oh, I don't know. I just hoped, I guess."

"Hoped." He nodded. "What's your son's name by the way?"

She played with her spoon, ran her fingers over the checkered tablecloth. "His name's Gabriel," she said softly, "and he's not my son. I told you that."

"You told me a lot of things," Danny said. "And you never mentioned this son who's not a son until Quentin Finn brought it up for you."

She raised her eyes and they were no longer bright, nor were they angry or wounded. She seemed to have reached a place beyond expectation.

"I don't know whose child Gabriel is. He was simply there the day Quentin brought me to the hovel he calls a home. Gabriel was about eight then, and a wolf would have been better tamed. A mindless, heartless child, our Gabriel. Quentin is a lesser creature among men, of that you've seen, but Gabriel? Sure now the child was molded from devil's clay. He'd crouch for hours by the hearth, watching the fire, as if the flames had voice, and then he'd leave the house without a word and blind a goat. That was Gabriel at nine. Would you like me to tell you what he was like at twelve?"

Danny didn't want to know anything more about Gabriel or Quentin or Nora's past. Her sullied, embarrassing (and that was it, wasn't it?) past. She was tainted now, a woman he could never acknowledge as his and look the rest of the world in the eye.

Nora sipped some more coffee and looked at him and he could feel it all dying between them. They were both lost, he realized, both floating away toward new lives that had nothing to do with one another. They would pass each other one day in a crowd and each would pretend not to have seen the other.

She put on her coat, not a word spoken between them, but both understanding what had transpired. She lifted her hat off the chair. The hat was as threadbare as the coat, and he noticed that her collarbone pressed up hard against her flesh.

He looked down at the table. "You need money?"

"What?" Her whisper was high-pitched, squeaky.

He raised his head. Her eyes had filled. Her lips were clamped tightly against her teeth and she shook her head softly.

454

"Do you—"

"You didn't say that," she said. "You didn't. You couldn't have."

"I just meant—"

"You . . . Danny? My God, you didn't."

He reached for her, but she stepped back. She continued shaking her head at him and then she rushed out of the café and into the crowded streets.

He let her go. He let her go. He'd told his father after he'd beaten Quentin Finn that he was ready to grow up now. And that was the truth. He was tired of bucking against the way things were. Curtis had taught him the futility of that in a single afternoon. The world was built and maintained by men like his father and his cronies, and Danny looked out the window at the streets of the North End and decided it was, most times, a good world. It seemed to work in spite of itself. Let other men fight the small and bitter battles against the hardness of it. He was done. Nora, with her lies and sordid history, was just another foolish child's fantasy. She would go off and lie to some other man, and maybe it would be a rich man and she'd live out her lies until they faded and were replaced by a matron's respectability.

Danny would find a woman without a past. A woman fi to be seen in public with him. It was a good world. He would be worthy of it. A grown up, a citizen.

His fingers searched his pocket for the button, but it wasn't there. For a moment, he was seized with a panic so severe it seemed to demand physical action of him. He straightened in his chair and set his feet, as if preparing to lunge. Then he recalled seeing the button this morning amid some change scattered atop his dresser. So it was there. Safe. He sat back and sipped his coffee, though it had gone cold.

On April 29, in the Baltimore distribution annex of the U.S. Post Office, a postal inspector noticed fluid leaking from a brown cardboard package addressed to Judge Wilfred

Enniston of the Fifth District U.S. Appellate Court. When closer inspection of the package revealed that the fluid had burned a hole in the corner of the box, the inspector notified Baltimore police, who dispatched their bomb squad and contacted the Justice Department.

By the end of the evening, authorities discovered thirty-four bombs. They were in packages addressed to Attorney General Mitchell Palmer, Judge Kenesaw Mountain Landis, John Rockefeller, and thirty-one others. All thirty-four targets worked in either industry or in government agencies whose policies affected immigration standards.

On the same evening in Boston, Louis Fraina and the Lettish Workingman's Society applied for a parade permit to march from the Dudley Square Opera House to Franklin Park in recognition of May Day.

The application for a permit was denied.

RED SUMMER

MID SUMMER

CHAPTER *twenty-six*

May Day, Luther had breakfast at Solomon's Diner before he went to work at the Coughlins'. He left at five-thirty and got as far as Columbus Square before Lieutenant McKenna's black Hudson detached itself from a curb across the street and did a slow U-turn in front of him. He didn't feel surprised. He didn't feel alarmed. He didn't feel much of anything really.

Luther had read the *Standard* at the Solomon's counter, his eyes immediately drawn to the headline—"Reds Plot May Day Assassinations." He ate his eggs and read about the thirty-four bombs discovered in the U.S. mail. The list of targets was posted in full on the second page of the paper, and Luther, no fan of white judges or white bureaucrats, still felt ice ice chips flow through his blood. This was followed by a jolt of patriotic fury, the likes of which he'd never suspected could live in his soul for a country that had never treated his people with any welcome or justice. And yet he pictured these Reds, most of them aliens with accents as thick as their mustaches, willing to do violence and wreckage to *his* country, and he wanted to join any mob that was going to smash them through the teeth, wanted to say to someone, anyone: Just give me a rifle.

According to the paper, the Reds were planning a day of national revolt, and the thirty-four bombs that had been intercepted suggested a hundred more that could be out there primed to explode. In the past week, leaflets had been pasted to lamp poles across the city, all of which bore the same words:

> **Go ahead. Deport us. You senile fossils ruling the United States will see red! The storm is within and very soon will leap and crash and annihilate you in blood and fire.**
> **We will dynamite you!**

In yesterday's *Traveler*, even before news of the thirty-four bombs leaked out, an article had listed some of the recent, inflammatory comments of American subversives, including Jack Reed's call for "the overthrow of capitalism and the establishment of socialism through a proletarian dictatorship" and Emma Goldman's anticonscription speech last year, in which she'd urged all workers to "Follow Russia's lead."

Follow Russia's lead? Luther thought: You love Russia so much, fucking *move* there. And take your bombs and your onion-soup breath with you. For a few, strangely joyous hours, Luther didn't feel like a colored man, didn't even feel there was such a thing as color, only one thing above all others: He was an American.

That changed, of course, as soon as he saw McKenna. The large man stepped out of his Hudson and smiled. He held up a copy of the *Standard* and said, "You seen it?"

"I seen it," Luther said.

"We're about to have a very serious day ahead of us, Luther." He slapped the newspaper off Luther's chest a couple of times. "Where's my mailing list?"

"My people ain't Reds," Luther said.

"Oh, they're *your* people now, uh?"

Shit, Luther wanted to say, they always were.

"You build my vault?" McKenna said, almost singing the words.

460

"Working on it."

McKenna nodded. "You wouldn't be lying now?"

Luther shook his head.

"Where's my fucking list?"

"It's in a safe."

McKenna said, "All I asked of you is that you get me one simple list. Why has that been so difficult?"

Luther shrugged. "I don't know how to bust a safe."

McKenna nodded, as if that were perfectly reasonable. "You'll bring it to me after your shift at the Coughlins'. Outside Costello's. It's on the waterfront. Six o'clock."

Luther said, "I don't know how I'm going to do that. I can't bust a *safe*."

In reality, there was no safe. Mrs. Giddreaux kept the mailing list in her desk drawer. Unlocked.

McKenna tapped the paper lightly off his thigh, as if giving it some thought. "You need to be inspired, I see. That's okay, Luther. All creative men need a muse."

Luther had no idea what he was on about now, but he didn't like his tone—airy, confident.

McKenna draped his arm across Luther's shoulder. "Congratulations."

"On?"

That lit a happy fire in McKenna's face. "Your nuptials. I understand you were married last fall in Tulsa, Oklahoma, to a woman named Lila Waters, late of Columbus, Ohio. A grand institution, marriage."

Luther said nothing, though he was sure the hate showed in his eyes. First the Deacon, now Lieutenant Eddie McKenna of the BPD—it seemed no matter where he went the Lord saw fit to place demons in his path.

"Funny thing is, when I started sniffling around back in Columbus, I found that your bride has a warrant out for her arrest."

Luther laughed.

"You find that funny?"

461

Luther smiled. "If you knew my wife, McKenna, you'd be laughing, too."

"I'm sure I would, Luther." McKenna nodded several times. "Problem is, this warrant is very real. Seems your wife and a boy by the name of Jefferson-Reese—that ring a bell?—seems they were stealing from their employers, family by the name of Hammond? Apparently, they'd been doing it for years by the time your beloved took off to Tulsa. But Mr. Reese, he got himself arrested with some silver frames and some petty cash, and he pinned the whole thing on your wife. Apparently he was under the impression that a partner in his enterprise made the difference between hard time and soft time. They slapped the hard charge on him anyway, and he's in prison now, but the charge is still pending against your wife. Pregnant wife, the way I hear it. So she's sitting there on, let me see if I remember, Seventeen Elwood Street in Tulsa, and I doubt she's moving around all that much, what with the loaf in her oven." McKenna smiled and patted Luther's face. "Ever see the kind of midwives they hire in a county lockup?"

Luther didn't trust himself to speak.

McKenna slapped him in the face, still smiling. "They're not the gentlest of souls, I can tell you that. They merely show the mother the baby's face and then they take that child—if it's a Negro child, that is—and they whisk it straightaway to the county orphanage. That wouldn't be the case, of course, if the father was around, but you're not around, are you? You're here."

Luther said, "Tell me what you want me—"

"I fucking told you, Luther. I fucking told you and told you." He squeezed the flesh along Luther's jaw and pulled his face close. "You get that list and you bring it to Costello's tonight at six. No fucking excuses. Understood?"

Luther closed his eyes and nodded. McKenna let go of his face and stepped back.

"Right now you hate me. I can see that. But today we're going to settle accounts in this little burg of ours. Today, the

Reds—all Reds, even colored Reds—are getting their eviction notices from this fair city." He held out his arms and shrugged. "And by tomorrow, you'll thank me, because we'll have us a nice place to live again."

He tapped the paper off his thigh again and gave Luther a solemn nod before walking toward his Hudson.

"You're making a mistake," Luther said.

McKenna looked back over his shoulder. "What's that?"

"You're making a mistake."

McKenna walked back and punched Luther in the stomach. All the air left his body like it was never coming back. He dropped to his knees and opened his mouth but his throat had collapsed along with his lungs, and for a terrifying length of time he couldn't get a breath in or out. He was sure he'd die like that, on his knees, his face gone blue like someone with the grippe.

When the air did come, it hurt, going down his windpipe like a spade. His first breath came out sounding like the screech of a train wheel, followed by another and then another, until they began to sound normal, if a little high-pitched.

McKenna stood over him, patient. "What was that?" he said softly.

"NAACP folks ain't Red," Luther said. "And if some are, they ain't the kind going to blow shit up or fire off guns."

McKenna slapped the side of his head. "I'm not sure I heard you."

Luther could see twins of himself reflected in McKenna's irises. "What you think? You think a bunch of coloreds are going to run in these here streets with weapons? Give you and all the other redneck assholes in this country an excuse to kill us all? You think we *want* to get massacred?" He stared up at the man, saw that his fist was clenched. "You got a bunch of foreign-born sons of bitches trying to stir up a revolution today, McKenna, so I say you go get them. Put 'em down like dogs. I got no love for those people. And neither do any other colored folk. This is our country, too."

McKenna took a step back and considered him with a wry smile.

"What'd you say?"

Luther spit on the ground and took a breath. "Said this is our country, too."

" 'Tis not, son." McKenna shook his large head. "Nor will it ever be."

He left Luther there and climbed into his car and it pulled away from the curb. Luther rose from his knees and sucked a few breaths into his lungs until the nausea had almost passed. "Yes, it is," he whispered, over and over, until he saw McKenna's taillights take a right turn on Massachusetts Avenue.

"Yes, it is," he said one more time and spit into the gutter.

That morning, the reports started coming out of Division 9 in Roxbury that a crowd was gathering in front of the Dudley Opera House. Each of the other station houses was asked to send men, and the Mounted Unit met at the BPD stables and warmed up their horses.

Men from all the city's precincts were dropped at Division 9 under the command of Lieutenant McKenna. They assembled on the first floor in the wide lobby in front of the desk sergeant's counter, and McKenna addressed them from the landing of the stairwell that curved up toward the second floor.

"We happy, happy few," he said, taking them all in with a soft smile. "Gentlemen, the Letts are gathering in an illegal assembly in front of the Opera House. What do you think about that?"

No one knew if the question was rhetorical or not, so no one answered.

"Patrolman Watson?"

"Loo?"

"What do you think of this illegal assembly?"

Watson, whose family had changed their Polish name from

something long and unpronounceable, straightened his shoulders. "I'd say they picked the wrong day for it, Loo."

McKenna raised a hand above them all. "We are sworn to protect and serve Americans in general and Bostonians in particular. The Letts, well"—he chuckled—"the Letts are neither, gents. Heathens and subversives that they are, they have chosen to ignore the city's strict orders not to march and plan to parade from the Opera House down Dudley Street to Upham's Corner in Dorchester. From there they plan to turn right on Columbia Road and continue until they reach Franklin Park, where they will hold a rally in support of their comrades—yes, comrades—in Hungary, Bavaria, Greece, and, of course, Russia. Are there any Russians among us here today?"

Someone shouted, "Hell no!" and the other men repeated it in a cheer.

"Any Bolsheviki?"

"Hell no!"

"Any gutless, atheistic, subversive, hook-nosed, cock-smoking, anti-American dog fuckers?"

The men were laughing when they shouted, "Hell no!"

McKenna leaned on the railing and wiped his brow with a handkerchief. "Three days ago, the mayor of Seattle received a bomb in the mail. Luckily for him, his housekeeper got to it before he did. Poor woman's in the hospital with no hands. Last night, as I'm sure you all know, the U.S. postal service intercepted thirty-four bombs meant to kill the attorney general of this great nation as well as several learned judges and captains of industry. Today, radicals of every stripe—but mostly heathen Bolsheviki—have promised a *national day of revolt* to take place in key cities across this fine land. Gentlemen, I ask you—is this the kind of country we wish to live in?"

"Hell no!"

The men were moving around Danny, shifting from foot to foot.

"Would you like to walk out the back door right now and hand it over to a horde of subversives and ask them to please remember to shut the lights out at bedtime?"

"Hell no!" Shoulders jostled off one another and Danny could smell sweat and hangover breath and a strange burnt-hair odor, an acrid scent of fury and fear.

"Or," McKenna shouted, "would you, instead, like to take this country back?"

The men were so used to saying "Hell no!" that several did so again.

McKenna cocked an eyebrow at them. "I said—Would you like to take this fucking country back?"

"Hell, yes!"

Dozens of the men attended BSC meetings alongside Danny, men who just the other night had been bemoaning the shoddy treatment they received at the hands of their department, men who'd expressed kinship for all the workers of the world in their struggle against Big Money. But all that, for the moment, was swept away by the tonic of unity and a shared purpose.

"We are going down to the Dudley Opera House," McKenna shouted, "right now and we are going to order these subversives, these Communists and anarchists and bomb throwers, to stand the fuck down!"

The cheer that rose up was unintelligible, a collective roar of the blood.

"We are going to say, in the strictest terms, 'Not on my watch!' " McKenna leaned over the rail, his neck extended, his jaw thrust forward. "Can you say it with me, gents?"

"Not on my watch!" the men shouted.

"Let me hear it again."

"Not on my watch!"

"Are you with me?"

"Yes!"

"Are you frightened?"

"Hell no!"

466

"Are you Boston police?"

"Hell yes!"

"The finest, most respected police force in these forty-eight states?"

"Hell yes!"

McKenna stared at them, his head sweeping slowly from one side of the crowd to the other, and Danny saw no humor in his face, no ironic glint. Just certitude. McKenna let the silence build, the men shuffling from side to side, hands wiping sweat on the sides of pants and the handles of nightsticks.

"Then," McKenna hissed, "let's go earn our pay."

The men turned in several directions at once. They shoved one another gleefully. They barked in one another's faces, and then someone figured out where the exit was and they turned into the rear corridor and moved in a sea through the door. They poured out the back of the station house and up the alley, some already rapping their billy clubs off the walls and the tops of metal trash cans.

Mark Denton found Danny in the crowd and said, "Just wondering . . ."

"What's that?"

"We keeping the peace," Mark said, "or ending it?"

Danny looked at him. "Fair question."

When they rounded the corner into Dudley Square, Louis Fraina stood on the top steps of the Opera House, speaking through a bullhorn to a crowd of a couple hundred.

". . . they tell us we have the right to—"

He lowered the bullhorn as he saw them enter the street and then raised it again.

"And here they come now, the private army of the ruling class." Fraina pointed, and the crowd turned to see the blue uniforms coming up the street toward them.

"Comrades, feast your eyes on what a corrupt society does to preserve its illusion of itself. They call it the Land of the

467

Free, but speech is not free, is it? The right to assemble is not free. Not today, not for us. We followed procedure. We filed our applications for the right to parade but those permits were denied to us. And why?" Fraina looked around at the crowd. "Because they fear us."

The Letts turned fully toward them. On the steps, up by Fraina, Danny saw Nathan Bishop. He seemed smaller than Danny remembered.

Bishop's eyes locked on his, followed by a curious cock of his head. Danny held the look, trying to will a pride he did not feel into his own eyes. Nathan Bishop's eyes narrowed with recognition. Recognition, followed by bitterness and then, most surprising, a crestfallen despair.

Danny dropped his eyes.

"Look at them in their domed helmets. With their night-sticks and their guns. These are not forces of law. These are forces of oppression. And they are afraid—terrified, comrades—because we hold the moral high ground. We are right. *We* are the workingmen of this city and we will not be sent to our rooms."

McKenna raised his own bullhorn as they got within thirty yards of the crowd.

"You are in violation of city ordinances prohibiting assembly without permit."

Fraina raised his bullhorn. "Your ordinances are a lie. Your city is a lie."

"I order you to disperse." McKenna's voice crackled in the morning air. "If you refuse, you will be removed by force."

They were fifteen yards away now and spreading out. Their faces were gaunt and determined and Danny searched for fear in their eyes and found very little.

"Force is all they have!" Fraina shouted. "Force is the weapon of choice for all tyrants since the dawn of time. Force is the unreasonable response to a reasonable action. We have broken no law!"

The Letts strolled toward them.

"You are in violation of city ordinance eleven-dash-four—"

"You are in violation of us, sir. You are in violation of our constitutional rights."

"If you do not disperse, you will be arrested. Come down off those steps."

"I will no more remove myself from these steps than—"

"I am ordering—"

"I do not recognize your authority."

"You are breaking the law, sir!"

The two crowds met.

For a moment no one seemed to know what to do. The cops mingled with the Letts, the Letts mingled with the cops, all of them interspersed, and few among them aware of how it had happened. A pigeon cooed from a windowsill and the air still carried a hint of dew. The rooftops along Dudley Square smoked with remnants of the early-morning fog. This close Danny had a hard time telling who was cop and who was Lett, and then a group of bearded Letts walked around from the side of the Opera House wielding ax handles. Big guys, Russians by the look of them, eyes clear of anything that could be confused with doubt.

The first of them reached the throng and swung his ax handle.

Fraina shouted, "No!" but that was lost in the sound of the wood connecting with the domed helmet of James Hinman, a patrolman at the One-Four. The helmet sprang up out of the crowd and hung in the sky. Then it clanged to the street, and Hinman disappeared.

The closest Lett to Danny was a thin Italian with a handlebar mustache and a tweed cap. In the moment it took for the guy to realize how close he stood to a cop, Danny snapped his elbow into his mouth and the guy gave him a look like he'd broken his heart instead of his teeth and hit the pavement. The next Lett charged Danny by stepping on his fallen comrade's chest. Danny cleared his nightstick but Kevin

469

McRae rose out of the crowd behind the big Lett and grabbed him by the hair, giving Danny a wild smile as he twirled the guy through the crowd and ran him into a brick wall.

Danny traded punches for several minutes with a small, balding Russian. Small as he was, the fucker could jab, and he wore a matching pair of knuckledusters over his fists. Danny concentrated so hard on slipping the jabs to his face that it left him open to body shots. The two of them went back and forth along the left flank of the crowd, Danny trying for the knockout punch. The guy was slippery, but then he caught his foot in the cracks between the cobblestones, and his knee buckled. He stumbled and fell on his back and tried to scramble to his feet but Danny stomped on his stomach and kicked him in the face and the guy curled up and vomited out the side of his mouth.

Whistles blew as the mounted police tried to wade into the crowd, but the horses kept backing up. It was all incestuous now, Letts and cops intertwined and the Letts swinging sticks, swinging pipes and blackjacks and, Jesus, fucking ice picks. They threw rocks and threw punches, and the cops started to get savage, too, gouging at eyes, biting ears and noses, banging heads off the pavement. Someone fired a pistol and one of the horses rose up on its hind legs and threw its rider. The horse tipped to its right and toppled, hooves kicking at anything in its way.

Two Letts got Danny by the arms and one of them butted the side of his face. They ran him across the cobblestones into a metal store grate and his nightstick fell from his hands. One of them punched him in the right eye. Danny stomped blindly and hit an ankle, drove his knee up and hit a groin. The breath blew out of the guy and Danny swung him into the grate and pulled one arm free as the other man sank his teeth into his shoulder. Danny spun with the biter draped over him and ran backward into a brick wall, felt the guy's teeth leave his skin. He took a few steps forward and then ran himself backward again, twice as hard. When the guy fell from his body, Danny turned and scooped up his nightstick and swung it into the guy's face, heard the cheekbone crack.

He added a final kick to the ribs and turned back to the center of the street. A Lett charged back and forth along the rear of the crowd on one of the police horses, swinging a length of pipe at any domed heads he saw. Several of the other horses roamed riderless. On the far side of the street, two patrolman lifted Francie Stoddard, a sergeant at the One-Oh, onto a loading dock, Stoddard's mouth wide and gulping, his shirt open at the collar, one palm pressed to the center of his chest.

Shots hit the air and Paul Welch, a sergeant with the Oh-Six, spun and grabbed his hip and then disappeared in the crush of men. Danny heard a scuffle of footsteps and turned in time to duck a Lett charging him with an ice pick. He speared the guy's solar plexus with his nightstick. The guy gave him a look of self-pity and shame. Spit popped out of his mouth. When he hit the pavement, Danny grabbed his ice pick and hurled it onto the nearest roof.

Someone had gotten a grip on the leg of the Lett on horse-back and he vaulted off the animal and into the crowd. The horse galloped up Dudley Street toward the el tracks. Blood poured down Danny's back and the vision in his right eye blurred as it began to swell. His head felt as if someone had hammered nails through it. The Letts were going to lose the war, Danny had no doubt, but they were winning this battle by a large fucking margin. Cops were down all over the street while burly Letts in their coarse Cossack clothing screamed in triumph as their own heads rose above the throng.

Danny waded into the crowd, swinging his nightstick, trying to tell himself he didn't love it, he didn't feel his heart swell because he was bigger and stronger and faster than most and could down a man with one blow from either fist or nightstick. He took out four Letts with six swings and felt the mob turn toward him. He saw a pistol aimed at him, saw the hole in the barrel and the eyes of the young Lett wielding it, a boy really, nineteen, tops. The pistol shook, but he took little comfort from that because the kid was only fifteen feet away, and the crowd opened up a corridor between them to give him a clean shot. Danny didn't reach for his own revolver; he'd never clear it in time.

The kid's finger whitened against the trigger. The cylinder turned. Danny considered closing his eyes but then the kid's arm shot straight up above his head. The pistol discharged into the sky.

Nathan Bishop stood beside the kid, rubbing his wrist where it had made contact with the kid's elbow. He looked reasonably untarnished by the fighting, his suit a little rumpled but mostly unstained, which was saying something for a cream-colored suit in a sea of black and blue fabric and swinging fists. One of his eyeglass lenses was cracked. He stared at Danny through the good lens, both of them breathing hard. Danny felt relief, of course. And gratitude. But shame larger than all that. Shame more than anything.

A horse burst between them, its great black body trembling, its smooth flank shuddering in the air. Another horse burst through the throng followed by two more, all in full charge with riders astride them. Behind them was an army of blue uniforms, still crisp and unsoiled, and the wall of people around Danny and Nathan Bishop and the boy with the pistol collapsed. Several of the Letts had fought in guerrilla campaigns back in the motherland and knew the benefits of cut-and-run. In the mad-dash dispersal, Danny lost sight of Nathan Bishop. Within a minute, most of the Letts were running past the Opera House, and Dudley Square was suddenly littered with blue uniforms, Danny and the other men looking at one another as if to say: Did any of that just happen?

But men lay crumpled in the street and against walls as the reinforcements used their nightsticks on the few that weren't brothers of the badge whether the bodies were moving or not. On the far fringes of the crowd, a small group of demonstrators, the last ones out apparently, were cut off by more reinforcements and more horses. Cops had cut heads and cut knees and holes that leaked from their shoulders and hands and thighs and swelling contusions and black eyes and broken arms and fat lips. Danny saw Mark Denton trying to pull himself to his feet, and he crossed to him and gave him his hand. Mark stood and applied weight to his right foot and winced.

"Broken?" Danny said.

"Twisted, I think." Mark slung his arm around Danny's shoulder and they walked to the loading dock on the other side of the street, Mark sucking oxygen from the air with a hiss.

"You sure?"

"Might be sprained," Mark said. "Fuck, Dan, I lost my helmet."

He had a cut along his hairline that had dried black and he gripped his ribs with his free arm. Danny leaned him against the loading dock and noticed two cops kneeling over Sergeant Francie Stoddard. One of them met his eyes and shook his head.

"What?" Danny said.

"He's dead. He's gone," the cop said.

"He's what?" Mark said. "No. How the fuck . . . ?"

"He just grabbed his chest," the cop said. "Right in the middle of it all. Just grabbed his chest and went all red and starting gasping. We got him over here, but . . ." The cop shrugged. "Fucking heart attack. You believe that? Here? In this?" The cop looked out at the street.

His partner still held Stoddard's hand. "Fucking guy had less than a year till his thirty, he goes like this?" The cop was crying. "He goes like *this*, because of *them*?"

"Jesus Christ," Mark whispered and touched the top of Stoddard's shoe. They'd worked together five years at D-10 in Roxbury Crossing.

"They shot Welch in the thigh," the first cop said. "Shot Armstrong in the hand. Fuckers were stabbing guys with *ice picks*?"

"There's going to be some hell to pay," Mark said.

"You goddamn got that right," the crying cop said. "You can make goddamn fucking book on that."

Danny looked away from Stoddard's body. Ambulances rolled up Dudley Street. Across the square, a cop rose from the pavement on wobbly feet and wiped at the blood in his eyes and then tipped over again. Danny saw a cop empty a metal trash can on a prone Lett, then drop the can on the body for good measure. It was the cream-colored suit that got Danny moving. He walked toward them as the cop delivered a kick so hard it lifted his other foot off the ground.

Nathan Bishop's face looked like a crushed plum. His teeth littered the ground near his chin. One ear was torn halfway off. The fingers of both hands pointed in all the wrong directions.

Danny put his hand on the shoulder of the cop. It was Henry Temple, a Special Squads goon.

"I think you got him," Danny said.

Temple looked at Danny for a bit like he was searching for an apt response. Then he shrugged and walked off.

A pair of paramedics were passing and Danny said, "We got one here."

One of the paramedics grimaced. "He ain't wearing a badge? He'll be lucky we get to him by sundown." They walked off.

Nathan Bishop opened his left eye. It was startlingly white in the ruin of his face.

Danny opened his mouth. He wanted to say something. He wanted to say, *I'm sorry*. He wanted to say, *Forgive me*. Instead, he said nothing.

Nathan's lips were sectioned into strips, but behind them spread a bitter smile.

474

"My name's Nathan Bishop," he slurred. "What's yours, eh?"
He closed his eye again, and Danny lowered his head.

Luther had an hour for lunch, and he hustled back across the Dover Street Bridge and over to the Giddreauxs' house on St. Botolph, which, these days, was the operating headquarters of the Boston NAACP. Mrs. Giddreaux worked there with a dozen other women pretty much every day, and it was in the very basement of the house on St. Botolph where the *Crisis* was printed and then mailed out to the rest of the country. Luther came home to an empty house, as he knew he would—on fine days, the girls all took their lunch in Union Park a few blocks away, and this was the finest day, thus far, of an often unforgiving spring. He let himself into Mrs. Giddreaux's office. He sat behind her desk. He opened her drawer. He lifted the ledger out and placed it on the desk and that's where it was sitting half an hour later when Mrs. Giddreaux came back through the door.

She hung up her coat and her scarf. "Luther, honey, what're you doing in here?"

Luther tapped the ledger with his finger. "I don't give this list to a policeman, he's gonna have my wife arrested, have our baby taken from her soon as it's born."

Mrs. Giddreaux's smile froze and then vanished. "Excuse me?"

Luther repeated himself.

Mrs. Giddreaux sat in the chair across from him. "Tell me all of it."

Luther told her about everything except the vault he'd built under the kitchen floorboards on Shawmut Avenue. Until he knew what McKenna intended it for, he wasn't going to speak of it. As he talked, Mrs. Giddreaux's kind, old face lost its kindness and lost its age, too. It grew as smooth and unmoving as a headstone.

When he finished, she said, "You've never given him a thing he could use against us? Never once played the rat?"

Luther stared back at her, his mouth open.

"Answer my question, Luther. This is no child's game."

"No," Luther said. "I never gave him anything."

"That doesn't make sense."

Luther didn't say anything.

"He wouldn't just get you under his thumb and not dirty you up a little bit in his filth with him. The police don't work that way. He would have sent you in with something to plant here or at the new building, something illegal."

Luther shook his head.

She looked back at him, her breaths coming soft and measured.

Luther shook his head again.

"Luther."

Luther told her about the vault.

She looked at him with such pained confusion Luther wanted to jump out the window. "Why didn't you just come to us the moment he approached you?"

Luther said, "I don't know."

She shook her head. "Don't you trust anyone, son? Anyone?"

Luther kept his mouth shut.

Mrs. Giddreaux reached for the phone on her desk and tapped the cradle once, tucked her hair behind her ear as she placed the receiver to her ear. "Edna? Girl, send every typist you've got up to the main floor. Get them all in the parlor and the dining room. You hear? Right now. And tell them to carry those typewriters with them. Oh, and Edna? You have phone directories down there, don't you? No, I can't use Boston. You have Philadelphia? Good. Send that up, too."

She hung up and tapped her fingers lightly off her lips. When she looked at Luther again, the anger was gone from her eyes, replaced by the shine of excitement. Then her face darkened again and those fingers stopped tapping.

"What?" Luther said.

"No matter what you bring him tonight, he may just have you arrested or shot."

"Why would he do that?" Luther said.

She stared at him, her eyes wide. "Because he can. Let's start there." She shook her head slightly. "He'll do it, Luther, because you got him the list. That's not something you'll be able to tell someone about from prison."

"What if I don't bring it?"

"Oh, then he'll just kill you," she said mildly. "Shoot you in the back. No, you'll have to bring it." She sighed.

Luther was still back at the "kill you" part.

"I'm going to have to call some people. Dr. Du Bois for starters." Her fingers tapped her chin now. "Legal Department in New York, that's for sure. Legal Department in Tulsa, too."

"Tulsa?"

She glanced back at him, as if just recalling he was still in the room. "If this blows up, Luther, and some policeman comes to arrest your wife? We'll have counsel waiting for her on the steps of the county jail before she even arrives. Who do you think you're dealing with here?"

Luther said, "I . . . I . . . I—"

"You, you, you," Mrs. Giddreaux said and then gave him a small, disappointed smile. "Luther, your heart is good. You never sold your people out and you sat here and waited for me when a lesser man would have been off down the street with that ledger. And, son, I do appreciate it. But you're still a boy, Luther. A child. If you trusted us four months ago, you wouldn't be in this mess, and neither would we." She reached across the desk and patted his hand. "It's okay. It is. Every bear was once a cub."

She led him out of the office into the living room as a dozen women entered carrying typewriters, their wrists straining from the weight. Half were colored women, the other half were white, college girls mostly, from money mostly, too, and those ones glanced at Luther with a bit of fear and a bit of something else he didn't care to think too much about.

"Girls, half stay in here, half of you get in that room yonder. Who has the phone directory?"

One of the girls had it on top of her typewriter and tilted her arms so Mrs. Giddreaux could see it.

"Take it with you, Carol."

"What we gone do with it, Mrs. Giddreaux?"

Mrs. Giddreaux looked up sharply at the girl. "What *are* we, Regina, *going* to do with it, Regina."

"What are we going to do with it, Mrs. Giddreaux?" Regina stammered.

Mrs. Giddreaux smiled at Luther. "We're going to tear it into twelfths, girls, and then we're going to type it all over again."

The cops who were able to walk on their own made their way back to the Oh-Nine and were attended to by paramedics in the basement. Before he'd left the Dudley Opera House, Danny had watched the ambulance drivers toss Nathan Bishop and five other damaged radicals into the back of their wagon like fish tossed on ice, before slamming the doors shut and driving off. In the basement, Danny's shoulder was cleaned and stitched and he was given a bag of ice for his eye, though it was too late to do much about the swelling. Half a dozen men, who'd thought they were okay, weren't, and they were helped back up the stairs and out onto the street where ambulances took them to Mass General. A team from Department Supply showed up with fresh uniforms that were handed out to the men after Captain Vance reminded them with some embarrassment that the cost of the uniforms, as always, would come out of the men's pay, but he'd see what he could do about getting a onetime reduction on the cost, given the circumstances.

When they were all assembled in the basement, Lieutenant Eddie McKenna took the podium. He bore a gash on his neck, treated and cleaned but unbandaged, and his white collar was black with blood. When he spoke, his voice barely above a whisper, the men leaned forward in their folding chairs.

"We lost one of our own today, men. A true policeman, a

copper's copper. We are lesser men now, and the world is a lesser place as well." He lowered his head for a moment. "Today they took one of our own, but they didn't take our honor." He stared out at them, his eyes gone cold and clear. "They did not take our courage. They did not take our manhood. They just took one of our brothers.

"We're going back into their territory tonight. Captain Vance and I will lead you. We are looking, specifically, for four men—Louis Fraina, Wychek Olafski, Pyotr Rastorov, and Luigi Broncona. We have photographs of Fraina and Olafski and sketches of the other two. But we won't stop with them. We will subdue, without quarter, our common enemy. You all know what that enemy looks like. They wear a uniform as obvious as ours. Ours is blue, theirs is of coarse cloth and scraggly beard and watch cap. And they have the fanatics' fire in their eyes. We are going to go out into those streets and we will take them back. Of this," he said, and his eyes found the room, "there is no doubt. There is only resolve." He gripped the podium, his eyes rolling slowly from left to right. "Tonight, my brothers, there is no rank. No difference between a first-year patrolman and a twenty-year gold shield. Because tonight we are all united in the red of our blood and the blue of our professional cloth. Make no mistake, we are soldiers. And as the poet wrote, 'Go tell the Spartans, thou who passest by, that here, obedient to their laws, we lie.' Let that be your benediction, men. Let that be your clarion call."

He stepped from the podium and snapped a salute and the men rose as one and returned the salute. Danny compared it with this morning's chaotic mix of fury and fear and found none of that. In accordance with McKenna's wishes, the men had turned Spartan, utile, so fused to their sense of duty that they were indistinguishable from it.

CHAPTER *twenty-seven*

When the first detail of officers showed up at the door of *The Revolutionary Age*, Louis Fraina was waiting for them with two lawyers in attendance. He was cuffed and led out to the wagon on Humboldt Avenue and his lawyers rode with him.

The evening papers had hit the streets by this time and outrage at the morning attack on police had been growing throughout the dinner hour while the streetlamps grew yellow. Danny and a detail of nineteen other officers were dropped at the corner of Warren and St. James and told by Stan Billups, the sergeant in charge, to spread out, taking the streets in four-man squads. Danny went a few blocks south along Warren with Matt March and Bill Hardy and a guy from the One-Two he'd never met before named Dan Jeffries, Jeffries inexplicably excited that he'd met another guy with the same first name, as if this were a favorable omen. Along the sidewalk stood a half dozen men in their work clothes, men in tweed caps and frayed suspenders, dockworkers probably, who'd apparently read the evening papers and been drinking while they had.

"Give those Bolshie's hell," one of them called, and the rest of them cheered. The silence that followed was awkward, the silence of strangers introduced at a party neither had much wished to attend, and then three men walked out of a coffee shop a few doors down. Two wore spectacles and carried books. All three wore the coarse clothing of Slavic immigrants. Danny saw it happening before it actually did:

One of the Slavic men looked over his shoulder. Two of the men on the sidewalk pointed. Matt March called, "Hey, you three!"

That was all it took.

The three men ran, and the dockworkers broke off in pursuit, and Hardy and Jeffries ran after them. A half block down the Slavs were tackled to the pavement.

Hardy and Jeffries reached the pile and Hardy pulled one of the dockworkers back and then his nightstick caught the glow of the streetlamp as he swung it down on the head of one of the Slavs.

Danny said, "Hey!" but Matt March caught him by the arm. "Dan, wait."

"What?"

March gave him a level gaze. "This is for Stoddard."

Danny pulled his arm free. "We don't know they're Bolsheviks."

"We don't know they're not." March twirled his nightstick and smiled at Danny.

Danny shook his head and walked up the street.

March called, "You're taking the narrow view, Officer."

By the time he reached the dockworkers, they were already turning away. Two of the victims crawled along the street while the third lay on the cobblestones, his hair black with blood, his broken wrist cradled against his chest.

"Jesus," Danny said.

"Oops," Hardy said.

"Hell you guys doing? Get an ambulance."

"Fuck him," Jeffries said and spit on the guy. "Fuck his friends, too. You want an ambulance? You find a call box and ask for one yourself."

Up the street, Sergeant Billups appeared. He talked to March, met Danny's eyes and then walked up the street toward him. The dockworkers had disappeared. Shouts

481

and breaking glass echoed from a block or two over.

Billups looked at the man on the ground, then at Danny. "Problem, Dan?"

"Just want an ambulance for the guy," Danny said.

Billups gave the man another glance. "He looks fine to me, Officer."

"He ain't."

Billups stood over the man. "You hurt, sweetheart?"

The man said nothing, just held his broken wrist tighter against his chest.

Billups ground his heel into the man's ankle. His victim writhed and moaned through cracked teeth. Billups said, "Can't hear you, Boris. What's that?"

Danny reached for Billups's arm and Billups slapped his hand away.

A bone cracked and the man let out a high sigh of disbelief.

"All better now, sweetie?" Billups took his foot off the man's ankle. The man rolled over and gasped into the cobblestones. Billups put his arm around Danny and walked him a few feet away.

"Look, Sarge, I understand. We're all looking to knock some heads. Me, too. But the right heads, don't you think? We don't even—"

"I heard you were seeking aid and comfort for the enemy this afternoon, too, Dan. So listen," Billups said with a smile, "you might be Tommy Coughlin's kid and that gets you some passes, okay? But if you keep acting like a pinko cocksucker? Tommy Coughlin's kid or no, I'll take it fucking personal." He tapped his nightstick lightly off Danny's tunic. "I'm giving you a direct order—get back up that street and *hurt* some subversive assholes, or else get out of my sight."

When Danny turned, Jeffries stood there, giggling softly. He walked past him and then back up the street past Hardy. When he reached March, March shrugged, and Danny kept walking. He turned the corner and saw three paddy wagons at the end of the block, saw fellow officers dragging anyone with a mustache or watch cap down the sidewalk and heaving them into the wagons.

He wandered for several blocks, came across the cops and their newly found working-class brothers going at a dozen men who'd wandered out of a meeting of the Lower Roxbury Socialist Fraternal Organization. The mob had the men pressed back against the doors. The men fought back, but then the doors opened behind them and some of them fell backward and others tried to hold back the mob with nothing more than flailing arms. The left door was wrenched off its hinges and the mob washed over the men and flowed into the building. Danny watched out of his good eye and knew there was nothing he could do to stop it. Nothing at all. This terrible smallness of men was bigger than him, bigger than anything.

Luther went to Costello's on Commercial Wharf and waited outside because it was whites-only. He stood a long time. One hour.

No McKenna.

In his right hand, he held a paper bag with fruit he'd slipped out of the Coughlin household to give to Nora, as long as McKenna didn't decide to shoot him or arrest him tonight. The "list," typed up from fifty thousand telephone users in Philadelphia, was tucked under his left arm.

Two hours.

No McKenna.

Luther left the wharf and walked up toward Scollay Square. Maybe McKenna had been hurt in the line of duty. Maybe he'd had a heart attack. Maybe he'd been shot dead by plug-uglies with an ax to grind.

Luther whistled and hoped.

Danny wandered the streets until he found himself heading along Eustis Street toward Washington. He decided he'd take a right when he reached Washington and cross the city until he reached the North End. He had no intention of stopping back at the Oh-One to sign out. He wasn't changing out of his uniform. He walked through Roxbury in sweet night air that smelled more of summer than spring, and all around him the rule of law was being enforced, as anyone who looked like a Bolshevik or an anarchist, a Slav, an Italian, or a Jew was learning the price of the likeness. They lay against curbs, stoops, sat against lamp poles. On the cement and the tar—their blood, their teeth. A man ran into an intersection a block up and took a police cruiser to his knees. Airborne, he clawed at space. When he landed, the three cops who'd exited the cruiser held his arm to the ground while the cop who'd stayed behind the wheel drove over his hand.

Danny considered going back to his room on Salem Street and sitting alone with the barrel of his service revolver propped over his lower teeth, the metal on his tongue. In the war, they'd died by the millions. For nothing but real estate. And now, in the streets of the world, the same battle continued. Today, Boston. Tomorrow, someplace else. The poor fighting the poor. As they'd always done. As they were encouraged to. And it would never change. He finally realized that. It would never change.

He looked up at the black sky, at the salted splay of dots. That's all they were. That, and nothing more. And if there was a God inveigled behind them, then He had lied. He'd promised the meek they would inherit the earth. They wouldn't. They'd only inherit the small piece they fertilized.

That was the joke.

He saw Nathan Bishop staring at him through a kicked-in face and asking his name, the shame he'd felt, the horror at his very self. He leaned against a streetlamp pole. I can't do this anymore, he told the sky. That man was my brother, if not of blood then of heart and philosophy. He saved my life and I couldn't even get him proper medical care. I am shit. I can't take another fucking step.

Across the street, yet another mass of police and workingmen taunted a small group of residents. At least this mob showed some mercy, allowing a pregnant woman to detach from the other victims and walk away without harm. She hurried along the sidewalk, her shoulders hunched, her hair covered by a dark shawl, and Danny's thoughts returned to his room on Salem Street, to the gun in his holster, the bottle of scotch.

The woman passed him and turned the corner and he noticed that from behind you'd never guess she was pregnant. She had the walk of the young, the unencumbered, not yet weighted down by work or children or graying wishes. She—

Tessa.

Danny was crossing the street before the word had even passed through his head.

Tessa.

He didn't know how he knew, but he knew. He got to the other side of the street and stayed a full block behind her, and the more he watched her walk with that confident languor, the more convinced he became. He passed a call box, then another, but never thought to unlock either of them and phone for help. There was no one in the station houses anyway; they were all out in the streets getting payback. He removed his helmet and coat and tucked them under his right arm, over his gun, and crossed to the other side of the street. As she reached Shawmut Avenue, she looked down the sidewalk, but he wasn't there, so she learned nothing, but he confirmed everything. It was Tessa. Same dark skin, same etched mouth jutting like a shelf above her chin.

She turned right on Shawmut, and he lagged for a few moments, knowing it was wide there and if he reached the corner too early, she'd have to be blind not to see him. He counted down from five and started walking again. He reached the corner and saw her a block down, turning onto Hammond Street.

Three men in the rear seat of a touring car were looking back at her while the men in the front seat looked at him, slowing, noticing his blue pants, the blue coat under his arm. They were all heavily bearded. They all wore watch caps. The men in back of the open car brandished sticks. The front-seat passenger narrowed his eyes and Danny recognized him: Pyotr Glaviach, the oversize Estonian who could out-drink any saloon's worth of men and probably outfight them all, too. Pyotr Glaviach, the veteran of the most vicious Lettish warfare in the motherland. The man who'd considered Danny his fellow pamphleteer, his comrade, his brother-in-arms against capitalist oppression.

Danny had found there were times when violence or the threat of it slowed the world down, when everything came at you as if through water. But there were just as many times when violence moved faster than a clock could tick, and this was one of those. As soon as he and Glaviach recognized each other, the car stopped and the men piled out. Danny's coat got caught on the butt of his pistol as he tried to clear it. Glaviach's arms closed over his, pinning them to his side. He lifted Danny off his feet and carried him across the sidewalk and rammed his back into a stone wall.

A stick hit his blackened eye.

"Say something." Glaviach spit in his face and squeezed his body harder.

Danny didn't have the air to speak so he spit back in the big man's hairy face, saw that his phlegm already had some blood in it as it landed in the man's eyes.

Glaviach rammed his skull into Danny's nose. His head exploded with yellow light and shadows descended on the men around him, as if the sky were dropping. Someone hit his head with a stick again.

"Our comrade, Nathan, you know what happened to him today?" Glaviach shook Danny's body as if he weighed no more than a child. "He lose his ear. Maybe sight in one eye. He lose that. What you lose?"

Hands grabbed at his gun and there wasn't much he could do about it because his arms were numb. Fists battered his torso, back, and neck, yet he felt perfectly calm. He felt Death on the street with him and Death's voice was soft. Death said:

It's okay. It's time. His front pocket was ripped from his pant leg and loose change fell to the sidewalk. The button, too. Danny watched with an unreasonable sense of loss as it rolled off the curb and fell through a sewer grate.

Nora, he thought. Goddammit. Nora.

When they were done, Pyotr Glaviach found Danny's service revolver in the gutter. He picked it up and dropped it on top of the unconscious cop's chest. Pyotr recalled all the men—fourteen—he'd killed, face-to-face, over the years. This number did not include an entire unit of czarist guards they'd trapped in the center of a burning wheat field. He could still smell that odor seven years later, could hear them crying like babies as the flames found their hair, their eyes. You could never lose the smell from your nostrils, the sounds from your ears. You couldn't undo any of it. Or wash it off. He was tired of the killing. It was why he'd come to America. Because he was so tired. It always led to more.

He spit on the traitor cop a couple more times and then he and his comrades returned to the touring car and drove away.

Luther had gotten good at sneaking in and out of Nora's rooming house. He'd learned that you made the most noise trying to be quiet, so he did his due diligence when it came to listening from behind her door to the hallway on the other side, but once he was sure there was no one out there, he turned her doorknob quick and smooth and stepped into the hall. He swung the door closed behind him, and even before it clicked against the jamb, he'd already opened the door into the alley. By then, he was in the clear—a black man exiting a building in Scollay Square wasn't the problem; a black man exiting a white woman's room in any building whatsoever, that's what got you killed.

That May Day night, he left the bag of fruit in her room after sitting with her about half an hour, watching her eyelids droop repeatedly until they stayed down. It worried him; now that they'd cut her hours, she was tired more, not less, and he knew that had to be about diet. She wasn't getting enough of something and he wasn't no doctor so he didn't know what that something was. But she was tired all the time. Tired and grayer, her teeth starting to loosen. That's what made Luther take fruit from the Coughlins this time. Seemed he remembered fruit was good for teeth and complexions. How or why he knew that, he couldn't say, but it felt right.

He left her sleeping and went up the alley, and when he came to the end of it, he saw Danny lumbering across Green Street toward him.

But not Danny, really. A version of him. A Danny who'd been fired from a cannon into a block of ice. A Danny with blood all over himself as he walked. Or tried to. Reeled was more like it.

Luther met him in the middle of the street as Danny fell to one knee.

"Hey, hey," Luther said softly. "It's me. Luther."

Danny looked up at him, his face like something someone had tested hammers on. One eye was black. That was the good one. The other was so swollen shut it looked to have been sutured. His lips were twice their normal size, Luther wanting to make a joke about it but feeling it was definitely the wrong time.

"So." Danny raised a hand, as if to signal the start of a game. "Still mad at me?"

Well, that was something no one had managed to take away apparently—the man's ease with himself. Busted all to hell and kneeling in the middle of a shit hole street in shit hole Scollay Square, the man was chatting all casual-like, as if this sort of thing happened to him once a week.

"Not at this *exact* moment," Luther said. "In general, though? Yeah."

"Take a number," Danny said and vomited blood onto the street.

Luther didn't like the sight or the sound of it. He got a

grip of Danny's hand and started to tug him to his feet.

"Oh, no, no," Danny said. "Don't do that. Let me kneel here a bit. Actually, let me crawl. I'm going to crawl to that curb, Luther. Gonna crawl to it."

Danny, true to his word, crawled from the center of the street to the sidewalk. When he reached it, he crawled a few more feet over the curb and then lay down. Luther sat beside him. Danny eventually worked himself up to a sitting position. He held on to his knees as if they were the only things keeping him from falling off the earth.

"Fuck," he said eventually. "I'm busted up pretty good." He smiled through cracked lips as a high whistle preceded his every breath. "Wouldn't have a handkerchief, would you?"

Luther dug in his other pocket and came back with one. He handed it to him.

"Thanks."

"Don't mention it," Luther said and something about the phrase struck them both funny at the same time and they laughed together in the soft night.

Danny dabbed at the blood on his face until the hand-kerchief was destroyed by it. "I came to see Nora. I got things to say to her."

Luther put an arm around Danny's shoulder, something he'd never ventured to do with a white man before but which seemed perfectly natural under the circumstances. "She needs her sleep, and you need a hospital."

"I need to see her."

"Puke some more blood and tell me again."

"No, I do."

Luther leaned in. "You know what your breath sound like?"

Danny shook his head.

"A fucking canary's," Luther said. "Canary with buckshot in its chest. You're dying here."

Danny shook his head again. Then he bent over and heaved his chest. Nothing came out. He heaved again. Again, nothing came out but a sound, the sound Luther had described, the high-pitched hiss of a desperate bird.

"How far's Mass General from here?" Danny bent over and vomited some more blood into the gutter. "I'm a little too fucked-up to remember."

" 'Bout six blocks," Luther said.

"Right. Long blocks." Danny winced and laughed at the same time and spit some blood onto the sidewalk. "I think my ribs are broken."

"Which ones?"

"All of 'em," Danny said. "I'm hurt kinda bad here, Luther."

"I know." Luther turned and crawled over behind Danny. "I can push you up."

" 'Preciate that."

"On three?"

"Fine."

"One, two, three." Luther put his shoulder into the big man's back, pushed hard, and Danny let out a series of loud groans and one sharp yelp, but then he was on his feet. Wavering, but on his feet.

Luther slid under him and draped Danny's left arm over his shoulder.

"Mass General's going to be filled," Danny said. "Fuck. Every hospital. My boys in blue going to be filling emergency rooms all over this city."

"Filling it with who?"

"Russians, mostly. Jews."

Luther said, "There's a colored clinic over on Barton and Chambers. You got any objections to a colored doctor working on you?"

"Take a one-eyed Chinese gal, long as she can make the pain go away."

"Bet you would," Luther said and they started walking. "You can sit up in the bed, tell everyone not to call you 'suh.' How you just regular-folk like that."

"You're some prick." Danny chuckled, an act that brought fresh blood to his lips. "So what were you doing here?"

"Don't worry about that."

Danny swayed so much he almost tipped the two of them to the sidewalk. "Well, I am." He held up a hand and they both stopped. Danny took a big breath. "She all right?"

"No. She's not all right. Whatever she did to any of you? She paid her debt."

"Oh." Danny tilted his head at him. "You like her?"

Luther caught the look. "Like *that*?"

"Like that."

"Hell, no. Most certainly, I do not."

A bloody smile. "You sure?"

"Want me to drop you? Yeah, I'm sure. You got your tastes, I got mine."

"And Nora ain't your taste?"

"*White women* ain't. The freckles? The little asses? Them tiny bones and weird hair?" Luther grimaced and shook his head. "Not for me. No, sir."

Danny looked at Luther through one black eye and one swollen one. "So . . . ?"

"So," Luther said, exasperated suddenly, "she's my friend. I look after her."

"Why?"

He gave Danny a long, careful look. "Ain't nobody else want the job."

Danny's smile spread through cracked, blackened lips. "Okay, then."

Luther said, "Who got to you? Size you are, had to be a few of 'em."

"Bolshies. Over in Roxbury, maybe twenty blocks. Long walk. I probably had it coming." Danny took a few shallow breaths. He leaned his head to the side and vomited. Luther shifted his feet so it wouldn't hit his shoes or trouser cuffs, and it was a bit awkward, him leaning off to the side, half sprawled over the man's back. The good news was that it wasn't half as red as Luther had feared. When Danny finished, he wiped his mouth with his sleeve. "All right."

491

They stumbled another block together before Danny had to rest again. Luther propped him up against a streetlamp and Danny leaned back against it with his eyes closed, his face wet with sweat.

He eventually opened his good eye and stared up at the sky, as if searching for something there. "I'll tell you, Luther, it's been one hell of a year."

Luther thought back to his own year and that got him laughing, laughing hard. He bent over from it. A year ago— shit. That was a whole *lifetime* away.

"What?" Danny said.

Luther held up a hand. "You and me both."

"What are you supposed to do," Danny said, "when everything you built your life on turns out to be a fucking lie?"

"Build a new life, I guess."

Danny raised an eyebrow at that.

"Oh, because you're bleeding all over yourself, you want sympathy?" Luther stepped back up to Danny, the big man lying back against the streetlamp pole like it was all he had left of friends in this world. "I ain't got that for you. Whatever's wearing you down, shit, throw it off. God don't care. Ain't nobody care. Whatever you need to do to make yourself right, get yourself out of pain? I say you do that thing."

Danny's smile was cracked, his lips half black. "Easy, huh?"

"Ain't nothing easy." Luther shook his head. "Simple, though, yeah."

"I wish it was that—"

"You walked twenty blocks, puking up your own blood, to get to one place and one person. If you need any more truth in your life, white boy, than *that*?" Luther's laugh was hard and quick. "It ain't showing up on this here earth."

Danny didn't say anything. He looked at Luther through his one good eye and Luther looked back. Then he came off the lamp pole and reached out his arm. Luther stepped under it and they walked the rest of the way to the clinic.

492

CHAPTER *twenty-eight*

D anny stayed in the clinic overnight. He barely
remembered Luther leaving. He did remember him
putting a sheaf of paper on Danny's bedside table.

"Tried to give that to your uncle. He never showed up for the meet."

"He was pretty busy today."

"Yeah, well, you make sure he gets it? Maybe find a way to get him off me like you said you would once?"

"Sure." Danny held out his hand and Luther shook it, and Danny floated off to a black-and-white world where everyone was covered in bomb debris.

At one point he woke to a colored doctor sitting by his bed. The doctor, a young man with the gentle air and slim fingers of a concert pianist, confirmed that he'd broken seven of his ribs and the others were badly sprained. One of those broken ribs had nicked a blood vessel and they'd had to cut Danny open to repair it. This explained the blood he'd vomited and made it highly likely that Luther had saved his life. They wrapped Danny's torso tightly with adhesive tape and told him he'd suffered a concussion and would piss blood for a few days from all the shots the Russians had delivered to his kidneys. Danny thanked the doctor, his words slurring from whatever they'd pumped into his IV, and passed out.

In the morning, he woke to his father and Connor sitting

by the bed. His father had one of his hands wrapped in both of his and he smiled softly. "Look who's up."

Con' folded the newspaper and smiled at Danny and shook his head.

"Who did this to you, boy?"

Danny sat up a bit in the bed and his ribs screamed. "How'd you even find me?"

"Colored fella—says he's a doctor here?—he called into headquarters with your badge number, said another colored fella brought you in here all banged to hell. Ah, it's a sight, you in a place like this."

In the bed on the other side of his father lay an old man with his foot hanging in a cast. He looked at the ceiling.

"What happened?" Connor asked.

"Got jumped by a bunch of Letts," Danny said. "That colored fella was Luther. He probably saved my life."

The old man in the next bed scratched his leg at the top of the cast.

"We've got the holding cells filled to the brink with Letts and Commies," his father said. "You go have a look later. Find the men who did it and we'll find ourselves a nice dark lot before we book them."

Danny said, "Water?"

Con' found a pitcher on the windowsill and filled a glass and brought it to him.

His father said, "We don't even have to book them, if you follow my meaning."

"It's not hard, sir, to follow your meaning." Danny drank. "I never saw them."

"What?"

"They came up on me fast, got my coat over my head, and went to work."

"How could you not see—?"

"I was following Tessa Ficara."

"She's here?" his father said.

"She was last night."

"Jesus, boy, why didn't you call for backup?"

"You guys were throwing a party in Roxbury, remember?"

His father ran a hand along his chin. "You lose her?"

"Thanks for the water, Con'." He smiled at his brother.

Connor chuckled. "You're a piece of work, brother. You really are."

"Yeah, I lost her. She turned onto Hammond Street, and the Russians showed up. So what do you want to do, Dad?"

"Well, we'll talk to Finch and the BI. I'll have some badges canvass Hammond and the rest of the area, hope for the best. But I doubt she's still hanging around after last night." His father held up the *Morning Standard*. "Front-page news, boy."

Danny sat up fully in the bed and his ribs howled some more. He blinked at the pain and looked at the headline: "Police Wage War on Reds."

"Where's Mom?"

"Home," his father said. "You can't keep putting her through this. First Salutation. Now this. It's a strain on her heart, it is."

"How about Nora? She know?"

His father cocked his head. "Why would she know anything? We've no contact with her anymore."

"I'd like her to know."

Thomas Coughlin looked at Connor and then back at Danny. "Aiden, you don't say her name. You don't bring her up in my presence."

Danny said, "Can't do that, Dad."

"What?" This from Connor, coming up behind their father. "She lied to us, Dan. She humiliated me. Jesus."

Danny sighed. "She was family for how long?"

"We treated her as family," his father said, "and look how she repaid us. Now it's the end of this subject, Aiden."

Danny shook his head. "For you maybe. Me?" He pulled the sheet off his body. He swung his legs off the side of the bed and hoped neither of them could see the price it cost.

Jesus! The pain blew up through his chest. "Con', hand me my pants, would you?"

Con' brought them to him, his face dark and bewildered.

Danny stepped into his pants and then found his shirt hanging over the foot of the bed. He slid into it, one careful arm at a time, and considered his father and brother. "Look, I've played it your way. But I can't anymore. I just can't."

"Can't what?" his father said. "You're talking nonsense." He looked at the old black man with the broken leg as if for a second opinion, but the man's eyes were closed.

Danny shrugged. "Then I'm talking nonsense. You know what I realized yesterday? What I *finally* realized? Ain't a fuck-ing thing made—"

"Ah, the language!"

"—made sense in my life, Dad. Ever. 'Cept her."

His father's face drained of color.

Danny said, "Hand me my shoes, would you, Con'?"

Connor shook his head. "Get 'em yourself, Dan." He held out his hands, a gesture of such helpless pain and betrayal that it pierced Danny.

"Con'."

Connor shook his head. "No."

"Con', listen."

"Fuck listening. You'd do this? To me? You'd—"

Connor dropped his hands and his eyes filled. He shook his head at Danny again. He shook his head at the whole ward. He turned on his heel and walked out the door.

Danny found his shoes in the silence and placed them on the floor.

"You're going to break your brother's heart? Your mother's?" his father said. "Mine?"

Danny looked at him as he pushed his feet into his shoes. "It's not about *you*, Dad. I can't live my life for you."

"Oh." His father placed his hand over his heart. "Well, I wouldn't want to begrudge you your earthly pleasures, boy, Lord knows."

496

Danny smiled.

His father didn't. "So you've taken your stand against the family. You're an individual, Aiden. Your own man. Does it feel good?"

Danny said nothing.

His father stood and placed his captain's hat on his head. He straightened it at the sides. "This great romantic notion your generation has about it going its own way? Do you think you're the first?"

"No. Don't think I'll be the last, either."

"Probably not," his father said. "What you will be is alone."

"Then I'll be alone."

His father pursed his lips and nodded. "Good-bye, Aiden."

"Good-bye, sir."

Danny held out his hand, but his father ignored it.

Danny shrugged and dropped the hand. He reached behind him and found the papers Luther had given him last night. He tossed them at his father and hit him in the chest. His father caught them and looked down at them.

"The list McKenna wanted from the NAACP."

His father's eyes widened for a moment. "Why would I want it?"

"Then give it back."

Thomas allowed himself a small smile and placed the papers under his arm.

"It was always about the mailing lists, wasn't it?" Danny said.

His father said nothing.

"You'll sell them," Danny said. "To companies, I'm assuming?"

His father met his eyes. "A man has a right to know the character of the men working for him."

"So he can fire them before they unionize?" Danny nodded at the idea. "You sold out your own."

"I'll bet my life that not a name on any of the lists is Irish."

"I wasn't talking about the Irish," Danny said.

His father looked up at the ceiling, as if he saw cobwebs there that needed tending. He pursed his lips, then looked at his son, a slight quiver in his chin. He said nothing.

"Who got you the list of the Letts once I was out?"

"As luck would have it," his father's voice was barely a whisper, "we took care of that yesterday in the raid."

Danny nodded. "Ah."

"Anything else, son?"

Danny said, "Matter of fact, yeah. Luther saved my life."

"So I should give him a raise?"

"No," Danny said. "Call off your dog."

"My dog?"

"Uncle Eddie."

"I don't know anything about that."

"Call him off just the same. He saved my life, Dad."

His father turned to the old man in the bed. He touched his cast and winked at the man when he opened his eyes. "Ah, you'll be fit as a fiddle, as God is my judge."

"Yes, suh."

"Indeed." Thomas gave the guy a hearty smile. His eyes swept past Danny and the windows behind him. He nodded once and then walked out the same door as Connor.

Danny found his coat on a hook against the wall and put it on.

"That your pops?" the old man said.

Danny nodded.

"I'd stay clear of him for a while."

Danny said, "Looks like I don't have much choice."

"Oh, he'll be back. His kind always comes back. Sure as time," the old man said. "Always wins, too."

Danny finished buttoning his coat. "Ain't nothing to win anymore," he said.

"That ain't the way he sees it." The old man gave him a sad smile. He closed his eyes. "Which is why he'll keep winning. Yes, sir."

* * *

After he left the hospital, he visited four more before he found the one where they'd taken Nathan Bishop. Bishop, like Danny, had declined to stay, though Nathan had slipped two armed policemen to do it.

The doctor who'd worked on him before his escape looked at Danny's tattered uniform, its black splotches of blood, and said, "If you've come for your second licks, they should have told you—"

"He's gone. I know."

"Lost an ear," the doctor said.

"Heard that, too. How about his eye?"

"I don't know. He left before I could hazard an informed diagnosis."

"Where to?"

The doctor glanced at his watch and slipped it back into his pocket. "I've got patients."

"Where'd he go?"

A sigh. "Far from this city, I suspect. I already told this to the two officers who were supposed to be guarding him. After he climbed out the bathroom window, he could have gone anywhere, but from the time I spent with him, I gathered he saw no point sacrificing five or six years of his life to a Boston prison."

The doctor's hands were in his pocket when he turned without another word and walked away.

Danny left the hospital. He was still in a fair amount of pain and made slow progress up Huntington Avenue toward the trolley stop.

He found Nora that night, when she returned to her rooming house from work. He stood with his back against her stoop, not because sitting down was too painful but because getting back up again was. She walked up the street in dusk yellowed by weak streetlamps and every time her face passed from dark into gauzy light, he took a breath.

499

Then she saw him. "Holy Mary Mother of God, what happened to you?"

"Which part?" A thick bandage jutted off his forehead, and both eyes were black.

"All of you." She appraised him with something that might have been humor, might have been horror.

"You didn't hear?" He cocked his head, noticing she didn't look too good herself, her face drawn and sagging at the same time, her eyes too wide and empty.

"I heard there was a fight between policemen and the Bolsheviks, but I . . ." She stopped in front of him and raised her hand, as if to touch his swollen eye, but she paused and her hand hung in the air. She took a step back.

"I lost the button," he said.

"What button?"

"The bear's eye."

She cocked her head in confusion.

"From Nantasket. That time?"

"The stuffed bear? The one from the room?"

He nodded.

"You kept its *eye*?"

"Well, it was a button, but yeah. I still had it. Never left my pocket."

He could see she had no idea what to do with that information.

He said, "That night you came to see me . . ."

She crossed her arms.

"I let you go because . . ."

She waited.

"Because I was weak," he said.

"And that kept you now, did it, from caring for a friend?"

"We're not friends, Nora."

"Then what are we, Danny?" She stood on the sidewalk, her eyes on the pavement, so tense he could see goose bumps in her flesh and the cords in her neck.

Danny said, "Look at me. Please."

She kept her head down.

"Look at me," he said again.

Her eyes found his.

"When we look at each other like this, right now, I don't know what that is, but 'friendship' seems kind of watery, don't you think?"

"Oh, you," she said and shook her head, "you were always the talker now. They'd have called the Blarney Stone the Danny Stone if they could have—"

"Don't," he said. "Don't make it small. It's not small, Nora."

"What are you doing here?" she whispered. "Jesus, Danny. *What*? I already have one husband, or haven't you heard? And you've always been a boy in a man's body. You run from thing to thing. You—"

"You have a *husband*?" He chuckled.

"He laughs," she said to the street with a loud sigh.

"I do." He stood. He placed a hand to her chest just below her throat. He kept his fingers there, lightly, and tried to get the smile off his face as he saw her anger rise. "I just . . . Nora, I'm just . . I mean, the two of us? Trying to be so respectable? Wasn't that our word?"

"After you broke with me"—her face remained a stone, but he could see the light finding her eyes—"I needed stability. I needed . . ."

That brought a roar from him, an explosion he couldn't stop that erupted out of the center of his body and, even as it punched its way along his ribs, felt better than anything he'd felt in a long time. "Stability?"

"Yes." She hit his chest with her fist. "I wanted to be a good American girl, an upstanding citizen."

"Well, that worked out tremendously well."

"Stop *laughing*."

"I can't."

"Why?" And the laugh finally reached her voice.

"Because, because . . ." He held her shoulders and the

501

waves finally passed. He moved his palms down her arms and took her hands in his and this time she let him. "Because all this time you were with Connor, you wanted to be with me."

"Ah, you're a cocky man, you are, Danny Coughlin."

He tugged on her hands and stooped until their faces were at the same level. "And I wanted to be with you. And the two of us lost so much *time*, Nora, trying to be"—he looked up at the sky in frustration—"whatever the fuck we were trying to be."

"I'm *married*."

"I don't give a shit. I don't give a shit about anything anymore, Nora, except this. Right here. Right now."

She shook her head. "Your family will disown you just like they disowned me."

"So?"

"So you love them."

"Yeah. Yeah, I do." Danny shrugged. "But I need you, Nora." He touched her forehead with his own. "I need you." He repeated it in a whisper, his head against hers.

"You'll throw away your whole world," she whispered and her voice was wet.

"I was done with it anyway."

Her laugh came out strangled and damp.

"We can never marry in the Church."

"I'm done with that, too," he said.

They stood there for a long time, and the streets smelled of the early-evening rain.

"You're crying," she said. "I can feel the tears."

He removed his forehead from hers and tried to speak, but he couldn't, so he smiled, and the tears rolled off his chin.

She leaned back and caught one on her finger.

"This is not pain?" she said and put it in her mouth.

"No," Danny said and lowered his forehead to hers again. "This is not pain."

* * *

Luther came home after a day at the Coughlin household in which, for the second time since he'd been there, the captain had invited him into his study.

"Take a seat, take a seat," the captain said as he removed his uniform coat and hung it on the coat tree behind his desk.

Luther sat.

The captain came around to the front of the desk with two glasses of whiskey and handed one to Luther. "I heard what you did for Aiden. I'd like to thank you for saving my son's life." He clinked his heavy glass off Luther's.

Luther said, "It was nothing, sir."

"Scollay Square."

"Sir?"

"Scollay Square. That's where you ran into Aiden, yes?"

"Uh, yes, sir, I did."

"What brought you over there? You've no friends in the West End, do you?"

"No, sir."

"And you live in the South End. As we know, you work over here, so . . ."

The captain rolled the glass between his hands and waited.

Luther said, "Well, you know why most men go to Scollay Square, sir." He tried for a conspiratorial smile.

"I do," Captain Coughlin said. "I do, Luther. But even Scollay Square has its racial principles. I'm to assume you were at Mama Hennigan's, then? 'Tis the only place I know in the square that services coloreds."

"Yes, sir," Luther said, although by now he knew he'd walked into a trap.

The captain reached into his humidor. He removed two cigars and snipped the ends and handed one to Luther. He lit it for him and then lit his own.

"I understand my friend Eddie was giving you a bit of a hard time."

Luther said, "Uh, sir, I don't know that I would—"

"Aiden told me," the captain said.

"Oh."

"I've spoken to Eddie on your behalf. I owe you that for saving my son."

"Thank you, sir."

"I promise he'll be a bother to you no longer."

"I really do appreciate that, sir. Thank you again."

The captain raised his glass and Luther did the same and they both took a drink of the fine Irish whiskey.

The captain reached behind him again and came back with a white envelope that he tapped against his thigh. "And Helen Grady, she's working out as a house woman, she is?"

"Oh, yes, sir."

"No doubts to her competency or her work ethic?"

"Absolutely none, sir."

Helen was as cold and distant to Luther as the day she'd arrived five months ago, but that woman could *work*, boy.

"I'm glad to hear that." The captain handed Luther the envelope. "Because she'll be doing the job of two now."

Luther opened the envelope and saw the small sheaf of money inside.

"There's two weeks' severance in there, Luther. We closed Mama Hennigan's a week ago for code violations. The only person you know in Scollay Square is one who used to be in my employ. It explains the food that's gone missing from my pantry these past few months, a theft that Helen Grady began to report to me weeks ago." He considered Luther over his scotch glass as he drained it. "Stealing food from my home, Luther? You're aware I'd be well within my rights to shoot you where you sit?"

Luther didn't respond to that. He reached over and placed his glass on the edge of the desk. He stood. He held out his hand. The captain considered it for a moment, then placed his cigar in the ashtray and shook the hand.

"Good-bye, Luther," he said pleasantly.

"Good-bye, Captain, sir."

* * *

When he returned to the house on St. Botolph, it was empty. A note waited on the kitchen table.

Luther,
  Out doing the good work (we hope). This came for you. A
plate in the icebox.
Isaiah

Underneath the note was a tall yellow envelope with his name scrawled on it in his wife's hand. Given what had just happened the last time he opened an envelope, he took a moment before reaching for it. Then he said, "Ah, fuck it," finding it strangely guilt-inducing to cuss in Yvette's kitchen.

He opened it carefully and pulled out two pieces of cardboard that were pressed together and tied off with string. There was a note folded underneath the string and Luther read it and his hands trembled as he placed it on the table and undid the knot to remove the top piece of cardboard and look at what lay underneath.

He sat there a long time. At some point he wept even though he'd never, not in his whole life, known this kind of joy.

Off Scollay Square, he went down the alley that ran alongside Nora's building and let himself in the green door at the back, which was only locked about 25 percent of the time, this night not being one of them. He stepped quickly to her door and knocked and heard the last sound he would have expected on the other side: giggling.

He heard whispers and "Sssh, sssh," and he knocked again. "Who is it?"

"Luther," he said and cleared his throat.

The door opened, and Danny stood there, his dark hair falling in tangles over his forehead, one suspender undone, the first three buttons of his undershirt open. Nora stood behind him, touching her hair and then smoothing her dress, and her cheeks were flushed.

Danny had a wide grin on his face, and Luther didn't have to guess what he'd interrupted.

"I'll come back," he said.

"What? No, no." Danny looked back to make sure Nora was sufficiently covered and then he opened the door wide. "Come on in."

Luther stepped into the tiny room, feeling foolish suddenly. He couldn't explain what he was doing here, why he'd just gotten up from the kitchen table in the South End and hurried all the way over here, the large envelope under his arm.

Nora came toward him, her arm extended, her feet bare. She had the flush of interrupted sex on her face, but a deeper flush as well, one of openness and love.

"Thank you," she said, taking his hand and then leaning in and placing her cheek to his. "Thank you for saving him. Thank you for saving me."

And in that moment he felt like he was home for the first time since he'd left it.

Danny said, "Drink?"

"Sure, sure," Luther said.

Danny went to the tiny table where Luther had left the fruit just yesterday. There was a bottle there now and four cheap glasses. He poured all three of them a glass of whiskey and then handed Luther his.

"We just fell in love," Danny said and raised his glass.

"Yeah?" Luther chuckled. "Finally figured it out, uh?"

"We've *been* in love," Nora said to Danny. "We finally faced it."

"Well," Luther said, "ain't that a pip?"

Nora laughed and Danny's smile broadened. They raised their glasses and drank.

"What you got under your arm there?" Danny said.

"Oh, oh, this, yeah." Luther placed his drink down on the

506

tiny table and opened the envelope. Just pulling out the cardboard, his hands trembled again. He held the cardboard in his hands and offered it to Nora. "I can't explain why I came here. Why I wanted you to see it. I just . . ." He shrugged.

Nora reached out and squeezed his arm. "It's all right."

"It seemed important to show someone. To show you."

Danny placed his drink down and came over beside Nora. She lifted off the top piece of cardboard, and their eyes widened. Nora slid her arm under Danny's and placed her cheek to his arm.

"He's beautiful," Danny said softly.

Luther nodded. "That's my son," he said while his face filled with warm blood. "That's my baby boy."

CHAPTER *twenty-nine*

S teve Coyle was drunk but freshly bathed when, as a licensed justice of the peace, he officiated over the marriage of Danny Coughlin and Nora O'Shea on June 3, 1919.

The night before, a bomb had exploded outside the home of Attorney General Palmer in Washington, D.C. The detonation came as a surprise to the bomber, who'd still been several yards short of Palmer's front door. Though his head was eventually recovered from a rooftop four blocks away, the man's legs and arms were never found. Attempts to identify him using only his head met with failure. The explosion destroyed the facade of Palmer's building and shattered the windows that faced the street. His living room, sitting room, foyer, and dining room were obliterated. Palmer had been in the kitchen at the back of the house, and he was discovered under the rubble, remarkably unscathed, by the assistant secretary of the navy, Franklin Roosevelt, who lived across the street. While the bomber's charred head wasn't sufficient to identify him, it was clear he'd been an anarchist by the pamphlets he'd been carrying, which floated over R Street in the moments after the attack and soon adhered themselves to the streets and buildings of a three-block area. Under the heading "Plain Words," the message was nearly identical to those plastered to street poles in Boston seven weeks before:

You have left us no choice. There will have to be
bloodshed. We will destroy and rid the world of your
tyrannical institutions. Long live social revolution.
Down with tyranny.
The Anarchist Fighters

Attorney General Palmer, described in the *Washington Post*
as "shaken but uncowed," promised to redouble his efforts
and entrench his resolve. He warned all Reds on U.S. soil to
consider themselves on notice. "This will be a summer of discontent," Palmer promised, "but not for this country. Only
her enemies."

Danny and Nora's wedding reception was held on the
rooftop of Danny's rooming house. The cops who attended
were of low rank. Most were acting members of the BSC.
Some brought their wives, others their girlfriends. Danny
introduced Luther to them as "the man who saved my life."
That seemed good enough for most of them, though Luther
noted a few who seemed disinclined to leave their wallets or
their women out of sight as long as Luther was in proximity
to either.

But it was a fine time. One of the tenants, a young Italian
man, played violin until Luther expected his arm to fall off,
and later in the evening he was joined by a cop with an
accordion. There were heaps of food and wine and whiskey
and buckets of Pickwick Ale on ice. The white folk
danced and laughed and toasted and toasted until they were
toasting the sky above and the earth below as both grew blue
with the night.

Near midnight, Danny found him sitting along the parapet
and sat beside him, drunk and smiling. "The bride's in a bit
of a snit that you haven't asked for a dance."

Luther laughed.

"What?"

"A black man dancing with a white woman on a roof. Yeah.
I'll bet."

"Bet nothing," Danny said, a bit of a slur in the words. "Nora asked me herself. You want to make the bride sad on her wedding day, you go right ahead."

Luther looked at him. "There's lines, Danny. Lines you don't cross even here."

"Fuck lines," Danny said.

"Easy for you to say," Luther said. "So easy."

"Fine, fine."

They looked at each other for some time.

Eventually, Danny said, "What?"

"You're asking a lot," Luther said.

Danny pulled out a pack of Murads, offered one to Luther. Luther took it and Danny lit it, then lit his own. Danny blew out a slow plume of blue smoke. "I hear the majority of the executive office positions of the NAACP are filled by white women."

Luther had no idea where he was going with this. "There's some truth to that, yeah, but Dr. Du Bois, he's looking to change that. Change comes slow."

"Uh-huh," Danny said. He took a swig from the whiskey bottle at his feet and handed it to Luther. "You think I'm like them white women?"

Luther noticed one of Danny's cop friends watching him raise the bottle to his lips, the guy making note which whiskey he wouldn't be drinking the rest of the night.

"Do you, Luther? You think I'm trying to prove something? Show what a free-minded white man I am?"

"I don't know what you're doing." Luther handed the bottle back.

Danny took another swig. "Ain't doing shit, except trying to get my friend to dance with my wife on her wedding day because she asked me to."

"Danny." Luther could feel the liquor riding in him, itching. "Things is."

"Things is?" Danny cocked an eyebrow.

Luther nodded. "As they've always been. And they don't change just because you want them to."

510

Nora crossed the roof toward them, a little tipsy herself judging by the sway of her, a champagne glass held loosely in one hand, cigarette in the other.

Before Luther could speak, Danny said, "He don't want to dance."

Nora turned her lower lip down at that. She wore a pearl-colored gown of satin messaline and silver tinsel. The drop skirt was wrinkled and the whole outfit a hair on the sloppy side now, but she still had those eyes, and that face made Luther think of peace, think of home.

"I think I'll cry." Her eyes were gay and shiny with alcohol. "Boo hoo."

Luther chuckled. He noticed a lot of people looking at them, just as he'd feared.

He took Nora's hand with a roll of his eyes and she tugged him to his feet and the violinist and the accordionist began to play, and she led him out to the center of the roof under the half moon and her hand was warm in his. His other hand found the small of her back and he could feel the heat coming off the skin there and off her jaw and the pulse of her throat. She smelled of alcohol and jasmine and that undeniable *whiteness* he'd noticed the first time he'd ever put his arms around her, as if her flesh had never been touched by dew. A papery smell, starchy.

"It's an odd world, is it not?" she said.

"Most certainly."

Her brogue was thicker with the alcohol. "I'm sorry you lost your job."

"I'm not. I got another one."

"Really?"

He nodded. "Stockyards. Start day after next."

Luther raised his arm and she swirled under it and then turned back into his chest.

"You are the truest friend I've ever had." She spun again, as light as summer.

Luther laughed. "You're drunk, girl."

511

"I am," she said gleefully. "But you're still family, Luther. To me." She nodded at Danny. "To him, too. Are we your family yet, Luther?"

Luther looked into her face and the rest of the roof evaporated. What a strange woman. Strange man. Strange world.

"Sure, sister," he said. "Sure."

The day of his eldest son's wedding, Thomas came to work to find Agent Rayme Finch waiting for him in the anteroom outside the desk sergeant's counter.

"Come to register a complaint, have we?"

Finch stood, straw boater in hand. "If I may have a word."

Thomas ushered him through the squad room and back to his office. He removed his coat and hat and hung them on the tree by the file cabinets and asked Finch if he wanted coffee.

"Thank you."

Thomas pressed the intercom button. "Stan, two coffees, please." He looked over at Finch. "Welcome back. Staying long?"

Finch gave that a noncommittal twitch of the shoulders.

Thomas removed his scarf and placed it on the tree over his coat and then moved last night's stack of incident reports from his ink blotter to the left side of his desk. Stan Beck brought the coffee and left. Thomas handed a cup across the desk to Finch.

"Cream or sugar?"

"Neither." Finch took the cup with a nod.

Thomas added cream to his own cup. "What brings you by?"

"I understand that you do, in fact, have quite a network of men attending meetings of the various radical groups in your city, that you even have some who've infiltrated a few groups under deep cover." Finch blew on his coffee and took a tiny sip, then licked the sting from his lips. "As I understand it,

512

and quite the contrary to what you led me to believe, you're compiling lists."

Thomas took his seat and sipped his coffee. "Your ambition might exceed your 'understanding,' lad."

Finch gave that thin smile. "I'd like access to those lists."

"Access?"

"Copies."

"Ah."

"Is that a problem?"

Thomas leaned back and propped his heels on the desk. "At the moment, I fail to see how interagency cooperation is advantageous to the Boston Police Department."

"Maybe you're taking the narrow view."

"I don't believe I am." Thomas smiled. "But I'm always open to fresh perspectives."

Finch struck a match off the edge of Thomas's desk and lit a cigarette. "Let's consider the reaction if word leaked that a rogue contingent of the Boston Police Department was selling the member rolls and mailing lists of known radical organizations to corporations instead of sharing them with the federal government."

"Allow me to correct one wee mistake."

"My information is solid."

Thomas folded his hands over his abdomen. "The mistake you made, son, was in use of the word *rogue*. We're hardly that. In fact, were you to point a finger at myself or any of the people I'm in congress with in this city? Why, Agent Finch, you'd surely find a dozen fingers pointing back at you, Mr. Hoover, Attorney General Palmer, and that fledgling, under-funded agency of yours." Thomas reached for his coffee cup. "So I'd advise caution when making threats in my fair city."

Finch crossed his legs and flicked ash into the tray beside his chair. "I get the gist."

"Consider my soul appropriately comforted."

"Your son, the one who killed the terrorist, I understand he's lost to my cause."

Thomas nodded. "A union man now, he is, through and through."

"But you've another son. A lawyer as I understand it."

"Careful with talk of family, Agent Finch." Thomas rubbed the back of his neck. "You're treading a tightrope in a circus fire about now."

Finch held up a hand. "Just hear me out. Share your lists with us. I'm not saying you can't make all the profit you want on the side. But if you share them with us, I'll make sure your son the lawyer gets plum work in the coming months."

Thomas shook his head. "He's DA property."

"Silas Pendergast?" Finch shook his head. "He's a whore for the wards and everyone knows you run him, Captain."

Thomas held out his hands. "Make your case."

"The preliminary suspicions that the molasses tank explosion was a terrorist act have been a boon for us. Simply put, this country is sick of terror."

"But the explosion wasn't a terrorist act."

"The rage remains." Finch chuckled. "No one is more surprised than us. We thought the rush to judgment over the molasses flood had killed us. Quite the opposite. People don't want truth, they want certainty." He shrugged. "Or the illusion of it."

"And you and Mr. Palmer are more than happy to ride the tide of this need."

Finch stubbed out his cigarette. "My current mandate is the deportation of every radical plotting against my country. The conventional wisdom on the subject is that deportation falls solely under federal jurisdiction. However, Attorney General Palmer, Mr. Hoover, and myself have recently come to the realization that state and local authorities *can* get more actively involved in deportation. Would you care to know how?"

Thomas stared at the ceiling. "I'd assume under the state antisyndicalist laws."

Finch stared at him. "How'd you arrive at that conclusion?"

514

"I didn't *arrive* anywhere. Basic common sense, man. The laws are on the books, have been for years."

Finch asked, "You wouldn't ever consider working in Washington, would you?"

Thomas rapped the window with his knuckles. "See out there, Agent Finch? Can you see the street? The people?"

"Yes."

"Took me fifteen years in Ireland and a month at sea to find it. My home. And a man who'd abandon his home is a man who'd abandon anything."

Finch tapped his boater off his knee. "You're an odd duck."

"Just so." He opened a palm in Finch's direction. "So the antisyndicalist laws?"

"Have opened a door in the deportation process that we'd long assumed closed."

"Local."

"And state, yes."

"So you're marshaling your forces."

Finch nodded. "And we'd like your son to be a part of it."

"Connor?"

"Yes."

Thomas took a drink of coffee. "How much a part?"

"Well, we'd have him work with a lawyer from Justice or local—"

"No. He works the cases as the point man in Boston or he doesn't work at all."

"He's young."

"Older than your Mr. Hoover."

Finch looked around the office, indecisive. "Your son catches this train? I promise you the track won't run out in his lifetime."

"Ah," Thomas said, "but I'd like him to board at the front as opposed to the rear. The view would be all the finer, wouldn't you say?"

"Anything else?"

"Yes. You call him to Washington to hire him. You make sure a photographer's in attendance."

"And in exchange, Attorney General Palmer's team will have access to the lists your men are compiling."

Thomas said, "Per specific requests that would be subject to my review, yes."

Thomas watched Finch give it some thought, as if he had a choice in the matter.

"Acceptable."

Thomas stood. He reached across the desk.

Finch stood and shook his hand. "So we have a deal."

"We have a contract, Agent Finch." Thomas gripped Finch's hand fast. "Do consider it inviolate."

Luther had noticed that Boston might have been different from the Midwest in a lot of ways—the people talked funny for one and everyone *dressed* in this city, dressed like they were going out to dinner and a show every day, even the children—but a stockyard was a stockyard. Same mud, same stench, same noise. And same job for coloreds—on the bottom rung. Isaiah's friend Walter Grange had been there fifteen years and he'd risen to the post of key man for the pens, but any white man with fifteen years on the job would have made yard manager by now.

Walter met Luther when he exited the streetcar at the top of Market Street in Brighton. Walter was a small man with huge white muttonchop sideburns to compensate, Luther guessed, for all the hair he'd lost up top. He had a chest like an apple barrel and short wishbone legs and as he led Luther down Market Street, his thick arms swung in concert with his hips. "Mr. Giddreaux said you were from the Midwest?"

Luther nodded.

"So you seen this before, then."

Luther said, "Worked the yards in Cincinnati."

"Well, I don't know what Cincinnati's like, but Brighton's a whole stock *town*. Pretty much everything you see along Market here, that's cattle business."

He pointed out the Cattlemen's Hotel at the corner of Market and Washington and the rival Stockyard Arms across the street and gestured in the direction of packing companies and canneries and three butchers and the various rooming houses and flophouses for workers and salesmen.

"You get used to the stench," he said. "Me, I don't even smell it no more."

Luther had stopped noticing it in Cincinnati, but now it was hard to recall how he'd accomplished that. The smokestacks emptied black spirals into the sky and the sky huffed it back down again and the oily air smelled of blood and fat and charred meat. Of chemicals and manure and hay and mud. Market Street flattened as it crossed Faneuil Street and it was here that the stockyards began, stretching for blocks on either side of the street with the train tracks cutting through their centers. The smell of manure grew worse, rising in a thick tide, and high fences with Cyclone wire up top sprouted out of the ground and the world was suddenly filled with dust and the sound of whistles and the neighing, mooing, and bleating of livestock. Walter Grange unlocked a wooden gate and led Luther through and the ground below grew dark and muddy.

"Lot of people got their interests tied up in the yards," Walter said. "You got small ranchers and big cattle outfits. You got order buyers and dealer buyers and commission agents and loan officers. You got railroad reps and telegraph operators and market analysts and ropers and handlers and teamsters to transport the livestock once it's been sold. You got packers ready to buy in the morning and walk those cows right back out the yard and up to the slaughterhouses, have 'em sold for steaks by noon tomorrow. You got people work for the market news services and you got gatemen and yard-men and pen men and weighmasters and more commission firms than you can shake a fist at. And we ain't even talking about the unskilled labor yet." He cocked one eyebrow at Luther. "That'd be you."

Luther looked around. Cincinnati all over again, but he must have forgotten a lot of Cincinnati, blocked it out. The yards were enormous. Miles of muddy aisles cut between wooden pens filled with snorting animals. Cows, hogs, sheep, lambs. Men ran every which way, some in the rubber boots and dungarees of yard workers, but others in suits and bow ties and straw boaters and still others in checked shirts and cowboy hats. Cowboy hats in Boston! He passed a scale the height of his house in Columbus, practically the width of it, too, and watched a man lead a dazed-looking heifer up there and hold up his hand to a man standing beside the scale with a pencil poised over a piece of paper. "Doing a whole draft, George."

"My apologies, Lionel. You go ahead."

The man led another cow and then a third and still another up onto that scale, and Luther wondered just how much weight that scale could take, if it could weigh a ship and the people on it.

He'd fallen back of Walter and hurried to catch up as the man took a right turn down a path between yet more pens, and when Luther reached him, Walter said, "The key man takes responsibility for all the livestock comes off the trains on his shift. That's me. I lead them to their catch pens and we keep 'em there, feed 'em, clean up after 'em until they get sold, and then a man shows up with a bill of sale and we release them to him."

He stopped at the next corner and handed Luther a shovel.

Luther gave it a bitter smile. "Yeah, I remember this."

"Then I can save me some breath. We in charge of pens nineteen through fifty-seven. Got that?"

Luther nodded.

"Every time I empty one, you clean it and restock it with hay and water. End of the day, three times a week, you go there"—he pointed—"and you clean that, too."

Luther followed his finger and saw the squat brown building at the west end of the yard. You didn't have to know what it was to sense its mean purpose. Nothing that squat and unadorned and functional-looking could ever put a smile on anyone's face.

"The killing floor," Luther said.

"You got a problem with that, son?"

Luther shook his head. "It's a job."

Walter Grange agreed with a sigh and a pat on the back. "It's a job."

Two days after Danny and Nora's wedding, Connor met with Attorney General Palmer at his home in Washington, D.C. The windows were boarded up, the front rooms had been obliterated, their ceilings caved in; the staircase just past the entrance hall was shorn in half, with the bottom half indistinguishable from the rest of the rubble and the top half dangling above the entranceway. D.C. police and federal agents had set up a command post in what had once been the parlor, and they moved freely through the house as Mitchell Palmer's valet led Connor to the office in the rear.

Three men waited for him there. The eldest and fleshiest of them he recognized instantly as Mitchell Palmer. He was round without being quite portly and his lips were the thickest part of him; they sprouted from his face like a rose. He shook Connor's hand, thanked him for coming, and introduced him to a thin BI agent named Rayme Finch and a dark-eyed, dark-haired Justice Department lawyer named John Hoover.

Connor had to step over some books in order to take his seat. The explosion had shaken them from their shelves, and the built-in bookcases sported great cracks. Plaster and paint had fallen from the ceiling, and the window behind Mitchell Palmer bore two small fissures in the panes.

Palmer caught his eye. "You see what they can do, these radicals."

"Yes, sir."

"But I won't give them the satisfaction of moving out, I assure you."

"Very brave of you, sir."

Palmer swiveled his chair slightly from side to side as Hoover and Finch took theirs on either side of him.

"Mr. Coughlin, are you happy with the direction in which our country is heading?"

Connor pictured Danny and his whore dancing on their wedding day, sleeping in their soiled bed. "No, sir."

"And why is that?"

"We seem to be giving away the keys to it."

"Well said, young Coughlin. Would you help us stop this habit?"

"With pleasure, sir."

Palmer swiveled his chair until he was looking at the cracks in his window. "Ordinary times call for ordinary law. Would you call these times ordinary?"

Connor shook his head. "I would not, sir."

"Extraordinary times, then . . . ?"

"Call for extraordinary measures."

"Just so. Mr. Hoover?"

John Hoover hitched his pants at the knee and leaned forward. "The attorney general is determined to rout the evil from our midst. To this end, he has asked me to head a new section of the Bureau of Investigation to be known from here on as the General Intelligence Division or GID. Our mandate, as the name suggests, is to gather intelligence against the radicals, the Communists and Bolsheviki, the anarchists and the Galleanists. In short, the enemies of a free and just society. You?"

"Mr. Hoover?"

"You?" Hoover's eyes bulged. "You?"

Connor said, "I'm not sure I—"

"You, Coughlin? You, sir. Which are you?"

520

"I'm none of those," Connor said and the hardness of his own voice surprised him.

"Then join us, Mr. Coughlin." Mitchell Palmer turned back from his window and extended his hand across the desk.

Connor stood and shook the hand. "I'd be honored, sir."

"Welcome to our table, son."

Luther was plastering walls on the first floor of the Shawmut Avenue building with Clayton Tomes when they heard three car doors slam outside and saw McKenna and two plainclothes cops exit the black Hudson and climb the stairs into the building.

In McKenna's eyes, as soon as he entered the room, Luther saw something far beyond the normal corruption, the normal disdain. He saw something so unhinged by rage it belonged in a pit, chained and caged.

The two cops he'd brought with him spread out into the room. One of them carried a toolbox for some reason. Judging by the way it pulled his shoulder down, it was heavy. He placed it on the floor near the kitchen doorway.

McKenna removed his hat and waved with it toward Clayton. "Good to see you again, son."

"Sir."

McKenna stopped by Luther and looked down at the bucket of plaster between them. "Luther, would you be offended if I asked you a rather arcane question?"

Luther thought: So much for Danny or the captain taking care of this problem.

"Nah, suh."

"I'm curious as to where you trace your ancestry," McKenna said. "Africa? Haiti? Or Australia, eh? You could be one of the aboriginals, yeah? Do *you* know, son?"

"What's that, suh?"

"Where you come from?"

"I come from America. These here United States."

McKenna shook his head. "You *live* here now. But where'd

521

your people come from, son? I ask ya—do you know?"

Luther gave up. "I don't, suh."

"I do." He squeezed Luther's shoulder. "Once you know what to look for, you can always tell where someone hails from. Your great-grandfather, Luther, based on that nose of yours and that kinky, tight hair and those truck-tire lips—he was from sub-Saharan Africa. Probably around Rhodesia'd be my guess. But your lighter skin and those freckles 'round your cheekbones are, God's truth as I'm standing here, West Indian. So your great-grandfather was from the monkey tree and your great-grandmother from the island tree and they found their place as slaves in the New World and produced your grandfather who produced your father who produced you. But that New World, it isn't exactly America now, is it? You're like a country within the country, I'll surely grant you, but hardly the country itself. You're a non-American who was born in America and can never, ever become an American."

"Why's that?" Luther stared back into the man's soulless eyes.

"Because you're ebon, son. Negroid. Black honey in the land of white milk. In other words, Luther? You should have stayed home."

"No one asked."

"Then you should have fought harder," McKenna said. "Because your true place in this world, Luther? Is back where you fucking came from."

"Mr. Marcus Garvey says pretty much the same thing," Luther said.

"Comparing me to Garvey, are we?" McKenna said with a slightly dreamy smile and a shrug. " 'Tis no bother. Do you like working for the Coughlins?"

"I did."

One of the cops sauntered over until he was directly behind Luther.

"That's right," McKenna said. "I'd forgotten—you were let

go. Killed a bunch of people in Tulsa, ran from your wife and child, came here to work for a police captain, and *still* you fucked that up. If you were a cat, I'd say you were near down to your last life."

Luther could feel Clayton's eyes. Clayton would have heard about Tulsa through the grapevine. He would have never guessed, though, that his new friend could have been involved. Luther wanted to explain it, but all he could do was look back at McKenna.

"What you want me to do now?" Luther said. "That's the point here—get me to do something for you?"

McKenna toasted that with a flask. "Coming along?"

"What?" Luther said.

"This building. Your remodeling." McKenna lifted a crowbar off the floor.

"I guess."

"Almost there, I'd say. 'Least on this floor." He smashed out two windowpanes with the crowbar. "That help?"

Some glass tinkled to the floor, and Luther wondered what it was in some people made feeding hate so pleasant.

The cop behind Luther chuckled softly. He stepped alongside him and caressed his chest with his nightstick. His cheeks were burned by the wind and his face reminded Luther of a turnip left too long in the fields. He smelled of whiskey.

The other cop carried the toolbox across the room and placed it between Luther and McKenna.

"We were men with an agreement. Men," McKenna said, leaning in close enough for Luther to smell his whiskey-tongue and drugstore aftershave. "And you went running to Tommy Coughlin and his overprivileged whelp of a son? You thought that would save you, but, Lord, all it did was curse you."

He slapped Luther so hard Luther spun in place and fell to his hip.

"Get up!"

Luther stood.

"You spoke out of turn about *me*?" McKenna kicked Luther in the shin so hard Luther had to replant his other leg so as not to fall. "You asked the royal Coughlins for special dispensation with *me*?"

McKenna pulled his service revolver and placed it to Luther's forehead. "*I* am Edward McKenna of the Boston Police Department. I am not someone else. I am not some lackey! I am Edward McKenna, *Lieutenant*, and you are remiss!"

Luther tilted his eyes up. That black barrel fed from Luther's head to McKenna's hand like a growth.

"Yes, suh."

"Don't you 'yes, suh' me." McKenna hit Luther's head with the butt of the pistol.

Luther's knees dropped halfway to the floor but he snapped back up before his knees could make contact. "Yes, suh," he said again.

McKenna extended his arm and placed the barrel between Luther's eyes again. He cocked the hammer. He uncocked it. He cocked it again. He gave Luther a wide, amber-toothed smile.

Luther was dog-tired, bone-tired, heart-tired. He could see the fear covering Clayton's face in a sweat, and he understood it, he could identify with it. But he couldn't touch it. Not right now. Fear wasn't his problem now. Sick was. He was sick of running and sick of this whole game he'd been playing since he could stand on two feet. Sick of cops, sick of power, sick of this world.

"Whatever you're gonna do, McKenna? Shit. Just fucking do it."

McKenna nodded. McKenna smiled. McKenna holstered his weapon.

The barrel had left a mark on Luther's forehead, an indentation he could feel. It itched. He took a step back and resisted the urge to touch the spot.

"Ah, son, you embarrassed me with the Coughlins, and

embarrassment is not something a man of my ambitions can abide." He spread his arms wide. "I just can't."

"Okay."

"Ah, if only it were as easy as 'okay.' But it's not. You'll need to be taxed." McKenna gestured at the toolbox. "You'll put that in the vault you built, if you please."

Luther pictured his mother watching him from above, a pain in her heart at what her only son had allowed his life to become.

"What's in it?"

"Bad things," McKenna said. "Bad, bad things. I want you to know that, Luther. I want you to know that what you're doing is a terrible thing that will immeasurably hurt the people you care about. I want you to realize that you brought this on yourself and that there is, I assure you, no way out for you or your wife."

When McKenna had the gun to his head, Luther had realized one truth beyond any: McKenna was going to kill him before this was over. Kill him and forget all about this. He'd leave Lila untouched simply because getting involved in a nigger prosecution over a thousand miles away was pointless if the source of his rage was already dead. So Luther knew this as well: no Luther, no danger to those he loved.

"I ain't selling out my people," he told McKenna. "Ain't planting anything in the NAACP offices. Fuck that and fuck you."

Clayton let loose a hiss of disbelief.

McKenna, though, looked like he'd been expecting it. "Is that right?"

"That's right." Luther looked down at the toolbox. He looked back up at McKenna. "I ain't—"

McKenna put a hand behind his ear, as if to hear better, pulled the revolver from his belt, and shot Clayton Tomes in the chest.

Clayton held up a hand, palm turned outward. He looked down at the smoke curling from the hole in his overalls. The smoke gave way to a stream of thick, dark fluid, and Clayton cupped his hand under it. He turned and walked carefully over to one of the cans of plaster he and Luther had just been sitting on while they ate and smoked and jawed. He touched the can with his hand before taking a seat.

He said, "What the . . . ?" and leaned his head back against the wall.

McKenna crossed his hands over his groin and tapped the barrel of the pistol against his thigh. "You were saying, Luther?"

Luther's lips trembled, hot tears pouring down his face. The air smelled of cordite. The walls shook from the winter wind.

"What the fuck is wrong with you?" Luther whispered. "What the fuck is—"

McKenna fired again. Clayton's eyes widened, and a small wet pop of disbelief left his mouth. The bullet hole appeared then, just below his Adam's apple. He grimaced, as if he'd eaten something that hadn't agreed with him and reached his hand toward Luther. Then his eyes rolled back from the effort and he lowered the hand to his lap. He closed his eyes. He took several shallow gulps of air and then the sound of him stopped.

McKenna took another sip from his flask. "Luther? Look at me."

Luther stared at Clayton. They'd just been talking about the finish-work that lay ahead. They'd just been eating sandwiches. Tears slid into Luther's mouth.

"Why would you do that? He didn't mean anyone harm. He never—"

"Because you don't run this monkey show. I do." McKenna tilted his head and bored his eyes into Luther's. "You're the monkey. Clear?"

McKenna slid the barrel of the gun into Luther's mouth. It was still hot enough to burn his tongue. He gagged on it. McKenna pulled back the hammer. "He was no American. He was not a member of any acceptable definition of the human race. He was labor. He was a footrest. He was a beast of burden, sure, nothing more. I disposed of him to prove a point, Luther: I would sooner mourn a footrest than the death of one of yours. Do you think I'm going to stand idly by while Isaiah Giddreaux and that clothed orangutan Du Bois attempt to mongrelize my race? Are you insane, lad?" He pulled the pistol from Luther's mouth and swung it at the walls. "This building is an affront to every value worth dying for in this country. Twenty years from now people will be stunned to hear we allowed you to live as freemen. That we *paid* you a wage. That we allowed you to converse with us or touch our food." He holstered the pistol and grabbed Luther by the shoulders and squeezed. "I will happily die for my ideals. You?"

Luther said nothing. He couldn't think of anything to say. He wanted to go to Clayton and hold his hand. Even though he was dead, Luther thought he could somehow make him feel less alone.

"If you speak to anyone about this, I will kill Yvette Giddreaux after she takes her lunch in Union Park some afternoon. If you don't do exactly what I tell you—whatever I tell you and whenever I tell you it—I will kill one nigger every week in this city. You'll know it's me because I will shoot them through the left eye so they will go to their nigger god half blind. And their deaths will be on your head, Luther Laurence. Yours and yours alone. Do we have an understanding?"

He let go of Luther and stepped back.

"Do we?"

Luther nodded.

"Good Negro." McKenna nodded. "Now Officer Hamilton and Officer Temple and myself, we're going to stay with you until— Are you listening?"

Clayton's body fell off the plaster can. It lay on the floor, one arm pointed at the door. Luther turned his head away.

"We're going to stay here with you until dusk. Say you understand, Luther."

"I understand," Luther said.

"Isn't that ducky?" McKenna put his arm around Luther. "Isn't that grand?" He steered Luther around until they were both facing Clayton's body.

"We're going to bury him in the backyard," McKenna said. "And we're going to put the toolbox in the vault. And we're going to come up with an acceptable story for you to tell Miss Amy Wagenfeld when she sends an investigator your way, which surely she will, as you will be the last person to have seen our Mr. Tomes before he absconded from our fair city, probably with an underage white girl. And once we've done all that, we'll wait for the announcement of the ribbon cutting. And you will call me the *moment* you know that date or . . . ?"

"You'll . . . you'll—"

"Kill a nigger," McKenna said, pushing Luther's head back and forth in a nod. "Is there any part of this I need to repeat for you?"

Luther looked into the man's eyes. "No."

"Magnificent." He let go of Luther and removed his coat. "Boys, take off your coats, the both of you. Let's give Luther a hand with this plaster, shall we? Man shouldn't have to do everything by himself, sure."

CHAPTER *thirty*

The house on K Street shriveled into itself. The rooms narrowed and the ceilings seemed to droop and the quiet that replaced Nora was spiteful. It remained that way through the spring and then deepened when word reached the Coughlins that Danny had taken Nora for a wife. Joe's mother went to her room with migraines, and the few times Connor wasn't working—and he worked around the clock lately—his breath stank of alcohol and his temper was so short that Joe gave him a wide berth whenever they found themselves in the same room. His father was even worse—Joe would look up to see the old man staring at him with a glaze in his eyes that suggested he'd been doing it for some time. The third time this happened, in the kitchen, Joe said, "What?"

His father's eyelids snapped. "Excuse me, boy?"

"You're staring, sir."

"Don't get lippy with me, son."

Joe dropped his eyes. It may have been the longest he'd dared hold his father's gaze in his life. "Yes, sir."

"Ah, you're just like him," his father said and opened his morning paper with a loud crackling of the pages.

Joe didn't bother asking who his father was referring to. Since the wedding, Danny's name had joined Nora's on the list of things you couldn't speak aloud. Even at twelve, Joe was all too aware that this list, which had been in place long before he was born, held the key to most mysteries of the Coughlin bloodline. The list was never discussed because one of the items on the list was the list itself, but Joe understood that first and foremost on the list was anything that could cause embarrassment to the family—relatives who'd engaged in repeated public drunkenness (Uncle Mike), who'd married outside of the Church (Cousin Ed), who'd committed crimes (Cousin Eoin, out in California), committed suicide (Cousin Eoin again), or given birth out of wedlock (Aunt Somebody in Vancouver; she'd been so completely banished from the family that Joe didn't know her name; she existed like a small stream of smoke that curled into the room before thought to shut the door). Sex, Joe understood, was stamped in bold at the top of the list. Anything to do with it. Any hint that people even thought about it, never mind had it.

Money was never discussed. Nor were the vagaries of public opinion and the new modern mores, both of which were deemed anti-Catholic and anti-Hibernian as a matter of course. There were dozens of other items on the list, but you never knew what they were until you mentioned one and then you saw from a single look that you'd wandered out into the minefield.

What Joe missed most about Danny's absence was that Danny couldn't have given a shit about the list. He didn't believe in it. He'd bring up women's suffrage at the dinner table, talk about the latest debate over the length of a woman's skirt, ask his father what he thought of the rise of Negro lynchings in the South, wonder aloud why it took the Catholic Church eighteen hundred years to decide Mary was a virgin.

"That's *enough*," his mother had cried to that one, her eyes welling.

"Now look what you did," his father said.

It was quite a feat—managing to hit two of the biggest, boldest items on the list, sex and the failings of the Church, at the same time.

"Sorry, Ma," Danny said and winked at Joe.

Christ, Joe missed that wink.

Danny had shown up at Gate of Heaven two days after the wedding. Joe saw him as he exited the building with his classmates, Danny out of uniform and leaning against the wrought-iron fence. Joe kept his composure, though heat flushed from his throat to his ankles in one long wet wave. He walked through the gate with his friends and turned as casually as he could toward his brother.

"Buy you a frankfurter, brother?"

Danny had never called him "brother" before. It had always been "little brother." It changed everything, made Joe feel a foot taller, and yet part of him immediately wished they could go back to how it had been.

"Sure."

They walked up West Broadway to Sol's Dining Car at the corner of C Street. Sol had just recently added the frankfurter to his menu. He'd refused to do so during the war because the meat sounded too German and he had, like most restaurants during the war, taken great pains to change the name of frankfurters to "Liberty Sausages" on his menu board. But now the Germans were beaten, and there were no hard feelings about it in South Boston, and most of the diners in the city were trying hard to catch up with this new fad that Joe & Nemo's had helped popularize in the city, even if, at the time, it had called their patriotism into question.

Danny bought two for each of them and they sat atop the stone picnic bench out in front of the diner and ate them with bottles of root beer as cars navigated horses and horses navigated cars out on West Broadway and the air smelled of the coming summer.

"You heard," Danny said.

Joe nodded. "You married Nora."

"Sure did." He bit into his frankfurter and raised his eyebrows and laughed suddenly before he chewed. "Wish you could have been there."

531

"Yeah?"

"We both did."

"Yeah."

"But the folks would never have allowed it."

"I know."

"You do?"

Joe shrugged. "They'll get over it."

Danny shook his head. "No they won't, brother. No they won't."

Joe felt like crying, but he smiled instead and swallowed some meat and took a sip of root beer. "They will. You'll see."

Danny placed his hand softly to the side of Joe's face. Joe didn't know what to do, because this had never happened. You slugged each other on the shoulder. You jabbed each other in the ribs. You didn't do *this*. Danny looked down at him with soft eyes.

"You're on your own in that house for a while, brother."

"Can I come visit?" Joe heard his own voice crack, and he looked down at his frankfurter and was pleased to see no tears fell on it. "You and Nora?"

"Of course. But that'll put you in the doghouse with the folks if you get caught."

"Been in the doghouse before," Joe said. "Plenty. Might start barking soon."

Danny laughed at that, a bark unto itself. "You're a great kid, Joe."

Joe nodded and felt the heat in his face. "How come you're leaving me, then?"

Danny tipped his chin up with his finger. "I'm not leaving you. What'd I say? You can come by anytime."

"Sure."

"Joe, Joe, I'm fucking *serious*. You're my brother. I didn't leave the family. The family left me. Because of Nora."

"Dad and Con' said you're a Bolshevik."

"What? To you?"

Joe shook his head. "I heard them talking one night." He

smiled. "I hear everything in there. It's an old house. They said you went native. They said you were a wop-lover and a nigger-lover and you lost your way. They were really drunk."

"How could you tell?"

"They started singing near the end."

"No shit? 'Danny Boy'?"

Joe nodded. "And 'Kilgary Mountain' and 'She Moved Through the Fair.' "

"You don't hear that one a lot."

"Only when Dad's *really* snockered."

Danny laughed and put his arm around him and Joe rocked against it.

"You go native, Dan?"

Danny kissed his forehead. Actually kissed it. Joe wondered if *he* was drunk.

Danny said, "Yeah, I guess so, brother."

"You love Italians?"

Danny shrugged. "I got nothing against 'em. You?"

"I like them. I like the North End. Just like you do."

Danny bounced a fist lightly off his knee. "Well, good then."

"Con' hates 'em, though."

"Yeah, well, Con's got a lot of hate in him."

Joe ate the rest of his second frankfurter. "Why?"

Danny shrugged. "Maybe because when he sees something that confuses him, he feels like he needs an answer right then. And if the answer ain't right in front of him, he grabs onto whatever is and makes *it* the answer." He shrugged again. "I honestly don't know, though. Con's had something eating him up since the day he was born."

They sat in silence for a bit, Joe swinging his legs off the edge of the stone table. A street vendor coming home from a day at Haymarket Square pulled over to the curb. He climbed off his cart, breathing wearily through his nostrils, and went to the front of his horse and lifted its left leg. The horse snuffled softly and twitched at the flies on its tail and the man shushed it as he pulled a pebble from its hoof and tossed it out onto West Broadway. He lowered the leg and caressed the horse's ear and whispered into it. The horse snuffled some more as the man climbed back up onto his cart, its eyes dark and sleepy. The vendor whistled softly and the horse clopped back into the street. When it dropped a clump of shit from between its flanks and cocked its head proudly at the creation, Joe felt a smile spread across his face he couldn't explain.

Danny, watching, too, said, "Damn. Size of a *hat.*"

Joe said, "Size of a *breadbasket.*"

"I believe you're right," Danny said, and they both laughed.

They sat as the light turned rusty behind the tenements along the Fort Point Channel and the air smelled of the tide and the clogging stench of the American Sugar Refining Company and the gases of the Boston Beer Company. Men crossed back over the Broadway Bridge in clusters and other groups wandered up from the Gillette Company and Boston Ice and the Cotton Waste Factory and most entered the saloons. Soon the boys who ran numbers for the neighborhood were dashing in and out of those same saloons, and from across the channel another whistle blew to signal the end of another working day. Joe wished he could stay here forever, even in his school clothes, with his brother, on a stone bench along West Broadway as the day faded around them.

Danny said, "You can have two families in this life, Joe, the one you're born to and the one you build."

"Two families," Joe said, eyeing him.

He nodded. "Your first family is your blood family and you always be true to that. That means something. But there's another family and that's the kind you go out and find. Maybe even by accident sometimes. And they're as much blood as your first family. Maybe more so, because they don't *have to* look out for you and they don't have to love you. They choose to."

534

"So you and Luther, you chose each other?"

Danny cocked his head. "I was thinking more of me and Nora, but now that you mention it, I guess me and Luther did, too."

"Two families," Joe said.

"If you're lucky."

Joe thought about that for a bit and the inside of his body felt splashy and ungrounded, as if he might float away.

"Which are we?" Joe said.

"The best kind." Danny smiled. "We're both, Joe."

At home, it got worse. Connor, when he talked, ranted about the anarchists, the Bolsheviks, the Galleanists, and the mud races who constituted their core. Jews financed them, he said, and Slavs and wops did their dirty work. They were riling up the niggers down South and poisoning the minds of the working whites back east. They'd tried to kill his boss, the attorney general of the United States of America, *twice*. They talked of unionization and rights for the working-man, but what they really wanted was violence on a national scale and despotism. Once turned onto the subject, he couldn't be turned off, and he'd just about combust when talk turned to the possibility of a police strike.

It was a rumor in the Coughlin home all summer, and even though Danny's name was never said, Joe knew that he was somehow involved. The Boston Social Club, his father told Connor, was talking to the AFL, to Samuel Gompers about an impending charter. They would be the first policemen in the country with national affiliation to a labor union. They could alter history, his father said and ran a hand over his eyes.

His father aged five years that summer. Ran down. Shadowed pockets grew below his eyes as dark as ink. His colorless hair turned gray.

Joe knew he'd been stripped of some of his power and that the culprit was Commissioner Curtis, a man whose name his father uttered with hopeless venom. He knew that his father seemed weary of fighting and that Danny's break from the family had hit him far harder than he let on.

The last day of school, Joe returned to the house to find his father and Connor in the kitchen. Connor, just back from Washington, was already well into his cups, the whiskey bottle on the table, the cork lying beside it.

"It's sedition if they do it."

"Oh, come on, boy, let's not be overly dramatic."

"They're officers of the law, Dad, the first line of national defense. If they even *talk about* walking off the job, that's treason. No different than a platoon that walks away from the field of battle."

"It's a little different." Joe's father sounded exhausted.

Connor looked up when Joe entered the room and this was usually where such conversation ended, but this time Connor kept going, his eyes loose and dark.

"They should all be arrested. Right now. Just go down to the next BSC meeting and throw a chain around the building."

"And what? Execute them?" His father's smile, so rare these days, returned for a moment, but it was thin.

Connor shrugged and poured more whiskey into his glass.

"You're half serious." His father noticed Joe now, too, as Joe placed his book sack up on the counter.

"We execute soldiers who walk away from the front," Connor said.

His father eyed the whiskey bottle but didn't reach for it. "While I may disagree with the men's plan of action, they have a legitimate beef. They're underpaid—"

"So let them go out and get another job."

"—the state of their quarters is unhygienic to say the least and they're dangerously overworked."

"You sympathize with them."

"I can see their point."

"They're not garment workers," Connor said. "They're emergency personnel."

536

"He's your brother."

"Not anymore. He's a Bolshevik and a traitor."

"Ah, Jaysus H," his father said. "You're talking crazy talk."

"If Danny is one of the ringleaders of this and they *do* strike? He deserves whatever's coming to him."

He looked over at Joe when he said this and swirled the liquor in his glass and Joe saw contempt and fear and an embittered pride in his brother's face.

"You got something to say, little tough guy?" Connor took a swig from his glass.

Joe thought about it. He wanted to say something eloquent in defense of Danny. Something memorable. But the words wouldn't come, so he finally said the ones that did.

"You're a piece of shit."

No one moved. It was as if they'd all turned to porcelain, the whole kitchen, too.

Then Connor threw his glass in the sink and charged. Their father got a hand on his chest, but Connor got past him long enough to reach for Joe's hair and Joe twisted away but fell to the floor and Connor got one kick in before his father pushed him back.

"No," Connor said. "No! Did you hear what he called me?"

Joe, on the ground, could feel where his brother's fingers had touched his hair.

Connor pointed over his father's shoulder at him. "You little puke, he's got to go to work sometime, and you got to sleep here!"

Joe got up off the floor and stared at his brother's rage, stared it straight in the face and found himself unimpressed and unafraid.

"You think Danny should be executed?" he said.

His father pointed back at him. "Shut up, Joe."

"You really think that, Con'?"

"I said shut up!"

"Listen to your father, boy." Connor was starting to smile.

"Fuck you," Joe said.

Joe had time to see Connor's eyes widen, but he never saw his father spin toward him, his father always a man of startling speed, faster than Danny, faster than Con', and a hell of a lot faster than Joe, because Joe didn't even have time to lean back before the back of his father's hand connected with Joe's mouth and Joe's feet left the floor. When he landed, his father was already on him, both hands on his shoulders. He hoisted him up from the floor and slammed his back into the wall so that they were face-to-face, Joe's shoes dangling a good two feet off the floor.

His father's eyes bulged in their sockets and Joe noticed how red they were. He gritted his teeth and exhaled through his nostrils and a lock of his newly gray hair fell to his forehead. His fingers dug into Joe's shoulders and he pressed his back into the wall as if he were trying to press him straight through it.

"You say that word in my house? In *my house*?"

Joe knew better than to answer.

"In my house?" his father repeated in a high whisper. "I feed you, I clothe you, I send you to a good school, and you talk like that in here? Like you're from trash?" He slammed his shoulders back into the wall. "Like you're common?" He loosened his grip just long enough for Joe's body to slacken and then slammed him into the wall again. "I should cut out your tongue."

"Dad," Connor said. "Dad."

"In your mother's house?"

"Dad," Connor said again.

His father cocked his head, eyeballing Joe with those red eyes. He removed one hand from Joe's shoulder and closed it around his throat.

"Jesus, Dad."

His father raised him higher, so that Joe had to look down into his red face.

"You're going to be sucking on brown soap for the rest of the day," his father said, "but before you do, let me make one

538

thing clear, Joseph—I brought you into this world and I can damn sure take you out of it. Say 'Yes, sir.' "

It was hard with a hand around his throat, but Joe managed: "Yes, sir."

Connor reached toward his father's shoulder and then paused, his hand hovering in the air. Joe, looking in his father's eyes, could tell his father felt the hand in the air behind him and he willed Connor to please step back. No telling what his father would do if that hand landed.

Connor lowered the hand. He put it in his pocket and took a step back.

His father blinked and sucked some air through his nose. "And you," he said, looking back over his shoulder at Connor, "don't let me ever hear you talk about treason and my police department ever again. Ever. Am I quite clear?"

"Yes, sir." Connor looked down at his shoes.

"You . . . lawyer." He turned back to Joe. "How's the breathing, boy?"

Joe felt the tears streaming down his face and croaked, "Fine, sir."

His father finally lowered him down the wall until they were face-to-face. "If you ever use that word in this house, it'll not get this good again. Not even close, Joseph. Do you have any trouble comprehending my meaning, son?"

"No, sir."

His father raised his free arm and cocked it into a fist and Joe saw that fist hovering six inches from his face. His father let him look at it, at the ring there, at the faded white scars, at the one knuckle that had never fully healed and was twice the size of the others. His father nodded at him once and then dropped him to the floor.

"The two of you make me sick." He went over to the table, slammed the cork back into the whiskey bottle, and left the room with it under his arm.

* * *

His mouth still tasted of soap and his ass still smarted from the calm, emotionless whipping his father had given it after he'd returned from his study half an hour later, when Joe climbed out his bedroom window with some clothes in a pillowcase and walked off into the South Boston night. It was warm, and he could smell the ocean at the end of the street, and the streetlamps glowed yellow. He'd never been out on the streets this late by himself. It was so quiet he could hear his footsteps and he imagined their echoes as a living thing, slipping away from the family home, the last thing anyone remembered hearing before they became part of a legend.

What do you mean, he's gone?" Danny said. "Since when?"

"Last night," his father said. "He took off . . . I don't know what time."

His father had been waiting on his stoop when Danny returned home, and the first thing Danny noticed was that he'd lost weight, and the second was that his hair was gray.

"You don't report into your precinct anymore, boy?"

"I don't really have a precinct these days, Dad. Curtis shit-canned me to every cold-piss strike detail he could find. I spent my day in Malden."

"Cobblers?"

Danny nodded.

His father gave that a rueful smile. "Is there one man who isn't on strike these days?"

"You have no reason to think he was snatched or something," Danny said.

"No, no."

"So there was a reason he ran."

His father shrugged. "In *his* head, I'm sure."

Danny placed a foot on the stoop and unbuttoned his coat. He'd been frying in it all day. "Let me guess, you didn't spare the rod."

His father looked up at him, squinting into the setting sun. "I didn't spare it with you and you turned out none the worse for wear."

Danny waited.

His father threw up his hand. "I admit I was a little more impassioned than usual."

"What'd the kid do?"

"He said *fuck*."

"In front of Ma?"

His father shook his head. "In front of me."

Danny shook his head. "It's a word, Dad."

"It's *the* word, Aiden. The word of the streets, of the common poor. A man builds his home to be a sanctuary, and you damn well don't drag the streets into a sanctuary."

Danny sighed. "What did you do?"

Now it was his father's turn to shake his head. "Your brother's out on these streets somewhere. I've put men on it, good men, men who work runaways and truants, but it's harder in the summer, so many boys on the streets, so many working jobs at all hours, you can't tell one from the other."

"Why come to me?"

"You damn well know why," his father said. "The boy worships you. I suspect he may have come here."

Danny shook his head. "If he did, I haven't been around. I've been working a seventy-two on. You're looking at my first hour off."

"What about . . . ?" His father tilted his head and looked up at the building.

"Who?"

"You know who."

"Say her name."

"Don't be a child."

"Say her name."

His father rolled his eyes. "Nora. Happy? Has *Nora* seen him?"

"Let's go ask her."

541

His father stiffened and didn't move as Danny came up the steps past him and went to the front door. He turned his key in the lock and looked back at the old man.

"We going to find Joe, or not?"

His father rose from the steps and brushed off the seat of his pants and straightened the creases of his trousers. He turned with his captain's hat under his arm.

"This changes nothing between us," he said.

"Perish the thought." Danny fluttered a hand over his heart, which brought a grimace to his father's face, then he pushed open the door into the front hall. The stairs were sticky with heat and they climbed them slowly, Danny feeling like he could easily lie down on one of the landings and take a nap after three straight days of strike patrol.

"You ever hear from Finch anymore?" he asked.

"I get the occasional call," his father said. "He's back in Washington."

"You tell him I saw Tessa?"

"I mentioned it. He didn't seem terribly interested. It's Galleani he wants and that old dago is smart enough to train 'em here, but he sends them out of state to do most of their mischief."

Danny felt the bitterness in his own grin. "She's a terrorist. She's making bombs in our city. Who knows what else. But they've got bigger fish to fry?"

His father shrugged. "It's the way of things, boy. If they hadn't bet the house on terrorists being responsible for that molasses tank explosion, things would probably be different. But they did bet the house, and it blew that molasses all over their faces. Boston's an embarrassment now, and you and your BSC boys aren't making it better."

"Oh, right. It's us."

"Don't play the martyr. I didn't say it was all you. I just said there's a taint to our beloved department in certain corridors of federal law enforcement. And some of that's because of the half-cocked hysteria surrounding the tank explosion, and

542

some of it's due to the fear that you'll embarrass the nation by going on strike."

"No one's talking strike yet, Dad."

"Yet." His father paused at the third-floor landing. "Jesus, it's hotter than the arse of a swamp rat." He looked at the hall window, its thick glass covered in soot and a greasy residue. "I'm three stories up, but I can't even see my city."

"Your city." Danny chuckled.

His father gave him a soft smile. "It is my city, Aiden. It was men like me and Eddie who built this department. Not the commissioners, not O'Meara much as I respected him, and certainly not Curtis. Me. And as goes the police, so goes the city." He wiped his brow with a handkerchief. "Oh, your old man might be back on his heels temporarily, but I'm getting my second wind, boy. Don't you doubt it."

They climbed the last two flights in silence. At Danny's room, his father took a series of breaths as Danny inserted his key in the lock.

Nora opened the door before he could turn the key. She smiled. Then she saw who stood beside him, and her pale eyes turned to ash.

"And what's this?" she said.

"I'm looking for Joe," his father said.

She kept her eyes on Danny, as if she hadn't heard him. "You bring him here?"

"He showed up," Danny said.

His father said, "I have no more desire to be here than you—"

"Whore," Nora said to Danny. "I believe that was the last word I heard from this man's mouth. I believe he spit on his own floor to emphasize the point."

"Joe's missing," Danny said.

That didn't move her at first. She stared at Danny with a cold rage that, while it encompassed his father, was just as much directed at him for bringing the man to their door. She flicked her gaze off his face and onto his father's.

"What'd you call him to make him run?" she said.

"I just want to know if the boy came by."

"And I want to know why he ran."

"We had a moment of discord," his father said.

"Ah." She tilted her head back at that. "I know all about how you resolve moments of discord with young Joe. Was the switch involved?"

His father turned to Danny. "There's a limit to how long I'll stand for a situation I deem undignified."

"Jesus," Danny said. "The two of you. Joe's missing. Nora?"

Her jaw tightened and her eyes remained ash, but she stepped back from the door enough so Danny and his father could enter the room.

Danny took off his coat straightaway and stripped the suspenders from his shoulders. His father took in the room, the fresh curtains, the new bedspread, the flowers in the vase on the table by the window.

Nora stood by the foot of the bed in her factory uniform—Ladlassie stripe overalls with a beige blouse underneath. She gripped her left wrist with her right hand. Danny poured three whiskeys and gave a glass to each of them, and his father's eyebrows rose slightly at the sight of Nora drinking hard liquor.

"I smoke, too," she said, and Danny saw a tightening of his father's lips that he recognized as a suppressed smile.

The two of them raced each other on the drink, Danny's father draining his glass one drop ahead of Nora, and then they each held out their glasses again and Danny refilled them. His father took his to the table by the window and placed his hat on the table and sat and Nora said, "Mrs. DiMassi said a boy was by this afternoon."

"What?" his father said.

"He didn't leave a name. She said he was ringing our bell and looking up at our window and when she came out on the stoop, he ran away."

"Anything else?"

Nora drank more whiskey. "She said he was the spitting image of Danny."

Danny could see the tension drain from his father's shoulders and neck as he took a sip of his drink.

Eventually, he cleared his throat. "Thank you, Nora."

"You've no need to thank me, Mr. Coughlin. I love the boy. But you could do me a courtesy in return."

His father reached for his handkerchief and pulled it from his coat. "Certainly. Name it."

"Finish up your drink, if you please, and be on your way."

CHAPTER *thirty-one*

Two days later, on a Saturday in June, Thomas Coughlin walked from his home on K Street to Carson Beach for a meeting regarding the future of his city. Even though he was dressed in the lightest suit he owned, a blue and white seersucker, and his sleeves were short, the heat soaked through to his skin. He carried a brown leather satchel that grew heavier every couple of hundred yards. He was a little too old to be playing the bag man, but he wasn't trusting this particular bag to anyone else. These were sensitive days in the wards, where the wind could shift at a moment's notice. His beloved Commonwealth was currently under the stewardship of a Republican governor, a transplant from Vermont with no love of, nor appreciation for, local mores or local history. The police commissioner was a bitter man of tiny mind who hated the Irish, hated Catholics, and therefore hated the wards, the great Democratic wards that had built this city. He only understood his hate; he did not understand compromise, patronage, the way of doing things that had been established in this town over seventy years ago and had defined it ever since. Mayor Peters was the picture of ineffectuality, a man who won the vote only because the ward bosses had fallen asleep at the switch and the rivalry between the two main and two true mayoral candidates, Curley and Gallivan, had grown so bitter that a third flank had opened up, and Peters had reaped the November rewards. Since his election, he had done nothing, absolutely nothing of note, while his cabinet had pillaged the till with such shamelessness that it was only a matter of time before the looting hit the front pages and gave birth to the sworn enemy of politics since the dawn of man: illumination.

Thomas removed his coat and loosened his tie and placed the satchel at his feet as he came to the end of K Street and paused in the shade of a great elm. The sea lay only forty feet away, the beach filled, but the breeze was desultory, the air clammy. He could feel eyes on him, the gazes of those who recognized him but dared not approach. This filled him with enough satisfaction to close his eyes in the shade for a moment, to imagine a cooler breeze. He had made it clear many years ago in the neighborhood that he was their benefactor, their friend, their patron. You needed something, you put the touch on Tommy Coughlin and sure he'd take care of it, he would. But never—ever—on a Saturday. On Saturdays, you left Tommy Coughlin alone so he could attend to his family, his beloved sons and beloved wife.

They'd called him Four Hands Tommy back then, an appellation some believed bespoke a man who had his hands in a lot of pockets, but one which actually took root after he'd apprehended Boxy Russo and three other plug-uglies of the Tips Moran gang after he'd caught them coming out the back of a Jew furrier's place off Washington Street. He'd been a beat cop then and after he'd subdued them ("Sure it must have taken four hands to fight four men!" Butter O'Malley had said when he'd finished booking them), he'd tied them together in twos and waited for the wagons. They hadn't put up much of a struggle after he'd snuck up and slapped his billy club off the back of Boxy Russo's noggin. The galoot had dropped his end of the safe, and so the others had been forced to do the same, and the end result was four mashed feet and two broken ankles.

He smiled to remember it now. Those were simpler times. Fine times. He was young and powerful-strong, and sure, wasn't he just the fastest man on the force? He and Eddie McKenna worked the docks in Charlestown and the North End and South Boston and there was no more violent place for a copper to be. No richer either, once the big boys figured out they weren't going to scare these two off, so they might as well all come to an accommodation. Boston was, after all, a port city, and anything that disrupted the entry to those ports was bad for business. And the soul of business, as Thomas Coughlin had known since he was a lad in Clonakilty, County Cork, was accommodation.

He opened his eyes and they filled with the blue glitter of the sea and he shoved off again, making his way along the seawall toward Carson Beach. Even without the heat, this summer was already taking on the feel of a nightmare. Dissension within the ranks that could lead to a strike on his beloved force. Danny in the midst of it. Danny, too, lost to him as a son. Over a harlot who, in his good graces, he'd taken in when she was little more than a shivering puddle of gray flesh and loose teeth. Of course, she'd been from Donegal, which should have been fair warning; you could never trust a Donegalan; they were known liars and fomenters of dissent. And now Joe, missing for a second day, out there somewhere in the city, eluding all attempts to recover him. He had too much Danny in him, that was plain to see, too much of Thomas's own brother, Liam, a man who'd tried to break the world open, only to see it do the very same to him. He'd died, Liam had, gone now these twenty-eight years, bled out in an alley behind a pub in Cork City, his assailant unknown, his pockets picked clean. The motive had been an argument over a woman or a gambling debt, both, in Thomas's mind, pretty much the same thing in terms of risk versus reward. He'd loved Liam, his twin brother, the way he loved Danny, the way he loved Joe—in confusion and admiration and futility. They were windmill tilters who scoffed at reason, who lived through their hearts. As had Liam, as had Thomas's father, a man who'd drank the bottle until the bottle drank him back.

Thomas saw Patrick Donnegan and Claude Mesplede sitting in the small gazebo that looked out on the sea. Just beyond it was a dark green fishing pier, mostly empty at midday. He raised a hand and they raised theirs as he began the trudge across the sand through families trying to escape the heat of their homes for the heat of this sand. He would never understand this phenomenon of lying by the water, of taking the entire family to engage in the mass indulgence of idleness. It seemed like something Romans would have done, baking under their sun gods. Men were no more meant to be idle than horses were. It fostered a restlessness of thinking, an acceptance of amoral possibilities and the philosophy of relativism. Thomas would kick the men if he could, kick them from the sand and send them out to work.

Patrick Donnegan and Claude Mesplede watched him come with smiles on their faces. They were always smiling, these two, a pair if ever there was one. Donnegan was the ward boss for the Sixth and Mesplede was its alderman, and they had held these positions for eighteen years, through mayors, through governors, through police captains and police commissioners, through presidents. Nestled deep in the bosom of the city where no one ever thought to look, they ran it, along with a few other ward bosses and aldermen and congressmen and councilors who'd been smart enough to secure positions on the key committees that controlled the wharves and the saloons and the building contracts and the zoning variances. If you controlled these, you controlled crime and you controlled the enforcement of law and, thus, you controlled everything that swam in the same sea, which was to say, everything that made a city run—the courts, the precincts, the wards, the gambling, the women, the businesses, the unions, the vote. The last, of course, was the procreative engine, the egg that hatched the chicken that hatched more eggs that hatched more chickens and would do so ad infinitum.

549

As childishly simple as this process was, most men, given a hundred years on earth, would never understand it because most men didn't want to.

Thomas entered the gazebo and leaned against the inner wall. The wood was hot and the white sun found the center of his forehead as a bullet to a hawk.

"How's the family, Thomas?"

Thomas handed him the satchel. "Tops, Patrick. Just tops. And the missus?"

"She's fit, Thomas. Picking out architects for the house we're building in Marblehead, she is." Donnegan opened the satchel, peered inside.

"And yours, Claude?"

"My eldest, Andre, has passed the bar."

"Grand stuff. Here?"

"In New York. He graduated Columbia."

"You must be fierce-proud."

"I am, Thomas, thank you."

Donnegan stopped rummaging in the satchel. "Every list we asked for?"

"And more." Thomas nodded. "We threw in the NAACP as a bonus."

"Ah, you're a miracle worker."

Thomas shrugged. "It was Eddie mostly."

Claude handed Thomas a small valise. Thomas opened it and looked at the two bricks of money inside, both wrapped tightly in paper and taped. He had a practiced eye when it came to such transactions, and he knew by the thickness that his and Eddie's payments were even larger than promised. He raised an eyebrow at Claude.

"Another company joined us," Claude said. "Profit participation rose accordingly."

"Shall we walk, Thomas?" Patrick said. " 'Tis diabolical heat."

"A sound suggestion."

They removed their jackets and strolled to the pier. At

midday it was empty of fishermen, save for a few who seemed far more interested in the buckets of beer at their feet than any fish they could jerk over the rail.

They leaned against the rail and looked out at the Atlantic and Claude Mesplede rolled his own cigarette and lit it with a cupped match that he flicked into the ocean. "We've compiled that list of saloons that will be converting to rooming houses."

Thomas Coughlin nodded. "There's no weak link?"

"Not a one."

"No criminal histories to worry about?"

"None at all."

He nodded. He reached into his jacket and removed his cigar from the inside pocket. He snipped the end and put his match to it.

"And they all have basements?"

"As a matter of course."

"I see no problem then." He puffed slowly on the cigar.

"There's an issue with the wharves."

"Not in my districts."

"The Canadian wharves."

He looked at Donnegan, then at Mesplede.

"We're working on it," Donnegan said.

"Work faster."

"Thomas."

He turned to Mesplede. "Do you know what will happen if we don't control point of entry and point of contact?"

"I do."

"Do you?"

"I said I do."

"The lunatic Irish and the lunatic dagos will organize. They won't be mad dogs in the street anymore, Claude. They'll be units. They'll control the stevedores and the teamsters, which means they'll control transport. They'll be able to set terms."

"That will never happen."

Thomas considered the ash at the end of his cigar. He held

551

it out to the wind and watched the wind eat the ash until the flame glowed underneath. He waited until it had turned from blue to red before he spoke again.

"If they take control of this, they'll tip the balance. They'll control us. At *their* leisure, gents, not ours. You're our man with the friends in Canada, Claude."

"And you're our man in the BPD, Thomas, and I'm hearing talk of a strike."

"Don't change the subject."

"It is the subject."

Thomas looked over at him and Claude flicked his ash into the sea and took another hungry puff. He shook his head at his own anger and turned his back to the sea. "Are you telling me there won't be a strike? Can you guarantee that? Because from what I saw on May Day, you have a rogue police department out there. They engage in a gang fight, and you're telling us you can control them?"

"I was after you all last year to get the mayor's ear on this one, and what happened?"

"Don't put this on my door, Tommy."

"I'm not putting it on your door, Claude. I'm asking about the mayor."

Claude looked over at Donnegan and said, "Ach," and flipped his cigarette into the sea. "Peters is no mayor. You know that. He spends all his time shacked up with his fourteen-year-old concubine. Who is, I might add, his cousin. Meanwhile, his men, carpetbaggers all, could make Ulysses Grant's gangster-cabinet blush. Now there might be some sympathy for your men's plight, but they pissed that all away, didn't they?"

"When?"

"In April. They were offered their two-hundred-a-year increase and they declined."

"Jesus," Thomas said, "cost of living has risen seventy-three percent. *Seventy-three.*"

"I know the number."

"That two hundred a year was a prewar figure. The poverty level is fifteen hundred a year, and most coppers make far less than that. They're the police, Claude, and they're working for less wages than niggers and women."

Claude nodded and placed a hand on Thomas's shoulder, gave it a soft squeeze. "I can't argue with you. But the thinking in City Hall *and* in the commissioner's office is that the men *can* be put on the Pay No Heed list because they're emergency personnel. They can't affiliate with a union and they sure can't strike."

"But they can."

"No, Thomas," he said, his eyes clear and cold. "They can't. Patrick's been out in the wards, taking an informal poll, if you will. Patrick?"

Patrick spread his hands over the rail. "Tom, it's like this—I've talked to our constituents, and if the police dare strike, this city will vent all its rage—at unemployment, the high cost of living, the war, the niggers coming from down South to take jobs, at the price of getting up in the damn morning—and send it straight at the city."

"This city will riot," Claude said. "Just like Montreal. And you know what happens when people are forced to see the mob that lives within them? They don't like it. They want someone to pay. At the polls, Tom. Always at the polls."

Thomas sighed and puffed his cigar. Out in the sea, a small yacht floated into his field of vision. He could make out three figures on the deck as thick dark clouds began to mass just to their south and march toward the sun.

Patrick Donnegan said, "Your boys strike? Big Business wins. They'll use that strike as a cudgel to fuck organized labor, Irishmen, Democrats, fuck anyone who ever thought of a decent day's pay for a decent day's work in this country. You let them turn this into what they'll turn it into? You'll set the working class back thirty years."

Thomas gave that a smile. "It's not all on me, boys. Maybe if O'Meara, God rest him, was still with us, I'd have more say

553

in the outcome, but with Curtis? That toad'll blow this city down to its foundations to stick it to the wards and the men who run them."

"Your son," Claude said.

Thomas turned, the cigar between his teeth pointing at Claude's nose. "What?"

"Your son is in league with the BSC. Quite an orator, we hear, like his father."

Thomas removed his cigar. "We stay away from family, Claude. That's a rule."

"Maybe in fairer days," Claude said. "But your son is in this, Tommy. Deep. And the way I hear it, he's growing in popularity by the day and his rhetoric grows exponentially more inflammatory. If you could talk to him, maybe . . ." Claude shrugged.

"We don't have that kind of relationship anymore. There's been a rift."

Claude took that information in, his small eyes tilting up in his head for a moment as he sucked softly on his lower lip. "You'll have to repair it then. Someone has to talk these boys out of doing anything stupid. I'll work on the mayor and his hoodlums. Patrick will work on the public sentiment. I'll even see what I can do about a favorable article or two in the press. But, Thomas, you've got to work on your son."

Thomas looked over at Patrick. Patrick nodded.

"We don't want to take the gloves off, sure now, do we, Thomas?"

Thomas declined to respond to that. He placed his cigar back in his mouth, and the three of them leaned on the rail again and looked out at the ocean.

Patrick Donnegan looked out at the yacht as the clouds reached it and covered it in shadow. "I've been thinking about one of those for myself. Smaller, of course."

Claude laughed.

"What?"

"You're building a house on the water. What would you want with a boat?"

"So I could look back in at my house," Patrick said.

Thomas grinned in spite of his dark mood and Claude chuckled.

"He's addicted to the trough, I'm afraid."

Patrick shrugged. "I'm fond of the trough, boys, I admit it. Believe in the trough, I do. But it's a small trough. It's a big-house trough. Them? They want troughs the size of countries. They don't know where to stop."

On the yacht, the three figures suddenly moved with quick jerky motions as the cloud above them opened.

Claude clapped his hands together and then rubbed them off each other. "Well, we don't want to be caught out," he said. "There's rain coming, gentlemen."

"God's truth," Patrick said as they walked off the pier. "You can smell it, sure."

By the time he got home it was pouring, a fine black unleashing of the heavens. A man who'd never been fond of a strong sun, he found himself invigorated, even though the drops were as warm as sweat and only added to the thickness of the humidity. The last few blocks, he slowed his pace to a fairgrounds stroll and tilted his face up into it. When he reached the house, he went in through the back, taking the path along the side so he could check on his flowers, and they seemed as pleased as he to finally have some water. The back door opened onto the kitchen and he gave Ellen a start as he came through it looking like something that had escaped the ark.

"Mercy, Thomas!"

"Mercy indeed, my love." He smiled at her, trying to remember the last time he'd done so. She returned the smile, and he tried to remember the last time he'd seen that as well.

"You're soaked to the bone."

"I needed it."

"Here, sit. Let me get you a towel."

"I'm fine, love."

She came back from the linen closet with a towel. "I've news of Joe," she said, her eyes bright and wet.

"For the love of Pete," he said, "out with it, Ellen."

She draped the towel over his head and rubbed vigorously. She spoke as if she were discussing a lost cat. "He's turned up at Aiden's."

Before Joe ran away, she'd been locked in her room, incapacitated by Danny's nuptials. Once Joe had gone on the run, she'd emerged and launched into a cleaning frenzy, telling Thomas she was back to her old self, she was, and would he please be so kind as to find their son? When she wasn't cleaning, she was pacing. Or knitting. And all the while, she asked him, over and over, what he was doing about Joe. She'd say it the way a worried mother would, yes, but the way a worried mother would to a boarder. He'd lost all connection with her over the years, made his peace with a warmth that lived occasionally in her voice but rarely in her eyes, because the eyes alit on nothing, seemed instead to always be tilted slightly up, as if she were conversing with her own mind and nothing else. He didn't know this woman. He was reasonably sure he loved her, because of time, because of attrition, but time had also robbed them of each other, fostered within a relationship based on itself and nothing more, no different from that of a saloon keeper and his most frequent patron. You loved out of habit and lack of brighter options.

He had the blood on his hands where their marriage was concerned, however. He was reasonably certain of that. She'd been a girl when they wed, and he'd treated her as a girl only to wake one morning, who knew how many years ago, wishing for a woman to take her place. But it was far too late for that now. Far too late. So he loved her in memory. He loved her with a version of himself he'd long outgrown because she hadn't. And she loved him, he supposed (if in fact she did, he didn't know anymore) because he indulged her illusions.

I'm so tired, he thought as she removed the towel from his head, but what he said was, "He's at Aiden's?"

"He is. Aiden telephoned."

"When?"

"Not long ago." She kissed his forehead, another rarity that defied recent recollection. "He's safe, Thomas." She rose from her haunches. "Tea?"

"Is Aiden bringing him by, Ellen? Our son?"

"He said Joe wished to spend the night and Aiden had a meeting to go to."

"A meeting."

She opened the cabinet for teacups. "He said he'd bring him 'round in the morning."

Thomas went to the phone in the entrance hall and dialed Marty Kenneally's house on West Fourth. He placed the valise under the phone table. Marty answered on the third ring, shouting into the phone as he always did.

"Hello? Hello? Hello?"

"Marty, it's Captain Coughlin."

"Is that you, sir?" Marty shouted even though, to the best of Thomas's knowledge, no one else ever called him.

"It's me, Marty. I need you to bring the car around."

"She'll be slipping in this rain, sir."

"I didn't ask you if she'd be slipping, Marty, now did I? Bring her 'round in ten minutes."

"Yes, sir," Marty shouted and Thomas hung up.

When he came back into the kitchen, the kettle was nearing the boil. He stripped off his shirt and used the towel on his arms and torso. He noticed how white the hairs had gotten on his chest, and that gave him a quick, mournful vision of his own headstone, but he vanquished the sentiment by noting the flatness of his belly and the hard cords in his biceps. With the possible exception of his eldest son, he couldn't picture a man he'd fear to go against in a fistfight, even today, in his golden years.

You're in the grave, Liam, almost three decades, but I'm still standing strong.

Ellen turned from the stove and saw his bare chest. She averted her gaze and Thomas sighed and rolled his eyes. "Jesus, woman, it's me. Your husband."

"Cover yourself, Thomas. The neighbors."

The neighbors? She barely knew any of them. And, of those she did, most failed to measure up to whatever standards she clung to these days.

Christ, he thought as he went into the bedroom and changed into a fresh shirt and trousers, how did two people vanish from each other's sight in the same house?

He'd kept a woman once. For about six years, she'd lived in the Parker House and spent his money freely but she'd always greeted him with a drink when he came through the door and she'd looked in his eyes when they talked and even when they made love. Then in the fall of '09, she'd fallen in love with a bellhop and they left the city to start a new life in Baltimore. Her name was Dee Dee Goodwin, and when he'd placed his head to her bare chest he'd felt he could say anything, close his eyes and be anything.

His wife handed him his tea when he came back into the kitchen and he drank it standing up.

"You're going back out? On a Saturday?"

He nodded.

"But I thought you'd stay home today. We'd stay home together, Thomas."

And do *what*? he wanted to ask. You'll talk about the latest news you've heard from relatives back in the Old Sod who we haven't seen in years, and then when I begin to talk, you'll jump up and start cleaning. And then we'll have a silent supper and you'll disappear to your room.

He said, "I'm going to get Joe."

"But Aiden said—"

"I don't care what Aiden said. He's my son. I'm bringing him home."

"I'll clean his sheets," she said.

He nodded and knotted his tie. Outside, the rain had stopped. The house smelled of it and it ticked off the leaves in the backyard, but he could see the sky brightening.

He leaned in and kissed his wife's cheek. "I'll be back with our boy."

She nodded. "You haven't finished your tea."

He lifted the cup and drained it. He placed it back on the table. He took his straw boater from the hat rack and placed it on his head.

"You look handsome," she said.

"And you're still the prettiest girl ever to come out of County Kerry."

She gave him a smile and a sad nod.

He was almost out of the kitchen when she called to him.

"Thomas."

He turned back. "Hmm?"

"Don't be too hard on the boy."

He felt his eyes narrow so he compensated with a smile. "I'm just glad he's safe."

She nodded and he could see a clear and sudden recognition in her eyes, as if she knew him again, as if they could heal. He held her eyes and broadened his smile and felt hope stir in his chest.

"Just don't hurt him," she said brightly and turned back to her teacup.

It was Nora who thwarted him. She raised the window on the fifth floor and called down to him as he stood on the stoop. "He wants to stay here for the night, Mr. Coughlin."

Thomas felt ridiculous calling up from the stoop as streams of dagos filled the sidewalk and street behind him, the air smelling of shit and rotten fruit and sewage. "I want my son."

"And I told you, he's wants to stay here for the night."

"Let me talk to him."

She shook her head and he pictured wrenching her out of that window by her hair.

"Nora."

"I'm going to close the window."

"I'm a police captain."

"I know what you are."

"I can come up."

"Won't that be a sight?" she said. "Sure, everyone will be talking about the ruckus you'll make."

Oh, she was a righteous cunt, she was.

"Where's Aiden?"

"A meeting."

"What kind?"

"What kind do you think?" she said. "Good day, Mr. Coughlin."

She slammed the window closed.

Thomas walked off the stoop through the throng of reeking dagos and Marty opened the car door for him. Marty came around and got behind the wheel. "Where to now, Captain? Home, is it?"

Thomas shook his head. "Roxbury."

"Yes, sir. The Oh-Nine, sir?"

Thomas shook his head again. "Intercolonial Hall, Marty."

Marty came off the clutch and the car lurched and then died. He pumped the gas and started it again. "That's BSC headquarters, sir."

"I know right well what it is, Marty. Now hush up and take me there."

A show of hands," Danny said, "for any man in this room who's ever heard us discuss, or even *say*, the word *strike*." There were over a thousand men in the hall and not one raised his hand.

"So where did the word come from?" Danny said. "How is it suddenly that the papers are hinting that this is our plan?" He looked out at the sea of people and his eyes found

Thomas's in the back of the hall. "Who has the motive to make the entire city think we're going to strike?"

Several men looked back at Thomas Coughlin. He smiled and waved, and a collective laugh rumbled through the room.

Danny wasn't laughing, though. Danny was on fire up there. Thomas couldn't help but feel a great swell of pride as he watched his son on that podium. Danny, as Thomas had always known he would, had found his place in the world as a leader of men. It just wasn't the battleground Thomas would've chosen for him.

"They don't want to pay us," Danny said. "They don't want to feed our families. They don't want us to be able to provide reasonable shelter or education for our children. And when we complain? Do they treat us like men? Do they negotiate with us? No. They start a whisper campaign to paint us as Communists and subversives. They scare the public into thinking we'll strike so that if it ever *does* come to that, they can say, 'We told you so.' They ask us to bleed for them, gentlemen, and when we do so, they give us penny bandages and dock our pay a nickel."

That caused a roar in the hall, and Thomas noted that no one was laughing now.

He looked at his son and thought: check.

"The only way they win," Danny said, "is if we fall into their traps. If we begin to believe, even for a second, their lies. That we are somehow in error. That asking for basic human rights is somehow subversive. We are paid below the poverty level, gentlemen. Not *at* it or slightly above it, but below it. They say we can't form a union or affiliate with the AFL because we are 'indispensable' city personnel. But if we're indispensable, how come they treat us as if we're not? A streetcar driver, for example, must be twice as indispensable, because he makes twice what we do. He can feed his family and he doesn't work fifteen days in a row. He doesn't work seventy-two-hour shifts. He doesn't get shot at either, last time I checked."

Now the men laughed, and Danny allowed himself a smile.

"He doesn't get stabbed or punched or beaten down by hooligans like Carl McClary did last week in Fields Corner. Does he? He doesn't get shot like Paul Welch did during the May Day riot. He doesn't risk his life every minute, like we all did in the flu epidemic. Does he?"

The men were shouting, "No!" and pumping their fists.

"We do every dirty job in this city, gentlemen, and we don't ask for special treatment. We don't ask for anything but fairness, parity." Danny looked around the room. "Decency. To be treated as men. Not horses, not dogs. Men."

The men were quiet now, not a sound in the room, not a cough.

"As you all know, the American Federation of Labor has a long-standing policy of not granting charters to police unions. As you also know, our own Mark Denton has made overtures to Samuel Gompers of the AFL and has been—several times in the last year, I'm afraid—rebuffed." Danny looked back at Denton sitting on the stage behind him and smiled. He turned back to the men. "Until today."

It took some time for the words to sink in. Thomas, himself, had to replay them several times in his head before the enormity of them took hold. The men began to look at one another, they began to chatter. The buzz circled the room.

"Did you hear me?" Danny smiled big. "The AFL has reversed its policy for the BPD, gentlemen. They are granting us a charter. Sign-up petitions will be distributed in every station house by Monday morning." Danny's voice thundered across the room. "We are now affiliated with the biggest national union in the United States of America!"

The men rose, and the chairs fell and the hall exploded with cheers.

Thomas saw his son up on the stage embracing Mark Denton, saw them both turn to the crowd and try to accept the outstretched hands of hundreds of men, saw the big, bold smile on Danny's face, caught up in the thrall of himself a bit, as it would be near impossible not to be, given the circumstances. And Thomas thought:

I have given birth to a dangerous man.

Out on the street, the rain had returned, but it was soft, caught somewhere between a mist and light drizzle. As the men exited the hall, Danny and Mark Denton accepted their congratulations and handshakes and shoulder pats.

Some men winked at Thomas or tipped their hats and he returned the gestures because he knew they didn't see him as The Enemy, knowing he was far too slippery to be caught holding fast to either side of a fence. They mistrusted him as a matter of course, that was a given, but he caught the glint of admiration in their eyes, admiration and some fear, but no hate.

He was a giant in the BPD, yes, but he wore it lightly. Displays of vanity, after all, were the province of minor gods.

Danny, of course, refused to ride in a chauffeured car with him, so Thomas sent Marty on to the North End alone and he and Danny took the el back across the city. They had to get out at Batterymarch Station because the trestle that had been destroyed in the molasses flood was still under repair.

As they walked back toward the rooming house, Thomas said, "How is he? Did he tell you anything?"

"Somebody banged him up a bit. He told me he got mugged." Danny lit a cigarette and held out the pack to his father. His father helped himself to one as they walked in the soft mist. "I don't know if I believe him, but what are you going to do? He's sticking to the story." Danny looked over at him. "He spent a couple nights sleeping on the streets. That'd rattle any kid."

They walked another block. Thomas said, "So you're quite the young Seneca. You cut a fine figure up there, if I do say so."

Danny gave him a wry smile. "Thanks."

"Affiliated with a national union now, are you?"

"Let's not."

"What?"

"Discuss this," Danny said.

"The AFL's left many a fledgling union hanging out to dry when the pressure got upped."

"Dad? I said let's leave it."

"Fine, fine," his father said.

"Thanks."

"Far be it from me to change your mind after such a triumphant night."

"Dad, I said quit it."

"What am I doing?" Thomas said.

"You know damn well."

"I don't, boy. Do tell me."

His son turned his head and his eyes were filled with an exasperation that gradually gave way to humor. Danny was the only one of his three sons who'd picked up his father's sense of irony. All three boys could be funny—it was a family trait that probably went back several generations—but Joe's humor was the humor of a smart-aleck boy and Connor's was broader and borderline vaudevillian on the rare occasions he indulged it. Danny was capable of those kinds of humor as well, but more important, he shared Thomas's appreciation for the quietly absurd. He could, in effect, laugh at himself. Particularly in the most dire hours. And that was the bond between them that no difference of opinion could ever break. Thomas had often heard fathers or mothers over the years claim they didn't favor any of their children. What a load of bollocks. Pure bollocks. Your heart was your heart and it chose its loves regardless of your head. The son Thomas favored would surprise no one: Aiden. Of course. Because the boy understood him, to his core, and always had. Which wasn't always to Thomas's advantage, but then he'd always understood Aiden, and that kept the ledger balanced now, didn't it?

"I'd shoot you, old man, if I had my gun."

"You'd miss," Thomas said. "I've seen you shoot, boy."

For the second time in as many days, he found himself in the hostile presence of Nora. She didn't offer him a drink or a place to sit. She and Danny went over to one corner of the room by themselves and Thomas crossed to his youngest son, who sat at the table by the window.

The boy watched him come, and Thomas was immediately shaken to see a new blankness in Joe's eyes, as if something had been hollowed out of him. He had a black eye and a dark scab over his right ear and, Thomas noted with no small regret, that his throat still bore a circle of red from Thomas's own hand and his lip was still swollen from Thomas's ring.

"Joseph," he said when he reached him.

Joe stared back at him.

Thomas went to one knee by his son and put his hands on his face and kissed his forehead and kissed his hair and pressed him to his chest. "Oh, Jesus, Joseph," he said and closed his eyes and felt all the fear he'd trapped behind his heart these last two days burst through his blood and his muscles and his bones. He tilted his lips to his son's ear and whispered, "I love you, Joe."

Joe stiffened in his arms.

Thomas released his grip and leaned back and ran his hands over his son's cheeks. "I've been worried sick."

Joe whispered, "Yes, sir."

Thomas searched for signs of the boy he'd always known, but a stranger stared back at him.

"What happened to you, boy? Are you all right?"

"I'm fine, sir. I got mugged is all. Some boys near the rail yards."

The thought of his flesh and blood being pummeled spiked his rage for a moment, and Thomas almost slapped the boy for giving him such fright and lack of sleep these past few nights. But he caught himself, and the impulse passed.

"That's it? Mugged?"

"Yes, sir."

Jesus, the chill that came off the child! It was the chill of his mother during one of her "moods." The chill of Connor when things didn't go his way. It wasn't part of the Coughlin bloodline, that was for certain.

"Did you know any of the boys?"

Joe shook his head.

"And that's it? That's all that happened."

Joe nodded.

"I've come to take you home, Joseph."

"Yes, sir."

Joe stood and walked past him to the door. There was no child's self-pity, no sense of anguish or joy or emotion of any kind.

Something's died in him.

Thomas felt the chill of his own son again and wondered if he was to blame, if this was what he did to those he loved—protected their bodies while deadening their hearts.

He gave Danny and Nora a confident smile. "Well, we'll be off then."

Nora shot him a look of such hatred and contempt, Thomas himself wouldn't have cast it on the worst jungle-bunny rapist in his precinct. It seared the organs in his body.

She smoothed Joe's face and hair and kissed his forehead. "Good bye, Joey."

"Bye."

"Come on," Danny said softly. "I'll walk you both down."

When they reached the street, Marty Kenneally got out of the car and opened Thomas's door, and Joe climbed in. Danny stuck his head into the car and said good-bye and then stood on the sidewalk with Thomas. Thomas felt the soft night around them. Summer in the city and the streets smelled of this afternoon's rain. He loved that smell. He reached out his hand.

Danny shook it.

"They're going to come after you."

"Who?" Danny said.

"The ones you never see," his father said.

"Over the union?"

His father nodded. "What else?"

Danny dropped his hand and chuckled. "Let 'em come."

Thomas shook his head. "Don't ever say that. Don't ever tempt the gods like that. Ever, Aiden. Ever, boy."

Danny shrugged. "Fuck 'em. What can they do to me?"

Thomas placed his foot on the edge of the step. "You think because you've a good heart and a good cause that it'll be enough? Give me a fight against a man with a good heart any day, Aiden, because that man doesn't see the angles."

"What angles?"

"You've proved my point."

"If you're trying to scare me, you—"

"I'm trying to save you, you foolish boy. Are you so naïve as to still believe in a fair fight? Did you learn *anything* as my son? They know your name. Your presence has been noted."

"So let them bring the fight. And when they come, I'll—"

"You won't *see* them come," his father said. "No one ever does. That's what I'm trying to tell you. You pick a fight with these boys? Jesus, son, you best be prepared to bleed all night."

He waved his hand in exasperation and left his son on the stoop.

" 'Night, Dad."

Marty came around to open his door and Thomas leaned on it for a moment and looked back up at his son. So strong. So proud. So unaware.

"Tessa."

"What?" Danny said.

He leaned on the door and stared at his son. "They'll come after you with Tessa."

Danny said nothing for a bit.

"Tessa?"

Thomas patted the door. "That's what I'd do."

He tipped his hat to his son and climbed into the car with Joe and told Marty to take them straight home.

BABE RUTH *and the* SUMMER SWOON

CHAPTER *thirty-two*

It was a crazy summer. No predicting it. Every time Babe thought he had a grip on it, it slipped free and went running off like a barnyard pig that smelled the ax. The attorney general's home bombed, strikes and walkouts everywhere you looked, race riots, first in D.C., then in Chicago. The Chicago coloreds actually fought back, turning a race riot into a race war and scaring the everloving shit out of the entire country.

Not that it was all bad. No, sir. Who could have predicted what Babe would do with the white ball, for starters? No one, that's who. He'd had an embarrassing May, trying to swing too big, too often, and still being asked to pitch every fifth game, so his average found the cellar: .180. Good Lord. He hadn't seen .180 since "A" ball with Baltimore. But then Coach Barrow allowed him to lay off the pitching starts until further notice, and Babe tweaked his timing, forced himself to begin his cuts a little earlier but a little slower, too, not rev up to full power until he was halfway into the swing.

And June was glorious.

But July? July was volcanic.

The month arrived with a curl of fear at its back when word spread that the goddamned subversives and Bolshies had planned another wave of national carnage for Independence Day. Every federal facility in Boston was surrounded by soldiers, and in New York City, the entire police force was sent to guard the public buildings. By the end of the day, though, nothing had happened except for the walkout of the New England Fishermen's Union, and Babe didn't give a shit about that anyway because he never ate anything that couldn't walk on its own.

On the next day, he hit two home runs in one game. Two of the fuckers—sky-high. He'd never done that before. A week later, he ripped his eleventh of the season straight at the Chicago skyline, and even the White Sox fans cheered. Last year he'd led the league with a *final tally* of eleven. This year, he wasn't even warm yet, and the fans knew it. Middle of the month, in Cleveland, he hit his second home run of the game in the ninth. An impressive accomplishment on its own, another twofer, but this was a grand slam to win the game. The hometown crowd didn't boo. Babe couldn't believe it. He'd just driven the nail straight through the fucking coffin and down into the funeral parlor floor but the folks in the stands rose to their feet as one joyous, addled mass and chanted his name as he rounded the bases. When he crossed home, they were still standing and they were still chopping the air with their fists and still calling his name.

Babe.

Babe.

Babe . . .

In Detroit three days later, Babe took an 0–2 pitch, down and away, and hit the longest home run in Detroit history. The papers, always a step or two behind the fans, finally noticed. The American League single-season home run record, set in 1902, by Socks Seybold, was sixteen. Babe, heading into the third week of that stupendous July, had already smacked fourteen. And he was heading home to Boston, to sweet, sweet Fenway. Sorry, Socks, I hope you've done something else for people to remember you by, because I'm just going to snatch up that little ol' record of yours, wrap my cigar in it, and set a torch to it.

He hit his fifteenth in the first game back home, against the

Yanks, plopped it high in the upper deck of the right-field bleachers, watched the fans up in those cheap seats fight for it like it was food or a job as he trotted down the first base line and he noticed how full the seats were across the entire park. Double, easily, what they'd had for the World Series last year. They were in third place right now, third and sliding toward the basement. No one had any illusions about a pennant this year, so about the only thing to keep the fans coming to the ballpark was Ruth and his dingers.

And, boy, did they come. Even when they lost to Detroit a few days later, no one seemed to care because Babe hit his sixteenth long ball of the year. Sixteen. Poor Socks Seybold now had company on the podium. The streetcar and el operators had walked off the job that week (Babe thinking, for the second time that year, that the whole fucking world was walking off the job), but the stands filled anyway the next day when Babe went for magic number seventeen against those wonderfully generous Tigers.

He could feel it from inside the dugout. Ossie Vitt was up and Scott was on deck, but Babe was batting third, and the whole park knew it. He risked a glance out of the dugout as he wiped down his bat with a rag, saw half the eyes in the stadium flicking his way, hoping for a glimpse of a god, and he ducked back in again as his whole body went cold. Ice cream cold. The kind of cold he imagined you only felt just after you'd died but before they put you in the coffin, when some part of you thought you still breathed. It took him a second to realize what he'd seen. What could have done this to him. What ripped the confidence from his limbs and his soul so completely that, as he watched Ossie Vitt ground out to short and went to take his place in the on-deck circle, he feared he might never get another hit the rest of the season.

Luther.

Babe risked another sideways glance from the on-deck circle, his eyes flitting along the row just past the dugout. The front row. The money row. No way any colored man would be sitting in those seats. Never happened before, no reason to think it would happen now. A strange optical illusion then, a trick of the mind, maybe some of the pressure getting to Babe, pressure he hadn't acknowledged until now. Silly, really, when you thought what—

There he was. Sure as summer, certain as dusk. Luther Laurence. Same light smattering of scars on his face. Same hooded, sullen eyes, and those eyes looking right at Ruth as a smile appeared in them, a tiny, knowing glint, and Luther raised his fingers to the brim of his hat, and tipped it at Ruth.

Ruth tried to smile back, but the muscles in his face wouldn't comply as Scott popped out to shallow right. He heard the announcer call his name. He walked to the batter's box, feeling Luther's knowing eyes on his back the whole way. He stepped up to the plate and hit the first pitch he saw straight back into the pitcher's glove.

So this Clayton Tomes was a friend of yours, wasn't he?" Danny caught the eye of the peanut vendor and held up two fingers.

Luther nodded. "He was. Musta had jackrabbit in him, though. Didn't say a word to me, just picked up and left."

"Huh," Danny said. "I met him a few times. He didn't strike me that way. Struck me more as a sweet kid, a boy really."

The oily brown bags came sailing through the air and Danny caught the first but let the second pass by, and it glanced off Luther's forehead and landed in his lap.

"Thought you were some kind of baseball player." Danny handed a nickel down the row of fans and the last man handed it to the peanut vendor.

"Gotta lot on my mind." Luther took the first warm peanut from his bag and flicked his wrist and it bounced off Danny's Adam's apple and fell into his shirt. "What Mrs. Wagenfeld say about it?"

"Just chalked it up to something you darker folk do,"

574

Danny said, reaching into his shirt. "Hired herself another houseman straightaway."

"Colored?"

"No. I guess the new prevailing theory on the east side after you and Clayton didn't work out is to keep it whiter up there."

"Like this here park, uh?"

Danny chuckled. Maybe twenty-five thousand faces in Fenway that day, and not a one besides Luther's any darker than the ball. The teams were changing sides after Ruth's line-out to the pitcher, and the round man trotted out to left on his ballerina toes, his shoulders hunched like he was expecting a blow from behind. Luther knew Ruth had seen him, and that the seeing had rattled him. Shame had filled the man's face like it had come from a hose. Luther almost pitied him, but then he remembered the game in Ohio, the way those white boys had soiled its simple beauty and he thought: You don't want to feel shame? Don't do shameful things, white boy.

Danny said, "Anything I can do to help you?"

"With what?" Luther said.

"With whatever's been eating you up all summer. I ain't the only one noticed. Nora's worried, too."

Luther shrugged. "Nothing to tell."

"I am a cop, you know." He tossed his shells at Luther.

Luther swept the shells off his thighs. "For *now*."

Danny gave that a dark chuckle. "That's a fact, isn't it?"

The Detroit batter banged a cloud-climber toward left and it made a loud clang off the scoreboard. Ruth mistimed the carom and the ball hopped over his glove and he had to go stutter-stepping after it in the grass. By the time he came up with it and threw it into the infield, a simple single had turned into a triple and a run had scored.

"You really play him?" Danny said.

"Think I imagined it?" Luther said.

"No, I'm just wondering if it's like them cactuses you're always going on about."

575

"Cacti."

"Right."

Luther looked out to left, watched Ruth wipe some sweat off his face with his tunic. "Yeah, I played him. Him and some of them others out there and some Cubs, too."

"You win?"

Luther shook his head. "Can't win against that type. If they say the sky's green and get their buddies to agree with them, say it a few more times until they *believe* it, how you going to fight that?" He shrugged. "Sky's green from then on."

"Sounds like you're talking about the police commissioner, the mayor's office."

"Whole city thinks you're going to strike. Calling you Bolshies."

"We're not striking. We're just trying to get a fair shake."

Luther chuckled. "In this world?"

"World's changing, Luther. The little man ain't lying down like he used to."

"World ain't changing," Luther said. "Ain't ever going to, neither. They tell you the sky's green until you finally say, 'Okay, the sky's green'? Then they *own* the sky, Danny, and everything underneath it."

"And I thought I was cynical."

Luther said, "Ain't cynical, just openeyed. Chicago? They stoned that colored kid 'cuz he drifted over to their side of the *water*. The water, Danny. Whole city's like to burn to the ground now because they think they own water. And they're right. They do."

"Coloreds are fighting back, though," Danny said.

"And what's that going to do?" Luther said. "Yesterday, those four white men got shot to pieces on the Black Belt by six coloreds. You hear that?"

Danny nodded. "I did."

"All anybody's talking about is how those six coloreds *massacred* four white men. Those white boys had a god-damned machine gun in that car. A machine gun, and they

576

were firing it at colored folk. People ain't talking about that, though. They just talking about white blood running 'cuz of crazed niggers. They own the water, Danny, and the sky is green. And that's that."

"I can't accept that."

"That's why you're a good man. But being good ain't enough."

"You sound like my father."

"Better than sounding like mine." Luther looked at Danny, the big, strong cop who probably couldn't remember the last time the world didn't work out for him. "You say you're not going to strike. Well, good. But the whole city, including the colored sections, think you are. Those boys you're trying to get a fair shake from? They're already two steps ahead of you, and it ain't about money to them. It's about you forgetting your place and stepping out of line. They won't allow it."

"They might not have a choice," Danny said.

"Ain't about choice to them," Luther said. "Ain't about rights or a fair shake or any of that shit. You think you're calling their bluff. Problem is, they ain't bluffing."

Luther sat back and Danny did, too, and they ate the rest of their peanuts and in the fifth they had a couple beers and a couple hot dogs and waited to see if Ruth would break the AL home run record. He didn't, though. He went zero for four and made two errors. An uncharacteristic game for him all around, and some fans wondered aloud if he'd come down with something, or if he was just hungover.

On the walk back from Fenway, Luther's heart was banging away in his chest. It had been happening all summer, rarely for any particular reason. His throat would close up and his chest would flood with what felt like warm water and then bang-bang-bang-bang, his heart would just start going crazy.

As they walked along Mass. Ave., he looked over at Danny, saw Danny watching him carefully.

"Whenever you're ready," Danny said.

Luther stopped for a moment. Exhausted. Wiped out from carrying it. He looked over at Danny. "I'd have to trust you with something bigger than anyone ever trusted you with something in their lives."

Danny said, "You tended to Nora when no one else would. That means more to me even than saving my life. You loved my wife, Luther, when I was too stupid to. Whatever you need from me?" Danny touched his chest. "You got."

An hour later, standing over the bump of land that was Clayton Tomes's grave in the backyard of the Shawmut Avenue building, Danny said, "You're right. This is big. Fucking huge."

In the house, they sat on the empty floor. It was almost done now, very little left but trim work and the painting. Luther finished telling all of it, every last bit, right down to the day last month when he'd picked the lock on the toolbox McKenna had given him. It had taken him twenty minutes, and one look inside told him everything.

No wonder it was so heavy.

Pistols.

He'd checked them, one by one, found that they were all well oiled and in good condition, though hardly new. Loaded, too. Twelve of them. A dozen loaded guns meant to be found on the day the Boston police decided to raid the NAACP and make it look like an army readying for a race war.

Danny sat silent for a long time and drank from his flask. Eventually, he handed it across to Luther. "He'll kill you regardless."

"I know it," Luther said. "Ain't me I'm concerned with. It's Yvette. She's like a mother to me. And I can see him, you know, just for the hell of it? 'Cause she's what he call 'nigger bourgeoisie'? He'll kill her for fun. He definitely want to jail her. That's what the guns are all about."

Danny nodded.

"I know he's like blood to you," Luther said.

Danny held up a hand. He closed his eyes and rocked slightly in place.

"He killed that *boy*? For nothing?"

"For nothing but being black and alive."

Danny opened his eyes. "Whatever we do from this point on . . . ? You understand."

Luther nodded. "Dies with us."

Connor's first big federal case involved an ironworker named Massimo Pardi. Pardi had stood up at a meeting of the Roslindale Ironworkers Union, Local 12, and proclaimed that the safety conditions at Bay State Iron & Smelting had better improve immediately or the company "might find itself smelted right to the ground." He'd been loudly cheered before four other men—Brian Sullivan, Robert Minton, Duka Skinner, and Luis Ferriere—had lifted him onto their shoulders and walked him around the room. It was that action and those men who sealed Pardi's fate: 1 + 4 = syndicalism. Plain and simple.

Connor filed deportation orders against Massimo Pardi in district court and argued his case before the judge on the grounds that Pardi had violated the Espionage and Sedition Act under the antisyndicalist laws of the Commonwealth and therefore should be deported back to Calabria where a local magistrate could decide if any further punishment were necessary.

Even Connor was surprised when the judge agreed.

Not the next time, though. Certainly not the time after that.

What Connor finally realized—and what he hoped would hold him in good stead as long as he practiced law—was that the best arguments were those shorn of emotion or inflammatory rhetoric. Stick with the rule of law, eschew polemic, let precedent speak for you, and leave opposing counsel to choose whether to fight the soundness of those laws on appeal. It was quite the revelation. While opposing counsel thundered and raged and shook their fists in front of increasingly exasperated judges, Connor calmly pointed out the logical strictures of justice. And he could see in the eyes of the judges that they didn't *like* it, they didn't *want* to agree. Their seepy hearts held for the defendants, but their intellects knew truth when they saw it.

The Massimo Pardi case was to become, in hindsight, emblematic. The ironworker with the big mouth was sentenced to a year in jail (three months time served), and deportation orders were filed immediately. If his physical eviction from the country were to occur before he finished his sentence, the United States would graciously commute the remainder of it once he reached international waters. Otherwise, he did the full nine months. Connor, of course, felt some sympathy for the man. Pardi seemed, in the aggregate, an inoffensive sort, a hard worker who'd been engaged to be married in the fall. Hardly a threat to these shores. But what he represented—the very first stop on the road to terrorism—was quite offensive. Mitchell Palmer and the United States had decided the message needed to be sent to the world—we will no longer live in fear of you; you will live in fear of us. And that message was to be sent calmly, implacably, and constantly.

For a few months that summer, Connor forgot he was angry.

The Chicago White Sox came to town after Detroit and Ruth went out with a few of them one night, old friends from the farm league days, and they told him that order had been restored to their city, the army finally cheesing it to the niggers and putting them down once and for all. Thought it would never end, they said. Four days of shooting and pillaging and fires and all because one of theirs swam where he wasn't supposed to. And the whites hadn't been *stoning* him. They'd just been throwing rocks into the water to warn him off. Ain't their fault he wasn't a good swimmer.

Fifteen whites dead. You believe that? Fifteen. Maybe the niggers had *some* legitimate grievances, okay, yeah, but to kill fifteen white men? World was upside down.

It was for Babe. After that game where he'd seen Luther, he couldn't hit shit. Couldn't hit fastballs, couldn't hit curves, couldn't hit it if it had been sent to him on a string at ten miles an hour. He fell into the worst slump of his career. And now that the coloreds had been put back in their place in D.C. and Chicago, and the anarchists seemed to have gone quiet, and the country might have been able to take just one easy breath, the agitators and agitation sprang up from the least likely of quarters: the police.

The police, for Christ's sake!

Every day of Ruth's slump brought more signs that push was coming to shove and the city of Boston was going to pop at the seams. The papers reported rumors of a sympathy strike that would make Seattle look like an exhibition game. In Seattle it had been public workers, sure, but garbagemen and transit workers. In Boston, word was, they'd lined up the firemen. If the cops *and* the jakes walked off the job? Jeepers Crow! The city would become rubble and ash.

Babe had a regular thing going now with Kat Lawson at the Hotel Buckminster, and he left her sleeping one night and stopped in the bar on his way out. Chick Gandil, the White Sox first baseman, was at the bar with a couple fellas, and Babe headed for them but saw something in Chick's eyes that immediately warned him off. He took a seat down the other end, ordered a double scotch, and recognized the guys Chick was talking to: Sport Sullivan and Abe Attell, errand boys for Arnold Rothstein.

And Babe thought: Uh-oh. Nothing good's going to come of this.

Around the time Babe's third scotch arrived, Sport Sullivan and Abe Attell removed their coats from the backs of their chairs and left through the front door, and Chick Gandill walked his own double scotch down the length of the bar and plopped into the seat next to Babe with a loud sigh.

"Gidge."

"Babe."

"Oh, right, right. Babe. How you doing?"

"Ain't hanging with mutts, that's how I'm doing."

"Who's the mutts?"

Babe looked at Gandill. "You know who the mutts are. Sport Sullivan? Abe Fucking Attell? They're mutts work for Rothstein and Rothstein's the mutt of mutts. What the fuck you doing talking to a pair of mutts like that, Chick?"

"Gee, Mom, next time let me ask permission."

"They're dirty as the Muddy River, Gandil. You know it and anyone else with eyes knows it, too. You get seen with a pair of diamond dandies like that, who's going to believe you ain't taking?"

"Why do you think I met him here?" Chick said. "This ain't Chicago. It's nice and quiet. And no one'll get wind, Babe, my boy, long as you keep your nigger lips shut." Gandil smiled and drained his drink and dropped it to the bar. "Shoving off, my boy. Keep swinging for the fences. You've gotta hit one sometime this month, right?" He clapped Babe on the back and laughed and walked out of the bar.

Nigger lips. Shit.

Babe ordered another.

Police talking about a strike, ballplayers talking to known fixers, his home-run-record chase stalled at sixteen because of a chance sighting of a colored fella he'd met once in Ohio.

Was anything fucking sacred anymore?

The BOSTON
POLICE STRIKE

CHAPTER *thirty-three*

D anny met with Ralph Raphelson at the headquarters of the Boston Central Labor Union on the first Thursday in August. Raphelson was so tall he was one of the rare men with a face Danny had to look up into as he shook his hand. Thin as a fingernail, with wispy blond hair racing to depart the steep slope of his skull, he motioned Danny to a chair and took his own behind his desk. Beyond the windows, a hot-soup rain fell from beige clouds and the streets smelled like stewed produce.

"Let's start with the obvious," Ralph Raphelson said. "If you have an itch to comment on or give me the rough work about my name, please scratch it now."

Danny let Raphelson see him consider it before he said, "Nope. All set."

"Much appreciated." Raphelson opened his hands. "What can we do for the Boston Police Department this morning, Officer Coughlin?"

"I represent the Boston Social Club," Danny said. "We're the organized-labor arm of the—"

"I know who you are, Officer." Raphelson gave his desk blotter a light pat. "And I'm well acquainted with the BSC. Let me put your mind at ease—we want to help."

Danny nodded. "Mr. Raphelson—"

"Ralph."

585

"Ralph, if you know who I am, then you know I've talked to several of your member groups."

"Oh, I do, yes. I hear you're quite convincing."

Danny's first thought: I am? He wiped some rain off his coat. "If our hand is forced and we have no choice but to walk off the job, would the Central Labor Union support us?"

"Verbally? Of course."

"How about physically?"

"You're talking about a sympathy strike."

Danny met his eyes. "Yes, I am."

Raphelson rubbed his chin with the back of his hand. "You understand how many men the Boston Central Labor Union represents?"

"I've heard a shade under eighty thousand."

"A shade over," Raphelson said. "We just picked up a plumbers local from West Roxbury."

"A shade over then."

"You ever known *eight* men could agree on anything?"

"Rarely."

"And we've got eighty thousand—firemen, plumbers, phone operators, machinists, teamsters, boilermakers, and transit men. And you want me to bring them into agreement to strike on behalf of men who've hit them with clubs when *they* struck?"

"Yes."

"Why?"

"Why not?"

That brought a smile to Raphelson's eyes if not his lips.

"Why not?" Danny repeated. "You know any of those men whose wages have kept up with the cost of living? Any who can keep their families fed and still find the time to read their kids a story at bedtime? They can't, Ralph. They're not treated like workers. They're treated like field hands."

Raphelson laced his hands behind his head and considered Danny. "You're pretty swell at the emotional rhetoric, Coughlin. Pretty swell."

"Thank you."

"It wasn't a compliment. I have to deal in practicalities. Once all the essential-dignity-of-the-working-class sentiments are dispensed with, who's to say my eighty thousand men have jobs to come back to? You seen the latest unemployment figures? Why shouldn't *those* men take my men's jobs? What if your strike drags on? Who's to keep the families fed if the men finally have the time to read those bedtime stories? Their kids' stomachs are rumbling, but glory hallelujah, they've got *fairy tales*. You say, 'Why not?' There are eighty thousand reasons *and* their families why not."

It was cool and dark in the office, the blinds only half open to the dark day, the sole light coming from a small desk lamp by Raphelson's elbow. Danny met Raphelson's eyes and waited him out, sensing a caged anticipation in the man.

Raphelson sighed. "And yet, I'll grant you, I'm interested."

Danny leaned forward in his chair. "Then it's my turn to ask why."

Raphelson fiddled with his window blinds until the slats let in just a bit more of the damp day. "Organized labor is nearing a turning point. We've made our few strides over the past two decades mostly because we caught Big Money by surprise in some of the larger cities. But lately? Big Money's gotten smart. They're framing the debate by taking ownership of the language. You're no longer a workingman fighting for his rights. You're *Bolsheviki*. You're a 'subversive.' Don't like the eighty-hour week? You're an anarchist. Only Commies expect disability pay." He flicked a hand at the window. "It's not just kids who like bedtime stories, Coughlin. We all do. We like them simple and comforting. And right now that's what Big Money is doing to Labor—they're telling a better bedtime story." He turned his head from the window, gave Danny a smile. "Maybe we finally have an opportunity to rewrite it."

"That'd be nice," Danny said.

Raphelson stretched a long arm across the desk. "I'll be in touch."

Danny shook the hand. "Thank you."

"Don't thank me yet, but as you said"—Raphelson glanced at the rain—" 'why not?' "

Commissioner Edwin Upton Curtis tipped the printer's courier a nickel and carried the boxes to his desk. There were four of them, each the size of a brick, and he placed one in the center of his ink blotter and removed the cardboard cover to consider the contents. They reminded him of wedding invitations, and he swallowed a sour and sad reflection of his only daughter, Marie, plump and dull-eyed since the cradle, now fading into spinsterhood with a complacency he found sordid.

He lifted the top slip of paper from the box. The script was quite handsome, utile but bold, the paper a heavy cotton bond the color of flesh. He placed the slip back on the top of the stack and decided to send the printer a personal letter of thanks, a commendation on such a fine job delivered under the stress of a rush order.

Herbert Parker entered from his office next door and said not a word as he crossed to Curtis and joined his friend at the desk, and they stared down at the stack of slips on the ink blotter.

To: _____

Boston Police Officer

By authority conferred on me as Police Commissioner, I hereby discharge you from the Boston Police Department. Said discharge is effective upon receipt of this notice. The cause and reasons for such discharge are as follows:

Specifications: _____

Respectfully,
Edwin Upton Curtis

588

"Who did you use?" Parker said.

"The printer?"

"Yes."

"Freeman and Sons on School Street."

"Freeman. Jewish?"

"Scottish, I think."

"He does fine work."

"Doesn't he, though?"

Fay Hall. Packed. Every man in the department who wasn't on duty and even some who were, the room smelling of the warm rain and several decades' worth of sweat, body odor, cigar and cigarette smoke so thick it slathered the walls like another coat of paint.

Mark Denton was over in one corner of the stage, talking to Frank McCarthy, the just-arrived organizer of the New England chapter of the American Federation of Labor. Danny was in the other corner talking to Tim Rose, a beat cop from the Oh-Two who pounded the bricks around City Hall and Newspaper Row.

"Who told you this?" Danny said.

"Wes Freeman himself."

"The father?"

"No, the son. Father's a sot, a gin junkie. The son does all the work now."

"One thousand discharge slips?"

Tim shook his head. "Five hundred discharge slips, five hundred suspensions."

"Already printed."

Tim nodded. "And delivered to Useless Curtis himself at eight sharp this a.m."

Danny caught himself tugging on his chin and nodding at the same time, another habit he'd inherited from his father. He stopped and gave Tim what he hoped was a confident smile. "Well, I guess they took their dancing shoes off, uh?"

"I guess they did." Tim gestured with his chin at Mark Denton and Frank McCarthy. "Who's the swell with Denton?"

"Organizer with the AFL."

Tim's eyes pulsed. "He bring the charter?"

"He brought the charter, Tim."

"Guess we took off our dancing shoes then, too, eh, Dan?" A smile exploded across Tim's face.

"We did at that." Danny clapped his shoulder as Mark Denton picked the megaphone off the floor and stepped to the dais.

Danny crossed to the stage, and Mark Denton knelt at the edge to give Danny his ear and Danny told him about the discharge and suspension slips.

"You're sure?"

"Positive. They got to his office at eight this morning. Solid info."

Mark shook his hand. "You're going to make a fine vice president."

Danny took a step back. "What?"

Denton gave him a sly smile and stepped up to the dais. "Gentlemen, thank you for coming. This man to my left is Frank McCarthy. He's your New England rep with the AF of L. And he's come to bring us something."

As McCarthy took the dais and the megaphone, Kevin McRae and several other officers of what was about to become the extinct BSC stopped at each row to hand out ballots that the men passed down the rows, their eyes pinwheeling.

"Gentlemen of the Boston Police Department," McCarthy said, "once you mark those ballots 'yay' or 'nay,' a decision will have been made as to whether you remain the Boston Social Club or accept this charter I raise before you and become, instead, the Boston Police Union Number sixteen thousand eight hundred and seven of the American Federation of Labor. You will, with some measure of sadness I'm sure, be saying good-bye to the notion and the name of the Boston Social Club, but in return, you will join a brotherhood that is two million strong. Two million strong,

590

gentlemen. Think about that. You will never feel alone again. You will never feel weak or at the mercy of your bosses. Even the mayor, himself, will be afraid to tell you what to do."

"He already is!" someone shouted, and laughter spread through the room.

Nervous laughter, Danny thought, as the men realized the import of what they were about to do. No going back after today. Leaving a whole other world behind, one in which their rights weren't respected, yes, but that lack of respect was at least predictable. It made the ground firm underfoot. But this new ground was something else again. Foreign ground. And for all McCarthy's talk of brotherhood, lonely ground. Lonely because it was strange, because all bearings were unfamiliar. The potential for disgrace and disaster lay ahead everywhere, and every man in the room felt it.

They passed the ballots back down the rows. Don Slatterly rounded up the stacks from the men collecting them like ushers at mass and carried the entire fourteen hundred toward Danny, his steps a bit soggy, his face drained of color.

Danny took the stack from his hands, and Slatterly said, "Heavy, uh?"

Danny gave him a shaky smile and nodded.

"Men," Frank McCarthy called, "do you all attest that you answered the ballot question truthfully and signed your names? A show of hands."

Every hand in the room rose.

"So that our young officer to stage left doesn't have to count them right here and right now, could I get a show of hands as to how many of you voted in favor of accepting this charter and joining the AF of L? If all of you who voted 'yay,' would please stand."

Danny looked up from the stack in his hands as fourteen hundred chairs pushed back and fourteen hundred men rose to their feet.

McCarthy raised his megaphone. "Welcome to the American Federation of Labor, gentlemen."

The collective scream that exploded in Fay Hall pushed Danny's spine into the center of his chest and flooded his brain with white light.

Mark Denton snatched the stack of ballots from his hands and tossed them high above his head and they hung in the air and then began to float downward as Mark lifted him off his feet and kissed his cheek and hugged him so hard his bones howled.

"We did it!" Tears streamed down Mark's face. "We fucking did it!"

Danny looked out through the floating ballots at the men toppling their chairs and hugging and howling and crying and he grabbed the top of Mark's head and sank his fingers into his hair and shook it, howling along with the rest of them.

Once Mark let him down, they were rushed. The men poured onto the stage and some slipped on the ballots and one grabbed the charter from McCarthy's hand and went running back and forth across the stage with it. Danny was tackled and then lifted and then passed across a sea of hands, bouncing and laughing and helpless, and a thought occurred to him before he could suppress it:

What if we're wrong?

After the meeting, Steve Coyle found Danny on the street. Even in his euphoria—he'd been unanimously voted vice president of Boston Police Union 16807 less than an hour ago—he felt an all-too-familiar irritation at Steve's presence. The guy was never sober anymore, and he had this way of looking into your eyes nonstop, as if searching your body for his old life.

"She's back," he said to Danny.

"Who?"

"Tessa. In the North End." He pulled his flask from a tattered coat pocket. He had trouble getting the stopper out. He had to squint and take a deep breath to get a grip.

"You eaten today?" Danny asked.

"You hear me?" Steve said. "Tessa's back in the North End."

"I heard. Your source told you?"

"Yeah."

Danny put his hand on his old friend's shoulder. "Let me buy you a meal. Some soup."

"I don't need fucking soup. She's come back to her old haunts because of the strike."

"We're not striking. We just joined the AF of L."

Steve went on like he hadn't heard. "They're all coming back. Every subversive on the Eastern Seaboard is raising stakes and coming here. When we strike—"

We.

"—they think it's going to be a free-for-all. St. Petersburg. They're going to stir the pot and—"

"So where is she?" Danny said, trying to keep his annoyance at bay. "Exactly?"

"My source won't say."

"Won't say? Or won't say for free?"

"For free, yeah."

"How much does he want this time? Your source?"

Steve looked at the sidewalk. "Twenty."

"Just a week's pay this time, huh?"

Steve cocked his head. "You know, if you don't want to find her, Coughlin, that's fine."

Danny shrugged. "I got other things on my mind right now, Steve. You understand."

Steve nodded several times.

"Big man," he said and walked up the street.

The next morning, upon hearing word of the BSC's unanimous decision to join the American Federation of Labor, Edwin Upton Curtis issued an emergency order canceling all vacations for division commanders, captains, lieutenants, and sergeants.

He summoned Superintendent Crowley to his office and

let him stand at attention before his desk for half a minute before he turned from his window to look at him.

"I'm told they elected officers to the new union last night."

Crowley nodded. "As I understand it, yes, sir."

"I'll need their names."

"Yes, sir. I'll get those immediately."

"And the men who distributed the sign-up sheets in each of the precincts."

"Sir?"

Curtis raised his eyebrows, always an effective tool when he'd been Mayor Curtis in the long-ago. "The men, as I understand it, were given sign-up sheets last week to see how many would be interested in accepting an AFL charter. Correct?"

"Yes, sir."

"I want the names of the men who brought those sign-up sheets into the station houses."

"That may take a little longer, sir."

"Then it takes longer. Dismissed."

Crowley snap-turned on his heel and headed for the door.

"Superintendent Crowley."

"Yes, sir." Crowley turned back to him.

"You have no sympathies in this area, I trust."

Crowley's eyes fixed on a spot a few feet above Edwin Upton Curtis's head. "None, sir."

"Look me in the eyes if you please, sir."

Crowley met his eyes.

"How many abstentions?"

"Sir?"

"In last night's vote, man."

"I believe none, sir."

Curtis nodded. "How many 'nay' votes?"

"I believe none, sir."

Edwin Upton Curtis felt a constricting in his chest, the old angina perhaps, and a great sadness filled him. It never had to come to this. Never. He'd been a friend to these men. He'd offered them a fair raise. He'd appointed committees to study

594

their grievances. But they wanted more. They always wanted more. Children at a birthday party, unimpressed with their gifts.

None. Not a single nay vote.

Spare the rod, spoil the child.

Bolsheviks.

"That'll be all, Superintendent."

N ora rolled off Danny in a heap, let loose a loud groan, and pressed her forehead into the pillow, as if she were trying to burrow through it.

Danny ran his palm down her back. "Good, uh?"

She growled a laugh into the pillow and then turned her chin to face him. "Can I say *fuck* in your presence?"

"I think you just did."

"You're not offended?"

"Offended? Let me smoke a cigarette and I'm ready to go again. Look at you. God."

"What?"

"You're just . . ." He ran his hand from her heel, up the back of her calf, over her ass and across her back again. "Fucking gorgeous."

"Now you said *fuck*."

"I always say *fuck*." He kissed her shoulder, then the back of her ear. "Why did you want to say *fuck*, by the way? Or, in your case, *fook*."

She sank her teeth into his neck. "I wanted to say I've never fucked a vice president before."

"You've limited yourself to treasurers?"

She slapped his chest. "Aren't you proud of yourself, boy?"

He sat up and took his pack of Murads from the nightstand and lit one. "Honestly?"

"Of course."

"I'm . . . honored," he said. "When they called my name out on the ballot—I mean, honey, I had no idea it was going to be there."

"Yeah?" She ran her tongue across his abdomen. She took the cigarette from his hand and took a puff before handing it back to him.

"No idea," he said. "Until Denton tipped me just before the first ballot. But, shit, I won an office I didn't even know I was running for. It was crazy."

She slid back on top of him and he loved the weight of her there. "So you're honored but not proud?"

"I'm scared," he said.

She laughed and took his cigarette again. "Aiden, Aiden," she whispered, "you're not afraid of anything."

"Sure, I am. I'm afraid all the time. Afraid of you."

She placed the cigarette back in his mouth. "Afraid of me now, are you?"

"Terrified." He ran a hand along the side of her face and through her hair. "Scared I'll let you down."

She kissed his hand. "You'll never let me down."

"That's what the men think, too."

"So what is it you're afraid of again?"

"That you're all wrong."

On August 11, with warm rain sluicing against the window in his office, Commissioner Edwin Upton Curtis composed an amendment to the rules and regulations of the Boston Police Department. That amendment to Rule 35, Section 19, read in part:

> No member of the force shall belong to any organization, club or body composed of present and past members of the force which is affiliated with or part of any organization, club or body outside of the department.

Commissioner Curtis, upon finishing what would become commonly known as Rule 35, turned to Herbert Parker and showed him the draft.

Parker read it and wished that it could be harsher. But these were upside-down days in the country. Even unions, those Bolsheviki sworn enemies of free trade, had to be coddled. For a time. For a time.

"Sign it, Edwin."

Curtis had been hoping for a bit more effusive reaction, but he signed it anyway and then sighed at the condensation on his windows.

"I hate rain."

"Summer rain's the worst, Edwin, yes."

An hour later, Curtis released the newly signed amendment to the press.

Thomas and the seventeen other captains met in the ante-room outside Superintendent Crowley's office in Pemberton Square. They stood in a loose circle and brushed the beads of water off their coats and hats. They coughed and complained about their drivers and the traffic and the miserable weather.

Thomas found himself standing beside Don Eastman, who ran Division 3 on Beacon Hill. Eastman concentrated on straightening his damp shirt cuffs and spoke in a low voice. "I hear they'll be running an ad in the papers."

"Don't believe every rumor you hear."

"For replacements, Thomas. A standing militia of armed volunteers."

"As I said, rumors."

"Rumors or no, Thomas, if the men strike, we'll see fecal gravity at work like never before. Ain't a man in this room who won't be covered in shit."

"If he ain't been run out of town on rails," Bernard King, the captain of Division 14, said, stubbing out his cigarette on the marble floor.

"Everyone keep calm," Thomas said quietly.

The door to Crowley's office opened and the big man himself walked out and gave only a desultory wave to let them know they should follow him down the hall.

They did so, some men still sniffling from the rain, and Crowley turned into a conference room at the end of the hall and the phalanx of captains followed suit and took seats at the long table in the center. There were no coffee urns or pots of tea on the sideboards, no slices of cake or trays of sweets, none of the amenities they'd become accustomed to as their due at meetings such as these. In fact, there were no waiters or junior staff of any kind in the room. Just Superintendent Michael Crowley and his eighteen captains. Not even a secretary to record the minutes.

Crowley stood with the great window behind him, steamed over from the rain and humidity. The shapes of tall buildings rose indistinct and tremulous behind him, as if they might vanish. Crowley had cut short his annual vacation to Hyannis, and his face was ruddy with the sun, which made his teeth seem all the whiter when he spoke.

"Rule Thirty-five, which was just added to the department code, outlaws affiliation with any national union. That means that all fourteen hundred men who joined the AF of L could be terminated." He pinched the skin between his eyes and the bridge of his nose and held up a hand to staunch their questions. "Three years ago, we switched from nightsticks to the pocket billies. Most of those nightsticks, however, are still in the possession of the officers for dress occasions. All precinct captains will confiscate those nightsticks starting today. We expect all of them in our possession by week's end."

Jesus, Thomas thought. They're preparing to arm the militia.

"In each of the eighteen precincts, an AFL sign-up sheet was distributed. You are to identify the officer who was in charge of collecting those signatures." Crowley turned his back to them and looked at the window, now opaque with moisture. "The commissioner will be sending me a list at day's end of patrolmen I'm to personally interview in regards to dereliction of duty. I'm told there could be as many as twenty names on that list."

He turned back and placed his hands on his chair. A large man with a soft face that could not hide the exhaustion that bulged from under his eyes, it was said of Michael Crowley that he was a patrolman mistakenly readorned in upper brass finery. A cop's cop who'd come up through the ranks and knew the names not only of every man in all eighteen precincts but also the names of the janitors who emptied the wastebaskets and mopped the floors. As a young sergeant, he'd broken the Trunk Murder Case, a front-pager if ever one existed, and the publicity that followed sent him shooting— quite helplessly, it was noted—to the top ranks of the department. Even Thomas, cynical as he could be about the motives of the human animal, fully acknowledged that Michael Crowley loved his men and none more so than the least of them.

His eyes found theirs. "I'm the first to acknowledge that the men have legitimate grievances. But a moving object cannot pass through a wall of greater mass and density. It cannot. And, as of this point, Commissioner Curtis is that wall. If they continue to lay down gauntlets, we will pass a point of no return."

"With all due respect, Michael," Don Eastman said, "what would you expect us to do about it?"

"Talk to them," Crowley said. "To your men. Eye to eye. Convince them that not even pyrrhic victory awaits if they put the commissioner in a position he finds untenable. This is not about Boston any longer."

Billy Coogan, a clueless flunky if ever there was one, waved a hand at that. "Ah, Michael, it 'tis, sure. This will all blow over."

Crowley gave him a bitter smile. "I'm afraid you're wrong, Billy. The police in London and Liverpool were said to take cues from our unrest. Liverpool burned, or did you not hear? It took warships of the English fleet—warships, Billy—to quell the mob. We've reports that in Jersey City and D.C., negotiations are afoot with the AFL. And right here—in

Brockton, in Springfield and New Bedford, Lawrence and Worcester—the police departments wait to see what we will do. So, with all due respect as well, Billy, it's far more than a Boston problem. The whole sodding world is watching." He slumped in his chair. "There have been over two thousand labor strikes in this country so far this year, gentlemen. Put your heads into that number—that's ten a day. Would you like to know how many of those turned out well for the men who struck?"

No one answered.

Crowley nodded at their silence and kneaded his forehead with his fingers. "Talk to your men, gentlemen. Stop this train before the brakes have burned off. Stop it before nobody can stop it and we're all trapped inside."

In Washington, Rayme Finch and John Hoover met for breakfast at The White Palace Café on the corner of Ninth and D, not far from Pennsylvania Avenue. They met there once a week unless Finch was out of town on Bureau business, and as long as they'd been doing so, Hoover always found something wrong with the food or the drink and sent it back. This time it was his tea. Not steeped enough for his liking. When the waitress returned with a fresh pot, he made her wait while he poured it into his cup, stirred in just enough milk to muddy the waters, and then took a small sip.

"Acceptable." Hoover flicked the back of his hand at her and she gave him a look of hate and walked away.

Finch was pretty sure Hoover was a fag. Drank with one pinky extended, finicky and fussy in general, lived with his mother—all the signs. Of course with Hoover, you could never be sure. If Finch had discovered he fucked ponies in the mouth while painting himself in blackface and singing spirituals, he wouldn't have been surprised. Nothing surprised Finch anymore. In his time with the Bureau, he'd learned one thing about men above all others: we were all sick. Sick in our heads. Sick in our hearts. Sick to our souls.

"Boston," Hoover said and stirred his tea.

"What about it, John?"

"The police have learned nothing from Montreal, from Liverpool."

"Apparently not. You really think they'll strike?"

"They're predominantly Hibernian," Hoover said with a delicate shrug, "a race that never let prudence or reason cloud its judgment. Time and again, throughout history, the Irish have boasted their way into apocalypse. I find no cause to think they'll do any different in Boston."

Finch sipped his coffee. "Nice opportunity for Galleani to stir the pot, if they do."

Hoover nodded. "Galleani and every other dime store subversive in the area. Not to mention the garden variety criminal element will have a field day."

"Should we involve ourselves?"

Hoover stared at him with those keen, depthless eyes. "To what end? This could be worse than Seattle. Worse than anything this country's seen thus far. And if the public is forced to question whether this nation can police itself at local and state levels, who will they turn to?"

Finch allowed himself a smile. Say what you would about John, that sleek ugly mind of his was gorgeous. If he didn't step on the wrong toes during his rise, there'd be no stopping him.

"The federal government," Finch said.

Hoover nodded. "They're tarring the road for us, Mr. Finch. All we have to do is wait for it to dry and then drive straight up it."

CHAPTER *thirty-four*

Danny was on the phone in the squad room, talking to Dipsy Figgis of the One-Two about getting extra chairs for tonight's meeting, when Kevin McRae wandered in, a piece of paper in his hand, a dazed look on his face, the kind a man got when he saw something he'd never expected, a long-dead relative, perhaps, or a kangaroo in his basement.

"Kev'?"

Kevin looked over at Danny as if he were trying to place him.

"What's wrong?" Danny said.

McRae crossed to him, extending his hand, the paper between his fingers. "I've been suspended, Dan." His eyes widened and he ran the piece of paper over his head, as if it were a towel. "Fucking suspended. You believe that? Curtis says we all have to attend a trial on charges of dereliction."

"All?" Danny said. "How many men were suspended?"

"Nineteen, I heard. Nineteen." He looked at Danny with the face of a child lost at Saturday market. "What the fuck am I going to do?" He waved the piece of paper at the squad room and his voice grew soft, almost a whisper. "This was my life."

All the chief officers of the nascent AFL–Boston Police Union were suspended except for Danny. All the men who'd distributed and collected sign-up sheets for the

AFL charter were suspended as well. Except for Danny.

He called his father. "Why not me?"

"What do you think?"

"I don't know. That's why I'm calling you, Dad."

He heard the rattle of ice cubes in a glass as his father sighed and then took a drink. "I've been after you your whole life to take up chess."

"You were after me my whole life to take up piano, too."

"That was your mother. I just enforced the idea. Chess, however, Aiden, that would have helped about now." Another sigh. "Far more than your ability to play a rag. What do the men think?"

"About?"

"About why you were given an exemption? They're all about to stand before Curtis for dismissal, and you, the vice president of your *union*, you're free as a lark. If you were in their shoes, what would you suspect?"

Danny, standing at the phone Mrs. DiMassi kept on a table in the foyer, wished he had his own drink as he heard his father pour a refill and add a few cubes to his glass.

"If I were in their shoes? I'd think I still had my job because I was your son."

"Which is exactly what Curtis wants them to think."

Danny placed the side of his head to the wall and closed his eyes, heard his father fire up a cigar and suck and puff, suck and puff, until he got it going.

"So that's the play," Danny said. "Dissension in the ranks. Divide and conquer."

His father barked a laugh. "No, boy, that's not *the* play. That's the opening act. Aiden, you silly, silly child. I do love you, but apparently I didn't *raise* you proper. How do you think the press is going to respond when they discover that only one of the elected union officials *wasn't* suspended? First, they'll report that it's proof the commissioner is a reasonable man and the city is obviously impartial and that the nineteen suspended men must have done something because the vice president himself wasn't suspended."

"But then," Danny said, seeing hope for the first time on this black day, "they'll see that it's a ruse, that I'm just a token symbol of impartiality, and they'll—"

"You idiot," his father said, and Danny heard the thump of his heels as they came off the edge of his desk. "You idiot. The press will get curious, Aiden. They'll dig. And fairly quickly they'll unearth the fact that you are the son of a precinct captain. And they'll spend a day talking about that before they decide to investigate further, and sooner or later, one honest scribe will run into one seemingly innocuous desk sergeant who mentions, quite casually, something along the lines of 'the incident.' And the reporter will say, 'What incident?' To which the desk sergeant will respond, 'I don't know what you're talking about.' Then that reporter will really dig, my boy. And we all know that your recent affairs will stand up dimly to scrutiny. Curtis designated you the staked goat, son, and the beasts in the woods have already started sniffing your scent."

"So what's this idiot supposed to do, Dad?"

"Capitulate."

"Can't do that."

"Yes, you can. You just don't see the angles yet. The opportunity will come, I promise. They're not as afraid of your union as you think, but they are, trust me, afraid. Use that. They will never yield, Aiden, on the affiliation with the AF of L. They can't. But if you play that chip correctly, they will yield on other issues."

"Dad, if we give up the AFL affiliation we'll have corrupted everything we—"

"Take what you will from my musings," his father said. "Good night, son, and the gods be with you."

Mayor Andrew J. Peters believed implicitly in the primacy of a single principle: Things had a way of working themselves out.

So many men wasted so much valuable time and energy placing faith in the canard that they could control their destinies when, in fact, the world would continue to entangle and disentangle itself whether they were part of it or not. Why, one just had to look back at that terrible foreign war to see the folly of making rash decisions. Any decisions, really. Think, Andrew Peters would say to Starr on late afternoons like these, what a different outcome would have been accomplished if, after the death of Franz Ferdinand, the Austrians had refrained from rattling their sabers and the Serbians had done the same. Think, too, how pointless it was for Gavrilo Princip, that hopeless fool, to assassinate the archduke in the first place. Just think! All those lives lost, all that earth scorched, and to what end? If cooler heads had prevailed, if men had had the temperance to refrain from acting until their countrymen forgot all about it and went on to other thoughts and other things? What a nice world we'd have today.

For it was the war that had poisoned so many young men's minds with thoughts of self-determination. This summer, colored men who'd fought overseas had been the main agitators behind the civil disorder that had resulted in the slaughter of their own people in Washington, Omaha, and most terribly in Chicago. Not that Peters was justifying the behavior of the whites who had killed them. Hardly. But you could see how it had happened, the coloreds trying to upset the applecart like that. People didn't like change. They didn't want to be upset. They wanted cool drinks on hot days and their meals served on time.

"Self-determination," he muttered on the deck as Starr, lying beside him, tummy down on a chaise, stirred slightly.

"What's that, Poppa?"

He leaned over from his own chaise and kissed her shoulder and considered unbuttoning his trousers. But the clouds were massing and the sky was low and the sea had darkened, as if from wine and grief.

"Nothing, darling."

Starr closed her eyes. A beautiful child. Beautiful! Cheeks that reminded him of apples so ripe they might burst. An ass to match. And everything in between so lush and firm that Andrew J. Peters, mayor of the great city of Boston, occasionally imagined himself an ancient Greek or Roman when he was inside her. Starr Faithful—what an apt name. His lover, his cousin. Fourteen years old this summer, and yet more mature and lascivious than Martha would ever be.

She lay nude before him, Edenic, and when the first raindrop hit her spine and splattered, he removed his boater and placed it on her ass and she giggled and said she liked rain. She turned her head and reached for his waistband and said, in point of fact, she *loved* rain. In that moment, he saw something as dark and stricken as the sea pass through her eyes. A thought. No, more than a thought, a doubt. It unsettled him—she was not supposed to feel doubt; the concubines of Roman emperors, he was reasonably sure, hadn't—and as he allowed her to unbuckle his belt, he felt visited by an ill-defined but acute sense of loss. His pants fell to his ankles and he decided it might be best to get back to the city and see if he could talk some sense into everyone.

He looked out at the sea. So endless. He said, "I am the mayor, after all."

Starr smiled up at him. "I know you are, Poppa, and you're the bestus at it."

The hearing for the nineteen suspended officers occurred on the twenty-sixth of August in the Pemberton Square office of Police Commissioner Curtis. Danny was in attendance, as was Curtis's right-hand man, Herbert Parker. Clarence Rowley and James Vahey stood before Curtis as the attorneys-of-record for all nineteen defendants. One reporter each from the *Globe*, *Transcript*, *Herald*, and the *Standard* was allowed inside. And that was it. In previous administrations, three captains and the commissioner made up the trial board, but under Curtis's regime, Curtis himself was the sole judge.

"You will note," Curtis said to the reporters, "that I have allowed the one nonsuspended officer of the illegal AF of L policemen's union to attend so that no one can claim this 'union' was underrepresented. You will also note that the defendants are represented by two esteemed counsel, Mr. Vahey and Mr. Rowley, both with prodigious experience representing the interests of labor. I have brought no counsel on my behalf."

"With all due respect, Commissioner," Danny said, "you're not on trial, sir."

One of the reporters nodded furiously at the comment and scribbled on his notepad. Curtis flicked a pair of dead eyes at Danny and then looked out at the nineteen men seated before him in rickety wooden chairs.

"You men have been charged with dereliction of duty, the worst offense a peace officer can commit. You have, more specifically, been charged with violation of Rule Thirty-five of the Boston Police Code of Conduct, which states that no officer may affiliate with any organization that is not part of the Boston Police Department."

Clarence Rowley said, "By that yardstick, Commissioner, none of these men could belong to a veterans' group, say, or the Fraternal Order of Elks."

Two reporters and one patrolman snickered.

Curtis reached for a glass of water. "I'm not finished yet, Mr. Rowley. If you please, sir, this is not a criminal court. This is an internal trial of the Boston Police Department, and if you are going to argue the legality of Rule Thirty-five, you'll have to bring a case before the Suffolk Superior Court. The only question to be answered here today is whether these men violated Rule Thirty-five, not the soundness of the rule itself, sir." Curtis looked out at the room. "Patrolman Denton, stand at attention."

Mark Denton stood in his dress blues and tucked his domed hat under his arm.

"Patrolman Denton, are you affiliated with Boston Police

Union Number Sixteen Thousand Eight Hundred and Seven of the American Federation of Labor?"

"I am, sir."

"Are you not, in fact, the president of said union?"

"I am, sir. Proudly."

"Your pride is of no relevance to this board."

"Board?" Mark Denton said, looking to the left and right of Curtis.

Curtis took a sip of water. "And did you not distribute sign-up sheets within your station house for affiliation with the aforementioned American Federation of Labor?"

"With the same aforementioned pride, sir," Denton said.

"You may sit back down, Patrolman," Curtis said. "Patrolman Kevin McRae, stand at attention . . ."

It went on for over two hours, Curtis asking the same monotonous questions in the same monotonous tone and each cop answering with varying degrees of petulance, contempt, or fatalism.

When it was time for defense counsel to take the floor, James Vahey did the talking. Long the general counsel for the Street and Electric Railway Employees of America, he'd been famous since before Danny was born, and it was Mark Denton's coup to bring him into this fight just two weeks ago at the urging of Samuel Gompers. He moved with an athlete's fluidity as he strode from the back and flashed a slim, confident smile at the nineteen men before turning to face Curtis.

"While I agree that we are not here today to argue the legality of Rule Thirty-five, I find it telling that the commissioner himself, the author of said rule, admits its nebulous status. If the commissioner himself does not believe firmly in the soundness of his own rule, what are we to make of it? Why, we are to make of it what it is—quite simply the greatest invasion of a man's personal liberty—"

Curtis banged his gavel several times.

"—and the most far-reaching attempt to restrict his freedom of action I have ever known."

Curtis raised the gavel again, but Vahey pointed directly at his face.

"You, sir, have denied these men their most basic human rights as workers. You have consistently refused to raise their pay to a level above the poverty line, provide them with safe and hygienic quarters in which to work and sleep, and have demanded they work hours of such duration that not only is their safety jeopardized but that of the public as well. And now you sit before us, as sole judge, and attempt to obfuscate the sworn responsibility *you* had toward these men. It is a low action, sir. A low action. Nothing you have said today has called into question these men's commitment to the populace of this great city. These men have not abandoned their posts, have not failed to answer the call of duty, have never, not a sole time, failed to uphold the law and protect and serve the people of Boston. Had you evidence to the contrary, I trust you would have produced it by now. Instead, the only failure—and, for the record, I use that term ironically—that these men are guilty of is that they have failed to capitulate to your desire that they not affiliate themselves with a national labor union. That is all. And given that a simple calendar will show that your insertion of Rule Thirty-five to be of rather dubious urgency, I am quite confident any judge in the land will deem that rule the naked gambit to restrict these men's rights that we all see it as here today." He turned to the men and the reporters beyond, resplendent in his suit and his grace and his white-white hair. "I am not going to *defend* these men because there is nothing to defend. It is not they who should have their patriotism or Americanism questioned in this room today," Vahey thundered. "It is you, sir!"

Curtis banged his gavel repeatedly as Parker shouted for order and the men hooted and applauded and rose to their feet.

Danny was reminded of what Ralph Raphelson had said about emotional rhetoric, and he wondered—even as he was

609

as swept up in and stirred by Vahey's speech as the rest of the men—if it had accomplished anything other than a fanning of the flames.

When Vahey returned to his seat, the men sat. Now it was Danny's turn. He took the floor in front of a red-faced Curtis.

"I'm going to keep it simple. The issue before us, it seems to me, is whether affiliation with the American Federation of Labor will lessen the efficiency of the police force. Commissioner Curtis, I say with full confidence that it hasn't thus far. A simple study of arrest records, citations given, and overall crime rate in the eighteen districts will bear this out. And I further state, with utter confidence, that it will remain so. We are policemen, first and foremost, and sworn to uphold the law and uphold the peace. That, I assure you, will never change. Not on our watch."

The men clapped as Danny took his seat. Curtis rose from his desk. He looked shaky, impossibly pale, his tie loosened at the throat, strands of hair pointing askew.

"I will take all remarks and testimony under consideration," he said, his hands gripping the edge of his desk. "Good day, gentlemen."

And with that, he and Herbert Parker walked out of the room.

ABLE-BODIED MEN NEEDED

Boston Police Department seeking recruits for Volunteer Police Force to be headed by former Police Supt. William Pierce. White males only. War experience and/or proven athletic ability preferred. Interested applicants apply at the Commonwealth Armory between the hours of 9 A.M. and 5 P.M., M–F.

Luther placed the newspaper on the bench where he'd found it. A volunteer police force. Sounded like arming a bunch of white men either too dumb to hold on to a regular job or so desperate to prove their manhood they'd leave the good jobs they had. Either way, a bad combination. He imagined the same ad soliciting black men to fill those jobs and laughed out loud, a sound that surprised him. He wasn't the only one—a white man one bench over stiffened, stood, and walked away.

Luther had spent a rare day off wandering the city because he was about to come out of his skin. A child he'd never seen waited for him in Tulsa. His child. Lila, softening toward him by the day (he hoped), waited there, too. He'd once believed the world was a sprawling party just waiting for him to join it and that party would be filled with interesting men and beautiful women and they'd all fill the empty parts of him somehow, each in their own way, until there was nothing left to fill and Luther would feel whole for the first time since his father had left the family. But now he realized that wasn't the case. He'd met Danny and Nora and felt for them a fondness so piercing it continued to surprise him. And, Lord knows, he loved the Giddreauxs, had found in them a pair of grandparents he'd often dreamed were out there. Yet ultimately it didn't make no difference because his hopes and his heart and his loves lay in Greenwood. That party? Never going to happen. Because even if it did, Luther'd just as soon be home. With his woman. With his son.

Desmond.

That was the name Lila'd given him, one Luther remembered half agreeing on back before he'd run afoul of the Deacon. Desmond Laurence, after Lila's grandfather, a man who'd taught her the Bible while she sat on his knee, probably gave her that steel in her spine, too, for all Luther knew, because it had to have come from somewhere.

Desmond.

A good firm name. Luther'd taken to loving it over the summer months, loving it in a way that brought tears to his eyes. He'd brought *Desmond* into the world and Desmond would do fine things someday.

If Luther could get back to him. To her. To them.

If a man was lucky, he was moving toward something his whole life. He was building a life, working for a white man, yes, but working for his wife, for his children, for his dream that their life would be better because he'd been part of it. That, Luther finally understood, was what he'd failed to remember in Tulsa and what his father had never known at all. Men were supposed to *do* for those they loved. Simple as that. Clean and pure as that.

Luther had gotten so sucked up, so turned around by the simple need to move—anywhere, anytime, anyhow—that he'd forgotten that the motion had to be put in service of a purpose.

Now he knew. Now he knew.

And he couldn't do a damn thing about it. Even if he took care of McKenna (one hell of an *if*), he still couldn't move toward his family because Smoke was waiting. And he couldn't convince Lila to move toward him (he'd tried several times since Christmas) because she felt Greenwood was home and also suspected—quite understandably—that if she did pick up and move, Smoke would send someone to follow.

Going to come out of my skin, Luther thought for the fiftieth time that day, right fucking out.

He picked the paper up off the bench and stood. Across Washington Street, in front of Kresge's Five & Dime, two men watched him. They wore pale hats and seersucker suits, and they were both small and scared-looking and they might have been comical—stock clerks dressed up to look respectable— if it weren't for the wide brown holsters they wore over their hips, the pistol butts exposed to the world. Stock clerks with guns. Other stores had hired private detectives, and the banks were demanding U.S. marshals, but the smaller businesses had to make do by training their everyday employees in the handling of weaponry. More volatile than that volunteer police force, in a way, because Luther assumed—or hoped anyway—that the volunteer coppers would at least receive a bit more training, be afforded a bit more leadership. These

612

hired help, though—these clerks and bag boys and sons and sons-in-law of jewelers and furriers and bakers and livery operators—you saw them all over the city now, and they were scared. Terrified. Jumpy. And armed.

Luther couldn't help himself—he saw them eyeing him, so he walked toward them, crossing the street even though that hadn't been his original intention, giving his steps just a bit of saunter, a dash of colored man's edge to it, throwing the glint of a smile into his eyes. The two little men exchanged looks, and one of them wiped his hand off the side of his pants just below his pistol.

"Nice day, isn't it?" Luther reached the sidewalk.

Neither of the men said a word.

"Big blue sky," Luther said. "First clean air in about a week? Ya'll should *enjoy* it."

The pair remained silent and Luther tipped his hat to them and continued on up the sidewalk. It had been a foolish act, particularly since he'd just been thinking about Desmond, about Lila, about becoming a more responsible man. But something about white men with guns, he was sure, would always bring out the devil in him.

And judging by the mood in the city, there was about to be a whole lot more of them. He passed his third Emergency Relief tent of the day, saw some nurses inside setting up tables and wheeling beds around. Earlier that afternoon, he'd walked through the West End and up through Scollay Square, and just about every third block, it seemed, he stumbled upon ambulances grouped together, waiting for what was starting to feel like the unavoidable. He looked down at the *Herald* in his hand, at the front-page editorial they'd run above the fold:

> Seldom has the feeling in this community been more
> tense than it is today over the conditions in the police
> department. We are at a turning of the ways. We shall
> take a long step toward "Russianizing" ourselves, or

Poor Danny, Luther thought. Poor honest, outmatched son of a bitch.

James Jackson Storrow was the wealthiest man in Boston. When he'd become president of General Motors, he'd reorganized it from top to bottom without costing a single worker his job or a sole stockholder his confidence. He founded the Boston Chamber of Commerce and had chaired the Cost of Living Commission in the days leading up to the Great War. During that conflict of waste and despair, he'd been appointed federal fuel administrator by Woodrow Wilson and had seen to it that New England homes never wanted for coal or oil, sometimes using his own personal credit to ensure the shipments left their depots on time.

He'd heard others say he was a man who wore his power lightly, but the truth was, he'd never believed that power, in any shape or form, was anything more than the intemperate protrusion of the egomaniacal heart. Since all egomaniacs were insecure to their frightened cores, they thus wielded "power" barbarically so the world would not find them out.

Terrible days, these, between the "powerful" and the "powerless," the whole absurd battle opening up a new front here in this city, the city he loved more than any other, and this front possibly the worst anywhere since October of '17.

Storrow received Mayor Peters in the billiards room of his Louisburg Square home, noting as the mayor entered that he was well tanned. This confirmed for Storrow the suspicion he'd long held that Peters was a frivolous man, one ill-suited to his job in normal circumstances, but in the current climate, egregiously so.

An affable chap, of course, as so many frivolous men were,

crossing to Storrow with a bright, eager smile and a spring in his step.

"Mr. Storrow, so kind of you to see me."

"The honor is mine, Mr. Mayor."

The mayor's handshake was unexpectedly firm, and Storrow noted a clarity in the man's blue eyes that made him wonder if there was more to him than he'd initially assumed. Surprise me, Mr. Mayor, surprise me.

"You know why I've come," Peters said.

"I presume to discuss the situation with the police."

"Exactly so, sir."

Storrow led the mayor to two cherry leather armchairs. Between them sat a table with two decanters and two glasses. One decanter held brandy. The other, water. He waved his hand at the decanters as a way of offering them to the mayor.

Peters nodded his thanks and poured a glass of water.

Storrow crossed one leg over the other and reconsidered the man yet again. He pointed at his own glass, and Peters filled it with water and they both sat back.

Storrow said, "How do you envision I can be of assistance?"

"You're the most respected man in the city," Peters said. "You are also beloved, sir, for all that you did to keep homes warm during the war. I need you and as many men as you choose from the Chamber of Commerce to form a commission to study the issues the policemen have raised and the counterarguments of Police Commissioner Curtis to decide which have wisdom and which, ultimately, should win the day."

"Would this commission have the power to rule or merely to recommend?"

"City bylaws state that unless there is evidence of reckless misconduct on the part of the police commissioner, he has final say in all issues regarding police matters. He can't be overruled by either myself or Governor Coolidge."

"So we'd have limited power."

"Power to recommend only, yes, sir. But with the esteem in

which you are held, not only in this state, but in this region, and at a national level as well, I feel confident that your recommendation would be taken to heart with the appropriate respect."

"When would I form such a commission?"

"Without delay. Tomorrow."

Storrow finished his water and uncorked the brandy decanter. He pointed it at Peters, and the mayor tilted his empty glass in his direction and Storrow poured.

"As far as the policemen's union, I see no way we can ever allow the affiliation with the American Federation of Labor to stand."

"As you say then, sir."

"I'll want to meet with the union representatives immediately. Tomorrow afternoon. Can you arrange it?"

"Done."

"As to Commissioner Curtis, what's your sense of the man, Mr. Mayor?"

"Angry," Peters said.

Storrow nodded. "That's the man I remember. He served his term as mayor when I was overseer at Harvard. We met on a few occasions. I remember only the anger. Suppressed though it may have been, it was of the most dire, self-loathing tenor. When a man like that regains authority after so long in the wilderness, I worry, Mr. Mayor."

"I do, too," Peters said.

"Such men fiddle while cities burn." Storrow felt a long sigh leave him, heard it exit his mouth and enter the room as if it had spent so many decades bearing witness to waste and folly that it would still be circling the room when he re-entered on the morrow. "Such men love ash."

The next afternoon, Danny, Mark Denton, and Kevin McRae met with James J. Storrow in a suite at the Parker House. They brought with them detailed reports on the health and sanitation conditions of all eighteen precinct houses, signed accounts from over twenty patrolmen that detailed their average workday or week, and analyses of the pay rates of thirty other local professions—including city hall janitors, streetcar operators, and dockworkers—that dwarfed their own pay scale. They spread it all before James J. Storrow and three other businessmen who formed his commission and sat back while they went over it, passing particular sheets of interest among them and engaging in nods of surprise and grumps of consternation and eye rolls of apathy that had Danny worried he may have overloaded their hand.

Storrow went to lift another patrolman's account off the stack and then pushed the whole thing away from him. "I've seen enough," he said quietly. "Quite enough. No wonder you gentlemen feel abandoned by the very city you protect." He looked at the other three men, all of whom took his lead and nodded at Danny and Mark Denton and Kevin McRae in sudden commiseration. "This is shameful, gentlemen, and not all the blame falls on Commissioner Curtis. This happened on Commissioner O'Meara's watch, as well as under the eyes of Mayors Curley and Fitzgerald." Storrow came around from behind the table and extended his hand, shaking first Mark Denton's, then Danny's, then Kevin McRae's. "My profoundest apologies."

"Thank you, sir."

Storrow leaned back against the table. "What are we to do, gentlemen?"

"We just want our fair lot, sir," Mark Denton said.

"And what is your fair lot?"

Danny said, "Well, sir, it's a three-hundred-a-year increase in pay for starters. An end to overtime and special detail work without compensation comparative to those thirty other professions we brought up in our analysis."

"And?"

"And," Kevin McRae said, "it's an end to the company-store policy of paying for our uniforms and our equipment. It's also about clean stations, sir, clean beds, usable toilets, a sweeping out of the vermin and the lice."

Storrow nodded. He turned and looked back at the other men, though it was clear his was the only word that really counted. He turned back to the policemen. "I concur."

"Excuse me?" Danny said.

A smile found Storrow's eyes. "I said I concur, Officer. In fact, I'll champion your point of view and recommend your grievances be settled in the manner you've put forth."

Danny's first thought: It was this easy?

His second thought: Wait for the "but."

"But," Storrow said, "I only have the power to recommend. I cannot implement change. Only Commissioner Curtis can."

"Sir," Mark Denton said, "with all due respect, Commissioner Curtis is deciding whether to fire nineteen of us."

"I'm aware of that," Storrow said, "but I don't think he will. It would be the height of imprudence. The city, believe it or not, is for you, gentlemen. They're just very clearly *not* for a strike. If you allow me to handle this, you may well get everything you require. The ultimate decision rests with the commissioner, but he is a reasonable man."

Danny shook his head. "I've yet to see evidence of it, sir."

Storrow gave that a smile so distant it was almost shy. "Be that as it may, the city and the mayor and governor and every fair-minded man will, I promise you, see the light and the logic just as clearly as I've seen it today. As soon as I am capable of compiling and releasing my report, you'll have justice. I ask patience, gentlemen. I ask prudence."

"You'll have it, sir," Mark Denton said.

Storrow walked around to the back of the table and began shuffling up the papers. "But you'll have to give up your association with the American Federation of Labor."

So there it was. Danny wanted to throw the table through the window. Throw everyone in the room after it. "And put ourselves upon whose mercy this time, sir?"

"I don't follow."

Danny stood. "Mr. Storrow, we all respect you. But we've accepted half-measures before, and they've all come to naught. We work at the pay scale of 1903 because the men before us took the carrot on the stick for twelve years before demanding their rights in 1915. We accepted the city's oath that while it could not compensate us fairly during the war, it would make amends afterward. And yet? We are still being paid the 1903 wage. And yet? We never got fittingly compensated after the war. And our precincts are still cesspools and our men are still overworked. Commissioner Curtis tells the press he is forming 'committees,' never mentioning that those 'committees' are stocked with his own men and those men have prejudicial opinions. We have put our faith in this city before, Mr. Storrow, countless times, and been jilted. And now you want us to forswear the one organization that has given us real hope and real bargaining power?"

Storrow placed both hands on the table and stared across at Danny. "Yes, Officer, I do. You can use the AFL as a bargaining chip. I'll tell you that fact baldly right here and now. It's the smart move, so don't give it up just yet. But, son, I assure you, you will have to give it up. And if you choose to strike, I will be the strongest advocate in this city for breaking you and making certain you never wear a badge again." He leaned forward. "I *believe* in your cause, Officer. I will fight for you. But don't back me or this commission into a corner, because you will not survive the response."

Behind him, the windows looked out on a sky of the purest blue. A perfect summer day in the first week of September, enough to make everyone forget the dark rains of August, the feeling they'd once had that they would never be dry again.

The three policemen stood and saluted James J. Storrow and the men of his commission and took their leave.

Danny, Nora, and Luther played hearts on an old sheet placed between two iron smokestacks on the roof of Danny's building. Late evening, all three of them tired—

Luther smelling of the stockyard, Nora of the factory—and yet they were up here with two bottles of wine and a deck of cards because there were few places a black man and a white man could congregate in public and fewer still where a woman could join those men and partake of too much wine. It felt to Danny, when the three of them were together like this, that they were beating the world at something.

Luther said, "Who's that?" and his voice was lazy with the wine.

Danny followed his eyes and saw James Jackson Storrow crossing the roof toward him. He started to stand and Nora caught his wrist when he wavered.

"I was told by a kind Italian woman to search for you here," Storrow said. He glanced at the three of them, at the tattered sheet with the cards spread across it, at the bottles of wine. "I apologize for intruding."

"Not at all," Danny said as Luther made it to his feet and held out a hand to Nora. Nora grasped his hand and Luther tugged her upright and she smoothed her dress.

"Mr. Storrow, this is my wife, Nora, and my friend, Luther."

Storrow shook each of their hands as if this kind of gathering occurred every day on Beacon Hill.

"An honor to meet you both." He gave them each a nod. "Could I abscond with your husband for just a moment, Mrs. Coughlin?"

"Of course, sir. Careful with him, though—he's a bit spongy on his feet."

Storrow gave her a wide smile. "I can see that, ma'am. It's no bother."

He tipped his hat to her and followed Danny across the roof to the eastern edge and they looked out at the harbor.

"You count coloreds among your equals, Officer Coughlin?"

"Long as they don't complain," Danny said, "I don't either."

"And public drunkenness in your wife is no cause for your concern either?"

Danny kept his eyes on the harbor. "We're not in public, sir, and if we were, I wouldn't give much of a fuck. She's my wife. Means a hell of a lot more to me than the public." He turned his gaze on Storrow. "Or anyone else for that matter."

"Fair enough." Storrow placed a pipe to his lips and took a minute to light it.

"How'd you find me, Mr. Storrow?"

"It wasn't hard."

"So what brings you?"

"Your president, Mr. Denton, wasn't home."

"Ah."

Storrow puffed on his pipe. "Your wife possesses a spirit of the flesh that fairly leaps off her."

"A 'spirit of the flesh'?"

He nodded. "Quite so. It's easy to see how you became enraptured with her." He sucked on the pipe again. "The colored man I'm still trying to figure out."

"Your reason for coming, sir?"

Storrow turned so that they were face-to-face. "Mark Denton may very well have been at home. I never checked. I came directly to you, Officer Coughlin, because you have both passion and temperance, and your men, I can only assume, feel that. Officer Denton struck me as quite intelligent, but his gifts for persuasion are less than yours."

"Who would you like me to persuade, Mr. Storrow, and what am I selling?"

"The same thing I'm selling, Officer—peaceful resolution." He placed a hand on Danny's arm. "Talk to your men. We can end this, son. You and I. I'm going to release my report to the papers tomorrow night. I will be recommending full acquiescence to your demands. All but one."

Danny nodded. "AFL affiliation."

"Exactly."

"So we're left with nothing again, nothing but promises."

"But they're *my* promises, son. With the full weight of the

621

mayor and governor and the Chamber of Commerce behind them."

Nora let out a high laugh, and Danny looked across the roof to see her flicking cards at Luther and Luther holding up his hands in mock defense. Danny smiled. He'd learned over the last few months how much Luther's preferred method of displaying affection for Nora was through teasing, an affection she gladly returned in kind.

Danny kept his eyes on them. "Every day in this country they're breaking unions, Mr. Storrow. Telling us who we have a right to associate with and who we don't. When they need us, they speak of family. When we need them, they speak of business. My wife over there? My friend? Myself? We're outcasts, sir, and alone we'd probably drown. But together, we're a union. How long before Big Money gets that in their head?"

"They will never get it in their heads," Storrow said. "You think you're fighting a larger fight, Officer, and maybe you are. But it's a fight as old as time, and it will never end. No one will wave a white flag, nor ever concede defeat. Do you honestly think Lenin is any different from J. P. Morgan? That you, if you were given absolute power, would behave any differently? Do you know the primary difference between men and gods?"

"No, sir."

"Gods don't think they can become men."

Danny turned and met the man's eyes, said nothing.

"If you remain adamant on AFL affiliation, every hope you ever held for a better lot will be ground into dust."

Danny looked back at Nora and Luther again. "Do I have your word that if I sell my men on withdrawal from the AFL, the city will grant us our due?"

"You have my word and the mayor's and the governor's."

"It's your word I care about." Danny held out his hand. "I'll sell it to my men."

Storrow shook his hand, then held it firm. "Smile,

young Coughlin—we're going to save this city, you and I."

"Wouldn't that be nice?"

D anny sold it to them. In Fay Hall, at nine the next morning. After the vote, which was a shaky 406 to 377, Sid
Polk asked, "What if they shaft us again?"

"They won't."

"How do you know?"

"I don't," Danny said. "But at this point, I don't see any
logic to it."

"What if this was never about logic?" someone called.

Danny held up his hands because no answer occurred to
him.

C alvin Coolidge, Andrew Peters, and James Storrow made
the drive to Commissioner Curtis's house in Nahant late
Sunday afternoon. They met the commissioner out on his
back deck which overlooked the Atlantic under a sallow sky.

Several things were clear to Storrow within moments of
their assemblage. The first was that Coolidge had no respect
for Peters and Peters hated him for it. Every time Peters
opened his mouth to make a point, Coolidge cut him off.

The second thing, and the more worrisome, was that time
had done nothing to remove from Edwin Upton Curtis the air
of self-loathing and misanthropy that lived in him so fully it
colored his flesh like a virus.

Peters said, "Commissioner Curtis, we have—"

"—come," Coolidge said, "to inform you that Mr. Storrow
may have found a resolution to our crisis."

Peters said, "And that—"

"—if you were to hear our reasoning, I'm sure you would
conclude we have all reached an acceptable compromise."
Coolidge sat back in his deck chair.

"Mr. Storrow," Curtis said, "how have you been faring since
last we met?"

"Well, Edwin. Yourself?"

Curtis said to Coolidge, "Mr. Storrow and I last met at a fabulous fete thrown by Lady Dewar in Louisburg Square. A legendary night, that, wouldn't you say, James?"

Storrow couldn't recall the night for the life of him. Lady Dewar had been dead more than a decade. As socialites went, she'd been presentable, but hardly elite. "Yes, Edwin, it was a memorable occasion."

"I was mayor then, of course," Curtis said to Peters.

"And a fine one you were, Commissioner." Peters looked over at Coolidge as if surprised the governor had let him finish a thought.

It was the wrong thought, though. A dark squall passed through Curtis's small eyes, taking the blithe compliment Peters had delivered and twisting it into an insult. By calling him "Commissioner," the current mayor had reminded him of what he no longer was.

Dear Lord, Storrow thought, this city could burn to its bricks because of narcissism and a meaningless faux pas.

Curtis stared at him. "Do you think the men have a grievance, James?"

Storrow took his time searching for his pipe. He used three matches to get it lit in the ocean breeze and then crossed his legs. "I think they do, Edwin, yes, but let's be clear that you inherited those grievances from the previous administration. No one believes that you are the cause of those grievances or that you have done anything but attempt to deal with them honorably."

Curtis nodded. "I offered them a raise. They turned it down flat."

Because it was sixteen years too late, Storrow thought.

"I initiated several committees to study their work conditions."

Cherry-picked with toadies, Storrow thought.

"It's an issue of respect now. Respect for the office. Respect for this country."

"Only if you make it thus, Edwin." Storrow uncrossed

his legs and leaned forward. "The men respect you, Commissioner. They do. And they respect this Commonwealth. I believe my report will bear that out."

"Your report," Curtis said. "What about my report? When do I share my voice?"

Good God, it was like fighting over toys in a nursery.

"Commissioner Curtis," the governor said, "we all understand your position. You should no more be beholden to the brazen demands of workingmen than—"

"Beholden?" Curtis said. "I am no such thing, sir. I am extorted. That is what this is, pure and simple. Extortion."

"Be that as it may," Peters said, "we think that the best course—"

"—is to forgo personal feelings at this time," Coolidge said.

"This is not personal." Curtis craned his head forward and screwed his face into a mask of victimization. "This is public. This is principle. This is Seattle, gentlemen. And St. Petersburg. And Liverpool. If we let them win here, then we truly will be Russianized. The principles that Jefferson and Franklin and Washington stood for will—"

"Edwin, please." Storrow couldn't help himself. "I may have brokered a settlement that will allow us to regain our footing, both locally and nationally."

Edwin Curtis clapped his hands together. "Well, I for one, would love to hear it."

"The mayor and the city council have found the funds to raise the level of the men's pay to a fair scale for 1919 and beyond. It's fair, Edwin, not a gross capitulation, I assure you. We've further designated monies to address and improve the working conditions in the precinct houses. It's a tight budget we're working with and some other public workers will not receive departmental funding they'd been counting on, but we tried to minimize the overall damage. The greater good will be served."

Curtis nodded, his lips white. "You think so."

"I do, Edwin." Storrow kept his voice soft, warm.

"These men affiliated with a national union against my express orders, in open contempt of the rules and regulations of this police department. That affiliation is an affront to this country."

Storrow recalled the wonderful spring of his freshman year at Harvard when he'd joined the boxing team and experienced a purity of violence unlike any he could have ever imagined if he wasn't pummeling and being pummeled every Tuesday and Thursday afternoon. His parents found out eventually and that put an end to his pugilism, but, oh, how he would have loved to lace up the gloves right now and pound Curtis's nose down to the rocks of itself.

"Is that your sticking point, Edwin? The AFL affiliation?"

Curtis threw up his hands. "Of course it is!"

"And if, let us say, the men agreed to withdraw from that affiliation?"

Curtis narrowed his eyes. "Have they?"

"If they did, Edwin," Storrow said slowly, "what then?"

"I would take it under advisement," Curtis said.

"Advisement of *what*?" Peters said.

Storrow shot him a glare he hoped was sharp enough and Peters dropped his eyes.

"Advisement, Mr. Mayor, of the larger picture." Curtis's eyes had moved inward, something Storrow had seen often in financial negotiations— self-pity disguised as inner counsel.

"Edwin," he said, "the men will withdraw from the American Federation of Labor. They'll concede. The question is: Will you?"

The ocean breeze found the awning over the doorway and the flaps of the tarp snapped against themselves.

"The nineteen men should be disciplined but not punished," Governor Coolidge said. "Prudence, Commissioner, is all we ask."

"Common sense," Peters said.

Soft waves broke against the rocks.

Storrow found Curtis staring at him, as if awaiting his final plea. He stood and extended his hand to the little man. Curtis gave the hand a damp shake of his fingers.

"You have my every confidence," Storrow said.

Curtis gave him a grim smile. "That's heartening, James. I'll take it under advisement, rest assured."

L ater that afternoon, in an incident that would have proven a profound embarrassment to the Boston Police Department if it had been reported to the press, a police detail arrived at the new headquarters of the NAACP on Shawmut Avenue. Lieutenant Eddie McKenna, armed with a search warrant, dug up the floor in the kitchen and the yard behind the headquarters.

As guests who'd come to attend the ribbon-cutting ceremony stood around him, he found nothing.

Not even a toolbox.

The Storrow Report was released to the papers that night.

Monday morning, portions of it were published, and the editorial pages of all four major dailies proclaimed James J. Storrow the savior of the city. Crews arrived to break down the emergency hospital tents that had been erected across the city, and the extra ambulance drivers were sent home. The presidents of Jordan Marsh and Filene's ordered employee-firearm training to cease and all company-provided weapons were confiscated. Divisions of the State Guard and platoons of the United States Cavalry, which had been mustering in Concord, found their alert status downgraded from red to blue.

At three-thirty that afternoon, the Boston City Council passed a resolution to name either a building or a public thoroughfare after James J. Storrow.

At four, Mayor Andrew Peters left his office at City Hall to find a crowd awaiting him. The throng cheered.

At five-forty-five, policemen of all eighteen precincts met for evening roll call. It was then that the duty sergeant of each precinct house informed the men that Commissioner Curtis had ordered the immediate termination of the nineteen men he'd suspended the previous week.

In Fay Hall, at eleven in the evening, the members of the Boston Police Department Union voted to reaffirm their affiliation with the American Federation of Labor.

At eleven-oh-five, they voted to strike. It was agreed that this action would occur at tomorrow evening's roll call, a Tuesday, when fourteen hundred policemen would walk off the job.

The vote was unanimous.

CHAPTER *thirty-five*

In his empty kitchen, Eddie McKenna poured two fingers of Power's Irish whiskey into a glass of warm milk and drank it as he ate the plate of chicken and mashed potatoes Mary Pat had left on the stove. The kitchen ticked with its own quiet, and the only light came from a small gas lamp over the table behind him. Eddie ate at the sink, as he always did when he was alone. Mary Pat was out at a meeting of the Watch and Ward Society, also known as the New England Society for the Suppression of Vice. Eddie, who barely believed in naming dogs, would never understand naming an organization, not once, but twice. Ah well, now that Edward Junior was at Rutgers and Beth was off to the convent, at least it kept Mary Pat out of his hair, and the thought of all those frigid biddies klatching together to rail against the sots and the suffragettes brought a smile to his face in the dark kitchen on Telegraph Hill.

He finished his meal. He placed the plate in the sink and the empty glass beside it. He got the bottle of Irish and poured himself a tumblerful and carried the tumbler and the bottle up the stairs with him. A fine night weatherwise. Good for the roof and a few hours' thinking because, with the exception of the weather, everything had turned to right shit, it had. He half hoped the Bolshevik policemen's union *would* strike, if only so it would keep this afternoon's debacle at the NAACP off the front page. Good Lord how that nigger had set him up. Luther Laurence, Luther Laurence, Luther Laurence. The name ran through his head like mockery defined and contempt distilled.

Oh, Luther. You'll have fair cause to rue the day you ever left your Momma's tired, old cunny. I swear that to you, boy.

Out on the roof, the stars hung fuzzy above him, as if they'd been sketched by an unsure hand. Wisps of cloud slid past wisps of smoke from the Cotton Waste Factory. From here he could see the lights of the American Sugar Refining Company, a four-block monstrosity that gave continuous birth to sticky pollutants and rodents you could saddle, and the Fort Point Channel smelled of oil, yet he couldn't escape the pleasure it gave him to stand up here and survey the neighborhood he and Tommy Coughlin had first worked as pups in their newfound homeland. They'd met on the boat over, two stowaways who'd been pinched on opposite ends of the ship the second day out and been forced into slave labor in the galley. At night, chained together to the legs of a sink the size of a horse trough, they'd traded stories of the Old Sod. Tommy had left behind a drunken father and a sickly twin brother in a tenant-farmer's hut in Southern Cork. Eddie had left behind nothing but an orphanage in Sligo. Never knew his da, and his ma had passed from the fever when he was eight. So there they were, two crafty lads, scarcely in their teens, but full of piss, sure, full of ambition.

Tommy, with his dazzling, Cheshire grin and twinkling eyes, turned out to be a bit more ambitious than Eddie. While Eddie had, without question, made a fine living in his adopted homeland, Thomas Coughlin had *thrived*. Perfect family, perfect life, a lifetime of graft piled so high in his office safe it would make Croesus blush. A man who wore his power like a white suit on a coal black night.

The division of power hadn't been so apparent at the outset. When they'd joined the force, gone through the academy, walked their first beats, nothing had particularly distinguished one young man from the other. But somewhere after their first few years on the force, Tommy had revealed a stealthy intellect while Eddie himself had continued with his combination of cajolery and threat, his body growing wider every year while Perfect Tommy stayed lean and canny. An exam taker suddenly, a riser, a velvet glove.

"Ah, I'll catch you yet, Tommy," Eddie whispered, though he knew it was a lie. He hadn't the head for business and politics the way Tommy did. And if he ever could have gained such gifts, the time was long past. No, he would have to content himself—

The door to his shed was open. Just barely, but open. He went to it and opened it fully. It looked as he had left it—a broom and some garden tools to one side, two of his battered satchels to the right. He pushed them farther into the corner and reached back until he found the lip of the floorboard. He pulled it up, trying to block out the memory of doing almost the exact same thing on Shawmut Avenue this afternoon, all the well-dressed coons standing around him with stoic faces while, on the inside, they howled with laughter.

Below the floorboard were the bundles. He'd always preferred thinking of them that way. Let Thomas put his in the bank or real estate or the wall safe in his office. Eddie liked his bundles and he liked them up here where he could sit after a few drinks and thumb through them, smell them. Once there got to be too many—a problem he happily ran into about once every three years—he'd move them into a safe-deposit box at the First National in Uphams Corner. Until then, he'd sit with them. There they were now, sure, all in their places like bugs in a rug, just as he'd left them, they were. He put the floorboard back. He stood. He closed the shed door until he heard the lock click.

He stopped in the middle of the roof. He cocked his head.

At the far end of the roof a rectangular shape rested against the parapet. A foot long, it was, and half that in height.

What was this now?

Eddie took a pull from his tumbler of Power's and looked

around the dark roof. He listened. Not the way most people would listen, but the way a copper with twenty years chasing mutts into dark alleys and dark buildings listened. The air that just a moment earlier had smelled of oil and the Fort Point Channel, now smelled of his own humid flesh and the gravel at his feet. In the harbor, a boat tooted its horn. In the park below, someone laughed. Somewhere nearby, a window closed. An automobile wheezed up G Street, its gears grinding.

No moonlight, the nearest gas lamp a floor below.

Eddie listened some more. As his eyes grew more accustomed to the night, he was certain the rectangular shape was no illusion, no trick of the darkness. It was there all right, and he damn well knew what it was.

A toolbox.

The toolbox, the one he'd given Luther Laurence, the one filled with pistols he'd spirited out of the evidence rooms of various station houses over the last decade.

Eddie placed the bottle of Power's on the gravel and removed his .38 from its holster. He thumbed back the hammer.

"You up here?" He held the gun by his ear and scanned the darkness. "You up here, son?"

Another minute of silence. Another minute in which he didn't move.

And still nothing but the sounds of the neighborhood below and the quiet of the roof in front of him. He lowered his service revolver. He tapped it off his outer thigh as he crossed the roof and reached the toolbox. Here the light was much better; it bounced upward from the lamps in the park and those along Old Harbor Street and it bounced from the factories off the dark channel water and up toward Telegraph Hill. There was little question that it was the toolbox he'd given Luther—same chips in the paint, same scuff marks over the handle. He stared down at it and took another drink and noticed the number of people strolling through the park. A rarity at this time of night, but it was a Friday and maybe the first Friday in a month that hadn't been marred by heavy rain.

It was the memory of rain that got him to look over the parapet at his gutters and notice that one had come loose from its fasteners and jutted out from the brick, canting to the right and tipping downward. He was already opening the toolbox before he remembered that it held only pistols, and it occurred to him what a harebrained instinct it had been to open it before calling the Bomb Squad. It opened without incident, however, and Eddie McKenna holstered his service revolver and stared in at the last thing he expected to find in this particular toolbox.

Tools. Several screwdrivers, a hammer, three socket wrenches and two pair of pliers, a small saw.

The hand that touched his back was almost soft. He barely felt it. A big man not used to being touched, he would have expected it to have taken more force to remove him from his feet. But he'd been bent over, his feet set too closely together, one hand resting on his knee, the other holding a glass of whiskey. A cool gust found his chest as he entered the space between his home and the Andersons', and he heard the flap of his own clothes in the night air. He opened his mouth, thinking he should scream, and the kitchen window flew up past his eyes like an elevator car. A wind filled his ears on a windless night. His whiskey glass hit the cobblestone first, followed by his head. It was an unpleasant sound, and it was followed by another as his spine cracked.

He looked up the walls of his home until his eyes found the edge of the roof and he thought he saw someone up there staring down at him but he couldn't be sure. His eyes fell on the section of gutter that had detached from the brick and he reminded himself to add it to the list he kept of household repairs that needed seeing to. A long list, that. Never ending.

We found a screwdriver on top of the parapet, Cap'."

Thomas Coughlin looked up from Eddie McKenna's body. "What's that?"

Detective Chris Gleason nodded. "Best we can tell, he was leaning over to remove an old fastener for that gutter, yeah? Thing had snapped in two. He was trying to get it out of the brick and . . ." Detective Gleason shrugged. "Sorry, Cap'."

Thomas pointed at the shards of glass by Eddie's left hand. "He had a drink in his hand, Detective."

"Yes, sir."

"In his *hand*." Thomas looked up at the roof again. "You're telling me he was unscrewing a fastener and drinking at the same time?"

"We found a bottle up there, sir. Power & Son. Irish whiskey."

"I know his favored brand, Detective. You still can't explain to me why he had a drink in one hand and—"

"He was right-handed, Cap', yeah?"

Thomas looked in Gleason's eyes. "What of it?"

"Drink was in his left hand." Gleason removed his boater and smoothed back his hair. "Captain, sir, you *know* I don't want to argue with you. Not over this. Man was a legend, sir. If I thought for one moment any foul play could be on the table? I'd shake this neighborhood 'til it fell into the harbor. But not a single neighbor heard a thing. The park was filled with people, and no one saw anything but a man alone up on a roof. No signs of a struggle, no hint of defensive wounds. Captain? He didn't even scream, sir."

Thomas waved it off and nodded at the same time. He closed his eyes for a moment and squatted by his oldest friend. He could see them as boys, filthy from their sea passage, as they ran from their captors. It had been Eddie who had picked the locks that had bound them to the galley sink. He'd done it on the last night, and when their jailers, two crewmen named Laurette and Rivers, came looking for them in the morning, they'd already insinuated themselves among the throngs in steerage. By the time Laurette spotted them and began pointing and shouting, the gangplank had been lowered and Tommy Coughlin and Eddie McKenna ran at top speed through a gauntlet of legs and bags and heavy crates that swung through the air. They dodged shipmen and customs men and policemen and the shrill whistles that repeatedly blew for them. As if in welcome. As if to say, This country is yours, boys, all yours, but you have to *grab* it.

Thomas looked over his shoulder at Gleason. "Leave us, Detective."

"Yes, sir."

Once Gleason's footsteps had left the alley, Thomas took Eddie's right hand in his. He looked at the scars on the knuckles, the missing flesh on the tip of the middle finger, courtesy of a knife fight in an alley back in '03. He raised his friend's hand to his lips and kissed it. He held on tightly and placed his cheek to it.

"We grabbed it, Eddie. Didn't we?" He closed his eyes and bit into his lower lip for a moment.

He opened his eyes. He put his free hand to Eddie's face and used his thumb to close the lids.

"Ah, we did, boy. We surely did."

CHAPTER *thirty-six*

Five minutes before the roll call of every shift, George Strivakis, the duty sergeant at the Oh-One station house on Hanover Street, rang a gong that hung just outside the station house door to let the men know it was time to report. When he opened the door late in the afternoon of Tuesday, September 9, he ignored a small hitch in his step as his eyes took note of the crowd gathered on the street. Only after he had rung the gong, giving it several hard hits from his metal rod, did he raise his head fully and take in the breadth of the mob.

There had to be at least five hundred people in front of him. The back edges of the throng continued to swell as men, women, and street urchins streamed in from the side streets. The roofs on the other side of Hanover filled, mostly kids up there, a few older ones who had the coal-pebble eyes of gang members. What immediately struck Sergeant George Strivakis was the quiet. Except for the scuffling of feet, the stray jangling of keys or coins, no one said a word. The energy, though, lived in their eyes. To a man, woman, and child they all bore the same pinned-back charge, the look of street dogs at sundown on the night of a full moon.

George Strivakis withdrew his gaze from the back of the crowd and settled on the men up front. Jesus. Coppers all. In civilian dress. He rang the gong again and then broke the silence with a hoarse shout: "Officers, report!"

It was Danny Coughlin who stepped forward. He walked up the steps and snapped a salute. Strivakis returned the salute. He'd always liked Danny, had long known he lacked the political touch to rise to a captaincy but had secretly hoped he'd become chief inspector one day like Crowley. Something shriveled in him as he considered this young man of such evident promise about to engage in mutiny.

"Don't do it, son," he whispered.

Danny's eyes fixed on a spot just beyond Strivakis's right shoulder.

"Sergeant," he said, "the Boston police are on strike."

With that, the silence shattered in a roar of cheers and hats thrown high in the air.

The strikers entered the station and filed downstairs to the property room. Captain Hoffman had added four extra men to the desk, and the strikers took their turns and handed in their department-issued property.

Danny stood before Sergeant Mal Ellenburg, whose distinguished career hadn't been able to surmount his German ancestry during the war years. Down here since '16, he'd become a house cat, the kind of cop who often forgot where he'd left his revolver.

Danny placed his own revolver on the counter between them, and Mal noted it on his clipboard before dropping it in a bin below. Danny followed the revolver with his department manual, hat number plate, call box and locker keys, and pocket billy. Mal noted it all and swept it away into various bins. He looked up at Danny and waited.

Danny looked back at him.

Mal held out his hand.

Danny stared into his face.

Mal closed his hand and opened it again.

"You gotta ask for it, Mal."

"Jesus, Dan."

Danny gritted his teeth to keep his mouth from trembling.

Mal looked away for a moment. When he looked back, he propped his elbow on the counter and flipped his palm open in front of Danny's chest.

"Please turn over your shield, Officer Coughlin."

Danny pulled back his jacket and exposed the badge pinned to his shirt. He unhooked the shield from its pin and slid the pin out of his shirt. He placed the pin back behind the hook and placed the shield in Mal Ellenburg's palm.

"I'm coming back for that," Danny said.

The strikers assembled in the foyer. They could hear the crowd outside and by the volume Danny assumed it had doubled. Something rammed into the door twice and then the door was flung open and ten men pushed their way inside and slammed the door shut behind them. They were young mostly, a few older men who looked like they had the war in their eyes, and they'd been pelted with fruit and eggs.

Replacements. Volunteers. Scabs.

Danny placed the back of his hand on Kevin McRae's chest to let him know the men should be allowed to pass unmolested and unremarked, and the strikers made a path as the replacements walked between them and up the stairs into the station.

Outside, the sound of the mob rattled and shook like a storm wind.

Inside, the snap of gun slides being racked in the first-floor weapons room. Handing out the riot guns, readying for a tussle.

Danny took a long, slow breath and opened the door.

The noise blew up from all sides and blew down from the rooftops. The crowd hadn't doubled; it had tripled. Easily fifteen hundred people out here, and it was hard to tell from the faces who was for them and who was against because those faces had turned into grotesque masks of either glee or fury, and the shouts of "We love ya, boys!" were intermingled with "Fuck you, coppers!" and wails of "Why? Why?" and

"Who will protect us?" The applause would have been deafening if it weren't for the jeers and the projectiles of fruit and eggs, most of which splattered against the wall. A horn beeped insistently, and Danny could make out a truck just beyond the fringe of the crowd. The men in back were replacements by the look of them, because the look of them was scared. As he descended into it, Danny scanned the crowd as best he could, saw some crudely fashioned signs of both support and condemnation. The faces were Italian and Irish and young and old. Bolsheviks and anarchists mingled with several smug faces of the Black Hand. Not far from them, Danny recognized a few members of the Gusties, the largest street gang in Boston. If this was Southie, the Gusties' home turf, it wouldn't have been surprising, but the fact that they'd crossed the city and spread their ranks made Danny wonder if he could honestly answer the shouts of "Who will protect us?" with anything but "I don't know."

A thick guy popped out of the crowd and punched Kevin McRae full in the face. Danny was separated from him by a dozen people. As he pushed his way through, he heard the thick guy shouting, " 'Member me, McRae? Broke my fucking arm during a nick last year? What you gonna do now?" By the time Danny reached Kevin, the guy was long gone, but others were taking his cue, others who'd shown up to do nothing more than pay back beatings they'd received at the hands of these no-longer cops, these ex-cops.

Ex-cops. Jesus.

Danny lifted Kevin to his feet as the crowd surged forward, bouncing off them. The men in the truck had dismounted and were fighting their way toward the station house. Someone threw a brick and one of the scabs went down. A whistle blew as the doors of the station opened and Strivakis and Ellenburg appeared on the steps, flanked by a few other sergeants and lieutenants and a half dozen white-faced volunteers.

As Danny watched the scabs fight their way toward the

steps and Strivakis and Ellenburg swing their billy clubs to clear a path, his instinct was to run toward them, to help them, to join them. Another brick sailed through the crowd and glanced off the side of Strivakis's head. Ellenburg caught him before he could go down and the two of them began to swing their billies with renewed fury, blood streaming down Strivakis's face and into his collar. Danny took a step toward them, but Kevin pulled him back.

"Ain't our fight anymore, Dan."

Danny looked at him.

Kevin, his teeth bloodied, his breath short, said it again. "Ain't our fight."

The scabs made it through the doors as Danny and Kevin reached the back of the crowd and Strivakis took a few last swooping cracks at the crowd and then slammed the doors behind him. The mob beat on the doors. Some men overturned the truck that had delivered the recruits and someone lit the contents of a barrel on fire.

Ex-cops, Danny thought.

For the time being anyway.

Good Lord.

Ex-cops.

Commissioner Curtis sat behind his desk with a revolver lying just to the right of his ink blotter. "So, it's begun."

Mayor Peters nodded. "It has, Commissioner."

Curtis's bodyguard stood behind him with his arms folded across his chest. Another waited outside the door. Neither was from the department, because Curtis no longer trusted any of the men. They were Pinkertons. The one behind Curtis looked old and rheumatic, as if any sudden movement would send his limbs flying off. The one outside the door was obese. Neither, Peters decided, looked fit enough to provide protection with their bodies, so they could only be one other thing: shooters.

"We need to call out the State Guard," Peters said.

Curtis shook his head. "No."

"That's not your decision, I'm afraid."

Curtis leaned back in his chair and looked up at the ceiling. "It's not yours, either, Mr. Mayor. It's the governor's. I just got off the phone with him not five minutes ago and he made it very clear, we are not to engage the Guard at this juncture."

"What juncture would you two prefer?" Peters said. "Rubble?"

"Governor Coolidge stated that countless studies have shown that rioting in a case like this never begins on the first night. It takes the mob a full day to mobilize."

"Given that very few cities have ever watched their entire police department walk off the job," Peters said, trying to keep his voice under control, "I'm wondering how many of these *countless* studies pertain to our immediate situation, Commissioner."

"Mr. Mayor," Curtis said, looking over at his bodyguard, as if he expected him to wrestle Peters to the ground, "you need to take your concerns up with the governor."

Andrew Peters stood and took his boater from the corner of the desk. "If you're wrong, Commissioner, don't bother coming to work tomorrow."

He left the office, trying to ignore the tremors in the backs of his legs.

L uther!"

Luther stopped at the corner of Winter and Tremont Streets and looked for the source of the voice. Hard to tell who could have called to him because the streets were filling as the sun flattened against red brick and the greens of the Common darkened with its passing. Several groups of men had spread themselves out in the Common and were openly running dice games, and the few women still on the streets walked quickly, most tightening their coats or cinching their collars close to their throats.

Bad times, he decided as he turned to walk down Tremont toward the Giddreauxs' home, are definitely coming.

"Luther! Luther Laurence!"

He stopped again, his windpipe grown cold at the sound of his true surname. A familiar black face appeared between two white faces, swimming its way out of the crowd like a small balloon. Luther recognized the face but it still took him a few anxious seconds to place it with certainty as the man split between the two white people and came toward the sidewalk with one glad hand raised above his shoulder. He slapped the hand down into Luther's and his grip was firm.

"Luther Laurence, I do declare!" He pulled Luther into a hug.

"Byron," Luther said as they broke the hug.

Old Byron Jackson. His old boss at the Hotel Tulsa, head of the Colored Bellmen's Union. A fair man with the tip pool. Old Byron, who smiled the brightest of all smiles for the white folk and cursed them with the nastiest shit imaginable as soon as they'd left his presence. Old Byron, who lived alone in an apartment above the hardware store on Admiral, and never spoke of the wife and daughter in the daguerreo-type atop his bare dresser. Yeah, Old Byron was one of the good ones.

"A bit north for you, isn't it?" Luther said.

"That's the truth," Old Byron said. "You, too, Luther. As I live, I never expected to find you here. Rumors had it . . ."

Old Byron looked out at the crowd.

"Had it what?" Luther said.

Old Byron leaned in, his eyes on the sidewalk. "Rumors had it you were dead, son."

Luther gestured up Tremont with his head and Old Byron fell into step as they walked toward Scollay Square and away from the Giddreauxs' and the South End. It was slow going, the crowd thickening by the minute.

"Ain't dead," Luther said. "Just in Boston."

Old Byron said, "What brings these folks out like this?"

"Police just walked off the job."

"Hush your mouth."

"They did," Luther said.

"I read they *might*," Old Byron said, "but I never would have believed it. This going to be bad for our folk, Luther?"

Luther shook his head. "I don't think. Ain't a lot of lynching up here, but you never know what'll happen someone forgets to chain the dog."

"Even the quietest dog, right?"

"Them most of all." Luther smiled. "What brought you all the way up here, Byron?"

"Brother," Old Byron said. "Got the cancer. Eating him alive."

Luther looked over at him, saw the weight of it pulling his shoulders down.

"He got a chance?"

Old Byron shook his head. "It's in his bones."

Luther put a hand on the old man's back. "I'm sorry."

"Thank you, son."

"He in hospital?"

Old Byron shook his head. "Home." He jerked a thumb off to his left. "West End."

"You his only kin?"

"Got a sister. She in Texarkana. She too frail to travel."

Luther didn't know what else to say so he said "I'm sorry" again, and Old Byron shrugged.

"What you gone do, am I right?"

Off to their left someone screamed and Luther saw a woman with a bloody nose, her face clenched, as if expecting another punch from the man who ripped her necklace off and then ran toward the Common. Someone laughed. A kid shimmied up a streetlamp pole, pulled a hammer from his belt, and smashed the lamp.

"This getting thick with ugly," Old Byron said.

"Yeah, it is." Luther thought of turning around, since most of the crowd seemed to be moving toward Court Square and then Scollay Square beyond, but when he looked behind him, he couldn't see any space. All he could see were shoulders and heads, a pack of drunk sailors in the mix now, red-eyed and pimple-faced. A moving wall, pushing them forward. Luther felt bad for leading Old Byron into this, for suspecting him, if only for a moment, of being anything but an old man who was losing his brother. He craned his neck above the crowd to see if he could find a way out for them, and just ahead, at the corner of City Hall Avenue, a group of men hurled rocks into the window of Big Chief's Cigar Store, the sound of it like a half dozen rifle reports. The plate glass broke into fins that hung in place for a moment, creaking in the moist breeze, and then they dropped.

A piece of glass ricocheted into a small guy's eye and he had time to reach for it before the crowd swarmed over him and into the cigar store. Those who couldn't make it inside broke the window next door, this one to a bakery, and loaves of bread and cupcakes sailed overhead and fell into the midst of the mob.

Old Byron looked frightened, his eyes wide, and Luther put an arm around him and tried to calm the old man's fear with idle talk. "What's your brother's name?"

Old Byron cocked his head like he didn't understand the question.

"I said what's—?"

"Carnell," Old Byron said. "Yeah." He gave Luther a shaky smile and nodded. "His name's Carnell."

Luther smiled back. He hoped it was a comforting smile, and he kept his arm around Old Byron, even though he feared the blade or the pistol he now knew the man had on his person somewhere.

It was the "Yeah" that got him. The way Old Byron said it like he was confirming it to himself, answering a question on a test he'd overprepared for.

Another window exploded, this time on their right. And then another. A fat white man pushed them hard to the left as he made his charge for Peter Rabbit Hats. The windows kept dropping—Sal Myer's Gents' Furnishings, Lewis Shoes,

644

the Princeton Clothing Company, Drake's Dry Goods. Sharp, dry explosions. Glass glittering against the walls, crunching underfoot, spitting through the air. A few feet ahead of them, a soldier swung a chair leg into the head of a sailor, the wood already dark with blood.

Carnell. Yeah. His name's Carnell.

Luther removed his arm from Old Byron's shoulders.

"What's Cornell do for work?" Luther said as a sailor with arms slashed to bits by a window pushed through them, bleeding all over everything he touched.

"Luther, we got to get out of here."

"What's Cornell do?" Luther said.

"He a meat packer," Old Byron said.

"Cornell's a meat packer."

"Yeah," Old Byron shouted. "Luther, we got to get free of this."

"Thought you said his name was Carnell," Luther said.

Old Byron's mouth opened but he didn't say anything. He gave Luther a helpless, hopeless look, his lips moving slightly as he tried to find the words.

Luther shook his head slowly. "Old Byron," he said. "Old Byron."

"I can explain." Old Byron worked a sad smile onto his face.

Luther nodded, as if ready to listen, and then shoved him into the nearest group to his right and quick-pivoted between two men who looked whiter than white and scareder than scared. He slid between two more men with their backs to each other. Someone broke another window, and then a few someones began firing guns in the air. One of the bullets came back down and hit the arm of a guy beside Luther and the blood spouted and the guy yelped. Luther reached the opposite sidewalk and slipped on some glass pebbles. He almost went down, but he righted himself at the last second and risked a look back across the street. He spotted Old Byron, his back pressed to a brick wall, eyes darting, as a man wrestled the carcass of a sow over a butcher's window frame, the sow's belly dragging across the broken glass. The man wrenched it to the sidewalk where he took several punches to the head from three men who kept swinging until they'd knocked him back through the open window. They availed themselves of his bloodied sow and carried it over their heads down Tremont.

Carnell, my ass.

Luther walked gingerly through the glass and tried to keep to the edge of the crowd, but within minutes he'd been forced toward the center again. It was no longer a group of people, it was a living, thinking hive that commanded the bees within, made sure they were all anxious and jangly and hungry. Luther pulled his hat down tighter and kept his head down.

Dozens of people, all cut up from the glass, keened and moaned. The sight and sound of them incited the hive even more. Anyone wearing a straw hat had it wrenched from his head and men beat the shit out of one another over stolen shoes and bread loaves and suit jackets, most times destroying the very thing they tried to possess. The packs of sailors and the soldiers were roving enemy squads, bursting out of the herd in sudden explosions to pummel their rivals. Luther saw a woman pushed into a doorway, saw several men press around her. He heard her scream but he couldn't get anywhere near her, the walls of shoulders and heads and torsos moving alongside of him like freight cars in the stockyards. He heard the woman scream again and the men laugh and hoot, and he looked out at this hideous sea of white faces stripped of their everyday masks and wanted to burn them all in a great fire.

By the time they reached Scollay Square, there had to be four thousand of them. Tremont widened here and Luther finally broke from the center again, made his way to the sidewalk, heard someone say, "Nigger got his own hat," and kept moving until he ran into another wall of men pouring out of a shattered liquor store, draining the bottles and smashing them to the sidewalk and then opening replacements. Some inbred-looking short sons of bitches kicked down the doors of Waldron's Casino, and Luther heard the burlesque show in there screech to an end. Several of the men came right back out pushing a piano in front of them, the piano player lying belly-down on top, one of the short sons of bitches sitting on his ass and riding him like a horse.

He turned to his right and Old Byron Jackson stabbed him in the bicep. Luther fell back against the wall of Waldron's Casino. Old Byron swung with that knife again, the old man's face a feral, terrified thing. Luther kicked out at him, then came off the wall as Old Byron lunged and missed, the knife sending a spark off the brick. Luther cuffed him in the ear but good, bounced the other side of his head off the wall.

"The fuck you doing this for?" he said.

"Got debts," Old Byron said and came at him in a low rush.

Luther banged into someone's back as he dodged the thrust. The man he'd bumped grabbed his shirt and spun him to face him. Luther jerked out of the man's grasp and kicked behind him, heard the kick connect with some part of Old Byron Jackson, the old man letting out an "oof" of air. The white man punched him in the cheek, but Luther had expected that and he rolled with it right into the crowd still dancing out in front of the liquor store. He broke through them and leapt up onto the piano keys, heard a smattering of cheers break out as he vaulted off the keys and over the piano player and the man riding him. He landed on the other side and kept his footing and got a quick glimpse of a guy's shock at this nigger dropping out of the sky and then he pushed into the crowd.

The mob moved on. They poured through Faneuil Hall, and some cows were set loose from their pens, and someone overturned a produce cart and lit it on fire in front of its owner, who dropped to his knees and pulled his hair out of his bleeding scalp by the roots. Up ahead, a sudden burst of gunfire, several pistols fired above the crowd, and then a desperate shout: "We are plainclothes police officers! Cease and desist at once."

More warning shots and then the crowd started shouting back.

"Kill the cops! Kill the cops!"

"Kill the scabs!"

"Kill the cops!"

"Kill the scabs!"

"Kill the cops!"

"Back off or we will shoot to kill! Back *off*!"

They must have meant it because Luther felt the surge change direction and he was spun in place and the swarm moved back the way it had come. More shots fired. Another cart lit afire, the yellow and red reflecting off the bronze cobblestone and the red brick, Luther catching his own shadow moving through the colors along with all the other shadows. Shrieking that filled the sky. A crack of bone, a sharp scream, a thunderclap of plate glass, fire alarms ringing so consistently that Luther barely heard them anymore.

And then the rain came, a fat pouring of it, clattering and hissing, steaming off bare heads. At first Luther held out hope it would thin the crowd, but if anything it brought more of them. Luther was buffeted along within the hive as it destroyed ten more storefronts, three restaurants, rushed through a boxing match at Beech Hall and beat the fighters senseless. Beat the audience, too.

Along Washington Street, the major department stores—Filene's, White's, Chandler's, and Jordan Marsh—had loaded up for bear. The guys guarding Jordan Marsh saw them coming from two blocks away and stepped off the sidewalk with pistols and shotguns. They didn't even wait for a debate. They set themselves in the middle of Washington Street, fifteen of them at least, and fired. The hive went into a crouch and then took another couple of steps forward, but the Jordan Marsh men charged them, guns booming and chucking, and the surge reversed again. Luther heard terror screams and the Jordan Marsh men kept firing and the hive ran all the way back to Scollay Square.

Which was an uncaged zoo by now. Everyone drunk and howling up at the raindrops. Dazed burlesque girls stripped of their tassels wandering around with bare chests. Overturned touring cars and bonfires along the sidewalk. Headstones ripped from the Old Granary Burying Ground and propped up against walls and fences. Two people fucking on top of an overturned Model T. Two men in a bare-knuckle boxing match in the middle of Tremont Street while the bettors formed a ring around them and the blood and rain-streaked glass crunched under their feet. Four soldiers dragged an unconscious sailor to the bumper of one of the flipped cars and pissed on him as the crowd cheered. A woman appeared in an upper window and screamed for help. The crowd cheered her, too, before a hand clamped over her face and wrenched her back from the window. The crowd cheered some more.

Luther noticed the dark bloodstain on his upper sleeve and took a look at the wound long enough to realize it wasn't deep. He noticed a guy passed out against the curb with a bottle of whiskey between his legs and he reached down and took the bottle. He poured some over his arm and then drank some and watched another window explode and heard more screams and wails but all of them eventually drowned out by the leering cheers of this triumphant hive.

This? he wanted to scream. This is what I kowtowed to? You people? You made me feel like less because I wasn't *you*? I've been saying "yes, suh" to you? "No suh"? To you? To you fucking . . . *animals*?

He took another drink and the sweep of his gaze landed on Old Byron Jackson across the street, standing in front of a whitewashed storefront, what had once been a bookstore, several years abandoned. Maybe the last window left in Scollay Square. Old Byron looked down Tremont in the wrong direction, and Luther tilted his head and drained

649

the bottle and dropped it to his feet and started across the street.

Glazed, white, maskless faces loomed all around him, drunk from liquor, drunk on power and anarchy, but drunk on something else, too, something nameless until now, something they'd always known was there but pretended they didn't.

Oblivion.

That's all it was. They did things in their everyday life and gave it other names, nice names—idealism, civic duty, honor, purpose. But the truth was right in front of them now. No one did anything for any other reason but that they wanted to. They wanted to rage and they wanted to rape and they wanted to destroy as many things as they could destroy simply because those things could be destroyed.

Fuck you, Luther thought, and fuck this. He reached Old Byron Jackson and sank one hand into his crotch and the other into his hair.

I'm going home.

He lifted Old Byron off the ground and swung him back in the air as the old man howled and when he got to the top of the pendulum, Luther swung it all the way back and threw Old Byron Jackson through the plate glass window.

"Nigger fight," someone called.

Old Byron landed on the bare floor and the glass shards popped all over him and all around him and he tried to cover up with his arms but the glass hit him anyway, one shard taking off a cheek, another carving a steak off his outer thigh.

"You going to kill him, boy?"

Luther turned and looked at three white men to his left. They were swimming in booze.

"Might could," he said.

He climbed through the window and into the store and the broken glass and Old Byron Jackson.

"What kinda debts?"

Old Byron huffed his breath and then hissed it and

650

grabbed his thigh in his hands and let out a low moan.

"I asked you a question."

Behind him one of the white men chuckled. "You hear? He *axed* him a question."

"What kinda debts?"

"What kind you think?" Old Byron ground his head back into the glass and arched his back.

"You using, I take it."

"Used my whole life. Opium, not heroin," Old Byron said. "Who you think supplied Jessie Tell, fool?"

Luther stepped on Old Byron's ankle and the old man gritted his teeth.

"Don't say his name," Luther said. "He was my friend. You ain't."

One of the white men called, "Hey! You going to kill him, shine, or what?"

Luther shook his head and heard the men groan and then scuttle off.

"Ain't going to save you, though, Old Byron. You die, you die. Came all the way up here just to kill one of your own for that shit you put in you?" Luther spit on the glass pebbles.

Old Byron spit blood up at Luther, but all it did was land on his own shirt. "Never liked your ass, Luther. You think you special."

Luther shrugged. "I am special. Any day aboveground that I ain't you or I ain't *that*?" He jerked his thumb behind him. "You're goddamned fucking correct I'm special. Ain't afraid of them anymore, ain't afraid of you, ain't afraid of this here color of my skin. Fuck all that forever."

Old Byron rolled his eyes. "Like you even less."

"Good." Luther smiled. He crouched by Old Byron. "I 'spect you'll live, old man. You get back on that train to Tulsa. Hear? And when you get off it, you go run your sad ass right to Smoke and tell him you missed me. Tell him it don't matter none, though, because he ain't going to have to look hard for me from now on." Luther lowered his face until he was close enough to kiss Old Byron Jackson. "You tell Smoke I'm coming for *him*." He slapped his good cheek once, hard. "I'm coming home, Old Byron. You tell Smoke that. You don't?" Luther shrugged. "I'll tell him myself."

He stood and crossed the broken glass and stepped through the window. He never looked back at Old Byron. He worked his way through the feverish white folk and the screams and the rain and the storm of the hive and knew he was done with every lie he'd ever allowed himself to believe, every lie he'd ever lived, every lie.

Scollay Square. Court Square. The North End. Newspaper Row. Roxbury Crossing. Pope's Hill. Codman and Eggleston Squares. The calls came in from all over the city, but nowhere more voluminously than in Thomas Coughlin's precinct. South Boston was blowing up.

The mobs had emptied the stores along Broadway and thrown the goods to the street. Thomas couldn't find even the strayest hair of logic in that—at least *use* what you looted. From the inner harbor to Andrew Square, from the Fort Point Channel to Farragut Road—not a single window in a single business stood intact. Hundreds of homes had suffered similar fates. East and West Broadway swelled with the worst of the populace, ten thousand strong and growing. Rapes—*rapes*, Thomas thought with clenched teeth—had occurred in public view, three on West Broadway, one on East Fourth, another at one of the piers along Northern Avenue.

And the calls kept coming in:

The manager of Mully's Diner beaten unconscious when a roomful of patrons decided not to pay their bills. The poor sod at Haymarket Relief now with a broken nose, a shattered eardrum, and half a dozen missing teeth.

At Broadway and E, some fun-loving fellas drove a stolen buggy over the sidewalk and into the front window of O'Donnell's Bakery. That wasn't enough revelry, however—they had to set it afire. In the process, they torched the bakery and burned seventeen years of Declan O'Donnell's dreams to soot.

Budnick Creamery—destroyed. Connor & O'Keefe's—ash. Up and down Broadway, haberdashers, tailors, pawnshops, produce stores, even a bicycle shop—all gone. Either burned to the ground or smashed beyond salvage.

Boys and girls, most younger than Joe, hurled eggs and rocks from the roof of Mohican Market, and the scant few officers Thomas could afford to send reported they were helpless to fire back at children. Responding firemen complained of the same thing.

And the latest report—a streetcar forced to stop at the corner of Broadway and Dorchester Street because of all the goods piled in the intersection. The mob added boxes, barrels, and mattresses to the pile and then someone brought some gasoline and a box of matches. The occupants of the streetcar were forced to flee the car along with the driver and most were beaten while the crowd rushed onto the car, tore the seats from their metal clamps, and tossed them through the windows.

What was this addiction to broken glass? That's what Thomas wanted to know. How was one to stop this madness? He had a mere twenty-two policemen under his command, most sergeants and lieutenants, most well into their forties, plus a contingent of useless frightened volunteers.

"Captain Coughlin?"

He looked up at Mike Eigen, a recently promoted sergeant, standing in the doorway.

"Jesus, Sergeant, what now?"

"Someone sent a contingent of Metro Park Police in to patrol Southie."

Thomas stood. "No one told me."

"Not sure where the order came from, Cap', but they're pinned down."

"What?"

Eigen nodded. "St. Augustine's Church. Guys are dropping."

653

"Bullets?"

Eigen shook his head. "Rocks, Cap'."

A church. Brother officers being stoned. At a church. In *his precinct*.

Thomas Coughlin didn't know he'd overturned his desk until he heard it crack against the floor. Sergeant Eigen took a step back.

"Enough," Thomas said. "By God, enough."

Thomas reached for the gun belt he hung on his coat tree every morning.

Sergeant Eigen watched him buckle the gun belt. "I'd say so, Cap'."

Thomas reached for the bottom left drawer of his overturned desk. He lifted the drawer out and propped it on the two upper drawers. He removed a box of .32 shells and stuffed it in his pocket. Found a box of shotgun shells and placed them in the opposite pocket. He looked up at Sergeant Eigen. "Why are you still here?"

"Cap'?"

"Assemble every man still standing in this mausoleum. We've got a donnybrook to attend." Thomas raised his eyebrows. "And we shan't be fooling about in that regard, Sergeant."

Eigen snapped him a salute, a smile blowing wide across his face.

Thomas found himself smiling back as he pulled his shotgun off the rack over the file cabinet. "Hop to it now, son."

Eigen ran from the doorway as Thomas loaded his shotgun, loving the snick-snick of the shells sliding into the magazine. The sound of it returned his soul to his body for the first time since the walkout at five-forty-five. On the floor lay a picture of Danny the day he'd graduated from the Academy, Thomas himself pinning the badge to his chest. His favorite photograph.

He stepped on it on his way out the door, unable to deny the satisfaction that filled him when he heard the glass crunch.

"You don't want to protect our city, boy?" he said. "Fine. I will."

When they exited the patrol cars at St. Augustine's, the crowd turned toward them. Thomas could see the Metro Park cops trying to hold the mob back with billy clubs and drawn weapons, but they were already bloody, and the piles of rocks littering the white limestone steps gave testament to a pitched battle these coppers had been losing.

What Thomas knew about a mob was simple enough—any change in direction forced it to lose its voice if only for a matter of seconds. If you owned those seconds, you owned the mob. If they owned it, they owned you.

He stepped out of his car and the man nearest him, a Gustie who went by the moniker of Filching Phil Scanlon, laughed and said, "Well, Captain Cough—"

Thomas split his face to the bone with the butt of his shotgun. Filching Phil dropped like a head-shot horse. Thomas laid the muzzle of his shotgun on the shoulder of the Gustie behind him, Big Head Sparks. Thomas tilted the muzzle toward the sky and fired and Big Head lost the hearing in his left ear. Big Head Sparks wavered, his eyes instantly glazed, and Thomas said to Eigen, "Do the honors, Sergeant."

Eigen hit Big Head Sparks in the face with his service revolver, and that was the last of Big Head for the night.

Thomas pointed his shotgun at the ground and fired.

The mob backed up.

"I'm Captain Thomas Coughlin," he called and stomped his foot down on Filching Phil's knee. He didn't get the sound he'd been after, so he did it again. This time he got the sweet crack of bone followed by the predictable shriek. He waved his arm and the eleven men he'd been able to pull together spread along the fringe of the crowd.

"I'm Captain Thomas Coughlin," he repeated, "and be of no illusion—we intend to spill blood." He swept his eyes across the faces in the mob. "Your blood." He turned to the

655

Metro Park Police officers on the stairs of the church. There were ten of them, and they seemed to have shrunk into themselves. "Level your weapons or stop calling yourselves officers of the law."

The crowd took another step back as the Metro Park cops extended their arms.

"Cock them!" Thomas shouted.

They did, and the crowd took several more steps back.

"If I see anyone holding a rock," Thomas called, "we shoot to kill."

He took five steps forward, the shotgun coming to rest on the chest of a man with a rock in his hand. The man dropped the rock and then urinated down his left leg. Thomas considered mercy and quickly deemed it inappropriate for the atmosphere. He opened the urinator's forehead with his shotgun butt and stepped over him.

"Run, you wretched curs." He swept his eyes across them. "RUN!"

No one moved—they looked too shocked—and Thomas turned to Eigen, to the men on the fringe, to the Metro Park cops.

"Fire at will."

The Metro Park cops stared back at him.

Thomas rolled his eyes. He drew his service revolver, raised it above his head, and fired six times.

The men got the point. They began to discharge their weapons into the air and the crowd exploded like drops from a shattered water bucket. They ran up the street. They ran and ran, darting into alleys and down side streets, banging off overturned cars, falling to the sidewalk, stomping on one another, hurling themselves into storefronts and landing on the broken glass they'd created only an hour before.

Thomas flicked his wrist and emptied his shell casings onto the street. He laid the shotgun at his feet and reloaded his service revolver. The air was sharp with cordite and the echoes of gunfire. The mob continued its desperate fight. Thomas holstered his revolver and reloaded his shotgun. The long summer of impotence and confusion faded from his heart. He felt twenty-five years old.

Tires squealed behind him. Thomas turned as one black Buick and four patrol cars pulled to a stop as a soft rain began to fall. Superintendent Michael Crowley exited the Buick. He carried his own shotgun and wore his service revolver in a shoulder holster. He sported a fresh bandage on his forehead, and his fine dark suit was splattered with egg yolk and bits of shell.

Thomas smiled at him and Crowley gave him a tired smile in return.

"Time for a little law and order, wouldn't you say, Captain?"

"Indeed, Superintendent."

They walked up the center of the street as the rest of the men dropped in behind them.

"Like the old days, Tommy, eh?" Crowley said as they started to make out the outer edge of a fresh mob concentrated in Andrew Square two blocks ahead.

"Just what I was thinking, Michael."

"And when we clear them here?"

When we clear them. Not *if*. Thomas loved it.

"We take Broadway back."

Crowley clapped a hand on Thomas's shoulder.

"Ah, how I missed this."

"Me, too, Michael. Me, too."

Mayor Peters's chauffeur, Horace Russell, glided the Rolls-Royce Silver Ghost along the fringes of the trouble, never once entering a street so strewn with debris or the throngs that they would have been hard-pressed to get back out again. And so, while the populace rioted, its mayor observed them from a remove, but not so much of a remove that he couldn't hear their terrible war cries, their shrieks and high-pitched laughter, the shock of sudden gunfire, the incessant shattering of glass.

Once he'd toured Scollay Square, he thought he'd seen the worst of it, but then he saw the North End, and not long thereafter, South Boston. He realized that nightmares so bad he'd never dared dream them had come to fruition.

The voters had handed him a city of peerless reputation. The Athens of America, the birthplace of the American Revolution and two presidents, seat to more higher education than any other city in the nation, the Hub of the universe.

And on his watch, it was disassembling itself brick by brick.

They crossed back over the Broadway Bridge, leaving behind the flames and screams of the South Boston slum. Andrew Peters told Horace Russell to take him to the nearest phone. They found one at the Castle Square Hotel in the South End, which was, for the moment, the only quiet neighborhood they'd passed through tonight.

With the bell staff and the manager conspicuously watching, Mayor Peters called the Commonwealth Armory. He informed the soldier who answered who he was and told him to get Major Dallup to the phone on the double

"Dallup here."

"Major. Mayor Peters."

"Yes, sir?"

"Are you currently in command of the motor corps and the First Cavalry Troop?"

"I am, sir. Under the command of General Stevens and Colonel Dalton, sir."

"Who are where presently?"

"I believe with Governor Coolidge at the State House, sir."

"Then you are in active command, Major. Your men are to stay at the armory and stand at readiness. They are not to go home. Is that clear?"

"Yes, sir."

"I will be by to review them and to give you your deployment assignments."

"Yes, sir."

"You are going to put down some riots tonight, Major."

"With pleasure, sir."

When Peters arrived at the armory fifteen minutes later, he saw a trooper exit the building and head up Commonwealth toward Brighton.

"Trooper!" He left the car and held up a hand. "Where are you going?"

The trooper looked at him. "Who the fuck are you?"

"I'm the mayor of Boston."

The trooper immediately straightened and then saluted. "My apologies, sir."

Peters returned the salute. "Where are you going, son?"

"Home, sir. I live right up the—"

"You were given orders to stand at the ready."

The trooper nodded. "But those orders were counter-manded by General Stevens."

"Go back inside," Peters said.

As the trooper opened the door, several more troopers started to file out, but the original deserter pushed them back inside, saying, "The mayor, the mayor."

Peters strode inside and immediately spied a man with a major's oak leaf cluster by the staircase leading up to the orderly room.

"Major Dallup!"

"Sir!"

"What is the meaning of this?" Peters's hand swept around the armory, at the men with their collars unbuttoned, weaponless, shifting in place.

"Sir, if I could explain."

"Please do!" Peters was surprised to hear the sound of his voice, raised, flinty.

Before Major Dallup could explain anything, however, a voice boomed from the top of the stairs.

"These men are going home!" Governor Coolidge stood at

the landing above them all. "Mayor Peters, you have no business here. Go home as well, sir."

As Coolidge came down the stairs, flanked by General Stevens and Colonel Dalton, Peters rushed up. All four men met in the middle.

"This city is rioting."

"It is doing no such thing."

"I have been out in it, Governor, and I tell you, I tell you, I tell you—" Peters hated this stammer he developed when upset but he wouldn't let it stop him now. "I tell you, sir, that it is not sporadic. It is tens of thousands of men and they are—"

"There is no riot," Coolidge said.

"Yes, there is! In South Boston, in the North End, in Scollay Square! Look for yourself, man, if you don't believe me."

"I have looked."

"Where?"

"From the State House."

"The State House?" Peters said, screaming now, his voice sounding to his own ears like that of a child. A female child. "The rioting isn't happening on Beacon Hill, Governor. It's happening—"

"Enough." Coolidge held up a hand.

"*Enough?*" Peters said.

"Go home, Mr. Mayor. Go home."

It was the tone that got to Andrew Peters, the tone a parent reserved for a bratty child having a pointless tantrum.

Mayor Andrew Peters then did something he was reasonably sure had never occurred in Boston politics—he punched the governor in the face.

He had to jump from a lower step to do it, and Coolidge was tall to begin with, so it wasn't much of a punch. But it did connect with the tissue around the governor's left eye.

Coolidge was so stunned, he didn't move. Peters was so pleased, he decided to do it again.

The general and the colonel grabbed at his arms, and several troopers ran up the stairs, but in those few seconds, Peters managed to land a few more flailing shots.

The governor, oddly, never moved back or raised his hands to defend himself.

Several troopers carried Mayor Andrew Peters back down the stairs and deposited him on the floor.

He thought of rushing up them again.

Instead, he pointed a finger at Governor Coolidge. "This is on your conscience."

"But your ledger, Mr. Mayor." Coolidge allowed himself a small smile. "Your ledger, sir."

CHAPTER *thirty-seven*

Horace Russell drove Mayor Peters to City Hall Wednesday morning at half past seven. Absent fires and screams and darkness, the streets had lost their ghoulish flavor, but stark evidence of the mob lay everywhere. Nary a window was left intact along Washington or Tremont or any of the streets that intersected them. Husks where once stood businesses. The skeleton frames of charred automobiles. So much trash and debris in the streets Peters could only assume this was what cities looked like after protracted battles and sporadic bombing.

Along the Boston Common, men lay in drunken stupors or openly engaged in dice games. Across Tremont, a few souls raised plywood over their window frames. In front of some businesses, men paced with shotguns and rifles. Phone lines hung severed from their poles. All street signs had been removed, and most gas lamps were shattered.

Peters placed a hand over his eyes because he felt an overwhelming need to weep. A stream of words ran through his head, so constant it took him a minute to realize it also left his tongue in a low whisper: *This never had to happen, this never had to happen, this never had to happen . . .*

The impulse to weep turned to something colder as they reached City Hall. He strode up to his office and immediately placed a call to police headquarters.

Curtis answered the phone himself, his voice a tired shadow of itself. "Hello."

"Commissioner, it's Mayor Peters."

"You call for my resignation, I expect."

"I call for damage assessment. Let's start there."

Curtis sighed. "One hundred and twenty-nine arrests. Five rioters shot, none critically injured. Five hundred sixty-two people treated for injuries at Haymarket Relief, a third of those related to cuts from broken glass. Ninety-four muggings reported. Sixty-seven assaults-and-battery. Six rapes."

"Six?"

"Reported, yes."

"Your estimate as to the real number?"

Another sigh. "Based on uncorroborated reports from the North End and South Boston, I'd place the number in the dozens. Thirty, let's say."

"Thirty." Peters felt the need to weep again, but it didn't come as an overwhelming wave, merely as a stabbing sensation behind his eyes. "Property damage?"

"In the hundreds of thousands."

"The hundreds of thousands, yes, I thought so myself."

"Mostly small businesses. The banks and department stores—"

"Hired private security. I know."

"The firemen will never strike now."

"What?"

"The firemen," Curtis said. "The sympathy strike. My man in the department tells me they are so irate about the countless false alarms they responded to last night that they've turned against the strikers."

"How does this information help us right now, Commissioner?"

"I won't resign," Curtis said.

The gall of this man. The gumption. A city under siege of its populace and all he thinks of is his job and his pride.

"You won't have to," Peters said. "I'm removing you from your command."

"You can't."

"Oh, I can. You love rules, Commissioner. Please consult Section Six, Chapter Three-twenty-three of the 1885 city bylaws. Once you've done that, clean out your desk. Your replacement will be there by nine."

Peters hung up. He would have expected to feel more satisfaction, but it was one of the more dispiriting aspects of this entire affair that the only possible flush of victory had lain in averting the strike. Once it had begun, no man, least of all himself, could lay claim to any accomplishment. He called to his secretary, Martha Pooley, and she came into the office with the list of names and telephone numbers he'd asked for. He started with Colonel Sullivan of the State Guard. When he answered, Peters skipped all formalities.

"Colonel Sullivan, this is your mayor. I am giving you a direct order that cannot be countermanded. Understood?"

"Yes, Mr. Mayor."

"Assemble the entire State Guard in the Boston area. I am putting the Tenth Regiment, the First Cavalry Troop, the First Motor Corps, and the Ambulance Corps under your command. Is there any reason you cannot perform these duties, Colonel?"

"None whatsoever, sir."

"See to it."

"Yes, Mr. Mayor."

Peters hung up and immediately dialed the home of General Charles Cole, former commander of the Fifty-second Yankee Division and one of the chief members of the Storrow Committee. "General Cole."

"Mr. Mayor."

"Would you serve your city as acting police commissioner, sir?"

"It would be my honor."

"I'll send a car. At what time could you be ready, General?"

"I'm already dressed, Mr. Mayor."

Governor Coolidge held a press conference at ten. He announced that in addition to the regiments Mayor Peters had called up, he had asked Brigadier General Nelson Bryant to assume command of the state response to the crisis. General Bryant had accepted and would command the Eleventh, Twelfth, and Fifteenth Regiments of the State Guard as well as a machine-gun company.

Volunteers continued to converge on the Chamber of Commerce to receive their badges, uniforms, and weapons. Most, he noted, were former officers of the Massachusetts Yankee Division and had served with distinction in the Great War. He further noted that 150 Harvard undergraduates, including the entire football team, had been sworn in as members of the volunteer police department.

"We are in good hands, gentlemen."

When asked why the State Guard had not been called out the previous evening, Governor Coolidge responded, "Yesterday I was persuaded to leave matters of public safety to city authorities. I have since regretted the wisdom of this trust."

When a reporter asked the governor how he'd suffered the bruise under his left eye, Governor Coolidge announced that the press conference was over and left the room.

Danny stood with Nora on the rooftop of his building and looked down at the North End. During the worst of the rioting, some men had blocked off Salem Street with truck tires they'd doused in gasoline and lit afire. Danny could see one now, melted into the street and still smoking, the stench filling his nostrils. The mob had grown all evening, restless, itchy. At about ten o'clock, it had stopped roiling and begun to vent. Danny had watched from his window. Impotent.

By the time it abated about 2 A.M., the streets lay as

smashed and violated as they had after the molasses flood. The voices of the victims—of assaults, of muggings, of motiveless beatings, of rape—rose from the streets and out of tenement windows and rooming houses. Moaning, keening, weeping. The cries of those chosen for random violence, bereft with the knowledge that they'd never know justice in this world.

And it was his fault.

Nora told him it wasn't, but he could see she didn't fully believe it. She'd changed over the course of the night; doubt had entered her eyes. About the choice he'd made, about him. When they'd finally lain down in bed last night, her lips found his cheek and they were cool and hesitant. Instead of going to sleep with one arm over his chest and one leg over his, her usual custom, she turned onto her left side. Her back touched his, so it wasn't a complete rejection, but he felt it nonetheless.

Now, standing with their coffee on the rooftop, looking at the damage strewn below them in the gray light of an overcast morning, she placed a hand on Danny's lower back. It was the lightest of touches and just as quickly removed. When Danny turned, she was chewing the edge of her thumb and her eyes were moist.

"You're not going to work today," he said.

She shook her head but said nothing.

"Nora."

She stopped chewing her thumb and lifted her coffee cup off the parapet. She looked at him, her eyes wide and blank, unreadable.

"You're not going to—"

"Yes, I am," she said.

He shook his head. "It's too dangerous. I don't want you out on those streets."

Her shoulders moved almost imperceptibly. "It's my job. I'm not getting fired."

"You won't get fired."

Another tiny shrug. "And if you're wrong? How would we eat?"

"This will be over soon."

She shook her head.

"It will. Once the city realizes we had no choice and that—"

She turned to him. "The city will hate you, Danny." She swept her arm at the streets below. "They'll never forgive you for this."

"So we were wrong?" A well of isolation sprang up inside him, as desolate and hopeless as any he'd ever known.

"No," she said. "No." She came to him and the touch of her hands on his cheeks felt like salvation. "No, no, no." She shook his face until he met her eyes. "You weren't wrong. You did the only thing you could. It's just . . ." She looked off the roof again.

"Just what?"

"They made it so that the only choice you had left was the one sure to doom you." She kissed him; he tasted the salt of her tears. "*I* love you. *I* believe in what you did."

"But you think we're doomed."

Her hands trailed off his face and fell to her sides. "I think . . ." Her face cooled as he watched her, something he was learning about her, her need to treat crisis with detachment. She raised her eyes and they were no longer moist. "I think you might be out of a job." She gave him a sad, tight smile. "So I can't be losing mine, can I now?"

He walked her to work.

Around them, gray ash and the endless crunch of glass. Scraps of bloodied clothing, splattered pies on the cobblestone amid chunks of brick and charred wood. Blackened storefronts. Overturned carts and overturned cars, all burnt. Two halves of one skirt in the gutter, wet and covered in soot.

It didn't get any worse once they left the North End, it just got more repetitive and, by the time they reached Scollay Square, larger in scope and scale. He tried to pull Nora to him, but she preferred to walk alone. Every now and then she would glance the side of her hand off his and gave him a look of intimate sorrow, and once she leaned into his shoulder as they climbed Bowdoin Street, but she never spoke.

Neither did he.

There was nothing to say.

After he dropped her at work, he walked back to the North End and joined the picket line outside the Oh-One station house. Throughout the late morning and early afternoon, they walked back and forth along Hanover Street. Some passersby greeted them with calls of support and others with shouts of "for shame," but the majority said nothing. They passed along the edge of the sidewalk with downturned eyes or stared through Danny and the other men as if they were ghosts.

Scabs arrived throughout the day. Danny had given the order that they were to be allowed entrance as long as they crossed along the outer edges of the picket line and not through it. Outside of one tense chest-bumping incident and a few catcalls, the scabs passed into the Oh-One station house without ado.

Up and down Hanover came the sound of hammers as men replaced windows with wood planks while others swept up the glass and rescued from the debris any goods the mob had overlooked. A cobbler Danny knew, Giuseppe Balari, stood for a long time staring into the wreckage of his shop. He'd stacked wood against his shop door and laid out his tools, but at the moment when he could have begun covering his storefront, he placed the hammer down on the sidewalk and just stood there, hands out by his side, palms up. He stood that way for ten minutes.

When he turned, Danny didn't manage to drop his eyes in time and Giuseppe's found his. He stared across the street at Danny and mouthed one word: *Why?*

Danny shook his head, a helpless gesture, and turned his face forward as he made another circuit in front of the station house. When he looked again, Giuseppe had placed a wood plank to the window frame and begun hammering.

Midday, several city tow trucks cleared the streets, the husks rattling and clanking over the cobblestones, the tow drivers repeatedly having to stop to retrieve pieces that had fallen off. Not long after, a Packard Single Six pulled to the curb by the picket line and Ralph Raphelson stuck his head out the back window. "A minute, Officer?"

Danny turned his sign upside down and leaned it against a lamp pole. He climbed into the backseat with Raphelson. Raphelson gave him an awkward smile and said nothing. Danny looked out the window at the men walking in circles, at the wood storefronts up and down Hanover.

Raphelson said, "The vote on a sympathy strike has been delayed."

Danny's first reaction was a chilled numbness. "Delayed?"

Raphelson nodded.

"For how long?"

Raphelson looked out his window. "Difficult to ascertain. We've had a hard time reaching several of the delegates."

"You can't vote without them?"

He shook his head. "All delegates must be present. That's sacrosanct."

"How long before everyone's rounded up?"

"Hard to tell."

Danny turned on the seat. "How long?"

"Could be later today. Could be tomorrow."

The numbness left Danny, replaced by an adrenal spike of fear. "But no later."

Raphelson said nothing.

"Ralph," Danny said. "Ralph."

Raphelson turned his head, looked at him.

"No later than tomorrow," Danny said. "Right?"

"I can't guarantee anything."

Danny sat back in his seat. "Oh, my God," he whispered. "Oh, my God."

In Luther's room, he and Isaiah packed the laundry Mrs. Grouse had brought up to them. Isaiah, a veteran traveler, showed Luther how to roll his clothing instead of folding it, and they placed it in Luther's suitcase.

"It'll give you a lot more room," he said, "and you're less apt to suffer wrinkles. But you have to roll it tight now. Like this."

Luther watched Isaiah, then brought the legs of a pair of trousers together and started rolling them from the cuffs.

"A little tighter."

Luther unrolled the trousers and made the first curl twice as tight and clenched his hands as he continued the roll.

"You're getting it now."

Luther cinched the fabric hard between his fingers. "She going to be okay?"

"It'll pass, I'm sure." Isaiah lay a shirt on the bed and buttoned it up. He folded it and smoothed the creases and rolled it up. When he was done, he turned and placed it in the suitcase and smoothed his palm across it one last time. "It'll pass."

When they came down the stairs, they left the suitcase at the bottom and found Yvette in the parlor. She looked up from the afternoon edition of *The Examiner*, and her eyes were bright.

"They may send the State Guard to the trouble spots."

Luther nodded.

Isaiah took his customary seat by the hearth. "I expect the rioting is near over."

"I certainly hope so." Yvette folded the paper and placed it on the side table. She smoothed her dress against her knees. "Luther, would you pour me a cup of tea?"

Luther crossed to the tea service on the sideboard and placed a cube of sugar and spoonful of milk in the cup before adding the tea. He put the cup in its saucer and carried it to Mrs. Giddreaux. She thanked him with a smile and a nod.

"Where were you?" she said.

"We were upstairs."

"Not now." She took a sip of tea. "During the grand opening. The ribbon cutting."

Luther went back to the sideboard and poured another cup of tea. "Mr. Giddreaux?"

Isaiah held up a hand. "Thank you, but no, I'm fine, son."

Luther nodded and added a cube of sugar and sat across from Mrs. Giddreaux. "I got hung up. I'm sorry."

She said, "That big policeman, oh, he was mad. It was as if he knew *exactly* where to look. And yet, he found nothing at all."

"Strange," Luther said.

Mrs. Giddreaux took another sip of tea. "How lucky for us."

"I guess that's how it turned out."

"And now you're off to Tulsa."

"It's where my wife and son are, ma'am. You know if there was any lesser reason, I'd never be going."

She smiled and looked down at her knees. "Maybe you'll write."

That damn near broke Luther, damn near brought him to his knees.

"Ma'am, you surely know that I will write. You surely must know that."

She gathered up his soul in her beautiful eyes. "You do that, my son. You do that."

When she looked back at her knees, Luther met Isaiah's gaze. He nodded at the great old man. "If I may impose . . ."

Mrs. Giddreaux looked back up.

"I still have a bit a business to clear up with those white friends I made."

"What sort of business?"

"A proper good-bye," Luther said. "If I could stay one or two more nights, it sure would make things easier."

She leaned forward in her chair. "Are you patronizing an old woman, Luther?"

"Never, ma'am."

She pointed a finger and wagged it slowly. "Butter wouldn't melt in your mouth."

"Might could," Luther said. "Depends if it got some of your roast chicken attached to it, ma'am."

"Is that the trick?"

"I believe it is."

Mrs. Giddreaux stood and smoothed her skirt. She turned toward the kitchen. "I have potatoes need peeling and beans need washing, young man. Don't be tarrying." Luther followed her out of the room. "Wouldn't dream of it."

It was sundown when the mobs returned to the streets. In some sections—South Boston and Charlestown—it was the same random mayhem, but in other areas, particularly Roxbury and the South End, it had a political tenor. When Andrew Peters heard about this, he had Horace Russell drive him over to Columbus Avenue. General Cole didn't want him to leave without a military escort, but Peters convinced him he'd be fine. He'd been doing it all last night and it was a lot easier with one car than three.

Horace Russell stopped the car at Arlington and Columbus. The mob was a block farther down, and Peters stepped out of the car and walked half a block. Along the way he passed three barrels filled with pitch, upended torches sticking out of them. The sight of them—the sense they gave of the medieval—stoked his dread.

The signs were worse. Whereas the few he'd seen last night were mostly crude variations on either FUCK THE POLICE or FUCK THE SCABS, these new ones had been carefully prepared in red lettering as bright as fresh blood. Several were in Russian, but the rest were clear enough:

REVOLUTION NOW!
END THE TYRANNY OF THE STATE!
DEATH TO CAPITALISM! DEATH TO SLAVE DRIVERS!
OVERTHROW THE CAPITALIST MONARCHY!

. . . and the one Mayor Andrew J. Peters liked least of all . . .

BURN, BOSTON, BURN!

He hurried back to the car and told Horace Russell to drive straight to General Cole.

General Cole took the news with a knowing nod. "We've received reports that the mob in Scollay Square is also growing political. South Boston is already bursting at the seams. I don't think they'll be able to hold them back with forty policemen, as they did last night. I'm sending volunteers to both areas to see if they can quell the disturbance. Barring that they're to report back with specifics about crowd size and the depth of the Bolshevik influence."

" 'Burn, Boston, burn,' " Peters whispered.

"It won't come to that, Mr. Mayor, I assure you. Why, the entire Harvard football team is now armed and standing by for orders. Those are fine young men. And I'm in constant contact with Major Sullivan and the State Guard Command. They're just around the corner, sir, standing at the ready."

Peters nodded, taking comfort in that, however small. Four full regiments plus a machine-gun unit and the motor and ambulance corps.

"I'll check in with Major Sullivan now," Peters said.

"Careful out there, Mr. Mayor. Dusk is near upon us."

Peters left the office that just yesterday had been occupied by Edwin Curtis. He walked up the hill to the State House, and his heart leapt at the sight of them—my god, an army! Under the grand archway at the back of the building, the First

673

Cavalry Troop paraded their horses back and forth in a steady stream, the clop of the hooves sounding like muffled gunshots against the cobblestones. On the front lawns facing Beacon Street, the Twelfth and Fifteenth Regiments stood at parade rest. Across the street, at the top of the Common, the Tenth and Eleventh stood at full attention. If Peters had never wanted it to come to this, he could nevertheless be forgiven for the swell of pride the sight of the Commonwealth's might birthed in him. This was the antithesis of the mob. This was calculated force, beholden to the rule of law, capable of restraint and violence in equal measure. This was the fist beneath the velvet glove of democracy, and it was gorgeous.

He accepted their salutes as he passed through them and up the front steps of the State House. His body felt utterly weightless by the time he passed through the great marble hall and was directed to Major Sullivan in the back with the First Cavalry. Major Sullivan had set up his command post under the archway, and the telephones and field radios on the long table in front of him were ringing at a furious pace. Officers answered them and scribbled on paper and handed the papers to Major Sullivan, who took note of the mayor as he approached, and then went back to scanning his latest dispatch.

He saluted Andrew Peters. "Mr. Mayor, I'd say you're just in time."

"For?"

"The volunteer police General Cole sent to Scollay Square walked into an ambush, sir. There have been shots fired, several injuries reported."

"Good Lord."

Major Sullivan nodded. "They won't last, sir. I'm not sure they'll last five minutes in truth."

Well then, here it was.

"Your men are ready?"

"You see them here before you, sir."

"The cavalry?" Peters said.

"No quicker way to break up a crowd and establish dominance, Mr. Mayor."

Peters was struck by the absurdity of it all—a nineteenth-century military action in twentieth-century America. Absurd but somehow apt.

Peters gave the order: "Save the volunteers, Major."

"With pleasure, sir." Major Sullivan snapped a salute and a young captain brought him his horse. Sullivan toed the stirrup without ever looking at it and swung gracefully atop his horse. The captain climbed onto the mount behind his and raised a bugle to his shoulder.

"First Cavalry Troop, on my command we will ride down into Scollay Square to the intersection of Cornhill and Sudbury. We will rescue the volunteer policemen and restore order. You are not to fire on the crowd unless you have no— *I* repeat, absolutely *no*—choice. Is that understood?"

A hard chorus of "Yes, sir!"

"Then, gentlemen, at-ten-tion!"

The horses swung into rows as sharp and straight as razors.

Peters thought, Wait a minute. Hold on. Slow down. Let's think about this.

"Charge!"

The bugle blew and Major Sullivan's mount burst out through the portico, as if fired from a gun. The rest of the cavalry followed suit and Mayor Peters found himself running alongside them. He felt like a child at his first parade, but this was better than any parade, and he was no longer a child but a leader of men, a man worthy of salutes given without irony.

He was almost crushed by the flank of a horse as they rounded the corner of the State House fence line, took a quick right and then streamed left onto Beacon at full gallop. The sound of all those galloping hooves was unlike anything he had ever heard, as if the heavens had unleashed boulders by the hundreds, by the thousands, and sudden white cracks and fissures appeared in the windows along lower Beacon, and Beacon Hill itself shuddered from the glorious fury of the beasts and their riders.

The breadth of them had passed him by the time they turned left on Cambridge Street and headed for Scollay Square, but Mayor Peters kept running, the sharp decline of Beacon giving him added speed, and when he broke out onto Cambridge, they appeared before him, a block ahead, sabers held aloft, that bugle trumpeting their arrival. And just beyond them, the mob. A vast pepper sea that spread in every direction.

How Andrew Peters wished he'd been born twice as fast, wished he'd been given wings, as he watched those majestic brown beasts and their magnificent riders breach the crowd! They parted that pepper sea as Andrew Peters continued to run and the pepper gained clarity, became heads and then faces. Sounds grew more distinct as well. Shouts, screams, some squealing that sounded nonhuman, the clang and thwang of metal, the first gunshot.

Followed by the second.

Followed by the third.

Andrew Peters reached Scollay Square in time to see a horse and rider fall through the storefront of a burned-out drugstore. A woman lay on the ground with blood seeping from her ears and a hoofprint in the center of her forehead. Sabers slashed at limbs. A man with blood all over his face pushed past his mayor. A volunteer policeman lay curled up on the sidewalk, clutching his side, weeping, most of his teeth gone. The horses spun in ferocious circles, their great legs stomping and clopping, their riders swinging those sabers.

A horse toppled, and its legs kicked out as it whinnied. People fell, people were kicked, people screamed. The horse kept kicking. The rider got a firm grip on the stirrup and the horse rose up in the crowd, its white eyes as large as eggs and wide with terror as it rose on its front legs and kicked out with its back legs and then toppled again with a squeal of confusion and abandonment.

Directly in front of Mayor Peters a volunteer policeman with a Springfield rifle and a face warped by fear leveled his weapon. Andrew Peters saw what was going to happen in the split second before it did, saw the other man in the black bowler with the stick, the man looking dazed, as if he'd taken a hit to the head, but still holding that stick, wavering. And Andrew Peters shouted, "No!"

But the bullet left the volunteer policeman's rifle and entered the chest of the dazed man with the stick. It exited his body as well, punching its way out and imbedding itself in the shoulder of another man, who spun and hit the ground. The volunteer policeman and Andrew Peters both watched the man with the stick stand in place, bent over at the waist. He stood like that for a few seconds, and then he dropped the stick and pitched forward onto the ground. His leg jerked, and then he sighed forth a gout of black blood and went still.

Andrew Peters felt the whole horrible summer coalesce into this moment. All the dreams they'd had of peace, of a mutually beneficial solution, all the hard work and goodwill and good faith, all the hope . . .

The mayor of the great city of Boston lowered his head and wept.

CHAPTER *thirty-eight*

Thomas had held out hope that the work he and Crowley and their ragtag band had performed last night would have sent the proper message, but it wasn't to be. They'd busted heads last night, they had. They'd gone in, fierce and fearless, and met the mob in Andrew Square, then met it again on West Broadway, and they'd cleared it. Two old warhorses and thirty-two bucks of varying experience and varying levels of fear. Thirty-four against thousands! When he'd finally arrived home, Thomas hadn't been able to fall asleep for hours.

But now the mob was at it again. In twice the numbers. And unlike last night, they were organized. Bolsheviks and anarchists moved among them, handing out weapons and rhetoric in equal measure. The Gusties and a variety of in-state and out-of-state plug-uglies had formed squads, and they were hitting safes up and down Broadway. Mayhem, yes, but no longer mindless.

Thomas had received a call from the mayor himself asking him to refrain from action until the State Guard arrived. When Thomas asked when His Honor expected that help to come, the mayor told him there'd been some unforeseen trouble in Scollay Square but the troops would be arriving presently.

Presently.

West Broadway was anarchy. The citizens Thomas had

sworn to protect were being victimized at this very moment. And the only possible saviors would arrive . . . presently.

Thomas ran a hand over his eyes and then lifted the receiver from the telephone cradle and asked the operator to patch him through to his home. Connor answered.

"All quiet?" Thomas asked.

"Here?" Connor said. "Sure. What's it like on the streets?"

"Bad," Thomas said. "Stay in."

"You need another body? I can help, Dad."

Thomas closed his eyes for a moment, wishing he loved this son more. "Another body won't make a shred of difference now, Con'. We're past that point."

"Fucking Danny."

"Con'," Thomas said, "how many times do I have to tell you about my distaste for profanity? Does anything get through your thick skull on that score, son?"

"Sorry, Dad. Sorry." Connor's heavy breath moved through the phone lines. "I just . . . Danny caused this. Danny, Dad. The whole city's tearing itself—"

"It isn't all Danny's fault. He's one man."

"Yeah," Connor said, "but he was supposed to be family."

That seared something in Thomas. The "supposed to be." Was this what became of pride in your offspring? Was this the end of the road that began when you held your firstborn, fresh from your wife's womb, and allowed yourself to dream of his future? Was this the price of loving blindly and too much?

"He is family," Thomas said. "He's blood, Con'."

"To you maybe."

Oh, Jesus. This was the price. It certainly was. Of love. Of family.

"Where's your mother?" Thomas said.

"In bed."

Not surprising—an ostrich always searched out the nearest pile of sand.

"Where's Joe?"

679

"Bed, too."

Thomas dropped his heels off the corner of the desk. "It's nine o'clock."

"Yeah, he's been sick all day."

"With what?"

"I dunno. A cold?"

Thomas shook his head at that. Joe was like Aiden—nothing knocked him down. He'd sooner poke out his own eyes before he took to his bed on a night like this.

"Go check on him."

"What?"

"Con', go check on him."

"Fine, fine."

Connor placed the receiver down and Thomas heard his footfalls in the hall and then a creak as he opened Joe's bedroom door. Silence. Then Connor's footfalls coming toward the phone, quicker, and Thomas spoke as soon as he heard him lift the receiver.

"He's gone, isn't he?"

"Jesus, Dad."

"When's the last time you saw him?"

"About an hour ago. Look, he couldn't have—"

"Find him," Thomas said, surprised the words came out a cold hiss instead of a hot shout. "You understand me, Con'? Are we clear?"

"Yes, sir."

"Find your brother," Thomas said. "Now."

Back in June, the first time Joe had slipped out of the house on K Street, he'd fallen in with Teeny Watkins, a boy who'd attended first and second grades at Gate of Heaven with him before he dropped out to support his ma and three sisters. Teeny was a newsie, and Joe, during those three days on the streets, had dreamed of becoming one himself. The newsies ran in tight packs based on whichever newspaper they were affiliated with. Gang fights were common. If Teeny were to be believed, so was breaking-and-entering on behalf of adult gangs like the Gusties, since newsies tended to run small and could squeeze through windows adults couldn't.

Running with the newsies, Joe saw a brighter world, a louder one. He became acquainted with lower Washington Street's Newspaper Row and all its saloons and shouting matches. He ran with his newfound gang along the edges of Scollay Square and West Broadway, and imagined the day when he'd cross over those edges and become part of that night world.

On the third day, though, Teeny handed Joe a canister of gasoline and a pack of matches and told him to set fire to a *Traveler* newsstand on Dover Street. When Joe refused, Teeny didn't argue. He just took the can and the matches back. Then he beat Joe in front of the other newsies, many of whom laid down bets. There was no fury to the beating, no emotion. Every time Joe looked into Teeny's eyes as he brought another fist down onto Joe's face, it was clear that Teeny *could* beat him to death if he chose. That, Joe realized, was the only outcome the other newsies were betting on. Whether Teeny did or not was an issue to which Teeny himself seemed indifferent.

It took him a few months to get over the coldness with which the beating had been delivered. The beating itself was almost forgettable by comparison. But now, knowing that the city was coming alive—and even coming apart—in a way it might not do again in his lifetime, any pains or lessons from that day receded and were replaced by his appetite for the night world and his possible place in it.

Once he left the house, he cut over two blocks and walked up H Street toward the noise. He'd heard it all last night from his bedroom—West Broadway making even more of a racket than usual. West Broadway was where the saloons were and the rows and rows of boardinghouses and the gambling dens and the boys playing shell games on the corners and whistling to the women who stood in the windows of rooms lit red or orange or dark mustard. East Broadway ran through City Point, the respectable part of South Boston, the section where Joe lived. But it was just a matter of crossing East Broadway and making one's way down the hill until you reached the intersections of East and West Broadway and Dorchester Street. There you found the rest of Southie, the vast majority of it, and it wasn't quiet and respectable and well tended. It jumped and exploded with laughter and quarrels and shouts and loud off-key singing. Straight up West Broadway until you hit the bridge, straight down Dorchester Street until you hit Andrew Square. Nobody had a car around these parts, much less a driver, like his father. No one owned a home; this was renters' territory. And the only thing rarer than a car was a yard. Boston proper had Scollay Square to provide its release, but Southie had West Broadway. Not as grand, not as brightly lit, but just as dense with sailors and thieves and men getting a load on.

Now, at nine in the evening, it was like a carnival. Joe made his way down the middle of the street, where men drank openly from bottles and you had to be careful not to step on a blanket where dice were being thrown. A barker called, "Pretty ladies for every taste," and upon seeing Joe: "All ages welcome! As long as you're stiff and not a stiff, come on in! Pretty ladies lined up for your delight!" A drunk reeled into him and Joe fell to the street and the guy gave him a glance over his shoulder and continued staggering. Joe dusted himself off. He smelled smoke in the air as some men ran past him carrying a dresser with clothes piled high on top. Just about every third man brandished a rifle. A few others held shotguns. He walked another half block and sidestepped a fistfight between two women, and he started thinking maybe this wasn't the best night to investigate West Broadway. McCory's Department Store burned ahead of him, people standing around cheering the flame and smoke. Joe heard a loud crash and looked up to see a body falling from a second story window. He stepped back and the body hit the street and broke into several sharp pieces and the crowd hooted. A mannequin. The ceramic head had cracked and one ear had broken into several shards and Joe looked up in time to see the second one sailing out of the same window. That one landed on its feet and snapped in half at the waist. Someone wrenched the head off the first mannequin and hurled it into the crowd.

Joe decided it was definitely time to head back. He turned and a small, bespectacled man with wet hair and brown teeth stooped in front of him, blocking his path. "You look like a sporting man, Young John. Are you a sporting man?"

"Name's not John."

"Who's to know from names? That's what I say. Are you a sporting man then? Are ye? Are ye?" The man put his hand on his shoulder. "Because, Young John, right down that alley there, we've some of the finest sports betting in the world."

Joe shrugged off the hand. "Dogs?"

"Dogs, aye," the man said. "We've got dogs fighting dogs. And cocks fighting cocks. And we've dogs fighting rats, ten at a time!"

Joe moved to his left and the man moved with him.

"Don't like the rats?" The man haw-hawwed. "All the more reason to see 'em kilt." He pointed. "Right down that alley."

"Nah." Joe tried to wave it away. "I don't think—"

"That's correct! Why think?" The man lurched forward and Joe could smell wine and egg on his breath. "Come now, Young John. Down yonder way."

The man reached for his wrist and Joe saw an opening and darted past the guy. The guy grabbed at his shoulder, but Joe snapped away from his hand and kept walking fast. He looked back and the guy followed him.

"A dandy, are you, Young John? So it's Lord John, is it? Excuse me all to heaven indeed! Are we not to your cultured taste, your lordship?"

The man trotted in front of him and swayed from side

to side, as if made jaunty by the prospect of fresh sport.

"Come, Young John, let's be friends."

The man took another swipe at him and Joe jerked to his right and darted ahead again. He turned back long enough to raise his palms and show the man he wanted no trouble, and then he turned forward again and picked up the pace, hoping the guy would tire of the game and spend his energy on an easier mark.

"You've pretty hair, Young John. The color of some cats I've seen, it 'tis."

Joe heard the man pick up sudden speed behind him, a mad scrabbling, and he hopped up onto the sidewalk and ducked low and ran through the skirts of two tall women smoking cigars who swatted at him and let loose high laughs. He looked back over his shoulder at them but they'd turned their attention to the brown-toothed barker who was still in pursuit.

"Ah, leave him alone, ya cretin."

"Mind yourselves, ladies, or I'll be back with me blade."

The women laughed. "We've seen your blade, Rory, and, sure, it's shameful small, it is."

Joe broke back out into the middle of the street.

Rory scuttled up alongside him. "Can I shine your shoes, Lord? Can I turn down your bed?"

"Let him be, you ponce," one of the women called, but Joe could tell by their voices that they'd lost interest. He swung his arms by his side, trying to pretend he didn't notice Rory making ape sounds beside him, the man swinging his arms now, too. Joe kept his head turned forward, trying to appear like a boy with a firm destination as he headed deeper into the thickening mob.

Rory ran his hand gently along the side of Joe's face and Joe punched him.

His fist caught the side of Rory's head and the man blinked. Several men along the sidewalk laughed. Joe ran and the laughter followed them up the street.

"Can I be of service?" Rory called as he trotted behind him. "Can I help you with your griefs? They looks a might heavy for ye."

He was gaining on him and Joe darted around an overturned wagon and through a group of men. He ran past two men with shotguns and through the doors of a saloon. He stepped to his left and watched the doors and took several gulps of air and then looked around at the men, many in their work shirts and suspenders, a majority with handlebar mustaches and black bowlers. They looked back at him. Somewhere in the rear of the saloon, beyond the crowd and the smoke, Joe heard grunts and moans and knew that he'd interrupted some kind of show back there, and he opened his mouth to tell them he was being chased. He caught the bartender's eye as he did, and the bartender pointed across the bar at him and said, "Throw that fucking kid out of here."

Two hands gripped his arms, and his feet left the floor and he sailed through the air and back through the doors. He cleared the sidewalk and landed on the street and bounced. He felt a burn in both knees and his right hand as he tried to come to a stop. And then he wasn't bouncing anymore. Someone stepped over him and kept walking. He lay there nauseated and heard brown-toothed Rory say, "No, allow me, your lordship."

Rory grasped Joe by his hair. Joe swatted at his arms and Rory tightened his grip.

He held Joe a few inches off the ground. Joe's scalp screamed and Rory's back teeth were black as he smiled. When he burped it smelled of wine and eggs again. "You've got trimmed nails and, sure, fine clothes, Young Lord John. You're quite the picture."

Joe said, "My father is—"

Rory squeezed Joe's jaw in his hand. "You'll be finding a new father in me, so ye might want to save your fucking energy, your lordship."

He drew his hand back and Joe kicked him. He connected

with Rory's knee first and the man's grip loosened in his hair and Joe got his whole body into the next kick and drove it into the man's inner thigh. He'd been aiming for his groin but it hadn't worked out. But the kick was sharp enough to make Rory hiss and wince and let go of his hair.

That's when the straight razor came out.

Joe dropped to all fours and scrambled between Rory's legs. Once he'd cleared them, he stayed that way, moving through the dense crowd on his hands and knees—between a pair of dark trousers and then a pair of tan ones, then two-toned spats followed by brown work boots caked with dried mud. He didn't look back. He just kept crawling, feeling like a crab, scuttling left, then right, then left again, the pairs of legs growing denser and denser, the air carrying less and less oxygen as he crawled ever deeper into the heart of the mob.

At nine-fifteen, Thomas received a call from General Cole, the acting commissioner.

"Are you in contact with Captain Morton at the Sixth?" General Cole said.

"Constant contact, General."

"How many men does he have at his command?"

"A hundred, sir. Mostly volunteers."

"And you, Captain?"

"About the same, General."

General Cole said, "We're sending the Tenth Regiment of the State Guard to the Broadway Bridge. You and Captain Morton are to sweep the crowd up West Broadway toward the bridge. You understand, Captain?"

"Yes, General."

"We'll pin them down there. We'll start making arrests and hauling them into trucks. That sight alone should disperse the majority of them."

"I agree."

"We'll meet at the bridge at twenty-two hundred, Captain.

You think that gives you enough time to push them toward my net?"

"I was just waiting on your orders, General."

"Well, now you have them, Captain. See you soon."

He hung up and Thomas rang Sergeant Eigen's desk. When he answered, Thomas said, "Assemble the men immediately," and hung up.

He called Captain Morton. "You ready, Vincent?"

"Ready and willing, Thomas."

"We'll send 'em your way."

"Looking forward to it," Morton said.

"See you at the bridge."

"See you at the bridge."

Thomas performed the same ritual he had the previous night, donning his holster, filling his pockets with shells, loading his Remington. Then he walked out of his office into the roll call room.

They were all assembled—his men, the Metro Park cops from last night, and sixty-six volunteers. These last gave him momentary pause. It wasn't the aged war veterans he was worried about, it was the young pups, particularly the Harvard contingent. He didn't like their eyes, the way they swam with the light of those on a lark, a fraternity prank. There were two sitting on a table in the back who kept whispering and chuckling as he explained their orders.

". . . and when we enter West Broadway, we'll be coming up on their flank. We will form a line stretching from one side of the street to the other and we *will not* break that line. We will push them west, always west, toward the bridge. Don't get caught up trying to push every single body. Some will remain behind. As long as they pose no direct threat, leave them. Just keep pushing."

One of the Harvard footballers nudged the other and they both guffawed.

Thomas stepped off the rostrum and continued talking as he worked his way through the men. "If you are hit with projectiles, ignore them. Just keep pushing. If we receive fire, I will give the order to fire back. Only me. You are not to return fire until you hear my order."

The Harvard boys watched him come with bright smiles on their faces.

"When we reach D Street," Thomas said, "we will be joined by the men of the Sixth Precinct. There we will form a pincer and funnel what's left of the mob straight at the Broadway Bridge. At that point, we will leave no stragglers behind. Everyone comes along for the ride."

He reached the Harvard boys. They raised their eyebrows at him. One was blond and blue-eyed and the other brown-haired and bespectacled, his forehead splattered with acne. Their friends sat along the back wall with them and watched to see what would happen.

Thomas asked the blond one, "What's your name, son?"

"Chas Hudson, Cap'n."

"And your friend?"

"Benjamin Lorne," the brown-haired one said. "I'm right here."

Thomas nodded at him and turned back to Chas. "You know what happens, son, when you don't take a battle seriously?"

Chas rolled his eyes. "Guess you'll be telling me, Cap'n."

Thomas slapped Benjamin Lorne in the face so hard he fell off the table and his glasses flew into the back row. He stayed down there, on his knees, as blood dribbled from his mouth.

Chas opened his mouth but Thomas cut off anything he might have said by squeezing his hand over his jaw. "What happens, son, is that the man next to you usually gets hurt." Thomas looked over at Chas's Harvard buddies as Chas gurgled. "You are officers of the law tonight. Understood?"

He got eight nods in return.

He turned his attention back to Chas. "I don't care who your family is, son. If you make a mistake tonight? I will shoot you in the heart."

He pushed him back against the wall and let go of his chin. Thomas turned back to the rest of the men. "Further questions?"

Everything went fine until they reached F Street. They were hit with eggs and they were hit with stones, but for the most part the mob moved steadily up West Broadway. When one didn't, he was hit with a billy club and the message was received and the mob moved again. Several dropped their rifles to the sidewalk and the cops and volunteers scooped them up as they continued forward. After five blocks, they were carrying an extra rifle per man and Thomas had them stop long enough to remove the bullets. The crowd stopped as well and Thomas found several faces who might have been making designs on those rifles, so he ordered the men to smash them against the pavement. The sight of that got the crowd moving again, and moving smoothly, and Thomas began to feel the same confidence he'd felt last night when he'd swept Andrew Square with Crowley.

At F Street, however, they ran into the radicalized section— the sign holders, the rhetoric spouters, the Bolsheviks, and the anarchists. Several were fighters, and a melee broke out on the corner of F and Broadway as a dozen volunteers taking up the rear were outflanked and then set upon by the godless subversives. They used pipes mostly, but then Thomas spotted a heavily bearded fella raising a pistol and he drew his own revolver, took one step forward, and shot the man.

The slug hit him high in the shoulder and he spun and dropped. Thomas pointed his revolver at the man who'd been standing next to him as the rest of the Bolshies froze. Thomas looked at his men as they fanned out beside him and he said one word:

"Aim!"

The rifle barrels came up in one swift line, as if choreographed, and the Bolshies turned and ran for their lives. Several of the volunteers were cut and bleeding, but none critically, and Thomas gave them a minute to check themselves for more serious damage as Sergeant Eigen checked on the man Thomas had shot.

"He'll live, Cap'."

Thomas nodded. "Then leave him where he lies."

From there they faced no further challenge as they walked the next two blocks and the crowd ran before them. The logjam started when they reached D Street, home of the Sixth Precinct. Captain Morton and his men had pushed from the sides and now the entire crowd was jammed and milling between D Street and A, just short of the Broadway Bridge. Thomas saw Morton himself on the north side of Broadway, and when their eyes met Thomas pointed to the south side and Morton nodded. Thomas and his men fanned out along the south side of the street while Morton's men took the north and now they very much did push. They pushed hard. They formed a fence out of their rifles and used that steel and their own fury and fear to manhandle the entire herd forward, ever forward. For several blocks it was like trying to push a pride of lions through a mouse hole. Thomas lost track of how many times he was spat on or scratched and it became impossible to tell which fluids on his face and neck were which. He did find one reason to permit himself a small smile in the midst of it all, however, when he spotted the formerly smug Chas Hudson with a broken nose and an eye as black as a cobra.

The faces of the mob, however, did not elicit anything near to joy in him. His people, the faces nearest him as Irish as potatoes and drunken sentiment, all twisted into repulsive, barbaric masks of rage and self pity. As if they'd a *right* to do this. As if this country owed them any more than it had handed Thomas when he stepped off the boat, which is to say nothing but a fresh chance. He wanted to push them straight back to Ireland, straight back to the loving arms of the British, back to their cold fields and their dank pubs and their toothless women. What had that gray country ever given them except melancholia and alcoholism and the dark humor of the habitually defeated? So they came here, one of the few cities in the world where their kind was given a fair shake. But did they act like Americans? Did they act with respect or gratitude? No. They acted like what they were—the niggers of Europe. How dare they? When this was over, it would take Thomas and good Irishmen like him another decade to undo all the damage this mob had done in two days. Damn you all, he thought as they continued to push them back. Damn you all for smearing our race yet again.

Just past A Street, he felt some give. Broadway widened here, opening into a basin where it met the Fort Point Channel. Just beyond was the Broadway Bridge, and Thomas's heart fairly leapt to see the troops arrayed on the bridge and the trucks rolling off it into the square. He allowed himself his second smile of the evening, and that's when someone shot Sergeant Eigen in the stomach. The sound of it hung in the air as Eigen's face bore a look of surprise mixed with growing awareness. Then he fell to the street. Thomas and Lieutenant Stone reached him first. Another bullet hit a drainpipe just to their left and the men returned fire, a dozen rifles discharging at once as Thomas and Stone lifted Eigen off the ground and carried him toward the sidewalk.

That's when he saw Joe. The boy ran along the north side of the street toward the bridge and Thomas made out the man chasing his son as well, a onetime pimp and barker named Rory Droon, a pervert and rapist, now chasing his son. Thomas got Eigen to the sidewalk and they lowered him so that his back was against a wall, and Eigen said, "Am I dying, Cap'?"

"No, but you'll be in a fair sight of pain, son." Thomas searched the crowd for his son. He couldn't find Joe, but he saw Connor suddenly, streaking up the street toward the bridge, dodging those he could, bulling his way through others, and Thomas felt a flush of pride for his middle son that surprised him because he couldn't remember the last time such a feeling had come upon him.

"Get him," he whispered.

"What's that, sir?" Stone said.

"Stay with Sergeant Eigen," Thomas said. "Slow the bleeding."

"Yes, Captain."

"I'll be back," Thomas said and headed into the mob.

The volleys of gunfire had whipped the crowd to a boil. Connor couldn't tell where the bullets were coming from, just that they were coming, pinging off poles and brick and street signs. He wondered if this is how men had felt in the war, during a battle, this sense of complete chaos, of your own death flying past you in the air, ricocheting off something hard and coming back for a second pass. People ran every which way, banged into one another, snapped ankles, shoved and scratched and wailed in terror. A couple ahead of him fell down, either from a bullet or a rock or just because they entwined their legs and tripped, and Connor vaulted into the air and cleared them. As he came down he saw Joe up by the bridge, the dirty-looking man grabbing him by the hair. Connor sidestepped a guy swinging a pipe at no one in particular, then spun around a woman on her knees, and the dirty-looking guy was turning his way when Connor punched him full in the face. His momentum carried him forward so that he finished the punch by landing on the guy and dropping him to the street. He scrambled up and grabbed the guy by the throat and raised his fist again but the guy was out, out cold, a small pool of blood forming on the pavement where his head had landed. Connor stood and looked for Joe, saw the kid crumpled in a ball when Connor had managed to knock them both over. He went to his little brother and turned him over and Joe looked up at him with wide eyes.

"You okay?"

"Yeah, yeah."

"Here." Connor stooped and Joe wrapped his arms around his shoulders and Connor lifted him off the street.

"Fire at will!"

Connor spun, saw the State Guard troops coming off the bridge, their rifles extended. Rifles from the crowd pointed back. A collection of volunteer policemen, one with a black eye and broken nose, leveled their weapons as well. Everyone was pointing at everyone else, as if there were no sides, just targets.

"Close your eyes, Joe. Close your eyes."

He pressed Joe's head to his shoulder and all the rifles seemed to go off at once. The air exploded with white puffs from the muzzles. A sudden, high-pitched shriek. A member of the State Guard grabbing his neck. A bloody hand raised in the air. Connor ran for a car overturned at the base of the bridge with Joe in his arms as the crack of rifle fire erupted anew. Bullets sparked off the side of the car, the clang of them like the sound of heavy coins thrown into a metal bowl, and Connor pressed Joe's face harder to his shoulder. A bullet hissed by on his right and hit a guy in the knee. The guy fell. Connor turned his head away. He'd almost reached the front of the car when the bullets hit the window. The glass slid through the night air like sleet or hail, translucent, a shower of silver rushing out of all that blackness.

Connor found himself on his back. He didn't remember slipping. He was just suddenly on the ground. He could hear the ping of bullets grow less insistent, could hear the yells and moans and people shouting out names. He smelled cordite and smoke in the air and the faint odor of roasted meat for some reason. He heard Joe call his name and then shriek it, his voice wracked with horror and sadness. He reached out his hand and felt Joe's close over it, but Joe still wouldn't stop screaming.

Then his father's voice, shushing Joe, cooing to him. "Joseph, Joseph, I'm here. Ssssh."

"Dad?" Connor said.

"Connor," his father said.

"Who turned out the lights?"

"Jesus," his father whispered.

"I can't see, Dad."

"I know, son."

"Why can't I see?"

"We're going to get you to a hospital, son. Immediately. I swear."

"Dad?"

He felt his father's hand on his chest. "Just lie still, son. Just lie still."

CHAPTER *thirty-nine*

The next morning, the State Guard placed a machine gun on a tripod at the northern end of West Broadway in South Boston. They placed another at the intersection of West Broadway and G Street and a third at the intersection of Broadway and Dorchester Street. The Tenth Regiment patrolled the streets. The Eleventh Regiment manned the rooftops.

They repeated the procedure in Scollay Square and along Atlantic Avenue in the North End. General Cole blocked off access to any streets entering Scollay Square and set up a checkpoint on the Broadway Bridge. Anyone caught on the streets in question without a viable reason for being there was subject to immediate arrest.

The city remained quiet throughout the day, the streets empty.

Governor Coolidge held a press conference. While he expressed sympathy for the nine confirmed dead and the hundreds injured, he stated that it was the mob itself that was to blame. The mob and the policemen who had left their posts. The governor went on to state that while the mayor had attempted to shore up the city during the terrible crisis, it was clear he had been wholly unprepared for such an emergency. Therefore control from this point on would be assumed by the state and the governor himself. In that capacity, his first order of business was to reinstate Edwin

Upton Curtis to his rightful place as police commissioner.

Curtis appeared by his side at the rostrum and announced that the police department of the great city of Boston, acting in concert with the State Guard, would brook no further rioting. "The rule of law will be respected or the consequences will be dire. This is not Russia. We will use every measure of force at our disposal to ensure democracy for our citizens. Anarchy ends today."

A reporter from the *Transcript* stood and raised his hand. "Governor Coolidge, am I clear that it is your opinion that Mayor Peters is at fault for the past two nights' chaos?"

Coolidge shook his head. "The mob is at fault. The policemen who committed gross dereliction of their sworn duties are at fault. Mayor Peters is not at fault. He was merely caught unawares and was thus, in the early stages of the riots, a bit ineffectual."

"But, Governor," the reporter said, "we've heard several reports that it was Mayor Peters who wished to call out the State Guard within an hour of the police walkout, and that you, sir, and Commissioner Curtis vetoed the idea."

"Your information is incorrect," Coolidge said.

"But, Governor—"

"Your information is incorrect," Coolidge repeated. "This press conference is completed."

Thomas Coughlin held his son's hand while he wept. Connor didn't make a sound, but the tears slid freely from the thick white bandages covering his eyes and rolled off his chin to dampen the collar of his hospital gown.

His mother stared out the window of Mass General, trembling, her eyes dry.

Joe sat in a chair on the other side of the bed. He hadn't spoken a word since they'd lifted Connor into the ambulance last night.

Thomas touched Connor's cheek. "It's okay," he whispered.

"How's it okay?" Connor said. "I'm blind."

"I know, I know, son. But we'll get through this."

Connor turned his head away and tried to remove his hand, but Thomas held fast to it.

"Con'," Thomas said, hearing the helplessness in his own voice, "it's a terrible blow. Of that there can be little doubt. But don't give in to the sin of despair, son. It's the worst sin of all. God will help you through this. He just asks for strength."

"Strength?" Connor coughed a wet laugh. "I'm *blind*."

At the window, Ellen blessed herself.

"Blind," Connor whispered.

Thomas could think of nothing to say. Maybe *this*, of all things, was the true price of family—being unable to stop the pains of those you loved. Unable to suck it out of the blood, the heart, the head. You held them and named them and fed them and made your plans for them, never fully realizing that the world was always out there, waiting to apply its teeth.

Danny walked into the room and froze.

Thomas hadn't thought it through, but he realized immediately what Danny saw in their eyes: They blamed him.

Well, of course they did. Who else was to blame?

Even Joe, who'd idolized Danny for so long, stared up at him with confusion and spite.

Thomas kept it simple. "Your brother was blinded last night." He raised Connor's hand to his lips and kissed it. "In the riots."

"Dan?" Connor said. "That you?"

"It's me, Con'."

"I'm blind, Dan."

"I know."

"I don't blame you, Dan. I don't."

Danny lowered his head and his shoulders shook. Joe looked away.

"I don't," Connor said again.

Ellen left the window and crossed the room to Danny. She placed a hand on his shoulder. Danny raised his head. Ellen looked in his eyes as Danny dropped his hands by his side and turned up the palms.

Ellen slapped him in the face.

Danny's face crumpled and Ellen slapped him again.

"Get out," she whispered. "Get out, you . . . you Bolshevik." She pointed at Connor. "You did that. You. Get out."

Danny looked toward Joe, but Joe looked away.

He looked at Thomas. Thomas met his eyes and then shook his head and turned his face from him.

That night, the State Guard shot four men in Jamaica Plain. One died. The Tenth Regiment cleared the dice players from the Boston Common, marching them up Tremont Street at bayonet point. A crowd gathered. Warning shots were fired. A man was shot through the chest trying to rescue a dice player. He succumbed to his wounds later that evening.

The rest of the city was quiet.

Danny spent the next two days marshaling support. He was assured in person that the Telephone & Telegraph Union was ready to walk off the job at a moment's notice. The Bartenders Union assured him of the same, as did the United Hebrew Trade Unions, and the Carmen and Electrical Workers Unions. The firemen, however, would not agree to meet with him or return his calls.

I came here to say good-bye," Luther said.

Nora stepped back from the door. "Come in, come in." Luther entered. "Danny around?"

"No. He's at a meeting in Roxbury."

Luther noticed she had her coat on. "You're going there?"

"I am. I expect it might not go well."

"Let me walk you then."

Nora smiled. "I'd like that."

On their way to the el, they got plenty of stares, this white

698

woman and this black man strolling through the North End. Luther considered staying a step behind her, so he'd appear to be her valet or something similar, but then he remembered why he was going back to Tulsa in the first place, what he'd seen in that mob, and he kept abreast of her, his head high, his eyes clear and looking straight ahead.

"So you're going back," Nora said.

"Yeah. Got to. Miss my wife. Want to see my child."

"It'll be dangerous, though."

"What isn't these days?" Luther said.

She gave that a small smile. "You've a point."

On the el, Luther felt his legs stiffen involuntarily when they crossed the trestle that had been hit during the molasses flood. It had long since been repaired and reinforced, but he doubted he'd ever feel safe crossing it.

What a year! If he lived a dozen lives, would he ever see another twelve months like these? He'd come to Boston for safety, but the thought of it now made him suppress a laugh— from Eddie McKenna to the May Day riots to the whole police force walking off the job, Boston had to be the *least* safe city he'd ever come across in his life. The Athens of America, my ass. Way these crazy Yankees had been acting since Luther arrived, he'd change the name to the Asylum of America.

He caught Nora smiling at him from the white section of the car and he tipped his hat to her and she gave him a mock salute in return. What a find she was. If Danny didn't find a way to fuck it up, he'd grow old a very happy man with this woman by his side. Not that Danny seemed intent on fucking it up, just that he was a man after all, and no one knew better than Luther himself how completely a man could step on his own dick when what he thought he wanted contradicted what he knew he needed.

The el car rolled through a shell of a city, a ghost town of ash and glass pebbles. No one on the streets but the State Guard. All that rage of the last two days gone corked up and bottled. Machine guns could have that effect, Luther didn't doubt it, but he wondered if there were more to it than just the show of power. Maybe in the end the need to postpone the truth—we are the mob—was stronger than the ecstasy of giving in to it. Maybe everyone just woke up this morning ashamed, tired, unable to face another pointless night. Maybe they looked at those machine guns and a sigh of relief left their hearts. Daddy was home now. They no longer had to fear he'd left them alone, left them for good.

They got off the el at Roxbury Crossing and walked toward Fay Hall.

Nora said, "How are the Giddreauxs taking your departure?"

Luther shrugged. "They understand. I think Yvette had taken a bit more of a shine to me than she'd counted on, so it's hard, but they understand."

"You're leaving today?"

"Tomorrow," Luther said.

"You'll write."

"Yes, ma'am. Ya'll should think of coming for a visit."

"I'll mention it to himself. I don't know what we're going to do, Luther. I surely don't."

Luther looked over at her, at the minute quiver in her chin. "You don't think they'll get their jobs back?"

"I don't know. I don't know."

At Fay Hall, they held a vote on whether to remain with the American Federation of Labor. The result was in favor, 1388 to 14. They held a second vote on whether to continue the strike. This was a bit more contentious. Men called out from the floor, asking Danny if the Central Labor Union would make right on their promise of a sympathy strike. Another cop mentioned he'd heard the firemen were waffling. They were pissed about all the false alarms during the riots, and the BFD had made a great show of advertising for volunteers to replace them. The turnout had been twice as large as expected.

Danny had left two messages with Ralph Raphelson's

office, asking him to come to Fay Hall, but he hadn't heard back yet. He took the podium. "The Central Labor Union is still trying to pull together all their delegates. As soon as they do, they'll vote. I've had no indication that they'll vote any other way but than how they told us they expect to. Look, they're killing us in the press. I understand. The riots hurt us."

"They're killing us from the pulpits, too," Francis Leonard shouted. "You should hear what they're saying about us in morning mass."

Danny held up a hand. "I've heard, I've heard. But we can still win the day. We just have to hold together, stay strong in our resolve. The governor and the mayor still fear a sympathy strike, and we still have the power of the AFL behind us. We can still win."

Danny wasn't sure how much of his own words he believed, but he felt a sudden glow of hope when he noticed Nora and Luther enter the back of the hall. Nora gave him a wave and a bright smile and he smiled back.

Then as they moved to their right, Ralph Raphelson stepped into the space they'd vacated. He removed his hat and his eyes met Danny's.

He shook his head.

Danny felt as if he'd been hit in the spine with a pipe and stabbed in the stomach with an ice-cold knife.

Raphelson put his hat back on and turned to go, but Danny wasn't letting him off the hook, not now, not tonight.

"Gentlemen, please give a warm hand to Ralph Raphelson of the Boston Central Labor Union!"

Raphelson turned with a grimace on his face as the men turned, saw him, and broke into applause.

"Ralph," Danny called with a wave of his arm, "come on up here and tell the men what the BCLU has planned."

Raphelson came down the aisle with a sick smile plastered to his face and a stiff gait. He climbed the steps to the stage and shook Danny's hand and whispered, "I'll get you for this, Coughlin."

"Yeah?" Danny gripped his hand tight, squeezing the bones, and smiled big. "I fucking hope you choke to death."

He dropped the hand and walked to the back of the stage as Raphelson took the podium and Mark sidled up to Danny.

"He selling us out?"

"He already sold us."

"It gets worse," Mark said.

Danny turned, saw that Mark's eyes were damp, the pockets beneath them dark.

"Jesus, how could it get worse?"

"This is a telegram Samuel Gompers sent to Governor Coolidge this morning. Coolidge released it to the press. Just read the circled part."

Danny's eyes scanned the page until he found the sentence circled in pencil:

> While it is our belief that the Boston Police were poorly
> served and their rights as workingmen denied by both
> yourself and Police Commissioner Curtis, it has always
> been the position of the American Federation of Labor
> to discourage all government employees from striking.

The men were booing Raphelson now, most on their feet. Several chairs toppled.

Danny dropped the copy of the telegram to the floor of the stage. "We're done."

"There's still hope, Dan."

"For what?" Danny looked at him. "The American Federation of Labor and the Central Labor Union both just sold us down the river on the same day. Fucking *hope*?"

"We could still get our jobs back."

Several men rushed the stage and Ralph Raphelson took a half dozen steps backward.

"They'll never give us our jobs back," Danny said. "Never."

* * *

702

The el ride back to the North End was bad. Luther had never seen Danny in so dark a mood. It covered him like a cloak. He sat beside Luther and offered hard eyes to the other passengers who gave him a funny look. Nora sat beside him and rubbed his hand nervously, as if to calm him, but it was really to calm herself, Luther knew.

Luther had known Danny long enough to know you'd have to be insane to take the guy on in a fair fight. He was too big, too fearless, too impervious to pain. So he'd never be dumb enough to question Danny's strength, but he'd never been close enough before to feel this capacity for violence that lived in the man like a second, deeper soul.

The other men on the car stopped giving them funny looks. Stopped giving them any looks at all. Danny just sat there, staring out at the rest of the car, never seeming to blink, those eyes of his gone dark, just waiting for an excuse to let the rest of him erupt.

They got off in the North End and walked up Hanover toward Salem Street. Night had come on while they rode the el, but the streets were near empty due to the State Guard presence. About halfway along Hanover, as they were passing the Prado, someone called Danny's name. It was a hoarse, weak voice. They turned and Nora let out a small yelp as a man stepped out of the shadows of the Prado with a hole in his coat that expelled smoke.

"Jesus, Steve," Danny said and caught the man as he fell into his arms. "Nora, honey, can you find a guardsman, tell him a cop's been shot?"

"I'm not a cop," Steve said.

"You're a cop, you're a cop."

He lowered Steve to the ground as Nora went running up the street.

"Steve, Steve."

Steve opened his eyes as the smoke continued to flow from the hole in his chest. "All this time asking around? And I just ran into her. Turned into the alley between

Stillman and Cooper? Just looked up and there she was. Tessa. *Pop*."

His eyelids fluttered. Danny pulled up his shirt and tore off a length of it, wadded it up and pressed it to the hole.

Steve opened his eyes. "She's gotta be . . . moving now, Dan. Right now."

A guardsman's whistle blew and Danny saw Nora running back down the street toward them. He turned to Luther. "Put your hand on this. Press hard."

Luther followed his instructions, pressed the heel of his palm against the wadded-up shirt, watched it redden.

Danny stood.

"Wait! Where you going?"

"Get the person who did this. You tell the guardsmen it was a woman named Tessa Ficara. You got that name?"

"Yeah, yeah. Tessa Ficara."

Danny ran through the Prado.

He caught her coming down the fire escape. He was in the rear doorway of a haberdashery on the other side of the alley and she came out of a window on the third floor onto the fire escape and walked down to the landing below. She lifted the ladder until its hooks disengaged from the housing and then latched onto the iron again as she lowered it to the pavement. When she turned her body to begin the climb down, he drew his revolver and crossed the alley. When she reached the last rung and stepped to the pavement, he placed the gun to the side of her neck.

"Keep your hands on the ladder and do not turn around."

"Officer Danny," she said. She started to turn and he slapped the side of her face with his free hand.

"What did I say? Hands on the ladder and don't turn around."

"As you wish."

He ran his hands through the pockets of her coat and then the folds of her clothing.

"You like that?" she said. "You like feeling me?"

"You want to get hit again?" he said.

"If you must hit," she said, "hit harder."

His hand bumped a hard bulge by her groin and he felt her body stiffen.

"I'll assume you didn't grow a dick, Tessa."

He reached down her leg, then ran his hands up under her dress and chemise. He pulled the Derringer from the waistband of her underwear and pocketed it.

"Satisfied?" she said.

"Not by a fair sight."

"What about your dick, Danny?" she said, the word coming out "deke," as if she were trying it out for the first time. Although, from experience, he knew she wasn't.

"Raise your right leg," he said.

She complied. "Is it hard?"

She wore a gunmetal-lace boot with a Cuban heel and black velveteen top. He ran his hand up and around it.

"Now the other one."

She lowered her right leg. As she raised the left, she bumped her ass back against him. "Oh, it is. Very hard."

He found the knife in her left boot. It was small and thin but, he had little doubt, very sharp. He pulled it out with the crude scabbard attached and pocketed it beside the gun.

"Would you like me to lower my leg or do you want to fuck me where I stand?"

He could see his breath in the cold. "Fucking you ain't in my plans to night, bitch."

He ran his hand up her body again and heard her take slow even breaths. Her hat was a broad-brimmed crepe sailor with a red ribbon across the brim tied off into a bow at the front. He removed it and stepped back from her and ran his hand over the trim. He found two razor blades tucked beneath the silk and he tossed them to the alley along with the hat.

"You dirtied my hat," she said. "Poor, poor hat."

He placed a hand on her back and removed all the pins

from her hair until it spilled down her neck and back and then he threw the pins away and stepped back again.

"Turn around."

"Yes, master."

She turned and leaned back against the ladder and crossed her hands at the waist. She smiled and it made him want to slap her again.

"You think you will arrest me now?"

He produced a pair of handcuffs from his pocket and dangled them from his finger.

She nodded and the smile remained. "You are no longer a police officer, Danny. I know these things."

"Citizen's arrest," he said.

"If you arrest me, I'll hang myself."

It was his turn to shrug. "Okay."

"And the baby in my belly will die as well."

He said, "Knocked up again, are we?"

"Sì."

She stared at him, her eyes wide and dark as always. She ran a hand over her belly. "A life lives in me."

"Uh-uh," Danny said. "Try another one, honey."

"I don't have to. Bring me to jail and the jail doctor will confirm that I am pregnant. I promise you, I will hang myself. And a child will die in my womb."

He locked the cuffs over her wrists and then yanked on them so that her body slammed into his and their faces almost touched.

"Don't fucking play me, whore. You pulled it off once, but twice ain't going to happen in your time on earth."

"I know that," she said, and he could taste her breath. "I am a revolutionary, Danny, and I—"

"You're a fucking terrorist. A bomb maker." He grabbed the cuff chain and pulled her close. "You just shot a guy who spent the last nine months looking for a job. He was of 'the people.' Just another working stiff trying to get by and you fucking shot him."

706

"Ex-officer Danny," she said and her tone was that of an elderly woman speaking to a child, "casualties are a part of war. Just ask my dead husband."

The metal shot from between her hands and into his body. It bit his flesh and then hit bone and chiseled through that and his hip caught fire and the bolt of pain shot down through his thigh and reached his knee.

He pushed her back and she stumbled and looked at him with her hair in her face and her lips wet with spittle.

Danny glanced at the knife sticking out of his hip and then his leg gave way and he dropped to his ass in the alley and watched the blood sluice down his outer thigh. He raised his .45 and pointed it at her.

The pain came in bolts that shook his entire body. It was worse than anything he'd experienced when he'd been shot in the chest.

"I'm carrying a child," she said and took a step backward.

Danny took a bite from the air and sucked it through his teeth.

Tessa held out her hands and he shot her once in the chin and once between her breasts and she fell down in the alley and flopped like a fish. Her heels kicked the cobblestones, and then she tried to sit up, taking a loud gulp of the air as the blood spilled down her coat. Danny watched her eyes roll back in her head and then her head hit the alley and she was still. Lights came on in the windows.

He went to lay back and something punched him in the thigh. He heard the pistol report a half a second before the next bullet hit him high on the right side of his chest. He tried to lift his own pistol. He raised his head and saw a man standing on the fire escape. His pistol flashed and the bullet chunked into the cobblestones. Danny kept trying to raise his own pistol but his arm wouldn't follow commands, and the next shot hit his left hand. The whole time, he couldn't help thinking: Now who the fuck is *this* guy?

He rested on his elbows and let the gun fall from his right

hand. He wished he could have died on any other day but this. This one had carried too much defeat with it, too much despair, and he would have liked to leave the world believing in something.

The man on the fire escape rested his elbows on the rail and took aim.

Danny closed his eyes.

He heard a scream, a bellow really, and wondered if it was his own. A clank of metal, a higher pitched scream. He opened his eyes and saw the man fall through the air, and his head made a loud pop against the cobblestones and his body folded in half.

Luther heard the first shot after he'd already passed the alley. He stood still on the sidewalk and heard nothing for almost a minute and was about to walk away when he heard the second one—a sharp pop followed immediately by another one. He jogged back to the alley. Some lights had come on and he could see two figures lying in the middle of the alley, one of them trying to raise a gun off the stone. Danny.

A man stood up on the fire escape. He wore a black bowler and pointed a gun down at Danny. Luther saw the brick lying by a trash can, thought it might be a rat at first even as he reached for it, but the rat didn't move, and he closed his hand over it and came up with, yup, a brick.

When Danny lay back on his elbows, Luther saw that execution coming, could feel it in his chest, and he let loose the loudest yell he was capable of, a nonsensical "Aaaahhhh" that seemed to empty his heart and soul of its blood.

The man on the fire escape looked up and Luther already had his arm cocked. He could feel grass underfoot, the smell of a field in late August, the scent of leather and dirt and sweat, see the runner trying to take home, take home against *his* arm, trying to show him up like *that*? Luther's feet left the alley, and his arm turned into a catapult. He saw a catcher's mitt waiting, and the air sizzled when he unleashed the brick into it. That brick got up there in a goddamned hurry, too, like it had been pulled from the fire of its maker but for no other purpose. That brick had *ambition*.

Hit that son of a bitch right in the side of his silly hat. Crushed the hat and half his head. The guy lurched. The guy canted. He fell over the fire escape and tried to grab it, tried kicking at it, but there wasn't no hope in that. He just fell. Fell straight down, screaming like a girl, and landed on his head.

Danny smiled. Blood pumping out of him like it was heading to put out a fire, and he fucking *smiles*!

"Twice you saved my life."

"Sssh."

Nora came running up the alley, her shoes clicking on the stones. She dropped to her knees over her husband.

"Compress, honey," Danny said. "Your scarf. Forget the leg. The chest, the chest, the chest."

She used her scarf on the left hole in his chest and Luther took off his jacket and applied it to the bigger hole in his leg. They knelt over him pressing all their weight into his chest.

"Danny, don't leave me."

"Not leaving," Danny said. "Strong. Love you."

Nora's tears poured down into his face. "Yes, yes, you're strong."

"Luther."

"Yeah?"

A siren bleated in the night, followed by another.

"Hell of a throw."

"Sssh."

"You should . . ."—Danny smiled and blood bubbled over his lips—". . . be a baseball player or something."

The BABE GOES SOUTH

CHAPTER *forty*

Luther arrived back in Tulsa in late September during a dogged heat wave and a humid breeze that kicked the dust up and caked the city tan. He'd spent some time in East St. Louis with his Uncle Hollis, enough time in which to grow a beard. He stopped grooming his hair as well and traded his bowler for a broke-down cavalryman's hat with a sloopy brim and a crown that the moths had gotten to. He even allowed Uncle Hollis to overfeed him so that for the first time in his life he had a little belly on him and some extra flesh beneath his jaw. By the time he got off the freight car in Tulsa, he looked like a tramp. Which was the point. A tramp with a duffel bag.

Most times he looked at the bag, he'd start laughing. Couldn't help it. Bundled-up stacks of money sat at the bottom, product of another man's greed, another man's graft. Years of corruption all stacked and tied up and smelling now of someone else's future.

He took the bag to a field of weeds north of the tracks and buried it with a spade he'd brought along from East St. Louis. Then he crossed back over the Santa Fe tracks into Greenwood and went down to Admiral, where the rough trade spent their time. It was four hours before he spotted Smoke coming out of a billiards parlor that hadn't been there when Luther left last year. Place was called Poulson's and it took Luther a moment to remember that this was Smoke's

713

given surname. If he'd thought of that before, maybe he wouldn't have lost four hours wandering up and down Admiral.

Smoke had three men with him, and they surrounded him until they reached a cherry red Maxwell. One of them opened the back door and Smoke hopped in and they drove off. Luther went back to the field of weeds, dug the bag back up, took what he needed, and buried it again. He walked back into Greenwood and kept going till he'd reached the outskirts and found the place he'd been looking for—Deval's Junkyard, run by an old fella, Latimer Deval, who'd occasionally done side work for Uncle James. Luther had never met old Deval in the flesh, but he'd passed his place enough back when he'd lived here to know Deval always kept a few heaps for sale on his front lawn.

He bought a 1910 Franklin Tourer off Deval for three hundred, the two barely exchanging words, just the cash and the key. Luther drove back to Admiral and parked a block down from Poulson's.

He followed them for the next week. He never went out to his house on Elwood, though it pained him more than anything to be this close after so much time away. But he knew if he saw Lila or his son, he would lose all strength and have to run to them, have to hold them and smell them and wet them with his tears. And then he'd surely be a dead man. So he drove the Franklin out to unincorporated scrub land every night and slept there, and the next morning he was back on the job, learning Smoke's routine.

Smoke took his lunch every day at the same diner but mixed it up for dinner—some nights at Torchy's, others at Alma's Chop House, another night at Riley's, a jazz club that had replaced the Club Almighty. Luther wondered just what Smoke thought about as he chewed his dinner in view of the stage where he'd almost bled to death. Whatever else you could say about the man, he definitely had a strong constitution.

After a week, Luther felt reasonably confident he had the man's routine down cold because Smoke was a man of routine. He might have eaten at a different place every night, but he always arrived at six sharp. Tuesdays and Thursdays, he went to his woman's place out in the sticks, an old sharecropper's shack, and his men would wait in the yard while he went about his business and came out two hours later, tucking in his shirt. He lived above his own billiards parlor, and his three bodyguards would all accompany him into the building and then come back and get into their car and return the next morning at five-thirty on the nose.

Once Luther got the afternoon routine figured—lunch at twelve-thirty, collections and package re-ups from one-thirty to three, back to Poulson's at three-oh-five—he decided he'd found his window. He went to a hardware store and bought a doorknob, lock assembly, and keyhole plate that matched the one on the door leading up to Smoke's apartment. He spent afternoons in the car, learning how to thread a paper clip through the keyhole, and once he could open the lock ten out of ten times in under twenty seconds, he started practicing at night, parked beside the dark scrub, not even the light of the moon to guide him, until he could pick that lock blind.

Of a Thursday night, when Luther knew Smoke and his men were at his woman's shack, he crossed Admiral in the looming dusk and was through the door faster than he'd ever stolen a base. He faced a set of stairs that smelled of oil soap and he climbed them to find a second door, also locked. It was a different lock cylinder, so it took him about two minutes to get the hang of it. Then the door popped open and he was inside. He turned and squatted in the doorway until he spied a single black hair lying on the threshold. He lifted it and placed it back against the lock and closed the door over it.

He'd bathed this morning in the river, his teeth clacking from the cold as he covered every inch of his stinky self with brown soap. Then he pulled the fresh clothes he'd purchased in East St. Louis from the bag on the front seat of the car and put them on. He commended himself on that now, as he'd guessed correctly that Smoke's apartment would be as orderly as his dress. Place was spotless. Bare, too. Nothing on the walls, only one throw rug in the living room. Bare coffee table, Victrola without a wisp of dust or even the tiniest smudge.

Luther found the hall closet, noted that several of the coats he'd seen Smoke wearing in the last week were hung precisely on wooden hangers. The hanger that was empty awaited the blue duster with the leather collar Smoke had worn today. Luther slipped in among the clothes, closed the door, and waited.

Took about an hour, though it felt like five. He heard footsteps on the stairs, four sets of them, and pulled his watch, but it was too dark to see, so he put it back in his vest and noticed he was holding his breath. He let out a slow exhale as the key turned in the lock. The door opened and one man said, "You good, Mr. Poulson?"

"I am, Red. See you in the morning."

"Yes, sir."

The door shut and Luther raised his pistol, and for one horrible moment he was seized by overwhelming terror, a desire to close his eyes and wish this moment away, to push past Smoke when he opened that door and run for his life.

But it was too late, because Smoke went to the closet straightaway and the door opened and Luther had no choice but to place the muzzle of the pistol against the tip of Smoke's nose.

"You make a sound, I'll kill you where you stand."

Smoke raised his arms, still wearing the duster.

"Take a few steps back. Keep those arms high." Luther came out into the hallway.

Smoke's eyes narrowed. "Country?"

Luther nodded.

"You changed some. Never would recognize you on the street with that beard."

"You didn't."

Smoke gave that a small upward tilt of his eyebrows.

"Kitchen," Luther said. "You first. Lace your hands on top of your head."

Smoke complied and walked down the hallway and entered the kitchen. There was a small table there with a red-and-white checkered tablecloth and two wooden chairs. Luther gestured Smoke into one of the chairs and took the one across from him.

"You can take your hands off your head. Just put them on the table."

Smoke unlaced his fingers and placed his palms down on the table.

"Old Byron get back to you?"

Smoke nodded. "Said you threw him through a window."

"He tell you I was coming for you?"

"He mentioned it, yeah."

"That what the three bodyguards are for?"

"That," Smoke said, "and some rival business associates too quick to the anger."

Luther reached into his coat pocket and came out with a brown paper bag that he placed on the table. He watched Smoke stare at it, let him wonder what it was.

"What'd you think about Chicago?" Luther said.

Smoke cocked his head. "The riots?"

Luther nodded.

"Thought it was a damn shame we only killed fifteen whites."

"Washington?"

"Where you going with this?"

"Humor me, Mr. Poulson."

Smoke raised another eyebrow at that. "Washington? Same thing. Wished them niggers had fought back, though. Chicago ones had some spirit."

"I passed through East St. Louis on my travels. Twice."

"Yeah? What it look like?"

"Ash," Luther said.

Smoke tapped his fingers lightly on the tabletop. "You didn't come here to kill me, did you?"

"Nope." Luther tipped the bag and a sheaf of money fell out, wrapped tightly in a red rubber band. "That's a thousand dollars. That's half what I feel I owe you."

"For not killing me?"

Luther shook his head. He lowered the gun, placed it on the table, and slid it across the tablecloth. He took his hand off it. He sat back in his chair. "For you not killing me."

Smoke didn't lift the pistol right away. He cocked his head at it, then tilted it the other way to consider Luther.

"I'm done with our kind killing our kind," Luther said. "White folk do enough of it. I won't be a party to any more of it. You want to still be part of it, then you kill me and you'll get that thousand. You don't, you'll get two thousand. You want me dead, I'm sitting across from you saying pull the fucking trigger."

Smoke had the gun in his hand. Luther had never seen him so much as flinch, but there was the gun pointed directly at Luther's right eye. Smoke thumbed back the hammer.

"You might be confusing me with somebody has a soul," he said.

"I might."

"And you might not think I'm the kind of man would shoot you right through that eye of yours and then go up the road and fuck your woman up the ass, cut her throat when I come, and then cook me a soup out of your baby boy."

Luther said nothing.

Smoke ran the muzzle over Luther's cheek. He turned the pistol to his right and drew the target sight down the side of Luther's face, opening the flesh.

"*You*," he said, "will not associate with any gamblers, any drinkers, any dope fiends. *You* will stay out of the Greenwood nightlife. All the way out. You will never enter a place where I could run into you. And if *you* ever leave that son of yours because the simple life is too fucking simple for you? I will take you apart, piece by piece, in a grain silo for a week before I let your ass die. Is there any part of this deal you have issue with, Mr. Laurence?"

"None," Luther said.

"Drop my other two thousand at the pool hall tomorrow afternoon. Give it to a man named Rodney. He'll be the one handing out balls to the customers. No later than two o'clock. Clear?"

"It ain't two thousand. It's one."

Smoke stared back at him, his eyelids drooping.

Luther said, "Two thousand, it is."

Smoke thumbed down the hammer and handed the gun to Luther. Luther took it and put it in his coat.

"The fuck out of my house now, Luther."

Luther stood.

As he reached the kitchen doorway, Smoke said, "You realize, your whole life, you'll never get this lucky again?"

"I do."

Smoke lit himself a cigarette. "Then sin no more, asshole."

Luther walked up the steps to the house on Elwood. He noticed that the railings needed repainting and decided that would be his first order of business tomorrow.

Today, though . . .

There wasn't a word for it, he thought, as he opened the screen door and found the front door unlocked. No word at all. Ten months since that horrible night he'd left. Ten months riding rails and hiding out and trying to be another person in a strange city up north. Ten months of living without the one thing in his life he'd ever done right.

The house was empty. He stood in the small parlor and looked through the kitchen at the back door. It was open, and he could hear the creak of a clothesline being pulled, decided that's something else he'd need to tend to, give that wheel a little oil. He walked through the parlor and into the kitchen and could smell baby here, could smell milk, could smell something still forming itself.

He walked out the back steps and she bent to reach into her basket and lift another wet piece of clothing from it, but then she raised her head and stared. She wore a dark blue blouse over a faded yellow house skirt she favored. Desmond sat by her feet, sucking on a spoon and staring at the grass.

She whispered his name. She whispered, "Luther."

All the old pain entered her eyes, all the grief and hurt at what he'd done to her, all the fear and worry. Could she open her heart again? Could she put her faith in him?

Luther willed her to go the other way, sent a look across the grass freighted with all his love, all his resolve, all his heart.

She smiled.

Good Lord, it was gorgeous.

She held out her hand.

He crossed the grass. He dropped to his knees and took her hand and kissed it. He wrapped his arms around her waist and wept into her shirt. She lowered herself to her knees and kissed him, weeping, too, laughing, too, the two of them a sight, crying and giggling and holding each other and kissing and tasting each other's tears.

Desmond started to cry. Wail actually, the sound so sharp it was like a nail in Luther's ear.

Lila leaned back from him. "Well?"

"Well?"

"Make him stop," she said.

Luther looked at this little creature sitting in the grass and wailing, his eyes red, his nose running. He reached down and lifted him to his shoulder. He was *warm*. Warm as a kettle wrapped in a towel. Luther had never known a body could give off such heat.

"He okay?" he asked Lila. "He feels hot."

"He's fine," she said. "He's a baby been setting in the sun."

Luther held him out in front of him. He saw some Lila in the eyes and some Luther in the nose. Saw his own mother in the jaw, his father in the ears. He kissed his head. He kissed his nose. The child continued to wail.

"Desmond," he said and kissed his son on the lips. "Desmond, it's your daddy."

Desmond wasn't having any of it. He wailed and shrieked and wept like the world was ending. Luther brought him back to his shoulder and held him tight. He rubbed his back. He cooed in his ear. He kissed him so many times he lost count.

Lila ran a hand over Luther's head and leaned in for a kiss of her own.

And Luther finally found the word for this day . . .

Whole.

He could stop running. He could stop looking for anything else. Wasn't anything else he wanted. This right here was the full measure of every hope he'd harbored since birth.

Desmond's wails stopped, just snuffed out like a match in the wind. Luther looked at the basket at his feet, still half full with damp clothing.

"Let's get those clothes hung," he said.

Lila lifted a shirt off the pile. "Oh, you gonna help, uh?"

"You give me a couple of those clothespins, I will."

She passed a handful of them to him and he hoisted Desmond onto his hip and helped his wife hang laundry. The moist air hummed with cicadas. The sky was low and flat and bright. Luther chuckled.

"What you laughing at?" Lila asked.

"Everything," he said.

Danny's first night in the hospital, he spent nine hours on the operating table. The knife in his leg had nicked the femoral artery. The bullet in his chest had hit bone, and some of the bone chips had sprayed his right lung. The bullet in his left hand had entered through the palm and the fingers were, for the time being anyway, useless. He'd had less than two pints of blood in his body by the time they got him out of the ambulance.

He woke from a coma on the sixth day and was awake half an hour when he felt the left side of his brain catch fire. He lost the vision in his left eye and tried to tell the doctor something was happening to him, something odd, like maybe his hair was on fire, and his body began to shake. It was quite beyond his control, this violent shaking. He vomited. The orderlies held him down and shoved something leather into his mouth, and the bandages on his chest tore and blood leaked from him all over again. By this time, the fire had raged all the way across his skull. He vomited again, and they pulled the leather out of his mouth and rolled him onto his side before he choked.

When he woke a few days later, he couldn't speak properly and the whole left side of his body was numb.

"You've had a stroke," the doctor said.

"I'm twenty-seven years old," Danny said, though it came out, "I'b wenty-vesen airs awl."

The doctor nodded, as if he'd spoken clearly. "Most twenty-seven-year-olds don't get stabbed and then shot three times for good measure. If you were much older, I doubt you would have survived. In truth, I don't know how you did."

"Nora."

"She's outside. Do you really want her to see you in your current state?"

"She I mife."

The doctor nodded.

When he left the room, Danny heard the words as they had left his mouth. He could form them in his head right now—*she's my wife*—but what had come out—*she I mife*—was hideous, humiliating. Tears left his eyes, hot ones of fear and shame, and he wiped at them with his right hand, his good hand.

Nora entered the room. She looked so pale, so frightened. She sat in the chair by his bed and took his right hand in hers and lifted it to her face, pressed her cheek to his palm.

"I love you."

Danny gritted his teeth, concentrated through a pounding headache, concentrated, willing the words to leave his tongue correctly. "Love you."

Not bad. Love ooh, really. But close enough.

"The doctor said you'll have trouble speaking for a while. You may have trouble walking, yeah? But you're young and fierce-strong, and I'll be with you. I'll be with you. 'Twill all be fine, Danny."

She's trying so hard not to cry, he thought.

"Love ooh," he said again.

She laughed. A wet laugh. She wiped her eyes. She lowered her head to his shoulder. He could feel the warmth of her against his face.

If there was a positive outcome to Danny's injuries, it was that he didn't see a newspaper for three weeks. If he had, he would have learned that the day after the shoot-out in the alley, Commissioner Curtis proclaimed all positions of the striking police officers to be officially vacant. Governor Coolidge supported him. President Wilson weighed in to call the actions of the policemen who left their posts "a crime against civilization."

Ads seeking the new police force contained within them new standards and rate of pay, all in keeping with the strikers' original demands. Base salary would now start at fourteen hundred dollars a year. Uniforms, badges, and service revolvers would be provided free of charge. Within two weeks of the riots, city cleanup crews, licensed plumbers, electricians, and carpenters began arriving at each of the station houses to clean and remodel them until they met safety and sanitation codes at a state level.

Governor Coolidge composed a telegram to Samuel Gompers of the AFL. Before he sent the telegram to Gompers, he released it to the press where it was published on the front page of every daily the following morning. The telegram was also released to the wire services and would run in over seventy newspapers across the country in the following two days. Governor Coolidge proclaimed the following: "There is no right to strike against the public safety by anybody, anywhere, anytime."

Within a week, those words had turned Governor Coolidge into a national hero and some suggested he should consider a run for the presidency the following year.

Andrew Peters faded from public view. His ineffectuality was deemed, if not quite criminal, then certainly unconscionable. His failure to call out the State Guard on the first night of the strike represented an unforgivable dereliction of his duties, and popular opinion held that it was only the quick thinking and steely resolve of Governor Coolidge and the unfairly maligned Commissioner Curtis that had saved the city from itself.

While the rest of the active police force found their jobs in jeopardy, Steve Coyle was given a full policeman's funeral. Commissioner Curtis singled out former Patrolman Stephen Coyle as an exemplar of the "old guard" policeman, the one who put duty before all else. Curtis repeatedly failed to note that Coyle had been released from the employ of the BPD almost a full year before. He further promised to form a committee to look into posthumously reinstating Coyle's medical benefits for any immediate family he happened to have.

In the first days after the death of Tessa Ficara, the papers trumpeted the irony of a striking police officer who, in less than a year, had brought about the demise of two of the most wanted terrorists in the land as well as a third, Bartolomeo Stellina, the man Luther had killed with the brick, who was reputed to be a devoted Galleanist. Even though the strikers were now viewed with the enmity once reserved for the Germans (to whom they were often compared), accounts of Officer Coughlin's heroics turned public sympathy back toward the strikers. Maybe, it was felt, if they returned to their jobs right away, *some of them*, at least those with distinguished records akin to Officer Coughlin's, could be reinstated.

The next day, however, the *Post* reported that Officer Coughlin might have had a prior acquaintanceship with the Ficaras, and the evening *Transcript*, citing unnamed sources in the Bureau of Investigation, reported that Officer Coughlin and the Ficaras had once lived on the same floor of the same building in the North End. The next morning, the *Globe* ran a story citing several tenants in the building who described the relationship between Officer Coughlin and the Ficaras as quite social, so social in fact that his relationship with Tessa Ficara may have crossed into unseemly areas; there was even some question as to whether he had paid for her favors. With that question in mind, his prior shooting of her husband suddenly looked as if it could have been colored by more than a sense of duty. Public opinion turned wholly against Officer Coughlin, the dirty cop, and all of his striking "comrades." Any talk of the strikers ever returning to work ended.

National coverage of the two days of rioting entered the arena of myth. Several newspapers wrote of machine guns turned on innocent crowds, of a death toll estimated in the hundreds, property damage in the millions. The actual dead numbered nine and the property damage slightly less than one million dollars, but the public would hear none of it. The strikers were Bolsheviks, and the strike had unleashed civil war in Boston.

When Danny left the hospital in mid-October, he still dragged his left foot and had trouble lifting anything heavier than a teacup with his left hand. His speech, however, was fully restored. He would have left the hospital two weeks earlier, but one of his wounds had developed sepsis. He'd gone into shock, and for the second time that month a priest had delivered last rites.

After the stories that defamed him in the papers, Nora had

been forced to leave their building on Salem Street and had moved their few belongings to a rooming house in the West End. It was there they returned when Danny was released from the hospital. She had chosen the West End because Danny's rehabilitation would be taking place at Mass General, and the walk from there to the apartment took a matter of minutes. Danny climbed the stairs to the second floor, and he and Nora entered the dingy room with one gray window that looked out on an alley.

"It's all we could afford," Nora said.

"It's fine."

"I tried to get the grime off the outside of the window, but no matter how hard I scrubbed, it just—"

He put his good arm around her. "It's fine, honey. We won't be here long."

One night in November, he lay in bed with his wife after they'd managed to make love for the first time since he'd been injured. "I'll never be able to get a job here."

"You could."

He looked at her.

She smiled and rolled her eyes. She slapped his chest lightly. "That's what you get, boy, for sleeping with a terrorist."

He chuckled. It felt good to be able to joke about something so bleak.

His family had visited the hospital twice while he was still in a coma. His father had come once after the stroke to tell him they would always love him, of course, but could never again admit him to their home. Danny had nodded and shook his father's hand and waited until he was five minutes gone before he wept.

"There's nothing to keep us here after my rehabilitation," he said.

"No."

"Are you interested in an adventure?"

She slid her arm over his chest. "I'm interested in anything."

* * *

726

Tessa had miscarried the day before her death. Or so the coroner told Danny. Danny would never know if the coroner lied to save him the guilt, but he chose to believe him because the alternative, he feared, could be the thing that finally broke him.

When he'd met Tessa, she'd been in labor. When he came across her again in May, she'd been pretending to be pregnant. And now, at her death, pregnant again. It was as if she'd had an overpowering need to remake her rage as flesh and blood, to be certain it would live on and pass down through the generations. This need (and Tessa, as a whole) was something he would never understand.

Sometimes, he woke from a sleep with the cold echo of her laughter ringing in his ears.

A package from Luther arrived. There was two thousand dollars in it—two years' salary—and a formal portrait of Luther, Lila, and Desmond sitting before a fireplace. They were dressed in the latest fashions; Luther even wore a coat with tails over his winged collar.

"She's beautiful," Nora said. "And that child, good Lord."

Luther's note was brief:

Dear Danny and Nora,
   I am home now. I am happy. I hope this is enough. If you need more wire immediately and I will send it.
Your friend,
Luther

Danny opened the packet of bills and showed it to Nora.

"Sweet Jesus!" She let out a noise that was half laughing–half weeping. "Where did he get it?"

"I have some idea," Danny said.

"And?"

"You don't want to know," he said. "Believe me."

* * *

On the tenth of January, in a light snow, Thomas Coughlin left his station house. The new recruits were coming along faster than expected. They were mostly smart. And eager. The State Guard still patrolled the streets, but the units had begun to demobilize. Within the month, they'd be gone, and the restored Boston Police Department would rise in their place.

Thomas walked up the street toward home. At the corner, under a streetlamp, his son leaned against the pole.

"Believe the Sox traded Ruth?" Danny said.

Thomas shrugged. "I was never a fan of the game."

"To New York," Danny said.

"Your youngest brother is, of course, distraught over it. I haven't seen him this beside himself since . . ."

His father didn't have to finish the thought. It pierced Danny just the same.

"How's Con'?"

His father tipped his hand from side to side. "He has good days and bad. He's learning to read by his fingers. There's a school in Back Bay that teaches it. If the bitterness doesn't overwhelm him, he could be all right."

"Does it overwhelm you?"

"Nothing overwhelms me, Aiden." His father's breath was white in the cold. "I'm a man."

Danny said nothing.

His father said, "Well, then, you look back to trim. So I guess I'll be going."

"We're leaving the city, Dad."

"You're . . . ?"

Danny nodded. "Leaving the state actually. Heading west."

His father looked stunned. "This is your home."

Danny shook his head. "Not anymore."

Maybe his father had thought that Danny would reside in exile but close by. That way Thomas Coughlin could live with the illusion that his family was still intact. But once Danny

728

left, a hole would open that not even Thomas could have prepared for.

"You're all packed then, I take it."

"Yeah. We're going to head to New York for a few days before Volstead kicks in. We never had a proper honeymoon."

His father nodded. He kept his head lowered, the snow falling in his hair.

"Good bye, Dad."

Danny started to walk past him and his father grabbed his arm. "Write me."

"Will you write back?"

"No. But I'd like to know—"

"Then I won't write."

His father's face stiffened and he gave him a curt nod and dropped his arm.

Danny walked up the street, the snow thickening, the footprints his father had left already obscured.

"Aiden!"

He turned, could barely see the man in all the white swirling between them. The flakes caked his eyelashes and he blinked them away.

"I'll write back," his father called.

A sudden boom of wind rattled the cars along the street.

"All right, then," Danny called.

"Take care of yourself, son."

"You, too."

His father raised a hand and Danny raised one in return and then they turned and walked in separate directions through the snow.

On the train to New York, everyone was drunk. Even the porters. Twelve in the afternoon and people were guzzling champagne and guzzling rye and a band played in the fourth car, and the band was drunk. No one sat in their seats. Everyone hugged and kissed and danced. Prohibition was now the law of the land. Enforcement would begin four days from now, on the sixteenth.

Babe Ruth had a private car on the train, and at first he tried to sit out the revelry. He read over a copy of the contract he'd officially sign at day's end in the offices of the Colonels at the Polo Grounds. He was now a Yankee. The trade had been announced ten days ago, though Ruth had never seen it coming. Got drunk for two days to deal with the depression. Johnny Igoe found him, though, and sobered him up. Explained that Babe was now the highest-paid player in baseball history. He showed him New York paper after New York paper, all proclaiming their joy, their ecstasy about getting the most feared slugger in the game on *their* team.

"You already own the town, Babe, and you haven't even arrived yet."

That put a new perspective on things. Babe had feared that New York was too big, too loud, too wide. He'd get swallowed up in it. Now he realized the opposite was true—he was too big for Boston. Too loud. Too wide. It couldn't hold him. It was too small, too provincial. New York was the only stage large enough for the Babe. New York and New York alone. It wasn't going to swallow Babe. He was going to swallow *it*.

I am Babe Ruth. I am bigger and better and stronger and more popular than anyone. Anyone.

Some drunk woman bounced off his door and he heard her giggle, the sound alone giving him an erection.

What the hell was he doing back here alone when he could be out there with his public, jawing, signing autographs, giving them a story they'd tell their grandkids?

He left the room. He walked straight to the bar car, worked his way through the dancing drunks, one bird up on a table kicking her legs like she was working burlesque. He sidled up the bar, ordered a double scotch.

"Why'd you leave us, Babe?"

He turned, looked at the drunk beside him, a short guy with a tall girlfriend, both of them three sheets to the wind.

"I didn't *leave*," Babe said. "Harry Frazee traded me. I had no say. I'm just a working stiff."

"Then you'll come back someday?" the guy said. "Play out your contract and come back to us?"

"Sure," Babe lied. "That's the idea, bub."

The man patted him on the back. "Thanks, Mr. Ruth."

"Thank you," Ruth said with a wink for his girlfriend. He downed his drink and ordered another.

He ended up striking up a conversation with this big guy and his Irish wife. It turned out the big guy had been one of the striking coppers and was heading to New York for a little honeymoon before moving on out west to see a friend.

"What were you guys thinking?" Ruth asked him.

"Just trying to get a fair shake," the ex-copper said.

"But it don't work that way," Babe said, eyeing that wife of his, a real dish, her accent sexy as all hell, too. "Look at me. I'm the biggest baseball player in the world and I got no say where they trade me. I got no power. Thems that write the checks write the rules."

The ex-copper smiled. It was a rueful smile and distant. "Different sets of rules for different classes of people, Mr. Ruth."

"Oh, sure. When wasn't that so?"

They had a few more drinks and Ruth had to say he'd never seen a couple so in love. They barely touched, and it wasn't like they got all gooey on each other, talked to each other in baby voices and called each other "dumpling" or anything. Even so, it was like a rope hung between them, invisible but electric, and that rope connected them more strongly than shared limbs. The rope was not only electric, it was serene. It glowed warm and peaceful. Honest.

Ruth grew sad. He'd never felt that kind of love, not even in his earliest days with Helen. He'd never felt that with another human being. Ever.

Peace. Honesty. Home.

God, was it even possible?

731

Apparently it was, because these two had it. At one point, the dame tapped a single finger on the ex-copper's hand. Just one light tap. And he looked at her and she smiled, her upper teeth exposed as they ran over her lower lip. God, it broke Babe's heart, that look. Had anyone ever looked at him like that?

No.

Would anyone?

No.

His spirits brightened only later as he walked out of the train station and waved good-bye to the couple as they went to stand in the taxi line. It looked to be a long wait on a cold day, but Babe didn't have to worry. The Colonels had sent a car, a black Stuttgart with a driver who held up a hand to acknowledge Babe as he walked toward him.

"It's Babe Ruth!" someone called, and several people pointed and called his name. Out on Fifth Avenue, half a dozen cars honked their horns.

He looked back at the couple in the taxi line. It sure was cold. For a moment he thought of calling to them, offering them a ride to their hotel. But they weren't even looking his way. Manhattan was cheering him, honking horns, yelling "Hurrah," but this couple heard none of it. They were turned into each other, the ex-copper's coat wrapped around her to protect her from the wind. Babe felt forlorn again, abandoned. He feared he'd somehow missed out on the most elemental part of life. He feared that this thing he'd missed would never, ever, enter his world. He dropped his gaze from the couple and decided they could wait for a taxi. They'd be fine.

He climbed into the car and rolled down the window to wave at his new fans as the driver pulled away from the curb. Volstead was coming, but it wouldn't affect him much. Word was the government hadn't hired nearly the manpower needed to enforce it, and Babe and people like him would be allowed certain exemptions. As they always had. That was the way of things, after all.

732

Babe rolled the window back up as the car accelerated.

"Driver, what's your name?"

"George, Mr. Ruth."

"Ain't that a kick? That's my name, too. But you call me Babe. Okay, George?"

"You betcha, Babe. An honor to meet you, sir."

"Ah, I'm just a ballplayer, George. Can't even read good."

"But you can hit, sir. You can hit for miles. I just want to be the first to say, 'Welcome to New York, Babe.'"

"Well, thank you, George. Happy to be here. Gonna be a good year, I think."

"A good decade," George said.

"You can say that twice."

A good decade. So it would be. Babe looked out the window, at New York in all its bustle and shine, all its lights and billboards and limestone towers. What a day. What a city. What a time to be alive.

THE END

ACKNOWLEDGMENTS

A City in Terror by Francis Russell is the authoritative account of the Boston police strike and its aftermath. It was an invaluable resource.

Other source material included *The Great Influenza* by John M. Barry; *Babe: The Legend Comes to Life* by Robert W. Creamer; *The Burning* by Tim Madigan; *Reds* by Ted Morgan; *Standing at Armageddon* by Nell Irvin Painter; *Dark Tide* by Stephen Puleo; *Babe Ruth: Launching the Legend* by Jim Reisler; *Perilous Times* by Geoffrey R. Stone; *The Red Sox Century* by Glenn Stout and Richard A. Johnson; *The Year the Red Sox Won the World Series* by Ty Waterman and Mel Springer; *Babe Ruth and the 1918 Red Sox* by Allan Wood; and *A People's History of the United States* by Howard Zinn.

A thousand thanks to Leonard Alkins, Tom Bernardo, Kristy Cardellio, Christine Caya, John J. Devine, John Dorsey, Alix Douglas, Carla Eigen, Mal Ellenburg, Tom Franklin, Lisa Gallagher, Federica Maggio, William P. Marchione, Julieanne McNarry, Michael Morrison, Thomas O'Connor (the dean of Boston historians), George Pelecanos, Paula Posnick, Jr., Richard Price, Ann Rittenberg, Hilda Rogers, Henry F. Scannell, Claire Wachtel, Sterling Watson, and Donna Wells.

Lastly, a particular debt of gratitude is owed to U.S. Army Sergeant Luis Araujo, whose selflessness and heroism lit the necessary fires.

